# ONE • THOUSAND • ONE

# PAPUA • NEW • GUINEAN • NIGHTS

# ONE • THOUSAND • ONE

# PAPUA • NEW • GUINEAN • NIGHTS

FOLKTALES • FROM
WANTOK • NEWSPAPER

VOLUME • 1 • TALES • FROM • 1972-1985

TRANSLATED • AND • EDITED • BY

THOMAS • H • SLONE

PUBLISHED • BY
MASALAI • PRESS
OAKLAND • CALIFORNIA
2001

This book is dedicated to Qiron Adhikary, my loving wife.

Published by
MASALAI PRESS
368 Capricorn Avenue
Oakland, California  94611-2058
U. S. A.

First Edition, 2001



*Publisher's Cataloging-in-Publication Data*
Slone, Thomas H., 1960-
One thousand one Papua New Guinean nights :
ancestor stories from Wantok newspaper
Volume 1 : Tales from 1972-1985 / by Thomas H. Slone.
p.  cm.
Includes bibliographical references and index.
ISBN 0-9714127-0-7 (Volume 1, pbk.)
ISBN 0-9714127-1-5 (Volume 2, pbk.)
ISBN 0-9714127-2-3 (2 Volume Set)
1. Tales — Papua New Guinea.
2. Folklore — Papua New Guinea.
3. Mythology — Melanesian — Papua New Guinea
4. Legends — Papua New Guinea
I. Thomas H. Slone II. Title III. Papua New Guinea Folklore Series 1

Papua New Guinea Folklore Series
1. One Thousand One Papua New Guinean Nights: Folktales from Wantok Newspaper.
    Volume 1: Tales from 1972-1985 (this volume)
2. One Thousand One Papua New Guinean Nights: Folktales from Wantok Newspaper.
    Volume 2: Tales from 1986-1997, Indices, Glossary, References, and Maps

"I know of no part of the world, the exploration of which is so flattering to the imagination, so likely to be fruitful in interesting results, whether to the naturalist, the ethnologist, or the geographer, and altogether so well calculated to gratify the enlightened curiosity of an adventurous explorer, as the interior of New Guinea. New Guinea! The very mention of being taken into the interior of New Guinea sounds like being allowed to visit some of the enchanted regions of the 'Arabian Nights,' so dim an atmosphere of obscurity rests at present on the wonders it probably conceals."

(Jukes, 1847: 291)

"'Am I to understand that you [Pandit Gananath Sastri] have translated the works of Molière, Rabelais, and Boccaccio into Sanskrit?' I asked, laughing at the outrageousness of the very idea... 'Who publishes the translations?'... 'No one,' he smiled with pleasure... 'Doesn't it bother you that nobody publishes your work, that nobody reads it?' He laughed again, flowers of laughter, 'What if you write this book on Indian comedy and nobody publishes it? What if somebody publishes it, but nobody reads it? What if somebody reads it, but nobody likes it? What if you knew your book would not be published? Would you write the book anyway? If your answer is 'no,' then you should not write this book. If the answer is 'yes,' then nothing can stop you from writing it. The only things that are important are necessities — eating, sleeping, breathing, defecating, urinating — these things our bodies compel us to do. Writing has to be like that. I have no choice in doing these translations. I have no choice,' he laughed, 'and if you have a choice about your book on humor, then don't write the book.'"

(Siegel, 1987: 90)

# Table of Contents

# Preface

As should be obvious, this book takes its name from Richard F. Burton's renouned translation, *The Book of The Thousand Nights and a Night: A Plain and Literal Translation of the Arabian Nights Entertainments*. Like Burton's magnum opus, this book aims to be a plain and straightforward, if not literal, translation of folktales written by Papua New Guineans in Tok Pisin. Tok Pisin is the pidgin English of Papua New Guinea, and the primary lingua franca of the country.

Burton's book was initially "privately printed by The Burton Club" more than a century ago (1885), not long after New Guinea's interior began to be penetrated by European explorers, most notably by Luigi D'Albertis (1880).

The folktales in this book were originally told orally in Papua New Guinea's hundreds of distinct languages. Without the existence of a lingua franca, or without the widespread literacy of modern Papua New Guinea, a diverse collection of tales such as these could not have been easily collected.

# Acknowledgements

I wish to thank Larry Orsak for supplying many issues of *Wantok* newspaper, and for general inspiration. I wish to thank Kathy Creely of the Melanesian Institute and the University of California at San Diego for facilitating access to the most recent issues of *Wantok*. I thank Joseph Nuwi Somp (Tok Pisin), Karl J. Franklin (Kewa), Wayne Warry (Chuave), Eugene Buckley (Manam), Chris Dal (Waskia and Gedaged), Eva Lindström (Kuot), and Lynus Yamuna (Tok Pisin) for translation assistance. For assistance with village locations, I thank R. M. Bourke (Embi and Kaiap villages), Don Mitchell (Wakupa), Hartmut Holzknecht (Bulesong and Zumanggurun), Duncan Foster (Disige), Ludwig Stuttgen (Urindogum and Nuigo), and Cathrine Paige West (story #294, Gimi People).

I also wish to thank librarians at the University of California (Berkeley, San Diego and Santa Cruz), the University of Papua New Guinea, the Papua New Guinea National Library, Word Publishing (Papua New Guinea), and the Papua New Guinea National Parliament Library.

The final quality of the translation of course rests with myself.

# Introduction

## I. Motivation

This book was motivated by my first two trips to Papua New Guinea (PNG) in 1988-1989 and in 1991. I had studied Tok Pisin beforehand and in PNG I found that I was able to read *Wantok* newspaper with little difficulty. I was intrigued by the idea that folktales (called *Stori Tumbuna* or "Ancestor Stories") were submitted by readers and printed by the newspaper, seemingly in every issue. The idea of collecting these tales into a book and translating them into English grew in my mind, so I began this project in 1993.

One of the motivations for editing the Tok Pisin edition of this book and translating it into this book has been to preserve and present cultural material that is not well preserved and that is not widely available. *Wantok* newspaper exists at relatively few libraries, and there is probably no complete set outside of PNG. Economic conditions in PNG have deteriorated substantially since my first visit in 1988, and institutional funding has declined dramatically. Concomitantly, the ability of PNG's libraries to assure the long-term preservation of material has also declined. Some of the dangers to libraries include tropical climate, vulnerability to natural disasters, irregular and makeshift plumbing and electricity supplies (Ryan, 1995: 158).

Another threat to folktales, a worldwide threat, is that of modernization. As mass media are disseminated to the farthest reaches of the earth, fewer and fewer people have the desire to tell stories as part of daily life. Currently, this is not a widespread problem in PNG, since televisions are still rare outside of the few urban areas. On the other hand, there is widespread knowledge of the world and there is often less interest in tradition among youth than there was a generation ago.

## II. Context

The *Stori Tumbuna* in *Wantok* newspaper have frequently been placed following the religion (Christian) section and preceding the sports section. The fact that the *Stori Tumbuna* column follows the religion section reflects the explicitly Christian orientation of *Wantok* newspaper, which is owned by Word Publishing, a consortium of the main Christian denominations in PNG. Alternatively, one can view the position of the *Stori Tumbuna* column as part of a series of cultural elements: the new religion (Christianity), the old religion (represented by the *Stori Tumbuna*), sports (which has partially supplanted traditional warfare), and two other columns that frequently occur in more recent issues of Wantok: *Laip Lain* (lit., "lifeline") and *Kanage*. *Laip Lain* is akin to the syndicated "Dear Abby" or "Ann Landers" column in English language newspapers. *Laip Lain* parallels the religion, sports and *Stori Tumbuna* columns, each being a method of problem resolution.

*Kanage* is a letters column in which the reader writes an account about a fictional person named "Kanage." "Kanage" is nearly homophonic with *kanaka* whose current Tok Pisin meaning is something like "hick" or "country bumpkin." In PNG, it was originally used by European colonists to refer to native Papua New Guineans; the etymological origin is from the Fijian language, meaning, "man." The Kanage column probably contains two types of stories thinly veiled accounts of actual incidents that are substantially factual and more fictionalized accounts that might be classified as urban legends. The incidents in the stories tend to be about embarrassing or funny situations. They are often told in the third person.  They show the unsophistication of Kanage and hence the relative sophistication of the letter writer.  The topics are sometimes scatological, but the intention is to depict a humorous and/or embarrassing situation.  Recently, this column has become the most popular feature of *Wantok*, and it is often placed on the front page as well as on several other pages.

The *Stori Tumbuna* column has also often appeared with the cross-word puzzle (*skruim tok*), comics, and the television schedule, suggesting that Stori Tumbuna is geared towards youth and young adults.

### III. Classificatory Methodology

This section details the methodology used in this book for creating the indices that follow the folktales.  Villages, languages and provinces that are indexed appear in bold throughout the text to facilitate finding them.  Author's names are also indexed, but these do not appear in bold because they always appear  at the end of each story when they are not anonymous.

### A. Villages

Some areas of PNG are centers of internal migration and hence are not indicative of the source of traditional folklore.  These areas include large towns and resource extraction areas such as Port Moresby, Lae, Rabaul, Kimbe, Ok Tedi, Panguna, Kieta, Arawa, Mt. Hagen, and Goroka (Jackson, 1985).  Smaller, individual institutions, such as high schools, missions and plantations are also centers of local migration.  Some towns are cosmopolitan in that most of their residents have been born elsewhere.  As of the 1980 census, the following towns had 70% or less of their inhabitants born outside of the province: Kundiawa (70%), Vanimo (68%), Bulolo (68%), Goroka, Popondetta (66%), Madang (60%), Lae (59%), Kavieng (57%), Kimbe (46%), Rabaul (44%), Port Moresby/National Capital District (41%), Kieta-Panguna (40%), and Mt. Hagen (36%) (Walsh, 1987).  For these towns, when only the address of the author is known and no origin of the story is stated, neither the town nor the province has been indexed, as it is assumed that there is a reasonable likelihood that the author is a migrant.  For other towns, when no place of origin is stated for the story, only the province is indexed, since intra-province migration to towns other than Port Moresby is common: Aitape (88%), Daru (87%), Kerema (82%), Alotau (81%), Kainantu (79%), Lorengau (75%), Mendi (75%), and Wewak (74%) (Walsh, 1987).  When no town is given in the address and no story origin is stated, the province has usually been indexed, since no province has more than 30% migrants from outside the province (Walsh, 1985).

Village and place names were often subject to short-term change and replacement due to changes in settlement patterns, e.g., among the Tairora People in Eastern Highlands Province (Watson, 1992: 187).  After the imposition of pax-Australiana (the Australian-imposed end to inter-village warfare), movement of entire villages became much rarer due to the general elimination of warfare, hence the renaming process was probably also greatly reduced.

### B. Languages

Rather than index culture group, which is not well standardized in PNG, the name of the local language used in the village from which each story originates is indexed.  The names used in the language index are primarily based on Dutton (1973), Laycock (1973), Wurm (1975), Wurm (1976), Wurm and Hattori (1983), and Z'graggen (1975). Generally, only distinct languages are indexed, not dialects. In some cases, there is ambiguity or linguistic gradation as to what constitutes a distinct language. In these cases, the more specific name was chosen. For example, "Gadsup and Agarabi; Auyana and Usarufa; Asaro and Gahuku; Kamano, Yate and Yagaria; and Kuman, Nagane, Sinasina, Marigl [now Golin] and Salt-Yui are technically dialects of single languages. However, in the existing literature, these communalects are mostly regarded as separate languages." (Wurm, 1983). These dialects are treated as separate groups in the index to this book. Furthermore, there is sometimes a difficulty even in defining linguistic communities in PNG, e.g. the Kewa (LeRoy, 1985b: 28-29).

The count of languages in the index is 273; the actual count of languages in the book may be slightly different because of uncertainty of village location for some stories. This represents 39% of PNG's total language count (about 700, according to Wurm, 1985).

Cultural groups in PNG, as elsewhere, should be regarded neither as static in time, nor as entirely isolated from other groups in PNG, nor as culturally homogenous. For example, some groups in PNG have traditionally made conscious efforts to import cultural elements from neighboring groups (Gewertz and Errington, 1991: 239). The people of the Sepik, in particular, have a strong tendency to borrow cultural elements from their neighbors (Mead, 1970). There is evidence of conflicting ideas of cultural history within the Chambri People (Gewertz and Errington, 1991: 162-163). The Oro Province tribes show great diversity as far as language, social organization, and ideology, even though there are many resemblances and borrowings in material culture, mythology and ritual (Schwimmer, 1984: 269, 287).

### C. Motifs

This motif index is based primarily on Thompson's *Motif-Index of Folk-Literature* (1993), with supplemental motifs from Kirtley (1955, 1971) and Hoffmann (1973). Motif classifications that end in "K" or "K+" refer to Kirtley (1955). Those that end in "K2" or "K2+" refer to Kirtley (1971). Those that end in "H" or "H+" refer to Hoffmann (1973). All others refer to Thompson (1993). Those classifications that end in "+" are new motifs, which are categorized to the closest classification in Thompson (1993), Kirtley (1955, 1971) or Hoffmann (1973).

In PNG, animals are often mono-gendered (e.g., cassowaries, marsupials). By implication, folk tales with transformations between animals and humans may imply such a gender. Consequently, motif classifications have been refined hereto indicate gender (and age): man (M), woman (W), child (C), boy (B), and girl (G) for the transformation motifs (D10-D499). When a story does not specify gender and it is not a child, or when transformation involves both genders, the classification is not specified.

The motifs listed in this book are more liberally defined than is ordinarily practiced, but still within Thompson's (1993) framework. For example, relationships ("P210. Husband and wife", "P231. Mother and son", etc.) are all categorized here, as they are in Thompson (1993). Thompson (1946: 415) defines a motif as "the smallest element in a tale having a power to persist in tradition." It is unclear whether Thompson actually considered these to be motifs, or whether there were merely useful markers for sub-categories that were truly motifs. In practice, such motifs are generally not listed in other indices (e.g., Wilbert & Simoneau, 1992). It was considered useful to list these because it would partially encapsulate the strong genderization of traditional PNG society, and becauseit was not known *a priori* whether this information would be useful for future analyses. An advantage of the intensive indexing used in this book is that the list of motifs following each story can be regarded as a non-sequential synopsis.

A problem with using a motif index that is primarily based on European folklore is that abstract mythological concepts do not necessarily translate well to distant cultures. This was recognized by Kirtley (1955), "One of the chief difficulties and one of the likeliest causes for error in preparing this work [a motif index of Oceanic folklore] has been the necessity of interpreting events in Polynesian narratives into a scheme basically designed to cope with European folklore. For instance, the divisions of supernatural creatures into separate species (demons, trolls, fairies, succubi, *et cetera*), each having its position in the motif-index, is irrelevant when applied to Polynesia, where frequently all categories of the supernatural (ghost, god, demon) are lumped under a term denoting 'spirit.'" However, this difficulty is not restricted to Oceania, since in Eurasia ghosts, devils, demons, vampires, ogres, and djinns are often confused (Thompson, 1946: 42). In PNG, *masalai* can have different meanings depending upon context. *Masalai* can mean: 1) a malevolent spirit associated with a specific location (such as a mountain) or specific natural feature (such as a whirlpool) or 2) an anthropomorph that is often a large and/or ugly cannibal, similar to an ogre. The anthropomorphic type of *masalai* is not always a cannibal, so in these cases a *masalai* is treated as a spirit rather than an ogre for purposes of motif classification. In this book, witches are treated as equivalent to ogresses.

In a few tales there is what appears to be confusion between the term *masalai* and the term *dewel* or ghost (e.g., #721). Fitz-Patrick and Kimbuna (1983: 22) describe <u>*uva poroi*</u>s, or spiritual beings of the Bundi People of Madang Province. <u>*Uva poroi*</u>s are able to manifest themselves as "ghosts, bats, dogs or deformed creatures." Hence for at least this culture in PNG, the ogre-type figure is not necessarily different from a ghost. For purposes of the motif index, both ogre and ghost are indexed when both terms are used in a story.

There is a danger interpreting symbols when the culture is not well known (LeRoy, 1985b: 12). However, because of the lack of substantial information on each culture, it has been necessary to make do with the data at hand.


### IV. Why Mourn the Disappearance of *Masalai*s?

*Masalai*s are of two general types; one type is the ogre-like anthropomorphs, which are typically cannibalistic. The other type is the non-anthropomorphic type of spirit associated with physical features of the environment, often found far from settlements, in forests or hazardous terrain. The *masalai* to the Papua New Guinean is a representation of the fear of the unknown.

The term *masalai* was not widely known in what is today PNG, prior to the spread of Tok Pisin. The term itself originated from New Hanover Island in New Ireland Province (Mihalic, 1971: 131), but similar concepts were widespread in pre-European contact times, as evidenced by the widespread use of the term in currently told folklore. The spirit world as represented in individual cultures is sometimes more complex than is easily representable in Tok Pisin. For example, Valentine (1965: 193) gives a table showing the relationship between *tambaran* and *masalai* as well as non-standard Lakalai (a.k.a. Nakanai in this book) Language terms for spirits. For example, Valentine defines *masalai* as a theriomorph (animal form), whereas elsewhere many *masalai*s are clearly anthropomorphic in the *Wantok* folktales.

*Masalai*s "were normally regarded as erratic, dangerous, and amoral creatures, worthy of fear but not respect. This complex of attitudes may help to explain how people who set great store by the observation of animal behaviour, from a combination of utilitarian and spiritual motives, can sometime exhibit what seems, to Western sensibilities at least, a wanton disregard for the well-being of these same animals, both as species and as individuals. It may also help to explain how villagers who fully understand the relationship between forest fallows and soil fertility are nevertheless prepared to sell their timber rights and permit the desecration of their 'sacred sites' for a relative pittance. Instead of inheriting a state of mystical harmony with their natural environment, landowners may well be accustomed to regard it, at least in certain contexts, as a source or form of evil power, especially if there is now a way to turn it into money and thus 'sacrifice' it to the spirit of 'development.'" (Sekhran & Miller, 1995: 192)

The anthropomorphic type of *masalai* represent, at least in pre-Pax Australiana times, those neighboring peoples with whom one had little or no knowledge, yet who were presumptively hostile. For example, the Tairora people of Eastern Highlands Province were only aware of some of their neighbors before European contact. The Batainabura subgroup of the Tairora considered "the Markham Valley to the east of them to be inhabited by naked, incestuous anthropomorphs who nest[ed] in trees, subsist[ed] entirely on bananas, and [were] probably indifferent to pollution by menstrual blood or other female contaminants." (Watson, 1983: 15–16) Watson did not label these anthropomorphs to be *masalai*s as such, but it is likely that a Tok Pisin speaker would do so. The anthropomorphic type of *masalai* has largely disappeared in the generative sense after the imposition of Pax Australiana. People may still believe in *masalai*s, and people still tell folktales about *masalai*s, but the root cause of their conceptualization is largely missing. Since the imposition of Pax Australiana, people are now intimately aware of their neighbors. Hostility between neighboring groups is still widespread, but inter-group warfare is infrequent compared to pre-contact times. Papua New Guineans are generally appreciative of the relative peace that Australians brought, but Papua New Guineans also appreciate their cultural diversity, at least in an abstract sense. Peace has brought a much higher rate of inter-group marriage. Contact with the wider world has increased the use of Tok Pisin and English, and has hastened the demise of indigenous languages and cultures.

The non-anthropomorphic *masalai*s are typically spirits associated with rivers, rocks, trees, caves, and other parts of the physical environment. These *masalai*s are typically found far from settlements, in forests or in rugged terrain. Village-dwelling Papua New Guineans frequently have ambivalent feelings about uninhabited areas. These are places of danger, where one can fall ill or become ambushed by enemies. These are also places full of bounty, sources of wild game, fruits, nuts, vines for ropes, medicines, and housing materials. Due to the introduction of foreign, unsustainable log extraction, deforestation in PNG has in recent years increased to an degree unprecedented (Barry, 1995) since at least the time of the sweet potato expansion into the Highlands about 400 years ago (Gagné, 1982: 248). As an example, the Wola (a.k.a. Mendi in this book) People of the Southern Highlands Province, who are surrounded by vast stretches of rainforest, have an ambiguous or paradoxical relationship with their environment (Sillitoe, 1993: 221, 230). Their forest is populated by an array of demons, and they generally interpret forest clearing positively since it deprives the demons of homelands. Yet, the Wola would think of the complete destruction of their forests as "horrendous" (Sillitoe, 1993: 230), at least in part because it would represent the elimination of a whole set of resources on which they depend and of which they are intimately aware (e.g., see Diamond, 1993).

## V. Translation Issues

Translation requires subjective interpretation, and this subjectivity means that the interpreter will convey a different idea than the original author had in mind. With this in mind, I have attempted to be as fastidious as possible in translating and disambiguating the Tok Pisin texts, while still maintaining readability for the casual reader. Nonetheless, it is important to bear in mind that these folktales are two translations away from the original tales, in all but a few cases. The vast majority of these tales were originally told in one of the local languages in the Language Index. A few of these tales may have been told in Tok Pisin, such as the modern stories listed in the Table of Folktales.

While it is possible to convey complex ideas in Tok Pisin, it can often be more laborious than in a non-pidgin language. One should therefore assume that nuance was lost in the translation from the original language to the Tok Pisin as published in *Wantok* newspaper because of the original author's desire for expediency. This book would have been nearly impossible to translate into English if the basal texts were in the original languages. This is because few non-Papua New Guineans are fluent in the many and complex Papua New Guinean languages, and because it would be a difficult task to contact a Papua New Guinean speaker of each of the hundreds of languages represented in this book. To get an idea of the high degree of grammatical complexity of some Papua New Guinean languages (the non-Austronesian ones), the interested reader might consult Foley (1991), which also includes three Yimas (East Sepik Province) folktales in simultaneous translation to English (Foley, 1991: 457-486).

When a word is italicized in the text, it indicates that it is either the scientific name of a plant or animal (e.g., *Spilocuscus maculatus maculatus*) or it is a Tok Pisin word that does not have a simple translation (e.g., *masalai*). In the case of the latter, definitions can be found in the Glossary. When a word is both italicized and underlined, it indicates that it is a word from a local language (e.g., *malga*).

## Crying for Nothing

(Wantok 48, July 19, 1972, page 4)

Long ago, there was a bad man. His name was Nothing. He never gave anything to the needy. If anyone ever asked him for something, he would get angry with him or her.

Sometime later, Nothing died and his wife was very troubled. This was because Nothing was good to his wife. His wife cried and saw that there was no other man or woman who cried for her husband. She went to get all of the yams from her house and cook them.

When the yams were done, she stood up and put all of them in a basket and carried them out to give to each child that she met who was playing. She told each of them to cry for her husband, Nothing.

So if you see a boy crying and you ask him, "Why are you crying?" The boy will tell you, "I'm crying for nothing."

[Anonymous]

A1319+. Origin of tears; P210. Husband and wife; W151. Greed

## Where Did Pots Come From?

(Wantok 49, August 2, 1972, page 4)

Long ago, there was no place where people cooked with pots. This was because no one knew how to make a pot. Also at this time in an area of **Madang** Province, there was a young man. His name was Bunag. This young man knew how to make many things, he also knew about many things.

One evening, Bunag got all his fishing gear and went to the beach. The sky was perfectly clear and he could see the stars as they came up. He soon thought of the stories that his grandmother had told him. She had told Bunag about the story of the stars, the moon and the sun when Bunag was still a boy. She had said that the stars were beautiful women who lived in the clouds. So now Bunag forgot about catching fish, and he lay down in his canoe and forgot about his cares. He thought and thought about the star women, then he closed his eyes and fell into a deep sleep.

He slept and dreamt that he saw a small bird that came to him and said, "Oh Bunag, the stars that you see here, they are actually women. If you truly desire one, you should do as I tell you. You should look for when the clouds are clear, then make a big fire. Wait and you will see one of these women come down. After you marry her, you must take care of her well."

Bunag heard this and was surprised. One day he saw that the sky was perfectly clear and he tried to do as the bird had told him. He made a big fire and waited. The smoke from this fire went directly up into the clouds. It was not long when he saw a ladder come down from a cloud into the smoke from the fire. Later he saw a woman begin to descend this ladder.

The woman's face was very pretty and Bunag was immediately attracted to her. Bunag brought her to his house. Later, Bunag gave her the name _Fonpain_, meaning "Star." The two of them married and had a boy.

At this time, Fonpain saw that they did not have a pot for cooking food. So she asked Bunag, "Why is there no pot for cooking?" But Bunag replied, "What is a pot?" He did not know about such things. So now, Fonpain took some earth and showed all of the women of the area how to make pottery. Now many people cook their food using pots, and the food is quite tasty. Many more people now know how to make pots.

[Anonymous]

A762.2 Mortal marries star-girl; A1451. Origin of pottery; B211.3. Speaking bird; B450. Helpful birds; D439.5.2W. Transformation: star to woman; D1810.8.2. Information received through dream; F52.2. Columns of smoke as ladder to upper world; P210. Husband and wife; P231. Mother and son; P233. Father and son; T111.2. Woman from sky-world marries mortal man

## Where Did Women Come From?

(Wantok 50, August 16, 1972, page 11)

Once there were no women in this land. They lived in the clouds and only men lived on the earth. Men did all of the chores of house and garden.

One day after the men finished looking for game in the forest, the women came down to the ground. They picked the yams and taros from the men's garden and cooked them. After they finished preparing the food, they immediately returned to the clouds.

When the men came back to their village, they were starving. They saw that the food was already cooked and they were surprised. They said, "Who cooked this food?"

This happened many times. One day, they hid one of the smaller men so that that he could find out who was responsible for cooking their food all of the time.

The little man hid and saw the women come down a rattan rope, gather up food, and cook it. When the women saw the men returning, they climbed the rope to return home.

The little man told about everything that he had seen to all of the men when they returned. So one day all of the men pretended to go to the forest, but instead they hid nearby and watched.

It was not much later when they saw the women descend the rope again. They waited for all of the women to finish their descent, and then they quickly cut the rope so that the women could not return. Right away each man grabbed a woman, went back to their houses and married her.

So now, these women help the men with housework and by cooking food for their husbands.

[Anonymous]

A1231+. First women descend from sky; A1455+. Why women cook; A1472. Beginning of division of labor; F51. Sky-rope; P210. Husband and wife; T111.2. Woman from sky-world marries mortal man

## The Children Who Turned into Stones
(Wantok 51, September 6, 1972, pages 4, 6)

Deep in the forest, there was a fruiting tree, and a huge eel that often ate this fruit. In the evening, the eel would come out of its hiding place to find something to eat.

One evening, a man was looking for some food, and he found this tree with fruit upon it. He saw that the base of the tree was cleared and that bandicoots had been eating the fallen fruits. So he waited for the bandicoots to come, but he was surprised when he saw a huge eel tossing about the leaves on the ground and eating the fallen fruit.

The man was scared out of his wits, so he did not make any noise that would stop the eel from eating the fruits and return to where it had come from. He wanted to see where this eel came from. When he saw the eel's hiding place, he returned home and told everyone in his village what he had seen. Another day, all of the men, women and children came to chase this big eel. They brought bows, arrows and many other things with which to kill the eel. They arrived at the eel's home in the river, then they gathered stones and leaves to dam up the river. When the dam filled up, they began to look for the eel.

They turned over many stones so that they could finally turn over the biggest boulder under which the huge eel had been hiding. They all stood around this boulder and some of the men lifted it up. When the eel ran out, all of the men, women and children called out and threw spears and arrows at eel's body, killing it. All of the men, women and children shouted with joy.

Later they wanted to carry the eel back home, but the eel was too big and heavy. So, they stayed there that night and cooked the eel in the forest. They heated stones in the fire, some men and women went to get some vegetables to cook with the eel, and the children with the elders stayed to watch the eel in the fire.

They sat around the fire and told some stories. Suddenly they heard a noise come from the fire. The eel arose and spoke to them, "You people called me an eel and you tried to kill me. Tomorrow night at this time you will see me traveling in the clouds." After the eel said this, it disappeared.

When the men and women returned from getting vegetables, they saw that the eel had disappeared. The old women told about the trouble that had come up, but the men did not believe them. They thought that the elders and children had cooked the eel and eaten all of it. The men were enraged, so they cooked a small eel with vegetables and ate it without sharing any with the elders and children.

The next day, the old women and children had nothing. There was no food for them, and they were very worried. At night the old women with the children went and stood on top of a boulder that was near a spring. They wanted to knock the boulder downstream. But immediately, they saw the moon for the first time amidst the clouds. They began to cry and sing and dance, and leapt down into the water.

The men and women from the village tried to stop them but it was too late. At the place where the old women and children jumped into the water, today you can still see where they had turned into boulders. The men and women of the village were very troubled by this, and they returned to their village.

Whenever they see the moon amidst the clouds, they always remember the huge eel and the old women and children who became stones.

Guksaluk Atolik
Madang Town
Madang Province

B211.5.2K. Speaking eel; B874.2. Giant eel; D231W. Transformation: woman to stone; D230C. Transformation: child to stone; D426.1+. Transformation: eel to moon; D562.1. Transformation by application of water; D2095. Magic disappearance; E168. Cooked animal comes to life

## How the Snake Lost Its Hair

(Wantok 52, September 20, 1972, pages 7, 10)

A long, long time ago, Marsupial (*Kapul*) and Snake lived happily together. The two of them were never angry, they were just good friends. The two of them often worked and played together.

One day, the king of the animals called for a big meeting of all of the animals so that they could hear his speech.

Snake said to Marsupial, "Friend, I think that we should dress up and go to hear our king's speech. We should cut our hair so that we will look handsome."

Marsupial replied, "Friend, cut my hair first, then I shall cut your hair."

But Snake demanded that Marsupial cut his hair first. So, Marsupial went to get a scissors and razor, then began to cut Snake's hair. Marsupial did not cut Snake's hair well. He did not leave a single hair, he had cut them all.

When he finished cutting, he said, "Friend, be careful. Don't go too close to women, otherwise you will give them a scare."

When Snake saw himself in the mirror, he knew that his friend had completely screwed up his hair. He was enraged, but he did not say anything to his friend Marsupial. When Marsupial asked him, "What's up friend, do you see yourself in the mirror?" Snake replied, "Yes, friend, you cut my hair very nicely."

Now it was Snake's time to cut Marsupial's hair. Snake said to him, "Friend, you have screwed up my hair, now I'm going to cut your hair just like mine."

Snake now got the scissors and razor and began to cut Marsupial's hair. He began first with the tail, then came to the middle of the tail when suddenly the conch trumpet was blown to signal that all of the animals should come to the meeting. So Snake said, "Friend, I haven't finished your hair yet. Now what? Should we go to the meeting, then after the meeting should I finish cutting your hair?"

When they came to the meeting, all of the animals had a good laugh at Snake who was completely bald and at Marsupial's bald tail. So today, you can see that Marsupial and Snake are both ashamed. When a marsupial sees a snake, it will go into hiding. And when a snake sees a marsupial, it will slither away.

Once, snakes had hair, but no longer. So too, marsupials had hair on their tails, but now their tails are hairless.

Stephen Gai

A2317+. Why snake is bald; A2317.12. Why opossum has bare tail; B211.2.12K+. Speaking marsupial; B211.6.1. Speaking snake (serpent); B240. King of animals; P310. Friendship

## The Moon in the River

(Wantok 53, October 4, 1972, page 6)

Once upon a time there was an old woman who went to fetch some water. When she was lifting her pot of water, she saw the moon lying in the water.

Immediately she picked up the moon, covered it in her loincloth and brought it back home. That night, the people did not have any light, they were completely in the dark. They did not know what had made the moon disappear.

So now, everyone was only able to work in the gardens during daylight. But the old woman slept during the day and worked in her garden only at night.

One day, the people saw that the woman's garden was weeded. They did not know why the woman just slept or who it was that worked her garden.

So, some of them hid at night at the old woman's garden. It was not long when they saw the old woman come to her garden. They watched and they saw the old woman take the moon out of her loincloth and light up the area. Then she put the moon on top of a tree buttress and she began to work at her garden.

All of the men saw this and were enraged. They got up and took the moon and threw it back up into the clouds where it stuck.

So now, if you see that part of the moon is dark, this is part of the old woman's loincloth that is covering it up. When you do not see the moon at all, this is when the old woman is still hiding the moon in her house.

[Anonymous]

A741+. Moon thrown into sky by person; A755.9K+. Causes of moon's phases: hidden by woman's loincloth; A758. Theft of moon

## Praying to the Sun

(Wantok 54, October 18, 1972, page 10)

Once upon a time, there was a man who lived in **Moge Nambaga** [**Hagen** People]. His name was Mit Kungil. This man was a good fighter and was very strong. There was no one who was capable of beating him.

One day, the people of Moge Nambaga were fighting their enemies. An arrow was shot up high and landed directly in Mit Kungil's forehead. He landed on the ground and lay there, blood came flowing across his face. Just before he was about to die, he told his kinsmen that he would not be able to leave them, but that his spirit would rise to where the sun is. He said, "You should think of me and ask me to help you whenever you are fighting." They buried Mit Kungil's body and made a big feast, they sang and danced in honor of his name.

Soon afterwards, their enemies came to fight again with the men of Nambaga. They fought, but not a single man thought of Mit Kungil and what he had said to them when he had died. So, ten of their men died in the fight. They continued to fight through the night until sunrise. When the sun rose, they spoke of Mit Kungil. They stood up and prayed to his spirit, they asked him to forgive them, and they asked for his help.

On another day, they prayed again and went to fight. The sun became intensely bright and hurt the eyes of their enemies, so the Nambaga People killed many of them.

So, now at this time, the people of this area frequently pray to the spirit of the sun, Mit Kungil, who helps them with all of their problems.

Anis Koma
**Western Highlands** Province

A711. Sun as man who left earth; F610. Remarkably strong man; S110. Murders; V52.3. Prayer before battle brings victory; V61.3+. Dead buried

## Where Did Languages Originate?
(Wantok 55, November 1, 1972, page 5)

Long ago, in the **Trobriand** Islands [**Milne Bay** Province, **Kilivila** People], there was only one kind of people and they spoke only one language.

One day, the men of one clan met together and decided to build a tower so tall that it would reach the clouds. They went to the forest and collected many kinds of trees and vines, then began to build this tower. They worked and worked until they came up to a cloud and then some of them climbed upon this cloud.

When they climbed upon this cloud, the tower broke and fell down. The men were stuck on the cloud; they were tied together with the vines that they had used to build the tower. They tried to remove the vines but when they did this they twisted about.

So now if you or I hear thunder, we are hearing these men inside the cloud trying to get rid of the vines entangled around their legs.

The other clans of the island fell down with the tower to the ground. When they fell, they came down on all of the other small islands near their original island. These men started new villages at all of the places that they landed. So now there are many other kinds of languages near this island.

Gibson Henry

A1142.3. Persons escape to sky and become thunder; A1333. Confusion of tongues; A1620. Distribution of tribes; F58. Tower (column) to upper world; F772.1. Tower of Babel: remarkably tall tower designed to reach sky; F941.3. Tower sinks into earth

## The Morning Star
(Wantok 56, November 15, 1972, page 14)

Long ago there was a family who lived on an island near the Finschhafen Peninsula [**Morobe** Province]. Their name was _Nola Nola_, meaning "The Men of Yore." In this family there were ten boys.

These boys always got angry whenever they came together. The youngest was always beaten up badly. So one day, he thought that he would run away from them and go to another place.

One day, he went with his father into the forest. The two of them went and arrived at a place with a betel nut palm tree. This boy left his father and climbed to the top of this tree.

When he went up, the tree began to grow up and up, toward the clouds. He was very high now. A strong wind arose that shook and shook the tree, throwing him out into the clouds.

The boy's father stood on the ground and saw his boy go and go. After a short time he saw a small fire become lit. He cried and went back to the village where he told his wife and his other children.

All of the children heard this story and they remembered all of the things that they used to do their youngest brother, so they were now very troubled. They began to cry, then went to the place of this betel nut palm tree. They too climbed this tree.

The tree began to grow and grow, going up to the clouds, just like before. When they reached the top, a strong wind arose, just like before and shook the tree. They were also thrown by the wind into the clouds, just like their young brother.

So now we can see the nine stars strongly lit up in the night and one that is very bright. We can see this as the morning star, and in the morning we can see water on the grass and on the leaves of the trees. These are fallen tears of the nine brothers from the night when they began to cry when they saw that their brother was lost.

Wanerao Bafafe
Morobe Province

A770. Origin of particular stars; A781.1. Origin of morning star; A1132. Origin of dew; D293B. Transformation: boy to star; F54.1. Tree stretches to sky; F963. Extraordinary behavior of wind; F1021. Extraordinary flights through air; P210. Husband and wife; P231. Mother and son; P233. Father and son; P251.5.3. Hostile brothers; P251.6.5+. Ten brothers; R213. Escape from home

## Where Did Coconuts Come From?

(Wantok 57, December 6, 1972, pages 6-7)

This is a story about the first time that coconuts came to eastern Papua. Long ago, in a village on the sea, there was a small woman who lived with her father and mother.

One day, this little woman went to the garden and picked some yams. She brought the yams home, then her mother told her to fetch some water.

Now the well was very far away. So when the little woman went to get the water, her mother cooked all her yams and ate all of them with her father.

When she returned, they told her that her maternal relative was hungry and they had given all of the yams to that person. They also said that this maternal relative had already left. The two parents said this sort of thing all of the time, they were always lying to their daughter.

One day, the little woman was very troubled and began to cry so hard that she could no longer listen to her parents. So, the parents left her and went to the garden. After they left, she began to gather all her belongings and put them in a net bag. Then she ran away to the beach and climbed a tree.

She stayed on top of the tree and threw something down into the sea. Immediately, some big fish came along and tore apart the thing that she had thrown into the sea. So later, she herself came down from the tree and went into the sea where the fish tore her apart too. [In the original version, these are crocodiles, not fish.]

When her parents came back from the garden, they tried to find her, they looked and looked but they did not see her anywhere. They thought that she had killed herself because they had mistreated her.

So one day, the little woman's mother went out from the village to catch some fish in the sea. Before long, she saw something approaching her. She picked it up and was shocked to see her daughter's head. She brought it to her husband and showed it to him. The parents waited awhile then carried the head outside and buried it.

Another day, they woke up and when outside, the parents saw a new kind of tree growing. Later, they saw that this tree had a fruit.

They picked the fruit from this tree and removed its skin. They saw that it was hard beneath the skin, but they broke it anyway and saw that there was blood inside. So, the parents put ashes on the fruit and buried it.

A little later, they saw yet another tree growing. This time when they broke open the fruit, they did not see blood and they tried to drink the liquid.

They found that it was delicious. So as we now know, these were the first people to eat the fruit that we call coconut.

Roselin Nebita
Holy Name High School
Dogura
**Milne Bay** Province

[A different version of this story was published in English in *Creation Legends from New Guinea* (Madang: Kristen Pres, 1972).]

A1423.3. Origin of coconut; A2611.3.1K. Coconut tree from head of human; E631. Reincarnation in plant (tree) growing from grave; M451.1. Death by suicide; P210. Husband and wife; P232. Mother and daughter; P234. Father and daughter; P290+. Maternal kin; R213. Escape from home; S11. Cruel father; S12. Cruel mother; V61.3+. Dead buried; W151. Greed

## Where Did Sugar Come From?

(Wantok 58, December 20, 1972, page 7)

Long ago, there lived a leader in a village. This leader had a very beautiful daughter. Many, many men worked for this leader as laborers. One of them saw the ruler's daughter and he fell in love. This woman also liked him but the leader found out. He was upset at this and wanted to kill his laborer.

In this village there was a snake with three heads that looked truly evil. This snake often killed young women and ate them.

One day, the snake spoke. It wanted the leader to give his daughter up for the snake to eat. It said that if the leader did not listen, the snake would destroy the village and everything else.

This leader did not want to give up his daughter to die. So he stood up and spoke to the laborer who loved his daughter. He said, "If you can kill this snake then I will let you marry my daughter."

So the laborer dressed like a woman and then went to the place where the snake lived. When the snake came out, he thought that he was a young woman and he wanted to eat him. Each person from the village was hiding and waiting to see what would happen, they were afraid and cried for the young man.

But the young laborer was not afraid. He quickly held one of the snake's heads and cut it right off with a knife. He also did this with the other two heads and killed the snake. Everyone who was hiding came and saw this and was happy that the evil woman-eating snake had died.

They carried the body of the snake to their village. They made a feast and danced and sang. The young laborer carried some of the snake's body back to show to the leader, his girlfriend's father. The leader followed through on his promise and gave his daughter to this youth.

The two of them married. Some days later, the two of them went to a garden and buried all of the pieces of the snake at various spots.

A while later, they saw a new kind of thing growing in the places where they had buried the heads of the snake. Tree-like plants were growing that looked like snake bodies. They cut these and tried eating them and they were deliciously sweet. So they called this "sugar" because it is sweet.

Mr. Nao Bazan
Asaroka High School
Goroka
Eastern Highlands Province

[A different version of this story was published in English in *Creation Legends from New Guinea* (Madang: Kristen Pres, 1972).]

A2684.4K. Origin of sugar cane; B15.1.2.2.2. Three-headed serpent; B16.5.1. Giant devastating serpent; B211.6.1. Speaking snake (serpent); B604.1. Marriage to snake; H335.3.4+. Suitor task: kill man-eating snake; G510.4. Hero overcomes devastating animal; K910. Murder by strategy; L113.1. Menial hero; P210. Husband and wife; Q53. Reward for rescue; S118.2. Murder by cutting throat; T10. Falling in love; T100. Marriage

## Where Did Salt Come From?

(Wantok 59, January 3, 1973, page 21)

Once there were two men who were maternal relatives, named Usinn and Gusuu. One day they went to the forest with their dogs. They collected some delicious edible greens and some leaves from the *tulip* tree. So Usinn said to Gusuu, "Let's take these tasty greens and get some salt so that we can cook them."

They talked and then went to the Arabag River. They followed the Arabag River and went to a place where there was boiling saltwater. Their dogs saw this first and barked.

The men thought that the dogs were barking because they saw a pig, so Usinn and Gusuu went to see the boiling water.

Usinn put a finger into the brine and then to his mouth. It was really salt. Usinn said to Gusuu, "Hey Gusuu, try this water, it's really salt." Gusuu tried it and it was good, so they cleared the water, cut a piece of bamboo and filled the bamboo with the water. They cooked the *tulip* leaves and then threw out the saltwater, they were very happy. They called it their saltwater and they were happy.

Mr. D. H. Belles
Begessin [**Bagasin** Village, **Girawa** People]
**Madang** Province

A942.2. Origin of salt springs; P290+. Maternal kin

## The Raven and the Well

(Wantok 60, January 17, 1973, page 6)

Ali is the name of an island, on this island there is a small village named **Malung** [**Ali** People, **West Sepik** Province]. This village once did not have a permanent water supply for cooking food. The ancestors were only able to get water from rain. When it did not rain, they had no water.

One time, there was an old man from Malung Village who went walking along the beach. He saw a black bird. It was a raven. The man went down to a place and hid while looking at this raven. This raven was making a small well. When the man saw this he walked closer to the well. Then the raven saw the old man and flew to the top of a tall tree, called *tau*. From the top of the tree, the raven looked at the man walking straight to the well.

The old man saw that there was still a stone in this well, which he tried to remove. The man removed the stone and when he saw the water inside it, he was ecstatic.

When the old man returned home, he did not tell the other people about this well. Each time he went to his garden or to any other place, he shut his house tightly. He did not like other people going inside his house.

So one time, some of the old men and women saw him shutting up his house to leave. He was going to get some water from the well again. One of the old men went to hide and saw him going straight to this well. After he finished getting water from the well, he hid the well with tree leaves. The old man who was hiding saw this and returned home where he told the other old people of the village.

So after they were told about the well, they all went to see it and they drank from it. The water was sweeter than the rainwater that they had been drinking.

When the old man returned, he was incensed at them because they had taken his water. But they told him that the water belonged to everyone.

This well still exists in Malung Village on Ali Island.

Mr. B. A. Mongalil
Ali Island
Aitape
West Sepik Province

A941.0.1+. Origin of particular well; W151. Greed

## The Men Who Were Reborn

(Wantok 61, February 7, 1973, page 6)

This is a short story about the ancestors. In the deep forest there were many young men who lived on top of a mountain. At the base of this mountain there was a house that belonged to a cannibal.

The young men who lived on top of the mountain threw some boulders down the mountain and destroyed the house that belonged to the huge cannibal. They did this not once, but often.

One time, the cannibal became completely enraged, so he began to search on top of the mountain for these young men. He saw the first brother and killed him, then carried him down to his house. He cooked and ate him, then he collected the bones that remained and hung them up inside his house.

The remaining brothers were not afraid of what had happened to their brother. So, again they threw some boulders down the mountain. After this, the huge cannibal came back and finished off all of the young men but one.

So then the last brother cried and cried and then he went down to the huge man's house. He hid himself well and then saw the man go into his garden.

So then the remaining brother went inside the house and saw the bones of his brothers together in one part of the house. He gathered them all up and put them into his net bag.

He then set fire to the giant's house and set off for another place. He came upon a nice pond where he took the bones of his brothers and put them into the pond.

He left the pond for a month and then returned to look for the bones. The bones had decayed and become frogs in the pond. Another month passed and he returned to the pond to see that the frogs now had the faces of men. He was happy to see this and fed the frogs with some food.

Later after another month had passed, the frogs had become small men. The brother wanted to take them with him, but they said to him, "No, we are not fully grown yet."

Yet another month passed, and the brother returned to the lake to look for them. Now he was able to take them with him back home where they lived happily and became young men again. They lived there and when their bodies became strong, they wanted to kill the huge man. They looked for him, then killed him and lived happily after that.

Tinam Sorewe

D395M. Transformation: frog to man; E234.3. Return from dead to avenge death (murder); E615.1. Reincarnation as frog; F531. Giant; F535. Pygmy; F562.7K. People live in mountain top; G11.2. Cannibal giant; P251.6. Several brothers; Q211. Murder punished; Q270. Misdeeds concerning property punished; Q411. Death as punishment; R155+. Brother recovers brother's bones; S110. Murders; S139.2.2. Other indignities to corpse; Z356. Unique survivor

## Where Did Coconuts Come From?

(Wantok 62, February 21, 1973, page 4)

Long ago there was a village near the beach. The people worked in their gardens, and they caught seafood from the sea. The men were the ones who went out to sea. Every day in the early morning, they went down to the sea to catch fish. One day, they brought their fishing lines and hooks and went to sea. The men worked hard to hook some fish, but they did not catch many. They only caught one.

However, one man brought many fish back to the village every day. This man had ringworm, so he did not walk with the other men or work with them at fishing. No, every day in the early morning, he would wake up and go to the beach to find fish. He did not carry a fishing line or hook. He did not carry a bow or a multi-pronged fishing arrow. The other men did not see him at work, but they thought a lot about him. They thought, "What does this ringworm man do to catch so many fish, while we catch so few? He is truly a fishing expert."

So, the village councilors met. While they met, one boy was listening to them. Right away he had a thought, he stood before the council and spoke, "I have a thought. Tomorrow before dawn, I will get up and follow this man. I can recognize him, but he won't be able to see me. After I see what he does, I will tell you how he catches so many fish."

The council listened to this and told the boy that it was a good idea. So, the boy woke up before dawn and waited near the house of the ringworm man. The ringworm man left his house and walked along the forest trail that led to the beach. The boy followed him, but he did not make the slightest noise. The boy watched everything that this man did.

He laid his net bag on the sand. He stood and held his head with his two hands. He pulled up hard on his head. His head loosened and came off into his hands.

The man laid his head near his net bag on the sand and he walked to the sea. He went into the sea until the water almost covered up his body. Then, the man shoved his neck under water. Immediately, many, many fish swam into the neck of this ringworm man.

After the man was filled with fish, he slowly walked back to the beach. He shook his body and vomited the fish onto the sand. After vomiting the fish, he took his head from the sand and put it back on top of his neck.

The boy did not wait any longer. He saw what the ringworm man had done and he ran back down the forest trail, arriving back at the village.

In the evening, the council brought the boy to the men's house to hear his story. They said to him, "OK, what did the ringworm man do?" The boy explained to them what he had seen the man do that morning. The councilors were surprised and said, "This man did wrong. We must get revenge against him."

So before dawn, the councilors followed the ringworm man down his forest trail. They waited and watched him. The man stood up on the sand and removed his head. He laid it on the sand and he went into the sea.

Quickly, one of the men ran and grabbed the ringworm man's head. He threw it into the forest.

Later, the ringworm man returned to the beach, shook himself and vomited all of the fish onto the beach. He wanted to put his head on again but he could not find it. He walked around on his hands and knees, but he could not find his head. So he stood up again and quickly ran back into the sea where he changed into a fish. He swam and swam, and his ringworm became fish scales.

After some days passed, the boy went to the beach where the men always went. The boy often thought about the man's head. He thought, "We didn't bury that man's head. That was a mistake."

He wanted to find the head and bury it. But at the place where the head was thrown, a new kind of tree was growing. The fruits of this tree were as large as the head of the man. The boy took a knife and cut off the skin of the

fruit. He found the man's face. He broke open the fruit some more and he found good liquid and good food inside.

So that is how coconuts came to us. When you remove the sin of the coconut with a knife, you can find that man's face.

[Anonymous]

[This story comes from the book, *Kisim Save Moa, Buk 2* (Madang: Literacy Literature New Guinea & Christian Missions in Many Lands, 1970).]

A2611.3.1K. Coconut tree from head of human; D170M. Transformation: man to fish; D2150+. Catching fish by removing one's head and letting fish enter body; F511.0.4+. Person with removable head; R260. Pursuits

## The Stars' Tears
(Wantok 63, March 7, 1973, page 4)

Many mornings we see small drops of water on tree leaves, on stones, and on grass. The ancestors say, "The dew on the tree leaves, stones and grass has an origin story."

The ancestors' story goes as follows: Long ago, before we existed, Star hung in the sky and spoke with Sand. The two had a contest.

Sand was stubborn. Sand spoke to Star, "You came from a stubborn group. You and I still must count how many of us there are. Who has more, sand or stars? Who will win?"

Star heard this and replied, "Good, you and I should count each of our numbers."

So, then Star and Sand began to count each of their numbers. Sand was stubborn and said, "Star, I want to count how many of you there are. After that you can count how many of me there are."

So Star heard this and waited. Sand counted how many stars there are in the sky. Then Sand spoke, "OK, you counted how many of me there are. Now I shall begin to count how many of you there are."

Star spoke and Sand lay down. Sand was stubborn and fell deep asleep. Star counted and counted the grains of sand. But Sand was too numerous for Star to count. Star was able to count the grains of sand on the surface, but could not count the grains of sand below the surface. So Sand won the contest, and Star was ashamed. Star was truly embarrassed. Tears welled up from Star's eyes and fell.

So in the morning we often see the stars' tears on grass, on stones, and on tree leaves.

[Anonymous]

[This story comes from the book, *Kisim Save Moa, Buk 2* [Madang: Literacy Literature New Guinea & Christian Missions in Many Lands, n.d.].

A1132. Origin of dew; H1144.5K+. Task: counting the grains of sand; H1144.7K. Task: counting the stars; W167. Stubbornness

## Thunder

(Wantok 64, March 21, 1973, page 4)

Once there was a short and strong man. He thought about going into the forest to find some wild game. He went to many places in the forest and became tired and hungry. He sat and rested, then ate some sweet potatoes that he had brought along.

Suddenly, a man with long hair appeared and wanted to kill him. The two of them fought fiercely. The short, strong man fought the longhaired man and the longhaired man said, "Stop! Enough! My brother! Come with me!"

So the two of them climbed a steep mountain. On the top of the mountain was a small, attractive house. This house was unusual and it belonged to the longhaired man. Surrounding the house was a small and well-maintained garden.

Later, this man of the forest said, "Today, you didn't catch any game because I did not desire it." And he said, "Bow your head down when I go outside." So the short man did this.

The man of the forest went outside and said an incantation, and then he told the other man to look above. The short man looked above and he saw many kinds of wild game.

The man of the forest gave the short man a charmed bow, a pig and some other kinds of things. Then he told him, "Now you can go home. But don't let your brothers see your bow. You should shoot this bow when you are fighting other men. Kill this pig and cook the heart to make a good aroma for me. But don't eat this pig's heart."

He gave a kind of leaf to him and said, "You should plant this leaf at the door of your new house."

The short man returned home and before long he got in a big fight. He fought and killed many, many men. At the point when he almost killed all of the other men, those that remained sized up their situation. They thought, "Where did this man get his bow from?"

One day, the short man's little brother stole and hid his bow. Later when he went to retrieve his bow, he saw that it was not there. He was enraged because he knew that only his little brother could have stolen it. Later he fought with his little brother, and his little brother ran away to another place.

At dawn the next day, the short man killed the pig that the man of the forest had given him. He cut out its heart and took it to the house of the ancestor's spirits. When he cooked this heart to give an offering to the man of the forest, he saw a small bird fly into the spirit house and perch inside. It was the man of the forest who was really the soul of his father who had died before.

When the two brothers had fought, there was a big explosion. So when we hear thunder, we know that it is the two brothers fighting again.

Sakaip

[The Ancestor Story in *Wantok* #118 is the same as this one, but is authored by Kurun J. Abegul of Madang.]

A1142. Origin of thunder; D1091. Magic bow; D1441.1.4. Magic song calls animals together; E613. Reincarnation as bird; P233. Father and son; P251.6.1. Three brothers; Q212. Theft punished; Q431. Punishment: banishment (exile); R213. Escape from home; S110. Murders; V112.1. Spirit huts

## Where Did Pigs Come From?

(Wantok 65, April 4, 1973, page 4)

Long, long ago, the first pig came to our district. The ancestors said that there were three men who were good friends and who lived together. They always slept together in the same house and shared their food with each other.

But every night a horrendous stink would waft through their house. They did not get angry about this because they were truly good friends. One man worked in the garden every day, and the stink came to him every day, and he brought it home with him every day. The second man fished every day, and the third man hunted in the forest for wild game every day. Each of them had their own job to do each day. That is how they cooperated.

One time, the gardener, the fisherman and the hunter sat together and talked about the gardener. The fisherman and the hunter wanted to find out from their friend where the stink came from.

One day, the gardener was at work just before dawn, one of the two others had followed him into the garden. The gardener did not know that there was someone watching him. When he went into his garden, he quickly removed his clothes and immediately turned into a huge insect and began digging the earth. When his friend saw this, he was terrified. But he shut his mouth and did not make a single sound from his hiding place in the forest. When the huge insect went into a hole in the ground, the man who was hiding ran into the open, took the clothes that were lying there and put them elsewhere. After the insect finished working, he looked and looked for the clothes but could not find them. He ate something then told his two friends that they should build a long house for him. They agreed to this. Later they began to work on this house for the insect. They finished the house at dusk. The insect brought something inside the new house. He told them to look for him in the morning. But the next morning, they heard a strange, new kind of noise coming from this house. When they went inside the house, they saw many baby pigs lying on the ground. But the two of them did not find their friend. They looked on the ground and they saw only his bones, the two of them had no idea what had happened to him.

Now, if you come to this district where I live in the Highlands, you will see that we take care of our pigs well and that the pigs are treated as if they are our own children.

Maris Waine

A1871. Creation of hog (pig); B211.4. Speaking insects; B873. Giant insects; D180M. Transformation: man to insect; P310. Friendship; R260. Pursuits

## Where Did Night Come From?
(Wantok 66, April 18, 1973, page 13)

Long ago, in the time of the ancestors, there was only daytime. The ancestors said that there was never night time. They never slept at night. No, they only sat under the big sun. They would go to get food in the forest and return to the village, they ate the food, and then went to get more food in the forest again, just like now.

One man went and cut a sago palm tree, he scraped and processed it with his wife. His wife rinsed the sago. The husband told his wife, "Rinse the sago."

Meanwhile, the husband went to find some marsupials (*kapul*) that often slept in caves. He went to find them, he looked and looked, but could not find a single marsupial.

So, he went to collect some water from the spur of a *ton* tree. Then the man wondered, "Is that water used by birds, do they come to bathe there?"

However, it was not a birdbath. No, it was the water where the sun came to bathe. Then this ancestor, who thought that it was just a birdbath, built a bird blind nearby then he returned home. At home he got his bow and arrows and returned to the bird blind where he hid and kept watch.

He watched and watched, then he thought, "If the birds come and bathe in this water, I will shoot them." Instead, he saw the sun arrive as if it were a real man while he was watching the water.

The man saw the sun bathe in this water, and the man trembled at the sun. After the sun finished bathing, he returned home. Later when the sun wanted to bathe, the man was sitting in the blind and watching.

The sun came down to bathe in the water, and the man stood and shot him. The sun died and darkness arrived everywhere.

That is the end of the story about the sun and how darkness came.

Frans Tetera
**Warapu** Village [**Warapu** People]
Aitape
**West Sepik** Province

A720+. Sun in form of man; A721.6K. Hero kills the sun; A722.5.1+. Sun bathes; A1174. Origin of night; P210. Husband and wife

## Where Did the Aerie Come From?
(Wantok 67, May 2, 1973, page 4)

There was a woman who used an axe to carve out a canoe. The axe was called Jambiagura. She carved the canoe often, but the woman never put away her axe properly. She would just throw her axe into the wind and rain, and the rattan wrappings that bound the axe blade to the handle would fall off.

This woman lived with a relative, named Gura. Gura always thought, "Why does she always throw away my axe in the wind and rain?" She worried about this and then another woman, named Kanda [lit., "Rattan"], said to her, "Let's go to the pond where we can catch some crayfish." So that night, Gura and Kanda went to the pond.

Gura came and woke Kanda, then the two of them went to look for crayfish in the pond. They searched and searched until dawn. Kanda paddled back to shore and saw Gura. Kanda thought, "Hey, this woman is not the woman that I spoke to before, she is not the one that I took to search for crayfish. No, this is another woman." Kanda had been paddling all night, and now she took a good look at the face of this woman.

Now Kanda spoke to the woman, "Hey, let's go catch some crayfish." The two of them worked some more, and then Kanda spoke to her again, "I'd like to take a dump." The other woman said, "OK."

So then Kanda jumped into the tall grass, the grass that had a huge *masalai*. She jumped up and said, "You always take that axe and throw it away into the wind and rain, then the rattan always falls off. What do you think it is, just an axe for carving canoes?" Then Gura left. She got up and took off in the canoe.

Kanda cried, "Oh friend, don't leave me, you must come back and take me." She cried and cried and the woman went outside and called for her to stay. The woman cried a long time, then a fish jumped out of the water and onto the woman, then stayed there.

Kanda said, "Oh, if you're a man, you should go tell your father to come and get me." So this fish went down into the pond and spoke to its father who was a river *masalai*. The fish said, "Papa, a woman is above in the grass and she said, 'If you are a man then you should tell your father to come and get me.'"

So the father said, "Why are you lying to me? You no-good fish, you're lying to me." After the scolding, another fish went up and spoke to Kanda.

Kanda told the fish, "Oh my, if you're a man, then go talk to your father to come get me." So the fish went to talk to the father and said, "This is the truth father, there's a woman in the grass who's talking about you." The father scolded the fish, "You no-good fish. You're lying to me."

Then another fish with a long neck went above the surface. But this time, the fish came back to the father and the father would not listen to the fish, he was too angry to listen. Then many more fish went up to the surface and came back down to talk to the father, but the father still did not listen to them.

Later, the father sent his first child to go to the surface. The child came back and said, "Yes papa, it's the truth. I went to the surface and a woman told me that I should tell you to go above and get her."

So the father dressed and went to the surface and saw this woman. When the father came to this woman, the woman was shocked and afraid.

The father said to the woman, "Don't be afraid. You sent a message to me and I came to get you." He wanted to get the woman to go into the water, but the woman said, "I shall drown in this water." However, the *masalai* told her, "You won't drown. I can help you." So, he carried her and the two of them came to the *masalai*'s home.

The two of them lived there, and the woman gave birth. She did not give birth to a child, but to two bird eggs instead.

The woman carried the two eggs in a pot, and later when the eggs hatched, they became two eagles. The two birds grew and grew and became big. But they had a big problem because they wanted to take their mother back to her home.

So they told her, "Mother, we should take you back." The mother replied, "Oh, you two can't carry me back to my home." So the big brother told her, "OK, look at me." He got up and flew down to the water and brought back a big log that was drifting in the water. He carried it back to show to his mother.

Now the mother believed. She said, "OK, you two can carry me." So the two of them got up and brought their mother back to her home. So now this is where the eagles live.

Joseph Angansuan
**Japandai** Village [**Iatmul** People]
Ambunti sub-District, Patrol Post Pagwi
**East Sepik** Province

A2431+. Origin of eagle's nest; B211.3.11K. Speaking eagle; B211.5. Speaking fish; F420.6.1.6. Offspring of marriage between mortal and water-spirit; F420.7.1+. Living underwater with water-spirit; F424. River-spirit; F490+. Masalai; K1900. Impostures; P210. Husband and wife; P230. Parents and children; P231. Mother and son; P250. Brothers and sisters; T111. Marriage of mortal and supernatural being; T554.10+. Woman gives birth to an eagle; T565. Woman lays an egg; T587. Birth of twins; T685. Twins

## The Axe that Returned

(Wantok 68a, May 16, 1973, page 4)

There was a man named Maima Poropaungabia who brought his axe into the forest. He saw a cluster of nuts on top of a pandanus tree (*karuka*). So he shook the tree, and then climbed the tree with his axe and cut off the cluster. However, there was a stream below him that he did not see. His axe slipped and fell into the water, so he closed his eyes and came down slowly.

He arrived at another place. He cried and cried, and searched the ground for his axe. Then he arrived at his house. At night, a river-*masalai* took the axe and hid it in some *tanget* leaves. The *masalai* took the axe that was wrapped in *tanget* leaves and put it in Maima Poropaungabia's hand as he was sleeping.

In the morning, he awoke and looked at his hand. Something had put a package in his hand. He shook and removed the *tanget* leaves. Inside was his axe, he trembled with joy to see that he now had his axe again.

Peter Kumai
Mul [**Nul**] Village, **Golin** People]
Gumine
**Simbu** Province

D1565+. Spirit causes things to seek their proper place; F424. River-spirit;
F490+. Masalai

## Dog Training

(Wantok 68b, May 16, 1973, page 4)

Long ago, the ancestors had many dogs. One man could get many dogs. Men often bought puppies for a big pig, not just a little pig.

Dogs were very poor at finding many marsupials (*kapul*), so there were many of these. The dogs were only able to find marsupials that were in the secondary forest. These marsupials would lie on the ground, eat green leaves and sleep. [Most marsupials in New Guinea are normally arboreal.]

The men would take the puppies and feed them small rats. The people did this for two to four months, and the dogs grew large.

If they cooked a rat in the forest, they would hide it in a tree. They tied up the dogs with ropes. After hiding the rat, they would let the dogs loose. Then the dogs would find the rat right away. So in this way, they learned how to quickly kill marsupials [that lived in trees in the primary forest].

Before, the ancestors had dogs and were happy. Now we only have small dogs. White people have many kinds of dogs. The Papua New Guinean sees this and worries that whites have better dogs.

Robert Laik
**Yampu** Village [**Enga** People]
Wabag
**Enga** Province

A2452.1. Why dogs hunt; W181. Jealousy

## White Dog, Black Dog

(Wantok 69, June 6, 1973, page 4)

In the time of the ancestors, there was a man with two dogs. One dog was white and the other black. These two dogs went with the man to sleep in the forest.

When it was time for the dogs to hunt for wild game, the white dog would kill the game and then bring it back to this man. But the black dog did not do this. The black dog never killed any game.

So the owner of the dogs only liked the white dog, and he gave food to this dog all of the time. The black dog just slept about, and the man never gave food to it because it never found any game. The dog just slept in the house.

So, the black dog was always hungry and it was always angry. The dog waited for the man to be asleep at night. When the dog saw the man sleeping, the dog made a big bonfire near the man's body to heat up the man. The man was sound asleep.

Then the dog went to get the sacred masks and returned with them. The dog raised the sleeping man along with his bed, carried him and put him in the pond. The man slept and slept, then he felt cold.

So, the man tried to find the fire to warm his body. He moved his arm to try to find the fire, but he could not find it. He put his hand into the water instead. He moved his other hand but could not find the fire either.

The man was surprised, so he woke up, took his hand-flute and blew it towards the village. The men of the village heard the flute playing and they came to see this man who was lying far below in the pond. They cut a large vine and threw it out to him. The man caught the vine, and he tied it to his bed, then the men pulled the man back to shore. The men were angry at this black dog. The dog knew this and went to hide in among some thorny sago palm trees. Because of this, the men could not kill the dog. But the white dog harried out the black dog, and the men killed the black dog, but instantly the owner also died.

Frans Tetera
**Warapu** Village [**Warapu** People]
Aitape
**West Sepik** Province

B857+. Dog avenges master by helping kill unfaithful dog; D2061.2.2.7. Animals abused or destroyed to cause death of person; Q261. Treachery punished; Q411.4. Death as punishment for treachery; W111. Laziness

## Why Do People Have Different Colored Skins?

(Wantok 70, June 20, 1973, page 4)

Among one group of people who speak the **Urat** language in the **East Sepik** Province, there is a story that came from the ancestors. The ancestors would tell this story about why men have different colored skins, such as white, yellow, brown, red and black. The story goes like this.

Long ago, there was a man named Noak with his wife named Hanuak. They had just one boy. No one lived anywhere else on earth, there was just forest. This man with his wife and child lived in a village that we call Moihauk [**Meiwhak**], near Dreikikir Station.

So Noak with his wife Hanuak thought a lot about raising men who would look after the trees, the earth and the wild game. They thought day and night. One day, Noak thought, "Oh yes, I shall kill my child, cut him into little pieces and throw them away to all of the places in the East, West, South and North so that many people will come up from the earth and take care of things."

One night, he pointed to his wife Hanuak to get his child, then the two of them [mother and child] went to sleep in a small house. While the two of them slept, Noak killed his child, cut him into very small pieces and boiled them with some vegetables. When it was nearly dawn, he very quickly cooked the child's body with vegetables. Some of the bloodied, incompletely cooked vegetables stuck to him.

Noak threw away these bloody vegetables, and now some men were created with red skin. Then he threw away some bloody vegetables that were lightly cooked, and these became yellow skinned people, just like mixed-race or Chinese people. Then he threw away bloody vegetables that were well cooked, and these became white men. Now if you look at the eyes of white men, they are just like those of cats, you will know that they were well cooked.

So for us New Guineans, he threw away the cooked vegetables, but the fire was low and you can see that our eyes are a little brown just like the fire had scorched us. And so our skin became darker.

But if you look at the people from Buka Island, they became very dark. Noak threw away the vegetables with the child's burnt flesh that was completely black. If you look at the eyes of people from Buka, they are black. You will know that the fire got them completely.

So when Noak had finished throwing things away, dawn broke. Hanuak awoke and saw all of the places with men. They shouted, they danced, they sang, they beat the hand drums, and they beat the signal drum. When she looked at all of the places, Hanuak saw the many, many people living in houses with their gardens. She asked her husband Noak, "Where did these people come from?"

He told her, "Your child created them." When Hanuak heard this, she was truly overjoyed.

Judah Akesim

A1600. Distribution and differentiation of peoples—general; A1611+. Origin of Buka People; A1614.6+. Origin of light and dark skin color: from slain and dismembered first son; A1614.9. Origin of white man; P210. Husband and wife; P231. Mother and son; P233. Father and son; S11.3.3. Father kills son; S139.2. Slain person dismembered; S139.2.2+. Corpse put into cooking pot or cooked

## How Did the Hornbill Get a Big Beak?

(Wantok 71, July 4, 1973, page 4)

Long, long ago Cassowary and Hornbill were very good friends. Hornbill only had a small beak, and Cassowary had a very big beak. One day, Cassowary was walking around and ran into a big boulder, losing his beak.

He saw his friend Hornbill walking towards him, so he said, "Good day, friend. You are a truly good friend. You are a nice man." The two were happy together, they joked and flattered each other, and they just laughed.

But a thought came to Hornbill. He thought, "I think that I will trick Cassowary and take his big beak from him. Because Cassowary has a big beak, he is able to kill men when they shoot at him."

So then, Hornbill told Cassowary, "Hey my friend Cassowary, I think that your beak is as good as an axe. Man, I think I'll get your beak and chop that tree."

Then Hornbill took Cassowary's beak and went to the foot of the tree. He began to chop a limb of the tree. He said, "My friend, your axe is quite good."

Cassowary began to laugh but then stopped. He thought that Hornbill had stolen his axe. But when Hornbill finished chopping the tree, he told his friend Cassowary, "Hey friend, I think that I would like to leave you now." But Cassowary said, "OK, take my axe and come here first." But Hornbill got up and flew away with Cassowary's axe.

When Cassowary saw this, oh boy, he was furious and he just began to cry. So then he took the small axe that was Hornbill's beak and began to strike a stone with it. He really wrecked the beak, then he took the beak and left. But Cassowary was very mournful because Hornbill had taken his good beak and carried it away.

So now we can see that hornbills a have huge beak. This beak was stolen from the cassowary. And cassowaries only have small beaks.

So what should we think, was what the hornbill did a good thing? No, I do not think so, because it was just like stealing. So, I think that many men in Papua New Guinea often do this. They like to trick other men and steal from them too. The cassowary and the hornbill were good friends at first, but then something came between them and they became enemies.

Before we were good friends with God, but bad behavior came between us, and now we are no longer friends of God. When the hornbill took the cassowary's axe, they became enemies. Similarly, if you or I sin in the eye of God, we will become enemies of God. Nowadays, we are far away from God. But if we truly believe in Jesus Christ, He will remove our sins and we will become friends of God.

Mantam Yomka

[The tract *Bel Bilong Man* ("Man's Soul") also anthropomorphizes animal behavior in a Christian context (Kulick & Stroud, 1990: 291). The tract associates the bird of paradise with stubbornness and vanity, the dog with promiscuity and dirtiness, the pig with theft and gluttony, the bandicoot with materialism, the snake with covetousness and dishonesty, the cassowary with belligerence, and the frog with laziness.]

A2343.1.4+. Why hornbill has big beak; A2343.1.4+. Why cassowary has small beak; B211.3.17K. Speaking cassowary; B211.3+. Speaking hornbill; K300. Thefts and cheats—general; K2297. Treacherous friend; P310. Friendship; W157. Dishonesty

# The Story of the Flood
(Wantok 72, July 18, 1973, page 4)

Long ago, the ancestors liked to catch fish, eels, and crayfish in the river. One time, as they were readying their nets, fishing spears and other things, the big chief said to spend a day at a river. So, the men and women went to this river.

This river was full of eels, big ones too. But the leader of the eels stayed in a hole at the source of the water. When the women went down to the river, they caught many small eels, crayfish and fish. When they had caught them, the men saw that the river [that had been dammed by them] was flowing slowly. The big, father eel was still there.

Because of this, the water did not flow quickly. The men said, "Ah! Why is the water not flowing? There is probably a big eel still there. We should try to find it." They found the father eel and the water flowed out of the dam, and the pond they had made dried up.

After they had shot the eel, they made a platform for carrying the eel. But it was not a real eel. It was an old man from before who had made a home in the water. The men carried the eel back, singing and playing flutes. The next day in the early morning, the village chief struck the signal drum for the men and women to go to the gardens. They must prepare this father eel to be eaten.

All of the men, women and children went to get food from the garden, while they did this, they told one old man to clean the eel. When they finished, the eel had come down from its platform. The eel spoke to the old man. The eel told the old man to give him betel nut, betel pepper, and lime (calcium oxide). The eel chewed on the betel nut mixture and told him, "Old man, do you think that I am an eel? I am not an eel. I am a man from long ago, from the time when the land had not yet risen. Men do not know anything about me. My skin is just like that of an eel. When the men cut me, you should go and stay at the base of a small coconut palm tree."

While the eel and the old man were speaking, they heard the men coming back from the garden, singing as they came. The man returned to the platform and turned back into an eel just like before.

After everyone returned from the gardens, the old man said, "You can't eat this eel. It is a man. It came down and spoke with me. The two of us spoke and he chewed betel nut with me. It would be better if you put him back where you caught him."

The men spoke to the old man, "You're lying to us. That's not a man. It's wild game." They went ahead and told the man to get the hell out. They cursed him and beat him up. The old man said nothing more. He went to sit alone at the base of a coconut tree, the one that the eel had told him about.

Later the men brought the eel down and cut it up into small pieces. They told the women to cook the pieces in pots and to roast them over the fire.

The men sang and danced with joy. As the meat cooked, the river was slowly rising, but they did not notice that a flood was coming.

The water crested the banks, it kept rising and it flooded over all of the men and women. The old man though stayed at the coconut tree and did not die. When all of the others had died, the flood began receding. When the river returned to the banks, the coconut tree with the old man came down slowly with the water. He threw a green coconut into the water to see how deep it was. He saw the coconut smash and said, "The water has receded." He saw the bones of the men and he was greatly saddened.

While he was still mourning, the eel saw him and brought him to the eel's home. So now at this place, the old man turned into a boulder that is still there. When you see this boulder in the river, you should think of this man.

Walter ToBungTabu ["ToBungTabu" is a **Tolai** male name **(East New Britain** Province)]
Karapi
Hoskins
[West New Britain Province]

14

A977.5. Origin of particular rock; A1011. Local deluges; A1015.2. Spirit causes deluge; A1018. Flood as punishment; A1023. Escape from deluge on tree; B211.5.2K. Speaking eel; B243.2.2. King of eels; D173M. Transformation: man to eel; D231M. Transformation: man to stone; D373M. Transformation: eel to man; F420.1.3.2+. Water-spirit as eel; J652. Inattention to warnings; J1050. Attention to warnings; Q211.6. Killing an animal revenged; Q428. Punishment: drowning; Q458. Flogging as punishment

## The Dolphin

(Wantok 73, August 1, 1973, page 4)

Long, long ago, among my ancestors, there was a brother and sister who lived on an island called **Dangtiti**. They left this island and wanted to go to another. When they rowed off, they came upon a reef. The name of this reef is *Aillwo*, meaning "Seaweed."

Then the two of them went directly towards an island while the waves began to come inside their canoe. The sister heard the water sloshing inside the canoe and looked behind her. She thought that her brother had broken wind. But no, it was just the waves going inside the canoe.

The brother saw that it was the sea, and his sister saw it too now and was quite ashamed. So the man told his sister, "I'm going to leave you now. You should tell the men of the village about me."

So the brother took his basket and spear and went into Aillwo Reef where he stood upon a piece of coral. He spoke to his sister again, "When you go to the village, tell the men to go to the top of the mountain and get a large piece of tree bark. Tell them to make a net from the bark and fetch me with the net."

The brother finished talking to the sister, then he dove into the sea and became a dolphin. The poor woman cried because she had thought that her brother would return right away after he jumped into the sea. But no, the boy turned into a dolphin.

The woman went to the village and spoke about what had happened. Then the men got up and went to the mountain, got some logs and began making nets from the bark.

This is a true story. If you go to **Pililo** Island, you will see a big net [**West New Britain** Province, **Arawe** People]. And if you go to Aillwo Reef, you will see the seaweed and the many *bonbon*, or dolphins. Whenever it is a holiday like Easter or Christmas, the men go in their large canoes with their large nets and catch dolphins in them.

The time to catch dolphins is only at night. If you want to find out for yourself about this story, you can go to Pililo Island and see the big nets that are there today.

Paul Areng

Rabaul

East New Britain Province

A1457+. Origin of dolphin hunting; D127.5M. Transformation: man to dolphin; P253. Sister and brother

## The Man Who Married a Bird of Paradise

(Wantok 74, August 15, 1973, page 4)

Before in my village, there were many married men. Among the men were two brothers. The big brother had married but the little brother had not. One day, the little brother went to build a bird blind in the forest. As he worked, the birds looked at him.

After he had finished the bird blind, he went there one morning to look for birds. He sat and peered through a hole in the blind and saw a vine hanging from a tree that was making a noise. He continued to look and saw the first bird of paradise coming down.

He watched and watched, then he saw many more birds come along this creek. While he watched them, he saw them lose their skins and he saw their eyes become round. So, it was at this creek that the birds of paradise became young women and bathed.

The man sat and thought and thought. Then said, "Hey, what is happening to them?" He thought again, "Oh, poor me, I have no wife. What if I can catch one of them?"

He looked at one of the women and decided to capture her. He quickly shoved his multi-pronged spear at her and grabbed her hair, and pulled her into the bird blind where he hid her.

All of the other birds finished bathing and wanted to return home, so the quickly left. But the poor woman in the birdhouse called out, "Hey, where is my bird skin?"

The other birds had found their skins, but not the one that the man captured. The others returned along the vine and went back to their home.

After they had departed, the man asked the woman, "Hey, where are you from?"

The woman said, "This is my only home. Where are you from?"

The man said, "This is my only home. Where are you from?"

The two of them spoke like this for some time, and then the bird-of-paradise woman asked him, "Hey, do you have my bird skin?" The man replied, "No, I don't know about it."

The woman continued to ask the man with more and more conviction. But the man had hidden the skin well. The man said to the woman, "Hey, let's go to my village."

The woman said that she would absolutely not go, but the man persisted. In the end, the man won and they went to the village.

The man had hid the feathers well and now he put them at the apex of his house. The woman married this man and the two of them had a child and lived happily thereafter.

Leo Manrip
**Yassip** Mission [**Kombio** People]
Wewak
**East Sepik** Province

B290+. Bird of paradise removes skirt or skin to bathe; B652. Marriage to bird in human form; D150+W. Transformation: woman to bird of paradise; D350+W. Transformation: bird of paradise to woman; D361.1. Swan Maiden; P210. Husband and wife; P230. Parents and children; P251.5. Two brothers; R10. Abduction; T192. Marriage by force

## The Deceitful Turtle

(Wantok 75a, September 5, 1973, page 4)

They told of the moon as follows: A man caught a turtle. He tied up its feet with vines, but he was not thinking of eating it. No, he put it into a palm frond basket.

One day, two children, a brother and sister, were processing sago. These two children lived alone at their house.

The boy was crying a lot when his sister asked him, "Would you like some fish?" The boy said, "No." The girl asked again, "Would you like some sago and banana?" The boy said, "I don't want any." He did not want this food because he was looking at his father's turtle.

His sister tired of this and gave the turtle to her brother. He began to cook it in the fire, but the vine that tied it broke, and it fell into the fire. The turtle got out of the fire and crawled along the ground, then climbed a betel nut palm tree. Then the turtle climbed a coconut palm tree. The turtle shot one of the moon's eyes with a multi-pronged spear. Now the moon only had one eye lit up.

But then the coconut palm began to climb. The two children thought, "What is it that we did to transform this turtle? We must get a coconut shell that will become a turtle, and we'll put it back in the palm frond basket."

The two children returned to cleaning the sago that was to be eaten with the turtle. Their parents returned in the evening. The father rested, then he thought again of his turtle and that he would like to cook it.

The coconut shell had not become a real turtle, it was still just a coconut shell. The father thought about this then said, "This is not a real turtle, it is just a coconut shell. Where is my turtle?"

The girl said, "It's little brother's fault. He cried and cried, so I gave it to him. Then the turtle climbed to the top of a coconut tree."

The father said, "Why did you two do this?" The girl replied, "We worked hard at processing the sago."

The father beat them badly. Then he said, "Never, ever do that again."

Inikio Sosmekul

B770+. Turtle climbs tree; B770+. Turtle shoots out one of moon's eyes; F54.1. Tree stretches to sky; P210. Husband and wife; P233. Father and son; P234. Father and daughter; P253. Sister and brother; Q212. Theft punished; Q458. Flogging as punishment

## Where Did Darkness Come From?

(Wantok 75b, September 5, 1973, page 4)

Long ago, there was no night like there is now, there was only sun.

One day, there was a man named Hiki who made a new garden for himself. After he finished clearing the trees for his garden, he went home. But there was a *masalai* woman named Hekep who came to the garden and replanted all of the trees again. The *masalai* woman always did this.

Eventually, the man who owned the garden became completely irate at this. He screamed, "Who is it that is destroying my garden?"

One time Hiki again cut the trees in his garden, but this time he waited with his spear rather than returning home. As Hiki was watching his garden, he heard a big noise come from the middle of his new garden. Hiki trembled and went closer to his garden, then he hit the *masalai* woman and his spear.

When the spear hit the *masalai* woman, it became pitch dark. Hiki went truly crazy, he climbed on top of a tree and fell asleep. After he slept he heard a rooster crow. He awoke and saw that it was dawn.

Now there is night and day. Before, there was only sun.

Jacob Hakon
P. H. D.
Wewak
East Sepik Province

A1174. Origin of night; F401.6. Spirit in human form; F490+. Masalai; H1115.1+. Task: cutting down forest, which is magically replanted

# Where Did Mushrooms Come From?

(Wantok 76, September 19, 1973, page 4)

A woman and her newborn child were staying in their house. Her husband went with some other people to a festival at another village.

At night there was a flying fox that was eating some fruit near the house. But it was not a real flying fox, it was a spirit in disguise. The woman thought it was a real flying fox so she scolded it.

The spirit told her, "Heat that pot in the fire." So, the woman heated the pot in the fire. The flying fox said, "Half will be cooked and the other half will not be." The woman said, "Oh my! The spirit is going to eat me." Then the flying fox came inside the house with her, and the two of them fought bitterly.

The flying fox killed her and ate her along with her infant, then the flying fox put their bones inside the house. His sister cut the bones and brought them to throw at her husband who was at the festival.

She threw the bones on top of his head. He thought, "What is this that's fallen on my head?" When he saw what it was, he said, "Oh, my wife is bad. I must leave."

He brought his sister with him and returned to their village. He went and saw a pile of sago pulp, then he shoved his sister underneath the sago pulp. He went to look for his wife, but she was not to be found. Then he went back to get his sister, but she was not there either. She had become like a mushroom.

So now, one can find mushrooms growing in the pulp of sago while women process it.

Magdalena N. Tango
C. M. [Congregation of Mission] **Yandugen** [**Mehek** People]
Nuku
**West Sepik** Province

A2686.1. Origin of mushroom; B211.2.11K+. Speaking flying fox; D210+W. Transformation: woman to mushroom; F401.3+. Spirit in flying fox form; F402.1.11. Spirit causes death; P210. Husband and wife; P253. Sister and brother; P264. Sister-in-law; S110. Murders

# Where Did the Cockatoo Come From?

(Wantok 77, October 3, 1973, pages 4, 12)

Long ago, in the Southern Highlands Province, there was an old woman who had a little boy. The boy's name was Ale. Whenever Ale was at home with his mother, he was tired.

One day Ale asked his mother, "Mother, I'd like to go for a little walk along the river." Ale's mother agreed to this. But his mother said to him, "Ale, do not be gone long. You must come back right away." Ale was very happy and began to walk along the river.

When Ale went to the river, oh my, he found many pieces of pig guts lying in the water! When Ale saw the pig guts, he did not know where they had come from. But he was happy because he had found some meat to bring to his mother.

So Ale gathered all of the guts in the water and brought them back to his mother. When his mother saw Ale bringing the pig guts, she was ecstatic. Ale's mother cleaned the guts and cooked them in an earth oven, then they ate them.

So after that, Ale went to the river at the same time every day. One day, he asked his mother, "I'd like to follow the river and go look on the other side." His mother agreed to this, so off he went. He went very far and then he saw a hanging vine. Ale climbed this vine to get a good view. He saw an old man eating a pig.

Ale went closer to look at the old man. The old man did not have a mouth, and he had no eyes. However, he was still able to eat the pig. Ale saw the old man open his head and shove the pork into his head, down and down it went. This is how the man ate.

Ale also saw the old man cooking pork in an earth oven. So Ale uncovered the earth oven and carried off the pork to his mother to eat. The old man came back a little while after Ale had left to uncover his earth oven, but when he arrived, there was no pork left.

The man thought and thought, then he thought he would capture the man who had stolen his pork. The old man put a huge net bag in the trail. When Ale and his mother finished the pork, Ale asked his mother if he could go back and steal some more pork from the old man. The mother agreed, and so Ale departed and followed the river. When Ale came to the place where the old man lived, he did not see the huge net bag in the trail. Ale went inside the net bag and was tied up by the old man.

The old man carried Ale off in the net bag and hung him up inside his house. He lit a fire underneath Ale so that the smoke would get into his eyes. Ale's mother waited and waited but her child did not return, so the old woman became worried and started to cry.

That night, the woman cried and cried and heard a flying fox eating ripe bananas. So the mother called out to the flying fox, "Please, nice flying fox, can you find my child and bring him to me?" The flying fox replied, "Yes I can find your child and bring him to you, but what will you give me?" The old woman said, "I will give you many pigs, shell money (*kina*) and other things too if you so desire." However the flying fox said, "I do not like those things. I only want one thing, *aalipu* (a very tough vine)." So the woman gave *aalipu* to the flying fox.

The flying fox was very happy, took the vine and went to find the boy, Ale. The flying fox went directly to the old man's house, tore apart the net bag, and brought Ale back to his mother. The old woman saw her child and was overjoyed. She thanked the flying fox profusely.

But the mother and child were ashamed of their bad behavior. Because of this they changed into cockatoos, and that is why we have cockatoos in Papua New Guinea.

Andreas Simbili
**Kagua** Village [**Kewa** People]
**Southern Highlands** Province

[See LeRoy (1985a: 9-15) and LeRoy (1985b: 198-221) for other Kewa tales about Ale (a.k.a. Pepana).]

A1998K+. Creation of cockatoo; B542.1.2+. Flying fox rescues person from height; B552+. Person carried by flying fox; D150+B. Transformation: boy to cockatoo; D150+W. Transformation: woman to cockatoo; F512.5. Person without eyes; F513.0.3. Mouthless people; K333. Theft from blind person; P231. Mother and son; Q53. Reward for rescue; Q212. Theft punished; Q469.5. Punishment: choking with smoke; R49+. Captivity in bag; R110. Rescue of captive; W27. Gratitude


# Now You Must Die

(Wantok 78, October 17, 1973, page 4)

Long, long ago there was a woman named Pipalnanr, but she was unmarried. She slept in a cave on a hill near a pond. She lived for a long time. One day, she traveled in the forest. It was not long before she met a *masalai* man.

But the *masalai* looked nice and did not scare the woman. So that morning the two of them arranged to become married. They spoke that morning, but at night Pipalnanr left him in the forest while she returned to her cave. At night, the *masalai* went to live with her, but during the day the *masalai* could smell the odor of the sun and he returned to the forest.

This marriage between the real woman Pipalnanr and the *masalai* man went on for some time. One day, the woman became pregnant. When it was time to give birth, the *masalai* said, "When the child cries at night you can't light lamps or make fires to pacify it. If the child defecates or urinates at night, you can't light a lamp to clean him. This you must do for five days after my telling you this."

When the child was born, the *masalai* man went far from his wife and child, so the wife was required to do the things that the *masalai* told her. She did well at first, but on the fourth day, she lit a lamp to clean the child. It was not long before the *masalai* returned. He was filled with anger and he said, "I thought you were really my wife, but it's not true. If you had done as I told you, you would have become a person of renown among the villagers. If you had done this, then when old people, children or middle aged people die, their spirits would have come to wash them in this river and they would have been reborn." He turned his back to her and left. Later he spoke, "But since you had not done as I had spoken, when men and women die they will not be reborn."

He finished his speech and went back to the forest, never to see her again. Today, if you go to this place, you can see four ponds. Three are nice and have water. But one is angry; it has stones and fights the trees that try to enter it. You will see the marks on the trees that live there. The trees that live there have stopped growing.

Peter Benjamin Pokawin
**Tingau** Village [**Kuruti** People]
**Manus** Island
**Manus** Province

A920.1.0.1. Origin of particular lake; A977. Origin of particular stones or groups of stones; A1335+. Origin of death from disobeying spirit husband; A2800+. Origin of marks on particular trees; E600. Reincarnation; F490+. Masalai; P210. Husband and wife; Q325. Disobedience punished; Q551.5+. End of reincarnation as punishment; T111. Marriage of mortal and supernatural being; T570. Pregnancy; T580. Childbirth; W126. Disobedience


# The Woman Who Worried
# about a Fish and then Ran Away

(Wantok 79, November 7, 1973, page 4)

This story comes from long ago, from a village called **Aibom** in **East Sepik** Province [**Iatmul** People]. There was a man married to two wives. His first wife had a son and daughter. His second wife had no children.

The man never bossed around his first wife. But he often bossed around his second wife. One day, the man had speared some fish. He gave the dead fish that he had caught to his first wife and he gave the fish that were still alive to his second wife.

The first wife was angry and hit the second wife with a fish that had poisonous spines. Then the two of them fought. After the fight, the first wife sent her child to go get her brother and to get a pig to slaughter.

The woman did not tell her brother that she wanted to run away. She said, "Your two maternal relatives are hungry." After they cut the pig, he gave half to the brother and then the child left. After the woman cooked the pig, she filled up a basket with the pork, and she and her children began to walk.

They walked for a while then sat on a stone. The two children began to eat the pork. But their mother began to cry. They got up again and walked some more. Then sat down again and the two children ate more pork while their mother cried. They continued in this manner, and eventually finished the pig as well as some sago.

They put the head of the pig on top of a stone and hung the basket on top of a tree branch, then they climbed a mountain. There they came upon a stone. The mother took a knife given to her by an ancestor and hit the stone five times. After the fifth blow, the stone opened like a door. They looked inside and saw men who had died before singing and dancing.

The two children were scared. The mother held them and shoved them down into the hole, then the mother went down too. The door closed upon them. The men of their village had been following them. When they arrived at the stone, they only found the knife. The woman's brother took the knife and cried and then returned to the village.

This old knife has since been ruined, but the stone is still there. If you go to Aibom Village, the people there can show you this stone.

An old ancestor of mine told me this story about a woman who worried about a fish and then ran away. She told me about my village, Aibom, when I was still a child.

Beno J.

F92.3 Visit to lower world through opening rocks; D1552.1. Mountain opens at blow of divining rod; F81. Descent to lower world of dead (Hell, Hades); P210. Husband and wife; P231. Mother and son; P232. Mother and daughter; P233. Father and son; P234. Father and daughter; P253. Sister and brother; P290+. Hostile co-wives; P290+. Maternal kin; P293. Uncle; R213. Escape from home; T145.0.1. Polygyny; W181. Jealousy; Z71.3. Formulistic number: five


## Where Did Fire Come From?
(Wantok 80, November 21, 1973, pages 4-5)

This story tells how fire first came to the men of Gope [**North-Eastern Kiwai**] People in the **Gulf** Province. Many hundred years ago, the men of Gope put their food in the sun to burn it first. They did not know about fire, but there were some insects and wild game who dreamt of fire.

Once, the sun was shining brightly and there were no clouds in the sky. At the seashore, it was high tide and the sea shone like a polished stone. The sun rose above all of the trees and mountains.

In one muddy pond, there was a small crab sleeping under a mangrove root. The crab was trying to molt into a new shell, and waiting for the new shell to harden. Suddenly, on top of the mangrove tree, the crab heard a "pop." A fruit of the mangrove had fallen on the crab's new shell.

The small, vain crab cried and cried, "Rat! Rat! Rat! Come here and eat this mangrove fruit. It has fallen on top of my new skin and has also broken my flesh."

The mangrove fruit is good food for rats, and so it was not long that a rat came and sat on top of the crab's shell and began to eat this fruit.

The mangrove fruit cried with pain, "Fire! Fire! Fire! Come and help me. Burn this rat who is trying to eat me."

However, there was no man who knew about fire, but the fruit had heard the insects talking about their dreams of fire coming to burn the rat.

Instantly, the rat's hair turned to ashes. The rat cried out, "Water! Water! Water! Where are you? Come and douse this fire that is burning my hair."

The Water heard this shouting, then came and doused the fire. Much later, the fire called out, "Snake! Snake! Snake! Where are you? Come and help me. Bring me to the other side of the pond. It is bad that water is making me die out." The snake came, fetched the fire and swam to another place.

The young men and women were sitting down and sunning themselves. They saw the snake swimming straight towards them with the fire. The women called this new thing, "fire."

Later the women said, "Fire, don't die out. Fire, don't die out. Fire don't die out."

But the young men competed with the women, and they sang out stronger, "Fire die! Fire die! Fire die!" Then the young women sang out stronger still, and the snake came ashore with the fire. A woman went to get the fire from the snake.

Then all of the girls gathered pieces of wood near the pond to make a bonfire. Later, each of them took a piece of the fire and brought it to their families.

The young women won the contest, so this made the young men angry at the snake. They brought some weapons to kill the snake. The snake was terrified and ran away into the forest.

So that is how fire came to the Gope People. Girls held the fire first, and they kept if from dying out, so now it is the job of women to cook food in the fire.

If the men had said, "Fire, don't die," then now it would be the men's job to cook food and not the women's job.

Oria Gemo
Kerema High School
Gulf Province

[A different version of this story was originally published in English in the book, *Creation Legends from New Guinea* (Madang: Kristen Pres, 1972: 19-22.)]

A1414. Origin of fire; A1455+. Why women cook; B211.8.1K. Speaking crab; B211.2.9. Speaking rat; B290+. Animal's dream; D1242.1. Magic water; D1271. Magic fire; D1610.10. Speaking fruit; D1610.39K+. Speaking fire; D1810.8.2. Information received through dream; H1500+. Speaking contest; J1813+. Cooking processes misunderstood: cooking with the sun; R220. Flights; W116. Vanity; Z41.1K. The mangrove and the crab

## Why Women No Longer Have Beards
(Wantok 81, December 5, 1973, page 4)

Long, long ago in the time of our ancestors, our men did not have beards, but the women did. Their beards were very long, some of them were so long that they touched their legs, or even touched the ground. When they walked, the beard would drag on the ground or they would get the beard out of the way by piling it atop their heads. Sometimes they would trip over their beards, fall down and bang their heads on rocks, sticks and things. This made them quite angry.

At this time, there was a woman ancestor who lived with her grandson. The parents of this young boy had died, so he lived with his grandmother. Small children did not know about the women's beards. They saw them, but did not know that they were beards.

So one time, this young boy sat with his grandmother, and they talked about all of the things that were growing in their garden. Then the boy looked at his grandmother's beard and asked her, "Grandma, what is that thing that hangs from your mouth and touches your legs?" The grandmother replied, "Boy, why do you ask? If you would like it, then you can have it." The boy said, "Yes."

So the grandmother told her young boy to close his eyes as she counted to ten, after she finished counting, he should open his eyes again. When the grandmother finished counting, the boy opened his eyes and he saw that he now had a long beard that touched his legs. Then he got a

scissors and cut some of it. So now, you can see if the boy had not done this, we men would not have beards. It was revenge against his wrong. It is good that he had cut some of his beard.

Kambar Gileng
**Karkar** High School [**Waskia** or **Takia** People]
**Madang** Province

A1315.3+. Why men have beards and women do not; F545.1+. Unusually long beard; F545.1.0.1. Beardless man; F545.1.5. Bearded woman; P292.1. Grandmother as foster mother; Q326. Impudence punished; Q580. Punishment fitted to crime

## Every Man Was Lost
(Wantok 82, December 19, 1973, page 4)

Once, a great sickness came to my island, Trowain [**Tarawai**] Island. Many people died all over the island [**Boiken** People, **East Sepik** Province].

At one village, everyone died except for two brothers and their two parents. The brothers' names were Haro and Laho. One day, Haro went to his garden to fetch some yams and taros. At the same time Laho went to spear many fish at the reef.

While Laho was coming back along the trail after he had finished catching fish, he met an old woman. The woman said to him, "Please fetch those coconuts of mine in that tree."

Laho was a good boy, so he climbed up the coconut palm. When he finished getting them, he wanted to come down. But the woman said, "You should come down head first with your feet up."

Poor Laho did this, and when he came down near the ground, the old woman took a stick and broke Laho's head. She took the head and went to eat it with her husband.

Brother Haro had been waiting for him, so he went to find him. When he came to the coconut tree, he saw the fish and the fishing spear. He also saw blood all around the coconut tree.

Another time, Haro returned to that place. He saw the old woman who said to him, "Go climb that coconut tree and fetch my coconuts." Haro climbed the tree and threw down many coconuts.

The old woman said to him, "You must come down head first." Haro was angry at that and said, "I know you. You were the one who killed my brother when he did this."

Haro came down quickly, fetched a stick and killed the old woman with it. He cut off a small piece of the woman and boiled it in one of the woman's pots.

Before long, the woman's husband returned. He was famished, and could not wait to eat. He began to eat his wife's cooked flesh.

After he finished eating, Haro went and climbed up the coconut tree and said to the old man, "You ate the flesh of your wife."

The old man came outside his house and looked around, then he looked up and saw Haro in the coconut palm. The old man said to him, "Hey! You killed my wife!"

After he finished speaking, he got his axe and started cutting the coconut tree. When the coconut tree was about to fall, Haro jumped to another tree, and the old man began cutting that tree too. Then just when that tree was about to fall, Haro jumped to yet another tree.

The two of them kept doing this until all of the coconut trees were like this, then all of the other trees too. Finally, there was just one was left standing, a breadfruit tree.

The old man began to cut this tree. He cut and cut, and when it was about to fall, Haro fell onto a rock and died. Then the old man ran towards Haro when he fell, but the tree fell on top of him, and he died too.

Now, everyone from this place was dead, and there were no coconuts or other trees there either. Yes, that is the end of my story.

Joseph Akulea
Aitape
West Sepik Province

G346. Devastating monster; G512.8.1. Ogre killed by striking with club; G650+. Ogre duped into eating spouse; J2244+. Climb down tree head first; K810. Fatal deception into trickster's power; N330. Accidental killing or death; P210. Husband and wife; P231. Mother and son; P233. Father and son; P251.5. Two brothers; S110. Murders


## Why Do People Get Gray Hair?
(Wantok 83, January 2, 1974, page 4)

Long ago, in the time of the ancestors, there was a man and wife who lived in a village with their son. One day they took their son and went to their garden. After they finished working, they returned to the village. The man went into his house and fell asleep because he had worked hard in the garden.

His wife began to cook some food, and their child went to play with a group of children. While the children were playing and walking around, they became hungrier. So, their child began to cry, and his mother called to him, "Don't cry. Your father worked hard and is sleeping. It would be bad if you woke him." But the little boy did not listen. He cried even harder.

The mother was quite angry because she was hungry too. She told her child again, "Don't cry. Look at the food in this pot, it is nearly done. We can eat soon."

But the child was completely stubborn, and he cried harder still. The mother was angry. So, she took the soup-spoon that she was using which was made from a seashell, and broke it over the child's head. The child received a big bump on his head and cried even harder, then he turned into a white cockatoo [sulphur-crested cockatoo (Beehler *et al.*, 1986: 117)].

The mother was sorry for the child, and tried to hold him. However, she was unable to do so. The bird flew on top of the house. The father went on top of the house too and tried to hold the bird, but he could not catch him. The bird flew away and perched on top of a breadfruit tree limb. When the father climbed this breadfruit tree, the bird flew higher. The bird's sore healed and yellow feathers formed where the sore had been. So now, you can see many men and women who have had head wounds get gray hair quickly in those places. It does not matter if they are not old yet, gray hair will come where the wound was because of this story.

John A. Skur
**Bogia** [Village, **Sepa** People]
**Madang** Province

A1315.1. Why men become grey-headed; A2321.12K. Origin of comb of white cockatoo; D150+B. Transformation: boy to cockatoo; D566. Transformation by striking; P210. Husband and wife; P231. Mother and son; P233. Father and son; Q325. Disobedience punished; Q551.3.2.2+. Punishment: transformation into bird; W126. Disobedience; W167. Stubbornness


## The Marsupial (*Sikau*) Who Stole the Baby
(Wantok 84, January 17, 1974, page 4)

Once there was a woman who went to her garden while carrying her baby in her net bag. She arrived at the garden and hung the net bag with her baby up on a tree branch, then went to work removing grass and weeds.

While she was working, the baby began to cry, but she did not go to check on him. The baby continued to cry. A marsupial (*sikau*) heard the crying and hopped along to go get the baby.

The marsupial came up to the net bag, looked inside and saw the baby. The marsupial took the baby and ran away. The marsupial looked after the baby, and the baby became big.

One day, the boy said to the marsupial, "We should go into the forest and find a *ton* tree."

The next morning, the two of them woke up and went into the forest with their net bag. They arrived at a *ton* tree, and the boy climbed it. He picked some fruits and threw them down to his mother, the marsupial.

The marsupial collected the fruits and put them in the net bag, then they went towards home. As they walked along the trail, some men took their spears and shot the marsupial, then took the boy with the marsupial to their village.

Kimoapa K.
**Usino** Village [**Usino** People]
**Madang** Province

B535.0.16K+. Marsupial as nurse for child; P231. Mother and son; P272. Foster mother; P275. Foster son; R13.1+. Abduction by marsupial

## Marrying a Mango Woman
(Wantok 85, February 6, 1974, page 5)

There were two brothers who lived happily together. Their parents had died, and there was no one who watched after them or who gave them food. The two brothers got their own food and did everything else for themselves.

One day, the big brother spoke to his little brother, "You should stay here until I come to look for you. All of your food is here, so don't go running about. You should stay here in the village, don't go into the forest. It would be bad if the enemies killed you."

The big brother prepared his things and put them in his sea-going outrigger canoe, then departed. He went to fish in the middle of the sea. He speared so many fish that his canoe was filled with them by the time evening approached. He was still at sea when it was nearly the time of sunset, so he scanned the horizon and saw an island. He paddled the canoe directly towards the island where he could see smoke coming from a fire.

He put the canoe ashore and an old woman came to see him. The old woman said to him, "Don't be afraid. I don't eat new things. I don't eat men. No. I'm alone here."

The boy heeded her and followed the old woman to her house.

The woman asked him, "Are you married or not?"

The boy said, "I'm not married. I'm single. I only live with my little brother. Our mother died. I left my little brother and came here."

The old woman told him, "Now, the young women will come to sing and dance. When the women come to sing and dance, don't look at them. You must sleep."

The women came and sang and danced until dawn. Everything that the women did was directed by this old woman.

After dawn broke, the old woman told the boy, "Go and climb that tree and fetch a mango. The young women are hiding inside the mango." He went to get the mango and then came back down.

The old woman told him, "You must put the mango in the back of your canoe, and then paddle back to your home." So, he paddled and paddled, and the mango turned into a woman. The woman was very young, and as beautiful as a red flower. When he saw her and was very happy.

When he returned and came ashore, his little brother saw him and coveted his big brother. The little brother said to him, "I should marry this woman. You can live alone."

So, the two of them fought and the big brother killed his little brother.

Mr. G. Womasi Beni
Madang
Madang Province

D431.4+W. Transformation: mango to woman; P210. Husband and wife; P251.5. Two brothers; P263. Brother-in-law; P264. Sister-in-law; Q301. Jealousy punished; Q411. Death as punishment; S73.1. Fratricide; S110. Murders; T117.7+. Marriage to a fruit; W181. Jealousy

## The Yam Woman
(Wantok 86, February 20, 1974, page 4)

In a village called Walingge [**Walingai**] in **Madang** Province [**Migabac** People], there was a man, a woman and their child. The child's name was Maho. Maho was a very nice girl, and her parents were very happy with her. The family was very happy together.

When she was still small, her parents often brought her line fishing at the river, to the forest, and to the garden. She was always happy to work in the garden. When she was a grown woman, she asked her parents if she could have a garden of her own.

Her parents agreed and they cleared a garden for her. The young woman worked very hard at her garden, weeding and planting. So, many things grew in her garden.

The young woman continued to work at her garden. One day, her parents told her that they would be going to visit a shaman who had died. The parents of this young woman wanted her to look after their garden, but the woman did not want to stay without them. She was afraid of the ghosts and pleaded to go with them.

Her parents did not like that idea, so they decided to leave her there. The afternoon that her parents left her, a man named Silivasi saw her and said to her, "I like you." Because the woman looked nice, the man slept with her that night.

When her parents returned, the woman told them about this man who had slept with her. The father was irate. He got his spear and stabbed his daughter as she was sitting on the ground.

The woman could not remove the spear. As she lay there with the spear in her chest, she told her mother, "Look at me, your husband stabbed me with a spear. If you bury me and work hard at your garden, when you harvest your food you will see that I have grown fat and long. If you do not work hard at your garden you will not see me fat and long."

And to her father she said, "You cannot look at me growing in your garden. If your wife plants me and takes care of me, and you see me growing, she will die and her body will break into tiny pieces."

So this is why it is very hard to plant yams. However, if you take good care and work hard, it will be just as this woman said, the one who worked hard in her garden from before.

Nai Kundi
Angoram Primary School
East Sepik Province

A2686.4.3. Origin of yams; C182. Tabu confined to men; C300+. Looking at yams; D1711. Magician; E631.5+. Reincarnation as yam; P210. Husband and wife; P232. Mother and daughter; P234. Father and daughter; Q240+. Premarital sex punished; Q411. Death as punishment; S11.3.3+. Father kills daughter; S115. Murder by stabbing

## The Two Brothers

(Wantok 87, March 6, 1974, page 4)

In a village, in the time of the ancestors, there were two brothers. They lived together in the same house. One night, when the moon was bright, they sat outside their house, gossiped and shot the breeze.

They did not know that a ghost was underneath their house listening to them. After the ghost heard them talking, the ghost returned to its home on top of a tree and went to sleep.

The two brothers went to sleep so that they could get up early in the morning to go spearfishing. While they slept, the ghost awoke before dawn and came to wake the big brother. The big brother woke up, got his spear and his oar, and departed. The big brother was in the front of the canoe and the ghost stayed in the rear and steered the canoe.

When they came to a lake, the big brother began spearing fish and putting them inside the canoe. While he speared big fish, the ghost would eat them and leave only the small fish in the canoe. When the big brother turned back to look at the fish, he saw only the small fish and asked the ghost, "Where are the big fish?"

The ghost replied, "They went into my belly."

The big brother was furious and now realized that this man was not his little brother, but a ghost.

They paddled and went a bit farther. The big brother threw his spear hard and hit a big tree trunk underwater. He turned and spoke to the ghost, "I speared a big crocodile and now my spear is stuck. Go into the water and get the spear out."

After the ghost retrieved the spear and came back to the surface, the big brother speared the ghost right in the face with the spear that the ghost had retrieved.

After the big brother had speared the ghost's face, he left him and paddled back home to see that his real brother was sitting at the river, waiting for him. The big brother was very sorry for his little brother. He held him and cried.

Roy N. Palan
**Angoram** Village [**Angoram** People]
**East Sepik** Province

E440+. Ghost laid by spear/arrow; E540.0.1K. Revenants eat fish as men catch them; E545. The dead speak; K910. Murder by strategy; K1930. Treacherous impostors; P251.5. Two brothers; S110. Murders

## The Cassowary and the Chicken

(Wantok 88, March 20, 1974, page 4)

Long ago, Cassowary and Chicken were friends, they traveled together in the forest. Once as they were traveling, Cassowary said to Chicken, "Let's carve a canoe." So, they looked for a tree and cut one down.

They began to carve the canoe. After they finished carving, they paddled it into the sea, then pulled up the mast. Cassowary said to Chicken, "Friend, sit down and I'll paddle."

So, Cassowary paddled and paddled. Cassowary went very far and said to his friend, Chicken, "Can you help me paddle?" But Chicken was lazy and Cassowary said, "If you are too lazy then I will hit the canoe." Cassowary asked Chicken again, but Chicken would not paddle.

Cassowary was angry and hit the canoe with its leg. The canoe broke and water came inside. What would these poor birds do? Chicken looked around, then flew to the beach. But poor Cassowary went crazy and stayed with the canoe.

Cassowary sat there and saw a turtle approaching, so Cassowary spoke to the turtle, "Friend, please take me." But the turtle replied, "You are still walking around." Cassowary looked at the turtle and spoke again. But the turtle replied, "You are still walking around."

Then at the last moment, the big turtle raised its dirty backside. Cassowary asked the turtle, "Friend, can you take me?" So, the turtle brought its backside to Cassowary, and Cassowary went on top.

The turtle carried Cassowary to the beach and Cassowary said to the turtle, "Good friend, wait here. I'll get you some food." But Cassowary was lying to the poor turtle. Cassowary went and cut a vine, then brought it and tied up the turtle to the foot of a tree.

Then Cassowary asked the turtle, "Now where are you going?" The poor turtle cried.

Cassowary went to find some fruit and brought the fruits back. Cassowary hit the turtle badly with the fruit. The poor turtle was close to dying.

Cassowary did this until there was no more fruit to be thrown. Then Cassowary went to find some that were farther away. Cassowary departed, then a little *siksik* bird came and broke the vines that bound the turtle, and the turtle fled.

Cassowary returned and saw that the turtle was not there anymore. Cassowary was incensed. Cassowary shouted, "Who broke the turtle's ropes?"

The little bird was on top of a tree and cried out, "I broke the ropes!"

Cassowary was irate and said, "Where do you shit?" The little bird said, "I shit on top of trees. Where do you shit?" Cassowary said, "I shit in the woods." The bird said to Cassowary, "If you shit in the woods, I'll ensorcell your shit."

So now little birds defecate on top of trees and their feces often stays there.

John Awola
**Karkar** Island [**Waskia** or **Takia** People]
**Madang** Province

A2480. Why a kind of bird only defecates on trees; A2494.13. Enmities of birds; A2494.13+. Enmity between cassowary and chicken; B211.3. Speaking bird; B211.3.17K. Speaking cassowary; B295.2K. Animals build canoe; B295.2.1K. Animals make voyage in canoe; B296.2K. Animal (who is land-dweller) crosses water on back of another animal; J2119.4+. Numskull puts hole in boat; K713.1.3. Animal persuaded to be tied by promise of food; P310. Friendship; R4. Surprise capture; R110. Rescue of captive; R220. Flights; W111. Laziness; X716.1H+. Birds and beasts (animal excretion)

## Why the Kangaroo Has Short Legs
(Wantok 89, April 3, 1974, page 4)

Long ago, Kangaroo and Dog were very good friends. The two of them worked well together. If one of them got into trouble, the other would work hard to help its friend. They were friends for a long time.

One morning, Kangaroo went into the forest. Meanwhile, Dog thought of ways to trick Kangaroo. Dog dug a hole then went inside and put its legs above the hole to make it look as if its legs were broken. Then Dog waited for Kangaroo to return from the forest.

In the late afternoon, Kangaroo returned and saw Dog's legs above the hole and asked, "What happened to your legs?"

"I cut them so that I can run faster," Dog replied.

"OK, then I'll cut mine too," said Kangaroo. Kangaroo did not twice about this. Kangaroo got its machete and cut off its legs. Dog then got up out of the hole and almost died laughing at his friend.

Now Kangaroo was sorry for what it had done. Kangaroo was angry. Kangaroo did not say another word, it just ran away into the forest. Kangaroo found some white earth and painted its face and chin. Then Kangaroo went back to find Dog. When Kangaroo met up with Dog, Dog tried to think what it was that made Kangaroo's mouth white. Kangaroo pointed to all of the garbage on the ground and said, "I ate all that sort of thing and it made me strong enough to fight. That's why my mouth is white."

Immediately, Dog ate the garbage on the ground. Kangaroo escaped into the forest and had a good laugh. Now, kangaroos and dogs are no longer friends. Kangaroos live in the forest and dogs eat garbage on the ground.

Otto Anduari
**Angoram** Village [**Angoram** People]
**East Sepik** Province

A2284. Origin of animal characteristics: animal persuaded into self-injury; A2371.2.10. Why kangaroo has short front legs; A2433.2.1+. Why kangaroo lives in forest; A2435.3.1+. Why dog eats garbage; A2494.4+. Enmity between dog and kangaroo; B211.1.7. Speaking dog; B211.2.12K. Speaking kangaroo; K1065+. Kangaroo persuaded into cutting off its front legs; K2297. Treacherous friend; P310. Friendship; R220. Flights; S160.1. Self-mutilation; S162. Mutilation: cutting off legs (feet); W157. Dishonesty

## The *Masalai* Who Obstructed the Garden
(Wantok 90, April 17, 1974, page 4)

Long ago in the time of the ancestors, in a place called **Bomai** Forest in **Simbu** Province, there lived a young man and woman [**Golin** and **Mikaru** Peoples].

They had a house and a garden. They worked near the river, planted food, and the food became ready for them to harvest and eat. However, they were not like man and wife, they were only like brother and sister.

One day, the boy told his sister, "I'm going into the forest now to find some vines for tying fences. Go into the garden and harvest the sweet potatoes, and get some greens for the earth oven. After you cook them, take them out and cool them for me to eat. Another thing, when you are in your garden, if you see many cucumbers, then pick them. You may eat the small and round ones, but don't eat the large and long ones."

After he said this to his sister, he went into the forest. His sister went to the garden. The sun was very hot and she picked all of the small cucumbers and ate them, but it was not enough. She went to the middle and ate more, but it was still not enough. She picked a huge cucumber in the middle of the garden and thought that it would be plenty.

"I picked a good cucumber to bring home that he would like to eat. He lied to me. I can still eat them," she said as she finished eating. She looked around in the river and saw a *masalai* woman coming to the surface. This woman thought, "I'm still here, and a woman is coming who will laugh at me."

The *masalai* woman did laugh as she approached and she said, "Carry me on your back as you weed your garden. Carry me as you wash your sweet potatoes. Carry me as you heat the stones for the earth oven. When you sit at your toilet, carry me. When you sleep at night, I must hold onto your neck while we sleep together." After she said this, the young woman lifted her up and carried her wherever she went. She felt miserable.

As the sister came back from the forest, she felt the weight of the huge *masalai* woman who did not loosen her grip and stayed on her back.

The boy spoke to his sister, "When you went to the garden, you didn't bring back any good cucumbers. Listen to me. You heard me before and you did wrong. Now you feel bigger and bigger pains."

So now the two of them slept together. However one day, early in the morning, the three of them walked down to the river where there was a bridge. The boy walked on top of the bridge first and said quietly to his sister, "When you get to the middle of the bridge, loosen the two *masalai*'s hands and she will fall into the river. Then the river will carry her away."

The woman listened to this and went to the middle of the bridge. She loosened the two hands and the *masalai* fell into the river, sweeping her away. The two young people were overjoyed and returned home.

Before, these two people did not know how to kill *masalai* women. Now, our parents make gardens near rivers when we want to get cucumbers, ripe bananas or other things. When we go to the garden and a *masalai* woman surrounds us we now know what to do to stop this kind of trouble, just like these two people did. This is a true story of the ancestors of yore.

George G. Nondri
Goroka
Eastern Highlands Province

E262+. Spirit rides on man's back; F405+. Spirit killed by pushing it into water; F401.6. Spirit in human form; F420.1.2. Water-spirit as woman (water-nymph, water-nix); F424. River-spirit; F531.0.4. Giant woman; F490+. Masalai; P210. Husband and wife; P253. Sister and brother; Q276+. Gluttony punished; Q325. Disobedience punished; R40+. Entrapment by sitting on shoulders/back; W125. Gluttony; W126. Disobedience; W157. Dishonesty

## The Mango Tree that Helped the Little Woman
(Wantok 91, May 1, 1974, page 4)

Before, there lived a little woman. Her parents had died and her maternal relative took charge of her. The name of this little woman was Wali.

When Wali's parents had died, her maternal relative said that he would give her food and a place to sleep. But her maternal relative was not a very good man. He was often angry and he gave much work to Wali. Every day, Wali worked very hard and carried water from the river. At the river there was a big mango tree.

One day, a big storm came, so Wali went to stand underneath the mango tree. Wali was not a woman to talk about herself or to worry about herself, but now she was quite worried.

After a little while, Wali turned to face the mango tree and told the story of her problems. She spoke about her maternal relative who was not nice to her. Wali felt happy inside as she told her story to the mango tree.

Every day, Wali would tell her problems to this mango tree. One afternoon she went to the river and a big storm came up again. This time, the mango tree talked to Wali.

First, the tree said Wali's name, then the tree said, "Wali, it has not been long since you came here to talk to me. A man bought me and he will cut me and make me into a canoe. After he makes me into a canoe, the people will come to see me when they push me through the river. I can't move. You must come and say, 'I have come to push you downstream.' The people will laugh at you. But you must hold me with your hand and call your name. After you call your name, I'll go downstream." The mango tree finished talking and Wali went home.

Some months later, the boys and their leaders cut this mango tree, then began to make a canoe. After they finished the canoe, the people came to look at it and push it into the river. Wali also went to look at the canoe. The boys and the leaders tried to push the canoe, but it would not even move a little bit.

So Wali said, "I can push the canoe into the water." Then the people who came to watch and the boys opened their mouths and stared at Wali. They thought Wali was not strong enough to push this big canoe. A leader came and told Wali to come and push the canoe into the water.

Wali came forth, held the canoe and said, "I am Wali." Then the canoe went into the water. The people were overjoyed for Wali. The leader called out to Wali, "I heard you talk to the canoe." Wali was not afraid because this leader did not get angry.

Wali told them the story and about her problems with her maternal relative. So, the leader became concerned about Wali and invited her to stay with his family. The leader had many things. He said that if Wali wanted something, he would give it to her. Wali was happy with her new family for many years, and then married a son of this man.

Wali lived happily until she died, and she never forgot the mango tree that helped her.

Leoba Kaugun

Yarapos High School

Wewak

East Sepik Province

D1610.2+. Speaking mango tree; D1774. Magic results from speaking; D1830. Magic strength; L102. Unpromising heroine; N815.0.1. Helpful tree-spirit; P210. Husband and wife; P271. Foster father; P275+. Foster daughter; P290+. Maternal kin; S36. Cruel foster father; T100. Marriage

## No More Ghosts
(Wantok 92, May 15, 1974, page 4)

Once, long ago there was a place where two brothers lived. After they lived together with their father and mother for many years, all of the brother's relatives and friends began to say that it was about time to purchase wives for these brothers.

Days passed, and various valuables were brought, such as axes, shell money (*kina*), black birds of paradise [probably the black sicklebill, *Epimachus fastuosus* (Beehler *et al.*, 1986: 227)], pigs to be slaughtered, and piglets.

After the preparations were completed, they gave these things to the relatives of the two women to be married to the brothers, and then they were married. The big brother had a boy and two girls. The little brother had a boy and a girl.

After some years, the younger brother became sick and died, and he was buried in a grave. The ancestors had a rule that if a man or child died, they would paint their faces with mud.

After a week had passed since the young brother's death, the older brother had not given a funeral party. He had many pigs and chickens, but he left them alone. He went inside his house and got a *kina* shell to trade for a pig so that he could give a party for his deceased brother. He took the *kina* and left.

He walked to a faraway place and traded this *kina* for a huge pig, then he brought the pig back with him. But his home was far away, so he found himself in the forest as the sun set. He made himself a shelter to stay for the night. He was in the deep forest, far from any people.

He made a bonfire and tied the pig up at one place while he slept at another near the fire. He wanted to close his eyes and sleep, but he could not. He just could not sleep. Many thoughts came to him, of dead men, of malevolent ghosts, of malign sorcery, of the ancestral spirits, and of his dead brother. He tossed and turned, and he wanted to forget these thoughts but he could not.

He heard something outside his shelter that sounded like a man walking around. He stared at the doorway, then he saw a man enter. He saw something fastened to the man's body. It was the same thing that was on his brother when he was buried. He now realized that he was seeing the ghost of his little brother. He trembled with utter fright, he urinated and defecated, and he broke into a sweat.

But then he got up, took a burning stick from the fire and thrashed his brother's ghost with it. He spoke to the ghost, "I had thought of you and I walked to that faraway place. Why have you come here?" He said this as he fought, and the ghost ran away. If the big brother had not chased away the ghost of his little brother, the ghost would have entered his shelter and continued to frighten him.

So now when we go into the forest, the ghosts will not frighten us. All of us should give thanks for the work of this big brother. Now we can walk freely into the forest to find wild game, edible mushrooms, and many other things. Men, women, children, and old people too, all of you can go into the forest.

Lucas Maglum Depo

Mt. Hagen

Western Highlands Province

A2800+. Why it is now safe to travel in the forest unmolested by ghosts; E226. Dead brother's return; E235.2+. Ghost returns because of improper mourning; E439.5. Revenant forced away by fire; E461. Fight of revenant with living person; P210. Husband and wife; P231. Mother and son; P232. Mother and daughter; P233. Father and son; P234. Father and daughter; P251.5. Two brothers; P253. Sister and brother; P253.0.2+. Two sisters and one brother; P681+. Mourning customs: earth on body; R220. Flights; T52. Bride purchased; T100. Marriage; V61.3+. Dead buried; W27. Gratitude


## The Tree That Helped a Man

(Wantok 93, June 5, 1974, page 4)

Long ago, there was an isolated island. This island had no men, there was only an old woman who lived there. This woman became pregnant and then gave birth to a boy. The boy grew up and took charge of the island.

His mother called him Tanepoa. This island had many kinds of trees that produced edible fruits, trees with nice aromas, and trees with flowers too. Many kinds of birds came to eat the tree fruits.

The old woman was called Nante. Old Nante became pregnant again and gave birth to another boy. But this time Nante gave birth to a baby that had a human head and a snake's tail. The mother of these two children gave the name Ruguraba to her newborn child.

Nante's first boy was now an adult and often gardened, but he was not married. His little brother was like a snake, so he did not work in the garden. But he fished and sang and danced, and was able to pull and remove things.

These two children, Tanepoa and Ruguraba, lived together and liked each other. Later, the young brother, Ruguraba, said to his big brother Tanepoa, "Brother, you are fully grown. Where can we find you a wife?"

The big brother, Tanepoa, said, "We do not have a woman on this island. So Ruguraba sang and danced at a tree that had a nice aroma. Then he sent the tree drifting in the sea, and it traveled to a place near a beach. The smell of the tree still wafted about and annoyed the people of this place, so they went to collect the flowers and leaves and vines of this tree.

However, one young woman was sick and did not go. A little later this woman felt better, and she went to go get some pieces of the tree. But there were no leaves or flowers to be obtained above water level, so she went to look on a branch that was submerged beneath the water. The woman found one and began to break off its bark.

While she broke off the bark of this tree, the tree began to move out to the sea. The men on the shore saw that this tree was moving, so they called out to her. The woman jumped, but then rested. Later, the tree sped up and brought the woman along to the shore of this island.

Before long, the old woman, Nante, with her two sons ran and fetched the woman for Tanepoa. Ruguraba saw the woman and spoke to his brother Tanepoa, "Brother, look at your wife. I worked hard to bring you your wife and now that you have a wife. We won't have anymore worries."

The big brother was overjoyed and made a huge welcome party for his little brother. So, Ruguraba called out to his friends, many kinds of birds, and his old mother for this party. All of the birds gathered and Ruguraba went among them. He explained to these, his friends, that his brother was now married and that his wife's name was Moaede.

Later he danced and sang, and Moaede was no longer worried about his village.

Herman Rupunae Moing

**Manam** Island [**Manam** People]

**Madang** Province

B29.2.1. Serpent with human head; D1520.1. Magic transportation by bough; D1781. Magic results from singing; D1781+. Magic results from dancing; P210. Husband and wife; P231. Mother and son; P251.5. Two

brothers; P263. Brother-in-law; P264. Sister-in-law; P310. Friendship;
T100. Marriage; T570+. Pregnancy without intercourse; T580. Childbirth


## Why Do Men Kill Rats and
## Marsupials (*Kapul*)?

(Wantok 94, June 19, 1974, page 4)

Long ago, Marsupial (*Kapul*), Rat and Man were three
good friends. They played, worked, and walked together.
Marsupial worked at cutting pandanus nuts (*karuka*) and
carrying them. Rat worked at turning the earth and planting
all kinds of foods. Man often ate a lot, but Marsupial and
Rat ate little.

One time, Marsupial and Rat talked. Rat said, "We always work hard but we don't get much to eat. Man only
works at filling his belly. I don't like this situation. I'm
tired of it."

Marsupial agreed with this and said, "Let's break off
with Man and become his enemies. If we are walking together in the sun, he'll be able to see us. So, when the sun
is out, we must hide and rest and sleep. Man sleeps at
night, so that is when we should walk and find food."

Marsupial and Rat did not know how to divide their
work. One went to the forest to find food. One knew how
to get food there. The other went close to Man's garden
and stole Man's sweet potatoes and other foods from his
garden.

Marsupial slept inside pandanus tree leaves. Rat became angry with Man. Rat hid inside Man's house and cut
up everything that belonged to him. When Man slept at
night, Rat stole his food.

When the pandanus trees were full of nuts, Marsupial
would cut off the nuts and eat them.

So then, Man cried when he saw all of these things that
Rat and Marsupial had ruined. Man had no way to kill
them so he thought hard.

One time, he was crying and he heard something
walking towards him. He looked and saw Dog approaching. Dog said, "Why are you crying?" Man told the story
about Marsupial and Rat. So then, Dog was very sorry for
Man and told him, "I can help you. But I'm not one who
works. If you look after me and give me food, then I'll be
your friend forever and I'll do whatever you tell me."
Man said, "I can give you food. Help me to kill Marsupial
and Rat." Dog agreed to this, then chased and surrounded
Marsupial and Rat. So now, Dog helped Man a lot. That is
how this relationship began.

Now dogs are man's good friends. Marsupials and rats
are enemies of man. When a marsupial or rat meets a man
somewhere, they do not like it. They see the man's face
and then run away. Men know how to send their dogs after
them and kill them right away.

Kingi Yakili
Mt. Hagen
Western Highlands Province

A2452.1. Why dogs hunt; A2493.4. Friendship between man and dog;
A2500+. Why rats are nocturnal; A2500+. Why marsupials are nocturnal;
A2585+. Enmity between marsupial and man; A2585+. Enmity between
rat and man; B211.1.7. Speaking dog; B211.2.12K+. Speaking marsupial;
B211.2.9. Speaking rat; B421. Helpful dog; K300. Thefts and
cheats—general; P310. Friendship; Q212. Theft punished; W125. Gluttony


## The Lazy She-Cockatoo

(Wantok 95, July 3, 1974, page 4)

Inside the deep forest there were two birds, a cockatoo
and a dove (or pigeon). The cockatoo was an enemy of the
dove. The dove was a hardworking female and the cockatoo was a talkative and lazy female who stole things from
the dove.

One time, the dove went to process sago. When the
cockatoo heard the crash of the sago tree falling, she was
surprised. She raced over and called out loudly, "Hey!
Hey! Who's that who is crashing about in the forest?" But
the dove did not reply. No, she closed her mouth and
worked.

Another day, the cockatoo again heard a crash and
called out, "Hey! Hey! Who's that down there in the forest?" But the dove was silent and continued at her work.
So the gabby bird asked the dove again, "Hey! Hey!
Who's that making all that noise? How can anyone sleep?
Do you only think of eating? You have a huge belly like a
cow. All you do is eat, night and day."

The dove became angry, just like water boiling over in
a pot. So, she brought her stone axe that she was using to
scrape sago. She went away, slowly and quietly, so that the
cockatoo would not see her. She traveled as silently as a
snake and hid inside some grass. Oh, poor cockatoo! She
was cooking food and did not realize what was happening

As the dove approached the house and saw the cockatoo, she quickly threw her axe at the cockatoo's head. The
poor cockatoo fell to the ground as blood gushed out. Then
the dove went back home.

Judah Akesim

C. L. T. C. [Christian Leaders Training College]

Banz Village

Western Highlands Province

A2494.13+. Enmity between cockatoo and dove/pigeon; B211.3+. Speaking cockatoo; B299.9+. Dove/pigeon processes sago; K300. Thefts and cheats—general; Q393.1. Punishment for talking too much; W111. Laziness; W125. Gluttony; W141. Talkativeness

## The Ghost Who Befouled the Sister

*(Wantok 96, July 17, 1974, page 4)*

There was a young man named Lyailelya with his sister named Tapieda Ipali. They lived together in a village called **Gulipyanda** in **Enga** Province [**Enga** People]. This is a true story about them.

One time the man told his sister, "Now is a good time for me to find wild game in the forest. Stay here at the house." But the sister said, "I don't like to stay home alone. I want to come with you." The brother said to his sister, "Who are you afraid of? You must stay at the house." After he told his sister this, he left to find game in the forest while the young woman stayed at their house.

A male ghost turned into an apparition that looked like the brother and carried game to the house. The ghost called to the young woman, "Sister, sister, I've returned. Come and look at the game that I killed." The woman thought it was her real brother, so she got up and went outside. The woman thought that her brother had returned too quickly, so she asked him, "Brother, how did you kill that game? Why did you come home so quickly?"

The ghost said to the woman, "I wanted to kill a lot of game, but something got in my eye, so I returned. Sister, come see what is in my eye. After you get it out, I'll go to find more game."

The young woman thought that he was telling the truth. So, the woman went very close to the ghost and looked in his eye. Then the ghost gave her a kiss. After they kissed, the woman cried and said to him, "I'm your true sister, why did you do that to me?" The ghost smashed his head and fell to the ground, but did not say anything. Then he got up and said to the woman, "That is the first time that I found game and that I did that. I think that something bad from the forest fouled me up and made me do that bad thing to you. But now after you said that, I'm ashamed. I'll return to the forest to find some more game."

The woman did not think that it was a ghost, she thought it was her real brother who did this, so she continued to cry.

After the ghost departed, the real brother returned with plenty of game. The brother awakened her, but she looked angry and did not get up. She told her brother, "Who wants your game anyhow? You're always shouting. You can eat it but I don't want it."

The woman's brother was very troubled, but he did not know that the ghost had come and done that bad thing to her. He went out and killed his pig to pacify his sister, but he could not make her happy because of what the ghost had done. The poor brother asked her to come and eat the food, but she was strong-willed and said, "You can eat your pig. You're the one who likes your good pig."

Her brother was angry and asked her, "What have I done that you are treating me this way? OK, if you don't want to look at me then I'll leave you." After he said this, he took a piece of pig's leg and stood outside. The grease from the pig fell to the ground and formed a pond.

The sister tried to come outside, but could not. There was a big lake surrounding her brother. The woman called out, "Come here and we can marry." But the brother was getting deeper. The woman wanted to hold him but was unable to do so. The area was flooded and her brother kept getting deeper. Later, she tried again, but she still was unable to do so. Then the water capsized a tree and killed her.

The ghost did this, and the brother and sister died at this time.

Benjamin Yapson

Wewak

East Sepik Province

A1012+. Flood from pork grease; D476+. Transformation: grease to lake; E217. Fatal kiss from dead; E425.2. Revenant as man; E545. The dead speak; K1330+. Woman kissed by inducing her to look at alleged object in man's eye; K1930. Treacherous impostors; P253. Sister and brother

## The Bird of Paradise That Became a Man

*(Wantok 97, August 7, 1974, page 4)*

This is a short story from the ancestors of my village that I would like to tell you. Long ago, before the white people came here, there were no people where my village is. However at this time, there lived two old people in the area of my village.

These two did not have a child, even though they were quite old. One day, they did not eat. They stayed inside their house and talked and thought. They continued talking and thinking until it was nearly dark. Then they went outside and said, "Oh, we're quite old, we don't have children, and we'll be dead soon." After they said this, they continued to worry.

A little while later, a bird of paradise came and perched on a casuarina tree near their house. The old man saw the bird first and pointed it out to the old woman. The old woman got up and talked to the old man. She said, "Oh, old man, climb that tree and catch that bird of paradise. Then come down and we'll take care of it." After the old woman said this, the old man climbed the casuarina tree. He caught the bird and came down. They brought the bird inside their house and freed it on their bed.

That night, the two old people slept. The bird of paradise slept with them in their bed. They slept until morning when they saw that the bird of paradise was not there. But in the bed, they saw a boy sleeping. They then knew that the bird of paradise had become the boy.

The old couple was very happy that they had a boy who could take care of them. They prepared many things to eat and they made a party for the boy. The boy grew into a big man, married and had many children. Now, there are many people who are my kin.

John Rutaikunda
Goroka
Eastern Highlands Province

D350+B. Transformation: bird of paradise to boy; N825.1. Childless old couple adopt hero; P210. Husband and wife; P230. Parents and children; P271. Foster father; P272. Foster mother; P275. Foster son; T100. Marriage

## The Ghost Who Killed the Selfish Man

(Wantok 98, August 21, 1974, page 4)

In one village, there was a man and woman who were satiated. However, they were short of food and worked hard to find more. There was a man among them who did not share his food. He was too selfish. None of the other men, women and children liked him.

One day, this man went to find wild game in the forest. However, he did not find game because a ghost also went along.

The man saw a tree fruit that a marsupial (*kapul*) had eaten at night. He said, "I will come back tonight and kill a marsupial." The ghost heard this and left.

The man returned to his house, fixed his bow and waited for the moon that night. When the moon rose, he left. The ghost asked him, "Maternal relative, where do you want to go?"

"I'm going to find a marsupial in the forest."

Then the ghost said, "I want to come with you."

The two of them came to the base of a tree and saw many marsupials fighting. "Maternal relative, go find a vine and I'll climb the tree," said the man.

The ghost said, "I found a vine, take it and climb."

The man thought that it was a real vine, so he took it and climbed the tree. He reached the top of the tree and put the vine around his neck. Then he shot marsupials that fell to the ground.

The man heard the bones of the marsupials cracking so he asked, "Maternal relative, what are you doing?" The ghost said, "I'm gathering the marsupials." However, he was not gathering marsupials, he was eating them.

The man was terrified. He broke a tree branch and prepared to throw it far away. He said, "Maternal relative, look carefully. I'm going to shoot a marsupial that is far away."

The man threw the branch far away, to a difficult place to get to. The ghost thought that it was a marsupial, and so went to get it. The man came down right away and ran home. However when the man tried to remove the vine that was around his neck, he was unable to do so. It was stuck.

The ghost came looking for the man and called out, "Muscle." Then the vine on the man's neck replied, "Yes." The man was shocked and tried again to remove the vine from his neck, but it was stuck fast.

He left the vine there and continued to run to the village. The man wanted to open the door to his house but he could not, then he died. The ghost came and removed the man's two eyes and ate them. The next morning, the people saw his body and the buried him.

W. Mano Lapa
**Rintebe** Village [**Benabena** People]
Goroka
**Eastern Highlands** Province

D1203. Magic rope; D1610.28+. Speaking rope; D1765. Magic results produced by command; E250. Bloodthirsty revenants; E425.2. Revenant as man; E545. The dead speak; G11.10. Cannibalistic spirits; K1930. Treacherous impostors; P290+. Maternal kin; Q272. Avarice punished; Q411. Death as punishment; Q425. Punishment: suffocating; R210. Escapes; S113.2. Murder by suffocation; V61.3+. Dead buried; W151. Greed

## The Dead Man Who Came to Life Again

(Wantok 99, September 4, 1974, page 4)

Once there was a young man named Nikint. His house was on top of a mountain. Whenever he looked towards a certain place, he saw smoke rising.

Nikint thought, "I think that I'll go find out what's causing that smoke." Then he went to his parents' house and said, "I would like to have my pig killed and then to bring it to that place." His parents said, "It would be bad if you got lost when you left home. Never mind that plan." Nikint said, "I can't get lost. I must go and return."

So, they killed this pig and cooked it in an earth oven. In the early morning, he woke up and carried the pig. He went far away to the place where the smoke rose.

He arrived at a river where a woman was coughing and blowing mucous from her nose while she was washing sweet potatoes. The man was sorry for her, so he cut off a piece of pig's leg and gave it to her.

The old woman said, "You're a very good man. They never gave me a piece of pork as you have. Will you marry a young woman named Rangapa?" The man said, "You saw what I did, but I didn't come to get married. I'm looking for the place where the smoke rises."

Nikint got up and went to the place from where the smoke came. There, he saw a very pretty woman. Nikint trembled at her beauty. The woman got up and looked at this man and she also trembled at the sight of him.

The woman took Nikint to her house. While they were walking along the trail to the house, they thought a lot. The man thought that the woman was very nice, and the woman thought that he was attractive too. They arrived at the woman's house and talked to her parents. "I brought my boyfriend here. You should shake hands with him." Her parents were happy and shook hands with Nikint. Nikint gave the pig to them, then they ate and slept.

In the early morning, the woman dressed up nicely and prepared to go with Nikint. They said good-bye to the parents, then the man took the woman and went to his village. They came to the mountain and looked at the woman's village in the distance, from where an enormous amount of smoke was coming.

The man spoke to the woman, "You should wait here. I'll go immediately and see what is happening there." The man ran and came to the woman's village. He saw a big fight happening between the woman's clan and another group of people. Nikint was a very strong man and he killed many men from the other group. He fought and fought, but a small man from the other group shot him and he died.

Nikint's ghost went to the woman and said, "A big fight came up between your clan and another group. I killed many men and then I came here." After he said this, he took the woman to his village. They came to his house and he said to her, "Go sit in the house. I must go and drink some water." But he was a ghost, so he did not return to the house.

The woman sat for a while then someone called out, "Nikint was killed in the fight and we have carried his body here." When the woman heard this, she became distressed and cried in the house.

They carried the man's body into the house and the woman said, "I want you to leave the man's body here in his unheated house." The men replied, "Never mind that idea. We must bury his body." However, the woman was stubborn, and they put his body in the cold house so that the body would not rot.

The woman heated some water and threw it on the man's skin. Then the man came to life again and began to eat. The people were ecstatic, they went and killed some pigs and had a party.

Thomas Mek
C. T. C. **Pumakos** [**Enga** People]
**Enga** Province

E80. Water of life; E321. Dead husband's friendly return; E425.2. Revenant as man; F610. Remarkably strong man; P210. Husband and wife; P231. Mother and son; P232. Mother and daughter; P233. Father and son; P234. Father and daughter; P261. Father-in-law; P262. Mother-in-law; P265. Son-in-law; Q42. Generosity rewarded; S110. Murders; T15. Love at first sight; T100. Marriage; W11. Generosity; W167. Stubbornness

## The Old People Who Found the Stone Axe
(Wantok 100, September 18, 1974, page 4)

Long, long ago, two old people went into the forest. They were looking for a marsupial (*kapul*) in the forest to kill. This marsupial is called *malga*.

When they found a marsupial, it was nearly dark. They killed the marsupial, brought it out of the forest and found a place to cook it. They started to prepare the marsupial, but they did not have a bamboo knife to cut out the guts. They tried to find some bamboo, but there was none nearby.

The man continued to look for some bamboo and the woman sat and waited. As the old woman sat waiting, she felt something poking her buttocks.

The woman stood up and saw that it was a long stone. The woman picked up another stone and hit the long stone. Then she saw that the stone was sharpened where she had broken it. She took the long stone and tried to cut some grass. The stone cut the grass well.

Then the old man came and the woman said to him, "I found something to gut the marsupial." So, the two of them were happy and removed the guts of the marsupial. They cooked it in an earth oven and ate it. They took the sharp stone with them when they returned home.

They told all of the men of their village about the sharp stone. The men broke this stone further and made a stone axe. The men called this axe, "Kunjun." It is the name of the place where the stone axe was found.

This place where the stone axe was found is forbidden to women, because the ghost of the old woman who found the stone axe does not want other women to see this stone that is used to make axes. If women come to this place, then the old woman's ghost will hide the stone axes.

When men cannot find stone for axes, they must find the _malga_ marsupial and cook it in an earth oven. This is so that the ancestors who found the first stone axe can eat the aroma of the marsupial and can give the stone axes back to men.

They cannot kill any other kind of marsupial, they must kill only the _malga_ marsupial. Until then, they will not be able to find another stone axe, and all of the existing stone axes will break quickly.

Karl Dimaua
C. T. C. **Pumakos** [**Enga** People]
**Enga** Province

A1446.2. Origin of the axe; C181. Tabu confined to women; C610+. Tabu: going to location where axes originated; D1766.2. Magic results produced by sacrifices; V12.4+. Marsupial as sacrifice

## How Two Mountains Were Named
(Wantok 101, October 2, 1974, page 4)

Long, long ago, there was an old man with two sons who lived in a village called Mungaro [**Mungoro** Village, **Kewa** People]. The old man's name was Gilwe; his sons' names were Yapai and Wayapa.

Each of these three men had a dog. They often planted many kinds of foods, wild game was plentiful, and they were happy.

One day, the old father told his two sons, "Tomorrow we'll go into the deep forest and cut trees to make a garden." The two sons agreed to this and they went to sleep.

They awoke in the early morning. They put some sweet potatoes in their net bags and went to cut trees in the forest. In the middle of where they were clearing their garden was a huge tree. The two brothers climbed this tree to cut the branches off.

When they stood high on top of this tree, they saw smoke coming from their house. They told their father, "It looks like our house is on fire, there's much smoke coming from our house." They came down quickly and shot off towards the house.

As they approached their house, the father told them, "Wait here while I go to see who is at our house." Gilwe went to the house and saw an old man there named Yalibu who had come from the **Western Highlands** [**Hagen** People]. He asked Yalibu, "Maternal relative, what have you come here to do?"

Yalibu said, "My village is having a big celebration and I came to get your two children. They can dance and sing at my village. Then I'll bring them back to you." Gilwe said, "But I don't have any children." "Don't lie to me," Yalibu said, "I saw three beds in your house."

Gilwe was ashamed and said, "OK, you can take them and go, but after the celebration is finished, you must bring them back to me." Gilwe told his two children to come to the house and then go to the celebration.

The two brothers dressed up nicely. They put bird of paradise feathers on their heads and then went with old Yalibu to his village. When they arrived at the village, the two brothers saw that there was no celebration, Yalibu had lied to them.

Yalibu put the two brothers with their two dogs into a huge hole. In this hole there were other men too. Yalibu had been eating them.

There was no easy way out of the hole, but Yapai and Wayapa's two dogs were determined and managed to get out. The two dogs found a big vine and gave it to the two brothers, then pulled them out. After they came out of the hole, they pulled all of the other men out too.

Then the two brothers ran home to their father. But the old Yalibu ran after them. He still wanted to kill and eat them. They ran and approached their village, then called to their father.

Old Gilwe heard this and quickly took his spear and stone axe. He came and met Yalibu in the trail. Gilwe found Yalibu, but Yalibu was strong and resisted. Then the brothers arrived and they killed Yalibu.

At the place where Yalibu died, Mount Yalibu [Ialibu] arose [Southern and Western Highlands Provinces]. Later at the place were Gilwe was buried, Mount Gilwe [Giluwe] arose [**Southern Highlands** Province]. Now you can see these two mountains standing. The dogs of Gilwe live on Mount Giluwe as wild dogs.

Cornelius Koya
Erave
Southern Highlands Province

A962.1. Mountain from part of deity's (hero's) body; A962.1+. Mountain from part of cannibal; A1617. Origin of place-name; B540+. Dog rescuer; G10. Cannibalism; K710. Victim enticed into voluntary captivity or helplessness; P233. Father and son; P251.5. Two brothers; P290+. Maternal kin; Q213. Abduction punished; Q411. Death as punishment; R100. Rescues; R210. Escapes; R260. Pursuits; S110. Murders; V61.3+. Dead buried; W157. Dishonesty

## The Man Who Only Had a Head

(Wantok 102, October 16, 1974, page 4)

Long ago, there was a pond. At this pond there lived a man who had only a head. Near the pond was a village. In the evening, the people of the village said that they would go look for wild game at the pond in the next morning.

When morning came, the people went and they found many fish. By evening, there was only one man who was still looking for game.

The man who only had a head was hungry, so he too went to the pond to look for game. The head saw the testicles of the man who was looking for game in the pond. The head thought that the testicles would be good meat to eat, so he took a bite.

However, the man was pained by this and shouted, "Let go of my balls!"

The head said, "I'm not letting go. This is my food." The man said, "If you let go of my balls, I'll give you a banana."

The man called out all kinds of foods to the head, but the head said, "I don't eat those kinds of foods."

So the man called out, "Breadfruit." The head said, "That's my kind of food."

The man said, "OK, let go of me and we will go find some breadfruit." The head said, "When we get some breadfruit, then I'll let go of you."

The two of them came to a breadfruit tree, and the head said, "Let's climb this breadfruit tree, then after you throw down some breadfruit I will go and get it." The man climbed the breadfruit tree with the head still hanging onto his testicles. The man picked a breadfruit and threw it down. Then the head went down and got the breadfruit.

The head said, "You must throw down one more." The man threw down one more far away. While the head went to get the breadfruit, the man came down as quickly as he could and ran back to his village. When the head came back, he saw that the man had run away. So, the head took his two breadfruits and ran home to his pond.

Emil Simangu

Brandi High School

Wewak

East Sepik Province

F501. Person consisting only of head; G10. Cannibalism; G80+. Cannibal eats breadfruit in lieu of man's testicles; G361.2. Great head as ogre; X712.3.1H. Injury to testicles

## How Pigs Arrived on Karkar Island

(Wantok 103, November 6, 1974, page 4)

Long ago, two men lived in a village called **Gial** on **Karkar** Island in **Madang** Province [**Waskia** People]. Their names were _Bega_ ["Mustard"] and _Muri_ ["Betel Nut" (Chris Dal, personal communication)]. One time, their friends who lived on the other side of the island sent a message to them that they should come to their party.

So, they walked for four days and nights on trails and came to their friends' village. Their friends brought them into the party where many people were making flattering remarks, playing, telling jokes, and having a good time.

When they divided the food, they forgot to give a dish of food to Bega. After the party finished, Muri and Bega went back to their village. While they walked along the trail, Bega was hungry, so he asked Muri to give him some food. But Muri did not want to give any food to Bega.

Near the trail, Muri went to defecate in the woods. After Muri returned to the trail, Bega went into the woods and ate Muri's feces.

Muri saw this and said to Bega, "Friend, you can't eat shit." Bega replied, "But when I asked you for food you didn't give me any." As Bega said this, he turned into a pig.

After they returned to their village, Muri called out for Bega to come up into their house, but Bega went underneath and slept. This is how pigs came to Karkar Island.

M. G. Mowan

Karkar Island

Madang Province

A1871. Creation of hog (pig); D136M. Transformation: man to swine; D551.6+. Transformation by eating excrement; P251.5.3. Hostile brothers; P310. Friendship; X716H+. The escoumerda; W152. Stinginess; W125. Gluttony; W158. Inhospitality

## The Marsupial (*Kapul*) that Struck the Sister's Breast

(Wantok 104, November 20, 1974, pages 4, 12)

Long, long ago, there was a brother and a sister. The brother's name was Kuta and the sister's name was Paiyali. They lived in a village called **Yango** [**Kewa** People, **Southern Highlands**]. They had a huge pig named Puramenalasa.

They divided their work between them. The young Paiyali cooked the food, cared for the pig, looked after the garden and took care of all of the things around the house. The young Kuta killed many kinds of wild game, made fences for the garden, cut firewood, and fetched water.

One day, Kuta went to the forest to look for game while Paiyali went to the garden and made mounds for planting sweet potatoes.

Kuta killed a marsupial (*kapul*) called _loke_. He gutted the marsupial and put it near the garden without telling his sister, then he went to find more game.

The marsupial looked up and saw the young woman making a mound for sweet potatoes. The marsupial took a tree fruit, aimed it at Paiyali's breasts and threw it straight at them.

The young woman was surprised. She saw the marsupial and beat it until it died. Paiyali was not happy and she began to cry, "Why didn't brother tell me he had put this marsupial here?"

When Kuta came to the garden and saw his sister crying, he asked her, "Hey, who hit you?" The sister did not reply, she just cried. Kuta was tired of asking questions, so he took the marsupial and went home to cook it. At the house, the brother told his sister to eat the marsupial, but his sister just kept crying.

So in the early morning, Kuta awoke and prepared to kill their big pig for themselves. After he finished cooking the pig in an earth oven, he took it out and divided it up well. He gave part to his sister who was still crying.

Kuta also divided different kinds of decorations between themselves. He put his share into a net bag with his share of pork. He got up and began to walk to a place near Erave where their maternal relative lived.

His sister stood up and spoke to him, "Please come back. You didn't tell me when you put the marsupial near the garden. The marsupial hit my breast and caused me to cry."

The brother replied, "Yes, I asked you many times and you didn't reply. Never mind. You can stay here while I go to look for my maternal relative."

Kuta left and came to the village of his relatives. One young man asked him, "Friend, why have you come here?" Kuta told him, "I came to look for my maternal relative."

The man said, "OK, come inside and sit in your maternal relative's room."

Then a large, old man came and told Kuta, "I haven't been looking for tree leaves [i.e., the branches of the family tree], so what have you come here to do?" Kuta did not have anything to say, so he kept his mouth shut. The old man brought a vine and tied him to one of the house posts.

His sister, Paiyali, had followed Kuta. She had come and hidden in the grass near the house where Kuta was.

When Kuta's maternal relative arrived, he saw that they had tied up Kuta with a rope. This angered him, so he told them, "This is my maternal relative, he isn't a pig and you have tied him up." He untied the vines, then killed two men and ran into the forest.

They tied up Kuta again, then they cut off some of his flesh and cut out his eyes and began to eat him. Paiyali heard them cutting Kuta and she began to cry. She thought that it was her fault.

An old woman who had gotten some [of his] blood in a bamboo tube was returning along the trail where Paiyali was sitting. She watched her and asked, "Child, what are you doing?"

Paiyali said, "I am Kuta's sister but they have eaten him." The old woman said, "OK, come and we will go to my house."

The old woman was the mother of Kuta's maternal relative. She said, "Child, I am the mother of your maternal relative." Paiyali heard this and she was happy.

At night the maternal relative came to the house of the old woman. The old woman told him, "Child, a maternal relative of yours has followed her brother here. You must take her back to her village quickly."

The old woman gave Paiyali the bamboo tube of blood and said, "You must put this in a cold place, this is the blood of Kuta."

So the maternal relative took the young woman, and they went to her village.

When Paiyali arrived at her village, she put Kuta's blood in a cold place. Then Kuta became a man again. She was happy and held tightly onto Kuta. The two of them lived in the village. Later Kuta married a woman who gave birth to his first child.

One day, the wife and sister went to the garden while Kuta was looking after his child. The two women returned home quickly, so Kuta was a little angry. When the women came home, Kuta scolded his wife and sister.

His sister told him, "They nearly ate you, but I carried your blood here. That is why you're still alive, so why should you be angry at me?"

Kuta listened to this and turned into the wind. They never saw him again.

The two women were sorry and they became birds. The child too became a small bird and tried to find his father in the garden.

Cornelius Koya

C. T. C. Erave

Southern Highlands Province

D150B. Transformation: boy to bird; D150W. Transformation: woman to bird; D281.1M. Transformation: man to wind; E3. Dead animal comes to life; E113. Resuscitation by blood; G10. Cannibalism; P210. Husband and wife; P233. Father and son; P253. Sister and brother; P253.4. Girl comes to brother's aid when he is attacked; P264. Sister-in-law; P290+. Maternal kin; P294. Aunt; P297. Nephew; R4. Surprise capture; R260. Pursuits; R350. Recapture of fugitive; S70+. Murder of kin; S110. Murders; S110+. Eaten alive; S160. Mutilations; S165. Mutilation: putting out eyes; T100. Marriage; T580. Childbirth

## How Kangaroos Lost their Arms

(Wantok 105, December 4, 1974, page 5)

Once there was a place near the beach where Kangaroo and Dog lived. [The northern pademelon, *Tylogale browni*, is the sole species of kangaroo on New Britain (Flannery, 1995b: 83-84).] One time, Kangaroo got up and went into the forest to find breadfruit. Kangaroo picked some, returned home, then cooked and ate them.

Dog came and asked Kangaroo, "Friend, what are you eating?" Kangaroo said, "I'm eating some breadfruit." Dog asked Kangaroo, "Can I try one?" Kangaroo gave one to Dog. Dog ate it and thought it was delicious.

Dog asked Kangaroo where he had gotten it, and Kangaroo said that he had gotten it in the forest. Later, Dog went to the forest, found some breadfruit and returned to cook it. Dog asked Kangaroo how to remove the skin to eat it.

Kangaroo said, "I rub it on my chest to remove the skin." Dog stood up and rubbed the breadfruit on its skin, which then came off. Kangaroo was not sorry for Dog. Kangaroo said that if Dog was in pain that Dog must rub it harder and not to be afraid. So, Dog rubbed it again and the skin came off completely.

Poor Dog felt a great pain and thought of how to get revenge. One day, Dog told Kangaroo, "Friend, come and we can go find some fish in the sea. Now is a good time for fishing." So they went to the beach, got a canoe and paddle, and went out to sea.

They paddled off and then Dog saw a [giant] clam. Dog went to get it to eat. Kangaroo saw this and asked, "What are you eating?" Dog said, "I'm eating a clam." Kangaroo said to Dog, "If you see another one, I'll go down and get it."

Dog saw a clam and told Kangaroo to go down and fetch it. Kangaroo said, "How should I get it?" Dog told Kangaroo, "When you see that the clam is open, shove your hands inside and pull it out."

Kangaroo went down into the sea and shoved its two hands into the mouth of the clam. Then the clam closed its mouth and cut off Kangaroo's two hands. Dog had lied to Kangaroo and Kangaroo lost his its arms. Now, kangaroos only have two short arms.

Walter Tobung Tabu ["ToBungTabu" is a **Tolai** men's name (**East New Britain** Province)]

Hoskins Village

West New Britain

A2284. Origin of animal characteristics: animal persuaded into self-injury; A2371.2.10. Why kangaroo has short front legs; A2494.4+. Enmity between dog and kangaroo; B211.1.7. Speaking dog; B211.2.12K. Speaking kangaroo; B874.6. Giant clam; K890+. Deceived into sticking body part into giant clam; K1065+. Kangaroo persuaded into cutting off its front legs; K2297. Treacherous friend; P310. Friendship; Q261. Treachery punished; Q451. Mutilation as punishment; S161. Mutilation: cutting off hands (arms); W157. Dishonesty

## Dog is Man's Good Friend

(Wantok 106, December 18, 1974, page 5)

Long, long ago, in the time of the ancestors, a brother and sister lived in a village called **Semin** [**Mendi** People, **Southern Highlands** Province]. The man's name was Hil and the woman's name was Naowe.

One day, Hil told his sister, "I want to look for some marsupials (*kapul*) in the forest." So his sister prepared some sweet potatoes, put them into a net bag, and gave it to him.

Hil went into the deep forest and saw a big tree. He came to the foot of this tree and saw a big hole. He put down all of his things and shoved his hand into the hole. Oh my! A big marsupial was inside and it bit onto his hand in such a way that he was unable to pull it out. He was also irritated by the cold wind, and he was wet.

A dog named Kanmap came by and asked him, "Friend, what are you doing at the foot of this tree?" Hil said, "Friend, a marsupial is chewing on my hand and I can't pull it out."

So the dog went inside the tree hole, killed the marsupial and pulled it out. The man was elated and grateful.

The dog said, "What will you do with this marsupial?" The man said, "Friend, I came out here to look for this. If you help me to kill 20 marsupials today, I'll bring you to my house and give you good food from the garden."

The dog listened to this and was pleased. The dog went with Hil that day. Then the dog told Hil, "Friend, I don't like that other food, I only like sweet potato."

Hil told the dog, "Yes, you will see some. My sister will cook some delicious sweet potato."

They cooked all of the marsupials in an earth oven at the house and the roasted the sweet potatoes in the fire for the dog. The brother and sister ate the marsupials and gave the sweet potatoes to the dog. The dog ate up all of the sweet potatoes.

So now, the dog was a good friend with Hil and helped him to kill marsupials. Now we can see the loyal manner of dogs.

Saimon Saiminal
Erave
Southern Highlands Province

A2493.4. Friendship between man and dog; B211.1.7. Speaking dog; B540+. Dog rescuer; P253. Sister and brother; P310. Friendship; R4. Surprise capture; R100. Rescues; W27. Gratitude

## Pembu Flew like a Bird
(Wantok 107, January 1, 1975, page 5)

Long ago, there was an old man and woman who lived in a village. They had one son named Pembu.

Pembu did not sleep with his parents at home. He would sleep in the forest, kill marsupials (*kapul*) and birds, and then bring them to his old folks.

One day, Pembu came home and heard many men talking in the house, so he asked them, "Who are you men who have come here?" He went inside and he saw a large man there. Pembu asked, "Father, when are you coming?"

The large man said, "Please, good man, there is a man at my village who has a spear in his heart and no one is able to remove it. I heard that you are knowledgeable about how to cut open men and remove spears."

His parents heard this and were strongly against Pembu going with this man. However, Pembu was stubborn and he decided to go. The big man was happy, he thought that he would eat Pembu, and so he would have plenty of meat to eat.

Pembu dressed up and put some bird feathers on his head, then went with this large man. They arrived at a place that had a big fence that held men to be killed and eaten.

All of the large man's relatives had red skin and Pembu was the only one with brown skin. Pembu went inside the house where the other men and women were waiting to be eaten. The people saw Pembu and were sorry for him.

Pembu asked, "Why did he bring you here?" They said, "He brought us here just as you have come here." Pembu told them, "Don't worry."

They went to sleep. In the middle of the night, Pembu had a dream in which an old woman told him, "Take three bird feathers and put them on your head. Put one on your buttocks and put one in each hand, then try to fly." He did this and tried to fly, and found that he was able to fly just like a bird.

He woke up everyone and gave everyone three feathers. They broke through the house and flew like Pembu. He sent them back to their homes. The people were happy and said that he was a very good man.

People heard this story and were very fearful of men with red skin. The first time that the white men came to the Highlands, the people were very fearful. They thought that the white men were cannibals.

Simon Kaump
C. T. C. **Pumakos** [**Enga** People]
P. O. Wapenamanda
**Enga** Province

D642.1. Transformation to escape from captivity; D670. Magic flight; F527.1. Red person; F531. Giant; G100. Giant ogre; G411. Person aids ogre and is captured; K710. Victim enticed into voluntary captivity or helplessness; P210. Husband and wife; P231. Mother and son; P233. Father and son; R4. Surprise capture; R210. Escapes; W167. Stubbornness

## How the New Clans Came into Being
(Wantok 108, January 22, 1975, page 5)

Once there was a man named Ikisakalimbu. At this time there were two beautiful women. Many young men wanted these women, and they would often fill the two women's house to dance with them.

Ikisakalimbu owned a huge piece of land. There was a ghost man who had a big rock. Ikisakalimbu and the ghost were good friends.

One time, many young men and the ghost went to dance with these two young women. All of the young men danced with the two women. However, when the ghost wanted to dance with them, the women spat on his face and told him, "Who wants to dance with you?" The women said that they did not want to dance with him three more times, so the ghost was ashamed and returned to his house.

One night, the ghost prepared a bed and carried it to the house of these two women. In the middle of the night, the ghost carried the two women to the Ikisakalimbu's house and put them on the very edge of the house. In the early morning, the women awoke and saw that they were not at their house, so they talked and talked.

The owner of the house came and said, "Who is this at my house?" They said, "We don't know who brought us to your house."

The man said, "OK, you two wait here and I'll kill a pig for you." He killed a pig and cooked it in an earth oven, then gave the pork to them to bring with them.

However at night, the ghost man had blocked their home with big stones. So, the two women could not go home and they returned to Ikisakalimbu's house.

The man asked them, "Why have you returned?" They said, "All of the routes home are blocked with stones and we can't leave." The man said, "I'm very sorry that I can't do anything to help you."

The two women thought and thought and said, "Never mind, we're not men. We're no longer thinking of returning. We'll stay here." So the young man married the two women. The women each gave birth to a boy. Their names were Waimba-Pembe [*waimba* means "pandanus tree" and *pembé* means "grass" (Lang, 1973: 84, 110)] and Yambarani. A third child was called Wamn-Kungu [*kúngu* means "tree", "vine" or "ridge" (Lang, 1973: 48-49)].

Now, Tsak Valley has three big clans that are named after these three children who are the ancestors of each of these three clans. So, you see that the ghost had helped Ikisakalimbu to become the founder of **Tsak** in **Enga** Province [**Enga** People].

Simon Es
Tsak-Pumakos
Enga Province

A1640+. Origin of Waimba-Pembe Clan; A1640+. Origin of Wamn-Kungu Clan; A1640+. Origin of Yambarani Clan; E390+. Ghost transports women to friend who marries them; E599.12. Human being transported by a ghost; F402.1.2. Spirit blocks person's road; P210. Husband and wife; P231. Mother and son; P233. Father and son; P310. Friendship; R10. Abduction; T10. Falling in love; T100. Marriage; T145.0.1. Polygyny; T580. Childbirth; Z71.2. Formulistic number: four

# Simbu Story
(Wantok 109, February 5, 1975, pages 5-6)

Long, long ago in the time of the ancestors, in a village called **Sinasina** inside **Simbu** Province, there lived an old man with a wife, a son and a daughter [**Sinasina** People]. The son's name was Dumun and the daughter's was Okenel.

At the time of Okenel's menarche, she just stayed inside her house for two or three weeks. In the custom of the ancestors, after a girl's menarche finishes, when she wants to come out of the house, her parents and kin must cook food and make a small party for her. Also, after menarche, she can begin to sing and dance and she can sleep with boys in the women's house.

So, when her brother Dumun heard about his sister, he got his bow and arrows and some fresh sweet potatoes. Then he began to walk into the deep forest to hunt for his sister's feast.

After walking for a long time, Dumun came to a big mountain in the deep forest. When he arrived at this mountain, it was getting dark, so he cut some firewood to cook his sweet potatoes. After he cut some branches, something crashed and Dumun's eyes bugged out as he fell to the ground and collapsed.

Later, he heard something like a human's voice. So, he got up slowly and saw a very beautiful woman who had never been seen in Sinasina. The woman asked Dumun to carry her net bag of sweet potatoes. However, Dumun did not want to do this. The ghost woman asked him again. Now Dumun was afraid, so he carried the net bag.

However while they walked, the ghost woman threw away the sweet potatoes, one-by-one into the deep forest. After the sweet potatoes were finished, she threw away the net bag. Dumun was incensed, but he did not know where the woman had come from so the two of them kept walking deeper into the forest.

When it was getting dark, they came to the base of a tree that my people call *karuka* [pandanus]. This *karuka* is different from the ordinary *karuka* in that it has long branches and hard fruits. The wild woman told Dumun to get two fruits. After he cut the fruits, they fell and opened, then they walked inside. They began to eat the food that the wild woman had cooked. They lived at this tree, which was the home of the ghost woman, for several months.

At Dumun's village his sister Okenel had come outside, and their relatives had completely forgotten Dumun.

One morning, Dumun, the wild woman and her son went to Dumun's village. The men, women and children saw Dumun and were shocked. They thought that he had died. So, everyone in the village had a pig feast.

However, the two of them did not believe in a woman sorcerer. So, the woman sorcerer stared directly at the ghost woman. The ghost looked back at her, and when she cut some pork, she cut her hand. The wild woman trembled and was afraid, so she had missed when she cut the pork. She cut her finger instead of the pork and blood gushed out like water.

Then the ghost woman got up and thought hard. Her thoughts were mixed up. She began to run fast, but Dumun was very sorry for her and followed her bloody trail. When Dumun returned to the village, he talked to the men of the village.

Now, there is a wild animal that we call _noko_. The meaning of this is, "men do not know where the woman came from." Now, there is a *karuka* tree called _dumun_. There is also a place that once had many _dumun_ *karuka* trees. And so today, there is a village called **Dumun**.

Yogomul Gaima

A991+. Origin of particular village; A2170. Origin of miscellaneous animal forms; A2681.15K2. Origin of pandanus tree; D1711. Magician; D2069. Death or bodily injury by magic—miscellaneous; D2071. Evil Eye; E425.1. Revenant as woman; E437. Revenants banished; E474. Cohabitation of living person and ghost; E540+. Ghost cuts self and flees in fright; F562.2. Residence in a tree; F567.1. Wild woman; P210. Husband and wife; P231. Mother and son; P232. Mother and daughter; P233. Father and son; P234. Father and daughter; P253. Sister and brother; P600+. Customs associated with menarche


## Cassowary Woman

(Wantok 110, February 19, 1975, page 5)

Long ago, cassowaries often bathed in ponds. Cassowaries would remove their skirts and enter the pond. Once, a man hid and saw that they had left their skirts behind.

One cassowary did not like this. Later, she saw another cassowary that was prettier than she was. She took the prettier cassowary's skirt and hid it. After the cassowaries finished bathing, they went to get their skirts. As the other cassowaries were putting on their skirts, the pretty cassowary looked for her skirt but could not find it.

Later, the man went up to the cassowary woman, took her to his village and married her. The cassowary woman bore two sons that were just like real boys.

When the two children were hungry, they told their mother, "After you finish cooking the top of the yam, we'll tell you where father hid your skirt."

After the children said this, the cassowary woman felt good. She cooked the top of the yam and gave it to the two of them. Then they showed her the "grass" skirt that their father had hidden.

The mother cassowary put on the skirt and became just like a cassowary, as before. Then she put the skirt back in the same place. Later, the father fought with her. The mother cassowary was angry, so she put on her skirt and ran away into the forest, becoming feral.

Another time, the cassowary mother came and took the children with her. The children went and stayed beneath a tree, and they fell into a deep sleep. The mother cassowary danced, and decorations and many kinds of food appeared.

The two children woke up and asked her, "Where are we?" The mother cassowary said, "If you are hungry, there is a banana here. You can eat the banana and mark this place."

While the children stayed there, the mother went down to the cassowary pond. The mother arrived and said, "You should make a spear, kill a cassowary and we shall eat it." The mother had tricked the two children. When they went down to look for their mother, she turned into a cassowary. The big brother said, "I know that is mother."

While the two children slept, the mother told them, "Shoot me. I belong to you. You must make a fence around me."

So in the morning, the two children went down to the water and made a fence. After they finished making the fence, the mother rotted away and many kinds of food came up from the mother cassowary. So, men came and took these foods. Some of the foods were eaten and others were planted.

Thomas Kwarunyala
**Maprik** Village [**Abelam** People]
**East Sepik** Province

A1420+. Origin of food from body of dead cassowary; B290+. Cassowary removes skirt or skin to bathe; B630+. Human offspring from marriage to cassowary; B652+. Marriage to cassowary in human form; D169.4W. Transformation: woman to cassowary; D350+W. Transformation: cassowary to woman; D361.1. Swan Maiden; D530+. Transformation by removing skirt; D1781+. Magic results from dancing; E631. Reincarnation in plant (tree) growing from grave; P210. Husband and wife; P231. Mother and son; P233. Father and son; P251.5. Two brothers; R213. Escape from home; R220. Flights; S22+. Matricide; S115. Murder by stabbing; T100. Marriage; W181. Jealousy

## The Woman Who Became a Snake

(Wantok 111, March 5, 1975, page 5)

In the place where the sun rose, there lived some men. An old woman and a girl also lived there.

Later, the young woman married a man, and they had three children: two girls and one boy. The husband and wife worked hard at planting a garden of taros and sweet potatoes.

They lived a little while longer and then the mother died. Her ghost became a pig and ate all of the taros and sweet potatoes in their garden. The father said, "What has eaten the taros and sweet potatoes in our garden? I should look and see."

So one day, the man went to watch the garden when the pig appeared. He killed the pig and carried it home.

They cut the pig and divided it among all of the men of the village, and they greatly enjoyed eating it. The man gave the head of the pig to his daughter to cook for their food.

The woman wanted to look inside the pot, and she saw the face of her old mother who had died. Immediately, her old mother's ghost transformed herself into a snake. After she turned into a snake, she traveled to the treetops, while her three children walked along the ground. They cried and cried as the mother snake told them, "Go back home."

But they said, "Mother, we want to be with you. Why are you trying to leave us?"

The mother replied, "I want to be with you too, but your father killed your ancestor. So, the ghost of your ancestor has turned into me, a snake."

After she finished speaking, she went into a cave. The three children were stunned and went home. They went to another village where the men of the village took them and lived with them.

Now, we see that the beach has many snakes, these originated from only this woman.

[Anonymous]

A2433.6.8+. Why there are many snakes on the beach; B211.6.1. Speaking snake (serpent); E611.3+. Woman reincarnated as swine; E614.1. Reincarnation as snake; P210. Husband and wife; P231. Mother and son; P232. Mother and daughter; P233. Father and son; P234. Father and daughter; P253.0.2+. Two sisters and one brother; S110. Murders; T100. Marriage; W125. Gluttony

## The Feast of the Birds

(Wantok 112, March 19, 1975, page 5)

At a mountain named Ambra, there was a bird named Ambra Mininga [**Hagen** People, **Western Highlands** Province]. This bird wanted to make a house, and so it went into the forest to find vines to make it. When the bird was still traveling in the forest, a strong rain fell that completely soaked the bird.

Then a big cassowary that was eating some tree fruits came towards the little bird. The cassowary thought that the bird was a tree fruit. It swallowed the bird and went off.

But the little bird did not die, it was still living inside the cassowary's belly. In the morning, the cassowary defecated and the little bird came to life again.

The little bird twisted and turned about, the sun heated its skin, and its feathers straightened out again. Then the little bird found some vines and returned home.

After the little bird finished building the house, it called to all of the birds and marsupials (*kapul*). The little bird had made a bow and arrows. The bird spoke, "I've finished making the house and I've made a big feast. Now all of you large birds and marsupials, come and eat."

All of the birds, including birds of paradise, and marsupials, and rats, came together through the sword grass to the little bird's big house. In the evening, the little bird bragged, "I'm a little bird without fame. But you are big birds of paradise and cassowaries and other birds and marsupials, you are my companions. However, you do not know about me because your father put you in the forest and my father put me in the sword grass. Now, why do you not know about me?"

After saying this, the little bird divided the food. The birds of the sword grass understood what was said, but the birds of paradise from the forest and the marsupials did not understand the secret meaning.

They just thought that the little bird had made the big house, given a speech, and that they would eat the food. But the little bird thought it would kill the big cassowary.

Then the bird lifted up its spear and killed the cassowary. All of the guests were surprised. They left the food and ran away; they left all of their things behind.

So now, all of the birds of paradise, cassowaries and marsupials do not live in the sword grass. This is because they are terrified of going there.

Mathias Nongur
Pumakos
Enga Province

[A similar story is told in *Wantok* #731, which involves a bird named Ambra Mininga.]

A2433.2.1+. Why marsupial lives in forest; A2433.4+. Why bird lives in forest; A2433.4+. Why cassowary lives in forest; B211.3. Speaking bird; B299.7. Festival of animals; B299.14K. Animals build house; F911.2+. Cassowary swallows bird and defecates it alive; K811.1.2+. Enemies invited to feast and killed; L315+. Small bird slays cassowary; R220. Flights; S110. Murders

## The Two Women Who Became Stones
(Wantok 113, April 2, 1975, page 5)

Long ago, in the time of the ancestors, men lived on an island called Adwi [**Pilelo**] in **West New Britain** Province [**Arawe** People].

One day, all of the young women told each other, "At night we'll spearfish on the reef using torches." At that time there would be a high tide.

So in the evening, all of the women went to get coconut-husk flares. When the women were ready to go, two sisters were still walking around elsewhere. While they were walking, they collected yellow coconuts that were very fibrous to use for torches. This coconut belonged to a *masalai* named Kaigon. When they finished collecting torch material, they returned to the village to get a knife and a basket.

That night, all of the women went out spearfishing. All of the other women went spearfishing first and the two sisters came later. While the two sisters spearfished, the other women finished their spearfishing and left.

However, sisters did not finish. They spearfished and walked slowly, following the other women. But before long, it got very dark and the women had trouble seeing. While they walked along the reef, the reef shook and moved away from them.

Later, their torch went out, they could not see anything because their eyes were used to the light of the torch from the yellow coconut belonging to Kaigon. They stood on top of the reef as the high tide came. They became submerged by the seawater at this reef and turned into stones.

If you want to see these stones, just go to Adwi Island near Pilio [Pilelo] Island and Kandrian Village in West New Britain Province.

Paul Areng
Ulamona
West New Britain Province

D231W. Transformation: woman to stone; F490+. Masalai; P252.1. Two sisters

## The Man Who Tricked the Ghost
(Wantok 114, April 16, 1975, page 5)

There was a man named Korakan who had a big grove of pandanus trees (*karuka*) in the forest. When it was pandanus season, there were many nuts on his trees.

When the pandanus nuts were ripe, he went into his grove and cut the nuts. After he cut some nuts he killed three marsupials (*kapul*).

He returned home and cut some firewood, then heated some stones for an earth oven to cook the marsupials. After the marsupials were cooked, he removed them from the earth oven and ate the marsupials and the pandanus fruits. He became bloated from the food and went to sleep.

Late at night, two ghosts came up to the sleeping man. The man opened his eyes slowly and saw the two ghost men, then he closed his eyes slowly and went to sleep. He had put the head of his stone axe under his head as a pillow and he had gone to sleep with the handle in his hands. The two ghosts saw hem and they said, "Oh my, there's a dead man."

The two ghosts smelled his mouth, while the man belched air that they could smell. They said, "Ugh! He stinks." Then the ghosts smelled his buttocks while the man loosened his bowels and broke wind. Now he smelled truly awful. One of the ghosts said, "Aha, he's been rotting here for a long time."

Quickly, the ghosts put all of the man's possessions on his bed and prepared to carry it away from the man's village. However, one of the ghosts noticed the axe and said, "Here, look, he's holding the axe handle!"

The other ghost said, "Never mind that. Go ahead. You're lying. That man is dead and rotting."

The two ghosts carried him near the man's house and then a little ways up a mountain, above his house. The two ghosts were terrified that the men would kill them.

On this mountain, the man slowly took his axe, raised it up and hit the ghost that was carrying his legs. The ear of this ghost broke off.

The two ghosts ran away together in fright. They said, "If a man dies in the forest, let him rot; we can't be friends with men."

This promise of the ghosts opened up a huge rocky cave in the mountain. This cave opened at the place where I live.

Simon Es
Wapenamanda
**Enga** Province

[Mr. Es comes from **Tsak** Village, **Enga** People. See the story in *Wantok* #108.]

A999.1K. Origin of caves; E266. Dead carry off living; E461. Fight of revenant with living person; E545. The dead speak; K1868. Deception by pretending sleep; R210. Escapes; X716.6H. Smell of breaking wind; X716.7H. Disastrous breaking wind

## The Bamboo Tube Filled with Women
(Wantok 115, April 30, 1975, page 5)

Before, there lived a man who did not have a wife. His name was Samb. He alone lived in Papyuk [**Papayuku** Village, **Enga** Province, **Enga** People]. He built a men's house and he slept there.

One time, he went far away. In the afternoon, he came to a village where there were many women who were making a garden. He saw that this village had no men, only women were making the garden. He hid and spied on them.

Near sunset, the women collected their belongings and returned to their house. The man stealthily followed them. As the women went inside their house, the man hid outside. The women talked and laughed and sat down to eat inside the house.

Night came and they went to their sleeping places. The man slowly opened the door of the house and went inside. He went far inside to the room where the women slept and tried to find them. However, the women were not sleeping on beds. No, they were hiding inside a huge piece of bamboo. That was how they slept.

Then the man carried the bamboo outside. He carried it all night long. When it was near dawn, he came to his home. He carried the bamboo inside his men's house and put it on top of his bed.

As dawn began to break, a ghost arose and spoke to one of the sleeping women, "Mangapuwan, wake up and leave." After the ghost spoke, the woman woke up and went outside. Later, each woman came outside and they talked.

The man then woke up and asked the women, "Who are you?" The women also asked him, "Who are you?" Then the man spoke again, "You're the women whom I brought to my men's house."

The women were afraid and shut their mouths. They saw that this house was not their house. They thought, "How did we arrive at this men's house?"

They were embarrassed now, they wanted to go back to their women's house, but they did not know how to get there. They were crazed, stunned and prideful at this man's house.

The man married all of the women together. Their first child was called Sambe [Sámbé (Lang, 1973: 214)], the second was called Kunalin [Kunálini is a clan name (Lang, 1973: 215).], and the third was called Lyein. This is the history of my ancestors from Lagaip sub-District.

Elias Pulye
Wapenamanda
Enga Province

E279.2. Ghost disturbs sleeping person; F564+. Person sleeps in bamboo tube; F566.1+. Village of women only; P210. Husband and wife; P230. Parents and children; R10. Abduction; T100. Marriage; T145.0.1. Polygyny; T192. Marriage by force

## You Would Not Die, If Only...
(Wantok 116, May 14, 1975, pages 5-6)

There was a woman who lived near Mount Mungaol. She lived long ago, before there were other people in this area. She lived alone there. Her house and her garden were near this mountain.

One time, a great, bright sun arose. While the woman worked in her garden, something was crashing in the forest near her garden. The woman went to look. A handsome young man had arisen there.

The woman was terrified because she had never lived with a man. So she did not say anything, she shut her mouth and just looked at this man. The man approached her. His hand went inside his net bag and produced a small piece of marsupial (*kapul*) meat from the bag.

He took it and gave it to the woman, then said to her, "Woman, eat this meat and later you shall become pregnant. I'll return after only five days. If you find a child, you can't give it your breast. Carry the child to the top of Mount Mungaol, and you'll find a man's house at the peak of this stone mountain. Open the fence of this house and go inside, but never mind opening the door right away. Just stand at the edge of the house."

After he told her this, he departed. After five days, the woman was pregnant and gave birth to a boy. The woman followed the man's instructions and carried the child to the top of this mountain, where she found this man's house. She did not give her breast to the child, she just hung him [in a net bag] at the edge of the house and waited for the man.

She waited until noon, and the child cried fiercely. The woman felt badly and thought hard, "Oh my, I've waited a long time and that man hasn't come. But if I wait longer, the child will die."

She thought and then gave her breast to the child. But then the man came to the top of the mountain. He was holding two containers of water with his two hands. One container was red and the other white. However, he had not arrived at the house quite yet. He was at the peak of the mountain and called out loudly and often, "Ever-living! Ever-living!" However, later he shouted with difficulty that life was finished. After he shouted this, the woman said, "Yes."

The man was irate. He threw the water down the mountain and asked, "Woman, you gave your breast to the child, huh? I forbade you to do this. But you did it and gave your breast to the child. OK, your child will have a bad life, and that is your fault."

After the man told the woman this, he fetched his good, strong bow from inside the house and strung it. He gave it to the woman and child and continued to talk, "Now, I wanted to do well for the child, I brought food for the child but it was wrong for you to give him your breast.

"Later, I will come to instruct his children. But now he'll have much pain and have a bad life." Then the man showed the woman a new, good place. The woman saw that this place had many nice children, who were happily playing together and finding good food.

Then the man said, "If you had not ruined your child, I would have sent him to be among those children. But you ruined him and I'm leaving. Later I'll come to take him." He said this and departed. The woman never saw him again.

Joseph Konona
**Wapenamanda [Enga** People]
**Enga** Province

[See *Wantok* #124 for a similar story with a more explicit relationship between the origin of death and breaking a tabu against nursing.]

A1335+. Origin of death: breaking tabu against nursing; C920.1. Death of children for breaking tabu; P231. Mother and son; P233. Father and son; Q402. Punishment of children for parents' offenses; Q325. Disobedience punished; T511.7.3. Conception from eating meat; T573. Short pregnancy; T580. Childbirth; W126. Disobedience

## Where Did Net Bags Come From?
(Wantok 117, May 28, 1975, page 5)

This story comes from the Finschhafen area in **Morobe** Province. Zacqarac was a **Mape** man.

One morning, Zacqarac woke up when it was still dark. Quickly, he prepared his bow and arrows. This day, he would go to find wild game and different kinds of birds. His wife roasted some taros, and he carried them with him. It would be bad if he became hungry in the forest.

"Wife," he said, "Today when the sun rises high in the sky, I must shoot some birds for us to eat." They finished getting ready, then Zacqarac hurried. It would be bad if the sun became too bright, then he would be unable to catch birds. He went directly into the deep forest. He went deeper and deeper into the forest, and came to the base of a huge tree.

Before, he had made a ladder going up to a crotch in the tree where rainwater collected. He would control this crotch, and if a bird came to bathe in it, he would shoot it. When he filled his carrying basket, he would return home.

He kept them inside a bamboo tube lest they become crooked. He put these arrows in his hiding place, in the water. Then he hid well in his hiding place on top of the tree. He sat and waited for birds.

Zacqarac took his arrows from the bamboo, and prepared to shoot. It was not like this before, but on this day more and more birds came. He did not fool around with shooting all of these kinds of birds. He shot them and they fell to the ground.

He sat on top of the tree until the sun set. After he shot the last bird, got ready to go home. He looked down and saw two women. Oh my, these were *masalai*s! They were cooking the birds in an earth oven and filling up their net bags with the cooked birds.

He was afraid and held tightly to the tree. He thought that there was not a long of talking, so they would just kill him that day. He perspired and was frozen with fear. They did not leave. No, they [would] finish his blood.

The two *masalai* women looked at him up there. They said, "Don't be afraid, you must come down. We won't do you any harm. We collected all of the birds that you shot.

Don't be afraid, we're at peace. You can carry some birds and we can carry some."

The two of them also gave a net bag to this man. The man was still afraid, when the two *masalais* left the bag and went off into the forest. Shortly after they left, he came down and ran home as fast as he could. He gave the birds and the net bag to his relatives in the village. Then they ate the birds, and started making net bags of their own.

Wawariec Qoroa
Kainantu
Eastern Highlands Province

A1453+. Origin of net bag; F490+. Masalai; N812. Giant or ogre as helper; P210. Husband and wife

[The ancestor story in *Wantok* #118 is the same as in #64.]


## The Crazy People
(Wantok 119, June 25, 1975, pages 5-6)

Long ago, on **Bagabag** Island in **Madang** Province, there were two clans [**Takia** People]. One clan had good and strong thoughts and the other had wrong and half-crazy thoughts.

They lived near a bay called Semanur [near **Semamur** Village], where the sun rises. The crazy people did not think much about growing food. They always watched the other clan who had good things and who caught birds and wild game.

Every day, they sat and watched the other good men with their good things making fishing baskets and catching many fish. However, the Ngiringar [Clan] had a different thought. They thought that the others were not catching fish correctly.

So they wanted to follow another idea. The other people always put their fishing baskets in the water with fish food, and caught fish in this manner. However, they thought that this was not correct.

One morning, an old mother called out to her two children, "Children, I want us to make a basket. However, we can't put fish food in the basket. We can put food for me in the basket, enough for two weeks. This is how we will catch many, many fish."

After the children listened to their mother, they helped her make a huge basket. They collected some food, water, firewood and things needed for sleeping.

One morning, they pushed off their canoe to go asea, they had put the big basket on the canoe and two big stones

too. The mother sat in the canoe and they paddled towards the deep sea. They paddled and paddled, and found a place that had many fish. They told their mother this, and she went inside the basket. The children tied the stones to each side of the basket, then they slowly lowered the basket with their mother inside into the sea.

They asked her, "Mother, everything you told us is alright, isn't it?" Their mother said, "Yes, everything is alright. However, you can't come here next week. Come here after two weeks. I think that this is enough food for two weeks."

After she said this, the children lowered her down about six feet below the surface. They lowered her with the heavy stones on the basket until she reached the sandy bottom. The children put a marker at the place that they left her.

They paddled back home and waited for their mother. They waited and waited for one fortnight, then they prepared to get their mother and return home. They awoke in the morning and shoved their canoe off into the sea. They paddled and paddled towards their mother. After about a mile, the sea began to change, but they were determined. They continued to paddle to the place where the marker was.

Quickly, they pulled their mother with the basket up towards the surface. They pulled up about six yards of rope and their hands were very sore. They could see the basket five feet from the surface, and they could smell their mother [rotting].

They remembered when they had let the basket down before that they had felt something and had heard a noise. It was their mother who was drowning and who was pulling the rope to come back to the surface. However, they had been determined and had let the basket down quickly.

The brothers were very troubled about their mother. They left her in the sea and returned to the shore. Now, they were alone in Semanur.

Galun wrote this story and Tamloi Saian translated it.

J1820+. Person drowns trying to catch fish in underwater cage; M451.2. Death by drowning; P231. Mother and son; P251.5. Two brothers


## The Man without a Face
(Wantok 120, July 9, 1975, pages 5, 10)

Once there lived a man named Napia who was making a garden near a river. After he cleared the trees he pulled out the roots of the wild sugarcanes (*pitpit*) and threw them downstream.

Then he went to his house and slept. In the early morning, he awoke and ate. He told his mother, "I'm going to work at the garden that I've been clearing." At the garden, he removed the wild sugarcane roots. The sun made him hot, so he wanted to drink some water. He thought that he would get a drink first, then work in the garden.

He went down to the river and threw some trash in it. However, he saw something white underwater. He put his hand down into the water and held some pig guts that were under the wild sugarcanes.

Then he followed the river upstream and discovered smoke coming from the forest. He walked slowly towards the smoke and saw an old man who was cooking a pig in an earth oven. Napia hid and looked at the face of this old man. The man did not have eyes.

He went a little closer and looked carefully at the man's face. The man did not have a mouth or eyes. He swallowed his food with his head.

Now he was very close, but the old man did not see Napia because he did not have eyes. Then Napia went back and waited a little while. The old man removed the pig from the earth oven and began to butcher it while Napia continued to watch him.

The man finished butchering the pig and prepared to eat it. Napia went closer and took the four legs. The old man did not see him. Napia took his net bag and filled it with pork, then carried it to his mother. He ate the pork with his mother and slept.

The next day, he again went to the old man's place. This time, he went early in the morning. He wanted to see where the man obtained his pigs. While he watched near the man's house, the man came outside. The man sang and danced near a pond, and a huge pig came out.

The man took this pig and killed it. He singed off its hair, then began to butcher it. Napia went closer, but the man did not see him. Napia again took the four legs, just as before, but the man did not see him.

Napia carried the pork to his mother. They cooked it in an earth oven and they gorged themselves on it. After Napia had left, the old man wanted to eat the pork, but he realized it was not all there. He was troubled and tried to find the missing pork, but he was unable to do so.

The old man thought and thought, he thought of the four pig's legs that were missing and he thought of the pig, "I just killed it. I've killed pigs many times before. What happened to the four legs?"

He thought some more, "I've eaten pork many times, but how did the pork disappear?"

He began to make a huge net bag. After he finished, he filled it with banana leaves. He tied up parts of the net bag to a tree. He trampled another part and sat upon it. He then killed a pig and cooked it in an earth oven.

Napia was standing in the distance and looking at the old man's place while he was cooking the pig. He saw the man cooking the pig, so Napia was quite happy. He went towards the man, but he did not see the net bag that the man had put in the trail. Unfortunately for him, Napia went inside the man's bag.

The man heard the noise from the bag and he quickly held the two handles of the bag. He sewed up the opening and took it to a tall tree that was standing near the river. The man tied up Napia to a crooked branch that went down to the water.

Napia stayed on this tree for two entire months. He had no real food, so he removed his hair and ate it. One night he heard a flying fox coming toward him. The flying fox threw two bananas at the bag. He caught and ate them with their skins.

The flying fox always gave food to Napia. Later, the bag broke. One of his legs came out and was nearly in the water. The flying fox saw this and called out for 500 flying foxes to come and help him return Napia to his mother.

They gathered together and opened the bag. Then they carried him and threw him at his mother's house.

Napia's mother was overjoyed at the group of flying foxes. She wanted to give them 500 pigs, but they did not want to take them. She tried to give them other things, but they did not want the other things that she tried to give them.

So Napia and his mother thought and thought, and they gave them a string that the mother had made into a net bag. The flying foxes were happy. They flew around and took the string that they had been given. They took it and broke it into little pieces for each flying fox.

Before, flying foxes did not have bellies. But Napia and his mother gave them string, so now flying foxes have bellies.

Alphonse Wi
**Pangia** Village [**Wiru** People]
**Southern Highlands** Province

A2354+. Origin of flying fox's belly; B449.3+. Helpful flying fox; B542.1.2+. Flying fox rescues person from height; B552+. Person carried by flying fox; D1781. Magic results from singing; D1781+. Magic results from dancing; D2074.1. Animals magically called; F511.1+. Faceless person; K333. Theft from blind person; P231. Mother and son; Q53. Reward for rescue; Q212. Theft punished; R4. Surprise capture; R49.1. Captivity in tree; R51.1. Prisoners starved; R110. Rescue of captive

## Pekabat and Tutupiok

(Wantok 121, July 23, 1975, pages 5-6)

Once there were some boys in a small village who played with their bows and arrows. When they played with their bows and arrows, one boy wanted to go into the forest to look for cuscus (*kapul*). [The northern common cuscus, *Phalanger orientalis*, is the only *kapul* on Bougainville (Flannery, 1995b: 96-99).] This boy's name was Pekabat.

Pekabat had called for his friends to go into the forest. When they arrived at a large fig vine, Pekabat smelled a "male" banana. This banana was buried underground. A man had put it there.

When the children saw the banana there, they were elated and ate the banana. After they finished eating it, they wanted to defecate. They wanted to go into the forest to defecate.

However, one boy spoke, "We must shit in the hole where the man buried the banana."

After they finished defecating, they covered their feces well. After they finished, they climbed the fig vine. They went very high and sat upon one of the branches.

The man who had hidden the banana that the children had eaten returned to look for his banana. His name was Tutupiok. Tutupiok came to the place where he had hidden it and he began to dig the ground. When he touched the feces, he was not happy. He said, "Aha! My banana has over-ripened, I'll fill myself up with it." However, he smelled the feces and then smelled his hand. He became irate and spoke again, "Where the hell are the men who ate my banana? I must find them and then I'll have some good food this evening."

After he said this, Tutupiok looked up the fig tree and saw the children. He said, "Aha! You're the ones that ate my banana." The boys laughed heartily. This made Tutupiok angry. He then said, "You little kids are delicious to eat."

He called for them to come down. As each child descended, Tutupiok shoved the child inside his mouth. Then Tutupiok went home. When he arrived home, his wife saw her husband's belly shaking and rumbling, so she asked him, "What did you eat?"

However, poor Tutupiok did not want to talk. The children kept running around inside his stomach. Tutupiok told his wife to heat a big stone in the fire. Tutupiok shoved the hot stone down his mouth to cook the children

that were in his stomach, but the children ran to another corner of Tutupiok's stomach.

After the stone had cooled, Tutupiok thought the children had died but they were not really dead. Tutupiok was exhausted, so he went to sleep. While he slept, the children inside his stomach asked, "Who has a small knife?" They found out that Pekabat had a small pocketknife.

Pekabat started to cut Tutupiok's stomach. Tutupiok did not feel it when the boys cut his belly. The children came outside and they killed Tutupiok's wife. Tutupiok also died. The children were elated and they returned home.

Bertha Hogun
**Wakunai** [**Rotokas** People]
Bougainville Island
**North Solomons** Province

F912.2. Victim kills swallower from within by cutting; G512.1. Ogre killed with knife (sword); G519.1. Ogre's wife killed through other tricks; G100. Giant ogre; G610. Theft from ogre; K1044. Dupe persuaded to eat filth (dung); P210. Husband and wife; Q212. Theft punished; Q215. Cannibalism punished; Q411. Death as punishment; R210. Escapes; S118. Murder by cutting; X716H+. Feces as gift; S110. Murders

## The Conch that Scared the *Masalai*

(Wantok 122, August 6, 1975, pages 5-6)

Long ago, there was a boy and his sister who lived in a small house near a river. One time when their firewood was depleted, the sister said, "Let's go and cut some firewood." So, they took a knife and axe, then put them in their canoe. They fetched their oar and paddled off.

They went towards the shore of an island. The boy wanted to pull the canoe up and tie it to a tree, then toss out the water. However, his sister got up and hit him with the paddle. The boy left the oar in the canoe and he swam to this island. He went ashore and saw his sister paddling.

His sister went ashore and tied up the rattan mooring of the canoe. She took the knife and axe, and went to cut some firewood. However, she did not see her brother hiding behind a tree looking at her. Before long, a *masalai* heard the chopping sound. The *masalai* took many vines from the *limbum* palm. The *masalai* saw the woman chopping firewood, then approached her and tied her up with the vines.

When the little brother saw this, he cried softly. The bad *masalai* heard him and tied him up just like his sister. The *masalai* carried the woman off. Her brother tried to hide for when the *masalai* would return. Later, the *masalai* came to his village and he told the men, "We will have a big celebration for this woman."

The little brother went someplace. After a week he departed. He arrived at the *masalai* village, then he turned into a lizard and went into the house to look for his sister.

His sister told him, "Why have you come? It would be bad if they killed you." The brother said, "I'm hungry and I've come!" So his sister gave him a plate of food.

He ate the food and asked his sister, "What day are they going to kill and eat you?" The sister said, "They will kill me on Thursday."

Her brother left and went to sit at the base of a tree where he played a conch trumpet. After he played the trumpet, he went to sleep on a ridge of the tree. Dawn came and he tried to play his trumpet, but it became dark again.

The *masalai*s woke up, and they danced and sang. They hung some betel nuts on a tree. The boy flew like a bird and sat on the tree. He chewed on the betel nuts and spat down upon the *masalai* men.

Dawn came and the little boy flew to the tree with the conch trumpet. He watched for the time that they would kill his sister. He saw them getting their spears, axes and knives, preparing to cut his sister's neck. One *masalai* carried the woman and put her on the ground.

They untied some of her ropes and the prepared to cut her neck. However, her brother got up and blew the trumpet. An earthquake occurred. This caused the *masalai*s to run off into the forest. The brother ran to her and held her hand. Then they raced back to their village.

Anton Waino

Ramu River

**Madang** Province

B211.6.2K. Speaking lizard; D197B. Transformation: boy to lizard; D1221. Magic trumpet; D1544. Magic object controls earthquakes; D2148. Earth magically caused to quake; F490+. Masalai; F1021. Extraordinary flights through air; G440. Ogre abducts person; G551.1. Rescue of sister from ogre by brother; G570. Ogre overawed; P253. Sister and brother; R4. Surprise capture; R156. Brother rescues sister(s); R220. Flights


## The People Who Tricked a *Masalai* Woman
(Wantok 123, August 20, 1975, pages 5-6, 10)

There was a woman from a small village named Wan [**Wanali**], near Sibilanga in the Nuku Patrol Post area [**Kayik** People, **West Sepik** Province]. One day, the woman left her husband at the village and went to look for her brothers at the village where she was born.

She was going to look for her brothers because they were giving a party with dancing and singing. They had sent a message to this woman to go with her child. If they came, they would get some pork and other food.

The woman left the village, and she saw her brothers and the other people from her village. They danced and sang until dawn. They divided the food in the morning. The woman with her child received their food and poured it into a *limbum* container. She shook hands with her parents and brothers, then returned to Wan Village.

They walked back and came to a village called Yolmbi [**Yambil**] where a *masalai* woman named Mukmak met them. Mukmak said, "Good evening, granddaughter. Where are you coming from?" The real woman said, "I went to my village to see my parents and now I'm returning to Wan Village."

Mukmak replied, "Granddaughter, it's getting dark now, let's sleep. Tomorrow when the sun comes up you can walk back to Wan and see your husband and other children."

But the woman said, "Never mind that Mukmak, I'll hold a torch to see the trail because it would be bad if the other men's children beat up my little children at Wan." The woman told this to Mukmak because she knew that Mukmak was a cannibal.

She wanted to run away quickly and she departed. She had not gone far when Mukmak turned her finger, then the woman turned around and went back to Mukmak's village.

Mukmak sat and watched the woman and child return. She said, "Oh granddaughter, you've returned, huh?"

The woman replied, "Grandma, I didn't leave, but I don't know why I've returned."

Mukmak said, "Granddaughter, never mind. We can sleep now. Tomorrow when the sun is out, you can go." So the two of them slept and in the evening Mukmak climbed a coconut palm tree. The real woman and her child were below on the ground holding leafy vegetables. They were cutting and counting the coconuts as they fell.

When the *masalai* Mukmak came down again from the tree, the woman and child were working at gathering and counting the coconuts. The real woman said that she wanted to go to a place on a mountain. The *masalai* woman spoke, "OK, you can go."

The woman went to find coconuts and she met Mukmak's *masalai* husband. The *masalai* man said, "Why did you come and sleep with that bad *masalai* woman? She has killed many people and eaten them raw. You should not go to sleep tonight. You should try to trick Mukmak and return to Wan Village with your child." After she heard this, the woman was terrified, her heart sunk, and she trembled with fear. She took the coconuts and went back to sleep with Mukmak, the *masalai* woman.

They went inside Mukmak's house, built a fire and put the *limbum* mat for the real woman to sleep with her child. Mukmak slept on a rack used for smoking meat. Mukmak went out to urinate. When she returned she wanted to close the door, but the real woman said, "Grandma, leave the door open, I'll shut it."

So Mukmak went on top of her rack to sleep. In the dead of night, the woman went out to urinate. Later she went inside to see that Mukmak had given her breast to her child and was sleeping on the rack. Mukmak looked at her child and it was like a flying fox on the real woman's mat. The woman saw this, took back her child and pretended to sleep to get Mukmak to go back to sleep.

When the real woman heard Mukmak snoring, she took her child and a small torch that she covered with a leaf. They ran back to Wan that night.

Mukmak took her spear and threw it where the woman had been sleeping, but the woman was not there. Mukmak was irate and said, "Hey, are you taking advantage of my mercy for you? If so, I'll still kill and eat you tomorrow." Mukmak's anger built up.

She slept until dawn, then made a long thread and tied one end to a *tanget* plant in Yolmbi Village. She held the other end and went to Wan Village to find the woman and child who had run away in the night.

After she tied the thread to the *tanget*, she spoke to her husband, "Stay here and keep your eye on this thread and *tanget*. If you see that the thread isn't taut and that the *tanget* is dead as if it were smoked from a fire then, you'll know that they've killed me. If you see that the *tanget* isn't dead and that the thread is still taut, then you'll know that I'm still alright."

Mukmak walked away. She called out and blew a conch trumpet to ask for the woman and child. She sang, "Oh granddaughter, why did you get up and walk away last night? You did not like sleeping till the morning. OK, you and I can go to Wan Village." She came to **Sibilanga** Village and hid her trumpet [**Aruop** People].

The men of Wan Village were ready with their bows, arrows and other fighting implements. They tried to trick her with some kinds of food, but Mukmak knew about this and said, "I have all of these kinds of foods at home."

She did not eat the food that the men of Wan had put out, but she was thirsty and asked them to give her some young coconut milk.

While she was drinking, the men said, "We always drink with our head, eyes and neck facing the sky. You must drink like this too."

When she faced skyward, the men cut her neck with a shield made of sago palm wood and she died. Then they buried her. Her husband saw the string slacken and the *tanget* dry up as if it had been smoked by fire. He knew that they had killed his wife.

Moses Nasam

Kabari

Lumi

West Sepik Province

D996.1. Magic finger; D1184. Magic thread; D1782. Sympathetic magic; E761.3. Life token: tree (flower) fades; E761.7+. Life token: string slackens; F419.4K. Spirits eat food raw; F490+. Masalai; G512.8+. Ogre killed by striking with shield; G530.1+. Help from ogress' husband; G560. Ogre deceived into releasing prisoner; G642K. Ogres eat raw flesh; J1050. Attention to warnings; K832. Dupe induced to look about: seized and killed; P210. Husband and wife; P230. Parents and children; P232. Mother and daughter; P234. Father and daughter; P250. Brothers and sisters; P291. Grandfather; P292. Grandmother; P293. Uncle; Q215. Cannibalism punished; Q411. Death as punishment; R220. Flights; R260. Pursuits; S110. Murders; V61.3+. Dead buried

## Why We Must Die

(Wantok 124, September 3, 1975, pages 5-6)

Long ago, a man and woman lived in a village called **Wamo**, near Nipa [**Mendi** People, **Southern Highlands** Province]. The man's name was Pelum and the woman's was Ralnu. Ralnu was pregnant. One day Pelum went to a small forest and built a birthing hut.

After he built the hut, Pelum told his wife Ralnu, "I finished making the house. You must sleep in the house and give birth. If your give birth to a boy then you can't give him your breast right away, you must talk to me first. If you give birth to a girl, then you must hold her in this house for a whole month. After that you must come back to Wamo Village."

In the afternoon, at about 5 o'clock, Ralnu gave birth to a boy. She thought about going to tell her husband because Pelum had told her to first tell him if she gave birth to a boy.

So, she began to walk along the trail. Ralnu had not given her breast to the child yet, she had not yet carried the child in her net bag yet either. She just held him in her hand as she walked.

She continued to walk and she wanted to go down a little farther. She did not see the big shaman, Yekilman, who had come and was standing at her home. The woman now saw him and trembled because she had never seen such a huge man before.

Yekilman spoke, "Woman, I want to give you this yellow fruit of the ancestors. It's a pumpkin. You must give it to your child just like milk. You can't give your breast to your child."

He also gave the woman a piece of bark and said, "You must put your child to sleep on this piece of bark. Don't carry the child in your net bag. That would be bad. You must carry your child only in this piece of bark."

The woman did not want to take these two things. The woman said, "Why should I take these two things? Never mind. I still have my breasts, and I still have my net bag and my pandanus (*karuka*) mat. I can still give my breast to my child, and I can still put him to sleep on my mat!"

Yekilman replied, "Woman! You asked me a question. OK, listen. I'm a big man from Mount Yalam, and I take care of forests, gardens, and everyone who lives in this land. It would be bad if you brought trouble upon your people."

The woman said, "Oh my, big man, what kind of trouble? In this land, we always have good times. We never feel troubled, not once!"

Yekilman said, "OK, if you disobey me, I want to tell you what will happen. Every person that is born to your clan will die. Furthermore, they must grow again and die again. This will be forever."

But if the woman had not disobeyed Yekilman, every person would be reborn. And when people became old, they could remove their skin and become young again. The land would be jammed with people. However, the woman still brought trouble because she said, "I can give milk."

So now we drink milk. It is a bad thing because when we do this we are eating our mother again. It is as if we are growing like an ignorant animal.

If we are people, we cannot eat people again. But long ago, this is what started it and now we drink our mothers' milk. This is why there is death.

Some of my people from the Southern Highlands Province still believe this. This is because though we are not animals, we still drink the "oil" of our mothers. This is the origin of death.

Simon Komet

Erave

Southern Highlands Province

A1335+. Origin of death: breaking tabu against nursing; D1711. Magician; D1889.6. Rejuvenation by changing skin; P210. Husband and wife; P231. Mother and son; P233. Father and son; T570. Pregnancy; T580. Childbirth; T611. Suckling of children; W126. Disobedience

[There was no ancestor story in *Wantok* #125 or 126.]

## The Custom of Revenge
(Wantok 127, October 15, 1975, pages 5, 12)

Once there were two brothers. Their parents had died and they lived alone. The big brother was married. He and his wife worked in their garden planting food. However, the little brother sat alone in the house making bows and arrows. He never helped in the garden.

They went on like this and then the big brother spoke angrily with his wife in secret about the little brother. They said, "He never helps us work in the garden. He always just sits alone in the house eating our food. What should we do with him?" Then the big brother spoke to his wife, "Tomorrow morning, we should go to the garden. He won't follow us. Then at night I'll cut his neck as he sleeps."

After they finished talking, the ghost of the brothers' father heard this. He quickly turned into a bird and flew into the house where the little brother lived. The bird told him, "You must get up in the night when the moon has risen. Gather all your things and run away to that ridge."

The little brother was surprised and said, "Why should I go to that ridge?" The bird said, "Because your big brother and his wife are angry at you. Your big brother said that at night when you are sleeping he will cut your neck."

That evening, the big brother with his wife went to the garden. They cooked some food, ate it and went to sleep. But the little brother only pretended to sleep. He moved as if asleep. When the moon rose, he saw the light and left. He went slowly to the place where his big brother's wife was. He carried her slowly and put her where he always slept. After he put her there, he went outside and ran away to the ridge.

Later that night, the big brother woke up, took his axe and slowly went to the place where his little brother always slept. He saw his wife but he thought it was his little brother, so he cut her neck. In the morning, the big brother woke up and looked there. No! He was irate. He took his bow and followed the trail of his little brother. However, his little brother already knew that his big brother would follow him, so he hid along the trail. When the big brother came near, he shot him in the liver with a spear.

So, the little brother went back home and later was happily married.

Gabriel Bar

Malala High School

Madang

Madang Province

A1336+. Origin of murderous revenge; E327. Dead father's friendly return; E363.3. Ghost warns the living; E423.3. Revenant as bird; J1050. Attention to warnings; K840. Deception into fatal substitution; K959.2. Murder in one's sleep; P210. Husband and wife; P233. Father and son; P251.5. Two brothers; P263. Brother-in-law; P264. Sister-in-law; P600+. Custom of retaliation; Q210.1. Criminal intent punished; Q411. Death as punishment; R220. Flights; R260. Pursuits; S73.1. Fratricide; S118.2. Murder by cutting throat; T100. Marriage


## The Pig Who Gave Birth to a Man
(Wantok 128, October 29, 1975, pages 5, 10)

Long ago, no one lived in **Enga** Province. However, in the Laiagam sub-District, there was an eagle called *kamp* [*kámbi* (Lang, 1973: 33)] in the **Enga** Language.

The eagle had a huge pig mother. The eagle slept in a hole in a large tree. The eagle's pig mother slept near the base of this tree.

One time, the pig had left, and the eagle tried to find her for three whole days. He found his mother, then approached and heard some small pigs crying in the forest. The eagle saw a boulder. Underneath the boulder, it saw the big mother pig nursing her piglets.

The eagle went even closer. The eagle stood and counted the piglets. The eagle also saw a boy drinking milk with the piglets. The eagle was overjoyed and took the boy underneath its wing.

The eagle tied his mother with a vine, put the piglets in its net bag and brought them home. The eagle tied the pig mother to the base of a big tree and left the piglets with her. The eagle carried the boy up to the hole in the tree where it slept. The eagle put the child inside the hole and killed each piglet to give to the boy.

The eagle also killed different kinds of marsupials (*kapul*) to give meat to the boy to eat. The boy grew and became a big boy. When he was about 12 or 13 years old, the eagle held him by his two hands and brought him down to the ground. The eagle gave him the name Tanjen and showed him the methods of making houses, gardens, spears, decorations, and everything necessary to take care of pigs.

When Tanjen was about 20 or 21 years old, he had many pigs and a big garden. He always slept in his men's house. Every morning at 4 or 5 o'clock, he would lay in bed and play his Jew's harp.

One night, while he was sleeping in his men's house, the eagle went to some places. He opened the door of a women's house where he saw a beautiful, young woman sleeping on her bed. The eagle put his two claws on the bed of the sleeping woman, carried her away, put her inside Tanjen's house and shut the door.

Tanjen did not hear or feel the noise, so he kept sleeping. The woman did not see or hear anything either and was also still asleep.

When it was nearly dawn, Tanjen took his Jew's harp and began to play it. The young woman awoke and said, "It's not even dawn yet and I want to sleep. Which crazy man are you to come to my house and play the Jew's harp like that?"

Tanjen was surprised, so he trembled with fear. He did not know who had come to sleep in his house and to become angry with him.

Later Tanjen asked, "Who are you? Why did you come to sleep in my house and get angry with me like that? This isn't your house." The two of them argued until dawn. Tanjen said, "Get up and go outside." So the beautiful, young woman went outside and looked. It was true, she was not at her house; she was not even in her village. She was terrified and sat near the house. Tanjen said, "I shall kill a pig and give it to you, then you can carry it back to your village."

Tanjen prepared some vegetables and killed a big pig. He cooked the pig in an earth oven, then gave it to the young woman. He said, "Carry this and leave." So, the woman carried the pig and left.

However, there was no trail back. A big boulder blocked the trail, and there was no other trail to her village, so she returned to Tanjen's house again.

Every day, Tanjen killed a pig and told the woman to carry it back to her village, but the boulder always blocked the trail and she returned each time. Later, Tanjen married this young woman and they had many, many children. These became the men of Enga Province.

Now, we who speak the Enga Language have the largest number of speakers of any local language in Papua New Guinea. There are many of us [more than 150,000 people (Wurm, 1982)]. The meaning of the word *tanjen* is "pig's blood raised man" in the Enga Language [*Tanjéná* means "blood" (Lang, 1973: 100).].

Alphonse Paliru
**Wapenamanda**
Enga Province

A1611+. Origin of Enga People; B535.0.7+. Eagle as nurse for child; P210. Husband and wife; P230. Parents and children; P231. Mother and son; P250. Brothers and sisters; R13.3.2. Eagle carries off youth; T100. Marriage; T566. Human son of animal parents; T589.7.1. Simultaneous birth of (domestic) animal and child; T611. Suckling of children

## The Marsupial (*Kapul*) That Stuck to a Man

(Wantok 129, November 12, 1975, page 5)

Not long ago, there was a man who went hunting for marsupials (*kapul*) with two "fathers" in the forest [father and uncle are often nominally the same]. When they went to the forest, their child saw two marsupials sitting together in a breadfruit tree. He called to them, "Hey, fathers, come here. There are two marsupials. Come here and I'll go kill them for you."

When their child went to climb the tree, he told them, "You should clear out from the place where the marsupials will fall." So, one of them went far away and the other whose name was Matina ignored him and just stood there. Matina thought he was smart, but he was also greedy.

The child shot the two marsupials. One of them died and the other did not really die: it jumped right on top of Matina and held tightly to his neck. The marsupial's eyes stared at Matina's eyes. Matina was afraid of the marsupial's stare, so he did not make a noise or call out. The other two men saw him and went home. Matina stood there with the marsupial in the forest for one-and-a-half days.

The marsupial died on Matina's body with its eyes open, so Matina thought that the marsupial had not died. Matina stood there, not making a noise or calling out. The other two men had gone to the village but they did not see Matina there, so they returned to the forest to find Matina standing there with the marsupial.

Matina was completely famished, his stomach was empty. The marsupial still held onto him and he was still afraid of the marsupial's stare.

The men pulled the marsupial from Matina's neck. When they did this, Matina, the good-for-nothing, sloughed off a big chunk of blackened blood. Then they gave him some water and food, and some tobacco to smoke. He ate, then they went to their village and cooked the marsupial. While they ate the marsupial, Matina said, "In the future, I can never hunt marsupials. I'll only sleep in the village." Thereafter, he never went far into the forest and he only slept in the village. Matina died not very long ago.



Miss Merry Anne Banau
**Tangu** Village [**Tangu** People]
**Madang** Province

J652. Inattention to warnings; J1050. Attention to warnings; J2700+. Hunter paralyzed with fear by dead marsupial; P233. Father and son; P293. Uncle; P297. Nephew; W151. Greed

## The Men Who Became a Flying Foxes

(Wantok 130, November 26, 1975, page 5)

In **Ilahita** Village, there lived a man and his wife who went to cut some forest [**East Sepik** Province, **South Arapesh** People]. There was also a wild woman who lived in a tree hole. She came outside her hole and replanted the forest that had been cut, then the forest came back just as before.

The man and woman wanted to return and see the work that they had done, cutting the forest. However, they saw that the forest was just as before, so they cut the forest again. After they finished, they returned to their village. The wild woman did just as before and the forest came back again.

The couple saw this again and they became very angry. The woman returned to the village, while the man stayed and watched. Then he discovered the wild woman replanting the forest. He scolded the wild woman, and the wild woman said, "You can't kill me. Come look at my home." The wild woman showed him some handsome net bags. She flattered him and flirted with him. He watched this and was impressed. Then he cut down the tree in which the wild woman lived and brought it to his village. He put the woman inside the men's spirit house and looked after her well.

The woman made many net bags and gave them to many men. The men liked the wild woman very much, and their wives became secondary.

Later, all of the men went to the forest to hunt pigs. Only the women stayed in the village. They sent one woman up a coconut palm tree to fetch a green coconut. Then the women burned the spirit house and the wild woman was burned with the house.

The men returned from the forest and they only saw ashes where the spirit house had been. The men were troubled and very worried about the wild woman. They took the wild woman's ashes and rubbed themselves with them. The men became flying foxes and flew away. Only the women were left in this village. That is how flying foxes came to Ilahita.

Kifas Kundalimuna

Ilahita

East Sepik Province

[See the ancestor story in *Wantok* #397 for a similar story.]

D117.5KM. Transformation: man to flying fox; D595+. Transformation by application of ashes; F567.1. Wild woman; H1115.1+. Task: cutting down forest, which is magically replanted; P210. Husband and wife; R1+. Wild woman captured; R10. Abduction; R220. Flights; S112.0.2. House (hostel) burned with all inside; V112.1. Spirit huts


## The Sun Does Not Cook Food

(Wantok 131, January 21, 1976, page 5)

Black Cockatoo [palm cockatoo (Beehler *et al.*, 1986: 117)] told his young wife, "OK, we are married now. It would be better if you cooked my food."

However, the young woman did not understand the words, "to cook food." So, she went to get some taros, yams and bananas, and washed them in the river. Then she removed their skins. She carried this food back to Black Cockatoo.

The young woman spoke, "I have prepared some good food for you, sit and eat." Cockatoo saw the food, held a piece of taro in his hand and said, "Hey! This taro is still hard and it's not hot. It's true that you removed the skin well, and all of the food is clean. But I don't like to eat cold food. It would be better if you cooked this food again."

So, the young woman took the food back and carried it away. However, she did not understand what her husband had said. So she thought and thought, "What is 'cooking food?'"

She felt the taro in her hand and she understood, "It was true that the food was cold. I think that my husband likes hot food." So, the woman carried the food under the sun and put the taro and yam and banana on top of a stone.

The food was under the sun long enough to heat it. Later the young woman carried the food back to Black Cockatoo. She said, "Now your food is hot. Now you can eat it." Cockatoo held a yam in his hand and felt that the yam was still hard.

"What have you done? I told you that you must cook this food of mine." Black Cockatoo was angry now and said, "Where is the fire?" The young woman replied, "What is fire?"

In the young woman's village, the people did not know about fire and they did not know how to cook food. They just ate everything. If they wanted to heat something, they just put it under the sun. Now the Black Cockatoo understood.

He thought, "It would be better if I taught my wife the way to make a fire." Cockatoo told the woman, "Go and find some tree branches that are very dry and carry them here." He taught her how to make fire and to cook food.

Pau Amep Pai

Vanimo

West Sepik Province

A1414. Origin of fire; A1455. Origin of cooking; B211.3+. Speaking cockatoo; B602+. Marriage to cockatoo; H383.4. Bride test: cooking; J1813+. Cooking processes misunderstood: cooking with the sun; P210. Husband and wife


## The Man Who Became a Tree

(Wantok 132, February 4, 1976, page 5)

Long ago, there were no men or women on the earth. There was only the earth, which was covered with forest and all kinds of trees, wild sugarcanes (*pitpit*) and grasses. Also, there were no good foods, such as what we find on the earth now.

There was a place called Mount Hagen that had a tree that grew big and beautiful. It grew directly on top of Mount Hagen and it was better than all of the other trees were. The name of this tree was *kapiapul*.

After the tree matured, it bore fruit. The first fruit that it bore fell to its base. The fruit broke open and became a male infant. The infant grew into a handsome boy whose name was Kapia Ulga. He became a man and he lived on top of Mount Hagen. He looked around and traveled the land. He saw that things grew nicely, so he was happy with the land.

He sat on the mountain and was tired. Kapia Ulga thought a lot that he would like to go down from the mountain. So, he began to walk down the mountain and he found a nice piece of land. He built a house and garden and slept there.

He was happy with the good land and he slept there. Many times he saw other lands that were just there. He thought a lot about this, "What if there's a man like me over on that land? That would be good," he thought, but there was no other man. He worried about this and thought more about finding a woman so that he could have a son.

One day he traveled in the forest to find some wild game. He went into the forest and found a nice, small house. In the house was a young woman.

Kapia Ulga was very happy and looked around the house. He found a long pigsty and many cassowary cages. He wanted to see who it was that slept in the house, so he waited. The young woman came and saw him. She was ecstatic and shook hands with him. The name of this woman was Hagen Multip.

She asked him, "How did you get here?" Kapia Ulga said, "I came to look for wild game in the forest and I came upon your house." Later they went inside the woman's house. They killed one of the man's [woman's?] pigs and they happily ate it in the house. They married and took all of the woman's possessions to the man's house.

After some months, they had many, many children and this place was jammed with people. They formed the two big clans. One clan is called Ulga Grunamp Agilimb and the other is called Ulga Grunamb Komb.

These two clans have become populous in the Western Highlands Province. My people call the mountain where the man came from Mount Hagen. The tree from Mount Hagen has spread to many places in Papua New Guinea.

John Kulda
**Togoba/Ulga Dan** Village [**Hagen** People]
**Western Highlands** Province

A1253.1. Creation of man from fruit; A1611+. Origin of Hagen People; A1640+. Origin of Ulga Grunamp Agilimb Clan; F562.7K. People live in mountain top; P210. Husband and wife; P230. Parents and children; T100. Marriage; T543.3. Birth from fruit

## The Ghost that Became a Cuscus
(Wantok 133, February 21, 1976, page 5)

There was a village where a man lived with his wife and children. The name of this village is Sauloku [**Soloku**, **Yil** People, **West Sepik** Province]. One day the husband died and the wife and two children were left alone.

In this village, the men did not look after this woman and her children. They always berated them.

One day, when it was still morning, the woman went to the forest with her children. When they were in the forest, she and her two children took some bananas from the hut gable. Then the three of them worked in the garden until the evening.

At about seven o'clock at night, the woman and her children made a fire and cooked the bananas that they had taken in the morning. The mother was still cooking the bananas while the children were playing on a cold bed that was not near the fire.

After two of the bananas were ready to eat, the mother peeled them. She ate one and put one on the bed. However, the two children did not get the banana that their mother had given them. No, the banana that had been given by their mother was taken and eaten by a ghost.

The third and last banana was still on the fire when the two children asked their mother, "Why did you eat the bananas and leave us nothing?"

The mother replied, "I already gave you a banana." Then the two children said, "You gave it to a man and we didn't get any."

So the mother took the third banana and yelled at them, "Here, the two other two bananas are gone." The ghost heard this and he shoved his hand out to try to take the banana, but the mother quickly grabbed the ghost's hand.

Then she asked the two children, "Whose hand am holding? Is it one of yours?"

"No, mother. We're over here."

The mother broke the ghost's hand and the ghost turned into a white cuscus [the spotted cuscus, *Spilocuscus maculatus maculatus* (Flannery, 1995a: 181-182)].

The mother told her children, "Light a fire and see what I'm holding." The children lit a fire and saw it. They told their mother, "Leave it there and we'll cook it tomorrow morning."

Then they tied it and hung it up. At dawn, they cooked this cuscus and feasted upon it.

James Meinik
Taingim
[West Sepik Province]

E423.2+. Revenant as marsupial; E425.2. Revenant as man; E446. Ghost killed and thus finally laid; E541. Revenants eat; K420. Thief loses his goods or is detected; P210. Husband and wife; P230. Parents and children; Q212. Theft punished; Q411. Death as punishment

## Why Did the Family Break Apart?
(Wantok 134, March 6, 1976, page 5)

Long ago, there lived a woman with her two children in a village. This village was not far from **Goroka** in the Eastern Highlands Province [**Gahuku** People]. The children, a girl and boy, were still very young.

Enemies had killed the children's father, and there was no father figure to look after them. There was no man to work in the garden or to help them. There was none at all. They had little food and they had nothing to cover their bodies. They had nothing like a loincloth or shirt. They grew up completely destitute.

One day these poor people had nothing to eat, so the mother was very troubled. What would her little ones eat? She thought for a while then told the children to stay while she alone would go to find food.

However, in this area there were huge men in the deep forest who were cannibals. Many times in the past they had killed and eaten people. So now, everyone in this area was afraid of them and did not travel around in this area.

The mother showed them a banana plant standing near their house. She said, "At that place, there are many enemies, but there is no food so I want to go there now!"

After she said this she got up and grieved with her children. Then she left to find food. The place where she went was very far, but she was not afraid, she just went there. She thought about finding fish first, then of finding some leafy vegetables with some food. She followed a creek up towards its source. Before long she met an old man. This man was sitting at the base of a tree, sharpening his stone axe.

The woman thought a lot and worried. It would be bad if the man killed her. She was completely famished. When the woman approached him, he asked, "Hey woman! Do you have some food? I'm famished." The old woman gave him some fish and the hungry man quickly ate it all, then asked for more. Before long, all of the woman's fish was gone. The man had eaten all of it.

"Where do you want to go now?" He asked the woman, "Do you want to follow me or do you want me to follow you?" The old woman was afraid, so she thought and thought. Then she said that she would follow him.

Before long, they found a different kind of yam in a garden. He told the woman, "This is a different kind of yam, but you don't have food, so you must dig it up." He said, "You must be careful not to break this yam in the middle. If you do that, it would be bad for you."

The woman began to dig while the man held his axe and watched carefully. The poor woman tried very hard to dig carefully, but the yam had grown very deep, so it was very hard to dig out. When the woman was very deep, it looked as if she was almost at the end of the yam. It was then that the woman moved in the wrong way and broke the yam. Oh my! The old man was extremely angry. He said, "Come on! Dig out all of that yam."

Quickly, the man cut her neck, and the poor woman died. He was very frightened, so he quickly buried her. He left the garden and ran far away, never to return again.

Peter Emong

Raipinka

Kainantu

[Eastern Highlands Province]

G11.2. Cannibal giant; H1100+. Task: digging a long yam without breaking it; P231. Mother and son; P232. Mother and daughter; P253. Sister and brother; Q325. Disobedience punished; Q411. Death as punishment; S118.2. Murder by cutting throat; V61.3+. Dead buried; W126. Disobedience

## The Woman Who Ate Two Children
(Wantok 135, March 20, 1976, pages 5-6)

Long ago, a man and a woman lived in a village called **Patil** near Mount Hagen [**Western Highlands** Province, **Hagen** People]. They lived well in their house, and the woman gave birth to two boys. The boys were good children, and their parents loved them. They heeded what their parents said. The names of the family members were Mopa, Kopsil, Kei and Kui. They never went to other villages. The two boys were nice, and their parents told them, "You two cannot go to other villages. You should stay at the house, go to the forest to kill marsupials (*kapul*), and return to the house."

There was a place where ceremonial dances were held, and their mother wanted to take them there to sing and dance with the others. The father said, "I don't want them to go there." The mother was persistent and took them. She brought all of the things that they would need for dancing. Before they left, the father spoke again, "When the songs and dances finish, come back. I'll tell you two more times. If you two get lost at the dancing place, you'll not be able to return home. I'm telling it to you plainly."

So, they went to the festival. The two boys had dressed smartly, and they sang and danced. The mother watched them sing and dance while she smoked and gave them water. They stayed for four days and spoke to everyone there. Many people had gathered to see the singing and dancing of two men. These people did not go to other places, but what they saw were these two boys singing and dancing. Then the festival was ending, and the mother collected all of the boys' belongings. They said that in two days, the festival would end. So the mother took their things and went to sleep in a house.

That night, the mother did not sleep because she was worried that her children would be taken from her. So she took her boys, Kei and Kui, and put them each inside a bamboo tube. She slept a little bit, then a woman came and took the two boys to her house. The mother woke up and saw that the two bamboo tubes were not in the room. She was surprised and said, "Where did they go?" She thought and thought about Kei and Kui, and she cried. Then she asked everyone where her boys were, "I'm looking for the two boys who sang and danced yesterday. They're lost." Mopa kept thinking and crying about his boys. Then a man said, "I know two children who went somewhere."

A cannibal woman asked, "Why don't we go get them?" The mother did not say anything to this, she went back to the house and cut off one of her fingertips [a traditional sign of extreme grief or mourning]. However, this was not enough, she cut the another one. This was still not enough, so she stayed in the house and the father asked her to come. He said, "The festival is finished are you coming?" The woman did not reply directly to her husband, she said, "Kopsil, listen to me or else you'll get sick."

Kopsil did not reply to this either. Mopa looked into Kopsil's eyes and cried about the places where she had cut herself. Then Mopa spoke, "Why did you cut your hands and why are you crying?" Kopsil replied, "Mopa, I lost our two boys, Kei and Kui. I had put them in two long bamboo tubes and I slept a little. I stayed inside, then near dawn I fell asleep." However, Mopa did not heed Kopsil. He cut off three of his fingertips, but this was not enough. Then Mopa became angry with Kopsil and said, "What did I tell you? I said not to bring them. Now go get them and come back. Why did you come here? What can I do now for Kei and Kui? Go get them and come back."

Kopsil did not reply to Mopa, so Mopa told Kopsil, "You must stay here. I'll go find them." Mopa left Kopsil at the house and he went to find Kei and Kui. Mopa asked a man where to go and the man told him, "Near that forest, go down to a river and then go above and near the river." He saw this place, then thought and thought. He said, "How will I get the two brothers?" Mopa saw a big garden where there was a cannibal woman who had many children. She called out, "You children, pick those cucumbers and come here. You are big children. Come bring them for the men." She was talking to a girl named Las.

"You still must get them for us." This woman did not eat big cucumbers, she only ate the small, round cucumbers that the children brought. Then Mopa went inside a cucumber and Las brought the cucumber to her mother who ate it.

When the woman ate the cucumber, blood spewed from her mouth. The mother thought, "What kind of cucumber could I have eaten?" So she berated her little girl, Las, "Just what kind of cucumber is this? I've never seen this kind of cucumber."

The cannibal woman had eaten Mopa because he was inside the cucumber. He wanted to get his two boys who were now inside the mother of Las. The cannibal woman's stomach was now in great pain. At night she could not sleep well because she had eaten Mopa. She was pregnant for four days. After two weeks, she gave birth to a boy named Kewa. She called out to all her other boys. She continued to talk, "I'm an old woman and I gave birth to a boy who can help me work around here."

This child became very big and said to [his mother], "I want to eat a pig." He cried, then Kewa's mother killed a pig and they ate it. The mother went to bring the pig to the other people. Kewa wanted to go with her. He cried, "Mother, where are you bringing the pig?" She said, "Stay here with the other children."

However, Kewa wanted to see his two children. The Mother said, "We can go." But Kewa did not say anything to her. Kewa took his pig inside of a cave and said, "Hello." The cave opened and the mother quickly went inside.

Kewa also went with her. Kewa understood what she had said. He gave the pork to everyone. Kewa put his pork inside the cave. Mopa slept with the other children and with Kewa. In the early morning, Kewa cried for pork inside the cave.

The mother said, "You know that you and I opened the hole in the cave." Kewa said, "Yes, I know it well." Kewa was happy to get two of his men. Kewa went again and said, "Hello," then the cave opened again. He said, "I belong to this place that they have spoken of." Kewa spoke to them, "Come and go outside." Then he called their names. He told them to run outside and to the mountain and yell out for many more to come.

"You, cannibal woman, eat well." After they said this, she brought everyone and she said, "Go now."

All three of them left, the father and the boy and the mother who was looking for her children. Then she was happy for everyone.

Kewa was another name for Mopa, the [father] of Kei and Kui. The two of them married but their parents died. Kei and Kui did not have children, they died inside the cave. I was told this story and I have seen this cave.

Paul Wama
C. T. C. Tsak
Enga Province

D1552.2. Mountain opens to magic formula (Open Sesame); D1774. Magic results from speaking; E600. Reincarnation; F564+. Person sleeps in bamboo tube; F910. Extraordinary swallowings; G10. Cannibalism; P210. Husband and wife; P231. Mother and son; P232. Mother and daughter; P233. Father and son; P251.5. Two brothers; P681+. Mourning customs: self-mutilation; S160.1. Self-mutilation; S161.1. Mutilation: cutting off fingers; T100. Marriage; T511.1+. Conception from eating cucumber; T573. Short pregnancy; T580. Childbirth; Z71.1. Formulistic number: three

## The Woman and the Snake

(Wantok 136, April 3, 1976, page 5)

Once upon a time there lived a woman with her baby who went over to a pond. The mother took her baby and hung it on a tree branch in a net bag, then the mother went to look for a pond. The pond that she found had plenty of fish in it and they were happy.

The woman went to block up the pond. She blocked the water and came down to the pond, then she started to scoop out the water. She tried very hard to finish scooping out the water. When she finished scooping out the water, she saw that it did not have any fish in it. She saw many other things in the pond. She took out all of the junk from the pond and continued to search for fish. Still there were none, just more junk.

When she was about to remove all of the junk, she saw a big snake, a python. The woman didn't kill the snake, she let it be.

Gently, she took her palm fiber basket and put it down. Then, she took the snake, tied it up, put it in the basket and carried it with her.

She went back to her village and hung up her baby in the net bag in her house. She came outside and took a stick that was standing up. She took the snake in the bag and hung up the bag on the stick. Then she took a knife and began cutting up the snake. However, the snake did not die. The snake just feigned death and went to sleep, so the woman thought that the snake was dead. She continued to cut up the snake. After that, she took a clay cooking pot and the knife. She cut up some edible leaves into little pieces and put them in the pot, then she began to make a

fire. After the leaves were done, she took them out and put them in a basket.

After the leaves were cold, she put them all into her net bag and hung them up on a tree. Later, she took her baby and came outside the house that evening. The two of them went by the fire and then went back inside the house to sleep.

While they were asleep, the snake began to reconnect itself. After it had finished putting itself together, it began to go around the house. Then it smelled the woman and came down to the ground level. The snake took the head of the woman and ate it along with her body. Then the snake went back to the pond where it had been taken. Later, the baby began to cry at the house. The men of the village heard the crying. They came and opened the house, then went inside and brought the baby outside until it was dawn. When dawn came, they all called out for the people to come gather, to talk and find out what had happened to the woman. They took a pig, some chickens, some coconut sprouts, and some yams. They took these, went down to the pond and threw them down. Then, they saw the woman's legs. They took the two legs and went back to their village. They cried and the buried the legs. She was dead.

W. Lawson
Negrie [**Negri** Mission [**Boiken** People]
Wewak
**East Sepik** Province

B765.7.2. Snake grows back together after it has been severed; F911.7. Serpent swallows man; P230. Parents and children; Q211.6. Killing an animal revenged; Q411. Death as punishment; V61.3+. Dead buried

## The Woman Who Became a Fish

(Wantok 137, April 17, 1976, page 5)

Long ago, there was a man and woman who had two children. The man only ate ginger roots from the forest. The woman and her two children only ate taro. The woman always hid the taro underneath firewood. When the man was not there, she would cook and eat it with her children. This is how it went every day.

One day, the woman went to the garden with her eldest daughter. They went to find firewood and food from the garden. The husband watched after the younger child at home. Near noontime, the child cried with hunger. So, the father cooked some wild ginger roots and gave them to the child. However, the child did not like them and continued to cry. The father thought, "Why isn't the child eating this food?" While the child cried, it pointed its finger to where the mother hid the taro. Then the father thought, "Why is the child pointing to that place?" He did not know that his wife hid taro underneath the firewood.

The father went and pulled up the firewood, then saw the taro there. He said, "Hey! You were always eating this good food, and I was like a fool. You only gave me wild things to eat." Then he took two pieces of taro and cooked them in the fire. After the taro was done, he gave one to the child. He smelled the other and vomited the ginger he had eaten as if it were garbage. After he had finished vomiting, he ate the taro.

In the afternoon, his wife and eldest child returned. The woman was famished and wanted to cook her taros, so she removed the firewood, but she did not find any taros. The woman did not say anything. She went out, took some bamboo skin [bamboo fishing gear?] and tried to catch some fish. Then she tried to swim in the water. She looked hard for fish. She left her bag and hid the bamboo skin. She returned home and asked her husband, "Who took my taro?" The man spoke, "I was always like a fool and you always gave me wild things from the forest, while you and the children ate good taro, huh?"

The woman spoke, "That's OK. Now you can look after the two children." She milked her breasts into a bamboo tube and gave it to her daughter. She said, "Take this and when your brother cries, give it to him. When the milk is done, bring your brother to the Ungu Pond and sing to him, '*Avo mao na mi pamo*.'" Then the woman took the bamboo skin. She turned into a fish and swam in Ungu Pond.

The girl looked after her brother until the milk was finished, then she brought him to Ungu Pond and sung to him as her mother had told her. The mother came and gave him some milk. This is how it went for a long time.

Then one time the father hid near the Ungu Pond. He saw that his wife was giving milk to the child. After he saw this, he went back home. He sent a message to all of the other villages, the message was for the men to gather and bring back his wife.

One day, the men came together, they built a fence around the Ungu Pond. When it was time for her to give milk to the child, the men quickly held her tightly. However, she quickly turned into a fish again and jumped back into the water, never to return again.



So, in my village, women worry about taro. They always leave it alone because they are afraid of turning into fish.

Bruno Malai
Josephstaal
**Madang** Province

C181. Tabu confined to women; C224+. Tabu concerning taro; D170W. Transformation: woman to fish; D370W. Transformation: fish to woman; K1892. Wife deceives husband by hiding food; P210. Husband and wife; P232. Mother and daughter; P253. Sister and brother; T611. Suckling of children

## How Cassowaries Obtained Their Colors
(Wantok 138, May 1, 1976, page 5)

There was a very tall mountain named Uria. On top of this mountain was a big village. In this village lived a woman named Hurianu. This woman did not have a husband, she was a young woman. There were no other men or women in this place.

The woman took care of a big pig. The pig was truly huge. One time, when the woman wanted to go to the garden, her pig watched after their house. The woman dug some sweet potatoes and cut some firewood. Then she gathered all of the things together and returned to the house. When she returned, she told her pig, "Go to the garden and carry my things back here."

Oh my, the pig heeded its mother and carried the things that she had said. After the pig returned with the things, they ate and slept. They did this routine every day.

One day, the woman went to the forest and took some vines to make a net bag, while her pig stayed at the house. The pig waited and waited, but the woman did not return home. At about three o'clock, a man came, opened the door and took all of the pieces of firewood that they used for cooking. Some of the pieces were lit. He took some water and threw it on the wood, extinguishing the fire. The pig saw this but did not say anything to this man, because the pig was afraid of the man.

The man carried the fire to his village. Much later, the woman returned to the house. The woman saw that the fire had died, so she and pig just went to sleep without eating anything. In the morning, the woman went outside and looked towards Ialibu, where she saw smoke.

The woman told the pig, "I want to get that fire. Stay here at the house." She took her net bag and walked. She thought, "Will I be able to return today?"

She walked and walked, then arrived at **Kagua** Village [**Kewa** People, **Southern Highlands** Province]. Near this village, she arrived at the place where the fire was. The poor woman wanted to go there, but she saw a man returning. She turned around but her leg tripped on a tree branch and she fell.

The man called out to her, "I see you. Come here." After he said that, the woman was terrified and slowly went towards him. The woman explained to the man that the fire at her house had died out and that she had just come to get some fire.

The man said, "It's alright, you can take it and leave. However first, I will cook some taro for you, then you can eat it before you return home." He gave two pieces of taro to her. She ate one piece and the other she held to take home to her pig.

The man said, "Tomorrow you can return this taro to me when I come to your house." The woman held a burning stick and returned home. When she arrived home, she gave the taro to her pig. The name of this taro is _kolapa_. The woman slept in her house and her belly swelled up. In the morning, the man came along the trail and called the name of this taro. When he did this, the woman's belly called out. This terrified the woman and caused her to worry.

The man was carrying a big bundle of bamboos when he arrived at the woman's house. He said to her, "Go to sleep." The man pulled out a long piece of bamboo and put it into the ground. The woman went to sleep on top of the bamboo, then he cut the woman's neck. After he cut off her head, he cut off her legs and arms. The woman died and the man returned to his village.

The woman's pig dragged the pieces of the woman's body over to the base of a tree. The fruits of this tree were ripe and cassowaries had been eating the fallen fruits. A young cassowary came and saw the woman's body, and mourned for her.

The cassowary saw some other cassowaries. All of them came and each kicked the woman's belly. The woman's belly burst open and joined with her arms and legs and head. She came back to life again and spoke with the cassowaries.

Then the cassowaries asked her, "Who killed you?" The woman said, "I took some fire from a man who gave me two pieces of taro. I ate the taro and my belly swelled up. Then I slept in my house. In the morning, that man came along the trail and called the name of the taro that I had eaten. The taro in my belly called back. The man heard it, came to my house and killed me."

A cassowary spoke, "We cassowaries can kill this man. Make a bonfire. This man will see it and come. When he comes, we can kill him."

Then, two cassowaries watched the door and a third watched the trail. The man saw the smoke rising and came to the woman's house. The man was carrying a big bundle of bamboos as he came and tried to enter the house. However, as he entered, the two cassowaries kicked his chest. Then all of the other cassowaries surrounded him, kicking him badly and killing him. Then they threw him into the creek.

The woman was ecstatic. She gathered pigs and _kina_ shells, and gave them to the cassowaries. The cassowaries spoke, "This is a big gift that you have given to us, but we can't take it." She wanted to give them a big pig, but the cassowaries said, "No." Then the woman asked them, "What would you like?" They said, "We would like to take something to decorate ourselves."

So the woman lined up all of the cassowaries and took two kinds of paints, one red and one yellow. She painted their necks, first red then yellow. The cassowaries were very happy about their handsome decorations.

When the woman finished painting them, they ran back into the forest. This man was able to kill everyone on the earth, but the cassowaries helped you and me so that now we live well. The cassowaries of long ago did not have handsome decorations on their necks as they do now. So now you can see all of the cassowaries have this kind of decoration on their necks.

Matyu Mali

Erave

Southern Highlands Province

A2411.2+. Origin of color of cassowaries; B211.3.17K. Speaking cassowary; B212. Animal understands human speech; B320. Reward of helpful animal; B469+. Helpful cassowary; B871.1.2.1. Giant hog; D1034+. Magic taro; D1419.4. Magic food brings eater into sender's power; D1619.2. Eaten object speaks from inside person's body; D1960. Magic sleep; E10. Resuscitation by rough treatment; E35. Resuscitation from fragments of body; P210. Husband and wife; P231. Mother and son; Q10. Deeds rewarded; Q211. Murder punished; Q411. Death as punishment; S118.2. Murder by cutting throat; S139.2. Slain person dismembered


## The Death of a Strong Man

(Wantok 139, May 15, 1976, page 5)

Once there was a man who worked in his garden in a village called **Airote**. At this time, there was another man who took a discarded piece of tobacco of his. He ensorcelled the tobacco and caused the man to get a little sick inside his belly.

Those who commit murders through sorcery are called _devara_ in my language. A _devara_ would learn that a man is sick and he would come to kill him. So, five men came to kill the man who was working in his garden. They fought with him and he killed all five. He was able to kill all of them with his axe because he was a very strong man.

All of the _devara_ were angry because of this, they came and knocked him down and beat him up. Afterwards, they picked him up and told him to wait in a village called **Tamoni**, where they would come and beat him up thoroughly at night.

His two eyes turned around and something brown came out. He slept in the forest for two entire days.

The next day a man named Aveni and his wife, Pirinave, went into the forest. They met him and carried him in a canoe and brought him to the beach.

Everyone came to meet him and cry for him. This man was now dead and they buried him at one o'clock.

Killian T. Naime
**Warapu** [Village, **Warapu** People]
Sissano
[**West Sepik** Province]

D1711. Magician; D2061.2.2.8+. Death from ensorcelled tobacco; F628.2.1. Strong man kills many men at once; P210. Husband and wife; Q211. Murder punished; Q411. Death as punishment; Q458. Flogging as punishment; S110. Murders; V61.3+. Dead buried

## Why Houses in Yangoru Do Not Have Fences
(Wantok 140, May 29, 1976, page 12)

Long ago, there lived a man named Manihia. One time he took his spear and walked into the forest. While he was walking, he did not see a snake that was well hidden in a tree near the trail. The poor man Manihia did not see the snake, so he walked directly into it. However, the snake had sensed him coming and was waiting for him. The snake bit him in the neck and the man fell in the trail. Then the snake prepared to devour him.

When Manihia awoke, the snake had already devoured him and he was in the snake's stomach. Poor Manihia had not died. He was still all right despite being inside the snake. However, the snake thought that the man had died. The man had stayed inside the snake for only a little while when the snake vomited up Manihia onto the ground. After that, Manihia went into the forest and found some wild taro that he could use to heal his neck.

After the snake had done this to him, Manihia kept his eyes open and thought a lot about returning. He knew that the snake had eaten him. So he thought, "I think that I should go to the village and tell the people to come. We'll kill that snake." After Manihia was ready to go, the snake returned quickly.

Poor Manihia was not able to run away. So, he took a big, strong branch and stood it up inside the snake's mouth. Then the snake could no longer eat or drink because of the branch in its mouth, this caused the snake to die.

Now if you go to the **Yangoru** area [**Boiken** People, **East Sepik** Province], you will see that all of the house posts stand up straight in the middle of the houses, and that the two outside walls of each of the houses touch the ground.

Tonny Willie
Brandi High School
Wewak
East Sepik Province

A1590+. Origin of house style; F911.7+. Serpent swallows man, then vomits him out

## Where Did Mosquitoes Come From?
(Wantok 141, June 12, 1976, page 12)

Long, long ago, there was an old woman who slept inside a house near a big village. She kept her door shut all of the time.

One day, the little boys heard a noise inside this old woman's house. One boy asked, "What's that?" Another boy said, "I don't know." Others said, "Let's ask the old woman." However, the old woman was not inside the house, so the boys searched for her everywhere.

Later, they saw her working in a garden. She asked the boys, "What do you want?" They said, "We heard a noise inside your house. Is there a bird inside your house?"

The old woman said, "There's no bird inside my house."

They asked, "Is there a man inside your house?" The woman said, "No, there's no man inside my house." Then she said angrily, "Go away!"

So, the boys went back to their village. They said, "One day we'll find out what's inside the old woman's house."

Three weeks passed, and some men stole bananas from the old woman's garden. She became angry, so she went to the village and asked the men about her bananas. She said,

"Who stole my bananas?" The men did not know. "Please help me to find my bananas," she said.

The men laughed. They said, "We don't know anything about your bananas." The old woman became irate and said, "I'll imprison you. I'll open the door of my house."

The boys said, "She can't imprison us." The boys decided to go inside the old woman's house and look. "Let's find out what is inside the old woman's house," they said. So, they followed the old woman and quickly went to her house, then opened the door. At this time, mosquitoes came outside the house.

The boys had never seen mosquitoes before. "What's that?" they asked. Later they found out that mosquitoes were like awful maternal relatives. They flew behind the boys and bit them. The boys quickly ran back to the village, but the mosquitoes flew after them. The elders saw the mosquitoes chasing the boys and then the mosquitoes started biting the men and women too.

The men and women were very concerned about the bananas and said, "We don't want to help the old woman find her bananas now that she unleashed these mosquitoes from her house. She was a very good old woman. She had put the mosquitoes far from us, but we didn't help her."

Now, for many years and months when it is the rainy season, the mosquitoes always bite men, women and children all over the place.

Peter Sospi
Congregation of Mission **But** [**Mountain Arapesh** People]
Wewak
**East Sepik** Province

A2034+. Origin of mosquitoes: from opening woman's house; J652. Inattention to warnings; K420. Thief loses his goods or is detected

## Where Did the Cucumber Come From?
(Wantok 142, June 26, 1976, page 12)

Long, long ago, in the time of the ancestors, two brothers lived in a village. One time, the brothers followed a branch of a river upstream until they found some tree fruits. The big brother took one and tried it. It was delicious so he took another. The little brother said, "Please don't take all of them, give me some." So the big brother gave him a piece.

They continued onward and arrived at the base of a tree. The big brother climbed one tree and the little brother climbed another. While they were eating the fruits, two pigs came along and ate the fallen fruits below.

When the big brother saw this, he took a fruit and broke it a little. Then he whispered a curse and blew on the fruit. He threw the fruit down and one pig ate the fruit and died. The little brother saw this, so he did the same thing. The other pig ate the fruit and died too.

After the two pigs had died, the brothers climbed down. The big brother sent the little brother to fetch fire from an old woman. The old woman asked him, "What is it that you want to cook?" The little brother said, "I want to cook mushrooms."

The old woman wanted to know what kind of mushrooms that they wanted to cook and the little brother said the names of all of the kinds of mushrooms. But the old woman said that those kinds of mushrooms were not good to eat. So finally, the brother named a kind of mushroom that was good to eat, and she gave him some fire. He carried the fire back and the two brothers cooked the pigs in an earth oven.

When the pork was ready, the old woman came and sat near the earth oven. She saw a piece of leg sticking out. When the two brothers asked her to go to her house, she pretended to be working on making a net bag.

The two brothers opened the earth oven and gave a leg of pork to the old woman who carried it home. After she put the leg in her house, she cut her hand on a piece of sword grass. She returned and told them that a dog had bitten her hand, and so the brothers gave her another leg of pork.

After the old woman left, the two brothers carried the pigs up a tree and ate them. When the old woman returned, she saw that they were not there so she watched for them while sitting in the sun. Then she saw their shadows and found them. When she saw them in the tree, they threw bones down and hit her head. The old woman cried and went back to her house. She took an axe and spear, then returned to the place where the two brothers were. She jabbed the spear around the tree to cut it. While she was cutting the tree, the brothers jumped to another, then they jumped again to another.

They continued to do this, and the little brother twisted his leg in a new branch. Then he held onto a big branch that broke and fell down with him. The spear killed him and the old woman carried him off to eat.

The big brother came down and cried and cried. He went to old woman's house with some others and burned the house down, killing the woman. Later, they saw something growing where the house was. This plant had flowers, and later it had fruit. One man took and ate the fruits, finding that they were delicious. He went to his village and told the men to come take the fruits back to the village. He told them to eat the fruits and to plant the seeds of the plant that we now call cucumber.

Wangakue Kesipik
Numoikum
[**Numoirum** Village, **Boiken** People]
Maprik
**East Sepik** Province

A2687.2+. Origin of cucumber; D981. Magic fruit; D1419.4. Magic food brings eater into sender's power; D1792. Magic results from curse; G10. Cannibalism; K812. Victim burned in his own house (or hiding place); P251.5. Two brothers; Q211. Murder punished; Q414.0.12. Burning as punishment for murder; R260. Pursuits; R311. Tree refuge; S110. Murders; S112.0.2. House (hostel) burned with all inside

# The Flood
### (Wantok 143, July 10, 1976, page 4)

One day, the women of Lonem [**Loneim** Village, **Mountain Arapesh** People, **East Sepik** Province] went to their gardens and pulled out taro corms. After they removed the taros, the corms were covered with dirt so they went to the river to wash them off.

While the women washed the taros, their children worked fishing in the river. The little fish went near a particular pond, but people never went near this pond because a *masalai* dwelled there.

A mudfish [?] had died there, but it was not a true mudfish, it was one of their men. His spirit had died and the small spirits had carried him up to this pond. However, the children did not know this and thought it was a real fish. They took this dead fish and gave it to their mothers. When the mothers had finished washing the taros, they took the dead fish with the taros and went to the village.

They cooked the dead fish and when they cut it to eat, the fish was full of blood. The blood was just like that of a man, so they cooked it again in the fire but the blood did not dry up. They removed the fish from the fire again and ate it with the blood.

After they finished eating, they went inside their houses and slept. That night, the rain came down. A strong wind blew and there was thunder. They did not know why the weather was like this.

Late that night, the water from the pond rose and flooded their village. The water went so high that it killed all of the people, dogs and pigs. The water went inside their houses, then it went above their houses and covered everything in the village.

Only two people were able to escape, a man with a woman who went up high. In the morning, they came down, went on top of a mountain and thought.

Now they call this village Lonem. Before, the people of Lonem lived in Malan [**Malin**] near Jlipain [**Japuain**] Village. One can stand in Jlipain and look at Malan. The land that the people of Jlipain use for gardens actually belongs to the people of Lonem.

So if you think that I am lying to you, go find a man or woman from Lonem or Jlipain. They can also tell you this story.

Leo Gilichibi
Maprik
East Sepik Province

A1011. Local deluges; A1015.2. Spirit causes deluge; A991+. Origin of particular village; D2142.1. Wind produced by magic; D2143.1. Rain produced by magic; D2149.1. Thunderbolt magically produced; D2151.8. Magic flood; E617. Reincarnation as fish; F490+. Masalai

# The Trick of the Worthless Man
### (Wantok 144, July 24, 1976, pages 12, 14)

This ancestor story comes from **Kaisap** Village, in the Lagaip area of Laiagam, **Enga** Province [**Enga** People]. Lemian is the subject of this story, he was a worthless man. He lived in a small forest on Kepau Mountain. On the other side of the mountain was a young woman. Many young men competed to befriend this woman. Whoever befriended her would be able to marry her.

Lemian was obsessed [lit., "tied up"] over this woman, so he wanted to try to talk and laugh with her. But the young woman mocked him and spit in his face. Lemian still looked at her, but he saw that he was truly worthless and that he could not get her. He remembered that he had neither pigs nor shell money (*kina*), "So I can't get this woman."

However, he thought that he would like to try to find a way to get her. One time he went on a trail and hid nearby. He saw that the young woman with her mother were searching for food far from their home. Lemian knew that they would be going to another place.

He went deep into the forest, killed two marsupials (*kapul*) and tied them tightly with a vine. Lemian carried the bundle of marsupials. He walked to the trail where the young woman and her mother had gone and where they would return. In the middle of the deep woods, Lemian had found a stone house.  He put the marsupial bundle high on top of a mountain.  He put a long rope from the bundle to the house.  He put a big pile of firewood, *tanget*, vegetables, and other good things on the long trail.  He found a good piece of bamboo to make a fire with his stick.  He tied it well with some leaves and marsupial skin to the marsupial hair.  He had truly made something and he put it inside his raggedy net bag.

Then he called out, "Come rainnnnn.  Come rainnnnn."  Oh my, then came a huge downpour.  However, he did not yet feel the rain washing over him [because of the forest cover], so he went to the trail.  The mother and the young woman came, and he stood up like a murderous sorcerer [*sangumaman*].  The rain poured and poured on the two women, making them cold.  Lemian said, "Heyyyy, where do you live?"  They replied, "We can't talk with you because the rain is drenching us terribly.  However, if you have a piece of bamboo for making fires, then you can help us."

So Lemian said, "Sorry, I have a piece of bamboo for making fire, but I don't have anything else.  Because this is very important, it's not easy [for me to do this for you].  I'm also cold, but I'll just stay here."

So, the old woman tried to think of things to give him.  She said, "We'll find a pig or a net bag of things to give to you.  Is that alright?"

Lemian said, "No."  The old woman said, "You can sleep with my daughter once, is that alright?"  Lemian agreed.

Lemian took the piece of bamboo from his net bag.  The two women saw the markings that covered it and felt that it was real.  Poor Lemian began to make the fire.  Lemian pulled hard and made a big fire, but there was no good firewood.

Lemian asked them, "Where can we get firewood?"  The two women thought and thought.  So Lemian said again, "You two must go and look out the door so that we all can see what is there."  They followed his instructions.

Then Lemian gently held the rope that tied the firewood, marsupial, vegetables, *tanget* leaves, and other things that he had prepared.  The women saw these at the door.  Then he shouted and called out, and the firewood, marsupial and other things fell down and he quickly pulled the rope.

Oh my!  Everything fell over.  Then he began to help them.  They thought that he was being genuinely nice, so the old woman just gave him her beautiful daughter.

[Anonymous]

D1711. Magician; D1774. Magic results from speaking; D2143.1. Rain produced by magic; K1350. Woman persuaded (or wooed) by trick; P160. Beggars; P210. Husband and wife; P232. Mother and daughter

## The Taboo against Women Spearfishing at Night
(Wantok 145, August 7, 1976, page 12)

Long ago, there were two sisters who lived in a village.  The big sister was married and had a child.  One afternoon, the big sister told the little sister, "Go home and cook some food.  When it's dark, go down and wait for me near the village, then I'll come with the child.  You can carry him while I spearfish in the river."

The little sister listened to this and went to cook the food.  Night came quickly, and a ghost woman was waiting where the big sister had told the little sister to wait.  When the big sister with her little baby went to the meeting place, they found this ghost.  She thought that it was her sister because the ghost looked like her.

Because she did not know that it was a ghost, she spoke to her.  The two of them with the little baby in a net bag walked along.  When they arrived at the river, the big sister gave the baby to the ghost and said to her, "If the baby cries, you must give the baby to me.  I'll give the baby milk and then I'll return the baby to you."  The big sister also gave her a bamboo tube to put fish in, saying, "When I spear fish, I'll give them to you.  You should put them in the tube."

After she said this, she began to spear the fish and give them to the ghost woman to put in the tube.  However, the ghost just took and ate them.  When they went a little farther upriver, the ghost woman put her hand inside the baby's net bag.  She pulled and broke off one of the baby's legs, eating it quickly.  The baby cried and its mother said, "Come, I'll give you milk and you'll sleep."

However, the ghost said, "I'll make the baby sleep," and the baby did sleep.  After the baby slept, the ghost broke and pulled off the other leg and ate it quickly.  The baby cried again and the mother said she would give it milk.  However, the ghost said, "I'll make the baby sleep now."

The ghost did this to the entire baby's body and put an old, short piece of wood inside the net bag with the baby's loincloth. The ghost had eaten the big fish that the sister had speared, so the ghost just held the empty tube.

They spearfished in the river until the morning. Then the big sister approached and said to the ghost woman, "Give me my baby and I'll give it milk. The baby did not have any all night."

The ghost gave the net bag to the big sister. She looked inside the net bag and saw the piece of wood. She asked the ghost woman, "Where is my baby? This is a piece of wood inside the net bag!"

The ghost woman heard this and fled. The woman saw this and ran after her. The woman chased the ghost who went inside a big boulder. Then the woman left her and went to the village, where she told all of the men and woman. They took their knives, axes and spears, and went into the forest. They arrived at the boulder where the ghost had entered. The woman told the people that this was where the ghosts entered. The woman spoke to them, "If we dig and the ghosts come out and they want to flee, you must kill one and cut her up. As they come out, you'll see one whose skin is entirely red. When you see this red-skinned one, you can kill her, you should let any others go."

They listened to this and then began to dig around the boulder. While they dug, they found ghosts. The ghosts began to flee, so the men and women watched. They saw the final one, the one who was red. They killed her and cut her into tiny pieces. Afterwards in the village, the men tabooed the women from spearfishing in the river at night.

Anton Akarigano

Bogia Catholic High School

C. M. [Congregation of Mission] Malala

P. O. Alexishafen

Madang Province

C181+. Taboo against women fishing at night; E250. Bloodthirsty revenants; E422.2.1. Revenant red; E425.1. Revenant as woman; E446. Ghost killed and thus finally laid; E545. The dead speak; G11.10. Cannibalistic spirits; K1930. Treacherous impostors; P210. Husband and wife; P230. Parents and children; P252.1. Two sisters; Q211. Murder punished; Q411. Death as punishment; R220. Flights; R260. Pursuits; R315. Cave as refuge; S139.2. Slain person dismembered

## The Custom of Hanging Oneself

(Wantok 146, August 21, 1976, page 14)

Once there was a husband and wife who lived in a village called Kurumul [**Kurumuil**, **Wahgi** People, **Western Highlands** Province]. They lived well and had no troubles. However, their house was not near the forest. No, it was deep in the sword-grass lands.

The man did not like the things in the sword-grass lands. He liked very much to just go into the forest and hunt marsupials (*kapul*). He often went to the forest to kill many marsupials, then he and his wife would cook the marsupials in an earth oven and eat them. But they never shared the marsupials with those who lived nearby. They never gave any to the man's brother.

One day, the man wanted to return to the forest. He told his wife to pull out some of her sweet potatoes to give to him to eat. However, the woman told her husband, "Hey, you always kill marsupials and bring them for us to eat. Now you want to go again to kill marsupials?"

The man told her, "Yes, I want to go to the forest." The woman replied, "You often kill marsupials and bring them for us to eat, but I don't know where you kill them. I don't know where the marsupials eat. Take me there, I want to see the place where the marsupials sleep."

So they went there, but on the main trail they arrived at a smaller trail. The woman was pregnant, so they walked carefully and came to a hut. It was dark and they slept in this forest hut. In the morning, they arrived at the place where the man killed marsupials.

The man showed her where he killed the marsupials. The woman told him, "You should carry me up this tree because I want to see the place where the marsupials sleep."

So, the man began to cut small pieces of wood. He tied them up with vines to the big tree [making a ladder]. After he finished tying them, he told his wife to get ready. Then he carried her up the tree. When they arrived at the place where the marsupials slept, they were high up in the middle of the tree.

The man looked at the place where the marsupials slept and told the woman, "Wife, I see one marsupial there." They killed this marsupial and took it out of its nest. They wanted to go down, but the big rope that they had used to tie to the tree had broken. So, they stayed on top of the tree and called out for someone to help them.

They called and cried. The man's brother came and helped them by retying the rope to the small pieces of wood. Then they came down to the ground.

When they came down, they told the man, "Later when we go home, don't say anything like, 'You carried your pregnant wife up the tree and didn't look after her.' Because if you speak like that I'll hang myself from a tree."

Later, the married couple's pig went inside the garden [and ate the produce] of the man [brother] who had helped them. The man mocked them and said, "You always just go to the forest and hunt marsupials! Your husband always carries you up the tree when you are still pregnant. You cried from on top of the tree and I helped you." Then he said, "This man's wife should be ashamed." So then the husband hanged himself and died.

Before, men did not know about this practice. Now they have the custom of hanging with a rope. This is a custom when people are angry and fight, this is why men hang themselves and die.

Joseph Yanga Walpe
Mt. Hagen
Western Highlands Province

A1599.9+. Origin of custom of committing suicide by hanging; J2100+. Pregnant woman becomes stuck climbing tree; P210. Husband and wife; P263. Brother-in-law; P264. Sister-in-law; P600+. Custom of hanging oneself; R155. Brothers rescue brothers; T570. Pregnancy; W152. Stinginess

## The Dog that Helped People

(Wantok 147, September 4, 1976, page 14)

Long ago, there was an old woman, a boy and a dog who lived near a mountain. The woman's husband had died and she did not have a husband. The boy's parents had also died. The two of them lived in the same house and worked together. The dog had come to their house. They gave food to him and took care of it well. They always did good things for each other and worked together every day.

When they made a new garden or did other tasks, they began in the early morning and returned to their house in the evening. The place where they lived was deep in the forest. There was no good place to plant real food because there were many stones and large trees. If you walked through this area you would become completely lost. The dog was very clever, it always walked well along the trails.

One time, they went to their garden to harvest taro. They worked at pulling out taro corms starting in the early morning. At about two o'clock in the afternoon, it began to rain. They gathered all of the taros and went someplace to sit down, but they could not find a hut to sit in.

As it began to pour, they hid underneath a boulder that was near the garden. It was almost as dark as night. They said, "How will we get to the house?" They continued to talk. They thought, "We left our house and came here, but who will husband the pigs at home?" Then it became pitch black and they could not see a thing.

The dog spoke like a man and said, "I see the house and the pigs. We should go to the house now." "How will

we get there?" they said. The dog replied, "Old woman, hold my tail and tell the boy to hold your hand." Then the dog said, "Let's go."

They listened to the dog and were terrified. Then they heard a pig squealing. Oh my, they arrived at their house! This place is near **Kumdi** in the **Western Highlands** Province [**Hagen** People].

So now, we take care of dogs well. When we lose a pig or something, the dog can smell the trail and find it quickly.

Thomas Rambul
Mt. Hagen
Western Highlands Province

A2493.4. Friendship between man and dog; B211.1.7. Speaking dog; B563.4.1+. Dog leads people back home; F965. Premature darkness

## The Grateful Snake

(Wantok 148, September 18, 1976, page 14)

There was a man who wanted to hunt wild game in the forest. He went to the middle of the forest, and then something made a noise nearby him. He looked at where the noise came from and saw nothing. Then he looked again and saw a snake. He was afraid and trembled at the sight of it, he wanted the snake to go away. The snake did not go, it just stayed there.

He thought about how to get rid of it. He went closer and looked at the snake. The snake went inside a snail's shell. The snail that had lived in the shell had died and just left the shell.

When the snake went inside, its head stuck out and the rest of its body was inside. The snail's shell stuck, so the snake stayed there and got smaller in the middle and bigger on the ends.

When the snake was nearly dead, the man held a stick and broke the snail's shell. The snake was very happy and left. After going a little ways, the snake turned and looked at this man. Then the snake thanked the man. The man then continued to hunt for game and later returned to his village.

Another time, the man's village was having a big battle. The man thought about going to the battle, then he went to the battle and was speared directly through his knee. It was too bad for him, what would he do now? He was near death. His kinsmen brought him back to the village. The poor guy gnashed his teeth, "Why did I go to the battle?" He could not walk because his leg was broken.

Now all he did was sleep in his house. Some men tried to cut and take out the piece of spear that was inside him. However, he said, "No, let me die with the spear in me." His kinsmen were sorry for him and wanted to remove the spear, but he did not want this. So then they left him there.

One time, he wanted to feel the sunshine warm his body, so he went outside. He went to a big grassland and hid there. The sun was hot. He went to sleep and became unconscious.

Then something came and scraped his leg. He woke quickly and looked. He saw a snake crawling on top of his wound and rubbing his wound with its tongue. The poor man was shocked and kicked his leg with the snake on it.

Then the piece of spear that was inside him came out. The guy was ecstatic. He was no longer afraid of the snake and was very happy.

The snake went to a clearing and the man looked at it. He saw that the snake was small in the middle and that its two ends were bigger.

Yes, he knew now that he had helped this snake before in the forest. "So now the snake came to save my life," he thought. He was happy. If he had not helped the snake, the snake would have died just as he would have been dead now.

Enos Pundu
**Kudjip** [**Nii** People]
Banz
**Western Highlands** Province

B375.9. Serpent released: grateful; B511.1. Snake as healer; R100. Rescues; W27. Gratitude

## Where Did Mount Giluwe Come From?
(Wantok 149, October 2, 1976, page 14)

Long ago, two women lived in a village called **Yombi** in Ialibu sub-Province [**Hagen** People, **Southern Highlands** Province]. Their names were Kiwame and Kawame.

One nice day, they woke up and said, "Let's go to the forest and find some vines to make net bags." So, they went to the forest and looked for some vines. They went deep inside the forest, and they came to a place where the ground was broken. They wanted to sit and rest there and to warm their bodies in the sun.

They found a nice stone to sit on and went there to sit. Later, when they wanted to get up and go to their village, one of them could not get up. She said to the other woman, "Get up first and help me stand up." The other woman replied, "Sister, I'm stuck here too."

The two women were stuck to the stone and tried hard to get up, but they stayed there sitting on the stone. Night came and they slept on top of the stone.

In their village, their parents searched for them and could not find them, so the next day in the early morning they followed the footprints that they had left. They followed them into the forest, and they found them sitting on this stone.

Their parents asked them, "What are you doing?" They replied, "We sat on this stone and the stone is stuck to us, so we're just staying here."

They tried to remove the stone, but the stone was very large and it was very hard work. Then they [the parents] left the stone and cried. They cut their hands [fingers off] and returned to their house.

This place where they sat, we call Mount Giluwe. It is the place where the two women turned to stone and became a mountain.

Pita Koyapu
Erave
Southern Highlands Province

[See *Wantok* #344 and 990 for similar ancestor stories.]

A960. Creation of mountains (hills); A974. Rocks from transformation of people to stone; D291W. Transformation: woman to mountain; D931. Magic rock (stone); D2171. Magic adhesion; P230. Parents and children; P681+. Mourning customs: self-mutilation; S161.1. Mutilation: cutting off fingers

## The Ripe Breadfruit that Saved a Life
(Wantok 150, October 16, 1976, page 13)

Long, long ago, there was a married couple with two sons. One day, the two boys went to the beach to catch fish with a hook.

When the brothers began to fish, they caught a piece of breadfruit that was drifting in the sea. The big brother told the little brother to swim and fetch the piece of breadfruit, but little brother said, "I'm too small, the current might carry me away."

So, the big brother swam out and got the breadfruit. When he returned, he gathered some pieces of wood and made a fire to cook it.

When the breadfruit was done, the big brother began to eat it. The little brother looked at him and called out, "Hey brother, give me a piece." The big brother said, "You didn't want to go in the water, so go eat your own shit." The poor little brother did not say another thing.

Another day, they went fishing again. When they came to the beach, the little brother took the canoe and went to the island where the breadfruit was. This island has *masalai*s that kill men.

The little brother threw down some breadfruits (from trees), then he put the breadfruits in his canoe. At this time, the *masalai*s smelled him. However, they came too late. The boy had quickly paddled the canoe and returned to his big brother.

When his brother saw that he had gotten a lot of breadfruit, he was happy, but the little brother told him, "Yesterday you said I should eat my own shit. Go find your own!"

So, the big brother took his canoe and paddled to the island. He went ashore and into the forest. The brother went up a breadfruit tree. Then he gathered some breadfruit. A breadfruit leaf flew directly into a hole where a *masalai* slept. The *masalai* saw this and knew that some man was stealing its breadfruit again.

The big brother was not fast enough in getting away, because the *masalai* arrived when he was still on top of the tree. The little brother knew that the *masalai* would fight with his big brother.

The little brother quickly paddled to the island. The *masalai* did not know that the little boy was hiding at the base of the breadfruit tree.

The boy gathered some ripe breadfruits and began to throw them at the eyes of the *masalai*. Because of this, the *masalai* could no longer see well. The little brother called out to the big brother, "Come down quickly, the *masalai* can't see. Its eyes are full of ripe breadfruit."

The brother came down, then the brothers took some breadfruits and ran to their canoes. They paddled toward their village. Later the big brother always treated his younger brother well.

Now, we always help anyone who wants something. Later on they will look after you too. The big brother mistreated his younger brother, but later the younger brother saved his life from the *masalai*.

Oxley Mike
**Tohatsi** Village [**Buka** Island, **Halia** People]
Arawa
**North Solomons** Province

A1590+. Origin of helpfulness; F490+. Masalai; K621. Escape by blinding the guard; P210. Husband and wife; P231. Mother and son; P233. Father and son; P251.5. Two brothers; F490+. Masalai; R155. Brothers rescue brothers; R210. Escapes; W151. Greed

## Before, People Did Not Sleep or Eat Fish
(Wantok 151, October 30, 1976, page 12)

Long, long ago, the ancestors did not sleep or eat fish. One old woman took her two young daughters to process sago. The pond where they used to rinse the sago had many large-mouthed fish that we call *karua* in my language.

The old woman watched the fish and wanted very much to eat one, so she told her two children, "You're big now, so you can take my place. I'll eat this fish and then become unconscious. So, don't worry about me." She cooked the fish; it had a good smell and was very oily. She ate it and it was delicious. She ate the entire fish, there was not a single piece of meat left.

She drank some water, then her eyes stopped functioning and she fell asleep. While she slept, the two children watched her. If she were dead, her heart would not function.

Long ago, the ancestors did not sleep. This was the very first time that the old woman had eaten fish or had slept. When she awoke, she beat the signal drum. She told everyone in the village to go into the forest to the pond, to catch a fish to eat, and then they would sleep.

Before, they had never eaten fish, nor had the ancestors ever slept. The old woman was the first to eat fish and the first to sleep. Now, everyone from every place eats the big-mouthed fish and sleep.

John Wisit
Kaindi [**Kainde** Village]
**East Sepik** Province

A1399.2.1. Origin of sleep; A1510+. Origin of fish eating; P232. Mother and daughter; P252.1. Two sisters

## The Cucumbers that Became Women
(Wantok 152, November 13, 1976, page 12)

Long ago, there were two brothers. The big brother often caught fish in the river and the little brother often found wild game in the forest.

One day, the big brother prepared his things to go fishing in the river, then he went to get a cucumber. He took one that was young and tender. He carried the cucumber and hid it near a boulder in the river.

Then he tried fishing in the river. He speared many. When evening approached, the boy returned and tried to find the cucumber, but he did not see it. There was a young woman sitting at the boulder.  So the boy asked her, "Woman, are you looking for my cucumber too?"

The woman said, "Never mind the cucumber.  Give me the fish and I'll carry them, then we'll go to your house." So, they went to the boy's house and cooked some food.

In the evening, the little brother returned from the forest.  He saw his big brother's woman and asked, "Brother, what did you do to get this woman?"  The big brother told what he had done to get the woman.

The little brother said, "I know what you did, so I'll do it too."  In the early morning, the little brother took his fishing spears and one ripe cucumber.  He went to the river and put the cucumber on top of the boulder.  Then he went to fish in the river.

Later, near evening, he returned.  He found his cucumber and he saw a wicked old woman sitting on top of the stone.  The old woman said, "Take me and put me on top of your shoulders."  The boy said, "No, you should still walk." But the old woman was stronger than the boy and made him carry her.

The old woman sat on top of the boy's shoulders and the boy carried her to his house.  The big brother saw his little brother and said, "I told you well about getting a woman.  But you disobeyed what I said and you got an old woman."

The old woman held tightly onto the boy's shoulders regardless of whether he wanted to sleep or bathe or go to the forest or urinate or defecate.  The old woman was really stuck on his shoulders.  The woman always urinated and defecated on top of the boy's shoulders.  The boy became emaciated and was approaching death.

One time, a snake heard this boy's story.  The snake's name was Pina.  Pina the snake sent a message to the boy. The message was, "You should carry your old woman to the base of a *tulip* tree.  Then you should pick some *tulip* buds."  Pina the snake lived at the top of this tree.

The boy went to the *tulip* tree, climbed it and picked some buds.  Quickly, Pina the snake jumped on top of the old woman's head and encircled her neck.  The snake fell with her to the ground, killing her.  The boy was ecstatic and paid the snake with money, such as cowry shells and shell rings.

Now, if you find this snake, *pina*, you will see a ring around its neck that is white.

Bruno Malai
Usino Village
**Madang** Province

B211.6.1. Speaking snake (serpent); B491.1. Helpful serpent; D431.4+W. Transformation: cucumber to woman; P251.4. Brothers scorn brother's wise counsel; P251.5. Two brothers; Q53. Reward for rescue; Q325. Disobedience punished; R40+. Entrapment by sitting on shoulders/back; R110. Rescue of captive; S110. Murders; W126. Disobedience; X716.1H+. Befouling with excrement

## The Black Woman and the Red Woman
(Wantok 153, November 27, 1976, pages 12, 15)

There was a man who was married to two women. One wife had black skin and the other had red skin.  One time, the red woman disliked her husband and fled to her parents' village.

Her husband wanted to get her and bring her back to his village, so he took some things for purchasing women, such as pigs, *kina* shells, and rock salt.  [The husband apparently kills her instead.]

The [red] woman's ghost went to a small pond.  This pond was where the women went to hunt for frogs.  The first [black] woman did not know that her husband had killed the second woman.  No, she did not know this.

At this time, the woman wanted to hunt for frogs in the little pond where the ghost of the second woman was staying.  She prepared a torch and went late at night.  When she arrived there, she caught many frogs.  While she was still there, something came and extinguished her torch.

It was just the red woman's ghost, whom the man had killed.  The ghost spoke, "Carry me to your house."  So, the woman who was hunting frogs carried the ghost to the woman's village.  She carried her and carried her, and she became very short of breath almost collapsing.

The ghost said, "Sit and open the door."  However, the woman who was carrying the ghost said, "Sit and make a fire."  The ghost said, "No, carry me on your shoulders and make the fire."  After the ghost said this, the real woman became irate.

The real woman put the ghost on top of her shoulders and made a huge fire.  The woman made the fire inside her house and burned the ghost on the fire that she had made.

The ghost said, "Oh I'm sorry sister, this is not a fight." The ghost then got up and fought the real woman.  However, the real woman was not gentle and she fought back.

They fought and fought until they were both short of breath and they just died. Their mouths were wide open as the lay near the house door. One was dead on each side of the door.

The husband of the real woman thought of bringing some pig fodder to the woman's house. He went there, but there was no smoke at the woman's house, so he thought that the woman had gone to find pig fodder in the garden.

He thought this then he opened the door of the house. The pigs inside were squealing, but the man did not know about the two dead women inside the door with their open mouths.

He opened the door and put his two hands into the mouths of the two dead women, then he died too. It was the fault of the ghost that the man and woman had died.

Kamares Kambeyapa
Kentagl [**Kendagl** Village, **Hagen** People]
Mt. Hagen
**Western Highlands** Province

E221+. Dead wife's malevolent return; E400+. Man puts hand in dead wife's mouth and he himself dies; E422.2.1. Revenant red; E425.1. Revenant as woman; E461. Fight of revenant with living person; E545. The dead speak; P210. Husband and wife; R213. Escape from home; R260. Pursuits; S63+. Husband kills wife; S110. Murders; T145.0.1. Polygyny

## The Pond Full of Grease

(Wantok 154, January 22, 1977, page 21)

Long ago, there was a man and woman who lived in a village. They were like sister and brother. The woman worked in a garden, planting various kinds of food. Her brother worked at hunting marsupials (*kapul*) in the forest.

One time, the boy told his sister, "I'm going now to find marsupials in the forest. Stay at the house." After he said this, he went into the forest. They husbanded a pig that was very large. [The boy] hunted for a marsupial in the forest and killed one near the garden. He put the marsupial in the trail and went to hunt more marsupials in the forest.

The first marsupial transformed in appearance into the woman's brother. He looked exactly like the woman's brother. He had sexual intercourse with the woman, then this marsupial returned and the woman was ashamed and cried.

Later, the woman's real brother returned. He had killed many marsupials and he brought them to his sister. The sister was angry, so the brother asked, "Why are you angry? I brought some marsupials, come and look." The sister did not say a thing. She was angry. Even after her brother had cooked the marsupials in an earth oven, she did not say anything. She just continued to be angry.

The brother asked, "What did I do to you that made you so angry at me?" The woman did not reply to him.

The marsupial had tricked the woman and the woman truly thought that it was her real brother who had had sexual intercourse with her. As the woman increased her rage at her brother, she tried hard to ask him to leave. Later, she was still angry while the brother removed the marsupials from the earth oven and divided them between himself and his sister. The sister did not take them or eat them, she was still angry.

The brother thought hard, "What did I do to make my sister angry at me?" The brother thought this and then he killed the pig that they had husbanded. The brother cooked the pig in an earth oven until it was done, then he took the pig out and divided it well. He took one half of the pig and some marsupials and he gave the other half of the pig and some marsupials to his sister.

The brother carried his side of pig on his shoulder and told his sister, "I gave some marsupials to you and you didn't eat them. I gave you some pork and you didn't eat that either. OK, stay here and I'll go somewhere else now."

The brother said this and walked away. Then the sister told him, "You did that to me, so I'm not eating the pork or marsupials."

The boy had left, so the woman followed him. He carried the side of pork on his shoulders and went far away. He arrived someplace and stood there.

The boy carried the pork and the grease from the pork fell on the ground, making a huge pond that surrounded him. His sister arrived and saw him standing in the middle of the pond. She stood near the water.

My people call the pond where the man stood Ipaper. A marsupial tricked two people and this is where they ran away and died.

Andreas Angale ["Ángale" is a male name from the **Enga** People (Lang, 1973: 214)]
**Enga** Province

A920.1.0.1. Origin of particular lake; D310+M. Transformation: marsupial to man; D450+. Transformation: fat to lake; K1930. Treacherous impostors P253. Sister and brother; P253+. Hostile sister and brother; R213. Escape from home; R260. Pursuits; T415. Brother-sister incest; T471. Rape

## Cooking Pig in an Earth Oven at a Grave

(Wantok 155, January 29, 1977, page 11)

In one village, there was a male ancestor. His name was Sinimai. One day, he went into the forest to find eggs. He looked near some stones and he saw a man sleeping.

Sinimai went closer to see him. He saw that a *masalai* man had died. When he saw this, he jumped back a little. Later he thought back about an ancestor story. So, he approached, carried the corpse and buried it in a good place.

He planted some beautiful "ancestor" flowers, then returned to his house and slept. At night he dreamt that he saw the *masalai* come speak to him, "My body was in the forest and you brought my body to a nice place, then buried me. Tomorrow, early in the morning, wake up, then take your bow and go to the place where you buried my body. You shall see a huge boar there. Shoot him with an arrow and he'll die. Don't take the boar elsewhere to cook. You should cook the boar in an earth oven there. Call that place, *Nanuwo Golik*."

The meaning of this name is "*Masalai*'s Grave." Later, when wild pigs are killed, they are always taken to this place, Nanuwo Golik, to be cooked in an earth oven.

This is what people do nowadays too. I am also from this place which is on the Jimi River, in a village called **Tabibuga** [**Narak** People].

Gola Pagai

Tabibuga

Mount Hagen

**Western Highlands** Province

A1510+. Origin of place of pig slaughter; E341.1.1+. Corpse grateful for being buried; F490+. Masalai; V61.3+. Dead buried; W27. Gratitude

## The Rat That Helped a Man

(Wantok 156, February 5, 1977, page 9)

Long ago, there were two brothers. The big brother was married, but the little brother was not yet married. They lived together and had a single garden. One night, the big brother went to watch for pigs in their garden. It would be bad if a pig ate their yams (*yam* and *mami*), so the big brother went to watch for and to shoot any pigs.

While the man was in the garden, the two brothers' mother was in the village. There was a wild *limbum* palm tree that stood near the old mother's house.

This wild *limbum* was not big or tall. It was just very small and short. At night the old mother woke up and climbed to the top of this wild *limbum*, then the *limbum* became very tall. It arrived at the garden where her first son was staying.

Then she became a pig and ate yams in the garden. She ate and ate, then she came up to the man [her son]. The man wanted to shoot this pig, but he could not conquer the pig. No, the pig was stronger. It conquered and ate him.

The pig ate the man's entire body, leaving only the head in the garden. This was not a true wild pig. It was the two men's mother who had transformed into this pig. Then she ate all of the food in the garden and finished eating her first son.

In the early morning, she went on top of the wild *limbum* and returned to her house in the village. She told her daughter-in-law and her second son, "Go to the garden and find this man. It would be bad if a pig ate him."

So they went to the garden and the searched for him. They did not find a man in the garden, but the saw all of the places where a pig had eaten, and they saw his head. They took the man's head and buried it in the village.

One time, the little brother said, "I'll try to go and watch the garden and shoot that pig." So he went to the garden and watched. He stayed there and saw a rat sleeping underneath the firewood. He wanted to kill this rat.

However, the rat spoke to him, "Hey, don't kill me. It would be bad if you died at night like your big brother. Who do you think killed your brother? It was your mother who killed and ate him." The man listened to this and told the rat that he would not kill it.

"Go and pick some yams, then we'll take them to my place. Your mother will come here soon. Do this quickly, then we'll hide," said the rat.

The man heeded the rat and took some *mami*, then they went to the rat's home. The rat went first and the man followed. They came to the base of a *ton* tree. The rat told the man, "Let's climb this *ton* tree. This is where my home is. Let's climb this vine."

However, the man said, "I'm afraid to climb. I see some big insects and I'm afraid. It would be bad if the insects bit me." The rat replied, "No, they are my friends. They won't bite you." So, the man climbed first and the rat followed. The rat carried their *mami* up the tree.

The rat told the man, "Peel the *mami* and cook it, then we'll sit outside and watch the garden. It's almost time for your mother to arrive."

They watched and watched, then they saw the woman enter the garden. The woman went on top of the wild *limbum* tree that was very tall, that had come into the garden.

The woman turned into a pig and entered the garden, then sniffed all of the places in the garden.

She smelled the path that the rat and the man had taken. She followed it and came to the base of the tree where the man and the rat were staying. The woman [pig] raised her head skywards and saw her child with the rat on top of the tree.

The man said, "Before, you ate my brother. Now you shall die." The woman tried to go up the tree to eat her child.

As she climbed, the insects bit her fiercely and her skin swelled up in various places. The insects did this to her all night long, and she did not hurry. She thought that she really wanted to eat her child, but she was unable to do so.

This went on until dawn. In the morning, the woman returned to the garden and climbed the wild *limbum* tree. Then she returned to her house in the village.

While it was still morning, she told her daughter-in-law, "You people should go to the garden and look for that man. It would be bad if the pig ate him." So the woman took her children and went to the garden.

They saw the man who was pulling out yams (*yam* and *mami*) in the garden. They went and stayed in a hut. The children who were his brother's, saw the rat and wanted to get it. However, the man told them, "Don't kill that rat. Just think, if it wasn't for that rat, I wouldn't be here now. The pig would have eaten me. Remember your father? Who was it that ate him? It was his and my mother who ate him."

So, they left the rat alone. Their uncle took some *mami* to the rat and put some for them too. His sister-in-law pulled up some food and they returned to the village. The man told the rat to go back to his home, and they went to their home too.

When they arrived at the village, the old woman told them, "Boil some water and wash me. Then cut my skin too [as treatment]. I had gone down to cut some firewood. The firewood fell down and hit my skin, that is why my skin is swollen." They said, "Yes, we'll boil some water."

They knew that she was lying to them, so they boiled water in two pots. One pot was not very hot and the other pot was boiling fiercely. They washed her with the water from the pot that was not too hot.

Then he [the son] took the other pot of water that was very hot and threw it on top of their old mother. The poor mother died. Then they took her and buried her among wild pandanus trees. Later, they cut some firewood and burned her till there was nothing left.

Miss Magdalene Kumbili
S. S. E. C. [South Sea Evangelical Church] **Arkosame** [**Kwanga** People]
**West Sepik** Province

B211.2.9. Speaking rat; B437.1. Helpful rat; D114.3+W. Transformation: woman to sow (wild); D336.1W. Transformation: pig to woman; D1520.1.1. Transportation by stretching and swaying tree; G352.2. Wild boar as ogre; P210. Husband and wife; P230. Parents and children; P231. Mother and son; P251.5. Two brothers; P262. Mother-in-law; P263. Brother-in-law; P264. Sister-in-law; P265+. Daughter-in-law; P293. Uncle; Q151. Life spared as reward; Q211.4. Murder of children punished; Q414. Punishment: burning alive; R311. Tree refuge; S12.2+. Cruel mother kills son; S22+. Matricide; S112.1. Boiling to death; V61.3+. Dead buried; W125. Gluttony

## We Cannot Disobey What a Dog Says
(Wantok 157, February 12, 1977, pages 9-10)

In a village, there lived two brothers and one woman, their sister. They lived together in one house.

One time, the eldest brother said, "I want to hunt marsupials (*kapul*) in the forest." He took his bow and arrows, and picked some sweet potatoes to put in his net bag. Then he prepared to go into the forest.

He walked away and darkness fell. He put his net bag of sweet potatoes in a hut and went to hunt for marsupials in the forest. A bright moon lit up the sky. He saw three marsupials. He took them and returned to the hut.

At the hut, he gutted the marsupials, removed the feces from the guts and ate the guts. He took some vines, tied up the three marsupials and carried them back to the village. The younger brother and their sister were there. Later, they cooked the three marsupials in an earth oven and ate them.

Some months later, the eldest brother said, "I want to go to the forest. I'll stay there for about a week and after that I'll return." After he told them this, he prepared his things for killing marsupials. He picked some sweet potatoes for his net bag, then he went to sleep. In the morning, he took his things and left. He walked and walked, then he came to a mountain.

He sat at the mountain and had a smoke. He caught his breath a little while he sat and he looked into the forest. He saw smoke rising in the middle of the forest. He thought that he wanted to go and look at this smoke. So after he finished smoking, he walked away. He heard a dog barking, then he saw a dog putting a breadfruit tree leaf in its mouth and barking. So, the boy came up to the dog and asked, "What are you doing here?"

The dog replied, "Can you help me?" The dog took the breadfruit tree leaf and other things used to cook pigs in an earth oven, then it went inside a house and brought a pig outside.

The boy saw this and took a big stick used to kill pigs. He took the stick and killed the pig, then singed off its hair. They cut up the pig and put it in an earth oven. They cooked the pig in small pieces. The sides and head of the pig were cooked separately.

Later, they removed the pig. The dog went to get just the head of the pig. The dog gave all of the pork to the boy and said, "Carry all the pork and leave." Then the dog gave a package to the boy and said, "Open this package on the mountain before you sit there."

The boy departed. He walked and walked, then arrived at the mountain. He took the small package that the dog had given him. He opened this package, then he stood at the door of his house.

The second brother and the sister were there. They said, "You said you were going to kill marsupials, so who gave you this pork that you brought?" He replied that a friend had given it to him. The second brother said, "You're always the one who goes and I'm always the one who stays at the house. So now I want to go see this friend."

The big brother said, "No." So, the little brother became angry and did not eat the pork. Then the first brother said, "OK, you can go tomorrow and you can prepare your things now. I'll be happy and eat pork."

They went to sleep. In the morning, the younger brother finished his preparations and his brother said, "You can't do other things. You must do as the dog says. You must follow its words." He walked and walked, then arrived at the mountain. He saw the smoke rising and went to where the smoke was. The dog was barking and holding a breadfruit tree leaf and other things used for killing pigs. The boy said, "Take all those things and just stand up like a policeman [i.e., at attention]." He took the stick and beat the dog badly. The dog thought, "Before, the boy did not do this, but you came and beat me badly." Then the boy took the pig from the house and broke its head while the dog whimpered.

The boy told the dog to remove the pig's hair. So the dog threw the pig's legs into the fire, and the pig's face too. But the dog did not turn the pig fast enough [to singe the

hair], so the boy clobbered the dog and the dog sat and cried.

The boy cooked the pig in an earth oven, then removed the pork and carried it all off. He arrived at the house. The elder brother saw the pig and said, "You did not give the head of the pig to the dog." The boy replied, "The dog said to me, 'You are a new boy, take all the pig.' After the dog said this, I carried it here."

The elder brother thought, "I think he fought and killed him or something. So, the dog didn't eat the pig. Tomorrow I'll go and see." In the early morning, he went to the mountain. The smoke was not coming from the place as before. He went to where the smoke used to come from. He cried when he came to the house. He saw the dog sleeping near the fire, the dog was nearly dead.

While he looked at the dog, the dog died. He cried and then he buried the dog. He returned to his home and killed his brother. His sister went off to marry. If the second brother had treated the dog well, they would have lived well. But the boy did wrong and their family was ruined.

Peter Kopen Muli
**Pumakos** [Village, **Enga** People]
**Enga** Province

[See LeRoy (1985a: 1-3; 1985b: 242) and *Wantok* #189 for similar stories.]

B211.1.7. Speaking dog; B331.2.2+. Helpful dog killed; P210. Husband and wife; P251.4. Brothers scorn brother's wise counsel; P253.0.2. One sister and two brothers; P310. Friendship; Q211.6. Killing an animal revenged; Q411. Death as punishment; S73.1. Fratricide; S110. Murders; T100. Marriage; W126. Disobedience

## The Marsupial (*Kapul*) that Lost a Toe
(Wantok 158, February 19, 1977, pages 13, 17)

We often kill terrestrial marsupials (*kapul*) [probably the ground cuscus, *Phalanger gymnotis* (Flannery, 1995a: 166-168)], and we always see something missing. Yes, we know that it does not have its first toe. Why is the toe missing? I want to tell you a story about the true origin of this. The story goes as follows. Long, long ago, a man and his wife lived in a village called **Naburume**.

One time, the man went into the forest to look for tree fruits. These tree fruits are the same kind that birds eat. He saw some and then built a bird blind on top of the tree. He returned to his village to get a bow and some multi-pronged arrows, and then he went back to watch the fruits.

When he went to watch the fruits, he saw a wild yam and dug it up. He took the root and wrapped it in breadfruit tree leaves. Then he took some breadfruits and went close to the fruiting tree, where he made a fire and cooked the breadfruit. The breadfruits were still in the fire and he went up the tree into the bird blind that he had made.

He watched the fruits and thought about the breadfruit: it would be bad if it burned. So, he went down the tree and turned the breadfruit. He thought the fire was doing well, so he turned the breadfruit around. He went back up the tree again and watched the tree fruits. He stayed for a little while, then he thought that it would be bad if the breadfruit burned. So, he went down again and saw that the breadfruits were ready to eat and that it was not burnt.

Then he thought hard, "Who had turned the breadfruits?" He went up the tree again, went inside the bird blind and watched the fruits. He also looked down and watched the fire. A hand came up from the bundle that held the wild yam that he had left near the fire. The hand came out of the package and turned the breadfruits, then went back inside the package.

The man was shocked and went down the tree. He went near the fire and said, "Who's the man that turned my breadfruit?" A nice woman appeared from the wild yam and said, "It's just me that turned your breadfruit. I'm your wife. You thought that a man ate your breadfruit? No, that is not so." He trembled at this woman because she better than his old woman.

The woman told him, "I am the origin of marsupials." Then the woman told him, "Go to the base of this tree." The man followed her instructions. He saw about ten marsupials at the base of the tree. The man took the marsupials and the woman too, and he went to the village. He told his old wife about what he had done and that he had found this woman. The old wife and the new wife were very happy.

The woman was like a dog. She and her husband went to the forest. The woman would reveal many marsupials, and she would tell her husband, "These are my family, don't kill them." The man would leave them alone. However, they did not leave alone other wild game; they ate those.

They were very happy. One time, they called for this man to go to a festival. The man told his new wife, "You should decorate yourself and we'll go the festival." The woman said, "I don't want to. I'll take care of the house. You and your old wife go to the festival."

They went to the festival, then dawn arrived. The man arrived and the woman began to run away. The man saw this, so he left his signal drum and followed her. However, the man was not quick enough, he could not grab her. The woman went up a big tree and the man followed her. The

woman went inside a hole in the tree and the man held her first toe. Her mothers and her family were strong and pulled her inside. The man just broke her toe off.

The man cried and yelled out. They replied to him, "We gave you a good woman who gave you food, but you didn't like her, so we can't give you any more. Now you must work hard to find your food." The man cried and cried, then circled around and around the base of the tree. Then he left and returned to his village.

So now if you kill a marsupial with a stone, you can see that its first toe was cut off and is shortened.

Mr. Urim S.

Madang

Madang Province

A1800+. Marsupials originated from a woman; A2371+. Origin of marsupials' missing toe; D179.6K+W. Transformation: woman to marsupial; D431.9+W. Transformation: yam to woman; P210. Husband and wife; P232. Mother and daughter; S162.3. Mutilation: cutting off toes; T145.0.1. Polygyny

## They Ate a Small Snake
(Wantok 159, February 26, 1977, pages 11, 13)

Long ago, there were two siblings who lived in southern Kambia [**Kombilinye** Village], in **Western Highlands** Province [**Hagen** People]. Their names were Kewa and Palt.

Kewa was the brother's name and Palt was the sister's name. Their parents had died during a battle with two families in the southern Kambia area.

The siblings lived very happily together and did not fight or get angry with each other. Whenever Kewa picked sweet potatoes and cooked them, she gave some to Palt. Kewa did various chores in and around the house, and this made Palt happy.

Kewa had put Palt inside a bamboo tube near their house. Kewa thought and told her, "I don't want to send you to marry a man." One time when Kewa was in the garden, Palt exited the bamboo tube and made some rope from vines.

When Kewa returned to the house, Palt immediately took the rope that she had made and went inside the bamboo tube. Kewa arrived at the house, cut some firewood, made a fire, and cooked sweet potatoes. When the sweet potatoes were ready, he called for Palt and gave her some sweet potatoes. When they finished eating, it became dark and they went to sleep.

In the morning, Kewa went to the garden again to pick some sweet potatoes. Palt stayed at the house and made some more rope. She thought about marrying a man. She tightened the rope that she had made on the fence near their house. She continued to tighten the rope [going farther and farther until] she arrived in the **Kiripia** area near Tambul.

At Kiripia, she married a man who often ate subterranean insects. His name was Kagul Kalua. Kalua knew a lot about small terrestrial snakes. A small snake lived underground and ate the people of Kiripia.

Kewa returned home and cooked some sweet potatoes, then he called for Palt to eat. However, Palt was not inside the bamboo tube. The good-for-nothing Kewa did not know where Palt was. Kewa tried to find her, but he was unable to do so. Darkness fell, and he went to sleep. In the morning, Kewa sat in the house and cried because his sister was gone.

He saw the rope that Palt had been tightening on the fence near their house and he followed the rope, but then it became night again and he went back to sleep.

In the early morning, he bathed in the river and then he came back to the house. He dressed nicely and began on the trail to Kiripia.

In a house he saw his young nephew. The boy said, "Uncle, come here." Kewa said, "Yes, nephew, I'm coming." So they stayed together. Kewa asked the little boy, "Where are your parents?" The boy said, "They went to find food in the garden." So the two of them waited in the house.

Then the parents came home. They said good day to Kewa. Kewa saw them carrying many bamboos filled with small ground snakes and many vegetables.

Palt and her husband, Kagul Kalua, heated some stones and cooked the small snakes in an earth oven. Kewa talked to them about the small snakes.

While Palt and Kagul Kalua were cooking the food, Kewa said, "I have never eaten this kind of food that you're cooking. I usually eat sweet potatoes that are cooked in hot ashes." So, Palt cooked some sweet potatoes in the fire and gave them to him. Kewa ate some but he hid some too.

The husband and wife removed the food from the earth oven. Then they cut it up and gave some to Kewa. Palt and Kalua thought that Kewa would eat it, but he only pretended to eat the sweet potatoes that he had put there. He threw away the pieces of small snakes outside the house.

After they ate, a big storm arose. Palt went outside and saw the snake pieces that Kewa had thrown out. Palt whispered to her husband that Kewa had not eaten the snake. Night arrived and they slept.

In the morning, Palt asked Kewa, "Do you want to stay in the house or go to the garden with me?" Kewa said that he wanted to go. They left and arrived at the garden where they removed snakes from inside stones.

Kewa stayed at the base of a tree while Palt and Kagul Kalua left him and went home. Kewa did not know how to find the trail, so Kewa was lost at that place.

Benny Embil

Tsak

Pumakos

Enga Province

F564+. Person sleeps in bamboo tube; P210. Husband and wife; P231. Mother and son; P233. Father and son; P253. Sister and brother; P263. Brother-in-law; P293. Uncle; Q260. Deceptions punished; Q438. Punishment: abandonment in forest; S143. Abandonment in forest; T100. Marriage


## A Dog Was the Source of Fighting
(Wantok 160, March 5, 1977, pages 11, 13)

Long ago, there was a man named Yandapo from **Lagaip** sub-Province who had two sons [**Enga** Province, **Enga** People]. The first son was named Sambe [Sámbé (Lang, 1973: 215)] and the second son was named Kunalin.

When the father was alive, the brothers lived well and shared the garden and other things amicably. Sambe had many children and Kunalin also had many children.

These two families became large clans. Sambe and Kumalin [Kunalin] were the ancestors of these two clans. There was a dog that lived in the Kumalin [Kunalin] family. This was not an ordinary dog. This dog had killed many marsupials (*kapul*).

When the dog was alive, it killed pigs and stole meat too. The dog's owner wanted to kill the dog, but when he brought the dog to the forest, the dog killed many marsupials, so the owner was too afraid of the dog. He found a strong tree, then he sharpened two sticks and made a hole. He put a rope on the dog and tied it to [a stick].

One time, the owner brought the dog to the forest to kill marsupials. They brought the marsupials back to the village. The man walked first and the dog followed.

The dog had the rope and a stick tied to its neck. The owner thought that the dog would follow him as he walked. A man was in the trail and saw that the dog had a rope on its neck. He only saw the dog approaching. The man called out quietly for the dog, then he held the stick and rope. He stole these and hid them in his house.

This man who stole the rope was from the Sambe family. The dog was free and followed his owner again, arriving at his house. The owner saw the dog and that the rope with the stick was not on the dog's neck.

He went back to look for them, but he could not find them. Then he shouted, "Who stole my dog's rope?" He yelled and yelled. The men from around the area said, "We haven't seen it." Then the dog's owner said, "Now I'll bring the dog to this trail. You from the Sambe family stole it. Please give it back to me."

He yelled this out and they did not return it. They hid well and did not answer him. The man became angry and he killed a man from the Sambe Clan [Sámbé (Lang, 1973: 214-215)].

Then the Sambe and Kunalin Clans had a battle. The clans fought for two months, and many men died from the two sides. Afterwards, the Sambe Clan was stronger and won the battle with the Kunalin [Kunálini (Lang, 1973: 215)] Clan. The Sambe burned the Kunalin houses and ruined their gardens and other things. The Sambe evicted all of the Kunalin people. Then the Kunalin went to many other places.

Now, some of the Kunalin Clan has joined the **Kandep** [Kandépe (Lang, 1973: 215)] Patrol Office, and some have joined other clans. The Kunalin Clan lives in Enga Province and only listen to this story. This is because before, the ancestors of the Sambe Clan won the battle. Now there is no way for the Kunalin to return to their ancestral lands. The Kunalin Clan has made contracts with other clans. This is a true story that was told to me by my father figure.

Elisas Puleya
C. T. C. Pumakos
Enga Province

A1640+. Origin of Kunalíni Clan; K420. Thief loses his goods or is detected; P230. Parents and children; P233. Father and son; P251.5. Two brothers; P555. Defeat in battle; Q211. Murder punished; Q212. Theft punished; Q411. Death as punishment; Q411.3. Death of father (son, etc.) as punishment; Q431. Punishment: banishment (exile); Q486. Criminal's property destroyed as punishment; Q486.1. Criminal's house burned down; S110. Murders


## The Frog That Turned into a Girl

(Wantok 161, March 12, 1977, pages 9-10)

Long ago, men worked with stone axes. Once there was a man who was sharpening his stone axe. A frog croaked near where he was working.

He heard this once, then twice, then he got up to find the frog. He searched and searched, but he could not find it. So, he sat down and worked at sharpening his axe again.

While he was sharpening his axe, he heard it again. Then he sat and sharpened it softly. He heard the frog croaking down in his testicles. He got up and cut off his testicles, then a little frog jumped to the ground.

He took the little frog and put it on top of a tree leaf, then he went home. After a week, he returned to see the frog. The frog had turned into a small girl who lived where he had put the frog.

The man saw the girl and asked her, "How did you come here?" The girl told him, "No. I just came from your balls, then you put me here. I stayed here and turned into a little girl."

The man listened to this, then built a house and placed her inside it. While she lived there, the man took care of her very well.

After the girl became big, he took her to the village and put her in the spirit house. While she lived in the spirit house, she made attractive net bags for the men of the village.

All of the men of the village carried these attractive net bags. The men's wives asked each of their husbands about the bags. They said, "We don't know who really made the men's beautiful net bags that they carry, nor why they are always happy about these beautiful net bags."

One time in the early morning, all of the men woke up and went into the forest. Only the women were left in the village. One woman climbed a coconut palm tree and threw coconuts to the ground. Some fell to the ground in other places, and one fell and rolled inside the spirit house.

The woman came down and fetched the coconuts, then looked for the one that went inside the spirit house. She searched and went inside the spirit house. She looked inside and saw a woman sitting there.

She told all of the women, "I saw a woman sitting in the spirit house." The women told her, "She's probably the woman who made our husbands' net bags."

They said, "We should burn this house." So, they lit a fire at the spirit house and the entire house burned. At this time, the men returned. The poor men saw this and were very worried that the woman inside was burned to a crisp.

They took the ashes from the fire that had burned the woman, and they put them inside a bundle made of *limbum* palm leaves. Quickly, they made a new spirit house and they put the ashes in the new spirit house.

That night, all of the men, women and children went inside to sing and dance. They sang and danced until it was nearly dawn.  Then all of the men, women and children turned into flying foxes and departed.  One girl who was not yet big was carried away by a she-frog.  Later, the girl cried and cried.

A cockatoo found her and took her to sleep near the cockatoo's nest.  So, every time you look at her, she [i.e., a flying fox] is flying near dusk.

Moses Kapirakuami
**Maprik** Village [**Abelam** People]
**East Sepik** Province

A2260+. Why flying fox flies at dusk; B535.0.7+. Cockatoo as nurse for child; D117.5K. Transformation: person to flying fox; D117.5KM. Transformation: man to flying fox; D117.5KW. Transformation: woman to flying fox; D395G. Transformation: frog to girl; D447+. Transformation: testicles to frog; P210. Husband and wife; Q414. Punishment: burning alive; R13.4+. Abduction by frog; S112.0.2. House (hostel) burned with all inside; S160.1. Self-mutilation; S176.1. Mutilation: emasculation; V112.1. Spirit huts; X712.3H. Testicles

## The Boy Who Was Deserted

(Wantok 162, March 19, 1977, page 15)

There was a man with two wives who lived in the forest.  They planted sweet potatoes, sugarcanes and other kinds of food.  They lived well in this semi-forested area.  The village where they lived is called **Tutos** [**Enga** People, **Enga** Province].

One time, the man heard about another village that was called **Tabires**.  They were killing pigs in this village, so the man from Tutos wanted to go eat pork in Tabires.  He cut some firewood and put it in his house.  The two wives were pregnant so he told them, "You are pregnant with my children.  Take care of yourselves well.  If you have a boy, then kill him and throw him into a hole.  I don't want a boy."

After he said this, he went to eat pork at Tabires.  The two women stayed at home.  One woman gave birth to a girl and the other gave birth to a boy.

The mother of the boy said, "Sister, I gave birth to a boy so should I kill him or what should I do?"  The mother of the girl said, "No, our husband's daughter belongs to us.  She will marry, so she will not help us cutting firewood and doing other work.  Only the boy will help us."

So she heeded her sister said and she did not kill her child.  They lived there and the husband did not return quickly, so the two children became big enough to walk.  The man still did not return home.  The children became big enough to cut firewood, to take care of themselves and their mothers too.

The girl worked at harvesting sweet potatoes, cooking them and giving them to her brother and her co-mothers.  Later, the father returned.  He was angry with the boy, "I talked about this when I left.  Why didn't you listen to what I said?"

He was irate, so he did not give pork to the boy.  He gave pork only to the girl.  He did not give pork to the mother of the boy either.  He only gave pork to the girl's mother.  He gave a small piece of pork to the girl and her mother, and they ate it.  The girl's mother saw that her sister did not have pork to eat, so she gave her some.

They slept, then late at night at about midnight, the father woke up and saw the boy sleeping quietly.  The father woke the two mothers and the girl.  They left the boy and went to another village, called **Liogtes**.  They went there in the dead of night.  The boy thought they were sleeping and did not know that they had left, so he slept.

In the morning, he woke up and saw that they were not sleeping in their beds.  They had left, and he did not know where they went.  He thought and thought, then he cried in the house.  The sun rose, and at about 8 o'clock he went outside and cried.  An eagle felt sorry for him.  It flew around and landed on the ground.

The eagle asked him, "Why are you crying?"  The boy said, "My father, my co-mothers and my sister left me for another place.  I don't know where they are and that is why I'm crying."  The eagle said, "Don't cry, I can help you."

The bird flew around to other places and caught a pregnant sow.  The eagle gave the boy this pig which then gave birth to twelve piglets.  The eagle helped the boy and he lived well under the wing of the eagle.  The eagle helped him and he did not think any more of his parents or sister.

Nikodimus N.
Tsak
Pumakos
Enga Province

B211.3.11K. Speaking eagle; B535.0.7+. Eagle as nurse for child; P210. Husband and wife; P231. Mother and son; P232. Mother and daughter; P252.1. Two sisters; P253. Sister and brother; Q211.4+. Punishment for not killing son; Q438. Punishment: abandonment in forest; Q450+. Punishment by withholding food; S110. Murders; S352+. Eagle aids abandoned child(ren); T145.1.3+. Man married to two sisters; T570. Pregnancy; T580. Childbirth; W126. Disobedience

## The Eagle that Was the
## Source of the Enga People

(Wantok 163, March 26, 1977, page 15)

In a village called **Lenke**, near Wabag [**Enga** Province, **Enga** People], there lived two young women who were sisters. They obtained their food from their own hard work.

One nice afternoon when the sun was setting, they made some mounds for planting sweet potatoes outside their house. The sisters were working in their garden when a big eagle came down and searched for the insects near where they were working.

The younger sister took the stick that she was using to make the mounds. She walked on her hands and knees close to the bird. She approached and broke one of the eagle's wings. The poor eagle could no longer fly well because the young woman had broken part of its wing. It jumped up poorly, flew over four of the sweet potato mounds and landed.

The two sisters ran to grab the bird. They approached the eagle, jumped and fell in the garden. Then they ran again to get the bird. The bird jumped and fell in the nearby scrub forest, leaving the sisters' garden and house.

The chase continued and the sisters went far from their home. The elder sister told the younger sister, "Never mind. We have come far and it will be dark soon. Let's go back to the house." The younger sister said, "No, you go home. I want to follow this bird and kill it. After I get it I'll go home."

The elder sister went back. The younger sister thought she could capture the bird, so she continued to run after it. It was dark now and the young woman could not see the eagle well that she had been following. At this point, she met a man in a village called **Wanepap** in the Laigam [Laiagam] area. The man asked her, "What are you looking for in the darkness?" The woman replied, "Hey, good man, I'm not from around here. I'm following a bird that I struck in my garden.. I'm chasing it and now I don't know where it is. Now I'm also confused as to which trail I came from."

"Never mind, it's too dark now," the man told her, "Come with me and sleep in my house. You can leave to-morrow." So the young woman went with this man to his house.

The next day, the man woke up in the early morning and cooked three sweet potatoes. When the sweet potatoes were done, he gave one to the woman and kept one for himself. The woman watched carefully what the man did with the other sweet potato. He took the third sweet potato and threw it outside. Right away, the woman heard thunder and she looked outside. She saw an eagle, the same kind that she had hit, come to eat the sweet potato.

The woman thought hard. The bird outside was not just another bird, it was the bird that she had been following. She was happy and told the man, "That's my bird. I followed it here. I had broken a piece of its wing."

The man replied, "There are many birds like that. You can't think that it is your bird. That is my bird. I don't think it went far."

The woman spoke more emphatically that the eagle belonged to her. She looked at her bird and was very happy. She forgot about returning to her village. The woman went to the man's garden, where she weeded and made a new garden. She stayed with the man for a month, later they married and had children.

The first of their children were named Sambe [Sámbé], Kunalin [Kunalíni] and Kandep [Kandépe (Lang, 1973: 214-215)]. If you, the reader, come to the Ambun Valley of Enga Province or the Sau [Sáu (Lang, 1973: 215)] Valley near Laiagam, you can see the Kunalin Clan. The other clans are named as if they originated from an eagle.

C. Kandamain

Tsikiro

Wabag

Enga Province

A1640+. Origin of Kandépe Clan; A1640+. Origin of Kunalíni Clan; A1640+. Origin of Sámbé Clan; P210. Husband and wife; P230. Parents and children; P252.1. Two sisters; R260. Pursuits; T100. Marriage

## Cassowary and Chicken Are Enemies

(Wantok 164, April 2, 1977, page 13)

Before, there were two animals who were good friends and who lived in the same place. Cassowary told its friend Chicken that they should go into the forest and cut a tree to make a canoe.

They talked at night, and Chicken agreed with Cassowary. At dawn, when it was time to go into the forest, Chicken did not want to go. Cassowary went alone into the forest and cut down a big tree to make a canoe. Cassowary returned home, then at night asked Chicken to go into the forest so that they could pull the tree home and carve the canoe.

Chicken agreed that night, but in the morning Chicken again did not want to go, just as before. Again, Cassowary alone went into the forest to pull the canoe home. Cassowary finished carving the canoe and then asked its friend, Chicken, to get some small trees for the outrigger. Chicken did not want to do this either. So, Cassowary went alone to get some wood for the outrigger and some material for the sail. Cassowary returned home and attached them to the canoe.

The canoe was ready and Cassowary pulled it down to the sea. The two of them jumped into the canoe. Cassowary sat in the back to steer while Chicken sat in the front. They sailed toward **Karkar** Island [**Waskia** or **Takia** People, **Madang** Province]. A wind came up and blew Cassowary's tail feathers. They sang and danced, then Cassowary saw that its tail feathers were missing. Cassowary asked its friend, Chicken, to give him a feather.

Cassowary took some feathers and wanted to replace the lost ones, but he missed and shoved them all up the shit hole. Cassowary turned around and saw that its tail plumage was not standing up as it should be. So, Cassowary asked its friend, Chicken, for another one. Chicken said, "I'm sorry. I'm not giving you any more." Cassowary said, "Sorry, I put them in but they are not standing up like yours."

Cassowary started to become angry. Cassowary told Chicken, "You lazy bird, you didn't help me make this canoe. You were just scratching shit around while I worked alone. I'll break the bottom of this canoe." Then Chicken said, "Friend, this is your canoe. If you want to break it, that's OK."

This made Cassowary very mad, so Cassowary lifted its leg and brought it down, breaking the bottom of the canoe. Water came forth and filled the canoe, then the canoe sank into the sea. Poor Cassowary could not fly or swim at sea. Chicken jumped and flew to Karkar Island.

Cassowary swam, then a turtle came and Cassowary asked the turtle to take it. The turtle quickly carried Cassowary away. Cassowary was afraid and defecated on the turtle's back.

Cassowary's feces splattered around, falling as if a squid had shot the turtle with ink. So Cassowary talked to the turtle and the turtle went slower to Karkar, whereupon Cassowary was deposited on the beach. Cassowary jumped off, then turned to the turtle and tied up its legs.

Quickly, Cassowary ran up to a village and told the men to come and carry the turtle to the village. They put the turtle there and then went to the garden. A rat [possibly the black-tailed melomys (Flannery, 1995b: 143-144)] came and cut the turtle's ropes, then the turtle escaped and went back to the sea.

It was at this time that cassowaries and chickens became enemies because of the canoe. One of them ran into the forest to live and the other lived in the village.

Ruth Aresop
Josephstaal
Madang Province

A2433.4+. Why cassowary lives in forest; A2433.2.4+. Why chickens live in the village; A2494.13+. Enmity between cassowary and chicken; B211.3.17K. Speaking cassowary; B211.3.2.1. Speaking chicken; B295.2K. Animals build canoe; B295.2.1K. Animals make voyage in canoe; B296.2K. Animal (who is land-dweller) crosses water on back of another animal; B336+. Helpful turtle killed by ungrateful cassowary; B437.1. Helpful rat; J2133.11+. Cassowary destroys boat in anger, but almost drowns while chicken flies away; P310. Friendship; R4. Surprise capture; R100. Rescues; R110. Rescue of captive; R210. Escapes; S110. Murders; W111. Laziness; W154. Ingratitude; X716.1H+. Befouling with excrement

## The Woman Who Tricked a *Masalai* Snake
(Wantok 165, April 9, 1977, pages 9, 11)

**O**nce there was a married couple who wanted to go to the reef to catch seafood. They told their young daughter to stay at home and look after her little brothers, since they would be going to the beach to fish.

Her father and mother told her, "When we go, you can't burn *galip* nut shells. If you do this, a *masalai* will smell it and come to the village." So, the little girl made a fire and cooked *galip* nutshells [anyway]. The wind brought the smell of *galip* to the *masalai*'s home, and a *masalai* came. The *masalai*'s head was like that of a man, and from the neck down it was like a python. When they saw the *masalai* coming, they were terrified. The young girl's little brothers fled into the forest and cried.

The *masalai* approached the house. He called out to the little girl, "Come and sit down girl, I'll play on your legs [a sexual allusion] while you look for lice and fleas on me." The girl was truly terrified but she did not run away. She followed his instructions and looked for bugs on him.

When the father and mother returned from the beach, they saw the *masalai* lying on their child's legs. They were irate, but they did not speak with the *masalai*. They approached the house and the *masalai* told them, "In-laws, you have returned." The two of them said, "Yes."

The two of them made a fire and cooked the seafood from the reef. While they watched, they called their little girl to come get her food with her husband, the *masalai*. While they ate, the *masalai* took a clam and ate it. He asked his wife, "This kind of shell is delicious. I like it very much. Was it obtained at the reef?" The girl said, "Let's go to the reef and I'll show you."

When they arrived at the beach, the girl pulled a canoe towards the sea. The *masalai* said, "Come, take my tail and put it into the canoe, then my head will jump in too."

The girl took a paddle and paddled very far away. The girl showed a giant clamshell to him and said, "Go down and shove your head inside that clamshell then pull it up to the surface."

When the *masalai* put his head inside the clam, the clam closed on his head. The *masalai* tried to pull himself out, but he was unable to do so. The clam had caught his head. When the girl saw this, she took the other end of the snake and threw it into the sea, then sharks came and ate him. The little girl returned to her parents and they were happy together again.

Dorothy Kepas

Arawa

North Solomons Province

B29.2.1. Serpent with human head; B604.1. Marriage to snake; B874.6. Giant clam; F401.3.8. Spirits in form of snake; F490+. Masalai; J652. Inattention to warnings; K890+. Deceived into sticking body part into giant clam; P210. Husband and wife; P230+. Daughter scorns parents' wise counsel; P231. Mother and son; P232. Mother and daughter; P233. Father and son; P234. Father and daughter; P250. Brothers and sisters; P261. Father-in-law; P262. Mother-in-law; P265. Son-in-law; R213. Escape from home; S63+. Wife kills husband; S110. Murders; T111. Marriage of mortal and supernatural being


## Why Porgera Has Gold

(Wantok 166, April 16, 1977, pages 15, 17)


Once, long, long ago, there lived a man and his wife in a village called **Yarika**. They lived together, and after a long time, they had a boy and a girl. The four of them lived together, then one time a group of kinsmen killed a pig and gave a party. They sent a message to everyone that they should come to the party, and the father and mother heard this.

They said, "The two of us will leave tomorrow. So now, we're bringing some sweet potatoes, cutting some firewood and bringing some water for the two children."

They finished preparing everything, then they slept. In the morning the two of them woke up and cooked food. They spoke to their two children, "You can sleep for just one night. You can't make a noise or say anything. You must close the door tightly and sleep. We'll return tomorrow."

After the parents told their children this, they took some sweet potatoes and left for the party. The two children did not make a single noise, and they did not say anything. No, they just stayed in the house. Later, at night, they closed the door tightly. They cooked food inside the house and ate it. After eating, they went to sleep in their room.

Late that night, they felt the ground tremble and they heard trees falling. They were very frightened and did not sleep. Their eyes were open, but they stayed there through the night. They heard a stick crack and they thought that a man was coming.

A little later, they heard a man speak, "Hey, my two children, don't be afraid. I'm your father and I've come to sleep with you."

The two children did not speak or make any noise. They held tight and just listened. Much later, this man opened the door and went inside. He told the two children, "I'm your parents' ancestor. Don't be afraid of me."

Then, the two children thought hard and came outside their sleeping room. This man did not look like a real man. His skin looked scaly, like a crocodile.

The man spoke to them, "I'm your ancestor. I've taken care of you well and now I've come to show my face to you. My name is Waigima. I sleep on top of Warokari Mountain."

After he said this, he gave them each a gold stone and said, "This will make you rich. You can obtain many kinds of things with these two stones. Your father and mother and you can find much gold beneath the ground, and in the river too."

Then he said, "Now it's dawn. I'm going to my house." When he went outside near the door, Waigima said, "You two can come with me and I can show my house to you." So, the two children got up and followed Waigima.

They walked and went on top of the mountain. He told them, "I'll go inside this cave. When I'm hungry, you can see that the breadfruit leaves are large and falling down. You must kill a pig then, and call my name and give the pig to me near this breadfruit tree.

"I'll eat and the breadfruits will be plentiful, then you can be happy. If you don't give food to me, I can ruin you and you won't be able to find gold either. The gold will disappear."

After he said this, he wanted to go inside the cave. He turned into a snake. As he went inside, the ground shook and stones and the earth broke all around.

Then the two children went back to their house. They waited there. Later their mother and father arrived. When the parents saw their children, the father asked them, "Who came at night?" "It was our ancestor, Waigima, who came and slept with us. Then we went with him on top of Warokari Mountain. We returned without him." Then they told the story that Waigima had told them.

After the father and mother heard this story from their children, they ate pork and brought a pig to him. They sat and waited until the breadfruit leaves were large, then they killed the pig and gave it to Waigima.

They did this, then later the father and mother died, and only the two children were left. They married each other and had a son. They called their son Tiyani and made a family. Now, the Tiyani Clan lives in Yarika Village. Now they find gold and work at mining gold. They obtain much money from gold.

The Tiyani Clan does as Waigima had told them. Nowadays, they still kill pigs and watch for when the breadfruit leaves are large.

Now the Mount Isa Mining Company (*Maun Aisa Main Kampani*) [now called MIM Holdings] has come here and has brought much employment. We still work at gold mining.

Joe Nandawa

**Porgera** [Town, **Ipili** People]

**Enga** Province

A978+. Origin of gold on mountain; A1640+. Origin of Tiyani Clan; D191M. Transformation: man to serpent (snake); E320. Dead relative's friendly return; J1050. Attention to warnings; P210. Husband and wife; P231. Mother and son; P232. Mother and daughter; P233. Father and son; P234. Father and daughter; P253. Sister and brother; T100. Marriage; T415.5. Brother-sister marriage; V12.4.3. Pig as sacrifice; W31. Obedience

## The Stone *Masalai* Women

(Wantok 167, April 23, 1977, page 13)

Long ago, my ancestors lived in a village named **Kalem**. There was a *masalai* named Tamaulpa who had two wives. One time, the people of Wampiu [**Wambiu**] Village had a big party with dancing and singing [**West Sepik** Province, **Yahang** People]. Tamaulpa heard the beating of the hand drums, so he told his two wives that he was sick. However, he was just lying to them. He got up, left his *masalai* skin behind, took his hand drum, and walked towards Wampiu Village.

Everyone from five villages was gathered in Wampiu. They were singing, dancing and looking each other over. They were all very short compared to the *masalai* Tamaulpa.

They continued to sing and dance while the *masalai* felt his skin burning, as if a fire was cooking him. He now knew that his two wives were burning his *masalai* skin, so he told the people, "I want to leave you now."

When was about to leave, everyone hung onto his arms and legs. *Masalai* Tamaulpa got up, threw out his legs. He left some men and women in **Inkiap** Village, some in **Impep** Village, and the last of them in **Termes** Village.

Then he went to **Kafle**, turned around and [contemptuously] showed his back to them. So now, this, my village, has many stone *masalai* women. If someone makes a fire on top of a stone *masalai* woman, all of the women in my village would die. Now, these stones lie near our houses. They were real women, but the *masalai* turned them into stone.

Martha Kamin

Nuku

West Sepik Province

C610+. Tabu: making fire on spirit stones; C920. Death for breaking tabu; D231W. Transformation: woman to stone; D531+. Transformation by removing skin; D793.2. Disenchantment made permanent by burning cast-off skin; F490+. Masalai; F495. Stone-spirit; F531. Giant; Q551.3.4. Transformation to stone as punishment; T145.0.1. Polygyny

## The Highlands Story about Coconuts

(Wantok 168, April 30, 1977, pages 13, 17)

Long ago, there were two brothers who lived in Oma [**Omai** Village?, **Southern Highlands** Province, **Kewa** People]. The first brother's name was Mampun, and the second brother's name was Kele. Their father had died long before. They lived together with their mother.

After a little while, the old mother of the two men became very sick and came close to death. However, the first brother, Mampun, did not worry about his mother.

He said, "I want to see the place of the sun." The second brother said, "Come, let's go together and see the place of the sun." So the two brothers left their old, sick mother, and they walked to the place of the sun. They arrived at a riverine area.

When they arrived at the river, they saw an old woman who looked like their old mother. The old woman asked them, "Where do you want to go?" They replied, "We want to go see the place of the sun."

The old woman replied, "The young men often like to go there, but they usually don't return. The sun usually kills and eats them." The brothers replied, "It doesn't matter that the sun kills them. It can eat us. We want to try to see this place."

The old woman said, "OK, you can go and see." So, the brothers left the old woman and walked toward the place of the sun. They walked and went a little closer, then they could see the place of the sun.

Oh my, the brothers saw that all of the trees, grasses, and leaves were completely dead. They were a little afraid, but they did not go back. They continued on and they arrived at the place of the sun.

They saw two houses, so they walked slowly and looked inside the houses. They saw a beautiful young woman sitting inside. The young woman saw the two brothers and was very surprised.

She told them, "I've never seen a man here. This is the first time that you two have come to our place. When men come, my father usually kills and eats them. Why have you come?" The brothers asked the young woman, "Where has your father gone now?" The woman said, "He went to the forest to hunt wild game." Then the woman said to them, "It's alright. I'll hide you two inside my house." So Mampun, the first brother, had sex with [lit., "befriended"] this young woman.

Then right away, the sun became dark and the earth quaked. The woman's father knew that something was wrong at home, so he hurried back home.

When he arrived home, he asked his daughter, "Why is it that before this sort of thing did not happen. Now the sun is dark and there was an earthquake. Why has this happened?"

The girl replied, "Father, I was a little hot, so I wanted to go down to the water and bathe for a short while. That's why the sun is dark and the ground shook. Don't worry, I'm alright. You know father that no man ever comes to our home."

The girl's father thought and thought, and he did not say anything. Then they slept.

In the morning, the woman called her father and said, "If much later, a man wanted to marry me, and he came here, would you eat him?"

The father replied, "You're not the child of a pig or dog, that I would eat your husband. No, I wouldn't eat him." So, Mampun and the woman married.

They lived in the place of the sun. They lived there for some years, until the father of the woman, the sun, was nearly dead. He told his child and his son-in-law, "When I die, you must cut my head off and plant it near your house. You must look at the place where you bury my head. If a *limbum* palm tree grows where you plant my head, you must take care of it. When it bears fruit, you must eat these fruits."

Today, we call this tree, "coconut." Because of this origin, coconuts only grow in hot places nowadays. They do not grow in cold places.

Martin Tege

Nipa

Southern Highlands Province

A711.2. Sun as a cannibal; A1423.3. Origin of coconut; A2611.3+. Origin of coconut: sun's head; A2778+. Why coconuts grow in hot places; D908. Magic darkness; D2148. Earth magically caused to quake; H1256. Journey to other world to obtain a wife; F17. Visit to land of the sun; K1900. Impostures; P210. Husband and wife; P231. Mother and son; P234. Father and daughter; P251.5. Two brothers; P261. Father-in-law; P265. Son-in-law; T111.2.3+. Marriage of man to sun's daughter; W157. Dishonesty

## How Many Laws Came About
(Wantok 169, May 7, 1977, pages 13, 17)

There was a man named Raringi. This man heard some men say that the bones of his father were in another clan's area. He thought about going to talk to them to get them back.

Raringi went to try to talk with this clan. However, they said, "We know nothing about this." So he went to another clan, and they said, "We know nothing about the bones." He went to yet another clan and asked about the bones. They too said, "No."

He went to another clan and asked, "Do you have the bones of the father of Kampani Raringi or not?" They said, "There isn't a single bone here. Go to the Ramui Clan and ask them. There are three bones at that place. We've just heard this as a rumor."

So, Raringi went to talk with this Ramui Clan. He talked about his father's bones. They asked Raringi, "What kind of man was he? Was he tall or short?"

Raringi said, "My father was a very tall man, but I was still small when he died. I never saw him with my own eyes, but some of my clansmen said that he was a very tall man. So, I'm searching for his long bones."

They said, "Look at this bone, it is very long." Raringi said, "This is my father's bone. I want to take it with me."

The men gave him his father bones. He took them back to his home. Raringi's family and the rest of his clan were happy that he had found his father's bones.

The next day, Kampani Raringi gathered together his clan and said, "Now listen just to what I say. Do as I say, because I have found my father's bones." So, they followed only the instructions of Kampani Raringi.

Raringi said to make a big party with only pork to eat. They followed his instructions and made a big party with pork.

He said, "Now is the time for a big one-week gathering." So, they followed him. He told them to go to all of the places to find salt, and they did this. Then he told them to find bird feathers in the forest. They followed his instructions and found them.

Then he said to eat and to play games at night, and they followed him. He told them to hold each other's hands and circle the house eight times. They did this as he stood in the middle of them.

Then he said, "Now, all of you come and sleep in my big house and tell stories." So they followed him. Then he said, "Now you can make a big festival ground, a place to line up and display *kina* shells and pigs." They followed his instructions.

Then he told only the leaders to come to his house and take the skull. They followed his instructions and came. Then he said, "Now, go and fight with the enemy clan." They followed his instructions and departed.

Then he said, "Make a big canal running up to a big river so that the water will come near my house." They followed his instructions and made the canal, connecting it to a big river, making the water run close to his house. Then Raringi called this canal *Nukumbukun*, meaning "My clan."

Kampani Raringi had only one son. His name was *Anda*, meaning "I am old and suffering."

Kampani Raringi became old. When he was near death, he gave his blessings to [his son]. He said, "You can take my place and work and follow my orders. The others can follow your orders."

He continued speaking, "When I die, bury me with my father's bones in a grave. On top of the grave, plant an ironwood tree. This is a strong tree. The base of the tree shall mark me as a strong man." Anda followed his father's instructions and did this.

Anda took his father's place and spoke to his clan. He spoke to them, giving them laws to follow. Some of the things he said were: "All food must be cooked in an earth oven with [hot] stones. It is forbidden to cook directly in a fire. Only pigs must be cooked in a fire. It is forbidden to cook them in an earth oven."

Then he said, "When you give birth to a boy, take him to me. I must give him his name. Girls must also be brought to me to be named. It is forbidden for you to give names to your children."

Then he spoke about his origin, "My mother gave birth to me on a bed in my father's big house. I lived on my mother's milk and grew bigger. My mother gave me ripe bananas. I ate these and became big. Then she gave me many vegetables and I ate these. These are the foods that my mother gave me: birds' eggs, red yams, taros, cucumbers, beans, pieces of pork, and red sweet potatoes. I ate these and I became as big as a man. I married one of my father's kin. Now I have taken the place of my father and I shall do his work."

After this he told the clan, "Go and count every tree that is standing near here." They went, but they could not finish counting the trees. So, he sent them to the river to count all of the stones in the river. However, they could not finish counting the number of stones either.

He told them to count the number of birds in the forest, but they could not finish counting the birds. Then he sent them to count the snakes, but they could not finish counting the number of snakes.

He told them, "All of you come and make a big house for me. This house must have seven doors. After that you can cut seven big trees and make seven posts to stand near the seven doors of my house." They followed Anda's instructions and did this.

Anda took the place of his father, Raringi, and instructed his clan until he became an old man and he died. He did not have a son. So his three daughters took him and buried him near his father's grave.

They instructed the clan about this, then enemies came and ruined the village. Now there are no more people there. Nothing is there at all.

Timoti Wangdui
**Rintebe [Benabena** People]
Goroka
**Eastern Highlands** Province]

A530. Culture hero establishes law and order; C200+. Cooking taboos; C437+. Leader must give names to children; F531. Giant; H1118+. Task: counting snakes; H1118+. Task: counting stones in a river; H1118.3+. Task: counting trees near village; P17.0.2. Son succeeds father as king; P17.3. Dying king names successor; P210. Husband and wife; P233. Father and son; P234. Father and daughter; P252.2. Three sisters; R154.2.2. Son recovers father's bones; T580. Childbirth; V61.3+. Dead buried; Z71.5. Formulistic number: seven; Z71.16.1. Formulistic number: eight

# The Kumdi Clan Came from a Frog

(Wantok 170, May 14, 1977, page 13)

A man lived alone on a mountain, his name was Ketpi. White people call this mountain Mount Hagen. Before, the ancestors only called it Mount Mul or Mount Kumdi.

Ketpi lived on Mount Hagen. Ketpi did not have an axe or any sharp tools. He used fire to cut big trees. One time, Ketpi was making a big garden. So, there was much smoke coming from the secondary forest where he was making the garden. Another man, named Pulingawirni, lived in **Kuli** Village, near Urup [**Western Highlands** Province, **Hagen** People].

One day he went to Kumdi Mountain. When he was preparing to leave, he brought an axe with him. This was a stone axe like those that the ancestors used. He woke up early in the morning at about six o'clock to go to Mount Hagen. He walked and walked for six hours. He kept walking until about six o'clock in the evening, when he arrived at Mount Mul. Poor Ketpi said "Good evening" to Pulingawirni. And he replied "Good evening" to Ketpi. They were happy to talk to each other.

Pulingawirni gave his axe to Ketpi and Ketpi gave vegetable salt to Pulingawirni. They were true friends and lived on Mount Mul. The two men brought a net into the river and caught fish. A frog went into Ketpi's net. In the morning they went to the river to look at the net. They took the frog that was in the water. The frog became a woman and Ketpi married her. They called the woman Rok. [*Rokrok* is frog in Tok Pisin.]

Ketpi and Rok had a daughter, then Pulingawirni married and had many children, both boys and girls. These siblings matured and married and had many more children. They became a big lineage on Mount Hagen. One clan of this lineage is called Kumdi Engafin, another is called Kumdi Engamai, and another is called Kumdi Kombla. Others are Witka, Rolimbo, Klimbi Aklka/Yatni, and Kunja Pandta. These are the clans of the Mount Hagen area.

This lineage came from Mount Hagen, down the Baya [Baiyer] River. This lineage has become large in the **Kumdi** area from the ancestors Ketpi and Pulingawirni.

Paul Peng

Baya Riva [Baiyer River]

Western Highlands Province

A1640+. Origin of Kumdi Clan; D395W. Transformation: frog to woman; P210. Husband and wife; P231. Mother and son; P232. Mother and daughter; P233. Father and son; P234. Father and daughter; P310. Friendship; T100. Marriage

# Who Was the First to Die?

(Wantok 171, May 21, 1977, pages 13, 15)

One day, a mother gave birth to twin boys. The two boys lived with their parents for three years. Then the parents died. The two boys grew up and became tall and stout.

One day, the two brothers were hungry for meat. So they went to the forest to find wild game. Inside the forest, Mai [one of the brothers] saw two trees like themselves. The trees were tall and fat and looked just like them. So Mai said to Ku [the other brother], "Look at those two trees that look like us. Let's try killing these trees. Ku! You remove the bark of one tree and I'll remove the bark of the other tree. Tomorrow we'll come back here and see which tree is dead. The tree that is dead will mean which one of us will die first."

So the two boys removed the bark of the two trees and then returned to their house to sleep. The next day in the early morning, they awoke and left for the forest. They looked at the trees from the previous day.

They looked for a long time and saw that Ku's tree had died. Ku's dead tree grew in a clearing. They were both sad now. Ku thought and thought about his death. He thought, "When will I die?"

Mai was very sorry that his brother would die. He said, "Whom will I live with afterwards?" Mai cooked much pork and gave it to Ku to eat.

After three days, Ku was dead. Mai cried and cried and buried him near the house. Four months later, Mai wanted to look and see whether his tree was dead, so he went into the forest. His tree was still alive. Ku's tree was completely dried out and it was full of insects that were eating it [probably beetle grubs].

Mai cut the tree to get out the insects and eat them. In back of Mai there was a noise, so he turned and saw Ku's ghost coming. Mai was afraid and trembled with fear. Ku said, "Brother Mai, don't be afraid. I came for us to cut the tree until the sun sets." Mai was still afraid as Mai spoke, and a house appeared where they were.

They slept in the house, but Mai was still afraid that Ku's ghost would do something bad and eat him in the night. Ku woke up and asked Mai, "Why are you afraid? Now is the time to sleep." Mai wanted to trick him by saying, "I'm thirsty for water." Ku said, "Good, I'll go and get some water for you to drink. But don't touch my net bag, I'll put it here before I go."

Ku left and Mai took the net bag and saw two pennies inside. He just looked at them and then left them where he found them. Ku returned with a bottle of water. Mai drank the entire bottle.

Then Ku said, "Brother, I saw that you held my net bag." Mai said, "Yes I took it, but I only looked. I didn't take anything from your net bag." Ku did not say anything more. They both slept again. As Mai slept, Ku quickly took the two pennies and put them on Mai's liver and left.

Mai slept for three weeks. Ku returned again and removed the two pennies from Mai and Mai said, "Man! I slept really well." Ku greeted his brother Mai and said, "You ignored what I said and you slept for three weeks. Now go home."

Mai did not say anything, he returned to his house.

Nikolas K. Zawie
**Rintebe** [Village, **Benabena** People]
Goroka
**Eastern Highlands** Province

D1964+. Magic sleep induced by twin brother's ghost; E326. Dead brother's friendly return; H1570+. Contest to see which tree dies first that will cause the corresponding twin brother to die; P251.5. Two brothers; T587. Birth of twins; V61.3+. Dead buried

## The Love-Charm Woman

(Wantok 172, May 28, 1977, pages 13, 17)

There was once place on top of a mountain where a man and his wife lived. One morning, the man went walking about in the forest. He saw a tree that had many fruits on it. He saw many birds coming to perch and eat the fruits. He climbed the tree and built a bird blind. When he finished in the evening, he returned home and slept.

In the morning, he woke up, strung his bow, took some arrows and departed. He arrived at the place where he had made the bird blind. He climbed the tree and watched the birds. He shot many birds, and they fell to the ground. The birds piled up at the base of the tree.

Quickly, a snake came and ate the birds that he had shot. The man in the tree saw this, went down and looked at the snake eating his birds. The man just looked at the snake.

The snake finished the birds and then encircled the tree where the man was sitting. The snake slithered up a tree branch and ate the birds that were on the tree leaves. The man was terrified. He had a four-pronged arrow and a blunt arrow for shooting lizards.

The man shot the snake down with an arrow. Then he shot the another arrow. He used all of his arrows to shoot the snake and the snake was completely down. The man had no more arrows to shoot the snake.

He wanted to hold a tree branch and jump up and down. But the snake told him, "If you jump up and down, you will fall and die." The man was afraid, so he did not jump up and down.

The snake told the man, "Come and sit on me, then I'll place you on the ground." The snake surrounded him and put its round head on the man's body. Then the snake told the man, "Come sit on me." So, the man sat on the snake and the snake carried him carefully, placing him on the ground.

Then the snake told the man, "Come follow me." So he followed the snake. The snake approached a love-charm, then told the man, "Take this love-charm and stand it up straight on the ground." The man did as the snake had told him to do.

The snake spoke to him again, "Watch the sun rising. When the sun is setting, look at the place where you placed the love-charm." The man did as the snake had told him.

When the man looked at where the love-charm was standing, he saw a beautiful young woman standing [there]. The man was elated. The snake told him, "I want to give you this young woman because I finished off your birds."

The snake told the man, "When you want to eat, don't eat in front of the love-charm. You must hide it while you eat." The man took the woman to his village. His first wife was there, so he took the other woman and told his first wife, "I have come with another friend of mine. Straighten the house, then I'll come and sit."

The first wife did what her husband had said. She finished straightening, then the two of them went inside. The first wife did not see the love-charm woman. She just heard some noise in the house.

While she cooked some food, the sweet potatoes turned around, but she did not see the hands of the love-charm woman turning them. When the two of them removed the sweet potatoes, it was just like that. The husband saw the love-charm woman, but the wife of the house did not see her.

One time, the man took the love-charm and forgot what the snake had told him. He took the love-charm in front of the love-charm woman. The man told his first wife, "Go fetch some water for my love-charm."

However, the first wife did not heed her husband. So the second wife, the love-charm woman, told him, "I'm going to get water for your love-charm." The man said, "Go ahead." The woman took a bamboo tube and went to fetch water with it. She put some green leaves in the water and sealed the bamboo tube well.

She stood up the bamboo tube in the creek. Then she went to the source of the creek, becoming a love-charm. Her husband waited and waited, then went to the creek. He saw the bamboo tube standing there, but he did not see the woman.

He looked at the source of the creek and he saw a new love-charm standing there. This love-charm was the woman who had transformed herself.

Daniel Basiya
**Aseki** [Village, **Hamtai** People]
Lae
**Morobe** Province

B211.6.1. Speaking snake (serpent); B491.1. Helpful serpent; C300. Looking tabu; D270+W. Transformation: person to love-charm; D434+W. Transformation: love-charm to person; D1355.3. Love charm; D1981+. Woman visible only to husband; P210. Husband and wife; T10. Falling in love; T145.0.1. Polygyny

## The Women Who Came from a Hollow Log
(Wantok 173, June 4, 1977, pages 11, 18)

Long ago, there lived a man who did not have any friends. His name was Sanguni [*Sángú* means "tree" and *ni* is the desiderative form (Lang, 1973: 75, 94).] he lived alone in **Pupuris** Village [**Enga** Province, **Enga** People].

One time, he thought about going far away. In the afternoon, he found a house and he heard many women talking. Some were harvesting sweet potatoes in the garden, and some were making fires or cutting firewood. He hid well and took a good look at these young women.

Near evening, the women returned to their house. They cooked some food, then talked and laughed inside their house. When it became dark, they went inside a hole in a log.

While they slept, Sanguni went inside and tried to find the young women, but he did not see them. He sat quietly and looked again. Then he held a log that was about eight feet long and took it outside. He carried this log directly to his house.

Late that night, he was returning to his house when he thought about looking at the log that he was carrying. He arrived at his house and put down the hollow log. After he put it down, he went to sleep. Near dawn, an insect cried out and the women woke up. Each of them came outside the hollow log.

The women made much noise and the man woke up and asked them, "Who are you?" The women replied, "Who are you?" the man got up and said, "Who is it that brought you to my house?" The women were afraid now and thought about going home, but they were confused.

They saw that the house was not theirs, so they thought about what to do. They were ashamed of what Sanguni had said to them. They wanted to go back to their village, but they did not know the way. They were very vain and stubborn at this man's house, but he was very happy.

This man married all nine of the women, and all of the women became pregnant. The first child was called Makui. The second was called Ambula. The third was called Tirandi. The fourth was called Petpet. Petpet is my father's ancestor. Petpet gave birth to my father, who is called Mamakin. My father and my kin originated from Sanguni and the women from the hollow log. This is how my female ancestors originated.

Thomas T. Pupaki
Pumakos
Enga Province

A1640. Origin of tribal subdivisions; F564+. Person sleeps in hollow log; P210. Husband and wife; P230. Parents and children; R10. Abduction; T100. Marriage; T145.1.1+. Man marries nine women; T570. Pregnancy; W116. Vanity; W167. Stubbornness

## Why Dogs Ignore What Men Say
(Wantok 174, June 11, 1977, pages 21, 24)

Once there was a man who lived in a village. His name was Yoroka and he had a dog. The men of Yoroka's village took his dog and went into the forest. They saw a tree that had fruit on it. Yoroka climbed the tree, built a bird blind and waited.

Yoroka waited and waited, but no birds came. So, Yoroka looked around and saw that all of the birds were eating at another tree across the river. Yoroka left this tree and tried to go across the river, but he could not find a way across.

He saw a duck swimming in the river and approaching him. The duck asked Yoroka, "Where do you two [Yoroka and his dog] want to go?" Yoroka said, "We want to go to the other side of the river, but we are unable to cross." The duck said, "I can carry you to the other side of the river."

The duck carried the dog to the other side of the river, then returned and carried Yoroka to the other side of river. Yoroka built a blind on top of the fruiting tree and shot some birds. Yoroka looked down and saw an old man walking closer to the tree. The old man said, "What are you doing here?" Yoroka said, "I have no bird feathers, so I want to hunt some birds to get their feathers."

The old man said, "I have many at home. Come and get them." Yoroka and the old man went to the old man's house. The old man gave some food to Yoroka and said, "I'm going to the women's house. Eat in this house." Yoroka's dog followed the old man to listen to what he said.

The old man told his wife, "I brought some meat. Tonight, you should prepare the food, stones, leaves, and other things to make an earth oven." The dog listened to this and returned to his owner. The dog told him, "Yoroka, tonight the old man wants to kill us, so don't tie me up tonight."

They slept that night. The old man woke up and wanted to kill Yoroka, so he took a cassowary bone dagger. The dog woke up and bit the old man badly.

The old man said, "I'm cold and I want to make a fire, but your dog is biting me. You must tie your dog up." Yoroka fooled him and tied the dog up to a banana plant. Late that night, the old man tried to kill Yoroka again. The old man got up quietly and tried to cut Yoroka with an axe, but the dog bit the old man badly again.

They did this until dawn, then they fought in earnest. Yoroka and the dog won, they killed the old man and burned the house. They took everything and returned to their village.

The dog told its owner, "Master, when you kill a pig for us, you must give me a just little grease." The owner killed a pig, then the dog came and sat near its owner. The owner said, "You worthless dog, get away."

The dog was angry with its owner. It went up Mount Ialibu and called to all of the other dogs, "We always listen to what men say, but they don't listen to us. Now you can't listen to men anymore."

This dog forbade all dogs from listening to men. Now, dogs cannot hear what men say.

Even E. Wapa
**Pangia** [Village, **Wiru** People]
**Southern Highlands** Province

[See LeRoy (1985a: 235-238) and LeRoy (1985b: 244) for a similar tale.]

A2422.1. Why dog lost his power of speech; B211.1.7. Speaking dog; B211.3.19K2. Speaking duck; B469.4.1. Helpful wild duck; B524.1.1. Dogs kill attacking cannibal (dragon); P210. Husband and wife; Q276. Stinginess punished; S110. Murders; W152. Stinginess

# Men with Different Kinds of Skins

(Wantok 175, June 18, 1977, page 21)

Once there were a man and his wife who were picking breadfruit in the deep forest. The man told his wife, "Climb that tree." The woman told her husband, "You climb it." So, the man climbed high up the tree. He went to the crown and showed her how to pick breadfruit.

The woman stood on the ground and saw a cassowary approaching, so she followed it deeper into the forest, arriving at a pond. She took a stick and struck the water, which splashed about, then she went to the cassowary's home. The man had finished getting breadfruits, so he told his wife to collect the breadfruits and put them in a pile.

The woman did not reply, so he came down and saw that a cassowary had gone into the forest with his wife. He followed their trail and arrived at the pond. He took the stick that they had used.

He too struck the water, then he followed their trail to the cassowary's home. The cassowary had changed his skin into that of a man. He had taken the woman, and they were planting yams (*mami*) in a garden. The man followed them to their home and looked around. He saw a large spirit house and went inside it. He saw all kinds of skins, from pigs, dogs, cassowaries, snakes, and other animals.

He came outside, then went to a house and saw an old woman. He took her fire and made it bigger, then he lit the spirit house. Then he went back and cooked the breadfruit that he had picked.

The skin of the men who were planting yams became very hot, so they sent the woman to fetch water. However, all of the water was dried up. The woman returned to the garden and saw that the men had died.

She returned to the village and saw that the spirit house was on fire, so she went back to her husband. They cooked the breadfruits and ate them, then they went home.

Gambiamu Minjwan
**Maprik** [Village, **Abelam** People]
**East Sepik** Province

D350+M. Transformation: cassowary to man; D531+. Transformation by removing skin; D793.2+. Killing by burning detached skin; P210. Husband and wife; R151. Husband rescues wife; S110. Murders; V112.1. Spirit huts

# Where Did Local Languages Come From?

(Wantok 176, June 25, 1977, page 19)

Long ago, everyone knew one language called Bukikundi. It was true that they had many villages, but they only had one language. So, the people were like brothers and sisters.

When they married, the parents of the boy would go to a faraway village to find a wife for their son. This was the custom of long ago.

Later, in a village called **Yamil**, there was a man named Aukejim [**Mountain Arapesh** People, **East Sepik** Province]. This man had many children. Most of his children married off, and only two lived with their parents. The names of these children were Lakito and Munapeihim; they were boys. Lakito was the last boy and Munapeihim was the second to last.

They always cooperated when their parents sent them to get food in the garden or to fetch water. They slept in the same room.

One day, their father told them, "You two children must leave behind your childish ways and become big men now." The younger one asked, "Why father?" The father replied, "Because you are big now and you should marry." The little boy was very worried because the big ones were married and he was still small and still worked for his parents.

After Munapeihim married, Lakito worked hard to help his parents. One day, the big brother told Lakito, "I want to get some betel nuts in the forest, can you come with me?" The little brother said, "OK, let's go."

They arrived at **Yaubul**, the place where they picked betel nuts. The little brother said, "Stay here, I'll climb the betel palm tree and pick the nuts." The big brother sat at the base of the betel tree while the little brother climbed the tree and picked betel nuts.

After Lakito climbed the tree, he was short of breath. His mouth was open as he stopped to catch his breath. Then when his mouth was open, an insect called *maliniti* bit his tongue.

Lakito went ahead and picked the betel nuts. On this tree were two clusters of betel nuts. Lakito called down to his big brother, "Do you want me to pick the first cluster or the second cluster?" The big brother replied, "I don't understand what you're saying." The little brother replied, "I didn't know that my tongue has changed. I can hear you talking to me, but when I want to reply, I do so in another language."

When they returned to their village, all of the men gathered and listened to this man speaking a new language. One old man said, "Lakito, you must leave us and go to another place and work there."

So nowadays, the people of Kalapu [**Kalabu** Village] call the men of Yamil "big brother." This is because this is the place where Lakito went to live and his language is called Tumakundi [**Abelam** People]. Also, the people of Kalapu can speak the language of Yamil.

Now, these two villages are nearby, but their languages are different and are called Tumakundi [Abelam] and Bukikundi [Mountain Arapesh].

Noel J.
Arawa, Bougainville
North Solomons Province

A991+. Origin of particular village; A1616+. Origin of Abelam Language; P210. Husband and wife; P230. Parents and children; P231. Mother and son; P233. Father and son; P251.5. Two brothers; T100. Marriage


# The *Masalai* Who Ate a Man

(Wantok 177, July 2, 1977, page 17)

There was a place that had no people, but was filled with sorcery and *masalai*s. Once there was a man named Tandaya who left **Margarima** and went to **Tari** [**Huli** People, **Southern Highlands** Province]. Tandaya carried some salt to exchange with red paint and tree oil [both used for body adornment] in Tari. He left Margarima and went into the forest where the *masalai*s dwelled. At this time, *masalai*s had not yet eaten men.

He followed a trail that was very long, so he slept along the trail for two nights before arriving at Tari. At Tari, he exchanged his salt for red paint and tree oil. He was very happy and carried the goods on the long trail back.

He prepared to sleep the first night on the trail. He made a shelter, then he wanted to make fire by rubbing a wooden stick and a piece of bamboo back and forth. However, he could not light a fire and he used up the bamboo. He was not near any friends.

Then he had an idea to trick the *masalai*s. Tandaya threw the tree oil into his nostrils, mouth, ear, and anus, then he threw the red paint there and it looked like blood. He went outside the shelter and lay on some soft ground as if he were dead. He slept until it was dark.

After it was dark, he heard a crash in the deep forest. He saw a huge man with hair down to his legs and a beard that went down to his legs too. It was just a *masalai*. The *masalai* came near and held Tandaya's hand, but Tandaya did not tremble or move. The *masalai* said, "Oh my! I just saw him when I was walking. I wonder who killed him?" Tandaya did not move at all.

This spirit [*masalai*] called out to all of the other *masalai*s, asking who had killed him, but no *masalai* replied. They all came and cried, showing their sorrow. However, the leader of the *masalai*s told them to make a bed and put Tandaya on it with all of his possessions. So, they carried him to Margarima and placed him near his house.

When they arrived at Tandaya's house, they put him very close to his house door. Then all of the *masalai*s went back to the forest, except for the leader of the *masalai*s and some others who stayed and watched.

Then Tandaya got up right away. Without taking any of his possessions on the bed, he ran inside the house and told his story to his kin.

The *masalai*s were angry and they decided to kill and eat people whenever they walk along the trail. This is the reason that *masalai*s now eat men in this area.

Howard Halu
Catechist Training Center
Erave
Southern Highlands Province

A1516+. Why ogres eat people; F441. Wood-spirit; F490+. Masalai; F531.1.6.3.1. Giant (giantess) with particularly long hair; F531.1.6.4. Giant with long beard; F555.3. Very long hair; G100. Giant ogre; K1861. Death feigned in order to be carried; Q260. Deceptions punished; S110. Murders

## Where Did Food Come From?
(Wantok 178, July 9, 1977, page 13)

Long ago, there lived a man from Finongan [**Finungwa** Village], near Erap and Boana in **Morobe** Province [**Finungwa** People]. He went into the deep, deep forest where there were no people. He cut a tree there to get the insects [probably beetle grubs] inside it [and to eat them]. While he was cutting the tree, a wild man heard the chopping sound and came to look for this man.

The wild man said, "These are my insects, why did you come to cut this tree?" The real man told him, "I saw these insects first, you are lying."

The two of them argued and argued, then the wild man said, "It's bad that we're arguing. Let's stop and share the insects." So, the real man said, "OK, I'll cut the tree, then you gather the insects for us. Later, we can divide them and take them away." The man began to cut the tree, and he gave some insects to the wild man.

The wild man pretended to put them inside a leaf, but ate them instead. The real man saw this and thought for a way to kill him and escape. He continued to cut the tree while he thought. Then quickly he struck the tree with a mighty blow, splitting it in two. He told the wild man, "Come and get these insects inside the tree here."

The wild man thought and then put his hand inside the tree while the real man pulled out the stone axe and escaped [thus trapping the wild man's hand inside the tree]. The real man went on top of a mountain and heard the wild man screaming.

He screamed, "O-o-oi-i! Why didn't I eat you first? Now you did this to me and escaped, ya-a! I didn't do anything to you and you did this bad thing to me i-i!" The man heard this, then went home to his village.

Later, after some years, the man returned to the forest to look for the bones of this wild man. He saw the place where this man had died. He stood and looked. Various kinds of nice things were growing in the forest.

These things had grown from the fat of the wild man who had died. He had never seen these kinds of things before, so he tasted each of them. Some of them were ripe and he ate these.

He carried some of them to the village and cooked them in a fire, then ate them. They turned out well, so he took some and tried to plant them in his garden. He grew many foods and shared them with other men in the area.

Dopenu S.
Kitip Commercial School
Mt. Hagen
Western Highlands Province

A1420.1+. Origin of food from body of slain ogre; E631. Reincarnation in plant (tree) growing from grave; F567. Wild man; G512+. Ogre killed by entrapment; K1111. Dupe puts hand (paws) into cleft of tree (wedge, vise); R210. Escapes; S110. Murders

## Fish Originated from a Cave
(Wantok 179, July 16, 1977, page 9)

Long ago, there was an old woman who lived near a river called Navarao. This woman lived with two small grandsons. Her name was Didikalom.

She always told her grandsons, "Don't go wandering about, just stay within sight of our house." The old woman often went to the garden and returned. When she did this, she would say, "*Mus-muskip*," meaning "Close, hole." Later she would say, "*Mus-mus pran*," meaning "Open, cave."

Later, the two young boys heard their grandmother saying these things. When the old woman was at the garden, the two boys tried to talk to the cave. After the cave opened, they took spears, went inside the hole and speared some fish.

Then all of the fish went out and splashed in the water. The old woman heard the fish splashing in the water. She ran and called out, "Hey you two, what are you doing in that stone?" Later, she could not catch the fish that had left the stone. She ran and jumped in the middle of the river. She wanted to stop the fish, but she was unable to do so.

All of the fish had escaped and now they live everywhere. The old woman was ashamed now and she sat in the Navarao River. She left her two grandsons and did not return. Now, when you see fish, you know that they originated from the Navarao River.

Elizabeth Taikura
**Ablingi** Village [**Gasmata** People]
Kandrian
**West New Britain** Province

A2100. Creation of fish; D1552.2. Mountain opens to magic formula (Open Sesame); D1774. Magic results from speaking; P292.1. Grandmother as foster mother; R213. Escape from home; W126. Disobedience

## The Son Who Confused His Father

(Wantok 180, July 23, 1977, page 13)

Once there was a father who was confused by his child. He wanted to go to the forest to hunt marsupials (*kapul*). At this time, the moon was bright like the sun. The father thought that his child was asleep, so he went to get his bow and arrows. Then he went to the forest to hunt marsupials.

However, the boy thought that his father would be getting him and that they would go together to the forest to hunt marsupials together. The boy had thought this, so he had not gone to sleep. He saw his father pretending to sleep and the father thought that the boy was asleep, but the good-for-nothing was not sleeping. He opened his eyes partway and watched carefully.

When his father went outside to go to the forest, the boy stayed in the house and secretly followed him. The father did not turn back to look at his son. He thought that the boy was asleep in the house, so he pushed ahead. He saw a marsupial sitting awkwardly, and he was ecstatic. He strung his bow, pulled back an arrow and tried to shoot the marsupial.

The boy was still trailing him and he saw a marsupial near the other one. The father had only seen one, so the boy said, "Papa, leave that marsupial and shoot the other one that's very close to you." The father thought, "Who's that? I left my son at the house."

The boy was persistent and called out to his father. The poor man thought it was a *masalai* who was tricking him, so he broke his bow and arrows, then fled. The child thought that his father had seen a *masalai*, so he fled too. The child followed his father and they ran away.

The father continued to run. When he looked backward and saw the boy running, he thought that the *masalai* was still chasing him. The good-for-nothing sped up, broke open the door and entered the house. He trampled over the men who were sleeping on beds. The men called out. Some thought that they were dreaming; others were still in a deep sleep.

His boy was still running after him, and he shouted that a *masalai* was chasing him. All of the men were sleeping, so their eyes were bloodshot and they were shouting.

Later, the father saw that his child was not there. His child was still following him. The father was irate, so he hung the child up on a rope as punishment. Then, because his father had run away and broken his bow and arrows, he beat his child badly.

So, the child did not go to the forest. He just stayed in the house and it was forbidden for him to go to the forest.

Joseph Dua Jerry
**Gembogl** Bendam [**Kuman** People]
**Simbu** Province

F402.1.10+. Imagined spirit pursues person; P233. Father and son; Q400+. Punishment: forbidden to go into forest; Q413. Punishment: hanging; Q458. Flogging as punishment; R220. Flights; R260. Pursuits

## A Story of the Deep Forest

(Wantok 181, July 30, 1977, pages 15-16)

Two maternal relatives went to the forest to cut some *limbum* palm to make bracelets or armbands for themselves. They walked into the forest, then looked up and saw a ghost woman sitting on a branch like a marsupial (*kapul*).

The younger kinsman told the older one, "Kinsman, I'm going up there to kill her." The elder kinsman said, "No, stay here on the ground."

So, the elder kinsman climbed the tree but he did not see the marsupial. He saw a house, went inside and saw a young woman there.

The woman asked Juebangu [the elder kinsman], "Why did you come up here?"

The man replied, "I saw a marsupial sitting on the tree branch, so I came up here."

The woman said, "It wasn't a marsupial. It was me sitting in the sun."

The younger kinsman called out to Juebangu. Juebangu replied, but his kinsman did not hear him. He only heard a _kambu_ bird calling. The younger kinsman called out again, then Juebangu replied.

A torrential rain with tornadoes came. The little relative cut a big tree and went in the middle of it to hide. The ghost woman hid Juebangu in a basket.

The father and mother of the ghost woman had left to process sago. When they returned to the house, the ghost woman was crying. The mother thought her child was crying because she was hungry. The mother quickly cooked some food and gave it to the ghost woman, but she did not want to eat it.

The mother asked, "Why are you crying?"

The daughter did not reply to her mother. So, the mother asked again, "Why? Are you hiding a man and crying because of that?"

The daughter said, "Yes, mama."

The mother called the father to come up to the house. The woman told him, "Our daughter is hiding a man and crying."

The ghost man called out to all his families. Some of them took spears and bone daggers for shooting the ghost woman. He pointed at the man [Juebangu]. The two of them were similarly tall and stout. So they did not shoot the man [Juebangu]. So then the two of them married [Juebangu and the ghost woman]. At this time, many of us often became lost in the forest.

Elias Gan
**Warimbi** Community School [**Sawos** People]
Torembi
**East Sepik** Province

D310+W. Transformation: marsupial to woman; D2143.1. Rain produced by magic; D2142.1+. Tornado produced by magic; E423.2+. Revenant as marsupial; E425.1. Revenant as woman; P210. Husband and wife; P232. Mother and daughter; P234. Father and daughter; P290+. Maternal kin; T111. Marriage of mortal and supernatural being

# To Light a Fire and Find a Woman
(Wantok 182, August 6, 1977, pages 13-14)

Long, long ago, before you or I were alive, there were two sisters who lived on a mountain near **Nondugl** Village, close to Minj [**Wahgi** People, **Western Highlands** Province]. The sisters' names were Muno and Wasep. They had no parents, they originated from beneath the ground, near a boulder.

At this time there were no men who lived there. The two sisters were afraid to walk far from their house. They often worked at fencing their garden in the morning. They did not return home until the sun set behind the mountain. They often cut firewood and cooked food for themselves.

One time in the afternoon, Wasep told Muno that she wanted to go hunt wild game in the forest. Muno told her to watch carefully when she went into the forest, lest a ghost killed her. She told her to come back quickly before the moon set.

Wasep said good-bye to her sister, then she went into the deep forest. She tried to hunt for wild game, but she did not kill a single animal. She searched far and wide, and she did not realize that it would be getting very dark soon.

She left the trail that returned to the house, then she came to the top of a mountain called Koimbol where she cried. She dried her eyes and saw a light from a fire at the base of the mountain. She thought that her sister had lit a torch to find her and was approaching. She went directly towards the firelight.

When she came closer, she did not find her sister, but she found the source of the light inside a house. She went quietly into the house, but she did not find the house owner. She felt cold and sat near the fire.

In this house, there lived two brothers. Their names were Koloika and Yambe. Yambe had gone to hunt wild game and had not yet returned. His brother, Koloika, had left to find him. Koloika called out to find him, but he was unsuccessful, so he returned to the house.

Koloika was shocked to find Wasep sitting near the fire. They were both surprised and they spoke to each other. Koloika asked Wasep to marry him and Wasep agreed, so they were very happy. They were talking about marrying when Koloika's brother returned.

Wasep told Koloika that her sister was living on the other side of the two mountains. She told them that she was hunting game and had left her sister there.

In the morning, the sun rose above some white clouds. The two of them awoke and walked into the forest to find their two lost relatives [story inconsistency noted].

They walked far away, then they heard a noise in the forest. They were surprised to find Yambe with Muno talking and approaching them. The two of them were happy to find the other two and they all went back to the house. They killed a big pig and made a big party, then married. Koloika married Wasep, Yambe married Muno, and they lived happily together.

Now in my village, we have two clans. One clan is called Muno Yambe *Kanem* [*Kekanem* (O'Hanlon, 1989: 25)] and the other clan is called Koloika Wasep *Kanem*. *Kanem* means clan in the Wahgi language [Ramsey, 1975: 104].

The men of this village always tell us unmarried men, "If you want to get married, then go make a fire at the base of this mountain where our ancestor Wasep cried. Then you'll be able to find women who will come to you to marry."

One boy in my clan tried this at night, but a woman did not come to him as they had said. He told me this and I almost died laughing. I laughed and laughed until my belly hurt and I could not eat that night.

I told him to go find a young woman in a clan with many women, and he too laughed and laughed. I do not think that I will ever make a fire like he had made.

Joseph Kasil Nuno

Nondugl

Minj

Western Highlands Province

A1280+. First woman; A1640+. Origin of Koloika Wasep Clan; A1640+. Origin of Muno Yambe Clan; P210. Husband and wife; P251.5. Two brothers; P252.1. Two sisters; T100. Marriage; T130+. How to find a wife: light a fire at the base of a mountain; T545. Birth from ground

## The Snake Mother

(Wantok 183, August 13, 1977, page 13)

Long ago, there was a man who lived on Tumeleo [**Tumleo**] Island [**Tumleo** People, **West Sepik** Province]. This man had a garden that was near a huge callophyllum tree. When he went to work in the garden and he wanted to urinate, he always urinated at the base of this callophyllum tree.

There was a snake that lived inside a hole in the callophyllum tree where the man urinated. The man urinated on this snake often and the snake became pregnant. Later, the snake gave birth to two boys named Kairoro and Lesautum.

The two boys lived in the hole in the callophyllum tree with their snake mother until they grew as big as five-year olds. One time their mother told them, "Look at that man who always works in this garden. He's your father. Go and ask him for some food."

The two boys went up to the man and said to him, "Father, mother sent us to you to ask you to give us some food." The man thought, "Where did these boys come from who are calling me father?"

So, whenever the two boys came to ask him for food, he would spy on where they returned to after he gave them food. He always saw them go down the hole in the tree where he urinated.

One time he asked them, "Where do you live and where do you come from? Where does your mother live? Who told you that I'm your father?"

They spoke, "Our house is in the hole at the base of the callophyllum tree. Our mother lives in the hole. She told us that you pissed on her and then she gave birth to us."

When their father heard this, he took them to the village. They often cooked food and brought some to their mother. This went on for some time, then the two boys became big men. One time their father told them, "Go get your mother and bring her here." So, they made a big basket and brought their mother to the village.

When their father saw the snake, he was terrified. He did not want them to put the snake mother in the house, so they put her underneath the house. One time, the two men went to see the ocean. They paddled far asea and they could not see their island. They caught some fish, then they saw a piece of ash blowing in the wind. The ash fell directly into the canoe. They saw this and they thought and thought. They felt queasy. They said, "There's probably something wrong in the village." So, they paddled back to the village.

When they arrived, they saw that their house had burned down. Their father had burned their mother. They cried together and made a basket from coconut palm leaves. They filled the basket with their mother's bones. They left the island and went to the mainland.

Felicity Fau

Tumleo Island

Aitape

West Sepik Province

B211.6.1. Speaking snake (serpent); B631.9. Human offspring of marriage of person and snake; B631.9+. Snake wife killed by human husband; B754.6.1. Unusual impregnation of animal; K812. Victim burned in his own house (or hiding place); P231. Mother and son; P233. Father and son; P251.5. Two brothers; S112.0.2. House (hostel) burned with all inside; T512.2.1. Child develops from man's urine; T570. Pregnancy; T587. Birth of twins; T685. Twins; X717.1H+. Urination on animal

## The *Masalai* That Was Tricked By Grass and Hair

(Wantok 184, August 20, 1977, pages 11-12)

Long ago, there was a man who woke up in the early morning and went to the forest for amusement. He walked around and went to a place where he saw a breadfruit tree that was laden with fruits that were nearly ripe. He cut some sago palm leaves and made a fence around the breadfruit tree, then he went back to his village.

This breadfruit tree belonged to a ghost who tended it. It did not belong to this man. When the man returned to his village, the ghost came and saw its breadfruit tree. The ghost was surprised to see that there was a man who had fenced the tree, thus putting a taboo against others from collecting the fruits. The ghost was irate and removed all of the man's fencing.

The ghost cut some new materials and fenced the tree again. A new day came and the man returned to see that his sago leaves were not there as before. He was furious and he removed all of the ghost's fencing. Then he cut some new materials, fenced the tree well and returned to his village.

Later, the ghost returned and saw that the things that it had used to taboo the tree were not there. So, the ghost removed all of the man's fencing and put up another fence. The two of them did this repeatedly until the breadfruits were ripe. One early morning, the man woke up and went to harvest the breadfruits.

When he arrived, he climbed the tree and threw the fruits down. The ghost heard this noise and came to see who it was that was stealing his breadfruits. The ghost arrived and saw a man on the tree, so it called out to him, "Ha! Now I know that it is just you doing this. When you take these breadfruits, which trail will you take?"

The man said, "I'll jump down and go into the forest where you live."

The ghost listened to this, then cut all of the grass that was around the breadfruit tree. The ghost made a big ring around the tree. After the ghost finished, it asked the man, "Now, which trail will you take?" The man said, "I'll jump down and go into the forest and the grass that you have cut."

The ghost listened to this and removed all of the trees and grasses. The ghost cut them and brushed the entire residue near the breadfruit tree. After that, the ghost asked him, "Which trail will you take now?" The man said, "I'll jump down and go into the hair [lit., "grass"] that is on top of your head."

The ghost listened to this and cut all of the hair on its head, making itself bald. By the time that the ghost had done this, the man had finished cutting all of the breadfruits, except for one that was at the top of the tree. He took this one and he sang to the fruit. The ghost saw this and tried to ask him something. But no, the man threw the breadfruit down near where the ghost was standing. The breadfruit rolled away and the ghost thought that it was the man who was running away. So, the ghost ran after the breadfruit.

The man saw this and came down immediately, gathering all of the breadfruits quickly. He took them and fled to his village. The ghost was still running after the breadfruit and had lost the man.

The ghost was irate when he realized that the man had tricked him. He returned and tried to follow the man again, but the man had reached his village. The ghost went near the village and then returned.

Xavierius Peter
**Maprik** [**Abelam** People]
**East Sepik** Province

E276. Ghosts haunt tree; F490+. Masalai; K525+. Escape by substituting breadfruit; R220. Flights; R260. Pursuits

## The Women Who Came from Coconuts

(Wantok 185, August 27, 1977, page 11)

Long ago, there were two men who lived in a place where there were no women, so they were married to frogs. The frogs did not know how to cook food for their husbands. No, they cooked awkwardly.

There was another village fairly far from them. The village is called **Nikavuvuya** [**East Sepik** Province]. In Nukavuvuya [Nikavuvuya], there was only an old woman. This woman often sang and danced for a long time. When she did this, her coconuts turned into women and came down the coconut tree trunk, then they sang and danced too. At dawn, the women went back up the coconut palm tree.

One night, one of the two men heard the beating of hand drums. In the morning, he awoke and went to Nikavuvuya. He only saw the old woman there. The man went and sat down in the old woman's house. The old woman told him, "Sorry, the nice singing and dancing is over, you have come too late." Then she said, "If you want to see the singing and dancing, then you must prepare all of the things that are necessary for it, such as food and water."

The man hurried and prepared these things. In the evening, the old woman told him, "You must shut every hole in the house. Shut the door, then sleep deeply. You can't wake up or make any noises. It would be bad if the women saw you, they would stop singing and dancing." The man heeded this and went quietly to sleep in the house, but he kept his ears open.

The man heard the women coming down the coconut palm and standing on the ground. He heard them begin to sing and dance. They sang and danced and sang and danced, then the old woman gave them food. They were still eating when the man stood up to look. He said, "I don't want an old woman to give me a dish of food. I want a young woman to give it to me."

So, he indicated a very young woman and she did not ignore what he had said. No, she gave him a dish of food immediately. Then the old woman took a dish of food and gave it to the man, and he ate it.

They sang and danced until it was dawn. The old woman was still looking at a young woman going up the coconut palm when she told the man to come outside. He came outside, then the old woman gave a net bag and rope to him. She said, "Climb the coconut palm and take a young coconut, but don't make any noise. You must climb very quietly." The man heeded her. He picked a coconut, then descended. The woman told him, "Take the coconut to the river. Put all of your things with the coconut in the trail, then go and bathe. After you finish bathing, go back and break the coconut, then eat it. After that, you can go home."

The man did as the old woman had said. After the man bathed, he returned to look for the coconut, but only a young woman was there. He looked around and the woman asked him, "What are you looking for?" The man said, "A young coconut." The woman said, "Never mind the coconut, let's go home." So, they went home and married each other.

Martin Mugumat
Catholic Church
Josephstaal
Madang Province

B604.5. Marriage to frog; D222+W. Transformation: woman to coconut; D431.11+W. Transformation: coconut to woman; P210. Husband and wife; T100. Marriage; T117.10. Coconut wife (in form of a woman)

# The Blood of the Garden
(Wantok 186, September 3, 1977, page 11)

Long ago in a village called **Menihegororo**, near Yufi Yufa [Yaviyufa Village], there lived two brothers named Hune and Pakure [**Yawiyuha** People, **Eastern Highlands** Province]. Their parents had died. Hune was the older of the two brothers.

One time when it was a good day for hunting, Hune said, "Pakure, you should stay in the village. I'll go hunt for wild game in the forest." So, he took some fresh sweet potatoes, and a bow and arrows for shooting birds and other game, then he left the village.

He arrived at a place where he saw a small boy. This little boy said to him, "Father, may I hold your things while we go into the forest to hunt game?" Hune said, "You can come." They came to the forest and the little boy scouted much game that Hune then shot. They filled their big bag with game, then late in the evening they returned towards the village.

The little boy said, "My home is in this cave." When he wanted to go, Hune gave him two marsupials (*kapul*). Then the boy went into the cave. When Hune returned to the village, Pakure cooked Hune's food. After the food was ready, Hune ate it.

The brothers slept, then in the early morning, they heated some stones for cooking the game in an earth oven. After the meat was cooked, Pakure told Hune, "Last time, you went to the forest and shot many animals. Now I should go to hunt."

When Pakure went on the trail, he saw the little boy waiting there. The boy said, "Father, may I hold your things while we go hunting?" But Pakure said, "I'm not your father. Who is it that you want to go with?" Pakure left him and walked a short way. Then the little boy said, "Father, may I come with you?" Pakure said, "I already told you, I'm not your father. If you persist, I'll shoot you with this arrow."

Pakure went a little farther and the boy again said, "Father, may I hold your things?" Now Pakure was angrier and he shot the boy in his belly. The little boy had the arrow inside him. He fell and went into the cave which was his home.

His home was like that of a prime minister: it was beautiful and it had a bed. He went to sleep, but then he died. Pakure went into the forest and did not shoot any animals. He did not get a single animal.

When Pakure returned to the village, Hune said, "I think that you're a woman because you didn't even shoot one or two animals. Tomorrow I'll go." The two brothers went to sleep. In the morning, Hune took his bow and he departed. When he arrived at the trail where the little boy lived, he was not there. Hune saw blood and he followed the trail of blood. When he arrived at the boy's home, the boy's throat was very dry. Hune cried and cried.

Hune removed the arrow and saw that it looked like Pakure had shot him. He was angry with Pakure. He dug a hole in front of the boy's home and buried him. Then he took his axe and ran to the village. He struck Pakure on the head, killing him.

Hune died as an old man. If you go to the Yaviyufa area in Konopiyufa [**Konoboyufa**] Village, near Goroka, you will see that there are two boys who stand and point to where the two brothers were from long ago.

Henry Wephew
Yufi Yufa [Yaviyufa Village]
Goroka
Eastern Highlands Province

J652. Inattention to warnings; P251.5. Two brothers; P251.4+. One brother acts wisely, another acts unwisely; Q211. Murder punished; Q411. Death as punishment; S73.1. Fratricide; S139.4. Murder by mangling with axe; V61.3+. Dead buried


## Where Did the Crocodile Come From?

(Wantok 187, September 10, 1977, page 11)

Many years ago, there was an old blind woman who lived on an island. The woman was lucky because she had a son who lived with her and took care of her.

[The mother said,] "I want you to take care of me." Her son agreed. One time, the man told his mother, "I've selected a woman that I shall marry." The mother said, "You can't leave. If you marry this woman, you two must live with me." So, they married and they went to live with the old blind woman.

The wife helped take care of the old woman very well. However after a long time, the woman began to get angry. [She told her husband,] "I hate this house. I don't like taking care of your mother. I want a house of my own." So the two of them made a house on the other side of the island.

The old woman became mournful because her son had left her. She could not catch fish because she was blind, and she could not work in the garden, so she had no food.

When the rainy season arrived, she was very cold because her house was falling apart and there was no man to fix her house. The married couple lived well in their house, but sometimes the son thought of his mother and was sorry.

Before long, his wife bore a son. The man heard his wife singing his son to sleep, so he spoke to her, "When I was still a little boy, my mother was old and she loved me." So, he thought about preparing to visit his mother. He took some food from the garden and brought it to her. He lived with his mother for two days. He caught fish and fixed the house well. Then he said good-bye to his mother and returned.

[When he returned, he asked,] "Will you, my wife, bring some food and firewood?" After he said this, the wife was furious, but she followed his request. The man told her to get two big fish and cook them for his mother. The two of them ate a little of it, then the wife carried the fish away.

While the wife was working on the old woman's house, she found three lizards. She made a fire and cooked them with some leaves from the deep forest. She took some banana leaves, then covered it up and took it to the old woman. She told her that it was fish, so the old woman said thank you and the wife left.

The old woman was not hungry at that time, so she left the food for another day. The man came to work for his mother. He brought his son to show to her. His mother was happy that she had a grandson. Then the man worked in the garden and he became very hungry. The mother gave him the lizard meat. He smelled a strange smell, but he was hungry and he ate it.

The mother told him, "Yesterday, a young woman came to see me and she told me that her husband had died. She asked me to live with her in her house. She spoke nicely, so I wanted to live with her."

As the mother told this story, the man was turning into a crocodile. His mouth became longer and longer and his skin became hard. [He asked,] "What kind of food did you give me?" The mother told him, "I don't know. Your wife gave it to me." She did not know where her son went or that her son had turned into a crocodile. Her son was angry now. He said good-bye to her, and returned home.

He was irate and he had not thought about bringing back his son. Before long, his wife saw the crocodile coming. She was afraid and fled.

"Don't run away," said the crocodile, "I'm your husband. What did you do with the fish that turned me into a crocodile?" However, the wife was still running away, so the crocodile followed her. She swam in the sea, but the crocodile still followed her.

They went down into the sea, so then there was no one to look after the old woman or the young boy. The blind woman did not know why her son did not return. So, the old woman took her grandson and lived with him. This is the origin of the crocodile.

Joseph Tom
**Buin** [**Buin** People]
**North Solomons** Province

A1710. Creation of animals through transformation; A2146. Creation of crocodile; B211.6.4K. Speaking crocodile; D194M. Transformation: man to crocodile; D551.3+. Transformation by eating lizard; K333. Theft from blind person; P210. Husband and wife; P231. Mother and son; P233. Father and son; P262. Mother-in-law; P265+. Daughter-in-law; P292.1. Grandmother as foster mother; R220. Flights; R260. Pursuits; S54. Cruel daughter-in-law; S140.1. Abandonment of aged; T100. Marriage; T580. Childbirth; W27. Gratitude

## The Woman Who Left Her Sister

(Wantok 188, September 17, 1977, page 11)

Once there were two sisters who went to look for leafy greens in the forest. They saw a _kwambi_ tree that was full of very ripe fruits, so they climbed the tree to collect the fruits.

While they were collecting the fruits, they saw two pigs approaching. They took some sago palm thorns and put them into the _kwambi_ fruits, then they threw the fruits down to the two pigs that ate them.

While the pigs ate, the sago thorns went into their necks and caused them to die. The two sisters saw this and went down. They took the pigs and bound them up. They carried the pigs home. Later, they saw an old woman who was carrying a fire.

When they saw the old woman, she asked them, "Do you two want to cook something?" They replied, "We want to cook our pigs." The old woman said, "Good, my granddaughters. These pigs belong to the three of us, so we can eat the pigs now."

Then the old woman gave the fire to them and said, "You cook the pigs, then I'll come later." So, the two sisters cooked the pigs. While one sister was beginning to cook the pigs, the other went on top of a huge _tulip_ tree and made a place to lie.

She descended, then they hurried and cooked the pigs in an earth oven. When the two pigs were ready, they prepared to carry them up the _tulip_ tree.

The old woman came and they gave her the pig guts. They told her to carry them down to the river and cut them open. When she left, the sisters took all of the meat and went up the _tulip_ tree. They hid well in the _tulip_ tree and ate the pork.

After the old woman finished cleaning the pig guts, she returned to look for the two sisters. However, when she returned, she did not see them.

She looked around everywhere. Then she saw their shadows and she said, "Hey, whose shadows are these?" Then she climbed the tree and saw them eating the pork on the tree.

She said, "My two granddaughters, you are eating the meat and throwing the bones down upon me."

They threw a bone down on her head. The old woman removed the bone and licked the blood off it.

After that, she went to her house and took her spears. She carried them over, then stood them up around the tulip tree and around other trees that were nearby.

After she stood the spears up, she began to cut the tulip tree. When the tulip tree began to fall, the sisters jumped to another tree. Then the old woman jumped to the other tree and cut that one too.

When that tree began to fall, they jumped again to another tree. The old woman jumped over to that one too and began cutting again.

Then as that tree began to fall, the sisters jumped to yet another tree. The first sister made a good jump, but when the second sister jumped, she bent the tree branch. The tree branch was dry and withering, so it broke.

She fell down to the ground and was impaled by the spears that were standing at the base of the tree, and she died. Then the old woman ate her.

Mr. [Tony] Sapin [Spian] Akipo
**Maprik** [Village, **Abelam** People]
**East Sepik** Province

G10. Cannibalism; K897.1+. Dupe killed by putting thorns in food it is about to swallow; P252.1. Two sisters; Q411. Death as punishment; R260. Pursuits; R311. Tree refuge

## The Dog That Befriended a Man

(Wantok 189, September 24, 1977, pages 11-12)

In a house, there lived two brothers named _Tauan_ and _Kuiman_. The meaning of both these names is "bamboo sprout." [_Taú_ is a kind of bamboo used for water containers and bowstrings. _Kuíma_ is a kind of wild bamboo (Lang, 1973: 47, 101).] They lived happily, they had good food, they made good gardens, and they had everything they needed.

One day, the big brother told the little brother, "Tomorrow, I want to go to the forest to find some marsupials (ka-

*pul*). I'll return on the third day. So, you must prepare everything for us to cook the marsupials in an earth oven."

The [elder] brother collected some food and departed. He walked and walked and climbed a mountain. Then he caught his breath. He heard a dog howl below, where he wanted to go.

This man, Tauan, heard the dog howling and he followed this sound. He left the mountain and went down. He found a black dog underneath a tree.

The dog was happy to see the man and made a noise by wagging its tail. The dog pointed with its leg to another tree where he saw a pig that was tied up with a rope. Then the dog showed him how to remove the ropes from the tree. The man did as the dog showed him.

The man removed the ropes from the pig, then held the pig in his hands. The dog made a wagging noise with his tail and right away he went past a rat. The man just followed the dog.

They arrived at a clearing and saw a nice place that had good food, a good house and other nice things. The man saw all of these things and was very happy. He just followed the dog.

The dog jumped and showed him a huge tree. The man thought, "The dog is telling me to cut the tree." So the man cut it. After he finished, the dog showed him leaves, vegetables and edible greens for cooking the pig in an earth oven. So, the man gathered all of these things that the dog had showed him.

Then the dog showed him a stick for hitting the pig on the snout and killing it. The man cut the stick and hit the pig on the snout. The man cut the stick and killed the pig, then they cooked it in the earth oven. While they were eating the pieces of meat, the man just ate the bones and gave the good meat to the dog.

The dog felt good. After the man finished removing the meat from the earth oven, he heard the dog doing something. The dog gave all of the pork and other meat to him. The dog only kept the pig's head.

He gave everything else to the man. The dog gave him many *kina* shells and other things, then sent the man away. The man went back to his village. His brother was very happy to see him.

He gave his brother much meat, but he did not want to eat it because he was strongly opposed to his brother going to that place. It would be bad to ruin the dog's place.

However the brother said, "If you send me to the place that you went to, then I must eat." No, he was strongly opposed to his brother going to this place. It would be bad if he ruined the dog's place.

So the next day, he learned well the things that his brother did, then he was sent away. He climbed the mountain and he heard the dog howling, then he ran down. He saw the dog right away and the dog was happy to see him, but then the dog felt bad because this man was not his friend.

The man shouted at the dog, "Where's the pig that you tied up?" The dog walked slowly and showed him. Then the man asked the dog, "Where's your home? I want to kill the pig and eat it." So, the dog walked slowly to its home.

The man shouted again, "Never mind this slow walking, run fast." So, the dog followed the man's instructions. They arrived at the home and the dog showed him all of the things that he had shown to the first brother.

However the man did not like this and he spoke, "I'm only working for my own desires. Never mind yourself." He killed the pig for himself alone and later he just gave the bones to the dog. The dog ate the bones, and the dog's mouth and teeth became bloody. The man injured the dog and the dog came close to death.

He listened to the dog, then he cooked the entirety of the dog's food and left. The man went back to his house and his brother saw that something was not right. His brother asked him, "What happened? Did the dog give things to you?" The man replied, "Yes, yes."

Then the brother cried and cried. In the early morning, he went to look for the dog, and the dog was near death. The man arrived and the dog told him, "You must send that man to me. He beat me and I waited for you because I'm going to die. We must kill his body."

The man cried and put the dog in a grave. Then he returned and killed his brother and he died too. The dog had made friends with a man, but the dog was ruined.

Simon Es
**Tsak [Enga** People]
Pumakos
**Enga** Province

[See LeRoy (1985a: 1-3), LeRoy (1985b: 242) and *Wantok* #157 for similar tales.]

B211.1.7. Speaking dog; B331.2.2+. Helpful dog killed; B421. Helpful dog; P251.5. Two brothers; P251.4. Brothers scorn brother's wise counsel; P310. Friendship; Q42. Generosity rewarded; Q211.6. Killing an animal revenged; Q411. Death as punishment; S73.1. Fratricide; S110. Murders; W11. Generosity

## The Snake That Became a Man

(Wantok 190, October 1, 1977, page 11)

This is a story about Mount Tonaiya. There was just a snake that lived on this mountain. This snake was named Kama Kama. It often killed and ate men, but sometimes it transformed itself into a man and had sex with women. This is what the snake did.

One time, a woman was going to her garden. The snake, Kama Kama, was watching and went down the mountain. The snake saw a woman pulling up sweet potatoes from the garden. The snake came towards this poor woman.

The snake changed into a man and the woman thought that it really was a man. The woman saw a very handsome man, so the snake said good day to her.

The woman said the same to the man. The snake told her, "I like you." The woman said "OK." Then the snake told the woman that he wanted to sit on top of her. The poor woman lay down and the snake placed himself on top of her. They had sex and then he kissed her. The snake departed, then the poor woman lay there. Then she got up and watched the snake leave.

The woman thought and thought. Later, she went to her village. She told her husband and the people of her village too. The woman told her husband, "Mount Tonaiya came and spoke with me then left." However, the men knew that the snake of Mount Tonaiya came and spoke with her. They wanted to go, but it became dark and they slept.

In the early morning, they walked to Mount Tonaiya. They arrived at the top of the mountain. They had carried some logs, and they made a ladder with them. The men looked at the ladder from both sides.

One man climbed the ladder and called to the snake, Kama Kama. Immediately, the snake heard the man calling his name.

The man ran down the steps of the ladder. Oh my! This huge snake was chasing him down the steps. The big group of men fought the snake and killed it. Then they brought the snake to their village. The women brought sweet potatoes, bananas, and cabbages. Their husbands carried the big dead snake. Some men cut some firewood and some heated stones for an earth oven. The women peeled the sweet potatoes. The men made a fire and put the stones on top of the fire.

They cooked the snake in the earth oven, then they uncovered it and ate the food. Oh my, the snake was very greasy. The people ate the grease with the snake's belly, then they slept.

However that night, the snake joined itself together again. After it rejoined itself, it went outside and cut a huge tree in to small pieces. It surrounded all of the houses. Its body was very strong and it broke all of the houses, killing all the sleeping people.

After the snake killed everyone, it slithered back up Mount Tonaiya. Now, the snake still lives on Mount Tonaiya.

Kevin Koatana B.

Wempamgo [**Wempangu**] Village [**Hamtai** People]
**Gulf** Province

B91+. Man-eating snake destroys houses; B211.6.1. Speaking snake (serpent); B613.1+. Snake paramour in form of man; B765.7.2. Snake grows back together after it has been severed; D391M. Transformation: serpent (snake) to man; P210. Husband and wife; Q211.6. Killing an animal revenged; Q241. Adultery punished; Q411. Death as punishment; R260. Pursuits; S110. Murders; T481. Adultery

## The Man Who Came From a Cassowary

(Wantok 191, October 8, 1977, page 10)

Once there was a man and a woman who walked into the forest to hunt wild game. They walked and walked, then arrived at the base of a *galip* tree. They had sex at this place. Later, a cassowary came and saw the *galip* nuts and ate them.

Then the cassowary laid some eggs. The eggs hatched, and what came out? They were cassowary chicks, except for one that was a boy.

The mother cassowary took the chicks around the forest. She found food for them for the first time by kicking a banana plant, causing ripe bananas to fall. The chicks were happy and cried out together, then ate the banana. However, the boy did not know how to eat wild banana, so he just stood there and held one.

The mother tried all of the kinds of cassowary food, but the boy did not eat them. The cassowary thought and brought them to someone's garden. She took some of the people's bananas, then gave them to the boy. She explained how to eat it, but the cassowary chicks just stood there in confusion, "What's he eating in the people's garden?"

The cassowary saw this [the boy eating the bananas] and took him to everyone's gardens. Then he finished off all of the food, and only one banana plant was left.

The owner of this garden had made a big hole and covered up the hole. He was hiding when the cassowary took her children to the banana plant. The chicks were standing in confusion.

The boy ate the bananas. He ate and ate. Then he wanted to get the ripe banana that was on top of the leaf that was covering up the hole. He fell down the side of the hole, and oh my, the mother was angry. She kicked her legs at the hole. But the boy was lost.

The man walked forward and the cassowary chased him. He ran away and told his brother, then the cassowary ran away and told her sister too. They fought and fought, then they shot the cassowary mother's eye. She said, "That boy is my child. I'm leaving now, take care of him well."

The men took him from the hole and returned to the village. He grew up and was given two wives.

Later, they angered him and he worried about his mother. So, he left for the deep forest. He came to his mother and she said, "Why have you come? They ruined my eye in the fight over you, so I ran away. Haven't they taken care of you well?"

The two wives ran away and followed him. They stayed with the man's mother. Later, the cassowary mother's son shot her again. He butchered his mother, then cooked the meat and bones for his clan.

Now, we people from **Nuku** Village and some people from the Dreikikir area have a name for these men, they are called *mami* (yam) and cassowary. They are numerous in the Nuku area [**Mehek** People, **West Sepik** Province].

Before, we did not have *mami*. When this son shot his mother, that was when we obtained it. Now there is a cassowary clan. They originated from this cassowary and her son. I am one of the people of this clan.

Tresia W. Nurkuminga
Nuku
West Sepik Province

A1640. Origin of tribal subdivisions; A2686.4.3. Origin of yams; B211.3.17K. Speaking cassowary; B631.16K+. Human offspring from cassowary; D985+. Magic *galip* nut; D1001+. Magic sexual secretions; K735. Capture in pitfall; P210. Husband and wife; P231. Mother and son; P262. Mother-in-law; P265+. Daughter-in-law; R213. Escape from home; R260. Pursuits; S22+. Matricide; T145.0.1. Polygyny; T511.8.4+. Conception from eating nut; T542. Birth of human being from an egg


## Mount Mul [Hagen] Is the Origin of Life

(Wantok 192, October 15, 1977, page 9)

Long ago, there were no people on earth. However, there were various kinds of birds that flew east and west, all day and night. They flew around and soared on the winds of Mount Mul [Hagen].

The word *mul* in the **Hagen** Language means, "A new sprout growing," or "The feces have broken and a seed is growing in it." So, Mul Mountain is where people originated and grew from.

Mul Mountain is the life of all people. Many, many people originated from Mul. Some of the people went to areas in Enga Province, some followed the Naiviler [Nebilyer] River and went to all of the parts of the Southern Highlands Province, and some went to all of the parts of Papua.

Some went to the headwaters and arrived at Banz, Bendwagi, and went to all of the places on the coast. Some still live on Mul Mountain. They like to go to other people's places and sleep. They all took some earth from the top of Mul Mountain, because this earth gives life to men.

They took this earth and they left our land, Papua New Guinea. From Mul Mountain they went to **Tambul** and **Tomba**, where we often have ice and cold.

All of the men took this good earth from the top of the mountain and brought it to the other parts of Papua New Guinea. That is why Tomba and Tambul have ice and cold. When it is sunny, they often go to Mul and hunt wild game to cook.

There was a beautiful men's house with good *tanget* plants growing around it. The village was beautiful and very clean. The men went to see Mul Mountain.

But they could not open their mouths or speak. They could only listen. The people spoke and a dog barked in another place, but these people could not see this. If one of the men had seen this, he would have died.

At this time, there was a man who had just cut the forest. He left Mul and founded **Minimb** and Keltiga [**Kutiga**] Villages, and **Hagen** Town proper. Later, he lived on Mul.

He had four boys, one was named Nining and another was named Mul Timb. Nining lived on the other side of the mountain and founded **Ningan** Village.

Later, the grandchildren went to these villages. From my eyes, I see this place. My brother went to the other side of the mountain and made a garden. He sleeps in a nice village.

Nining left his house and went with a tree called *kerakapiapul*. He took this tree and planted it in **Arowa** on the Naviler [Nebilyer] River. This tree is still in this village.

Nining had another boy that he called Naminga. Grandchild 1, grandchild 2, grandchild 3, Awil. Awil and brother Kamugil 4. Merua and father 5, these were Abura, Duwa and Oga.

These are old fathers who are still alive. The fifth grandchild founded the clan of my father and brothers who live in the Naiviler [**Nebilyer**] Valley. I live there with them.

Now, Timb's house is cleaned and fixed by the fathers in the area of Mul Timb.

John Kulda
Mount Hagen
**West Highlands** Province

A991+. Origin of particular village; A1135+. Why it gets cold in certain places; A1260+. Origin of people from excrement; A1640. Origin of tribal subdivisions; P233. Father and son; P251.6.2. Four brothers; P291. Grandfather; T541.8.1. Birth from excrement

## Fighting in the Highlands

(Wantok 193, October 22, 1977, page 13)

Long, long ago, there was no fighting in the Highlands. There were two brothers with the same father and mother. The elder was named Sambe [Sámbé (Lang, 1973: 214)] and the younger was Kunalin. The brothers did not have wives. They each had a dog.

One time, when there was a bright moon, they prepared some food. They carried the food, bows [and arrows], then went away to hunt marsupials (*kapul*) in the forest with their dogs. They went into the deep forest and put their food in a hunting hut.

They walked around in the forest and killed many kinds of marsupials. They carried the marsupials back to the hut. They cooked some of the marsupials in an earth oven and ate them. In the morning, they wrapped up the marsupials and returned home.

They walked very far. They approached a trail and had a smoke. Their dogs had ropes tied to their necks.

After they finished smoking, they got up and continued walking. The young brother, Kunalin, went first with his dog, and his big brother, Sambe, followed.

The first brother saw his dog get loose of his rope and go ahead, so he asked his brother, "Hey! Hey! Sambe, can you get my dog's rope? It came loose nearby and I lost it."

The big brother Sambe said, "No, I can't get it. I think it's lost in the forest." The little brother said, "No, I had it at the place where we sat and smoked, so it's not in the forest.

"If you get it, give it back to me." The big brother Sambe said, "No, I don't see your worthless dog's rope." After he said this, he ran past his brother. The little brother, Kunalin, followed him, then held onto him and took his net

bag. He looked inside, then he found and took back his dog's rope.

The big brother, Sambe, was ashamed that he had stolen this, so he strung his bow and shot [at] Kunalin. Then [Kunalin] too took his bow out and the two brothers fought.

The two brothers fought and fought. The people along the trail and the village watched them fighting with bows and arrows and shouting at each other.

The men from around the village and gardens heard their shouting. They also took their bows [and arrows], then went to the fight. Many people helped Sambe, and many others helped Kunalin. The fight continued on to the whole of **Enga** Province.

The big brother, Sambe, chased away the group that was fighting with Kunalin to Sirungi [**Sirunki**] Village, near the border between Wabag and Laiagam [**Enga People**].

Now, they call this clan Kunalin [Kunálini (Lang, 1973: 215)]. The big brother's clan is in **Papayuku** Village. This clan is large now and is called Sambe. These two brothers had started the fighting; it was the first time in Enga Province. They continued this fighting, and so fights have arisen many times and have spread to other places, such as Mount Hagen, Simbu Province, Eastern Highlands Province, and the rest of Papua New Guinea.

Alphonse Paliru
C. T. C. Pumakos
Wapenamanda
Enga Province

A1599.11.1. Origin of war; A1640+. Origin of Kunalíni Clan; K420. Thief loses his goods or is detected; P210. Husband and wife; P231. Mother and son; P233. Father and son; P251.5. Two brothers; P251.5.3. Hostile brothers; Q212. Theft punished

## Using a Man as Lime (Calcium Oxide)

(Wantok 194, October 29, 1977, page 13)

Once there was a young woman who was menstruating. She slept until morning, then woke up to go to the forest. She arrived at the base of a *ton* tree. She saw that the base of the tree had mushrooms and some bamboos.

She thought and thought, and then she asked herself, "Is this edible?" She took the bamboos and mushrooms, then she called to a cockatoo, "Hey, can you cut down some *ton* fruits for me?"

The cockatoo listened to this and cut off many *ton* fruits for the woman. She ate some and carried some home to her village. She finished eating the bamboos, mushrooms and *ton* fruits, but she did not know that she had taken a *masalai*'s decorations. The bamboos were the *masalai*'s spears, and the mushrooms were the *masalai*'s adornments.

In the evening, she slept. Meanwhile the *masalai* took on a man's face and went inside the house, then slept with her. He did this for three nights. On the fourth night, the woman awoke and was angry with her husband. Her husband said, "Hey! It's not me!"

So, she kept watch that night and saw a man going inside the house. It was a man who closed the door and became a huge python. Then it departed. In the morning, the husband asked his wife, "Where are you going?" The wife replied, "I'm going to get something over there."

The husband said, "Can't you stay in the village? This is wrong for you. After a while, you will be married to the *masalai*." Then the *masalai* told them, "If I marry this woman, it will be alright. Nothing will be ruined."

The men of the village heard this indirectly. They killed a pig and cooked it, then they called out and the *masalai* came to the village. The woman and the *masalai*, ate the pig.

After they ate, the *masalai* got up and carried his spears. He went to the pond with the woman. Then the *masalai* told the woman, "Do you see a cockatoo?" She looked up and he cut off her two breasts. The two breasts drifted on the water and sank.

The woman's sister was standing and hiding near them. She was also carrying a spear. She shot her sister's two breasts and carried them to the village. The villagers cried over the two breasts.

After they buried the breasts, they cut a *jaket* [?] that fell at this place. Later, they heated stones and threw them into the pond. The pond boiled and they saw the python.The woman left him. When the man [*masalai*] arrived, they killed him and cooked him. Later, he became lime (calcium oxide), and they sent this to every village. This lime is used only for yams (*yam* and *mami*). This story comes from Kumphun [**Kumbuhum** Village, **Boiken** People, **East Sepik** Province]. The name of the *masalai* is Miaka.

Mr. Joris M. S.

Arawa

North Solomons Province

B212. Animal understands human speech; B469+. Helpful cockatoo; D42.2. Spirit takes shape of man; D191M. Transformation: man to serpent (snake); D230+. Transformation: ogre's corpse to calcium oxide (lime); F350. Theft from fairies; F389.4. Fairy killed by mortal; F420.1.3.9. Water-spirit as snake; F490+. Masalai; K420. Thief loses his goods or is detected; P210. Husband and wife; P252.1. Two sisters; S139.2.2+. Corpse put into cooking pot or cooked; S176+. Mutilation: breasts cut off; T475.2.1. Intercourse with sleeping girl; V61.3+. Dead buried

## How Did Kremendin Village Originate?

(Wantok 195, November 5, 1977, page 11)

Long, long ago, in the time of the ancestors, there was a woman named Newa who lived in Hanyiak [**Hanyak** Village, **Boiken** People, **East Sepik** Province].

This woman went and lived at a place on the beach where the sea crashed and swirled. The ancestors took this land by my village and covered it over, making a hill, then they fenced it off.

There is no sea that goes to my village. This woman, Newa, wanted to return to her place that was closed off by a hill that blocked the sea. There was no path to go to this place, so she became confused and turned into a lizard.

There was also a man who came from near **Passam** Village. He transformed into a tree's shadow. This man stayed at the tree and descended to ask the woman, "Hey, what are you, a ghost or a woman?"

The woman asked him, "And you too, what are you? Are you a tree spirit or a real man?" Then the two of them married. The man's name was Mifariki.

The man and woman came to live on this land called **Huasufawu**. They were the first man and woman who lived on this land. They lived there and raised children.

Now you can see Yake with his brother Muruki living there. Their maternal relatives left to live at **Wom**. This is how Kremendin [**Kremending**] Village originated. The women of my village originated from this place.

Johnny Kriosaki

Kremendin [Kremending]

Wewak

East Sepik Province

A967. Origin of mounds; A991+. Origin of particular village; D197W. Transformation: woman to lizard; D270+M. Transformation: man to tree's shadow; P210. Husband and wife; P251.5. Two brothers; P290+. Maternal kin; T126+. Marriage between lizard and tree's shadow

## Where Did Coconuts Come From?

(Wantok 196, November 12, 1977, page 11)

Yes friends, long ago, we did not have coconuts. There was a place where only two brothers lived. Their father and mother had died. The first brother often went to the sea to catch fish and the second brother often caught wild game in the forest.

When the first brother returned home, oh my, he often brought many fish. When the second brother returned, he never had many fish. It often happened like this. One time when they were at home, the second brother asked the first, "What is it that you know that you always catch so many fish?"

The first brother replied, "I often go fishing with a hook and catch many fish." One day, the first brother said to the second, "You go. I'm sick. I'm going to sleep in the house."

However, he was not sick, he was lying. When the first brother went towards the sea, he removed his head and tied it to a tree leaf that we call _huanawiok_. Then he put it at the base of the tree and went down into the sea.

The second brother stayed home for a long time, then he followed the first brother into the sea. When the second brother returned from the sea, he hid in the forest and watched the first brother come out of the water carrying many fish.

When he wanted to go to the sea, the second brother called out, "What is it that you do to catch so many fish? I asked you this before and you lied to me."

The first brother heard this and was ashamed. He went into the sea and turned into a log that lay in the water. The second brother returned to the house. At night, the first brother came and spoke to him in a dream.

In the morning, the second brother followed his dream. He went to the sea to find his brother's head at the base of a tree. He carried it and put it underneath the house. Many months passed, then he saw that a seedling was growing from the head's mouth.

He cut some sword grass, burned it and buried the head there. He saw the seedling grow and he did not take it. He left it and it became big, then [nuts] fell down. He took them and placed them carefully.

The second time that there were nuts, he took them and tried to eat them. As he was eating, he found them to be increasingly delicious. He cleaned the base of the tree and the tree bore many nuts. He took them and planted them.

Now, there are many large coconut trees with nuts. People from faraway saw this and took them with them. So now in every place, there is something that is called coconut.

Gabriel Panjiva
Kimbe
West New Britain Province

A2611.3.1K. Coconut tree from head of human; D216M. Transformation: man to log; D1810.8.2. Information received through dream; D2150+. Catching fish by removing one's head and letting fish enter body; F511.0.4+. Person with removable head; P251.5. Two brothers; W157. Dishonesty

# One Man and Two Women Founded a Village
(Wantok 197, November 19, 1977, page 15)

Long ago, there was an old man who lived in a village. One day, he crossed a river named Bale. After he crossed the river, he went into the sea and began to catch fish. The river ran strongly into the sea with many fish, sea grasses, and plenty of trash.

At this time, there was a village named Sera [**Serai**]. Every one of Sera was butchering a turtle on a Mam Beach. The turtle is called _nausa_ in our language. Two of the women wanted to eat some turtle.

When the two went down to the beach, they saw many, many fish that the waves had thrown ashore. They did not think any more about eating turtle with the others. No, they began to follow the shoreline and pick up all of the fish. While they were collecting the fish, they arrived at the river that the old man had crossed. Then the sun set.

The old man saw the two women and he asked them, "Are you real women or ghost women?" The women said, "We're real women." They asked the old man, "Are you a real man or a ghost?" The old man said, "I'm a real man."

So, the three of them married and lived together. They had many descendants who populated this place. In this village called **Leitre**, the people originated from this man and these two women [**Rawo** People, **West Sepik** Province].

Augustine Kaiyon
Erave
Southern Highlands Province

A991+. Origin of particular village; P210. Husband and wife; T100. Marriage; T145.0.1. Polygyny

# The Dog that Turned into a Man
(Wantok 198, November 26, 1977, page 13)

Once there were two sisters who went to process sago. While they were processing sago, a big flood arose. They took their belongings and they tried to cross the water. Try as they might, they could not cross the water. The current was too strong.

As they stood there, they saw a dog standing on the other side of the water. They said, "Oh dear! If you were a man, you could come and take us to the other side of the water." The dog heard this and went into the forest, then changed himself into a man. Then he returned and crossed the water to get the two women.

They crossed the flood, and in the middle of the water, the man held the big sister's body. When they reached the other side, the man told them, "You two go to my house."

The man went to the forest and removed the bark of a sago palm tree, then sharpened it so that he could kill them. While the sisters were walking along the trail to the man's house, they began to talk.

The big sister told the little sister, "That man is yours." The little sister said, "That man is yours because he held your body."

They talked like this, then they arrived at the man's house as he had instructed. They opened the door and went inside. They closed the door and planted a spear in the door, then they went to sleep. While they slept, the little sister heard a man talking and making noises. The spear was in the door to shoot him. The man said, "You two in there, I shall come inside and open your two mouths."

The little sister heard this and tried to wake her big sister, but she was unable to do so. She was dead asleep because the man had held her body from before.

The little sister tried again to wake her, but she was still unable to do so. So she broke the sago palm thatch wall of the house, took a coconut and ran up a big mountain. She stood there and saw the man go inside the house to kill her big sister.

After the man killed the big sister, he went outside the house and chased the little sister up the mountain. While he chased after her, she threw the coconut down the mountain. The man thought that the woman was running down the mountain, so he chased after the coconut.

While he chased the coconut, the woman returned to her village and told the men of the village about what had happened. Later, the man went to the village and the men killed him. If the men had not killed him, he would have finished off all of the women of the village.

Paula Kamak

**Maprik** [Village, **Abelam** People]

**East Sepik** Province

B212. Animal understands human speech; D341M. Transformation: dog to man; D1964. Magic sleep induced by certain person; K525+. Escape by substituting coconut; K950+. Rescued from flood, only to be murdered by rescuer; K959.2. Murder in one's sleep; P252.1. Two sisters; Q211. Murder punished; Q411.6. Death as punishment for murder; R100. Rescues; R210. Escapes; R260. Pursuits; S110. Murders



# The Yam that Turned into a Snake and then Became a Man

(Wantok 199, December 3, 1977, page 13)

Long ago, in the time of the ancestors, there were two women who lived in a place. There was not a single man there. The women usually just performed garden work, planting and harvesting yams.

One time, the big sister told the little sister, "It would be better if we went to a new garden and took some yams there." So, they went to the new garden, taking the big, long and good yams to put there. They slept that night. While they slept, a yam turned into a big, sleeping snake.

In the morning, they woke up and saw that the yam had turned into a sleeping snake. They said to the snake, "Snake, you listen. We are asking you what you want. Whatever it is, we'll give it to you."

The snake kept its eyes closed and continued to sleep. The big sister told the snake again that they would like to give him things, but he did not open his eyes, he just slept.

The big sister asked him if he wanted her little sister. Then the snake opened his eyes and saw them there. The snake married this woman. The names of these women were Yang and Yambiak. The snake married Yang, and became a real man who lived with these two women and had many descendants.

Now people have these two names, Yang and Yambiak. This story comes from **Ambu** in **Madang** Province [**Monumbo** People].

M. E. Kawe

Heldabach [Heldsbach]

Finschhafen

Madang Province

A1640. Origin of tribal subdivisions; B656.2. Marriage to serpent in human form; D391M. Transformation: serpent (snake) to man; D441.4+. Transformation: yam to snake; P210. Husband and wife; P252.1. Two sisters; T100. Marriage

# Friend Helps Friend

(Wantok 200, December 10, 1977, page 17)

There was a small village named **Suap** in the Erap area [**Madang** Province]. There were two old men who lived there with their wives. They each had a son.

One evening, they decided that the next morning their two boys should wake up and dam the creek. When the boys arrived at the creek, one dammed the creek near the source and the other dammed it at the base of the mountain.

Muddy water came to the Serop River. An enemy man from **Sugu** Village came and saw this muddy water, then followed it upstream [**Numangang** People]. When the enemy approached them, he hid and watched the two boys.

The man did not see the boy's friend, and so he thought that the boy was alone. They boy's friend did not see this enemy, and the boy thought that he was alone with his friend. The enemy came quietly and shut the boy's mouth, then carried him away.

The enemy had some sort of weapon such as a spear, or a bow and arrows. He also had some *limbum* palm fronds and cassowary feathers, so he tied the boy up with the *limbum*. The enemy took the boy to his village, Sugu, and stood him next to a post in the middle of the village. They tied up his legs and hands with ropes.

In the evening, everyone of this village prepared for a celebration. They dressed up and began to sing and dance.

The boy's friend looked for him and called out for him, but he did not reply. The friend went down to the place where the boy had made a dam, but he did not see him.

A little later, he looked on the ground and saw a big man's footprint. The boy was very angry with his friend. A little later, he heard the men of Sugu singing and blowing conch trumpets. He thought that the enemies had taken his friend, that they were singing and dancing with joy, and that they would kill him in the morning.

After the boy thought this, he hurried home. His parents asked him, "Where's your friend?" The boy did not reply to his parents. The boy thought that he must hurry and sharpen his arrows, but the two fathers and two mothers berated him.

They told him, "If you're a real man, go get your friend from the hands of the enemies." So, the boy hurried at sharpening his arrows. He tied them well with rope and carried them. Then he took some decorations for celebrations: cassowary feathers and some other bird feathers. He tied these with his *limbum* to a wooden shield.

He left home and went towards the enemy village. He arrived at the side of a mountain, then he climbed the mountain. When he approached the village, he hid and carefully looked over the village. He saw a good place where he could stand and shoot people and block the trail of the men at the celebration. Then he went inside the festival with the enemies.

When the villagers pretended to cut the boy at the post, his friend pretended to do this too, but instead he cut a rope each time. They continued to sing and dance like this.

When dawn was approaching, the friend asked him, "Have I cut all of your ropes or is one still binding you?" The boy answered, "You have cut all of the ropes except one on my side that you have not cut." So the friend told him, "Don't worry about that rope, I'll get you and we'll run away."

When it began to become light, a big, hairy-chested man went past the dancers. When the dancers came by, the friend told the boy, "When we dancers return to you again, get ready to run away." The next time they came by, the friend shot the big man with his bow and arrow, then he pulled the boy off the post and they ran away home. Their parents were ecstatic to see their two children return.

Boni Nogudong

Lae

Morobe Province

K647. Confederate cuts rope almost in two so that prisoner breaks it and flees; K2357. Disguise to enter enemy's camp (castle); P210. Husband and wife; P231. Mother and son; P233. Father and son; P310. Friendship; R4. Surprise capture; R10.3. Children abducted; R110. Rescue of captive; R169.5+. Rescue by friend


## The Two Enemy Birds

(Wantok 201, December 17, 1977, page 13)

Long, long ago, there lived two birds who were good friends. Their names were Malip and Kau. They often played, laughed and flew together. They walked together every day.

Kau had beautifully colored plumage, but Malip did not have beautiful plumage. Malip saw that its plumage was bad, that it was too dark, but that Kau's feathers had grown very nicely.

Because of this, Malip had bad thoughts of his friend Kau. Malip did not want to look as before. Malip wanted to look nicer, like Kau.

At this time, Malip tried very hard to think of a way to obtain Kau's beautiful feathers. So one day when they were talking, Malip asked Kau whether Kau wanted to bathe together in the river someday. Kau listened to this and said, "Oh, it would be very nice to bathe in the river."

The next afternoon, the two birds walked down to the river. Poor Kau did not know that Malip wanted to play a trick.

When they arrived at the river, Malip told Kau to bathe first, then Malip would bathe. Malip had been thinking of stealing Kau's beautiful feathers.

Kau's friend departed and bathed first. Malip told Kau that it would look out for Kau's feathers while Kau was bathing lest someone came and took their feathers.

Kau stayed and watched while Malip went to bathe. At this time, Malip finished bathing then Kau got up to go into the water. While Kau was still bathing, Malip told Kau to go deep into the water.

When Kau was beneath the water, Malip quickly exchanged its plumage with Kau's beautiful plumage, then flew away.

When Kau came up again, Kau found that its beautiful feathers were not there. Malip had taken them and left its poor plumage for him. Kau saw this and was irate. Kau took Malip's feathers and threw them on the ground. But poor Kau could not do a thing now, so Kau just put on Malip's rotten feathers because Kau did not have another set of beautiful feathers.

Malip had departed and was quite happy with Kau's handsome feathers. He showed them to other birds and people. But poor Kau was not happy with Malip's plumage.

So from that time until today, Kau and Malip are no longer friends. If the two of them meet, they always become angry and fight because Kau is still unable to get back its feathers from Malip.

Today, they are still enemies. Because of Kau's anger, Kau always wakes up everyone and all of the other birds in the early morning before the sun has risen.

Luke Silopita

Lunga Lunga School

Rabaul

[East New Britain Province]

A2494+. Enmity between birds; A2489.1.1+. Why bird calls before dawn; B211.3. Speaking bird; K634.2. Master thief persuades captors to dive into water: steals their clothes; P310. Friendship; R220. Flights; W195. Envy

## The Marsupial's (*Sikau*'s) Revenge
(Wantok 202, January 21, 1978, page 13)

In a little place called **Dukutam**, there lived just one woman [**Madang** Province?]. She had a small boy who was still a baby.

One time when the tree fruits were ripe and falling, the woman thought of getting some fruits in the forest. She carried her child and departed. She followed a river called Urer. On the other side of the river, she saw many, many tree fruits falling. She said, "It would be better if I hung up my child [in a net bag] on a lizard's groin/armpit." Then the woman walked far away to find tree fruits.

The poor lizard's groin/armpit became quite weary, and the lizard called out, "Hey woman, come fetch your child. My leg is in great pain. It would be bad if I lost your child, and he fell and died." However, the woman did not hear the lizard.

A marsupial (*sikau*) was warming its body in the sun. The marsupial heard the lizard calling and calling, so the marsupial carefully ran and took the child, then fled into the forest.

The marsupial took care of the child in the forest, enabling the child to become a big boy. The marsupial showed him many kinds of things, such as axes, bows, fire and knives. The marsupial had traveled around, stealing these things from men. So, the boy had all of these kinds of things. The boy made a house for the two of them and a garden too.

One time, the marsupial traveled around and found two young women who were fishing inside the water. The women's young brother was with them too.

The marsupial jumped up quickly and stole the first woman's "grass" skirt, then ran away. The women came out of the water and ran naked after the marsupial. The women sent the brother back to the village. The women continued to follow the marsupial and then married the boy whom the marsupial had cared for.

The women's elders sent a little boy back to the forest to find the two sisters. The poor little boy went and found that the sisters had married this man. In the morning, the two women and their husband killed a pig, then gave it to the little boy to send back to the village.

Some years passed, then there was a desire to have a big party in the village for the two women. The women's parents sent a message to obtain payment from the man in the forest who had married them. The women's little brother sent the message to the marsupial who was the mother of the man who had married the women.

The day was ending, and they got up to go to the party. The women tied the marsupial's legs and hands together, then put her in a net bag. Their husband did not know about the marsupial: the women had put the marsupial [in the net bag] and hidden it well. Then they carried the bag and departed.

At the time of the party, there was much singing and dancing. The singing and dancing went until late at night, close to midnight. The women's little brother lifted up the marsupial and said, "This marsupial is the payment for my two sisters [i.e., the bride price]. I want to eat it now." So, he took a knife and cut the marsupial's neck.

The poor women's husband saw that they were killing his mother, so he felt truly awful. He cried terribly, because the marsupial had taken care of him from the time that he was a baby until he had married. While it was still night, the man fled back towards his home. Along the trail, he made a big and deep hole, then covered it with tree leaves.

Later at the party, the men wanted to return home. A long line of people followed the trail. All of them fell into the hole and died. The next day, the man saw this and covered up the hole with dirt again. This place is called "The Marsupial's Revenge."

Bruno Malai

Usino

Madang [Province]

B211.6.2K. Speaking lizard; B535.0.16K+. Marsupial as nurse for child; K735. Capture in pitfall; P210. Husband and wife; P231. Mother and son; P232. Mother and daughter; P234. Father and daughter; P253.0.2+. Two sisters and one brother; P262. Mother-in-law; P265+. Daughter-in-law; P272. Foster mother; P275. Foster son; Q211.6. Killing an animal revenged; Q411. Death as punishment; R13.0.1. Children carried off by animals; R220. Flights; R260. Pursuits; S50. Cruel relatives-in-law; S54. Cruel daughter-in-law; S110. Murders; T52. Bride purchased; T100. Marriage; T145.0.1. Polygyny

## Why Do Dogs Sniff Each Other's Tails?

(Wantok 203, January 28, 1978, page 13)

In the deep forest, there was a place where men did not often travel. In this place, many kinds of dogs gathered. This was the dogs' home. They each had a house where each dog family lived. When the dogs had a big meeting or when they had a party, they always gathered in the house of a family. They also had a playground where they often played soccer, volleyball, basketball and other games.

One beautiful afternoon, a dog thought that it would be a good day to play soccer. So, the dog spoke to the other groups of dogs about this. After they all heard this, they agreed to play soccer.

The young and strong dogs sent their children and the aged to sit in their houses. The young dogs divided themselves up well, then began to play. On one side, there were one hundred dogs. These were both strong he- and she-dogs. They had five goalies.

The other side had strong dogs too. There were no rules. They often just kicked with their legs and moved the ball with their snouts. The ball was not very large, because they used tree fruits.

They played hard and diligently, but some dogs were not happy. While they played, some dogs held others by the tail. When one dog shook the leg of another, ten or twenty others would awkwardly fall on the other side.

So, they all stopped playing. They agreed to remove their tails and hang them on the soccer ground's fence. After they had hung their tails, they began playing again. The poor dogs were not just fooling around, the sun was hot. Some were badly injured, but they continued to get hotter.

In the middle of the game, a dog looked back at their tails that were hanging on the fence. At first the dog thought the tails were OK. But no, he saw a pig digging in the ground near the fence. Then the pig moved the fence and all of the tails fell.

The poor, strong dogs tried to find their tails immediately. However, the pig had mixed all of the tails and the dogs could not find their own tails. These dogs were not boys, they were a big group. So, they just put on whichever tails they could find.

Now we can see that when one dog sees another, the dog will run to smell the tail of the other. That is because the dog is trying to find its lost tail from the time when the dogs played soccer. We often see each dog looking for its tail like this.

If a dog smells another dog's tail that does not belong to the first dog, we often see that the dog just smells it and leaves. However, if this dog finds that the dog has put on its tail, we will see them fight.

George Makaja

P. O. Box 14

**Tari** [Town, **Huli** People]

**Southern Highlands** Province]

A2471.1. Why dogs look at one another under tail; B221+. Dog society; B298+. Dogs play sports; B770+. Dog removes tail

## How the Eagle Marked Hagen

(Wantok 204, February 4, 1978, page 13)

Long ago, there were no men in **Eglem** Village [**Hagen** People]. There were many women who lived there. One time, after sunrise, it was a good time to go to the forest to hunt marsupials (*kapul*). The women thought about searching for vines to make net bags. They prepared to leave. They took plenty of sweet potatoes, then they went to sleep.

Early the next morning, they awoke and walked into the forest to find vines for making net bags. While the women were walking in the forest, they arrived at a foothill, then they divided themselves. Some went along the stream while the others went through the forest. One woman who went along the stream took her vines with her. She saw a bird's nest. The woman took the bird's nest and saw an egg inside. The woman took the egg, but it broke, so she ate it.

Later, she took some vines and went to find her friends. She went to their house. She did not explain to her sisters that she had eaten an egg. She just went to the house. Three months later, the young woman's belly swelled up. Her sisters said to her, "Sister, you've eaten a lot and now your stomach is swollen." But the woman said "No."

After nine months, the woman was close to giving birth and was having labor pains. She lay on the ground and rubbed the earth on her skin. She cried and was near death. Her sisters had never seen anything like this before. Her sisters said, "I think that she'll die like this." They continued to look, then the woman gave birth to a baby boy. The women saw that this boy was shaking badly. The women were ecstatic for the boy. They kissed the mother.

They took him and looked after him for three months. Then his mother and his aunt took him to the garden. They put him at the base of shady tree while they went to get cucumbers.

An eagle flew by and perched on a tree branch above where the baby was. The two mothers saw this. Quickly, the eagle swooped down and snatched the baby boy with its two talons and flew back to a tree branch. The two mothers shouted and called out loudly, but the eagle said, "The baby is mine now. I've taken him away from you. You two, go back to your house."

After the eagle said this, she continued to perch on the branch. The mothers cried and threw a stick up, but it was ineffective. They shouted again, but this was ineffective too. Near dusk, the eagle told them, "You two, go home. The baby is mine now, I've taken him away from you."

The two mothers cried terribly and rubbed mud on their faces [a sign of mourning]. They returned home and [the mother] told the other women, "Once, when we went to the forest to find vines to make net bags, I took an eagle's egg. I think that because of this, I gave birth to the baby boy. This eagle spoke to us and took the baby away."

The mothers cried mournfully. Later, they had a party for their baby. They worked in the garden to stop thinking about their only child.

The eagle took the young boy to the forest and put him in a tree hole. The eagle flew around the forest and killed marsupials (*kapul*), then brought them back to give to her boy. Every time the eagle did this, the boy became bigger. Eventually, the boy could no longer fit in the tree hole. So when the sun set, the eagle brought the young boy down to the place where his mothers lived. The mothers were cooking sweet potatoes in an earth oven and telling various stories.

They heard a bird's wings flapping. They saw the eagle bringing the young boy closer to them. The mothers were surprised and held tightly to the boy. Then the eagle flew back to the forest.

The boy became an adult and married his mothers, who gave birth to many boys. This clan of men is called Munjika. They live near Tiria [**Tiri**] in **Western Highlands** Province.

When this clan sings and dances, they always decorate themselves with eagle feathers. The men of this clan grow to be stout. Men from other clans often say, "The Mujika [Munjika] Clan came from the eagle and has grown well."

Mr. Zawie Kaepni

Mt. Hagen

Western Highlands Province

A1465.3+. Origin of eagle feather decoration; A1640+. Origin of Munjika Clan; B211.3.11K. Speaking eagle; B535.0.7+. Eagle as nurse for child; B552. Man carried by bird; F112.2. City of women; P210. Husband and wife; P231. Mother and son; P252. Sisters; P1. Aunt; P681+. Mourning customs: earth on body; R13.3.2. Eagle carries off youth; T100. Marriage; T145.0.1. Polygyny; T412. Mother-son incest; T421. Man marries his aunt (mother's sister); T511.7.2. Pregnancy from eating an egg; T570. Pregnancy; T580. Childbirth

## The Dog That Found a Pond

(Wantok 205, February 11, 1978, page 11, 13)

Long ago, there was no water in Lake Kutubu in **Southern Highlands** Province. At that time, many people did not have water and they hungered for it.

There is a place near Kutubu called Topua Village [**Tobua** Village, **Mendi** People]. This place did not have many people, there were just a young woman and a dog. They had plenty of food in the their garden. They often ate various kinds of food, but they had no water to drink.

The dog always tricked the young woman, because the dog often went to the forest to drink water. One day, the woman told the dog to go find water in the forest, but the dog told her, "You're crazy, woman. Where am I going to find this water that you're talking about?"

The young woman was ashamed and said, "Never mind, let's go into the house." They went into the house, then the young woman cooked some sweet potatoes. The dog finished eating, then went into the forest to get some water. Afterwards, the dog returned to their home.

They went to sleep. In the morning, they awoke, cooked sweet potatoes and ate them. Later, the dog again went to get some water. When the dog returned to the house, the young woman looked at the hairs around the dog's nose. She saw that a little water was still on its hairs.

This time, the young woman thought hard. The young woman worked at winding a rope. She worked at making the rope for one month. Then one time after the dog had eaten and was about to leave, the young woman took the rope and tied it to the dog's tail. She followed the dog closely and she saw the dog go close to a rotting tree.

The dog went up a big fig tree, then drank some water. Later when the dog tried to get down, it was unable to do so. The young woman shouted to the dog, "Hey, hey, what are you doing?" The dog was ashamed and said, "I drank some water." Then the young woman held onto the big tree and it fell apart. Oh my! Water fell everywhere. The young woman was near the water and wanted to get it.

The dog said, "*I pu Kutubu yura yu tengteng*." This means, "Lake Kutubu, you can't become larger." Then the water was still. The name of the dog was Nol and the name of the woman was Temoki.

When we go to Kutubu, we often see this big fig tree in the very middle of the lake. The dog's marking is on this tree. When you go to Kutubu, you can see many dogs in the area around the lake.

If this young woman had not done as she had in the Southern Highlands, we would not be able to drink water there. We would only be eating sweet potatoes, and only the dogs would be drinking water. You would not be able to see the water, and you would not be able to see Lake Kutubu where it is now.

[Anonymous]

A920.1.0.1. Origin of particular lake; A1429.3. Acquisition of water; B182.1. Magic dog; B211.1.7. Speaking dog; D1774. Magic results from speaking

[The Ancestor Story in *Wantok* #206 is the same as that in #172.]

# The Heron and the Crab

(Wantok 207, February 25, 1978, pages 9, 14)

A heron is the name of a kind of bird that hunts fish to eat. In a place named **Pahang**, there was a heron that was quite old. The heron often went to a pond and saw many fat fish. The heron threw its beak into the water to catch the fish, but the fish swam away too quickly for it to catch them. So for many days, the heron did not catch a single thing. The heron became as thin as a bone and its skin became loose. The heron was very worried.

The heron continued to worry, but later it thought of a way to fool the fish. After it thought of this scheme, it went to find a turtle. Near the pond, the heron saw a turtle, so the heron said, "Have you heard what the two men said?" The turtle said, "I didn't hear what the men said. What did they say?" The heron said, "They'll come to this pond after one month. They want to remove all of the water and quickly take all of the fish away on the next night. This is what I heard them say."

The turtle left the heron and went to talk to the fish. A short while later, the heron walked close to the pond. The fish came to ask the heron, "What can we do? The men are coming to remove the water and all of us will die."

The heron thought a lot then said, "I think that I can carry each of you. I can fly to another pond on the side of the mountain and put you there."

The fish replied, "That's a good idea." So, the heron carried the fish away. However, when the heron carried the fish away, it did not bring them to the pond. No, it ate them until there were no more fish.

An old crab lived in this place called Pahang. The crab saw the heron and thought, "Before, the heron was just skin and bones. The heron was always worrying about catching fish. I think that the heron has eaten all of my friends."

When the heron returned to get more fish, the crab called out, "Take me!" So the heron took the old crab and carried it away. While the heron was carrying the crab, it tried to eat the crab, but the crab held tightly onto the heron's neck and strangled the heron. Pahang is a nice place now with fish in the lake.

Pius Aunal
**Yassip** [Village, **Kombio** People]
**East Sepik** Province

B211.3.10K. Speaking heron; B211.5. Speaking fish; B211.8.1K. Speaking crab; B211.6.3K. Speaking turtle; B299.1+. Animal takes revenge for animal friend; K484. Cheating by raising an alarm; K953.3+. Crab carried by heron, clings round his neck and strangles its head with pincers; P310.

Friendship; Q211.6. Killing an animal revenged; Q424.0.1. Strangling as punishment for murder; S113. Murder by strangling

## The Python that Defeated the Crocodile

(Wantok 208, March 4, 1978, page 13)

A very long time ago, the Fly River ran between **Olsobip** [Village] and Telifomin [**Telefomin** Village, **Telefol** or **Faiwol** People, **West Sepik** or **Western** Province]. At this place, there was a lake with a she-crocodile that was guarding her eggs. This crocodile's husband was hunting for food, and he had killed a wild pig. The husband ate some of the pork, then cut a piece of leg and carried it back to his wife.

There was also a big python that lived at this lake. The python was also hunting for food, but it was unable to find any. So, near dawn, the python returned home.

The crocodile husband returned and gave the food to his wife, then he wanted to go down to the lake. The python's head was already in the lake, but its body was on the shore.

There was only one path that the crocodile liked to take, so the crocodile followed the path and came down to the lake. Oh my! The python was already there, so the python grabbed the crocodile and the two of them wrestled. The python defeated the crocodile and killed him. Then the python drank some water and swallowed the crocodile. The python wanted to go down in the water, but it could not do so because it was stuck where it had eaten the crocodile.

Three men from the Telifomin area followed the Fly River and arrived at this place, finding the python. They slaughtered the python and left it to die and rot at this place. Then the three men returned home.

Kraolus K. Ayam
K. T. S. Erave
Southern Highlands Province

B299.12K. Animals go hunting; B875.1. Giant serpent; P210. Husband and wife

## There Was No Sago

(Wantok 209, March 11, 1978, page 13)

Long ago, in a village called **Pindup**, there were some *masalais* [**East Sepik** Province]. At this time, the people still did not have real sago. They only ate wild sago, yams (*yam* and *mami*), taros, and *gamak*.

One time, a married couple went directly towards the Sepik River, carrying sago seedlings. They planted the sago seedlings, and then returned. They planted and planted until they came towards Pindup. When they were almost at Pindup, they sang and danced together.

A *masalai* of Pindup heard a very loud noise and wanted to see what was causing it. Oh my, the two people were not quietly singing and planting the sago. The *masalai* spoke, "You can't just take that junky sago and plant it here. Its leaves are very noisy, and it will taste bland. It's truly worthless sago, it's not good to plant it here. This is a place for taros, yams, *gamak*, and sugarcanes. Sago can't be planted here."

Then the *masalai* said, "Carry that worthless sago and go." After the *masalai* said this, the two people did not continue to work. They ran back, breaking stones with their legs.

These footprints are still there. My people often drink water at this place. The two people carried all of the sago seedlings back and they planted them on the Ramu and Sepik rivers.

So now, my people do not have much sago. Only on the Ramu and Sepik rivers is there much sago.

Martin Mugumat
C. M. [Congregation of the Mission] Josephstaal
Madang Province

A901. Topographical features caused by experiences of primitive hero (demigod, deity); A2681+. Origin of sago; F490+. Masalai; P210. Husband and wife; R220. Flights

## Why Is There a Red Pond?

(Wantok 210, March 18, 1978, pages 13-14)

A long time ago, in the time of the ancestors, in the area near **Erap**, there were two villages [**Munkip, Numangang, Sauk, Gusan, Finungwa, Nimi** or **Urii** People, **Madang** Province]. One village was small and high up, and the other was big and down below. When the people of these two villages all went to their gardens, there was a *masalai* snake that turned into a small boy and played with the other little boys of the villages. In the evening, the little boy would return home, turn back into a python and go to sleep.

When the adults went back the gardens, the *masalai* snake already would have turned into a little boy and be coming to play with the little boys in the villages. The *masalai* snake did this many times.

There was an old woman who lived with her grandchildren. One day while her grandchildren were playing, the *masalai* python turned into a little boy and went inside to play with them. The grandmother saw that there was another face, and she thought, "This boy, whose child is that?" She looked at him, and then she looked harder.

In the evening, the old woman did not see this boy. She looked but she only saw her grandchildren. This was the first time that she had seen him, so she spoke unclearly to the big men that she had seen him and lost him.

Another day, the *masalai* snake returned and played with the little boys again. The old woman saw him and said, "Hey you there. You tricked me. Now I know about you." In the evening, the adults returned from the gardens and she told them, "When all of you go to the gardens, a *masalai* python often comes to play with your children." After the old woman said this, the adults were truly irate.

One day, they decided to kill the *masalai*. The old woman stopped them and said, "Don't kill it. Let it be. It's the same as my ancestor."

However, the men did not believe what she said. They told the old woman, "You're a bloody old worthless woman. You leave it alone. What will you do about it?" The old woman just cried.

They decided to prepare food, edible greens, and firewood, and to clean the pots. After they finished the preparations, one of them sharpened his stone axe. He sharpened it until it was very sharp. Then he tried to cut a rope, and he cut it in one attempt.

After they finished all of the preparations, they called the python to come eat with them. The snake did not know that they wanted to kill him. The poor old woman and one of her grandchildren were crying and crying. When they left, their explanations finished. The man who had sharpened the axe put a tree branch on the path that the snake had to cross. The *masalai* snake did not know about this. The snake just came and put his head on the branch, then the man put his axe down and cut the snake's neck.

After they killed the snake, they cut him into little pieces and cooked him with food in a can. When the water boiled, the snake's head did not die. It was still moving its eyes. The poor old woman [and] her grandchild took the snake's belly. She took the belly to the stream and removed the guts. The water was dirty and she told the men, "Men, this water is too dirty." Some women told her, "The pigs dug the earth at the headwaters, so the stream is dirty."

However, the old woman and her grandchild were through. They did not want to eat what had been cooked. It was becoming dark, then the python came and spoke to two old women and their grandchildren, "You two can't sleep here. Wait for me." Everyone who ate appeared at the village. The snake sent the two of them to a small mountain to stay and watch. While they were watching, a big lake arose and killed the people from these two villages.

If you go to this area near Erap and look, there is a small place with a pond that marks the place where the snake ruined the villages. Inside the pond, it is pitch black. In the second place where they killed *masalai* snake, there is a red pond because of the snake's blood. If you go to this place and look, you will see some short snakes without heads.

Now there are two ponds, they call these ponds *Guankaya*. In our language, this means "Fighting ponds."

Boni Nangudang
Popondetta
Oro Province

A920.1.0.1. Origin of particular lake; A1018. Flood as punishment; A1022. Escape from deluge on mountain; A1617. Origin of place-name; B15.1.1+. Headless snake; B91.6. Serpent causes flood; B211.6.1. Speaking snake (serpent); D191B. Transformation: boy to serpent (snake); B211.6.1. Speaking snake (serpent); D391B. Transformation: serpent (snake) to boy; E783. Vital head; F401.3.8. Spirits in form of snake; F490+. Masalai; F401.6. Spirit in human form; J652. Inattention to warnings; J1050. Attention to warnings; K914. Murder from ambush; P292.1. Grandmother as foster mother; Q211.6. Killing an animal revenged; Q428. Punishment: drowning; S139.4. Murder by mangling with axe

## Why the Eagle Is Finely Adorned!
(Wantok 211, March 25, 1978, pages 9, 12)

Once there was a man who lived on a mountain named Kemanemanda. This man had a kind of bird called *kambi* [*kámbi* (Lang, 1973: 33)], or eagle. The eagle and the man were good friends and lived on Mount Kemanemanda.

The other men lived near the mountain and liked them. The eagle flew to other places and brought good things to help his man. He often brought bark for loincloths, bracelets, bellies or *matapu* [*Matápu* means "belt" (Lang, 1973: 67).], *kina* shells, *gam* shells, stone axes, and hand drums. This eagle flew to all of the other places and brought these good things back to his man. The man truly liked this eagle.

One day, the eagle flew to a place and saw people singing and dancing. Quickly, the eagle returned home and told his man, "I saw something over there."

The man asked the eagle, "What did you see?"

The eagle replied, "I said, 'I saw people singing, dancing and jumping.' Do you want to go sing and dance there or not?"

The man said, "Yes, I want to go sing and dance."

After the man replied, the eagle was very happy for the man and dressed him nicely. The eagle went to get *tanget* leaves and a tree leaf that the Enga People use for decoration called _maryoko_.

After the eagle finished, it looked at the man and was very happy. The eagle called the man's name, Pandaiakali Lela. The eagle liked Pandaikali [Pandaiakali] Lela, so the eagle told him, "Don't be afraid or worry. Look at me when I fly away. When I fly, you should follow me to the dance."

Wow, Pandaiakali Lela was dressed better than the other men were dressed. This eagle flew slowly to the place where the men had been singing and dancing.

The bird flew above the dance. The people beat their hand drums, sang, danced and watched the eagle. Then they saw a finely dressed man approaching from behind. The people saw this man, Pandaiakali Lela, who was dressed better than any other person was dressed. The women held their breasts and milk came out of them. They trembled for this man and said, "I want to sing and dance with him."

The young women fought among themselves because this man was not the same as the other men. He was better than all of the other men and women were. He sang and danced, then the eagle returned home and prepared food for this man. When the food was ready, the eagle returned to the dance grounds. The eagle flew slowly and came to rest on his man's head. The people saw this and were happy. They got up and flew around, singing and dancing.

It was evening, and the eagle saw two women who were holding tightly onto Pandaiakali Lela. The eagle told the women, "Why are you two holding so tightly onto my brother? Look, there's no woman that takes care of this man. I alone take care of him. Let go of him. The two of us want to go home."

The two women did not want to heed what the eagle said, so the eagle shoved its talons at the two women. The two women were afraid and left the eagle's brother. The eagle took his brother, and the two of them flew home. One of the women cut her hand [a sign of mourning, probably meaning cutting off a finger] and the other pulled her ear [another sign of mourning]. They cried and cried on the dance grounds.

One day, the eagle flew to a garden. The eagle saw five women who were pulling out sweet potatoes. The ea-gle approached them. They thought that the eagle was coming to kill them, but the eagle approached slowly. They walked around, but the eagle continued to follow. They continued walking.

Four women became exhausted and gave up. Only one woman continued. The eagle [pulled back] the women. Then the eagle took one woman to the house and gave her to Pandaiakali. This man liked the woman very much that the eagle had brought. He called her Litin Puim.

Pandaiakali and Litin Puim married. The eagle still called their names. They were good friends, living on Mount Kemanemanda. The man and the eagle often went to the forest to hunt marsupials (*kapul*). They would bring them back home to cook in an earth oven and eat.

One day, the man went alone into the forest, he walked three miles. The woman and the eagle stayed home. The woman told the eagle, "Go find your brother."

The eagle replied, "I don't want to. He'll be able to return home. Don't worry so much."

This made the woman angry, so she pointed at the eagle with a kind of stick that is used by women to dig sweet potatoes. The eagle trembled and trembled, and cried and cried.

The man returned home, and the eagle told about what the woman had done to him. The man listened to this story and saw the eagle crying. The man beat the woman very badly.

The eagle told the woman, "Every bird can hear the speech of men, women and children. But you angered me, so I'll tell the other birds. There was no other man who took you here to marry Pandaiakali Lela. It was I who took you here, but you argued with me too much, so I shall tell the other birds. They too will be afraid of you people. I too am afraid of you. I'll give one of my feathers to your husband. He can put it on when he sings and dances, and during the time of _moka_. [*Moka* is a Hagen exchange system, whereas _tée_, is an Enga exchange system (Lang, 1973: 102, Feil, 1984: 1).]

This eagle's feather, we **Enga** [People] put on during the times of dances and of _moka_. So, the eagle departed and became feral in the forest. Today, no kind of bird listens to what people say. They are all afraid. The eagle forbade it, so all of the little birds listened to what the eagle had said. Now they know about us men and women. Because of this, the birds are afraid of us.

Thomas P. Tum

C. M. [Congregation of Mission] **Tsak**, Pumakos
**Enga** Province

A1465.3+. Origin of eagle feather decoration; A2494.13+. Enmity between birds and people; B211.3.11K. Speaking eagle; B212. Animal understands human speech; B455.3. Helpful eagle; B552. Man carried by bird; P210. Husband and wife; P310. Friendship; P681+. Mourning customs: self-mutilation; Q458. Flogging as punishment; R13.3.2. Eagle carries off youth; S160.1. Self-mutilation; T10. Falling in love; T192. Marriage by force

## Why the Dog Does Not Talk

(Wantok 212, April 1, 1978, page 9)

Long ago, dogs talked. But now, they do not. Why is it that they do not talk? What is the origin of speech? OK, this is how the story goes.

Long ago, men and women did wrong and stole something from a man. Oh my! The man did not know who had stolen from him, but there was a man who slept and watched. His name was Dog. In my language, this is *Koluwi*. It was Dog who often spoke out about every little thing that men did.

One day, a man had had sex with a woman. The woman's parents did not know who had done this. Dog alone had seen this and spoken out. The man was truly irate and said, "Oh, is that so? The dogs see something and talk about it every time."

The man went into the forest to get some thin pieces of rattan. He returned, took the dogs and sewed their mouths. The poor dogs could not speak any longer.

So now you see that dogs have long hair on their snouts and they can no longer talk.

John Wisit

**Torembi** (Number 1) [Village, **Sawos** People]
**East Sepik** Province
A2335.4.3+. Why dogs have whiskers on snouts; A2422.1. Why dog lost his power of speech; B211.1.7. Speaking dog; B290+. Dog as tattler/gossip; K420. Thief loses his goods or is detected; Q393.2. Gossiping punished; Q451.12. Lips sewed together as punishment for slander

## Probably Just the Phantom

(Wantok 213, April 8, 1978, page 11)

Long ago, before the white people had come to Papua New Guinea (PNG), there was a single white man named Magruai. He had gone to every place in PNG. He often listened to the local languages from every place in PNG. He often went to the Chimbu [Simbu] area. He helped them fight, and helped them with other things.

However, he often felt mixed up inside himself, so he went to Mount Hagen. Magruai often ate many forest foods. His wanderings also took him to Daru [Western Province], to the edge of Papua, and all of the places where white people lived. The white people killed this man, Magruai.

So, we Papua New Guineans have suffered a true loss. The white people killed Magruai and took his power from PNG. Now, there are many white people who come to PNG and give examples and knowledge to the people.

If Papua New Guineans had killed Magruai, we would have had power and we would have gone to the places where the white people live.

Joseph Dua Jerry
**Bendam** [Village, **Kuman** People]
Gembogl
Chimbu [**Simbu** Province]

[Note: The motif "cargo cult" is listed below not because this story implies that there was one at Bendam necessarily, but rather because the ideas in this story are similar to those expressed elsewhere in PNG in relation to cargo cult formation. For example, see Berndt (1992: 74-75) for an example from the Eastern Highlands Province.]

A536. Demigods fight as allies of mortals; D1720+. Magic obtained by killing; D1740. Loss of magic power; D2121. Magic journey; F527.7K+. White person; S110. Murders; V450+. Cargo cult

## The Southern Cross

(Wantok 214, April 15, 1978, page 13)

Long ago, in a place called Mount Bi, there was a woman and a man. After a while, they had two children named Gemo and Marua.

They continued to live there, then one time they did not have any good food left at home. So, the woman said to her husband, "We don't have food in the house, we should go to the forest to find some food."

Her husband said, "Get your machete and net bag, then we'll go." When they were ready to go, they told their children, "We don't have food at home, so the two of us are going to find some food in the forest. You two must close the door tightly and just stay inside the house. You can't go outside."

Although they said this, the boy, Gemo, did not want to do this. So, the two of them walked over a mountain. Gemo took his little sister, Marua, and carried her off into the deep ocean.

Later, their parents returned from the forest. They looked at the house and saw that the two children were not there. They left the food at the house, then followed their children's trail into the sea. They followed and followed, swimming and swimming. Then they found the two children.

Gemo and Marua were quite happy to be with their parents.

The waves and wind became strong, then Gemo, Marua and their parents died.

Something bad came and turned them into lights. Four lights arose from the sea and went up into the sky. Now, they are always there in the sky. If you look up in the sky at night, you will see four bright stars in the South. These are Gemo, Marua and their parents. We see these every night, they are called the Southern Cross.

Ludwig S. Dolmbi Onguglo
Port Moresby
National Capital District

[Mr. Onguglo wrote the Ancestor Stories in Wantok #239 and 317. So, this story probably comes from **Dunuabanma**, **Kalam** People?, **Madang** Province?]

A771.1. Origin of the Southern Cross; D293B. Transformation: boy to star; D293G. Transformation: girl to star; D293M. Transformation: man to star; D293W. Transformation: woman to star; P210. Husband and wife; P231. Mother and son; P232. Mother and daughter; P233. Father and son; P234. Father and daughter; P253. Sister and brother; R260. Pursuits; W126. Disobedience


# Cucumbers Growing
(Wantok 215, April 22, 1978, page 15)

Long ago, there were two boys and a mother and father. The mother and father died and they buried the father's body far from the house. They buried the mother's body beneath their house. They put nothing [else] underneath the house. The poor boys did not have food to eat.

There were no other people where the boys lived, it was just the two of them. Oh my, they were hungry! They waited for their mother's body to rot first. They wanted to go to another place, but they waited for their mother. Their mother rotted, but they saw that her head did not rot.

After a while, the first brother looked at his mother's head. He looked carefully and he saw a little thing coming out from inside his mother's head. Quickly, he told his brother, then two of them looked.

Some days later, they went there. Something big was growing. Another time they went to looked again and saw a cucumber plant (called *kimit* in my language). So, they stayed and watched the cucumber. Soon, it was bearing fruit. The two of them decided not to eat the first cucumber that the vine was bearing. They waited and they were starving to death. They wanted to cut the first cucumber.

The first brother tried to cut it but it fell to the ground. He tried to get it, but it rolled away. They followed the cucumber. They wanted to quickly block the cucumber's path and grab it, but the cucumber tricked them. It kept rolling and came to a stream where the cucumber followed the water downwards. They wanted to grab the cucumber, but they were unable to do so.

They continued to follow it, but again the cucumber tricked them. They kept going for about 200 miles, then came to a waterfall. The first brother raced at 60 [kilometers] but he passed the water. So, the cucumber did not have a way out and it turned into an old woman. The brothers were furious and beat the old woman to death, breaking her into little pieces.

They left and went a short distance. The old woman got up and went looking for them again. They were irate and killed her again.

They broke her into very small pieces and put her flesh far away (about a mile). This old woman got up and looked for them yet again. They treated her the same, and this went on fifteen times.

The first brother had a good idea and found a long stone, about 2 [meters?] long. He told his brother, "Carry this stone and heat it up on one end. Then hold the other end that is not heated." He carried this stone, while the first brother waited for the old woman. When the old woman arrived, he asked her, "Are you hungry or not?" The old woman told the boy, "I'm very hungry." The boy told her, "Let's wait here for my brother who is bringing food."

Oh my, the old woman thought about the food and was happy. When the first brother saw his brother carrying the hot stone, he told the old woman, "Open your mouth and close your eyes, then I'll give you food." Oh my, the woman thought that she would be getting food, so she opened her mouth. The brothers put the hot stone into her mouth, killing her.

The brothers returned to the house and ate the cucumbers. They became intoxicated and fought for a long time, then they died.

Mr. Sakiba Sanameng
[Mr. Sanameng wrote the Ancestor Stories in *Wantok* #282 and 330. He is probably from the **Faiwol** People, **Western** Province.]

A2687.2+. Cucumber from head of ogre; D441.2+W. Transformation: cucumber to woman; D450+. Head of corpse grows into cucumber plant; D2121. Magic journey; E30. Resuscitation by arrangement of members; F810+. Traveling cucumber; K951.1. Murder by throwing hot stones in the mouth; P210. Husband and wife; P231. Mother and son; P233. Father and son; P251.5. Two brothers; R260. Pursuits; S122. Flogging to death;

S139.7. Murder by slicing person into small pieces; S112. Burning to death; S401. Unsuccessful attempts to kill person in successive reincarnations (transformations); V61.3+. Dead buried; Z71.16.11. Formulistic number: fifteen

# Water Came from the Stone

(Wantok 216, April 29, 1978, pages 9 and 13)

Long, long ago, there was a small village without water. This village is called Tipinini [**Tibinini** Village, **Ipili** People, **Enga** Province]. In this village, there lived a man named Lemeyan and a woman named Lakeyam. At this time, they did not have any children, it was just them who lived there.

Lemeyan worked at fetching water and cutting firewood. Lakeyam worked in the garden and husbanding a pig. Lameyan [Lemeyan] often fetched water from a place that Lakeyam did not know about. Lakeyam often thought, "There's no stream here, where does Lemeyan get the water from?"

One time when the sun was very bright and it was a beautiful day, Lemeyan and Lakeyam were near the entrance of their house. They sat and watched a bird flying towards them. The bird perched on a tree near their house entrance and dropped a pig's toenail. Lemeyan saw it fall to the ground and fetched it.

Lemeyan asked the bird, "Why did you carry this pig's toenail here and give it to us? Did you see a dead man coming, or a lost pig, or a man who killed a pig and sent a message for you to bring me? What's the real reason that you came?"

The bird turned around and said, "No." Lemeyan asked the bird again, "Did a clan make a big party and kill their pig, then send a message out to all the villages? Did they send you here to bring me, or what?" The bird heard this and lowered its head, then flew around the house. It lost a tail [feather] in front of Lemeyan, then flew away.

Lemeyan took this bird's tail [feather] and said to Lakeyam, "The bird explained it to us. I'll go to this party. You should stay at the house. Take care of your pig." Lakeyam said, "OK, but you must prepare the firewood and water for me before you go."

Lemeyan heeded Lakeyam, and he quickly cut the firewood, making a big pile by the house. Then he cut four long pieces of bamboo and went quickly to fill them with water at the place that he knew about. After he filled them, he placed them by the house. He sat for a little while and told Lakeyam, "Now I'll walk off. I'll sleep in the middle of the trail. Tomorrow, I'll continue walking and will arrive at the place of the party. I'll sleep there, then the next day they'll begin the party. I'll eat one day, then the next day I'll return along the trail. After six days, I shall come home."

Then he said to Lakeyam, "Don't drink the water too quickly. It's enough for five days. On the sixth morning, you should finish the water."

Lemeyan took his stone axe and his bow [and arrows]. He took his festive decorations, and carried them in his net bag. Then he walked until it was night, and he slept in the trail. The next day, he woke up in the early morning and cooked some food. After he ate, he continued walking until the late evening when he arrived at the village with the party. This village is called Lhiyama [**Leyalam** Village, **Enga** People].

There were many men from other villages. They came there and just slept together in men's house. Lemeyan slept with them too. The next day, all of the men woke up in the morning and lined up. The clansmen who made the party lined up many pigs. The other clans of men from other villages had come to see this.

The men who were giving the party divided the pigs: two pigs for each man from another village. They had come to see the party for this. After they finished dividing the pigs, they killed all of the big pigs. Lemeyan butchered one pig. A bird came and perched on top of his leg, and Lemeyan trembled slightly. He saw that this bird had a piece of *purpur* shrub and a sweet potato leaf with water on it. Lemeyan saw this and felt that he was done. The water had come and flooded his house and garden.

He told all of the men, "The water has ruined my garden and home, so I'm leaving. Stay here." He took his net bag and departed. He ran off and arrived at a mountain, from which he looked out. He saw that his home was white and blue, and he was terrified.

He hurried off, holding his rattan stick. He ran and ran, then arrived at the flooded area. He hit the water with his rattan stick and the water flew about. He did this repeatedly and he arrived at his house. He saw that his wife, Lakeyam, and her pig were not there. So, he climbed to the place where he used to fetch water. He saw the two of them on top of a mountain, and he saw them coming down.

He climbed up and said to Lakeyam, "Why did the water ruin the place?" Lakeyam told him, "I looked for the stream and followed the trail that you used to bring water. I came there and I prepared to fill the tube that you gave me with water. After I filled it, I tried to close it. But no, the water shot out all over very strongly and I lost it. Then the water ran and ran and there was water all over."

Lemeyan was irate and told Lakeyam, "You and the pig can sit on the mountain. I'm going down to fix the water again. I'm calling the name of the water. Much later, all men will know the water's name."

He called the names of the water, Kaiya and Komaiya. These are the two streams that come through Tipinini, even now. Also Lakeyam Stream comes out of stone. The woman Lakeyam and her pig live on Stone Mountain.

Joe Nandawa
Enga Province

A934.9. Stream unexpectedly bursts from side of mountain; A1022. Escape from deluge on mountain; A1111. Impounded water; A1617. Origin of place-name; B211.3. Speaking bird; B291.1. Bird as messenger; C615. Forbidden body of water; D1766.7. Magic results from uttering powerful name; P210. Husband and wife; Q325. Disobedience punished; W126. Disobedience

## Blowing the Flutes Caused a Flood

(Wantok 217, May 6, 1978, page 15)

Long ago, in **Torembi** Number One in the Ambunti sub-District of **East Sepik** Province, the ancestors had a spirit house called Sai [**Sawos** People]. Sai was a spirit house where the men of yore cut [scarified] the skin of uninitiated boys.

One time, they decorated this spirit house very nicely. At this time, everyone in Torembi went down to the pond in the **Korogo** area to catch fish [**Iatmul** People]. There was no other man or woman at this place, so they only left three men in the village, one of whom was mute.

Two men went on top of the spirit house and blew flutes. The poor mute man sat underneath the spirit house. Clouds thundered the wind blew, and the rain came, but the two men who blew the flutes continued.

The water began to rise up to the holes where the posts of the spirit house were. The poor mute man ran up and told the two others with his hands that the water had risen to the base of the posts of the spirit house.

However, they did not believe what the poor man had said, they just continued to blow their flutes. The water rose higher. The poor man ran up to talk to them again, but they did not pay attention to the mute man.

The water continued to rise. It covered the spirit house, so the three men were within the flood. Now this place is called Seleapankraku.

If you go to Torembi Number One and ask about this place, they will show you. If you go to this place Seleapankraku at night, you will hear two men blowing flutes in this area that was flooded.

You cannot go near there. If you go near there, the big spirit house will defeat you. Only the men of this area are able to go there. This area is between **Yamok** Village [Sawos People] and Torembi Number One Village.

Tobias Anggan
Vanimo
West Sepik Province

A920.1.0.1. Origin of particular lake; A1011. Local deluges; C615. Forbidden body of water; D1223.1. Magic flute; D2142.1. Wind produced by magic; D2143.1. Rain produced by magic; D2149.1. Thunderbolt magically produced; D2151.8. Magic flood; E402.4. Sound of ethereal music; P600+. Initiation of boys: scarification; V112.1. Spirit huts

## How Did People Originate?

(Wantok 218, May 13, 1978, page 15)

Long, long ago, there were no people anywhere on earth. There were only three people who lived in the middle of the earth. In the middle of all of the land was the sea. There was also a long [mountain] that was completely filled with all kinds of animals, large and small.

These three people were women. The mother was an old woman, her first daughter was a big woman, and her little daughter was a young woman. One time, the old woman and her two daughters went up the long mountain. They stood on top of the mountain and looked at all of the earth. However, they did not see any people on the other side. The old woman thought that when they returned to their home, she would study her thoughts about wanting to make people and sending them to all of the other places on earth.

When the old woman finished thinking, she thought, "If I burn them, I'll kill my two children. Their ashes would make many people arise in all of the places of the earth, then I myself would be their great ancestor." The three of them went to the center of the earth and made a trap for all of the kinds of wild game.

When they made traps, they did not just make an ordinary trap for pigs, nor did they just make it for the size of pigs. They thought of cattle, birds, snakes, and every kind of wild game, and then they made different sized traps for them.

The old woman said, "If the cassowary's trap or the pig's trap shuts, or if the snake's trap or the bird's trap shuts, it would be bad. If the animals go directly to their traps, we'll not be able to bring forth people all over the earth." They finished the traps and they slept. The next morning, they went to look at their traps. They saw that the pig's trap had shut. All kinds of wild game had gone directly into the traps. The three women were happy together and carried the animals back to their home.

The mother made a round house and closed it tightly with strong fences. When the house was finished, she put the two children with the net bag of game inside this house. She gave an order to the children to eat all of the game. Then she closed the door of the round house very tightly. The mother left them and went to live far away from these places.

The first sister looked after the bag of game and ate them. When the mother came to check on them, the big sister said, "We're still eating." However, she was lying, the little sister had not eaten. The little sister was very hungry. The second time that the mother came to check on them, the second sister said, "We finished eating all of the game. Now we're starting to eat the net bag."

The old woman heard this and started to burn the round house. She made a fire on four sides. The old woman burned her two children inside the round house, then she went far away to the other side of the sea. She lived in the middle of the earth. She lived there for some days, then returned again to see the frogs turning into people. She was their ancestor now, but these descendants began to fight among themselves. Because of the ashes of the sister who had not eaten the game, two groups of siblings were beginning to fight. The old woman saw this and returned home. She thought again, and she wanted to give a name to each group of people, and give them each a style of dress. The old woman studied and thought, then she returned to see her groups of descendants threatening each other with bows and arrows. They were severely punishing each other in battle. The origin of this anger was the group that had come from the little sister who had not eaten the game. The group that had come from the little sister was fighting with the group from the big sister.

The old woman saw this and returned to her home. She began to make bark loincloths, "grass" skirts, knives and axes. [She] thought of the people who live by the sea who would make canoes, those who live who live in the forest who just exist, and the white people who would make ships, cars, and airplanes. The old woman finished thinking and took all of this cargo, then sent it to each of all of the peoples on the earth.

When the old woman returned, the descendants were not there. They had voyaged upon the sea. The old woman stood up and called out. They replied, calling out from the other sides of the water. She called out again to them. They called out again to her sides. This is because when she had made a fire at the round house, she made a fire on four sides. So, the descendants called out from four sides.

Along the sea, there was a big tree in the ground that had a hole in it. The old woman's descendants went inside the hole and the old woman found them. The old woman took an axe and first cut the sides of the native people. Then she pulled them out from the tree hole. She gave names to the groups of people and divided them up. She gave styles of dress to each group. She shot them [out?] and put them in all of the places on the earth.

After she divided all of the natives, she cut the old tree again and pulled all of the white people out of the tree hole that the axe had made. The old woman divided them and gave them their style of dress. She took a scrap of wood that had fallen from the tree when she had cut it and gave it to them. She put them on top of the water and sent them across the water, saying, "You can use this piece of wood from the axe on the sea. When you want to see another person of your group, you will sit on this tree and it will take you to see other people on the other side of the sea." Then they departed.

The sea took them to a shore where they lived. These three people are our three ancestors.

When I was a small boy, I lived in my village. My grandfather told me this ancestor story. His name is Hapo, from **Wantini** Village, Upper Watut River [**Hamtai** People, **Morobe** Province].

My ancestor told me, "When you are big, you can go to different places and see people who speak different languages. They have round houses in these places. The men who live by the sea have _yempa_ (meaning ship), boats and canoes. Now they speak all over the earth that they'll still fight. Brothers will still fight. You'll see." He told this to me, so now if we look at all of the places of the earth, there are many round houses and ships on the sea. And brother still fights with brother all over the earth.


James Hamigau
Henganofi
Eastern Highlands Province


A1268+. People created from ashes of two daughters of primeval woman; A1440+. Primeval person distributed crafts to all tribes; A1599.11.1. Origin of war; A1620+. Tribes distributed in ashes of primeval ancestor's daughter's ashes; A1620+. Tribes distributed by primeval ancestor; D395. Transformation: frog to person; F527.7K+. White person; K812. Victim burned in his own house (or hiding place); P232. Mother and daughter; P252.1. Two sisters; Q325. Disobedience punished; S12.2+. Cruel mother kills daughter; S112.0.2. House (hostel) burned with all inside; W31. Obedience; W126. Disobedience

## Where Did Murderous Sorcery Come From?

(Wantok 219, May 20, 1978, pages 19-20)

Long, long ago, there were many, many men. But no man knew how to kill another. Men died in their own time, so the village was filled with people.

Near the village was a worthless man who was just a lizard. The lizard lived on a big tree near the stream from where the women obtained water. The lizard also had a hiding place on the top of tree.

This tree had a vine that climbed up it. The vine had made a big pile of fruits. The fruits were like round pots, and the lizard always slept in these pots.

When the women wanted to fetch water at the place where the lizard lived, the lizard slowly killed them, one-by-one. When the women went to this place, they died. This place was a cemetery.

The men of the village did not understand the reason for these women's deaths. They did not know that the lizard lived near the stream and killed the women. Every man was going crazy because of this.

One time, a young boy shared his thoughts and said, "I always see women going to fetch water at that place." So one day, a woman went to the stream, while the young boy hid and followed the woman. When the woman was about to fill her container with water, the lizard quickly ran down the tree and put a death spell upon this woman.

The young boy saw the lizard and quickly ran to the village. He said, "I saw something kill one of us. It was a lizard. Oh my, the lizard was not boy-sized, it was huge and had two heads and tongues." The men of the village listened to this and prepared their spears, bows and other things for killing this lizard. One day, they told an old woman, "Go down to the stream and we'll follow you." The old woman took some bamboo tubes and put them in her net bag, then she went down to fill them up with water.

The men were prepared to kill the lizard. When the lizard saw the woman, he came and held tightly onto her. He wanted to kill the old woman, but the men surrounded this sorcerer [lizard] and shot him with their spears. When they were ready to kill the lizard, he told them, "Hey! Wait, don't kill me quickly. I have a marvelous thing to tell you."

So, they waited and the lizard explained about the methods of murderous sorcery, other kinds of sorcery, and love spells to the leader men of the village. This was truly something new and they were very happy to get these secrets from the lizard. After the lizard told the entire story of murderous sorcery, they killed him. So, this is the origin of sorcery and evil [!] love spells, it was a lizard that originated them.

All parts of the earth have various kinds of evil things to ruin men. So too, Papua New Guinea is the true origin of sorcery and other evil things that ruin people. This is something that the ancestors began and continues until today.

Joe Arovong

Madang

Madang Province

A1336. Origin of murder; A1459.3. Acquisition of sorcery; B15.1.2.1+. Two-headed lizard; B191.7+. Lizard as magician; B211.6.2K. Speaking lizard; D2061. Magic murder; G354.3. Lizard as ogre; G346. Devastating monster; G512. Ogre killed; K914. Murder from ambush; P160. Beggars; Q211. Murder punished; Q411. Death as punishment; S110. Murders

## The Boy Who Conquered the *Masalai*

(Wantok 220, May 27, 1978, page 18)

In a village called Waragan [**Warekam**], there were many people [**Mikarew** People, **Madang** Province]. A *masalai* went to this place, and each time the *masalai* would eat one of the people. This went on for a while, until the people were nearly gone. The *masalai* had done this in the forest where there was a mountain, so the remaining people left this village and wanted to go to the beach. They followed a trail that crossed over a big mountain. One poor woman was pregnant. The woman thought, "Never mind this. I'm finished on the earth." So she went back to the village that they had left.

It was close to the time when she would give birth. She saw a cave and went inside to look for a good place. Then she went out to get firewood and something to eat. She went inside again and made a bonfire. Then she went out and saw the smoke rising high. She went back in again and gave birth to a boy.

She was ecstatic and she took care of the boy, who grew bigger. The mother made a toy bow and gave it to the boy.

The poor little boy became bigger. Some men had lost their bow. He took the bow and shot marsupials (*kapul*) and various kinds of birds. His mother said, "Don't go far from the mountain. Before, there was a *masalai* who killed and ate many people. The people became fearful and went to the beach. I was one of those people. I was pregnant with you and was nearly ready to give birth when I left them."

The mother told all of the stories that she had been told, but the boy did not think any more of this. He went out and made a big house in a clearing. He fenced his house with three fences. Then he made a bow and sharpened some arrows until they were very sharp. Then he brought his mother inside his nice house.

The youth made fire with much smoke to attract *masalai*s that he could kill. They saw the smoke and came. So they fought and fought. The man was strong and he killed them. The second group came, and then the third. He killed off these *masalai*s too. The mother was ecstatic and congratulated him. Then she sent a message to the beach. The men came and the mother told them the story. They were all very happy and congratulated the youth. They carried him and sang and danced.

They gave him pork, spears and other things. Later they gave a beautiful and fine woman to him. They lived well for a long time. Now they lived in the place called Waragan Village.

Wavem Dingor

Heldsbach

Finschhafen

Madang Province

F490+. Masalai; G346. Devastating monster; G510.4+. Hero overcomes devastating ogre; G512.1+. Ogre killed with spear/arrow; P210. Husband and wife; P231. Mother and son; R213. Escape from home; R315. Cave as refuge; S110. Murders; T570. Pregnancy; T580. Childbirth; Z71.1. Formulistic number: three

## Two Kinds of Marsupial (*Kapul*)

(Wantok 221, June 3, 1978, page 15)

Long ago, there were two marsupials (*kapul*). Their names were Pore and Pesalo. Pore had a long nose and black fur. Pore had many thorns [quills?] in its hair.

Pesalo was fairly long and had a short, plump nose. Pesalo ate tree leaves all day long. Pore ate ants all day long [probably an echidna, not a *kapul*, *Tachyglossus aculeatus* (Flannery, 1995a: 66-73)].

One time, when they were telling stories, Pesalo hid its tail in a hole then said, "Pore, I cut my tail. You still have a long tail, why is that?" Pore said angrily to Pesalo, "Why didn't you tell me?"

So, Pore took a machete and cut its tail off. Pesalo got up and took its tail from the hole then said, "I lied to you. I still have my tail."

Pore yelled at Pesalo, "Why did you anger me, huh? It's too bad that the men will not be able to catch me quickly. But you, they can kill you quickly because you live on the tree branch and the dogs can find and kill you quickly. I don't have this problem. I live inside a hole in the ground and it is very hard for them to catch me."

It was true that it was hard work for them to catch this kind of marsupial, *pore*. But men, and dogs too, do not have trouble killing *pesalo*.

If Pesalo had not tricked Pore, they would be two good friends. Then we would be able to see, hunt and quickly kill both of them. However, now it is hard work for us to kill the one kind.

Dominik Moka

**Angoram** [Village, **Angoram** People]

**East Sepik** Province

A2284. Origin of animal characteristics: animal persuaded into self-injury; A2378.2+. Why a kind of marsupial has no tail; B211.2.12K+. Speaking marsupial; K1065+. Marsupial persuaded into cutting off its tail; W157. Dishonesty

## Where Did Mother Come From?

(Wantok 222, June 10, 1978, page 15)

Long ago, two brothers lived in a village in the **Mendi** [People's] area of **Southern Highlands** [Province].

One of them was a farmer and the other was a hunter. Their garden was very big and was filled with various kinds of foods.

One day, they were working in the garden. The farmer told his brother, "I think that we don't have any meat now, it would be good to hunt for some game tomorrow."

They prepared their food: they cut some edible greens, and they dug up some taros and sweet potatoes. They cut some wild sugarcanes (*pitpit*), firewood, and tea leaves. They finished cooking in their earth oven, then they prepared their multi-pronged spears, arrows, axes, bows, *tanget*, and some ragged bark loincloths. After these things were ready, they removed the food from their earth oven and divided the food up. They divided everything between them.

The next day, the hunter put on his *tanget* and his ragged loincloth, then he held his hunting gear. He began to walk into the forest. He walked and sprang up a mountain, arriving at the other side of yet another mountain. At this place, there was a trap that was full of marsupials (*kapul*).

He killed many marsupials and carried them in a net bag. He walked and went fairly far, then arrived at a fallen tree. He turned and looked. Oh my, the ground was soft and very soggy at this tree.

He thought and thought, "What is this? I think I'll look, then return home."

He went underneath the tree. He did not let any part of his body show from under the tree, not even a little. He was not there very long when, oh my, the tree moved and shook. He shouted. He made a trap at this place and slept there. The next day, he sat and sat at this place.

Singing women came and they just jumped over this trap. The man saw a bad eye, a bad leg and a good one. It was bad that he had his hands full and could not spring the trap. One of the women saw him, and the others ran away. The man got up to look, but he did not see which trail they had taken. The man thought and thought, "What should I do? I think it would be better if I just laid the trap."

The man carried his net bag of marsupials and walked back home. When he arrived home, his brother was happy that he had returned. He was happy for the meat too.

However, he did not tell about what he had seen. Another day, he went back to the place where he had been before. He did as he had done before. The young women came singing, and the very last woman was very young and beautiful. They saw him again and ran away. But this time, he worked his trap. The last, beautiful woman came and became hung up on the trap. The boy [man] got up and held her tightly.

The woman turned to stone, but the boy held her tightly. She worked at turning herself into something else, but the boy still held tightly. So the woman said, "The two of us can go to your home." The two of them had a big family. All of my people are children from just these two people.

Samuel Sengi
Erave
Southern Highlands Province

D231W. Transformation: woman to stone; D610. Repeated transformation; P210. Husband and wife; P251.5. Two brothers; R4. Surprise capture; R220. Flights; T192. Marriage by force

## Hagen and Wabag Are Brothers

(Wantok 223, June 17, 1978, page 13)

Long ago, there were no men. There was one man who lived between Hagen and Wabag. He was completely alone. He lived there and was fed up. He wanted to go into the forest, so he took some food and departed.

He traveled and entered the deep forest. He looked around and he saw a young woman. He very quietly went towards her. Then he approached her and held her. The woman turned into water, but he held tightly.

The woman turned into a tree, but the man still held tightly. The woman turned into dirt, but the man still held tightly. The two of them did this for some time. The man was not afraid, he kept looking and holding tightly.

Then the woman became a real woman again. The woman said, "I'm tired of this. You and I can go to your home." The man was happier than ever. He took the woman to his home and they lived there a long time. The woman gave birth to a boy, and the two of them called the boy Hagen.

Hagen grew up, and the mother gave birth to another boy. The parents called this boy Wabag, and Wabag grew up.

The father and mother died, and the two children continued living. They grew to adulthood. Hagen said, "I'm going down. Wabag, you go up." So Hagen went down and lived below. Wabag went up and lived above.

Hagen had one kind of language and Wabag had another. So now, people of Hagen speak a different language than those of Wabag do.

Now, we speak different languages in **Hagen** [People] and Wabag [Town, **Enga** People]. This is true in every part of Papua New Guinea, there is a different language, just like Hagen and Wabag.

John Jongapen
**Par**, Wabag
**Enga** Province

A1270. Primeval human pair; A1333. Confusion of tongues; A1611+. Origin of Enga People; A1611+. Origin of Hagen People; A1616+. Origin of Enga language; A1616+. Origin of Hagen language; D215W. Transformation: woman to tree; D283W. Transformation: woman to water; D287+W. Transformation: woman to dirt; D610. Repeated transformation; P210. Husband and wife; P231. Mother and son; P233. Father and son; P251.5. Two brothers; T192. Marriage by force; T580. Childbirth

## Where Did the Bird of Paradise Come From?

(Wantok 224, June 24, 1978, page 11)

This ancestor story won the second prize from the big contest held at the National Museum of Papua New Guinea. The contest was held to find different stories about PNG's national bird, the bird of paradise.

The author, Daniel Kita Pari, is from **Amboin** in the upper Sepik River area, near the place where the mountains of Enga [Central Range] meet the Sepik River [**Karawari** People, **East Sepik** Province].

Long ago, there were no birds of paradise in my people's forest, nor were there the kinds of calls that birds of paradise make now. There lived a married couple with two children, a boy and a big girl. The parents died and there were just the two children.

The girl thought and thought, "I think that I should marry now. It would be easier for the two of us. With a husband, I could take care of my little brother." So she married. The man that she married was a very good man. He always took care of his brother-in-law. But the sister was often angry with her little brother.

One time, the woman and her little brother went into the forest to drain a small stream to catch fish. They caught many fish. The little brother was hungry and took some fish to cook. The sister saw this, so she took a huge pile of sticks and beat her little brother badly.

She tried to grab his neck and break it, but he hid his neck too quickly. He cried and cried, then went into the forest, greatly in pain. He found a place with various kinds of colored earth: yellow, red, brown and black.

He sat and cried. Immediately he thought of something. He took a little red earth and some black and yellow earth, then rubbed his skin. He took the brown earth and rubbed his two hands with it. He took a little black earth and put it around his two eyes.

Then he found a place with some sunshine. He sat on a log that was once a huge tree. While he sat there, his eyes spun around and he collapsed. At the same time that he collapsed, he turned into what we now a call a bird of paradise. He stayed there for some time on the ground. A little rain came down and washed his head. He was surprised and flew up to a tree branch, then called out.

The sister heard this call and thought hard, "[I should] chase after my little brother who went into the forest." So, she began to look for him. She arrived at the place where he painted his skin and became a bird of paradise. The bird of paradise began to call out again. The woman saw him sitting on a tree branch. She thought and thought, then asked him, "Are you my little brother?"

He called out stronger. The sister cried out loudly. She shouted to him, "Never mind that, come down here."

But he flew to another tree. He made the sister more worried and she cried harder. She went back to the place where they had caught the fish. She took all of the fish and threw them away. She cried and returned home.

Her husband asked her what happened, and she told him about what had happened in the forest. Her husband was angry with her and beat her badly until she was half-dead. This was because the man liked his brother-in-law very much. He went to the spirit house and quickly explained to the men, "If you hear a different kind of call from a forest bird that has yellow coloring like the *purpur* shrub, do not kill it. I will kill the man that shoots this bird."

So they asked him, "Did you make this happen?"

He told them, "No. It was my little brother-in-law, he went with my sister."

Then he told them about the story of how he had turned into a bird. After they listened to him, they went to the other houses and warned the women and children.

They made an important law against shooting birds of paradise, which if broken would result in death. They began to shoot some, but only in secret. When they shot them, they were very worried and cried. So now, in my village, we usually do not shoot birds of paradise without a good reason. When we want to sing and dance, we shoot one. Regarding selling them, we often think of them as men. Why would we sell [a man] and take money? If you want to give one to a friend, you must give it without recompense. You must not get something in return.

Daniel Kita Pari
Amboin [Village]
East Sepik Province

A1970+. Creation of bird of paradise; C92.1.6+. Tabu: killing bird of paradise; D150+M. Transformation: man to bird of paradise; D560+. Transformation by application of paint; D671. Transformation flight; P210. Husband and wife; P231. Mother and son; P232. Mother and daughter; P233. Father and son; P234. Father and daughter; P253. Sister and brother; P263. Brother-in-law; Q212. Theft punished; Q285. Cruelty punished; Q458. Flogging as punishment; R220. Flights; S70+. Cruel sister; T100. Marriage; V112.1. Spirit huts

## The Man Who Came from a Blood Egg
(Wantok 225, July 1, 1978, page 15)

Long, long ago, in **Sara** Village, there was a young unmarried woman [**Boiken** People, **East Sepik** Province]. One day, she took her knife and went into the forest to cut some wild sugarcanes (*pitpit*) to use to fence her garden. While she was cutting the wild sugarcanes, she slipped and cut her hand.

After she cut her hand, she took a coconut shell and let the blood go into the shell [probably to prevent the blood from being ensorcelled]. After the blood stopped, she cut a wild taro leaf, covered up [the wound] and went home.

When she returned in the morning, she found that the blood had changed into a round egg. The woman saw this and put the coconut shell with the egg in her house.

The egg broke on the third day and the woman found that a boy had come out of the egg. The woman was ecstatic. She took the child and looked after him. The boy became big and very tall. He liked to travel to other places by jumping on one leg with the other folded up.

One day, the boy left his mother and went to a stream. When he arrived at the stream, he climbed a tall tree and slept. While he was sleeping, two young women came to fetch water. When they were approaching, the little sister saw a man's shadow and looked around to find him. After she saw the man, she told her big sister to look too.

While they were watching, they threw away their bamboo tubes and ran to the garden to tell their father. They arrived at the garden and told their father, "Papa, we saw a very nice man at the stream and we came to tell you. We want to take him and bring him here."

The father said, "Go take him and return so that he will help me plant yams (*mami*)."

The sisters heeded their father, so they ran to the stream and asked the man to come with them to the garden. When they arrived at the garden, the sisters' father gave the man two sticks with which to plant yams. But every stick that he used just broke. The sisters' father was angry and chased him away.

The man ran away and saw an old woman taking out a stone from a hole in the ground. After the woman removed the stone, the man went down into the stone and disappeared.

Bruno Takulamini

Maprik

East Sepik Province

[See *Wantok* #422 for a story that starts like this one.]

D457.1.14K. Transformation: blood to eggs; F682.0.1+. Person only one leg; F949.2. Man falls underground through hole; P231. Mother and son; P234. Father and daughter; P252.1. Two sisters; R210. Escapes; R260. Pursuits; T534. Conception from blood; T542. Birth of human being from an egg



# The Old Ways [The Story of Dawia Plomb Pond]

(Wantok 226, July 8, 1978, page 15)

Long, long ago, two people lived in a village. At this time, they did not have food where they lived. So, one day the man asked his wife, "Can we cut a sago palm or not?"

The woman said, "Good. We'll cut a huge sago palm for ourselves lest we became hungry."

The next day, they went together to cut a sago palm. They removed the spines from the trunk of the sago palm and the man struck the tree with a traditional [stone] axe.

This place was high on a mountain. The two of them did not have European-style clothing, so they were wearing their traditional clothing. The man was wearing a penis gourd, his two testicles [scrotum] were just hanging out in the open. On his backside hung an old black net bag. He had an armlet on each arm and he had two pig tusks through his nose. The two tusks were curved and very long.

While he was cutting the sago palm, his clothing got into a very awkward position. His wife too had poor clothing, she had a "grass" skirt covering her back and front. She had put bird of paradise feathers on the front of her head and the man had done this too.

His wife had prepared the things needed to process the sago. She put some small sticks in the ground near a pond. Afterwards, she carried the sago palm leafstalks and put them on top of the sticks that she had put in the ground [thus making a sluice for rinsing the sago].

It was almost noon and she went to see her husband at the base of the sago palm. Her husband pulled up two sago palm flower sheaths and she carried a sago palm leafstalk. She put a long sago palm leafstalk underneath the bag for rinsing the sago pith.

At about three o'clock, the man stopped working and went to the house. He made a cigarette, then he took his bow and arrows and went to hunt wild game. His wife finished processing the sago and went to the house to cut some firewood. In the late afternoon, at about five o'clock, her husband brought back a white marsupial (*kapul*) [the spotted cuscus, *Spilocuscus maculatus maculatus* (Flannery, 1995a: 181-182)].

They butchered the marsupial and cooked it in an earth oven. At the same time they cooked plain sago in a fire and ate it with the marsupial. In the early morning, he went to hunt birds in the forest. He hunted and hunted, but he did not shoot a single bird. He returned to the house, but near the house he shot one bird called a wildfowl. He carried this bird to the house.

The woman had gone to wash a sago palm leafstalk. The man cooked the bird and ate the entire thing. He did leave some for the wife, none at all. He just left the feathers. She was still pounding the sago pith. His wife returned to the house and saw the bird feathers, so she went back to the place where she was processing sago.

At this time, the wife killed a red ground snake. She cooked this snake and then quickly, a big flood arose and covered her up. She drifted in the water, but she was dead. At this time, her husband ran away into the deep forest.

This flooded area is still there today. The name of this place is called _Dawia Plomb_ in my language, meaning, "It snatched one woman." Today, some white people go to visit this pond. This pond is near **Imonda** [Village, **Waris** People, **West Sepik** Province]. The man's name was Maiva and the woman's name was Sawa.

Daniel Mai

Erave

Southern Highlands Province

A920.1.0.1. Origin of particular lake; A1011. Local deluges; A1018. Flood as punishment; A1617. Origin of place-name; B91.6. Serpent causes flood; P210. Husband and wife; Q211.6. Killing an animal revenged; R220. Flights; X712.3H. Testicles

## The Revenge of the Snake
(Wantok 227, July 15, 1978, page 13)

The woman's name was Tuwai. Tuwai went to get firewood so she could fry some sago. She saw a snake that was laying still. The name of this snake was Pumakua.

Tuwai picked up the snake and bound it with breadfruit tree leaves, then put it in her net bag. The snake was not dead. Tuwai had an ulcer on her back. The snake saw Tuwai's sore, then went inside her ulcer.

Tuwai went to the house and put down the firewood. She told her child, "Hey, hey child, come and look at what has gotten inside my ulcer." Tuwai's child ran to her and saw that the snake had gone inside the mother's ulcer. The mother said, "Get this snake out and throw it away."

The child tried to hold the snake, but it jumped into Tuwai's belly. The snake was inside and cut Tuwai's belly. The snake ate her and killed her. Tuwai's child dug a hole and buried her. After one month, Tuwai's first child dug the hole again and saw that the snake was still there. Her child killed the snake and carried it to the father's house. They cooked the snake in a pot and ate it.

Joseph Whisky [Wiski]

Warimb [**Warimbi**] Community School [**Sawos** People]

Torembi

**East Sepik** Province

B765.5+. Snake kills by entering person's ulcer; E150+. Snake survives burial; P230. Parents and children; Q385. Captured animals avenge themselves; Q411. Death as punishment; S110+. Eaten alive; V61.3+. Dead buried

## The Marsupial (*Sikau*) and the Rat
(Wantok 228, July 22, 1978, page 17)

Long, long ago, there were two friends, a marsupial (*sikau*) and a rat, who were indeed very good friends. When they wanted to eat, they often searched for food in the forest and ate it. When they defecated, their feces always just came out black.

However, one time the rat left its friend, the marsupial, and went to a place that had coconuts. The rat quickly ran to the top of a coconut palm, cut some coconut and carried it down to the ground. The rat took it and hid it near their house. The rat did this all of the time, and did not show this to the marsupial or share any.

Every time the rat did this, the rat it did not give even a tiny piece to the poor marsupial. One time, the rat defecated, and the rat's feces were very white. The marsupial saw this and thought, "What did my friend do that made shit like that?"

The marsupial tried and ate the rat's feces. Wow, the marsupial ate the rat's feces and they were delicious, so the marsupial ate all of them. Later, the marsupial saw the rat and asked, "Friend, why is it that we are good friends, but you didn't tell me or give me a piece? If you had told me, I could have gotten some for us." The rat had not wanted to do this because the marsupial could not climb trees. So, the rat tried to teach the marsupial to climb trees. After the rat finished the training, the rat explained where to find the coconuts.

After a while, when everyone was sleeping, the marsupial climbed up but did not get just one. The marsupial was very surprised because it cut many stems and the coconuts fell to the ground. The owner of the coconut tree woke up, then woke all of the other people of the village. They watched the base of the coconut palm and one man went to the top. The marsupial took one big coconut and hit this man badly, knocking him down. The marsupial ran down, but the men watched the marsupial. They grabbed it and tied its legs and arms.

At dawn, everyone went to the gardens. They removed taros, yams, and bananas to eat with this marsupial and to make a big party. Everyone returned to the village and sent a message to all of the villages to come for joyful singing and dancing. At dawn, they would kill the marsupial.

This message went around and the rat heard it too. The rat made a feather headdress for itself and one for its friend, the marsupial. At night the men chose an old man to watch the marsupial. They made a bonfire and he watched the marsupial. At this time, all of the other people from other villages had gathered and were singing and dancing. They were happy and waiting for dawn.

The rat took the headdresses, a hand drum and other adornments, then arrived at the place where everyone had gathered. The rat met an old woman who was the wife of the man guarding the marsupial. The rat asked her, "Hey, do you know which house they put the marsupial?"

The old woman said, "They put it in this house." The rat went inside the house and saw the old man watching the marsupial. Oh my, the rat jumped up and fought the old man, throwing him into the fire. Then the rat took its friend, the marsupial, and they went to where they were singing and dancing. They were still singing and dancing because it was not yet dawn. The two of them left for their home. At dawn, the men wanted to kill the marsupial and went to look for it, but they saw the man in the fire. They were irate. But where were they? They were happy at their home.

Kongango from **Saidor** Village wrote this story [**Dahating** or **Wab** People, **Madang** Province].

W. Roy Kongango

Wewak

East Sepik Province

B211.2.9. Speaking rat; B211.2.12K+. Speaking marsupial; B540+. Rat rescuer; K420. Thief loses his goods or is detected; K521. Escape by disguise; K1822. Animal disguises as human being; K2061.10+. Marsupial detects coconut by eating rat's white excrement; K2357. Disguise to enter enemy's camp (castle); P210. Husband and wife; P310. Friendship; R4. Surprise capture; R110. Rescue of captive; R210. Escapes; W151. Greed; X716H+. The escoumerda

# Women's Stolen Beards

(Wantok 229, July 29, 1978, page 15)

Long, long ago, there lived many people. This group of people lived beneath a big mountain, Mount Piora, near **Kainantu** [**Agarabi** People, **Eastern Highlands** Province].

At this time, the women were not quiet, they had a different kind of happiness because of their long beards. Some very smart women washed and combed their beards well. Their beards came down to their chests.

At one time, the women gathered at the women's house for a meeting. They talked about having a festival at the women's house on the next night. When the next night arrived, all of the strong women, old and young, gathered and called out to sing and dance at the women's house.

They played that night, doing various things, such as holding breasts, and pulling each other's beards. They sang and danced near the bonfire while their sweat poured out. They ate, sang, danced and sweated all at once. On this night, too, there was a joker who listened in on the women from the men's house.

He thought about going to see them. He went to the door, but the fire was too bright for him. The women were roughly pulling their beards. So he put a false beard on and covered his skin well with reeds [*purpur*]. The good-for-nothing was ready and he stood at the door.

The good-for-nothing was angry and went inside the house. Two women stood near him. He struck and pulled off a beard then sped outside again. The good-for-nothing kept running and put the beard on his face.

When he put on the beard, the good-for-nothing became completely unconscious [or dead] from the beard. The women also immediately became completely unconscious. At night, beards went to each man. Because of this one man, men have beards and women do not.

Robin Taka U.

Kudjip Hospital

Mt. Hagen

Western Highlands Province

A1315.3+. Why men have beards and women do not; F545.1.5. Bearded woman; K311. Thief in disguise; K1821.4+. Disguise by applying false beard; R220. Flights

## The Trick at the Fig Tree

(Wantok 230, August 5, 1978, page 13)

Long, long ago, there were two brothers who lived on a mountain called Bumui. They always went into the forest to hunt for wild game to eat. Their parents had been eaten by a *masalai*.

One day, the big brother carried his bow and went into the forest. The little brother stayed at home. He got firewood and water ready, then waited for his brother. When the brother returned, he brought game. After they cooked and ate, they slept.

Late that night, the big brother woke up and cooked two yams (*mami*) in the fire. After the yams were done, he scraped them off well and took them into the forest. The little brother did not know that the big brother had departed.

The big brother went to the base of a fig. The fig had many wild pigs that were eating the fruits. The man hid among the fig vines and watched. He sat a little while, then he heard many men, women and children running towards him. When the man heard this, he hid well among the fig vines and watched. This was serious. Many men, women and children went up the fig and ate the fruits.

When they had arrived at the base of the fig, they removed their loincloths and "grass" skirts, then put them down. They went bare-assed and ate the fig fruits.

The man watched this. The very last to arrive were two beautiful young women who came and removed their skirts, then ascended. Quickly, the man took the first woman's skirt and hid it.

The *masalai*s were still eating and it was getting close to dawn. Then each of them descended, put on their loincloths and skirts, and ran away to their homes. Much later, the two young women descended. One of them took her skirt and left. The other woman tried to find her skirt. But her skirt was not there. The poor woman searched until it was almost noon.

Then the man gave the skirt to her. The woman wanted to run away, but the man jumped and held her tightly. He took a small knife, then cut off the woman's long fingernails and toenails. The woman tried hard to run away, but the man held her tighter. The woman lost her strength and she told the man, "You're too strong for me, huh? Now you have parts of my body [that you could use for sorcery]. OK, I'll go with you to your house and I'll marry you."

The man took his two yams and gave one to the woman. The woman smelled the yam and began to vomit the fig fruits. She kept vomiting until her stomach was completely empty. Then she began to eat the yam. After she ate it, they went to the man's home.

They arrived at the house and rested. In the late afternoon, the little brother returned from the garden. As he approached the house, he heard his brother talking with his wife. He said, "Hey, what? Who's that talking with my brother? There's no [other] person in our house."

When the little brother entered, he saw his big brother with his wife. The little brother was ecstatic and worked to help his brother.

They cooked some food. When it was nearly time to sleep, the boy asked his big brother, "Brother, how did you get this woman?" The big brother wanted to tell him the story, but the little brother said, "Brother, don't tell me so much. I understand everything you say. I can do those things. I don't like it when men tell me long stories."

In the early morning, the little brother did as the big brother had done. He went and hid among the fig vines, then he waited. He watched the *masalai*s ascend the fig. The last young woman arrived and ascended. Quickly, the boy hid the woman's skirt. After all of the *masalai*s finished eating, they descended and left for their homes. When the woman descended, she did not find her skirt.

The woman cried and called out. She said, "My big sister left from this place and I want to leave too. Whatever happened to my sister yesterday has happened again to me."

However, the *masalai*s were hiding nearby. They were waiting for the woman. The boy did not know this; he thought that the *masalai*s had left. He gave the skirt to the woman. Then the woman called out loudly. She jumped and took away the boy's two eyes. Then all of the *masalai*s came. They removed his legs and arms and carried him to their home to eat.

The big brother waited until it was dark. Then he said, "The *masalai*s are eating my brother. I told him well, but he disobeyed me and left."

The man asked his wife, "Wife, where do your kin live?"

The woman said, "We live in a hole in a wild pandanus (*karuka*) tree."

The man asked, "OK, how can we kill them?"

The woman said, "If you burn this wild pandanus, they'll all die. There will be no escape for them."

The man sent a message to his maternal kin to meet. They prepared many, many torches. The next day at exactly noon, they surrounded the wild pandanus and burned it. No *masalai*s escaped, they all died in the fire.

The ashes of the fire have not disappeared, they are still there now. If you go to Ungu's mountain, you will see the ashes from this fire.

Bruno Malai
C. M. [Congregation of Mission] Usino
**Madang** Province

F238. Fairies are naked; F441.2. Tree-spirit; F490+. Masalai; F515.2.2. Person with very long fingernails; G512.3. Ogre burned to death; K812. Victim burned in his own house (or hiding place); P210. Husband and wife; P251.5. Two brothers; P251.4. Brothers scorn brother's wise counsel; P252.1. Two sisters; P263. Brother-in-law; P264. Sister-in-law; P290+. Maternal kin; Q211. Murder punished; Q414.0.12. Burning as punishment for murder; R4. Surprise capture; R220. Flights; S70+. Wife betrays her kin to her husband; S112.0.2. House (hostel) burned with all inside; S139.7. Murder by slicing person into small pieces; S165. Mutilation: putting out eyes; T115+. Man marries ogress; T192. Marriage by force; W126. Disobedience

# The Marsupial (*Sikau*) that Stole a Woman
(Wantok 231, August 12, 1978, page 15)

There lived a woman named Manu. Manu went to the garden to get *mami* and other kinds of yams. A marsupial (*sikau*) was hiding among the sugarcane leaves. Manu went closer to the sugarcanes, then the marsupial jumped and held her tightly, carrying her to its house.

The marsupial carried Manu away. It took some rattan and tied her tightly to the house. The woman's husband was looking for her when Juwe asked him, "What are you looking for?" The husband said, "I'm looking for my wife."

Juwe said, "I saw your wife. A marsupial carried her to its house." Juwe told the husband, "Go to the village and beat the signal drum. All of the men must gather, then you should come. I'll cut the trail to the marsupial's house."

After Juwe cut the trail, he returned and waited for them. The men were ready to fight. Juwe took two of his spears and went down the trail. The marsupial saw the men approaching. The marsupial was prancing belligerently (*samsam*) for a fight.

The marsupial shot all its spears at the men, but the woman's kin were not hit by any. They shot at the marsupial a little. The marsupial dodged the spears well. They continued to fight, then Juwe ran and pulled the woman from the marsupial's house and hid her on the trail. After that, Juwe leapt up a tree and watched. The marsupial was about to jump when Juwe shot it.

The marsupial said, "Never mind burying me in a grave. You should eat me." Then the marsupial died and

Juwe ran to the marsupial's house and took everything from it. After that Juwe burned the marsupial's house.

The men took the woman and carried the marsupial to the village. They cooked the marsupial, then butchered and ate it.

Joseph Wiski
**Warimbi** Community School [**Sawos** People]
Torembi
**East Sepik** Province

B211.2.12K+. Speaking marsupial; P210. Husband and wife; R13.1+. Abduction by marsupial; R100. Rescues

# The Mother's Mistake
(Wantok 232, August 19, 1978, page 13)

Long, long ago, there lived a married couple who had a son. This boy became big and often walked around.

His father made a little bow and gave it to him to play with. One day, they went to their new yam garden to clean and straighten it, and to make posts for the yams to climb on.

The two parents cleaned the garden and the boy went to shoot the yam sprouts with his bow. The yam sprouts broke and fell apart, so he laughed hard and was very happy. He did this for a while, then the mother thought, "He's playing around and laughing." She continued to remove the grass from around the yams.

His father got up and saw his child. Oh my, oh my, the yam sprouts were lying roughly on the ground. He told his wife, "Look at your child, he's weeding the grass and he's excelled us." (He spoke a code language to the woman.) The woman thought and got up to look. No, the yam sprouts were ruined and lying about on the ground.

The child thought, "They don't see me." So, he continued to shoot the yam sprouts, shouting and laughing and being very happy. His mother shouted very loudly at him and hit him badly. She turned around and spoke angrily at her husband, "You. It's your fault. You made the bow and gave it to him, so he ruined the yam sprouts. Now you two can't eat. I won't be able to cook food for you. Find it yourself in your garden and cook and eat it." After she finished her tirade, she went to the house, cooked her food and ate it herself.

The father called out to his child and said to him, "Mother is angry at us, so we can't go home. We must go to a place where there are no people." The boy listened to his father, then they began to walk into the very deep forest.

122

The mother waited until late afternoon. She noticed that they did not come home quickly. She went to the yam garden again and called out for them, but they were not there. The mother called out very loudly, calling their names, but they were far away. She saw that their footprints went into the forest and she followed them. She kept walking until it was quite dark. She called out for them but they did not reply to her. She listened but they did not reply.

They heard her approaching a little closer. The father told the boy, "Your mother's coming closer now, so turn into a tree. I'll turn into a snake and go into a cave." They talked and the mother came very close, so the boy turned into a tree and the father turned into a snake and fled into a cave.

The mother came and looked for them, but they were not there. She began to cry for them. She could not look for them any more. So, she slept under the tree until dawn and then returned home.

Dopenu Sawiembe
L. C. **Boana** [Village, **Sirak** People]
**Morobe** Province

D191M. Transformation: man to serpent (snake); D215B. Transformation: boy to tree; D671. Transformation flight; P210. Husband and wife; P231. Mother and son; P233. Father and son; R213. Escape from home; R260. Pursuits; R315. Cave as refuge

## The Man Who Killed a *Masalai*

(Wantok 233, August 26, 1978, pages 17, 22)

Long, long ago, there was a man named Gouboro who lived in a village called **Maipani** [**Dibiri** Island]. This village is near Daru in the **Western** Province [**Wabuda** People]. Gouboro was a man who shot wild pigs in the deep forest at night.

One time, he went to the forest and cut a sago palm tree so that he could shoot pigs there. After Gouboro cut the sago palm in the forest, he returned home. Gouboro stayed at the village for a month because he was waiting for the sago to rot and for the pigs to begin eating it.

After a month passed, he went to look for the sago palm. He wanted to know whether the pigs were eating it or not. The pigs had indeed been eating the sago. So one night, he prepared his bow and arrows and his multi-pronged spear. He would watch for the pigs at this place. He went to the forest very late at night and approached the sago, then heard a pig eating.

Gouboro shot the pig dead. Gouboro left the pig and returned to his house.

However, before he came to his house, he saw a wild man in the middle of the trail. This wild man had a bow and arrows and a multi-pronged spear too. That night, there was a bright moon without a cloud in the sky.

When Gouboro saw this *masalai* man, he thought, "It's just a *masalai*." So he jumped quickly into the shadows. The *masalai* jumped into the shadows too when he saw Gouboro.

Then the two men watched. Gouboro watched from one place and the *masalai* watched from another. Between the two men was just the moonlight; they stood in the shadows. They waited and waited in the darkness. Who would come out of the darkness into the clearing?

The two men stayed like this for many hours. Then the wild man, or *masalai*, thought that the man had run away on another trail. The *masalai* left the shadows and came into the clearing.

Gouboro saw that the *masalai* had left the shadows and come into the clearing too. The man spoke, then Gouboro pulled his bow back far and shot the *masalai* man. After he had shot him, the *masalai* was badly wounded, so he threw away all his belongings, the bow, the arrows and the spear. He felt that he was near death, so he went to the place that he often went to, a place where there was a big tree.

The *masalai* arrived at the tree, climbed it and died. After Gouboro shot the man, he did not leave him. Instead, he followed him to the big tree. When he arrived there, he heard the cry of the *masalai*'s two wives.

Later, he left this place and went back to his village. He sat for a while at his house. Dawn came. That morning, he told the people that he had shot a pig and that they should get it. He also told the people that he had shot a *masalai* man.

Before, there were many of this kind of real *masalai* that lived in the forest in the Western Province area. Now, there are not even a few. If one sees you in the forest, too bad! It will kill and eat you. My people are truly terrified of this kind of *masalai*. There is one of this kind of forest *masalai* that lives at the mouth of each of the Fly and Bamu rivers. Sometimes we see them, and we run away quickly.

Abel Naia A.
Catechist Training Center
Erave
Southern Highlands Province

F490+. Masalai; F567. Wild man; G512.1+. Ogre killed with spear/arrow; P210. Husband and wife; S110. Murders; T145.0.1. Polygyny

## The Dog-Man's Scabies

(Wantok [2]34, September 2, 1978, page 13)

Once there were some people who were processing sago. A completely worthless dog with scabies came and walked on top of their sago. When they saw this, they took the dog and threw it on some sago palm thorns. The people, an old woman and her husband, told the good dog to kill a bandicoot and then they would take the dog and remove the sago thorns from its body. Afterwards, they would take the dog to the house.

At night, they ate food and they gave some to the dog to eat. The dog ate the food and looked at its plate. It was a pig's plate. The next morning, the dog woke up and went to the forest. The dog removed his worthless skin, became a handsome man and returned to the house. When he came to the house, the old woman jumped in surprise. She cooked some food and took a plate that she used for friends. The man noticed this.

He asked, "Whose plate is that?" The woman said, "It's for you to eat with." He said, "Yesterday, I ate on that one." The woman said, "That's the plate of a worthless dog that has departed." The man said, "No, that's my plate." After he said that, the old man told his wife that the dog had changed his skin.

After they finished eating, the man went outside. He saw a coconut palm and he spoke to the couple. It was a tall coconut palm, and he told them to make a house on the top of the coconut palm. They went and built a house on top of the palm tree, then prepared all of their possessions to go up the palm tree. The man spoke and the old man listened, then the couple went on top of the coconut palm.

The couple sat on top of the coconut palm and the man told them, "After you two hear my voice, something will happen." Then he went down into a hole in the ground. The couple saw a big flood arise. People died all over. Some people tried to climb the tree, but they died. The flood almost came to the top of the coconut palm, but it crested.

The man took a small, young coconut and said all of the things that the man had told him before. After he said these things, he blew on the coconut and threw it towards the ground. But the coconut hit the flooded area. They waited and the water receded until there was very little. The man took another coconut and threw it down again. This time, it fell on the ground and bounced far away.

They took all of their belongings and went down to the ground. They saw that everyone in the area was dead.

They traveled to all of the houses that had been destroyed and took all of the rings from the people who had died.

Later, the man made a house and put the rings in this house. Another day, he went to cut an ironwood tree to use to carve people. He cut the tree, then it fell and broke apart. Some fell in a small pond that was nearby. He returned home and slept. In the morning, he went to carve people's faces.

When he arrived at the place where he had cut the ironwood tree, he saw a young girl sitting on top of the stump of the ironwood tree. He asked her, "Where did you come from?" The girl told him about everything that had happened to her. The man learned about her and took her home. He put her with her mother at the house.

The man returned to carve people and threw them into the pond. He continued carving and as he carved women, they became real women. As he carved men, they became real men. Then the man wanted to make a spirit house. The people that the man had carved at night only worked on the house at night. After the spirit house was finished, he marked a day for a festival.

This was the first time ever for a festival. The man and his wife and the child came to sing and dance with the others for the second time when they heard them call out from the forest. In the morning, the man took them. He made a man friends with [i.e., have sex with] a woman, and a woman friends with a man. He did this for everyone, then they married and lived in this village.

Tony Spian Akipo
**Maprik** [Town, **Abelam** People]
**East Sepik** Province

A1011. Local deluges; A1023. Escape from deluge on tree; A1540. Origin of religious ceremonials; B421+. Saved from flood by dog in form of person; D341M. Transformation: dog to man; D435.1.1. Transformation: statue comes to life; D531+. Transformation by removing skin; D1774. Magic results from speaking; D2151.8. Magic flood; P210. Husband and wife; P232. Mother and daughter; Q45. Hospitality rewarded; Q151.6. Life spared as reward for hospitality; T100. Marriage; V112.1. Spirit huts

## Why Women Do Not Shoot Wild Game in the Forest

(Wantok 235, September 9, 1978, page 15)

Once there lived a man named Kome and his wife Duma. One night, Kome told Duma to go find some food for him so that he could carry it with him into the forest. In the morning, Duma went to find food for him. After the food was ready, she brought it to Kome.

In the very early morning, Kome woke up, took his bow and arrows and his net bag of food, then got ready to go to the forest. Duma saw Kome standing and asked him, "Where are you going?" The wife told him that she wanted to go with him and carry his net bag of food. So, they went together and entered the deep forest. Kome left his bow and cut some saplings to make a hut.

After he finished making the hut, he took some food and ate it. He finished eating, then took his bow and told his wife to wait at the hut. However, Duma insisted on going with Kome. At night, the wife also followed her husband into the forest. They arrived at a huge tree. Kome saw the nest of a marsupial (*kapul*) and told Duma to wait.

Duma told him that she had never seen a marsupial sleeping in its nest. So, Kome agreed that Duma could go with him. Kome carried Duma up the tree. As they climbed, the marsupial transformed itself into a huge bird.

The bird flew down and plucked Duma from the middle of the tree, then carried her into the deep forest. Kome cried terribly. He went back and told the people of the village. So now, women are afraid and do not go into the forest to hunt for pigs or marsupials.

[Anonymous]

B31.6. Other giant birds; C181.2+. Tabu: women hunting in the forest; D411+. Transformation: marsupial to bird; P210. Husband and wife; R13.3. Person carried off by bird

## Why Did the Ancestors Use Trees?

(Wantok 23[6], September 16, 1978, page 19)

Long ago, there was a man named Repes who lived in **Embi** Village [**Pembi** Village, **Mendi** People, **Southern Highlands** Province]. This man never defecated or urinated; he was closed up.

When he ate, his belly swelled up terribly. One time, he went over to a tree and climbed to a branch. He sat on the branch and bounced up and down. Then he vomited and his belly loosened. Every time he ate, he would go on this tree, then bounce up and down.

He did this all of the time, so the tree was like his toilet. He always bounced and vomited his food to loosen his belly. When he worked, it was not the same as us who stand up to work. He always worked sitting. When Ripes [Repes] wanted to cut grasses or wild sugarcanes (*pitpit*), he shoved his legs under the grasses or wild sugarcanes. He would cut his legs with the grass or wild sugarcane and be in great pain and shout, "*Amooe*!", meaning "I mourn for myself!" He cut his legs many times and his legs were filled with sores.

He used big animals, such as cassowaries and pythons, as firewood. He ate bananas only when they were ripe. Some kinds of foods that are normally eaten cooked, he would eat before they were done. He made his house using a stone axe and traditional salt.

One day, his maternal relative, named Muripumb, saw him. Muribumb [Muripumb] went to a mountain and heard his maternal relative's shouting in the garden. He went quietly and arrived at his relative's house. He looked inside the kitchen and saw cassowary meat and python meat and other kinds of meat from big animals on the fire. He thought hard.

He thought, "What kind of man is this?" He removed all of the meat from the fire, heated some stones and cooked all of the meat in an earth oven using the stones. After this, he destroyed his relative's house and made a new house for Repes.

When he was done, Muripumb found Repes' toilet. He followed a small trail and arrived at the tree. He looked at the tree and thought, "This is my relative's toilet." He cut a *komb* tree and sharpened two branches well. He stood one up in front and one in back.

After he finished, he went to his relative's garden. Muripumb went quietly to the garden, hid by the base of a tree and watched. Repres [Repes] shoved his legs beneath the grasses and wild sugarcanes. He cut his legs and shouted, "*Amooe*."

Murpumb [Muripumb] said, "What are you doing?" Repes was a little ashamed and said, "Hello, kinsman." Muripumb said, "Give me your knife first." He gave it to him. Then he said, "Repes, look at me, OK?" So, Muripumb stood and shoved a stick underneath the grass and cut the grass. He said, "Do you see this? Now you should do this work like me."

Repes said, "Yes, kinsman, I understand." After he finished, Muripumb told Repres that he had cooked some food in an earth oven at the house, and that they should uncover the oven and eat. They went to eat. They uncovered the earth oven and Repres said, "Oh my, what did you cook? You cooked my firewood, huh?"

Muripumb said, "Try to eat a piece of meat." He took a piece of meat and ate it. "Man-oh-man, that's my firewood, but it tastes delicious," Repes said. They ate and ate, then Repres said, "I've had enough." Muripumb said, "No, we must finish this food that I cooked."

They finished and their bellies were bloated. Repes got up and went to his tree to loosen his gut. He sat on top of the branch, then bounced up and down. When he bounced, the two sticks pierced his loins. He shouted, "*Eyiye!*" meaning, "I've been badly injured!"

Muripumb said, "*Amnei i ya i komb pu komb.*" This means, "Kinsman, I opened your shit and piss holes." If Muripumb had not opened Muripumb's anus and urethra, we people of the Southern Highlands Province would not be able to defecate or urinate. This man opened these holes for all people.

The two men went inside a cave. All of the people of Southern Highlands Province honor these two men at their cave and say to them, "Open our shit and piss holes."

They often take a pig and go to this cave. Now still, they honor these two men at this cave.

Colman Nika
Erave
Southern Highlands Province

A992+. Sacred cave of primeval ancestors; A1318K. Origin of anal orifice (wound made by culture hero); A1318K+. Origin of urethra (wound made by culture hero); F529.2. People without anuses; J1813+. Cooking processes misunderstood: eating partly cooked food; J1813+. Cooking processes misunderstood: using animal flesh as firewood; J1971+. Legs used as knife to cut sugarcane; P290+. Maternal kin; V12.4.3. Pig as sacrifice; X740.1H+. Symbolic pedicatory rape while at stool

## Wild Game or Man?

(Wantok 237, September 23, 1978, page 17)

Long ago, men lived in a village named **Mnamgimgi**. They worked in gardens and one of them lived in **Kogrikargo**. This man turned into a pig and often came to eat their food. They followed the trail of this pig, then they would return.

They did this all of the time. One time, they sent a message around to men who lived nearby. They came to meet and again follow the pig's trail. They followed and followed, then saw the pig wallowing in the mud and turn into a lizard that went into a tree hole. They found him and looked at the ground by the tree hole. They cut the tree and saw a huge lizard.

They held the lizard, tied it up and carried it back. After they brought the lizard back, they slept. At dawn they went to look for food. When they wanted to leave, they left two small boys and an old woman to watch the lizard. While they were watching, the lizard turned into a man again. The man told the two boys to untie the ropes that bound him.

So the boys untied the ropes. After they untied him, he asked them, "Is there a hand drum and paint?" They said, "Yes." He told them to bring these things. After they brought them, he asked them again, this time for marsupial fur and for bird-of-paradise feathers. They brought these and gave them to him. Then he decorated himself and sang and danced. He sang, "*Ihmgumgu manamgumgu, managat, managimura.*"

The men were in the garden. They heard the hand drum and said, "Those two boys like to eat meat, and sing and dance." So, the men went towards the village. When they were approaching the village, the man told the two boys and the old woman, "They want to kill and eat me. Don't let them come near me or eat me. You must stop them far away and look at various colors coming from the pot. After a while, a tree fruit with a stick for cutting sago will appear. Later, when the signal drum comes, you must go stand at the base of a coconut palm, then hold me by the tail of the signal drum." [Some signal drums are shaped like animals.] After he said this, he turned back into a lizard and said, "You two tie me up tightly again." So they tied him up.

The men came to eat and the two boys told their elders, "Elders, you think that this is wild game. No, he's a man." They told about everything that the lizard-man had done. The elders spoke, "Ah, shame on you two. This isn't a man, it's wild game. You two like to eat meat and be happy, yet you say this." They ignored what the boys said. They killed the lizard and butchered it. After they butchered the lizard, they divided it up for all of the houses to cook.

They cooked the lizard, then the three saw various colors come and go. They saw the tree fruit and the stick for cutting sago. Finally the signal drum came and ran towards the three of them. They held the signal drum's tail. The signal drum raised the three of them and put them on a mountain ridge. Then the signal drum destroyed the men of the village called Mnamgimgi.

So now, this is a swampy region with sago palms that is about five miles from my village.

Aravigara Endru
Pangasev Village [**Bangasav** Village, **Katiati** People]
C. M. [Congregation of Mission] Josephstaal
**Madang** Province

A920.1+. Origin of swampy area; A1011. Local deluges; A1022. Escape from deluge on mountain; B211.6.2K. Speaking lizard; B875.5K2. Giant lizard; D114.3.2M. Transformation: man to boar; D197M. Transformation: man to lizard; D397M. Transformation: lizard to man; D412.3.5+. Transformation: pig to lizard; D425.2K+. Transformation: lizard to drum; D670.

Magic flight; D1211. Magic drum; D1609.1+. Running drum; D2188+. Objects magically appear and disappear inside cooking pot; J652. Inattention to warnings; J1050. Attention to warnings; K311.6.5. Thief disguised as pig; Q211.6. Killing an animal revenged; Q212. Theft punished; Q411. Death as punishment; R260. Pursuits; S110. Murders

## The Pig that Killed a Father

(Wantok 238, September 30, 1978, page 15)

Long, long ago, there was a pig that often ate in a garden. One time a father told his child, "Tomorrow evening, you and I will go watch for the pig in the garden." So in the evening at about half past six o'clock, they walked toward the garden.

When they approached the garden, the father told the child, "If you see the pig coming, you must stand and hide. I'll try to shoot the pig." After the father said this, they walked inside the garden. They stood for a little while, then they heard a pig making a noise in the forest and coming towards them. Quickly, the father hid his child at the base of a banana plant and covered his child with banana leaves.

He stood and watched for the pig. When the pig came to a clearing, he quickly said to his child, "Child, stand and look at me when I shoot at the pig. If I shoot at the pig and the pig kills me, that's OK. You can go back and tell mama."

He left the child and took a bamboo arrow with his bow. He pulled back hard on the bow and shot straight at the pig. Oh my! The pig just turned and broke the arrow, then ran straight at the man. The pig gored the man and killed him. The pig went back home. When the child saw this, he turned into a bird and flew after the pig. The bird flew and flew until the pig went into a tree hole.

When the pig went into the hole, the bird perched at the entrance to the hole. Then the bird turned into a boy again and went home. He walked and walked. When he came close to his village, he began to cry. He told his mother and they both cried.

In the morning, the people came to gather and mourn. Everyone brought their spears, axes, stones, fire, bows, and other things to the place where the pig lived. When they arrived at the place where the boy had seen the pig, the boy spoke to them and they began to cut the tree where the pig lived.

They cut the tree until it fell over, then they cut it into little pieces. After they cut the tree, one man cut more pieces and the others watched. After much cutting, the pig came forth and they beat it with axes. Later they made a big fire and cooked the pig. After they cooked the pig, they went home.

Pius Aunal

C. M. [Congregation of Mission] **Yassip** [**Kombio** People] Wirui, Wewak

**East Sepik** Province

D150B. Transformation: boy to bird; D350B. Transformation: bird to boy; B784+. Pig lives in tree; P230. Parents and children; P231. Mother and son; R260. Pursuits

## The Man Who Stole a Pig from a Snake

(Wantok 239, October 7, 1978, page 15)

In a village called **Dunuabanma**, there lived many men [**Kalam** People?, **Madang** Province]. One time, there was a bright moon rising, so two men wanted to go to the forest. These two men were named Kuruba and Gile. In the early morning, Kuruba and Gile woke up and walked far into the deep forest that men did not know about.

When they arrived there, Kuruba told Gile, "Make a fire and get ready to go into the forest a little to hunt some wild game." After Kuruba said this, he went into the forest while Gile made a hut for them to sleep in. Kuruba found a pig that was already dead, so he just took it.

Gile thought that Kuruba had killed the pig when he brought it. But no, a huge snake had killed the pig and had left to wash its mouth before eating the pig. The snake washed its mouth and began salivating. It returned and saw that the pig was not there. The snake was surprised that the pig was not there, so the snake followed the trail.

While Kuruba was carrying the pig, Gile noticed that it was a snake that had killed the pig, not Kuruba. Gile did not say anything, he just watched as they cooked the pig and ate it. They slept that night, but Gile thought that the snake must have been still following the pig. So, he heated three round stones and a pot of hot water, preparing to kill the snake. Gile did not sleep because he was afraid of the snake and was thinking. A big noise came from the forest from where Kuruba had carried the pig.

Gile was surprised and woke up Kuruba, but Kuruba did not listen, so Gile kept thinking. Oh my! A big snake came to the door of the hut and everything in its wake was ruined. The snake came closer and put its head inside Kuruba and Gile's hut.

The snake opened its mouth and quietly entered. Gile tried to wake Kuruba, but he did not listen. Gile got up, took a long stick and pushed each of the three stones into the snake's mouth. Then Gile spilled the hot water on the snake. The snake rolled around and died near a pond.

Gile took the big stick and hit Kuruba who was still sleeping. Kuruba was surprised and Gile told him that he had killed the snake that had been following the pig. "Tomorrow, go get it to cook and eat," he said. They were ill humored that night as they slept.

In the early morning, they searched for and saw the dead snake dead near a pond. They butchered the snake and gave it to the people of the village. They cooked and ate it. They put the skin of the snake on their hand drums and sang and danced.

Ludwig Onguglo
Simbai [Madang Province]
Port Moresby [National Capital District]

B875.1. Giant serpent; K951.1. Murder by throwing hot stones in the mouth; S112. Burning to death


# The Python that Swallowed a Man
(Wantok 240, October 14, 1978, page 7)

Once there lived a man with his wife and child. They went to their garden to dig up yams (*mami*). When they arrived at the garden, the man began to dig up yams.

In the evening, they finished one area. He told his family, "You can go home and I'll sleep in the garden."

So, they left and he slept. Late at night, a huge python smelled the man and went to the garden hut where he slept. The snake entered and tried to wake the man to see if he was sleeping or dead.

When the snake poked the man's head, he belched. When the snake poked the man's buttocks, he broke wind. So, the snake went down to the stream and ate some snake's leaves that are poisonous.

The snake returned and poked the man again. The man did not feel anything that the snake did because he was in a deep slumber. The snake tried to knock the man again on the head and buttocks. The man did not make a sound. So, the snake rested at the man's head, then opened a net bag, put the man in it and brought him outside. Afterwards, the snake swallowed the man.

The man thought that he was sleeping in his bed. He wanted to turn and sleep on another side, but the man could not turn. He wanted to turn his hands and legs but they were bound by the snake's belly.

The man thought, "Oh, I'm sleeping in a snake's belly." The man felt around his body and felt the stick that

he had used to remove yams. It was hanging from his armlet. He took the stick, called *boge* in my language, and cut the snake's belly.

The snake felt a great pain and went into the stream. The man cut the snake's belly, then came outside and swam in the *masalai*'s stream. He swam and arrived at the source of the stream, then he went to his garden and slept in the middle of the yam field. In the morning, they went to look for him and saw him near the source of the stream. They saw the python's body. So, the people do not like to sleep in the garden hut near the *masalai* place.

Christine K. Hualing
**Yangoru** [Village, **Boiken** People]
Wewak
**East Sepik** Province

B765+. Snake eats leaves; B765+. Snake uses net bag; B875.1. Giant serpent; C735.2. Tabu: sleeping in certain place; F490+. Masalai; F424. River-spirit; F911.7. Serpent swallows man; F912.2. Victim kills swallower from within by cutting; P210. Husband and wife


# The Woman Who Gave Birth to a Baby Snake
(Wantok 241, October 21, 1978, page 17)

There was a woman who gave birth to a girl. The name of this baby girl was Korikuku. Her mother often took her to the stream and bathed her. Poor Korikuku would cry.

There was a *masalai* man named Tomaiang, but Tomaiang had turned into a little bird. He began to sing, then Korikuku's mother replied, "I see your wife." The women were fishing at the stream, so Korikuku often took many fish. Some poor women did not know that Korikuku took many fish. Korikuku felt cold and went to sit on top of the *masalai* [in the form of a] stone. The stone held Korikuku tightly. She could not follow the other women back to the village.

When the women returned to the village, the *masalai* turned into a man and took the woman. They went down to Tomaiang's home. He was like Korikuku's husband. Korikuku's husband said, "When you and I go, my brothers will come up and you will call out to them."

So, Korikuku cooked food and put some for all of Tomaiang's brothers. Poor Korikuku would only drink soup. She became like skin and bones. She talked with her husband that she would go to her real home. When she went home, Tomaiang sent one of his brothers to follow her there.

The brother was a small lizard that you see which has a blue tail. This lizard followed the woman to her village.

The woman had given birth to a snake and brought it with her. Korikuku's mother told her child, "I want to see your child."

The mother saw the child and laughed. It was not a child, it was a snake and the mother threw it away. So, Korikuku went to get back her child.

After Korikuku's mother threw away the snake child, Tomaiang's young brother saw this and went back to tell his brother. His brother said, "Never mind, let her come."

When Korikuku wanted to go, [she said,] "I'm leaving. When you hear a strong wind and rain, you'll know that Tomaiang has cut me." Then she told her father, "In the early morning, you should look at my hair and tie it with rattan. You should take it and put it in a clay pot, then look after me."

Korikuku's father tied her hair well. When she became a girl, her father just put her in the house. Then she became a woman.

Tomaiang saw her again and climbed up two stones. He called out, "Korikuku, Korikuku, _Taribusne_." This meant that he was calling out for men to follow Korikuku and come back with him.

However, the men of the village fooled him and threw young coconuts. Tomaiang said, "You must send my wife to me."

So, the men of the village made a big fence and stood their spears inside it. The men fooled Tomaiang and put lime [calcium oxide], betel nuts, and betel peppers on a mat with a torch. They called out for him to come and sit on the mat.

The poor men called out for Korikuku to come and sit on the mat. And they called out for Tomaiang to come. He was very happy and went to sit down. But no, he fell through a hole and water capsized on top of him. Then he ran away to live at **Gila Gila** [**Baining** People?, **East New Britain** Province?].

This is a story that I cannot finish. I married at this village, but I do not belong to this village. I married a woman from the place to which the _masalai_ had walked.

Peter K. Kiwari
Coltba Ent[erprises]
Mt. Hagen
Western Highlands Province

D150M. Transformation: man to bird; D432.1M. Transformation: stone to man; D2171. Magic adhesion; F401.3.7. Spirit in form of a bird; F401.6. Spirit in human form; F401.3.13K2. Spirit in form of lizard; F490+. Masalai; F495. Stone-spirit; K735.1. Mats over holes as pitfall; K1601.1. Pitfall arranged but victim escapes it; P210. Husband and wife; P232. Mother and daughter; P234. Father and daughter; P251. Brothers; P292. Grand-mother; R210. Escapes; T111. Marriage of mortal and supernatural being; T554.7. Woman gives birth to a snake; T580. Childbirth

## The Brother Rose from Death
(Wantok 242, October 28, 1978, page 15)

This is the story of two sisters. Young men came to ask these sisters to marry them all of the time, but the two sisters did not want to marry them.

One time, the two sisters went to cut some forest for a new garden. A handsome man named Mremengie was hiding and spying upon them as they worked. After they stopped working, they returned home and Mremengie went to finish the work that they had started. The next day, the sisters returned to finish their work, but they were surprised. The forest had been cut, but they did not know who it was that had come and worked after they had.

Their brothers and maternal relatives said that on the next day, they would cut trees in the sisters' garden. In the morning, the women went to get food from the gardens and see the new garden where someone had cut all of the trees. They asked around, "Who was it that went and worked? We'll give him food for his hard labor."

The brothers asked the two sisters, "Was there a man who came and found one of you?"

They replied, "No. If that were true, one of us would be pregnant. But that's not true."

There was a little water for the two sisters, which was located in a tree hole. The two were working and feeling the heat of the sun, so wanted to wash. However, Mremengie had gone and washed with the water, finishing it. Later, he dressed very nicely and climbed to the top of the tree. He sat and waited for the sisters.

They went and saw that the water was gone. They cursed the man who had taken it. Mremengie spat some betel nut juice from his mouth that fell between them. They looked at him and trembled. They asked him to come down so that they could marry him.

However, the man did not want to do so. The two sisters were angry and made a big fire underneath the tree on which the man was sitting. The fire was burning him.

Mremengie sang and called the name of his brother, Peit. He called for him to hear him and come to help. Peit heard him and ran over there, but Mremengie fell on top of the fire and died.

Peit made it rain and put the fire out. Then he gathered his brother's bones and put them in the water. He said, "If I see a small bubble come up first, that means that my brother will be all right again. If a big bubble comes first, that means that he won't be alright."

He did this, but then removed the bones from the water. He ate a piece of ginger root and spat upon the bones. Immediately, his brother jumped and stood up.

Peit went to his village. He told his mother and sister that they should make a party because their brother had died and was resurrected. He told his mother that she should sit under the gable of the spirit house and wait for him.

In the evening, when they had prepared the food, their brother came home. The two sisters saw him. They ran and held him and said, "You are our husband. We two shall meet to marry him."

The man's mother said, "No. Why did you two burn him in the fire and kill him?"

The sisters replied, "It wasn't this man that we burned in the fire. It was another man."

The sisters were persistent, so Mremengie married the two sisters and they lived happily.

Mrs. C. Maspnulin
P. O. Box 133
Goroka
Eastern Highlands Province

D2143.1. Rain produced by magic; E100+. Resuscitation by ginger; E114. Resuscitation by spittle; M364.8+. Prophesy: resuscitation by disposition of bones; P210. Husband and wife; P231. Mother and son; P232. Mother and daughter; P250. Brothers and sisters; P252.1. Two sisters; P253.0.2. One sister and two brothers; P290+. Maternal kin; Q287. Refusal to grant request punished; Q414. Punishment: burning alive; R155. Brothers rescue brothers; S112. Burning to death; T100. Marriage; T145.0.1. Polygyny; T570. Pregnancy; V112.1. Spirit huts

## The Boy that Tricked the *Masalai*

(Wantok 243, November 4, 1978, page 17)

Long, long ago, there was a boy who lived with his old grandmother in a village. On a mountain near this village, there lived a *masalai*.

One time, the boy took his bow and arrows and told his grandmother, "Stay here. I'll go hunt birds for us." After he said this, he went into the forest. He walked and walked. He was confused by the trail and instead followed a *masalai* man's trail.

He kept walking and saw a small black bird that was caught in a spider's web [probably the orb-weaving spider, *Nephila* spp.]. He was sorry for the bird, so he took the bird and held it.

He walked farther still and he met the *masalai*. He asked him, "Old father, where did you come from?"

The *masalai* said, "I was hunting for wild game for myself. And where did you come from?"

The boy said, "I was hunting birds for my grandma."

The *masalai* asked the boy again, "Do you think that you're half a man to go out shooting that bow?"

The boy said, "Yes."

The *masalai* said again, "Let's test our muscles. Who can throw a stone the highest?" The boy told the *masalai* to throw the stone first.

The *masalai* took the stone and said, "If my stone goes the highest, I'll eat you. If your stone goes higher, I'll let you go."

After he said this, he threw the stone upwards. They waited, and the stone came down again. He told the boy, "Now it's your turn."

The boy threw the bird that he had in his hand. They waited a very long time and the bird did not return. So, the *masalai* let the boy go back home.

E. Conneber
**Finschhafen** [Town, **Yabêm** People]
**Morobe** Province

F490+. Masalai; G572. Ogre overawed by trick; H1562.5.2K. Contest to determine who can throw (toss) the highest; K18.3. Throwing contest: bird substituted for stone; P292.1. Grandmother as foster mother

## Where Did the Bird of Paradise Get Its Colors?

(Wantok 244, November 11, 1978, page 15)

Long, long ago, there was a woman with her ten children who lived in a garden hut amidst the deep forest. One time, a woman from another place came and made a garden in the same forest in which the woman with her ten children lived.

While the woman was making the garden, a *masalai* man came who killed and ate her. The poor woman was pregnant, so when the *masalai* ate her, the fetus fell to the ground, went underneath a big tree leaf and slept. On the same day, the woman with ten children was walking around. She came and saw the forest where the other woman had been making a garden. She saw the blood and looked around. She was surprised to see something underneath a tree leaf. She saw that it was a baby boy. The old woman was happy, so she took the baby and brought him to her house.

When she arrived at her house, she told her ten children to prepare everything in the house for her, such as firewood, food and water. The children prepared these things and fixed up the house. She told her children to leave the house and go far away. She alone would stay and take care of the baby in the house. When it was sunny, she often went outside and taught the child. She worked at teaching him, and he grew to become a man.

A very long time passed. The ten children thought, "It's been a long time since mama began taking care of that baby and kicked us out of the house. We've lived here a long time now. We should try to hide and spy on her."

When they went to look, there was a big boy who was living with her. The ten children called out together and ran inside the house. They were very happy to see their brother. They lived, worked and played together all of the time.

When the last boy became big, about twenty years' old, there was a big festival about to happen near the shore. The poor old woman worked hard to make fineries for the festival, such as "grass" skirts for the women and hand drums and spears for the men. For the last boy, she made a special hand drum, spear and loincloth, and she gave him two cassowary bones. After everything appeared to be ready, they waited for the time of the festival to arrive. The ten children dressed up and the old woman helped them dress the last boy. She told him, "You should stay behind, and then you should go. Your ten brothers and sisters should go first, then you should follow them. After the festival has begun, then you should go."

After the ten children left, she adorned the last son well. She put on green, yellow and black paint on his face. She gave him a hand drum, a spear, and two cassowary bones that she put through his [nose]. After she finished adorning the boy, she instructed him, "When you go to the festival, you can't go inside or among the other dancers. When you sing and dance and hit your drum, you must do it in a separate area. Before it is dawn, you must leave the festival grounds and hit your hand drum as you follow the trail to the beach. If two young women follow you and call for you, you can't stop. You must go and sit on the beach near a big ironwood tree. Hit your hand drum and sit down. If the two young women go down to bathe and call out for you to bathe, you can't bathe with them. If they ask why, then get up and hit the ironwood tree with this piece of cassowary bone, then go inside. Just leave your face there, giving enough time for the two women to find you. Then you can disappear."

After the old woman finished her instructions, the boy walked towards the festival. When he arrived, the singing and dancing had started, so he just sang and danced. When he hit his hand drum, every man, woman and child were envious for the sound of his hand drum. They saw his face and talked, "We wish that dawn were here so that we can see this man." Before it was light, the man followed the trail to the beach. He hit his hand drum while two beautiful young women followed him. They arrived at the beach and the women went down to bathe. He sat on the beach and sang. The two women were burning with desire for him. He did not go down to bathe with them, so they told him, "You worthless bumpkin, don't you bathe in the sea?"

This made him ashamed so he got up and hit the ironwood tree with a piece of cassowary bone, then went inside. The women watched and followed him. One woman saw him and called out to the other. They ran after him and tried to hold him. But they could not catch him, so they kept running after him.

He went up and turned into a bird of paradise and called out, "Kokk kokk," and flew to another tree. So now you can see that birds of paradise have green, black and yellow on their heads. They also have a hand drum and spear [on the national emblem].

John S. Mufoia [Mufola]
Purina [**Parina**] Point, Parpur [Village, **Boiken** People]
Wewak
**East Sepik** Province

A1970+. Creation of bird of paradise; A2411.2+. Origin of color of bird of paradise; D150+B. Transformation: boy to bird of paradise; D1013+. Magic cassowary bone; D1355.1. Love-producing music; F490+. Masalai; G370+. Ogre eats pregnant woman, fetus survives; P230. Parents and children; P250. Brothers and sisters; R260. Pursuits; P272. Foster mother; P273. Foster brother; P275. Foster son; R260. Pursuits; S110. Murders; T10. Falling in love; T549.4. Child born from miscarried fetus; T570. Pregnancy; W31. Obedience; W195. Envy

## The Sky Woman
(Wantok 245, November 18, 1978, page 15)

Long ago, there lived a man. One time, he wanted to go into the forest. He went into the forest and a hard rain fell. He stood at the base of tree [to keep drier]. A strong wind arose and clouds covered the sky.

He kept standing there. He heard something flying above the top of the tree. He looked up and he saw many young women in the sky. He hid and kept looking at them. The young women came down to the ground and took some yellow earth, called _ambu_ in my language. Some women took the earth and went back to the sky.

The very last one to descend was a beautiful woman. The man held this beautiful young sky-woman tightly. She turned into something with thorns, but he held tight. The woman turned into a snake, but the man still held tight. The woman kept transforming herself, but then she tired and said, "If you're a man of the forest, leave me be. If you're a villager, then let's go to your village."

The man took the woman and went to his village. The woman said, "If they have a festival somewhere, you can't go." The man said, "I won't go." The woman turned this worthless man into a handsome young man and they lived together.

Their home was filled with all kinds of things. One room was filled with _kina_ shells, another room was filled with money. They continued to live together. One time, the man said that he wanted to go to a place where there was going to be a festival. The woman dressed him very nicely. Then she said, "Go ahead. I'll stay at the house."

The man went to the festival and the woman went to her place in the sky. After the festival ended, the man returned home. He found that his wife was not there. The man had often promised to her that he would not go to a festival.

He built a long ladder up to the sky. He was nearly at the point of being able to touch the sky when it became dark and he returned. At night, the woman broke the ladder and it fell to the ground. In the morning, the man saw the broken ladder on the ground. He was angry. He ran away into the forest and became an outcast.

Yawe Pu
**Tindua** Com[mercial] School [**Wiru** People?]
Kerapali
P. O. Pangia
**Southern Highlands** Province

D56+. Person made younger; D191W. Transformation: woman to serpent (snake); D213.5W. Transformation: woman to thorns; D610. Repeated transformation; F52. Ladder to upper world; F205+. People from the sky; J652. Inattention to warnings; L160. Success of the unpromising hero (heroine); P160. Beggars; P210. Husband and wife; Q325. Disobedience punished; R213. Escape from home; T111.2. Woman from sky-world marries mortal man; T192. Marriage by force; W126. Disobedience

# An Island in Madang Province

(Wantok 246, November 25, 1978, page 15)

Long ago, there was a small place called **Biliau** [Island] in **Madang** Province [**Bilbil** People]. This village was close to the beach. At this time, they made big sailing canoes to travel along the Rai Coast. Once, the men of the Rai Coast announced that there would be a big feast and traditional festival. So, the men of Biliau prepared various things to put in their canoes.

The men took their wives and children and set off along the Rai Coast. When they arrived at the place on the Rai Coast where the festival would be, they went ashore and pulled their canoes up on the beach. They told their children to watch the canoes while they were gone.

The children waited and waited. They became very hungry. They called out for their parents to hurry, but ghosts replied to them saying, "We're coming." They ghosts made their faces like those of the parents. They took plates of food and came to give the food to them to eat. However, two children hid underneath a canoe platform and watched them.

When the children ate, they became ghosts. Shortly thereafter, their real parents came. They saw that all of their children had turned into ghosts. The two children that had hidden under the canoe platform came and told what had happened. So, they took one canoe and went back toward Madang with the two children. They left one canoe for the children who had become ghosts. These children climbed onto the canoe. The high tide brought them out to sea and they returned to Madang. When they arrived in Madang, the high tide brought them shoreward. Their canoe broke at Kalibobo Point. They shoved hard and came to an island where they stayed and died.

This island is uninhabited, even today. The island lies between the airport and **Kerosin** Island.

Edward Misob
P. O. Box 80
Lae
Morobe Province

E425.1. Revenant as woman; E425.2. Revenant as man; E425.3. Revenant as child; E481.2.0.1. Island of the dead; E540+. Ghosts feed people who then turn into ghosts too; K1930. Treacherous impostors; P210. Husband and wife; P230. Parents and children; W196. Lack of patience

## Where Did Fighting Originate?

(Wantok 247, December 2, 1978, page 15)

Long, long ago, there lived two brothers in Wapinam [**Wabinama**] Village [**Mendi** People, **Southern Highlands** Province]. The brothers' names were Inja and Murini. One brother worked in the garden and the other hunted marsupials (*kapul*) in the forest. They ate together and were very happy. They never had an argument between themselves and were of the same mind.

One time, they wanted to cook some food, so they prepared some stones, firewood and leaves [for an earth oven]. One brother took some good food from the garden and the other took some marsupial that he had killed.

They cooked much food. They removed the food from the earth oven, then they began to eat it. They ate their fill, and there was still some left, so they saved it to eat in the morning.

When darkness fell, they slept deeply. Inja woke up in the dead of night and finished all of the food that they had put aside, then Inja went back to sleep. In the morning, Murini woke up and looked for the food that was put aside. Oh my! The food was not there.

Murini was irate, so he burned their house and a big fight arose between the brothers. They took spears and axes and did battle. Inja won over Murini and evicted him to Meki [**Megi**] Village.

So now, a big river is between them. The river is called Kombu or Lai; it has two names. The two brothers married and had many children who populated the land. They still teach their children about this, and the children follow after their ancestors, fighting each other.

Pita Rombua

Erave

Southern Highlands Province

A1599.11.1. Origin of war; P210. Husband and wife; P230. Parents and children; P251.5. Two brothers; P251.5.3. Hostile brothers; Q270. Misdeeds concerning property punished; Q431. Punishment: banishment (exile); Q595. Loss or destruction of property as punishment; T100. Marriage; W151. Greed

## There Is No Fighting

(Wantok 248, December 9, 1978, page 15)

Once there were two women who were good friends. They lived in a village called Koiya [**Kauwo** Village, **Wiru** People, **Southern Highlands** Province]. One day, they thought about marriage, but they had not found a potential husband or boyfriend.

They tried walking to a village called **Lega**. At this village, they found two handsome young men whom they thought of marrying.

They began to befriend these two men. The two men gave their hearts to them and thought of marrying the two women. They were friends for a very long time and were near marriage.

One time, when they were close to marriage, the men called for their clan to give valuables to the two women [bride price]. They called on the women's clan too, for them to see the valuables for purchasing the two women. Everything was agreeable, so they married and lived together.

Some months later, one of the women was pregnant. The parents had twin boys. They were very happy and named the two children, Koiyama and Lekama. The children grew well and did not get sick or have problems. The boys kept growing and became men.

They became men of renown in the area. All of the men of the village had a big party and called for all of the men of the area to come and see the party for the two men.

At this time, the twins wanted to give a small name to their clans. They finished speaking and began to give a name to their clans. One of them spoke. Lekama got up and gave the name Lekarii to his own clan. Then Koiyama got up and gave the name Yoarene to his own clan. Now, in this village, there are two big clans, named Yoarene and Lekarii.

Sometimes, these two clans get angry with each other, but they never get angry enough to battle each other. They argue, but then they make amends. This shows that there are not big fights between these two clans. This is a true ancestor story of my clan. We use the clan names Lekarii and Yoarene.

Henry Angue

P. O. Box 456

Mt. Hagen

Western Highlands Province

[The ancestor story in *Wantok* #288 is a variation of this story and was written the same author.]

A515.1.1. Twin culture heroes; A1640+. Origin of Lekarii Clan; A1640+. Origin of Yoarene Clan; A1641+. Origin of peaceful relations between two clans; P210. Husband and wife; P231. Mother and son; P233. Father and son; P251.5. Two brothers; P310. Friendship; T10. Falling in love; T52. Bride purchased; T100. Marriage; T570. Pregnancy; T587. Birth of twins; T685. Twins; Z210. Brothers as heroes

## The Cassowary and the Chicken

(Wantok 249, December 16, 1978, page 13)

Long, long ago in Finschhafen, there were two very good friends Cassowary and Chicken. One time, these friends wanted to go to an island, so they took their canoe. Chicken sat on a bench and paddled the two of them away.

A strong wind arose and made Chicken's feathers dance about. The people saw this and said various things, joking about Chicken. Chicken's friend, Cassowary, sat on the canoe bench and was ashamed and angry.

So, Cassowary broke the canoe with its leg and water filled the canoe. Chicken flew up and over to the beach where the people were. Cassowary was too heavy to fly, so Cassowary sank into the sea. Cassowary went down and found a crab. Cassowary asked the crab for help.

The crab said, "I know how to get to the top of the water. I can carry you up." So, the crab carried Cassowary to the place where Cassowary wanted to go. Cassowary did not thank the crab. Instead, Cassowary killed the poor crab.

Now, the people of this place call it *Qeraharuc*, meaning "Cassowary and Chicken" in my language. The missionaries called this place **Sattelberg**, where there is a mission station for Finschhafen [**Kâte** People, **Madang** Province].

J. R. Kugeva
Igam Barracks
Lae
Morobe Province

[See the stories in *Wantok* #289, 676 and 1184, which are similar.]

A1617. Origin of place-name; A2494.13+. Enmity between cassowary and chicken; B211.3.17K. Speaking cassowary; B211.8.1K. Speaking crab; B295.2.1K. Animals make voyage in canoe; B296.2K. Animal (who is land-dweller) crosses water on back of another animal; B336+. Helpful crab killed by ungrateful cassowary; B495.1. Helpful crab; J2133.11+. Cassowary destroys boat in anger, but almost drowns while chicken flies away; P310. Friendship; S110. Murders; W154. Ingratitude

## A Big Flood

(Wantok 250, January 20, 1979, page 17)

Long ago, many people lived in a village named **Ipaiva** [**Southern Highlands** Province?]. However, these people were not good people, they often did various bad things. Among this group of people were one good man and woman and their child. They never did bad things to the other people.

One day, they said, "Let's go to the stream and look for fish." So, they went to the stream and fished. They saw a big fish that was like a snake. The nice man said, "Let's not kill it. If we kill it, a big flood will come here and all of us will die."

However, the bad men said, "You're lying. This is not God or a *masalai* that will cause us to die. No, it's just a fish."

So, they killed the fish and took it to the village to eat. The nice man dreamt at night that a man told him, "Don't eat that fish. I'll kill whoever eats that fish." So, this man did not eat the fish.

After they ate, they cooked the medicinal part of the fish that comes from its innards. This medicine spilled onto the fire and caused a deep black smoke to rise into the sky, causing a heavy rain to fall.

The nice people knew that a rain would fall, so they took two chickens, a cock and a hen, two pigs, two dogs, their daughter and some fire. They climbed a coconut palm.

When the flood came high, the coconut palm rose high in the sky. While they were on top of the coconut, they did not know about the state of the water. They broke off a new coconut and threw it down to the water. They did this three times, then the fourth time, they broke another young coconut, threw it and it hit the ground.

They knew that the flood had finished, so they left the coconut palm and descended to the ground. All of the people and animals on the ground had died; the flood had killed them.

Now, we live here. We have descended from these two people. And the animals also [came from these survivors].

Francis Momori
K. T. S.
Erave
Southern Highlands Province

A1011. Local deluges; A1015.2. Spirit causes deluge; A1018. Flood as punishment; A1023. Escape from deluge on tree; D1810.8.2. Information received through dream; D1810.8.3.1. Warning in dream fulfilled; D2143.1. Rain produced by magic; F54.1. Tree stretches to sky; J652. Inattention to warnings; J1050. Attention to warnings; P210. Husband and wife; P232. Mother and daughter; P234. Father and daughter; Q211.6. Killing an animal revenged; Q320. Evil personal habits punished; Q428. Punishment: drowning; R311. Tree refuge; Z71.2. Formulistic number: four

## Why Is There Thunder

(Wantok 251, January 27, 1979, page 11)

Long ago, there were many men who lived in a village named **Luwi** [**Foe** People, **Southern Highlands** Province]. They had things to eat, but when it was time to fight, they did not have a bow.

Oh my, the enemies had come to the people of Luwi. Everyone was finished, just one man and one woman were left in Luwi. All of the others were killed.

About a month later, the man thought, "What can I do to kill those enemies?"

At this time, the man told his wife, "First, you and I must kill a pig and eat it."

They killed a pig and ate it. The man told the woman, "You should stay home."

The woman said, "Yes, I can stay."

The man adorned himself and went to **Kutubu**. For two nights, he slept in the forest. On the third day, he went to the top of Mount Kesu. The man stayed on this mountain and thought hard.

He stayed there for a while, then he heard an explosion. He left the mountain and went close to the Kutubu men's house. Inside the house, the men were still noisy. [Note: *pairap* means "noise" or "explosion"; *klaut i pairap* means "thunder"]. The men were very happy. When everyone was asleep, he went inside and found something. He took this thing and left.

He looked at the thing, and it was truly beautiful. It was a bow. He left Kutubu, then went to Luwi Village. This time, it would be his enemies that would be defeated. This man's name was Kepi.

Kepi defeated all of the men [who came], but there were still many others. He wanted to kill a pig, so he sent a message to all of his friends. Just in time, his bow fired. Many men coveted Kepi's bow. In one month, he had killed eighty-one pigs.

At this time, he became quite famous. Many people came to eat the pigs that he had killed. They cooked them in an earth oven and he told about how he had stolen the bow.

After he told about the bow, he uncovered the pork. He divided all of the pork among his friends. They ate the pork and everyone went to their homes.

Kepi wanted to herd the pigs inside, so he went to get the pigs. At this time, he saw a young boy. Kepi asked the boy, "Where are your parents?"

The boy said, "They left me here and went away."

Kepi said, "OK, come with me. Let's sleep."

They slept and the little boy took the bow. Then something took him up into the clouds. So, [now] this bow fires all of the time. If the boy had not done this, there would be no thunder. The boy would have just fired the bow on the ground.

Philip Pesue

Erave

Southern Highlands Province

A1142.3+. Person escapes to sky and shoots bow that makes thunder; A1459.1.1. Origin of bows and arrows; D1091. Magic bow; F61. Person wafted to sky; K400. Thief escapes detection; P210. Husband and wife; P310. Friendship; Q211.11. Punishment for wholesale massacre of tribe; Q411. Death as punishment; S110. Murders; W195. Envy

## Where Did Mount Rabaul [Saruwaged] Come From?

(Wantok 252, February 3, 1979, page 13)

Long, long ago, the ghosts often lived at the source of a stream. At this time, they did not know about eating meat from wild game. No, they just ate the fur and threw away the meat into the stream. One woman took this meat all of the time.

Later, she thought hard and she wanted to see what it was that was killing the game. So one morning, the woman woke up and followed the stream up and up. She saw that the ground was broken and jagged. She saw many entangled vines like a sword-grass house.

The woman worked hard to keep going upstream. She saw something there. Much later, she arrived at the tangled vines and saw an old woman. She went inside. The old woman was shocked and asked sternly, "Why did you come and what do you want?"

The woman told her that she often saw bandicoots and other marsupials (*kapul*) carried by the stream. She asked, "Can I stay with you people and teach you how to eat the meat of wild game?"

The old woman said, "Oh my, I have seven children. If you speak, they'll come and scold me. So, I don't want you to stay."

They continued to talk, and the boys arrived. They saw the woman and were very happy. They asked her why she had come. The woman was happy too and she told them her story. So, the first brother married her.

Later, they had a baby boy. One day, the fathers [father and uncles] went to the forest to hunt for food and wild game. After they had left for the forest, the little boy made a ditch. As the sun was setting, a little rain fell. The rain went into the ditch and directly towards the house. The boy's mother scolded him badly, saying, "Oh my! Your fathers are just ghosts. They're ignorant, so they made the house in a bad location. Why did you make a ditch that caused the water to come and wreck the house?"

The woman said this at home, but the ghosts heard her in the forest. They were irate and decided to leave the woman and flee.

In the early morning, the six brothers and the old woman turned into birds and flew away. The father carried the child and went upwards. The woman woke up and cried out. The child heard her and told his father, "Papa, I think mother is calling and following us."

But the father said, "No, it's a bird calling."

The father and son continued climbing a tall mountain called Mount Sarowaga [Saruwaged Mountains, **Morobe** Province?]. The mother stood on a short mountain called Sarowaga's Wife.

At this time, the father put the boy down and said, "Son, you love your mother too much. OK, stay here and when your mother finds you, look for the trail and leave. Otherwise, you two stay here. The sun will see you in the early morning at about five o'clock. It will see you first, then later it will see me."

The poor father said this, then departed. He turned into a stream that we call Magi which flows down Mount Sarowaga.

The mother took the child, and the father left them and went straight to the sea. The mother carried the child and found the trail, but it was entirely impassable.

So the mother turned into a black stone. On top of the stone the child turned into a red fig, called _wifu_ in my language.

You who live near Sarowaga, look at this story. I think that it is correct. You will worry just a little.

R. N. Nupo Kani
Rabaul
East New Britain Province

A934.11. River from transformation; D215+B. Transformation: boy to fig plant; D231W. Transformation: woman to stone; D283.1+M. Transformation: man to river; D671. Transformation flight; E332.1+. Ghost haunts stream; E423.3. Revenant as bird; E425.1. Revenant as woman; E425.2. Revenant as man; E426+. Revenant as river; E474.1. Offspring of living and dead person; E495.2. Marriage (ceremony) to a ghost; E541+. Ghost eats fur, not flesh; P210. Husband and wife; P231. Mother and son; P233. Father and son; P251.6.3+. Seven brothers; P293. Uncle; R213. Escape from home; T100. Marriage



# A Story of Two Brothers

(Wantok 253, February 10, 1979, page 15)

In the time of yore, two brothers lived in a village called **Napoga** [**Madang** Province]. These two poor brothers did not have parents. Their parents had died in a fight with enemies. The brothers lived well.

One time, they swept the house and as they were sweeping, they found something like a bullet; it was small and round. They took this and planted it near the house. They went to look at it every morning.

One morning, they looked and saw something growing, so they took a long stick and planted it nearby. They waited a week and looked. Oh my, something was climbing the stick that had many fruits, both long and short. The name of this plant is the winged bean. They counted twelve beans on it. One time, the big brother wanted to go to another place, so he told his little brother, "You should take care of the winged bean well." Then he departed.

The little brother wanted to try to count them. He counted and there were thirteen beans. He took one, then cooked and ate it. He thought that the two of them had counted twelve, but he counted thirteen, so he took one to eat. But now there were really eleven. His big brother returned with a pig. He went to the house and counted the beans. He left the house and counted the winged beans. He counted eleven, so he thought that he had counted them wrong. He counted them three times more but one was gone.

He went and took a knife, then went to the forest to cut thorny sticks. He cut ten thorny sticks, then returned to the house where his little brother was. He beat the poor little brother badly. Every thorn on the sticks went inside the little brother's skin. The little brother climbed a mountain and stood in the middle of the mountain. Blood flowed like water from every part of his body and filled the place where he stood. He walked to the other side of the mountain. He stood and hid near a stream.

A young woman came and fetched some water in a pot. He had seen a bird's tail and had put it in the grass. The woman saw this and said, "Did I follow you or did you follow me?" The boy said, "I followed." He told the woman, "My brother beat me." They went to a house and the woman hid the boy where she kept the firewood. The woman's father had died. She lived with her mother. She cooked some sweet potatoes in the fire and pretended to eat some. She gave these to the boy. In the morning, she took him into the sun and pulled the thorns from the boy's skin. Then her mother came into the garden, so she took and hid him. The woman did this for four days and the mother thought, "I don't know what you're doing, but I must find out." The mother pretended to get her net bag but she hid instead. The woman took the boy outside into the sun. So, the mother ran quickly and grabbed the woman and said, "Why didn't you want to show him to me? It's just the two of us that live here." So, the two of them together pulled the rest of the thorns from the boy. The woman married him and they lived happily together.

Juwankele Lou A.
Holy Spirit Com[munity] School
P. O. Box 112
Madang
Madang Province

A2686.6+. Origin of winged bean; J2030. Absurd inability to count; P210. Husband and wife; P232. Mother and daughter; P251.5. Two brothers; P251.5.3. Hostile brothers; P262. Mother-in-law; P265. Son-in-law; Q325. Disobedience punished; Q458. Flogging as punishment; R213. Escape from home; T100. Marriage; W126. Disobedience; Z71.2. Formulistic number: four; Z71.16.2. Formulistic number: ten


## Where Did the Moon Come From?

(Wantok 254, February 17, 1979, page 19)

Long ago, there was no moon in the sky. This is the story of the moon from the Aitape area. There was a village named **Malol** [**Sissano** People, **West Sepik** Province]. In this village, there lived a man and his wife. They lived there and raised only two children. The first child was a boy and the second was a girl.

One night, they did not have food for themselves. The father and mother told the two children, "You two stay here and we'll go find fish in the stream. We'll bring sago and other food." The two children agreed. The father and mother went to the stream. This place had a land *masalai* that lived in the area.

When the parents returned, they had not fooled around with fishing. They had "stolen" a lot. The two of them cooked the food. The man told his wife, "Don't call the children, leave them alone. They're sleeping and we can finish this food. When they ask you in the morning for food, say, 'We didn't get any fish. We came home empty-handed.'"

The boy heard their parents talking. When dawn arrived, the little boy woke his sister and said, "We must leave our parents." The sister agreed. They got up and went down [through the window] and arrived at the area of the land *masalai*. They asked the *masalai* to help them.

The land *masalai* asked them what they wanted. The land *masalai* turned them yellow. The little boy asked the *masalai* why it did this. The *masalai* told them, "To give you light." They said "Yes" to the *masalai*.

So when you want to look at the moon and you see something black, it is the little boy and his sister.

Lambert Sayaw
Madang
Madang Province

A747. Person transformed to moon; D683.7. Transformation by fairy; F490+. Masalai; P210. Husband and wife; P231. Mother and son; P232. Mother and daughter; P233. Father and son; P234. Father and daughter; P253. Sister and brother; R213. Escape from home; S11+. Cruel father refuses children food; S12.6. Cruel mother refuses children food; W151. Greed


## Three Brothers

(Wantok 255, February 24, 1979, page 17)

Once, in a village called Ormikoan [**Omkalai**] in Gumine sub-Province in **Simbu** Province, there lived three brothers [**Golin** People]. The first brother was named Amil, the second Koba, and the third Dimin.

One morning, the first brother, Amil, looked and saw the sun rising. He saw that the village looked very nice. He looked at the forest and the trees turned blue, all of the clouds turned blue too. He thought of going into the forest to hunt for birds and marsupials (*kuskus*). He took his bow and arrows, then departed.

He arrived at a place in the forest and saw a tree with many birds eating fruits on it. He worked at shooting the birds. He was running short of arrows and it had become evening, so he thought of finding and collecting the birds that he had killed.

However, there was not a bird to be found. He was angry, so he went to his right. He tried to hold a cut branch but could not. He tried to hold a house fence. He trembled and wanted to run away, but he could not. An old woman had coiled a rope around his leg. His leg was burning as if it was on fire. The woman told Amil to come inside. She said, "Men often come in. Don't be afraid to come. I've cooked and eaten the birds that you shot. I gathered your arrows. You can take them and I'll cook some food for you. You can eat and the leave." Then the old woman went inside the house.

He went in, then the old woman cooked two sweet potatoes for Amil and cut two pieces of sugarcane for him. He ate the sweet potatoes and drank the juice from the sugarcane, then the old woman's husband arrived. Amil saw that his teeth were unusual. The old man's teeth were fastened to bark and his "young" [small?] teeth were bright white, like white cloth. Amil was terrified and wanted to run away, but the man said, "Don't be afraid and run away. I'm your old man, huh? Come hold this log and I'll cut some firewood." So, Amil went and held the log. The old man gave one chop at the wood. Amil thought that he would chop at the wood again, but no, he cut Amil's neck and killed him.

The wife came and held her man's legs tightly and said, "I'll eat your ass, my good man." She said, "Thank you" to her husband and they butchered Amil's body. After they butchered him, they cooked Amil and ate him.

When they finished eating, they took the bones and scraps, and then gave them to a woman named Temnegi who had no husband or children.

Koba and Dimin waited for Amil for two days. Koba, the second brother, went to the forest with a bow and some arrows. He searched for Amil and called out near the house of the two old people. A man said, "Yes." So Amil said, "Is that Amil?" The man said, "Yes!"

Koba said, "Did you kill some wild game or not?" Amil [the man] said, "A lot, and you must try to hunt for some too." Koba thought hard and began shooting birds at the same tree that was filled with birds where Amil had shot them. Koba kept shooting the birds until he was running out of arrows. Then he said, "Enough." He looked for the birds that he had shot and held the same tree that Amil had held. Then he saw the old woman and she said, "Amil came and he slept with me. Come find him." Koba said, "Yes." [She said,] "Come inside." So he went.

The old woman flattered him, then her husband arrived. Koba looked at the woman's husband and he wanted to flee like Amil had wanted to before. The old man said, "Don't be afraid, I'm your old father." The old man did as he had done with Amil and killed Koba. The old man and woman cooked and ate him as before. They took the bones and scraps, and gave them to the woman named Temnegi, just as they had done with Amil.

However Temnegi was tired of eating the bones and scraps, so she threw them into a small stream and she did not eat.

Now the third brother, Dimin, was waiting for his two brothers who had not returned. He thought that they were still hunting marsupials (*kapul*) and birds in the forest. However, this was not the case. The two old people had killed and eaten them, but Dimin did not know this.

He waited for a long time, about three days. He became angry and said that he would go look for them in the forest. He took his bow and arrows and an axe, then departed. When he entered the forest, he called out for his two brothers, but nobody replied. He kept calling and calling until he arrived at the same place. He heard two men say, "Yes."

He thought that his two brothers had said, "Yes." Now he felt better. However, he came to a cut tree and tried to hold it. Then he held the house fence just as his two brothers had held it and entered the house.

Then the old woman said, "Your two brothers came and we stayed here. They went to hunt birds in the forest." He went inside and the old woman did as before with Dimin's two brothers. They stayed there until the evening when the old man came and told the young man, "Come, I want to cut some firewood. Come and hold the log." So, he went and held the log and the old man cut it. After he made one cut, he raised the axe again and was about to cut Dimin's neck. However, Dimin dodged the blow and he killed the old man. Then he killed the old woman.

Then he went to kill Temnegi, but Temnegi said, "The two old people killed your two brothers and ate them. They gave me the bones but I didn't eat them. I put them in this small stream. I'll give you this flute. Go to the water and blow this flute. When you blow the flute, your two brothers, Amil and Koba, will come forth. Take them and you can go home."

Dimin did as Temnegi said and his two brothers came and they went home.

Before, men went into the forest and the two old people killed and ate them. However, Dimin was strong and killed the two old people. So now, you can travel around the forest and return to your house.

Are John
Hohola No. 4
Port Moresby
National Capital District

See LeRoy (1985a: 159-192) and LeRoy (1985b: 170-180) for similar tales.

D492+. Clouds turn blue; D492+. Trees turn blue; D1203. Magic rope; D1223.1. Magic flute; D2144.3. Heat produced by magic; E55.2. Resuscitation by playing flute; F513.1. Person unusual as to his teeth; G413. Ogre disguises voice to lure victim; G512. Ogre killed; K910. Murder by strategy; K1930. Treacherous impostors; P210. Husband and wife; P251.6.1. Three brothers; Q211. Murder punished; Q215. Cannibalism punished; Q411. Death as punishment; R4. Surprise capture; R155.1. Youngest brother rescues his elder brothers; S139.2. Slain person dismembered; S139.2.2+. Corpse put into cooking pot or cooked; S139.4. Murder by mangling with axe

## Where Did the Cockatoo Come From?

(Wantok 256, March 3, 1979, page 21)

Long, long ago there were families who lived on top of a mountain called Aseonka in the **Kainantu** area [**Agarabi** People, **Eastern Highlands** Province]. These families only ate sweet potatoes and taros. They never ate them with meat.

One time, the father angrily said, "Why is that that we only eat sweet potatoes with taros everyday." He said that the next day, he would take his son and they would hunt for wild game, then eat it with taros and sweet potatoes.

The father woke up in the early morning and began to cook some sweet potatoes to carry into the forest. Dawn arrived. He put the sweet potatoes in a small net bag and took his bow and arrows. At about six o'clock in the morning, he woke his son and they began to walk into the forest.

They walked and walked. In the middle of the forest, the son became very hungry and ate some sweet potato. The father turned back and saw the boy eating. He said, "Son, stop eating. We have not arrived in the deep forest yet." However, the boy was hungry, so he finished eating. They kept walking and arrived at the [deep] forest.

The father sat under a tree and told the boy, "I'm hungry now. Get some of the sweet potatoes that we cooked and brought here. We'll eat first, then go hunt for wild game."

The boy told his father that the he had finished the food on the trail. The father asked him again. He asked whether he was telling the truth or just fibbing. The boy was telling the truth. When the father heard this, he became irate. He told the boy, "Boy, you must stay here and I'll go shake that tree. When I return to the forest, I'll have killed many marsupials (*kapul*) at that tree." The boy said he would stay there. However, the father tricked his son and quickly ran back home.

The child waited and waited for his father, but his father did not return quickly. He called out, "Papa! Papa!" But his father did not reply. He called out again, "Papa! Papa!" But the boy's voice "missed", and he became a cockatoo.

Now if you see a cockatoo and say, "Hello cockatoo," the cockatoo will say "Hello" to you. This is because that boy became a cockatoo. However, men cannot do this, so they cut a *tanget* and plant it.

Tiko Thomas Bai

Kainantu

Eastern Highlands Province

A1998K+. Creation of cockatoo; A2490+. Why cockatoo can speak; D150+B. Transformation: boy to cockatoo; F561+. People only eat tubers; F562.7K. People live in mountain top; P233. Father and son; Q325. Disobedience punished; Q438. Punishment: abandonment in forest; S143. Abandonment in forest; W126. Disobedience

## An Eagle's Story

(Wantok 257, March 10, 1979, page 21)
(Wantok 258, March 17, 1979, page 21)

Long ago, there was a big eagle that flew in the forest. When this eagle saw pigs, dogs, men, women or children, it never left them alone. It would fly down, pick them up and carry them to its aerie, then eat them.

When the people made gardens and made fires, the eagle would see the smoke, then fly down and snatch them with its legs, carrying them away. The eagle did this until the people were almost all gone.

One time, all of the men gathered and wanted to escape to **Karkar** Island [**Waskia** or **Takia** People, **Madang** Province]. All of the men went to the forest, cut some huge trees and made canoes from them to escape from their enemy.

When the canoes were ready, all of the men helped each other push off the canoes toward the sea. The canoes were ready and the women prepared food, water, firewood and everything else to take with them to Karkar Island. After everything was ready, the people decided that they would pull the canoes into the sea at exactly six o'clock in the evening [dusk]. They said, "If we go in the daylight, the eagle will see us in the middle of the sea and fly down and kill us." So, they waited for night. When nighttime arrived, they began to walk to the sea and pull the canoes into the sea.

A poor old woman had left her bracelet at her house. She went back to her house to get it. When she returned, everyone had gone asea. When she reached the beach, she did not find anyone. She looked for them, but they were far from shore. This poor old woman was a childless widow, so she had no one to help her. The woman slept at the base of a huge callophyllum tree that had a hole in it.

The woman often slept at the base of this tree by the beach, and it was also like her house. She would sleep during the day, and she went to her garden to get food at night. She cooked her food at night and prepared it during daylight. She was afraid of the eagle, so she did not want to make a fire during daylight lest the eagle would see the smoke from her fire and kill her.

139

The woman lived like this for a while, then she became pregnant and gave birth to a boy named Kinim. Later, she gave birth to another boy, called Wiwil. The last child that she gave birth to was named Rukas. When the three boys became big, she went to the men's house where she found bows, arrows and spears that she gave to her sons. After the boys were fully-grown, they began to train at fighting. The first boy took a spear, ran and shot it at a tree. The tree split in two and he named it after himself. He said, "Aha Kinim." The second and third boys did likewise. The boys' mother told them, "Don't go to the forest, you must stay nearby."

When the boys returned to their mother, they asked her, "Why did you stop us from going far into the forest?" Their mother said, "There's a big eagle that lives there which kills and eats people."

She said, "This eagle killed and ate your father. All of the other people fled to Karkar Island." She said, "I was the only one here; they left me. I stayed under the callophyllum tree and I gave birth to you." The three boys listened to this and were very troubled. They said, "We'll kill this eagle." However, their mother said, "You're just boys. You can't kill the eagle." She said, "Your elders tried and couldn't, so they escaped."

One day, the three boys began to cut some very strong trees and build a house. When everything was ready, they began to make a very large and strong house. On the roof of the house, they made a small hole for smoke to exit. When everything was ready, the three boys told their mother to cook some food for them.

However, their mother was afraid. She said, "It would be bad if I made a fire and the eagle saw the smoke. The eagle will come and kill us." The three boys said, "Mama, don't be afraid, we'll kill the eagle."

So the boys' mother began to make a fire. She made a bonfire. When the smoke went out, the eagle saw it. The eagle quickly went down to this house. When the eagle perched upon the house, the house shook violently. Their mother was terrified. When the eagle landed on the house, one of its claws went inside the post at the front of the house. The eagle wanted to pull its leg out, but it could not. It was stuck inside the post. The eagle's two huge wings flapped on top of the house.

The three boys took their clubs and ran outside. They climbed the house and broke the eagle's wings with the clubs. The boys killed the eagle. They could not lift the eagle, so they rolled it down to the ground. Their mother was happy. She sang and danced and jumped about. She was very happy for her three sons.

On the next day, they worked at gathering firewood. When the firewood was ready, they made a bonfire. They cooked the eagle on the fire and burned the eagle completely. While the fire was burning, some sparks flew about. They held the [ashes] and put it back inside the pyre, but some small pieces flew about that they did not see. These became the small eagles that we see flying around nowadays.

When you make a garden [by burning the forest], you often see eagles flying in the smoke from the fire. It is as if they were coming from the ashes from when the three boys had burned the big eagle. So, they are often very happy for the smoke from the fire.

The boys' mother turned into a stone that stands at the beach. Her three sons turned into stones too, and they stand in the sea. When the white people came to our area, there were no people or boats that had come to this area. If a ship came by, it would break apart and sink. When people, pigs or dogs approached, they would kill them. Then the missionaries made the Catholic Mission at **Mugil**, and there is no more trouble there [**Mugil** People].

If you want to see the mother of the three boys, go to the Catholic Mission at Mugil (N. G. R.) and ask some men to show you. However, you cannot see the three boys because they are beneath the sea.

Joe Baduk

Wabag

Enga Province

A974. Rocks from transformation of people to stone; A977. Origin of particular stones or groups of stones; A1937+. Origin of eagles; A2471.3+. Why eagle hovers over fire; B16.3. Devastating birds; B33. Man-eating birds; B872.1. Giant eagle; D231B. Transformation: boy to stone; D231W. Transformation: woman to stone; D1402.21+. Magic stones kill; E658. Reincarnation: animal to other animal; F614.8+. Tree split in two by arrow/spear; G510.4. Hero overcomes devastating animal; P231. Mother and son; P251.6.1. Three brothers; R213. Escape from home; S140.1. Abandonment of aged; T510. Miraculous conception; T538. Unusual conception in old age; T570. Pregnancy; T581.9. Child born on beach; V331. Conversion to Christianity


## The Boy Who Had a Dog-Father
(Wantok 259, March 25, 1979, page 25)

Once there was a pregnant woman. She went into the deep forest to hunt for wildfowl eggs [probably the common scrubfowl, *Megapodius freycinet* (Beehler, 1986:72-74)]. She saw a wildfowl nest and worked at removing the leaves from the nest, taking some eggs.

She had labor pains [and gave birth]. She covered up the baby inside the wildfowl nest with broken leaves. She went to her husband at home. The baby did not die, it lived well and grew two teeth.

There was a big dog that traveled far and wide in the forest. Every time the dog came near the baby, it would stop. The dog smelled the baby's odor and thought, "What's that?" The dog worked at removing the leaves, then scraped against the baby's head. The baby cried loudly. The dog was surprised. It ran away and hit its head on a stone, falling down.

The dog returned quietly and saw the beautiful baby sleeping there. The dog took the baby in its mouth and carried it to a boulder. It was spacious underneath the boulder and there was shelter from the rain. The dog left the baby there and ran to a house. The dog stole bananas and returned to give them to the baby to eat. The dog did this for a long time and the baby grew up.

Another time, the dog went to steal a loincloth and returned to give to the baby for clothing. Another time, the dog stole a bow and gave it to the boy to use. The boy became a handsome young man. The boy's father, the dog, took him to a village.

The dog went first and the boy followed the dog. The dog went inside the house of the dog's owners together with the boy. The dog's master saw them and was very happy about the boy. In the evening, he called on his two young daughters to bring firewood to him.

However, the first daughter did not want to bring firewood. She spoke vainly, "You'll get a husband for me, then I'll give firewood to you. Very sorry." The old man called out to his second daughter, "OK, bring some firewood here."

The second girl heeded her father and brought some firewood. She saw the young boy and giggled at him. The girl left the firewood, but she held tightly to the boy. She was very happy. The father let them marry and they were happy together.

One time, the dog stole a chicken, so the old father was angry and killed the dog.

The boy and his wife went to the village. They went into the garden and the boy saw that his father, the dog, had died. He cried and cried until he could not cry any longer. He took a spear, then stabbed and killed himself. His wife came and saw this. She hanged herself from a rope and died with him.

Kisi V. Bambok
Morobe Province

B535.0.4. Dog as nurse for child; K420. Thief loses his goods or is detected; M451.1. Death by suicide; P210. Husband and wife; P214.1. Wife commits suicide (dies) on death of husband; P233+. Son commits suicide on death of father; P234. Father and daughter; P252.1. Two sisters; P271. Foster father; P275. Foster son; Q212. Theft punished; Q411. Death as punishment; S143. Abandonment in forest; T10. Falling in love; T100. Marriage; T570. Pregnancy; T581.1. Birth of child in forest; W31. Obedience; W126. Disobedience

## The Man Who Was Afraid of Breasts
(Wantok 260, March 31, 1979, page 21)

Long ago, there were only forty young women who lived in the deep forest between Indonesia and Papua New Guinea. At this time, there were no men, and the women did not think about men or know what they were. They only thought of themselves. This is how things were before.

They made houses and gardens, and they took care of pigs. They did all of the work with their own hands. However one time, a young woman wanted to drink some water because they had made a big garden and the sun was very hot. The woman left the others and went to where they usually drank.

A very handsome young boy was hunting marsupials (*kapul*) in the forest and he heard a very loud noise. He had heard the women working and laughing in the garden. The boy also did not think that there were other women or men. He thought that there were only marsupials and cassowaries and other kinds of animals in the forest. This is how it once was. The boy had also left his home which was about one hundred miles away from where he was hunting.

When he arrived at this place and heard the noises, he went very quietly and sat, then he watched and listened to them. He was shocked because he had never seen this kind of thing before. He looked at his body and their bodies; his was different. There were two things on them that were different. They had two long things hanging from their bodies, their breasts. Also, he had never heard their kind of speech before. He was afraid, but not too afraid.

When he saw the woman go down to the stream to drink, the boy ran down and sat at the head of the stream. When the woman put her mouth to the water, the boy turned into a mosquito and flew along the water. The woman drank him with the water. After she finished drinking, she went back to work with the others in the garden. In the evening, they completely finished working in the garden. They sang and danced in a row towards their house. When they arrived at the house, they prepared much food. They were happy together and they ate.

However, the one woman did not want to eat. She told her friends, "I have a big pain in my belly, so I can't eat." She tried to just sleep in a room for two entire weeks. Her belly began to swell and the young women said, "Come outside." They looked at her belly and were shocked because they had never seen anything like this before. After three weeks, the woman began to cry in the sleeping room. They went to look at her and she gave birth to a boy. They were afraid, but they took care of the boy and he became bigger. He got up, pulled the two breasts and began to drink. It was not long before he became a big boy, and a smart one.

The boy married one of them and she had a boy again. When all of the young women saw this, they said, "Do that to me." One said, "Me first." They all seduced the boy and he impregnated all of the women. Some had boys and some had girls. Now there are many of us.

Jackett Yaponai
Enga Province

A1290+. Primeval forty women and one man; D185.1+B. Transformation: boy to mosquito; P210. Husband and wife; P231. Mother and son; P232. Mother and daughter; P233. Father and son; P234. Father and daughter; T100. Marriage; T145.0.1. Polygyny; T511.5.3+. Pregnancy from swallowing mosquito; T570. Pregnancy; T573. Short pregnancy; T580. Childbirth


## The Sister's Fault

(Wantok 261, April 7, 1979, page 17)

In the time of yore, a brother and sister lived in a village named **Kwipage Nokiake** [**Madang** Province?]. The brother's name was Perkagel, and the sister's name was Direduruagele.

One day, the brother told his sister Direduruagele, "You and I always stay home, that's bad. When the sun rises, it would be better if you dig some sweet potatoes in the garden and prepare them. Then you and I shall go to the forest to hunt for some wild game for ourselves." So, the sister went to the garden and took the good sweet potatoes from the garden.

The brother, Perkagel, sharpened his arrows and his multi-pronged spear, and he tightened his bow. Things were ready, so the next morning they woke up and went to the forest. When they arrived at a place to sleep, the brother told his sister, "Stay here and make a fire, clean off a place to sleep, and prepare some food for us. I'm going to the forest to hunt for some wild game for us tonight." When he was ready to go, he told his sister, "Please, don't travel around the area. You must just stay in the hut here." The brother went to the forest, and the sister stayed. She tired of staying at the hut, so she went a little ways away and found a good vine for making a net bag. While she was taking the vine, she heard a man hitting a hand drum, singing and coming toward her. He was dressed beautifully, his name was Digindagan.

He told the woman, "Get your net bag and come here." The man was filled with adornments, and he had decorations of many colors inside his net bag. When the woman saw this, she was startled. Her heart jumped and she nearly wanted to go with him. Digindagan made an offer to her, then he got up, hit the hand drum, sang and departed. The woman got up and went to the hut to stay. When the brother returned, the sister was crying. She did not eat. The brother gave her some marsupial (*kapul*) meat, and he too did not eat. She was still crying, so the brother said, "Now I know. I told you that you couldn't go outside the hut. You should have just stayed at the hut, but you ignored what I said and you saw Digindagan. OK, finish crying and eat, then you can go to him." The woman finished crying, then she ate. In the morning, they went back home. The brother cut firewood and gathered stones. He took a huge pig, then killed and cooked it [in an earth oven]. After the pig was done, he removed it [from the oven] and butchered it.

He decorated his sister very nicely: a pretty "grass" skirt, bracelets, necklaces, beautiful bird feathers for her hair, and many marsupial furs. After he finished, he took the pork ribs, put much salt on them and gave them to his sister. When the sister held them, a bolt of lightning flashed, then rain came and took the woman away. Now, we often send women away to be married. It is the fault of this woman, Direduruagle [Direduruagele], because she ignored her brother. At first, we often worry when our sisters leave us and go with a new man.

Peter Yaga
Maiwara [School]
Madang [Province]

A1550+. Origin of virilocality; D1032. Magic meat; D2120. Magic transportation; D2143.1. Rain produced by magic; D2149.1. Thunderbolt magically produced; P210. Husband and wife; P253. Sister and brother; P600+. Virilocality; W126. Disobedience

# The Story of the Ramu River

(Wantok 262, April 14, 1979, page 25)

Long ago, the men of Ramu lived well and were happy together. However one time, there was a big festival in a village. This village was fairly far away, and a young woman lived there. The men competed at singing, dancing and hitting their hand drums to get her attention.

Two young men with their mother were quite late. An old woman was sitting on the trail. Mucous fell from her and she had ringworm. The foul old woman asked the two young men and their mother, "Children, are you coming to the festival? I have some taros and sweet potatoes in my net bag. Do you want to eat it or not?"

The old woman had asked many young men but they spat at her and ridiculed her. However, the these two men and their mother said, "Old mother, we want to go to the festival, but we're famished. We'll eat. After we regain our strength we'll go to the festival."

So, the old woman divulged a secret, "When you go to the festival, stay on your own side. Let the other men sing and dance inside while you two and your mother sing and dance on the side. The beautiful woman will tremble and come to you two. Many men will have thought that she trembled at them, but they will lose and the woman will come directly to you and your mother." So, they sang and danced excellently, and all of the other men lost and were very troubled.

The two young men with their mother and the beautiful young woman went home. The old woman threw away her stick, and a heavy rain fell. The river rose and rushed towards the sea. Many people tried very hard to make a bridge across the river, but the water was too strong and carried the logs away.

Everyone stayed on one side of the river, they could not get to the other side. The two young men with their mother and the [young] woman stayed on the other side.

So now, this is called the Ramu River. Before, the Ramu River did not flow. This story comes from where the Ramu River is near **Madang** Province.

Joseph Dua
Upper Chimbu
[Simbu Province]

A934.4+. Origin of river: magic stick; D956. Magic stick of wood; D2143.1. Rain produced by magic; P231. Mother and son; P251.5. Two brothers; Q41. Politeness rewarded; T50. Wooing

# How Did the First Yam Come About?

(Wantok 263, April 21, 1979, page 21)

Long, long ago, there was an old woman with her young son. At this time, they did not work in the garden. They lived together until the boy married a young woman from another village. They then lived together and had four children. The man, his wife and their four children did not look after the man's old mother. No, the poor old woman often went to sleep hungry.

One time, the man went to the forest to build a bird blind. Then he watched from the blind. While he was watching, his old mother was approaching death at her home.

While she slept in her bed, her spirit became a cassowary and followed her son into the forest. She approached the bird blind and ate tree [fruits] near her son's bird blind. When her son saw her, he thought that it was a real cassowary, so he quickly shot her. When the cassowary was approaching death, she spoke as a person would, "You killed me. You can't eat me. You must cut a tree on top of me, then go home. Stay there for one or two months, then return. When you see something growing on top of the place that I am lying, you must take care of it. It's food for you." The man heeded this and did as his mother's spirit told him to do.

After two months, he went and saw a new thing growing on top of the place where his mother's spirit rested. He looked at it and he took care of it. Later, the man tried eating it and it was delicious. So, they took care of it and planted it.

This is the beginning of gardening. They planted these yams, took care of them and they were prolific. So now in **Nuku**, we often plant yams [**Mehek** People, **West Sepik** Province].

Mathias Yawur
St. Ignatius High School
Aitape
West Sepik Province

A1441. Acquisition of agriculture; A2686.4.3. Origin of yams; B211.3.17K. Speaking cassowary; D169.4W. Transformation: woman to cassowary; E631. Reincarnation in plant (tree) growing from grave; F401.3.7+. Spirit in form of cassowary; P210. Husband and wife; P230. Parents and children; P231. Mother and son; S22+. Matricide; S115. Murder by stabbing; T100. Marriage

# Fire Came from Manam Island

(Wantok 264, April 28, 1979, page 17)

Long ago, there were two animals, Dog and Marsupial (*Sikau*) who were very good friends. They were friends for a very long time.

They never became angry or fought. Never. They were friends who often cooked their food just using the heat of the sun. They always saw smoke coming from a volcano called **Manam** Island [**Manam** People, **Madang** Province].

They often thought about who was making the smoke, "We should go see what is over there and get what is making that smoke." They talked some more, then Marsupial told Dog, "Friend, [I'll] get it and come. If I encounter an enemy, I won't be able to reach you. If you wait too long, you must know that it's ruined." Marsupial finished speaking, then swam to the island.

Dog waited on the beach for its friend, Marsupial. Marsupial swam and swam, then arrived at the beach of Manam Island. Marsupial rested and then climbed to the place where the smoke came from.

Marsupial went to a place where there was firewood, then worked at igniting it. Marsupial returned to the beach and swam back. While Marsupial swam, the waves almost extinguished the fire. But the flame was strong and did not go out. Marsupial came very close to shore, then a big wave came and extinguished the fire.

When Dog saw this, Dog became irate and told Marsupial, "Now I'll go to get it." So Dog swam away. Dog tried the same thing. Dog rested, then took a piece of firewood, lit it and returned. The waves almost extinguished the fire again, but Dog was very good and the fire did not go out.

Dog reached the shore and told Marsupial, "Now you must still find your fire and cook food." Poor Marsupial listened to this and was ashamed, then Marsupial went into the forest to live. So now, marsupials live in the forest and dogs live with people in villages. Now too, we who live in villages have fire.

Ignatius Kumala

Bogia [Town]

Madang Province

A1414. Origin of fire; A2433.2.1+. Why marsupial lives in forest; A2433.3.2+. Why dog lives in village; A2494.4+. Enmity between dog and marsupial; J1813+. Cooking processes misunderstood: cooking with the sun; P310. Friendship; R213. Escape from home

# The Old Woman Who Gathered Cockatoos

(Wantok 265, May 5, 1979, page 21)
(Wantok 266, May 12, 1979, page 21)
(Wantok 267, May 19, 1979, page 17)

Long ago, a young man took his bow and arrows and went into the forest. He arrived at a tree that had many fruits on it. The tree was full of big fat birds too. The birds were cockatoos. When the man saw them, he built a bird blind on top of the tree. He went inside the blind and waited.

He sat and watched. Many more birds came to eat the tree fruits. When he shot the birds, they fell with the arrows on top of a *limbum* palm. He continued to shoot the cockatoos. They did not fall straight to the ground, they became stuck on this *limbum* palm.

He did this for a while, then finished. He went to go home and sleep. In the morning, at about six o'clock [dawn], he awoke, carried his bow and went back to watch from the same bird blind.

He watched the cockatoos fill the tree. The man shot the birds but they did not fall to the ground. No, they became stuck again on the *limbum* palm. He continued to do this and became irate. He shot a cockatoo again and it fell again on the *limbum* palm.

He went down to the ground and left his bow and arrows on the ground. He made a rope and climbed high up the *limbum* palm. The *limbum* palm carried him up to the moon.

The *limbum* palm went inside [the moon]. It left the man there and shrank back down to earth again. The *limbum* was very short now and the poor man was still up at the moon. The poor man was terrified. He tried to hide at various places. An old woman took some trash and threw it at him while he was hiding.

The old woman took him and brought him to her house. The old woman told him, "I removed the feathers of all of the cockatoos that you shot and gathered them up. I smoked their edible parts and put them on top of the bed."

The old woman and the man sat down together. The man saw a bonfire burning. The old woman was in charge. The man went up and looked at the fire and was afraid.

However, the woman told him, "Don't be afraid." You should come and warm your body by the fire. The man went and sat by the fire, warming himself. The old woman went to the garden, took some food and cooked it. She and the man ate it. The old woman told him, "At night, the people will come to sing and dance." So they waited.

They waited through the evening until it was night. They were not fooling around. The people came and sang and danced. The man asked the old woman, "Hey grandma, where did these people who are singing and dancing come from?" The man continued, "When I came, I didn't see many people. There were no houses for them. Where do these people live?"

### The Star People Who Sing and Dance

The old woman tricked him and said, "They live at another place. They came here to sing and dance." She tricked him because there were not real people. No, they were stars that had turned into people and had come to sing and dance.

The people wanted to sing and dance, but they each broke off one of their legs and smoked them of the fire. The old woman controlled them. So, they continued to sing and dance with their other legs. When these legs tired, they changed their legs again. Then these legs were smoked in the fire again.

They did this until dawn. Then the old woman put the man inside the house and she controlled the others' legs. The man stayed for about four weeks with this old woman.

The man's parents searched and searched for him but they could not find him. So, his parents and the rest of his family made a big feast. They ate and mourned for him. They cried for him because they thought that he was dead.

However, the man was still alive and living with this old woman. Later, the old woman wanted to send him back again to his village. When she was ready to send him back, she prepared everything for him and sent him down.

Before he departed, the old woman told him, "You must go on top of that tree and take the fruits from the vine growing on it, but you can't take the red or yellow fruits. You must take those that are pure green." So, the boy followed the old woman's instructions. He took the green fruits from the vine. He took them slowly then climbed down to the ground. [...He scraped] his skin and his tears flowed. He took them [the fruits] and gave them to his grandmother. The grandmother told him, "Take them and hide them well. Cover them up well." So he covered them well, as his grandmother had instructed.

The two of them went around the garden. At about five o'clock, they went back to the village. When they arrived, the old woman told the boy, "Open the door." The man opened the door and saw two beautiful young women sitting there. The boy was very surprised, his teeth chattered at the sight of these two women.

The women were very beautiful. The old woman told him, "These are your wives." So the boy was very happy to have these two wives. However, one of his eyes was ruined because of the time that he had climbed the tree and his hand had poked his eye out.

They slept until dawn, then the old woman wanted to send the man with his two wives back down to the ground.

The old woman pulled a *limbum* leaf, then it went up and brought the man with his two wives back down to the ground. The man took his two wives and went to his village.

They walked and approached the village. The man hid the two women at the base of a banana plant. He went alone to the village. He went to his parents and cried loudly to them. They had thought that their child was dead.

### The Boastful Brother Became a Flying Fox

The child told his parents about his family. They gathered food and prepared a very big party. They killed pigs and cooked them for eating. The man went to get the two women. He went to the clearing. The parents watched and the family was very happy that he had two wives.

One eye was bad and one was good. They made a big party and were happy for the two women and the man too. The man's little brother saw his two wives and he trembled.

He said to his older brother, "Yes brother, it would be better if you gave one woman to me and I married her. Then you'll still have one to marry."

The big brother told him, "No, I'm determined on this matter. I found them, I shall keep them. If you want a wife, come sit and listen carefully to this story. I must instruct you first, then you can find a wife for yourself."

The little brother was very happy about what his big brother told him. He sat nearby. His big brother told him the story, but the boy did not sit still and he did not absorb the story that his brother told him. He woke up at dawn, took his bow and went to the forest. His brother's bird blind was still there.

He watched and shot a cockatoo. The cockatoo fell on the *limbum* palm. The boy went down and climbed the *limbum* palm, as his brother had done. When he climbed the *limbum*, it brought him up high to the moon. When he reached the moon, the *limbum* returned to the ground.

He stood there and the old woman came, the one who had come to his big brother. His grandmother brought him to the house. When he arrived at the house, his grandmother cooked some food and gave it to him. He ate it. The old woman told him that at night there would be people coming to sing and dance.

[The old woman said,] "I'm in control of this fire. They will come and lose one of their legs in the smoke. I'm teaching you. You're a real man and you came up here. You must do as your big brother did."

So at night, they came and sang and danced. They all removed their legs and smoked them. They danced on only one leg. The little boy saw their legs and he salivated [lit., "swallowed his saliva"]. He wanted to take a leg and eat it.

He took a man's leg and ate it. They sang and danced until dawn. Then they all returned to get their legs and put them back on. However, one poor man could not find his leg. The boy had eaten it. He killed this boy and threw him down to the ground.

The boy turned into a flying fox. He flew around to his brother's view. He now knew that his little brother was killed, so he was saddened and cried for him. This ancestor story comes from Kaiapit, **Pupuk** Village [**Adzera** People, **Morobe** Province].

Mr. Kissip Joseph
Heldsbach
Box 217
Finschhafen
Madang Province

A751.8. Woman in the moon; A767. Stars sing together; D439.5.2. Transformation: star to person; D1520.1.1. Transportation by stretching and swaying tree; D2174+. Dancer removes one leg and smokes it on fire while dancing with other leg; D2198. Magic control of spirits (angels); E612.4.1K. Dead men transformed into flying-foxes; F16. Visit to land of moon; F215. Fairies live in star-world; G70+. Dismembered leg eaten; P210. Husband and wife; P231. Mother and son; P233. Father and son; P251.5. Two brothers; P251.4. Brothers scorn brother's wise counsel; P292. Grandmother; Q215. Cannibalism punished; S110. Murders; T100. Marriage; T145.0.1. Polygyny

## Where Did the Sea Come From?

(Wantok 268, May 26, 1979, page 25)

Long ago, there lived a man named Mairua. He lived on Mount Marien[berg?]. Later, he went to a place named **Amunu**. Then he went to see the men turning the earth.

At one garden, named Waiberav, he called out, "If a man is married, the man's little brother cannot marry." The men of the garden heard what *Masalai* Mairua said and they were irate.

They sent a child named Pupu. He went to this place, Amunu, where he saw a huge, bad man who was only wearing arm and leg bands. His head also had a big band around it.

Pupu went back and told the men at Waiberav garden. He told them about the *masalai* man, then he told them, "He's not a small man. He is a huge man who is only wearing leg, hand and head bands." The men who had not seen the *masalai* place often sat on *tanget* shrubs. So, they made a hole at the base of a *tanget* shrub.

*Masalai* Mairua wanted to come and sit on this *tanget* shrub, but he broke it and fell into the hole. The men took their digging sticks and killed him.

Pupu called two friends and said to them, "Cut off Mairua's head and put it inside a signal drum." So the two friends, Kabayui and Kabadidi, cut off his head and put it in a signal drum.

While they slept that night, the clouds thundered and a heavy rain poured down. The sea arose inside the signal drum. Two fish, named Memel and Dui, also arose inside the drum.

Memel was a white fish and Dui was a black fish. Kabayui was working in his garden and he told his friend Kabadidi, "I don't have any meat to give to men [in exchange for] helping me make my garden."

So Kabadidi told Kabayui, "Go shoot the black fish Dui." Kabayui went to shoot Dui, but missed and shot the white fish, Memel. At night, the sea inside the signal drum crashed and jumped about. The two fish also jumped about. The sea capsized out of the drum and the two fish capsized with it. The sea took them to the beach.

Now, the sea is adjacent to people who live near the beach. Now, the sea is full of fish. Those who live by the beach travel in canoes and eat fish from the sea. However, I want to tell those of you who live by the sea that the sea does not belong to you. No, it belongs to my people who live in the forest. The sea came from my forest at Amunu.

Francis Verek
Bogia
Madang Province

A920. Origin of the seas; A1550. Origin of customs of courtship and marriage; A2100. Creation of fish; D2143.1. Rain produced by magic; D2149.1. Thunderbolt magically produced; E540+. Spirit dictates marriage rules, then is killed by mortals in revenge; E617. Reincarnation as fish; E636. Reincarnation as water; F401.6. Spirit in human form; F401.8. Gigantic spirit; F405+. Spirit killed by spear/arrow; F238. Fairies are naked; F490+. Masalai; K735.1. Mats over holes as pitfall; P210. Husband and wife; P310. Friendship; Q411. Death as punishment; S115. Murder by stabbing

## The Flying Fox Killed Kaiwaru [the Snake]

(Wantok 269, June 2, 1979, page 21)

Long, long ago, there was a huge snake named Kaiwaru that lived up in the sky. This was a snake that ate people, pigs, dogs and other things on the earth.

Every day, Kaiwaru came straight down from above to kill people, then went back up to eat them. Kaiwaru did this for a long time until there were no people anywhere except for just one woman. This young woman fled to the forest and went inside a cave. She lived there and gave birth to a baby flying fox. The woman was irate and wanted to kill the flying fox, but she was surprised to hear a small voice say, "Don't kill me, I'll help you mother. Let me stay with you."

As the flying fox grew, it often flew and went down to find food for itself and its mother. They lived for a while, then the mother gave birth to a baby boy. The flying fox was ecstatic. The flying fox worked hard to find water, food and firewood for the mother and boy. The flying fox also watched carefully for Kaiwaru. It would be bad if Kaiwaru found them and ate them.

One morning, the flying fox flew very far to find food. The mother and baby were hungry, so the baby cried very loudly and incessantly. Kaiwaru heard the crying, and so the snake came down and said, "Who's that? This place doesn't have any people, or maybe there's a person hiding in a hole for me." Kaiwaru laughed loudly and went down to earth.

The woman was surprised to look outside the cave. No, it was the huge head of Kaiwaru making a noise at the entrance. The woman knew that Kaiwaru would kill her and her son, so she began to cry and sing a song of mourning. The flying fox heard this singing, "Come quickly, come quickly home, flying-fox child." So, the flying fox sped back to the cave.

The flying fox looked at the cave, but there was no one there. The flying fox went to what was a village, but no one was there either. The flying fox looked up and saw its mother and brother hanging. The flying fox left the food behind, took a stone axe and flew upwards.

The flying fox missed its mother and brother, then went to the middle of Kaiwaru and began to cut. The flying fox cut the snake into two pieces, which fell to the ground. Its mother and brother were all right now.

The flying fox cut the snake into many small pieces. The flying fox threw the head into the forest. Kaiwaru's head became all of the kinds of snakes that we see on the ground. The flying fox threw some pieces of Kaiwaru into the sea and these became eels, lizards, octopuses, sea snakes and other things. The flying fox threw Kaiwaru's blood into the sea and this became red fish. Now you can see many red fish in the sea.

Later, when the flying fox finished, it looked at its mother and brother. It left them at the village and went back to the cave where it grew up. Kaiwaru was dead and the mother and boy lived well. Now, we can see flying foxes that live in caves.

Robert Mai

P. O. Box 433

Wewak

East Sepik Province

A522.3+. Flying fox as culture hero; A2110. Creation of particular fishes; A2131. Creation of eel; A2145. Creation of snake (serpent); A2148. Creation of lizard; A2139.1K. Creation of octopus; A2433.3+. Why flying fox lives in cave; B16.5.1. Giant devastating serpent; B91.4. Sky-traveling snake; B211.2.11K+. Speaking flying fox; B211.6.1. Speaking snake (serpent); B290+. Flying fox kills snake with axe; D447.3+. Transformation: blood to fish; E658. Reincarnation: animal to other animal; G510.4. Hero overcomes devastating animal; P231. Mother and son; P250. Brothers and sisters; Q211.11. Punishment for wholesale massacre of tribe; Q429.3. Cutting into pieces as punishment; R220. Flights; R315. Cave as refuge; S118.1. Murder by cutting adversary in two; S139.4. Murder by mangling with axe; S139.7. Murder by slicing person into small pieces; T510. Miraculous conception; T554.0.2K+. Woman gives birth to flying fox; T581.1. Birth of child in forest; Z356. Unique survivor

## The Two Spirit Dogs

(Wantok 270, June 9, 1979, page 17)

Long, long ago, there was a place where a man lived. The man's name was Ari Paiyabe. His family was worthless, they had no possessions. One time, a man called out to Ari Paiyabe.

The man said he wanted to kill a pig, and so he had called to Ari Paiyabe. Ari Paiyabe walked along the trail and went to where the pig was to be killed. He found two dogs lying on the trail and said to them, "I'm going to eat pork. What if you two dogs were real men who had turned into dogs?" Ari Paiyabe believed this, that these were not real dogs.

He told the two dogs, "If you are men, then follow me. I'm going to where a pig will be killed. The men called me and I'm going." The two dogs followed Paiyabe and went.

They arrived at the place for killing pigs. When they stopped, the men ridiculed the two dogs. But Paiyabe believes that the dogs were not real dogs, that they were men.

The men gave pork to Paiyabe and Paiyabe shared some of the pork with the two dogs. After he shared the pork, Paiyabe took the two dogs and went to the trail where he gave a package of pork to the dogs. Then he went home.

The next day, he went to the garden. In the evening, he returned to the house. He saw that the door of the house was open slightly, so he looked inside and saw a huge bundle of cowry shells lying on his bed. Ari Paiyabe looked carefully and saw the legs of the two dogs from the day before.

He carried the cowry shells, bought two pigs and took care of them. The two pigs became bigger and bigger. Then he purchased a wife. The pigs became plentiful and he became well off. Paiyabe's descendants were plentiful and became leaders.

This story comes from **Komo** Village in Mendi District [**Huli** People, **Southern Highlands** Province].

Konrad Tigi

Erave

Southern Highlands Province

B421. Helpful dog; D141M. Transformation: man to dog; P160. Beggars; P210. Husband and wife; Q111.2. Riches as reward (for hospitality); T52. Bride purchased; T100. Marriage

# Lunganga
(Wantok 27[1], June 16, 1979, page 21)

Long, long ago, there was an old woman with her grandson. They lived in a village called **Lossu Number One** near Kavieng in **New Ireland** Province [**Notsi** People].

These people took care of a pig name Lunganga. They took care of the pig for a while, but one time the little boy ate a piece of sweet potato.

The pig saw him eating and squealed for the boy's sweet potato. The little boy wanted to give the pig a piece of the sweet potato, but the little boy overshot it a little and shoved his hand inside the pig's mouth.

The pig chewed and broke the boy's hand, drinking the boy's blood. The pig then ran away into the forest. But now, the pig had tried human blood. This was when the pig began to only eat people. It often lived in the forest and killed the people of Lossu Number One.

Everyone was afraid of this pig and escaped to **Tabar** Island [**Tabar** People]. Everyone paddled their canoes and left the old woman behind.

When the canoes were almost out of the old woman's sight, she said, "I want to go with you." But the men lied to her and said, "The canoes are filled up. Wait for this canoe to come later."

They lied to her that the canoes were entirely filled. After the canoes left, the old woman cried and escaped to a small island that is very near Lossu Number One [probably the small island in Lossu Bay, about 0.1 kilometers from shore].

The old woman began to cry, then a bird came and asked her, "Why are you crying?" The old woman replied, "I'm crying because I'm afraid that the bad pig will come and eat me. Everyone escaped to Tabar Island. I'm the only one here now."

The bird said, "OK, I'll marry you." After they married, the old woman gave birth to twin boys, named Daururu and Damaremare.

The boys grew up and became big boys. One time, the old woman told them, "The other people had escaped to Tabar Island." They asked their mother, "Why did they run away?" The mother told them, "They ran away because of the man-eating pig."

They asked their mother, "Will you let us kill pigs with spears?" The mother asked, "Why?" They said, "We want to kill the man-eating pig." The mother told them, "You absolutely cannot." However, the boys were stubborn and the mother let them go shoot spears.

When they were ready to kill the pig, they asked, "Where's the pig? We want to go kill it now." The mother told them, "The pig lives over there."

In the early morning, they awoke with their father and went to hunt the pig. They approached the pig. They stood up and called to the pig. The pig ran towards them and wanted to eat them, but the boys' father flew and shut the pig's eyes.

They fooled the pig into going toward the beach. When they went close to their home, Daururu threw his spear and shot the pig. The pig felt the spear and tried to eat them. But their father flew quickly and covered the pig's eyes. Damaremare threw another spear at the pig and the pig died.

They pulled the pig to the other side of the beach. An old man who was hiding in a cave saw them pulling the pig and said, "If you cook the pig in an earth oven, I'd like you to give me the head."

They prepared to cook the pig in an earth oven. They cut of the pig's hair, put it inside a callophyllum fruit and sent it to Tabar Island. At this time, the men of Tabar Island were fishing with nets.

The callophyllum fruit went inside the net of one man. He took it and threw it outside the net. But the fruit returned to the net.

This time, the man looked inside the fruit. He saw pig hair. He told the men, "They killed Lunganga." The men did not believe him, so he showed them the pig's hair. Everyone jumped with joy. But they did not know who it was that had killed the pig. After they found out that the pig had died, they paddled back to their true home at Lossu.

They approached Lossu and saw the old woman standing on the beach with her two sons. However, they did not know these two boys. The old woman and her two sons saw the canoes approaching the shore, so they went down to the beach.

Everyone asked about the old woman, so a man told them, "This old woman married a bird and she gave birth to two sons. It was these two boys who killed Lunganga."

This is a true story, and today if you go to Lossu Number One, you can still see the earth oven, the pig's blood, and the firewood used to cook the pig on the island near Lossu Number One.

Michael Lamasuk

Malcom Section

Kieta

North Solomons Province

A515.1.1. Twin culture heroes; B16.1.4. Devastating swine; B211.3. Speaking bird; B602. Marriage to bird; B631.16K+. Human offspring from bird; G36.2. Human blood (flesh) accidentally tasted: brings desire for human flesh; G510.4. Hero overcomes devastating animal; K957. Murder by blinding; P210. Husband and wife; P231. Mother and son; P233. Father and son; P251.5. Two brothers; P292.1. Grandmother as foster mother; R213. Escape from home; S140.1. Abandonment of aged; S371+. Abandoned woman's son becomes hero; T100. Marriage; T587. Birth of twins; T685. Twins; W157. Dishonesty; W167. Stubbornness; Z210. Brothers as heroes

# Tamuaiang

(Wantok 272, June 23, 1979, page 21)

Long ago, there was a village named **Bualibual**. The men were cultivating the earth using digging sticks made from the ironwood tree. Their necks were dry and they called out for water, "Hey you boys, get some water for us to drink."

There was a man named Tamuaiang, he was a man who seduced women, and he was filthy as soot. He said, "I'll get the bamboo tubes of water. It would be bad if the boys came too slowly with the water."

So, he went to go get the water. He arrived at a stream called Kalewiang. He dropped his loincloth and put it below. He dressed nicely by putting a tube around his hair to make a topknot, then he jumped on a *mangas* tree. He called out, "*Palugama ilombune palugama ilombune*." Then he made the water very dirty, filled up the tube and brought them to the men to drink.

"No, the water is dirty," they said. He told them, "You're crazy. A heavy rain fell and flooded the stream. I couldn't get any clean water." He often did this and the men knew about his behavior. So, the next day, they sent a man to go hide where he fetched the water. The man hid and waited. Tamuaiang dropped his loincloth and put a topknot in his hair. Then he put chicken feathers in his hair.

He jumped up on the ironwood tree and sang. The man who was hiding got up and went to garden. He told everyone, "No, the good-for-nothing came." He told them that there was a big rain down below and the stream flooded, then he ran back. Another time, the man went to remove the ironwood tree. He cut it in the middle and completely removed it.

He put the tree bark back, tidied up the area and left. Another time, Tamuaiang jumped upon the tree to sing, but no, the "tree" fell and broke into the stream, carrying him down to the sea.

He went ashore at a point called Tabelena, then turned into a log. A man from a village called **Mabuan** was walking with a dog and he saw this very straight log. He carried the log away, it was used for shaving [?]. He put it at the head of his house.

He thought that it was an ordinary log. No, it was the man from the garden who had turned into someone that was killing all of the chickens, pigs, and dogs and eating them. The men asked, "Why are our animals disappearing?"

One old woman said, "No, a very handsome man has jumped down to this house and he is the one who is killing pigs, chickens and dogs and eating them."

So, they removed the house and threw the log into the sea where it drifted ashore on **Manam** [Island, **Manam** People]. There too, he did the same sorts of things.

The people of Manam tried to remove him too, but he told them, "You people will not have a good songs or dances in this village, you will only have poor songs and dances." So now, the people of Manam do not have good songs or dances, only poor ones. The people of Manam threw him back into the sea where he drifted and missed his mountain. This mountain is named Banivitapa.

He went ashore on a beach called Gauat, by a village called **Buanaputa**. He stayed there on the beach and sang,

"*O nisaluwane saluwakomo*." This means, "I'm ashore on the beach." Two men, from a village called Paria Kanam [**Pariakinam**] wanted to go asea [**Saki** People]. They went down and heard this singing.

But there was no man in this place, just a log lying on the beach. It was strange, as if it was the log singing. So the man shot the log with his spear. When he pulled out the spear, no! He saw yams, taros and bananas inside the log.

He took some leaves from vines that grow on the beach. We call these plants *kalikal*. He stuffed the tree hole with leaves and carried it home.

So now, my people come from these three places, **Muap**, Bualibual and Buanaputa. We originated from this story called "Tamuaiang." Tamuaiang is the man who originated the song called Binambina and other songs too. This story comes from the Bogia District in **Madang** Province.

Bunam Kamaia
Mt. Hagen
Western Highlands Province

[Note: the above songs are not in the Manam Language (F. Lichtenberk, personal communication).]

A1542+. Why particular place has poor songs; A1542+. Why particular place has poor dances; A1543. Origin of religious songs (chants); D216M. Transformation: man to log; D451.1+. Transformation: log to banana; D451.1+. Transformation: log to taro; D451.1+. Transformation: log to yam; D1615.2. Magic musical branch; E402.1.11.2+. Evil spirit kills and eats domestic animals; K983.2+. Dupe lured onto tree that collapses; Q280. Unkindness punished; W115. Slovenliness; W157. Dishonesty

## The Stone from Ablingi Island
(Wantok 273, June 30, 1979, page 21)

Long, long ago, my ancestors from **Ablingi** Island had fishing nets [**Gasmata** People, **West New Britain** Province]. If they wanted to have a big party or feast, they would always go get some fish. They fished at night, in the morning or in the afternoon.

Every time they did this, they would fish with nets. One night, they went to get their nets for fishing. They took their canoes and paddled to an island. They came approached the island and put their nets in the sea. This island is named **Arili**.

They began to chase the fish into the nets and were surprised to see a big light falling from the sky. It was as if a star was falling into the sea, straight into their nets. They ran towards it like it was a big fish and held it in the net.

The men jumped on top of the star. They held it tightly and looked closely to see whether it was a fish or a star. It was a big stone. They took the rock with the net and put it at the bow of the canoe.

They began to be afraid, so they trembled and thought that it was a *masalai* that was making them afraid and argumentative. Their thinking was confused, so they questioned each other.

Some said that it was a stone from the sky and some said, "It's not a stone. It's probably a *masalai* or an ancestral spirit." They became afraid of the stone and no one approached it. They went home and brought the stone to their village. They woke up everyone and told everyone to come look at what they had brought.

The people came and looked at the big stone that was placed in the middle of the village. Another clan asked them, "Why did you take this stone? Did you think that it was a *masalai* or an ancestral spirit?" No, they said, this was a stone and it had fallen from the sky, it was lit like a star, and it had fallen into their net like a big fish.

So, they all carried the stone and put it near the village. In the morning, they sent the women to get taros from the garden. They made a big feast for the stone. Today, you can still see this stone. We boys grew up looking at this stone. Today we put the stone under our church gable. If you come to Ablingi, you will see this stone.

Mr. Roydet Kapopong
Ablingi Island
West New Britain Province

A977.5. Origin of particular rock; F490+. Masalai; F960+. Meteor falls into fishing net; V1.11.2. Worship of stone idols

## The Woman Who Became a Mermaid
(Wantok 274, July 7, 1979, page 20)

Long ago, on **Karkar** Island, on the side where there is a village named **Kulubob**, there lived a man and his wife [**Takia** People, **Madang** Province]. The man's name was Kulubob and his wife's name was Manub. They were married for a long time, but did not have any children.

One time, they had just awoken at their beds in the morning. Kulubob's wife asked him what they would do. Her husband said, "We don't have meat to eat for the evening, so let's go to the garden. You get some taros and bananas, then I'll go to the forest to hunt for wild game."

Kulubob took his bow and his wife took a net bag, then they walked away. They followed the trail to the garden.

His wife went to the garden while Kulubob went into a piece of forest where he wanted to hunt for game. Kulubob followed the forest trail and arrived at a garden. In the garden, he saw a very young woman. Kulubob leered at her and he forgot hunting. He just stared at the woman while he sat on a tree.

Kulubob shot an arrow into the garden at the young woman who was removing grass from the taro garden. The spear landed near her and she was shocked. She stood up and tried to see who it was that had tried to kill her, but the young woman did not think of running home. She said, "If you're a real man, then come inside the garden and talk, otherwise kill me."

When Kulubob heard this, he jumped down to the ground and went into the garden. He walked up to the woman and held her. They flattered each other. Kulubob was talking with the woman and thought about not going home.

However, Kulubob's real wife had returned home and was waiting for him to bring some wild game for her to cook for themselves. The poor wife waited, but he did not show up, so she just cooked the food. She did not eat quickly, she continued to wait for her husband.

Kulubob and the woman continued to talk until it was late evening. They went out of the garden and he sent the young woman home while he walked slowly. When he arrived home, his wife was furious at him because he had traveled in the forest and had not returned quickly.

His wife knew that he had spoken with a young woman, because he did not find any game and did not come home quickly. Kulubob knew that he had done wrong, so he did not want to say much. He just sat and listened. His wife said, "You're not a man. I think you're a cur. You have the face of a woman. I know that you always find game and that when you don't find any, you return right away. What happened this time?"

Kulubob's wife finished scolding him and said, "I finished cooking, but there's no meat. Let's just eat." His wife went into the house and poured the food onto wooden plates. She put spoons made from coconut shells on the plates and went to give one to her husband.

Her husband was not happy with the food, so he thought and did not eat quickly. He told himself, "Why did my wife call me woman-faced?" He thought about making his wife run away from him. He was very sad about what his wife had said to him. Kulubob pretended to take his spoon from the food, but he did not eat. He let the spoon drop through a small hole in the floor of the house.

Kulubob called his wife to go down and fetch it. His wife said, "I don't want to." She went down to get the spoon anyway. When Kulubob's wife was still underneath the house, Kulubob spilled the hot soup on his wife. The woman cried and shouted with pain. She said to her husband, "Why did you hurt me? Now I can't come back to see you. You are a bad husband, so now I'm leaving you." After the woman said this, she jumped into the sea.

When she jumped into the sea, she immediately turned into a mermaid, just as now in some places you can see women in the sea that are half-woman and half-fish. This is not a fish, it is Kulubob's wife.

S. Tab
Enga Province

A2170+. Origin of mermaid; D199.4K2W. Transformation: woman to mermaid; D576. Transformation by being burned; D671. Transformation flight; P210. Husband and wife; Q304. Scolding punished; Q469.10.3. Scalding as punishment for insult; R213. Escape from home; R227.2. Flight from hated husband; S62. Cruel husband

# Modaged and Gerail
(Wantok 275, July 14, 1979, page 20)

Long, long ago, there were two birds, Modaged and Gerail. Gerail had a short tail and lived in the forest. Modaged had a long tail and lived in a village and did not like to go in the forest much.

Modaged was a bird that flew around villages and hunted for feces. It went inside latrines and under houses. It dug and ate the feces and some trash too.

Gerail wanted to grow up as a clean bird of the forest. One time, Gerail went to the village. Near the village was a big tree. Gerail went to the top of this tree, perched and watched Modaged's tail.

Gerail worried a lot that its tail was not nice and long. Gerail knew that it would be ruined on the feces and on the ground too.

Gerail sat and sat. Gerail thought hard. Then Gerail said, "Never mind. I'll try and ask my friend if we can quickly exchange tails." Quickly, the short-tailed bird jumped in front of its friend Modaged, and said, "Can we exchange tails or not? I saw yours, but aren't you a little straight?"

Modaged replied, "Why, Gerail? You have a nice tail, but you often throw it around on the ground. On the other hand, I have a bad tail though I take care of it well." Modaged told his friend, "I think this is true because I'm not a forest-dwelling bird. I'm just a village-dwelling bird.

We must exchange tails quickly. Take mine and save it well on the tree. You must come to me and throw your tail around the village."

They exchanged tails. So now you see a kind of bird that is in the forest with a long tail. If you go to New Guinea, you will see many men who shoot this kind of bird with guns and make head decorations from their feathers for use in festivals [probably a bird of paradise]. If you look at another kind of bird that lives in villages, it has a short tail. This bird goes around latrines and under houses. It digs feces and eats them. The feathers of both birds are black.

Paul Tangal
Port Moresby
National Capital District

A2378.8.7+. Why particular bird has long tail; A2378.8.7+. Why particular bird has short tail; P310. Friendship; K140.1+. Trick exchange of feathers; W181. Jealousy; X716H+. The escoumerda

## The Boy Who Scared His Father

(Wantok 276, July 21, 1979, page 17)

Long, long ago, there was a man who lived with his son. When the father wanted to go somewhere, the son always followed his father. Whether it was day or night, the son still followed.

One time at night, they were together in the men's house. There was a bright moon rising, so the father thought of going to hunt marsupials (*kapul*) in the forest. So, the father took the son to bed.

The father thought that his son was sleeping, but he was not really asleep. The father got up quietly and went outside. Later, his son got up and saw that his father had left, so he followed him.

The father did not think to look behind himself, so his son continued to follow him. However, the son did not talk to his father because he was afraid of him. They entered the very deep forest. The father looked up at a tree and saw a marsupial sitting on top of a branch.

The father climbed the tree. He heard a little noise, looked down and saw a man coming up the tree.

The father was terrified, but the son did not talk to his father. The father was so scared that he immediately threw his bow and arrows down, then left the tree. The father met his son in the middle of the tree and they both went down the tree. When the father reached the ground, he did not wait around, he ran off. The son ran behind him towards the men's house.

When the father arrived, he ran right into his bed and the child did the same. A little later, the father said, "Man, a ghost chased me all over." But some men said, "No, you ran with your son." The father was angry and said, "That was not another man's son. No, it was my son, so I must kill my son."

At this time, the father beat his child. The other men of the village broke up the fight between the father and son.

Dominik Andana
**Kawanigle** Village
**Simbu** Province

E261.4+. Imagined ghost pursues man; P233. Father and son; Q325. Disobedience punished; Q458. Flogging as punishment; R260. Pursuits

## The Vegetables that Spoke

(Wantok 277, July 28, 1979, page 21)

Once there were a man and his wife who returned from **Bomai** to **Amia** Village in the Gumine sub-Province [**Golin** and **Mikaru** Peoples, **Simbu** Province]. The man's name was Olimi, and the woman's was Dimaima. They brought with them many things, like pandanus nuts (*karuka*), pandanus fruits (*marita*) and other things.

When they were in the middle of the forest, Olimi told Dimaima to wait on top of a mountain called Olmukul. Olimi went to cut a vine to make a fence. However, while his wife Dimaima was waiting, she felt dizzy. She saw a nice house that had many good edible greens near it. Dimaima became covetous, and approached the house.

At the house, there was an old woman. The old woman saw Dimaima and said, "Hey woman, who told you to come here?" Dimaima replied, "I came to sleep. I'll leave tomorrow." The old woman was very happy because she wanted to kill and eat Dimaima.

When it became dark, the old woman prepared her spears, then she took some greens from the garden. The old woman cooked the vegetables and gave them to Dimaima. Dimaima thought they were delicious and wanted more, so she finished all of them.

At night, Dimaima wanted to sleep. She looked up and saw the spears. When she saw the spears for killing people, she got up and said, "I want to go to the latrine." Dimaima took some ashes from the fire and went all of the way up the trail to Mount Olmukul.

The old woman thought that Dimaima was at the latrine, but she had departed. So, the old woman took a spear and ran to kill Dimaima. She called out, "Edible greens." The edible greens inside Dimaima's belly replied, "Yes," because these were the old woman's vegetables that were inside Dimaima's belly.

Dimaima's belly kept saying, "Yes" when the old woman called to them. Dimaima arrived at Mul [**Nul**] Village and told the story about the old woman to Olimi [Golin People, Simbu Province]. Olimi trembled violently because of the old woman. When she approached Olimi, he cut the old woman's neck and she died.

Now at this time, men and woman often go along this trail to Bomai because the old woman was killed.

Kobila Kaupa
Gumine
Simbu Province

D1610.31+. Speaking vegetables; D1619.2. Eaten object speaks from inside person's body; G512. Ogre killed; P210. Husband and wife; Q215. Cannibalism punished; Q421.3. Punishment: cutting throat; R260. Pursuits; S118.2. Murder by cutting throat; W195. Envy

## Cutting the Pregnant Woman's Belly
(Wantok 278, August 4, 1979, page 21)

Long, long ago, there was a village where there were many men. This group of men took care of a little boy named Panagah. This boy did not have parents. He grew and became a big man.

At that time, he married in this village. In those days, the men often cut the women's bellies when they were about to give birth. When they cut their bellies, they killed them.

One time, when Panagah's wife was pregnant and about to give birth, he sat at the door of the house. He watched and he saw the men cutting his wife's belly. Immediately, Panagah shouted, "You can't cut my wife's belly!"

However the men replied, "We must cut your wife's belly so that all of her pain will be over with." Panagah did not want to reply, so he closed the house door and sat.

After a little while, Panagah called to the men who cut the belly, "Now the woman has given birth." Then he went outside and said, "You men must go to the forest, get some traditional medicine and give it quickly to the women when they give birth."

At this time, before the white people arrived, they began to follow Panagah's instructions. Now we have a birthing house ("infirmary") in which women give birth.

Mr. Thomas Sonnu
**Korikunu** [**Siwai** People]
N. S. P. [**North Solomons** Province]

A1560+. Origin of birthing house; A1562. Origin of medical treatment during pregnancy; P210. Husband and wife; S110. Murders; T100. Marriage; T584.3. Cesarean operation upon a woman at childbirth as a custom; T570. Pregnancy; T580. Childbirth

## The Child Who Turned into a Cockatoo
(Wantok 279, August 11, 1979, page 17)

Long, long ago, a man and woman married and lived together. They had just one child. When the woman went to the garden, she often took the child with her.

When they arrived at the garden, the woman did not usually give her breast to the child and then work in the garden. She usually went directly to work in the garden. When the child was hungry, it would cry.

When the woman heard the crying, she did not come quickly to give her breast to her child. No, she just worked. She often said, "You want to work in the garden too, huh?" The woman would say this and the poor child would still cry until it nearly choked. Then she would come and give her breast. When she gave her breast, she would hit the child. The woman did this all of the time to her child. One time, when they went to the garden, her husband went to the forest to hunt. When the woman took the child and departed, she did something bad in the garden. So when the child cried, it changed into a bird that is called cockatoo.

Its skin became the cockatoo's feathers, but its mouth did not yet turn into a cockatoo's beak. Then it flew up on a yam (*mami*) vine and called out to its mother. It said, "Mother, look at me." When its mother turned, she just saw the cockatoo, she did not see her child.

The mother began to cry for her child. The child told its mother, "Mama, it's OK. Your breasts are still there. You can give them to another child. I'm not your real child. That's why you treated me badly."

Then its mother wailed and tried to hold the cockatoo, but it turned completely into a cockatoo and flew into the deep forest. The bird called out like a real cockatoo and flew away. When it called like a cockatoo, its father tried to follow it in the forest. He heard the call and thought, "Hmm, what kind of bird is that?"

He heard the call and was terrified, so he ran back home. When he arrived, he saw and heard his wife crying. He asked her, "Why are you crying?" The woman told him the story.

The man listened, then he cried and cried. The two of them died inside the house. They turned into the "Womponko Stones."

Tobias Walop Korupu
**Dreikikir** [Village, **Urat** People]
**East Sepik** Province

B211.3+. Speaking cockatoo; D150+C. Transformation: child to cockatoo; D231M. Transformation: man to stone; D231W. Transformation: woman to stone; D681. Gradual transformation; P210. Husband and wife; S12+. Mother withholds breast from child; T100. Marriage

## The Snake Looked at His Hair

(Wantok 280, August 18, 1979, page 17)

Long ago, when it was still the time of the ancestors, the **Tolai** People called it "The Time of Darkness." At this time, there was a snake and a cuscus (*kapul*) who were very good friends. [The northern common cuscus, *Phalanger orientalis*, is the only bare-tailed marsupial on New Britain (Flannery, 1995b: 96-99).]

They played and traveled in the forest, on the beach, in the village, and in people's gardens. They often joked about the animals and fish in the sea.

Once there was a drought. The grass died and the trees did not flower or fruit. All of the small ponds dried up under the hot sun. So, all of the birds and other animals were hungry and thirsty.

One day, the snake and cuscus went to play on the beach. They were very hot in the sunshine, so they sat under a *talis* tree.

The snake said, "Hey, my brother and friend, Tokapul. We have hair, so we're too hot. Look at the Tolai People, they don't have hair like us and they're not hot. The wind blows and cools their skins. Look, if we just went in our skins without fur, our skin would be cool, even in this heat." Tokapul said, "Is that true, my brother and friend, Tokaliku?"

The cuscus, Tokapul, said, "You're telling a lie." The snake, Tokaliku, said, "Brother and friend Tokapul, I have only one plan and thought." Tokapul asked, "What kind of plan?" Tokaliku replied, "You and I must remove our fur."

Tokapul replied, "That's good. We'll follow this plan. Let's go ahead. Let's do it now." Tokapul said, "Let's re-move your fur first." Tokaliku replied, "That's OK if we remove my fur first."

Tokapul told the snake, Tokaliku, "Brother and friend, you go and wrap your neck around this tree. You must wrap your tail around that tree over there." Then Tokapul said, "When I count, you must tighten your body and lie flat."

Tokapul began to count, "*Tikai*, *aurua* [*a ura*], *autul* [*a utula*] (1, 2, 3), tighten strong." While Tokapul counted, he walked into the forest to find bamboo for removing Tokaliku's fur. However, Tokapul did not return quickly, so Tokaliku tired and fell to the ground.

Tokapul returned and told Tokaliku, "Hey brother and friend, why did you give up? I told you to stay taut between the two trees." Tokaliku replied, "I saw some Tolai People coming, so I hid." Later he said, "OK, I'll become taut again between the two trees."

So, Tokaliku tautened himself between the two trees as before. Then Tokaliku told Tokapul, "Go ahead and do your work." Tokapul told Tokaliku, "Brother, close your eyes." Tokapul started at the head with the piece of bamboo, and began to remove Tokaliku's fur, finishing at the tail.

After Tokapul removed Tokaliku's fur, Tokaliku's skin looked like a tree called *golom* that is used to make houses. When Tokapul finished, Tokapul told Tokaliku to open his eyes slowly and look at himself. Tokaliku opened his eyes slowly, looked and said, "Oh my, is this really me?" Tokapul said, "Brother, it's just you. Congratulations!"

Tokaliku replied, "I'll never go on the trail again. No, I'll just hide in the grasses because this has shamed me greatly. I look like a tree called *mangas* from which the bark has been removed."

Tokapul said, "This is something that you yourself know, but I don't like it." Tokaliku was angry and wanted to eat Tokapul, his brother and friend. So Tokaliku held Tokapul's tail. But Tokapul was too strong and just left his fur in Tokaliku's mouth. Then Tokapul ran away and climbed a tree.

Tokapul [*ToKapul*] always lives on top of trees because he is afraid that Tokaliku will eat him. So now, cuscuses live on the top of big trees. Also, cuscuses don't have fur on their tails. The snake that is called *tokaliku* [*ToKaliku*] always hides in the dense grass because he is ashamed. They are no longer friends.

Michael Tobung
**Tamanairik**
**East New Britain** Province

A2317+. Why snake is bald; A2317.12. Why opossum has bare tail; A2433.2.1+. Why marsupial lives in forest; A2433.6.8+. Why snake lives in grass; A2494.16+. Enmity between snake and marsupial; P310. Friendship; R210. Escapes; R311. Tree refuge

## The *Masalai* Woman Ate Feces

(Wantok 281, August 25, 1979, page 21)

Once, there was a little boy who took his bow and arrows and followed a stream to hunt for crayfish and eels. As he went along, he saw a huge *tulip* tree's shadow in the water.

The *tulip* tree was ruined, and so the little boy went to get some *tulip* leaves [to eat]. He went to defecate at the base of the tree, then he climbed the tree.

While he was still gathering the leaves, a *masalai* woman was following the stream. The *masalai* woman smelled the little boy's feces, so she looked up into the forest and saw the little boy on top of the *tulip* tree.

The *masalai* woman climbed the tree and told the little boy, "Little boy, go along this small branch to get some *tulip* leaves." But the little boy was afraid to go along the small branch.

The *masalai* woman tricked the boy and he fell. Later, the *masalai* woman put the little boy into many net bags, about nine or ten.

The *masalai* woman ate the little boy's feces. She covered up a piece of excrement and carried it to her husband. Her husband was sharpening his arrows and tightening his spear. The *masalai* woman went and looked at her husband. She took the bow in her hand, broke it and threw it away.

The *masalai* woman told her husband, "You're just working on your bow and arrows. You never go to find wild game." After she said this, she threw the covered excrement at her husband and said, "Where do you hunt? You left this shit that was covered and eaten." Her husband immediately uncovered the excrement and began to eat the little boys' feces.

The *masalai* woman had hung up the poor little boy in their house. The married couple went to find some bananas and other food to cook with the little boy.

After they departed, the little boy put his hand on his loincloth and felt a *kina* shell. He took this *kina* shell and began to cut the net bags. The old mother of the married couple saw this and called out, "Hey, what are you doing? It would be bad if you fell. Just go to sleep." The married couple went to the garden to get some bananas. [The old woman said,] "We'll cook and eat first, then later you'll go back to your village."

However, the little boy kept cutting the net bags and he fell down. He took a yam (*mami*) and hit the old woman in the guts, killing her. The boy got up and ran home. When the married couple returned to the house, they did not see their old mother.

The *masalai* woman got up and checked the trailhead. She smelled or sensed the boy going along the trail, so she followed him and went towards the little boy's village.

When the little boy arrived home, he spoke to his parents and the other people of the village. After he told them his story, all of the men of the village prepared to kill the *masalai* woman. When the *masalai* woman arrived at the village, she asked the people, "Hey did you see a crazy boy come here or not?"

The *masalai* woman lied and said, "Yesterday, I took a little boy to my house and he just slept. In the morning, my husband and I went to the garden to find some bananas to cook and eat. But the crazy boy got up and ran away, so I came to get him and return."

When the *masalai* woman tried hard to get the boy, the boy's father shot the *masalai* woman dead.

Peter Hamin
**Maiwara** [School; **Rempi**, **Garuh**, or **Gedaged** People]
**Madang** Province

F490+. Masalai; G411. Person aids ogre and is captured; G441. Ogre carries victim in bag (basket); G512+. Ogre killed with yam; G512.1+. Ogre killed with spear/arrow; J1772.9+. Man eats someone else's feces, believing that they are his own; P210. Husband and wife; P230. Parents and children; P233. Father and son; Q215. Cannibalism punished; Q411. Death as punishment; R11. Abduction by monster (ogre); R210. Escapes; R260. Pursuits; S110. Murders; W157. Dishonesty; X716H+. The escoumerda

## Brother Married Brother

(Wantok 282, September 1, 1979, page 21)

Long, long ago, there were two brothers. One brother worked in a taro garden and the other grew fruit trees.

One day, the brother who was the taro gardener wanted to go into the deep forest to hunt wild game. He went deeper and deeper into the forest, but he did not kill any game. He thought about returning home. He kept walking and arrived at a garden. Inside the garden were many cucumbers, but he did not touch the cucumbers. Absolutely not.

He walked through the garden and saw a house with smoke coming from within it. He went closer to the house. He looked inside the house and saw an old woman there.When the old woman saw this man, she was very happy to see him. The old woman took the man inside and told him, "When I saw you, I went into the house. When I leave you, I'll go to the garden. You must go and cut some leaves. When I come and stand on the trail, I'll call out to you, then you can remove the taros from the ashes of the fire."

The old woman went to the garden, and the man cut some firewood and leaves. When the old woman came and called to him, the man removed the taros. When the old woman came, she told him, "Go below and look for a house. Inside the house there are some pigs." Then the old woman said, "You can kill one white pig and bring it to me."

Quickly, the man went down to the house and took a white pig. He brought it to the old woman. They made a fire and singed off the pig's hair. Later, they cooked the pig in an earth oven. In the evening, they uncovered the earth oven. The old woman gave some food to the man. She took some food, and they ate. They kept eating the pork until it was very dark.

The old woman got up and stoked the fire. The man slept well by the side of the fire. While the man was deep asleep, the old woman removed her skin. She put on the skin of a young woman and became a very beautiful woman.

She dressed herself very nicely. She went outside and called to the cucumbers. All of the cucumbers in the garden changed into very young women who sang and danced with the old woman. When the man saw these young women singing with the old woman, he was angry. They sang and danced until it was nearly dawn, then the cucumber women went back to the garden.

The man pretended to sleep, but he kept looking at them. The old woman went back inside the house, took off her young skin and put on her old skin. Then she woke the man and said, "Get up, it's morning." The old woman told him, "We slept well last night, but you can go back to your village." The old woman gave him a new net bag and put a piece of pork inside it.

The old woman told him, "You can go now, but when you come to the garden, you can take two cucumbers with you. You must cut them well and carry them away." So, he got up, cut two cucumbers and carried them with him.

As the man was walking on the trail, he heard some small birds calling. He put his net bag down and climbed a tree. When he climbed the tree, he saw a marsupial (*kapul*) sitting there. The man wanted to kill the marsupial, but the marsupial jumped down to the ground. Later, he again heard a noise on the ground, so he went down and saw two women taking a short cut.

He took the two young women to his brother's home. His brother saw the two young women and was very happy. The brother said, "Give me one woman." But the man said, "No." So the brother asked, "How did you find these two women?" The man told the story of the cucumbers and the old woman, and everything that he had seen when the cucumber-women transformed themselves and sang and danced.

The brother said, "Never mind, I'll become a woman and my brother shall marry me." So, he turned into a woman and his brother married him. Since this time, many people have descended from these people in this area.

Sakiba Sanameng
**Olsobip** [Village, **Faiwol** People]
**Western** Province

D12. Transformation: man to woman; D56.1. Transformation to older person; D211+W. Transformation: woman to cucumber; D431.4+W. Transformation: cucumber to woman; D520. Transformation through power of the word; D531+. Transformation by removing skin; D1774. Magic results from speaking; D1881. Magic self-rejuvenation; P210. Husband and wife; P251.5. Two brothers; T100. Marriage; T415.5+. Man marries brother in form of woman; W31. Obedience

## The Man Who Became a Bird
(Wantok 283, September 8, 1979, page 21)

Long, long ago, in my village, **Tigina**, there was an ancestor named Tiginakuo Tulagu Yea. He was like a real man, but he was a *masalai*.

Tiginakuo had a boy named Pokuka. He and his son did not have a garden, so they often stole food from other gardens. One time, it rained and rained, and they were very hungry.

At this time, Tiginakuo told his son, "Let's travel around and find some food." He brought his son and they left. They walked and walked. After about fifteen miles, they arrived at a garden.

They rested and saw some bananas. They wanted to get the bananas, so Tiginakuo took his axe and cut the bananas. Later, they took the bananas and carried them along the trail.

After a little while, the garden's owner arrived. He was shocked to see that his bananas were gone. He was very angry. Later, he saw their footprints, but they had already returned to their home. When they arrived at their house, Tiginakuo told his son, "Son, you must sit and watch for men. I'll cook the bananas in the fire."

His son, Pokuka, sat on a stone and watched. As he was watching, his eyes closed and he slept a little, forgetting about watching.

After a little while, the owner of the garden saw the smoke from the fire. He pulled out his axe and walked quietly towards the house. He looked inside the house and saw Tiginakuo sitting and cooking the bananas on the fire. He stood up and said, "Tiginakuo." When Tiginakuo turned and saw the owner of the garden, he was surprised.

When Tiginakuo called out to Pokuka, the owner of the garden put his axe right through his back. As he was dying, he said, "Pokuka, son, you ran away and I'm dying now." Then Tiginakuo's head went forward to a cave and he died.

When Pokuka heard his father calling out, he jumped and ran away. However, when he jumped down, he was no longer a boy. No, Pokuka turned into a bird and flew towards the big stone called Tulu in the deep forest.

Now, he lives at a stone that we call Homainige. I am from Tiginakuo's little village in **Madang** Province [**Gende People**].

R. M. Mande

Gindi

Madang Province

D150B. Transformation: boy to bird; D671. Transformation flight; F401.6. Spirit in human form; F405+. Spirit killed by axe; F490+. Masalai; K420. Thief loses his goods or is detected; P233. Father and son; Q212. Theft punished; Q411.13. Death as punishment for thievery; R220. Flights; R260. Pursuits; S139.4. Murder by mangling with axe; W126. Disobedience


## The Flying Fox that Helped a Man

(Wantok 28[4], September 15, 1979, page 11)

Long, long ago, there were many people who lived in **Tikil** Village in the area around Mount Hagen [**Hagen** People, **Western Highlands** Province]. In this village, there just lived a woman and her son.

The woman and her son planted many sweet potatoes, leafy vegetables, beans, and corn in their garden. They barely got by, and they were wasting away. They did not have pigs or meat, so they only ate sweet potatoes.

In the early morning, the man took his bow, arrows and axe and told his mother, "Every day, we just eat sweet potatoes. So now I want to go hunt for wild game for us in the forest. You should get some greens and sweet potatoes ready, then wait for me."

The son followed a stream. He walked very far. He saw something like a python lying on top of a stone. He looked at it and thought that it was a huge python, so he stood there, strung his bow tightly and shot.

When he went closer to look, he was surprised. He turned and looked, it was not a python. No, it was the innards of a pig. Some man had removed them and left them there about a week before.

The man took these innards, cleaned them and carefully removed the pig feces. He was very happy. Later, he carried the pig guts back home. When his mother saw him, she ran and held her son. His mother was very happy. They cooked the pig guts in an earth oven with greens and sweet potatoes, then ate them.

Another morning, the son took his bow, arrows and axe, and returned to hunt for game. He followed the stream and bypassed the place where he had found the pig guts. He continued to walk and he again saw something that looked like a python. So, he stood and took his bow. He strung his bow tightly and shot at it.

When he went closer, he saw something that was not a python. No, it was the innards of a pig that some man had just removed the previous day. So he did as before, he removed the feces from the pig's innards and washed the innards well. He was very happy. Later, he carried the pig guts back home. He and his mother again cooked the guts in an earth oven with some greens and some sweet potatoes.

The next morning, the man again woke up, took his bow, arrows and axe, and went to the forest to hunt for game. He followed a small trail. As he walked, he arrived at the place where he had found the pig guts the second time. The sun was beating down strongly. He saw something that was like a python again.

When he was ready to shoot this thing, he saw a foot print near the pig's innards. He saw a vine that had been trampled by a man. He climbed this vine upwards and saw a good place that was high above.

Still looking, he saw a man sitting there. He went closer and saw that the man was blind and mute. He stayed up there and when he looked down, he saw a very big hole. The blind and mute man cut up pigs and threw them down into the hole.

The son stole some of the blind and mute man's pigs, carrying them to his mother. They cooked and ate them. The blind and mute man continued to eat pigs, but his belly was not full, so he said [!], "Who is it that ate my pigs? I don't know." The blind and mute man made a long hole that went far below. At night, he finished the hole and put a long net bag down the hole. He covered part of the hole with some tree leaves.

In the early morning, the woman's son walked towards this place. He climbed and went to sit down, but he fell into the hole. But he did not die, he fell into the net bag. The blind and mute man raised the net bag and hung it up in a bad place. The tree had two branches, one went north and the other south.

The blind and mute man was famished, so he began to eat the son's loincloth and *tanget*. Later, he ate his fingernails, toenails and hair. The poor son was approaching death.

The mother cried and cried when her son did not return at night. She heard a flying fox come and eat her ripe bananas. She continued to cry as she asked the flying fox, "Are you a man or a flying fox that's eating those bananas? I'm crying for my son who went to the forest and has not yet returned." When the flying fox heard this, it flew closer to the door.

In the morning, the flying fox saw the son sleeping in the net bag. The flying fox flew and called upon all of the big and small birds in the forests and grasslands for help. They gathered around this tree and sang. The birds of the forest held one part of the net bag, and the birds of the grasslands held the other part of the net bag. All of the birds carried the net bag and put it near the house door. Then all of the birds flew to their homes.

The mother came and saw the net bag with her son that had been brought to the house. She laid him near the fire and gave him ripe bananas. She did this for a month, and her son became well again. The son was angry at the blind and mute man, so he told his mother, "Mama, I'll go and kill that blind and mute man."

In the early morning, the son took his bow, arrows, and axe, then went into the forest. He followed the stream to the place where the blind and mute man lived. He looked up and saw him sitting and eating pork.

The son made a big hole near the stream. When the blind and mute man finished eating, he climbed down to drink some water. He went to sit and drink, but he fell into the hole.

The blind and mute man fell directly on a stick and cried out. The son made a fire and heated some stones. When the stones were hot, he threw them down on top of the blind and mute man. The man cried out and later he died.

The man went home and lived happily with his mother. So now we, the people of Tikil, never eat flying foxes. These holes are still at this place. If you go to Hagen, you

can see them. The helicopters land near this place in the deep forest.

Tomi Bopi

Finschhafen

Morobe Province

A983+. Origin of holes in ground; B212. Animal understands human speech; B542.1.4K. Bird rescues boy from tree top; B542.1.2+. Flying fox rescues person from height; B552. Man carried by bird; B552+. Person carried by flying fox; C221.1+. Tabu: eating flying fox; F216.1+. Blind and mute man who lives in tree; K333. Theft from blind person; K420. Thief loses his goods or is detected; K735. Capture in pitfall; P231. Mother and son; Q212. Theft punished; Q215. Cannibalism punished; Q429.1. Punishment: culprit eaten by cannibals; Q414. Punishment: burning alive; Q433. Punishment: imprisonment; R49.1. Captivity in tree; R51.1. Prisoners starved; R110. Rescue of captive; S112. Burning to death

## Why Man Is the Boss
### (Wantok 285, September 22, 1979, page 17)

Long, long ago, an old woman and her five sons lived in a village called **Nebira** [**Central** Province].

One day, the children told their mother, "Mama, go get some *nonu* for us. We'll go to the forest and hunt for wild game." This food, called *nonu*, is a good fruit for cooking and eating.

That morning, the old woman went into the forest to get these fruits that are called *nonu*. The sons went to hunt for game. The old woman walked and walked, then saw a *nonu* tree. She went closer to look, but there were no fruits on the ground. So, she sat and sang to the *nonu*.

The old woman sang, "*Nonu rua nonu toi, taura rua taura toi, nou o moru moru o.*" While she sang this, many *nonu* fruits fell down to the ground. She saw this and was very happy.

The old woman gathered the *nonu* fruits and carried them home. When she arrived home, her sons had also arrived. At this time, there was no fire, so they put the *nonu* fruits and marsupial (*sikau*) meat in the sun. When the *nonu* and sikau were done, they sat and ate together.

They did this every day, but one day, the sons asked their mother, "Mama, is there some *nonu* or not?" The mother replied, "Sorry, children, there's no more *nonu*."

The sons told their mother, "Mama, there are some *sana* (taros) growing in the river. Will you go and get it?" This name, *sana* means taro in the Koitabu Language [**Koita** People].

In the morning, the mother went to dig up the taro corms. Her sons went to the forest and hunted for wild game. The old woman dug up many taros and brought them home.  Her sons killed many, many marsupials.  They put these in the sun.  When the taros and marsupials were done, they ate them.

They did this every day.  But one morning, the sons asked their mother, "Mama, is there some taro, or not?"  The mother replied, "Sorry, there's just one taro plant left."

The sons told their mother, "Mama, go remove it.  We'll go and hunt for wild game."  So in the morning, the mother left them and went to the river to dig up the taro plant.

When the old woman was about to dig up the taro corm, the land slid and fell into the river.  She tried to swim, but she was unable because the river was too swift and carried her completely away.

The old woman drifted in the river and arrived at a village.  At this village, there were five young women who were standing by the river.  She saw them and called out, "Children, please help me."  The fifth sister wanted to help her, but the other four sisters did not want to, so the river swept her away.

The old woman drifted past many villages, but the people all did the same.  They did not help her, so the water kept carrying her farther.  She drifted and arrived at a village that was very far away.  She raised her head and saw five young women standing by the river.

The old woman called out, "Hey children, help me."  The women were surprised to see the old woman calling out.  The fifth sister saw the old woman and threw a stick into the water.  The old woman grabbed onto the stick and the fifth sister began to pull her closer.

The five young women took her to their home.  They washed her and gave her food.  Later, the women made a big fire and the old woman sat near it.

The old woman told the five women, "I have five sons. Look at the river.  After a little while, they will come to find me."  When the women heard this, they were very happy.

The old woman's sons were very worried because they could not find her, so they dressed themselves.  They made a canoe from a tree and paddled it downstream.

They paddled and arrived at the first village.  When they saw the five women, they called out, "Is our mother here or not?"  The fifth sister replied, "I wanted to help your mother, but my four sisters did not want to, so the water carried her down to another village."

They paddled farther and passed by many villages, but the people said, "No, we did not see your mother."  They continued to paddle and they arrived at the village where their mother was.

They saw five women and called out, "Hey, is our mother here?"  The women quickly replied, "Yes, your mother is here."  When the women saw the old woman's sons, they became very lustful.

When the men saw their mother, they cried with joy.  The first brother was the most handsome of the five, so the mother told him, "Son, you will marry the fifth sister because she helped me and pulled me out of the water."

So, the first brother married the fifth sister.  The four other sisters were very worried, but later, the four brothers married the four sisters.

They lived in this village for about a month.  However, the old woman was not very happy.  So at night, she swallowed all of her sons with their wives.  After she swallowed them, she walked into the night.

When the old woman, Nebira, arrived at her old home, she vomited her sons and their wives through her mouth.  In the morning, the women were surprised to hear a noise from a *toaro*.

A *toaro* is something that people use during festivals.  The women heard this noise and were very worried.  They lived in this village and begat many people.  So now my kin from this place are called Iarohaga [Iarogaha].  There are many people from **Iarogaha**.  One of my kin from Korobosea Village lives in Port Moresby.

So now, we follow the customs of our ancestors.  If we, the people of Iarogaha, marry a woman from another place, we never live at that woman's village.  Now, we give a bride price for [lit., "purchase"] the woman and take her directly to our village.  This is because our ancestors did this.

Kuruku Tabu

Korobosea

National Capital District

A1550+. Origin of virilocality; A1555.2. Origin of custom of purchasing wives; D1275. Magic song; D1781. Magic results from singing; D2105.7. Fruit obtained from tree by magic; F910+. Extraordinary vomitings; F911.1.2K2+. Woman swallows her sons and their wives whole; J1813+. Cooking processes misunderstood: cooking with the sun; P210. Husband and wife; P231. Mother and son; P251.6.2+. Five brothers; P252.2+. Five sisters; P600+. Virilocality; Q53. Reward for rescue; T10. Falling in love; T52. Bride purchased; T100. Marriage

# Burning the Ghost

(Wantok 286, September 2[9], 1979, page 17)

Not long ago, about four generations ago, the ancestors of Wabute [**Wabutei**] Village went into the deep forest called Emrium to look for wild game [**Olo** People, **West Sepik** Province].

They searched for about four or five weeks in the deep forest. Their supply of sago was finished and they were famished, so they saw a breadfruit tree with many fruits. They went to gather the fruits and to cook and eat them. Some men climbed the tree, others cut firewood, and others collected the fruits, putting them in a pile to be cooked.

When the firewood was ready, they made a big bonfire. When the fire was burning, they took the breadfruits and cooked them. After they were done, they removed them from the fire and let them cool before eating. The leaders were very muscular men.

They sat and ate. At the same time, they talked and shouted and made much noise. While they were eating, they heard a hand drum from somewhere in the forest, near the stream where they were eating breadfruit.

It was the hand drum of a big ghost man. He sang and approached them. He asked them, "Hey, grandchildren, what have you been cooking?"

They said, "Oh grandfather, we cooked some breadfruit. Come and eat with us."

The big ghost agreed. He sat amongst them and they gave him some breadfruit. The real men ate slowly, but their ancestor just ate the breadfruit like it was nothing. They watched and whispered to each other so that the ghost would not hear them. They passed along the message, "Let's carry him and throw him into the fire."

The men made a bonfire. They prepared two big logs to throw on top of the ghost after they threw him onto the fire. When all of the men were ready, they asked the ghost, "Grandfather, is it all right if we carry you and dance?"

The crazy ghost said, "Yes, that's OK, grandchildren. I like dancing very much."

All of the men made a big ring. They stood around the fire and lifted the crazy ghost in their arms. They danced and sang around the bonfire. They sang and danced for a long time, then they threw him into the fire.

Quickly, a man took the two heavy logs. He threw one on the ghost's head and the other on the ghost's legs. They quickly carried their game meat and ran home.

On the trail home, they heard a big explosion from the ghost's belly. They took the ghost's stone axe and returned home. Now if you want to see this axe, ask the men of Wabute Village and they will show it to you.

John Woni

Wabute [Wabutei], Lumi

West Sepik Province

E422.3.2. Revenant as a very large man (giant); E425.2. Revenant as man; E446.2. Ghost laid by burning body; E545. The dead speak; F610. Re-



markably strong man; K816. Dupe lured to supposed dance and killed; K925. Victim pushed into fire; P291. Grandfather; R220. Flights

## The Silent Place
(Wantok 287, October 6, 1979, page 17)

Once, long ago, a man from **Wilbeite** Village and his two children went to a mountain far away from his village to hunt wild game [**Olo** People, **West Sepik** Province]. They took bows, arrows, food and a dog with them.

They arrived at a mountain hut and the father told his children, "You two stay in the hut. Just myself and the dog will go into the forest to hunt for marsupials (*sikau*)." The children made a fire and stayed in the hut. They joked and laughed.

The sister told her brother, "You stay here. I'm going to find some vegetables." When the sister returned from finding vegetables, her brother got up to find some firewood. He cut and cut the firewood. While he was cutting, he heard a dog barking and chasing a marsupial. He stood up and saw a marsupial running towards him. He killed it and his father killed another.

The sister was alone in the hut and thought of the things left at home, such as ropes, yams, bananas, and bamboo tubes. She thought of these things and spoke to herself, "Oh please, I'd like those things very much. Who will bring those things here to me?"

As she spoke, those things just appeared before her eyes.

Right after the things arrived, all of the things in the forest transformed themselves. The place became pitch black. The insects in the forest chirped and sang, and it became very noisy. Soon, a big flood arose from the ground.

When the father saw the transformations, he asked his two children, "Which one of you spoke when these things changed?"

The brother told his father, "It was sister who spoke when these bad things happened."

The water was rising quickly. The father noticed this, so he quickly took a long piece of rattan and used it for them to climb a tall tree. However, a big *masalai* fish shot the girl [with a jet of water?] and carried her down into the water.

The father cut the girl's pinkie finger and gave it to the dog to carry home. The dog jumped down to the ground and went home.

When the dog arrived home, the girl's mother was stirring sago. The dog threw the finger into the dish of sago. The mother saw this and thought that something bad had happened to her two children and her husband on the mountain.

Now, because of this, if we go on top of this mountain, we can see yams and bamboo growing near this pond. Also, if we go to the summit, we cannot speak, point at food or call out. We are terrified there.

John Woni

Lumi

West Sepik Province

A1011. Local deluges; A1023. Escape from deluge on tree; A2800+. Why certain plants grow in certain place; B874. Giant fish; C400. Speaking tabu; C843+. Pointing at food in certain place; D521. Transformation through wish; D908. Magic darkness; D2151.8. Magic flood; D2074.2.3. Summoning by wish; F402.1.11. Spirit causes death; F420.1.3.2. Water-spirit as fish; F490+. Masalai; P210. Husband and wife; P231. Mother and son; P232. Mother and daughter; P233. Father and son; P234. Father and daughter; P253. Sister and brother; R311. Tree refuge

## The Story of the Kinsmen Lekare [Lekari] and Yoarene

(Wantok 288, October 13, 1979, page 20)

Long, long ago, there were two women who lived in a village named Koiya [**Kauwo** Village, **Wiru** People, **Southern Highlands** Province]. One day, they thought about marriage, but they could not find a husband or even a friend.

One time, they walked and walked to a village called **Lega**. In this village, they found two very handsome young men. They thought and thought because they wanted to marry these two young men.

At this time, the women were friends with these two men. The men gave their hearts to the woman, so they thought of marriage. They were friends and they were approaching marriage.

Later, they agreed to marry, so the men called to the women's clan to come and receive the bride price. They called to their own clan to come and help them give the bride price for these two women.

Everything was agreeable, so the two men married these two women. Later, after some months, the women became pregnant. They gave birth to two boys. The women were very happy and named the boys Koiyama and Lekama.

Koiyama and Lekama grew up well. They did not get sick or get into trouble. They grew and grew, and became very big men.

Koiyama and Lekama became leaders of the village. They became men of renown. All of the men of the village followed their speech and manners. One time, they planned to host a party, so they called out to all of the men of the village to come and see their party.

At this time, Koiyama and Lekama thought of giving a small name to their lineage. Koiyama stood up and gave the name Yoarene to his lineage. Then Lekama gave the name Lekari to his lineage.

So now in my village, we have two big clans of people. These two clans have the big names Yoarene and Lekari.

Sometimes, these two clans argue, but they never have a big argument and fight. They only just talk and then forget about their disagreements. Now we, the young clan members, still use these two names Yoarene and Lekari in the village.

Henry Ague [Angue]

Mt. Hagen

Western Highlands Province

[The ancestor story in *Wantok* #248 is a variation of this story and was written the same author.]

A1640+. Origin of Lekarii Clan; A1640+. Origin of Yoarene Clan; A1641+. Origin of peaceful relations between two clans; P210. Husband and wife; P231. Mother and son; P233. Father and son; T10. Falling in love; T52. Bride purchased; T100. Marriage; T570. Pregnancy; T580. Childbirth

## The Crab Helped the Cassowary in the Water

(Wantok 289, October 20, 1979, page 17)

Long, long ago, in the Finschhafen Peninsula, there was a cassowary and a chicken that were very good friends. One time, the friends thought about going to an island. So, they took their canoe and paddled off. The chicken sat in the bow.

While they were paddling, a strong wind arose and made the chicken's feathers dance about. Everyone saw chicken's feathers and they gossiped. When they gossiped, they made the chicken very unhappy. However, the chicken's friend, the cassowary, was ashamed and very angry at the chicken.

So, the cassowary stood up and broke the canoe with its leg, then the water filled the canoe. As the water rose, the chicken flew to the beach where everyone was standing.

The cassowary was too heavy and found it too hard to fly. So, the cassowary sank beneath the water where it found a crab and asked the crab for help. The crab said, "I often go above the water." So the crab carried the cassowary upwards and placed the cassowary where it wanted to go.

When the crab put the cassowary down, the cassowary did not say thank you. No, the cassowary did something bad. It killed the crab.

So now, the people of this area call this place *Oeraharuc*. In English, this means, "Cassowary and Crab." Now, there is a mission station there that is called **Sattelberg**, in the Finschhafen Peninsula [**Kâte** People, **Morobe** Province].

J. R. Kugeva
Igam Barracks
Lae
Morobe Province

[See the stories in *Wantok* #249, 676 and 1184, which are similar.]

A1617. Origin of place-name; A2494.13+. Enmity between cassowary and chicken; B211.3.17K. Speaking cassowary; B211.8.1K. Speaking crab; B295.2.1K. Animals make voyage in canoe; B296.2K. Animal (who is land-dweller) crosses water on back of another animal; B336+. Helpful crab killed by ungrateful cassowary; B540+. Crab rescuer; J2133.11+. Cassowary destroys boat in anger, but almost drowns while chicken flies away; P310. Friendship; R100. Rescues; R220. Flights; S110. Murders; W154. Ingratitude


## Where Did Shells for Lime Come From?

(Wantok 290, October 27, 1979, page 17)

Long, long ago, the people did not have lime (calcium oxide), so they always chewed betel nut with just ashes from the fire. The women had one huge, round shell. They never put the shell outside. No, they always hid it inside a clay pot.

When the men wanted to chew betel nuts, they always chewed them with ashes, but their saliva did not turn red. When they chewed betel nuts, their mouths became very yellow.

When the women wanted to chew betel nuts, they usually each took a piece of sago palm midrib and the shell. Then began chewing the betel nuts. After they chewed, they went outside. The men said to them, "You women were chewing betel nuts with something and now your mouths are very red."

The women replied, "We only chewed betel nuts with ashes and now our mouths are very red."

One time, the women went to the forest. The men hid a little boy in the house where the women chewed betel nuts. The boy's name was Embangeba.

In the evening, the women returned from the forest and went inside their house again to chew betel nuts. The boy saw them chewing betel nuts. He hid well and just watched the women. The women removed the shell from the clay pot and began to chew the betel nuts.

One day, the women went to fetch some water. The boy hid and took their betel nuts, then chewed them with the women's shell. After he chewed, his mouth became very red.

When the women returned, they saw the little boy sitting there. His mouth was very red. The women saw this and thought, "The boy has ruined our shell."

The women said, "What should we do about this little boy who ruined our shell?"

One day, all of the men went to hunt for wild game. The women made a big party. They quickly divided the food. they took their shell and put it in the middle.

They called to the little boy, Embangeba. All of the women surrounded this boy. They took their sago palm midribs and beat the boy, killing him. Later, they told the children, "This is your father's food plate. When he arrives, you can eat with him."

After the women spoke to the children, they pulled an "eagle" betel nut and a flying fox bone, then hit the base of a coconut palm tree. Later, all of the women climbed this coconut palm. However one woman was pregnant, so she did not climb with the others.

Runga Saimon
Madang Province

A2691+. Lime (calcium oxide) initially hidden by women; Q200+. Revealing secret punished; Q422.0.1. Punishment: beating to death; S122. Flogging to death; T570. Pregnancy


## The Dog Found Water

(Wantok 291a, November 3, 1979, page 21)

Long ago, there lived a man and his wife. The place where they lived did not have water. None. They usually just cooked their food in the fire and ate it. They did this for a long time, then the wife gave birth.

The man was very worried for his wife and child. They slept and the next morning, he woke up and took his dog to the forest to hunt for wild game. They arrived at a mountain and the man saw a fig tree.

On top of the fig tree were many marsupials (*kapul*). The man left his dog on the ground and he climbed the fig tree. He killed many marsupials. He thought, "If there was water, I could make a good soup for mama and baby." He thought this and continued to kill the marsupials while singing on the tree.

His dog was walking around on the ground. Then the dog quickly dug a hole. The man went and called out to his dog. The dog came up the hole and shook its body, splashing water on the man. The man carried the dog and rubbed its skin. They turned and looked. No! There was water shooting to the top of the hole that the dog had made.

The man was very happy and went to cut a piece of bamboo to fill with water. He returned home with his dog. The woman saw this and was very happy for her husband and their dog.

In the morning, they woke up and oh my, the water was flowing down. This place is called Kanome [**Kanomi**] in Sialum sub-Province, in the Finschhafen Peninsula of [**Morobe**] Province [**Ono** People].

If you go to this place, you will see many streams and think that there is a lake there. It is very high in the forest, not near the beach. This lake is where the dog dug the hole.

The dog's master came down from the fig tree and he tried to make other springs, but there was only one spring that could be made. The men of this place often make gardens inside the water. The people also often defecate in the water. When they want to plant taros (*taro tru* and *taro kongkong*) and bananas, they will talk in the language used in **Pindiu** Village and the water will go where they planted [**Kube** People]. The water goes back to lie in the garden.

Gewing K. Pongke
Rintebe
Eastern Highlands Province

A920.1.0.1. Origin of particular lake; D1774+. Magic results from speaking foreign language; D2151.2. Magic control of rivers; P210. Husband and wife; T580. Childbirth

## The Man Who Pulled Fish from His Head

(Wantok 291b, November 3, 1979, page 21)

Long ago, there was a man who had many small sores on his head. When he went to catch fish, he would put his head in the sea. Many fish came and hung onto his sores and ate them.

This man often caught many fish this way, more than all of the other men did. He often shared his fish with all of the men of the village.

He did this for a while, then one day the men found him and saw how he caught fish. They were very angry with him, so he was quite ashamed. He transformed his body and became a reef in the sea.

So now, we can see that reefs have many little holes and spikes like sores, and that reefs are very sharp. If we walk on top of a reef, we will scratch our legs and be in pain.

Jamalak Oscar
P. O. Box 89
Bulolo
Morobe Province

A958K. Origin of reefs; A2872+. Why reefs are sharp; D237+M. Transformation: man to reef; D671. Transformation flight; D2150+. Catching fish with ulcer as bait

## Marsupial (*Sikau*) Was Ashamed of Chicken

(Wantok 292, November 10, 1979, page 21)

Long ago, Marsupial (*Sikau*) and Chicken were friends. They lived in a village of people. They often played and ate together.

One time, Marsupial told Chicken, "Friend, come with me to the forest to look for breadfruits." They went to get breadfruits, then they went to the beach. They made a fire, cooked the breadfruits and ate them.

After they ate, they talked and played. They sang and danced happily. Later, Marsupial told Chicken, "Friend, come and we'll cut a tree and make a canoe." So they went to cut a tree and they made a canoe.

After the cut the tree, they began to hew the log. They made various carvings and images of people. They made various images at the bow of the canoe too. After they finished, they went to cut an outrigger. After they cut the outrigger, they began to fasten their canoe together. They made a seat and a sail, then they prepared to go asea.

Marsupial told its friend, "Chicken, friend, let's go to the forest to find some betel nuts and betel peppers." So, they went to get some betel nuts and peppers, then they returned. They paddled their canoe into the sea. Chicken steered the canoe while Marsupial sat on the seat, chewing betel nuts and peppers.

While Chicken steered the canoe, a strong wind arose and blew Chicken's plumage, making the canoe go faster. They sped along and Chicken said to Marsupial, "Oh Friend, come change positions with me so that I can rest a little." They changed positions and Marsupial steered the canoe. Chicken sat on the seat, chewing betel nuts and peppers, while singing and hitting a hand drum.

While Marsupial steered, the canoe did not go so swiftly because Marsupial's tail was in the water and fastened to a stone. Marsupial said, "Friend, I'm tired. Come and change with me." So, Chicken steered the canoe again, and the canoe sped along very rapidly.

Chicken told Marsupial, "Oh friend, I'm a little tired, come and take my place." So, Marsupial steered the canoe again. They continued to do this and Chicken became angry, so Chicken took an axe and cut the canoe. When the canoe broke, Chicken flew away and Marsupial sank with the canoe.

Marsupial asked the big fish for help to go back up towards the sun. The fish replied, "Oh, sorry, we don't have time to help you." Later, a turtle came and Marsupial asked the turtle, "Please, can you help me and carry me towards the sun?" The turtle told Marsupial, "Climb on my back and I'll bring you to the beach."

When the turtle left Marsupial on the beach, Marsupial ran straight back into the forest. This was because Marsupial was ashamed of its friend, Chicken.

So now, only chickens live in villages, and marsupials live in the forest. If the two had not gotten angry or traveled around, they would probably both live in villages now.

M. Yukul
Arawa
North Solomons Province

B211.2.12K+. Speaking marsupial; B871.2+. Giant marsupial; D12. Transformation: man to woman; J652. Inattention to warnings; P210. Husband and wife; P230. Parents and children; Q211.6. Killing an animal revenged; Q223.5. Neglect to attend church punished; Q551.3. Punishment: transformation

A2433.2.1+. Why marsupial lives in forest; A2494.13.10+. Enmity between chicken and marsupial; B211.2.12K+. Speaking marsupial; B211.3.2.1. Speaking chicken; B211.5. Speaking fish; B211.6.3K. Speaking turtle; B214.1+. Singing marsupial; B540+. Turtle rescuer; P310. Friendship; R100. Rescues; R220. Flights

## The Man Who Became a Woman

(Wantok 293, November 17, 1979, page 20)

Long ago, there was a village. At this time, God began to speak. The name of this village is Molom [**Morom**] in the Markham Valley [**Silisili** People, **Morobe** Province].

In this village, they worshipped every Sunday. There was a man named Guwos who never worshipped on Sunday. His wife and children did worship. Every Sunday, Guwos would go to hunt for wild game, and his wife always scolded him for not worshipping on Sunday.

One Sunday morning, Guwos woke up, took his bow and multi-pronged arrows, and went to the forest to hunt for game. He saw a huge marsupial (*kapul*) sitting down. He approached very quietly and drew back his bow to shoot at the marsupial. The marsupial turned and told him, "Hey,

you can't shoot me. If you shoot me, something will happen to you." Guwos said, "You're lying. You're my meat."

Then he let the arrow fly and he shot the marsupial. Immediately, he became a young woman. His breasts changed and stood up like those of a woman.

When he returned to the village, his wife saw him and said, "Hey, woman, why are you coming here?" He replied, "No, it's just me coming." So, he was a woman and they just lived in one house.

Elisah P. Benny
Markham
Morobe Province

B211.2.12K+. Speaking marsupial; B871.2+. Giant marsupial; D12. Transformation: man to woman; J652. Inattention to warnings; P210. Husband and wife; P230. Parents and children; Q211.6. Killing an animal revenged; Q223.5. Neglect to attend church punished; Q551.3. Punishment: transformation

## Tabo Married the Woman from a Cave

(Wantok 294, November 24, 1979, page 21)

Long, long ago, an old man and his old wife lived in **Aoaveloi** Village in the **Gimi** [People's] area, near Okapa [**Eastern Highlands** Province].

They had a beautiful child named Tabo. Tabo always went to the forest to hunt for marsupials (*kapul*). One day, he was tired of going to the forest, so he took his bow and arrows, then followed the Olaotu River upstream.

In the middle of Olaotu River stood a boulder. Tabo approached the boulder and a light came over his entire body. He followed the light and saw a beautiful woman sitting on top of the boulder, making a net bag.

Tabo looked up at a tree and saw a tree branch that went close to the boulder. He quietly climbed the tree and followed the branch towards the boulder. He jumped down and stood in front of the woman. The woman was surprised and wanted to run away, but Tabo held her hand tightly. The woman trembled. Tabo asked her, "Who made this bracelet and gave it to you?" The woman said, "You think that I don't have a father, huh?" Tabo asked again, "Who made this hat and gave it to you?" The woman said, "I don't have a mother, huh?" The boulder opened and the woman ran inside, but quickly Tabo ran inside too. The two of them killed an old man who was watching the door. Tabo did not have a way to get out, so he married the woman. The woman's parents made a big party for them.

Tabo's parents thought that he was gone for good, so they put much mud on their bodies [a sign of mourning] and cried.

After the woman's parents gave the party, the woman's father took a big stick and hit the stone, opening it. Tabo and his wife went outside. Tabo took the woman to his house. His parents had thought that he was gone for good, so when they saw Tabo with the woman coming, they were happy.

They lived for a fairly long time, and his wife had a baby boy. Tabo left the house and his wife went to the garden, so they left the boy with his grandmother. While they were gone, the boy cried loudly. The grandmother scolded him, "You're not the son of a man, you're the son of a cave woman. You can't cry."

The boy's mother went closer to the house and heard him. The woman went there, held her boy and she took some fire. They went down to the boulder where she used to sit, and she cried. Tabo went to the house. He searched and searched for his wife. His wife was not there, so he followed her footprints and went down to see the woman sitting on top of the boulder with their son. Tabo said, "First, give me the boy." The woman replied, "He's not the son of a cave woman." After she said this, the boy turned into a bird of paradise and flew towards the source of the river, then went inside a cave. Tabo cried and cried, then went back to the house and killed his mother.

Aisip N. Egadi
Oradatu Village
Gimi, Okapa
Eastern Highlands Province

D150+B. Transformation: boy to bird of paradise; D1162. Magic light; D1552.1. Mountain opens at blow of divining rod; P210. Husband and wife; P231. Mother and son; P232. Mother and daughter; P233. Father and son; P234. Father and daughter; P261. Father-in-law; P262. Mother-in-law; P265. Son-in-law; P265+. Daughter-in-law; P292. Grandmother; P681+. Mourning customs: earth on body; Q235. Cursing punished; Q304. Scolding punished; Q411. Death as punishment; R210. Escapes; R260. Pursuits; S22+. Matricide; S110. Murders; T100. Marriage

## The Cassowary Tricked the *Masalai* Clam

(Wantok 295, December 1, 1979, page 17)

This is a true story about a cassowary [the dwarf cassowary (*Casuarius bennetti*) is the only species on New Britain Island (Beehler *et al.*, 1986: 45)] and a *masalai* clam. Long, long ago, in the time of the great men, there was a very bad *masalai* clam. The clam swallowed men who paddled canoes or logs that drifted in the sea. If the men of my area near Hoskins wanted to go there, no, this *masalai* clam often swallowed them. The *masalai* clam did this for many years. The people of the area became fewer and fewer.

One time, a cassowary stood on top of its home and saw a canoe coming towards **Hoskins**, so the cassowary thought that it would arrive. But no, the bad clam ate the canoe. The cassowary thought and thought, something did not look right. The cassowary was very angry. So the cassowary thought of a trick with which to fool the clam. The cassowary finished thinking and said, "OK, I'll go try the trick on the clam." One day, the cassowary went down to the sea and called out to the *masalai* clam. The cassowary said, "Hey, friend, I always stand at my place and watch you eating a lot of food. It just makes me salivate. I often find it hard to find food. What do you think, can we change places? Come up here, and I'll take your place and eat some meat?"

The *masalai* clam thought for five minutes then said, "That's just fine. We can change places. Come help me, then eat some meat." So they changed places. The clam went up and the cassowary went to the *masalai* clam's place.

They stayed for a very long time. The clam saw some canoes coming from the Biala [**Bialla**] area and the clam called down to the cassowary, "Hey friend, get ready now, a canoe's coming from Biala." The *masalai* clam thought that the cassowary would swallow the canoe. But no, the cassowary just let them paddle past. The clam saw this and was very angry. The clam said, "Why did you let them go? Are you blind?" The cassowary said, "It's a bad thing that you always do. Before, I often saw you swallow and eat many of my men, women and children. I'm very sorry for them, so I talked to you about changing places. Now I'll let them go." The clam was very angry and wanted to go down to its home, but it was too late. The vines of the forest were growing around the clam and holding it tightly. The clam could no longer move. The clam stayed there, then large red ants and other ants of the forest urinated in its "eyes", and the clam died. The cassowary lived entirely in the sea.

If you go to the **Tarobi** area in **West New Britain** Province, you can see this *masalai* clam shell. Its opening is about fifty feet [**West Nakanai** People].

Now too, if it is a good day with calm seas, you can see our friend, the cassowary, walking on the reef in the home of the *masalai* clam. If you take an airplane from Hoskins to Biala, you can see this, the shell of the *masalai* clam, and the big hole in the reef. I have seen the cassowary walking on the reef with my own eyes. The cassowary is a *masalai* too, before and now. You can not play with it, it is a very bad boy.

Andrew Eddi Woodee

Wewak

East Sepik Province

A983+. Origin of holes in ground; B16.5.3. Devastating shell-fish; B211.3.17K. Speaking cassowary; B211.9K+. Speaking clam; B469+. Helpful cassowary; B750+. Cassowary lives in sea; B874.6. Giant clam; D1402.18+. Urine kills animal; F401.3.7+. Spirit in form of cassowary; F420.1.3.2+. Water-spirit as clam; F490+. Masalai; F911.4.1.1. Party in canoe swallowed by great clam; G510.4. Hero overcomes devastating animal; K910+. Cassowary persuades clam to exchange places, clam is trapped by vines and killed by ants; X717.1H+. Urination on animal


# A Man Who Found a Woman

(Wantok 296, December 8, 1979, page 17)

Long, long ago, there was a man with ringworm. His two brothers did not have ringworm. They went to hunt for wild game in the forest. They traveled until it was dark, then they slept. At dawn, they continued hunting. The ringworm man went up a mountain. He saw a tree called *surum* in the language spoken in **Pindiu** Village, meaning fig tree [**Kube** People].

He took a leaf and put it in his hair. He continued walking and arrived at a forest hut. His two brothers had run away and gone home. The ringworm man was looking for them and he was worried. He took the leaf from his hair and put it in the hut, then went to find some fire. The tree leaf turned into a pretty woman. The woman made a fire and cooked some food. The man arrived, saw the woman and was terrified. The woman said to him, "Don't be afraid of me. I'm your wife. You yourself carried and left me here."

The man was terrified, so he did not sleep. He stayed there and the woman cooked some food, then went to sleep. The ringworm man climbed a tree. At dawn, the woman looked for the ringworm man. When she saw him on top of the tree, she said, "Come down, we're going home." The ringworm man did not want to do this, so the woman said, "Yesterday, you yourself brought me here. Why did you do this?" Then the woman walked up the mountain. The ring-worm man wailed, then came down the tree and followed her.

He followed her up the mountain, and she turned into a fig tree. The man climbed the fig tree and took a leaf, but he was very high up the tree.

The poor ringworm man wailed and turned into a stone. If you want to see this fig tree, take an airplane to Lae, then go to Pindiu in the Finschhafen Peninsula of **Morobe** Province and you will see it.

I am from the Pindiu sub-District of Finschhafen in Morobe Province. Now I live in Kimbe.

U. S. Shonggy Erick

Kimbe

West New Britain Province

A974. Rocks from transformation of people to stone; A977.5. Origin of particular rock; D215+W. Transformation: woman to fig tree; D231M. Transformation: man to stone; D361.1+. Forest Spirit Bride; D431.3W. Transformation: leaf (of tree) to woman; D516. Transformation through excessive grief; D671. Transformation flight; L140+. Ugly marries beautiful; P210. Husband and wife; P251.6.1. Three brothers; R220. Flights; R260. Pursuits; R311. Tree refuge; S143. Abandonment in forest


# A Snake Turned into the Fly River

(Wantok 297, December 15, 1979, page 17)

Once when people lived in Boliny [**Bolim**] and Alsobip [**Olsobip**], there was no river between them. One time, the men wanted to go up a mountain to hunt for marsupials (*kapul*) and pandanus nuts (*karuka*) [**Faiwol** People, **Western** Province]. So, they went up the mountain for three days. All of the men returned home except for one man that they left on the mountain. This was because he had not killed any marsupials. He had told the other men that he would continue to hunt for marsupials while they went down the mountain.

He continued to hunt for marsupials. In the evening he went to a hut. A strong wind blew and a heavy rain fell. He made a fire. He was there for only about five minutes when he saw a huge python putting its head by the door. He was surprised.

He offered a piece of marsupial, but the snake did not want it. He offered his dog, but the snake did not want it. So, he tried to offer other things. He offered his leg, then the snake flicked its tongue and came and swallowed him, becoming a lake on this mountain. The villagers waited and waited for this man, but he did not come. They went up to look for him and saw this lake, so they went home.

His two brothers wanted to do something to kill the snake. They went to the other side of the lake and saw part of the snake lying underwater. The big brother just grabbed this part of the snake. He told his little brother, "Go cut a piece of rattan and come back."

The little brother went to find this, but he just cut an ordinary vine. His big brother scolded his little brother and told him, "Come hold it." The big brother went to the forest and cut a piece of rattan. The little brother held the snake, and the snake's smell got stronger and stronger. The little brother let the part of the snake back into the water. Then he went to go check the water. The lake had burst and was flowing down the mountain. When the big brother heard the noise from the waterfall, he came to see it. He kicked his little brother who changed into a little bird. We call this bird _wanik_. The big brother became a mountain.

Samuel Daken

Ok Tedi Training Centre

Tabubil

Western Province

A920.1.0.1. Origin of particular lake; A934.11. River from transformation; B875.1. Giant serpent; D150M. Transformation: man to bird; D283.1+. Transformation: person to lake; D291M. Transformation: man to mountain; D425.1+. Transformation: snake to lake; D551.3. Transformation by eating flesh; F911.7. Serpent swallows man; P251.6.1. Three brothers; Q325. Disobedience punished; Q551.3.2.2+. Punishment: transformation into bird; W126. Disobedience

## The Bird of Paradise that Became a Woman

(Wantok 298, January 19, 1980, page 15)

Mr. Kuri lived under Mul [Hagen] Mountain [**Hagen** People, **Western Highlands** Province]. One morning, Kuri took his bow and multi-pronged arrows, then went to the forest to shoot birds that were eating tree flowers. [Pollinating flowers? The crested berrypecker (_Paramythia montium_) picks flowers, but does not eat them. Sunbirds (family Nectariniidae) and some honeyeaters (family Meliphagidae) drink flower nectar.] One tree had beautiful flowers, and so it had many birds eating them.

Mr. Kuri watched and saw a very beautiful bird of paradise sitting nearby. Kuri took a good shot at the bird with a multi-pronged arrow that had a hole. The beautiful bird of paradise fell down with the arrow. When Kuri wanted to hold the bird, it flew away. Kuri watched and saw this bird of paradise land in Hagen Town. Kuri bit his fingers and broke his bow. He said that it would be bad if he went home to sleep.

In the morning, he killed a pig and cooked it in an earth oven. He carried the pork and went to find the bird of paradise. In the evening, Kuri said good-bye to his clan and walked off. He walked and walked... then arrived at a garden. In the garden, he saw a woman picking edible greens.

The woman called to her daughter, "Sick daughter, which kind of cucumber do you want to eat, the big one or the small one?" The little girl replied that she felt the pain of a multi-pronged spear, so she wanted to eat the small cucumber.

Kuri heard this, and was happy. He waited for the mother to leave the house first. The mother took a cucumber and some greens, then left the house. Kuri carried the pork and followed her. Near the door, the woman turned, saw Kuri and asked, "Hey, why did you come here?" [He replied,] "No, I shot a bird of paradise, but I came down here to look for it. It's nearly dark, so I came to sleep with you two. Tomorrow I'll leave."

This was the mother of the young woman who had transformed from a bird of paradise and who Kuri had shot. So, Kuri gave the pork to the woman to eat as payment [bride price]. The woman gave her beautiful young daughter to Kuri. When they wanted to marry, the mother gave a piece of ginger root to them and blessed them, "Put this ginger in a dry place, so that you two will have many good things for yourselves." They took it and put it in a dry place, then they slept in the men's house. In the morning, they went to look for the place where the ginger was. The mother was not fooling around. They found a good house and garden with cassowaries, pigs, money, wild bamboo, and fine clothing. These things filled the place.

They left their old place and went to sit in their new place. They lived there for a while, then the woman gave birth to a baby boy.

One afternoon, the woman went down to the garden while the man took care of their son. However, the mother did not return quickly and the baby cried a lot. The father scolded this boy, "I did not buy your mother with pigs and cassowaries. No, I shot her with an arrow and got her for free. I'm not boasting." The mother returned, stood outside and heard the father talking. She became irate. The poor mother felt ashamed and cried loudly.

Later, she went inside and gave her breast to the boy. She cooked food and they ate. After eating, she told them to stay while she went to the latrine. The mother went outside, took the ginger and went back to her home. They waited and the boy cried. The father called and called, but there was no reply. They slept, then in the morning, the father went outside and saw that the place had become entirely forested. There was no garden and no animals. The place looked very bad. They were very hungry. The father was all right, but the baby was near death.

One night, the mother cooked two taro corms and carried them to them. Near the door, she put a big pile of feces and put the two taro corms on top of the feces. In the morning, they woke up and saw this, but they were famished. So, the father washed the taros and they ate them.

After a while, the woman felt sorry for them, so she returned with the ginger and all of the good things returned. The three of them lived there until the ends of their lives.

Zawi Kapen
Mt. Hagen
Western Highlands Province

B652. Marriage to bird in human form; D350+W. Transformation: bird of paradise to woman; D361.1+. Forest Spirit Bride; D967+. Magic ginger; D1774+. Magic results from blessing; D2100. Magic wealth; P210. Husband and wife; P231. Mother and son; P232. Mother and daughter; P233. Father and son; P262. Mother-in-law; P265. Son-in-law; Q304. Scolding punished; Q438. Punishment: abandonment in forest; Q585. Fitting destruction (disappearance) of property as punishment; Q595. Loss or destruction of property as punishment; R260. Pursuits; T52. Bride purchased; T100. Marriage; T580. Childbirth; X716H+. Feces as gift


## How One Language Came About

(Wantok 299, January 26, 1980, page 17)

Long, long ago, there was a man who lived in the area between Wewak Town and Yangoru Village. His name was *Numbo Duo*. This name means, "Man of the Mountain."

He lived alone and took care of a big place that is now called the Prince Alexander Mountains [**Boiken** People, **East Sepik** Province].

One day, he took his spears and other things, then went to the forest to hunt wild game. He went very far. When it was becoming dark, he found a trail. He slept under an ironwood tree. At night, as he was sleeping, a heavy rain fell and made the river rise and flood. The ironwood tree was near the river. When the flood came, it broke off the ground and the tree and carried Numbo Duo towards the sea. It was the Hawain River that carried him on and on.

When the morning arrived, the tree had drifted into the middle of the sea. When Numbo Duo awoke, he looked around and saw only water. He just drifted and drifted on the tree. He became famished. In the evening, he drifted towards an island called **Walis**. He swam to the island. When he went ashore, he saw a huge garden. He went inside it, took some food, then went to hide and eat. On this island, there were only women. Their husbands were flying foxes.

Another day, two sisters went to their big garden and saw that some of their things were ruined. They said, "Who was it that came and stole things from our garden?" They

talked about which one of them should stay and watch the garden. After a while, the little sister won the discussion. The big sister shut her sister in among the sugarcanes. The big sister went home and the little sister stayed in the garden.

When evening arrived, Numbo Duo left his hiding place and went to the garden. He went to break off a piece of sugarcane. Quickly, the little sister held his hand and asked, "What are you doing in my garden?" Numbo Duo told her what had happened to him. So the woman said, "I'll take you to my house." The woman put him inside her net bag, put some vegetables and taros on top and covered him up well. She carried him home. When she arrived home, she quickly went inside the house and closed the door. She latched the door and removed the things from the net bag, then said, "Fix this net bag, then I'll fetch some water and cook some food."

As she was leaving, she put a branch against the door. Numbo Duo worked on the net bag. A piece of string from the net bag fell through a hole and lay upon the palm-thatch flooring (*limbum*). The big sister saw this and thought, "Who is it that's in the house?" It was then that she went to open the door to go inside. When she tried to open the door, the branch against the door fell. She went in and saw Numbo Duo sitting there. She ran towards him and they fornicated [lit., "did something shameful"]. After they finished, the woman left.

The little sister returned and saw that the branch was not there, so she knew that something bad had happened. She went inside and Numbo Duo told her what had happened.

They stayed there for a while, then Numbo Duo asked her about her husband. The woman told him about the flying foxes. Then Numbo Duo told her to tell all of the women to kill their husbands and carry them to him. That evening, Numbo Duo cooked and ate some of them, and he threw some away.

The other women married the children of these two [Numbo Duo and the little sister]. They gave birth to children who went to various islands to live. Some of them also went to the mainland.

So now, the people of [some of] the islands near Wewak and [some of] the coastal areas near Wewak, and people from the forests near Wewak speak the same language (Boiken).

Jack Miki
Boystown, Wewak
East Sepik Province

[See *Wantok* #499 for a similar story from Walis Island.]

A1011. Local deluges; A1021.0.4. Deluge: escape on floating tree; A1616+. Origin of Boiken language; B601.14.1K. Marriage to flying foxes (in village without men); F112. Journey to Land of Women; F610.0.1. Remarkably strong woman; L111.2.2. Future hero found on shore; P210. Husband and wife; P230. Parents and children; P252.1. Two sisters; S63+. Wife kills husband; S110. Murders; T100. Marriage; T145.1.3. Man married to several sisters; T580. Childbirth; T481. Adultery

# The Man Who Married a Fish-Woman

(Wantok 300, February 2, 1980, page 17)

Once there was a young man who followed a river into the forest. He walked and walked, and he saw a very beautiful young woman. However, it was not a real woman, it was a fish that had turned into a woman. She was on top of a stone and making a net bag. The man saw this woman and trembled. He said, "Ha ha, now I'll go grab that woman and bring her home. I shall marry her." After he said this, he hid well and approached quietly. The fish-woman on top of the stone saw him. She left the net bag on the stone, then turned into a fish and jumped back into the river. The man was irate and angrily went back home. He took the fish-woman's net bag. This net bag was very beautiful, so he thought that he could not display the fish-woman's net bag. It would be bad if he told his story and the others stole his woman. He did not tell his friends or brothers his story.

The next morning, he forgot his thoughts and wanted to go to his garden. However, he saw the net bag again and said, "Never mind the garden. I'll go down to the river and look for my fish-woman." He quickly went upriver. His thoughts of grabbing the fish-woman returned, so he said, "I'll quickly hide very close to where she made her net bag, then I'll grab her."

He ran and hid very near the stone where the woman had made the net bag. He did not make any noise while he was hiding. He looked up and down the water. As he watched, a very big fish jumped up on the sandy shore and immediately turned into a beautiful young woman. She went up to the stone where the man was hiding. Oh my, the man did not wait any longer. He quickly grabbed her. The poor woman screamed and said, "Leave me. Leave me. I'm not a woman, I'm a fish from the river. It would be bad if you killed me." The man said, "No. You're my woman. I see your face, hands, hair, legs and breasts and I'm troubled. Please, I won't kill you or rape you. Please, I'll marry you. Please tell me the truth and I'll bring you home." They talked and talked until their mouths hurt.

It was nearly dark and the woman was sorry for the man. She said, "My man, if you truly love me, then take me and marry me. You must never bring me near the river. If you don't do this, then you will be sorry and cry for me." The man said that he understood. They married and lived very happily together in the man's village.

Kipau Manami
**Saidor** [Village, **Dahating** or **Wab** People]
**Madang** Province

D361.1+. Forest Spirit Bride; B654. Marriage to fish in human form; B874. Giant fish; D170W. Transformation: woman to fish; D370W. Transformation: fish to woman; P210. Husband and wife; P251. Brothers; P310. Friendship; T10. Falling in love; T100. Marriage

# Sabaou Stole Rako's Meat Rack

(Wantok 301, February 9, 1980, page 17)

Long ago, there were two men who lived in two villages, **Paup** and **Yakamul** [**Ali** People, **West Sepik** Province]. The men's names were Sabaou and Rako. Sabaou lived in Paup Village and Rako lived in Yakamul Village. Sabaou did not know that Rako lived in Yakamul. One time, Sabaou went to a mountain and called out his own name. On the other side of the mountain, Rako stood up and called out his own name.

Rako was a hunter. In Rako's area, there was plentiful wild game, such as pigs, cassowaries, marsupials (*sikau*), and various kinds of birds. Rako was married, but he did not have children. Poor Sabaou, there was no wild game in his area. He always just ate vegetables and sago beetle grubs.

One afternoon when there were no clouds on the mountain, Sabaou stood on top of the mountain and saw smoke rising from Rako's mountain. He thought, "There must be someone on that mountain."

Later, he thought about going to see who it was that lived over there. He walked over there and found Rako in Yakamul. He looked inside Rako's house and saw that it was jam-packed with meat. Rako gave some meat to him and he carried it back to his house in Paup. When Sabaou was about to return home, he told Rako, "Friend, I think that I would like to come and see you again." He did not say when.

Another time, Sabaou went to Yakamul to see Rako, but Rako was not at the house. He had gone to the forest to hunt game. Only Rako's wife was home. Sabaou had brought some vegetables and sago grubs, and he gave them to Rako's wife.

They were at the house when Sabaou told Rako's wife that he was thirsty and wanted to drink some water. Rako's wife told him that there was no water at the house. So Sabaou told her, "Go get some." The woman urinated in a bucket and brought it to Sabaou. But Sabaou looked at it and told the woman, "This is not water. This is your piss in a bucket." The poor woman went back again to fetch some real water. The water was far away, about a mile. While the woman was fetching water, Sabaou stood up and took a rack of meat, then ran away to Paup.

When Rako and his wife returned home, they did not talk. They just ate vegetables and sago grubs. Sabaou went to Paup and ate the meat. So now, we people of Paup Village have more wild game in our forest, and the people of Yakamul just eat vegetables and insects.

If you go to Aitape in West Sepik Province, and you arrive at Paup, you can see two mountains called Sabaou and Rako.

Paul Cosmas Aitong
Aitape
West Sepik Province

A1617. Origin of place-name; A2582+. Why wild game is plentiful at particular place; K343.1. Owner sent on errand and goods stolen; P210. Husband and wife; P310. Friendship; R220. Flights; X717H+. Urine as gift


## Taro Woman and Grass Woman

(Wantok 302, February 16, 1980, page 17)

Long, long ago, there were two women. Their names were Grass Woman and Taro Woman. They were good friends who lived, slept and ate together, but they traveled in two different places.

Taro Woman always worked in a taro garden. Grass Woman only walked in the grasslands, digging the grass roots. She cooked and ate the roots every night. Taro Woman went around her garden, digging up the roots and cooking the food every afternoon.

One afternoon, Taro Woman arrived quickly, then she cooked and ate. She gave some food to her children, then she gave some to Grass Woman's children. Grass Woman's children did not eat properly, so some food fell into the ashes. Taro Woman saw this and scolded them, "Hey, hold the food properly and eat. Your mother can't give you this kind of food. She'll just give you grass roots, and your bellies will just be filled with grass."

While Taro Woman was scolding Grass Woman's children, Grass Woman arrived and stood near the house.

Grass Woman heard Taro Woman's scolding, and she was quite ashamed. She waited a little while, then went inside, cooked some food and ate. She finished and went down to the river where she called out to the frogs. Later, she returned to the house and called the other woman, "Hey friend, light a torch and we'll go catch frogs." They lit torches and followed the river quietly. They caught many, many frogs. After a while, they came to a bad place where the water fell. Grass Woman went up first and told Taro Woman, "Friend, give me your hand and I'll pull you up." So the other woman put her hand up and Grass Woman slowly pulled her up. She pulled her slowly, then let go. Poor Taro Woman fell right onto a boulder and died.

Grass Woman pulled her and threw her into a lake. Taro Woman became a boulder in the middle of this lake.

Grass Woman returned home and told Taro Woman's children, "The river flooded and carried your mother away." They thought that this was true, but the woman was lying.

Grass Woman was alone and took care of her children and Taro Woman's children. She also looked after the taro gardens. The male leaders told me this, "If a man or woman wants to be good friends with you, travel with you, and sleep and eat with you, you can't speak badly to your friend or speak behind your friend's back. If you do this then one time, something bad will happen just like Taro Woman."

Junamu Iyakung
Kainantu
**Eastern Highlands** Province

E642. Reincarnation as stone; P230. Parents and children; P272. Foster mother; P310. Friendship; Q304. Scolding punished; Q411. Death as punishment; S127. Murder by throwing from height


## Kantaure Confused Mataio

(Wantok 303, February 23, 1980, page 17)

Long, long ago, there were two brothers. They were married and lived on an island named **Udaha** in **Goru** Village, near Vitu [**Witu**] Island in West New Britain Province [**Vitu** People]. Kantaure was the first brother and Mataio was the second. Peburuburu was the first brother's wife and Galiki was the second brother's wife. The first brother's wife had not given birth, but the second brother's wife had. The four [adults] lived happily on Udaha Island.

One time, the leaders of **Vambu** Island gathered and talked about making a big feast with singing and dancing.

When the two brothers heard this, they prepared their hand drums, their feather headdresses, and their "grass" skirts to take to the feast. When they arrived at the place of the feast, they put their headdresses on their heads. The second brother's headdress was crooked, but the first brother's headdress was in good order. The big brother said, "I put on my feathers." Mataio said, "I also put on my feathers, but they're crooked. I think that you made a hole in your head, so you're lying to me."

When the singing and dancing finished in the morning, the two brothers went back to their home on Udaha. In the afternoon, they paddled off again to the feast. When they dressed to go to the feast, the same thing happened, so the little brother asked the big brother again. The big brother was tired of him and said, "Go tell your wife to make a hole in your head so that your feathers will stand up straight." So, Mataio told his wife to make a hole in his head. Poor Mataio died and they carried him back to the island, then buried him.

Mataio's wife and Peburuburu's husband were alone on Udaha Island. They lived there for a while, then they married. After a little while, they paddled a canoe to another island, called **Nagara**. They populated this island, but later everyone on this island died and now no one lives there.

This is a true story. If you go to the Goru or Ningau Island group, you can see this island.

Stephen Pirika
Goru
Vitu Island
West New Britain Province

A991+. Why particular island is deserted; A1640. Origin of tribal subdivisions; J2130+. Numskull has wife put hole in his head to attach feathers; K1000. Deception into self-injury; P210. Husband and wife; P230. Parents and children; P251.5. Two brothers; P263. Brother-in-law; P264. Sister-in-law; T100. Marriage; V61.3+. Dead buried

## The Man Who Married a Cassowary Woman

(Wantok 304, March 1, 1980, page 17)

Long ago, there was a village with an old man and his wife. The man was called Yakewe and his wife was called Amayanuwewei. They had a son named Yagukedi. The two old people worked hard at taking care of their son, and he became a very big man. One time, his father and mother told him, "Tomorrow we'll go to the forest with you and stay for about two or three weeks." Their son said, "Yes papa, that's good. I too want very much to go and sleep in the forest so that I'll be able to find out how to trap pigs and shoot cassowaries." The family finished their preparations and put everything in the part of the canoe that is called _peka_ in the language spoken at **Leitre** [Village, **Rawo** People, **West Sepik** Province]. The boy's father asked his two co-mothers, "Do you think that we'll leave the three mountains and make a house near a big fig tree near a lake?" This lake is where the cassowaries bathe and where they come to eat the fig tree fruits. The parents said, "That's good. We'll paddle until the sun sets." They went inside the canoe and paddled. As they paddled, the son asked his father, "Are we near or far now?" The father replied, "It's still very far. After we pass four river forks, then we'll arrive at the place that I spoke of." After they passed three forks, the father said, "I'll tell a story for you and your mother." The son said, "OK, father, tell us." The old man told them about the time before he was married. He and his father went to sleep at this place. He dreamt and saw many thousands of cassowaries running towards the lake. They removed their skins and became women.

He spoke quietly. He dreamt and saw the beautiful women, but one was more beautiful than all of the others were. Her skin was lighter, like that of a white woman. She was the best. The father said that he saw this in his dream, but he had thought that it was real. Then he got up and said, "Why did you call out? I told my father that I had dreamt that I saw something very nice. My father asked me to tell him whether it was something real that had caused me to call out. I told my father and then he said, 'Ha, you ate a lot of cassowary meat and you just had a dream.' So father did not believe my story."

As the three of them were still paddling, the sun began to set. It was not long when they came to this place. They paddled the canoe up to a huge boulder. A big flood arose and took the canoe away. It was night now, and they took their things to a place and went to make a house. They lit a fire from a big piece of bamboo, then they made a house from wild _limbum_ leaves. When the house was finished, the old mother cooked some sago and they ate it with dried fish.

In the early morning, the boy took his bow and arrows and went to watch for what his father had told him and his mother. He believed everything, so he thought that he too would see this. As he was thinking, he felt the ground shake and he heard a loud noise coming from a mountain. He was terrified, and he trembled. But he thought back to the story and said, "I can't be afraid because if this really happens, I will really see it with my own eyes." So he went and hid at the base of a tree and watched. It was not long when he saw many cassowaries running, removing their skins and jumping into this lake.

He watched and saw a very beautiful woman. Her skin was like coconut meat. He said, "Oh my, what can I do to get this beautiful woman?" He crawled on his hands and knees and he zigzagged towards them. The women did not see him, so he quickly took the beautiful cassowary's skin. After he took the skin, he quickly fled on his hands and knees back to the base of the fig tree. When he arrived at the fig tree, he shouted and shouted. The women were surprised and ran to get their cassowary skins. They put them on and ran away, but the beautiful woman did not find her skin, so she was very ashamed and sat and cried. The boy came out of hiding and asked her, "Hey, why are you crying? Don't cry. Come with me and we'll go to my home on the beach."

So, the woman stopped crying and said, "I'm ashamed because I don't have a bark skirt." The boy told her to wait and he would go ask his mother to give him a bark skirt, then he would bring it to her. He ran and told his parents to bring him a bark skirt. They looked at him and gave him a bark skirt. Later he married this woman.

The four of them returned home and they lived well together. The young boys of this village saw the beautiful woman. They were very troubled, and they lusted for her [lit., "swallowed their spit"].

This story is too long, so I will stop now after the first part.

Luke Hooker Kesi

C. M. [Congregation of Mission] Leitre

Vanimo

Sandaun [West Sepik Province]

B290+. Cassowary removes skirt or skin to bathe; D361.1. Swan Maiden; B652+. Marriage to cassowary in human form; D169.4W. Transformation: woman to cassowary; D350+W. Transformation: cassowary to woman; F527.7K+. White person; P210. Husband and wife; P231. Mother and son; P233. Father and son; R220. Flights; T100. Marriage; W181. Jealousy


## The Cassowaries that Helped a Woman

(Wantok 305, March 8, 1980, page 17)

Long ago, a man and his two wives lived near Mount Kiliwe [Mount Giluwe]. They lived there for a while, but they did not have children yet. Then the man died and the woman was there alone. At this place, there were no other people nearby.

The woman made various kinds of things. The author no longer mentions [the two wives.] She made a house and gardens, and she husbanded pigs. She did both men's and women's work. Because of this, her garden was substantial; it had various kinds of food, such as sweet potatoes, bananas, leafy vegetables, sugarcanes, taros, yams, and many other things that she had planted.

This woman lived there for a while like this. Then one evening, she prepared her things to work in the garden. In the morning, she woke up and went directly to the garden. She did her work in the garden, then near noon, she returned home to cook some food. However, it was too bad for her, her fire had died out and she did not have a way to cook food any more. The poor woman just slept. She went out and saw smoke rising from a mountain that was very far away.

She ran to try to get the fire, but when she arrived at the mountain, she saw that the smoke had come from another mountain. She ran again towards the other mountain, but when she arrived at that mountain, she saw that the smoke was coming from yet another nearby mountain.

The poor woman wanted very much to get some fire, so she did not think anymore. She ran again to the other place where the smoke was rising. She ran about three miles then saw a *masalai* making a fire in his garden, but she was not afraid of the *masalai*. She took a dry stick and snapped it so that the *masalai* would look at her. The *masalai* saw her and asked, "What is it that you want?"

The woman said, "Please, I want to get some fire from you." The *masalai* told her, "That's OK, you can get some. I have some food too if you want to eat." The woman said, "Yes, I'm famished." So the *masalai* gave her a vegetable that is called <u>okai</u> in my language. The woman finished eating and took the fire back to her home.

When she arrived, she made a bonfire and cooked some food for herself. After she finished eating, it was about seven o'clock. The *masalai* stood on top of the mountain and called out, "<u>Okai, okai.</u>" After he called out, the <u>okai</u> inside the woman's stomach spoke, "I'm here. I'm here." The woman was shocked and wanted to run away, but she could not do so because the vegetable was still calling to the *masalai*. The woman sat there and the *masalai* brought a big package of rattan. The *masalai* whipped the woman's legs [with the rattan]. The woman felt a terrible pain but there was no one to help her. The *masalai* did this for three nights. A cassowary came and asked the woman, "Why are you in such terrible condition?" The woman said, "A *masalai* man has been whipping my legs with rattan and raping me. Now I'm in truly wretched condition. Can you help me?" The cassowary said, "Yes, I'll help you, but you must repay me." The woman said, "Yes,

I'll repay you if you'll help me." So, the cassowary ran into the forest and called out for all of the cassowaries to come and tightly surround the woman's house. Two cassowaries watched the door while the others hid at the bases of various trees and banana plants.

At seven o'clock exactly, the *masalai* man arrived and called out. When he came to the door, the two cassowaries kicked him right in the belly with their legs. The *masalai* man wanted to run away to the forest, but the other cassowaries liquidated him. After he died, the cassowaries ran and asked the woman for payment. The woman told them that she would give them her pigs, but they did not want them. She said that she would give them everything from her garden, but they did not want such things. So the woman asked them whether they wanted to marry her. The cassowaries said, "We would marry you but we're not men."

The woman thought and thought. Then she told them that she would turn into a wild pandanus tree (*karuka*) so that they could eat its fruits. The cassowaries said, "That is terrific." They thanked her and she turned into a wild pandanus tree.

Cassowaries often eat these pandanus fruits, and my people often make rope [snares] to catch these cassowaries.

The fruits are from the woman's head, and the leaves are from the woman's "grass" skirt. If you go to the Southern Highlands Province, you will see many cassowaries.

Paulus Buka Waik
C. M. [Congregation of Mission] **Pomberd [Hagen** People]
**Southern Highlands** Province

A2435.4+. Food of cassowary; B211.3.17K. Speaking cassowary; B469+. Helpful cassowary; D215.10KW. Transformation: woman to pandanus tree; D1419.4. Magic food brings eater into sender's power; D1610.3. Speaking plant; D1619.2. Eaten object speaks from inside person's body; F401.6. Spirit in human form; F405+. Spirit killed; F490+. Masalai; P210. Husband and wife; Q53. Reward for rescue; Q244. Punishment for ravisher; Q411.7. Death as punishment for ravisher; R100. Rescues; S180+. Torture by whipping; T145.0.1. Polygyny; T471. Rape; W27. Gratitude


## The Boys Who Tricked a Ghost
(Wantok 306, March 15, 1980, page 17)

In my home area, **Malol** Village, in the area near Aitape in **West Sepik** Province, the young boys often like to bathe in the sea [**Sissano** People]. Sometimes, they bathe from morning until night.

One time, long ago, many boys awoke in the morning and went to get their things for swimming, then they walked to the beach. The boys usually did not return to get food, so they took various foods with them. Some took young coconuts for drinking, and other foods too.

They went down to the beach and went bathing. They were very happy and forgot everything else. When a boy became hungry, he would go on top and cook something, then bring it to eat. After he finished eating, he would run back down to the sea and bathe. They continued to bathe until the sun set and it became dark. The boys were very tired when it was time to go back up, so they each made a fire on the beach and slept. Not one boy thought of returning home. A gentle breeze blew from the forest, and they all were sound asleep by the heat of their fires.

After a while, at about two o'clock when everyone was asleep, a huge ghost followed the shoreline from the east. The ghost wanted to go to his home where the sun set. The ghost had gone around looking for food, but had not found any and was returning home.

The ghost was still far away when it smelled the boys and their fires. The ghost had a huge net bag and was holding a big spear too. The ghost came to the first boy and put him inside his bag. The ghost put all of the boys inside the bag, but the bag was still not completely filled. The ghost man was very happy because he and his family would have a big party because of these boys.

The ghost carried the boys and followed the seashore, crossing the mouths of rivers, too. He went very far and wanted to cross a big river. While he was swimming, the water hit one of the sleeping boys and made him cold. This boy was sleeping with a piece of shell (*kina*) when the ghost had taken him. The boy thought that a ghost had taken them and carried them off. Quietly, he began to cut the ghost's net bag. They boys began to exit the net bag, and as they left, they put a boulder inside the net bag in their place. The ghost swam on another side, towards his home.

All of the boys ran away to their homes and told their parents what had happened to them. The men of the village knew that the ghost would return to look for the boys, so all of the men of the village took their bows and arrows and waited for the ghost.

The ghost arrived home and called out to his family to wake up and boil some water to cook the boys. They did not wait. They took a big pot, put water in it and started it boiling. Later, they took the net bag with the boulder that had been put inside it. The boulder went down and broke the pot. The ghost family saw that it was not little boys, but a boulder. They were irate at this ghost man.

The ghost man told them that he had carried real boys, but that he thought they escaped and tricked him. He told them not to worry, that he would return and find the boys. The big ghost man walked and walked and came to the village of the little boys. He did this just by following their scent. When he arrived, he saw many men standing near a bonfire with their bows and arrows. The ghost stood up and wanted to fight these men, but when he approached, all of the men shot him with their arrows. They were standing-by with yet more arrows. The poor ghost could not continue, he fell and died.

The men took their axes and cut the ghost into little pieces, then threw them into the fire. The fire burned him until all of the bones were gone.

Nowadays, the little boys always finish bathing and return to the village because they are terrified that a ghost will take them if the sleep on the beach.

John T. Alosi
Taurama Barracks
National Capital District

E422.3.2. Revenant as a very large man (giant); E425.2. Revenant as man; E440+. Ghost laid by spear/arrow; G11.10. Cannibalistic spirits; G441. Ogre carries victim in bag (basket); G572. Ogre overawed by trick; K525+. Escape by substituting stone; Q213. Abduction punished; Q411. Death as punishment; R11. Abduction by monster (ogre); R260. Pursuits; S139.2. Slain person dismembered

## The True Origin of Why Everything Dies
(Wantok 307, March 8, 1980, page 17)

Long ago, Snake and Rat were good friends. They hunted for wild game together and for other things to eat.

One morning, they talked about going to a mountain. This mountain went right up into the sky. They walked and crossed three rivers and three foothills, then they arrived at the big mountain where they wanted to go.

They stayed there for a whole week. Then Snake asked Rat, "Can you follow what I'll tell you now?" Snake told Rat, "We'll try jumping off this mountain and see who will die and change their skin." Snake wanted to jump first, but Rat said, "No, I'll jump first." The two of them talked and talked. Rat thought some more and did not wait for Snake to jump first. Yes, crazy Rat jumped and died immediately. However, Snake was not afraid and jumped too. Snake did not die, but changed its skin and slithered happily away.

We men and women today can die, but snakes will not die. Snakes change their skins and slither away. Rats also die. Rat first demonstrated the origin of death.

Michael W. Endin
C. M. [Congregation of Mission] Sassoya [**Sassoia**, **Boiken** People]
Wewak
**East Sepik** Province

A1335.5+. Origin of death: serpent given immortality instead of rat; A2253. Animal characteristics from jumping contest; B211.2.9. Speaking rat; B211.6.1. Speaking snake (serpent); B765.7.3K. Snake is immortal; F55.1. Mountain stretches to sky; P310. Friendship

## The Worthless Man Who Helped the Good Men
(Wantok 308, March 29, 1980, page 17)

Long ago, there was a clan in **Wabag** [Town, **Enga** People, **Enga** Province]. The name of this clan was Depau. They lived there a long time. One day a man said, "I'm just living here and I'm tired of it. I want to go to the forest." After he said this, he took his bow, arrows and things, then went into the forest.

The Depau Clan waited and waited, but this man did not return. Three days passed, and another man went into the forest to find him. He walked and walked, trying to find him while the other men waited and waited. However, the second man did not return either.

Another man went to try to find them. The people waited and waited for three days. Then a fourth man said that he would go try to find the other men. He went and he did not return, making it four men who did not return.

The whole Depau Clan decided to go and find these four men. They told one man to stay. This man did not own a single pig or anything else worthwhile. He was a complete pauper. So, he stayed and the other men went into the forest. He waited for an entire month, but the men did not return.

He waited and said that he would go to find the other men. The worthless man departed. He walked and walked into the very deep forest. He heard singing coming from somewhere in the forest. He walked towards the place where the singing was originating. He arrived there and saw many women singing and talking in a garden. The man looked carefully at them and he saw a beautiful woman among them. This woman was more beautiful than the others were.  He watched as they went to get some water to drink.

He thought and thought about how he could get this woman.  He thought some more, then he thought that he would become a mosquito and go inside the beautiful woman's belly.  He quickly went inside her belly.  She told the other women, "Something has gone inside my belly." She waited for one month, then she felt as if she was pregnant.  After two months, she gave birth to a boy.

The other women asked her, "Where did you marry a man that caused you to give birth to a baby?"  The woman told them, "I didn't marry a man.  I just gave birth."  The boy grew up and lived with them.  The boy saw many taro plants and he marked one for himself.  He told his mother, "When you dig up the taro corms, the taro that I marked is mine."

After a while, the women said that the next day they would dig up the taros.  So the little boy took a stick and went to the taro that he had marked and began to dig the ground around the taro plant.  After he dug the ground around the taro plant, he went back to his house.  In the morning, they went to dig the taros, and the little boy went to remove his taro.  When he was removing his taro, he watched it break apart.  He cried and cried.  He began in the morning and was still at working it in the afternoon, after the others were finished.  His mother saw this and lovingly said, "Stop crying.  Let's go home."

The little boy asked her, "Where is your home?"  His mother told him, "My father lives there.  When we go to my home, you'll see my father."

The little boy finished his small task, then happily ran and ate some taro.  He filled his belly and went to sleep.  In the morning, he awoke and told his mother, "Wake up and we'll go to your home."  His mother woke up and took their things, then they walked towards her home.  They walked and walked, then arrived at the mother's home.  The woman's father saw the child and asked him, "Whose child is this?"  The woman said, "This is my son."  The woman's father was very happy.

After they stayed there for two days, the mother told the boy, "Stay with your grandpa and I'll go to the garden." So, the boy stayed with his grandfather at home.  While they stayed there, the grandfather told him, "You just stay and play here.  Don't go in back of the house."  This made the boy think hard, so he played and played there.  But he tricked his grandfather and went in back of the house.

He went there and saw [another] house.  This house was beautiful and it was very neatly kept.  He went closer and saw a group of men from his village there.  The men saw this little boy and liked him right away.  They thought that he was another boy, but this little boy already knew that is was just the Depau Clan.  He left them there, then ran in back of the house.  He saw a beautiful multi-colored tree.  He quickly ran back to his grandfather's house, took an axe and went back to cut the tree.  He cut the tree once then sap shot out of it.  He cut the tree a second time and it fell right over.  The tree fell directly on top of his grandfather's house, killing him.

After the old man died, the door of the men's house opened up.  The men went out of the house.  At that time, the little boy turned into the [worthless] man from the village.

The men saw his face; some of them were happy and some of them cried.  They thought that they were going to stay there until they were dead, but this man had come and helped them.  Later, they went back to their home and saw their wives and children in the village.

This story is from the days of yore when this ghost wanted to finish off all of the men, but this worthless man tricked the ghost, so that now there are still people.

John Yongapen Taun

Wabag

Enga Province

D56.1. Transformation to older person; D185.1+M. Transformation: man to mosquito; E437.5. Ghost laid under tree; P160. Beggars; P210. Husband and wife; P231. Mother and son; P234. Father and daughter; P291. Grandfather; R50+. Whole village captured by ghost(s); R150+. Rescue by pauper; T511.5.3+. Pregnancy from swallowing mosquito; T573. Short pregnancy; T580. Childbirth

## The Lizard that Ruined Its Friend
### (Wantok 309, April 5, 1980, page 17)

Long, long ago, Large Red Ant and Little Lizard were very good friends.  One time, they talked about going to hunt some wild game in the forest.

One morning, very early, they woke up and went to the forest.  They walked and walked, and Little Lizard saw a pig.  Lizard walked quietly and swiftly, grabbing the pig. Lizard had caught the pig and called out to its friend.  Lizard's friend, Ant, quickly ran over to them.  Ant jumped up and went right into the pig's eye.  The ant urinated into the pig's eye, and the pig died immediately.

The two friends pulled the pig over to a river.  They made a big earth oven for the pig.  While they were cooking the pig in the earth oven, Lizard told Ant that they should go and wash.

They arrived at the river and Lizard told Ant, "Let's throw a stone into the river, then we'll try to swim down and get it." Ant was the first to try. But poor Ant was not heavy, so Ant just drifted on top of the water. Ant could not swim beneath the water.

After a while, it was Little Lizard's turn. Lizard just jumped down into the water and swam underneath, then Lizard went to the place where they had made the earth oven. Lizard jumped on top, then started to eat the pork, just leaving the bones. Lizard finished eating, then went back to Ant.

They had been bathing for a long time. They began to feel hungry, so they ran directly to their earth oven.

They arrived at the place of the earth oven, but only the pig bones and stones were there. Lizard jumped and asked its friend, Ant, "Hey, who ate all of the pork?" Lizard was the one who had actually left the bones and stones.

Ant said, "I think it was just you who ate all of the meat." However Lizard said, "I think it was just you who ate it, because I was swimming in the water to get the stone." Ant was irate and said, "I think it was just you. You swam underneath the water, then came out, ate and returned to me."

Poor Ant was famished. What Ant had said to its friend, Lizard, made Lizard angry. Lizard wanted to eat Ant, but Lizard's little friend was very smart. Ant jumped up and urinated directly into Lizard's eye. Lizard was in pain and Ant quickly fled a tree.

When Ant reached the crown of the tree, it made a nest from tree leaves. [This is the weaver ant, *Oecophylla smaragdina* (Hölldobler and Wilson, 1990: 618, plates 22 and 24).] After building the nest, Ant hid well. Lizard was afraid of Ant and did not want to follow Ant to the crown of the tree. Lizard just slept at the base of the tree.

So now you can see that large red ants make leaf nests on top of trees, and that lizards often hide under leaves at the bases of trees.

John S. Mufola

Wewak

**East Sepik** Province

[Mr. Mufola (or Mufoia) wrote the ancestor story in Wantok #244. He is probably from the **Boiken** People.]

A2433.5.5+. Why weaver ant builds nest in tree; A2533.6+. Why lizard lives in leaf litter; A2494.16+. Enmity between lizard and ant; B211.4.1. Speaking ant; B211.6.2K. Speaking lizard; B299.12K. Animals go hunting; D1402.18+. Urine kills animal; H1543. Contest in remaining under water; K16.2+. Diving match: trickster eats food while pretending to be underwater; K2297. Treacherous friend; P310. Friendship; R210. Escapes; R311. Tree refuge; W125. Gluttony; W157. Dishonesty



# The Spirit Fish Dance
(Wantok 310, April 12, 1980, page 14)

Long ago, in **Fatima** Village in **West Sepik** Province, a man and his wife lived with two daughters [**Olo** People]. Every night, the man would take his bow and arrows to go hunting. Wherever he went, he took his hand drum and headdress to sing and dance. This dance is called "Spirit Fish."

He left home and followed a fork of the river into the deep forest. At the place where he put his bow and arrows, he would put on his headdress and then sing and dance. He jumped and jumped and made a spectacular dance and song. He sang and danced at the source of the stream, then came back down below to begin again. The man did this song and dance, going up and down the stream until the birds of the morning began to sing.

At this time, he removed his headdress and put his hand drum down. He took his arrows and his bow and shot around the base of a fig (*mal*) tree. He did this until the arrows were broken and there was sap flowing from the tree where the arrows had entered.

Quickly, he carried his dancing equipment and hid it, then he went back to his house. When he returned to the house, he told his kin to wait because he had shot plenty of game, but he had broken his arrows and run away. He showed his arrows and the red "blood" [i.e., red tree sap] to his wife and children. The first time he did this, they believed him, but he did this too many times and they knew that he was lying. His wife told the two children that she would follow him and try to find out what he really did.

One night, the man took his things and prepared to go into the forest. The woman also went outside the house. She ran quickly to a place with muddy ground. She put the mud all over her skin. After she finished, she heard singing coming from a branch of the river, so she ran and hid. She wanted to see who was singing.

The woman went right over there and found her husband beginning to jump up towards the source of the stream. The man was singing and dancing fervently and did not see his wife who had walked over quietly. The man jumped and jumped. When he turned his head, the poor man was terrified. He saw his wife, but he thought that it was a ghost [because of the mud].

The man got up but he did not run slowly. He wanted to run to the source of the stream. The woman followed him, so he thought that a ghost was chasing him. While he ran, his headdress fell and broke apart. He was just holding his hand drum. They kept running together until his hand drum fell and broke. The woman did not stop. She kept chasing him until rattan thorns bloodied her poor husband.

The woman left him and ran back home. She quickly washed off the mud from her skin, then she slept and waited for dawn. When dawn arrived, the poor man walked like a sick man. He walked very slowly. When he arrived, he threw away his bow and arrows and walked to bed. His wife was still asleep. When he saw his wife, he saw some mud in her armpits and her breasts. The man knew that it was just his wife who had tricked him because his wife did not completely wash off the mud. She was completely exhausted and was still sleeping. The man whispered, "I thought it was a real ghost. Now it's your turn, so I'll get revenge and you'll suffer."

One time, the man told the woman that the *galip* nuts in the forest were ripe. He said that they must go break them open and give them to her brother. The man told his daughters that they should stay, and that he and their mother would go to break open *galip* nuts, then give them to their uncle.

The woman took her things and they went into the forest. They arrived at a *galip* tree and the man said that he would climb the tree and shake the branches so that the ripe *galip* nuts would fall. The man carried his spear so that he could hit the ripe *galip* nuts. He knocked down many *galip* nuts. He called out to his wife and asked her where she was standing. He wanted his wife to show him where she was, so that he would know where to throw down the *galip* nuts. The woman said, "Here." However, the man asked her to shake the underbrush so that he would know exactly where she was.

The woman shook the underbrush and the man knew exactly where she was. The man took his multi-pronged spear that he had carried and threw it down. The spear went straight threw the woman's head, exited her anus and planted itself in the ground. The woman did not scream or make any noise because the spear took her and she died immediately. However, the man thought that he had not hit her. He saw a black lizard on a tree branch, so he told the lizard to go down and see what had happened.

The lizard went down and saw that the spear had impaled the woman into the ground. The lizard took a piece of the woman's blood and put it in its armpit to show the man. When the lizard went back up, the man asked it, "What happened? Did I hit or miss?" The lizard replied, "Don't think any more about it. You're a marksman. Your spear went straight through her head and impaled her into the ground. She is dead, look at this blood." The man was ecstatic and went down immediately.

He took his knife and cut off the woman's two breasts. After he cut them off, he cut a wild taro leaf and tied the breasts up in the leaf. He carried this bundle back home. When he arrived home, he put the bundle inside a signal drum. The two daughters saw him and asked him for their mother. The father told them that their mother was carrying the *galip* nuts to give them to their uncle.

In the afternoon, the father told them to go get edible mushrooms to cover up the wild taro leaf that he had put in the signal drum. He told them to fetch them and return. They raced off and gathered the mushrooms. When they returned and opened the covering of the signal drum, they saw two breasts. They knew that these were their mother's breasts. It was now that they knew that their father had killed their mother.

They went and hid in back of the house. They cried softly until it was dark. They stayed there and decided to avenge their mother's death. They lived with their father, but they did not ask about their mother anymore.

One time, the father brought them to the garden. The father was hard at work and he became thirsty. The two girls went down to the river to fetch some water. After they filled the bamboo tube, the big sister took a huge grasshopper and put it inside the tube of water. The little sister took a centipede and put it inside too. They carried the tube and gave it to their father to drink. The man was very thirsty, so he did not look inside. He drank all of the water and the two bad things too.

In the afternoon, they returned home and cooked some food. The two bad things inside the man's stomach began to eat all of the food in his stomach. After he finished eating, they began to eat his belly. They kept eating and ate his liver, killing him.


Francis Rapi

Taurama Barracks

National Capital District


[For a similar story, see *Wantok #517*.]

B211.6.2K. Speaking lizard; B491.2. Helpful lizard; F402.1.10+. Imagined spirit pursues person; K1833. Disguise as ghost; P210. Husband and wife; P230+. Daughters avenge father's murder of mother; P232+. Daughter avenges mother; P234. Father and daughter; P252.1. Two sisters; P253. Sister and brother; P293. Uncle; Q211. Murder punished; Q262. Impostor punished; Q418. Punishment by poisoning; Q461. Impalement as punishment; S22+. Patricide; S63+. Husband kills wife; S110. Murders; R260. Pursuits; S111.8+. Murder by feeding poisonous invertebrates; S115.2.1+. Murder by driving spear through head; S176+. Mutilation: breasts cut off; W157. Dishonesty

## The Bird's Child

(Wantok 311, April 19, 1980, page 15)

Long, long ago, there was a bird that stole children. The name of this bird was Masianagai. It was a huge bird, like an eagle. But it was actually a real man that had turned into a bird.

One day, a newly married couple had a baby. They went to work in their garden. The baby was hung up in a net bag nearby, while they knelt and worked in their garden.

While they were kneeling in the garden, the huge bird quietly came and removed the baby from its net bag. The bird quickly removed the baby and flew away with it.

They saw this and cried out, "Hey, you're carrying our baby, come back!" However, the bird did not heed them. It flew high up to a big *talis* tree.

They saw this and cried and cried until they were out of breath. They stood and shook their arms. They did this until their arms were stiff. They were there until darkness came, then they went home to sleep.

The baby cried for milk. The bird tried to feed the baby and give it different kinds of food, but the little baby did not stop crying. Later, the bird gave its ball to the baby. The baby stopped crying. It sat quietly and babbled.

They lived like this for some years. The baby grew up to be a strong young man.

When he was completely grown, he asked his father, "Hey papa, where's mama?" His father said, "Your mother died when you were still young."

Then he asked his father again, "What is it that I ate that made me grow?" His father said, "Look over there. That is my garden. Do you think that you are just big?"

The man was very happy with his father. He followed the branches of the *talis* tree and arrived at his true place on the ground.

Later he asked his father, "Hey, papa, where should I sit and comb myself?" His father said, "Follow this tree branch and go sit there to comb your hair."

As he was sitting and combing himself, he saw two young women drawing water. He did not know that his reflection was in the water.

The big sister saw the man's reflection in the water and the man looked very handsome. So, the first sister got up and quickly dirtied the water. She was very worried that her little sister would see him too. The little sister got up and helped her big sister make the water dirty. They did this for a while, then they let the water clear. The two of them both saw the man sitting and laughing at them.

They ran home and told their father. They asked him, "Papa, can you send a message to your clan to come and cut down a tree for us? We want to see something beautiful. We want to marry a nice man."

Their father killed some pigs, gathered some betel nuts and tobacco, and then he sent these to his clan. His clan set aside a big day for cutting down this tree.

When the day arrived, they went to cut the tree. They cut and cut the tree until some weeks passed. When the tree began to fall, the man jumped underneath the tree leaves and hid. The men tried to find him, but they were unable to do so. So, they left for their homes.

The two women hid near the base of this tree. They stayed there for a while. As evening approached, the man thought that everyone had left home. He got up from the place where he was hiding and went outside. He sat right at the base of the tree, where the two women were hiding.

While he was sitting, the women approached quietly and grabbed him. He said, "Please let me go." But the two women said, "Please come with us to our home."

He heeded them and went with them. They walked along a trail, and the big sister asked the little sister, "Who shall marry him, you or me?" The little sister said, "Never mind that. We saw him at the same time, so we should both marry him."

They argued and then approached their father. Their father listened to their arguments and said, "You, the big sister shall marry him." So, the big sister married him and the little sister did not.

So now, you can see that the first child often marries at home, and that the second or third often marries far away.


Maryanne Dubanau
**Wagi** Village [**Tangu** People]
Bogia
**Madang** Province


A1550+. Origin of first child marrying at home and others leaving home; B31.6. Other giant birds; B211.3. Speaking bird; B535.0.7. Bird as nurse for child; D150M. Transformation: man to bird; P210. Husband and wife; P233. Father and son; P234. Father and daughter; P252.1. Two sisters; R13.3.2. Eagle carries off youth; T10. Falling in love; T100. Marriage

## The Stone that Covered Up the Men

(Wantok 312, April 26, 1980, page 15)

One day, eleven brothers wanted to go hunting in the forest. All of the brothers took their axes, bows and arrows, and some sweet potatoes. They also took their dogs to help them find some wild game. At this time, the sun was very hot. Rain had not fallen recently. At night, the moon was very bright.

Ten of the brothers did not take their wives with them, but one did. His wife was pregnant, she was nearly ready to give birth.

While they walked, the other brothers went quickly into the deep forest, but the married couple followed them slowly because the woman was about to give birth. She was not strong enough to go very fast up a mountain.

The other brothers arrived first at the place where they wanted to sleep. The married couple arrived there at about five o'clock in the afternoon. They all straightened out their sleeping places for the night.

They made their sleeping places under a big boulder. This boulder was as like a house. It had a big space inside it where many people could sleep. The men of the village often slept there when they went hunting. So on this night, the brothers wanted to sleep at this stone house.

All of the brothers and the woman slept underneath this boulder. In the morning, the ten brothers woke up and went to hunt wild game. The other brother stayed and made a hut where his wife could give birth. After he finished, he told his wife to sleep. Then he followed the other brothers who were hunting.

After a while, his wife gave birth to a boy. She lay there and saw the boulder coming down and covering up the place where the men had slept. After it came down, it stopped for little while, then went back to where it was.

The woman saw this and was terrified. She did not breast feed her baby anymore. No, she lay there and just watched the boulder.

She was afraid. A little later, her husband and his brothers returned. They carried meat and were laughing happily when they arrived.

When they were all there, the woman told them what the boulder had done. However, the men shouted, "You're lying. We have often come to this boulder and hunted for game. Why are you lying to us like that, telling us that the boulder moved? We think that you're just talking nonsense."

The woman got up and said, "I'm not lying to you. What I said is absolutely true. I saw it with my own eyes, so don't go to sleep under this boulder."

The ten brothers were stubborn and disregarded what the woman said. The woman did not argue further and said, "That's OK. You're too persuasive. You can sleep there, but my husband will sleep with me and our baby."

The woman's husband believed her, so he carried his wife and baby to sleep in the hut. The other brothers ignored what she said and so they slept under the boulder.

Late that night, the boulder shook and came down, covering up all of the brothers. When the boulder came down, it made a crashing sound like a big gun.

The men inside woke up in shock and began to run. They looked for the exit to go outside, but they were unable to go outside.

They shouted and tried to move the boulder to find the exit. They kept trying. They cried and shouted too. They thought that they would be heard and rescued from the boulder.

The married couple heard the crashing and later they heard their cries. They looked and saw the boulder coming down and covering them up. They did not wait any longer. They took their things and went quickly to the village to find help.

They went swiftly down the trail and arrived in the village. They spoke to the men of the village. Then all of the men of the village took their axes and ran to this place. They arrived and heard the cries and shouts of the ten brothers. The brothers shouted for the men to rescue them.

The men of the village each cut a tree and tried to move the boulder. They pulled hard, but the boulder did not budge.

They rested a little, then heard the brothers crying and shouting louder. One brother was dead and only nine were left.

The men outside the boulder were crying too. They waited a little longer, then they heard that a second brother was dead. Only eight were left.

The third brother died, then the others died until only one was left. He shouted, "I'm the only one alive now. All my brothers are dead." After a little while, he shouted, "Good-bye to all of you. I think I'm dying now."

Then the men did not hear any more, he was dead. They fell on the ground and cried loudly. They knew that they would never see their faces again.

They cried and cried and sent a message back to the village. They got up quietly and cried on the way back to the village. They were very troubled.

They returned to the village and slept fitfully. In the morning, they gathered food and carried it to make a feast in the area by this boulder. The wives of the dead men were upset, so they did not eat well. After the feast, they returned to the village.

This boulder is still there. We call this place, "The Place of Ten!" The real name is "Tumon." We call it "The Place of Ten" because of the ten men who died there.

Nason Bob Du
**Kudjip** [Village, **Nii** People]
**Western Highlands** Province

A1617. Origin of place-name; D931. Magic rock (stone); J652. Inattention to warnings; J1050. Attention to warnings; M341. Death prophesied; P210. Husband and wife; P251.6.6. Eleven brothers; P263. Brother-in-law; P264. Sister-in-law; T570. Pregnancy; T581.1. Birth of child in forest; W167. Stubbornness

## The Cassowary Got New Legs
(Wantok 313, May 3, 1980, page 19)

Long, long ago, Cassowary flew higher than the other, little birds. At this time, Cassowary was a very big bird. Cassowary was king of all of the birds.

At one place, there was a tree. This tree was always filled with little birds. It was their home.

Whenever the birds rested there, Cassowary flew and perched on one of the tree branches. The branch would sag so far that it would touch the ground. This made the little birds angry at Cassowary.

They were very troubled by what Cassowary did, but Cassowary did not say anything. Cassowary would fly around and then come back to perch on this branch. Cassowary was very happy.

One time, they saw Cassowary flying around. They sent a message around that there would be a meeting. They wanted to try to find a way to ruin Cassowary.

They met and said, "We'll talk to the insect that eats sago and coconut palm trees to come and help us." [Probably the sago beetle *Oryctes centaurus*, and the coconut beetles, *O. rhinoceros*, *Scapanes australis grossepunctatus*, and *Xylotrupes gideon*, (Gressitt and Hornabrook, 1977: 34-35).] So they spoke to this insect.

The insect came and began to cut the tree branch where Cassowary often perched. The insect cut and left just a little piece of the branch.

They waited for Cassowary to return. Before long, Cassowary flew quickly and perched on the branch. Cassowary held tightly and wanted to rest.

However, the branch broke and carried Cassowary down to the ground. Cassowary fell awkwardly and broke its two legs. Poor Cassowary no longer had a means to get around. Cassowary felt sad for itself and cried loudly.

Cassowary cried and cried, then Kangaroo came to look. Kangaroo asked Cassowary, "Hey what did you do to cause you to fall down here?" Cassowary replied, "Oh my brother, I broke my legs. I'm famished because I don't have good legs to walk and find food." Cassowary asked Kangaroo, "Can you give me your legs for me to try?"

Kangaroo was sorry for Cassowary and said, "That's OK, but you can't go far." Cassowary said, "No, I'll just try them and give them back to you." So, Cassowary gave its broken legs to Kangaroo, and Kangaroo gave its good legs to Cassowary. When Cassowary put on the good legs, it pretended to walk slowly. But Cassowary just left and quickly ran away.

Poor Kangaroo called out, "Ss, ss, ss. Give me my legs back." But it was too late. Cassowary ran and hid.

So now, you can see that kangaroos have the bad legs that Cassowary had broken, and that cassowaries have their strong legs from Kangaroo.

If you kill a kangaroo, you will hear it talk, "Ss, ss." It is angry at Cassowary who wronged it, and at you who boastfully shot it.

Daniel N. Kuna
Arawa
North Solomons Province

A2370+. Why cassowary has strong legs; A2371.2.10+. Why kangaroo has bad legs; B211.2.12K. Speaking kangaroo; B211.3. Speaking bird; B211.3.17K. Speaking cassowary; B242.1+. Cassowary as king of birds; B449+. Helpful kangaroo; B482. Helpful insects—coleoptera; K300+. Cassowary steals kangaroo's legs after exchange; K1110+. Cassowary returns to usual perch that has been cut, cassowary falls and breaks legs; R220. Flights

## A Marsupial (*Sikau*) Found a Baby Boy
(Wantok 314, May 10, 1980, page 15)

One day, when the sun was bright, everyone went to the forest. They went to hunt wild pigs, marsupials (*kapul*), and other wild game. One woman who was pregnant was among them.

This woman left the other people and went alone into the deep forest. The other people did not know where she went. The woman walked and searched for wild game. As she was walking, a huge tree fell right on top of her.

She was silent. She lay there dead, but her baby came out of her belly. The baby lay there and cried loudly.

The poor baby cried and cried, but there was no man or woman nearby to hear it and come to its rescue. However, an old he-marsupial (*sikau*) was eating vegetation and heard the crying. He heard the crying distinctly and followed the sound.

He came close to the fallen tree and saw the baby crying and moving its hands and legs about. The old marsupial was terrified and ran and hid at the base of the tree. He stood and watched for a while then said, "That's just a baby, so there's no need to be afraid."

After a little while, the old marsupial went and carried the baby in his mouth. He carried the baby to the base of a big tree where he usually slept. He put the baby there and they stayed there.

The marsupial took care of this baby well. He often went to the forest and searched for various kinds of fruits and other foods to give to the baby. After a while, the baby grew up.

The baby became a very handsome boy. One day, the young boy went up a tall tree and looked across the land. He looked and saw smoke coming from one place.

The young boy turned into a red parrot. He flew directly to the place where the smoke was rising. He flew down and took some fire from two young women who were working in their garden.

They were shocked, but one of the women quickly pulled out a feather from this beautiful bird. The bird took the fire and flew away, back to where he came from.

He returned home and made a bonfire. His father smelled smoke and almost died, but the boy took his marsupial father and put him near the fire. Before long, the heat of the fire resuscitated his father. The boy used the fire and made a huge garden for themselves where they lived.

At the real village, the woman that pulled out the parrot feather thought about him and cried for him. She knew that it was not a bird, it was a man that had taken her fire.

When the people had a feast or a party, the young woman went looking around. She tried to match this hair (or feather) with the boys to find whose it was. She did this all of the time, but she did not find whose it was.

She did this often and was very troubled about this boy. One time, the villagers had another feast, and the boy of the forest came too. The woman convinced her brother into taking the hair and matching it with all of the other boys at the gathering.

Her brother checked and checked, but he could not find a match. Then he approached the last boy and the hair matched. It was the boy from the forest.

He ran quickly and told his sister. While they were eating, he told her what he found. The woman took some vines and tied them to all of the trails that led into the forest, then she returned and slept.

In the very early morning, she went to check all of the trails to see which vines had been broken. She looked and looked then she went to one trail where the vine had been broken. The woman followed this trail. She walked and walked and arrived at a huge garden.

She stood and looked around, but no one was there. Her eyes were heavy, so she slept at the base of some sugarcane plants. She was dead asleep when the young boy returned from the forest and found her sleeping.

He went quietly to the woman's head and turned himself into a beautiful red *tanget* plant. When the wind blew, the *tanget* plant threw water on the woman's face. The woman woke up in surprise and said, "Oh my, that's a beautiful *tanget*, just like a real man. You blew on me and sprayed me with water, making my skin very cold."

Later, he turned back into a real man and took the woman to his father. He took her to live with his old marsupial father.

The woman's family waited and waited, but she did not return home. On the next morning, they followed the trail that she had taken. They walked and walked until they arrived at the place where the three of them lived. It was deep in the forest.

Her kin took her back to the village. At the village, they made a big feast and everyone in the village ate. The next day, they tied up the woman and brought her back to the man's home.

They let her live there and returned to the village. Only the woman's old mother went to live with the three of them at the man's home. This old woman saw the marsupial and wanted very much to eat the marsupial.

So, she told the married couple to kill the marsupial and she would carry it back to the village to cook and eat. The married couple were stubborn and said that they would not do this. They said that it was the boy's father, so they could not kill him.

They talked and talked, but the old woman was more persistent. The old marsupial told his son, "That's OK. The old woman is too angry with you two. Tell your wife that you can take a piece of the outside of a sugarcane and strike my leg with it, then I'll die."

The man told his wife this. So, they killed his poor father and carried him to the village to be cooked and eaten.

The young man just stayed in their village, and he and cried and cried. He took dancing adornments and dressed himself. Then he went to a clearing.

He took a rope and went on top of a tree. He tied one end of the rope to his neck and one end to the tree. The poor man jumped down and died.

His wife came and just watched this. She was very troubled. She did the same thing and hanged herself near her husband. The next day, the woman's brothers came and saw them, oh my!

They saw what they had done and they knew what had happened. It was their mother who had done wrong. They went back to the village, took their axes and killed their mother immediately. Afterwards, they buried the three of them together.

Kenny H. Aveo

Kainantu

**Eastern Highlands** Province

B211.2.12K+. Speaking marsupial; B535.0.16K+. Marsupial as nurse for child; D157B. Transformation: boy to parrot; D213+B. Transformation: boy to tanget plant (*Taetsia fructicosa*); D357B. Transformation: parrot to boy; D431.6+B. Transformation: tanget plant (*T. fructicosa*) to boy; M451.1. Death by suicide; P214.1. Wife commits suicide (dies) on death of husband; P233+. Son commits suicide on death of father; P253. Sister and brother; P261. Father-in-law; P262. Mother-in-law; P265. Son-in-law; P265+. Daughter-in-law; Q211.6. Killing an animal revenged; S22+. Matricide; S22+. Patricide; S51. Cruel mother-in-law; S139.4. Murder by mangling with axe; T100. Marriage; T570. Pregnancy; T581.1. Birth of child in forest; T584.2. Child removed from body of dead mother; V61.3+. Dead buried; W167. Stubbornness


## The Nokondi Ghost

(Wantok 315, May 17, 1980, page 15)

Long, long ago, there was a ghost man who lived on Mount Kefeya [Gesega]. His name was Nokondi. This ghost, Nokondi, lived with his *nokondi* ghost wife, and his *nokondi* child. They lived in a hole in a boulder at the base of Mount Kefeya.

This ghost man, Nokondi, had a body. He had half a head, half a nose, half a mouth, one ear, one eye, one leg, and one arm. In the language of Korepa [**Koreipa** Village], *nokondi* means "half body" [**Siane** People, **Eastern Highlands** Province].

In their boulder house, there were two rooms. One room was where the *nokondi* man slept. The other room was where the *nokondi* woman and child slept. The boulder was divided into two rooms, and in between them was a hole that was like a window.

The *nokondi* woman and child cooked food in their room and gave it to the *nokondi* man. They often gave it to him through the window, then the *nokondi* man would eat. After he finished eating, he would give his plate of food back to them.

The *nokondi* man never entered their room, and they never entered his room. The *nokondi* woman and child never went outside. No, they just lived inside. There was no door to exit their room, nor was there one to go into the *nokondi* man's room. Only the *nokondi* man had a door in his room. So, only he went outside.

At night, the *nokondi* man often went out to hunt for food in the forest. Sometimes, the *nokondi* man came down to the village and cut the people's bananas. After he finished cutting, he would whistle on his way back to his stone house.

When he came close to his house, he whistled loudly. The woman and child would hear this, and they would know that their food was coming. He would carry the bananas inside and give the bananas to them. They would take these and quickly cook them for a big meal. After they cooked the bananas, the *nokondi* man would sleep awkwardly in his bed. This is because he only had half of a body and [carrying] the bananas hurt him. If he had had a good body, then he would have been able to carry heavy things. After they cooked the food, they would call for him to eat. He would eat the food and be satiated, then he would go back to bed and have a good sleep.

This group of people, ghost *nokondi*, woman *nokondi*, and child *nokondi*, they still live in a hole in a boulder that is at the base of Mount Kefeya.

Robert Wane

Goroka

Eastern Highlands Province

F490+. Nokondi; F525. Person with half a body; K300. Thefts and cheats—general; P210. Husband and wife; P230. Parents and children; R45.3. Captivity in cave


## The Python that Killed the Big Brother

(Wantok 316, May 24, 1980, page 15)

Long, long ago, two brothers lived in a village named Tororo. The brothers' names were Lagola Gurijai and Tanaip Kavani. Once they went to hunt for wild game in the forest. They went into the forest and slept overnight in a hut.

The next morning, they went to a place where they saw a dead marsupial (*kapul*). The little brother said, "Oh brother, that's wonderful. Some man killed that marsupial for us and left it there. Now we can go get it." But the big brother told him, "Don't say anything. Shut your mouth." The big brother went to find a rattan to use for rope.

He tied up the marsupial with this rope and told his younger brother, "You must hide on this tree." After he said this, the little brother hid and watched.

When the [big] boy took the marsupial and went up the tree, a big noise came from the forest. He looked to see what it was. Oh my! It was not a small thing. They saw that it was a huge python.

This snake looked for the place where it had left the marsupial, but it did not find it. So, it spit water to see if it could find it. The snake turned and looked for the marsupial. The snake became angry, then it went to get water again.

The snake came back to look for the marsupial, but it was not there. It spit water again, three times, to try to find it.

The snake knew that it was probably a man or something like a snake [that had taken the marsupial]. It hid on the side and looked up the tree. It saw a man holding the marsupial. The snake saw this, then hid in the area. It went and climbed high up a tree, then slowly went to the tree where the boy was sitting.

The boy held tightly onto the snake, and they both fell to the ground. The snake broke the boy's bones and he died. The little brother saw this and cried and cried. He went home and told all of the men of the village about what had happened. They knew that he was a stubborn boy. So, the men of the village took Tanaipa [Tanaip] Borowai Kavani and buried him in Tororo Village.

I am a man from **Tororo** Village in the Goilala area, **Central** Province [**Kunimaipa** People], but now I live in Buimo.

M. Roy Moroi Koiro & Anton Sule
Corrective Institution Buimo
Lae
Morobe Province

B765.20. Snake kills man who has killed its prey; B875.1. Giant serpent; P251.5. Two brothers; V61.3+. Dead buried; W167. Stubbornness; Z71.1. Formulistic number: three

## The Men Who Ate a Dead Person

(Wantok 317, May 31, 1980, page 15)

In the days of yore, there was a man named Aulanagle. This man caused trouble and made various kinds of tricks too.

One day, he killed one of his pigs. He cooked it in an earth oven, then he and his daughter ate it. Afterwards, he gathered some banana leaves and edible greens, and cooked them with the fatty parts of the pork. He gathered this together and went to a grave. He dug up a boy who had died and was buried not long before.

After he disinterred the body, he took it back to the place where he had cooked the pig and greens. He arranged everything carefully, and he put the dead boy inside the earth oven with the pork and greens. After the body was cooked, he saw that it was just like pork.

He took the flesh, covered it with fresh banana leaves and put it in a net bag. Then carried it to the men's house. This was the house where the men of the village slept.

He carried this large net bag and gave it to the men. He said, "This is my white pig. The pig was always breaking the fences and eating in the garden. So, I killed and cooked it. My daughter and I ate some. I brought some to give to you to eat." Then he gave the flesh to the men in the men's house.

When they took the bag and opened the bundle inside, Aulanagle was not nearby. He was near the door. They opened the bundle and began to eat the vegetables with the real pork. But when they went to cut some more pork, they pulled the boy's leg. They got up and opened the whole bundle. Oh my! They saw that it was the boy that had died. They jumped and trembled.

One man said, "I ate some greens." Another said, "I ate something bad, so now I'm furious." They began to look for this man because they wanted to fight him.

Aulanagle ran away to a mountain. He said, "So, you never gave food to me. You were always angry with me. Do you understand now or not? Did you eat pig or man?" He shouted like this to them, then fled completely.

They took the little boy that had died and put him back in his grave. They slept, and in the morning, each of the men killed a pig and carried it to the men's house to cook and eat.

Ludwig Ongoglo Simbai
Port Moresby
National Capital District

[Mr. Onguglo wrote the ancestor stories in *Wantok* #214 and 239. He is probably from **Dunuabanma** Village, **Kalam** People?, **Madang** Province?]

G60. Human flesh eaten unwittingly; P234. Father and daughter; Q276. Stinginess punished; Q580+. Punishment for not sharing food: tricked into cannibalism; R220. Flights; V61.3+. Dead buried; W152. Stinginess

## _Tongangakoai_ [Dugong]

(Wantok 318, June 7, 1980, page 19)

This story comes from the ancestors of Duke of York Island. It is the story of a sea creature named Tongangakoai. This sea creature was a dugong. One day, two girls went to Uranging, a point on Duke of York Island.

The two girls climbed a mango tree that was near the sea. Later, they sat on this tree and ate mangos, throwing the peels and pits into the sea. Later, the second girl thought, "Why is it that the mango peels that we threw in the sea are not drifting there? Only one of the peels that we threw is drifting."

This girl told the other, "I want to tell you something to look at. The peel from one of our mangos fell. It went into the sea, but the other is drifting. Whose peel is that, yours or mine? I don't know. OK, wait. I'll eat a mango first and see if the peel drifts or sinks in the sea." Then this girl ate a mango and threw the peel into the sea.

They watched. The second girl spoke again, "Look, my mango peel just sank. It went into the sea. It did not drift. I'll throw this mango pit now. Look, the pit sank too. OK, now you eat a mango."

The first girl ate a mango and threw the peel and pit into the sea. However, the mango skin and pit drifted, they did not sink. They finished eating. Later, the first girl said, "Which one of us will jump into the sea first? You should go first." However, the other girl said, "No, I can't jump first. You go first."

Later, the first girl jumped. She jumped into the sea and then came up. The second girl said, "Ah, you came up alright. Now, I can jump. Look at me, I'm jumping now." This girl jumped into the sea. However, she went all of the way down, she did not come up.

The other girl waited, and waited, and waited, but the second girl stayed beneath the sea and did not come up again. Later, the girl's body became like that of a fish.

The name of this sea creature is Tongangakoai. Some time later, the men of **Inolo** Village on **Duke of York** Island used a fishing net in the sea near this place [**Duke of York** People, **East New Britain** Province]. Tongangakoai with her child went inside this net at night and were caught.

The child was six months old. Its name was Misikorai. Tongangakoai told Misikorai, "OK, stay here and I'll jump. Stay in the net, then come back to our home."

Then Tongangakoai jumped out of the net and Misikorai stayed. Later, some [m]en from Inolo found Misikorai in the net. They took Misikorai to the beach.

They held Misikorai, but they were surprised when the dugong shouted to an important man. This leader came and told them, "Carry the dugong to the house."

They took some coral tree leaves and burned them in a fire. They put the leaves on the dugong's skin and burned its skin. Later that night, Misikorai's hands and legs came off. They hung Misikorai in a basket in a tree. At dawn, they took Misikorai and went to **Piritop** Village. At Piritop, a woman took care of Misikorai and breast-fed her. Later, Misikorai became a beautiful woman who became pregnant and gave birth.

The name of this baby was _Nembenepai_. The meaning of this name is "They caught her in a net."

Later, a man from **Makada** Island bought her [gave bride price] and took Nembenepai with him to Makada. At Makada, she gave birth to many children.

Some children live on Makada. But some children went to many other places, such as **Tavui**, near Nonga. All of the people from this place are from the Dugong Clan.

If they take and kill this dugong, _tongangakoai_, it would be taboo to eat it at this place because it is their ancestor. This sea creature is like a man and like a woman too. And, it is still like us.

John Landi
Inolo Village
Duke of York Island
East New Britain Province

A1640+. Origin of Dugong Clan; A1890+. Origin of dugong; B211+. Speaking dugong; B631. Human offspring from marriage to animal; B650+. Marriage to dugong in human form; D127+G. Transformation: girl to dugong; D327.4K+W. Transformation: dugong to woman; P210. Husband and wife; P230. Parents and children; P232. Mother and daughter; T52. Bride purchased; T570. Pregnancy; T580. Childbirth

## The Two Brothers that Married the Two Fruit Women

(Wantok 319, June 14, 1980, page 19)

Long ago, two brothers lived together. Their names were Teka and Poka. There was no one else who lived nearby them. The brothers were very desirous of becoming married, but there was no woman who lived nearby.

One time, the brothers wanted to go hunt some wild game in the deep forest. They woke up at six o'clock in the morning, took some food to eat in the forest, then departed. In the deep forest, the brothers worked very hard at hunting game, but they did not find anything. So, they went deeper into the forest.

When it was getting dark, the first brother, Poka, told Teka that they must go home. However Teka told Poka, "Our home is too far and it is nearly dark. We must find a place to sleep, such as a cave. If we don't find a cave, we should make a hut to sleep in."

Poka agreed with Teka and they tried to find a cave. They searched and searched, then arrived at a hut. They were very happy that they had found a hut to sleep in.

As they approached the hut, an old woman came outside and saw them. She told them that she was happy to see them and told them to come inside. They told her that they had become lost in the forest while they were hunting for game.

[They told her that] it was nearly dark when they began to search for a cave to sleep in, and that they were lucky to have found her. The old woman said, "OK, you can come and sleep in my house, then tomorrow you can go."

The three of them went inside the hut, and the old woman gave them food. After they finished eating, she showed them the place where they would sleep. In the early morning, the brothers woke up to go back to their home. The old woman gave them fruits to take with them.

This fruit is what we call pandanus fruit (*marita*). She told them to just carry the fruits back to their home. While they were carrying the fruits along the trail, the first brother, Teka, became very angry. He was angry because the fruit was too heavy, so at times he threw the fruit onto the ground.

He did this and caused the fruit to be ruined. Poka did not care that his fruit was heavy. He followed the old woman's instructions and carried the fruit into their house.

When Teka and Poka arrived at the house, they saw two young women in their house. The first brother was very troubled by these women. He ran up and held the hand of one of them. One of the women was beautiful and the other was not so beautiful.

The big brother held the hand of the beautiful woman, but the woman said, "I'm not your wife. I'm your little brother's wife." So, Poka married the beautiful woman and Teka married the woman that was not so beautiful. Teka's wife was not very beautiful because he had not followed the old woman's instructions.

He had thrown the fruit onto the ground and as a consequence ruined the woman's skin. Poka's wife was beautiful because he had heeded the old woman's instructions and carried the fruit all of the way home, so her skin was not ruined.

If the two brothers had carried the fruit well into the house, every man and woman on the earth would be beautiful. But one brother did not follow the instructions, so some men and women are not very attractive.

Dominic Daugl

St. Fidelis College

Kap

Alexishafen

Madang Province

A1310+. Why some people are ugly; D215.10K+W. Transformation: woman to pandanus fruit; J652. Inattention to warnings; J1050. Attention to warnings; P210. Husband and wife; P251.4+. One brother acts wisely, another acts unwisely; P251.5. Two brothers; T100. Marriage

## The Man Who Found Tobacco
(Wantok 320, June 21, 1980, page 19)

Long ago, there was no tobacco to smoke in **Irafo** Village in the Kainantu sub-Province of **Eastern Highlands** Province [**Usarufa** People].

One time, everyone went into the forest to hunt wild game. At this time, the sun was very hot. At night, the moon was very bright.

All of the men, women and children brought their kin into the forest. Only one man and his child stayed in the village. The two of them stayed there, and the boy asked his father, "All of the men and women went into the forest to hunt for wild game. Why did you and I stay here?" The father said, "Oh yes, son, we should follow them."

They strung their bows and took their arrows, then walked into the forest. They searched and searched for game, but it was almost dark and they had not shot anything yet. So, they made a fire and slept.

The next morning, they woke up and hunted for game again. They searched and searched, then they shot a marsupial (*kapul*). The name of this marsupial is called *wanume* in my language.

The boy told the father, "Let's go cook this marsupial at home." However the father said, "No. We must cook it here and eat it at home." Then he said, "What are you worrying about?"

The two of them began to make a fire. The boy gathered firewood and his father went to cut a tree to remove its bark and cook the marsupial in the bark. They came together and thought about what to cook with the marsupial.

The father traveled and saw a fallen tree. This tree was already rotten. On top of the tree was a tobacco plant growing right out of it. The leaves of the plant were nice and big.

The old father thought that these would be good leaves to eat. He took many leaves. Then he and his child cut open the marsupial's belly and removed its guts. After that, they put the marsupial meat inside the leaves and made a bundle.

They put it into the tree bark and placed it in the fire. They waited quietly and turned the bundle around. After a little while, they knew that the food was done, so they removed it from the fire.

The boy's mouth began to salivate and he told his father, "Papa, I'll try the soup first. Is it delicious or not?" The little boy opened the food bundle. He took two tobacco leaves and just shoved them into his mouth.

The tobacco leaves were extremely bitter, so the boy spit them out. His father asked him, "Son, how is it?" The little boy was irate and said, "This soup is dreadfully bitter."

The father had a good laugh at his son. He said, "Son, if you eat the marsupial meat, it will not be as bitter as the soup. It is good meat."

The father took the marsupial and ate. He tried it and said, "Ugh! This is bitter too because the juice from the leaves went inside it." So, the poor father and son did not eat.

The father told his son to get some tobacco leaves and return. The boy fetched them and the father heated them on top of the fire. When the leaves dried, he smoked them.

He tried inhaling it. It was not ordinary smoke: it was wonderful. They removed the tobacco plant and brought it to their village.

When the tobacco plant went to seed, all of the other men of the village took the seeds and planted them. Now all people know about tobacco, and it is abundant.

K. Kenawi
Kimbe
West New Britain Province

A2691.2. Origin of tobacco; J2134. Numskull makes himself sick (uncomfortable); P233. Father and son


## *Masalai* Naiwa

(Wantok 321, June 28, 1980, page 15)

This is a true story. This story began on April 12, 1980, when a *masalai* snake killed a piglet. The *masalai* snake killed the piglet near Madang's highway.

It killed the piglet in the early morning. When the piglet squealed, the people of **Ileike** village ran down to look at the pig [**Madang** Province]. They went and saw the poor pig dead and lying awkwardly. It was lying at the base of a tree near the highway.

The people also saw the *masalai* snake and they screamed. The people shouted, but the snake did not care. The snake did not slither away. It stayed there, showing its tongue and flicking its tail.

The men went to kill the snake, but a young woman told them not to kill it. The woman said that it was not an ordinary snake, "It is a man. Look at him, he makes a noise with his tail. He is a *masalai* snake."

So the men left the snake and carried the piglet back to the village. They cooked the piglet and ate it. On April 15, 1980, the snake returned to the village. The snake killed five chickens in one man's chicken coop.

The man got up quietly, took his flashlight and went outside. He found the same *masalai* snake there. He shouted loudly and his kin ran towards him.

They came and killed the *masalai* snake. They cut the snake up into little pieces, then put the pieces by a tree in the middle of the village. In the morning, they went there and found that the snake was not there. They thought that a dog or a pig had eaten it.

But no, the pigs and dogs had not eaten it. In the early morning of April 14 [16?], 1980, the *masalai* snake's kin had come and carried its body away. An old man also went with them to the home of the snakes. They carried the snake right into the snake hospital.

The old man saw all kinds of snakes. Some were big and some were small, others were multicolored. The boss of the *masalai* snakes was huge. It just stayed in one place and did not move around.

Later, they tied up the parts of the snake that the men had cut up before. He saw that they had finished, and the snakes told him, "You people, why do you always kill us such that we are your enemies? We are not snakes. No, we are men just like you."

They also told him, "If we snakes want to fight with you, too bad. You're no match for us. We'll destroy all of you."

The old man listened to them and was terrified. He saw all of this with his own eyes. He stayed with them and then the snakes brought him back to the village.

The next morning, he explained to his family what had happened. They were terrified. Before long, the snake returned to the village and took six chickens.

This was on [April] 19, 1980. The men came and saw the snake, then killed it. They took a piece of metal and hit the snake right on its head. They let it lay there. In the morning, the men woke up and killed a pig and some chickens.

They dug a hole and threw the snake's body into it. Then they butchered the animals that they had killed and threw the blood into the hole along with the pig. One man also took a *tanget* leaf and called out the *masalai* snake's name. Then he tied the *tanget* leaf and threw it into the hole.

The name of this *masalai* snake was Naiwa. This *masalai* snake does not come to Ileike Village any more. It really does not. The men are no longer afraid. They live happily.

Mr. Koul
Usino
Madang Province

B211.6.1. Speaking snake (serpent); B225.1. Kingdom of serpents; B244.1. King of serpents (snakes); B290+. Serpents' hospital; B765.7.2. Snake grows back together after it has been severed; B875.1. Giant serpent; F401.3.8. Spirits in form of snake; F127.1. Journey to serpent kingdom; F405+. Snake spirit killed by burial and propitiation; F490+. Masalai; S110. Murders; V12.1. Blood as sacrifice; V12.4.3. Pig as sacrifice; V12.4.11+. Chicken as sacrifice

## Tari and Enga
(Wantok 322, July 5, 1980, page 19)

Long ago, there were two brothers who lived in the region of the Star Mountains where the **Ok Tedi** Copper Mine is now located [**Tifal** or **Kauwol** People, **Western** Province]. The brothers' names were Huli and Opene. These two brothers were friends and traveled with each other. They never had an argument between themselves.

One time, they went into the deep forest to hunt for wild game. They walked and walked and they arrived at their forest hut. Opene told Huli to stay by the house and prepare some stones, leaves and edible greens [for an earth oven].

Opene went away to hunt for game. He went just a little ways when he saw a cassowary. He shot it and carried it back to the hut. He told Huli, "Cook this entire cassowary in an earth oven, then just cook the guts."

Opene said to Huli, "After you cook the guts, you must wait for me. Don't eat yet, wait for me. After I return, we'll eat together."

Opene left his brother and went right into the deep forest to hunt for more game. Huli cooked the cassowary. After he finished, he heated some small stones to cook the guts in an earth oven in another hole in the ground.

He put all of the things in the hole, then waited for Opene. He waited and waited a long time. Huli was worried that the cassowary guts were becoming overcooked, so he removed some of the food from the earth oven.

After he removed it, he tried a piece. Oh my, it was delicious, more delicious than anything else was. So Huli ate all of the cassowary guts. After he was finished, he removed the food from the big earth oven. Then he waited for his brother.

A little later, Opene came and talked to Huli about the cassowary, "Bring the guts over here, then we'll eat." Huli said, "I'm very sorry, brother. I ate all of the cassowary guts. Please don't be angry."

Opene was irate and told Huli, "That's OK, brother. You ignored what I said. I can't do anything bad to you. But I can't live with you any longer, and you can no longer look for me."

After he told this to Huli, he left. He went fairly far from this place and went to live elsewhere. Now you can see that Tari is far from Enga.

These two brothers had an argument over cassowary guts and then they went separate ways. They live far away from each other. This story shows how **Tari** started the **Huli** People [**Southern Highlands** Province] and Opene started the **Enga** People [**Enga** Province].

J. Pangari Pirai
North Solomons Province

A1611+. Origin of Enga People; A1611+. Origin of Huli People; P251.5. Two brothers; P251.5.3. Hostile brothers; W125. Gluttony; W126. Disobedience

## Manting, the Stone and the Bird
(Wantok 323, July 12, 1980, page 15)

Long, long ago, there was a man named Manting who was from **Tararan** Village [**Adzera** People, **Morobe** Province]. This man was a true gossip. In my language, we call a gossip, *manting manting*.

This man was also belligerent. He lived with his family in **Ologuangin**. He was past marriage age and he was still not married.

He fought all of the time. When he tried his luck with women, they just spat at him. The poor man often tried hard, but he never found a wife.

Manting searched and searched, but he could not find a wife. One time, he fought with all of the men of the village. They beat him badly and then he went to the Erap River.

He sat and rested and saw a beautiful stone. He took it, put it in his net bag, and carried it to Tararan Village. Manting brought it there and put it in his house.

He stayed there for a fairly long time, then went and caught a dove. He put the dove with the stone. He called these his two wives. Manting had married a stone and a bird. This bird is called _wampon_ in my language.

Now Manting was very happy because he had married two wives. One time, he went and fought and fought and fought. The men gave him a real woman to marry [for his efforts at fighting]. But Manting did not want to marry her.

He told them, "Where were you men before? Your women lived with you and were married. I'm already married." Manting told them that he had married a stone that lives in a river house and a bird that flies in the sky.

Manting went back to his house in the village. He often said that it was taboo to eat any bird, and so he never ate them. He also said that it was taboo to cross the Erap River, and so he never crossed it. He never drank from the Erap River either, because the Erap River was taboo for his soul (lit., "true liver").

One other thing about him was that he often spoke as a man. Later, he would speak as a woman would.

When he went to the garden, he would take a branch and hang on it his net bag with the stone. He would take the bird, tie it up and let it perch on a tree. Then he would carry them to the garden.

He would very carefully put his two wives in the garden and then he worked hard. If he saw some man approaching his wives, he would scold the man unmercifully.

He would become angry and just fight the base of a banana plant in the garden. First he would talk angrily as a man, then later he would talk angrily in the voice of a woman. However, the poor man never fought his two wives. Never. He lived well with them until the bird died, then he died too.

Michael Ching

Tararan Village

Markham Valley

Morobe Province

B602.3. Marriage to pigeon; C221.1.2. Tabu: eating bird; C265K2. Tabu: to drink from a certain brook; C833.1+. Tabu: crossing river; F556. Remarkable voice; P210. Husband and wife; T117+. Marriage to stone; T145.0.1. Polygyny

# The Big Brother's Friend

(Wantok 324, July 19, 1980, page 15)

Long, long ago, there was a place where there were no people except for two brothers. One time, the big brother went into the forest to kill some marsupials (_kapul_).

The big brother told the little brother, "Stay here and get some firewood. Also, please cook some food for me." After the big brother told his little brother this, he took his bow and arrows, then went into the forest to hunt.

He went high up a mountain and killed many marsupials. When he saw that he had killed many marsupials, he went to a trail and sat down to count them.

While the man was sitting, he looked down the trail and saw a he-dog approaching. This dog was wagging his tail and coming to where the man was sitting.

Later, the dog went fairly far away and returned to see the man there. This went on for a while, then the man thought, "I'll try to follow him." The man tied up all his marsupials well and followed the dog.

The two of them walked and walked, then they arrived at a house. They went inside the fence that surrounded this house. Oh my! Plenty of food was at this house, but no one was home.

The dog sniffed an axe and looked back at the man. The man took the axe and just followed the dog. The dog sniffed at a fireplace and looked back at the man. The man cut some firewood.

The man was cutting firewood, while the dog went to bring stones, one by one, to the fireplace. When the man finished cutting firewood, he made a fire and heated the stones. The dog ran inside the house, fetched a rope and brought it back to the man.

The man took the rope and just followed the dog. The dog went directly to the pigsty. The dog made a signal to open the fence of the sty. The man understood and opened the door. The dog ran right in and sniffed at a pig, then the dog looked at the man.

The man went and tied the rope to the pig's leg. The pig was not a juvenile. No, it was truly huge. The man cut up the pig well along with some marsupials and cooked them in an earth oven.

Later, he removed all of the meat from the earth oven, giving the marsupial and pig livers to the dog. The dog ate them and was very happy. The dog quickly went and brought a big net bag to give to the man. The man filled the net bag with the meat from the pig and the marsupials and brought it all back to his little brother.

The big brother and the little brother were both very happy. They ate the pork and the marsupial meat.

They stayed there for a while, then the little brother asked his big brother to show him where he found all of the meat. The big brother told the story to his little brother. His little brother listened carefully to everything that he was told.

The little brother followed his big brother's instructions. He shot many marsupials and continued onward as he was told. While he rested, he saw a dog approaching. The dog came closer to him and sniffed his skin.

The man opened his mouth and spoke angrily at the dog. The poor dog was afraid and put his tail between his legs, then slowly walked to his home. The man followed this dog.

When they arrived at the house, the dog did the same things that he had done with the big brother. However, the dog killed a mangy pig for this man. Because of this, the man shouted angrily at the dog.

He told the dog, "My big brother came and you killed a huge pig for him. Now I've come and what have you done for me? This pig that you killed for me is a mangy pig." The poor dog just stood and listened to the man's curses.

When the food in the earth oven was ready, the dog approached slowly. The man gave him the pig and marsupial livers, but the man was irate and he killed the poor dog. He took all of the meat and livers together, then carried them to his big brother.

When he arrived, his big brother asked him, "Why are you also carrying the pig and marsupial livers? Didn't you give them to the dog?" The little brother said, "Your friend didn't want to eat them, so I carried everything here."

The big brother knew that his little brother was probably lying, so he ran to the dog's house. He arrived there and saw young women crying for a young boy who had died.

Kelepus Walane
Buvusi [Buvasi] Settlement [Block]
Kimbe
West New Britain Province

B331.2.2+. Helpful dog killed; D341. Transformation: dog to person; P251.5. Two brothers; P251.4. Brothers scorn brother's wise counsel

# The Man Who Turned into a Snake

(Wantok 325, July 26, 1980, page 15)

Long, long ago, there were once no true snakes. At one place, there lived two brothers. The first brother often worked in the garden, took care of housework and husbanded pigs. The second brother hunted wild game in the deep forest.

The second brother was a real man at killing game. He would kill them quickly and bring them back to the house. The first brother would cook the meat with edible greens, and they would eat together. They lived happily for many years.

One time, the first brother told the second brother, "Now you can take my place at doing housework and husbanding the pigs. Also, don't forget about making a new garden. I'll try to take your place and become a little man of the forest and kill wild game for us."

Early one morning, the first brother woke up and took the bow and arrows and an axe. Then he called to his dog and they went right into the deep forest.

He went into the middle of the deep woods and heard his dog howling. The man thought that the dog had found some game, so he quickly jumped over stones and logs and ran quickly to where the dog was howling.

The man arrived there and he saw that his dog was carrying a woman's "grass" skirt. He looked to his left and saw a beautiful woman standing there naked.

The poor woman was ashamed and covered her breasts with her hands. She was terribly ashamed and turned her back to the man. The man told the dog to give the skirt back to the woman, then they would all go back.

The dog wagged its tail and gave the skirt back to the woman. The man did not want to hunt for game any more. He took the woman and his dog, and they went directly home.

The second brother was working in the garden. When he saw the three of them, he was very happy and ran towards them. They cooked food, ate and went to sleep.

When they lay down, the second brother asked his sister-in-law, "Were you alone, or do you have some sisters where you lived?" The woman said, "There is one last sister who lives at my home."

The woman said, "I didn't tell about her when I came here. The dog stole my skirt and I followed the dog to get it back, but your brother found me and I came to your home." The woman told her brother-in-law, "If you want to get my sister, OK. Tomorrow, we can go and bring her here." The man was very happy.

In the early morning, the two in-laws left the first brother and went to the woman's home. They told the first brother that they would return another day with a wife for the second brother.

They walked off to a place where there was a very big mountain. They walked toward the top. Near the top, the boy became sick. He told his sister-in-law to go first and that he would rest a little then follow her. Afterwards, he followed her.

His sister-in-law went first and then waited for him. She waited and waited, but her brother-in-law did not arrive. The woman was a little worried and turned back to look for her brother-in-law.

The woman looked for her brother-in-law, but did not find him. The man had turned into a snake. The two arms and head were still human. The belly down through the legs had turned into a snake.

The sister-in-law cried and cried, then quickly went to tell her husband. When they returned to look, only the face and head were left. All of the other parts had turned into a snake.

The big brother saw this and was very troubled. He just went to touch the face, but his brother turned entirely into a snake. The snake chased after them.

The snake continued the chase and sunk its fangs into his big brother. As the big brother was dying, he told the woman, "Now we will be married."

So they married and had many little snakes, and big snakes too. So now, we can find many kinds of snakes all over our land.

Wambe Epano

I. L. Hospital

[Wabag]

Enga Province

A2145. Creation of snake (serpent); B29.1+. Body of snake, face and arms of human; B29.2.1. Serpent with human head; B632. Animal offspring from marriage to animal; B646.1. Marriage to person in snake form; D191M. Transformation: man to serpent (snake); D681. Gradual transformation; P210. Husband and wife; P251.5. Two brothers; P263. Brother-in-law; P264. Sister-in-law; R260. Pursuits; S73.1. Fratricide; T100. Marriage


## The Story of the Moon

(Wantok 326, August 2, 1980, page 15)

Long ago, the moon lived with a man. The moon helped this man kill pigs, cassowaries, and other wild game at night. The man used the moon like a flashlight at night.

This man took the moon and poured it into a small bamboo tube, then covered up the opening of the tube well.

He carried the tube with him. When the sun was out, he hid the tube carefully in his net bag or in his house. The man had a friend who lived with him in this village, but the friend did not know what he had.

The man who took care of the moon killed many more pigs than the others did. At night, he would go to hunt for game. He would go to the place where he had fenced in sago palm trees, or to the place where there were tree fruits.

When he heard the pigs eating, he would slowly open the bamboo tube. The moon would come out and give light, then the man would shoot the pigs. After that, he would let the moon clean the blood and then return to the bamboo tube.

He would close the opening of the bamboo and they would go to hunt for pigs again. Then they would do the same thing. When he opened the bamboo, he would not entirely open it.

The moon would come out of the opening of the bamboo just enough to give him enough light to shoot the pigs. One time, the man went to a festival at a village. His wife was menstruating, so she stayed at home and only he went.

When he was about to leave, he gave the bamboo with the moon in it to his wife. After he gave it to her, he said, "Listen well to what I say. It is absolutely forbidden for someone to come and ask you questions or to flatter you to get something and give to that person. You must say, 'I don't know,' because when the person leaves, they will not give me anything or tell me about what happened."

The man spoke sternly to his wife. After he left, the woman made a hole in the ground where she was sitting and buried the bamboo inside it. After she buried the bamboo, she sat on top of it.

She was sitting there for a fairly long time when a friend of her husband arrived. The friend came quietly and asked the woman, "Hey, do you know about your friend's [husband's] strength too? It's the thing that helps him shoot many pigs."

The woman said, "I'm a woman, and I can't know about men's things." The man replied, "I think that you know but that you're just lying to me." The woman said, "I've no idea what you're talking about. He didn't give me anything nor did he tell me anything about it."

The man spoke more forcefully, "I think that you're sitting on top of it. You had better get up so that I can examine whatever is there."

The woman did not want to get up, but the man was forceful and pushed her off. He then began to dig the ground where she was sitting. The ground where the woman was sitting looked like a man after he finished digging, so the man thought that something was there.

He kept digging and found something. He removed the bamboo with the moon in it. He was very happy and carried it to his home. The woman cried and cried.

The woman said, "That's OK. You're strong and you've taken it away. But please, you must take care of it well. It belongs to your friend. If he finds that something's wrong with it, he'll beat me to a pulp." The man carried it off without delay. He went directly into the forest and tried it out.

He heard a pig eating. As he listened, he removed the covering of the bamboo tube entirely. The moon came out and lit up. The man shot the pig. The man pushed the moon back into the bamboo and covered it up again. The man trembled and wanted to shoot more pigs, but he did not allow the moon to clean the pig's blood. He carried the bamboo and shot a pig. Again, he did not let the moon drink the pig's blood.

The moon was angry with this man. He carried the moon and wanted to shoot a third pig. When he opened the covering of the bamboo, the moon quickly jumped out and jumped onto a vine with red flowers.

The man tried to grab the moon, but the moon climbed higher up the vine. The man took his bow and hit the moon, but was only able to remove a piece of skin.

The moon went up and up, then jumped onto a tree branch. Then it went very high and jumped onto a cloud. Now the moon lighted every place. The moon's owner was singing and dancing at the festival. He saw the moon's light in the clouds.

The poor man left the festival, then sat and waited for dawn. When it was almost dawn, he went quickly to his house and castigated his wife. The woman told him what had happened.

The man went and spoke angrily at his friend. He told him that they were no longer friends because he had ruined their friendship. So, their friendship ended.

When you look at the moon, you can see that part of it is not well lit. This is the place where the man hit it with his bow.

Gabinus Gandgomal
Ulis Church
**Josephstaal [Pondoma People]**
**Madang Province**

A750+. Moon escapes to sky when man does not let it drink blood of pig that he killed using moon's light; A754. Moon kept in box; A754.1. Moon buried in pit; A755+. Moon's phases caused by being hit; A758. Theft of moon; K300. Thefts and cheats—general; P210. Husband and wife; P310. Friendship; Q212. Theft punished

## The Sexy Sago Woman
(Wantok 327, August 9, 1980, page 27)

Long, long ago, in one village, there were no women. Only men lived in this village. They married pigs or dogs or other things.

One morning, a man took his bow and arrows, then went to the forest to hunt for wild game. He walked and walked into the very deep forest. He heard a woman singing.

The man stood up to get a better idea where the woman's singing was originating. He thought, "Ah, sweetheart! That's a good wife for me."

The man listened carefully to where the singing was coming from, then he ran in that direction. He ran and ran, then the singing stopped. The man had arrived too late.

The sago woman had gone to the top of a sago palm tree and she began to sing again. The man came closer and walked quietly to search for this woman. The woman sat and hid well in the sago tree leaves, she sang stronger. He did not find this woman, so he gave up and sat down.

While he sat, he thought, "Ah, too bad about my good woman. How can I manage to marry her?" The poor man stayed there and saw the sun setting.

He got up and walked slowly home. He arrived at the village, went directly into his house and went to sleep. He did not sleep very well. He was very troubled, and he tossed and turned.

The poor man woke up in the early morning and walked into the deep forest to try to find the woman again. He walked and walked into the deep forest. Again, he heard the voice of this woman. He began to run towards where the singing was originating.

He ran and ran, but he was too late again. The sago woman was already on top of the sago tree and she was well hidden as she continued to sing. The poor man searched and searched until the sun set. Then he went back to the village.

The poor man thought and worried. What could he do to marry this woman? He cooked some food and ate, then went to sleep.

He slept and then he thought of a plan. He thought, "Tomorrow morning, before it's too light, I'll go and hide at the base of the sago tree. Then I'll see this woman."

The man slept that night and kept his ears open for the birds that sing in the morning. He slept and slept, then he heard the morning birds sing. He got up from bed, then walked and walked. When dawn began to break, he was at the place where the woman sang.

He stayed there, and when dawn finally arrived, he heard the woman's singing. He listened and hid well at the base of the sago tree. The woman's singing came closer. She stood at the base of the sago tree and was about to climb it.

The man jumped up quickly and grabbed this woman. The sago woman trembled in shock and cried out loudly. But the man held onto her and did not let her go.

The man told her, "Stop crying. We will marry now." However, the sago woman said, "Sorry. Please let me go. It would be bad if my mother and father found me. I'll go explain to them first then I'll return."

However, the man did not want to let her go. He told her, "No. You go first and I'll follow you. Let's go now. We'll be married right away."

So, the two of them walked to the village. They followed the trail and went directly to the village. They went directly inside the house. The poor man was now ecstatic.

The sago woman told him, "Now we'll be married, but you'll do all of the work and I'll just stay here." The man just laughed and said, "That's alright. I can do all of the work and you can just stay here."

The next day, the man went to the garden and brought some food back. After that, he made some sago and brought that back. Then the two of them ate happily. They lived like this for a while and the woman became pregnant and gave birth to a child.

The man did all of the work, but one time he was tired of working. He spoke angrily at his wife, "Why is it that I always do all of the work?" The woman told him, "Didn't you listen to me before when I told you that I'd just stay here and you'd do all of the work?"

The man said, "I'm tired of that. I do all of the work and you just stay there. Come on, get up and take all of the baby's shitty things and wash them." The woman truly did not want to do this. The man was irate, then he got up and hit his wife.

So, the woman took the baby's soiled things and carried them to the stream to clean. As she threw the soiled things into the water, she cried.

The man was waiting and waiting, then he followed her. He came close to the stream and called out, "Hey, what are you doing? Hurry up and bring the baby." The poor woman called back, "My husband, come and look at me first."

The man went quickly to the stream. The woman jumped down into the stream. She turned to liquid, just like when sago turns to a mushy liquid when one rinses it.

The poor man saw this and cried terribly. He said, "Oh I'm sorry, my good wife. I ruined you." He cried and returned to the village. He stayed there until he died too.

Norman Gorea
**Dami** Village [**Bola** People]
**West New Britain** Province

B601. Marriage of person to beast; B601.2. Marriage to dog; B601.8. Marriage to swine; D215.11K+W. Transformation: woman to sago; D361.1+. Forest Spirit Bride; D1355.1.1. Love-producing song; F113. Land of men; M451.1. Death by suicide; P210. Husband and wife; P230. Parents and children; P232. Mother and daughter; P234. Father and daughter; T10. Falling in love; T117.5+. Marriage to sago woman; T192. Marriage by force; T570. Pregnancy; T580. Childbirth


## We Are Children of the Snake
(Wantok 328, August 16, 1980, page 19)

In one place, there lived a man and his wife. They lived with their daughter. This young woman was very smart and beautiful. Oh my! I am not lying. If you saw her, you would fall down right in front of her.

At this place where they lived, their garden was not small. No, their garden was packed with sweet potatoes, bananas, sugarcanes, wild sugarcanes (*pitpit*), various kinds of edible greens, and many other foods. Their pigsty was huge too, and their pigs were not just worthless. They lived well and nothing bad happened to them.

At the place where they lived, there were no other people. The three of them lived amidst the forest. One time, the two elderly parents told their daughter, "We'll kill pigs at a particular place."

They made a row house for killing pigs. They spoke to the young woman, but the woman said, "Never mind, let's go together." But the two parents were insistent because they wanted her to live in the house and take care of the pigs and other things.

The next morning, the parents woke up and left. The woman was there alone. She stayed there for two days. On the third night, she gave sweet potatoes to the pigs.

She also ate, then she made a fire and got ready to sleep. It was getting dark so she shut the door. After a while, she wanted to go outside to get a little air because she had shut the door.

While she was outside, she looked around. When she looked in the direction where the sun rises, she saw a small light. The light looked like a star and she thought that it was just a star, so she went back into the house and went to shut the door. But she had not put all of the wood inside to shut the door.

She let the door open. She looked out and saw that the light was bigger, like a torch. She watched and saw the light coming closer, then it looked like a lamp.

She kept looking, and it became as big as a burning house. Oh my, the poor woman was afraid and she trembled terribly. She thought and thought, but there was no one who lived nearby that she could call to come and help her.

She cried and when she went to look at the light again, it looked like the light from five burning houses. Oh my, it was truly huge. She just sat there because there was no place to hide. She cried sadly and said, "Papa and mama don't love me, so they left me here. They went away and they left me here to die."

The light came closer to the house, then the woman opened the door and looked out. Oh my! The woman saw a huge snake.

The snake's mouth was as big as a big water tank. The poor woman ran back inside and hid underneath her bed. The snake opened the door and came inside, then stayed on the other side of the room.

The young woman thought that the snake had not seen her. The snake lay in wait while the woman lay underneath the bed. They continued like that until dawn. When the woman looked at the snake, oh my! She saw its long forked tongue flicking outside its mouth.

The woman was terrified. It was light now. The woman said, "Never mind, I can die." So she went outside. She left the snake there and went to give food to the pigs. While she worked, she kept an eye on the snake.

However, the poor snake did not do anything to her. She was confused, but she had one thought. She spoke with conviction, "Later, I'll come and cook food but now I must first find some sweet potatoes." She told this lie, then left. When she was fairly far from the house, she sped up. She ran very quickly and got very far away until it was nearly dark. When she looked back, she saw that the snake had followed her. The woman was out of breath from running and said, "OK, snake, come and eat me."

After she said this, she got a second wind and began to run again. She ignored the darkness and kept going. She kept running and the snake slowly followed her. The snake shot its light at the woman to see where she was running.

The heat of the light began to affect her, but she did not care. They continued onward until dawn, and onward until dusk again, and then on until dawn again when they came directly to the place where they were killing pigs. The poor woman just collapsed on top of her father's legs. After she collapsed, she said, "Now that I see you two, I can die."

After she told them this, they were very worried. The father asked her, "Why?" The woman said, "Look at the base of the sugarcanes and you'll see. What's really there?"

At this time, many people came to look. After they heard the story, they looked at the base of the sugarcanes. Oh my, they were shocked because they had never seen anything like this before. The woman's father took his axe and ran to cut this snake.

The axe broke the snake's skin. All of the men saw this, and they took their axes and cut the snake into small pieces. They threw the pieces around, but the pieces came back together again. The people trembled in fright.

The men divided the pigs up, then the family of three took their share and returned to their house. The snake followed them back to their house. When they arrived at the house, the woman's father saw this and told his daughter, "Never mind the snake, you must go with it."

But the young woman said, "I don't want to." The parents were adamant that she must go with the snake. After a while, she consented and walked toward the snake.

They went together. The snake went first and the woman followed. They went far and came to a certain place. This place was filled with houses, food gardens, and pigs in their sties. The place looked very attractive.

They went inside a house, then the woman took an axe and went out to cut firewood to cook food. After she finished, she pulled up some taros, yams, sweet potatoes, and various edible greens. She brought these and cooked them in an earth oven. After the food was ready, she got up to find the snake so that they would eat.

However, the snake was not there, so the woman sat and waited. She heard a kind of bamboo flute music crying out. A man was blowing a flute and terrifying the woman.

The man came inside, sat on the floor and smoked. He got up and told the woman, "Remove the food from the earth oven now. We shall eat." The woman did not reply and she did not look at the man either. The man got up and shouted, "You think that I'm another man, huh?"

The woman got up and spoke, "I didn't come with a man. I came with a snake." He showed the axe mark where the woman's father had cut him. He spoke, "I truly loved you, so I transformed from a snake and came to get you."

The woman was very happy that she would marry a real man.  She removed the food from the earth oven and they ate.  Later, they had many children in the place that is my village.

Now they call us children of the snake, and my clan's marking is the snake.

Don Tukayu
Catholic Church
**Erave** [Village, **Kewa** People]
**Southern Highlands** Province

A991+. Origin of particular village; A1640. Origin of tribal subdivisions; B656.2. Marriage to serpent in human form; B720+. Luminous snake; B765.7.2. Snake grows back together after it has been severed; B875.1. Giant serpent; D391M. Transformation: serpent (snake) to man; P210. Husband and wife; P230. Parents and children; P232. Mother and daughter; P234. Father and daughter; R260. Pursuits; T10. Falling in love; T100. Marriage


## The Angry Mountain

(Wantok 329, August 23, 1980, page 19)

In a village named Papayuk [**Papayuku**], there stand five stone mountains [**Enga** Province, **Enga** People].  There is a story that long ago they were brothers.  This is the story of the little mountain brothers.  The names of the stone mountains are Liane, Kumbali, Welen, Yango, and Kupitu.  Kupitu is the last [smallest] of them.

One time, the other stone mountains of Papayuk Village killed a pig and prepared it to eat.  They called to the five brothers to come and eat with them.  All of the brothers were gathering and still looking for the other stone mountains.

They went, then the others gave food to the brothers.  They divided it and later ate the food.  All four big brothers took their big pieces of meat and shoved them inside their mouths.  They did not think about their little brother, not at all.

Their little brother, Kupitu, was thinking and thinking, but his thoughts were not clear.  He was a little troubled because of his big brothers and because of the group that had killed the pig.

Kupitu stopped thinking and turned his back to the others and began to cry.  He cried and cried, then his skin sloughed off.  His head turned entirely black.  He was troubled because his big brothers had not treated him well.

He cried hard, coughed and began to fall, all at once.  The brother that the mother had given birth to first, Yango,

was sorry for his little brother.  So, he threw away his pig bone and went to him.

Kupitu took the pig bone and saw that it had no meat.  The poor brother still felt sorry for him.  He cried harder and said, "I think that we have come together.  Let's all eat together.  It's all right, I'm not worried now."

He also told them, "You treated me as if I was the child of a hick or the child of a *masalai*.  I can't travel with you or laugh with you any longer.  I shall live by myself."

After Kupitu told them this, a heavy rain fell and water began to fall from his head.  The water fell and completely ruined all of the food.

This stone mountain, Kupitu, is still at this place, Papayuk.  Even during droughts, water falls down from the top of this mountain.  It is always raining at the top of this mountain.  The top of this mountain is completely black.  This shows that this mountain is still troubled.

Joseph Kama
Transport and Civil Aviation
Konedobu, Port Moresby
National Capital District

A965. Origin of mountain chain; A1617. Origin of place-name; F490+. Masalai; F755+. Mountain that eats; F755.1. Speaking mountain; P251.5.3. Hostile brothers; P251.6.2+. Five brothers; W152. Stinginess


## The Clever Dogs

(Wantok 330, August 30, 1980, page 19)

In the Telefomin area, we believe that Karikunip is our God.  We believe that Karikunip made the earth and us and other people too.  But that is not all.  Our God, is a woman.  So one day, this false-god woman, told the people, "I made the earth and I made you too, so you must worship me."

So, in **Min** Village, in the Telefomin area, they often call this woman their god [**Faiwol** People, **Western** Province].  Even to this day, they make spirit houses and worship Her.

However one day, God Woman Karikunip told the people, "I made everything.  Now I want all of you to close your eyes, then the marsupials (*kapul*) will hide.  After that, you can open your eyes again."

They heeded what She said, and everyone closed their eyes.  However, the dogs did not shut their eyes completely.  They left them open just a little bit.  This was because the dogs wanted to find out where the marsupials hid.

They looked and saw Karikunip sending the marsupials to hide.  Some hid in the trees and some hid in caves.

When the marsupials were well hidden, She told the people to open their eyes again. Then she asked them, "Did all of you close your eyes well or not?" All of the men and dogs said that they had closed their eyes well.

The people were telling the truth, they did close their eyes well. The people did not know where the marsupials were hiding.

The dogs were very clever. So now, dogs can easily find marsupials. Even in the dead of night, they can find marsupials.

The men were foolish to have closed their eyes. Now, they cannot find marsupials like dogs can. This is because they do not know where marsupials hide. Some men know this, so they often bring dogs with them to go hunting for marsupials. When dogs go with them, they do not miss.

When dogs sleep, they open their eyes a little. If a person or something comes when a dog is asleep, they will wake up very quickly and bark. Regardless of whether they are sleeping, they notice things very quickly.

So we, the people of Min near Telefomin, like dogs very much. This is because dogs can protect us from enemies during the day as well as during the night.

Sakiba Sanameng

S. I. L. [Summer Institute of Linguistics]

Ukarumpa

Eastern Highlands Province

A15.1. Female creator; A2452.1+. Why dogs are good hunters; B211.1.7. Speaking dog; V112.1. Spirit huts; W157. Dishonesty

## The Cloud that Sank the Island

(Wantok 33[1], September 6, 1980, page 19)

This ancestor story tells of how an island sank in the sea. This island was about a mile long in the mouth of the Yalingi River, near **Malol** Village in **West Sepik** Province [**Sissano** People]. Only on good nights, does the island surface, and whoever paddles a canoe nearby can see it.

Long, long ago, there were many, many people, dogs and chickens [on this island]. When they wanted to make sago flour, the people paddled to the mainland. In the evening, they took the canoes and paddled back to the island. The people also made their gardens on the mainland.

One time, a man cut down a sago palm tree and prepared it for pigs to eat. He let it lay there for about a week, then he made a fence around this sago tree. Later he returned and stayed until the next day to rinse the sago pith.

While he was working on the fence, he saw that the pigs had nearly finished the sago. Oh my! They had taken a big piece of the tree out and eaten it. He said, "Tomorrow, one pig will be soup for me."

He stayed there through the next evening, when he took his canoe and paddled to the mainland. He paddled the canoe upriver. He took his bow and arrows and walked toward the sago tree that he had fenced.

The poor man searched and searched, but there was no pig eating the sago, none at all. The place was very dark, since it was late at night. It was nearing dawn and it was getting darker.

The man looked up and saw something like a cloud obscuring all of the stars. He felt the hairs on his body stand up and he felt sweat come from his armpits. He rose and spoke, "Why am I afraid? The leaders of yore were never afraid of such a thing."

He chewed some ginger and spat it out. Before long, he saw a very big light descend from above a nearby sago tree.

The light fell directly towards the sago tree that the man had fenced. The man now knew that it was a spirit cloud. It was coming to eat the sago. The man waited for the cloud to eat its fill of sago. After that, the cloud would be speared.

The ghost [spirit] cloud did not stay and eat nicely. It broke apart the sago trees. It was happily eating the sago and did not see the man drawing back his bow.

The man drew back the bow and shot the arrow right into the spirit cloud's groin. Oh my! This thing did not call out quietly. It thundered, "You are a man who likes meat too much. You never eat vegetables, not even a little. You wait and the two of us will try your bones."

This thing spun around and around, then the man quickly looked for a hole that a pig had dug. He threw away his bow and other things, then jumped inside the hole. He still held his small net bag with ginger and things in it. He took some sago leaves and covered himself up.

The spirit cloud felt a terrible pain and went to suffocate the man who had shot it. It searched and searched, but only saw his bow and things. The man was just lying quietly, chewing ginger and spitting it out. This was so that the spirit could not smell him.

The poor thing could not find the man, and it fell down dead. The man listened and did not hear anything, so he came out of the hole. It was nearly dawn.

He looked and found a dead piglet. This spirit was the piglet. The man tied a *tanget* leaf to it, cut its tail and went back to the island.

He told the men of the island to carry the pig that he had killed, then to cook and eat it. The men brought the pig and cooked it. The man who had killed the pig brought his kin to the mainland. They did not return. They left the pig and all of the other people on the island who were eating.

The father of the young cloud waited and waited for his child, but the child did not return. The big spirit cloud knew that his child had probably encountered enemies.

It was almost evening when the spirit cloud began to come and look for his child. The people of the island saw that it was dark and they thought that it would rain. They quickly divided the pork and went inside their houses.

The spirit-cloud father searched and searched, but could not find his child. He looked in the all of the places, but could not find his child. Only the little island was left for him to check. He went towards the island and he smelled his child.

Now the big spirit cloud knew that this group of people on the island had killed his child. The poor spirit began to cry. A heavy rain fell.

The islanders were happily eating pork in their houses. A heavy rain fell and there was thunder and lightning. It was nighttime when the spirit cloud father came down brutally upon the island.

He took the little island and the island sank. The sea came and covered everything. The spirit cloud stood up and shoved the island until all of the people and animals were dead. Then he left and returned to his home where the sun sets.

Now this island is underneath the sea, even today.

Armela S. Alosi

Moem Barracks

Wewak

East Sepik Province

D440+. Transformation: cloud to pig; D2143.1. Rain produced by magic; D2149.1. Thunderbolt magically produced; F401.3.10K. Spirit in form of boar; F405+. Spirit killed by spear/arrow; F431. Cloud-spirit; F473.6.4. Spirit eats food; F944.3. Island sinks into sea; P230. Parents and children; Q552.2.3.2.3+. Island sinks for offense; Q428. Punishment: drowning; Q211.6. Killing an animal revenged; R213. Escape from home; R220. Flights; R315. Cave as refuge; S110. Murders

## The Spirit Woman Created a Food

(Wantok 332, September 13, 1980, page 19)

Long, long ago in the Markham Valley, there were not any good foods. None at all. The people just ate ashes.

Once there was a man from **Samaran** Village who went to cut insects out of a tree [**Adzera** People, **Morobe** Province]. This tree was deep inside the forest.

He arrived at this place and began cutting the tree. The tree was completely rotten and was filled with insects [probably beetle grubs]. He broke off pieces of the tree, took out the insects and threw the pieces of wood into the stream.

The pieces of wood drifted in this branch of the river, went to another branch, then arrived at the river itself. In this river, there was a *masalai* woman. She saw the pieces of wood drifting, and she wanted to find out who it was that had broken the tree apart early in the morning.

The name of this river is Amaimoa. This *masalai* woman followed the river and arrived at Mangiang River. She did not yet find out who it was that had broken the tree apart. She continued to follow the Mangiang River.

She just followed the pieces of wood that were drifting in the water. She traveled and traveled, then arrived at a stream named Mami. It was then that she heard the man breaking apart the tree.

The *masalai* woman went a little farther and immediately met the man who was breaking apart the tree for insects. The man was surprised and asked her, "Are you a real woman or a *masalai* woman?"

However, the *masalai* woman did not reply to him. No, she asked the man, "And you, are you a real man or are you a *masalai* man?" The man did not reply to the *masalai* woman's question either. No.

The man said, "You're probably a *masalai* woman. As for myself, I came in the very early morning to break apart this tree to get insects from it." The *masalai* woman said, "That's alright. You can break apart the tree and get the insects. I'll sit down and look for all of the bad insects that get away."

So, the man continued to break apart the tree, throwing insects at the *masalai* woman. When the *masalai* woman got the insects, she just tossed them into her big mouth. The *masalai* woman did this, but the real man did not know about it.

Finally, he came to the last insect. The man threw it and saw the *masalai* woman immediately eat it. Now he knew what the *masalai* woman had done. He knew that she was not a real woman.

Deep inside the tree, it was not rotten. The man took his axe and split the tree, then called out for the *masalai* woman to come and get an insect that was deep inside the tree. The *masalai* woman ran and shoved her hand inside.

Quickly, the man removed the axe and the tree closed on the *masalai* woman's hand. The *masalai* woman could not remove her hand. The man left her crying and he ran to the village.

He went there and did not tell anyone what had happened, not a sole. He just stayed there by himself. The *masalai* woman defecated all over and burned all of the underbrush. The *masalai* woman's feces burned the bushes just like fire.

Three months later, the man returned to see the *masalai* woman. He arrived there and looked at the place. Oh my! Many kinds of food filled this area. There were corn plants, melons, various kinds of taros, sweet potatoes, beans, cucumbers, bananas, and many other kinds of foods.

He took one of each and tried eating them. Some, like cucumber and melon, were good to eat raw. Others, like yam and taro, made his mouth itch. So he took those, and cooked and ate them.

All people know about these things now. They take them and plant and grow them in their gardens everywhere. So now, in Markham Valley, there are many kinds of food. This is the origin of foods.

Magai Upabini
Panguna
North Solomons Province

A1420.1+. Origin of food from captured spirit burning forest with her feces; A2685.1.1. Origin of maize; A2686.4.1. Origin of sweet potato; A2686.4.2. Origin of taro; A2686.4.3. Origin of yams; A2686.6. Origin of beans; A2687.2. Origin of melons; A2687.2+. Origin of cucumber; A2687.5. Origin of banana; D1002. Magic excrements; F401.6. Spirit in human form; F420.1.2. Water-spirit as woman (water-nymph, water-nix); F490+. Masalai; H46.1+. Spirit recognized when it devours raw flesh; K1111. Dupe puts hand (paws) into cleft of tree (wedge, vise)

## The Frog in the Light

(Wantok 333, September 20, 1980, page 19)

Once there was a place where a handsome boy lived. The poor boy's mother and father had died. So he lived with his grandmother.

His grandmother never got angry with him. They lived happily together. After a while, it was time for young people to *karim lek* with each other. [The term *karim lek* is a kind of culturally sanctioned caressing between unmarried youths (see glossary). In this story, it indicates a probable origin from the Middle Wahgi Valley (Mihalic, 1971: 107): **Wahgi**, **Kuman** or **Golin** People; **Western Highlands** or **Simbu** Province.]

This young boy often finished eating in the evening, then walked to his girlfriend's place. When it was dark, he would find himself right in the middle of his girlfriend's place. He went to the other young people, and they showed him how to *karim lek*.

When he walked along the trail, something always happened to him. He went directly to a puddle where a frog called, "Buu, buu, buu" to him. Every time that he went to this place, the frog would call out.

One time, the man thought, "I think that the frog watches me. When I go to that place, the frog calls me."

It was evening again, so the boy went walking because he wanted to *karim lek*. He arrived at the place, and the frog began to call again. The boy stopped and said, "Every time I come here, you're calling me. If you're a man or woman, then come with me."

The frog listened to what the boy said and jumped towards him. The boy did not wait. He held the frog and carried it with him. After he finished *karim lek*, he returned to his house with the frog. He put the frog in a corner of the house.

After a while, it was time for a big festival at his girlfriend's village. His grandmother dressed him finely. Afterwards, the boy checked on the frog. He looked and the frog was not there... only its skin was there. The boy took the skin and threw it in the fire.

The frog turned into a very beautiful young woman who sang and danced with the other women [at the festival]. The boy went to the festival. The festival lasted until dawn. At the festival, the beautiful woman kept by the boy's side.

It was light now and the boy walked back towards his house. As he walked back, he thought hard about the woman who had sung and danced at the festival with him on the previous night. He had never seen her before.

This beautiful woman left the festival before it became light. She went back to the boy's house and began to look for her skin. She searched and searched, but the poor woman could not find her skin, so she just sat down.

The boy came inside the house and saw the woman sitting there. Oh my, he quivered. He asked her, "Where did you come from?" The woman replied, "I was at the festival and I came here."

The boy truly lusted for her. He told his grandmother that he wanted to marry this beautiful woman. His grandmother agreed.

He prepared things to pay the woman's clan [bride price]. The boy asked the woman, "Who's in your clan?"

The woman replied, "I have no parents and I have no clan either."

The boy now knew. He thought to himself that it was just the frog that had turned into a woman. He was very happy but he did not tell his clan. No, they just lived together and married. They had a big feast with much singing and dancing for their marriage.

Francis Ben
S. T. C. [Steamships Trading Company]
Port Moresby
National Capital District

B655+. Marriage to frog in human form; D395W. Transformation: frog to woman; D531+. Transformation by removing skin; D793.2. Disenchantment made permanent by burning cast-off skin; P210. Husband and wife; P292.1. Grandmother as foster mother; P600+. Courtship customs: *karim lek*; T10. Falling in love; T50. Wooing; T52. Bride purchased; T100. Marriage


## A Village Obtained Singing and Dancing

(Wantok 334, September 27, 1980, page 19)

In my home, **Ali** Island in **West Sepik** Province, the people once did not have singing or dancing [**Ali** People]. However, one woman brought song and dance to us, and now we have singing and dancing. This is the story of the woman who brought singing and dancing to my island.

One time, long, long ago, there was a woman on my island who married a man from another place. This woman lived with her husband for a while and became pregnant.

One time, late at night, she felt that she was about to give birth. She got up, woke her husband and said, "Come, let's go to the beach. I feel like I'm about to give birth."

However, her husband said, "Ah, go by yourself. I want to sleep." So, he fell asleep again and the poor woman walked by herself down to the beach.

The poor woman looked for a place to give birth. She searched and searched, then she saw a big tree with a big hole in it. So, she went inside the hole and gave birth.

After she gave birth, she let the baby sleep and she went outside to gather leaves to make a bed for themselves. After she gathered the leaves, she returned and made a bed. The two females sat there and heard *masalai*s singing and approaching them. The woman's skin quivered and she quietly told her baby, "Oh, sorry my baby. The *masalai*s are singing and coming now."

She said, "I don't know if they're coming nicely or if they're coming to kill us. It's all right, we'll just stay and watch. If they come to look at us, that's all right. If they come to kill us, that's all right too."

The *masalai*s sang and went around the base of the tree. One of them called out, "Woman in the hole, don't be afraid. We are *masalai*s from your homeland."

A *masalai* also told her, "We came to congratulate you for your new baby. Also, we want you to take these songs and dances and teach them to our clan in the village."

The *masalai* finished speaking, they taught her well a song and dance. After they began the first song and dance, the woman broke a tree leaf and performed the first song and dance.

They finished, then began the second song and dance. The woman broke two tree leaves and marked this as the second song and dance. She did like this to mark all of the songs and dances. Dawn arrived and the *masalai*s returned to their home.

The woman got up and carried her baby back to her husband. When she returned, she told her husband about what the *masalai*s had done in the night. The man was happy and said, "Show all of us this place that you sang and danced."

However, the woman replied, "At night, I called you but you didn't want to come with me. Now I'll take the songs and dances, and only teach them to my clan."

The woman left her husband and returned to her home. She arrived there and taught the people these songs and dances. After she finished, she took her child back to her husband's village.

She lived there a little while and then died, but my clan has obtained the songs and dances. If she had not come to teach my clan these songs and dances, we would not have had them.

Steven J. Jarvis
Catholic Mission Ali
Ali Island, Aitape
West Sepik Province

A1464.2.1. Origin of particular song; A1542.2. Origin of particular dance; F261. Fairies dance; F262.1. Fairies sing; F490+. Masalai; P210. Husband and wife; P232. Mother and daughter; Q280. Unkindness punished; T570. Pregnancy; T581.3. Child born in tree; T581.9. Child born on beach


## How a Pond Came to Wangkatubure

(Wantok 335, October 4, 1980, page 23)

Long, long ago, in a village named **Itnera** in the Erap area of **Morobe** Province, there were few people. One woman from this village went to marry a man from the sword-grass lands.

The woman's brother often brought fruits and thatch shingles made from palm leaves to give to his in-laws and to his sister in the grasslands. When he went to this place in the grasslands, he would go along a trail that crossed the deep forest.

There were some short people who lived in this deep forest. This group of people never grew tall. No, they stayed as they were.

When the man arrived at this place, he asked them, "Boys, where have your parents gone? Are you just boys here?"

The people replied, "They went to the gardens." He went by this place many times, and he often asked them this question. He did not know that they were adults. No, he did not know this.

He asked them again and again, so they became angry and said, "We aren't boys. We're adults." However, the tall man always asked this question and humiliated [them]. So, the short people looked for a way to kill this man.

One time, he came again and asked them the same question. Afterwards, they asked him, "What time will you return?" He folded all of the fingers on his two hands, indicating ten days. [This is a common method of indicating the number ten in PNG (Murphy, 1985: 34).]

He went to the place in the grasslands while the short people made preparations. They counted the days, and the day of his return approached. They dug a huge hole that went very deep. After that, they killed pigs, cassowaries and various kinds of wild game, and prepared a big feast.

On the tenth day, the man was coming. The short men took a big piece of bark and covered the hole. After that they sat around the bark and kept it taut like a stretcher. Some of the others arranged food in the middle and called out to the man to come and sit and eat.

He sat and ate his fill of all of the foods. The people helped him [eat] too. They ate and ate, then they started to speak in their own language [which was unintelligible to the tall man]. They all got up at the same time and the bark brought the man down into the hole.

Inside the hole, there was firewood already prepared. They burned the man and butchered him, then divided him up to eat. One poor old woman was given the head of this man.

The old woman did not eat it. She just left it. On the next morning, they went to fetch water. But no, they saw that the water was dirty. A big flood had come and covered up the short people.

Only the poor old woman had escaped to the grasslands. She told everyone that the short people had killed their in-law. After she told them this, she turned into a pond.

The short people that were covered in water also turned into a pond. Now, these two ponds are still there. We call the pond up in the forest, Wangkatubure. We call the pond down below, Yaronge.

Fury Tuguram
Finogam [Finungwa] Village
Erap
Morobe Province

A920.1.0.1. Origin of particular lake; A1011. Local deluges; A1018. Flood as punishment; D283.1W. Transformation: woman to pool of water; F535.6. Kingdom of pygmies; G11.1. Cannibal dwarfs; K735.1. Mats over holes as pitfall; P210. Husband and wife; P253. Sister and brother; P260. Relations by law; Q215. Cannibalism punished; Q326. Impudence punished; Q429.1. Punishment: culprit eaten by cannibals; S112. Burning to death; T100. Marriage

## The Boulder Covered People Up
(Wantok 336, October 11, 1980, page 19)

This story comes from a village named **Weleki** [**Weleki** People, **Morobe** Province]. This is a place on Finschhafen Peninsula. Long ago, there were many men and women in this place.

They lived there and did various kinds of bad things. One time, all of the women and children went down to the beach. They wanted to catch fish, clams and things in the sea.

They went there and put their net bags and things at the base of a boulder. The women arranged a place to sleep. After that, they went around the beach, then returned to eat and sleep.

Dawn arrived, then they ate and went to the sea to catch fish, clams and other things. They left an old woman. This old woman had not slept with them.

She had slept at a place fairly far from where the others had slept. All of the others slept right at the base of this boulder. While she was sitting in the sun, she saw the boulder expand and become huge.

It kept expanding, then fell and covered everyone's things. After it fell and covered the things, it went directly back to where it had been standing before. The old woman saw this and went a little ways away. She sat and waited for everyone to come.

It was nearly dark and everyone returned. The old woman told them not to sleep at the base of the boulder. They told the old woman that she was lying and said many bad things to her.

They cooked some food that they had taken from the sea and ate happily. That night, they slept. When it was very late, the boulder expanded and became huge.

After it enlarged, it fell down and covered all of the men, women and children. They were surprised and tried to find a way out. They searched and searched, but there was no way out.

The poor people were trapped there and died under the boulder. Only one girl had heeded the old woman. She was afraid, so she had not slept with the others. She had gone to sleep with the old woman.

In the morning, they saw that the boulder had fallen and covered everyone. They were very saddened and cried. They stayed there and then went home.

They lived there and the girl grew up. A man from another place came and married her. They had children and their children married and had more children. But in this village now, there are not many people.

This boulder is still there. The name of this boulder is Bobondi, near Wasu, in the Finschhafen District of Morobe Province.

Vathort Wama
Finschhafen
Morobe Province

A1617. Origin of place-name; D931. Magic rock (stone); F802. Growing rocks; J652. Inattention to warnings; M341. Death prophesied; P210. Husband and wife; P230. Parents and children; P272. Foster mother; P275+. Foster daughter; T100. Marriage


## The Man Who Conquered a Snake

(Wantok 337, October 18, 1980, page 19)

Long, long ago in Gievi [**Gueibi**] Village, in the Bundi area in **Madang** Province, there were two brothers [**Gende People**]. The name of the first brother was Konaria, and name of the second was Muranaba.

They lived there a while. Once when the pandanus fruits (*marita*) were ripe, the second brother, Muranaba, wanted to go hunt wild game and to gather pandanus fruits. He took his bow and arrows then called his dog, and they walked into the forest.

Muranaba and his dog hunted and hunted, but did not find any game. The man was very angry, so he decided to turn and go back home. While they were walking back, they found a marsupial (*kapul*).

They killed the marsupial and brought it back. Muranaba arrived at the place where two clumps of bamboos grew together, making a good path to walk under. He walked through it, but he did not know that a big bad thing was lying on top and looking at him.

It was a big, evil snake. It smelled the marsupial and quietly came down. It came closer, then leapt and wrapped itself around Muranaba's body.

Muranaba was a real man of the forest, and he clearly knew how to get out of the way of various enemies. So, he very quickly broke a big piece of bamboo and held it near his right hand.

The snake completely encircled the poor man. The snake squeezed its tail end tighter and the big piece of bamboo broke. The snake squeezed its middle tighter, and the middle of the bamboo broke. The snake squeezed itself tighter near the man's shoulders, and the bamboo near the man's shoulders broke.

Muranaba had tricked this snake. He just stood there quietly, not making a noise. The snake thought that the man had died. So it slowly began to loosen its grip.

The snake let go of the man. Then the snake lay there waiting to see if the man was really dead. Muranaba did not move or make a sound. None. The snake slowly returned and smelled the man's nose.

This man was a real man of the forest, and he knew what he was doing. So he held his breath and just lay there quietly. The snake thought that the man was completely dead.

The snake left him there. It went to drink water and find something to make its mouth slippery. When the snake sped towards the stream, Muranaba got up, cut a sapling and sharpened it so that it was as sharp as a spear.

After he sharpened the wood, he brought his marsupial up a tree. The snake returned with its mouth moistened. Its mouth was packed with the things that it used for lubrication, which fell out when it came to eat the man.

The snake came and saw that the man was not there. It smelled the man up the tree and it looked up.

Muranaba was just quietly waiting. When the snake raised its head, Muranaba threw the sharp stick directly at the snake's head. Then he came down and began to fight with the snake.

The point of the stick had impaled the snake and the man finished the snake off. The snake was dead and the man sat, resting a little. He had fought with the snake and he was exhausted.

After Muranaba got his wind back, he followed the trail back to the village. He told the men to come and cut its skin and to use the skin on hand drums.

Francis Yoga
Bundi
Madang Province

B11.11+. Fight with giant snake; B875.1. Giant serpent; K1860. Deception by feigned death (sleep); P251.5. Two brothers

## The Highlands Did Not Have Salt

(Wantok 338, October 25, 1980, page 23)

In the time of yore, there was an old woman and her young son. One time, the boy told his mother that they should make a new garden. The mother agreed and they decided that they would make a new garden on the next day.

The next day, they woke up and went to make the garden near a stream. They cut the underbrush to dry, then they returned to burn it. After they burned the underbrush, they prepared the earth to plant food.

They gathered the food plants and prepared them to be planted on the next day. The next day, the boy took the taro and banana plants and planted them. The mother took the edible greens, bean plants, and sweet potatoes and planted them.

While the mother was planting, she left her net bag and "grass" skirt on top of a tree branch. They planted the food plants until the afternoon when a heavy rain came down. They forgot the net bag and raced back to the house.

Later, after the rain stopped that evening, the mother wanted to return and dig up some sweet potatoes from the garden. She went and dug some sweet potatoes, then remembered her net bag. She told her son to stay while she went back to the new garden to get her net bag and skirt.

The mother ran and found the place where she had put the bag and skirt. But they were not there. She looked near where they had been planting. She trembled and almost fell down dead.

The woman looked and saw a huge lake where they had been planting. She was terrified and wanted to run back to the house. But when she was about to run, she heard a man calling her name.

The poor old woman looked back and shook terribly. She saw an old man standing and holding some kind of package. The old woman looked at him and the man waved his hand for her to come.

The old man said, "Don't be afraid. Come." So, the woman came and the man put out his hand, giving her the package that he was holding.

The woman was afraid and did not take it quickly. She stood and just looked. The man gave it to her. He said, "Don't be afraid. Take this package and bring it to your son. You must tell him not to open it. He must kill a white pig first, then he can open the package."

The old woman took the package and ran quickly back to her house. She gave the package to her son. After she gave it to him, she told him what the man had said.

The boy said, "Ah, I think you're lying and that you were whoring with an old man, weren't you?" The boy did not wait. He just opened the package. Inside the package were various kinds of shells from the reef and the beach.

So, what this story says is that if the boy had not opened the package, the Highlands would have cowry shells and other kinds of shell wealth. He opened it and so now the lake does not have these kinds of shells in it.

The lake is still there. I have seen it with my own eyes. In the area of the lake, there are bananas, taros, and other foods. However, a man had not planted these. These are from when the old woman and her son had planted them.

Lukas Kela
Mt. Hagen
**Western Highlands** Province
[Lukas Kela also wrote the ancestor story in *Wantok* #344. He is from Keltiga (**Kutiga**) Village. The story in *Wantok* #344 takes place in **Wurup** Village, so he is probably from the **Hagen** People.]

A920.1.0.1. Origin of particular lake; A1433.3+. Why there is no local source of shell money: broken promise; D2136.4+. Lake magically appears; P231. Mother and son; Q266. Punishment for breaking promise; Q325. Disobedience punished; Q595.4. Loss of money as punishment; W126. Disobedience

## Taro Created Two Mountains

(Wantok 339, November 1, 1980, page 19)

In the time of yore, there was a brother and his sister who lived in **Muli** Village, near Ialibu in **Southern Highlands** Province [**Kewa** People]. They husbanded a pig that lived with them. In their village, Muli, they also had a huge garden.

The woman was not like other women of the Highlands. She did not make raised mounds for planting sweet potatoes, nor did she plant other foods. No, only her brother worked in the garden and he planted all of the foods.

His sister just sat in the house. She stayed in the house and made arm and leg bands, "grass" skirts and net bags. She also took care of their pig. She sat and did these things, leaving all of the other garden work for her brother's hands.

The brother said, "This sister of mine just sits in the house, and I don't see her doing a thing. What does she really do in the house?" Then he thought, "It would be better if I found out what my sister does."

So the next day, when the boy went to the garden, he just pretended to go, hiding instead. He watched his sister. His sister began to make a net bag, then she put it on and made a "grass" skirt. After she finished that, she worked on making an armband.

After she finished that, she took a new net bag and carried it down to the river. She sat on top of a boulder and made a new net bag for herself. Before long, her brother heard a big splashing in the river.

A big fish came out and drank from his sister's breasts. In the evening, she returned to the house. Her brother also returned to the house. He came and talked to his sister, "I'm tired of working in the garden. It would be better if tomorrow you worked in the garden."

So the next day, the sister went to work in the garden. The brother went to the river and sat. He waited there and the fish came out of the water. The boy let the fish find his breasts.

The fish found that there was no milk, so the boy killed it right away. He carried the fish and cooked it in an earth oven by the house. In the evening, the sister returned and the uncovered the earth oven. When the sister saw her child, she cried terribly.

The sister was very troubled. She got up and took all of their things and went to the **Erave** area. Only the boy and the pig stayed there. They lived there for a while and the boy became worried about his sister. One time he cried in sorrow for her.

He woke up in the morning and killed his pig. He cooked it well in an earth oven, filled a big net bag and brought it to take care of his sister. He walked and walked, then finally he found his sister.

The sister saw him and they were very sad. They cried and cried. After they finished crying, the sister told him, "My husband is a *masalai*. You must be careful. It is nearly time for him to return."

Before long, the *masalai* man returned. He smelled the boy and salivated profusely. But the woman said, "That's my brother." The *masalai* man pretended to be very happy.

The sister told her brother, "Very late at night, you must look out. I think that he'll eat you."

So, the boy slept with his knife. In the dead of night, the *masalai* man came. The boy woke up and they fought. They fought until dawn and continued on until dark again. A little bird told the boy, "Cut the sapling that is near you."

When the boy cut it, the *masalai* man fell down dead. Then the sister came and told him to take a big taro that was near the house, and to take it to their village. The sister told the brother, "Carry it with you and when you are hungry, cook and eat it."

The boy carried it towards his home. At Kendeal [**Kendagl**] Village, he felt hungry [**Hagen** People, **Western Highlands** Province]. He sat and cooked the taro, but the taro fell back down on the ground. The taro made the boy angry and the two of them fought.

They fought for five whole months. The boy called out to his maternal relative who came and cut the taro into two pieces. When the taro broke, the blood flowed like a torrent.

These two pieces of taro became Mount Ialibu and Mount Gilua [Giluwe]. Today, in the place where they had fought, there are no trees or grasses. The ground is soft. The blood of the taro became two lakes. The names of these lakes are Buna and Walumi.

B. Ane Kalunda
Muli Village
Ialibu
Southern Highlands Province

A920.1.0.1. Origin of particular lake; A960. Creation of mountains (hills); B211.3. Speaking bird; B450. Helpful birds; B874+. Giant fish, child of woman; D451.9+. Transformation: taro to mountain; D451.9+. Transformation: taro juice to lake; D983.2+. Fight with magic taro; D1402.1. Magic plant kills; E765.3.3. Life bound up with tree; F490+. Masalai; G512. Ogre killed; P210. Husband and wife; P230. Parents and children; P253. Sister and brother; P263. Brother-in-law; P290+. Maternal kin; S110. Murders; T111. Marriage of mortal and supernatural being


# The Old *Masalai* Woman
(Wantok 340, November 8, 1980, page 19)

Long, long ago, the people in a village gathered their pigs for a feast. After the pigs were assembled, they slaughtered them and cooked them well in earth ovens.

They uncovered the earth ovens and divided the food among the men, women and children. The children received their food and went down to the stream. This was the children's custom.  They bathed and ate their meat together.

The children were very happy as the bathed and played.  While they were bathing, an old blind woman came towards where they were bathing.  She arrived there and told them, "If you fill up my net bag, I'll carry you around."

This was music to the children's ears.  They wanted to get inside the net bag so that the old woman would carry them around.  They did not wait.  They filled her net bag up, and she carried them to her home that was in a cave.

The old *masalai* woman's belly was very happy.  She had found some meat.  She worked very quickly at getting to her home.

When she arrived, she called some magic words, and the hole in the stone opened.  When the door opened, she carried the children inside.  After she went in, she put the children down and told them, "Stay here.  I'm going to the garden to get some food for us."

The old *masalai* woman spoke some magic words and the door [opened].  She went out and the door closed again.  The children came out of the net bag and began talking.  One said, "I think that the old woman has tricked us.  She's getting edible greens and is coming to eat us."

All of the other children listened to this and were terrified.  The poor children wanted to go out, but they did not know how to open the door.  One little boy had heard the *masalai* woman's magic words and still remembered them.

He got up and spoke them, then the door opened.  Oh my, were they happy.  They sped back to the village and told their parents what had happened to them.  All of the children's fathers decided to come and kill this old *masalai* woman.

They took their bows and arrows, went into the forest, and waited for the *masalai* woman.  The *masalai* woman had gotten the food from the garden, and was singing happily as she returned.  She said, "Oh sorry, my little pieces of meat will fill up my belly.  I'll sleep well tonight."

The men heard this and they knew that it was a *masalai* woman.  She was singing loudly and did not know that the men were lying in wait to finish her off.  The poor *masalai* woman came, then the men fought her and shot her with arrows.

The old woman did not have an escape.  She just stood there and the men completely pulverized her.  She stood and turned into a boulder.  Then the boulder broke into pieces and fell about.  So today, we see many stones scattered about on this side of the mountain.

Waikisa Emos
Mainyanda D. T. P. School
**Aseki** Village [**Hamtai** People]
**Morobe** Province

A974. Rocks from transformation of people to stone; A977. Origin of particular stones or groups of stones; D231W. Transformation: woman to stone; D1552.2. Mountain opens to magic formula (Open Sesame); D1774. Magic results from speaking; F490+. Masalai; G370+. Blind ogre; G422. Ogre imprisons victim; G441. Ogre carries victim in bag (basket); G512.1+. Ogre killed with spear/arrow; K711. Deception into entering bag; K914. Murder from ambush; P230. Parents and children; R11. Abduction by monster (ogre); R45.3. Captivity in cave; R210. Escapes; R260. Pursuits; S110. Murders

## The Trick at Yassa Village
(Wantok 341, November 15, 1980, page 19)

One time, long ago, there was a man who lived in a village on Manam Island in Madang Province.  The man did not have a family.  He lived alone.

This man's name was Kongoroki.  He was very lazy.  He never worked in the garden or hunted for wild game.  No, he just lived there and stole from the other men and from their gardens.

This man also sometimes turned into something like a pig and ate in the others' gardens.  When he saw the other men coming, he quickly turned into a stone again.  He was truly a trickster.

One time he was stealing food in a garden, and he noticed that he did not have a plate or anything to put his food on.  So he went to the village, emptied some clay pots, and took some wooden plates and some spoons made of coconut shell.

Kongoroki often stole like this.  He was able to get everything.  The food did not say anything.  One time when he was hungry, he just went to the men's garden and stole something that he wanted.  The people noticed this; they had lost many things by now.

So one time, the people decided to catch this thief.  All of the men and women hid in their gardens, trying to see this thief.  They waited while the thief slept and slept until he was dying of hunger.

Kongoroki woke up.  He wanted to go to a woman's garden.  He had seen ripe bananas there the on the previous day. He went directly to the garden. When he arrived, he wanted to break off a bunch of bananas and take it to eat.

The people were watching their gardens. This woman had come to watch her garden too. When she saw this man about to steal, she shouted very loudly.

When the woman called out, all of the other people in the area came running. They came and tried to hold this Kongoroki, but they were unable to do so. The man had already sped off. While he ran, the men chased him.

They ran and ran, and the thief ran completely out of breath. He went directly into a hole that a pig had made, but the hole was not very deep. When he ran into it, he turned into a pig, and sat in the hole.

The people came and put their axes, knives, and spears into the back of this pig. They stabbed and stabbed, then they watched the blood run. After a little while, the blood stopped running. The knives were broken and the axes were scattered about. The spears were broken, bent and scattered about.

This man had turned into a stone. The people were very angry with him. But what could they do now? There was nothing to do, so they left him and went back to the village.

This stone is still there, at Mount Yassa near **Yassa** Village on **Manam** Island in **Madang** Province [**Manam** People]. This stone is named Kazi and is still there.

Francis P. Saku
Manam Island
via Bogia
Madang Province

A974. Rocks from transformation of people to stone; A977.5. Origin of particular rock; D114.3.2M. Transformation: man to boar; D422.3.2K. Transformation: pig to stone; D642.7. Transformation to elude pursuers; J1110. Clever persons; K420. Thief loses his goods or is detected; Q212. Theft punished; R260. Pursuits; W111. Laziness

## The Old Woman with the Torch

(Wantok 342, November 22, 1980, page 19)

Not long ago, about fifteen years ago, there was an old woman who lived near **Gembogl** sub-Province [**Kuman** People?, **Simbu** Province]. One day, the old woman brought food to the men at the men's house. When she gave the food to the men, she listened to the men's story about the time when a great darkness came.

The old woman's pigsty was not nearby, about one or two miles away from the men's house. The old woman quickly thought, "It would be bad if I listen to the men's story and the pigs break their tethers, ruining my house."

The old woman wanted to leave the men's house, but not one of the men wanted to bring her back to her house. They had eaten the food, so they were bloated and just wanted to sleep. Also, these men did not have torches.

However, the old woman's son had a new torch (or flashlight). A man showed the old woman how to shut off the flashlight when she brought it to her house. Along the trail, the old woman thought about shutting off the flashlight, but she became confused.

When she arrived at the house, she did not remember how to turn off the light, so she sat and thought about what to do with the flashlight. Her son had put new batteries into the flashlight, so the light was still bright. When the old woman put the flashlight in the house, she saw that the light just went in one direction.

The old woman thought, "If the light burns the house, it will burn me with the pigs." The old woman tried to talk to the flashlight to turn it off, but the flashlight was not a man. The old woman asked the flashlight if it was hungry, but it was not. The light kept shining. The old woman moved the flashlight to another place, but it kept shining. The flashlight had the old woman on the verge of tears.

A thought came to her head. The thought was that she should close the "eye" of the flashlight so that it could no longer look out and burn the house. The woman took the cloths, towels, blankets, and breadfruit tree leaves, then covered the flashlight. She kept covering up the flashlight, then put [the whole bundle] into an [empty] copra bag. She put the bag outside her house and she went to sleep. In the early morning, the old woman woke up and looked outside the house. The bag was still there.

Right away, she untied the pigs' tethers and chased them out to forage. The old woman took the bag to the men's house. The men saw the old woman coming with this bag and they thought that it was a huge bundle of more food that she was bringing. When the old woman stood at the front of the door of the men's house, she said, "It was good that you gave me that 'man,' but it nearly burned down my house and my pigs. So, I covered his eye so that he could no longer see or make trouble."

The men were very surprised that the old woman had covered the flashlight. She had not just covered it a little bit, either. Then many of the men began to laugh. Some men removed the coverings from the flashlight. When they got the flashlight, the batteries were dead.

This was the first time that the poor old woman had seen a flashlight.  Later, the old woman's child taught her how to use one if she ever used one in the future.

Jerry Martin
Upper Simbu
Gembogl
[Simbu Province]

F965. Premature darkness; J1806+. Flashlight mistaken for torch; J1880+. Flashlight spoken to as if human; P231. Mother and son

## The Young Brother Killed Bibeo

(Wantok 343, November 29, 1980, page 19)

Long, long ago, there were three brothers, Mekuri, the eldest, Tufuve, the second eldest, and Vegagofa, the youngest.  The three brothers left their big village and went to live very far away on a big mountain.  This is because the three were afraid of a ghost woman.

This ghost woman was named Bibeo.  Every time that she came down to the big village, she would kill a man or woman and eat them if she was hungry.  So the three brothers were afraid and made a little camp on the big mountain, far from the big village.

They lived there and thought of things to kill this ghost woman.  One afternoon, the big brother, Mekuri took his bow and arrows and went to hunt for wild game in the forest.  He said that if the ghost woman Bibeo met him, he would knock her off.

Mekuri went into the deep forest.  The ghost woman Bibeo smelled him and came to ambush him.  Mekuri did not know this.  He saw a huge bird sitting on top of a tree branch.

He aimed and hit the bird right in the breast.  The arrow brought the bird straight down to Bibeo's hand.  The ghost woman took the bird and just ate it.

Bibeo wanted to trick Mekuri, so she turned into a very beautiful young woman and sat awkwardly [seductively?].  Mekuri came and saw her, and he trembled.  Mekuri asked her, "Sister, did you see the game that I shot?"

Bibeo said, "I ate it.  Whenever I try to hunt wild game, the animals run away from me.  Can you kill one for me?"

The ghost woman said, "There is a marsupial (*kapul*) on that tree.  I'll go up there and shake it and make it fall, then you kill it.  However, you must draw your bow back and watch as it falls to the ground."

Mekuri listened to this and drew his bow back, just watching the ground.  Bibeo went up the tree and quickly took the axe that she used to kill people.  She threw the axe down and split open Mekuri's head.

Bibeo was ecstatic.  She came down and carried the man off to eat.  The two brothers were waiting and waiting.  For three days and three nights, their brother did not return.  One evening, Tufuve wanted to go to the forest to hunt for game and also to try to find his brother.

He took his bow and arrows, then departed.  Immediately, the ghost woman Bibeo smelled him.  She again turned into a very beautiful young woman and came to ambush him.

Tufuve also killed an animal and the animal fell right by Bibeo.  So, the ghost woman took the animal and ate it.  The second brother came and met this beautiful young woman who was sitting down.  He trembled too.

He asked Bibeo about his animal.  The woman said the same thing that she had told his big brother.  Tufuve did not understand what was going on, so Bibeo tricked and killed him.  Then she carried him off to eat.

The young brother Vegagofa waited and waited for three nights.  Then he took his bow and arrows, and went to hunt for game.  No, he wanted to find his two brothers and this ghost woman Bibeo.

He walked and walked into the forest.  The ghost woman knew that a man was coming, so she went and waited for him.  Vegagofa arrived and saw a bird.  He shot the bird and it fell right by the ghost woman.

Bibeo took it and ate it.  Vegagofa went and met the beautiful young woman in the deep forest, and his skin jumped.  He knew that it was just the ghost woman.

Bibeo said the same thing that she had said before to his two brothers.  However, Vegagofa replied, "We always look right at the animal when we want to shoot it."

The ghost woman was afraid now.  She knew that this man was not like the other men before.  He had replied and it looked as if he knew the ghost woman's trick.

Vegagofa had replied to her, but he had a plan.  He took his best arrow and looked down.  The ghost woman began to climb the tree, then she shook the animal and it fell.

The man put his eyes to the ground, but he also kept an eye on the ghost woman.  He saw the ghost woman ascend and he saw her throw the axe at his neck.

When Vegegofa [Vegagofa] saw the axe come down, he jumped very quickly and the axe missed him.  He got up and shot the arrow at the ghost woman Bibeo's back.  The ghost woman felt the pain.  She bared two fangs and fire shot out from her.

Bibeo came down and Vegagofa shot all of the spears that he had. The poor ghost woman fell down with all of the spears in her back. She fell to the ground and died.

Vegagofa cut off the ghost woman's head and carried it to the big village. The people saw this and were ecstatic. They took the head and buried it in the middle of the village.

Nickie V. Susuve
June Valley
Port Moresby
National Capital District

B872. Giant bird; E425.1. Revenant as woman; E440+. Ghost laid by spear/arrow; E421.3+. Fire shoots from ghost; G11.10. Cannibalistic spirits; G346. Devastating monster; G510.4+. Hero overcomes devastating ogre; G512.1+. Ogre killed with spear/arrow; K917. Treacherous murder during hunt; P251.3.1. Brothers strive to avenge each other; P251.6.1. Three brothers; Q211. Murder punished; Q411. Death as punishment; S139.2.1.1. Head of murdered man taken along as trophy; S139.4. Murder by mangling with axe; V61.3+. Dead buried

## The Two Women Who Became Mountains

(Wantok 344, December 6, 1980, page 19)

Once there were two women who lived near **Wurup** Village in the Hage [Hagen] area [**Hagen** People, **Western Highlands** Province]. The names of these women were Mekal and Tekal. These women were very beautiful and smart.

Many men from all parts of the Hagen area came and courted (*tanim het*) with them. One time, the men came at six o'clock in the evening and *tanim het* with them until six o'clock in the morning.

The men got up and went back to their houses. The two women slept soundly. They slept and slept until ten o'clock in the morning, then woke up.

Tekal got up and told Mekal that they should go bathe and then cut some vines to make net bags for themselves. Mekal got up and they went down a stream in the deep forest.

After they bathed, they began to cut the vines. They cut many, many vines. They felt cold, so they went to a place in the sun and sat on two stones. They sat there and made their net bags from the vines that they had cut.

Tekal and Mekal told each other good stories. They stayed there until three o'clock in the afternoon. Mekal said, "Let's go." So, they decided to get up and go back to the village.

The young women wanted to stand, but they were stuck. Mekal looked at Tekal and Tekal looked at Mekal. Their buttocks were both stuck to the stone.

The poor women tried very hard to stand, but they were unable to do so. They cried and cried, but the village was far and no one could hear them. They had no way out, so they just stayed there.

At night, it rained very heavily and they became completely drenched. They stayed there for four whole days. They had no food. They were famished and they ate the vines that they had cut.

After the vines were gone, they ate their "grass" skirts. After that, they ate their net bags. After they had eaten everything they had, they ate the grasses that were near them.

Oh my, now they had finished all of the grasses. They had nothing to eat. The women died. They died and their bodies rotted. Grasses sand trees grew on top of them.

After a while, they became two big mountains. These two mountains are still there. So now when it rains, we often watch these two mountains rise. When there is a drought, they sink.

Lukas Kela
Keltiga [**Kutiga**] Village
Mt. Hagen
Western Highlands Province

[See the ancestor stories in *Wantok* #149 and 990 for similar stories. The one in #990 is also from Wurup.]

A960. Creation of mountains (hills); E649.1+. Reincarnation as mountain; D931. Magic rock (stone); D2171. Magic adhesion; P600+. Courtship customs: *tanim het*; T50. Wooing

## How Eagles Obtained Their White Necks

(Wantok 345, December 13, 1980, page 19)

Long, long ago, there were two brothers who were married and lived in their village. However, the brothers' marriages were not very good because the big brother lusted after the little brother's wife. The little brother did not know that the big brother lusted after his wife. No.

One time, the big brother told his little brother, "Come, let's travel and hunt for wild game in the forest." So, they hunted for game until the evening, but they had not found any yet.

After a while, the brothers saw a white marsupial (*kapul*) [the spotted cuscus, *Spilocuscus maculatus maculatus* (Flannery, 1995a: 181-182)] sitting on a *galip* tree branch. The big brother watched and told his little brother, "Climb the *galip* tree, then kill that white marsupial."

The little brother listened to what the big brother said, but he did not want to climb the tree. He tried to find a place to climb the tree, but the base of the tree was too big. So, he grabbed a vine and followed it upwards.

He climbed it, then his big brother cut the vine that he was using to climb the tree. The poor little brother saw this and he cried. He was very worried.

The poor brother was famished, so he ate the flesh of the ripe *galip* nuts. Later, he killed the marsupial and removed its guts. He tied the skin to a branch of the *galip* tree and he ate the meat.

The boy was entirely alone now. There was no way down. He saw a bird come and perch. It looked at the white marsupial skin.

The bird looked desirously at the skin for a while, then it spoke to the boy, "Please, I want that white marsupial skin." However, the boy said, "No." They spoke like this for a while, then the boy had an idea.

The boy told the bird, "Friend, if you help me, I can give you that white marsupial skin." The bird said, "How do you want me to help you?" The boy said, "I want you to help me get down from this big tree."

The bird alit and said, "OK, stay there. I'll go and call all my brothers and sisters, then we'll come to help you." The bird flew away and called out to all of the big and little birds, saying, "I saw something nice on a *galip* tree branch. If we help a boy, he'll give us this nice thing."

After the bird said this, all of the other birds followed it and flew to the *galip* tree. They arrived and asked the boy, "Do you want us to help you?"

The boy said, "Go down to the river and get a big shiny stone, then bring it here." All of the birds flew down, took a bright stone and brought it to the boy. Then he spoke to them again, "I'll sit on [the stone] and you carry me to my village."

Each of the birds carried a side of the boy, who was sitting [on the stone], and they flew away. They put the boy directly at his house. They wanted to fly away then, and the boy called for them to wait. He wanted to make a party for all of the birds.

The boy told everyone to go to their gardens and to get sweet potatoes, taros, edible greens, and other kinds of foods, then to bring them to make a party for the birds. They got these and brought them, making a big feast.

All of the birds ate and were very happy. Afterwards, the boy gave the marsupial skin to the birds and they carried it away. Only two birds did not have a piece of skin, and they were very troubled and angry. These two birds went to the garden, took some fresh ashes from a fire, and they rubbed themselves with the ashes.

All of the other birds put the white marsupial skin on their necks and flew away happily. So now, we can see the white markings on the necks of eagles, and the necks of other birds are just black.

The stone that the birds used to carry the boy is still there in Nokori [**Nungori**] Village, near the area of the Sassoya [Sassoia] Catholic Mission, in the Wewak Area, **East Sepik** Province [**Boiken** People].

Arnold Wafi

Arawa

North Solomons Province

[Mr. Wafi also wrote the ancestor story in *Wantok* #653. This story is similar to that one.]

A977.5. Origin of particular rock; A2411.2. Origin of color of bird; A2411.2.2. Origin of color of falconiformes; B211.3. Speaking bird; B450. Helpful birds; B455.3. Helpful eagle; B542.1.1. Eagle carries man to safety; B552. Man carried by bird; D1520.36. Transportation by magic stone; K2211.0.1. Treacherous elder brother(s); P210. Husband and wife; P251.5. Two brothers; P251.5.3. Hostile brothers; P263. Brother-in-law; P264. Sister-in-law; Q53. Reward for rescue; R49.1. Captivity in tree; R51.1. Prisoners starved; R110. Rescue of captive; S73.1.4. Fratricide motivated by love-jealousy; S143.2. Abandonment in tall tree; T92.10. Rival in love killed; W181. Jealousy

## The Smoke Helped the Boy
(Wantok 346, December 20, 1980, page 19)

One time, long, long ago, there were seven brothers who lived in a village. They lived in **Wagri** Village in the Bundi area of **Madang** Province [**Gende** People].

These seven brothers lived together and cut down a big piece of forest. After the cuttings were dry, they planted a big taro garden. After a while, the taro was ready to be harvested.

They each removed their taros, then went to cook and happily eat them. While they were eating, they argued about going to hunt wild game to mix with the taros. The eldest brother thought about going fishing for eels with a net in the Ibrum River.

The eldest brother took the nets, brought them down to the stream, and put them in. He put the nets high in the headwaters where there was a pond.

The name of this pond is Kavaiavo-Kuai. The eldest brother put the last net in and the returned to the house to sleep. The next morning, he would return to check on the nets.

In the morning, the big brother woke up very early to look at the nets. He followed the stream until he came to the last net in the pond. A tree with many fruits was near this place.

The man was about to remove the net when a ripe fruit fell near him. He looked up and saw a very beautiful young woman. Oh my, she was more beautiful than all of the other women were.

He looked at this woman and he left the net where it was. He jumped up quickly and tried to climb the tree that held this woman. However, he slipped and the woman jumped down into the pond, then went inside her house.

The poor man jumped and followed this woman inside the pond. He searched and searched until it was dark, but he could not find this woman. So he returned to his house.

This man had a great stomachache. When he arrived at the house, his brothers gave him food, but he did not want to eat. He slept hungry that night.

The next morning, his six brothers had a very long smoke, but the eldest brother did not want to smoke. The other six brothers argued about getting this woman.

They made a decision to go down to the pond to find her. All seven brothers wanted to go there, but the six elder brothers spoke angrily to the youngest, "You're too little. You can't do anything, so it would be better if you stayed here and took care of the house."

So, the six brothers departed and the youngest brother stayed to watch the house. When they left him, he thought a lot. The poor boy watched and watched the smoke in the ashes of the fire.

The poor boy took the ashes and said, "If I ignite you and you light up, will you help me find this beautiful young woman or not?" When the ashes ignited, the little boy saw a picture of the trail and the beautiful woman's house.

The boy saw that the woman often jumped down into the pond and climbed onto a lily pad in the pond.

After the little brother saw this, he left the ashes and sped down to the pond. All of the other brothers were hiding, so the little brother hid too.

After a while, the woman came, went up the fruit tree, and ate the fruit. The eldest brother very quietly came and tried to grab her, but he slipped again and the woman jumped into the pond.

The woman jumped right into the youngest brother's hands. There was silence. The little boy carried the woman and they went to the house of the seven brothers.

He took her into the house and set her down at the head of the eldest brother's bed. Then he went to his own bed and quietly waited.

All of the brothers came and were very troubled. When they arrived, they went directly to their beds. The eldest brother came and saw this beautiful thing sitting at the head of his bed.

The big brother was ecstatic. He shouted and shouted, and all of the other brothers ran towards him. They came and carried the youngest brother, speaking joyfully because he had helped the eldest brother get this beautiful thing.

John Negi Toma
Kindagovel [**Kindogoveki**] Village
Bundi
Madang Province

D931.1.2. Magic ashes; D1300. Magic object gives supernatural wisdom; L31. Youngest brother helps elder; P210. Husband and wife; P251.6.3+. Seven brothers; T192. Marriage by force

## The Woman Who Came from the Sea

(Wantok 347, December 27, 1980, page 19)

Long, long ago, a young boy finished working in the forest and returned in the afternoon. When he returned, he went to bathe in the sea. After he finished bathing, he sat on the beach.

The afternoon sun was very hot. A gentle wind blew and the boy sat happily. While he sat, he watched a tree drifting in the sea.

The young boy sat watching. The tree was coming ashore right where he was sitting. The sea tossed the tree right onto the beach and he quickly ran down to get it.

It was almost dark, so the boy took the tree and carried it up to the village. When he arrived at his house, he saw his mother cooking food.

His mother saw the tree and said, "Child, you're carrying a tree that I can use as firewood." But the boy said, "Why? I want to make a spear from this tree."

The mother said, "That's alright." So, the boy took the tree and put it away in the cookhouse. The mother doled out the food, then they ate and went to sleep.

While they were sleeping late at night, the young boy heard crying coming from the cookhouse. He got up and went out to look around.

He looked and saw a woman standing there. The boy ran back and woke his parents to come and see this beautiful young woman.

The boy and his father asked the woman, "Where did you come from?" The woman told the father, "Your son just brought me from the beach and carried me here."

Oh my, the young boy's eyes popped open. He felt very happy inside. His father said, "OK, come and sleep in the room."

The woman went with them. She lived with them for a little while, then they made a big party and the two of them married. The young boy married this woman and they lived happily until they died.

If you go to **Nissan** Island, you will see that for some clans it is forbidden for them to eat from the tree that is called _husing_ [**Nehan** People, **North Solomons** Province]. This is just the tree that became the woman.

Anthony Tedi

Nissan Island

Arawa

North Solomons Province

C226. Tabu: eating certain plant; C621. Forbidden tree; D431.2W. Transformation: tree to woman; P210. Husband and wife; P231. Mother and son; P233. Father and son; T100. Marriage

## We Came from the Simbu People

(Wantok 348, December 27, 1980, page 19)

Long, long ago, in a village called **Womkama-Sumbrokai** in **Simbu** Province, there were two brothers and a woman. The names of the brothers were Monde and Gande. The name of the woman was Bomai-Kambia.

One time, there was a big party held by the clans of the tribe. When they sang and danced, they were dressed very finely. The two brothers were also dressed well, but Gande was more finely dressed than his brother and than all of the others were.

Before long, they said, "Gande will become a leader of the village."

The clans of the village sang and danced strongly. They kept going through the afternoon. Gande left his brother and the woman, and walked into the deep forest. There had never been a man who had been to this place before. Never.

When Gande entered the deep forest, he transformed himself and became a boar, then worked at digging the earth and eating insects. In the evening, he had eaten enough. He turned back into a man and walked back to the house.

Monde was waiting and waiting, and his brother had not returned yet. He said, "Oh my, what happened to Gande? He left at noon, and now it's evening and he hasn't returned."

However, when Monde went to look down by the stream, he saw Gande walking slowly home. Gande's belly was distended like a pumpkin.

When Gande came close to Monde, Monde asked him, "You were away for a long time in the forest. What did you do that you did not come back quickly?" Gande said, "I just went walking around."

So, Monde called out to his wife to cook some food and bring it for them to eat. When the woman finished cooking, she brought the food and Gande said that he did not want to eat. His belly was full.

Monde and the woman ate, then they all went to sleep. At night, Monde and the woman heard Gande's belly growling and growling. They thought, "This man's going to die now."

However, he did not die. Gande slept until morning. In the morning, Gande woke up and went back to the forest to find some more food. When he left, the two others followed him to find out what he would do.

They followed him into the deep forest. They saw him turn into a pig and work at digging the earth, searching for food. It was then that the two of them left and want back to the village.

It was almost dark when Gande returned to the house. This time too, he did not want to eat. He just slept. At night, his belly made various kinds of loud noises.

Gande slept and died that night. Monde and the woman were afraid and did not cry for him. They quietly took him and buried him.

On another night, Monde went and kept a mournful vigil, sitting at his brother's grave. He stayed there until daybreak. His eyes hurt and he rubbed his eyes.

After he rubbed his eyes, he saw two huge, white pigs standing there. He quietly ran and called his wife to come capture them and to bring them to the house. They thought and said that they would kill the pigs, then send away their two daughters. Their daughters' names were Geregl and Kuman.

So one day, Monde killed the first pig and sent his daughter Geregl to Geregl [**Gereglkane**] Village on the Bundi side [**Gende** People, **Madang** Province]. Then the other pig was killed and the daughter Kuman was sent to the **Kuman** [People's] side [Simbu Province].

Now we can see that Simbu has many, many people who live in Simbu Province and in all of the other places too.

Aimos Gene
C. M. [Congregation of Mission] Bomai
Simbu Province

[Note: the Gende and Kuman languages are not closely related. They are from separate families (Central and East-Central, respectively) within the same Stock (East New Guinea Highlands), according to Wurm's classification (1975: 468).]

A1611+. Origin of Gende People; A1611+. Origin of Kuman People; D114.3.2M. Transformation: man to boar; D336.1M. Transformation: pig to man; P210. Husband and wife; P232. Mother and daughter; P234. Father and daughter; P251.5. Two brothers; P252.1. Two sisters; P263. Brother-in-law; P264. Sister-in-law; V61.3+. Dead buried

## A Fish Woman Gave Us a Song and Dance

(Wantok 349, January 17, 1981, page 19)

Long, long ago, there was an old man and his wife who lived with their son in a small place deep inside the forest. Their son was a big boy. The three of them were very happy.

Every night, they heard people singing. The three of them tried very hard to find out who it was that was always singing. However try as they might, they could not find this out.

One day, the boy woke up and told his two old folks, "If you wait for me until it gets dark, don't worry. I want to go find out what it is that we hear every night."

The man took his bow and walked off. He went into the deep forest. He walked and walked. When it became dark, he found himself by a river, and he made a hut by the water and went to sleep.

When he was about to fall asleep, the fish came up from the water and began to sing. Oh my, the fish-men befriended the fish-women and danced [lit. "bent their knees"]. Clear out, the place was hot!

The young man hid and spied upon them. While he watched, his bones and skin and all of the parts of his body trembled terribly. He almost fell in the midst of them.

The fish danced and sang and danced and sang, then rested for a little while. They sat and rested, smoking and chewing betel nut. Then a young woman came directly towards the place where the bone-shaking man was lying.

The man saw this woman coming and he was no longer afraid of the fish-men. He gnashed his teeth and stretched out, then shut the woman's mouth. The woman wanted to call out, but she was helpless.

The woman tried to fight the man, but the good-for-nothing held her too tightly. His hands were like glue.

They struggled like this for a while, then the woman gave up and said, "Let go of me and I'll tell you something."

The woman said, "If I promise to go with you, you can't get angry with me and call me a fish-woman. If you say this, I'll leave you and run away. So, promise me this and I'll go with you."

The woman's skin was hot, so she slept under the trees. After one month, she told her husband that they should go get something of hers from home.

They walked and walked, then the woman pulled out vines and grasses. After a while, they came close to the river. The woman chewed some betel nut. Afterwards, she told her husband, "If I spit in the river and the river opens, you must hurry and come inside with me."

However, the man was afraid, so the two of them turned around to go back home. As they walked, the woman taught the man the song and dance of the fish. The man learned this song and dance well.

They had a son and later they had a little girl. The two children married and later the two of them had many more people who all learned this song and dance of the fish.

This song and dance is only performed in this one place. They never go and compete with this song and dance [e.g., at the Highlands Show]. They only perform it in their village. This is a very beautiful song and dance, and many men would copy it.

Miss Marryanne [Maryanne] Dubanau
Catholic Mission Tangu [**Tangu** People]
**Wagi** Village, Bogia
**Madang** Province

A1464.2.1. Origin of particular song; A1542.2. Origin of particular dance; B214.1+. Singing fish; B290+. Fish that chews betel nut; B290+. Fish that smokes; B293.7K2. Dancing fish; B654. Marriage to fish in human form; D370. Transformation: fish to person; P210. Husband and wife; P231. Mother and son; P232. Mother and daughter; P233. Father and son; P234. Father and daughter; P253. Sister and brother; T192. Marriage by force; T415. Brother-sister incest

## Watuwatu Married a *Sela* (Heron)

(Wantok 350, January 24, 1981, page 19)

Long, long ago, a mother often took her son and went fishing in a pond. The mother would paddle and the boy would sit at the bow of the canoe. When they arrived at the middle of the pond, the mother would cast a hook out and pull up fish. The boy would just sit nicely at the bow of the canoe.

This boy, Watuwatu, often went with his mother, until he became a man. One time, the two of them paddled out, and a bird looked desirously at him. We people of the Sepik River call this bird _sela_ [**East Sepik** or **West Sepik** Province].

This bird is like a duck, but it has a long neck [a heron or egret]. Many _sela_s always came and watched this boy and his mother. However, one _sela_ looked lustfully at this young man.

One time, Watuwatu and his mother went back to the village. At night, he had a dream. His dream was that the next day, he must get his canoe and paddle to the place where the _sela_s perched.

His dream said that when Watuwatu paddled to the place where the _sela_s perched, they would come and give him sago, betel nuts, betel peppers and other things. So in the early morning, he took his canoe and paddled out. He went to the place where the _sela_s perched, then birds came and gave him various kinds of food.

His canoe was completely filled and he paddled back to the village. Watuwatu called out to his friends or playmates to come and eat the sago, and betel nuts and betel peppers that the _sela_s had given to him. He told them what had happened to him, but his friends said that it was a lie and that they did not want to eat those things.

Poor Watuwatu took these things and gave them to his mother and sister. The next morning, Watuwatu paddled back to look at the _sela_s. The _sela_ that liked him was very troubled and wanted to go with him now. But her parents told her to wait and they would settle things first.

The _sela_s decided to bring their daughter to Watuwatu. At night, Watuwatu would have to take a new canoe and put a paddle for their daughter inside it. Watuwatu could not put his legs at the place where their daughter would sit. The _sela_s would bring her to him.

The man did not sleep well. In the early morning, he woke up and paddled out. He went far and saw many _sela_s sitting in the grasses. The place was entirely black. The parents, brothers, sisters, and maternal relatives came to bring the girl to Watuwatu.

Watuwatu came and saw the _sela_s. He looked in the middle and saw a girl. He paddled towards them and they flew up, only the girl was sitting now. The canoe came close to the girl, then the girl jumped inside the stern of the canoe and paddled in earnest. The boy sat at the bow and he paddled too.

They arrived at the village, and the people came to ask the boy where he had found this smart girl. Some men lusted for Watuwatu's wife. The two of them always went fishing with the women. Watuwatu's sisters often took care of their child at the village while the _sela_ woman went and fished. She was the best of all of the women at fishing. She often caught scorpionfish [order Scorpaeniformes], tilapia [_Tilapia mossambica_], groupers and cod [family Serranidae], and all other kinds of fish.

Their house was completely filled with fish. So her female in-laws were very happy and often lived at their place and took care of their child. After a while, there was a bad time when Watuwatu's wife strung up the fish and brought them back. When she came back, Watuwatu said, "How did this woman get these fish?" It was a bad time now.

One time, his wife wanted to go fishing again. She took the canoe and departed. She paddled and arrived somewhere. She tied up the canoe and climbed a tall tree, then sat on top of it and looked out.

After a little while, she saw women paddling closer and closer. She looked around and took a _sela_ head from a bamboo tube, then took off her real head and put on the _sela_ head. She put the real head in the canoe and jumped into the water.

She went down in the water and caught fish. Watuwatu sat looking and said, "Why did she take off her nice face and put it in the canoe. Oh my, the sun is burning her nice face. She did not tell me to come sit and hold her head so that she can catch fish."

Watuwatu sat a little then went to the village. In the evening, his wife put the _sela_ head inside the bamboo and put on her real head, then she came to the village. When she arrived, Watuwatu stared at her.

As he stared, the woman looked at him and asked, "Why are you staring at me? I'm your wife. I don't belong to any other man." After a little while, Watuwatu told her what he had seen.

Watuwatu's wife took the _sela_ head and put it on. After she put it on, she flew outside. Watuwatu was very troubled. He chased his wife and came outside, but his wife just flew around the house, then flew to her _sela_ kin.

Now people are tabooed from going to this place where the _sela_ perch. This is the place where the _sela_ lay their eggs. So we never see the eggs of the _sela_s (herons or egrets). We never see their chicks either. No, we only see the adults.

Augustine Duma Yalwan

Vanimo

West Sepik Province

B211.3.10K. Speaking heron; B463.2. Helpful heron; B652.2+. Man marries heron in human form; C610+. Tabu: going to heron nesting ground;

D162+W. Transformation: woman to heron; D350+W. Transformation: heron to woman; D1011.0.1+. Woman puts on heron head to go fishing; D1810.8.2. Information received through dream; F511.0.4+. Person with removable head; P210. Husband and wife; P230. Parents and children; P231. Mother and son; P232. Mother and daughter; P234. Father and daughter; P250. Brothers and sisters; P260. Relations by law; P290+. Maternal kin; P310. Friendship; R260. Pursuits; T10. Falling in love; T100. Marriage; W181. Jealousy


## The Ghost Wanted To Kill the Child

(Wantok 351, January 31, 1981, page 19)

Once there was a man, his wife and their child. At this time, it was the custom to bury dead people in the house to rest. One day, the man's wife died, so they buried her inside the house.

The man and his daughter lived together for a while, then the father married another woman. The three of them lived happily together. One day, the husband and wife told the girl, "Stay here and gather the coconut shells to fill up the bamboo tubes. Then fetch water and bring it to the house. We'll go to the garden and get some food."

The husband and wife went to the garden and the girl just stayed there. Before long, she heard a spirit bird approaching and crying out. It said that the married couple went to the garden and that one is still there. The girl heard this, so she took her things to fill up the water containers and left.

As she walked along the trail, she felt strange, and her skin trembled. She thought, "I think that my mother's ghost has come and is holding me now." So, she did not fill up the water containers. She turned around and went back home. When she arrived home, she did not make a single sound. She went inside the house and put down the net bag, coconut shells, and bamboo.

Later, she went outside the house again and went up a big tree. After she climbed the tree, she looked down and saw her mother's ghost. The ghost took a spear and pranced belligerently (*samsam*) toward the stream, looking for her daughter. Her daughter was not there, so she returned to the house. The ghost wanted to kill her daughter. The poor girl hid well on top of the tree.

Her ghost mother searched and searched, but could not find her. The ghost went inside the house, then broke the clay pots and the coconut shells that were used to fetch water. After she finished breaking things, she went back down into the hole in which she dwelt.

What the girl had seen had terrified her. Also, the smell of the ghost had become very strong. She stayed on top of the tree until late at night when her father and step-mother returned. They tried to find her and called out to her. They called and called, then the father heard a quiet reply from on top of the tree. He told her to come down, but the girl replied, "I can't come down."

The father lit a torch made from coconut fibers and climbed the tree and brought her down. The girl did not speak, not at all. She was half-dead and her father put *salat* on her [to revive her]. Then she told them that her mother's ghost wanted to kill her. They went inside the house and saw that everything was broken. So, they asked some men for their pots, and the men gave them some.

The three of them boiled water and threw it down the hole where the ghost woman was hiding. They threw boiling water down the hole until the hole was filled with hot water. The ghost woman was boiled to death. The ghost never came out of the hole again.

This was the beginning of when men were too afraid to bury corpses inside houses. This story came from the Maprik area.

Rainford Naulaw
**Bainyik** Village [**Abelam** People]
P. O. Box 122
Maprik
**East Sepik** Province

A1591+. Why corpses are buried away from houses; B211.3. Speaking bird; E253+. Ghost mother tries to kill daughter; E299.4+. Ghost breaks objects; E446.2+. Ghost laid with boiling water; E481. Ghost lives in hole; E542. Dead man touches living; F401.3.7. Spirit in form of a bird; G11.10. Cannibalistic spirits; P210. Husband and wife; P232. Mother and daughter; P234. Father and daughter; P282. Stepmother; P600+. Corpses buried away from houses; R311. Tree refuge; S112.1. Boiling to death; T100. Marriage; V61.3+. Dead buried


## The Orphans

(Wantok 352, February 7, 1981, page 19)

Long, long ago, in the deep forest, there were two children. Their parents had died. They did not have a garden from which to get food, and they did not have a house in which to sleep. They slept underneath a tree. The tree had broken and fallen down with the many vines that had climbed it. The rain did not go inside it.

They did not have fire or anything else to help themselves. The little boy often just sat. He never moved or walked around. He never defecated, not even the slightest thing. Nothing. The boy was small, but he had facial hair. He had not grown big. When his mother bore him, he was very small.

The little girl often walked around. She did not make gardens or build a house. No, she often hunted for food in the forest. These foods were things such as wild edible greens, mushrooms, and various kinds of tree seedlings.

The girl did not care whether it was rainy or sunny. The deep forest was big enough for her to find food. One time, she was tired because there were no more tree leaves. She searched and searched until the sun set, and did not return before sunset to their home. When she finally returned home, she was angry with her brother.

She said, "You're a boy who never even works a little bit. I'm like your mother or father, and it's only me who works. You never help me, not even a little."

The boy replied to his sister, "You'll see me later. You still have father's power over me. I don't know the day or time when I'll grow up. Now I can't do anything. Don't get angry with me."

The girl listened to this and was no longer angry. Another day, she looked for food, but she did not find any. She climbed a mountain and then went down it.

At the bottom of the mountain she found a tree that had just been cut. The little girl trembled and trembled. When she went a little farther, she saw a grass house. It was a very beautiful house.

The little girl had not seen this kind of house before. She went very quietly to the house. There were many ripe bananas there, as well as taros, chickens, birds, pork, sweet potatoes, sugarcanes, and various kinds of edible greens. The little girl did not know about these kinds of foods. She just looked at all of them.

She smelled the nice smell of meat, but she was afraid and just stood at the base of a tree, watching. The girl was getting warm all over. While she was watching, a young boy came. He was a very handsome boy.

However, the girl was terrified and hid inside the base of the tree. The boy saw her, quietly went to her and held her. He said, "Hey, what are you doing at my home? Did you want to steal or what?"

The girl was terrified at what the boy had said, but he took her to the house and gave her some food. After she ate, she took some food to give to her brother. However, on the trail she ate a taro and vomited fiercely. She vomited all of the meat and vegetables that she had eaten at the boy's house.

When she arrived home, she gave a taro to her brother. Her brother saw this and said, "What did you bring?" The girl told him about the boy and the food at his house.

She told her brother about this, and their traditional food, "We eat rubbish from the forest, just like wild people. Now I've found something to make us very strong."

They ate and ate, and the girl became a woman. However, her brother did not grow, not even a little. He just stayed a little boy. The young woman went to look for her friend. He brought plenty of food, fire and decorations, then came to their home. When her brother saw this, he knew that the man liked his sister. He told his sister, "I still have my father's power, but my day has not arrived yet. You can't marry quickly."

His sister listened to this and said, "I'll do as I please. If I want to marry, I shall. You can't boss me around." They fought bitterly, then the woman left her brother there and went to live at the man's house. She stayed there for one night.

In the morning, she wanted to return to her home. However, she could not find the way. The place where she lived had a big sago palm tree growing there. This sago tree grew and grew, until the crown reached the sky. His sister looked at this and cried for her brother. She stayed at the base of this sago tree for a whole year.

After a year, she wanted to return to her husband, but she found a pond there. When she looked at the pond, it turned red. The woman just stayed in the area of the pond. Later she married a big fish from the pond.

Later, there was a battle, and many, many people died. It was because of the wrongs of this woman that these bad things happened. If she had not disobeyed her brother, her brother would have left many good things on the earth.

Mark Kiugili
C. M. [Congregation of Mission] **Porandaka**

B603. Marriage to fish (whale); B874. Giant fish; D215.11K+B. Transformation: boy to sago tree; D283.1M. Transformation: man to pool of water; D492. Color of object changed; F54.1. Tree stretches to sky; J652. Inattention to warnings; P210. Husband and wife; P231. Mother and son; P253+. Sister disobeys brother's wise counsel; Q325. Disobedience punished; T100. Marriage; W126. Disobedience

## The Lizard that Became a Child
(Wantok 353, February 14, 1981, page 19)

Long, long ago, a married couple lived in **Kofena** Village in **Eastern Highlands** Province [**Asaro** People]. The husband was named Ewa and the wife was named Meu.

They were married for a long time, but they did not have any children yet. They worked hard at trying to have a child. One day, the woman told her husband, "My husband, my breasts are sore and full of milk. What should I do?" Her husband did not reply, so the woman kept asking from the afternoon until it was dark. Her husband was tired, so they went to the house to slept.

They lay there and decided that in the morning they would wake up and go looking for pandanus nuts (*karuka*). They would go quickly and return quickly because it was the rainy season and it would be bad if they became caught in the afternoon rains.

In the early morning, Meu woke up and cooked some food. After it was done, she filled a net bag, and the two of them walked to the place where the pandanus trees were. They arrived at a big mountain, then they sat and rested a little.

They ate and rested, then they got up and followed the trail again. They walked and walked to the place where the pandanus trees were. The woman was carrying the net bag and sat to wait for Ewa.

Her husband, Ewa, began to clear the underbrush by the pandanus trees. After he cleared the underbrush, Meu sat and felt her breasts that were full of milk. They were causing her great pain.

Meu called out to her husband, Ewa, "Hey, my breasts are full of milk and causing me pain. What should I do?" Ewa was busy working and did not want to listen to her.

The woman called and called. A little lizard heard this, jumped and drank Meu's milk. Meu did not remove the lizard. No, the lizard drank and drank, and the woman felt good again.

The woman did not tell her husband about what was happening. No, she told the little lizard, "If you're human, then jump inside the net bag." Right away, the lizard jumped inside the net bag.

Meu was ecstatic. She pretended that she was sick. Meu told her husband not to get the pandanus nuts now, and they went back home.

They walked along the trail, and the woman looked inside the net bag. She saw that the lizard was now half-human and half-lizard. They continued to walk, and they arrived home. She looked inside the bag again. Now the lizard was now entirely human.

The woman hid the baby inside a barrel. She told the baby, "If I come throw something heavy on the ground and you hear it, then come and drink from my breasts."

So every day, the woman gave her breasts to the baby. One day, the woman went to the garden and the man went to cut firewood.

The man carried the firewood and threw it on the ground with a crash. The little baby thought, "That's the woman." So, the baby came out to drink milk.

Oh my, the man thought hard, "I think this woman befriended another man." He thought wrong, took an axe, and cut open the baby's head. After that, he threw the body on the fire.

The woman returned and made a big noise, but the baby did not come out. She went to look inside the barrel, but it was empty. She looked and looked, and saw that the fire had burned the baby and only its bones were left.

Meu hanged herself. Her poor husband returned and saw this. He was speechless. He saw that the woman was dead. The poor man stood and tears welled from his eyes, but all he said was "Why?" The woman was dead.

B. T. J.

Lae

Morobe Province

B765+. Lizard drinks milk from woman's breasts; D397C. Transformation: lizard to child; D681. Gradual transformation; M451.1. Death by suicide; P210. Husband and wife; P231+. Mother commits suicide on death of son; P272. Foster mother; P275. Foster son; S32+. Murderous stepfather; S139.4. Murder by mangling with axe; T611. Suckling of children; T676. Childless couple adopt animal as substitute for child


## A New Woman Came from the Ground
(Wantok 354, February 21, 1981, page 19)

Long, long ago, there was a village where only men lived. There were no women. The men did not know what women looked like.

This village where the men lived had many bamboos growing in it. One day, a man had to defecate very badly, so he sped over to the place where the bamboos grew.

He went there and jumped on top of the bamboos. He wanted to defecate, but when he sat down to defecate, a bamboo cane broke and cut his posterior.

The man's posterior was cut and became the same as a woman's private parts [lit., "a woman's shame"]. The man was ashamed to tell the others. He hid this from them.

When his friends traveled to places, he never went with them. He only went places by himself. He did this for a while, then one day, his friends met together in their spirit house and argued.

They said, "This friend of ours, why doesn't he travel with us any more? He's probably angry with us." They said this, then their leader said, "Never mind this. I think that one of us can go quietly to him and ask him."

So, they chose a boy to go and ask him. This boy went and asked him, "Friend, why is it that you never travel with us?"

The man who had cut his posterior on the bamboo said, "Friend, I went and sat on top of the bamboos and a bamboo cut me terribly. Now I have a huge sore. Because of this, I'm ashamed to travel with you."

The boy said, "Never mind. Don't be ashamed. Come, then you and I will show your sore to our leader." So the two of them went to show all of the men. However, they did not understand.

They thought it was just an ordinary sore, so they began to travel together. This continued for a while, and they forgot about the sore. One day, a man from another village came to their village.

He sat and told stories with their leader, then the leader told the story about this sore. The other man said, "Bring the man here and I'll look at this sore." A boy ran to get the man who had cut himself on the bamboo.

The man saw this and spoke, "This isn't a sore. No, it's a woman's private parts. In my village, there are women such as this. He is your woman."

Then he told them, "We marry the women and they give birth to babies. You can marry your woman and she'll give birth to your children."

So now, the men of this village understood that it was a woman. They married and had both baby boys and girls in their area.

Stanley Husai [and] H. C. Teiminal
P. O. Box 332
Goroka
Eastern Highlands Province

A1313.2.2K. Origin of woman's vagina; D12. Transformation: man to woman; D566+. Transformation by cutting; F529.2. People without anuses; F566.1. Village of men only; P210. Husband and wife; P230. Parents and children; P310. Friendship; T100. Marriage; T580. Childbirth; V112.1. Spirit huts; X712.1H. Female genitals; X740.1H+. Symbolic pedicatory rape while at stool

## The Wildfowl Puts Its Eggs in the Forest

(Wantok 355, February 28, 1981, page 19)

Long, long ago, there were two sisters who lived in a house. The parents of these poor sisters had died. They lived alone.

One day, the sisters went down to wash their dirty things in the river. While they were washing, they saw wildfowl eggs drifting on top of a platform that was floating downstream.

The big sister saw this and told her little sister, "Hey sister, look at the wildfowl eggs drifting down." The big sister told the little sister to swim out and pull the platform closer, so that they could get the eggs.

The little sister pulled the platform and the big sister took all of the good eggs. The little sister took all of the bad eggs that were left. After they took the eggs, the big sister hurried her little sister, so that they could go to the house and cook the eggs.

They went and cooked the eggs, but the little sister's eggs were bad. So, she told her big sister, "Please sister, my eggs are bad. Can you give me some of your eggs?"

The big sister did not give any to her little sister. None. The little sister was very troubled and went to sleep. The next day, the little sister pretended that she was sick, so only the big sister went down to the river.

The little sister who had pretended that she was sick and sleeping then rose and dressed quickly. She went and took some tree fruits and put them in a net bag, then she went off into the deep forest. Along the way, she arrived at a pigsty.

She stood and heard a woman asking, "Hey, who are you coming to my place?" The girl said, "It's just me." The woman said, "OK, wait a minute."

She stood for a fairly long time, then saw the old woman approaching. The old woman asked her, "Where do you want to go and where are you coming from?" The little sister began to explain to her.

She said, "My big sister and I were doing the wash in the river. I saw wildfowl eggs drifting on a platform towards us. I told my sister this: she took all of the good eggs, and I took all of the bad eggs. I want to marry this wildfowl. That's why I have come here."

The old woman told the girl, "That's alright. First come here and look for lice [or fleas] in my hair."

The poor girl looked through her hair for lice. While she was looking through her hair, she saw a snake and a lizard. She kept looking through the hair, then she put her hand in the net bag, took a tree fruit and ate it.

She kept doing this, then she told the old woman that she had finished the delousing. The old woman got up and said, "OK. If you want to see this 'man,' you must not go on the trail of the other birds. The other birds' trails are very bad. These are very cold places that are uninhabited. If you want to go to the wildfowl's home, you will see a very nice place. Just follow the way to that place."

So, the woman just followed the trail and found the 'man.' The girl saw him and said, "Ah, you are the one who knows how to make a platform, put eggs on it and send it downstream, aren't you?"

The wildfowl said, "Take this net bag. Bring the net bag into the taro garden and fill it with eggs, then go cook and eat them." The woman did this. Later she and the wildfowl married.

The big sister wanted to do what her little sister had done. However, when she came to the old woman, she cried out, "These aren't lice." The old woman had snakes and lizards in her hair.

So the old woman said, "Follow the birds' bad trail." The big sister did what the old woman said. She arrived at a cold place.

That afternoon, the birds came and excreted all over her. The poor woman listened to lizards running about. The bird droppings ruined her and she just stayed in place.

After a little while, she heard a child say, "I'm the wildfowl's child. My mother married a wildfowl." The big sister called out to this child to come. She told the child to bring her mother and come see her.

The woman knew that the child's mother was actually her own little sister. The child ran to bring its mother to remove the bird droppings from her sister's body.

The little sister took the big sister and put her to sleep with them in the house. The four of them lived there for a while. The wildfowl often defecated in the taro garden, and they often cooked and ate this taro.

One day, the little child went and saw its father defecating. The child returned home, then told its mother and aunt that it had seen that its father's anus was bright red when it defecated.

The father heard this and was ashamed, so he did not put eggs in the garden. He was ashamed and put the eggs in the very deep forest. He was ashamed and changed his body into a [different kind of] bird, then flew away forever.

Mickey Poruta Bogino
**Bovera** Village [**Binandere** People]
Northern [**Oro**] Province

B211.3. Speaking bird; B602. Marriage to bird; B631. Human offspring from marriage to animal; D413+. Transformation: one kind of bird to another; F555+. Hair with snakes and lizards in it; P210. Husband and wife; P230+. Father ashamed of being seen defecating, runs away; P252.1. Two sisters; P252+. First sister acts wisely, another acts unwisely; P294. Aunt; Q10+. Obedience rewarded; Q287. Refusal to grant request punished; Q325. Disobedience punished; R100+. Person buried in excrement rescued; T100. Marriage; W31. Obedience; W126. Disobedience; W151. Greed; X716H+. Feces as gift



# Red Sago

(Wantok 356, March 7, 1981, page 19)

This is a story that explains why sago becomes red when we rinse it during processing.

Long, long ago, there were two brothers. One day, they left the village and went to a place in the forest to process sago. When they arrived at this place in the forest, they made a hut for themselves.

After they made the hut, they cut down a sago palm tree. After the tree fell, they cleaned off and removed the bark.

After that, they cut the sago tree with a very sharp stone. They broke up the tree for a while, then the big brother told the little brother, "Go rinse the sago. I'll continue breaking up the sago." The little brother agreed with what his brother had said and went to rinse the sago. While they were working, the little brother did not know that a hermit had come and was talking to his big brother. The hermit asked the big brother, "Hey boy, is that your sago, or whose is it?"

The big brother said, "Hey you hick, never mind that nonsense. This here is my sago!" The hermit was angry because the big brother spoke angrily with him. The hermit was irate and broke the big brother's head, killing him. The hermit dragged his body and hid him underneath the sago leaves.

The big brother's ghost went and told the little brother, "Little brother, go help me break the sago, and I'll take your place rinsing the sago." The little brother thought that it really was his brother, so he went to break up the sago.

The big brother's ghost rinsed the sago and the blood from his head fell into the place where he was rinsing. The little brother finished breaking up the sago, then returned to see that his big brother had finished the rinsing.

He saw the blood and asked the big brother, "Hey, whose blood is it that fell into the sago?"

The big brother said, "I don't know." He just listened from then on and no longer replied. They kept working at making the sago until it was dark, then they went to sleep.

While the little brother slept, the big brother worked at burning the leaves in the fire along with his head. He did this until daybreak.

At daybreak, the big brother's ghost got up and said, "Little brother, carry all of our sago and go to the village. After you bring it to the village, you can return and we'll go together to the village." The little brother agreed and carried the sago to the village.

He put it down in the village, then returned to his big brother's ghost. The big brother's ghost said, "Brother, I want to tell you something."

He said, "Go remove the sago leaves and you'll really see me." The big brother's ghost finished. The little brother went down, removed the sago leaves and saw that his brother was dead.

The poor brother saw this and was very disturbed. He called out and cried and cried, then returned to the village. He told the men of the village, then they came and took his body, burying it in the village.

So now when we make sago, we see that the sago water becomes red like blood. This is the blood of the big brother.

Wesley E. Jimmy
Finch Enterprises
Finschhafen
P. O. Box 132
**Morobe** Province

[Mr. Jimmy wrote the ancestor story in *Wantok* #376. He is probably from the **Bukawac** or **Tami** People.]

A2791+. Why sago pith turns red when rinsed; E226. Dead brother's return; E231. Return from dead to reveal murder; E545. The dead speak; P251.5. Two brothers; Q327. Discourtesy punished; Q411. Death as punishment; P251.5. Two brothers; P426.2. Hermit; S116.4. Murder by crushing head

## Mount Geluwa [Giluwe] Dog Trading

(Wantok 357, March 14, 1981, page 19)

Long, long ago, Mount Geluwa [Giluwe] did not have many people. At this time, there lived a man and his dog. They lived in a small forest. They had a house and some gardens. They hunted and ate marsupials (*kapul*) and other wild game in the forest.

They went around hunting and when it became dark, they made a hut, cooked food and went to sleep. They did this all of the time.

One time, they traveled and saw a nice place. They were very worried about this place. They made a house there. They quickly made a garden and a good house for themselves. There was no [food from the] garden, so they hunted for wild game in the forest and they ate this.

The "businessman" thought and thought, then he cut a big piece of forest near his house. He cut down the forest to plant food. He made a garden, and the dog hunted for marsupials and other wild game in the forest. The man returned to the house but there was no food. He saw his dog coming and carrying game. He was very happy. They did this every day.

Later the man finished cutting the forest and making gardens. He had no food for planting. He thought hard. He thought and thought, then lost his breath, "Why do I do this hard work? There is no food to plant. Where will I find some?"

The dog saw this and went to look for food to plant in the garden. The dog went through the forest towards a village. The dog walked for about four days and four nights. The dog arrived at a small village. The dog hid and looked at the people going to their gardens. The dog went inside a house and took some sweet potatoes, taro leaves, and sugarcanes. Then the dog just hid and went to its friend.

The dog returned to their home. When the man saw the dog, he was ecstatic. He planted in the forest. After some time, the food from the garden was ready. They ate and were happy. The man cut forest and planted more food. The food rotted and was ruined.

The dog left him and went to a village where some clans were singing and dancing. They had tied pigs to a house. The dog turned and saw that no one was there, so the dog took two pigs, a boar and a sow. The dog took the pigs to its friend. They were very happy because now they had pigs.

The man was happy and husbanded the two pigs. The sow had many piglets. The man was happy and he made a new house. He took care of the pigs. The food in the garden was rotten and the pigs liked this.

The dog saw that the pigs were plentiful and that there was no one to help this man. The dog felt sorry for the man and went to a village. The dog walked and walked and arrived at the village. The dog walked and walked and arrived at another village. The dog hid there and saw some young women. The dog saw the women go to a garden. The dog hid and saw the women removing their "grass" skirts. The dog grabbed a skirt and watched the women working in the garden. The dog was still hiding while watching the women working in the garden. The dog kept the skirt nearby while it watched.

The women finished working and wanted to go home. They went to put their skirts back on and leave. One of the women came and saw that her skirt was not there. She searched and searched, but could not find it. She thought hard. She said, "Which man or woman took my skirt? Whoever took it must give it to me so that I can leave."

The dog was in the forest and brought the skirt. The woman said, "Why did you take my skirt? Give it back to me so that I can leave." The dog listened to this, but did not give back the skirt. The woman talked and talked, then than grew tired and said, "If you want to take me to your house, then you must give me the skirt, then we'll leave."

The dog listened to this and then gave the skirt to the woman. Then they left. They walked and walked then came to the man. The man saw the woman and they were happy together. They lived together for a while, then the man paid a bride price to her kin.

The woman took her kin and went to her husband's place. The man saw her kin approaching and he was very happy that they came to look at him.

They married and the woman became pregnant. She gave birth to a boy. They lived together for a while, then the boy grew up and had his first two teeth come out.

One time, the woman wanted to work in the garden. She gave the boy to the dog to take care of. The dog took care of the boy while the mother worked.

While the dog was taking care of the boy, a fly came and landed on the baby's head. The dog went to remove the fly, but missed and scraped the baby's head, killing him. The dog was very afraid and worried.

When the mother came and saw that the baby was dead, she scolded the dog terribly. The baby's father heard that the baby was dead, and he too hit the dog terribly.

The poor dog cried and the said, "I worked hard at arranging your marriage. You two have hit me again and again." Then the dog ran away to live on a mountain called Mount Geluwa.

The husband and wife lived there and planted much food, but the food did not grow well and the pigs that they husbanded did not grow well either. They just kept working hard at planting food, but they did not eat a single thing from this garden. They worked hard for nothing, and the dog only lived on the mountain called Mount Gelawa [Giluwe].

Now at this time, they used the name, "Geluwa Dog Trading." This is the story of how the people got this name.

Alkena, a young agronomist
**Tambul** sub-Province [**Hagen** People]
Mt. Hagen
**Western Highlands** Province

B211.1.7. Speaking dog; B340+. Dog runs away after being beaten for accidentally killing baby; B421. Helpful dog; B582.1.1. Animal wins wife for his master (Puss in Boots); K401.1.1. Trail of stolen goods made to lead to dupe; N333. Aiming at fly has fatal results; P210. Husband and wife; P233. Father and son; P231. Mother and son; R220. Flights; T52. Bride purchased; T100. Marriage; T570. Pregnancy; T580. Childbirth

## Sugarcane Tore Apart the Brothers

(Wantok 358, March 21, 1981, page 19)

Long, long ago, there were two brothers who lived in a place far from other people. They lived happily. One time, the big brother wanted to go to a village far away. This was a place where they were slaughtering pigs. He told his little brother to stay and plant his big sugarcane garden. The little brother agreed with what the big brother had said.

The big brother went to the village where they were slaughtering pigs. The little brother worked at planting the sugarcanes. The big brother had told the little brother not to cut the little sugarcanes and eat them. He said that he must leave these alone, so that they would grow too. The little brother heeded his big brother and did not eat a single sugarcane. He planted the sugarcanes, and the canes grew tall.

However, in one corner of the garden, a small piece of sugarcane had broken and fallen to the ground. The poor brother went and planted it, but it fell again. He planted it again and it fell again. He did this repeatedly, but he could not plant it. He got up and said, "Man, I planted all of the sugarcanes in the garden. My big brother won't be angry if I eat this little cane, after all of the work that I've done for him." So, he broke the sugarcane and drank the juice. After he finished, he was terrified that his brother would see the remnants of the sugarcane that he had eaten, so he dug a big hole that filled with water. Then he threw what was left of the sugarcane into the water.

Afterwards, he went back to the house. Before long, his big brother returned. He carried a big net bag of pork. The little brother saw this and was very happy. They gathered stones and cooked all of the pork in an earth oven. After the pork was done, the big brother asked the little brother, "Did you finish planting all of the sugarcanes?" "Yes, brother, I did what you told me to do," [said the little brother]. "That's good," said the big brother, "Now, let's just wait for the food in the earth oven to be ready."

They waited a little while, then a small insect went onto the little brother's leg. The insect was carrying a piece of the sugarcane that the little brother had eaten and discarded. The little brother was afraid and told the big brother that he had had some sugarcane. The big brother was irate. He took the little brother and put him right into the bonfire. The little brother turned and turned in the fire. The fire burned him terribly.

Later, the big brother threw him out. After that he evicted him up to a grass house. The little brother worried and worried. One day, when he was still alone, two small birds flew to him. The little brother said, "If you are men, can you please bring me food."

The birds found some tree fruits and after they finished eating, they carried two of them to the little brother. The little brother often waited for the two birds. Every day, they would come and give him fruits, such as mangos, papayas, or ripe bananas. The three of them continued like this until the rainy season arrived at this place and the rain ruined all of the food in the gardens. This was the time of hunger.

However, the two birds helped this poor man who had been burned by the fire. The three of them were not short of food, so one time, the big brother was famished and he went to his little brother. He went and asked him for some fruit or other food, but the little brother did not give him any. He waited and waited, but the little brother did not give his famished brother a single thing. He looked at his little bother, but his brother did not give him anything. The big brother did not have any more strength because he had not eaten for many days, then he died.

Theresa Rema
Pupu Business Group
P. O. Box Koiangil [**Kendagl**] Village [**Hagen** People]
Ialibu
**Southern Highlands** Province

B450. Helpful birds; L111.1. Exile returns and succeeds; P251.5. Two brothers; P251.5.3. Hostile brothers; Q285. Cruelty punished; Q325. Disobedience punished; Q431. Punishment: banishment (exile); Q411. Death as punishment; S73.2. Person banishes brother (sister); S132. Murder by starvation; S326.1. Disobedient child burned; W126. Disobedience

## The Two Children Became Birds
(Wantok 359, March 28, 1981, page 19)

Long, long ago, there was a village that had a husband and wife, and their son and daughter.

One day, they and their children woke up and went to the garden to plant yams. When they arrived at the garden, they worked noisily. They worked and worked until the sun was high in the sky.

At noon, the sun was terribly hot. The two children were dying of hunger and asked their parents to give them two yams to eat. However, the parents ignored them, so the two children held their bellies and continued to work.

When a person has food in one's stomach, the person will do good work, so it was not long when the two children asked again for food. This time, the parents were angry and said, "You two talk too much about eating. Get the bamboo tubes, fill them with water and bring them here."

The poor children took the bamboos and went down to the stream. When they arrived at the stream, they sat and hit the bamboos on stones.

The noise of the bamboos was very loud. They continued this, and the boy told his sister, "Sister, look." After he said this, he jumped into the stream and became a fish.

However, his sister said that she did not see it well. So, the boy got up again and tried turning into many things, but the sister did not like these.

Finally, he turned into a big bird that made the sound of the bamboo smashing on the stones. His sister liked this bird very much and she too became a bird. They jumped about and made this sound, "Kringgg — kringgg — keng kong — kringg kringg — keng kong."

They jumped and flew to the garden, then made this sound near their parents. The husband and wife listened to this, then they sped to the stream. They just saw the bamboos there. They were speechless.

They did not know what to do. They just went back to the garden and removed all of the yams that they had planted. They cooked all of them in the fire and they cried going back to the village.

So now in my area, when children cry for yams, the parents never withhold the food. They just give it to them.

Peter Las
L. N. H. S. [Lutheran National High School]
P. O. Box 323
Madang
Madang Province

B31.6. Other giant birds; D150B. Transformation: boy to bird; D150G. Transformation: girl to bird; D170B. Transformation: boy to fish; D610. Repeated transformation; P210. Husband and wife; P231. Mother and son; P232. Mother and daughter; P233. Father and son; P234. Father and daughter; P253. Sister and brother; S11+. Cruel father refuses children food; S12.6. Cruel mother refuses children food

## How Mount Ialibu and Mount Gilue [Giluwe] Arose
(Wantok 360, April 4, 1981, page 21)

Long, long ago, there was a man who lived alone in a place in the Ialibu District of Southern Highlands Province. At this place, there were no people, the man was alone and did all of the work himself.

He had a huge garden, and he planted many kinds of food in it. The foods often just rotted, because there was no one to help him eat the foods.

The man never worried that he was alone in this place. No, he was always happy and he did his work.

One day, the rain began to fall when it was still morning, so the man stayed in his house. The rain stopped when it was about noontime, so he took his large knife and walked to the garden.

He made a fire by the garden hut, cooked some bananas and ate them. Later, he cut a sugarcane and drank the juice. Insects had eaten the base of the cane, so the man took his knife and cut off the bad part.

However, the poor man missed and cut his little finger. The finger came right off. The man mourned for his finger and went to get some taro leaves to bandage it. He left the garden hut and walked to his house.

About three days later, he went back to the hut and opened the taro leaves to look at his finger. He was surprised to see that the finger had turned into a bird's egg.

He was ecstatic, and went to the garden and took some big banana leaves. He made a good place [for the egg], then he went back to the house. After about a week had passed, he went back to the garden hut to look at the egg. To his surprise, he saw that the egg had broken and a handsome boy was sleeping there.

Oh my, oh my, he became happier and happier. He began to trample the ground and run around the house. He took his good sleeping things and fixed up the baby in the garden hut.

Every day, he watched this little boy, and did not think about other work. When the boy had become bigger, he gave him soft foods like bananas, pumpkins, edible greens, and other things to eat.

### Growing Bigger

They lived there for a while, and the boy became very big. He began to help his father in the garden, making fences and other kinds of work. They made a nice house near the garden, and the young man often slept there. The father often went to sleep in his old house.

They lived happily for many years. One day, they were still in the garden when a heavy rain and strong wind arose. The father told his son, "I think trouble's coming. I'll go back home and find out. You must hide in your house. If I find trouble, don't come to help or show your face. You must just hide there."

The father removed all his good clothing and put on ragged clothes. He cut some new pieces of firewood, then walked towards his house.

He stood on the trail and looked towards his house. He saw that the door of the house was open, also much foul smoke was emanating from the house. He sped back to his child and said that some men were at the house. He told the child that he must go back to the house. When he returned, he threw the firewood hard upon the ground and said, "I don't know who the men are that are in my home. I alone live here. Are you a real man or a ghost that has come to my house?"

He did not see the man's face yet, but he heard a voice that was like that of a giant or a wild man. The man replied, "I'm a real man that has come here." The poor man went inside and saw a huge hunk of man there. He had two heads, two mouths, four eyes, and everything doubled on his body.

### Fearful Father

The father was terrified, but he went inside and shook hands with him, then they told each other stories. Later, the father asked this man why he had come to his house. The man replied, "I have many marsupials (*kapul*) in my area, but there are no young men who can climb the trees to kill them. So, I came to look for some young men to help me kill wild game."

The father said, "I too am alone. There are no other men who live with me." They continued to tell stories and then went to sleep.

The next morning, the wild man woke up and told the father, "I want to see the places where you have made gardens. I think that we should go to your gardens." So, the two of them went to a garden. He told the owner of the garden to go around the garden and finish working on all of the fences.

The poor man worked and worked until it was evening, and he had not finished the fences. So the wild man told him, "I think that you have some men who work with you, but you're hiding them."

### Working Slowly

The real man said, "I don't do all of the work in one day. I work slowly and finish one job in a week or two."

They stayed there for one week. The wild man worked at giving a very hard time to this man, but the real man did not flinch. He worked diligently because he did not want the wild man to see his child and take him away.

The wild man tried various kinds of tricks, but the real man gave all of the right answers to him.

After the second week, the wild man wanted to return to his home. He walked to a hill and called out that he had left behind his stone axe. The man looked and looked, but did not find a stone axe in his house.

After a little while, he called out to say that he had left his spear in the man's house. The real man did not find it, so he took his own spear and gave it to the wild man. The wild man kept calling out like this, and the poor father gave him everything that he had, then everything in the house was gone. He was out of breath and called out to his child to come out.

### The Wild Man

When his child came out, he told him about the wild man. The child listened to this and said that he would go with the wild man. The child was ready and shook hands with his father. His father gave him two dogs, spears, a bow, an axe, and a wooden spade.

The father tied a long rope to his son's hand and he held the other end. He told his son, "If you encounter trouble, you must shake the rope so that I can pull you."

The child and the wild man left and walked away. When they approached the deep forest, the wild man wanted to eat the boy, so he sent the boy up a tree to kill a marsupial. However the boy said, "You go first, then I'll follow you and get the marsupial." The wild man listened to this and sprang up the tree, going to the crown.

The young boy drew back his bow and shot at him. When the wild man looked down, the young boy shot again, but the wild man turned his head and said, "Child, a little insect scratched my skin." The young boy worked harder still at shooting him.

The wild man called out, "Child, do you want to fight? Just wait!" So he began to descend the tree. The young boy shook the rope with his hand and his father began to pull the rope. The wild man came down and began to chase the young boy and his dogs.

They ran and arrived at a stream. The wild man killed one of the boy's dogs and ate it with its hair and blood. The other dog again tried to help the boy at fighting the wild man. When they arrived at another stream, the wild man grabbed this dog and killed it too.

The young boy then arrived at the hill. He did not have any more strength to run. He took the spade that his father had given to him and hit the wild man right between his two heads.

One head broke and formed Mount Gilue [Giluwe]. The other head broke and formed Mount Ialibu. These two mountains are in the Ialibu District of **Southern Highlands** Province [**Hagen** or **Kewa** People].

W. Keme

Box 8

Pangia

Southern Highlands Province

A961.5+. Mountains (cliffs) from severed head(s) of killed giant; D457.9+. Transformation: finger to egg; D2142.1. Wind produced by magic; D2143.1. Rain produced by magic; F531.1.2.2.1. Two-headed giant; F567. Wild man; G100. Giant ogre; G361.1.1. Two-headed ogre; G512.1.2. Ogre decapitated; P233. Father and son; R260. Pursuits; T542. Birth of human being from an egg; W157. Dishonesty

## The Two Old Men Ate Soap (A Modern Story)
(Wantok 361, April 11, 1981, page 21)

Hepo is an old man from **Kasokasa** Village near Okapa [**Fore** People]. One time, the old man went over to **Okapa** Station. He went inside a store and bought a can of [cooking] oil. Then he went back to the village.

When he returned to the village, he went directly to a garden to get some edible greens. He cooked the greens in a bamboo tube, then opened the tin of oil and put it on the greens.

He ate. Then he gave some to an old friend of his. This old man had not seen or eaten this kind of thing before, so he ate the greens, then he waited to eat his meat.

He waited and waited until late that night, then he slept. In the morning, he woke up and spoke angrily at Hepo, "Why did you just give me greens? You didn't give me any meat with it. What do you think of me? Am I a dog that you only feed greens?"

The old man Hepo said, "No. That was another kind of thing that the Europeans brought. You just use it to put on greens."

His friend listened and said, "Is that so? I didn't know that there is a lot of that at the store. OK, I'll go talk to the storekeepers and they'll give me some."

The old man Hepo said, "Go and tell the storekeepers, 'I want oil,' then they'll give it to you."

So the old man said, "OK, I'm going." He followed the path to Okapa. Old man Hepo said, "You must think and ask for oil."

The old man said, "Oil, oil, oil," and walked along the road. When he entered the store, he forgot what he had been saying to himself. Another thought entered his head.

This thought was soap. So he went to the storekeeper and said, "I want soap." He bought the soap and was happy with it. Then he went to the village.

He went directly to his garden and took some edible greens. He went to the house, scraped the soap and cooked it with the vegetables in a bamboo tube. After the soap boiled over, he went to get old man Hepo. He told him, "That thing that you brought, that European food, I brought some too. Here it is."

So the two old men sat down and ate the soap, then passed out.

This is a true story. It came from Okapa in the **Eastern Highlands** Province. I want to draw a lesson here. Christian brothers and sisters, go to Jesus. You must be faithful to Jesus' name. If you forget Jesus, you will be fouled up.

Kuma Manoba

Box 787

Port Moresby

National Capital District

J1772+. Soap thought to be food; P310. Friendship

## The Girl's Mistake

(Wantok 362, April 18, 1981, page 21)

Long, long ago, an old woman, and her granddaughter lived in a village. They would always go to the garden and pick sweet potatoes, then go to the stream to wash them. One day, the girl left her grandmother and followed the stream upwards. The girl kept following the stream and saw pieces of pig guts and pig fat. The girl took them and brought them to her grandmother. They cooked the sweet potatoes with the pieces of pork, then they ate.

Later, they slept. In the early morning, the girl woke up and cooked some food. Then she put some in a net bag. She gave some to her grandmother and said, "Yesterday I went upstream and saw this pig fat and pig guts. I want to see who it is that lives upstream."

The girl left the house and went to the stream. She began to follow the stream, eventually arriving at a small place.

The little girl saw an old man in this place. This old man did not have a mouth or eyes. The girl saw this and quietly approached the old man. The old man was preparing to remove his food from an earth oven, so the little girl sat quietly and watched. The old man removed the pork from the earth oven then put it out to cool so that he could eat it later. The girl looked at the old man and thought,

"How will he eat?" Then, she saw the old man removing something like a lid from his head.

He took the meat and put it into the hole in his head. The girl went closer, took some good pieces of meat from the man, and put them in her net bag. She carried them to her grandmother. The girl did this all of the time, so the old man often thought that his meat was getting lost. However, the poor old man did not know who was taking his meat.

One time, the old man made a hole. Inside the hole, he put some spears, then he placed leaves and grasses to hide the opening of the hole. The next day, the girl returned to this place. However, she did not know that the old man had ruined the place. The poor girl was looking up while she was walking. When she arrived there, she went on top of a fence, stood and watched. She saw where the old man was. After she saw him, she jumped down. Oh my, it was not an easy jump off the fence. She jumped into the hole and died.

Maria Talom

Holy Spirit Convent

Alexishafen

Madang Province

F512.5. Person without eyes; F513.0.3. Mouthless people; K333. Theft from blind person; K420. Thief loses his goods or is detected; K735.1. Mats over holes as pitfall; P292.1. Grandmother as foster mother; Q212. Theft punished; Q411.13. Death as punishment for thievery; Q461. Impalement as punishment

## The Sergeant Ate a Snail (A Modern Story)

(Wantok 363, April 25, 1981, page 21)

One Friday, a payday, the supervisor of the A. C. O. [warden's] mess hall of Kerevat [Keravat], Sergeant Dingo Dempier went to the office and took the money for buying food for the unmarried soldiers. The officer of the jail told Sergeant Dempier, "There's no car available now to go to Rabaul and get food for the single soldiers. Tomorrow, you can go and buy food in Rabaul. So for now, try and find some food in the garden, such as sweet potatoes, taros, cassava, and edible greens. Send your prison cooks to the forest and get some edible grasses and watercress."

Sergeant Dingo did as his officer had told him. He sent two prisoners to go to the forest and find some edible grasses, and two to get some food from the garden. The four prisoners left and got the things that Sergeant Dingo asked them to get. They took the food, came together and cooked the food. At four o'clock in the afternoon, all of the single soldiers came and ate in the mess hall, then they went out. Sergeant Dingo was the very last man to come and eat in the mess hall.

He called a prisoner from North Solomons Province to give him some food. The man from Buka [Buka is an island in North Solomons Province, "Buka" is sometimes used to refer to anyone from the whole province.] dished out some food, such as sweet potatoes, taros, cassava, *aibika*, *tulip*, and watercress, then brought it to Sergeant Dingo's quarters. There was much food, so he took some to his leader.

### A Big Snail

In Sergeant Dingo's place, there was a big snail. This snail was on the edible grasses. When the prisoner had cooked the greens, he did not see that he had cooked this with it. Sergeant Dingo took his plate with his knife and fork and went to sit at the table. He began to eat.

While Sergeant Dingo was eating, he did not see the huge snail. He shoveled the food inside his mouth, and the huge snail broke in two pieces with a crack.

Poor Sergeant Dingo heard the crack, and he quickly spit out all of the food from his mouth back onto the plate from which he was eating. He got up, looked carefully and saw two big pieces of snail amidst the food.

When Sergeant Dingo saw this, he called the prisoner from the Buka. He told him, "Look at this plate of food. What kind of food did you shoot and give me?" The poor man from Buka looked carefully and said, "I see sweet potato, taro, cassava, some *aibika*, *tulip*, beans, watercress, and two pieces of snail on your plate."

Sergeant Dingo Dempier asked him, "Do the people from Buka eat snails, or which place in Papua New Guinea do people eat snails? Can you tell me or not?" The poor prisoner told the jailer, "I'm very sorry, sir, there's not one man on Buka, or one man in Papua New Guinea who eats snails. So, you are the first man in Papua New Guinea who has eaten a snail."

The sergeant told him, "Do you know that you were wrong to cook the snail and give it to me to eat? It could have made me sick and killed me."

The prisoner replied, "Yes, I did cook it, and I understand everything that you said. However, you are bringing this complaint against me alone and that is not correct. There was not just one person who cooked the food with this snail. We four prison cooks had cooked this food. So, if you want to bring forth a complaint, then do it to the four of us together. It is not fair to make a complaint against me alone."

After his jailer listened to what he said, he called for the other three cooks to come. He told the men, "I know that you together cooked this snail in the food for us soldiers. We could have eaten it, gotten sick and died. So, now that I've found out, I'm making a complaint and you will get [prison] time for this. However, I'll ask you two things first before I bring a complaint. 1) If all of you agree and eat this snail that I ate, then I can't bring a complaint against you. 2) If you don't want to eat the snail, then I'll bring you to court and you'll have your prison time lengthened. Do you want to eat the snail or do you want to just go to the officer of the court?"

### Checking Carefully

The poor prisoners thought and thought, then told Sergeant Dingo, "We're very sorry, sir, we didn't mean to cook and give this snail to the soldiers. We didn't see that we had cooked it with the food. We were wrong, so the four of us have agreed that we'll eat this snail."

Their jailer listened to this, took a knife and cut the snail into two more pieces. He gave the each of the prisoners a piece, and they ate it.

After they finished the snail, Sergeant Dingo said, "Now you have learned a lesson. Later when you cook food, you must check carefully and wash the food well before you cook it. If you do this again to us, you won't be able to eat the snail [as penance]. Do you understand me or not?"

The poor prisoners told their sergeant that they understood what he had explained. The four men went out towards the mess hall. They spat and spat, then vomited the entire snail from their stomachs. They vomited the other food too, and they just lay about.

When their jailer, Sergeant Dingo, came and saw this, he too began to vomit with the four prisoners. They lay there for about fifteen minutes. The prisoners got up first, then met in the mess hall and laughed and laughed until their bellies were in great pain. They thought back about eating snails and laughed again.

Their jailer, Sergeant Dingo, got up, entered and met the four of them. He too laughed inside the mess hall. He saw their faces and he laughed too.

When the four prisoners finished their work in the compound and told the story to the other prisoners (men and women), they laughed at the four men. They were afraid of having their sentences increased, so they ate the snail.

Frank N. Mathaias

C. I. S. [Corrective Institute Services] Kerevat [Keravat]
Rabaul

East New Britain Province

J200+. Choices: eat the food contaminant or face more jail time; Q580+.
Person must eat food contaminant that was served to another

## The Woman Who Married a *Masalai*

(Wantok 364, May 2, 1981, page 21)

Long, long ago, an old woman named Kauki lived on a
mountain named Walmu. She often planted taros, wild sugarcanes (*pitpit*), and other foods.

She slept in cave on the mountain. On the other side of
the mountain lived a *masalai*. However, the woman did not
know this.

One time, the woman was making a new garden. She
cut all of the trees, then went to her home. About three
weeks passed, and she returned to this place to burn the
scrub for her garden.

The *masalai* was at his home and saw the smoke rising
from the fire. When he saw this, he began to think hard because he had thought that he was alone at this place. He
said, "I think I should go and see who it is that is over there
that lit that fire. If I see a man, I'll kill him. If I see a
woman, I'll return."

The *masalai* left his home. He walked over to the
other side of the mountain. When he arrived at the place
where there was smoke, he saw the woman working hard at
cleaning her garden. When she finished, she sat down and
made a net bag. He came very close and watched her.
However, the woman had her head down while she was
making the net bag and did not see the *masalai* who was
spying upon her.

The *masalai* finished watching, then turned back and
walked to his house. He stayed there for three days then returned to the woman's garden. At this time, the woman
was carrying food [plants] from her old garden and bringing
it to her new garden. It was nearly dark. She took some
*limbum* palm leaves and covered the things that she was
would plant. She said, "Tomorrow morning, I'll come and
plant these food plants. It's almost dark now."

The *masalai* hid and listened to what she said. He was
sorry for the poor woman and said, "I think that I'll come
and help this woman with her planting."

In the morning, the woman returned to plant her food
plants. She was surprised to see the *masalai* working at
planting. She asked, him, "Who are you? Are you a man
or a ghost?" The *masalai* said, "No, I'm a real man, but I
live very far away."

The woman listened to the *masalai* who said that he
would help her work inside the garden. They finished
planting the food in the garden, then they rested. The

woman asked the *masalai*, "Would you like to get married?" The *masalai* said, "That's OK." So, they went to
where the woman lived.

The woman gave birth to a daughter first, then later she
had more children. Their children grew up, married and
produced many, many people. This place is still there, and
it is called **Manu** Village [**Yaul** People, **East Sepik** Prov-
ince].

Francis Sami
Steamship [Trading Company]
Box 79
Vanimo
West Sepik Province

A991+. Origin of particular village; F490+. Masalai; G81. Unwitting marriage to cannibal; P230. Parents and children; P232. Mother and daughter;
P234. Father and daughter; T111. Marriage of mortal and supernatural
being; T580. Childbirth

## The Beer's Fault (A Modern Story)

(Wantok 365, May 9, 1981, page 17)

There was a man named John K— from Kaindi Village, near Wewak [East Sepik Province]. He was married
and had five children, three girls and two boys. The eldest
was a girl named Hilda. John's wife was Lorna. The father
worked at the Labor Department in Wewak.

The family lived in their house, and they never fought
or got angry with other men or women. They just lived
happily. Each fortnight [payday], John K— would come
and put all his salary into his wife Lorna's hand. Mrs.
Lorna K— managed the house well. She supplied good
food, and bought the clothes for the children and her husband. Lorna's husband, John, was very happy with how his
wife took care of the family. So, they were all happy in
their house.

One day, John K—'s wife told him that she was going
to see her maternal relative in Madang. She took three
children and took an airplane one Sunday morning. When
the airplane left, John, Hilda, and the other child took the
bus to Wewak Town.

They went around town and met Tom Mat, one of John
K—'s beer buddies. Tom saw John and called out, "Hey
friend, it's eleven o'clock now. Let's go and have a drink."
However John K— said, "I'm sorry friend, I came with my
children and I can't follow you now." However Tom said
again, "Friend, it's not a carton of beer. You're cowering
like a crab on the beach." John K— had been buttered up,

so he told his friend that what he thought was good. John K— sent his children back to the house.

The two of them went to a store, bought ten loose bottles, and went to Wewak Market by the beach to drink. They finished the beer and they still thirsted for more. They pooled their money and went to buy a whole carton. Then they went back to the same place and drank and drank. They finished at about six o'clock, when it was nearly dark. They walked back to Kaindi Village.

In Kaindi, John K— said goodnight to his friend and walked towards Nuigo Community Beer Club. He bought some more beer, and drank and drank until eleven o'clock at night. He felt completely drunk and went back to his house.

When he arrived at his house, he saw the two children. Hilda and the other child were asleep. The girl Hilda slept where her mother usually slept. Father John saw his daughter and he trembled. He did not think that it was his daughter. No, he just jumped down on top of his daughter. Hilda called out, "Papa, papa, papa." But the father did not listen to her, his ears were shut.

Later, Hilda got up and was completely ashamed. She ran to the police station and filed a complaint against her father. The police came, took the father and locked him in a guarded room. On Monday, father John stood in court. The court removed the charge when the father said that he saw the child sleeping in her mother's place and he thought that it was his wife when he did what he did.

Later, John's wife returned and heard what her husband had done to their daughter. She was irate and made a huge fight. Everything in the house was broken. All of the pots, the clothes, the radio, the silverware, the plates and cups were entirely ruined and went into a fire. All of their happiness and their good life were destroyed.

Lorna went and filed a complaint with the Welfare Office. She took all of the children and went to Madang. Her husband was very troubled. He cried and cried for three whole days.

It was just like that. A little beer can cause a family to become destroyed. All of the good life and happiness were ruined when John K— did this. Now he has a truly rotten existence. Other women will not marry this kind of man because the news goes around to the ears of all of the men and women. How very, very sad.

Anton Manda

Box 106

Wewak

East Sepik Province

J1485. Mistaken identity; N365.2. Unwitting father-daughter incest; P210. Husband and wife; P231. Mother and son; P232. Mother and daughter; P233. Father and son; P234. Father and daughter; P250. Brothers and sisters; P290+. Maternal kin; Q242.2. Father-daughter incest punished; T411. Father-daughter incest; T471. Rape

## The Sun Arose
(Wantok 366, May 16, 1981, page 21)

Long, long ago, there was no sun in the sky. Every place on the earth was dark. In a village called **Saulaku**, there were two men. Their names were Maiku and Maikien.

One time, two maternal relatives were fighting over some wildfowl eggs. They fought in the very deep forest, but they made such a noise that it was as if a smoke bomb had been ignited.

The two men heard this, and so Maiku sent his son, Miken [Maikien] to look. He said, "It's bad that the two maternal relatives are fighting and making a big racket in the forest. I think you should look at them." After the father said this, he took a big portion of tobacco and some ripe bananas, and gave them to his son to bring with him.

When he arrived at the place where the noise was coming from, he saw his two maternal relatives fighting.

They were not pretending to fight: they were smoking. When Maiken saw this, he stood in between them to stop them. However, one of the maternal relatives stood up, took a piece of wild *limbum* palm tree and swung it at his maternal relative. He missed and broke Maiken's head. Blood spurted out all over like a flowing river. When the maternal relatives saw this, they stopped fighting.

Miaken [Maikien] took a noxious plant (*salat*) from the ground that we call <u>*aislu*</u> and tied it to the place where the blood was spurting. Then he walked back home.

He felt terrible, but he was still strong enough to walk. When he arrived home, his father saw him and was shocked. He was very angry and asked his son [about what had happened]. Miaken said, "You sent me, and I went to see the two maternal relatives fighting. I went between them to break up their fight. One of them broke open my head with a wild *limbum*."

The father saw that his son was going to die, so he asked him, "What should I do with you? Should I bury you or put you on top of the clouds?"

Miaken said, "If you bury me, it will still be dark. Raise me up so that your place will be light."

When his father heard this, he went to gather some scents from ginger, scents from the *purpur* shrub, bark, and other things from the forest. He took these things, then he took some betel nuts and betel peppers and returned. He went to a village called Talpepi [**Talbipi** Village, **Olo** People, **West Sepik** Province].

He took a hard and thick piece of bamboo. This village is very far from Lumi Village. He took this bamboo and brought it. When he returned to the village, his son was dead.

The father broke the bamboo and made it into something like a net. He put his son inside the bamboo and tried to put him up into the clouds. When he tried, the clouds broke. While he was trying to put his son there, he "pulled" water from his son's two wives.

One of these women was pregnant and the other was not. When they saw that the water had dried up, one said to the other, "How will we process the sago without water? All of the water has dried up. I think that our husband has been defeated and his father is pulling water from us." So, they took the sago and their wash and walked to the village. They saw the betel nuts in the middle of the trail. They took the food and went directly to the village where the father was now raising the child into the clouds. Oh my, the sky was broken and the sun went inside it. The father lost the bamboo and it fell down onto the house. He slept and slept, until about five o'clock in the morning when he heard crying. He opened his eyes and saw the sun was bright red.

Before, we lived in the dark. We only worked at night. We did not have a moon or sun. There was only darkness. The men worked at night. They got food, cooked and ate it only at night. We call the sun _wpli_ [_epli_] in my language.

Paul Suar
Catholic Mission Laingim
Yancok sub-District
West Sepik Province

A605.1. Primeval darkness; A711. Sun as man who left earth; D2151.2.3. Rivers magically made dry; F61. Person wafted to sky; N730+. Relative accidentally killed when intervening in fight; P210. Husband and wife; P233. Father and son; P261. Father-in-law; P265+. Daughter-in-law; P290+. Maternal kin; T145.0.1. Polygyny; T570. Pregnancy


## The Ground Broke (A Modern Story)

(Wantok 367, May 23, 1981, page 17)

It was February 16, 1981 when I saw something happen in a village with my own eyes. It was something else, the thing that happened at this time.

At 6:30 in the evening, on Monday the sixteenth, we finished eating and were getting ready to sleep. My grandparent, Dabanau [Dubanau] went to the toilet and my parents were listening to the radio with my sister. I was playing on the verandah of the house by myself.

It was all too true, a powerful earthquake began to shake. My grandparent saw that the trees, coconuts, breadfruits, and flowers had begun to slowly fall. My grandparent jumped. Our house was beginning to fall. We heard this and shut the doors of the house. We pushed the house back and my father pushed hard against the house wall as it fell.

He and the others began to jump. When we all jumped away, the house fell completely and was ruined. The things in the house were gone and so was the house. We would never see the house again. The suitcases, the pots, the plates, the radio, the guitar and everything else of ours were trashed.

There were two things that came before my eyes. Two coconut palms fell down on the ground and the ground covered them over. A _limbum_ palm from very far away came and stood in the middle of where the ground had broken open. When the coconuts fell to the ground, we found a leader, who was the landowner, to come and curse the _masalais_. We men removed our waistcloths, stood butt naked and killed chickens. We threw the chickens and coconuts down into the place where the ground had broken open.

Immediately, the coconut palms slowly stood up straight again. A little later, something huge came to our village. It was black and had a tail. However, it was dark and we could not see it well. It had wings, and a long nose, and it had a tail. We saw it and we trembled with fear. It went back immediately.

The people saw this and everyone collected their things. If you had looked at this place there were no people walking around. It was as if the Japanese soldiers [were there] and there was not a single boy or girl. Everyone lay down with his or her rubbish. They followed the long trail to their two villages.

Some men were all right, but two old people, Mudua and Palaua, could not carry their rubbish. If you had seen this, I think that any one of you would have laughed at this strangeness, or you would have laughed and vomited or pissed yourself.

This place where the ground broke open is about 130-150 feet deep and 180 feet wide. If you would like to see this, when you go to **Wagi** Village, near C. M. [Congregation of Mission] Tangu, ask them to show you what happened on February 16, 1981 [**Tangu** People].

Rex T. Dubanau
Catholic Mission Tangu
Wagi Village
Bogia
**Madang** Province

B871. Giant beasts; D1602.2. Felled tree raises itself again; D1643. Object travels by itself; D1766.2.2. Magic power from sacrificing a cock; F438+. Spirit of earthquake: black with wings, long nose, and tail; F490+. Masalai; V12.4.11+. Chicken as sacrifice

## The Man Stole a *Masalai* Baby

(Wantok 368, May 31, 1981, page 21)

In 1980, a man named Mirin took his dog and traveled in the forest. He went around and around, and when he arrived at one place, the rain began to fall down. Mirin saw this and looked for a place to hide from the rain. He looked and looked, then he saw a boulder that was like a house, and he went to hide there.

When the rain had nearly stopped, he saw a woman approaching. He thought that it was a woman from the village, so Mirin stood and watched her approaching. However, he was at the woman's house. Oh my, the *masalai* woman did not quietly bring her food. She saw Mirin and she thought it was her husband, so she gave her baby to him. Mirin stood and watched. He saw the woman open the boulder and go inside.

Mirin saw this, took the *masalai* baby and went to his village. The *masalai* woman did not think any more about her baby. No, she did not wait to cook her food. When the food was ready, she called out to her husband, but her husband was still in the forest. She called and called. Then she went outside and looked for the man to whom she had given her baby.

When she went outside, no one was standing there. Oh my, the *masalai* woman was shocked and said, "I must have given the baby to a man from the village." So, the *masalai* woman went to find her baby. She searched and searched, then she found her baby with Mirin. The *masalai* woman tried and tried to take her baby, but she was unsuccessful, so she returned to her house and told her husband that Mirin had taken the baby. The *masalai* man was irate.

He took his spear and the two of them went back to their house. Another morning, they did not go to their home. Very late at night, they went to Mirin's village, but Mirin was not asleep. He was watching for them. The *masalai*s were irate, so the *masalai* man hid nearby in a place where men did not go. They kept watching for their baby.

The *masalai* waited and waited. He tired and went back home. He beat his wife terribly and said, "You did wrong and they took our baby. I tried to get the baby back many times, but the men were too strong. What should I do now?"

The *masalai* man just went like a river and took the baby. This river flows and still meets a certain place. If you travel to this place, you will die immediately.

Febian Ambasi
P. O. Box 20
**Nuku** [Village, **Mehek** People]
**West Sepik** Province

A934.11. River from transformation; C615. Forbidden body of water; D283+. Transformation: spirit to river; D1552. Mountains or rocks open and close; F401.6. Spirit in human form; F408.3. Spirits dwell at tabu place; F490+. Masalai; J1485. Mistaken identity; P210. Husband and wife; P230. Parents and children; Q430+. Carelessly giving child away punished; Q458. Flogging as punishment; R153.4+. Mother rescues child

## The Man Taught by a Log (A Modern Story)

(Wantok 369, June 6, 1981, page 17)

There was a man who lived in a town. He was married and had three children. This man's habits were not good ones in the eyes of his peers. He worked, and every payday he would spend all his money to buy beer. One fortnight (payday), he took his money at 3:30 [p.m.] then went to his brother and said, "Now it's time for us to be happy." When he took the money, he did not go home from that Friday until the next Saturday evening.

His wife worked too, in a warehouse. When she was paid on the fortnight, she divided her money up. Part went to her savings account, and part to the children. The woman's habits were good in the eyes of her peers. When her kin came, she would talk nicely to them, and she would cook food and feed them. She was happy for people to come to their house.

The man drank and got blind drunk all of the time. The leaders of the village talked about collecting money to build a church made of sheet metal. So, they sent a letter to their children who lived in the town that they should collect money and send it to the village. The man's wife told him about the letter.

Oh my, the man's eyes popped out and he said, "Oh man, who's really going to give a hand to the people in the village for this kind of work? My money is just for helping me. There's money in the village, so why are they calling out for money? I don't work to give money to them."

His poor wife judged that what he said was bad. She told him directly, "It's too bad that you can't think that God's spirit is in you. No, Satan's spirit is controlling you now. So I'm telling you directly, it won't be long before you'll be miserable."

The woman's husband listened to what she said, and he knew that she was furious. The next fortnight, the man took his salary and went to a club. The woman knew this and prepared a piece of firewood. Her husband returned home at about one o'clock at night. He was drunk and demanded food, "I'm hungry." His wife hammered his head and said, "When will you stop drinking beer?"

The man was half-dead. Later, he got up and thought clearly. His wife said, "You must think about your children. Later when you're old, your children will take care of you." The man was terribly ashamed at what his wife said to him. It was as if he was being taught in school.

So now, this man's habits have completely changed. He never drinks. His habits have changed and he is very good. This man is from Mabumb Village.

Paul Yatu

Gobmasun

Box 80

Lae

Morobe Province

P210. Husband and wife; P230. Parents and children; Q276. Stinginess punished; Q458. Flogging as punishment; W152. Stinginess; X800. Humor based on drunkenness

## Cassowary Woman

(Wantok 370, June 13, 1981, page 17)

One day, a leader traveled in the forest, hunting for wild game. He carried his magic object with him into the forest. While he was hunting, his magic object fell. He did not know this and he continued to hunt for game.

Later, he returned to the village and gave his game to his wives. He then looked for his magic object. His two wives could not find it, so he went back into the forest. However, he could not find his magic object in the forest.

This man's name was Dafa. His magic object had fallen in the forest and a cassowary had come and eaten it. The cassowary saw the magic object and thought that it was a tree fruit, so the cassowary had eaten it.

After a while, the she-cassowary had babies. All her babies were cassowaries, except for one who was a girl. The cassowary's children grew up.

Whenever they traveled with their mother, they ate tree fruits. The girl also traveled with them.

One time, a man from the village went into the forest and saw this girl going around with the cassowaries. The man's name was Saga. Every day, Saga went into the forest and saw these cassowaries and the girl eating fruits. He saw this and made a fence around the base of the tree. After he finished the fence, he went back to the village. When it was still at night, he woke up and went back to this place and looked for the cassowaries eating the tree fruits. However when they saw him, they all fled. Quickly, he jumped and grabbed this little girl.

He was very happy and brought the girl back to the village. The leaders of the village made some rope [rattan?] and gave it to the girl to swallow. She swallowed the rope, then vomited all of the tree fruits out.

Saga and his wife gave some ripe bananas to the girl and she ate them. Later, they gave her other kinds of human food, and the girl ate these. Now they knew that the girl would not die. She lived with the husband and wife as their real daughter.

The girl lived there, growing up and speaking like the other children. Later, she became a woman and married. She gave birth to a boy, and later she had more children. Her sons became very smart and many women wanted them. Men were lustful after her daughters too. Later, these children married and they had children. This family became very large. The people of the village were never angry with this family. It is forbidden.

Paul Kuna

P. O. Box 1210

Arawa

North Solomons Province

A1640. Origin of tribal subdivisions; B631+. Cassowary gives birth to girl and cassowaries after swallowing magic object; B754.6.1. Unusual impregnation of animal; C680+. Forbidden to get angry with those humans descended from cassowary; D800. Magic object; L111.2. Foundling hero; P210. Husband and wife; P231. Mother and son; P232. Mother and daughter; P234. Father and daughter; P271. Foster father; P272. Foster mother; P275+. Foster daughter; R220. Flights; T100. Marriage; T145.0.1. Polygyny; T511. Conception from eating; T580. Childbirth

## A Radio Confused the Old Man (A Modern Story)

(Wantok 371, June 20, 1981, page 17)

Atoka is an old man from Mugayamuti Village [Mugaiamuti Village, Eastern Highlands Province]. He is a good man. He takes life easy and he never gets angry with other people.

His eldest child works in Goroka [Eastern Highlands Province]. He lived in Goroka for a long time without returning to the village. One time, Atoka's child thought about returning to the village to see his parents. So, he bought clothing and other presents for his family, and he bought a huge radio with a cassette player.

The next day, he took a P. M. V. [Public Motor Vehicle or bus] to his village. When he arrived, his parents and siblings were very happy to see him. He gave presents to his whole family. Then he opened the new radio. Everyone came to listen. The poor old man Atoka thought that it was some man there inside the radio that was talking and singing.

After the old man thought this, he went to his garden and cut some sugarcane to give to this man inside the radio. [Offering sugarcane is a sign of hospitality.] He took some sugarcane, returned to the village and gave some to his child. He put some by the radio.

He said, "OK, that's enough talking, telling stories and singing. You must get up and eat some sugarcane now. You must be thirsty and very hungry."

After he said this, he went back to the garden. Later her returned to the house. He saw the things were still there. No one had eaten them. The old man did not feel well. He was furious and told the radio, "What kind of food do you people want to eat then? You did not eat my sugarcanes." While he was saying this, he peeled some sweet potatoes. He cooked the sweet potatoes and threw it on a big dish. Then he told the radio, "OK, you people get up and eat now."

The old man Atoka said this, but nothing happened. The old man was irate.

He said, "You men from Goroka came with my child. Now you must eat my food. I worked hard and you don't like the food or anything else that I gave to you. What do you usually eat?"

The old man finished talking. He took an axe, broke the radio and threw it around. Later his child returned to the house and saw the pieces of the radio lying about. He did not say anything about the radio to his father because he was at fault and the old father had broken his radio. He did not want to talk first.

It is true that many young people today often confuse the old people in the villages. Please do not do this. You should explain what all of the new things are so that they understand.

Manoba Kuma
P. O. Box 787
Port Moresby
National Capital District

J1850+. Radio thought to contain humans; P210. Husband and wife; P230. Parents and children; P250. Brothers and sisters

## Paroko Took out a Woman
(Wantok 372, June 27, 1981, page 17)

Long, long ago, there was a village that was about to have a festival. The name of this village is **Sirumpa**. One man lived down below on a mountain called Malamuga.

He was not a good man. He was a crazy man. His name was Paroko. All of the good people prepared their things for the festival. This bad man, Paroko, was still making a huge headdress. He made a small hand drum with *tanget* leaves. He killed a wild rat that was fairly large.

He skinned it and brought it home. He covered one end of the hand drum's opening [with the skin], then got everything ready.

Night had come and the good people were still trying their singing and dancing. The bad man, Paroko, tried singing and dancing too.

Oh my, his hand drum was completely different. Everyone was singing and dancing, and he alone followed them. While they sang and danced, he went among them and sang and danced too.

Everyone looked at him and said, "We have all come here, but where has he come from?" The sound of the hand drum was like this, "Mini toriyuo. Mana troviyo, vivivivi..." All of the young women fell for this sound.

They took fire and warmed the bodies of those who were singing and dancing. They gathered all of their pieces of trash by their legs, [?] just Paroko's.

Paroko called the name of a young woman and sang, "*Saye-e* Kimiti, Kimiti *saye*." The name of this woman was Kimiti. Then she sang, "*Saiye-e saiye-e* Paroko *naroko saiye*." Oh my, they sang this song for a while, angering the people very much.

The woman, Kimiti, got a needle and thread ready then she followed him. Near dawn, at about 5:30 a.m., he left and ran away. He followed a trail. The sun rose brightly and he became dizzy. He put his hand drum underneath his head like a pillow. He fell dead asleep.

All of the women were shocked because he had run away in the dead of night. They checked all of the trails and did not see him. They checked a small trail that the man Paroko had used. All of the young women followed this trail. They traveled and traveled, then they became tired and returned to the village.

Only one woman, Kimiti, continued to follow this trail, and then she saw him dead asleep. She tried to inject a small needle into Paroko's skin, but he did not feel it. The woman took the other end of the thread and used it attach herself to him. One needle was inside Paroko's skin and another was inside her skin.

Paroko wanted to turn in his sleep, but he felt something strange, so he woke up and saw this. He left the thread and ran away.

The woman got up too and chased him. But as Paroko went along, the woman took a shortcut and met him.

He took another trail, and they continued on like this for some time. Paroko made a big hole and went down into it. Kimiti said, "I love you. I'm coming after your strength, but you keep running away. So at **Untitega**, I'll become a nice tree and bear much fruit that you shall eat. Behind me, there shall be much water."

The man became a flying fox. So, every time that the flying foxes go to Untitega, they eat the tree fruits. The place where the man made a hole for himself is a place that we call **Henganofi** [**Kamano** People, **Eastern Highlands Province**]. This cave (hole) is filled with flying foxes, and the Europeans go to see this cave. It is still there.

This is the end of my little ancestor story. If you want, I will write again. I have many ancestor stories. I live in Kundiawa in Simbu Province.

Yossy H. Manuo
Yohotegaw [Yohotegave] Village
Goroka
Eastern Highlands Province

A999.1K. Origin of caves; A2430+. Why flying foxes eat tree fruits; A2433.3+. Why flying fox lives in cave; D117.5KM. Transformation: man to flying fox; D215W. Transformation: woman to tree; D1181. Magic needle; D1355.1. Love-producing music; R260. Pursuits; T10. Falling in love

### The Champion Won a Medal (A Modern Story)

(Wantok 373, July 4, 1981, page 17)

One Saturday morning after payday, military police A. C. O. [Warden] Baining Taulir told his wife that he would go diving for fish in the river. This river is three miles away from the beach at Keravat [Kerevat] Prison and is called Kindam (lit., "Crayfish" or "Shrimp") [East New Britain Province]. The river is between Kerevat National High School and the Kerevat Prison fence.

This champion, A. C. O. Baining Taulir told his wife, B. T. Sidamun, to go to Rabaul Town and get food for themselves for two weeks. So, his wife went in the prison truck with the other police wardens' wives and went to the market in Rabaul Town.

I called Baining, "Champion," because among all of the A. C. O.s or police wardens in Kerevat Prison, he is the best at catching fish and eels in the river near the prison. All of the men, officers, and wardens, know this man well, A. C. O. Baining Taulir, and they call him Champion.

Champion has five children, three boys and two girls. But he never takes his children with him when he wants to go swimming to catch fish.

Yes, and he also keeps the heat on the prisoners when they are working. If you are a prisoner, you must look out for this man, Champion A. C. O. Baining. If you are not looking, he will go near you and shout at you. Oh my! You will be shocked and have the soul scared right out of you. He is a very fiery man, and all of the prisoners shake at his presence.

Champion caught big fat fish, huge golden fish, big *mukmuk*, big eels, and big crayfish. When his fishing line was filled with fish, he left it on a tree near the water. Then he found another line and swam far away to the edge of the road.

When he arrived at a lake, he looked at his watch and saw that it was half past three p.m. already. He said, "OK, I'll swim in the water, then go back and wait for the truck to the prison." After he said this, he quickly killed some fish in this lake. He killed many fish in this lake, he did not fool around. Then he swam to a tree that had fallen and was lying in the water. When he swam underneath the tree, he saw a huge eel. He did not see it well and he thought that it was just a big eel. No, it was the mother of the eels. It was small like a snake and it had white marks on its black skin.

### The Eel Pokes Out Eyes

The mother eel often broke swimming goggles and removed men's eyes if she got them good. Champion surfaced and caught his breath. He set his spear gun and went back to kill this eel. When he went, he was ready, but the eel came quickly and broke his goggles on his good side. The poor fish-shooting champion found his match in the lake. He was completely stunned. He dropped everything in his hands, bumped the tree, went to the other side and bumped a big stone. The poor man had found his match.

He looked to see what happened. One eye was all right and the other was ruined.

The poor man was lucky that he came up to the surface of the lake. He groped about, feeling the stones, and found a little place that had sand. He lay there and turned about. The pain in his eye was tremendous. He lay there for about an hour and it became dark. Then he got up and looked for a stick. He removed the leaves and used it to walk and find the road. The poor man thought that he was walking downstream, but he was not, he was walking upstream. He walked a long way, but he did not know that he was going the wrong way. The poor man kept listening for the sound of the truck, but he did not hear it. He just heard the sound of frogs, small birds, and insects in the deep forest. These are the things that cry out when it gets dark.

The poor man felt very cold and he was still in pain. He fell down on a log and into a hole. He wrecked his leg and lost his strength. He went down close to the river and slept until daybreak. The place where he had slept was about six miles from the road on which the truck traveled.

It was daylight. The sun rose and it became very hot. Baining walked down, followed the river and found some men. The men met him, cut some branches and made a platform with vines. They carried him to the prison. All of the wardens were shocked to see him. The poor man was a wreck, and the wardens' wives cried for Champion.

Some of the men ran to find his wife. They told her that her husband had died at Kindam River, and that some men had found him and carried him to the office. The woman cut off two of her fingers on her right hand and her ear [a sign of morning]. She carried a big axe and cried on the way to the office. She cried out, "I don't care if I die or if I'm imprisoned. I want you to show me who killed my husband. I don't care, I'm going to cut his neck and he'll die just like my husband." The officers told her, "Your husband is not dead and no one killed him. The mother eel of Kindam River broke his goggles and removed his good eye when he was spearfishing yesterday. He slept by the Kindam River. In the morning, the men from the village met him and brought him here."

### The Man Rests

One officer told a warden who was a driver to take Champion to the hospital at Nonga. Champion's wife took the four men who carried him. She took them to her house, made tea and served them. They drank and she said, "Now my husband is unable to work, so we have no money, but next fortnight [payday], we'll have money. For now, I'll just give you half the money [for bringing him]."

She gave them something and they departed. However, on the road, they sat, rested and argued. One of them wanted the money and another wanted the bag of taro that Champion's wife had given to them. They argued and fought, wrecking the taros. They finished fighting, then carried back the bag of food to their home at Balabonga Number 7.

Poor Champion, who had killed fish and eels in the sea and river was finished with work. Queen Eel of Kindam River was very happy with Champion's good work at killing fish and eels, so Queen Eel gave a new name to Champion. Now they call him Sir Baining. Queen Eel also gave him a big medal. This "medal" was pinned on him by the doctors on his eye when he left the hospital.

The medal that Queen Eel gave to Sir Baining is called a glass eye, or a false eye, where the doctors at Nonga Hospital put it where Champion's real eye was.

Peter Mathaias

C. I. S. [Corrective Institute Services] Kerevat [Keravat] Rabaul

East New Britain Province

B17.2.1.2. Hostile eel attacks hero; B243.2.2+. Queen of eels; B874.2. Giant eel; P210. Husband and wife; P230. Parents and children; P681+. Mourning customs: self-mutilation; R130. Rescue of abandoned or lost persons; S110. Murders; S160.1. Self-mutilation; S161.1. Mutilation: cutting off fingers; S168. Mutilation: tearing off ears

## Shooting Koramau's Eye
(Wantok 374, July 11, 1981, page 17)

Long, long ago, two brothers lived in a small village called Gani [**Gunakane**] in the Sinasina area [**Sinasina** People, **Simbu** Province]. Their names were Koramau and Sipa.

One night, the brothers decided to go to the forest and hunt marsupials (*kapul*) and birds. They told their father about what they thought. Their father, Korul, made two bows and some arrows. He gave three arrows and a bow to Koramau then told him, "In the early morning, go up the Polule River and shoot some birds and marsupials, then return."

He turned and told his other son, Sipa, "I'm giving you seven arrows and a bow. In the morning, you'll go towards Kawikane [**Kwikane**] to **Waragelu**."

In the morning, the two brothers woke up when it was still half-dark. They took the bows and arrows, then went walking off. When they arrived at Ganikama [Gunakane], the big brother, Sipa, told the little brother, Koramau, "Papa made two bows, giving one to you and one to me. I'd like you to try aiming your first arrow at my eye. If you shoot my eye and my eye comes out, then you'll shoot a lot of wild animals. If not, you will not shoot many animals."

After he said this, he took some bark and put it inside some sweet potato leaves, then he took [his eye] out. He told his brother to shoot his eye. Koramau stood about eleven meters away and aimed at Sipa's eye. He drew back his bow and shot, but his arrow missed and hit the bark, falling down.

The big brother Sipa said, "Now it's time for me to try to shoot your eye." Koramau took the bark and sweet potato leaves and placed his eye [there]. He called to Sipa to shoot at his eye.

Sipa aimed the arrow at his eye. He drew back his bow and shot. The arrow flew and removed Koramau's eye. He was in pain and he cried. He called out, "*Aia abe abe mina mina*." In the Kere Language [**Golin** People], this means, "Aia, papa, papa, mama, mama."

Their parents came and when they saw this, they took a big stick and beat Sipia [Sipa]. They mourned for Koramau, killing a big pig and making a party. Everyone in the village came and ate the pork.

The two brothers lived a very long time. Sipa is still alive and his brother, Koramau, died last year.

Malan Sula, Line Operator

P & T [Post & Telekom]

Arawa

North Solomons Province

F541.11. Removable eyes; M300+. Contest: whoever shoots the other's eye out will be a good hunter; P231. Mother and son; P233. Father and son; P251.5. Two brothers; Q458. Flogging as punishment


## Poeka Gave a Party (A Modern Story)
(Wantok 375, July 18, 1981, page 17)

There is a man named Poeka. He is a worthless man. He lives in his house. He does not have kin, a wife, children, or friends. He is entirely alone in his home.

Also, the men do not like him. They do not give him food or help him with his work. He is just completely alone. However, this man, Poeka, is a hard worker. In his garden, he had various kinds of food plants that were just rotting because he did not have anyone to help him eat the food.

Poeka had one pig. He often gave food to the pig and the pig became very big. The pig's two tusks grew and came outside its mouth in a loop. It was a huge pig. Poeka often heard the men talking, "Party, party." So he thought about giving a little party for himself. He thought of killing his pig and making a party. Then he thought about making a party with some men who often helped him work, and walked with him, and did other things.

He took some edible greens, cabbage, breadfruit tree leaves, and other things for making an earth oven. Then he slaughtered his pig, singed off the hair and butchered it. He finished the butchering and the cooked it in the earth oven, then he went to wash up. When he returned, he uncovered the earth oven. He removed the pork and cut it up, then he filled a net bag with the pork. Now he wanted to begin the party.

The first party, he wanted to give for his "brother leg." So he told his leg, "You're here and I go to all of the other places. I often go to the forest. I often go to the garden and all of the other places. It is because of you that I'm able to walk around and do these things. That's why I have made a party for you." Then he shoved his leg inside the net bag of pork and rubbed his leg around in the pork.

He wanted to make the second party for his arm. He told his arm, "You're here and I cut firewood, I sharpen house posts, and I cut the forest to make gardens. I cook food and eat it too. Now I want to make party for you." Then he shoved his arm in and held the pork and mashed it up. He rubbed his arm in the pork and shoved it about.

The third party he made was for his ear. He said, "You're here and I often hear talking. In the morning, I hear the birds sing and then I know that it's dawn. I know when an airplane is coming and when a car is coming. Also, I hear when men are calling out because of you, ear."

Then he made a party for his ear. He took all of the pork fat and shoved inside his ear. His ear was stuffed with grease. He said, "Now I have made a party for you."

Later, he made a fourth party for his eye. He told his eye, "You're here and I can see. I see the trees, the streams, the mountains, and all of the other things. So now I'm making a party for you." He took the pork fat and rubbed it in his eye.

The fifth party that he made was for his nose. He told his nose, "Because of you, I smell corn, sweet potatoes, pork, leafy greens, and rotten things. Now I want to make a party for you." He shoved the grease into his nose.

Then he made a party for all of the parts of his body. There were still two friends. He brought his axe and said, "You're here and I cut trees, make houses, cut firewood, and cut all of the other things. So now I'm making a party for you." Then he shoved the axe into the net bag of pork and rubbed it around.  He finished, then brought another one of his friends.  This friend was a shovel.  He told the shovel, "You're here and I dig the earth and make gardens. I dig the earth to make houses.  Now I'm making a party for you."

After he finished making the party, he wanted to scold one.  He said, "Mouth, you never do any work.  You always just eat food.  No, you just swallow food.  All of the other parts work hard for you, and you just eat."  Then he hit his mouth.  He hit it hard and it swelled up quite a bit.
Eno P. Napa
**Tambul** [Village, **Hagen** People]
**Western Highlands** Province

J1856. Food given to object; J1856+. Food given to body part; J1867. Man punishes offending part of his body; P160. Beggars; P426.2. Hermit


# The Signal Drum Came to Finschhafen
(Wantok 376, July 25, 1981, page 21)

Long ago, an old man and his wife lived in a small village named **Robalong**, near the Muigsung River on Finschhafen Peninsula [**Morobe** Province].

The two old people made a huge taro garden by their home.  There were many pigs in the village, so they made a big fence around the taro garden.

However, there was a man who lived in this village.  At night, he often turned into a pig and went to eat their taros. He would jump the fence, crossing over two rails.  Then he would scatter the taros about the garden.  When dawn approached, he would run back to his house and sleep.  This man lived on a mountain named Kulung Kongkong [*Kongkong* means "Chinese" or "Chinese taro" in Tok Pisin].

In the early morning, the two old people went back to the garden and saw that the taros were strewn about.  They were horrified and said, "Which worthless pig removed our taros?"

They finished talking and they replanted the taros.  At night, the man returned again and ruined the taro garden. They went to see this and again said, "What kind of pig is coming to our garden?  It did not break the fence.  It must be a huge pig that jumps the fence and comes inside."

They reconnected the fence and made it go very high. Then they made a huge hole near the fence.  At night, the pig came back to the garden.  He wanted to jump over and go inside.  But no, he fell right into the big hole.  When he fell into the hole, he hit the ground, and it was like the beating of a signal drum.  The two old people heard this

sound and said, "What's that noise?"  The noise came from their garden, so they thought it was a big tree that had fallen into the garden.

They lit a torch, then walked towards the garden. When they arrived at the garden, they went inside and saw something lying there.

They saw a half-man, half-pig in the hole.  They were shocked and took a piece of rope to tie up the pig.  However, when the rope touched its neck, it was like the sound of a signal drum.  They said, "What kind of new thing is this?"  Then they put the rope down slowly and pulled the pig-man out of the hole.  They tied him up and carried him to the village.

They arrived at the house and hid this thing well in a corner of the cookhouse.  In the morning, the old man woke up and told his wife, "I'll go hunt for some wild game in the forest.  Stay home, then go to the garden and get some yams.  However, if someone comes to our house, you must not tell the person about this thing.  It's just our new thing."

After he finished explaining this to his wife, he went into the forest.  When the old man departed, his wife straightened things around the house.  While she straightened the house, she did not see the crooked leg of the pig-man.  Oh my, there was a booming sound.  The **Tami** People heard this and said, "Hey, what's that booming sound?" They took their canoes and paddled towards the big village.

The Tami arrived at the big village and left their canoes near a village near Tigidu [Tigedu], called **Waolong** [**Bukawac** People].  They followed the Bulosong [Bulesong] River.  They left the Bulusong [Bulosong] and followed the Bume [Bumi] River to the old woman's house. When they arrived at the house, they asked, "Where's your old husband?"

The old woman said, "I don't know."  They said, "Did you hear a loud noise or not?"  The old woman lied to them and said, "No."  The men from Tami said, "OK, stay at your house, we're going to find out what made this noise."

### The Tami People Heard It
However, the old woman told them to stay at the house and she would give them some food first.  The men from Tami stayed at the house and the old woman went to get some yams from her garden.  When the old woman left the house, the men from Tami began to look around inside her house.  They wanted to thoroughly search the house first lest the old woman was hiding something inside.

They searched and searched, then they saw the pig lying underneath the cookhouse.  When one of them held the pig's leg, there was a loud booming sound.  They knew that they had found this thing. They quickly took a piece of rope, tied the pig to a stick, carried it and ran away.

While the old woman was removing yams from her garden, she heard a loud booming sound from the pig. She knew that the Tami men had found this thing. She left her net bag and the food there in the garden, then ran back to the house. However, it was too late. The men of Tami had already run away with the pig.

The old man also stopped hunting for game when he heard the booming sound from the pig. He stopped thinking about game. He began to run back to the village. When he arrived at his house, no one was there and he knew that whoever had taken the pig had run away.

The men of Tami had run to the beach. They put the pig on top of their canoe. They were beginning to shove the canoe into the sea when the old man arrived.

The old man was furious and he began to throw spears at the canoe. However, the young men paddled quickly and the old man's spears missed.

The old man saw that they had beaten him and he sorrowfully went back to Raboling [Robalong] Village.

The Tami men arrived at their island and carried the pig onto the beach. When the boys played with it, it made loud crashing sounds. The sounds went out to [the mainland of] Madang [Province] too.

The clans of **Madang** [Province?] heard this, took their canoes and paddled to Tami. They arrived at **Tami** Island, stole the pig and carried it back to their village.

So now, the people of [the mainland of] Madang [Province?] often hit the signal drum, and the people of Tami do not do so very much. The place where the half-man half-pig came from is called Kulung Kongkong. When you hit the signal drum, you will hear this sound.

This is the story of the first signal drum that came from Fins[c]hhafen Peninsula and went to Tami Island and Madang.

Wesley E. Jimmy
P. O. Box 132
Finschhafen
Morobe Province

A1680+. Why one place plays drum more often than another; A2824. Origin of drum; B29.3+. Man-hog makes sound of drum when touched; B871.1.2.1. Giant hog; D136M. Transformation: man to swine; D336.1M. Transformation: pig to man; D422.3+. Transformation: pig to drum; K420. Thief loses his goods or is detected; K735. Capture in pitfall; P210. Husband and wife; R220. Flights; R260. Pursuits; W157. Dishonesty



# An Airplane Came to Okapa (A Modern Story)

(Wantok 377, August 1, 1981, page 17)

In the year 1942, the Second World War came to Papua New Guinea [then the Territories of Papua and New Guinea]. At this time, the people of Okapa sub-District did not know about white men [Eastern Highlands Province].

One time, the Japanese Army took an airplane and flew over the area around Okapa. There were four men inside this airplane, two young and two a little older. They were trying to find American soldiers.

This airplane followed the Iratopindi River and went slowly. When the people of this area saw this airplane, they were terrified. Many of them ran and hid in the forest because they thought that it was an ancestral spirit.

There are many boulders and mountains in this area, and the pilot of the airplane did not look carefully. He crashed the airplane directly into some rocks.

When the airplane crashed, the two young men died. The two older leaders [officers] came out the opposite side and looked around. They saw some people of the village and they made a sign for them to come. However, the men of the village thought that these two men were ancestral spirits, so they were afraid and stayed far away.

Yes, it was true, these people of the village had not seen a white person [or Asian] before. This was the very first time that many of them had seen some light-skinned men.

After a little while, they people slowly approached and carefully looked at these two men. One-by-one they approached the two men. However, many still stood far away and looked at their airplane. They looked covetously at it. Some of them said, "It is the first thing that made a spirit axe."

Two men said, "Don't go near that dove. [Dove and airplane are conflated in Tok Pisin.] There is something there." However, the people of the village were not clear about what the two men said.

The people went inside this airplane, took two bombs and carried them out. They did not know that these things could explode and kill them.

They carried the bombs on top of a mountain. About two hundred people followed them and came to see this thing that came from the airplane. When the crazy people brought the bomb up the mountain, they knocked it. Oh my! The bomb exploded and killed those people.

My parents had also seen this bomb. They broke apart the wings of the airplane and distributed them. They brought them to a stream called Nigonisi. They thought that they could make axes from these pieces of the airplane's wings.

The two soldiers stayed in the village. Later, the people made stretchers and carried them to Kainantu, leaving them there. The men of the village called these two men Onesawa and Hesegi.

This story comes from Irasa [**Ilesa**] Village near Okapa, South **Fore** [People, **Eastern Highlands** Province]. The old people of the village can tell you good stories about this event.

Kuma Manoba
P. O. Box 787
Port Moresby
National Capital District

J1770+. Airplane misunderstood; J1770+. Bomb misunderstood; W195. Envy

# Buarlah Mountain

(Wantok 378, August 8, 1981, page 17)

Long ago, there was a man. His name was Malet and he had only two children, a boy and a girl. He and his wife and children lived in a village together. One time, the men of another village were preparing for a festival.

So, Malet with his children got prepared too. On this day, the father made a headdress and the mother made "grass" skirts for the two children. After they finished their preparations, it was evening. They left their home and walked to the village of the festival.

They arrived at the area of the village and heard it. They were not fooling around, there was not a single man, woman, old person, or child, or even a man with a bad leg, who was not dancing. Everyone was moving his or her head at the dance. The man and woman with their children just went inside and danced with them.

### Lust For the Woman

At dawn, the singing and dancing finished, and the men told all of the clans to go back to their villages. However, the boy told his father and mother that he would go later and that they could go first.

The boy was lusting for a girl from this village. After the festival finished in the morning, the boy saw the face of this girl, and he did not think clearly. He just sat, watching her and feeling sorry for her. The boy's family had already returned to their village. The boy stayed there until the af-

ternoon, then he left the village and walked slowly in sadness. However, he often turned and looked behind.

He arrived at the base of a big mountain. This big mountain has various stories. It is a place of *masalai*s, and at the peak of the mountain is a cave where *masalai* men live.

Oh my, a *masalai* saw that he was not walking smartly. He walked with sorrow for the girl that he had seen and left. So, the *masalai* man sent his own daughter down to follow him. The *masalai* girl turned her face into the face of the girl that the boy had seen.

The boy walked and walked. When he wanted to look back, the *masalai* girl laughed quietly at him. The boy threw away his hand drum and headdress, then ran quickly to her. He grabbed the *masalai* girl and told her, "You're bad. Why did you follow me? Don't you want to marry the young boys in your village? I'm a good boy. Do you want to marry me because you followed me here?" The girl told him, "I don't like to talk much. I just like you. All my love is for you. You're smarter than all of the boys of my village are. Now I'll just marry you."

The boy took the *masalai* girl and they approached the village. The boy hid the *masalai* girl. He went alone to his parents and sister. He rested a little, then told his mother and sister, "Dish out some food for me. I'm famished, but get two leaves [for plates]. One will be for me and one will be for my friend. My friend came with me and is hiding in the forest."

The two women dished out some food, as the boy had wanted, and gave it to him to eat. He held the other food, then he went and gave it to the *masalai* girl. Then he returned and waited for night.

### *Masalai* Girl

The *masalai* girl's father made it rain heavily, and the wind blew, and the clouds thundered. It was a big storm. The wind blew off tree branches that fell about. The boy's parents told him to bring his friend lest his friend became drenched. The poor boy listened to them and went to the place where the girl was.

Quickly, the *masalai* pulled the boy into the cave where they lived. Malet and his wife waited and waited, but he did not return, so they sent their daughter after him. She followed the trail that her brother had taken and arrived at the place where the *masalai* girl had been hiding. She saw plenty of rubbish from net bags in this place. However, the [*masalai*] girl had gone home with the boy and her parents.

The poor girl looked for her brother, but it was dark so she went to the house and told her parents. The two of them cried hard that night until dawn.

### The Man Became an Eagle

They stayed there, the *masalai* girl and her parents had carried the boy up to their home. The *masalai* girl told them, "Papa and mama, this is my man. I shall marry him." However, the parents of the *masalai* girl told her, "We know that he's your man, but we want your man to get meat for us to eat." After they said this, they took the poor boy and broke him open from his head to his buttocks, making two pieces. They smoked him in the front of their home. Night and day, they smoked the boy for a whole month. The boy's fat and blood dried up entirely.

They kept smoking him. One month passed, then another came and went. They looked at him and saw some feathers growing from the boy's skin. Two wings stood from his shoulders, and he began to become a bird, but they kept smoking him.

Another month came and went, and a new moon came. When they looked at the boy again, his feathers and wings were nearly strong. So, they worked at putting two bundles of firewood for the rest of the month. Now his feathers and wings were completely strong. His two legs and arms had become like that of a big bird. They looked at him and took him outside. They decorated his body with various kinds of adornments that they had. They did this and then they looked at him. They saw that his feathers were beautiful.

Now they made a sleeping place for the boy outside in the sun. They carried him and put him outside. The sun heated the poor boy's skin very much. He stayed there until the afternoon, then the boy made a noise. They watched, and it was not long when the boy got up and looked around himself. He saw that he had become something else, he was not as before. Before he was just a man, now he had become a big eagle. They took him and went inside, then he married their daughter. They gave him food and after he ate, they slept. In the morning, they taught the boy how to find wild game.

They gave him an iron *limbum* [spear?]. This iron *limbum* was not small like the *limbum*s that we often carry and hold. No, it was huge and terribly heavy. Then the *masalai*s sent the boy away. He flew a long way, to all of the villages. He went very far from their home. He hunted for wild game, he took people's children, dogs, pigs, cassowaries, and bandicoots. After he finished all of these things, he began to take the young men and women until he finished off all of them. Then he began to take all of the adult men.

After he took the men, he flew back. He had not killed them. He carried them to a breadfruit tree near the mountain where the *masalai*s dwelled. He rested on top of the tree, then he took his piece of iron and killed them, spilling their blood. Later, he hung them up on the iron *limbum*, then carried them to give to his in-laws and his wife in the cave.

The *masalai*s' only work was eating. They never really rested from eating because they kept eating people. The boy worked at taking people from far away and finishing them off. But he did not take any from nearby. No, whenever he flew, he would leave these people alone, and hunt for people in faraway places. The people from nearby saw that this boy never rested at taking people. They said, "Oh my! This will finish off the people." So, they sent a message around to the villages about the boy who was taking people. They asked them if they were all right or not. The villages said, "We're very sorry, but we're finished now."

They spoke to all of the villages from which the eagle was taking people. They told them to leave their villages. They must all take their bows, arrows, multi-pronged spears, and *limbum*s and to get ready. On that day, they met together. The next day, they all went and fenced in the breadfruit tree. At dawn, all of the men hid at the base of the breadfruit tree. They saw the eagle-boy leaving the hole in the mountain. He flew far away, to the sea. Oh my, they saw him very close. They bit their fingers and shook their heads about.

However, they called out, "Don't tremble and be afraid, just be ready. When he carries someone and returns, don't make a sound. Let him perch and rest first. When he wants to lift the person onto the breadfruit tree branch to kill, that is the time to shoot him." They made their decision and were ready. When the sun was coming out, the eagle-boy carried a big woman. The woman was pregnant. They did not see him flying. They were whistling and ready. The eagle-boy perched with his prey.

### The Eagle Strikes

He finished resting and carried the woman to the breadfruit tree. He pulled a piece of his *limbum* and broke open the woman's head. However, he had not yet killed her. They began to shoot their arrows, sticking to the boy's body. The arrows weighed down the eagle-boy's body and he left the woman. However, he did not die yet. He kept fighting with the men.

Near the base of the breadfruit tree stood a left-handed man who drew back his bow and shot his multi-pronged arrow right into the boy's ear. Now the boy died. All of the men rested and caught their breaths. After they rested, they began to cut up the eagle, dividing the flesh among themselves. However, the men of the local village told the others, "We'll take the blood and scraps and leafy greens." The men from the other villages took the piece of the iron *limbum* because it came from the mountain and the eagle. The villager Marahiri cooked the scraps, greens and blood in an earth oven. The villager Mulan took the iron *limbum*.

These two villagers had big families and now we have filled four whole villages. Some live around the [mission] station. The people made a house for the *limbum* and put it inside. When the talk of the mission came from the mission at Gamazun, our leaders were taking care of this piece of iron *limbum*. However, it is not there. It disappeared and is no longer in this house.

When the talk from the mission crossed the Markham River and followed the Wuwut River, it came to two villages, Walem [**Warom** Village, **Sukurum** People] and Wulup [**Wuruf** Village, **Silisili** People, **Morobe** Province].

My family is from these "eagles", Marahiri and Muran [Mulan].

J. Y. Timothy
Lower Wuwut
Markham [Valley]
Morobe Province

A991+. Origin of particular village; B16.3. Devastating birds; B33.0.2K. Man-eating eagle (osprey); B872.1. Giant eagle; D2142.1. Wind produced by magic; D2143.1. Rain produced by magic; D2149.1. Thunderbolt magically produced; E613.3.1. Reincarnation as eagle; F490+. Masalai; G440. Ogre abducts person; G510.4. Hero overcomes devastating animal; K1930. Treacherous impostors; P210. Husband and wife; P231. Mother and son; P232. Mother and daughter; P233. Father and son; P234. Father and daughter; P253. Sister and brother; R10. Abduction; R45.3. Captivity in cave; S118.1. Murder by cutting adversary in two; T10. Falling in love; T100. Marriage; T126+. Marriage of ogre and eagle; T570. Pregnancy

## A Cassowary Took out Yagoe (A Modern Story)

(Wantok 379, August 15, 1981, page 17)

There is a man at Kerevat [Keravat] Police Station named Manda Kaima [East New Britain Province]. He has just one brother. The policeman loves his brother, so he sent a message to him that he should come. The boy left his village and went to Rabaul. His name is Yagoe Kaima.

He stayed with his brother for three months, then Yagoe told his big brother, Manda, "The sun is high. Let's sit at the station for now. I want to travel around the forest in the Baining area. Can you find some food for me?" Manda said, "What will you do around there?" Yagoe told his brother that he wanted to hunt cassowaries and wild pigs for themselves [the dwarf cassowary (*Casuarius bennetti*) is the only species on New Britain island (Beehler *et al.*, 1986: 45)].

The big brother said, "OK, I'll get a boy from a local village, then tell him that you two will go together and hunt for game." The big brother prepared food for the two boys. He bought three packages of rice, six tins of fish, two tins of [beef], one jar of coffee, one package of sugar, and five boxes of matches. He took this food, filled up a handbag and gave it to them.

The little brother said, "Can you find a spear for me." The policeman went to the Works and Supply workshop, then sharpened two pieces of iron, one of them like a knife. He gave these to his brother and the boy from the local village. The two youths prepared themselves to go, but their walk would not be easy. They would sleep on the trail. The policeman helped them and brought them in the police car. He left them in a village.

The two said, "We'll stay for two days. On the third day, we shall return. You should get us from this same place that you're leaving us." The place that the policeman left them is called North Baining. They walked away.

They followed a river, walking until three o'clock in the afternoon. They followed a creek again and they made a camp someplace. They made a hut and cooked food. Yagoe told the boy, "We walked and our legs are tired. You should sleep and I'll travel a little, following this creek."

He took a spear, a knife, a flashlight, tobacco, and matches, then began to walk. At this time, there was a bright moon rising and the area was very clear. The boy was quite happy and said, "Now is a good time for me to find game." He went fairly far, then heard something breaking branches. The wind arose and the poor boy was frightened as he stood next to a big tree.

He saw something walking on the ground approaching him. He trembled as he stood there. When he saw it, he thought, "Now I'm done for. That thing is going to take me out." He watched and watched, then he saw a huge pig.

When the pig walked closer, a strong wind arose and the trees broke. He was terrified. The pig came closer and the boy held the spear tightly, waiting. The pig came closer still and saw Yagoe holding the spear. He was small and the pig was bigger than he was. He continued to stand there, then the pig left Yagoe and went down one step. Yagoe saw this and said, "I'll try to shoot. If it turns back and eats me, that's alright." Then he threw the spear.

Oh my! He raised one leg and loosed the spear. The pig took the spear directly and fell. It did not move. Yagoe stood and did not say anything. He went closer to the pig. He was afraid and stood there. He waited one hour, and went closer to the pig. Then the pig died, just like that.

He took a rope and put it around the pig's neck. He pulled it closer and he called out to the boy, "Come here and look at me!" He sat and rested. The boy came and the two of them pulled the pig closer to the stream. They began to look for some firewood. They singed the hair off the pig, butchered it in the water and left it there. They took a little to cook. They ate it, then they slept. "Tomorrow morning, we'll wake up, make a rack and smoke the pig."

The next day, Yagoe went back and saw a cassowary standing. He looked at the cassowary approaching and he killed it. Oh my, he was ecstatic and carried it away. He told his friend, "We've been here two days, and we've killed much game." The friend told Yagoe, "Let's camp for two days, then depart." After he said that, they cooked the cassowary in an earth oven for themselves. Later, they uncovered the earth oven and ate. They slept for the second night.

In the morning, Yagoe went to hunt for game. He went and stood fairly far away in the deep forest. He saw a pig approaching, and he killed it. He carried it and left it in the stream. He went back and saw a black-feathered cassowary with an entirely blue neck.

Yagoe stood next to a tree. The cassowary came and was scavenging for fig fruits. The cassowary came closer and Yagoe shot at it, but the cassowary saw Yagoe.

The spear missed the cassowary. Yagoe got up to run and get the spear, but no, the cassowary turned and shot [kicked at] Yagoe. Yagoe took his knife and cut the cassowary's neck. However, the cassowary came back and kicked him in the belly, breaking it open and causing his guts to fall out. Later, the cassowary kicked again and removed an eye. Yagoe cried out and fell down.

The cassowary defecated on Yagoe, making a complete wreck of him. The cassowary's feces wrecked the poor boy, and then the cassowary fled. The poor boy got up and removed his shirt. He shoved his guts back in and bandaged himself up with his shirt. He walked back to his friend.

When the friend saw him, he was very sorry for him. They prepared their things to go back, and the friend told Yagoe, "You're still carrying your guts. We can't tie you up like that, so I'll carry some pork and food for us." They spoke like that then they walked and walked, sleeping along the trail.

However, Yagoe's belly and head were in pain, so he cried as he slept. In the morning, they walked again and they arrived at the road. Yagoe's belly was stinking and they waited for his brother. Yagoe's brother was thinking of him, so he took the police car and departed. He went directly towards them. Manda thought that he would be eating pork with cassowary meat, so he was very happy. But no, he saw Yagoe's belly and eye, and Manda began to cry. The three of them together cried, then he took the two of them directly to the hospital.

As they approached the hospital, Yagoe cried out to Manda, "Brother, I think I'm ruined." When he said this, Manda turned to look at him and ran into a post. The glass broke and shot at Manda's eyes. At the same time, the nurses came and pulled out the three of them into the hospital. They examined the two brothers together. The nurses and doctors were very sorry for them.

However, there were some people who were hiding and laughing hard. The two brothers stayed at the hospital. The two of them watched and watched, then they told their story to the doctors and laughed with them.

If you want to take an airplane to Rabaul, OK go ahead. Then take a taxi to Noga Hospital. You will hear this story about the two brothers and see the pig tusks. The two of them live together and you can come see them.

Mr. Robert Evagulo
Kerevat [Keravat] C. I. S. [Corrective Institute Services]
P. O. Box 571
Rabaul
East New Britain Province

## The Ancestral Ghost of Ngorongoro
(Wantok 380, August 22, 1981, page 17)

Long ago, there was an ancestral ghost that lived in the Ngorongoro area. During low tides, the ghost would go down to the reef and catch fish.

When the ghost went out of the sea to catch fish, it would take coconut shells and put them on its breasts, and put on a "grass" skirt too. Then it would be like a woman and catch fish in the sea.

However, it did not catch real fish. No, it usually caught sea cucumbers). These were like fish for the ghost. The ghost did this all of the time.

One time, twelve women from my village, **Nambariwa**, went fishing at Ngorongoro Beach [**Sio** People, **Morobe** Province]. The ancestral ghost was dressed like a woman, had caught some sea cucumbers and was drying them in the sun.

The women from the village saw the ghost and thought that it was a real woman. The ancestral ghost fooled them and asked them for fire. So, the woman gave some fire to the ancestral ghost.

The ancestral ghost carried the fire and made a bonfire from it. A heavy rain began to fall. The twelve women saw this and hid in a cave. The rain kept falling, preventing them from returning to the village. So, they slept in the cave.

While they were sleeping, the cave closed up and they no longer had an exit. They starved to death in this cave. A long time passed and their women's bodies rotted away.

The caved opened up again. They call this cave, "Matawari Ngonza." Later, some men of the village went and found the bones of these twelve women. They took the bones back to the village and buried them in a grave.

The men of the village knew that the ancestral ghosts had tricked the women into going inside the cave in which they had died. So, they decided to kill this ancestral ghost.

The leaders of the village made a decision. The women went to get food from the gardens and brought food back. They began to cook the food. After they finished preparing all of the food, the men of the village began beating their hand drums, singing and dancing. All of the men were dressed finely. They sang and danced vigorously.

Oh my! The ancestral ghost saw the women's sisters and trembled. They had dressed well. They were not fooling around about dressing well. The women had various kinds of arm and leg bands and "grass" skirts. The ancestral ghost saw the beautiful ornaments on the women's bodies and coveted them.

All of the men and women of the village sang and danced until very late at night. The leader of the village blew a flute, then they ate and caught their breaths. The ancestral ghost went directly to the leader of the village and said, "Friend, can you dress me like that? I like your clothing very much."

The leader of the village knew that this man must be an ancestral ghost. The leader lied to him and told him to go to the spirit house. He told him to lie down, then he would

dress him. The leader of the village took some strong ropes and tied up his legs. He bound up the ancestral ghost's legs tightly, then he told him to go out to sing and dance.

However, the ancestral ghost could not get up. The man called out to everyone in the village to come and look. They burned the house and this ghost burned with the house.

Jerry Nonny
Sio Number 2 Village
Yumalos Trade Store
Morobe Province

D1552. Mountains or rocks open and close; E422.4.4. Revenant in female dress; E422.4.5. Revenant in male dress; E425.1. Revenant as woman; E425.2. Revenant as man; E446.2. Ghost laid by burning body; E259+. Ghost seals people in cave, killing them; K713.1. Deception into allowing oneself to be tied; K1810. Deception by disguise; Q211. Murder punished; Q414. Punishment: burning alive; R45.3. Captivity in cave; R51.1. Prisoners starved; R315. Cave as refuge; S112.0.2. House (hostel) burned with all inside; S146.2. Abandonment in cave; V61.3+. Dead buried; V112.1. Spirit huts; W195. Envy; W157. Dishonesty

# A Ghost from Kerevat [Keravat] (A Modern Story)
### (Wantok 381, August 29, 1981, page 17)

Near the prison in East New Britain Province, there is a big river. They call this river Keravat. This river is very big, about 120 feet wide. Near the river is a pump. There is a machine that pumps sewage from the prison to this place.

Near the place where there is a pump, it is very swampy and there is a bridge. However, it is not a real bridge, it is a tree that fell which people walk on as a bridge. If someone misses the bridge, the person will fall into the swamp up to his or her belly. If a short person falls into the soft ground, the bad water will go up to their chest. The machine that carries sewage from the prison throws it into this swamp.

Near this place, there lives a man. The man's name is Peter Aikat. The man is from Miniamia Village. He is a man that is terrified of snakes and ghosts. He looks like a man from Western Province because he is tall and fat. Peter has three children, and his wife is from his village.

One time, on Peter's day off, he woke up in the early morning and took his family to work in the garden. Their garden was on the other side of the river. They worked in the garden until it was two o'clock. A light rain began to fall. Peter saw this and sent his family back to the house.

Peter worked in the garden alone. He worked until it was almost half past four and the prisoners were walking back to the prison. Peter also left the garden and prepared to go back to his house.

He arrived at the river and saw that the river was a little flooded, so he quickly jumped over to the other side. He carried a stalk of bananas with him. When he arrived at the other side of the river, he put the bananas on the sand and washed up.

While he was washing, he saw the water rising. He looked up towards the headwaters and saw something following the river. Peter looked hard and saw a man coming downstream. The man's head was turning from side to side. The man was jumping and prancing belligerently (*samsam*) as he went. Also, he held a spear in his hand. Peter was terrified, so he closed his eyes as this man descended the river. It began to become dark and Peter could not see the man's face well.

He was entirely afraid and called out to the man, but the man did not reply to him. He pranced closer. Peter saw him and did not wait any longer. Right away, he fastened his waistcloth, quickly carried his stalk of bananas and ran away. While he ran, he heard the man making noises and coming downstream.

He did not think to turn and look behind him. No, he just looked in front of himself and kept going. He was afraid, and it would be bad if he turned and saw the ghost's face that was prancing belligerently downstream.

When he arrived at the swamp, he turned and looked back, but he did not slow down. His legs kept running as he turned his face to look back.

When he did this, he did not see the bridge well. His legs missed the crooked bridge and he went headfirst into the swamp. Oh my, the swamp was very watery and he fell in up to his belly. The poor man wanted to call out, but he did not because he was afraid. It would have been bad if he had called out because the ghost man would then follow and kill him.

He turned about in the swamp until he could jump out. He got out and when he wanted to turn again, he saw a man coming behind him. Peter forgot about standing up; he ran to the main road.

He ran and ran. He did not see a big stone in the middle of the road. The stone hit his leg and he fell badly. It was too bad the skin on his knees came off and six of his teeth fell out.

His body was in pain, but he did not think about stopping. He cried and called out at the same time, and he kept running away.

The man called out to Peter, but Peter's ears were shut because he thought that the ghost man was chasing him, and he did not want to turn and look.

The man came closer to Peter, and poor Peter ran entirely out of breath, then fell down. Everyone heard him cry out and they came running.

They saw that his skin was full of dirt and that he smelled horrible. Blood was coming from his legs and mouth. They thought that some man had killed him.

They asked this man about Peter. He told them, "I don't know. I went close to the swamp and I saw Peter coming to the swamp. When he saw me, he cried out and ran, crashing through the forest. I thought that a bad snake or something bad was chasing him, so I followed him here. However when I called to him, he called out more and went faster."

When Peter heard the man tell this story, he opened his eyes, looked around and got into a sitting position. He asked the man for his name.

The man was a policeman too, and he was working in his garden. When he had seen the water flooding, he cut across to where Peter was.

Then Peter asked, "Who was it that was following the river and moving belligerently?"

John [The policeman] said, "No one was following the river and jumping along. I just saw a big tree that the flood was carrying downstream."

No, Peter did not want to hear any more talk. He said, "I think that I saw this tree. I was afraid and ran away, wrecking my body."

He showed his teeth, arms and legs to the people. Too bad, the people had fits of laughter. They laughed and laughed, and Peter laughed with them too. He slowly got up and went to the house. He washed and got rid of the stink from the swamp that was on his skin.

Later, his friends told the other people about this so that they could tell their friends. After three whole months, the people were still laughing when they saw Peter. They thought back to his story about when he saw a big tree and he fled, ruining his body.

Robert Evagulo
Keravat C. I. S. [Corrective Institute Services]
P. O. Box 571
Rabaul
East New Britain Province

E261.4+. Imagined ghost pursues man; J1782+. Floating tree thought to be ghost; P210. Husband and wife; P230. Parents and children; R220. Flights; R260. Pursuits; W115. Slovenliness

## The Little Boy Was Cleverer

(Wantok 382, September 5, 1981, page 17)

Long ago, inside **Simbu** [Province], there was a huge house where all of the young women slept. The young men from other villages often went to the young women's house. They often caressed (*karim lek*) and slept alongside the women. [The term *karim lek* is a kind of culturally sanctioned caressing between unmarried youths (see glossary). In this story, it indicates a probable origin from the Middle Wahgi Valley (Mihalic, 1971: 107): **Wahgi**, **Kuman** or **Golin** People; **Western Highlands** or Simbu Province.] At dawn, they would return to their villages.

At this house, there lived fifty young women. They were just the right size for this house. One of the women among the fifty was very beautiful. So, many young men competed to *karim lek* with this woman when they went to sleep there. However, this woman never slept with or *karim lek*ed with the other men. This was because when this woman found the men *karim lek*ing, there was not one nice man among them.

After a long time, the young men went to the women's house where this woman slept. There was no man among them who looked handsome, and she did not like them. The men tried to find a way to change her mind, but mucous was always running from their noses. The woman did not like them.

One evening, some young men went to this village from another village that was far away. When the young women saw them, they took them inside the house. They gave food to the young men and they sated themselves.

The handsomest boy was among them. When the beautiful woman saw him, she pointed to him, then the two of them *karim lek*ed. At this time, the women began to find men, and these two sat on the woman's bed. They *karim lek*ed for a while and the woman said, "Where do you live, that you did not come around to the house before? I've never seen you before, not even a little. Oh my, you're a very nice boy. I'd like to be friends with you right away, and then get married."

### Liking the Other Boy

However the boy said, "My parents only had me. I don't have a brother or a sister. So my parents forbade me to travel to the women's house. Now is the very first time that I've come to the women's house. You're the very first woman that has *karim lek*ed with me, so you must teach me how. You asked me to marry you. That's alright, but first I'll return to the village and ask my parents."

The two of them made a decision that night. They *karim lek*ed until ten o'clock at night. The leader of the women told them to fix the bed so that they could sleep. All of the women fixed their beds, and they slept.

The beautiful woman told her boyfriend that they would sleep together. However, the boy fooled the girl. He got up later, ran away to his village and did not sleep with her. The girl cried for the boy until dawn.

The women saw her and said, "Hey, gorgeous, why are you crying?" The girl told them that she was troubled about the boy. He had said that they would sleep together, but he had run away to his village.

When a boy saw this, he was sorry for the girl and said, "Don't worry. I'll get the boy and bring him." The boy finished speaking, then went to the boy's village. He told him, "You ran away from that girl and she's crying for you. I came to get you and go back so that you can *karim lek* with her."

After he told the boy this, the two of them went back to the girl's village. They arrived at the women's house that night. The other boy told the girl that he had brought the boy back, "He's waiting for you outside the door. Go and get him." So, the girl went outside and met him. She saw him and was very happy. They talked and the girl fixed up her bed to sleep.

### Fooling the Girl

However, it was just like the night before. The boy fooled her and ran away from her again. He returned to his village that night. The girl cried again until dawn. The boy did this and made the girl very troubled.

One time, the girl went to her parent's house. She stole a long vine for making net bags and "grass" skirts that her mother had hidden away. She put it in her net bag, then followed a trail to a big stream from which people drank. She followed the stream upwards. She saw a tree with many branches near the water. She climbed the tree, tied one end of the rope to a tree branch and another end to her neck. Then she jumped down and died.

The girl's ghost appeared just like the real girl and went to the village. It was evening and the boys had come to *karim lek* with the girls. The handsome boy had come too.

### The Girl Hanged

The boy saw the ghost girl and thought that it was the real one. No one knew that the real girl had died, so the ghost girl told all of them not to *karim lek*, but to go spearfishing with torches by the stream. They killed crayfish, fish and eels. Later they returned to the house.

Everyone was very happy. The girl told the boy, "You fooled me many times by running away. You don't want to sleep with me. Also, you often told me that your parents have just one child. You made me very troubled, but I know that your parents are very happy because you now have a sister. Go and look now. Bring her to your village and show her to your parents. They'll take care of her."

The ghost girl told the boy to untie the rope around the girl's neck. The ghost told him to carry the rope too and to bring it down. The poor boy was speechless. He just followed all of the ghost girl's instructions. He carried the girl towards the village. The ghost girl helped the boy with carrying. The boy carried her to a garden and went inside a garden hut.

The ghost girl told the boy to look for a bamboo knife and to cut the girl. The boy began to butcher the girl while the ghost girl began to heat some stones. The two of them would cook the girl in an earth oven. The boy finished butchering the girl and he removed her guts. After he cut the girl into small pieces, the ghost girl spoke to him. The boy did as she said and took the liver and lungs out of the girl. The ghost cooked them, then she gave part to the boy and she ate the other part.

They finished eating. Then the ghost girl told the boy, "I'll go to the stream and remove the feces from the girl's guts. I'll return later. You must wait here." Then she went down to the stream. When she left, she called out to all of the ghosts and ancestral spirits to surround the boy and to eat him.

However as the boy was butchering the girl, a flying fox flew by. The flying fox went noisily to the hut and called out to the boy. The flying fox told him to run away because the ghosts were coming to eat him. It told the boy to run away quickly and go back [to his village].

The boy ran away to his village. When he arrived, he went to the men's house. He woke his father and all of the men that were sleeping there. He told them about everything that had happened to him. All of the men saw blood on his hands and skin. It was the blood of the girl that he had butchered. They hid the boy well inside the men's house. They made a big [fire] and sat around the boy.

### Hiding in the Men's House

The ghost girl had gathered the ghosts and ancestral spirits. She went to the garden hut, but the boy had run away. She followed the boy and arrived at the boy's vil-lage. She went to the men's house. She looked inside and saw the boy, but she saw him amongst a group of men.

The ghost girl called into the house, "Hey, men, my friend left me at the garden hut. He went to the village and I followed him here. Let him come and we two shall go to my village."

The men hid the boy and told the ghost girl, "The boy has not arrived yet. He's probably still in the garden." Then they told the ghost to go back to the garden to find him. However, the ghost girl knew that the boy was in the men's house, and that the men were just lying to her. So, the ghost girl asked them who it was that they were hiding amongst themselves. She said that she had already seen the boy. She said that she would be going to the garden and she asked the men to tell the boy to go to the garden. Then the ghost girl departed. After about ten minutes, the boy died.

The parents of the boy and of the real girl gathered together and took their two young bodies. They were mourn-ful and cried. Their kin just buried them in a hole.

Peter N. Mathias [Mathaias]
C. I. S. [Corrective Institute Services] Kerevat
P. O. Box 571
Rabaul
East New Britain Province

B211.2.11K+. Speaking flying fox; B449.3+. Helpful flying fox; E231+. Return from dead to reveal suicide; E232. Return from the dead to slay wicked person; E234. Ghost punishes injury received in life; E261.4. Ghost pursues man; E380. Ghost summoned; E425.1. Revenant as woman; E541.2+. Revenant eats own corpse; G11.10. Cannibalistic spirits; G77+. Boyfriend eats girlfriend; M451.1. Death by suicide; P233. Father and son; P600+. Courtship customs: *karim lek*; Q411. Death as punishment; R220. Flights; R260. Pursuits; T10. Falling in love; T75.2.1. Rejected suitors' revenge; T50. Wooing; T81.2. Death from unrequited love; T81.2.1. Scorned lover kills self; T86. Lovers buried in same grave; V61.3+. Dead buried; W157. Dishonesty

## A Way to Find a Woman (A Modern Story)
(Wantok 383, September 12, 1981, page 17)

There is a man named Kokomili who lives in the Dei Council [Census Division] area. Long ago, when the white people first came to the Highlands, one of them gave a looking glass to Kokomili.

Kokomili was very happy with this new thing that the white men had given to him. He knew that many people from the other villages had not seen such a thing before, so Kokomili thought he was going to trick some people.

The Jimi [**Maring**] People had never seen this kind of thing, and Kokomili went to the villages to try to trick them [**Western Highlands** Province].

Kokomili walked and walked, then he saw a woman and her child washing. Kokomili saw them and waited for them to come out of the stream. He told the mother that he liked her daughter, but the mother was angry and cursed Kokomili.

Oh my, Kokomili became irate and showed the glass to the old woman.

The old woman and her daughter saw the glass and were terrified. They thought that a ghost was looking at them. Kokomili hid the mirror from them. He fooled the old woman and said, "If you don't want to give me your child, then I'll hold tightly onto your spirit. You and your child will die."

The poor old woman thought that Kokomili was telling the truth. She was terrified and cried. She just thought about her child, and was afraid that she would die quickly. She told Kokomili to marry her child. The old woman cried and cried, and Kokomili took the young woman to his house.

Latang Kenowa Pena
Kapita Youth Group
P. O. Box 246
Mt. Hagen
Western Highlands Province

J1795+. Image in mirror mistaken for ghost; K1372. Woman engaged to marry by trick; P232. Mother and daughter


## Kambeya Brought His Sister Back to the Village

(Wantok 384, September 19, 1981, page 17)

Long, ago, a brother and sister lived on a piece of land. The man's name was Kambeya and the woman's name was Kambeino.

All of the other men were often angry with them and wanted to kill them. However, they watched over themselves very carefully and avoided their enemies.

One time, when the sun was bright, the man told his sister that they would go to the forest to hunt marsupials (*kapul*). So, they carried their food and walked into the forest.

Kambeya killed many marsupials and they cooked some in an earth oven with food from the garden. They lived for some days in the forest.

The brother told his sister, "Tomorrow, we'll return to the village. Then you'll stay at the house and I'll go back to the forest to hunt more marsupials."

They went back to the village. The sister stayed there and her brother went back to the forest. However, his enemies were waiting for him in the forest. He went alone into the forest. His enemies grabbed him and killed him.

Oh my, his sister was staying in the village and did not know that her brother had died. The brother's ghost returned to the village and the sister thought that it was her real brother who had come.

The brother brought more marsupials and said, "I feel sick, so you should cook these marsupials in an earth oven. Tomorrow, we'll go back to our real [natal] village." The sister took the marsupials, butchered them and cooked them in an earth oven. She gave some to her brother, but the brother said, "I feel sick and I don't want to eat. Never mind, just eat it yourself."

The sister thought hard and ate. However she was tired, so she put back her head and went to sleep. At night, while she was lying down, the sister turned and saw that her brother looked like a log. However, when the fire was brighter, he looked like a man sleeping in the bed. The sister worried a little, and turned back to sleep.

Dawn came. They woke up, filled a net bag with marsupials and went back to the village. The sister walked first and the brother followed her. They approached their natal village and heard the men of the village crying and calling out.

Her brother knew what this was and he wanted to fool his sister, so he said, "Hey, sister, they're crying. I think that a man must have died. Let's go quickly and look." When they were very close, the brother told his sister, "I'm going to find a *tanget* first, wait for me."

However, his sister already knew. She said, "No, I'll come with you." They continued on with this conversation until evening came. Then the brother spoke strongly, "You walk ahead. I'll go and find some *tanget*, then you shall meet me on the other side of the trail."

The sister turned her head and began to walk. She turned her head again to look at her brother, but he was not there.

Her brother had disappeared. She did not know where he went. She looked for his footprints to follow them, but they did not look like a man's footprints. They were the footprints of a ghost. The poor woman saw this, then cried and walked to the village.

She arrived at the village and she listened to the people tell her that Kambeya was dead. They had hung his body up and were mourning. The sister had thought, "My brother and I came together. Who is it that died, that they're crying for?"

She cried too, rolling on the ground. Late that evening, the men of the village took the boy's body and buried it.

One time when the woman was crying and worrying about her brother, her brother's ghost came and told her, "Don't worry about me. If you want something, I can come and help you." His sister listened to this and lived without worry. After a while, she too died. Her ghost dwelled with her brother, and they traveled around together.

Theresa Rema
Paphy [Pupu?] Business Group
P. O. Box 27 [**Kendagl** Village, **Hagen** People]
Ialibu
**Southern Highlands** Province

[Ms. Rema also wrote the story in *Wantok* #358, so she is probably from Kendagl Village.]

E326. Dead brother's friendly return; E425.2. Revenant as man; E421.2.1+. Ghost leaves unusual footprints; E553+. Ghost becomes log in dim light; K914. Murder from ambush; P253. Sister and brother; S110. Murders; V61.3+. Dead buried

## The Woman Tricked a Man (A Modern Story)
(Wantok 385, September 26, 1981, page 21)

In the **Kompiam** area of **Enga** Province, there is clan named Yaup [**Enga** People]. There is a young woman from this clan named Pyakom.

One time, she went to a faraway village that belonged to another clan called Yoktin. She went to get leafy greens from a garden.

The garden was large and she picked the vegetables when it was near nightfall. Then she walked back to her village. When she was in the middle of the trail, it became completely dark. She saw a house near the trail and went towards it.

She went inside, putting her net bag of greens outside. When she went in, there were no matches to make a fire, so she put her hand in the ashes of the fire to feel if there were any embers. She felt some heat, so she took a big leaf or something like that and fanned the fire. When the fire brought a little light, she saw that a man's blood had fallen down there. She made the fire bigger, then she looked up and saw a man's body that they had killed and placed up in the back, so as to stop the fire from going up and reaching the sword grass.

The woman saw this and tried to call out, but the man told her, "Don't call out, take your bag of greens and come inside. Then put out the fire and sit quietly. Two men will be coming here. When they arrived, I'll talk to you. When they come inside, climb on this door and get ready. When one of them comes inside, jump on his neck. He'll carry you to his house."

The woman was afraid, but she heeded what the man said. She put out the fire and sat quietly. While she sat, the man told her, "Get ready. The two men that I told you about are coming now." So, the woman quickly went on top of the door of the house and got ready to jump.

One man came inside first. The woman arranged her bag of greens above his head and she jumped down on the neck of this man.

The man thought that the dead man had jumped onto his neck and was holding on to it. He was afraid, so he called out and ran to his house. While he ran, the woman held very tightly onto his neck. When the man arrived at his house, the woman let go and went inside.

The man thought that he had carried the ghost of the dead man and was completely afraid. It was still night time. He went inside the pigsty, cut off a piece of pig's ear, and ate it. At dawn, he killed the pig. He and his kin ate it.

Later, he wanted to become married, so he asked this woman that he had carried on his neck to marry him. The woman knew that it was this man that had carried her on his neck, but the man did not know this. He still thought that he had carried a ghost that night.

The two of them married and lived together. One time, they wanted to cook some edible greens in an earth oven, so the woman sent the man into the forest to get some leaves. The woman waited and waited. The man did not return quickly. She became irate. After she became angry, the man returned with the leaves.

The woman scolded her husband, "That night, I tricked you and you carried me here. Now you want to show off to me." The man listened to this and he became irate. He did not eat that night, he just sat. While his wife was sleeping, he took an axe and quietly cut his wife's neck. Then he went outside and put fire to the house, burning his wife's body inside. Later, he told the people, "My wife burned with my house."

Peter Mendai
Catholic Mission of Pipares
P. O. Box 217
Kompiam
Enga Province

E262+. Presumed ghost rides on man's back; E300+. Ghost arranges marriage; E425.2. Revenant as man; K1310+. Marriage from pretending to be ghost; P210. Husband and wife; Q260. Deceptions punished; Q411. Death as punishment; S63+. Husband kills wife; S110. Murders; S118.2. Murder by cutting throat; S139.4. Murder by mangling with axe; T100. Marriage

## The Man Brought a *Masalai*

(Wantok 386, October 3, 1981, page 17)

This story takes place near the Pindiu Patrol Post on the Finschhafen Peninsula [**Morobe** Province]. Long ago, there was a man named Gonzan. He went to the forest to look for a tree.

The tree was fruiting, but the fruits were not ripe yet. He thought and said, "I should try and make a platform and ladder. Later, the tree fruits will ripen and animals will eat them. I should come quietly, stand on the platform and shoot the animals." So, he made a platform and went back to the village.

Gonzan went back to his village, Kizeng [**Kwenzenzeng** Village, **Kube** People]. After about five weeks passed, he told his wife that she should stay at the house and that he would go to the forest. When the sun was about to set, he began to walk into the forest. When he arrived at the place where he had made a platform, he saw that the tree fruits were ripe and that the animals were eating them. Some had fallen, but not one was littering the ground.

The poor man stood and thought, "Oh my, the animals have been eating, and some of the fruit discards have fallen, but where? There's no litter at the base of the tree." He kept thinking, and the *masalai*s walked towards him, surrounding him. They cried out from every corner. Gonzan stood his bow up and stood like a tree, so the *masalai*s did not see him.

He stood and watched all of the *masalai*s climb the tree. They left their little children underneath the tree and ate. Later, a *masalai* ghost woman, who was carrying her baby in a net bag, hung the bag right on Gonzan's shoulder. The *masalai* thought that Gonzan was a piece of a tree. After she put the net bag there, she went up the tree.

Gonzan stood on the platform and just looked at the children on the ground. He said, "I'll go down and fool them. I'll go down with the sleeping baby, then run away." So he carried the baby *masalai* down. The *masalai* children on the ground saw him and he threw a fruit at them. They gathered at one place and he ran back to the village, carrying the baby.

The mother of them *masalai* baby came down the tree and forgot her baby. She went with the other *masalai*s back to their village.

Gonzan brought the baby to the village. He and his wife took care of the baby *masalai*. After a while, the baby became a woman. Gonzan gave the woman to his second son, Dino, and he married her. Later, she became pregnant. When she was about to give birth, she felt a pain that almost killed her. She called the name of her *masalai* mother, Rotou. Then she gave birth to a girl. When the baby girl cried, everyone in the village closed their doors and stayed inside.

Dino gave a blessing to his mother and daughter, then he called out for everyone to come see the baby. When they went to look, the baby girl became a rattan root. These rattans are still there at the Bureson River. And all of us [from this village] came from this *masalai*.

Soloba Siarong
Sonon [Sananga] Village
Pindiu Patrol Post, Lae
Morobe Province

A991+. Origin of particular village; D215.11K+G. Transformation: girl to rattan root; F490+. Masalai; P210. Husband and wife; P232. Mother and daughter; P233. Father and son; P271. Foster father; P272. Foster mother; P273. Foster brother; P275+. Foster daughter; R10. Abduction; T415.5+. Foster brother-sister marriage; T570. Pregnancy; T111. Marriage of mortal and supernatural being; T580. Childbirth

## Sorcery Shut Someone's Eyes (A Modern Story)

(Wantok 387, October 10, 1981, page 21)

In the **East Sepik** [Province], there is a small village named Monji [ **Mundjiharanji**], near Kubalia Village [**Boiken** People]. In this village, live a man and his wife. The man's name is Jacob and his wife's name is Bertt. They have lived well with their parents, brothers and sisters.

The two were newly married and did not have children yet. Jacob was twenty-one years old at the time. He has a young brother named Lukas.

They all lived well in this village. However one time, on Monday, November 28, 1978, they found that they did not have meat in the house. So Jacob and his wife thought about going to hunt wild game for themselves. They made a decision and told the other brothers and sisters.

They left the village at about two o'clock in the afternoon. They walked very far away. After about three kilometers, they entered the deep forest. They were not too concerned about finding game, they just walked slowly and looked around. When they left the village, they thought that it was just them who had left that afternoon. However, Lukas also thought about hunting for game.

A little while after Jacob and his wife left the village, Lukas followed them. But before he left, he went to his father's house and brought a shotgun from his father. He was thinking of going to hunt and shoot a big pig.

However, enemies were waiting for Lukas. His thinking and eyesight were not clear when he left the village, because some bad men had performed sorcery and ruined his head. He had become completely confused. He did not clearly understand what he was doing with his father's shotgun.

As Lukas walked, the sorcery began to affect his head. He walked and walked, then found his brother Jacob and Jacob's wife resting beneath a tree.

However, when Lukas looked at Jacob's head, it was no longer Jacob. He had turned into a big and black wild pig. Lukas did not see Bertt, Lukas' wife, anymore. So, he thought that it was just a wild pig sitting underneath the tree. Immediately, he fired the shotgun at this "wild pig."

Too bad, it was not really a wild pig. It was Jacob's brother. The sorcery had ruined Lukas' head, causing him to think that his brother was a wild pig. Lukas was standing only about seven meters from Jacob, so the cartridge hit him directly, causing Jacob to fall down dead.

Lukas was happy now. He thought that he had shot a wild pig. He walked slowly to check and make sure that the pig was dead, and if not he would shoot it again. However, when Bertt saw that her husband had fallen, she cried out wildly and cried on top of him. This changed Lukas' thinking, and his head became clear. He saw his brother lying in blood.

He put his hand to his mouth and he trembled. Jacob's wife saw Lukas and called out, "Aiyo! Lukas, you killed your brother." She cried louder. Lukas was afraid and turned his back and cried. He sped back to the village. He left his father's shotgun in the house and ran to the highway that goes to Wewak.

Lukas ran and ran, then arrived at Tuonunbu [**Toanumbu**] Village. Some men held him and hid him. They heard that Lukas had killed his brother, so they held him until the police arrived. The police put Lukas before the court and charged him with killing his brother. But Lukas won his case. Many people did not believe that Lukas could have won this case because Lukas still talks about how he killed Jacob. But when the C. I. B. [Criminal Investigation Branch] Police went to show a photo, it showed that Jacob had really changed into a wild pig.

They had determined that Lukas' head and eyes were not confused. Sorcery had taken hold of Jacob and changed him into a wild pig. Lukas now lives in the village. He won the case, but he is often still troubled about his brother. He still talks about having killed his brother.

Mathis Huasi

Box 332

Goroka

Eastern Highlands Province

D114.3.2M. Transformation: man to boar; D683. Transformation by magician; D1711. Magician; K929+. Man deceived by magician into killing brother; P210. Husband and wife; P250. Brothers and sisters; P251.5. Two brothers; P263. Brother-in-law; P264. Sister-in-law; S73.1. Fratricide; S110. Murders

## How Did Tumleo Island Arise?
(Wantok 388, October 17, 1981, page 21)

Long, long ago, there were three mountains. The first was Sualkalia, on one side. The second was Sulkan in the middle, and the third was Sararai. These three mountains were very solid.

There were two *masalai* men who lived on these three mountains. These two *masalai* men were named Sumbiar and Runu. One day, they prepared food for themselves.

Sumbiar prepared food for himself, sago and meat, while Runu prepared yams (*yam* and *mami*). Another day, they began to cook food. When the food was done, Sumbiar filled a *limbum* basket with his food, while Runu filled a net bag with his yams.

After the food was ready, they began to argue. Runu told Sumbiar, "Go stand on Mount Sararai and look at me. I'll stand on Mount Sulkalia [Sualkalia] look at you." So, Sumbiar listened to Runu and they each stood on a mountain.

Sumbiar called out and asked Runu, "*Malihil* (friend), what shall we do now?" Runu called out to him, "*Malihil*, we shall close our eyes and point our hands to the mountain that we like. Listen, when I call out, open your eyes and look at my hand. I too will open my eyes and look at your hand."

When Runu called out, they shut their eyes. Sumbiar did not close his eyes quickly. He looked at Runu's hand, then closed his eyes.

When Runu called out, they opened their eyes and looked at each other's hands. When the looked, they were both pointing to the same mountain. They were pointing to the mountain in the middle, Sulkan. They left the mountains that they were standing on and met at Mount Sulkalia.

Runu stood on a bad piece of ground, while Sumbiar stood on a good piece of ground. They brought their cooked food, and they began to sing and dance. They called for rain. While they sang and danced, a torrential rain and strong wind arose. The clouds thundered and there was lightning all over. A big flood came, cutting Mount Sulkan into two halves.

The water carried away the ground that the two *masalais* were standing on, bringing it out to sea. The flood brought them right into the deep sea. The waves came up and shook them. The half of the mountain that Sumbiar stood on was good. Sumbiar lived well there.

The part of the mountain that Runu sat on was not good. The ground was too soft. When the waves washed the earth, it broke apart. When the ground broke apart, Runu looked for a place in the sea. He swam when the sun rose. He swam and swam to **Yuo** Island [**Kairiru** People] and to Karasau [**Keresau**] Island [**Boiken** People, **East Sepik** Province]. Sumbiar lived well on his part of the mountain. The waves had carried him to **West Sepik** Province.

After a while, a hair comb fell down in the **Paup** area [**Ali** People]. He returned, bringing the comb. At dawn he went to a reef. This reef is named Tamoar. A piece of Sulkan Mountain passed by the reef and stuck there. It is there now, near Aitape. The white men came and called this island Tomeleo [**Tumleo** Island, **Tumleo** People].

Tomeleo Island is well known. The *masalai* man Sumbiar had a short snake wife. Her name was Suhanar. They were married on Mount Sulkan. This is an ancestor story from the **Ulau** [**Ulau-Suain** People] Aitape, Sandaun Province.

Peter M. Hayak

Box 1448

M. V. [Motor Vessel] Provincial Chief

Lae

Morobe Province

A955+. Origin of islands from contest between spirits: mountain moves to sea; A955.3.1. Origin of an island's shape; B800+. Marriage of spirit to snake; D1542.1.5. Magic song brings rain; D1542.1.5+. Magic dance brings rain; D1781. Magic results from singing; D1781+. Magic results from dancing; D2142.1. Wind produced by magic; D2143.1.2. Rain produced by singing; D2143.1.2+. Rain produced by dancing; D2149.1. Thunderbolt magically produced; D2151.8. Magic flood; F490+. Masalai; K90+. Contest won by opening eyes and cheating; T100. Marriage

# Do Not Anger a Woman — You Will Die

(Wantok 389, October 24, 1981, page 17)

Long ago, there was a man who lived with his dog. He was not married. He and his dog lived in a small house.

One day, the man took his dog and went into the deep forest. They walked and walked, and arrived at a river. They sat and rested. The dog left its master and went along the edge of the river.

The dog saw a nice flower standing by the water. The dog went back to its master and sniffed him. The man saw this and knew that the dog had found something on the other side of the river. He followed his dog and they arrived there, then the dog smelled the flower. The man watched and then he too smelled it. Immediately, the flower turned into a woman.

The woman had big, long hair. The man looked at her and lusted for her. He wanted to marry her. The woman agreed and said, "Yes." The man and his dog brought the woman back to their house.

They lived well for a very long time. One time, the man became angry with his wife. They argued and argued, then she thought, "I'll run away back to my place, then he'll come looking for me." She thought this and stayed. Then after one day, she really ran away.

The man looked for the woman, but he could not find her. He cried terribly. He found that his dog was not there either. The next day, he went and looked for his wife and dog. He went to the river and saw the dog whining by the river.

The man took his dog and they went back. However, the dog smelled a snake sleeping in a tree hole. The dog dug at the base of the tree but it was not enough. He thought that it was a marsupial (*kapul*) lying inside the tree hole. He did not know that it was a snake inside. The man was sorry for the dog and he climbed a young tree to see what it was inside the tree hole.

The branch of the tree broke and the man fell inside. The snake woke up and wanted to kill the man, but the man immediately took his *kina* shell [as a blade] and was ready.

He held it, but the snake wrapped itself around his legs and wound itself up to his head. The snake constricted itself until the man died.

His dog saw this and went back to a village where there were many people. The dog sniffed a man and barked. The man noticed this, took some other people and followed the dog to the tree hole.

They broke apart the tree and saw that the man was dead. They took him back to the village and buried him.

Then they returned and waited for the snake. The snake was washing its mouth so that it could swallow the dead man. The men waited, and they heard something making a noise and approaching. They knew that something bad was coming closer and they went back to the village.

The man's dog stayed near his grave. This was near that of his father. This is a story that my grandparent told me, that I remembered it and wrote it down.

Josep Komako
Madang
Madang Province

B421. Helpful dog; B301.1+. Faithful dog keeps vigil at master's grave; B582.1.1. Animal wins wife for his master (Puss in Boots); B875.1. Giant serpent; D431.1W. Transformation: flower to woman; D564. Transformation by smelling; P210. Husband and wife; R213. Escape from home; T10. Falling in love; T100. Marriage; V61.3+. Dead buried

## The *Masalai* Tricked Maka (A Modern Story)
(Wantok 390, October 31, 1981, page 17)

In the month of August, Mr. Maka, a young man from the forest near **Telesea**, had been married for just a month. The name of his new bride was Tina Maka.

During this month, their marriage was very good. Everyone in the village saw the good things that they did and they were happy for them.

Maka's parents saw that their daughter-in-law, Tina, worked hard in the garden and at doing other work. Oh my, they were very happy. They looked after their daughter-in-law very well.

Maka worked as a P. M. V. [Public Motor Vehicle or bus] truck driver. The P. M. V. belonged to his father. The P. M. V. that Maka drove took twenty-four passengers on the Kokopo Highway. Sometimes he would travel to the edge of the prison or to Kerevat High School. Every day he made K150 [150 Kina was about US$230 in 1981], up to K200. Every evening, he went to his village in the Baining area and looked at his new wife [**Baining** People, **East New Britain** Province]. He slept with her and he did not sleep anywhere else. Never mind whether the truck was broken at another place, he would forge ahead and go home to the village.

Maka did this because he thought much of his wife. So regardless of heavy rain, or darkness, or a broken truck, he would forge ahead to Tina every time.

In August, Maka's truck was broken, so he left his truck at a workshop in Rabaul. He returned to the village

and brought his wife to the garden. The garden was in the very deep forest.

They arrived at the garden and weeded it. At about two o'clock in the afternoon, they finished working in the garden. Tina began to make a fire to cook some bananas and taros (*taro singapo* and *taro tru*). Maka went to the forest to hunt for some wild game. He walked and arrived at the home of a *masalai*. However, he did not know that it was a *masalai*'s home because it was the first time that he had been to this part of the forest.

He looked at the base of a fig tree and saw two big eggs. He went closer and he thought that they were cassowary eggs [the dwarf cassowary (*Casuarius bennetti*) is the only species on New Britain Island (Beehler *et al.*, 1986: 45)]. But they were not, they were *masalai* eggs. He finished looking, then he cleared a trail to return there that night to kill the cassowary. He cleared the trail very far, so that when he returned he would not make a noise and scare away the cassowary. He cleared it well, then he returned to the garden. He told his wife that they would stay until about eight o'clock, then they would go kill the cassowary.

His wife listened to this and was very happy that her husband would kill a cassowary to give to her. They finished eating and waited until about eight o'clock that night. They got up and left the garden. They walked and walked, then arrived at the *masalai* place where Maka had seen the eggs and had cleared the trail.

When they arrived at the place where the fig tree and the eggs were, Maka told his wife not to make a noise, not to talk or to cough. She must sit quietly and wait for him. He would go and kill the cassowary. After he killed it, his wife would get it.

His wife sat in a place covered with bird excrement. Maka walked quietly and went to the place. He searched around the fig tree, but he did not find the eggs or the cassowary.

The *masalai* had fooled him and was just walking around this area. He did not know where he had gone or where his poor wife was.

Maka walked quietly and saw his wife covered in black bird excrement, sitting in the place where he had left her. Maka saw this and thought that it was the cassowary sitting there, so he quietly walked closer to his wife. He did not see well and the *masalai* had mixed his head up.

His wife saw him raise a stick for killing the cassowary, but she thought that her husband knew that it was just her sitting there. But no, the stick broke right on his poor wife's head. The woman jumped up, then fell down and jumped and jumped. All her brains began to fall about.

When Maka saw this, he thought that he had killed a big cassowary, so he threw another hard one on top of his wife again. Then the woman slowed down and died.

He put his hand to feel his wife's skin and he was surprised. He stood and thought. He called out for his wife, but she did not reply. He took some matches from his pocket and struck one. He looked down and saw that he had not killed a cassowary. It was his wife that was dead.

Maka hugged his wife, shouting and crying until about midnight. He carried his wife back to the village, arriving at about three o'clock in the morning. He woke up his parents and told them that he had thought that his wife was a cassowary and had killed her and brought her body there. Everyone in the village was shocked and went outside to see the woman who had died.

Everyone in the village cried and asked Maka exactly where they went when he had killed his wife in confusion. Maka told them the whole story. All of the old people of the village told him that this was a *masalai* place and that the *masalai* confused him so that he had killed his wife.

They finished talking, and buried Tina. Then they brought Maka to the police station in Rabaul.

Mr. Frank Mathaias
C. I. S. [Correctional Institute Services] Kerevat
P. O. Box 571
Rabaul
East New Britain Province

F441. Wood-spirit; F490+. Masalai; K929+. Man deceived by spirit into killing wife; P210. Husband and wife; P231. Mother and son; P233. Father and son; P261. Father-in-law; P262. Mother-in-law; P265+. Daughter-in-law; S122. Flogging to death; V61.3+. Dead buried

## Two Women Arose

(Wantok 391, November 7, 1981, page 17)

Long ago, there lived a man, his wife and their son. There were no other people who lived with them in their place.

One time, the parents went to the garden. They left their son at home. Near their house was a big *tulip* tree. At this time, the *tulip* fruits were ripening and falling on the ground.

The young boy sat at the house and saw two doves (or pigeons) flying closer and perching on the tree. The two birds began to eat many *tulip* fruits. While they ate the fruits, they jumped down to the other branches and eventually arrived at the base of the tree.

The young boy saw this, ran inside the house and took a bow and arrows. He began to shoot at the two birds. He shot at the birds, but all of the arrows missed. The birds did not die, and they did not become frightened or fly away. No, the two birds ate their fill of the *tulip* fruits.

When all his arrows were gone, the boy went and took some of his father's arrows then again tried to shoot the birds. However, he kept missing until all of his father's arrows were gone too.

He ran to get the spears (*limbum*) and tried shooting them with these, but he kept missing. He finished the spears and looked for other things to shoot at these birds until everything in the house was gone.

He looked and looked until he just saw his father's wooden headrest [used for sleeping]. He ran inside, took this piece of wood and also threw it at the two birds. When the two birds saw this wooden headrest, they left the tree branch, flew down and carried the headrest away.

The birds brought the headrest far away. They flew past many villages until they arrived at a tall coconut palm tree. The tall tree stood on top of a hill. The two birds took this headrest and put it up there with the coconuts.

Below the hill was a forest hut. An old woman lived in this hut. Her eyes were shut and crust from her eyes covered them up completely. There was not another man who lived at this place. The old woman was entirely alone.

The young boy who had thrown his father's headrest was afraid now. He knew that his father would be very angry with him. In the evening, the parents returned from the garden. They saw things lying about the house and by the *tulip* tree too. They asked the boy about this, but he was entirely afraid and did not tell them the story about the two birds.

His father was irate when he heard that the birds had carried his headrest away. He told his son, "Tomorrow, you'll just wake up and look for my headrest. If you don't, I'll kill you."

The poor boy listened to this and was very worried. He did not eat, he went to sleep hungry.

At daybreak, he woke up and left his parents' house, following the path that the two birds had flown. He walked and walked until he arrived at a village. He asked the people, "Did you see two birds that were carrying a headrest come here?" The men of this village said, "No."

He left this village and walked to the next one. At the second village, it was the same thing. The people said that the birds had not come there, so he went to the next village.

The poor boy kept going until he arrived at a small side trail. The trail was overgrown and covered up with forest.

The boy stood and thought, should he follow this trail or not? He thought yes, so he followed the side trail.

He followed the forest trail and heard an old woman call out, "Grandson, wait. I'm changing my 'grass' skirt first, then you can come." The young boy listened to this, then stood and waited.

The old woman finished changing her skirt and called out for the young boy to come. The boy walked towards the old woman's hut, then the old woman told him to sit and rest. The old woman cooked some food for him. He ate, then he told the old woman his story.

The old woman listened and told the young man, "Sleep now. Tomorrow morning when you wake up, I'll tell you where you can find your father's headrest."

The man heeded the old woman and went to sleep. In the morning, the old woman told him to climb the tall coconut tree. She said, "When you arrived at the crown of the coconut tree, you'll find the headrest. When you take the headrest, take a green coconut too then come down. Don't throw it, you must carry it down slowly."

The young man climbed the tall coconut tree and found his father's headrest. He took the headrest and a young, green coconut, then carried them down to the ground.

When he came down to the ground, the old woman told him to put the coconut inside the house and rest. The old woman cooked some food and gave it to him. When he finished eating, the old woman told him to go inside the house, take his coconut and go back to the village.

The young man went to get his coconut, but it was not there. He saw a beautiful young woman sitting where he had put the coconut. He saw this and searched for the coconut. The old woman was waiting and told him, "That coconut is the young woman who is sitting there. Take her and go. She is your wife now."

The young boy listened to this and was ecstatic. He took the woman and his father's headrest, then walked back to the village. His friend saw the beautiful woman and trembled. He asked, "Friend, how did you get this woman?"

The young boy told the story of how the birds took his father's headrest to the place where the old woman lived. His friend listened to his story and followed after him. He sat in the house, and when the two birds came to eat *tulip* fruits, he tried to shoot them. He did this until everything was gone. Then he took his father's headrest and threw it at the birds. The birds took the headrest and flew away. The man followed the two birds until he arrived at the place where the old woman lived.

When he approached the old woman's hut, he heard the old woman call out to wait until she changed her "grass" skirt. However, the man did not heed the old woman. He shook at the woman and his ears were shut to whatever she said. He went closer to her and saw that the old woman's skirt was broken and that her buttocks showed through openings. The man just went and raped the old woman. Later, the old woman gave food to him. He ate it and told the old woman his story. The old woman listened to his story and said, "OK, sleep now. In the morning, you'll find your father's headrest."

The man slept. In the morning, he woke up quickly and woke the old woman at the same time. The old woman told him, "Climb that tall coconut tree and you'll find the headrest on top of it. Then take a coconut that is nearly ripe and carry it down."

The man followed the old woman's instructions. He took the headrest and the coconut, then descended. The old woman told him to rest and smoke. The coconut turned into a woman, but it was not a young woman. No, an old woman came and sat waiting for the man. When the man went to get the coconut, he saw that an old woman was sitting there. The woman told him, "What are you waiting for? Get up and we'll go to your village."

The man took his old wife and they went to the village. When they arrived at the village, his friend saw him bringing the aged woman with him. He knew that his friend had not followed the old woman's instructions, and that he had married an old woman.

They lived together in the village. After a while, his friend always thought badly about his wife. One time when there was a bright moon, the old woman's husband told his friend, "Let's go hunt marsupials (*kapul*) in the forest."

The two of them carried their things to hunt wild game, then went into the forest. They walked and walked, and hunted for marsupials in the deep forest until they arrived at a fruiting tree. The tree had grown in a sword grass area, or near a stream. Flying foxes were flying around its branches. They hung about and ate the fruits.

The men watched this and they shot at some. They shot flying foxes, then the old woman's husband told his friend, "Climb the tree and sit at the crown, then shoot some down. I'll watch at the base and kill them."

His friend climbed the tree. The old woman's husband just spoke to his hand and held the tree. The middle of the tree grew very large.

Later, his friend wanted to come down, but he was unable to do so. He was stuck on top of the tree, and his friend went back to the village. Later, at dawn, the woman's husband asked him about her husband. The man lied and said, "I don't know. He's probably lost in the deep forest. I called and called but he didn't reply, so I came back alone."

The poor woman listened to this and cried for her husband. She cried and cried. The man said, "Don't cry for him. I'm your husband now." However, the woman kept crying for her husband.

John Pamuser
Arawa
North Solomons Province

D431.11+W. Transformation: coconut to woman; D482.1. Transformation: stretching tree; D1774. Magic results from speaking; K1113. Abandonment on stretching tree; K1371. Bride-stealing; K2297. Treacherous friend; P210. Husband and wife; P231. Mother and son; P233. Father and son; P310+. Friend scorns friend's wise counsel; Q244. Punishment for ravisher; R260. Pursuits; S143.2. Abandonment in tall tree; T145.0.1. Polygyny; T471. Rape; W31. Obedience; W126. Disobedience; W157. Dishonesty


## The Bird of Paradise Woman Won
(Wantok 392, November 14, 1981, page 17)

A man made a house by the river where the birds went. Whenever he went to watch, various birds came to drink at the river. He often shot many birds when they came to drink water. The kinds of birds that he shot were hornbills, and small birds like doves (or pigeons), and birds of paradise.

One day, he was watching from his house and he saw a bird of paradise flying. It came, drank water and bathed. The bird of paradise looked into the house and saw an armlet on the man's arm. The bird of paradise flew directly to it, cut the armlet off the man's arm, and carried it away.

The man was surprised and he stopped thinking about killing birds. He ran and stood outside to see which way the bird of paradise went. He watched for this bird and saw that it flew over five whole mountains, then he could see it no longer. The bird of paradise went down to its home, below the fifth mountain.

The bird of paradise was not a real bird of paradise. No, it was a very beautiful woman. When she arrived at her home, she showed the armlet to her kin. Her kin were only young women.

After the man saw the bird of paradise fly over five mountains, he worried about his armlet. He did not eat, he just went to sleep when he went back home.

In the very early morning, he woke up and filled his basket with food. He lit a piece of firewood and walked away. He followed the path that he had seen the bird of paradise follow when it took his armlet and flew away.

He walked and walked, arriving at the mountains. He went to the top of one mountain, down the other side, then up the second mountain. He kept doing this, then arrived at the fifth mountain.

When he arrived at the fifth mountain, the sun was setting. He looked down and saw the bird of paradise woman's home. He went to this place and was surprised to see only beautiful young women there.

He asked the women for his armlet. Some women showed him the house of the woman that had taken his armlet. The man went to the woman's house and saw that the woman had put the armlet on her arm.

The man asked her, "Was it just you that came to my house and took my armlet?" The woman said, "Yes, it was just me who took your armlet." The man said, "I came to take back this armlet and to go back to my home."

However, the bird of paradise woman insisted that the man should live with her. The man was happy and agreed. They married and lived in the woman's village.

Felix Melipa
Wamsis [**Womisis**] Village [**Mountain Arapesh** People]
Aitape
**West Sepik** Province

B652. Marriage to bird in human form; D350+W. Transformation: bird of paradise to woman; K420. Thief loses his goods or is detected; P210. Husband and wife; R260. Pursuits; T100. Marriage; Z71.3. Formulistic number: five


## None of the Young Women Wanted To
(Wantok 393, November 21, 1981, page 21)

Long ago, an old woman and her child lived in a village called **Mambina**. The child's name was Bilo. They lived there for a while, then Bilo became a big man and thought of marriage.

His mother went to the house of a young woman and asked her to marry her son. The young woman laughed at the old woman and said, "Who would want to marry this child of yours? Get out of my house and leave!" The old woman turned her back and went to her house. Another day, she went to another woman and asked her to marry Bilo. This young woman also shamed the old woman and her son. All of the other women of the village did this same thing to the old woman when she asked them to marry her son.

None of the young women of the village liked Bilo, and the poor man was all alone. One day, his mother went to the forest to process sago.

She went to the forest and saw that a sago palm tree was ready to harvest. She cut the sago tree down. Then she cut the sago tree's leaf stalks and brought them over to make a platform for processing the sago. She cut the branches of the tree, put them into the ground, and finished making the platform for rinsing the sago. Then she went back to the village.

In the morning, she woke up and brought the things to scrape the sago into the forest. She arrived at the tree and scraped the sago until the sun became very hot. She left the tree and began to rinse the sago that she had scraped. She rinsed and rinsed until the sun set. She removed the water and carried the processed sago back to the village.

Another morning, she went back to scrape and rinse the sago again. She did this for two days until all of the sago was finished. She removed all of the water and there was much sago in the *limbum* basket. The old woman was very happy. She left it and went back to the village. She went back the next day. She cut leaves and tied up the sago. After she finished packaging the sago, she carried it back to the village.

She brought it back and put it on top of a platform inside the cookhouse.

One day, the old woman sat inside the house and heard something inside the cookhouse making noises. The old woman thought that rats were making noises. Oh my! She was shocked to see a beautiful young woman sitting on the platform where she had placed the sago. The old woman was very happy to see her and asked her to live with herself and her son. The woman agreed and lived with them. It was not long when Bilo married her and they lived with his old mother.

Josuwa B. Saii
Maprik
East Sepik Province

D431+W. Transformation: sago to woman; P210. Husband and wife; P231. Mother and son; P262. Mother-in-law; P265+. Daughter-in-law; T100. Marriage

# Befriending [Having Sex with] a Ghost Woman

(Wantok 394, November 28, 1981, page 17)

Long, long ago, there lived a man. He had two wives. When he wanted to go to the forest, they would often cook food for him. Then he would take his two dogs and depart.

One time, a heavy rain fell, so he hid inside a tree hole. The poor man did not have fire for a smoke and he was freezing cold. He began to talk, and a ghost woman heard him. She threw down some fire, then the poor man stoked the fire and warmed his body. Afterwards, he went to the village.

His two wives gave him some food. After he ate, they asked him, "Where's our meat?" The man told them, "Sorry, I just went to the base of a tree and returned."

He told them to cook food for him a second time. After that, he called his two dogs. The man went and took much wild game, and gave it to the ghost woman. He only brought a little back to the village.

The man befriended [had sex with] the ghost woman. One time, his son wanted to go with him, but he chased him away. The boy followed him and saw the ghost woman and his father.

The boy went back to the village and told his co-mothers, "Papa has a wife in the forest. I have seen his wife. She's very beautiful." The two told the boy, "Tomorrow, we'll go with you and see this woman."

At dawn, the three of them went to see the ghost woman. They told her, "The two of us want to cut your hair." They lied to her and cut off her head, killing her. Then two women went back to the village.

The woman's blood spurted over a vine. The women's husband returned to the forest and saw the ghost woman's blood. He thought, "I think that my wives killed this ghost woman."

He cut a *limbum* palm tree and used it to carry the ghost woman's body to the river. He put the body there, then went to the village. One time, he told the two women that they should go net fishing at the river.

They fished and fished. The fish had eaten much the soft parts [lit., "fat"] of the ghost woman. The two women continued to fish, and the shadow of the ghost woman hit the leg of one of the women. The woman said, "There's a big fish here." However, when she raised the net, the ghost woman's body came up.

Then, the women's husband told them to eat the body. They looked at each other. The first woman asked, "What should we do?" The second said, "You go downriver and

I'll go upriver." That is what they did. Their husband called out to them, but they had left.

He took his children to the village. It was dawn, and the second woman's child took his little sister to the beach. The sister said, "Is that our mother or is it a piece of a tree drifting towards the sea?" The piece of tree came directly towards them, giving her breasts to them. The tree said, "Come to the beach tomorrow and wait for me. I'll come to look for you again."

Their mother left and they went back to the village. Another day, they went back to the beach. Their mother gave them milk and spoke to them. Later they went back to the house. They told their father. He said, "Tomorrow we'll go. I'll hide in the sand."

At dawn, they went to the beach. The father hid while the little ones waited. When their mother came, the father asked them if they could come closer. Their mother came and gave the children milk while her husband came and tried to grab her. She was surprised and flew away like a bird. The man called for her to come back, but the woman had left and no longer thought of her children.

Theresia Venak
Domestic School
P. O. Alexishafen
Morobe Province

D215W. Transformation: woman to tree; D441.1+. Transformation: tree to bird; D1610.2. Speaking tree; E323.1.1+. Dead (transformed) mother returns to suckle child; E425.1. Revenant as woman; E440+. Ghost laid, then returns as a ghost; E446.3. Ghost laid by decapitating body; G50. Occasional cannibalism; K810+. Beheading rather than haircut; P210. Husband and wife; P231. Mother and son; P232. Mother and daughter; P233. Father and son; P234. Father and daughter; P253. Sister and brother; Q241. Adultery punished; Q411.0.1.1. Adulterer killed; R210. Escapes; S133. Murder by beheading; T91.3. Love of mortal and supernatural person; T145.0.1. Polygyny; T481. Adultery; T611. Suckling of children; W157. Dishonesty; W181. Jealousy

## The *Masalai* Ate a Baby

(Wantok 395, December 5, 1981, page 25)

Long, long ago in a village were two women. At night, they talked about looking for *gam* shells on the beach. A *masalai* woman was eating rubbish near their house and overheard them. The *masalai* heard another woman say that her friend would go wake her.

The *masalai* finished listening, then late that night, she woke the woman up. She said, "Wake up, wake up, let's go now." The woman woke up and carried her child outside the house, then they departed.

They walked along and the *masalai* woman said, "I'll carry your child." So, the woman gave the baby to the *masalai* woman. She looked at the *masalai* woman and thought that it was her real friend. It was not. The *masalai* told the woman to go first and they would follow her. They walked and arrived at the beach.

The real woman told the *masalai* woman, "You two sit there and I'll go look for *gam* shells." The *masalai* woman watched the baby while the real woman looked for *gam* shells on the beach.

The *masalai* woman broke one of the baby's arms and the baby began to cry. The baby's mother asked, "Why is baby crying?" The *masalai* woman said that mosquitoes were biting the baby, causing it to cry. The *masalai* woman then finished eating the baby. The real woman found many *gam* shells, then went to the *masalai* woman. She said, "Give me my baby, and I'll nurse my baby."

The *masalai* woman got up to give the baby, but only its head was inside the net bag. The woman took the net bag and gave her breast, but she felt that her baby was dead. She took her net bag of shells and ran away with it. The *masalai* woman chased her.

The *masalai* woman approached her and the woman threw a *gam* shell into the forest. The *masalai* woman looked for this *gam* shell, and the real woman ran away. The *masalai* woman found the shell and followed the woman again. She approached the woman and the poor woman threw a shell into the forest. The *masalai* looked for it again, and the woman kept running away. They did this until all of the shells were gone.

It was then that the woman saw a tree. She ran and climbed the tree, removing all of the bark of the tree and making the tree very slippery. The poor woman went up and sat down. The *masalai* arrived and tried to climb the tree, but it was too slippery and she fell down. The *masalai* asked the woman how she had gotten up there. The woman said, "Put your legs up and your head down." The *masalai* tried this but she fell down again. She kept trying until dawn arrived, then she ran away.

The woman saw the *masalai* go inside a hole. When the sun rose, the woman climbed down and went to her village. She told her whole clan to take their axes and other things, then go. They went by the hole and made a bonfire. They began to dig at the hole, then they saw the *masalai* woman there. They grabbed her, cut her into little pieces and threw her into the fire.

However, one finger went into the forest. So now, we have a kind of short snake in our forest.

Joe G. Irakau

C. M. [Congregation of Mission] **Bieng**, Baliau

**Manam** Island [**Manam** People]

P. O. Bogia

**Madang** Province

A2145. Creation of snake (serpent); D447+. Transformation: finger to snake; F490+. Masalai; G413+. Ogre disguises self to lure victim; J2244+. Climb up tree feet first; K1930. Treacherous impostors; P230. Parents and children; Q211.4. Murder of children punished; Q429.3. Cutting into pieces as punishment; R260. Pursuits; R311. Tree refuge; S110+. Eaten alive; S139.7. Murder by slicing person into small pieces; T611. Suckling of children

## He Only Liked Heads

(Wantok 396, December 12, 1981, page 25)

Long ago, there lived a married couple with had many children who lived in a village, but the children did not live with their parents. Two lived in one place and the others lived in another place.

When the children wanted to go to the forest, they did not fool around with killing wild game. They killed many animals. When they killed animals, their father sent their mother to see what kinds of animals they had killed.

She would look and say, "Pig, bird of paradise, bandicoot, kangaroo." The old man would say, "Just give the heads to me." Every time he would send his wife to get only the heads. The children wanted to give him legs, arms and rumps, but he did not want these, so his children became angry.

One time, the boys said, "Let's do something about this. Let's eat the animals' heads." So all of the little children said, "If we kill wild game, we'll eat the heads first. If papa sends mama, we'll scold her. If she asks why, we'll give an arm or leg for her to carry away."

In the early morning, the big brother wanted to go urinate. He saw a huge white pig digging the earth at the base of a tree near the house. When he saw this, he did not hesitate. He threw a spear at the pig, killing it. His brothers saw this and they said, "Now eat the head." So, they butchered the pig and their old mother came. They only gave a leg to their mother and she said, "No. Your father likes the head." The children gave the leg to her and chased her off. Later, they cooked the pig's head and ate it.

The two poor old people were sad. They were sad until it became dark, then they took torches and went to the river to search for fish. However, their children were ready for them in the forest. They wanted to light their torches, but the boys had tricked them and made crashing sounds all around them. The two old people did not know what was happening.

The boys went back, washed and went to sleep. In the morning, their mother arrived and told them that she wanted to look for lice on her babies' heads. However, all of them said that they were not babies. Only one little boy let his mother look for lice on his head.

The mother wanted to start looking for lice, but no. She looked on the ground and saw the boy's head [from the pig]. The mother said, "Hey, you just tricked me and papa." When the father heard this, he asked again, "Wife, what did you say to your baby?" The mother lied and said that she did not say anything, but the father had heard it.

The father was angry and said, "Now, I'll send a hot sun to kill you." However, the children said that they were not worried. So, the father said that he would send wind and an earthquake, but the children said that they were not worried. Then he said that he would send rain and that a big flood would arise. The boys did not reply to him.

Their mother immediately turned into a long vine, giving herself to the little boy. He used it to climb a coconut palm tree. Then a heavy rain arose, and it flooded and flooded. The flood came and washed away all of the gardens and houses. All of the young coconut trees were carried away into the Uyaban (Sogeram) River, then thrown into the Ramu River, and then thrown towards the sea. All of the men, women, children, pigs, dogs and chickens were gone.

So now, if you go to the **Koromasarik** area, you will not see many coconut trees. Men had planted many, but they cannot grow well there.

Peter Las

**Mis** Village [**Kamba** People]

P. O. Box 323

**Madang** Province

A1011. Local deluges; A1018. Flood as punishment; A1023. Escape from deluge on tree; A2730+. Why coconuts do not grow well in one area; B871.1.2. Giant boar; D213.4W. Transformation: woman to vine; D2143.1. Rain produced by magic; D2151.8. Magic flood; P210. Husband and wife; P230. Parents and children; P231. Mother and son; P233. Father and son; P250. Brothers and sisters; Q325. Disobedience punished; R311. Tree refuge; S11.3. Father kills child; W31. Obedience; S110. Murders; W126. Disobedience; W157. Dishonesty

## Why Are Net Bags Multicolored?

(Wantok 397, December 19, 1981, page 25)

Long ago in Mahapitum Village, the men were clearing the forest to make a garden. After they cleared the forest, they returned to the village then ate and slept.

At daybreak, they woke up and returned to the place where they were making a garden. When they arrived, they saw that the place was still dense forest. The men said, "Hey, we cleared this place yesterday, then we went to the village. How did it become dense forest again?"

The men finished talking then cut the forest again. After they finished working, they went back to the village. Another day, they returned to this place and saw that the same thing had happened. This happened many times until the people became tired of cutting the forest.

One day, they decided to find out who it was that put back the forest that they had cut. They sent a boy to hide near this part of the forest and to see who did this.

In the afternoon, when all of the men went back to the village, the boy climbed a tree. This tree had an ant's nest in it [the weaver ant, *Oecophylla smaragdina* (Hölldobler and Wilson, 1990: 618, plates 22 and 24)], but the boy did not care. He lay on a tree branch against the nest and watched.

He saw an old woman coming to the cleared forest. She took the forest and put it back again. She saw the ants' nest that the boy was lying against. She thought that he was just the nest's shadow.

She worked very quickly at putting the forest back until all was dense forest again. The ancestral ghost woman went down to her home underground. The boy saw this and quickly went down. He looked for a stick, then planted it where the woman had descended. He went directly back to the village and told all of the men about what he had seen. All of the men decided not to talk to the women because this was something only for men. Then they went to sleep.

In the very early morning, they woke up and took stones, knives and axes to dig up the ancestral ghost woman. They began to dig. They dug and dug, then saw the fiery place where the moon goes. They kept digging and saw the fiery place from the day before yesterday and from that morning. They kept digging.

They kept digging, then saw the ancestral ghost woman sitting and making a net bag. They held her, took a log and tied her to it. When they tried to carry the log, it broke. They tried again, but every log broke. Then the old ghost woman sang in our language, "*Pera mueri wata ikil*." This means, "Cut the ironwood tree." They found an ironwood tree, then cut it and brought it. They tied the woman up to it and carried her to the village where they put her in the spirit house. Then they cut the trees and fenced in their garden.

The women did not know that this ancestral ghost woman was in the spirit house. When the real women wanted to work in the garden, they would often take fire and food for the boys to cook and eat. After they departed, the ancestral ghost woman would come out and chase the boys who were cooking and eating. The ghost woman would go back to the spirit house to cook and eat.

When the mothers returned to the village, the boys told them about the old ancestral ghost woman. However, they did not know where she really lived. The mothers decided to find out who it was that took their little boys' food. One day, when all of the women went to the garden, they left one woman there. She saw the old ghost woman chase the boys, take their food and fire and go back to the spirit house.

When all of the women returned to the village, she told them about what had happened. They decided to kill this old ancestral ghost woman. They went and took all of their things from the forest, such as *salat*, biting ants and other insects. They put these around the spirit house while the ghost woman was making a net bag.

She finished making a net bag for her big brother, then began to make some more. The poor woman did not know that the women were trying to kill her. The women put fires around the spirit house. She was surprised. She jumped to one side and beat a signal drum. Then she jumped to another side and beat a signal drum. She did this until she died.

The spirit house burned down and a piece of fire shot straight out to the place where the men were working. It fell on top of a net bag and the net bag burned.

The men saw this and said, "The signal drum was struck and now that net bag is on fire. The women probably killed the old ghost woman." Then they went to the village. They saw that the spirit house had burned down and that the old woman was dead. The men did not say anything. They were very troubled. They climbed coconut palm trees, took green coconuts and drank the milk. They took ashes from the burned spirit house and put them into the green coconuts, making something like salt.

They ate, then they took some taro leaves. They put forth their right hands and climbed the coconut trees. They told the women, "You have ruined this for us. Come get it." Oh my, the women cried and said, "You, our husbands, come down now. Don't worry." However, all of the men jumped. Some became flying foxes and some became marsupials (*sikau*).

Now if you go to **Mahapitum** Village, in **East Sepik** Province, you will see women making multicolored net bags.

Augustine Awa Leket
Waigani Service Station
Port Moresby
National Capital District

[See the ancestor story in *Wantok* #130 is similar to this one.]

A310+. Ancestral spirit who lives in fiery underworld; A750+. Moon beneath the earth; A1590+. Why net bags are multicolored; D179.6K+M. Transformation: man to marsupial; D117.5KM. Transformation: man to flying fox; E425.1. Revenant as woman; E446.2. Ghost laid by burning body; E591. Ghost travels under ground; H1115.1+. Task: cutting down forest, which is magically replanted; K420. Thief loses his goods or is detected; P210. Husband and wife; P231. Mother and son; Q212. Theft punished; Q414. Punishment: burning alive; R10. Abduction; S112.0.2. House (hostel) burned with all inside; V112.1. Spirit huts

## The *Masalai*'s Forest

(Wantok 398, December 26, 1981, page 25)

Long ago, there was a married couple that lived in the area around **Okapa**, **Eastern Highlands** Province [**Fore** People]. The man's wife was pregnant. When the woman was about to give birth, the man took his bow, arrows and dog and went to hunt for wild game.

He entered the very deep forest. He made a hut and left his food in this hut. He went to hunt marsupials (*kapul*) in the forest. In the evening, he returned to his hut.

He cooked his food. When he was about to eat, his wife came with his baby. Oh my, he was surprised to see her. However, he knew that this woman was not really his wife. So, the man thought hard and thought that his wife had died and that her ghost had followed him there.

He asked the woman, "Where did you two come from?" The ghost woman said, "You came alone into the forest and we felt very sorry for you, so we followed you here." After she said this, he gave her a bamboo tube and told her not to fill it at the first stream because people never drank there. He told her that she must fill it up at the second stream where people often drink.

The ghost woman very quickly filled the tube and returned. So, the man asked her where she had filled the tube. The ghost woman said that she filled it nearby. The man told her to spill out the water because people never drank from there.

The man told her to go past the first stream, then to go a little farther to the second stream to fill the tube. He told the woman to go back and fetch the water.

Then the man quickly tied up his dog and carried it to a big wild pandanus tree (*karuka*). When the woman returned, she saw the man with his dog on top of the big wild pandanus tree. The woman was irate. She took a stick and cut the aerial roots of the pandanus tree until only one was left at daybreak. At daybreak, the woman departed.

The man took his dog and they went to their village where they saw that his wife had died. The man shot his wife's corpse with arrows, filling her corpse with them. Then the man broke the arrows off the corpse and buried his wife in a grave.

This is not an ordinary story. No, it is a true story. This forest is called Damugoi. It is near Okapa, Eastern Highlands. Many people who go to Damugoi Forest do not return.

Sipha Tusuke
Port Moresby
National Capital District

C612. Forbidden forest; E261.4. Ghost pursues man; E425.1.4. Revenant as woman carrying baby; E440+. Ghost laid by spear/arrow; P210. Husband and wife; P230. Parents and children; R220. Flights; R260. Pursuits; R311. Tree refuge; T570. Pregnancy; T580. Childbirth; V61.3+. Dead buried

## The Place of Bones

(Wantok 399, January 9, 1982, page 25)

Long, long ago in Genai [**Gena**] Village, in **Simbu** Province, there was a *masalai* named Yokond [**Kuman** People]. He often slept by Agmbo Kombugo Stream. He killed many men, women and children when they went by this stream.

Because of this, all of the men, women and children had to go in a group. If someone went alone to this stream, the *masalai* would kill and eat the person. After the *masalai* finished eating them, the *masalai* would gather all of their bones and put them in a cave. The name of this cave is Yokond Kombugo.

No man, woman or child went close to Yokond Kombugo because they were terrified of seeing the bones. There were so many bones that no one could count them. They were as many as the leaves that fall from trees.

One day, all of the men, women and children of Genai held a big meeting. At this meeting, they talked about finding and killing this Yokond.

One nice day, all of the men carried their bows, arrows and stone axes then went to Yokond Kombugo. However, they did not find the *masalai*. They were furious and said, "If we find this murderous sorcerer, Yokond, we'll cut Yokond up into little pieces then burn them in a bonfire."

They looked for the *masalai* in all of the parts of the stream and forest. They searched and searched, but they did not find the *masalai*. When they arrived at Yokond Kombugo, they saw the bones piled high inside the cave. When they saw the bones, they said, "Hah, let's leave and return home. It would be bad if the *masalai* ate some of us again." Yokond was hiding inside the pile of human bones, but the men did not see him. They thought that it was just a pile of bones from people that the *masalai* had killed.

When they went outside the cave, Yokond was very happy and said, "Friends, you didn't want to kill me, huh?" Then Yokond went inside again. All of the men were angry and said, "You murderous sorcerer, Yokond, are you bragging? We'll find and kill you later." They all went back home to sleep.

Later, after two or three months, the men held a big meeting again. They said, "This time, we'll kill that murderous sorcerer right away." They all called out, "Kill Yokond, cut Yokond and burn Yokond!"

One day, in the very early morning, all of the men took their bows, arrows and stone axes, then they took three little boys and went into the forest.

The men told these three boys to go and pretend to kill birds in the forest. All of the men went to hide about in the forest. They readied their bows and arrows to shoot Yokond.

The three boys pretended to kill birds near Yokond's cave. Two of the three ran down and said, "Yokond, if you're nearby, come and kill that boy." When Yokond heard this, Yokond quickly ran and grabbed the boy.

As Yokond held onto the boy, he called out, "Let me go! Let me go!" When the men heard the little boy calling out, they quickly readied their bows, arrows and stone axes then ran from all of their places, surrounding Yokond.

One of the leaders said, "Yokond, today you'll die." He took his stone axe and split open his head. Everyone was very happy and jumped about.

They carried Yokond to the cave and cut Yokond into little pieces. They burned the pieces in a bonfire. They had finished him off. All of the men were happy to see Yokond burn. They cried out, "Listen, murderous sorcerer Yokond! You're burned now!"

After Yokond's death, the men, women and children often went by this stream and forest whenever they desired. They were no longer afraid.

At this time, all of the men, women and children were happy and traveled as they wished. Also, from this time onwards, whoever died in Genai Village was brought to Yokond Kombugo and buried. They thought that all of the ancestors looked after this cave, which caused people to fall down and urinate in fear.

My father told this story to me. I will tell my children, and they will tell their children. This story is still told and has not yet disappeared.


Joseph H. Kau
Kemeng Community School
P. O. Box 35
Mount Hagen
Western Highlands Province



The Institute of Papua New Guinea Studies gave awards to people who won a contest for writing stories and plays. This is Joseph Kau's story. He won first prize for ancestor stories in Tok Pisin.


D2061. Magic murder; F490+. Masalai; F490+. Nokondi; G200. Witch; G512.1+. Ogre killed with axe; K914. Murder from ambush; S110. Murders; S139.4. Murder by mangling with axe; S139.7. Murder by slicing person into small pieces; V61.3+. Dead buried

## The Child that Came from a *Wailbal* Tree Fruit

(Wantok 400, January 16, 1982, page 27)

Long, long ago, in the time of the ancestors, there was a man who lived in a village. His name was Viaui. He and his wife were married when they were young. They did not have children and they had become old, so they were very worried. They tried all kinds of ways to make the woman pregnant but none worked.

One day, old Viaui woke up in the early morning because it was a very good day. The sun rose quickly and made the morning very bright. He told his wife, "It's a very good day for me to rest. I always work very hard in the garden, digging the earth and planting food. I often work hard to raise a lot of food, but I have no child to give this food. Never mind that, I'm tired. Today, I'll travel around the forest a little first."

His wife prepared some betel nuts, betel peppers and other things for Viaui to bring with him.

Their little village was very close to the deep forest, and when Viaui went inside the forest, he became confused.

He walked a long way and arrived at a hill. At that place, he thought about taking a little rest.

He sat and wanted to chew some betel nuts. Immediately, something caught his eyes. On top of a small _wailbal_ tree, he saw a small, green _wailbal_ fruit. However, the outside of the _wailbal_ fruit's body was bright, like the sun. He looked at this and trembled a little. He did not chew on the betel nuts. He threw the betel nuts away, took a basket and climbed the little tree to get the _wailbal_ fruit.

After he climbed the tree, he took the fruit. However, he found that it was very heavy and it was too hard on the outside. If he threw it away, the _wailbal_ fruit would break like an egg. So, he looked after it carefully as he climbed down. On the ground, he felt the _wailbal_ fruit become heavier and heavier.

He did not think of resting or chewing betel nuts. No, he just took this thing and walked off towards home. As he walked, he did not walk straight because the _wailbal_ fruit was too heavy. So, he walked a little crookedly. When he came to a difficult place, such as a ditch or a big tree, he would jump over. His basket would shake and the _wailbal_ fruit shook with it. He did this all along the way, then he heard the cry of a little baby. He thought that some people must have been following him. He walked a little farther, then he thought that he should hurry because it would be bad if they came and saw him. He walked a little farther and he heard the cry again. So, he kept going until he arrived home.

He went inside the house and saw that his wife was cooking food and waiting. They ate the food, then they heard the baby's cry again, they cry that Viaui had first heard on the trail. They heard the cry coming from inside their house and they were surprised. Viaui's wife put her ear close to the basket and she heard that the cry was coming right from her husband's basket. They took the _wailbal_ fruit and broke it with the small stone axe that they used to cut firewood. When they cut it open, a baby came outside.

Oh my! The old couple was very happy to see the baby. It was a very beautiful baby boy. They jumped and jumped and were happier and happier. They called the baby Kuluban, meaning "Green _Wailbal_." The old man Viaui changed his name to Ban, meaning, "The Little Tree Had a Green _Wailbal_."

They took care of the baby well until he became a big man. He married and raised a family, from which I came. The name Kuluban is the ancestral name of my clan. This name is still used. We have always believed that our ancestors came from a wailbal fruit, and that he married and made the family from which we came, we from

**Numamaka** Village [**Abelam** People, **East Sepik** Province.]

Francis Kipandu
J. Camp Trading
P. O. Box 166
Maprik
East Sepik Province

A511.1.9+. Culture hero born from fruit; A1640+. Origin of Kuluban Clan; D211B. Transformation: boy to fruit; D2035. Magic heaviness; F813+. Extraordinarily bright fruit; N825.1. Childless old couple adopt hero; P210. Husband and wife; P231. Mother and son; P233. Father and son; T100. Marriage; T570. Pregnancy

## A Woman Tricked a Wild Man
(Wantok 401, January 23, 1982, page 25)

Long, long ago, the men wanted to make a big party in a village. They finished preparing all of their things, then on the day of the party, a man died. The leader of the village said, "Let's forget the party. We'll make it tomorrow."

So, they made a box, put the man's body inside and carried him to his grave. The next night, the women cooked the food for the party. In the evening, everyone gathered for the party. However on this day, one woman gave birth. Her husband wanted to go to the party, so he left the baby with its mother and he departed. He told his wife that he would not stay for long.

The man went to the party and had a good time with the other men. He forgot about home. It was late at night when he went back towards the house. A wild man from the forest went to the grave and dug out the casket of the man who had just died. He carried it to the village of the woman who had just given birth. He put down the casket and began to eat.

The man was still at the party and had not yet returned. The woman was terrified that the wild man would finish eating the dead man, then eat herself and her baby. The wild man ate until he came to the middle of the body, then he asked the woman for meat. The woman gave him two taros (_singapo_). He put them next to the dead man.

The wild man finished, then asked the woman for water. The woman said, "There's no water. I'll go fetch some water nearby." So, the woman put the baby in a box. She put the bottles on top of the box and she put the box near the window. She went outside, took the box with the baby and bottles, then departed. She entered the forest, removed the baby and left the bottles in the forest.

She ran with the baby and found the father walking on the trail. The woman told her husband about everything that had happened to them. The three of them went to the village of the party. The man told everyone that the wild man had eaten the corpse.

Everyone went to this man's village. They surrounded the house, and this man alone went to the wild man. He asked him why he had taken the corpse. Then everyone grabbed the wild man and killed him. They took his body, put it in the house and burned him with the house. Later, they took the bones and put them back in the box and buried them in the grave. The man took his wife and child and they went to live in a new house in another village.

Elizabeth Sukunkun
**Tanga** Island [**Tangga** People]
**New Ireland** Province

F567. Wild man; G512. Ogre killed; K914. Murder from ambush; P210. Husband and wife; P230. Parents and children; Q215. Cannibalism punished; Q212.2. Grave-robbing punished; Q411. Death as punishment; R220. Flights; S110. Murders; T580. Childbirth; V61.2. Dead burned on pyre; V61.3+. Dead buried


# A *Masalai* Married a Real Woman

(Wantok 402, January 30, 1982, page 25)

Long ago, there was a *masalai* who lived in Kumbuhin [**Kumbuhum**] Village, near Yangoru in **East Sepik** Province [**Boiken** People]. The name of this *masalai* was Walemiska.

One time, a woman from Kumbuhin Village traveled and bathed near the area where the *masalai* dwelled. The *masalai* saw this woman and liked her. He turned into a cockatoo, then flew and perched on top of a tree.

The woman finished bathing and wanted to go back home when she saw the cockatoo. The cockatoo was eating. While the cockatoo ate, the peels of its food fell right on top of the woman.

The woman turned and called out to the cockatoo that if it was a good bird, it should down some *ton* fruits to her. The cockatoo heard this and threw down a cluster of *ton* fruits to where the woman was standing.

The woman turned to get the *ton* fruits and the cockatoo turned into a man. He broke off many *ton* fruits and threw them down to the woman. The place where the woman stood filled with *ton* fruits. The woman did not know that the cockatoo was a *masalai* and she told the cockatoo that it was a good bird. The cockatoo replied, "Cockatoo eats." Then the woman ate some food and carried a net bag of fruits back to the village.

At night, the woman slept and the *masalai* changed his appearance to that of the woman's husband, then he slept with the woman. The woman thought that it was just her husband.

In the morning, the woman asked her real husband whether he had slept with her. The man said no. The woman spoke strongly, "It was you. I saw your face. You said that it wasn't you, so who was it that slept with me?" Now the man was irate.

Another night, the man slept in the house with his wife and watched carefully with his spear. He saw the *masalai* approach, remove his snakeskin, and come inside the house to sleep with the woman.

The real man threw the spear at the *masalai*, but he missed and the *masalai* fled. The *masalai* did this every night and the woman became pregnant. The *masalai* wanted very much to marry this woman.

It was at this time that the men killed a pig and made a big feast for the woman to go marry the *masalai*. After they prepared the feast, they called out for the *masalai* to come to the village. They finished eating, then the *masalai* took the woman and they left together.

They walked a little ways and the woman's little brother followed them. He went up a tree and sat.

The *masalai* and the woman arrived at a stream and the *masalai* said, "Look up the tree and see what is there." The woman looked and the *masalai* cut off her breasts. The woman turned into a snake, then went inside the water.

The boy saw all of this. He also saw his sister's breasts drifting on top of the water like two pieces of wood. The boy shot the breasts and carried them to the village. He told all of the men, then they cried and buried the breasts. They were very sorry because they were wrong to have given the woman to the *masalai* to marry, but not one of them knew that the man was a *masalai*.

Tobias Wafi
Peru Village
Yangoru
East Sepik Province

[See the book, *The Mountain Arapesh II: Arts and Supernaturalism*, by Margaret Mead (1970). There is a story about a woman who marries a *masalai* on pages 307-312.]

B211.3+. Speaking cockatoo; B469+. Helpful cockatoo; D150+. Transformation: spirit to cockatoo; D191W. Transformation: woman to serpent (snake); D191+. Transformation: spirit to serpent (snake); D350+M. Transformation: cockatoo to man; D566.4+. Transformation by cutting or dismemberment; F401.3.7+. Spirit in form of cockatoo; F401.3.8. Spirits in form of snake; F490+. Masalai; K1311. Seduction by masking as woman's husband; K1910. Marital impostors; P210. Husband and wife; P253. Sister and brother; R220. Flights; S62. Cruel husband; S176+. Mutilation: breasts cut off; T111. Marriage of mortal and supernatural being; T570. Pregnancy; V61.3+. Dead buried

## The Old Man Became a Baby

(Wantok 403, February 6, 1982, page 21)

Long, long ago, there was a man and woman who were childless. One time, the man stayed at the house and the woman went to the garden. She dug some sweet potatoes and put them in a net bag. Later, she carried the sweet potatoes to a stream where she dumped them into the water.

She finished washing the sweet potatoes, then put them back into the net bag. She heard a noise. When she turned to look, she saw a little man in the water who said, "Ata ata." She was surprised and ran to get him.

However, this boy was not a little baby, it was old man Umanei. It was this old man who had turned into this little baby. Oh my, the woman was very happy. She quickly put the sweet potatoes in the net bag and went home.

When she arrived at the house, her husband was very happy. He said, "We didn't have a child." The woman gave the baby her breast.

The next day, the man told his wife to stay with the baby and he would go hunt for wild game for the baby. He departed. When the man returned, he brought a marsupial (*kapul*). The woman quickly cooked it and gave the guts to the dog. However, the little boy cried terribly to eat the guts.

You would have thought that the little boy was two years old, and that he would not have cried for marsupial guts. But the little boy did cry for them. The woman gave the meat to the boy, but he did not want it and he cried again. He wanted to swallow it with the skin and bones, and he continued to cry.

They gave him the bones and skin, and he finished the marsupial. Another day, he cried again for meat, so the woman told her husband to stay with the boy and she would go spearfishing at night with a torch.

The woman spearfished only for frogs and not for fish because the boy cried too much for meat. The woman caught many and brought them back to the village. She cooked some and gave them to the boy. She dried some on top of the fire like fish. The next day, she hunted for more.

After she finished fishing, she returned to the house and saw that the dried frogs were not there. She put some frogs on the fire and went to look for her husband. She asked for the frogs that she had dried, she asked whether he had taken them or whether the boy had. The man said that the boy had taken them.

The two of them said, "Let's pretend to hunt for frogs." So they lit torches and went to the forest. They spearfished again then returned to the village. They saw the boy rise from the net bag and become an old man. He went down and blew on the fire. When the fire lit up, they saw the man's white hair. He broke the frog bones. They saw this and they were very angry. They did not catch any more frogs.

In the morning, they told the boy to sleep and they would find game for him. They closed the door tightly and lit a torch. The boy thought they really were going to find game.

They went to the other side and lit the house on fire with the torch. The [little boy] became an [old man] and jumped down from the net bag. He just said, "Eat my shit! You hunted game for me to eat and I drank your wife's milk." He did not know that they had put fire to the house.

When the woman heard the boy talking like this, she became irate and said, "You can eat our shit too! We've set fire to the house. You're going to roast." They were still angry, but they did not have any more to say to the old man. The fire burned and killed him.

They went to another village and slept until dawn. They returned and there was not one log of the house standing. The fire had burned it entirely. The man had also burned up and only his soul was left.

The two of them began to make a new house. They slept and were happy.

Cypriana Bauai Etau
Camp 9
Panguna, Arawa
North Solomons Province

D56.1. Transformation to older person; D1881. Magic self-rejuvenation; D1890. Magic aging; F321.1.4.3. Changeling thrown on fire and thus banished; K1930. Treacherous impostors; P210. Husband and wife; P231. Mother and son; P233. Father and son; Q262. Impostor punished; Q414.0.6. Burning as punishment for impostor; S112.0.2. House (hostel) burned with all inside; T611. Suckling of children

## An Old Woman Helped them Run Away

(Wantok 404, February 13, 1982, page 17)

Long, long ago, in the time of the ancestors, there were no pigs in the village. People often killed the children and ate them like pigs. There lived a man and his wife who had two children.

One day, the married couple wanted to kill their children. So, they went to the garden to get some things: taros, yams, bananas, leafy vegetables and such. When they finished in the garden, the two children were playing in the village.

The boy had made a little bow and was sharpening his marksmanship by aiming at a coconut palm leaf.

He and his little sister were walking around the village, coming and going. Later, some boys saw them and joined them. They shot at insects, played around, called out, coming and going.

Later, the children's old grandmother told them, "You who are calling out back and forth, your parents want to eat you. They're in the garden getting some food." The two of them ran to their grandmother, cried and asked her, "What can you do for us?"

The old woman told them to run to the nearby garden and look for red sugarcane in the center of the garden. Then they should remove it with its roots and leaves and bring it back. They took it and returned, then the grandmother said, "Dig a hole nearby and plant the sugarcane with its roots and leaves together."

They finished planting and told their grandmother, "Granny, we planted it." The old woman told them, "Climb the sugarcane and you'll go and go, up to the clouds." They climbed and climbed. The sugarcane became very tall and brought them along. The sugarcane grew and grew, arriving at the clouds, where the children stayed.

Later, the parents returned from the garden. They rested, then it was time to eat. They wanted to kill the children, so they called for them. They called and called, but they did not come. They searched for them in the forest and the village too. They asked the old woman, "Did you see where your grandchildren went?"

The old woman said, "My grandchildren are in the clouds. Later in the evening, you'll see that they'll become stars and rise above you while you watch." The old woman had helped her grandchildren anger their parents. She said, "My grandchildren are not pigs for you to come and eat. Don't you want to hunt pigs and kill them?" The old woman finished scolding them and said, "If you want pigs, then pigs will come now for you to see." Various kinds of colored pigs from the deep forest came: black, white, red, yellow, and blue. Green pigs came much later and the old woman told them to go back to the forest. So now there are white pigs and village pigs.

Later, when it was dark, the children turned into stars and rose high above the clouds. The old woman told the children's parents, "The years come and go, and each year the stars are in the middle there, marking Christmas Day. The children have turned into stars and have risen above the clouds. When you follow these stars to that point, it marks a new year." We can still follow this way of marking each year.

Joe Muyat
Arawa
North Solomons Province

A770. Origin of particular stars; A1485. How people learned about calculating time and the seasons; A1520. Origin of hunting and fishing customs; A2513.3. How pig was domesticated; D293C. Transformation: child to star; F54.2+. Sugarcane grows to sky; F60+. Ascent to upper world by climbing; G72. Unnatural parents eat children; P210. Husband and wife; P231. Mother and son; P232. Mother and daughter; P233. Father and son; P234. Father and daughter; P253. Sister and brother; P292. Grandmother; R213. Escape from home; S110. Murders

## The Old Man Who Became Young
(Wantok 405, February 20, 1982, page 25)

Long ago, in a village called **Tolofon**, near Drekikir [Dreikikir], **East Sepik** Province, there was an old man who had two wives [**Urat** People]. The three of them lived together.

When they worked in the garden, the two women worked very hard. But their husband just slept. At night, when the two women went to sleep, the man transformed himself and become new again, then went to work. However, the two women did not know that their husband often did this.

If there were a festival in one place, the man would tell the two women to go first. He would say, "You go and let me sleep. Tomorrow, bring the pork [from the festival] back for us. I'm old and I'll just sleep."

However when they would leave, he would go hide. Then he would change into a handsome young man. He would dress finely, go to the area of the dancing and wait for the festivities to begin. Then he would sing and dance with the men. He would be very worried that the two women would dance hotly (*samsam*).

When the man would see them, he would hide among the people and they never saw him. They would sing and dance until dawn approached, then the man would go back to their home. He would change back to an old man and pretend to be asleep. Later, the two women would arrive home.

He would trick them by asking them what had happened at the festival or party, and they would tell him. This sort of thing happened for a while, then one time, there was another festival. He sent the two women first. Darkness arrived and there was singing and dancing.

However this time, he did not hide well and the two women saw him and lusted for him. This was their husband, but they did not know it. They said, "We don't like being married to an old man."

The two of them planned to marry him. They waited until dawn to get a good look at his face. However before dawn, the man returned to their home.

When the two of them returned to their old husband, they were always lusting for the young man. They always talked about and lusted for the young man. They wanted to marry him.

One time, they went to a festival, but they did not sing or dance. They just stood and looked around at the men. They saw him come then sing and dance. They said that one of them should go look carefully at his face. However, the man hid his face among the many dancers.

They wanted find out the village from which this man came, but no one knew.

The two of them said that they should watch him carefully, but they could never catch him. They saw the path that he followed. They saw him approaching. They took a rope and some sword grass, then sat ready to grab him.

They waited and the man came running. He came and removed the sword grass that they had put there. The two of them said, "It's only you that we've lusted for!" The man saw them and quickly changed back to an old man again. They saw him and they went back to the village. They transformed themselves too.

The first woman became a bird of paradise and the second woman became a Victoria crowned pigeon [*Goura victoria*]. They of them perched on a tree and made noises when the man arrived at the village. They shook their feathers. The man was very troubled and said, "It was me who was wrong." So, now many men like the feathers of the bird of paradise and the Victoria crowned pigeon when they want to go to festivals.

William Wokumel

Raval Settlement

Kavieng

New Ireland Province

[Mr. Wokumel retold this story in *Wantok* #669.]

A1680+. Why men wear feathers at festivals; D56.1. Transformation to older person; D150+W. Transformation: woman to bird of paradise; D154.2+W. Transformation: woman to Victoria crowned pigeon; D1881. Magic self-rejuvenation; K1814+. Man in disguise wooed by his faithless wife; K1910. Marital impostors; K1930. Treacherous impostors; P210. Husband and wife; T10. Falling in love; T145.0.1. Polygyny; W111. Laziness

# A *Masalai* Killed a Brother
(Wantok 406, May 27, 1982, page 25)

In the time of yore, there were two brothers. Their father had died and they lived with their mother. One time, the brothers told their mother that they would go to hunt for marsupials (*kapul*). Their mother told them not to go to a particular place because it was a *masalai* place. She carefully explained to them about this place that they should avoid.

The two brothers were big and very strong. The brothers ate some food, then carried some food and fire into the forest.

They walked to a faraway place and they arrived at a big tree. The tree had many marsupials on it. They began to make a hut for themselves. After they finished, the big brother climbed the tree. The little brother stayed below and lit a fire.

The big brother was on top of the tree. He called out to the little brother so that he could throw marsupials down to him. He threw them, then the little brother took them and singed off their fur in the fire. They worked like this for a while and the marsupials piled up below because the big brother had killed many. However, while the little brother was receiving marsupials, the fire began to die out. When he brought a marsupial back to cook, the fire died out completely. He did not see any fire.

The little brother called out to the big brother and told him that the fire was out. Oh my, the big brother was irate, "What did you do to put out the fire? You're still strong, go find some fire so we can singe off the marsupial fur."

His brother came down from the tree. They sat in their hut and felt sorry for themselves. They looked up a mountain. The little brother saw smoke and told the big brother, "Stay here. I see smoke from a fire. I'll go get fire from that place." The big brother told him to go get the fire from there. The big brother told him to go and return quickly while there was still sunlight.

The little brother began to walk towards the mountain, but it was not nearby. He walked and walked, then arrived at the place from which the smoke was coming. He saw some meat. He thought that it was pork and he ate it, but it was human flesh that the *masalai* had partially eaten. The big brother was very tired and was waiting for him. He got up and followed his little brother.

He walked for a long time, then arrived and saw his little brother eating meat. He was surprised and asked the little brother, "What are you eating?" The little brother said, "Meat." Then the big brother helped the little brother eat the meat. When darkness arrived, they did not have a place to sleep, so they climbed trees. The little brother went up one tree and the big brother went up another. The clouds thundered and rain fell. They saw a *masalai* come out of a hole.

The *masalai* tried to find his meat. He said, "Oh my, who ate my meat? Today I'll kill the man that stole my meat." The little boy heard this. He was terrified and cried. The *masalai* heard the boy crying. The *masalai* climbed the tree and was very happy.

After the *masalai* climbed the tree, it threw the boy down to his death. The *masalai* went down to the ground and began to eat the boy.

The *masalai* began to eat from the legs upwards. When he arrived at the neck, the big brother called out, "Hey, leave my brother's head and I'll carry it home." The *masalai* heard this and said that he would eat him too. Now the boy was afraid and began to say, "Hurry dawn." The *masalai* began to say, "Darkness, don't get light."

They continued to talk like this, then dawn broke. The *masalai* ran away and went back down his hole. The boy went down, took his brother's head and returned home. He cried and arrived at their village.

The mother saw him and asked him what he was crying. The big brother told the story to his mother. They mourned together. In the morning, they buried the boy's head near their house so that they could keep the boy's grave clean all of the time.

One morning, they saw a tree seedling growing directly from the grave. They tended the seedling well. The seedling became a tree and bore fruit. The fruits grew large and fell down. They took these, removed the husk and broke them open. They saw the white meat inside it. This is what we now call coconut.

Joe Tosi

Guru Plantation

Box 2

Wakunai

North Solomons Province

A1423.3. Origin of coconut; A2611.3.1K. Coconut tree from head of human; C612. Forbidden forest; F408.3. Spirits dwell at tabu place; F490+. Masalai; F610. Remarkably strong man; G60. Human flesh eaten unwittingly; G570. Ogre overawed; G610. Theft from ogre; G632. Ogre who cannot endure daylight; K420. Thief loses his goods or is detected; P231. Mother and son; P251.5. Two brothers; Q212. Theft punished; Q411. Death as punishment; Q429.1. Punishment: culprit eaten by cannibals; R220. Flights; S127. Murder by throwing from height; V61.3+. Dead buried

## The In-Laws Ruined a Woman

(Wantok 407, March 6, 1982, page 21)

**B**efore, in a place near **Kainantu**, there lived a boy and his sister [**Eastern Highlands** Province, **Agarabi** People]. Their father and mother had died when they were still nursing. They did not have any kin to take care of them.

However, an old woman took them and looked after them. They lived with the old woman until they grew to be a man and a woman. They often helped the old woman, doing all of the work that she wanted to be done.

One day, the boy asked the woman if she would listen to his concerns and whether she could help him. The old woman said, "If I can, I'll help you." The boy told the old woman that he wanted to be married. The old woman was very happy and gave her approval to the boy.

The boy married and went to live with his in-laws. He raised a house and he lived there with his wife. Then only the woman lived with the old woman. She lived there until the old woman died. She told her brother that the old woman had died, and that they should bury her. They mourned for the old woman and they made a big feast.

Later, the woman went to live with her brother. They lived there for a while and the woman went to marry a man from Komano [**Kamano**], near Kainantu. The woman went to live at her husband's village. She did not see her brother for a very long time.

One time, her brother wanted to make a big feast, so he sent a message to his sister. His sister prepared everything, then went to his village. She arrived with her little daughter.

They arrived in the evening, but her brother was still at the spirit house. The brother's wife told her to sleep in the pigsty. The brother's wife did not speak about giving food.

The woman took her daughter and went to sleep in a man's pigsty. They were famished. They ate two of the pigs' sweet potatoes. The woman was very ashamed of her brother.

At dawn, her brother went to the house and asked his wife, "Did my sister come or not?" The woman said, "Yes, the two of them came. I told them to sleep with me, but they said that you weren't here, so they slept in someone's pigsty." The woman lied to her husband in this manner.

The man thought that it was true, so he went back to the spirit house. He made some arrangements about killing the pigs. In the morning, he took his spear and killed a big pig. Then he told the men to help him carry and butcher the pig. They butchered the pig, then the man's wife took the guts and cleaned them well.

She cooked them in bamboo tubes, then she and her children ate in the house. After they finished eating, she told the children to carry some to their aunt. While the children were bringing it to them, they began to eat it. After they finished the food, they returned to their house. When their father asked them about the food, they said that they had given it to their aunt, but they were lying.

The poor father thought that his wife and children were behaving well towards his sister. When he asked his wife, the woman lied again and said that she gave them food. She told him, "You think that I waited for you, but she's my dear in-law, so I gave her food right away."

They waited until evening, then uncovered the earth oven. The man removed the pork and butchered it. He gave a leg to his wife, telling her to give it to his sister. However, his wife took it to the house and gave some to her children. Then she took a big piece of the leg and went to give it to the woman. However, she only pretended to do this. She hid behind a big house, ate all of the meat and returned to the house.

When her husband asked her if she had given meat to his sister yet, she said, "Yes, I did." The man's sister saw this and was very ashamed at what her sister-in-law had done to herself and her daughter. She slept with her daughter in the pigsty. They were famished. They kept eating the pigs' sweet potatoes.

In the early morning, she woke up, took her daughter and they walked back to their village. It was then that her brother saw them and called out for her to wait. He wanted to give them some meat and other food to bring back.

However, his sister did not wait. She and her daughter kept walking, so her brother followed them. The two of them crossed a mountain, and the brother also crossed the mountain. The two of them stood on one mountain and the brother stood on another.

They did this until the two of them arrived at a big mountain. The brother stood on another mountain. He called out for his sister to wait. He wanted to go with them, but his sister called out, "I'm ashamed at what your kin did to me and my daughter." So she threw her baby into a hole, then she died.

She began to tell her brother about what had happened at the village when they were there. She said, "I've lived well in my husband's village. Then you called for me to come. Because I'm your sister, my daughter and I crossed mountains and trails to come. However when we came, your wife put us in the pigsty. We didn't eat even a little piece of food. Your wife lied to you. She didn't give us food. You told her to give us food, but she hid behind a house and ate it. Your children are just like their mother. They lied and they ate the pig guts."

Her brother listened and was very troubled. She spoke again, "I threw away my baby because she was starving. I too am starving. Your kin are boors. Go to your village and tell every man not to leave their sisters like this." She finished speaking, then jumped into the hole with her baby and she also died.

Her brother heard this and went to see that his sister and niece were indeed dead. He cut off one of his ears and threw it into the hole [a sign of mourning]. He walked back to the village. He took a pig, then locked it up with his children and wife. He told them to eat the whole pig.

After three whole days, they ate the pig. When they finished, he opened the door and let them out to urinate and defecate. Then he prepared his bow and arrows. He told them to go hunt for wild game in the forest.

They followed the trail that his sister and her daughter had walked upon. They arrived at the mountain where his sister had died. They went to that place, then the man asked his wife how she had treated his sister. The man told her everything that his sister had told him. When the woman heard this, she was afraid and wanted to run away. However, the man drew back his bow and killed her.

Then he killed all his children too and threw them all into the hole where his sister had died. Later, he walked slowly back to the village. He called out for everyone to gather in the village. Then he spoke to them:

"I killed my children and my wife, then threw them into a hole on top of the mountain where my sister and her daughter died. I did this because when my sister came here, they didn't take them into my house. They told them to sleep in the pigsty. They stayed there in hunger for four whole days. All of you, if your sister comes from a faraway place, your wife must not do this. You must take good care of her and give her food. You cannot do what my wife did."

After he said this, he killed himself.

William Beiyabi
P. O. Box 31
Kainantu
Eastern Highlands Province

K2213. Treacherous wife; K2214. Treacherous children; M451.1. Death by suicide; P210. Husband and wife; P230. Parents and children; P231. Mother and son; P232. Mother and daughter; P253. Sister and brother; P253.5+. Brother avenges sister's death; P253.5+. Brother commits suicide on sister's death; P260. Relations by law; P264. Sister-in-law; P272. Foster mother; P275. Foster son; P275+. Foster daughter; P293. Uncle; P294. Aunt; P298. Niece; P681+. Mourning customs: feast; P681+. Mourning customs: self-mutilation; Q261. Treachery punished; Q292. Inhospitality punished; Q411. Death as punishment; Q433.7. Imprisonment for treachery; R260. Pursuits; S11.3. Father kills child; S12.2. Cruel mother kills child; S55. Cruel sister-in-law; S63+. Husband kills wife; S70+. Cruel cousin; S70+. Cruel nephew; S70+. Cruel niece; S72. Cruel aunt; S110. Murders; S127. Murder by throwing from height; S160.1. Self-mutilation; S168. Mutilation: tearing off ears; T100. Marriage; V112.1. Spirit huts; W125. Gluttony; W157. Dishonesty; W158. Inhospitality

## The Two Thieves

(Wantok 408, March 13, 1982, page 21)
(Wantok 409, March 20, 1982, page 21)

Very long ago, two brothers lived in a village called **Muloga** [**Agarabi** People?, **Eastern Highlands** Province]. The two men were great tricksters and they often stole many things from people. The name of the first brother was Kugut and the name of the second brother was Geat.

One afternoon, Kugut told Geat, "I found a pigsty, let's go and steal some pigs from the house."

They left at about four o'clock in the afternoon. They walked about twenty miles and arrived at the pigsty at about six o'clock in the afternoon [!]. They went inside the house and killed a huge pig.

They tied the pig to a log and they carried it back. However along the trail, they met a heavy rain. They found an open-air house along the road where no one was sleeping. They brought the pig in and waited for the rain to stop. They would leave later.

However Kugut told Geat, "Never mind. Let's singe off the pig's hair and cook it in an earth oven inside this house." They wanted to make a fire, but they did not have matches or anything. They took a long piece of bamboo string and drew it taut around a piece of dry wood. They pulled the bamboo back and forth and made a fire.

Kugut wanted to find some firewood to singe off the pig's hair. He put his hand into the corner of the house to try to find some firewood. However, he put his hand on top of a pregnant woman who had died and was placed in the house. They had not known that a dead woman had been put in the house.

Kugut was terrified, but he did not tell Geat that the dead woman's body was in the corner of the house. He slowly rose and told his brother, "We don't have firewood in the house. I must go outside to look for some." So, he ran away, leaving his brother with the pig. He went back to their house.

Geat waited for Kugut to return, but Kugut did not return, so Kugut thought hard. He also went to look for firewood in the corner of the house. He too put his hand on top of the dead woman's belly. Geat jumped up high. Now he knew why Kugut had run away, because he had touched the dead woman.

Geat found a piece of firewood, made a fire and singed off the pig's hair. When the smell of burning hair became strong, Geat heard something fall in the corner of the house. He turned and saw the dead woman's ghost. The ghost told him, "I want to sleep. Which man is making a smell inside my house?"

Oh my, Geat was terrified and he made a bonfire. He worked at butchering the pig. When the fire began to die down, the tongue of the dead woman came very close to Geat's back. Geat made the fire bigger again and cut some pieces of pork to give to this woman. When Geat looked at her, she was eating slowly. However, when he did not look at her, the woman swallowed the pieces of pork just like a cassowary eats [i.e., without chewing].

Geat went on top of the house to look for some stones to use for the earth oven. While he heated the stones, he put the pig's big belly near the fire. When fire heated the belly, it swelled up and boiled inside.

Geat cooked the pig in the earth oven and he made a big fire. A little later, he uncovered the earth oven. He gave some pork to the woman and he put some in his net bag.

It was about four o'clock in the morning and he wanted to go to the village, but the dead woman was near him. Geat was terrified. He took the pig's belly and hit the dead woman right in the face, then he ran away.

However, the dead woman did not leave him. No, she followed Geat. She called out and spoke to Geat, "You, the man who wants to steal my pig, where are you going? You must wait for me!" Geat raced swiftly and arrived at his house. Dawn came and the ghost woman returned.

Geat saw Kugut and was irate. Kugut told Geat, "Don't be angry at me. It's very good that you cooked the pig and brought it for us to eat." So Geat was not angry, but he tried to think of a way to trick his brother because he had run away and left him with the dead woman.

Some time later, Geat saw that it was a good time to trick his brother Kugut. Near their village, there was an old man who had become sick and had died from sorcery.

However, Kugut did not know this. Only Geat knew about this dead man.

The dead man's clan came to dig a hole for his grave where they would bury his body. However it became dark before they finished, so they just put the body in the hole without covering it up. Then they went back to the village.

Geat went quickly to the hole and put some big leaves and some tree branches on top of it. Then he returned to the house. He told his brother Kugut to look for a bird's nest near the grave, then they would go kill some birds to cook and eat. Geat told Kugut, "You should stand directly on the big _kaviyako_ tree [leaves] and look up. You'll have a good view and you can kill the birds that come."

Poor Kugut heeded Geat. He took his bow and went to the grave at about seven o'clock at night. He stood directly on top of the big _kaviyako_ leaves, then fell on top of the body of the old dead man.

Oh my! Kugut was terrified and he did not have a way to get out of the hole. It was dark in the hole, so he raised the body of the old dead man and he slept underneath it.

At about twelve o'clock at night, the ghost of the dead man wanted to find some food. Two ghost men came and stood on top of the hole where Kugut was sleeping. They told the old man, "You should come on top and we'll go find some food." However, the old man told them, "I can come, but there's a man with me, so I'm ashamed of coming."

Kugut heard this and was terrified. He defecated and urinated when the ghost spoke from the body of the old dead man. He thought that dawn must be coming quickly, but the ghost men did not leave. They continued to ask the old man to come up and look for food with them.

Finally dawn arrived and the old man's clan wanted to bury him. So, they took a pig along with the women and children. They went to the grave, to the place where they would cook the pig in an earth oven and eat it. They also brought a male sorcerer to find out the cause of the old man's death. Kugut hid well under the body of the dead man and waited.

The group of people killed the pig and gave the pig grease to the sorcerer. The sorcerer and two men carried a wooden ladder to the grave of the old man. The people cooked the pig in the earth oven. Two men put the ladder down into the hole and the sorcerer went down with the pig grease and a bamboo knife.

Kugut saw the bamboo knife. He grabbed it and cut the sorcerer's hands. When the two men saw this, they ran away. The sorcerer also went out of the grave. His hands were bleeding profusely. When the people saw this, they ran away to the village, leaving the food there.

Kugut went out of the hole. His skin was full of red mud. At the same time, his brother, Geat, went to the grave and laughed hysterically at him. Kugut was angry and wanted to kill his brother. But Geat told his brother Kugut, "Don't be angry with me. It's very good that we'll uncover the earth oven and eat."

Geat told Kugut, "First, you tricked me and now I've tricked you. So now we must live well. We must not make tricks and steal other people's pigs anymore." So, the two of them stopped stealing and they lived well for the rest of their lives.

Joel Tagabara

Kainantu

Eastern Highlands Province

D1711. Magician; D2061. Magic murder; D2122. Journey with magic speed; E261.4. Ghost pursues man; E425.1. Revenant as woman; E425.2. Revenant as man; E541. Revenants eat; E545. The dead speak; E568. Revenant lies down and sleeps; E587.3. Ghosts walk from curfew to cock-crow; E587.5. Ghost walk at midnight; J1110. Clever persons; K301.2. Family of thieves; K307. Thieves betray each other; K735.1. Mats over holes as pitfall; P251.5. Two brothers; Q380+. Abandonment punished; Q456+. Punishment: trapped in grave with corpse/ghost; R212. Escape from grave; R220. Flights; R260. Pursuits; T570. Pregnancy; V61.3+. Dead buried; W157. Dishonesty

## Huli Started a Village

(Wantok 410, April 3, 1982, page 21)

Long ago, in the area of the Southern Highlands Province, there were two brothers. There was no other person who lived near them. They were alone.

One day, the big brother told his little brother, "We've lived here for a long time and we've not eaten any meat. Today, I want to go hunt for wild game, so stay here." The little brother said, "OK, go ahead. I'll stay here and wait for you."

The big brother prepared his bow and arrows and some food. Later, he told the little brother that he would stay in the forest for five days. On the sixth day, he would return home. After he told his little brother this, he departed.

He walked and arrived at a river, but he could not swim and go to the other side. So, he walked downriver. He walked and walked, then saw a bridge. He jumped to the other side of the river.

He began to walk again. He walked and walked, then saw smoke from a fire. He began to hunt for marsupials (_kapul_), but he did not find a single marsupial. He rested then he got up and walked towards the smoke. When he arrived at this place, he saw a village.

He did not go directly to the village. He hid by a tree. However, a man saw him immediately. The man walked up to him and asked, "What are you looking for in this area? You don't belong to this place." [He replied,] "I just came to hunt for game because we have not eaten any meat. I saw your smoke and I came here."

The boy's name was Opena. The man told him that he must go back to his place with his brother. The boy was angry and thought that the man was alone, so he wanted to kill him. But no, the man called out and all his brothers heard him. They came out and grabbed Opena.

They carried Opena to the river. They cut the bridge and threw Opena into the water. They had tied his hands and legs so that Opena could not swim, and he drowned.

However, Opena's ghost returned home and told the little brother that he had died. He told him that the men had killed him and thrown him in the water. So now, he could no longer stay with his little brother.

The little brother was named Huli. He listened to what his big brother's ghost said, then he cried. He cried and cried until dawn, then he slept a little. In the morning, he woke up and was a little afraid because he was alone.

The two of them had a dog. The dog had very long ears. The dog had stayed with Huli when Opena went hunting for game. The dog slept. In the early morning, Opena's ghost told the dog to go find a woman for Huli.

The dog heeded him. In the early morning, the dog woke up, went to a village, and then went above a house. The dog saw a young woman going up to the house. The dog tied up the woman and carried her in the night to the Huli's home.

The dog put the woman in Huli's house while she was sleeping. She thought that she was still sleeping in her house. At dawn, she woke up and saw that she was sleeping with a man. Huli had felt the woman, but he thought that he was sleeping with his dog.

When he woke up, he saw the woman sleeping with him. Huli was very happy because the young woman was very beautiful. The woman also looked at Huli and she almost fainted with desire to marry him. When Huli asked her, she was very happy to marry him.

They married and lived there. They had very many children. All of them lived there and grew big. They all lived there on their father's land. One time, a child went to hunt for game. He went into the deep forest and found many marsupials. He also found a good piece of land. He brought the marsupials back home.

When he arrived home, he told his brothers about the good land that he had found. In the early morning, all of them went to this land. The big brother became angry and they fought. Then, the **Huli** People became strong and they killed off the other groups of men.

Later, they carried them and threw them into the Fly River. Now they live well and are happy all of the time. Today, we often look at the Fly River. It is a long river that passes near Kiunga.

Openi
Muritaka [**Muri**] Village
**Southern Highlands** Province

[See *Wantok* #410 for another story about Obena and Huli.]

A1611+. Origin of Huli People; B421. Helpful dog; B582.1.1. Animal wins wife for his master (Puss in Boots); E226. Dead brother's return; E231. Return from dead to reveal murder; E326. Dead brother's friendly return; E545. The dead speak; P210. Husband and wife; P230. Parents and children; P231. Mother and son; P233. Father and son; P251. Brothers; P251.5. Two brothers; Q270+. Trespassing punished; Q428. Punishment: drowning; R10. Abduction; S131. Murder by drowning; T10. Falling in love; T100. Marriage

[There was no *Wantok* #411.]


## Pots Fell from the Sky
(Wantok 412, April 10, 1982, page 17)

Long, long ago, an old man and his wife lived in a little village. The old folks had a son. The son was married to a woman from another village. The young couple also had a son.

The five of them lived for a while then the old father died, leaving four of them. They made a big garden, they processed sago, and they hunted wild game for themselves. The old mother lived for a very long time until she could no longer walk. She just stayed in the house and looked after her grandson when the married couple worked in the garden or made sago.

One day, they did not have any pots to cook food. All of the pots had broken. The man told his wife that they would prepare some food and send it to the people who make clay pots. These are the **Bilbil** and Yobob [**Yabob** Islands, **Bilbil** People, Madang Province]. They finished their preparations then the man told his mother to take good care of her grandson.

The married couple began to walk away. Their son stayed with his grandmother at home. The little boy played and played by the house. Before long, the boy went to the place where his father made sago. He took some sago beetles and went back home. He gave them to his grandmother.

His grandmother took the insects and put them in the fire. She sat down nearby and worked at making a net bag. The little boy went around nearby. Later, the little boy came and asked for the package of insects. However the insects were burned up, so the little boy began to cry. The old woman tried to soothe him, but he continued to cry.

He cried and lay in the ashes of the fire. The soot made him very dirty. He kept crying then his parents returned home. They carried a big net bag filled with clay pots. They saw their son crying on the ground.

The boy's father picked him up and asked him why he was crying. The boy told him the story about his grandmother. The man listened to this and was angry. He picked up everything that belonged to the boy. Later, he took the boy and the net bag of pots, leaving nothing, and [they] went up into the clouds.

The boy's mother and grandmother stayed on the ground. When they were in the middle of the clouds, the boy's mother took a knife and cut the string of the net bag. Then all of the pots fell to the earth and broke, falling all over.

So now, if you go into the forest or make a garden in the Madang area, you can see these pieces of broken pottery lying on the ground.

Jorin Bonny
Ayab [**Aiyap**] Village
**Madang** Province

A990+. Why there is broken pottery all over the ground; F61. Person wafted to sky; F962+. Pots fall from sky; P210. Husband and wife; P231. Mother and son; P233. Father and son; P261. Father-in-law; P262. Mother-in-law; P265+. Daughter-in-law; P291. Grandfather; P292. Grandmother

## A Dead Man Ruined a Man
(Wantok 413, April 17, 1982, page 21)

Long ago, in the time of the ancestors, in the area near Drekirkir [Dreikikir], **East Sepik** Province, they often put corpses in old garden huts [**Urat** People]. If there were no old huts available, they would make a platform on top of a tree and put the corpse there.

One time, a man had died somewhere and they went to put him in a garden hut. Two days later, two men from a village went to hunt for wild game in the deep forest. However, they did not know that the corpse was in the garden. They did not know that someone had died.

They went into the deep forest and caught many marsupials (*kapul*). When they were ready to return to the village, the sun had already set and it was dark. They went directly to the garden where the people had put the corpse. The two of them said that they would sleep in the hut.

They put the game down. One of them kept watch and the other went to sleep. When the man who wanted to sleep went inside the hut, he touched the corpse's leg. He knew that he was holding a corpse's leg, but he did not tell his friend. No, he quietly went back outside and ran away.

His friend waited and waited. His eyes grew heavy and he wanted to sleep. He called out to his friend to change places. The ghost of the dead man replied and told him to wait until he straitened something out first. So, the poor man waited some more.

While he waited outside, the ghost untied a rope that had been tied around the corpse. Then the ghost stood up the corpse in the clearing. Later, he opened the corpse's groin and the place was lit as if from a fire.

The real man who was outside saw this and thought that his friend had made a fire, so he asked his friend if he had finished making the fire. The ghost replied that he was finished making the fire. The friend brought the marsupials over to be cooked and eaten. The real man thought that it was really his friend, so he brought the marsupials inside.

He wanted to look around, and he looked directly at the groin and eyes of the corpse which were lit up like fires. He saw this and threw away everything, then began to run. He was terrified, so he ran in a crazy manner. His friend too had run crazily. It was late at night and the two of them just crashed through the forest, they did not care about being scratched or injured.

The first man thought that the ghost had eaten his friend. The second man thought that when his friend had gone inside the hut, the ghost had eaten him. But no, they were both crashing though the dense forest.

The first man arrived at a garden, lost his breath and fell asleep in the garden. The other man was running behind him and also entered the garden. He also lost his breath and he thirsted for water. He broke off a sugarcane to drink the juice. After he broke it, he looked for a log where he could sit and drink.

The man with the sugarcane walked directly to the place where his friend was sleeping. He saw this man and thought that he was a log. When he went to sit down, he sat directly on top of him. The poor man called out and began to run again. They each thought that the other was the ghost of the corpse.

The first man began to run. His friend left the sugar-cane and he too began to run again. They were both terrified and ran about, crashing through the forest. They ran and ran, then went directly to their village. Each one went directly to their own houses.

However, they did not sleep well. Each of them thought about the other. They each thought that the other had died.

At dawn, one of them came out of the house with sores on his face. The men asked him, "Why is your face all scratched up?" He did not reply because he was afraid. He sat for a little while, then his friend came outside. He saw him and said, "Hey friend, I thought you were dead." The other man replied that he had thought the same of him.

They told their stories and everyone in the village died laughing at them. However, they were both badly scratched up. So from that point onward, people began to bury corpses in the ground. They no longer put corpses in garden huts.

William Wokumel
Raval Settlement
Kavieng
New Ireland Province

A1591. Origin of burial; E261.4+. Imagined ghost pursues man; E425.2. Revenant as man; E421.3+. Ghost/corpse with glowing groin; E421.3.3+. Ghost/corpse with glowing eyes; E545. The dead speak; P310. Friendship; R220. Flights; R260. Pursuits; V61+. Dead placed in garden hut; V61.3+. Dead buried; V61.10. Corpses exposed in tree

## The Wild Woman Who Died in a Fire

(Wantok 414, April 24, 1982, page 17)

Long, long ago, there was an old woman named Japetururu. She had only one daughter. The two of them lived together. One time, the old woman went to go and kill men from another village.

At this time there was a young boy walking towards Japetururu's home. The boy came and hid nearby, but the place where he hid was the place where the old woman's daughter usually went defecate and urinate.

The boy hid for a long time, then saw the girl approaching. She was dying to urinate, so she went directly towards the boy who was hiding. She did not see the boy. She went closer to the boy and the boy grabbed her.

The girl was surprised and she asked him why he had come there. The boy replied, "I came to marry you and take you back to my village." The girl said, "You must sleep with me tonight first, then tomorrow we'll go to your village." So, they went to the girl's house.

At the house, the girl told stories to the boy. She told about the bad things that her mother did. The boy was afraid and wanted to run away to his village, but the girl stopped him. She told him that she would lie to her mother.

While they talked, the clouds thundered and it became dark. Then the girl told the boy, "That's my mama coming now, so I'll hide you in my room. When mama comes, just be quiet. I'll lie to her."

When the old woman arrived home, she smelled the boy and called out to her daughter, "Where are you?" The girl replied, "Yes mama, I'm here." The old woman told her that she smelled the odor of a man. The girl replied, "I think it's the smell of an old man that you had killed." So, the mother said that she was just asking.

They slept until morning, then the old woman left home and went to another place to kill some men. At dawn, after the old woman left, the two young people prepared some food for themselves and began to run away to the boy's village.

They arrived at the village and called to the people to gather. The boy told them to dig a hole and heat some stones because the bad old cannibal woman was coming. Everyone did as the boy had instructed. They made a platform on top of the hole and waited.

The old woman went back to her daughter's home. She called to her daughter, but her daughter did not reply. Immediately, the old woman went into her daughter's room, but nothing was there. She sniffed around and smelled her daughter.

She finished sniffing, then began to follow them to the boy's village. The clouds thundered and it became very dark. The girl told everyone, "My mama's approaching. When she arrives at the village, show her where to sit. Get ready now."

They stayed there, and before long, the woman arrived. She was completely overheated. The people shouted, "*Oro, oro, oro kaiva, oro.*" Then they showed her the place to sit. As the woman walked, she asked them if her daughter had run away to this village. They told her no, but then she said, "You're liars. I think you're hiding my daughter."

As she spoke, she walked towards the place where they showed her to sit. When she arrived there, she fell right into the hole. The people took the stones and fire and threw them into the hole. The stones burned her and she died. The people made a big feast. They sang, danced and were very happy.

Reginald Faho
Hanuiri [**Hanjiri**] Village [**Hunjara** People]
Kokoda
**Oro** Province

D2149.1. Thunderbolt magically produced; G84. Fee-fi-fo-fum; G512.3. Ogre burned to death; K735.1. Mats over holes as pitfall; P210. Husband and wife; P232. Mother and daughter; R260. Pursuits; S112. Burning to death; T115. Man marries ogre's daughter; W157. Dishonesty

## The Origin of Rain

(Wantok 415, May 1, 1982, page 21)

Long, long ago, two brothers lived in a village. The name of this village was Wanu [**Wamu**, **Anggor** People, **West Sepik** Province]. The first brother was named Eatif and the second brother was Ankas. Their parents had died by this time. They lived with their old grandmother.

They lived happily for a while. One time, their old grandmother became deathly ill. However the first brother, Eatif, was not worried about his old grandmother. He said that he wanted to go look for the place of the rain.

His poor little brother, Ankas, said, "That's alright for you to look for the place of the rain. I'll stay and take care of our old granny."

At the place where the rain comes from, there was a huge mother of the trees that stood nearby. This tree tore apart the land. This place, where the tree stood, was where was the rain originated. It was completely forbidden for men, women or children to go near this place.

This tree had a big hole in it. The rain would turn into a real woman, then go and get food for herself near the huge tree. If little children, pigs or dogs went close to this place, the rain would turn into a woman. The woman would capture them and bring them into the tree hole. This was her home because she always lived there.

The big brother, Eatif, wanted to go look at this place. In the very early morning, he woke up, took some food for himself and began to walk away. The place was fairly far away from Wanu, where they lived. He walked and walked, then in the afternoon, he arrived at the place.

When he arrived, the rain jumped and became like a real woman. The woman asked the big brother, "What did you come to look for?" When the rain said this to Eatif, Eatif immediately stood, trembling and trembling. The rain took him and went inside the big tree's hole. Then Eatif turned into a hailstone.

Now, this place is still forbidden for men, women or children to go to, so this tree has never been cut.

The poor little brother, Ankas, cried and cried for his big brother. He was very troubled because only he and his grandmother were left. It was not long when the old grandmother died.

Ankas was alone. He married and had many children. So now, only descendants of Ankas can go to this place in the forest without being destroyed. The other people cannot go there. If they go there, they will become sick and die. Some will not be able to find their way back to their villages.

Willy Sek Terry
C. M. [Congregation of Mission] Wumi
Wanu Village
West Sepik Province

A1131+. Rain comes from huge hole in tree; C612. Forbidden forest; C621. Forbidden tree; C920. Death for breaking tabu; C961+. Transformation to hail for breaking tabu; D281+M. Transformation: man to hail; D281+W. Transformation: woman to rain; D430+W. Transformation: rain to woman; F811.14+. Giant tree; P210. Husband and wife; P230. Parents and children; P251.5. Two brothers; P292.1. Grandmother as foster mother; R4. Surprise capture; T100. Marriage

## The Man Who Stole a Ghost Woman's Skin

(Wantok 416, May 8, 1982, page 21)

Long, long ago, there was a woman who lived with her son and daughter. One day, the mother and her two children went to the garden. The three of them stayed at this place which was far away from other people or villages.

The boy looked at a tree that was near their garden. He went to climb the tree. The tree had many birds that often gathered on it at night and ate its fruits. The boy climbed the tree and made a small shelter on a tree branch. After he finished making the shelter, he went down to the garden where his mother and sister were working. They continued to work in the garden until the afternoon, then they went back home.

When the three of them were ready to go back home, the boy told his mother and sister that they should go back without him. He told them that he would go up to the shelter that he had made on the tree branch, then in the morning when they return, they would find him again.

He took a bow and arrows, then went up the tree and sat, watching for the birds. When it was nearly dark he heard a noise. He was sitting very quietly... then... he heard people walking quietly... and then the sound of talking approaching from a distance. Later, their sounds came close. He heard their loud talking and laughing below the tree where he was sitting. When he looked down, the place was completely different. He shut his eyes. Later, he lifted his hand from an eye and looked down again. He looked with just one eye and kept the other shut.

He saw the ghost people dressed very finely, preparing to go to the ghosts' festival someplace. The nighttime was the ghosts' daytime.

The man sat on top of the tree and watched carefully. He listened to the ghosts talking. He was terrified. His body trembled. However, he was very strong and did not make a noise on that tree branch lest they saw him up there.

He listened and he heard a ghost man tell the women, "Go to that hiding place and change your clothes. Then dress well for the festival. We men will change our clothes first at the base of this tree." It was the tree where the man was sitting and watching.

After the ghost men changed their things, they told the women to put their "grass" skirts and other adornments under the base of the tree where it was clear. The men went fairly far away from this tree. When the women were changing, the real man was sitting on top of the tree. He did not move, not even a little. His heart went out to the women as he watched them dress.

The women removed their ghost skins. These looked like their shadows. They became just like real women when they removed their dresses and skins. They put down their dresses and painted their faces. They decorated their heads, legs and arms. Now they were adorned. They had become very beautiful women, more so than any others had. The man sitting on top of the tree saw this and trembled clumsily.

The women finished dressing, then went with their husbands to the ghost festival. They left their ghost skins underneath the tree. They had hidden them well, but... the man on top saw them.

Later, two ghost women went back to this place to dress. It was just themselves and no one else. One of them was very beautiful, more so than all of the others were. You could see that her skin was very bright. The woman removed her skin and hid it underneath the tree. Then the two of them went to the festival.

The real man who was on top of the tree went down, took the skin of the most beautiful woman and carried it up into the tree. Near morning, the ghosts finished their festival and returned to get their skins. They talked and were happy. They sang and danced to the place where they had left their clothing. The festival was very hot.

They sang and danced and sang and danced. It was nearly dawn when they had finished. They all took their skins and put them back on. They turned back into ghosts and went to their homes. Then the two friends returned. When they arrived there, one of them put on her skin. The beautiful woman began to look for her skin. They called out to other ghost women. They told her, "That's your problem. Who walked with you and saw where you hid your skin?"

The woman's friend searched and searched [for her friend's skin], but she did not find it. It was nearly dawn, so she ran away lest they find her. The other woman did not find her skin, so she sat and cried at the base of the tree.

While the woman sat and cried, the man descended from the tree and saw her. The woman was surprised. The man lied and asked her, "What are you doing here?" The woman also asked him what he was doing in the deep forest.

The ghost woman said that it was her land. The man also spoke and said that he had come to hunt for birds. The ghost woman called out, then many birds came. However, the man did not shoot at them because he was nervous and trembling. Also, he thought that the woman did not want him to look at the birds.

The birds piled up and just died where they were standing. The man told the woman, "I'll tie some birds for you, then carry them to your parents. I'll take some and bring them to my mama and sister." The woman did not want this. She wanted the man to tie them up and to take all of them. The man heeded the woman. He tied all of the birds and the woman carried all of them on her head. They walked together to the man's village.

While they were walking, his sister and mother were in the garden. They called out for him to come. The man told them that a beautiful woman was hiding in the forest. He went to his sister and mother in the garden. [The three of] them together worked for a little while, and later they cooked some food. The poor woman sat down and hid in the forest. While the three of them sat and ate, the man told his mother to leave some yams (*mami*). After they finished sitting, the man told his sister, "Go get some sugarcanes near the base of the banana plants. I broke them earlier and left them there. I want to drink some now."

When the sister went there to look, oh my, she was very surprised to see a beautiful woman sitting at the base of the bananas. The sister took the woman and went with her. All of them were very happy. First, they did not say anything. Later, the mother gave some yams for her to eat. All of them finished working in the garden and returned to the village.

They sat with everyone from the big village. Many men liked this woman. They often asked the man what kind of woman she was, but he did not want to tell them. "It's each one's strength," he often said in his thoughts. At the time of the village festival, the woman wanted to sing and dance. The people were knocked out by her adornments. Her singing and dancing went directly to the men's hearts. Later, the man and woman married. They had many children and they were very happy in the village.

Charles Wang

P. O. Box 838

Rabaul

East New Britain Province

D531+. Transformation by removing skin; D2074.1.3. Birds magically called; E402.1.1.4. Ghost sings; E421.4+. Ghost's skin as shadow; E425.1. Revenant as woman; E425.2. Revenant as man; E493. Dead men dance; E495.2. Marriage (ceremony) to a ghost; E540+. Ghost removes skin and appears human; E545. The dead speak; E587.3. Ghosts walk from curfew to cockcrow; F610. Remarkably strong man; F981. Extraordinary death of animal; P210. Husband and wife; P230. Parents and children; P231. Mother and son; P232. Mother and daughter; P253. Sister and brother; P310. Friendship; R220. Flights; T111. Marriage of mortal and supernatural being; W157. Dishonesty

## The Ghost Woman Lied to a Man

(Wantok 417, May 15, 1982, page 21)

Long, long ago, in the time of the ancestors, we people from Drekirkir [Dreikikir], **East Sepik** Province, had a place named Kokap [**Urat** People]. Inside this place were two newlyweds. The man and his wife lived alone in this ancestral place. There was no other man or woman who lived with them.

When the man wanted to go hunt for wild game, he often took his wife with him. He did not want his wife to be alone at home, so the man would take his wife and their dogs, then all of them would go into the forest together.

One time, the married couple and the dogs went to hunt for food in the forest. The forest where they went had a *masalai* marsupial (*sikau*) that lived there. The two of them thought that it was an ordinary forest, they did not know that the *masalai* dwelled there. They built a forest hut there.

One time, the man left his wife at the forest hut while he hunted game in the forest with the dogs. When the man returned to the hut, he saw that his wife had cooked sago. The man skinned and gutted the game. The two of them finished cooking, then sat to eat.

Another time, the man went to hunt for game and he wife stayed at the hut. Later, the woman went to collect some *tulip* tree leaves. While she was collecting the *tulip* leaves, the *masalai* marsupial turned into a woman and went to collect some *tulip* leaves at a tree near where the real woman was collecting them.

When the real woman saw her, she was shocked because in this area, there were no other people except for her husband. She looked carefully and asked her, "Who are you and why have you come here?" The *masalai* woman mumbled and the real woman did not hear her. The *masalai* told her, "I also want some *tulip* leaves." The *masalai* woman had confused the real woman, and the real woman did not ask her any more questions.

The two women worked together at collecting *tulip* leaves, the real woman on one side and the *masalai* woman on the other. Near the *tulip* tree was a big tree.

In this tree, there was a big hole. The *masalai* woman had confused the real woman's thinking, so she went towards the tree hole. The two of them did not talk to each other. They were quiet, with their mouths shut, just working at collecting the *tulip* leaves and putting them in their net bags.

When the real woman approached the tree hole, the *masalai* woman shoved her in and she fell very far down into the hole. There was no way for her to get out, and it was pitch black.

The *masalai* marsupial woman went down to the ground. She transformed herself into this real woman. She took the net bag of *tulip* leaves and went to the hut. She cooked the sago well, making something called _nangu_ in my language. She prepared it for the man who was returning from the forest.

When the man and dogs returned with the game, they were happy that the sago was ready. The woman was also ready to cook the meat with the *tulip* leaves. The two of them removed the skins and guts from the game, then cooked the meat with the *tulip* leaves. Afterwards they ate.

### The Food Did Not Taste Good

When they sat down to eat, it was dark. The *masalai* woman ate very quickly. When she finished, she asked the man to giver her some of his food. The man gave her some of his food. The woman was not quiet while she ate.

She ate very quickly, just like the first time. She ate the bones, too. Then she asked for food a second time, but the man said, "Hey, I gave you some already. There's not much left now and I've not eaten my fill yet. It's time for me to eat. I gave you plenty the first time. How did you eat?"

The man just ate the sago, but it did not taste good like his wife usually cooked it. He asked her, "Why is this sago not like the way you usually cook it?" The *masalai* woman said, "Just eat it. I think it didn't turn out well this time." The man said, "That must be it." He ate it, but he thought hard.

Another day, the man went into the forest. In the afternoon, something else happened. He thought hard. He saw that the things in the hut had changed. The woman had arranged the hut to her desire, but it was not the same as his real wife had done before. No. This made the man more troubled.

When these things happened at the hut, his real wife was still sitting inside the big hole in the tree. She shouted and shouted until she could shout no longer. She was famished and ate the tree bark. What would the man do? He had thought that this woman was really his wife, but he had another idea.

He and the *masalai* woman had not lived together for long, and the woman had made many kinds of changes. These things made the man stop asking questions. He swallowed his saliva [stopped speaking] and just thought. He often thought, "What kind of woman is this? My real wife never did this. Where did she get these habits?" This is what he thought.

One time, he took the dogs and went into the forest again. When he returned to the hut, the woman had finished making the sago. The man went into the hut. He butchered the game and told the woman to go to the stream, clean the feces from the guts and remove the skin. When the *masalai* woman went to the stream, she turned into a *masalai*.

**The Man Found Out**

She had four ears, four eyes, and many legs and arms. Her children were plentiful, and they came to eat the meat scraps and to speak with her. The man went quietly and hid near a big tree that was near the stream. He saw everything that happened, then he quietly went back to the hut.

The man was furious and he just thought, "This *masalai* woman just killed my wife, so I'll try to kill her." The *masalai* has many ways of killing people.

He took all of his things from the forest hut and ran far away. He found a tree that had many branches on it, where he could make a platform. He climbed the tree, put his things there and made a platform.

He took a big piece of earth, some sago leaves with thorns, and some tree leaves. He tied these with rope and put them underneath the tree.

He rubbed two pieces of dry firewood and made a fire. He took the fire, climbed up and put it in his little shelter. Then he went down, carried up his dogs and put them in the little shelter. They stayed tight. The *masalai* woman was by the stream, back at the shelter. She did not see the man there. [She said,] "He ran away from me. I'll find him."

After the *masalai* said this, she took all of her children under her armpits and sniffed around for the man. She went and went, then arrived at the tree where he was sitting. She spoke to him, "Friend, where are you now? I'll eat you right up. Did you find your wife? I pushed her down a tree hole near the *tulip* tree. That's your wife's problem. She's probably dead. You'll be like the wild game that you brought from the forest for us to eat. Now, I'll eat you just like the wild game."

Then the *masalai* opened up her two armpits and the *masalai* children came out. One-by-one, they climbed the tree. However, the man danced and sang, then many kinds of ants (including red ants) and black insects of the forest came and filled the tree shelter. When a *masalai* child reached the shelter, the insects would eat and kill the *masalai*. This happened to each of the *masalai* children. One-by-one, they died.

Now it was time for the mother. At first, she laughed at him. Then she said, "Friend, I'll see you yet." When she went up the tree, the insects bit her, urinated into her eyes and all over her skin, killing her. She fell down to the base of the tree.

Very quietly, the man took the dogs and descended. The poor dogs had howled when the *masalai*s were climbing the tree. They wanted to scare the *masalai*s. They had helped their master. There was nothing to worry about now. The *masalai*s were in their graves. The man sang and danced for the dogs to find his wife. They showed him the way to the *tulip* tree and the place that the *masalai* woman had spoken about before she died.

**The Dogs Showed the Way**

He went with the dogs, and he saw the hole in the tree. He called down. He heard something like insects making a noise. She was nearly dead. The man told her to hold the rope that he threw down. She tied it around her middle and the man pulled her up slowly. His real wife was emaciated. Her eyes were completely yellow and so was her skin. He took her and gave her water. Then he took a little piece of food and gave it to her. Later, the man took her with the two dogs and went to their house at their real home.

Much later, they never went to this forest, and the man never left his wife at home. He always took her with him. They lived long ago, in the time of the ancestors.

William Wokumel
Raval Settlement
Kavieng
New Ireland Province

B421. Helpful dog; B480. Helpful insects; B481.1. Helpful ant; D40.2. Transformation to likeness of another woman; D310+W. Transformation: marsupial to woman; D1781. Magic results from singing; D1781+. Magic results from dancing; D2000+. Magic confusion; D2074.1+. Insects magically called; F490+. Masalai; G213+. Four-eared ogress; G213+. Multilimbed ogress; G213.1+. Four-eyed ogress; G229.2+. Ogress carries her children under her armpits; G352+. Marsupial as ogre; G512+. Ogre eaten alive by insects; K735. Capture in pitfall; K1919+. Ogress poses as wife; K1930. Treacherous impostors; P210. Husband and wife; P230. Parents and children; Q262. Impostor punished; Q411. Death as punishment; R49.1. Captivity in tree; R51.1. Prisoners starved; R110. Rescue of captive; R260. Pursuits; R311. Tree refuge; S110. Murders; S110+. Eaten alive by insects; V61.3+. Dead buried; W157. Dishonesty


## A *Masalai* Made Three Islands

(Wantok 418, May 22, 1982, page 19)

By the shores of **Kandrian** in **West New Britain** [Province], there are three nice islands that stand in a row [**Moewehafen** People]. The three islands are the same size. Each is flat on top like an airfield. Before, they did not look like this. There was just one island and something divided it into three pieces.

This is the truth. The old people tell the story like this. A leader from a place called **Ais** [Island] sat down and told the story to a *Wantok Newspaper* reporter about this place. An old woman sat at the door of her house by the beach and told it too. The name of this woman is Selseme Martina.

The story goes like this. Long, long ago, there was a *masalai* man. He had huge bones. His name was Koran Rainge. He left the forest and went down to the place called Ais. This is a trick name because it was near a river's mouth. The sea filled this [part of the] river, but when it rained, a big flood would come down from the forest and the water would be as cold as ice. [In Tok Pisin, *ais* means "ice."] So that is how it got this name, Ais. The real name is Aruba.

*Masalai* Koran Rainge wanted to play a little, so he took his stone axe and cut a long island into three parts. Before, it looked like a long loaf of bread. The *masalai* cut it into the islands **Kangro**, **Pugi**, and **Aviglo** [**Aweleng** Islands]. The *masalai* shoved them out fairly far into the sea, looking as if [it was the mouth of] a river. However it was not a river, it was just the sea. Today, the big ships come directly between these islands.

After *Masalai* Koran Rainge had cut Aviglo Island, he wanted to go to other places in the Kandrian area. This time he wanted to cut Mount Aiwo. But the *masalai* woman from this part of the forest banished him. The name of this *masalai* woman was Arung. Arung was angry and told him that she did not like these islands. She wanted some mainland to remain. So now there is Kandrian, **Aiwo** and Yumelo [**Iumielo**].

The *masalai* man trembled and returned. His hard work made him weak and thirsty. So he went to the Ais River. This river is part seawater and part cold [fresh] water, the two waters mix together. After he drank, Koran Rainge wanted to clear the forest and make a garden. However, the poor *masalai* had two kinds of water inside him. They fought and he was in pain.

He walked to the place where the sun rises and he loosened the pain is his belly. He was dying to urinate, so he urinated eight whole times, then he walked away. So today, there are eight nice cold springs that come out of the earth in this area. The names of these eight springs are: Apolo, Ariep, Arunkenekit, Sikinlo, Amulo, and Atimere [Only six names were given].

Later, the *masalai* turned back to the Kandrian area and he began to urinate again. So in this area today, there are eight streams. Their names are: Ayalao, Amatun, Emilo, Auyamo, Kasiglo, Kalamlo, Aralo and Amalo.

Even though he urinated a lot, Koran Rainge's illness was not over. He went back into the forest and died. So now, people of Kandrian have three islands and sixteen cold streams, and they never drink from the River Ais.

[Selseme Martina
Ais Island
West New Britain Province]

[Caption of photo in *Wantok*:] "Elder Selseme Martina sits her house door and tells stories to people."

A933+. River from urine of deity/spirit; A941.1.1+. Spring from urine of deity/spirit; A955.3.1+. Islands cut by axe; A955.3.2.1. Primeval hero moves islands into their present position; A1617. Origin of place-name; F490+. Masalai; Z71.16.1. Formulistic number: eight

## The *Masalai* Marsupials (*Kapul*)

(Wantok 419, May 29, 1982, page 17)

Long, long ago, in the time of the ancestors, in the Teptep area of **Madang** Province, there was a village named **Megan** [**Nokopo** People].

One day, two men from this village took their dog and went to hunt for food in the forest in the very early morning. They walked into the forest and set traps to kill pigs or marsupials (*kapul*). They set many of these all over. Later, they went back to the village.

In the afternoon, they returned to the forest to check on their traps. They had killed many marsupials all over. When they arrived at a trap, they would only see the head there. Something had eaten their legs and tails. They did not know what it was that had eaten these marsupials. The two men and the dog carried many marsupials. It was nearly dark, so they went to stay at a cave. Many people knew to go there when it rained or became dark and there was not a quick way home.

The men made a fire and cooked the marsupials. The marsupials did not cook well. They were still bloody when they ate them, so they gave one to the dog too. After they had eaten, they thought about sleep. They heard a little noise coming from outside the big cave.

They slept, then the *masalai* who had been eating the marsupials' heads and tails came to get them. They fought. Quickly, the dog ran fairly far away and watched. The *masalai* was stronger, so he killed the men and threw them into the fire, burning them.

Their dog ran and ran, then arrived at the village. The dog sat there, barking and howling. In the early morning, the men of the village awoke. The dog showed them the way to where the two men had been burned. The village men took the remains of their bodies and brought them back to the village. They made a small house and decorated it well. They put their remains inside the house.

Later, the men of the village stretched a rope from the house to another place on the mountain called Finstret. Then all of the men of the village carried their bows, sticks, arrows, axes, and stones, then hid around and inside the house that contained the dead men's remains. They sent one very strong man from the village to stand on top of Mount Finstret and to call out for the *masalai*s to come.

All of the *masalai* men, women and children from the forest came and gathered. These ghosts turned into marsupials and walked on the rope towards the place where the two men's bodies were. When the marsupial ghosts arrived at the village, the men in charge of the rope cut it and all of the marsupials turned into real people.

However, they looked like something else. They looked like very wild people from the deep forest. After the real men cut the rope, all of the wild people fled and went inside the little house. They rejoiced in the bodies of the two men whom the *masalai* had burned in the fire. Then the men of the village swept all of the rubbish around into a pile near the little house. They raised a fire and lit the house with it. The bodies of the two men and those of the wild people burned completely.

Luckily, there was a *masalai* woman and her child who had gone inside this house. They lived very far away. When the house and all of the wild people were burning, only they escaped into the forest.

So now, the people of Megan Village in the Saidor District go to the forest to hunt for wild game and other kinds of food. They often vomit violently if they go to the place where the *masalai* woman with her child had escaped.

Sometimes, when someone holds a fire and goes into the forest, if the person holds it awkwardly, the fire will burn their body. So people often say that these kinds of things happen, because before the ancestors killed the wild people at this place.

Sayaba Willinut

Teptep Sub-District

Madang Province

C612. Forbidden forest; C927. Burning as punishment for breaking tabu; C980+. Vomiting as punishment for breaking tabu; D179.6K+C. Transformation: child to marsupial; D179.6K+M. Transformation: man to marsupial; D179.6K+W. Transformation: woman to marsupial; D310+C. Transformation: marsupial to child; D310+M. Transformation: marsupial to man; D310+W. Transformation: marsupial to woman; F401.3+. Spirit in marsupial form; F401.6. Spirit in human form; F408.3. Spirits dwell at tabu place; F490+. Masalai; F567. Wild man; F567.1. Wild woman; F610. Remarkably strong man; K914. Murder from ambush; Q211. Murder punished; Q411. Death as punishment; Q582+. Fitting death as punishment: burning; R210. Escapes; R260. Pursuits; R310. Refuges; S110. Murders; S112.0.2. House (hostel) burned with all inside

## The Stones of the Ancestors

(Wantok 420, June 5, 1982, page 21)

Around each village in West New Britain Province, there is a spirit house. Inside the spirit house, or nearby it, are ancestral stones. Christians also think that these stones have power.

Many stones have been found in the rivers or in the forests. Some have names and stories. Some mark each family or clan. When there are ancestral dances, or dances with ceremonial headdresses (*dukduk*), the dancers sit and catch their breath at the places where the stones stand.

Some stones look like chairs; they have flat seats and straight backs. The ancestors often sat and rested on these kinds of chairs. Sometimes, the leaders would stand these chairs near schools. You can see these at **Aimaga** Community School inside the forests of Gloucester and Kilenge of **West New Britain** [Province, **Kilenge** People].

When the leaders taught boys about the ancestral customs and the village laws, they often sat on these stone chairs. People believed that these chairs gave power to their speeches when they brought complaints against someone.

A big stone that stands outside the spirit house of **Kilenge** Village has a story and a name. Airipi is the name of the stone. The story goes like this.

In Kilenge Village, there were two angry men. This was because one had borrowed a pig from the men of the village spirit house. However, they had not eaten this pig. No, they gave some of it to other men. The man named Riayu was angry and ran away from Kilenge. He went to **Gi** Village.

After six months, Raiyu's temper cooled off. The people of Gi wanted to give a present to him before he returned to his village. At this time, someone would give a dog or chicken, or something like that. However, Raiyu did not want these. He was covetous of a special stone that stood in Gi Village. The stone was like a blackboard. The people of Gi gave this stone to Raiyu and he gave the name Airipi to this stone.

Today, you can find Airipi standing outside the Kilenge spirit house. On top of it, some men have put a row of small, beautiful, special stones that they found on the beach or in the forest. This is an adornment of the big stone, Airipi.

There is another kind of stone story in Bougainville. In a small village near Buin, there is a row of special stones. The name of this place is Leitaro [**Laitaro** Village, **Buin** People, **North Solomons** Province].

Among the rows of cacao trees, near the village, there is a big boulder. It sits on top of a row of small stones. Today, there is no bulldozer that can move this boulder; it is too heavy. However, the strength of the ancestors moved this kind of boulder many times around Leitaro Village.

The story of this stone goes as follows. Fairly far from Leito [Laitaro], there is a small mountain that looks like a table. Its name is Kangu. It is near the beach. The men still say that the ancestors made this mountain. They had found a boulder in the forest then pulled and rolled it, and brought it forward with rattans from the forest. They worked long and hard.

When the men were turning the boulder, named Bokie, a message came forth: Mount Kangu is finished now. The men pulled the boulder forward. They could throw it away now. There was no more work, so they left Boike [Bokie] Stone by Leitaro Village. However, they did not leave it lying on the ground. No, they hoisted it up and placed small stones underneath Boike, like a bed.

Now, the ancestors did one more thing in the Buin area. They began in the forest and lined up a long row of stones to show the way to the beach. They took these stones from the source of the Nkumu River. These stones are also large, and there are slightly bigger ones on top of the smaller ones. This means that they are special stones, but they do not have power. They are like signposts that show where the "highway" of yore is located.

[Caption of first photo in *Wantok*:] This photo shows the Boike Stone in Bougainville. On the left is Nopetau Timoti, the man who told the story to *Wantok* newspaper.

[Caption of second photo in *Wantok*:] Some stones mark the ancestral highway. They also sit on top of these stones. Here are three people who are sitting in a row.

A962. Mountains (hills) from ancient activities of god (hero); A977. Origin of particular stones or groups of stones; A990+. Origin of road/path; D931. Magic rock (stone); D1151.2. Magic chair; P600+. Special seats for teaching customs; R220. Flights; V112.1. Spirit huts; W195. Envy

## The Cloud-Man Helped the People from Sio
(Wantok 421, June 12, 1982, page 26)

Long, long ago, in the time of the ancestors, there was a big village named **Kambuntina**. The old people from Kambuntina Village still lived on **Sio** Island in **Morobe** Province [**Sio** People].

One time, there was a heavy rain falling. The rain began in the afternoon and continued until the morning of the next day. An old man and his wife took a canoe and paddled it away from the island. These people from Sio went ashore to the mainland called Talagiwa. They paddled their canoe up to the beach and went to a garden.

When they approached the garden, they looked up and saw a tree. They saw a man tied to a branch of the tree. This man was very black and was holding a gun. The old woman looked at this man. She thought that it was a ghost and she screamed.

The old woman told her husband to look up and see the black man hanging on a tree branch. The old man looked and saw the black man on the tree branch.

This was not an ordinary man. He was a man who could make clouds thunder when it rained. The woman was afraid. She told the old man to leave the man there on the branch and to run away. But the old man did not heed her. The old man tried to talk to this man who could make the clouds thunder, but the man did not reply to him. The old man told him to come down to the ground. The black man went down to the ground and followed them to the village on Sio Island. [How] did the cloud-man stay on that tree branch? The old couple talked to themselves all of the time about this.

The two of them did not know that the cloud-man had fled to avoid being killed by them. He was hiding on top of the tree branch.

He often made clouds thunder at night when it rained. On that night, the rain fell until dawn. The man had descended when the clouds thundered. When the clouds broke in the middle, he could not return to his home. So, when the rain finished, he was hanging onto the tree branch like a ghost. He held onto something that was like a gun. When it shot, the clouds thundered.

The two old people took him, went to the village and put him in the house. The old woman cooked yams. She removed the yam peels and gave them to the cloud-man to eat. The man ate the yams. He did not look like a real man from the village. He looked like something else. His fingers were very long. His toes were crooked. Some of his teeth were long and some were short. His hair twisted about and was very long. If another man had seen him, he would have been terrified.

He did not have a way to return to the clouds, so he just stayed in the old couple's house for three whole months. He was not a man of the earth. He belonged in the clouds and he had only traveled with the clouds, so his power was strong and his life was ruined. The food was not his kind of food. Everything was different to him, so he wanted to go back to the clouds.

But how could he return? One way was for him to make a huge fire and for the smoke to rise past the clouds. Then the rain would descend and the man would make the clouds thunder. He would ascend when the rain was still falling.

The people of the village did not know that the man was living inside the old couple's house. They had hidden him well so that the other people would not kill him. When he wanted to return, the couple was worried because they still had to go to the village leaders and speak with them. The old man spoke to them and they were very surprised. They helped the old man arrange a way for the cloud-man to return.

They burned all of the sword grasses of **Labutina** Village on Sio Island, but the smoke was not strong enough to make the rain come down. They sent a message to the small village called Nambariwa [**Nambariwa**]. These two villages together burned a huge amount of sword grass. This sword-grass area had a name, because they often burned it to kill pigs. It was called Ngongoba.

The people sang and danced, then burned a huge amount of sword grass that afternoon. A heavy rain fell that night. They brought the cloud-man out into the rain. He shot the gun up into the clouds and the clouds thundered terribly, down towards where he was. The people ran away from the clouds and hid in their houses. Later they checked on the place where the man was sitting, but he was not there. He had ascended with the great thunder of the clouds.

The man had told the old couple, "When I live above and I hear that you are having trouble finding fish when there is a drought, I shall send rain down for you. If you do not want rain, I shall make the water dry up."

Later, the people had various troubles and they talked about them. The cloud-man heard this and followed through on his promise to them. Henceforth, they were never hot and they were often happy. It was not hard to catch fish, the water was good and the food in the gardens grew well. The rain often fell on time. The cloud-man took good care of them. There were no big thunderstorms to ruin the coconut palm trees or other good things of the village.

When the people of other places were angry that the rain had ruined something, the people of Sio Island were just content. They never told about this thing to other people lest their good fortune would be ruined again.


Nonga Donga

W. D. H. O. [Wills Distributors Head Office] Wills

P. O. Box 678

Madang

Madang Province


A284+. Cloud-man falls from sky, people aid his return; A1142.5+. Thunder is sound of cloud-man's gun; D2143.1. Rain produced by magic; D2149.1. Thunderbolt magically produced; F60+. Person falls from sky; F61. Person wafted to sky; F527.5. Black man; F431. Cloud-spirit; F434. Spirit of thunder; F515.1+. Remarkably long fingers; F544.3.5. Remarkably long teeth; F551.2+. Crooked toes; F555.3. Very long hair; P210. Husband and wife; Q190+. People rewarded with good weather after aiding cloud-man; R220. Flights; R311. Tree refuges

## A Woman Arose from Blood

(Wantok 422, June 19, 1982, page 17)

Long ago, there was a husband and wife without children. All of the other people of the village had many children, but these two had none and they often worried about this.

One day, the two of them went to work in the garden. They worked and worked. When the sun stood at high noon, they rested. The man's wife said, "I'll go over there and cut some sugarcanes for us to eat." While she was cutting the canes, she cut her hand on a sugarcane leaf. She put the blood from her hand onto a taro leaf.

Later, she went back to her husband. They drank the sugarcane juice and began to work again through the afternoon. The woman went to get food for them to put in the house for a whole week. After that, they went back to the village. They just stayed in the village for a whole week. Her husband went line fishing in the sea.

After one week, they returned to the garden. When they arrived there, they heard a baby crying in the garden. They went very quickly into the garden and saw the baby sleeping under the taros.

The woman told her husband about when she had cut her hand on the sugarcane. The blood that she had put on the leaves had become a baby. They were very happy that they had a baby.

They worked quickly and returned to the village. They worked at taking care of the baby who quickly became a woman.

One time, the woman saw the young women going to the forest to fetch water. She asked to go with them. They told her to get a coconut shell for fetching water and to follow them. She heeded them and took something for drawing water, then she went with them.

While they were fetching the water, a man came and told them, "I'm thirsty," and he pointed to one woman to get water for him. When she brought him water, he said, "The water isn't clean." Then he told another woman to get water for him. The man said, "The water's dirty." He told this to all of the women until he told the woman who had arisen from blood. The woman fetched the water and he said, "That's it. This is real water: sweet and very clean."

While the women went to the village, the man hid the woman's "grass" skirt. When the woman came very close to the village, she remembered it. She asked the other women to go back with her to get her skirt, but they did not want to do this. She returned alone to get her skirt. When she arrived there, she met the man immediately. He was waiting for her.

The man asked her, "What are you looking for?" The woman said, "I'm looking for my skirt." The man said, "It's here." When the woman wanted to return, the man grabbed her and blocked her path from the forest. He made a path through the forest and carried her into the deep forest, then married her.

The woman's parents went to the village and found that she was not there. They searched and searched but did not find her. They were very worried. They were alone again.

This story comes from Ruprup [**Blupblup**] Island in **East Sepik** Province [**Bam** People].

Jeffry Ogen
c/- Phillip Sowar, Lae City Council
P. O. Box 1335
Lae
Morobe Province

[See *Wantok* #225 for a story that begins like this one.]

H360+. Bride test: fetching clean water; P210. Husband and wife; P232. Mother and daughter; P234. Father and daughter; R10. Abduction; T100. Marriage; T192. Marriage by force; T534. Conception from blood

## Jit Tricked the Greedy Cassowary

(Wantok 423, June 26, 1982, page 17)

Long, long ago, the little birds and the huge birds often flew up to the sky. At this time, Cassowary also flew and ate tree fruits.

When the birds filled a tree and ate its fruits, Cassowary would often chase them away. The other birds were afraid of Cassowary, so they would flee. Cassowary was very greedy. Cassowary often took its fill from the tree fruits.

When the birds fled, they often gathered again on another tree and ate there. When Cassowary finished the tree fruits, Cassowary would fly directly to the other tree where the other birds had gathered.

Cassowary often chased the little and big birds away. After a while, the birds became furious at Cassowary. The birds thought hard for a way to stop Cassowary from chasing them. They thought and thought, then a little bird, called Jit, thought of an idea for stopping Cassowary from flying on top of the tree. The little bird Jit went to sleep. In the early morning, Jit woke up and flew to the place where Cassowary was sleeping.

Jit told Cassowary, "Hey friend, I want to bathe there. I'm alone, so I'm afraid to bathe in the stream."

After Jit gave Cassowary a good flattering, Jit told Cassowary, "You're a big bird. If someone tries to kill me, go kill them." After Jit flattered and flattered Cassowary, then they went to the stream.

After they arrived at the stream, Jit bathed first. Later Jit sat next to the stream. Then Cassowary bathed. While Cassowary was still bathing in the stream, Jit quickly took two dry sticks. After Cassowary came out of the stream, Jit sat next to Cassowary.

Cassowary told little Jit, "I'm freezing." Jit took two little dry sticks and broke them. Jit fooled Cassowary into thinking that Jit had broken its wings while drying off.

Little Jit said, "Later, I'll rejoin my wings after I dry them." Then Jit told Cassowary, "You too should break your wings and dry them. Later, we'll rejoin them and we can fly away."

Cassowary really believed Jit, so Cassowary broke its wings. When Cassowary saw Jit fly up to a tree, Cassowary tried to rejoin the wings, but Cassowary was unable to do so.

Poor Cassowary was very mad because Jit had tricked Cassowary. Jit warmed its belly as it flew away.

Cassowary was furious and told Jit, "If your shit falls on the ground, I'll take your shit and ensorcell it. Then I'll kill you."

When the little bird Jit defecated on a tree, Jit would bend its legs and go. So Jit's feces make big piles on top of tree branches.

Now you can see the feces of this bird, _jit_, on top of all of the big and little trees all over the place.

This is Atuak Dandom's story. I, Aurenu Trowit, wrote it down.

Zurenu [Aurenu] Trowit
Markham Road, P. O. Box 1709
Lae
Morobe Province

A2284. Origin of animal characteristics: animal persuaded into self-injury; A2320+. Why cassowary is flightless; A2480. Why a kind of bird only defecates on trees; B211.3. Speaking bird; K1065+. Dupe persuaded into mutilating wings; L315+. Small bird overcomes cassowary; R220. Flights; R260. Pursuits; W151. Greed; W125. Gluttony; X716.1H+. Birds and beasts (animal excretion)

# The Brother Hid the Water

(Wantok 424, July 3, 1982, page 17)

Long, long ago, [two] brothers lived in a village named **Ampaonga** in the area of Kamano Village Number Two, by Kainantu [**Kamano** People, **Eastern Highlands** Province].

They lived well together. One time, they went to the garden and brought back some leafy vegetables to cook in an earth oven.

They heated the stones. When the stones were hot, they removed them from the fire and began to cook the vegetables in an earth oven with them. Later, they uncovered the earth oven and looked at their food.

The little brother's food was completely burnt and the big brother's was cooked just right. The little brother asked the big brother, "What did you do to make your food turn out well?" The big brother lied and said, "I cooked it just like you did." He lied, but the little brother thought that he was telling the truth.

After a while, they decided to make another earth oven. In the morning, they woke up quickly and went to the garden to get some leafy vegetables.

When they returned from the garden, they heated the stones. When the stones were ready, the big brother told the little brother that he would go to find something near the forest and then return. However, he did not go to get something. No, he lied and went to get water from a pond.

When he returned, he hid the water carefully in a bamboo tube. The little brother did not see the bamboo that the big brother had used to hide the water.

When the stones were ready, they cooked their vegetables in the earth oven. After the food was in the oven, they waited for a little while then uncovered the earth oven and looked. Something had happened to their food.

The little brother's food did not turn out well, but the big brother's food came out well just like before. The little brother thought that the next time he would follow his big brother into the little forest.

They lived there for a while, then another time, they talked about cooking their vegetables in an earth oven. So, the two brothers heated the stones and the big brother told the little brother that he would again go to the forest near their house.

He said that after he returned, they would remove the stones and make the earth oven. The little brother said, "That's OK, go ahead." He stayed and then he followed his big brother.

The big brother left quickly and looked around for his little brother. He quickly filled the bamboo with water.

Then he returned to the house. However, the little brother had seen the place where the water was. He too quickly drew up the water, finishing it all.

Later, he returned with his bamboo tube of water, but the big brother did not see him.

They removed the stones and cooked their vegetables in the earth oven. They waited a little, then uncovered the earth oven and saw that both of their vegetables did not turn out well.

The big brother recognized the little brother's food and he knew that the little brother had stolen water from him, so he was very angry. He went to the pond and he saw that the water was gone.

He returned and asked the little brother, "Who went there and returned?" The little brother said, "It was just me." Then he said, "Many times before, when we cooked in an earth oven, you lied to me and told me that you cooked the food just like me. But you had spilled water on your vegetables causing yours to come out well. Because of this, I followed you and finished off the water. After that, I spilled the water onto my food so that it would turn out like yours."

The big brother was not sorry after what the little brother had told him. No, he took a big log and broke the little brother's head. The blood flowed profusely from the little brother's head.

The little brother fell down and passed out. In the early morning, he prepared his things. Then he left his big brother and went to an area near **Okapa** where there were many streams [**Fore** People].

In the morning, the big brother woke up and looked for his little brother, but he could not find him. He cried and cried and mourned. He said, "Oh my, I hit my little brother and treated him poorly. Now I'm all alone."

The big brother hanged himself from a tree near their house, killing himself.


Harnon Sautha
P. O. Box 711
Arawa
North Solomons Province


M451.1. Death by suicide; P251.5. Two brothers; P251.5.3. Hostile brothers; Q212. Theft punished; Q458. Flogging as punishment; R213. Escape from home; W157. Dishonesty

# Why the Clouds Thunder

(Wantok 425, July 10, 1982, page 17)

Long, long ago, there were some men who lived near Aurik [**Aupik**] Village in the Maprik District [**Abelam** People, **East Sepik** Province].

One time, the men went spearfishing. One of them, a man named Jatdu went to the mouth of the river and spearfished. None of the men speared many fish, but this man, Jatdu, speared very many. This was because he would often remove his head and put it nearby, then he would go down into the river. When he was in the water, the fish would go inside his body. When he would come outside of the water, he would spill them out onto the ground and kill them. Later, he would put his head back on, then carry the fish back to his house and share the fish with his friends.

Some people noticed and said, "How is it that he spears so many fish?" Some went and asked him, and he told them, "I often drink all of the water, leaving the fish on the sand. Then I kill them." After he told them this, some of the men went to sleep.

In the early morning, before it was very light, these men went and drank from the river, but they did not finish it off. They went back to the village and told Jatdu. Jatdu listened to their troubles and he told them, "I think you're lying. You didn't finish off the river like I told you to do." Then they replied, "We tried, but we couldn't finish all of the water. Our stomachs ached and we left." They chatted until it became afternoon.

One day, when Jatdu went spearfishing, the people of the village had a meeting to find out how it was that he caught so many fish. They told a boy to go hide and spy on him.

In the morning, Jatdu went to the river. The little boy went to hide and spy upon him. He saw Jatdu removing his head and hiding it at the base of a tree. The boy was terrified, but he was well hidden.

When Jatdu went inside the water, the boy went and grabbed his head. He hid it and ran away to the village. When Jatdu came out of the water, he tried to find his head. He searched and searched. He became furious and exploded like thunder from the clouds. He broke a tree and went up to the sky. Now, if you hear the clouds thunder, it is just Jatdu trying to find his head.


Moses Ramu
Brandi High School, P. O. Box 108
Wewak
East Sepik Province

A1142+. Thunder from man searching for his head; D281.3M. Transformation: man to thunder; D2150+. Catching fish by removing one's head and letting fish enter body; F61. Person wafted to sky; F511.0.4+. Person with removable head; W157. Dishonesty

## The Ancestral Spirits Tangled with Sailas
(Wantok 426, July 17, 1982, page 17)

Long ago, there was a man named Sailas. He lived in a village called **Marmar**. Marmar Village is right on Lambom Point, at the tip of **New Ireland** [Province, **Siar** People].

One time, Sailas told his wife that he would go to the beach and look for some small sea creatures. He took his fishing line and began to walk down to the beach.

When he arrived at the beach, he pushed his canoe towards the sea. He put all of his fishing gear inside the canoe and jumped inside. He paddled the canoe towards the deep sea.

When he was far from shore, he threw out his fishing line and hook down, then waited. He waited and waited, but there were no fish biting the hook. He pulled the hook up again.

He threw the hook down for a second time, but there were no fish. He waited a long time again then pulled up the hook. He threw the hook down for a third time.

Then he was surprised. Something very big tugged on the hook. He tried to pull it up and check on the line, but the huge fish pulled him along with the canoe. He pulled tight and tried to pull in the line, but he unable to do so.

The fish pulled Sailas with the canoe directly towards Lambom Point, then it went back. The fish turned again and shot directly towards Kulan Point, near Arura Point. Later, it turned again and went back to the place where Sailas had hooked the fish.

Later, the huge fish pulled the canoe with Sailas directly towards the Warangoi River. They turned again and went back. Oh my! Sailas was shocked as he watched the canoe flying on top of the water.

The fish stopped pulling the canoe. Sailas sat inside the canoe, then the two of them flew and landed at the place of the ancestral ghosts. Poor Sailas was shocked to see this place.

Sailas went to stand up. The ancestral ghosts of this place came and held him firmly. They tied him up with his canoe. Then they tied him and his canoe firmly to a tree. Poor Sailas was in great bodily pain.

How could he get away? He tried to stand up. He did not know that the ancestral ghosts had decided to eat him.

When he stood, he thought hard. Then his maternal relative came and spoke to him.

This maternal relative of his had died before and had become an ancestral ghost. Sailas' maternal relative asked him, "How did you get here? The ancestral ghosts already met and decided to eat you, but now I'll loosen your ropes and you must flee quickly back to the village."

Sailas' maternal relative loosened the ropes around him and his canoe. The maternal relative told him again that he must run away quickly lest the other ancestral ghosts come and finish his bones.

Poor Sailas took his canoe and sped back to Marmar Village. Later, he told about what had happened to him.

This man, Sailas, was my father's grandfather. He told this story to his children. Later, these children told their children, and so on until now when I have put this story down on paper. All of the kin of this man, Sailas, still live in Marmar Village.

Janet O. Simon
George Brown High School
via Kerevat [Keravat]
Rabaul
East New Britain Province

B874. Giant fish; D1532.11. Magic journey in flying boat; E320. Dead relative's friendly return; F129.4. Journey to otherworld island; G11.10. Cannibalistic spirits; P210. Husband and wife; P290+. Maternal kin; R49.1. Captivity in tree; R100. Rescues; R210. Escapes; X1303.1. Big fish pulls man or boat; Z71.1. Formulistic number: three

## The House Underneath Lake Ivea
(Wantok 427, July 24, 1982, page 17)

Long ago, a young man lived in a village called **Sirunki**, near Laiagam, inside **Enga** Province [**Enga** People]. This village is near a lake called Lake Ivea. The lake is still there today.

Long ago, there were no people who lived there. There was only the one man who lived in the deep forest. One time, he wanted to make a garden, so he worked at cutting down the big trees.

He cut down all of the trees, then he waited for two whole months. By then, all of the trees were dry. One day, when the sun was bright, he burned all of the fallen trees.

The fire burned brightly and burned all of the trees. There was not one tree left. Afterwards, he prepared his things for making his garden.

One day, he worked at breaking the earth. He worked and worked, then he slept and got his rest at night. The

next morning, he woke up and returned to plant sweet potatoes and other things in his new garden.

When he arrived at the garden, oh my! Everything was
already ready. All of the foods, such as sweet potatoes and
other things were already there, and these foods had grown
well.

The young man was surprised. He thought hard and
said, "Who was it that came late at night and made my garden? There's no one else in this place. There are only forest animals here. I think these animals came and helped me
arrange my garden."

He thought hard and worked at breaking the earth
again. He broke the earth, then he went to sleep. The next
morning, he woke up and returned to his garden. Oh my!
He saw that everything was completely ready.

"Some man has probably planted everything at night."
He thought hard now, "Who really did this? I'll try to
watch at night to find out who it was that did this."

The man finished thinking then worked at breaking the
earth. After he finished cultivating, he quickly returned to
the house. Later, at about six o'clock in the evening, he
returned to his garden.

He went and hid near the place where he had broken
the earth. He waited and waited until it was about ten
o'clock at night. He heard some talking coming from the
forest. He hid well and watched. Oh my! He heard much
talking and laughing approaching, so he just sat quietly.

The talking and laughing entered the clearing where
the garden was. Oh my! There were more than one hundred very beautiful women who were dressed finely. All of
them carried many kinds of foods and came to plant them in
the garden.

The man sat and watched them. He watched and
watched, then he saw a very beautiful woman working at
planting food and approaching him. The woman planted
sweet potatoes and came closer still.

The man jumped and grabbed this woman. The others
saw the man and ran away. The poor woman wanted to run
away too, but the man held her tightly. The woman tried to
remove the man's hands, but she was unable to do so.

The man kept holding on to the woman. Then the
woman turned to stone. The poor man was holding onto
stone. Later, the stone became a tree and the man held onto
the tree. Then the tree turned into dog feces, but the man
held onto the feces.

The poor man was nearly gagging and he said, "I saw a
beautiful woman and I held onto her. Why am I holding
onto this dog shit?" Then the woman came up and told
him, "That's enough now."

The woman said, "My body's tired. Let go of me and
let's go to your house." The man let go of her hand, then
the two of them walked to the house.

They lived together for some time then the woman told
the man, "From now on, you can't hit me or anger me.
Don't call me the daughter of a bitch or a duck. If you become angry with me, you must just hit me. Don't call me
any kinds of names."

They lived together for a while, then they had a baby
boy. One day, they went to their garden. They brought
plenty of good leafy greens back to the house. They arrived
at the house, then the man chopped firewood and made a
fire.

The fire burned strongly, then the man heated the
stones to cook the greens in an earth oven. After the stones
were hot, he told the woman, "Go get some *tanget* leaves
and bring them here. We'll cook the greens with them."

So, the woman went into the forest and looked for
*tanget* leaves. The man stayed at the house and watched the
baby and the stones. The woman worked at gathering
*tanget* leaves. A bird called *yai* [*yái* (Lang, 1973: 115)]
was singing on top of the branch of a tree.

The woman listened to the bird's singing for about two
hours. The bird sang, "Leaf *yai*-i. I am leaf *yai*. I'm singing now. Tomorrow, the next day, and all of the time, I'll
be singing. It's bad that you're cutting sticks and feeling
pain. Go to the house."

The woman was surprised at hearing this kind of singing. She carried the *tanget* leaves and quickly went to the
house. However, the baby had been crying for a long time.
Her husband was furious. He was completely angry and
sitting down.

When the woman arrived at the house, the man spoke
angrily at her. He said, "You're a daughter of a bitch.
What is it that you were doing while the baby was crying
for so long?" The man gave a hard punch to his poor wife.

The woman was in pain and furious. She thought, "Before, I told him not to call me the daughter of a bitch. Why
did this man call me a bitch's daughter and hit me?"

The woman was irate and just sat quietly. When her
husband removed the greens [from the earth oven] and gave
some to her, she did not eat. The man finished eating and
went to sleep in the house.

The woman sat and worked at making a long rope.
The rope was about one hundred yards long. When the man
was dead asleep, she put the little baby in a net bag.

Then she took the rope and tied it around the man's
leg. She tied it tightly and lit a torch. She had prepared this

torch before and left it there. She carried the baby with her and went outside the house.

She walked and walked and stood near Lake Ivea. She pulled the other end of the rope and walked away with it.

She pulled the rope. Her husband was surprised and held onto the rope. He held the rope and went outside. He watched and saw his wife carrying the baby and standing near the lake. The torch was bright.

The man watched and he ran. He ran and tried to approach her. But no, the woman jumped with the baby down into the water. Oh my! The man jumped down into the water too, but he resurfaced.

The big waves of the lake carried him ashore. He jumped and went down again, but the water carried him back to the shore. He just stood there and watched. He watched and watched. He saw his wife and child go inside a house underneath the water.

The man tried again to jump down into the water. But no, the water carried him back and just threw him ashore. The man was tired, so he went back to his house and slept. He did not sleep well that night. He thought about his wife and child.

In the early morning, he woke up, brought his sticks, logs, and axe, and went down to the lake. He stood near the shore and dug a big ditch. He thought that he could remove all of the water and get back his wife and child.

He worked at digging the ditch around the lake. It became dark, then he went back to the house to sleep.

The next morning, he woke up again and went to the lake to continue digging the ditch. He looked and saw a boulder blocking the place where he had made the ditch. He said, "Where did this big white boulder come from? I think that a man must have carried it at night and put it there."

Also, two big logs stood on each side of the ditch. The man did not have a way to continue digging the ditch, so he would not see his wife and child again. He stood, watching and watching. He was finished.

Now, we can see this big ditch, the boulder, and the two logs still standing there. My ancestors also told us that there is a man and a woman who live inside Lake Ivea. We believe that this is true.

Martin Kupea
P. O. Box 498
Konedobu
National Capital District

A977.5. Origin of particular rock; A983+. Origin of holes in ground; B214+. Singing bird; D231W. Transformation: woman to stone; D361.1+.

Forest Spirit Bride; D437.4W. Transformation: excrements to woman; D451.1+. Transformation: tree to excrement; D452.1+. Transformation: stone to tree; D610. Repeated transformation; D1667. Magic garden grows at once; D2136.1. Rocks moved by magic; F725.3.2+. House under lake; F725.4+. People live under lake; P210. Husband and wife; P231. Mother and son; P233. Father and son; Q235. Cursing punished; R213. Escape from home; R227.2. Flight from hated husband; R260. Pursuits; S62. Cruel husband; T192. Marriage by force

## The Stubborn Daughter
(Wantok 428, July 31, 1982, page 17)

Long, long ago, there was a young woman who lived in a village called Masandanai [**Masandenai**, **Karawari** People, **East Sepik** Province]. She was the only one with white skin, all of the other women had black skin.

One morning, the married women wanted to cast their fishing nets in a stream. When this woman heard this, she also wanted to go with them. She asked her mother, and her mother said, "You can't go with them because they're married and you're single. You can't go."

The woman did not heed her mother. She took her sago basket and fishing net, then followed the married women. She arrived at the place to get a canoe, and she saw her canoe was not there. She went to get her mother's canoe, then she put her sago basket and fishing net into the canoe.

When she wanted to paddle away, she heard a man's voice. The man said, "Where do you want to go?" She was very surprised and looked around, but she did not see a man. So, the woman paddled after the other women who had gone ahead.

When she arrived at the fishing place, she told the other women what had happened to her. They listened to her and told her, "When we go to chase the fish down the water, stay on the [high] ground. Don't come down to the stream." The woman agreed to stay there, so the other women left her and went to the source of the stream to remove the fish.

After they had left, the woman again heard them calling her name, Kundiarim. She turned and looked, but she did not see anyone, so she sat down again. However, something called out again.

The woman knew that it was a *masalai* behind her, so she began to cry when she thought of what her mother had told her. While she cried, the women were working and chasing the fish downstream. When she saw them, she stopped crying and went down to the women's baskets. However, she did not see them there. She followed the women who were chasing the fish. Later, the women removed the nets with the fish. An old woman saw her and told her, "Go back up there. Why are you down here?" Kundiarimai [Kundiarim] replied, "I was up there, but a man called my name, so I came down here." However, one woman was angry and said, "You're a liar." The women on the land told her, "Let's go to the village now."

It was afternoon now and Kundiarimai was still standing there. The women knew that the *masalai* held her, so they told the *masalai* to let go of the young woman. The women told the *masalai*, "If you want the woman, then wait first." Later, a woman went down to the water and brought Kundiarimai back.

When Kundiarimai returned, blood was coming from her leg. The women saw this and quickly brought her back to the village. When they arrived at the village, an old woman quickly told Kundiarimai's mother what had happened to her daughter.

When the mother heard this, she and her husband quickly prepared adornments for their daughter and waited for the *masalai*. However, it was too late. The *masalai* had taken her away.

Later, Kundiarimai's mother heard the voice of her daughter singing a mournful song and crying. The mother told her, "You didn't heed what I said, so this has come upon you." While the two of them cried, a strong wind and rain arose.

The mother told her [daughter], "You have come, now go." She fell down and cried harder. While she was crying, the *masalai* came and took her daughter away. When the *masalai* took Kundiarimai, Kundiarimai tied *tanget* leaves and put them on the trail until they jumped into a canoe.

In the morning, the men and women woke up and saw that the woman had gone. They were very worried in the village.

P. Kamban
Masandanai Village
Angoram
East Sepik Province

D2142.1. Wind produced by magic; D2143.1. Rain produced by magic; F490+. Masalai; F527.7K+. White person; P210. Husband and wife; P232. Mother and daughter; P234. Father and daughter; Q325. Disobedience punished; R14+. Abduction by spirit; W126. Disobedience; W167. Stubbornness

# The *Masalai* of Lep Island

(Wantok 429, August 7, 1982, page 44)

Long, long ago, in **Manus** Province, there was a small island behind **Baluan** Island [**Baluan-Pam** People]. This island was called Lep.

On Lep Island, there was a *masalai* who had exactly ten heads. This *masalai* had two wives. The three of them lived happily together on their island. There were many kinds of foods and fruits. Tree fruits filled the island.

There was no other person who lived on this island. It was just the *masalai*, his two wives, the animals, and the birds that lived there. The people of the big island, Baluan, often heard stories about Lep Island.

Many men would say, "Lep Island is just behind Baluan. There are many kinds of foods and wild animals there." Sometimes, the people of Baluan would wake up in the morning and search the many good tree fruits that were lying about in the grasses and areas around their houses.

They would take these fruits and eat them. The fruits were very sweet. Some men took the fruits and tried to plant them near their houses, but the fruit trees did not grow well.

Many men of Baluan wanted to try to find this Lep Island. So one day, an old man and his little boy wanted to try. They took their canoe and paddled off to find Lep Island.

They paddled the canoe for ten whole days. Later, they saw a small island. They boy said, "Hey papa, I think that's Lep Island over there!"

The father said, "Sssshhh, don't talk loud. It would be bad if some man hears you then comes to kill us." So, the two of them paddled very quietly and approached the small island.

It was becoming dark when they went towards the shore of the island. They did not go up on the beach. No, they were completely exhausted and slept in the canoe. Late that night, they heard the sweet bird songs of the island.

Oh my! The father and son heard bird songs and they salivated [lit., "their mucus fell"] for this island. They did not know yet that a *masalai* dwelled on this island because they had gone ashore on one end, and the *masalai* dwelled on the other end.

In the morning, they paddled up to the beach. They walked up the island and they gorged themselves on fruits.

Later, the father said, "Son, let's try to see the other side of the island." So, they walked around the island and arrived at the other side. They were surprised to see smoke rising from a fire in the forest.

They said, "There must be some people living here. Let's try to go closer and see this fire." They walked closer very quietly and they saw two young women making a garden.

They did not show their faces. They hid and watched. The old father told his son, "We must hide and see where they go."

The women finished working then got up to walk away. The old man and the boy followed them to their home. They went there and saw a house standing there.

The old man said, "I think that the they live with their husband in that house." But no, the two of them were married to a *masalai* with ten heads, and they lived in that house.

Later, the women walked down to the beach to bathe. The old man walked very quietly and went inside the house. He heard a man breathing heavily inside a room.

The old man wanted to go closer, but he heard the two women returning. He sped outside and spoke to his son. He said, "We must hide inside the shed." Then they went and hid inside the firewood shed.

They stayed there quietly until it was night. They did not sleep well that night. They tried to hear all of the noises inside the house.

In the morning, the women woke up and cooked food. They left it there for their husband. They walked into the forest and continued to work in their garden. In the late afternoon, they would return to the house.

When the *masalai* woke up, he said, "Ah hah! I can smell a new kind of smell inside the house." Then the ten heads looked everywhere inside the house.

The *masalai* got up and walked around outside. Oh my! When the old man and boy saw the *masalai*, they gnashed their teeth and were terrified. They trembled fiercely inside the firewood shed.

They did not tremble quietly. The firewood trembled with them and fell about. The *masalai* looked and said, "Ah hah! I think that this smell is in the firewood shed."

So the *masalai* asked them, "Why did you two come here?" The old man said, "We came to look for fish in the sea and a strong wind arose. The waves carried us ashore on this island."

The *masalai* listened to the old man's story and he was sorry for them. He took the food and gave it to them. Then he hid them in his room. They hid in the *masalai*'s room until the afternoon.

The two women returned from the garden and cooked some food. Later, they served the food, leaving some for their husband. They finished their food and went to sleep.

In the morning, the women woke up. They wanted to look, but no! All of their food was gone. They cooked again. They left some for their husband and went back to the garden.

The women returned in the afternoon and saw that all of the food was gone. Some days later, they saw what was happening: the food was being finished very quickly.

They spoke to each other and said, "Oh my! This *masalai* is not like before. Is he getting hungry too quickly? It would be bad if he found the food to be bad, then killed and ate us."

The women said, "We must find a way to escape to another place." The poor women did not yet know that the old man and boy were in their house. They only knew that the *masalai*'s food was being eaten.

One woman told the other, "I know a kind of vine in the forest. Let's take it and cook it, then give it to the *masalai* to drink. This liquid or soup from the vine can kill the *masalai*."

The next morning, the women went to work in the garden. Later, they removed the vine from the forest and brought it back to the house. They cooked the vine with the food.

The two women did not eat that night. The *masalai* ate and later he gave some to the old man and his son. They were famished and they finished the food right away.

They all slept that night. The next morning, the *masalai* felt a great pain in his stomach. The poor old man and his son had died because the poison from this vine was very strong and killed them quickly.

The ten-headed *masalai* cried and turned about. When he called out and cried, the clouds in the sky broke and thundered. He wanted to cry, but no. A heavy rain fell. When his body trembled, all of the places on the island shook with him.

The two women looked for a place to go, but they did not have a way to escape. A strong wind arose. The clouds thundered. A heavy rain fell. A strong earthquake shook the island. Then the *masalai* died.

Water flooded over Lep Island. The two women, the ten-headed *masalai*, the old man and the boy all went down into the sea with the island.

If today you travel to the far side of Baluan Island, you can see a small reef in the sea. On Baluan, you can also see various kinds of good fruits and foods. People had planted these when the birds carried them from Lep Island to Baluan.

I believe that this story from the ancestors is a true story.

Mike Soanin

Box 174

Manus Province

A958K. Origin of reefs; D2142.1. Wind produced by magic; D2143.1. Rain produced by magic; D2148. Earth magically caused to quake; D2149.1. Thunderbolt magically produced; D2151.8. Magic flood; F490+. Masalai; F944.3. Island sinks into sea; F960.2.5.2+. Earthquake at ogre's death; G361.1.5. Ten-headed ogre; N332. Accidental poisoning; P210. Husband and wife; P233. Father and son; Q211. Murder punished; Q428. Punishment: drowning; S111. Murder by poisoning; T145.0.1. Polygyny

## The *Masalai* Stone of Genai

(Wantok 430, August 14, 1982, page 17)

Long, long ago, there was a *masalai* stone that ate men. This stone was near Genai [**Gena**] Village in **Simbu** Province [**Kuman** People]. The name of this stone is Maigl Mur.

When a bright moon arose, all of the men of Genai would prepare their bows and food. Later, they would go to the forest to kill marsupials (*kapul*). They would sleep by Maigl Mur for two or three whole weeks.

When they returned to Genai, they would bring back many marsupials. All of the men, women and children would eat these marsupials until they were bloated. The village would reek of marsupial.

One time, two leaders and a boy wanted to go hunt marsupials. The names of the two men were Kauga and Kawage, and the little boy's name was Kogma. The three of them wanted to go hunt marsupials near Maigl Mur.

They woke up in the early morning, then prepared their bows and food. In the late afternoon, everything was ready. At about four or five o'clock, they carried their things with net bags of food and walked away. They walked and walked, then arrived at a place called Yomba Yaundo and slept.

The next day, they woke up again and continued walking into the deep forest. On the second day, at about noon, they arrived at Maigl Mur. They went inside this cave and put all of their things down.

They made a big fire inside Maigl Mur and prepared things for sleeping. They gathered tree leaves and made beds on which to sleep. They sat and straightened their bows.

After they straightened their bows, they ate their sweet potatoes and walked away. The two leaders, Kauga and Kawage told Kogma to stay in Maigl Mur and to look after their food.

The little boy was afraid, but he heeded them and stayed back at Maigl Mur. Kauga and Kawage left him and walked into the deep forest. Kogma went inside the cave and worked at sharpening a stone to make a stone axe for himself.

While he was working, he heard a loud noise at the cave entrance. He left the axe and ran out to look, but he could not see a thing. His skin jumped but he could not do anything about it.

Kauga and Kawage did not return quickly, so Kogma went inside again and worked at sharpening his axe. Then he heard a loud noise a second time.

He threw the axe down, ran outside and looked again. However, he did not see a thing. He was afraid and began to call out to Kauga and Kawage. They did not reply to him, so he was furious.

He walked inside and pretended to slowly sharpen his axe. He put his ear and two eyes towards the cave entrance. Before long, a loud noise came for the third time.

Immediately, he saw a big stone door close, and then reopen. Oh my! Something had closed and opened the house door! Kogma urinated right there. His tears spilled out. He called out while he was still inside and sped outside with his axe.

His voice jumped again. He called for the two leaders, "Kauga and Kawage! You must run back here now! Something bad has happened to meeeee! I should eat pork first, then I'll die!"

Poor Kogma, the two leaders could not hear him. Kogma walked outside. He quickly cut down some trees and made a hut.

He made the hut outside, near Maigl Mur. The hut was made quickly. He made a big fire and sat down. He sat and thought very hard.

At about midnight, Kauga and Kawage returned. Kogma heard them coming and was a little happier, but his legs, arms and whole body were trembling.

Kogma told his story to the two leaders. He said, "When I was in Maigl Mur, the cave door closed and then reopened. I heard a loud noise three times."

He spoke out about everything that had happened to him. He told them that the three of them must sleep in his hut and that the next day they must quickly wake up and return to Genai.

Kauga and Kawage's mouths and eyes were just wide-open. They did not believe anything that Kogma had said. They said, "Our ancestors slept here long, long ago. Nothing like that happened to them. You just came and made this blather up, right? We don't believe you."

Kogma was insistent and said, "It's absolutely true! I really heard those things and I saw it with my own eyes." However, the two leaders did not believe him. This made Kogma even angrier.

Kogma told them, "If you don't believe me, OK. One of you must sleep inside Maigl Mur." They looked and looked then asked, "Who wants to go?"

Kauga stood up and said, "Don't worry, I'll go sleep inside and see if Kogma's lying." Kogma turned and told him, "When you go to sleep inside, you must pretend and keep an eye open."

That night, Kogma and Kawage slept in the hut. Kauga went to sleep inside the cave. Before long, Kauga heard the stone making a loud noise. He looked at the door and the cave was completely shut.

It was very dark inside the cave. Poor Kaug [Kauga] tried to call out, but it was too late. Kawage and Kogma barely heard his voice.

They quickly lit a fire to see. No! The cave was completely shut. How could they open it? There was no way. They just looked and cried as they stood outside.

Kauga stood inside and cried sorrowfully for himself. The three of them just stood there and cried. The two of them could not see Kauga's face. They mourned that night, crying and crying until dawn.

In the early morning, they left all of their things and ran back to Genai. They called out for all of the men, women and children to come gather, then they told their story. However, none of the people of the village believed their story.

Kawage and Kogma said, "All of us must take one of Kauga's big pigs and go and slaughter it near the cave Maigl Mur. This will open the cave and Kauga will come out. It would be bad if we wasted time, since poor Kauga will die inside the cave."

Every man agreed to this idea and took a pig. In the afternoon, all of the men, women and children together took the pig and walked away. They walked and walked and arrived at Maigl Mur.

They saw that the cave was completely shut, but there was a small hole where the men could put only one hand inside. All of the men tried to break the stone with their stone axes, but they were completely unsuccessful.

They tried and tried, but their stone axes just broke. They were very sorry. They killed the pig and rubbed its blood on the stone, but the cave did not open.

They cooked the pig in a fire. When the pig was ready, they removed the liver and shoved in inside to Kauga. They took the pig fat and rubbed it on the stone again, but the cave did not open.

They called the names of all of the *masalai*s and ancestral ghosts who had died before, but the cave still did not open. All of the men, women and children sang, danced and cried together as they stayed outside Maigl Mur.

Poor Kauga heard the cries of his kin. He too cried and cried inside the cave. His kin stood and shoved their hands inside and shook hands with them. It was too bad, Kauga could not get outside.

As each of them shook hands, [they would say,] "I, Kawage, am shaking hands with you... I, Agmba, am shaking hands with you..." Every man, woman and child did this.

Then all of them sang, danced and cried together. They said good-bye to Kauga and they walked back to Genai Village. They could not forget what had happened to poor Kauga.

Kauga stayed inside the cave until he died. His body broke into small pieces and stuck to the stone. One year later, the cave opened again.

The mark of Kauga's body is still inside this cave. One part of the stone has something like a head, two arms, and two legs. This piece of stone is still there.

Now, if the men go to this area, they do not sleep inside Maigl Mur. When they go there, they often take a piece of tobacco, some food, a stick or tree leaves and throw it inside the cave.

This is a story from the ancestors. But, this cave, Maigl Mur, is still there. Every man who goes there, gives these sorts of things inside the cave.

Joe H. Kau
Genai Village
P. O. Box 299
Mt. Hagen
Western Highlands Province

C735.2+. Tabu: sleeping in certain cave; D1552. Mountains or rocks open and close; F401+. Spirit in cave form; F408.3. Spirits dwell at tabu place; F490+. Masalai; F495. Stone-spirit; F757. Extraordinary cave; J652. Inattention to warnings; J1050. Attention to warnings; R45.3. Captivity in cave; R51.1. Prisoners starved; V12+. Food as sacrifice; V12+. Tobacco as sacrifice; V12+. Tree leaves as sacrifice; V12.4.3. Pig as sacrifice; Z71.1. Formulistic number: three

## Men Killed the Moon

(Wantok 431, August 21, 1982, page 14)

Long, long ago, there was a huge moon in the sky. His size was much bigger than the moon that we see nowadays.

One time, the moon thought about coming down to the ground. He left the sky, jumped on his rope and descended to Tarata [**Tarara**] Village in **North Solomons** Province [**Torau** People].

The moon descended when it was exactly noon. The moon only saw little children playing in the village. All of the big people had gone to the gardens. The moon salivated and thought about eating the children. The moon carried some ripe bananas and left them near the houses, then the moon hid.

The children saw the ripe bananas and they gathered to eat them. The moon grabbed some of them and swallowed them down into his belly.

In the afternoon, the parents returned to the village. Oh my! They found that their children were gone, so the parents thought hard. One day, everyone gathered and had a big meeting. They told one man to watch the village and find out what had caused this to happen.

The next morning, everyone went to the gardens. One man hid and watched. At exactly noon, he saw the moon descending from the sky.

The moon jumped on his rope and went down to the ground. The moon tricked the children into going near a house, then the moon swallowed all of them. The moon's belly was filled, so the moon jumped on the rope again and returned to the sky.

That afternoon, the man spoke to the villagers. He said, "The moon is a very big man with a huge head. He often takes his big rope, jumps on it, comes down, and then returns to the sky. His belly is not ordinary, it's truly huge!"

All of the men of Tarata Village listened to this, then prepared to fight with the moon. They appointed one man to cut the rope and two men to cut one of the moon's legs. Two men would cut the moon's other leg. Many of the others would stand by to cut his neck and belly.

All of the men took their axes, spears, and many other things to fight. They were ready. They sent the women to go to work in the gardens. They told the little children to play around the village.

At exactly twelve o'clock noon, they saw the moon jump on his big rope and come down. He saw the little boys and he was very happy. He quickly jumped down and hid near a house.

He tried to grab the children, but they called out and ran away. The men got up quickly. One sped over and cut the rope. Four men cut the moon's two legs. Then they cut the moon's body into tiny pieces, like rubbish. The moon was completely dead.

Now at night, the village was completely dark. There was no moon to light the sky. So, all of the people in all of the lands were very sorry. The men, women and children could not walk around at night.

All of the men were very worried, so they met one day to fix this problem. They argued about finding something to put up in the sky to take the place of the moon.

They wanted to find out who was truly able to fly up to the sky. They pointed to an eagle, who was the only one able to do this kind of thing. This was because the eagle is a strong bird that can fly very high.

The eagle flew and shot up into the sky. It flew up and up, but lost its breath because the sky was still far away and the eagle was tired. So, the eagle flew down again to the ground.

The men sent another little bird up. The bird tried, but could not get there, so it returned again. Later, they sent another big bird, but this bird lost its breath again and flew back down to the ground.

All of the different kinds of birds tried, but they could not get there. Then they decided to send two birds together. They took a bird called a swiftlet [*Collocalia vanikorensis* or *C. esculenta*]. This is a kind of bird that is like a sea eagle [*Haliaeetus leucogaster*], but it often makes its nest inside caves [These birds are actually unrelated].

They took the swiftlet with a bird called *pentanug*. This little bird *pentanug* has a red neck and a long tail full of red plumage. The two birds carried a small piece of stone like the moon and flew with it up to the sky.

They went up very high, up to the point of the other birds. They kept on going. Never mind their pained bones, never mind the big sun, never mind starvation, they kept going. They kept going and reached the sky.

They affixed the small piece of moon to the sky. The little bird *pentanug* burned its tail feathers. Then they lit the moon's fire and they flew down to the ground again. Now the moon was relit and the people of the earth were very happy.

The people of all of the places on the earth gave a great thanks to these two birds. They gathered together and made a big party. However, the group of people from Tarata Village who had killed the moon ran away.

They made a new village at **Loloho** and lived there. This tribe is still around now. If you go to Loloho in North Solomons Province, you can see this group of people.

Try to look at the moon one night. You can see marks on it. These marks came from the time when they worked and formed a new, little moon. This moon cannot come back down to the ground because the men had cut its rope.

Matthew Playo Andrew

P. O. Box 732

Arawa

North Solomons Province

A715.3. Moon as ogre; A741+. Moon from object brought by birds into sky; A751.11. Other marks on the moon; A753. Moon as a person; A759+. Moon comes to earth; A759+. Moon killed by people; A759.5. Formerly moon was larger; A991+. Origin of particular village; B450. Helpful birds; B455.3. Helpful eagle; B469. Helpful swiftlet; F51. Sky-rope; F56.2+. Birds fly to sky; F911.5. Giant swallows man; G100. Giant ogre; G512. Ogre killed; K914. Murder from ambush; P230. Parents and children; Q211.4. Murder of children punished; Q215. Cannibalism punished; Q429.3. Cutting into pieces as punishment; R220. Flights; S139.7. Murder by slicing person into small pieces; W27. Gratitude

## Leklachem Lap Made the Day Long

(Wantok 432, August 28, 1982, page 14)

Long ago, in a little village, there was an old woman and her two sons. The first son was Arubu Keklacho [Laklaxo] and the second was Leklachem [Laklaxem] Lap. These two sons were usually very good at hunting wild game in the forest. When they went to the forest, they often returned with various kinds of game, such as pig, marsupials (*kapul* and *sikau*), and birds.

Their mother was a real farmer. In her garden, there were various foods, such as yam, taro, sweet potato, banana, sugarcane, and cassava. However many times, the men would come and steal the old woman's food. Beautiful flowers surrounded the little house, and there was a little pond. These things made the people of the village terribly jealous of them.

Each time that there was a celebration, they would have a contest to see who could get more game from the forest and return home with it. Every time, these three people would win. One time, the two sons told their mother, "We're going to the forest to hunt for game now. We won't be returning quickly. If the men anger you or do something bad to you, don't do anything until we return."

The poor old woman heeded her two sons and stayed. When they came to steal her food and flowers, she just watched. They did this for a while, then one morning, the women from another village came and took her water. Then they took the beautiful flowers.

When the old woman saw this, she shouted, "Which pig stole my things?" The women replied and told her, "Shut your mouth or we'll break your mouth!" However, the old woman did not heed them.

She shouted again. The women were furious and went up to her house. They beat her terribly, killing her.

Later, they made a fire and burned her. She burned up entirely except for a little finger. This finger fell down and drifted on top of the water that was near the fire.

A month passed, and her two sons returned. When they returned, they saw that their mother was not there. They looked around and saw a little finger floating on top of the water.

They were very troubled and decided to avenge the death of their mother. They put their words together. The name *Arubu Leclacho* [*Laklaxo*] means "at night." This first son, Arubo [Arubu] Lechlachem [Lakalaxem], performed a magic spell and the night became very long. This made the people of the other village famished.

This was because there was no light to find food and game. They thought that the ghosts of the earth were angry and had done this. This made them terrified, but later they thought of the big brother's name, the first son of the old woman that they had killed.

The men called out to the two brothers to come to a big feast. They told them to marry all of the women of the village. The two of them were happy and listened to the men of the village. *Leklachem* [*Laklaxem*] *lap* means, "long day." So he made a magic charm and the day was very long. The people saw this and were very happy that everything was normal again.

Anton Kinsim

**Naiama** Village [**Kuot** People]

Kavieng

**New Ireland** Province

[There are no ponds in this part of New Ireland, so this story may have originated elsewhere, even though the names in the story are Kuot (E. Lindstrom, personal communication).]

D1273. Magic formula (charm); D2146.1.1. Day magically lengthened; D2146.2.2. Night magically lengthened; K300. Thefts and cheats—general; P231. Mother and son; P251.5. Two brothers; Q211. Murder punished; Q235. Cursing punished; Q411. Death as punishment; S122. Flogging to death; T145.0.1. Polygyny; V61.2. Dead burned on pyre; W181. Jealousy

## The Brother Died in Hot Water

(Wantok 433, September 4, 1982, page 18)

Long, long ago, there were two brothers who lived on an island in the middle of the sea. Their mother and father had died.

The big brother's name was Mumuro and his little brother's name was Morukas. They lived well. They had their garden and they planted various foods, such as edible greens and things like taros and yams.

One day, Mumuro wanted to go to another island near the island where they lived. So, he took his canoe and paddled away. He arrived on the island and he walked around. He saw a good tree standing straight up. It was a breadfruit tree. In the **Buin** language, this is called _oleu_ [**North Solomons** Province]. The breadfruit tree belonged to a _masalai_ named Ogulonu.

Mumuro took a breadfruit and went back to their island. He cooked the breadfruit, sat and ate it. His brother Morukas came and asked him for a piece. However, his big brother replied, "Sorry brother, I'm not filled up yet." The little brother asked again. When his brother replied again, Morukas said, "If you don't want to give me a piece, then just give me the skin."

Brother Mumuro replied, "Sorry brother, I'm not filled up yet." Every time that the little brother Morukas asked, Mumuro replied, "Sorry brother, I'm not filled up yet."

So, Morukas took his canoe and went to the island that his brother had gone to before. When he arrived there, he met a crayfish. The crayfish told him, "Hey, tie your canoe with this rope." The crayfish gave him a rope and he tied up his canoe.

When he went up the breadfruit tree, large red ants bit him. He wanted to kill them, but he heard them say, "Don't kill us." So he did not kill them.

As he worked at getting the breadfruits, he broke off a leaf too. The breadfruit leaf flew down on top of the _masalai_'s head. The _masalai_ knew that a man was stealing his breadfruits. He went to his house and took his fighting implements.

Then the _masalai_ went to the place where the breadfruit tree was and he saw Morukas on top of the tree. The _masalai_ thought of what he could do to Morukas. Morukas also tried to find a way to come down the breadfruit tree and quickly flee.

The _masalai_ thought of a way to kill this little boy. When he saw Morukas trembling on top of the breadfruit tree, he told him, "Throw down all of the breadfruits, then we'll cook and eat them." Morukas listened to this and he threw down the breadfruits while the _masalai_ gathered them.

While the _masalai_ gathered the breadfruits, Morukas defecated and covered up the feces with a breadfruit leaf. When the _masalai_ finished gathering the breadfruits, he told Morukas that he would also go up the breadfruit tree and get some more breadfruits.

The _masalai_ made a rope and went up. While he was still climbing, Morukas told him to look up at him. The _masalai_ looked up at Morukas and the boy blasted the _masalai_'s eyes with his feces.

The _masalai_ sped down the rope and fell half-dead. Quickly, Morukas jumped down from the breadfruit tree. He took the breadfruits, filled his canoe, and rapidly paddled home.

When he arrived home, he made a big fire and cooked his breadfruits. His brother Mumuro saw him eating breadfruit and asked him for a piece of breadfruit. Brother Morukas replied, "When I asked you for breadfruit, you were angry at me and almost hit me." Morukas chased him away.

The next day, the big brother Mumuro took the canoe and paddled to the _masalai_'s island. When he arrived, a crayfish told him, "Tie your canoe with this rope." However, Mumuro killed the crayfish and threw it inside his canoe.

He also wanted to kill the ants when it went up the breadfruit tree. When the ants told him not to kill them, he did not heed them. He taught them a lesson and killed them.

Then he worked at getting the breadfruits and he heard the _masalai_ approaching. The _masalai_ heard him too and went to the base of the breadfruit tree, then looked up. The man stood and blasted the _masalai_ with a huge breadfruit. The _masalai_ fell down half-dead.

Quickly, Mumuro jumped down and worked at putting the breadfruits into the canoe. When the _masalai_ got up again, he took his spear and the two of them fought fiercely.

They fought and fought, then Mumuro's little brother arrived. He took his bow and put an arrow through the _masalai_'s flesh. The big brother was quite surprised when the _masalai_ fell to the ground.

The big brother, Mumuro, looked towards the beach and saw his little brother Morukas was escaping with his canoe. The poor big brother called and called until darkness came. He slept on the beach.

In the morning, he went inside the _masalai_'s house and saw a pot on top of the fire. He looked inside the pot and saw water boiling. The big brother Momoru [Mumuro] jumped inside the pot of hot water and died.

Andrew Donald
Saint Joseph's High School
North Solomons Province

B211.4.1. Speaking ant; B211.8K+. Speaking crayfish; B336. Helpful animal killed (threatened) by ungrateful hero; B479.1K+. Helpful crayfish; F405+. Spirit killed by spear/arrow; F490+. Masalai; K2211.0.2. Treacherous younger brother(s); M451.1. Death by suicide; P251.5. Two brothers; P251.5.3. Hostile brothers; R155.1. Youngest brother rescues his elder brothers; R210. Escapes; S112.1. Boiling to death; S145. Abandonment on an island; X716.1H+. Befouling with excrement; W152. Stinginess; W154. Ingratitude

## Why Does Markham Valley Have Many Wild Pigs?

(Wantok 434, September 11, 1982, page 18)

Long, long ago, there was a man who lived on a mountain called Netine. The man's name was Miluno. There was much wild game on this mountain.

This man did not have a mouth. His mouth was on top of his head, and the door of his house was on top of its roof.

One time, a man was on Mount Sunivi and looked over to the top of Mount Netine. He saw this man, Netine, cooking food and he saw the smoke from his fire rising high above the mountain. The man from Sunivi was named Komogofafe.

Komogofafe went to see who this man was that had made the fire and made smoke rise above the mountain. Komogofafe took a piglet, a dog, and some food, then walked and walked. He walked and approached Miluno's house. He smelled some food.

Miluno often just ate food without throwing the bones outside. He often just put them inside the house. Komogofafe went very close and he saw that there was no one inside the house.

He also saw that the house did not have door. He searched for the door and he became very angry. He sat on the ground for about two hours.

Later, he looked up above the house and he saw a stick hanging down from the roof of the house. He went up to the stick and removed it. When he looked inside, oh my, it was filled with animal bones, it was just filled with such rubbish.

Miluno was not at his house. He was in the forest hunting for wild game, so Komogofafe went inside Miluno's house. He ate and ate the meat that was there.

When Miluno was approaching but still far away, he smelled a man inside his house. He went quickly, then threw the food down and went up the ladder.

He removed the wood, went down and saw Komogofafe inside his house. Komogofafe was sitting well. He turned and looked up to see Miluno descending the ladder. Miluno came down and the two of them began to fight.

They fought and fought, and then Komogofafe tried to talk to Miluno. However, Miluno did not reply. His mouth was shut. The two of them lost their breath and stopped fighting.

They lived well there for a week. One time, Komogafafe [Komogofafe] made a bamboo knife. He took a vegetable leaf called _kifinae_ and he hid them.

One morning, after they cooked and ate, Komogofafe told a nonsense story. Miluno wanted to laugh and part of his mouth moved a little. However, his real mouth was on top of his head. The two of them slept, and late that night, Komogofafe took the bamboo knife and the _kifinae_ leaf. He grabbed Miluno and began to cut him a mouth. Miluno was surprised. He held Komogofafe and fought him, but Komogofafe overcame him and cut his mouth. After he finished cutting, Miluno had a mouth and the two of them lived together at this place.

One time, Miluno sent Komogafofe [Komogofafe] down to the Bafo River to cut some sugarcane. So Komogofafe went and called out, "Miluno, Miluno, which tree did you say that you pulled?" Miluno said, "I planted the sugarcanes by Komofafe." [Komogofafe] called out, "Say it again." So he said, "I tied it to Komogofafe." The man listened to Miluno call his name, "Komofafefe," and he was furious. So he did not cut the sugarcanes, he just went back.

He went to the house and asked Miluno, "What did you say? I've returned." Miluno said, "I didn't say anything bad. It was just me who was talking. Why are you mad?" Komogofafe said, "I cut your mouth so that you can talk. Now you want to bullshit me."

After he said this, they fought terribly. The fire burned their house, and they kept fighting and fighting. They fought past the first mountain and towards the second mountain. In the middle, they completely lost their breath.

Later, they were sorry and they cried and cried. They said, "We don't live with other men. We're by ourselves and that's our problem." The two of them turned into wild pigs in Markham Valley. Now, there are many wild pigs in Markham Valley.

Itoto Jumao

Kesavaka [**Kesawaka**] Village [**Kamano** People]

Heganofi [Henganofi]

**Eastern Highlands** Province

A2434+. Why there are many pigs at certain place; D114.3.2M. Transformation: man to boar; F513+. Person with mouth on top of head; F513.0.3+. Mouth cut open for mouthless person

## Simiji Got His Eyes back from the *Masalai*

(Wantok 435, September 18, 1982, page 18)

Long ago, there was a man named Simiji. He worked at a garden, planting various kinds of foods. He had a small house. He never ate much. He only ate a little and let the other food plants grow.

One night when he was sleeping, he heard a noise from the other side of the valley. He put his ear out to listen to this kind of speech, "To-be-nol-de." For four whole nights, he heard this kind of speech.

On the morning of the fifth day, Simiji tried to make a trap to put on the other side of the valley. He made a rat trap, then he made a marsupial (*kapul*) trap. He began working near his house, then he went to the other side of the valley. When he went closer, he saw a trail. Later, he returned to the house.

At night, Simiji slept and heard the noise again, "To-be-nol-de," going up and then coming back down.

In the morning, Simiji woke up, carried his small net bag and began to check the traps. When he arrived at the last trap, he saw a *masalai* woman inside.

The *masalai* looked at Simiji and said, "This is my trail. Why did you make a trap?" Simiji shook terribly, cut the trap and let the *masalai* stand. The *masalai* took her two fingers and removed Simiji's eyes. Then she exchanged them with two pumpkin seeds and planted them inside Simiji's eye [sockets].

Simiji found it very difficult to return to his house because he did not have eyes to see the way. He arrived at his house and just stayed there. The pumpkin seeds in his eyes grew and many pumpkins grew outside his house. The grasses and forest also grew, covering up his big garden.

One time, a woman came and put her child on the fence while she took the pumpkins. Simiji felt that something was pulling him. He called out, "Who's pulling my pumpkins?" The woman heard this, forgot her child and ran away.

In the afternoon, Simiji heard a baby crying, so he went outside to felt around with his hands until he felt a net bag.

He put his hand down and felt a boy inside the net bag. He carried the boy inside the house and gave him the name Yombi.

Simiji put the baby on the other side of the fire and slept opposite him. When Yombi was hungry and cried, Simiji would cook a pumpkin and give it to him. Eventually, Yombi became a big man.

One time, Yombi looked at his father and asked, "Why is it that you have no eyes?" Poor Simiji told him the story of the *masalai* who had taken his eyes. Yombi listened to this story and became furious, so he made a trap again on the *masalai*'s trail. At night, he slept and heard the noise again, "To-be-nol-de." This noise went up and then came down.

In the morning, Yombi took his things to kill the *masalai* then he departed. When he arrived at the last trap, the *masalai* saw him and said the same thing that she had said to his father. However Yombi replied, "I'll let you go if you tell me where you put my father's eyes."

The *masalai* woman said, "Follow this trail and you'll arrived at a small house. There is a box inside the house. Your father's eyes are inside it. When you return, you must let me go." But Yombi did not believe what she said, so he killed the *masalai*. Then, he took his father's eyes from the *masalai*'s house. He put back Simiji's eyes and they lived happily at their home.

John Michael Monda

Fatima High School

Box 67

Banz

Western Highlands Province

D2161.3.1.1. Eyes torn out magically replaced; F405+. Spirit killed; F441. Wood-spirit; F512+. Person with pumpkins growing out of eye-sockets; F490+. Masalai; K730. Victim trapped; P231. Mother and son; P233.6. Son avenges father; P271. Foster father; P275. Foster son; Q210+. Trespassing punished; Q411. Death as punishment; Q451.7. Blinding as punishment; S110. Murders; S165. Mutilation: putting out eyes

## The Dog Took Care of a Baby Boy

(Wantok 436, September 25, 1982, page 18)

Long, long ago, there was a place called **Yamade** in the Rai Coast area [**Madang** Province]. There was a married couple there named Turi and Tari. They had a baby boy and a dog that lived with them. The four of them lived alone in a house.

Their routine was as follows. The two of them would go to the garden and leave the baby in the house. They would tell their dog to look after the baby until they returned home.

One day, the married couple told the dog this again, and the two of them went to the garden. After they left, oh my, a gigantic snake came, encircled the house and wanted to eat the baby. The poor married couple did not see the snake.

Their dog went and saw this snake that had come to eat the baby. The dog also saw that there was no one in the house to fight with the snake. So the dog fought with the snake. They fought and fought until the dog killed the snake. The snake's blood splattered all over the dog.

Before long, the married couple returned home. They saw that the dog was full of blood and so was the house. They were very surprised and they trembled together. They thought that their dog had killed their baby.

The man was furious and he killed the dog. After he killed the dog, he went around the house and he saw something lying down. Oh my, it was the huge dead snake.

When he saw this, he quickly came and told his wife. A little later, they heard their baby boy crying underneath the house. When they turned, they saw their baby. They saw this and they wailed for their dog. They were torn apart emotionally. It was too bad that they could not get their dog back.

Nelson Karayo
Ogeibeng S. T. C. [Steamships Trading Company]
P. O. Box 447
Mt. Hagen
Western Highlands Province

B11.11+. Fight with giant snake; B331.2. Llewellyn and his dog; B421. Helpful dog; B535.0.4. Dog as nurse for child; P210. Husband and wife; B875.1. Giant serpent; P231. Mother and son; P233. Father and son

## A Python Swallowed a Man

(Wantok 437, October 2, 1982, page 18)

Long ago, there was a tall man from a village called Kualmip [**Gwalip**] in the Maprik District of **East Sepik** Province [**Abelam** People].

This man had two dogs, and the two dogs often hunted wild game in the forest such as pigs and bandicoots. The dogs would get these and return with them. The man was very happy because the dogs caught plenty of game and brought it to him.

One time, they went to the forest to hunt for game. They went and the man killed a big pig immediately. He carried it and put it with the other game. The poor man sat and thought, "Who will help me carry this game home? The sun has set. If I walk home now, it will be too dark along the trail. What should I do? Home is still far away."

He thought and thought, then he stopped. He was hungry. He was also angry. He got up and made a big fire to cook all his meat. After he singed off the hairs, he removed the guts and smoked them.

He made a hut and a meat rack. As he worked, he took all his meat and put it on the rack.

When he was done working, he sat and ate. The place was pitch black. He sat for a while, then felt sleepy. He got up, went to his hut and went to sleep. He slept until late that night when a huge python came up from a lake, looking for food. The man was sleeping. Then, the python came and saw him. The python went to find some edible grasses to make its throat slippery. This would help the snake swallow the man.

After it ate the greens, it returned to swallow the man. It swallowed the man and returned to its lake. It went down to the bottom and slept.

The poor man was sleeping and felt terribly cold, so he woke up and tried to stretch his bones and straighten out his legs. However, when he tried to raise his feet, he felt that they were stuck together. He thought, "Where am I now?" After a while, he thought that he was in a snake's belly.

He said, "What shall I do to kill this snake and get out of it?" He felt a piece of bamboo in his hand and he began to cut the python's belly. He cut and cut, then came close to the outside. The python was in pain and vomited out the man who fell nearby.

Later, he got up and went up to his forest hut. He took his two dogs and the meat, then went home. He arrived home and told the men the story of how the python had swallowed him.

After the men heard this, they went with him to the forest and then down to the lake. They saw that the snake had died and was drifting on top of the lake, so they took the snake and went to the village where they made a big party. At night, they sang, danced and were very happy that the snake had died.

This was the beginning of when people ate big snakes. Even now, at this village, people eat snakes.

Jacob W. Wash
Maprik Catholic School
East Sepik Province

A1681.3+. Why one village eats snakes; B875.1. Giant serpent; F911.7+. Serpent swallows man, then vomits him out

# A Man Married a Mango Woman

(Wantok 438, October 9, 1982, page 18)

Long ago, there were two brothers. Their parents had died. There was no one to look after them and give them food. They themselves worked in the garden and did everything.

One day, the big brother told his little brother, "Stay here until I return. All our food is ready, so don't go walking around. You must just stay here at the house, don't go into the forest lest the enemies kill you."

His big brother prepared all his things, put them in his canoe and left. He worked at spearing fish and while he was in the middle of the sea, the fish filled his canoe. He was still asea when darkness fell. He looked around and saw an island. He paddled directly towards where there was a fire. He put up the canoe and an old woman immediately came to see him. The old woman told him, "Don't be afraid, I've never eaten anything new or any men. No, I'm alone here."

The boy listened to her and followed her to her house. The old woman asked the big brother, "Are you married or not?" The boy replied, "I'm not married. I just live with my brother. Our parents died awhile ago. I left my little brother and I came to catch fish."

The old woman listened to him and told him, "Now, the young women will come to sing and dance. Don't look at them, you must sleep."

He slept and heard the women who came and sang and danced until dawn. The old woman directed their singing and dancing. When dawn arrived, the old woman told the boy, "Go up and get a mango." The young women were hidden inside the mangos. So he went up, took a mango and came down to the ground.

The old woman spoke to him again, "You must put this mango in the back of your canoe and paddle towards home until this mango becomes a beautiful young woman." He listened to this, then paddled off and the mango became a woman.

The mango woman was very young, like a red flower. The big brother saw this and was very happy. When the boy went ashore, his little brother saw the woman and coveted his big brother's woman.

He told him, "I must marry this young woman, you can just do without." The two of them fought. The big brother killed his little brother and married the mango woman.

John Patu
P. O. Box 141
Bulolo
Morobe Province

D431.4+W. Transformation: mango to woman; P210. Husband and wife; P251.5. Two brothers; Q301. Jealousy punished; S73.1.4. Fratricide motivated by love-jealousy; S110. Murders; T92.10. Rival in love killed; T100. Marriage; W181. Jealousy

# The People Who Turned into Birds

(Wantok 439, October 16, 1982, page 18)

Long, long ago, in a small village named Nengan [**Nengamp**] in the Mount Hagen area, there was a brother and sister [**Hagen** People, **Western Highlands** Province]. Their names were Saing and Joni. The two of them also had a male cousin named Wana.

They were just poor children without any elders. The big girl, Joni, was only four years old. They had a little piglet. Their mothers and fathers had died.

When they lived in this village, there was no one to give them food, so they were very hungry. One bright day, all of the men and women with their children went around to the gardens and only they were left in the village. Their poor big sister, Joni, put all of their things into a net bag and told her two younger brothers [brother and cousin], "We'll leave this village and go to another."

She took the two of them, put them inside another net bag, and carried them on her head. She carried them and held the piglet in her arm and walked away.

They walked and walked, then arrived at a small village, a hundred miles away from Nega [Nengamp]. This village is called Tegai [**Tega**]. At this village was a long house. Inside the house were twelve whole rooms where each woman lived.

That afternoon, a heavy rain fell and darkness came quickly. The girl and her two brothers sat near the women's house. The girl heard that many young women were walking in a line and singing down the mountain. The girl listened to this and covered the two boys well with her skirt, hiding them. She just held the pig in her arms.

The young women arrived at the house. They saw the girl and the pig sitting by the house. They all gathered and asked the girl, "Where did you come from?" The girl told them her story, but she did not tell them about her two brothers.

All of the young women were very happy and they gave her many things, such as beads, skirts, *kina* shells, taros, sweet potatoes, bananas, leafy greens, and many other small things. They gave her a bedroom. They lived in this village, and the two boys and the pig grew up. But the young women did not know that the girl had two boys with her.

One day, all of the women said, "Let's check on all of the things in our house and see who has many things." They counted the things and said, "Now it's time to count Joni's things." She counted all her things that they had given to her, but she did not count the things that she had brought from her village. All of the women said, "These are the things that we gave you. We want something that is really yours."

However, Joni did not want to show them her two brothers, so she lowered her head. All of the women spoke and grabbed her. They checked her net bag. While they held the poor girl, they checked and found the two boys sitting in the net bag. When they saw this, they took back all of the things that they had given to Joni and they scolded her badly.

Later, they did not have food or adornments. So every day, Joni and her two brothers would go down to a stream and catch fish. The three of them and their little pig would just eat their fish at this stream. They would always take their pig with them to this stream.

One time, when the sun was very bright, the girl and her two brothers began at the source of the stream and went to the other end. They caught many fish, both big and small. They gave the small fish to the pig and they put the big ones inside a bamboo tube for them to eat. While they carried the fish, their poor backs were breaking [under the weight], so they sat on the sand and caught their breaths.

While they were catching their breaths, they heard a loud noise coming from the source of the stream. The poor children were terrified and just sat quietly. When they looked downstream, they saw a man cooking pork, carrying it in a net bag and coming towards them. They kept watching. The man went up to them and left the net bag of pork in front of them.

They were ashamed and just sat there. The young man told them to eat and then he would go to his home. They ate the meat of this pig, giving the bones to their pig. Later, they went to the house and slept. Whenever they went to catch fish at this stream, the man would cook pork in an earth oven and go to them.

They lived in this place for a while and they grew up. One day, the young man went to the woman and told her, "Tomorrow, you and I shall marry at my village. So, you must follow the trail and meet me in the sugarcane garden."

The young man showed the woman the trail and went back to his house.

However while they were making this decision, they did not see a red-skinned *masalai* woman who was hiding behind them and listening to their secret. After the young woman went to explain to her two brothers that she would marry the next day, the two brothers prepared stones and leafy greens for killing their pig [and cooking it in an earth oven].

They slept then early the next morning, the *masalai* woman went to their house and said, "I came to take the woman to the man's village." They thought that this was true, so they killed the pig quickly and cooked it in the earth oven. They sat for a little while, then uncovered the earth oven and divided the meat between the two women to carry to the man's village. When the two women wanted to leave, the two brothers cried and shook hands with their sister.

The two women walked and walked along a very long trail. The real woman felt thirsty and wanted to drink water, so she asked the *masalai* woman, "Where is there drinking water?" The *masalai* woman said, "Put your net bag down and follow me." The two of them went a little ways. She told the real woman to jump down onto the wild sugarcanes (*pitpit*) that she had cut and laid down. When the woman jumped onto the wild sugarcanes, the poor woman jumped down into a huge hole underneath it.

The woman went very far down and then she landed on top of a forest garden. At this forest garden, there was a hut and many kinds of foods. The poor woman went inside the garden hut and tried to find something such as an axe and fire.

After she found an axe, she took it, went outside and cut some sugarcanes, bananas, yams, taros and all of the other things that grew in the garden. After she had cut these things, she looked for a big and tall tree. When she found one, she began to remove the tree bark and to make a hole for herself to sit in. After she removed the bark, she began to grease the tree with traditional [tigaso tree] oil. Then she sat in the tree hole that was very high up the tree.

After the real woman went down the hole, the *masalai* woman had taken the net bag and all of the real woman's adornments. She decorated her skin well so that she looked just like the young woman. Then she carried the net bags of pork and walked along the trail until she arrived at the garden.

She saw the young man who was tying sugarcanes. The *masalai* woman called out to the man and said, "Friend, I've come." The man looked at her and thought that it was really his woman, so he went to shake hands with the woman and talk with her. He was very happy and he took this woman to the house. They arrived at the house where they made a big feast and they ate.

At this time, the real woman made a big fire. She burned the whole food garden and the house with all of the things that were in the hole with her. She sat in the tree house and made a net bag. One day, the young man went to look for wild game in the forest. He went back towards the house. The poor man was caught in a huge downpour along the trail that drenched him completely. He felt very cold, so he went inside the house and told his wife to get some firewood from on top of the roof to make a big fire.

When the woman put her arm up to get the firewood, the man saw red hair on the *masalai* woman's hand. He was furious that the *masalai* woman had tricked him.

The man just drew back his bow and shot the *masalai* woman dead. Then he burned the house with the *masalai* woman and everything that belonged to them. The man just walked around, went down to the garden and saw that all of the things in the garden with the house had burned. He saw this and was furious at whichever man had burned his hut and garden. So, he searched and searched, and arrived at the tree where the woman was staying.

At the tree where the woman had removed the bark, he heard her sitting inside it and making a net bag. After he heard this, he cut a vine and circled the tree with it so that he could use it to climb the tree and see her. However the tree was greased too much, so he slid back down. The poor man tried to climb, but he kept slipping down and his body became tired and pained.

He tried again and the grease had completely dried, so he went up the tree and saw his real wife sitting in the tree hole, making a net bag. The man saw his wife and quickly went inside the tree hole. The poor woman got up and fought him. Then the two of them turned into birds.

Now we often see these birds sleeping in tree holes. Near dawn, you can hear this bird cry, "Kaooo, kaoo."

Samson Mugare
P. O. [B]ox 494
Mt. Hagen
Western Highlands Province

A1900. Creation of birds; A2431.2+. Abode of particular bird as tree hole; D150M. Transformation: man to bird; D150W. Transformation: woman to bird; D615. Transformation combat; D1830. Magic strength; D2122. Journey with magic speed; F490+. Masalai; F527.1. Red person; F949.2. Man falls underground through hole; K735.1. Mats over holes as pitfall; K1911. The false bride (substituted bride); N741. Unexpected meeting of husband and wife; P210. Husband and wife; P253. Sister and brother; P295. Cousins; Q262. Impostor punished; Q411. Death as punishment; Q431.17. Banishment for lying; T111. Marriage of mortal and supernatural being

## The *Masalai* Eel Often Became a Wild Pig
(Wantok 440, October 23, 1982, page 18)

Long, long ago, there was a village near a pond. In the pond lived a *masalai* eel. At the village, the people often worked in their gardens. When they returned to the village, a wild pig often went and broke their garden fences and finished off all of the food of these poor people.

They often cut trees and made new fences, but at night the wild pig would come and ignore the fences that they had made. The pig would break the fences, go inside the gardens and eat food again. The men of the village discussed this, but they did not know what it was that finished off their food.

One time, a man took his dog and spear, woke up at three o'clock in the early morning and went to the garden. They hid and watched. They saw a huge eel come and change itself into a wild pig.

Then the wild pig broke the fence and ate the food inside the garden. Then the pig returned and changed into the eel. The man hid and followed the eel to the pond near the village. He saw what the *masalai* eel did.

He ran to the village and told the men, "I found out what it was that has been finishing the food in our garden. It's a huge eel that lives in the pond near the village. We must go kill and eat it. If you go, you must carry big stones and spears to kill it."

At this time, the people tried to find the eel. They killed all of the eels in this pond. By the side of the pond, the eels piled up. They worked and worked and found the eel lying underneath a small eel. They killed the eel, cut it into small pieces and divided it up among all of the houses of the village.

They gave the eel's head to a boy. The boy's parents had died and he lived with his grandfather. When his grandfather went to the forest to get some tree bark and leafy greens, the *masalai* eel told the boy, "Don't eat me. At about six o'clock in the evening, take my head and put it outside. Then close your door. You two must stay inside the house."

When his grandfather returned, the little boy told him what the eel head had told him to do. The two of them heeded the *masalai* eel. They put the head outside the house and shut the door tightly.

That night, they heard men's bellies breaking. When their bellies broke, the pieces of the eel came outside and joined back with the eel head outside the house. Later, the eel went back to its pond. Everyone was dead.

In the morning, the boy and his grandfather left the village and went to another village. Now, no one lives at this place.

Joel Ben Kokoso
c/- Aisack Marum
P. O. Box 351
Kimbe
West New Britain Province

B16.4.2K. Man-eating eel; B874.2. Giant eel; D410+. Transformation: eel to swine; D412.3.2+. Transformation: swine to eel; D1610.5. Speaking head; E32.0.2K. Eel cooked and eaten comes to life; E168. Cooked animal comes to life; E783.5. Vital head speaks; F420.1.3.2+. Water-spirit as eel; F490+. Masalai; J1050. Attention to warnings; P291.1. Grandfather as foster father; Q211.6. Killing an animal revenged; Q212. Theft punished; Q411. Death as punishment

## A Woman Married a *Masalai* from Taga

(Wantok 441, October 30, 1982, page 14)

Long, long ago, in the **Morobe** [Province] area, there was a village named **Moubus** where a man and his wife lived. The man was named Sapi and the woman Beroditi. The two of them were farmers.

One time, they were working in their garden near a *masalai* stone. The name of this stone is Taga. One night, the *masalai* of the stone turned into a pig, then came and finished off their taros. This happened many times, so one time, Sapi made a trap near the garden. In the morning, Beroditi wanted to go to the garden, so Sapi told her to go check on the trap. She returned home, then told Sapi and some men that a pig was caught in the trap. After she told them this, she ran to be the first to see the trap. However, when she went to the pig, she did not see the pig. She saw a man who was dressed finely who was chewing his [betel nuts (lit., lime or calcium oxide)] and sitting in the trap.

When the *masalai* man saw Beroditi, he said, "I'm not a pig and you two entrapped me. You came first, so we'll go to my home." When the men of Sapi's village came, they saw the *masalai* man taking Beroditi and leaving. They called out to Beroditi to stand up, but the *masalai* took her away.

They came to the boulder named Taga. The man hit the boulder, the boulder opened and they went inside. The man hit the stone again and it closed tightly. When Sapi and the men arrived at the boulder, it was too late, the boulder was closed. So, they tried to dig underneath the boulder

and tried to break it. However, the boulder shook and enlarged. They worked at digging. Then they became tired and went back to Moubus.

When the *masalai* took his wife inside, the *masalai* man's mother was ecstatic. They lived inside the boulder house for a long time and Beroditi gave birth to two boys. The two boys lived with their grandmother inside the boulder. A betel nut palm tree grew inside the boulder. The betel palm broke open the boulder and grew out of it. When the *masalai* man and Beroditi wanted to go to the garden, the man would climb the palm, take its ripe leaves, come down and give them to his two sons. Then the two mothers [parents] would go to the garden. The two boys would play with the palm leaves until the mother and father came back from the garden.

They did this until one time, the father and mother wanted to go to the garden, but the father did not go up the betel palm. He forgot and the two of them just went to the garden. The two boys stayed and the big brother saw the ripe betel leaves. He told his little brother, "Brother, papa did not get the betel leaves for us. Find a rope, then I'll go up the betel palm and get the leaves." So, the little brother took a rope and gave it to the big brother. The big brother climbed the betel palm. When he reached the top, he took the betel leaves, looked down and saw the people of Mou [Moubus] Village bathing. He saw some boys playing in the water, he saw some men making fires near the water, and he saw some people in their gardens.

When the big brother saw them, he told the little brother to come up and look at these things. The two of them watched then they went down and waited for their parents to return from the garden. When they returned, the two boys ran to their mother and told her, "Mama, you two often leave us here where we can't see our village, but we just went up the betel palm and saw the men, women, and children in the village. They were very happy. Some went to the gardens, some bathed and some made fires near the nice water. We don't have water. We want to go to your village."

After the two boys said this, the father was not very strict, so he prepared all of the things and the boys' adornments. He carved a canoe for them and their mother. After he prepared all of the things, he sent the two boys and their mother in the canoe. He told them, "If you arrived at the village in the afternoon, tell everyone that you're going up a mountain. In the evening, I'll cry for my two sons."

After he said this, he sent them to Mou. When they arrived at the village, Beroditi told everyone about what her husband had told her. The people of the village did not heed her. They said, "You went and married a *masalai* then came to lie to us." She told her kin, and only they went up the mountain where made a pretend house to live in. At night, her husband cried for his sons. The clouds thundered and a heavy rain fell, killing all of the villagers.

The woman told her kin, "You thought that I was lying to you." Then the kin multiplied and became plentiful. They became the people called **Yekora** in the Morobe area. This is a true story. If you go to Mou Village, you will see that this boulder Taga is still there.

Poyo Gamato
Sappa [Sapa] Village
Morobe Province

A1011. Local deluges; A1022. Escape from deluge on mountain; A1131.1. Rain from tears; A1611+. Origin of Yekora People; D336.1M. Transformation: pig to man; D442.1+. Transformation: stone to swine; D489+. Boulder gets larger; D1552. Mountains or rocks open and close; D2143.1. Rain produced by magic; D2149.1. Thunderbolt magically produced; F401.3.10K. Spirit in form of boar; F490+. Masalai; F495. Stone-spirit; F979. Tree grows from within boulder; J652. Inattention to warnings; J1050. Attention to warnings; P210. Husband and wife; P231. Mother and son; P233. Father and son; P251.5. Two brothers; P262. Mother-in-law; P265+. Daughter-in-law; P292. Grandmother; T111. Marriage of mortal and supernatural being; T192. Marriage by force; T580. Childbirth


# A Girl Came from a Malay Apple
### (Wantok 442, November 6, 1982, page 18)

Long, long ago, on the far [west] side of the **Gulf** Province, there was a village called **Urika** [**Purari** People]. There was a big Malay apple tree that grew near the branch of a river called Uripa.

On this Malay apple tree, there was just one big fruit that grew on it. There were no other fruits on this tree.

This fruit was there for a while and it became completely ripe. However one day, a very strong wind came and shook the tree, then the big fruit fell down into the Uripa River. The fruit was in the water for about two entire weeks. It was too bad that there was no man or woman who knew to go to this place where the tree stood because this was very deep forest.

Two weeks passed, then the ripe fruit broke open and a beautiful baby girl came outside. For two whole years, the baby girl sat at the base of the Malay apple tree and just ate its fruits. She just stayed at this place. After eight years, she made a net for catching fish. When she caught fish, she just ate them raw. She did not know how to make a fire or how to cook fish.

When the girl was fourteen years old, she did not know that many men, women and children lived on the other side of the water. However near the side of the water where she lived, there was a man and woman with their son who was fourteen years old, the same age as the Malay apple girl.

One time, the girl went to get some Malay apple fruits. When she was on top of the tree, she saw much smoke on the other side of the mountain. After she saw this, she immediately descended the tree and quickly swam to the other side. She walked and walked towards the source of the smoke. She walked butt-naked. This was the first time that she had ever seen things such as houses and smoke. She had not seen these things before.

This woman walked very quietly and went inside the people's house. She was afraid, so she trembled and just urinated. She looked around inside the house, but the owner of the house was not there. All of them had gone to the garden. While she was in the house, she looked at all of the good food and salivated. She took some sago, some bananas some sweet potatoes, and some lit pieces of firewood, then she quickly carried them back to her home. She cooked all of the sweet potatoes and ate them.

She tasted that the good food was more delicious than hers was, so she woke up the next day and went back to steal some more food from the other people. She did this three times. The poor owner of the house and his son were furious each time, because the food disappeared quickly.

One day, the son took an axe and spear, then hid near the house to see what it was that finished their food. When the woman went to get the food, the boy heard the woman's footsteps. The woman walked inside the house and worked at getting some bananas, sago, and taros. She put them into her net bag and went outside. But no, the boy quickly came and blocked her way. The woman was surprised and wanted to run away, but the boy held her tightly.

The boy told her, "I can't do anything bad to you if you'll become my sister." The girl just listened and sat. She told the boy about what she had done in her life until that time. They talked and worked at cooking food for the evening. Then the boy's parents came home.

The parents were very happy to see the girl. The boy's mother made a "grass" skirt and gave it to the girl. They lived for many years. One time, the boy and girl were playing. The boy tired and slept, then the girl continued playing and became a butterfly. The boy woke up and followed the butterfly to an island. At this island, he saw the girl sitting. When the boy saw the girl again, they were very happy. They made love.

On another day, they married and went back to see their parents. Their parents saw them and were very happy. As time passed, the woman gave birth to many children. If you go to Uripa River now, you can see the huge Malay apple tree that still stands near the water.

Mat[t]hew Playo Andrew
P. O. Box 732
Arawa
North Solomons Province

D186.1G. Transformation: girl to butterfly; D380+G. Transformation: butterfly to girl; F567.1. Wild woman; K300. Thefts and cheats—general; P210. Husband and wife; P230. Parents and children; P231. Mother and son; P233. Father and son; P273. Foster brother; P271. Foster father; P272. Foster mother; P274. Foster sister; P274.1. Love between foster sister and foster brother; P275+. Foster daughter; T100. Marriage; T415.5+. Foster brother-sister marriage; T543.3. Birth from fruit; T580. Childbirth; Z71.1. Formulistic number: three

## The Man with Twelve Children in His Stomach

(Wantok 443, November 13, 1982, page 15)

Long, long ago, there was a man who lived on **Lou** Island in **Manus** Province [**Lou** People]. At this time, there were no people who lived there; only *masalai*s dwelled there.

The man did not have a wife, but he had an enormous belly. Inside his belly were twelve children. When the children were hot and wanted to bathe, they made a loud noise inside the man's belly.

One time, when the sun was bright, he saw and felt his belly making a racket, so he knew what it was. He got up, hit his belly and said, "One." A boy came out. Then he said, "Two", and a man big enough to be married came out, but he lived inside his father's belly. Then he hit his belly for the third time and a woman came out. Her breasts were developed, but she was not married. He hit his belly eleven times and all his children came out except for one. When he hit his belly for the twelfth time, a beautiful young woman came out.

The twelve children stood in a line and he asked them, "What do you want?" They said, "We want to bathe." He told them, "You can go bathe, but come back quickly when you see that the sun is setting."

The twelve children bathed, sang, laughed and played with a crude ball. They made much noise. When they saw the sun setting, they quickly ran out of the water, tied on their "grass" skirts, rested and then ran back to their father's belly. They did this every time.

One time, they came outside their father's belly and they went to bathe. They bathed and sang vigorously, played with a ball, and made much noise. However, they did not know that up above in a cave, there was a *masalai* sleeping. When the *masalai* heard the noise that the children made, he woke up and said, "Who is that making all that noise? There wasn't all this noise before like this. I'll go look outside and see who it is that's making this noise."

When the *masalai* saw them, he said, "Oh my, that's very good food." He aimed a crude ball and threw it down to them. None of the children saw this. Only the young woman saw it and she told them. However, they did not listen. They were bathing and coming and going. The *masalai* saw this. He threw another down and the first boy saw it. Quickly, he called out to the others. They all ran home, leaving the little girl crying and coming from behind.

The *masalai* came behind her, then held her and carried her. Then he followed the scent of the other children. He sniffed and followed and followed, then arrived at the man's house. The *masalai* told the man, "Friend, did you see the children running by here or not?" The big-bellied man said, "No, I did not see the children running by here." The *masalai* told him again, "Don't lie to me or I'll kill you."

The big-bellied man was afraid now and said, "They live inside my belly." The *masalai* spoke to him and he hit his belly eleven times, then the children came outside. The *masalai* took all of them to his home and told them to stay in the cave above the pond. After he spoke to them, he went to grate some sago.

The poor big-bellied man cried and cried for his children. While he was crying, a *masalai* woman turned into a little bird and flew to him. The bird asked him, "Why are you crying?" The big-bellied man said, "A *masalai* man came and stole my children. They went to his home which is a cave near the pond." The *masalai* woman listened to this, flew to the *masalai* man's home and saw that he was not there. The *masalai* woman knew that the *masalai* man had gone to grate sago and that he would return to eat it with the children.

Each part of his body was working. His two hands were working, one grating the sago and the other carrying it. One leg was rinsing the sago and the other was carrying water for rinsing.

His belly and head were there, and his mouth was chewing betel nut. When the *masalai* woman saw this, she flew back and worked at breaking the cave door. After she broke it, she sang and danced, then the inner door opened and the children came outside. She took all of them, decorated them and told them to go up a small tree. She sang and danced and took a *tanget* sprout, then very quickly, the tree grew very big and tall. She told the children to sing, and they sang vigorously.

The *masalai* man carried the sago back to the village and saw that his home had been broken into. He was furious. He took his axe then went and saw the children singing. He called out, "Hey, you there! Now I'll cut the tree and eat all of you." So, he chopped and chopped. When the tree was about to fall, the *masalai* woman made a song and dance again and the tree stood up. The *masalai* man was furious and began to climb the tree. As he approached them, the *masalai* woman immediately took the axe and cut his neck. He fell down to the ground.

The *masalai* woman sang and danced again then they went directly to their home in the big-bellied man. When the big-bellied man saw his children, he was very happy and cried with them. When all of the children came down from the tree, they thanked the *masalai* woman, then the tree became small again.

Peter P. Kago

Yangoru High School

P. O. Box 2

Yangoru, Wewak

East Sepik Province

B211.3. Speaking bird; B450. Helpful birds; D150W. Transformation: woman to bird; D150.0.1K. Transformation: ogre to bird; D1552. Mountains or rocks open and close; D1576.1. Magic song causes tree to rise to sky; D1781. Magic results from singing; D1781+. Magic results from dancing; F54.1. Tree stretches to sky; F548. Remarkable legs; F529.6. Person with enormous belly; F562+. Children live inside father's belly; F490+. Masalai; G422. Ogre imprisons victim; G440. Ogre abducts person; G512.1+. Ogre killed with axe; P233. Father and son; P234. Father and daughter; P250+. Twelve brothers and sisters; Q215. Cannibalism punished; Q411. Death as punishment; R45.3. Captivity in cave; R110. Rescue of captive; R311.4. Stretching tree refuge for fugitive; R260. Pursuits; S139.4. Murder by mangling with axe; W27. Gratitude

## How Did the Sea Arise?

(Wantok 444, November 20, 1982, page 18)

Long, long ago there was a man who lived in **Giri** Village, in the Bogia area of **Madang** Province [**Giri** People].

The man was married to two women. At this time, his mother-in-law came and lived with them. The husband of the two wives had two skins. His outer skin was mangy,

but his inner skin was very beautiful. His two wives and his mother-in-law did not know that the man had two skins.

The man usually just slept by the fire, he never went to the forest or worked in the garden. No, he often just lived in the house and his two wives often went to work in the garden. After a while, at one village, the people wanted to have a festival.

The husband heard this information about the festival and he told his two wives to prepare the decorations for the festival. When the time of the festival arrived, the man told them, "Go to the forest and get some wild betel nuts and some betel peppers for me then come back. After that, go to the festival with the others."

They quickly went into the forest to get the wild betel nuts and betel peppers for their husband to chew. The two women gathered the betel nuts and peppers, then brought them to their husband. Then they put on their decorations for the festival and they went to the village where it was to be held. When they arrived at the festival site, they showed their talents to the people of this village.

They sang and danced while their husband stayed at the house. After a while, he told his mother-in-law, "Stay here. I'll go and watch my two wives at the festival site." After he said this, his mother-in-law watched him remove his bad skin and his good skin was revealed.

His mother-in-law was quite surprised by this. In her mind she said, "Oh my! I think that my two daughters married this bad man, but no, he's just like a bird of paradise. They married a real man."

The man took a big basket with the betel peppers inside and he went to find his two wives. When he arrived at the festival site, he saw his two wives working very hard at singing and dancing.

He removed the peels of the betel nuts and pelted them with the peels. When they turned to look at him, he looked elsewhere. He hit them a second time. One of them, then the other saw the betel nut husks falling near them. They told each other, "These betel nut husks are like our husband's, and some man here has this kind of betel nut."

While they were talking, their husband overheard them and immediately went back to their house where he put back on his bad skin. Then he went to sleep by the fire. The two women sang and danced until the evening, then their eyes went towards their home. They saw their husband sleeping very close to the fire.

They sat down, not having caught their breath yet, and their mother told them, "You think that your husband is bad. You often say, 'Why did we marry him? This mangy dog never works.' However, you haven't seen him with your eyes. I saw him clearly with my eyes. He isn't a man, he's like a spoon. His outer skin has scabies, but his inner skin is good."

While she was talking to her daughters, the husband heard her. He was furious at his mother-in-law, so he prepared his bow and multi-pronged arrows. He wanted to kill his mother-in-law. After he was ready, he called out to his two wives and told them, "It's been a long day and I'm hungry. What if you bring some sago, break it open and put it on a plate? Also, I don't want one of you two to bring it to me. My mother-in-law must bring it to me directly to my room."

They heeded their husband, broke open a bamboo container of sago and put it on a plate. The sago was ready to eat. They gave the plate to their mother and told her to take it directly to his room.

When their mother went inside the room, their husband shot her with the multi-pronged arrow and killed her. The man came outside and told his two wives that he had killed his mother-in-law. The man took an axe and cut all of the things around his house. He also ruined everything inside the house.

Later, he put his mother-in-law's body on a *limbum* palm fiber mat and tied it with rope. Then he told his two wives to follow him. They went very far and it was nearly dark. He put the mother-in-law's body on the ground. He wanted to sleep a little.

When he put his mother-in-law's body down on the ground, the body began to boil and water came out of its skin. The water came forth more and more, splashing back and forth and becoming like the sea. After two weeks, the *masalai* of this area where the sea had arisen became angry. The *masalai* said that it was tired of listening to all of the noises that sounded like the beating of signal drums.

The poor man listened to this, took his mother-in-law's body and went to a place in the Bogia area called Numbia [**Nubia** Village, **Awar** People]. Then he threw his mother-in-law's body away at this place.

The woman's body boiled up again, just like the sea, and it became bigger. So now, if you go to Giri, in the Bogia area, you can see the place where the sea arose. Now there are large sword grasses that grow at this place.

Bened W. Sagim
P. O. Box 787
Brahman High School
Madang
Madang Province

A924+. Ocean from corpse; D531+. Transformation by removing skin; D1860. Magic beautification; E636. Reincarnation as water; F490+. Masalai; K914. Murder from ambush; P210. Husband and wife; P232. Mother and daughter; P252.1. Two sisters; P262. Mother-in-law; P265. Son-in-law; Q340. Meddling punished; Q411. Death as punishment; S56. Cruel son-in-law; S110. Murders; T145.0.1. Polygyny; W111. Laziness

## The Man Who Only Liked Daughters
(Wantok 445, November 27, 1982, page 14)
(Wantok 446, December 4, 1982, page 18)

Long, long ago, in Genai [**Gena**] Village in **Simbu** Province, there was a man who only liked daughters [**Kuman** People]. His name was Agua, and he had two wives named Agmba and Daka.

Agua loved his daughters and he did not like his sons. When his wives were pregnant, he looked forward to seeing whether they would bear girls. When he saw that they had given birth to girls, he would be very happy because he wanted to get a large payment [bride price] for them.

When they gave birth to boys, he tired of them and killed them because he did not want to give his land to them. Agua would kill the boys and throw them down a cave called Mullkun Kambugo.

He sent his first and second daughters to go marry at **Giraiku** in the Koronigle area.

One time, Agmba and Daka were pregnant and Agua waited to see whether they would have boys or girls. He made them call out to their ancestors that they must give them two girls.

When the time was near, Agua thought hard and said, "Will my two wives have one girl, two girls, or none?"

Agua waited and waited, then he became very tired. He wanted them to give birth to two girls, but they did not give birth quickly.

One afternoon, Agua asked the women, "When will you give birth? I'm waiting and waiting and I'm tired." The women said, "Tomorrow or the day after, we'll give birth. Just wait quietly and watch. What do you want to do with the children that you talk of so much?"

That night, the two women both gave birth. Agmba gave birth to a beautiful boy and Daka gave birth to a girl. The boy was very beautiful and already had teeth.

The boy's mother saw that he was very beautiful. She took the boy to a place called Miane that night. She hid the little infant until he became a smart and strong boy.

Both the brother and sister grew up. The boy's name was Mua and the girl's was Munome. They were five years old. Their parents were very happy, but Agua did not know where Mua lived.

He always asked Agmba where she had hidden her son, but Agmba always told Agua, "The boy lives someplace. I can't tell where. You'll see him one day when he comes."

The boy grew to be strong, smart and very big. If you had seen him, you would be have been afraid of him. Agma [Agmba] had worked at hiding Mua until he became a smart and strong boy. His mother worked at giving him good food so that he would look handsome and would be strong. He never saw his father or the other people until he became big.

One time, Agua asked Agmba to bring Mua, but she did not want to get Mua. Agua was furious, so Agmba told him, "Just wait a little longer, then I'll bring him."

One day, there was a big party at Genai, so Agua told his wife to bring Mua. This day, his mother dressed him finely and brought him. Agua saw Mua and was afraid of him, but he was very happy because he had not seen Mua for six years.

Agua said, "My son! My son! Come and hold me." Mua said, "Shut up, you! I'm not your son. I'm the son of forest ghosts. The ghosts of the forest gave me food. I grew up from their hands alone. You thought of killing me, but fortunately you didn't kill me. Now I've grown up."

Agua was terribly ashamed and did not say anything. He put his head down and thought of a way to kill Mua. Immediately, he told his two wives to quickly put their things into net bags.

They would go to a big festival that would happen in the Koronigel [Koronigle] area, where the two daughters had married. The two wives quickly prepared the things. Agua took his axe and cut two pieces of bamboo, then made a hole in each of them. He gave the good one to the girl and he gave the bad one with the big hole to the boy.

He told them to go to the Bokun Dugo River and fill them with water. He told them, "Whoever has their water fill up first must bring the water back quickly." Agua knew that the girl would come back quickly because hers did not have a hole at the tip.

The brother and sister sped off with the bamboos to the river. They put the bamboos inside the water. Munome's filled quickly because it did not have a hole, but Mua's did not fill quickly because it had a hole.

The poor boy did not know that the bamboo had a hole, so he worked and worked at filling it while the water kept spilling out. Munome told Mua, "My bamboo has filled quickly, so I must go to the house first. Wait and come behind when your bamboo has filled."

Munome was happy and ran to the house with her bamboo. They asked her, "Where's your brother Mua?" She replied, "His bamboo has not filled yet, so he's still there."

Agua said, "Never mind, let him come behind and find us on the trail. OK, take the net bags and things, and then let's go. The village is very far away and we must hurry to go to Koronigel." He hurried the two women and Munome, and they passed a mountain.

Poor Mua tried hard to make his bamboo fill up, but it was still not filled. He tried and tried then he grew tired. He turned the bamboo and saw a huge hole underneath it. He was furious and he broke his bamboo on a stone, then ran back to the house.

When he arrived at the house, his kin were not there and everything else was gone too. He was shocked and called out to them, but they were not nearby. They had already passed a mountain. He called out a second time. This time, they replied to him from on top of the mountain, "We'll go slowly, you must run and come meet us."

Mua ran and went up the mountain, but they had already gone to the next mountain. Then he called out to them, "I, Mua am coming! Wait for me!" But they replied, "We'll go slowly. You must run and come meet us."

Mua ran and arrived at the mountain, but they had already crossed a big river. He stood again on the other mountain and called to them, "I, Mua am coming. Wait for me." However, they did not say anything.

Mua ran to the river, but they had already crossed to the other side. He came very close to them, but he did not yet find them. They kept going. Mua had entirely lost his breath, but he kept following them.

They walked and walked, then came right to the Waghi [Wahgi] River. They sat there and ate their sweet potatoes, waiting for Mua. He was completely out of breath and went to meet them at the Waghi River. He lay down awkwardly on the ground and caught his breath.

Agua got up and said, "Whose child are you? Who knows about you? Who told you to follow us here?"

Then he shoved Mua into the Waghi River, and the water carried him down. Agua and his two wives began to walk again. But Munome was very sorry for what Mua had done to her [half-]brother, so she cut off one of her fingers [a sign of mourning] with an axe and threw it down the Waghi River.

The river carried Mua down and down, past a piece of wood. He grabbed onto the log. That afternoon, a man was looking for firewood and found Mua in the river. He left all his firewood, swam into the river, took Mua and brought him to the other side. He brought Mua to the house, gave him food and took care of him.

Mua stayed there for a while and grew to be a strong young man. Everyone in the village was very worried for Mua. They wanted to know where the man had taken him, but the man did not tell them. He left Mua for a long time and Mua became a man.

After he had become a man, there was a big festival about to happen at his village. Mua dressed very finely with various kinds of bird feathers then went to the festival with a beautiful hand drum.

Everyone wanted to know this man. They tried to look at him because he was very handsome and because his dancing and singing were excellent.

Also at this time, his sister Munome came to see the festival. Munome had become a beautiful young woman too. When she saw Mua dancing, she did not know that this man was her brother.

She thought that Mua was another man, and she stared at Mua. Munome thought hard about flirting with him and going to *karim lek* with him that night. She also thought strongly about marrying him.

After the festival ended, Munome went and pulled Mua's hand hard. She said, "Let's go to my house. I love you and I want you to marry me." The other women also went to flirt with Mua, but it was too late. Munome was already holding his hand. The women were angry and spoke behind her back.

That evening, they went to Munome's house. She cooked good food and gave it to Mua. They ate and told stories.

They *karim lek*ed with each other that night, but when they held hands, Munome did not give her left hand to Mua. She tried to hide it and she gave her right hand to him. She did not give her left hand because she was ashamed of the finger that she had cut off.

Mua discovered her trick and asked Munome, "What is wrong with your [left] hand that you're not giving it to me. My left hand is 'dying.' We should change hands and hold our [left] hands."

They changed hands and held left hands. When they did this, Mua felt that one of Munome's fingers was not there. He asked Munome, "What did you do to your finger? I felt that it's missing." Munome was sorry and too ashamed to talk, but she told the story to Mua anyway:

"Before, in a village called Genai, there lived a man. His name was Agua. He married two women. One time, the two women were both pregnant. One gave birth to a

girl; that's me. The other gave birth to a boy. His name was Mua, he was a very beautiful boy.

"Papa wanted to kill this boy, so he tricked him into staying back and fetching water. I came to the house quickly and left my brother Mua at the river. When I came to the house, we all left the house and went to this village to see the festival.

"When the boy went to the house, there was no one there. He followed us and met us on the trail. We all had walked and arrived at the Waghi River. Papa carried Mua and threw him into the river. The water carried him very far down.

"When I saw this, I was very sorry for my brother. I cut my finger off and threw it into the river, where my brother went."

Mua replied, "Ah! It was just you with your parents that threw me down the Waghi River. Did you think that I was dead? I laugh at you people. I haven't died yet. The river carried me downstream. A man found me and took care of me. Now I'm a man."

After Munome heard this story, she was speechless. Her neck was completely dry and her mouth was shut. She could not say a word. She looked down at the ground and cried and cried.

After this story, Munome spoke out to everyone. They gathered pigs, bird feathers, stone axes, and *kina* shells and then the two of them married. This was the first time that a brother and sister had married in the Simbu area. The news went to all of the places in the Simbu area that the brother and sister had married.

From this time onwards, men never killed their sons. So if you go to Genai Village in Simbu Province, you will see many men and boys. There are more of them than there are women and girls. Now, there are not many females.

Joe H. Kau

Kaip Community School, P. O. Box 229

Mount Hagen

Western Highlands Province

A2850+. Why there are more males than females: fathers no longer kill sons; E540+. Revenant as foster parent; F513.1+. Baby born with teeth; H1023.2.4. Task: filling a bottomless water tube; P210. Husband and wife; P231. Mother and son; P232. Mother and daughter; P233. Father and son; P234. Father and daughter; P252.1. Two sisters; P253. Sister and brother; P271. Foster father; P275. Foster son; P290+. Half-brother; P290+. Half-sister; P600+. Courtship customs: *karim lek*; P681+. Mourning customs: self-mutilation; R213. Escape from home; R260. Pursuits; S11.3.3. Father kills son; S11.3.6. Father throws boy into river (sea); S110. Murders; S143. Abandonment in forest; S160.1. Self-mutilation; S161.1. Mutilation: cutting off fingers; T10. Falling in love; T50. Wooing; T52. Bride purchased; T100. Marriage; S142. Person thrown into the water and abandoned; T145.0.1. Polygyny; T415.5. Brother-sister marriage; T570. Pregnancy; T580. Childbirth; T589.7. Simultaneous births; W151. Greed

## Why Do Highlands Men Often Marry Many Women

(Wantok 447, December 11, 1982, page 19)

Once upon a time, two little boys lived on a mountain. Their names were Sop and Soponda. Sop was the big boy and Soponda was the little one.

They lived together for a while, then one time, they lived in the forest. They killed some bandicoots and other marsupials (*kapul*). They carried some firewood and began to walk back to the house. They walked and when they arrived at a mountain, they stood and looked towards their house. They saw that a man or woman had made a fire there.

The little boy, Soponda said, "I think a man came around to look for us." However the big boy, Sop, replied, "We don't have any kin or friends. Our house is on fire and the fire just started. We must run there."

They thought hard and quickly ran to their house. When they went very close to the house, they saw a huge pig tied to a rope that was surrounded by a fence.

They heard a man inside the house speak, "My two sons, don't be afraid. I'm a good man. I know that you often work very hard finding food, so I brought a big pig for you to kill and eat. So, give me your bandicoots and other marsupials that you hunted in the forest then I'll cook and eat them when you kill the pig. You can make a big feast in an earth oven for us."

After they listened to this and went inside the house, they saw an old man with a huge white beard and long white hair sitting down. They were happy about the old man. They gave him all of their bandicoots and other game to him because they were very happy to be able to just eat the pig.

They listened to the old man and began to make a fire for heating stones to cook the meat in an earth oven. The old man waited for the earth oven. They waited and waited. When the food in the earth oven was ready, they removed it. The old man had a huge net bag and said, "Boys, let's eat under the house. Put all of that inside the net bag."

The two boys agreed and filled the bag with all of the food. The man said, "You two worked hard at the earth oven, so I'll carry this to the house." The man took the net bag and carried it on his head, but he did not bring it under the house. No, he carried it to the big trail and fled.

The poor boys saw the man carrying the pork away and were very troubled. They did not have anything to eat. All of the game that they had brought, the old man had already eaten. They were famished and just slept in their house that night. In the morning, they hunted for insects and ate them.

They stayed there for a while. They often hunted for food and firewood in the forest just as they had always done. After a while, they went to the forest. When they finished hunting for game, they walked back to the house. On the mountain that they had been on before, they stood and saw smoke rising from their house, just as before.

The little boy, Soponda said, "I think that old man came again." However Sop said, "No, it's another man." They finished talking and quickly ran to their house to see. When they arrived, they saw the same thing as before, they saw a pig. Immediately, they heard an old man in the house say, "My sons, don't be afraid. I came before and befuddled you. Now, I've returned to say that I'm very sorry. I've brought a pig again. This really belongs to us."

When they heard this, they knew that he would carry all of the meat away. So the big boy, Sopi [Sop] told Soponda to hide some meat when they made the earth oven. This time, Soponda hid plenty of meat all over. They put the meat in the hole [of the earth oven] and waited for it to be cooked.

When the earth oven was ready, the man told them to put all of the meat inside the net bag. The man told them that he would carry it inside the house. But no, he carried it all away. This time, however, they did not worry because Soponda had hidden plenty of meat and they ate it happily.

The old man did this kind of thing to the boys many times. One time, the boys went to the forest and hunted for wild game. They hunted and hunted, then went to an old house in the forest that was completely covered over. They went inside and saw an old woman making a fire.

The old woman was shocked when the two boys went inside and said, "Boys, this is a bad house. It's quite old. Why did you come inside? It would be bad if the house fell and killed you."

The big boy said, "Sorry, ma'am, we thought that there was nothing in here and we came inside. We were hunting for food. We saw this old house and just came inside." The old woman said, "That's all right, but I'm worried about your safety." The old woman also told them that she did not have a garden, food, children or a husband, so she just stayed in the bad house.

When the two boys heard all of the old woman's stories, they were sorry for her. Quickly, they cut some wood and stood it up. Before long, they erected a new, beautiful house for the old woman.

After the boys finished all of the work, they wanted to return. They told the old woman about all of the things that the old man had done to them. The old woman listened to them and was sorry to hear that the old man had tricked them.

The two of them wanted to return to their house, so they went outside. However, the old woman called for the little boy, Soponda, to return. The old woman gave him something that she tied with rope and said, "When you two return to the house and the old man is there, you must remove this rope near him."

The little boy took this thing and he ran quickly to catch up to his brother. They arrived at the house and saw a huge pig again. They knew that it was just the old man who had come. The old man said the same thing that he always did. They listened to him. The two of them killed the pig and made an earth oven.

They waited for the earth oven to be ready. When they uncovered the earth oven, the little boy, Saponda [Soponda] followed the old man. He called out near him and removed the thing that the old woman had given to him. He put it very close to the old man's backside and he quickly went far away. The little thing went inside the old man's buttocks. The man put his hand back to scratch his buttocks, but something pulled his hand inside.

The man turned into a ball. He called out to the two boys to help him, but the two brothers laughed hysterically at him and said, "You're a greedy man. Sorry, we can't help you."

The man turned and turned like a ball. He said, "I'm very sorry that I befuddled you, but at my house there are many girls. Also, there is not a single boy to kill our pigs and make earth ovens."

The old man died at this place. They carried the pork and other things and followed the mountain down. At the bottom, there were many pigs, chickens, and cassowaries, and it was filled with garden food. They found out that the old man was the real leader. In the middle was a long house with many young women.

Henceforth, they had many wives. They were free [of the man, and spoke] little. They did this until now when many [High]landers often [try to] marry [many] women.

Nelson H[...]

Moem B[arracks]

D. Coy, [...] Bag

Wewak

East Sepik Province

[There is apparently only one publicly accessible copy of this issue. It is at Word Publishing in Boroko, National Capital District, Papua New Guinea. The quality of the copy is poor.]

A1559+. Origin of polygamy; D270+M. Transformation: man to ball; D817. Magic object received from grateful person; D821. Magic object received from old woman; D1402. Magic object kills; F545.1. Remarkable beard; F555.3. Very long hair; F917+. Person swallowed up through own anus; K360+. Man exchanges pig for game meat with boys, then dupes boys and takes all; P210. Husband and wife; P251.5. Two brothers; P426.2. Hermit; Q42. Generosity rewarded; Q212. Theft punished; Q272. Avarice punished; Q411.13. Death as punishment for thievery; Q551.3. Punishment: transformation; R220. Flights; T145.0.1. Polygyny; W27. Gratitude; W151. Greed

## Malevolent Water Consumed a Man
(Wantok 448, December 18, 1982, page 27)

Long, long ago in **Dengia** Village, there were many men, women and children. One time, when it was the time of the doves (or pigeons), all of the men went to the forest to make huts and to watch for the birds.

The men did not fool around with shooting doves. They did well until it was afternoon when they returned to the village. At this village, only one man did not go with them to the forest. He had stayed in the village.

In the morning, the other men's children ate birds and ran around the village. This man's child saw this and cried. The father asked him, "Why are you crying?" The poor little boy told him that he wanted to eat the birds that the other little boys were eating.

The father said, "Don't cry. Tomorrow morning, I'll go shoot some birds for you. So, don't cry for others' things." The father said this, but the boy did not stop crying. No, he cried until dark, then slept.

The father told the mother, "Cook some sweet potatoes for me because before dawn, I'll go to the forest and find some water where the birds are bathing, then I'll shoot some birds for our son. The other men's children never give any bird meat to our son."

The mother prepared food for the father and put it down. Before it was light, the father woke up and departed. He walked and walked, then dawn broke. He was near the water where the men had already made a hut, so the poor man kept going and going. He entered the very deep forest. There had never been a man who had gone there before.

He saw some water. The birds were plentiful and drinking the water. The man began to make a hut.

While he was still making the hut, the birds did not flee. No, they stood by. After the man made the hut, he went in and watched. When he was ready to go inside, he heard a bird flying and coming down to drink water. He sat down and the bird came down to the water. Then he shot it.

At this time, he did not fool around with shooting birds. He strung them up until it was about four o'clock in the afternoon. Then he heard something explode in the clouds.

It was not thunder. It was just the water making noise. The water smelled him and the blood of the birds that he had shot. The water exploded to consume him.

The man sat for a little while, then he felt the hut shaking. The ground softened. The water rose very high, and he was surprised. He went out to see. But no! The water had surrounded him.

The poor man did not have a way out, so the water consumed him with all of his birds. It was nearly dark and the poor little boy asked his mother, "Mama, it's dark now and papa did not bring the birds to me yet." The mother said, "I think that there are no birds or there was no water, and papa did not shoot any birds to bring back for you."

The mother spoke to the boy and they slept. They did not know that the water had consumed the father. No, in the early morning, the mother woke up and put her little baby into a net bag. She told the big boy, "You stay here. The baby and I will go."

They went and followed the father's footsteps. The father had often broken saplings, so that the two of them could follow his markings. They walked and walked, and they saw a lake.

The mother thought that the source of the water had become like human blood. The mother said, "The water has eaten father."

She looked and looked, then saw the bones of her husband lying there. She was very troubled and said, "Never mind. I can't go back to the village. Father's lost in this water, so I must go into the water. The water can eat me with father."

She broke a tree branch and hung up [the net bag with] her baby. She took a tree leaf, milked herself into it [lit., "turned" her breasts], and put it with her baby. She told the baby, "Papa is lost in this water, so I'm going with him. You can stay in the net bag with the milk that I've given to you. You can drink it and stay hung up there."

After she said this, she jumped into the water. The water consumed her and she died. The poor baby stayed hanging in the net bag.

The other child was waiting in the village, but the mother, father and baby did not return quickly. The poor little boy stayed for two nights. His maternal kin asked him, "Where's your papa and mama?" The little boy replied, "I think that the lake in the deep forest swallowed them. They've not come since yesterday morning."

The little boy's maternal kin listened to him and departed. He followed the markings where his father had broken saplings. He followed them, entered the deep forest and saw the lake that was swollen. He stood and thought.

He went closer and he saw the poor baby hanging in the net bag. He thought that the water had eaten his father and that his mother was sorry and went with him.

After the boy thought this, he carried the baby in the net bag and returned to the village. Another big boy saw this and asked, "Where has your father and mother gone that you're carrying the baby?" The boy told the big boy, "The lake in the deep forest ate them, so I'm carrying the baby back."

His father and mother saddened the poor little boy, so he continued to talk, "Who will take care of me and my little brother?" He was still saddened by them. Later, their maternal kin fetched them and took care of them.

Late at night, the lake often became bigger, then rests. Then at dawn it recedes, and the trees and forests cover it up again.

Philimon Gedisa
P. O. [B]ox 84
Bulolo
Morobe Province

D915.6. Magic flood; D921. Magic lake (pond); F421. Lake-spirit; G11.5. Water cannibal; M451.1. Death by suicide; M451.2. Death by drowning; P210. Husband and wife; P214.1. Wife commits suicide (dies) on death of husband; P230. Parents and children; P231. Mother and son; P233. Father and son; P251.5. Two brothers; P290+. Maternal kin; T611. Suckling of children; W151. Greed; W181. Jealousy

## Why Manam Island Exploded
(Wantok 449, December 25, 1983, page 24)

[Westerners] have various ways of showing that **Manam** [Island] and other mountains can explode [**Manam** People, **Madang** Province]. However, the villagers think differently. The old people of Manam Island think that Manam Island is a volcano.

Manam's fire came from Boem [**Aris**] Island, not far from Manam, in the middle of the sea, looking towards Manus [Island].  A *masalai* woman, named Oadamoungabia, was often in control of fire.  Long, long ago, she was angry with a *masalai* man who controlled fire, so the woman took the fire and went to Manam.

Before long, Manam exploded three times.  Some people died and **Bokure** Village was completely ruined.

The *masalai* woman, Oadomoungabia [Oadamoungabia], taught each man how to make Manam explode.  The men gave this knowledge to their sons.  So today, there are still some who have this power.  However, they do not meet and work together.  Some are against the others and their power is lost.

The manner of raising fire from Manam is as follows.  Sorcerers have this power.  The sorcerer must completely abstain from food for six days.  It is completely forbidden to drink water, to chew betel nuts, to smoke, or to eat anything [during this time].  The sorcerer's throat must be completely dry, so that he cannot salivate or swallow.  If this sorcerer wants to perform the song and dance of the mountain and he still has saliva in his mouth or neck, he will be killed.

On the sixth day of the eating taboo, the sorcerer goes to a place where he had planted a special little tree.  The name of this tree is *oatalatala*.  Then he stands close to this tree.  He calls out, "This must come from the mountain."

Then he holds the small tree and shakes it.  This makes the fire arise from Manam.  If he shakes the tree strongly, the fire will come up stronger.

If the sorcerer forgets and does not do this precisely, a big fire will not come out of Manam.  If he does not shake the tree or if he does not pray, the fire will only come up partly.

Some ordinary men can also shake the tree, and Manam will explode.  However if they do this, the *masalai* woman will do something bad to them in revenge.  They will be covered with various sores and they will die.  When the sorcerer who raised the fire wants to stop it, they must plant a tree called *mombosa* near the *oatalatala* tree.  One is to make the other cold and to remove its power.

During the big explosion of 1957, a sorcerer said that he had not raised the fire.  Another, stronger sorcerer had made it, so he could not make it die out yet.

Later, a sorcerer revealed another story.  He said that one day he was angry at his *mombosa* tree and he spat betel nut juice on top of it.  So, the tree almost died and lost its strength.  Henceforth, he could no longer make the fire die in Manam.

[Anonymous]

A493. God of fire; A493.1. Goddess of fire; D950. Magic tree; D985.5. Magic betel-nut; D1001. Magic spittle; D1275. Magic song; D1741. Magic powers lost; D1733.3.1. Magic power by fasting; D1733.3.1+. Magic power by abstaining from drinking water; D1766.1+. Volcano explodes from prayer; D1781. Magic results from singing; D1781+. Magic results from dancing; D2152+. Magic control of volcanoes; F490+. Masalai; F497. Fire-spirits; Q380+. Misuse of magic punished; Q411. Death as punishment; V50. Prayer; Z71.1. Formulistic number: three

## A Dog Stole Fire from a *Masalai*
(Wantok 450, January 8, 1983, page 16)

Long, long ago, there was no fire, and people often just dried their food in the sun then ate it.  There was an island where there was fire, but the people of this village were afraid of an old *masalai* woman who controlled the island.  So, the people were afraid to go get fire from the island.

One day, the chief of the village sent word to all of the men, "If a real man gets the fire from the *masalai* island, that man can marry my daughter."  When the leader of the village said this, all of the men's souls were in great pain because the leader's daughter was not an ordinary woman.  She was better than everything.  She was a queen.  So at night at the spirit house, none of the men slept.  They did not sleep even a little bit.  They just told stories about marrying this woman.

In the early morning, before daybreak, an old man with his dog went to see the leader of the village.  He told him, "We want to compete to get the fire."  The leader of the village told the old man, "You're too old.  Never mind, go back and stay here."  However the old man was stubborn about going, so the leader told him, "That's alright, you can try.  If you lose, so what?"  The old man said, "That's alright.  If I lose, the *masalai* woman can eat me.  I'll send my dog back, then you'll know that I'm dead."

They finished speaking.  Then when the sun was nearly overhead, the old man and his dog left the village.  They went asea when the sun was high.  You know that long ago, dogs listened to what men told them.

So the old man told the dog, "You must hide near the fire and watch the wind.  It would be bad if the wind carried your smell so that the *masalai* woman smelled you and came to kill you.  If the wind comes from you, then you must go downwind so that the *masalai* woman cannot smell you.  You must wait patiently.  If the old *masalai* woman gets up to go inside her house, then you must speed off and carry a piece of fire in your mouth."

After the dog heard this, it began to swim in the sea until its master could no longer see it.  The old man waited for the dog for two days. He thought that the old *masalai* woman had eaten his dog, or that a big fish had eaten it.

However on the third day, in the morning when the sun was rising, the old man saw something black coming from far away. He was a little bit happy. He kept looking and he saw his dog approaching with a piece of fire in its mouth. He was very happy and walked on the reef. He grabbed his dog in one hand, took the fire in the other hand and carried them to the shore.

The fire was nearly out, but the dog's master quickly stoked it and cooked some food. They ate the food and, oh my, it was delicious. They were very happy. In the early morning, they left the beach and went to the village.

When they arrived at the village, they went directly to the chief's house and woke him. He awoke and looked. He was very happy. He hit the signal drum and called out for everyone to come and see. Oh my, they were very surprised and happy. The chief divided [the fire] among the people. The women went to the gardens and killed plenty of wild game. They appointed some young boys to find pieces of firewood.

In the afternoon, the village was filled with people, and the women and men prepared a big feast. They sang and danced, then everyone made a bonfire. They danced around the fire until dawn.

In the early morning, the leader of the village wanted to give his daughter to the old man, but the old man said, "I'm too old to marry, so never mind. You can give your daughter to the other young men." So, the old man just stayed with the leader of the village. The leader took care of him and his dog.

So if you see a dog that is sleeping by the fire, do not chase it away, because dogs brought us fire.

John Damge
Brandi High School
Wewak
East Sepik Province

[This story is very similar to the one in *Wantok* #606. John Daniels sent in the story in #606.]

A493.1. Goddess of fire; A1415.2+. Theft of fire by dog; A1455. Origin of cooking; A2422.1+. Dog once understood human speech; B212. Animal understands human speech; B421. Helpful dog; C830+. Tabu: chasing dog from fire; F490+. Masalai; K300. Thefts and cheats—general; P14.13+. Chief gives his own daughter as reward; P234. Father and daughter; V112.1. Spirit huts; W167. Stubbornness

# A Man Married a Fruit Woman

(Wantok 451, January 15, 1983, page 16)

Long ago, there were two brothers. Their parents had died. They lived with their grandmother.

One morning, the big brother woke up and told his little brother, "Stay with granny at home. I'll go hunt for wild game for us." So, the big brother brought his bow into the forest.

After he left, their old grandmother turned into a cockatoo then flew away and perched near a tree branch. The big brother saw this and shot at the bird with his bow. The cockatoo carried the arrow and went directly to the grandmother's garden.

The big brother followed and went to the garden too. The old woman asked, "Hey, grandson, what did you find?" The big brother said, "I found a cockatoo that I shot with the bow. The cockatoo carried the arrow and went to the garden, so I came looking for it."

The grandmother said, "That was just me. Wait and I'll get a little food for us first, then we'll go home." The big brother listened to his grandmother and waited for her.

It was getting dark, so he went home with his grandmother. The grandmother told him, "If you sleep and hear people coming to sing and dance at night, don't get up and look at them. You must just sleep inside the house."

The big brother listened and he slept. Before long, the young men and women came from the fruit of a vine, jumped down then sang and danced. They sang and danced until it was nearly dawn, then they all went inside the vine fruits. The old woman quickly swept their rubbish, and dawn arrived.

In the early morning, the grandmother asked the big brother, "Hey, grandson, do you want a vine fruit or not?" The big brother said, "Yes, granny, I'd like one." So the grandmother told him, "If you climb [the vine], you must come down carefully, don't throw [the fruit] on the ground. You must carry it down carefully."

The big brother climbed the vine, removed a fruit and carried it carefully. He put it in the house and went to the toilet. When he returned to his house, he looked inside where he had put the vine fruit. He saw a beautiful young woman sitting there.

The brother asked the woman, "Hey, where's my fruit?" The young woman got up and told him, "It was just me." The man listened to her and was ecstatic. He took the woman and they went to his little brother.

His little brother saw the woman and he was very jealous. He thought, "I must marry this woman." When he explained this to his brother, they were angry. They argued and argued, then the little brother shot the big brother with a bow, killing him. The little brother married this young woman and they lived together.

Bill Mala

P. O. Box 1275

Lae

Morobe Province

D150+W. Transformation: woman to cockatoo; D211W. Transformation: woman to fruit; D350+W. Transformation: cockatoo to woman; D431.4W. Transformation: fruit to woman; P210. Husband and wife; P251.5. Two brothers; P292.1. Grandmother as foster mother; R260. Pursuits; S73.1.4. Fratricide motivated by love-jealousy; S110. Murders; T92.10. Rival in love killed; T111. Marriage of mortal and supernatural being; W181. Jealousy

## A Ghost Chased Mende

(Wantok 452, January 22, 1983, page 19)

Long, long ago, there was a man named Mende. His mother had died and his father was old.

One time, Mende wanted to go hunt some marsupials (*kapul*) in the forest. He took his bow and arrows then began walking away. He went into the deep forest and approached to the base of a boulder. He went closer and found a hole in the boulder. He sat and made a fire.

When it was nearly dark, he went to hunt marsupials. He searched and searched, going into the deep forest. However, he did not find a single marsupial. Poor Mende was angry. He thought about returning to the cave. He heard something falling on his head. He looked up and he saw the ghost of his mother hanging like a marsupial and urinating onto his face.

Mende thought that it was a real marsupial, so he opened his good eye and looked up. He left his bow and all his arrows then sped away. His mother jumped on top of him and they both ran to the cave.

Mende sped into the cave, took his axe and stood there. The ghost woman was still at the door and said, "Before I died and was still alive, you didn't like to kill marsupials to give to me. After I died, you wanted to kill marsupials and give them to whom? My son, I'm just going to eat you."

Poor Mende fell down, urinated and defecated. The ghost woman stayed by the door, and Mende did not sleep. They stood there until dawn. Then the ghost woman departed. Mende left all his things and very slowly went to his house.

He took a huge pig of his and cooked it in an earth oven [for] his kin. After the food was ready, poor Mende went to sleep and died. They carried him off and buried him.

So nowadays, when the men want to go hunting for marsupials in the forest, they never go to sleep at the place where Mende had slept.

John Guande Mangrawai

Genaiwame Village [**Gena** Village, **Kuman** People]

**Simbu** Province

C735.2. Tabu: sleeping in certain place; E222. Dead mother's malevolent return; E234. Ghost punishes injury received in life; E262. Ghost rides on man's back; E423.2+. Revenant as marsupial; G11.10. Cannibalistic spirits; P231. Mother and son; P233. Father and son; Q272. Avarice punished; Q411. Death as punishment; R260. Pursuits; V61.3+. Dead buried; W151. Greed; X717H+. Urine as gift

## Secha — Good Man — Good Mali

(Wantok 453, January 29, 1983, page 19)
(Wantok 454, February 5, 1983, page 19)

### Secha, Son of a Tree, Lived to Kill Urachi

Long ago, there was no one in all of the places of the Mali People. A *masalai* woman named Urachi had killed everyone. Only one man had run away and was still alive. This man turned into a live tree [shrub] called *lagunchi* or *tanget*.

The tree bore a single fruit and when the fruit was ripe, it broke in two and fell down to the ground. A baby boy came out of the fruit. The father tree named him Secha. Secha became a very strong boy.

One day, he took his little knife and he wanted to travel inside the deep forest, but his father the tree said, "Don't go far, there is a *masalai* woman that lives nearby. She killed everyone. Only I escaped and am still alive." The boy replied to his father, "I know what happened."

He broke trail through the forest, leaving his father. The father did not know where his son went. Secha went very deep into the forest and found Urachi's house.

He quickly went inside the house. He took all of the taros, long bamboo tubes of water and all of the other things in the house, then threw them outside. He ate just a little taro, then he had a good rest inside the house and waited for Urachi.

Urachi walked right into the house and Secha pretended to sleep quietly. Urachi walked very quietly inside the house, took his [her?] log and lifted it up. However when he heard her, Secha ran away. He ran back to his father and told his father, "I saw Urachi." Later, he did this to Urachi two more times.

One day, Secha took his log, left his father and went to Urachi's house. He ruined everything inside the house and threw it all outside. Then he saw Urachi coming and he again pretended to quietly sleep.

Urachi walked inside the house and had a very strong desire to kill Secha with her log. She was furious because Secha had already run away from her three times. She took her log and threw it hard at Secha's head, but she missed. Urachi was even angrier and ran directly towards Secha. She tried again with all her strength to hammer Secha's head, but she just missed. Quickly, Secha took his log then broke open and pulverized Urachi's head. He took a piece of firewood and left the house, then lit it on fire. The house burned with the woman inside it.

Secha took Urachi's bones and broke them up well. He went back to his father and told him, "I killed Urachi." Secha and his tree-father took one of Urachi's bones and cut it in two. Later, they hit stones and trees and called the names of everyone who had died to come to life again.

Everyone was happy with Secha's work, so they made a big feast with singing and dancing. They married amongst themselves and the men were no longer afraid because Urachi was dead.

### Secha Married Sechi

One time, the men of the village prepared their wooden masks for dancing. The women saw the men making masks.

When it was time for the festival, the men went to the dance grounds. They covered their heads and bodies with the masks.

One woman, named Sechi, wanted to marry a man, but she did not think clearly about which man would take her. Secha's little brother, Lelcha told him, "Let's go inside the forest and make masks for ourselves." They had made a forest trail from the village, but they had not cleared the trail near the dance grounds. They had left the forest there.

In the late afternoon, when it was nearly dark, Secha put on his mask, came and danced. The men did not see him because of the bonfire and because there was much smoke. The woman, Sechi, watched and chewed betel nuts. All of the men who were dancing left the dance grounds, but the smoke still covered them. Sechi looked for their footprints on the ground and followed them.

Secha finished washing in a stream, then went to his house and rested. The woman crossed a stream and arrived at a big tree called *airima*. She stayed at the tree and looked directly at the house of the man whose footprints she had been following. She went close to the house, then went inside and sat with Secha and Lelcha, his little brother.

At night, Secha married Sechi. At dawn when the [cock] crowed, everyone awoke and went to work in the gardens. Sechi gave birth to two of Secha's children, a boy named Chumescha and a girl named Levopchi.

One day, Secha and Sechi went to the garden, but they met an enemy on the trail and they were entirely lost. The little boy and his sister were afraid, so they stayed in a hole in a bamboo. This became their home.

### The Life of Secha and Sechi's Two Children

Chumescha and Levopchi both lived inside the piece of bamboo. During the day, Chemecha [Chumescha] went to his father's garden to look for a cluster of ripe bananas and bring them back for them to eat at night. The two of them always did this.

One day, the brother and sister went to the garden. The woman picked taros and *achil* (*aibika*), and the man again picked a cluster of ripe bananas. When they arrived at their home, they saw that their fire had died out. Chumescha said, "Food, go above the fire." Immediately, the fire was lit again. They cooked their food and at night they ate and slept.

One day again, Chumescha went to walk around the forest and he heard the daughters of the she-snake, Ulanchi saying that they would fetch their water. On this day, he returned to his sister when it was dark. Levopchi was a little worried and asked him what it was that had detained him until the evening.

He told his sister, "I didn't go far into the forest." His sister told him sternly, "If you walk like that again, a man will kill you." However in the morning, Chumescha went walking again and he met the women fetching water. When he saw them, they all ran away, leaving one woman behind. The women told their mother, "A man tricked us and grabbed our sister."

The next day, the mother Ulanchi carried her big log and followed her daughters to Chumescha. She asked the boy, "Was it you who tricked my daughters?" Chumescha replied, "I didn't trick them. No, I tried to talk with them, but they ran away." Ulanchi believed the boy and told him, "OK, come follow us."

They all went together and mother Ulanchi killed a huge pig for her in-law, Chumescha. The next day, his sister, Levopchi, killed a big pig that belonged to Ulanchi, along with the sow's piglets. From then on, Cheumescha

[Chumescha] lived with his wife and they made themselves many gardens.

One day, Chumescha saw a man. This man asked for the hand of his sister, Levopchi. Chumcha [Chumescha] agreed and the man lived with Levopchi. They too made many food gardens. Now, men plant *tanget*s or *luguncha* [*lagunchi*] with a story. It is the father of the good Mali, the good man Secha.

Bart Advent and Michael Kennikiso won the prize for the ancestor story section in the 1982 Annual Literature Competition. Mr. Advent's story is from the Mali People in Baining [**Bainings**], **East New Britain** Province [**Baining People**].

B211.6.1. Speaking snake (serpent); B656.2. Marriage to serpent in human form; D213+M. Transformation: man to tanget plant (*Taetsia fructicosa*); D522. Transformation through magic word (charm); D1007. Magic bone (human); D1610.3. Speaking plant; D2158.1. Magic kindling of fire; E64. Resuscitation by magic object; E79+. Resuscitation by saying victim's name; F490+. Masalai; F562.2+. Residence in a bamboo; F610. Remarkably strong man; G346. Devastating monster; G510.4+. Hero overcomes devastating ogre; P210. Husband and wife; P231. Mother and son; P232. Mother and daughter; P233.6. Son avenges father; P234. Father and daughter; P251.5. Two brothers; P252. Sisters; P253. Sister and brother; P262. Mother-in-law; P265. Son-in-law; Q411.6. Death as punishment for murder; R210. Escapes; S110. Murders; S116.4. Murder by crushing head; T100. Marriage; T543.3. Birth from fruit; T580. Childbirth; Z71.1. Formulistic number: three; Z356. Unique survivor

## Why Dogs Never Talk

(Wantok 455, February 12, 1983, page 19)

Long, long ago, in a little village called Klelpuf [**Klelbuf**] inside the Lumi District, there was a man named Filef Fale and his two dogs [**Olo** People, **West Sepik** Province].

At this time, the dogs often spoke, so this man had two good friends. Filef Fale was not an ordinary man. No, he was a great hunter. Every day, he would kill wild game in the forest and bring it back with his two dogs, then they would eat. What they did not eat, they smoked, until there was plenty of dried meat inside their house.

His dogs often sniffed out game and would quickly tell Filef Fale to kill the game. So, he found it very easy to hunt game, not like now when we often work very hard at hunting.

Sometimes, the two dogs would go with him to the forest and sometimes he would tell the dogs to stay and watch the house lest some group came to steal their dried meat.

Many times, men would come to Filef Fale's house and try to steal the dried meat, but the dogs would watch very carefully for these men. The men would ask the dogs, "Is your master still in the forest or is he returning now?" Sometimes, they would ask, "Is your master here or where did he go?" However the dogs usually replied to these men, "Why did you come looking for master? Master went to the forest and we are staying home, watching after our house." The men were usually shocked to hear the dogs reply to what they said.

Their talking often angered the men very much. When their master returned to the house, they would tell Filef Fale what had happened while he was away in the forest.

The two dogs and their master often worked together, but after a while, all of the men of the village would come and try to steal the dried meat from them. Filef Fale would tell his two dogs to watch carefully and not to leave the house and go outside. The dogs usually heeded what Filef Fale said.

One time, two thieves thought of a very good idea of tricking the two dogs and getting inside the house to steal the dried meat. They finished talking and they waited.

Another day, the sun was high and it was a perfect day. Falef [Filef] Fale told his dogs, "You two stay and watch the house, I'm going to the forest, but I won't be back quickly." Filef Fale woke up in the early morning, took his bow and multi-pronged arrows, and then went into the forest.

He was still in the forest when the two thieves came to his home. They brought a poisonous vine to poison the two dogs. They scraped ripe coconut and mixed it with the poisonous vine and other things for the dogs to eat. This would make the two dogs' stomachs turn and make them vomit.

The two men went inside the house and flattered the two dogs well so that they would eat the food that they had brought. The two dogs saw the great food and did not wait. The dogs both ate it all, then sat down and vomited. Then the two thieves went into the house and stole all of the meat. There was not the smallest piece of dried meat left in the house. The thieves took everything. They left the house and went to their home.

Filef Fale was still in the forest and did not know what had happened in the village at his house. He thought hard about his two dogs and the dried meat. When he arrived in the village, he called out to his two dogs, but they did not reply.

He [went] up to the house. The two dogs saw him and howled and howled. He tried to talk with them, but they did not talk. He went inside the place where the dried meat was. Oh my, there was not even the smallest piece of dried meat.

The poor man, Filef Fale, was very troubled about his two dogs because they no longer spoke like men. These good dogs just howled. The poison had made the dogs unable to speak like men.

Arthur Mopin

Mark Trading Company

P. O. Box 23

Wewak

East Sepik Province

A2422.1+. Why dog lost his power of speech: poisoned by thieves; B211.1.7. Speaking dog; K330+. Thief poisons guard; P310. Friendship; W31. Obedience

## The Child of a Flying Fox

(Wantok 456a, February 19, 1983, page 19)

Long, long ago there were many people who lived in a place called **Selepet** [People]. There was a village called **Kabwum** in **Morobe** Province.

One time, they wanted to make a big party in their village. So, all of the men of the village decided to send all of the women to the beach to look for adornments and "grass" skirts to decorate their bodies for singing and dancing. The women walked about twenty miles and arrived at the beach. Dawn was breaking in the early morning, and they went from the forest to the area of the beach, then worked at finding adornments.

One of the women was pregnant. When all of the women were still around in the forest, this woman felt birth contractions. Before long, the woman gave birth to a baby boy. The poor woman got up, took her baby and slept under a huge rotting tree. The baby's mother left him there and ran away to where the other women were.

The poor baby was hungry. He cried and cried and drank water from the rotting tree. He cried and cried until it was completely dark. Then a flying fox flew by and heard the baby crying.

The flying fox flew down near the ground and saw the baby. Very carefully, the flying fox carried the baby, went up, put him in a seat on a tree, and put him to sleep. The flying fox left the baby, flew to the men's garden, stole ripe papayas and bananas and gave them to the baby. The flying fox often did this, and the baby became a big and strong man.

One time, two women followed a stream. The two young women saw his shadow in the water. They just jumped and jumped in the water. After a while, one of their backs was in pain. She wanted to look, but no, she looked directly at the son of the flying fox sitting on top of the tree.

Oh my, the two women jumped and called out to the man, but the man just laughed. They made a ladder, went up the tree, brought him to their house and they married him.

The man told his two wives, "When you see my father, the flying fox, in the garden among the bananas and papayas, don't kill him. Leave him alone."

One time, the two women went to the garden and gathered leafy greens. Among the leaves, they saw the flying fox. They took a log from the side and hit the flying fox. The poor flying fox just cried, but they did not listen. The women killed him, covered him well with banana leaves and carried him to their house.

They left their net bags of food, took some cucumbers and gave them to their husband. He ate and they made a fire to cook some food. One woman told her sister to get the flying fox to give to their husband. She told her to singe off its hair and butcher it. Then they cooked it. When the man saw the face of the flying fox, he cried and cried and said, "Why the hell didn't you listen to me?" The poor man cried and cried until it was completely dark.

The two women saw this and were speechless. Quietly, they took the net bags and went to their garden.

After they had departed, the man prepared his things, such as bows and spears. He sharpened them well on the house verandah. Then he jumped down [upon them], killing himself. When they returned from the garden and saw that their husband was dead, they killed themselves and then everyone was dead.

Nelson Dapepe

P. O. Box 173

Arawa

North Solomons Province

B535+. Flying fox as nurse for child; K300. Thefts and cheats—general; M451.1. Death by suicide; P210. Husband and wife; P214.1. Wife commits suicide (dies) on death of husband; P231. Mother and son; P252.1. Two sisters; P261. Father-in-law; P265+. Daughter-in-law; P270+. Son commits suicide on death of foster father; P271. Foster father; P275. Foster son; S54+. Daughter-in-law kills father-in-law; S110. Murders; S143. Abandonment in forest; T100. Marriage; T145.0.1. Polygyny; T570. Pregnancy; T580. Childbirth; W126. Disobedience

## The Man Who Became an Eel

(Wantok 456b, February 19, 1983, page 19)

Long, long ago, a man and his wife and baby lived in **Kagarik** Village in the Umandam area. Near their house, they had a garden.

One time in the morning, the woman went to clear their garden that was near the house. Her husband watched their baby at the house. However, the baby cried for its mother's milk, so the father called out for the mother. The mother did not come quickly, so the father worked hard at taking care of the baby.

The father removed some bamboo peels and tried to create an eel. He put it inside a wooden plate. He called out to the mother again, but the woman cursed at her husband. The poor man did not speak. He looked and saw his wife come closer to the door of the house. Then the man went inside the bamboo peels, transformed into an eel and followed the stream.

The woman saw her husband. She followed the stream and said, "Hey, husband, I was lying. Come back." But no, the man left for good and did not return.

So now in this village where the man had turned into an eel, there is a lake. The men never go near it or go spearfishing there. If a man goes near and spears fish, oh my, a strong wind and rain and clouds will arise, like you have never seen. Also, when we spearfish at night with torches and see an eel with two tails, we never spear it. This is because it is the man who turned into an eel with two tails. At my village, the women never say bad things to their husbands.

Bruno Malai
C. M. [Congregation of Mission] Usino
P. O. Walium
Madang Province

B720+. Eel with two tails; C494. Tabu: cursing; C615.1. Forbidden lake (pool); C841.9+. Tabu: killing particular eel; D173M. Transformation: man to eel; D2142.1. Wind produced by magic; D2143.1. Rain produced by magic; P210. Husband and wife; P230. Parents and children; R213. Escape from home; R260. Pursuits; S12. Cruel mother

## How Did the Snake Come into Existence?

(Wantok 457, February 26, 1983, page 19)

Long, long ago, a man and woman lived in a village. They had two children, a son and a daughter.

One day, the father and mother went to the garden and just left the two children at home. They felt terribly hungry and they said, "Come on, let's follow our parents to the garden."

They got up and followed their parents. On the trail to their garden, there lived a wild man who often tricked people, then killed and ate them. They followed this trail to the garden and became a little confused, so they followed another side trail directly to the house of the wild man.

They saw him sitting there. He had turned into an old man and was sitting there. When they went closer to him, he lied and said, "Grandchildren, where do you want to go?" They told him, "No, we want to follow our parents and go to the garden, but we became confused on the trail and followed your trail here."

Then he told them, "OK, stay and rest first, then you can go." He tricked them. They rested and then they wanted to get up and go. However he told them, "Grandchildren, why do you want to go so quickly? Never mind that. Stay here and we'll cook some food first, then you can go. It's not far."

He went inside the house, took a yam and a clay pot, and gave them to the girl to make soup. He told the boy, "Climb that coconut palm tree and fetch some ripe ones. When you're on the coconut tree, don't throw them down."

The boy climbed the tree, fetched all of the coconuts and did not throw a single one down. No, he carried all of them right down to the ground. However, one fell down to the ground. A [coconut] crab [*Birgus latro*] grabbed it and put it in its home. The crab was an old woman.

When the little boy descended from the tree, he searched for the ripe coconut that had fallen. He searched and went to the old woman who was sitting down. The crab woman asked him, "Grandson, what are you looking for?" The boy said, "No, that man sent me up the coconut tree and one fell down, so I came to look for it."

Then the old woman told him, "I took it and put it here. I want to tell you two that that man is a no-good. He's killed many people and eaten them. You must leave this man quickly and run away. It would be too bad if he killed and ate both of you."

After the boy heard this, he quickly took all of the coconuts, put them down and sat down. When he saw that the wild man was not there with them, he quickly told his sister, "You thought that this was a good man and you sat with him. Get up and we'll run away. It would be bad if he killed and ate us." However, his sister did not listen to him. She said, "You're lying. This old man is nice. He can't kill us."

Her brother listened to this then told the sister and the old man, "I want to go pee. You two stay here." He lied to them and went down to see the old crab-woman who had told him about the man's habits.

The old woman lit a bamboo [torch] and showed him to a latrine that was by her house. She just left the lit bamboo outside the latrine.

The old man waited and waited, but the boy did not return. So, he called down to the old woman, "Wala'amu… Wala'amu… Wala'amu o…"

The bamboo was lit at the [latrine] and there was a reply, "Wait a little, I'm still at the latrine." The man said, "O — o — o." He stood a little, then called out again, and the bamboo said something until the old man came and took the bamboo and went to the house.

Then the old man asked the old woman, "Oe — e — e, old woman, did you also see a boy or not?" However the old woman Wala'amu lied and asked the old man, "How did he go?" The old man said, "No, he wanted to go to the latrine and he left, but he hasn't returned yet."

The old woman told him, "I think he's run away." The old man replied, "That's OK, I'll just eat his shit. How will his sister go?"

He went back to his house and the two of them ate. The old man and the boy's sister finished eating. Then the man told the girl, "I feel sick and want to go to sleep first. You can go to sleep later." The girl told the old man, "That's OK, go and sleep. If I want to sleep, I'll come inside and sleep."

The old man went inside the house, transformed himself, put on a python's skin, and went to sleep by the door of the house. When the girl wanted to go inside the house, the python rose up and blocked her way. The girl tried to call out awkwardly.

She called out, but no one came to help her. The old woman who had saved her brother went and said, "Come on, show him. I told both of you to run away, but you were stubborn and you stayed with him. Show him." The girl kept calling out until she died.

Later, the python turned back into an old man and ate her. When her brother went to tell their parents, they were very worried and they cried. Later, they told all of the men of the village.

At that time, they knew which man it was that had killed the men of the village and eaten them. They said, "Tomorrow, we must go and kill him." They prepared all of the stones. They made a fire and heated the stones.

The "friend" disregarded this. He slept awkwardly and did not know that the men would come to try to kill him. He was soundly asleep. When the stones were red hot, they took them and spilled water onto them until the water went

onto the python's body. They saw that the body did not move anymore, so they took the python to the top of a mountain and threw it down.

When the python was rotting, little insects came outside it. Each of the insects turned into a little snake. So now, we often see many snakes in the forest and not in the water.

Peter Gabriel Marakus
Amahup [**Amahop**] Village [**South Arapesh** People]
   S. S. E. C. [South Sea Evangelical Church]
Walahuta
via Balif, Brungam
**East Sepik** Province

A2145. Creation of snake (serpent); A2433.6.8. Habitat of snake; B94.1+. Crab-person; B211.8.1K. Speaking crab; B495.1. Helpful crab; D92. Transformation: wild man to normal; D191M. Transformation: man to serpent (snake); D391M. Transformation: serpent (snake) to man; D415. Transformation: insect to snake; D531. Transformation by putting on skin; D1610.3+. Speaking bamboo torch; D1891. Transformation to old man to escape recognition; F567. Wild man; G11+. Wild man as cannibal; G354.1. Snake as ogre; G512.3+. Ogre boiled to death; P210. Husband and wife; P231. Mother and son; P232. Mother and daughter; P233. Father and son; P234. Father and daughter; P253+. Sister scorns brother's wise counsel; Q211. Murder punished; Q414.0.12. Burning as punishment for murder; R210. Escapes; S110. Murders; S112.1. Boiling to death; W167. Stubbornness; X716H+. The escoumerda

## The Fish-Woman Helped a Boy

(Wantok 458a, March 5, 1983, page 21)

Long, long ago, there was a boy and his mother who lived on an island. The name of this island is **Biak** in West Irian [**Biak** People, **Irian Jaya**, Indonesia].

The father of this boy had died, so it was just he and his mother who were there. The boy was nine years old. He and his mother lived by themselves because the others of the village were often angry with them and said, "You're trash."

They lived on an island where there were few things and little food. However, the little boy often went to town to go to school. Every morning, he took his canoe and went to sea to catch fish. He also did this in the afternoons.

One time, when he went fishing, he cast his hook down, held the string and sat waiting for the fish to bite. He waited and waited, but the fish did not bite. So he said, "This is the last time." He threw the string down and he felt a big fish pulling the string taut. He pulled the string up quickly, but there was no big fish on his hook. He saw a little stone affixed to the hook. He was furious and threw the stone into his canoe. He paddled back to the beach.

He paddled his canoe up to the shore and he ran to school. His mother had gone to the garden. When the boy finished school in the afternoon, he went back to the house. He followed his mother to the garden.

The two of them were working in the garden. When it became completely dark, they walked back to their small house.

When they were still far from the house, they saw that their house had a light in it. They said, "Who's that in our house?" They whispered and walked quietly then arrived at the house.

The old mother opened the door and they went inside the house, but no one was inside. They looked inside the house and saw that it was perfectly clean and that their food was ready. The boy's bed was made and there was a light in his room.

They looked and said, "Who did this?" They did not know that it was the stone that the boy had caught in the sea and left in the canoe that had done this work.

The stone that was inside the canoe had turned into a beautiful mermaid. She had gone to their house and she did this work.

After she did the work, the mermaid went back to the canoe and turned back into a stone. The mermaid did this all of the time. After a while, she tired and said, "Never mind this, I'll go into the open and reveal myself to those two."

One day, the boy and his mother went to work in their garden until dark. Then they walked back. When they were still far away, they saw a bright light, and the boy's room was particularly bright.

They went closer and saw the mermaid sitting on the boy's bed, combing her hair. Quietly, they went inside the house and the boy's mother said, "Let's grab this woman, I think that she's the one who comes and does our work."

However the woman knew and said, "Don't grab me. I know. I can't run away. I'll stay here. I want to help you because I know that you live in poverty, so I came to help you."

She spoke to the boy, "I always saw you fishing in the sea, so I fooled you and became a small stone. You threw me into the canoe, so then I came to help you two."

She told the boy's mother, "Cook taro for me and leave it by the door. Don't lock the door, I'll come back late at night. I must go see my father first."

The boy his mother ate and slept. The woman went to the sea and swam down under. She went to her father and told him about these two poor people. Her father gave a little stone to her and she carried it back.

In the dead of night, she went to their house and entered. She took her taro and ate it. She woke the boy and his mother.

She told them, "I went to see my father and he gave me this small stone to help you two. I'll return now. If you want something, then hold this stone and think of my face and ask for whatever it is that you desire."

The next day, the two of them did as the mermaid told them to do and they became very rich. They had more things and more money than the townsfolk. They were quite happy. The mermaid looked like a real woman, but her legs were like a fish's tail.

Ronnie Ireuw
Ongu Store
Aitape, P. O. Aitape
West Sepik Province

B81.13.4+. Mermaid gives mortals wealth; B81.13.11.1. Mermaid caught by fishermen; D231+. Transformation: mermaid to stone; D432.1+. Transformation: stone to mermaid; D610. Repeated transformation; D931. Magic rock (stone); D1466. Magic stone furnishes wealth; D1719.7. Magic power of mermaid; D2100. Magic wealth; L143. Poor man surpasses rich; P231. Mother and son; P234. Father and daughter

## How Did the Asaro Mud Men Come About?
(Wantok 458b, March 5, 1983, page 21)

Long ago, there were two clans. Their names were Gimisave and Gomunive. These two clans were enemies.

When they fought, the Gimisave Clan won every time. They had almost finished off the Gomunive, and only a few of the clan were remaining.

One time, the Gimisave chased the Gomonive [Gomunive] into the deep forest where the ground was muddy. The Gomonive were completely out of breath and ran into the forest. They thought hard and said, "What should we do to our enemies?" They talked and talked, then decided to make face [masks] like ancestral spirits. When the enemies came, they had rolled about in the mud and put on faces like the ancestral spirits, so they chased the enemies backward. They won.

After this, the Gimisave no longer came to fight. The Gomunive lived for a long time and had many children until now. If you go to the Goroka Show, you will see these "Mud Men" who are just the Gomunive [**Asaro** People, **Eastern Highlands** Province].

Francis G.

Box 1011

Goroka

Eastern Highlands Province

A162.1.0.1. Recurrent battle (everlasting fight); A1542.2. Origin of particular dance; F402.1.10+. Imagined spirit pursues person; K1833. Disguise as ghost; L310. Weak overcomes strong in conflict; P230. Parents and children

## Dogs Spoke like Men

(Wantok 459, March 12, 1983, page 22)

Long, long ago, there was a man with his wife and two children who lived in the forest that they call Kumbai. The married couple's names were Dame and Timba. Their daughter's name was Mani, and their son's name was Boga. The married couple often scolded and beat their children when they made the smallest mistake.

One morning, Dame and Tiba [Timba] went to the garden. The two children thought about a plan to kill their parents. So, Mani and Boga took some bird feathers and attached them to their bodies. After they did this, they flew to the garden. When they arrived at the garden, the parents were removing grasses, and digging yams and sweet potatoes. The children saw them and flew down to hit the two parents. They came and perched on a tree and watched, but their parents just thought that they were ordinary birds.

The children went quickly and hit their parents. They hit their parents until they were half dead, then they flew back to the house, quickly boiled water, washed their bodies, and removed the bird feathers. After they removed the feathers, they went to sleep. However, Boga's poor sister did not wash well. A bird feather was still attached near her eye.

When their parents returned to the house, they saw their children sleeping. The parents went to see their children and saw that their daughter had a bird feather near her eye. So, they discovered that their children had gone and beaten them.

When it was still at night, Dame and Tiba took the woman's big net bag, and put Mani and Boga inside the net bag along with each of their things. They carried them to a river and threw them into the water.

The water carried them until dawn arrived and they were in a place where no people lived. They got up and saw that they had come to another place.

Boga quickly went to the other side of the river and told his sister Mani to gather sword grasses and some leaves. Quickly, Boga cut some trees and found some vines. They made a little house for themselves.

However, they had a hard time obtaining fire. They saw smoke rising from a mountain. Boga told his sister Mani to go and get the fire on the mountain then bring it back to their house. Mani replied that she was a girl and wanted her brother to go, but Boga was insistent and sent his sister away.

His sister listened to him and quickly went to the mountain from which the smoke was rising. Mani went closer and saw an old woman sitting and spinning rope. The fire was lit from part of the old woman's leg.

Poor Mani thought hard about getting this fire. She trembled a little then pulled off the piece of the old woman's leg and ran away. When she took the piece of the old woman's leg, the old woman told her that when she went to her house, she would die.

Mani returned to the house and she told her brother what the old woman had told her. She also told Boga that when she dies, Boga must bury her behind the house. From her innards, a dog would arise, and her brother must take good care of the dog because the dog would be the same as Mani.

After Mani told her brother this, she died. Boga was very sorry for his sister and cried terribly. He took her body, buried her near the house, and put a fence around the grave.

After one week, a beautiful dog with various kinds of things came to this place where he had buried his sister. Boga held the little dog and cried. He lived with his dog until the dog grew up.

One time, the young people went to splash in the river, and the dog told her master, "Stay in the house. I'll go to the river and watch the people splashing in the river."

When the dog wanted to go, she told her master to stay in the house, cook food and get ready because the dog would go and find a wife for her master. The dog left Boga and went to the river.

When the dog went to the river, the dog saw many beautiful women splashing in the water. The dog sat upon the net bag of one beautiful woman and watched. After the women finished splashing in the water and wanted to return to their houses, the dog got up, took the beautiful woman's net bag and ran away.

The woman thought that it was just an ordinary dog and chased it, but the dog was still speaking. [She said], "If you're a person and you came to steal my net bag, OK then, stop and give me back my net bag and we'll go to your house."

The dog listened to the woman and stopped. The woman came and took her net bag. They went to the dog's house. When the woman arrived at the house with the dog and saw the dog's master, she fell for him completely. The man completely fell for this beautiful woman too. Boga and the woman married and lived together.

After the dog brought the woman to the house, the dog told her master that she would die because she was just a dog and had broken a promise to the big man above by speaking like a person. The little dog died.

So, since this time, dogs never spoke like men. They always shut their mouths. When you call your dog's name, the dog will come wagging its tail and come right up to you. Dogs know that you are calling their names, but they cannot reply to you.

Bravo Bolui
**Bolen** Village
P. O. Box 70
Kundiawa
**Simbu** Province

A200. God of the upper world; A2422.1. Why dog lost his power of speech; B211.1.7. Speaking dog; B581. Animal brings wealth to man; B582.1.1. Animal wins wife for his master (Puss in Boots); C400. Speaking tabu; D150B. Transformation: boy to bird; D150G. Transformation: girl to bird; D350B. Transformation: bird to boy; D350G. Transformation: bird to girl; D531. Transformation by putting on skin; D1021. Magic feather; E611.6+. Woman reincarnated as dog; F570+. Person with part of body on fire; K401.1.1. Trail of stolen goods made to lead to dupe; M451. Curse: death; P210. Husband and wife; P231. Mother and son; P232. Mother and daughter; P233. Father and son; P234. Father and daughter; P253. Sister and brother; Q212. Theft punished; Q411. Death as punishment; Q451.3. Loss of speech as punishment; Q458. Flogging as punishment; R260. Pursuits; S11. Cruel father; S11.3.6. Father throws boy into river (sea); S11.3.6+. Father throws girl into river (sea); S12. Cruel mother; S12+. Mother throws boy into river (sea); S12+. Mother throws girl into river (sea); S142. Person thrown into the water and abandoned; T10. Falling in love; T100. Marriage; V61.3+. Dead buried

## The Tree People of Marayang

(Wantok 460, March 19, 1983, page 23)

Long, long ago, there was a group of people who made themselves a village on top of a big tree. These were the people of Marayang, in the Ngaruapum [Narawapum] area of Kaiapit. At this time, there were still clans of the Marayang People.

Long ago, men from other villages often went around killing men. They often ate their bodies and decorated the houses or villages with skulls. The men often carried spears and *limbum* [spears] for fighting and walking around.

The people of Marayang were completely different from other villages. Their house was on top of a huge tree. The people from other villages did not know where this tree was.

In the morning, each man and woman of Marayang went down to the base of the tree and walked to the gardens. Later, another man and woman among them would go down to the base of the tree. But they did not follow the trails to the gardens. No, each man had to go on his own trail.

In the afternoon, each man or woman followed his or her own trails back and went up the tree. They gathered at the base of the tree and quietly sprang up the ladder to each of their houses on the tree branches. They did not make much noise.

They did not like to walk on one trail lest people from other villages saw their village and came to kill them. At this time too, the men often walked "naked." Some men wore small loincloths and the women wore "grass" skirts. When they walked around, they could not make noise. It would be bad if the enemies heard their noises and followed them.

When the men went to fight at another village, they went down to the base of the tree very quietly. They would follow each other and meet in a corner. They would spit ginger on their fighting equipment and follow each other into the village to kill people.

The other villages customarily fought too. Sometimes, they killed men from Marayang and chased them. But later the men from Marayang would each crash through the forest and go to their tree. The groups followed them and found that there was no real trail.

The other villages were very angry with these people from Marayang because the men of Marayang had killed many, many people from the other villages. The other villages wanted to get revenge [lit., "reply to their obligation"], but they did not have a way to find this Marayang Village.

What the Marayang People did made the other villages terrified. The men of the other villages gathered and decided to follow the men of Marayang to find out where they lived.

The men of the other villages traveled and arrived at the Marayang's place in the forest, then spied upon them. They hid in the forest and waited. When the people of Marayang returned from the garden, the other groups of people followed them and went close to their home.

When the Marayang People continued and went up the tree, the other people saw them. However, they were not afraid to fight. They went back and told their kin. The warriors prepared their fighting equipment and gathered together to go to Marayang.

The Marayang were still asleep in the early morning and were surprised. Many called out and went up. The trees shook back and forth. A big battle took place on top of the tree.

Many men, women and children of Marayang were injured. They tried to fight, but it was too late. The people from the other villages filled their home and ruined them.

Many men, women and children from Marayang died, pressed up the tree and went down to the ground. Some men were standing-by on the ground and finished them off. However, some just pretended by just falling down to the ground and running away. Some women and children also did this and escaped.

Some men from other villages also died on the branches of Marayang, but Marayang Village on top of the tree was ruined. There was not a single person left inside the houses. Every house was broken into pieces and fell down to the ground.

The Marayang People ran away and gathered again at another place then made a new village. Right away, the people from the new village proliferated. They fought and fortified their new home, but they no longer made a village on top of a tree.

When the other villages came to fight, the men of Marayang stood and broke bones with them, but the Marayang never lost. They still had strong power from their ancestral spirits. The medicine men and sorcerers obtained their knowledge from the ancestral spirits and watched over the village.

Long ago, the men were very, very tall. They became strong warriors. But now, time has changed and many men in the Kaiapit area are very short men. Some men are just tall, but they are not strong like the men of yore.

Now there are still ten clans among Marayang. Some people have married around. Each lives in the middle of the Ngaruapum [**Narawapum**] area, but the Marayang clans have not forgotten this place on top of the trees. They still tell stories about their ancestral village.

Salmon Apagu Umi
Maiemsariang [**Maiamsariang**] Village [**Adzera** People]
Ngaruapum [Narawapum]
Kaiapit
**Morobe** Province

A162.1.0.1. Recurrent battle (everlasting fight); A991+. Origin of particular village; A1101+. Formerly men were taller; D1711. Magician; D1810.11. Magic knowledge from mythical ancestor; F765+. Village on top of a tree; F811.14+. Giant tree; K914. Murder from ambush; Q211. Murder punished; Q411. Death as punishment; R210. Escapes; R260. Pursuits; S110. Murders

# How Did Yams Arise?
(Wantok 461, March 26, 1983, page 19)

Long, long ago, the people of Maprik District in **East Sepik** [Province] did not have yams. The people of **Yahigoma** Village near Maprik often just ate wild taros and other kinds of leafy greens from the forest. The other people of this area only had one kind of food.

One man from this village, Yahigoma, always woke up and urinated near his house. He would wake up each morning and always urinate in the same place. One morning, he wanted to go urinate and he saw a small child. This child was sitting at the place where the man urinated.

The man saw this, took the boy and looked after him. The boy became a man, but he was very short and did not have a long beard. However, the man did not care. He took care of this short man as if he was his true son.

One time, there was a big festival for lining up [displaying] wild taros in another village that was near Yahigoma. The father and his short, bearded son went to see the festival. The father called his son Anowahim.

The people of the other village did not fool around at lining up taros. The village was filled with wild taros and many kinds of foods from the forest. The father and the son Anowahim walked and walked and went to see the food.

The son, Anowhim [Anowahim] did not look carefully and he trampled a wild taro. The taro broke into two pieces and the leaders of the village excoriated Anowahim along with his father. They cursed them and shamed them badly in front of the eyes of many people.

Anowahim and the father did not stay to see the festival any longer. They went and stood near the village and worried. They hid near the village in the evening until late at night.

In the early morning, they woke up and walked back to Yahigoma. Anowahim told the father to cut the deep forest and to make a garden. The father listened and cut the forest. When the father went to sleep and rest at night, the son woke up, cut a big piece of forest and finished the corners.

The father woke up in the morning and wanted to go see the forest, but no! This part of the forest was gone. He said, "Hey! Who came and finished cutting the forest?"

However, the son kept his mouth shut. He did not say anything.

The father woke up the next morning and went to clear the rubbish and put it elsewhere. He worked and worked until it was evening, then he slept and rested that night. His son, Anowahim, woke up that night and finished all of the work.

The father went to look at the garden again in the morning and he was surprised. He thought hard. He burned all of the rubbish in the garden and the fire burned it well.

Another morning, Anowahim told his father, "Don't plant anything in this garden. I'll find the food and plant it there." So the father heeded his son.

At night, Anowahim removed his entire beard and threw it around inside the garden. Three days later, many new seedlings were growing in the garden. These were yam bulbs.

The yams grew large and were ready to be harvested. Anowahim and his father dug and dug the yams until it became too hot. Oh my! These were really yams. They had only removed very long yams.

The father and Anowhim [Anowahim] prepared to make a festival to show the people the food and to rejoice in the new garden. They sent a message to all of the villages, and the people came to see the festival of Yahigoma Village. They began singing and dancing in Yahigoma Village. They sang and danced in the hot sun until it was late at night and then until dawn.

In the morning, Anowhim [Anowahim] spoke. He called out, "You people look now. I have planted these wild taros too. You berated my father and me for ruining your taro. OK, come, take these and look. Are my 'taros' better than yours or not?"

The people did not have anything to say. They took the yams and brought them to their villages. Later, they planted the yams in each of their gardens and the yams grew plentiful.

One time, the father sent Anowahim to fetch water and carry it back to the house. When the son arrived at the house, he saw his father sleeping with his mother. The breath (or spirit) of his parents inside the house took Anowahim and he called out and cried. Anowahim cried and said, "Can I come inside the house or not?" The father did not reply to him.

Anowahim sang, "*Ihuka a-a wak wak, Ihuku a-a- wak wak, Ihuku a-a wak wak.*" He took a hand drum then sang and danced with it until a heavy rain fell. The river flooded. The flood carried him by the house into the Sepik River.

The river defeated Anowhim, but his yams became plentiful in Yahigoma and the other places inside Maprik District. His festival is still there too. Now the yams are plentiful in Maprik.

Anton Aneka
Division of Primary Industry
B. M. S. Free Mail Bang
Wewak
East Sepik Province

A1011. Local deluges; A1540+. Origin of yam festival; A2686.4.3. Origin of yams; D457.4+. Transformation: beard hair to yam; D915.6. Magic flood; D1002.1. Magic urine; D1275. Magic song; D1781. Magic results from singing; D1781+. Magic results from dancing; D2143.1.2. Rain produced by singing; D2143.1.2+. Rain produced by dancing; D2151.8. Magic flood; P210. Husband and wife; P231. Mother and son; P233. Father and son; Q270+. Damaging food punished; Q470+. Public excoriation; T182+. Death from witnessing parents' intercourse; T512.2.1. Child develops from man's urine

## Long Ago, Dog and Kangaroo Were Friends
(Wantok 462, April 2, 1983, page 19)

Long, long ago, Dog and Kangaroo (*Sikau*) were very good friends. They often slept together, hunted wild game together, and played together. They became the best of friends.

If Dog was sick, Kangaroo would go and work hard at finding whatever kind of game that Dog liked to eat. Dog did the same kind of thing when Kangaroo was ill. They often did this nice custom between themselves.

One time, in the very early morning, Kangaroo just woke up without waking Dog. Kangaroo went to hunt wild game in the forest without informing Dog where it was going.

Kangaroo went into the deep forest, and Dog awoke in bed. Dog looked for Kangaroo and began to call out Kangaroo's name, "A... oooooo, friend Kangaroo. A... oooooo, Kangaroo." But who could hear Dog's call and reply to it? Kangaroo was in the deep forest.

The sun climbed high in the sky then Dog saw Kangaroo's footprints and began to follow them into the deep forest.

At this time, Kangaroo was also following the wild game in the forest, but even after a while, Kangaroo did not find any game. The sun went up behind the clouds then Kangaroo tired and slept under a tree. The tree was a huge breadfruit. This breadfruit tree was bearing fruit and the fruits were falling to the ground.

Kangaroo hunted for food and became very hungry. There was no other food, so Kangaroo sat on the ground and began to eat the breadfruits. When the sun was setting, poor Dog found Kangaroo eating the breadfruits. Oh my, Kangaroo was quite surprised when Dog came to the base of the breadfruit tree.

Dog called out, "Hey friend, I've been looking for you from the early morning until now when the sun is setting." Kangaroo looked for a time to reply to Dog. Dog asked Kangaroo, "What is that that you are eating?" Then he shut his mouth. "I want to eat some."

Kangaroo told Dog, "Friend, what I'm eating is people's shit from this place." Oh my, Dog asked Kangaroo, "Is that good food?" Kangaroo told Dog, "O yoooo… Friend, this food is delicious. If you eat it, you'll turn your back on your in-laws [i.e., not share it]."

It was nearly dark when the two friends went to their home. While they were walking, they found two big pieces of excrement on the trail. Kangaroo told Dog, "Will you eat that or not? I'm filled up."

Dog went over to the two big turds by the trail. While Dog was eating, Dog told Kangaroo, "Oh my, friend, this food is most delicious. I love it."

When they arrived at their house, Kangaroo revealed the lie to poor Dog. Kangaroo told Dog, "Hey friend, when you saw me eating something in the forest, it wasn't shit. I was eating breadfruits. I'm very sorry that I lied to you and that you ate people's shit on the trail."

This made Dog furious, but Dog did not speak angrily at Kangaroo. Dog just stayed quietly and kept his thoughts to himself.

After some time passed, Dog and Kangaroo traveled again, this time to the beach where they looked for *kina* shells, fish and other things from the sea that we often eat. Kangaroo worked very hard at finding *kina* shells while Dog dug in the sand, covering over its front paws with sand. When Kangaroo turned and saw Dog, Dog's front paws were completely shortened.

Oh my, Kangaroo threw away the *kina*s and fish that it was holding, then went to see what it was that had happened to Dog. Kangaroo asked Dog, "Hey, friend, why have your front paws become so short?"

Dog told Kangaroo, "I cut them on a *kina* shell because I was tired of those long arms. I wanted my arms to be short, so I cut them."

Kangaroo told Dog, "I too shall cut my arms so that they're short like yours. Then we'll be alike." Dog replied to Kangaroo, "Friend, if that's what you want."

Kangaroo just got up, took a *kina* shell, and cut off the two front arms, shortening them in the way that we now see them. After Kangaroo cut off the arms, Dog slowly pulled its front legs out of the sand. When Kangaroo saw this, it was furious at its friend. Kangaroo said, "Why did you trick me so that I cut off my arms?"

Dog told Kangaroo, "And you too, why did you trick me so that I ate human shit?"

They talked and talked, then they had a big fight. Dog chased Kangaroo into the very deep forest. Their friendship ended at this time.

When you see dogs and kangaroos, they no longer live together. You will see dogs looking for feces and eating them. They are delicious to dogs. Also, you will see that kangaroos' front legs are short. If you take a dog into the forest and you find a kangaroo, you will see that the kangaroo immediately speeds away. Their friendship is over and they are enemies.

Mathew Kapi
c/- Wama Marine Products
P. O. Box 308
Wewak
East Sepik Province

A2284. Origin of animal characteristics: animal persuaded into self-injury; A2371.2.10. Why kangaroo has short front legs; A2435.3.1+. Why dog eats excrement; A2494.4+. Enmity between dog and kangaroo; B211.1.7. Speaking dog; B211.2.12K. Speaking kangaroo; J1772.9+. Excrement thought to be food and therefore eaten; K1044. Dupe induced to eat filth (dung); K1065+. Kangaroo persuaded into cutting off its front legs; P310. Friendship; S160.1. Self-mutilation; S161. Mutilation: cutting off hands (arms); W151. Greed; W157. Dishonesty; X716.1H+. Birds and beasts (animal excretion); X716H+. The escoumerda

## Sons Killed their Co-Mother
(Wantok 463, April 9, 1983, page 18)

Long ago, a man from **Simbu** [Province] married two women. The first woman had two sons. The [third] son was still in her belly. At this time, the woman's husband left her to go to the beach. He stayed there for two whole years. The man's second wife stayed with his first wife at the village.

At his village, the two women argued and fought, and argued and fought. One time, the first wife went to a garden high on top of a mountain. The second wife stayed for a little while in the village, then thought that the first wife was nearby and would return to the house before long. She also went to the garden and stood at the fence gate. She saw the first wife gathering food, putting it in the net bag and carrying it towards the gate.

When the first wife came to the garden gate, the second wife shoved her back and she fell down. The second wife ran towards her, cut off her two breasts, and carried them together. The first wife died. The second wife took her net bag of food, put the two breasts inside it, and took them back to the house.

The first wife's two sons were waiting for their mother until darkness came. When their co-mother came to the house, they asked her about their mother.

The woman lied to them, saying that their mother was still giving food to the pigs and that she would be at the house in a little while.

She told them that their mother told her to give them food and to go to her house. The boys listened to her and they went to her house. At the house, the woman told them to go to sleep.

While the two boys slept, their co-mother who had cut off their mother's breasts, put the breasts into a bamboo container and put it on the fire. When it was ready, she put it on top of a banana leaf then woke the two boys to come and eat.

The two boys' eyes were still sleepy and they ate. The first boy ate and did not know what it was that they were eating, but the second boy ate and felt that something did not taste right. So, the little boy covered up the piece of breast that he was eating, put it nearby and slept.

In the morning, they woke up and saw that the woman was not in the house. The little boy saw that their co-mother was no longer in the house. The woman had run away, back to her parents' village. The little boy saw his mother's breasts. He told his brother. They went to the garden where their mother had died and was lying. They cried and returned to their house. They told the men of the village to go get their mother from the garden. The men went and buried her.

Another day, in the early morning, the two of them went to their mother's forest hut and tried to find a way to avenge their mother's death and kill their co-mother.

The first brother turned into a marsupial (*kapul*) and the second brother turned into a cat. They went to their co-mother's village, to the woman's garden. They saw the woman walking around in the middle of the food garden.

They hid quietly near the fence gate. In the afternoon, the woman walked towards the fence. The cat ran close to the woman. She was surprised and shouted. She left her

net bag and ran over to hold this cat. However, the cat tricked the woman again. It jumped down to the ground and went up a tree. When the woman went closer to the base of the tree and looked up at the cat, the cat urinated into her eyes. The urine burned the woman's eyes and she fell down on the ground. The cat and marsupial laughed and laughed at her.

The cat went down to the ground. His brother, the marsupial, also went to where the woman was lying. The two of them killed the woman. They were very happy. They ran back to their village and explained what had happened to the people of their village. The woman's kin also heard about this. They went to the garden to find the woman who had died and was lying there.

After some time passed, their father left the place on the beach and returned to his village. When two sons saw their father, they were very sorry for their mother and they cried again. Another morning, their father asked them what had happened. His two sons told him the story of how their mother had died.

Their father was sorry for his two sons and told them, "If one of your mothers was still here, you could live with her, but they're both dead, so we must go to the beach and live there." Their father took them to the beach and they lived with him. Later, their father also died and they lived alone at their place on the beach.

Gorom Gek

Siromba Hotel

P. O. Box 122

Kieta

North Solomons Province

D179.6K+B. Transformation: boy to marsupial; D142B. Transformation: boy to cat; D310+B. Transformation: marsupial to boy; D342B. Transformation: cat to boy; G60. Human flesh eaten unwittingly; G61.1. Child recognizes relative's flesh when it is served to be eaten; P210. Husband and wife; P231. Mother and son; P233. Father and son; P251.5. Two brothers; P290+. Hostile co-wives; Q211. Murder punished; Q411. Death as punishment; R213. Escape from home; R260. Pursuits; S70+. Cruel co-wife; S70+. Cruel co-mother; S110. Murder; S176.1K2+. Murder by cutting off breasts; S322.3. Jealous co-wife kills woman's children; T100. Marriage; T145.0.1. Polygyny; V61.3+. Dead buried; X717H+. Urine as gift

## Ipapaya Helped Two Boys

(Wantok 464, April 16, 1983, page 18)

Long ago, in the time of the ancestors, there was an old man. His name was Wanabokobombom. This man lived in a village named **Genana** [**Milne Bay** Province]. One day, the man paddled and paddled his canoe. He asked two boys to paddle it to a village named **Wedau** [**Wedau** People].

The two boys told their grandfather to wait, that they wanted to get their food ready. However their grandfather said, "Grandsons, never mind that. I've prepared everything. I have food, green coconuts for drinking, sugarcanes, betel nuts and peppers, and everything else. Just jump in the canoe and we'll go."

The two poor boys just jumped in and they paddled away. The sea was not too choppy, so they lay on the water easily, and the two boys paddled seawards. The little brother was thirsty so he asked their grandfather, "Grandpa, can you give me some coconut milk?"

His grandfather told him, "Sorry, you two did not get your food ready when you came." The poor boys just sat quietly. Their grandfather did not give them food.

The two of them were hungry now, but they kept paddling and arrived at Wedau Island. They stayed on this island for one week. During this week, their kin on Wedau Island killed pigs and gave them to the two boys. Their grandfather went to eat the food that they had given to him.

Another day, they went back to their village. When they were going back in the middle of the sea, a heavy rain fell and drenched them. When the sun came out, it baked them. Then their grandfather felt very thirsty.

He asked the young boys, "Grandsons, can you give me a green coconut to drink?" The little boy said, "Sorry grandpa, you can't. Think of when we went to Wedau and I asked you for a drink from a green coconut. What did you reply? So now, we can't give coconut milk or food to you either."

Their poor old grandfather was dying of thirst. The other grandparents of these two young boys lived on a mountain named Mount Ganuvinoa. A woman was angry with the boys' old grandfather. The woman took a stone, blocked the water and the water no longer came from the top of the mountain. The water gathered where it was blocked and became a pond.

When the three of them went to their village, their old grandfather did not think of his grandchildren. He ran to drink water and found that the water was dry.

This stream had two sources. He followed the two sources of the stream together and went up the mountain. He thought that if one stream were completely dry, then the other would have still have some water. He went far up and tired then just followed one branch. He left the stream named Dodonaia and followed the Oua Stream.

The old man followed Oua and arrived at the place where the woman blocked the water with a stone. The water did not run even a little bit. However, the water ran like a man's urine stream where the stone stood. He ran very quietly, and the old man put his mouth to the place where the water was originating. Immediately, the woman removed the stone from the water source. The flood carried the poor old grandfather down into the sea.

At this time, the two boys were eating fruit from a tree that belonged to the old woman. When the woman went to the garden to work, she cut her leg. Because of this, she knew that some clansman was probably stealing something of hers.

The woman called all of the things that belonged to her, but she did not call the things that were stolen from her, so the blood was still falling from her. Later, she thought of the tree that the boys were eating from and said, "I think they're eating from my tree." The name of this tree in my language is _makita_.

This tree looks like a pandanus (_karuka_) and grows by the beach. When the woman called the name of this tree, her bleeding stopped. She went and tried all of her "grass" skirts, but each of the skirts that she tried on was very heavy, so she took banana leaves and affixed them like a skirt, then went directly down to the beach.

As she ran, she flew like the wind. She came to the beach and saw the two boys who were eating the tree fruits. The woman called out to them. She said, "Ah ha, you are eating from my tree, huh?"

They called out, "Oh, grandma, it would be bad if you ate or killed us." The woman said, "No, I'm not a murderess, but you two come down here." The two boys went down from the tree.

The woman took them and they went up a mountain to her home. They lived there happily together. So now at this time, this woman still lives on top of our mountain. This woman is our ancestor. She lives in a cave. Now we try to follow this custom: we often paddle our canoes to Wedau to see our kin there, and they often make food and kill pigs for us. And the water too, when it is rainy and it floods, you cannot cross and go to the other side. When the sun is strong, and the water dries up, go up the mountain.

That is the end. This story comes from my village, Ibonaniu [**Ibwananio**] in West **Fergusson** Island, in Milne Bay Province [**Kukuya** People]. This was the story of the two boys whose parents died and who were all alone. The grandfather was Wanabokabombom [Wanabokobombom] and the grandmother was Iapapyaya [Ipapaya]. This is a true story that is still told.

Mesak Teguya
Ibonaniu [Village]
West Fergusson [Island]
Milne Bay Province

A1011. Local deluges; A1018. Flood as punishment; D670. Magic flight; D1774. Magic results from speaking; D1812.5. Future learned through omens; D1830. Magic strength; D2069. Death or bodily injury by magic—miscellaneous; D2122. Journey with magic speed; D2161. Magic healing power; K420. Thief loses his goods or is detected; P251.5. Two brothers; P291. Grandfather; P292. Grandmother; Q272. Avarice punished; Q411. Death as punishment; Q582. Fitting death as punishment; S42. Cruel grandfather; W151. Greed; W157. Dishonesty

## A Woman Gave Birth to a Baby Crocodile

(Wantok 465, April 23, 1983, page 18)

Long, long ago, in a village of the **Siwai** [People] in the Buin District, there was a married couple [**North Solomons** Province]. They lived together and were happy. After a while, the woman became pregnant.

The custom of the Siwai people is to hide babies when the mother gives birth. Not one man or woman in the village can see the baby until the parents and grandparents make a big feast, then bring the baby out of the house and show them. Then they call the baby's name. At this time too, the people of the village can know whether it is a boy or girl.

The baby's mother followed this village custom. When she gave birth to the baby, she saw that the baby was not human, it was a crocodile. The mother hid her baby well. The other people did not know that she had given birth to a baby crocodile.

The woman's husband also thought that their baby was human, so he worked hard to take care of them. Every day, he went to the garden and carried firewood to cook food for his wife.

One morning, when the man was ready to go to the garden, his wife came and said, "Today, you must cut a tree that is a fair bit longer than the bed that we sleep in. Our baby is growing very quickly and can't sleep in this bed."

The man listened and did what his wife had asked him to do. Later, the woman often told him to cut long trees and to carry them to the house where she and the baby slept. The man listened to her, but he did not ask his wife why she kept asking him to cut these trees.

One day, the man was ready to go cut a tree, but his wife called out for him to come back. She said, "Stay outside the house and keep an ear out for the baby. I'm going quickly to the stream, then I'll return. If the baby cries, you must call for me. You still mustn't go inside the house."

The woman left her husband sitting there and she went down to the stream. Her husband sat and thought of the baby then said, "Our baby, what kind of baby is it? There is no baby that grows as quickly as this. Never mind custom. I'll hide inside the room and look at the baby."

He got up and just went inside the house. He went directly to his wife and baby's room. The man was shocked to see the baby crocodile sleeping on a log that he had cut in the forest. The man immediately ran outside, fetched his axe and cut the crocodile.

When his wife returned, she heard her husband calling out and she knew that her husband had seen the baby. The mother cried and ran into the house. When she came into the house, she saw that the crocodile was not yet dead.

The woman took the crocodile, carried it and put it in a pond. The name of this pond is *Kotu*, meaning "She brought it from there."

Every day, the woman went to the pond then she gave food and spoke to the crocodile. Her husband did not know that the crocodile was in this pond.

One day, when the men of the village were preparing to go to a festival in another village, the crocodile's mother told it, "Tonight, the men of our village will go to a bird-of-paradise festival in another village. They will follow this trail. Your father's adornments are more handsome than those of all of the others. Also, he will walk exactly in the middle of the others. When they are walking by the water, jump on top of him, pull him into the water and kill him. He did a bad thing to you."

That night, the men walked to the festival at the other village. The crocodile's father had dressed finely and he walked in the middle of the other men. When they passed by Kotu Pond, the crocodile jumped on top of its father and killed him.

So now, if you travel to this place in the Siwai area, you can see this pond called Kotu.

Louise Ann Attracta
P. O. Box 343
Kieta
North Solomons Province

A1617. Origin of place-name; K914. Murder from ambush; P210. Husband and wife; P230. Parents and children; P600+. Babies secluded after birth; Q285.3. Cruel mutilation punished; Q411. Death as punishment; Q582. Fitting death as punishment; S11.1. Father mutilates children; S22+. Patricide; S110. Murders; T554.0.3K+. Woman gives birth to crocodile; T570. Pregnancy

## The Boys Killed Three Enemies

(Wantok 466, April 30, 1983, page 19)

Long, long ago in the Point Lutu area [**Lutu Busama**], near Salamaua, our ancestors saw three bad things [**Kaiwa** People, **Morobe** Province]. They were terrified of these things.

Samba was a shell in the sea, Gulik was an octopus that lived in the sea, and Bokwalam was a wild pig whose skin was white.

These three things often killed many people. So, the men of the village near Lutu Point near Salamaua took their women and children, then fled to the **Lababaia** area [**Labu** People], to the areas near **Lae** [Labu People], and to **Bukaua** [**Bukawac** People].

The people who went to Lae left a woman behind in their old village. The woman's name was Mokwanyeyewe. The woman was pregnant and her husband had died. She had tried to go with the other people, but she found it too hard to go inside the other's canoes. When she went inside the canoes, she was too heavy because she was pregnant and the canoes almost sank in the water. Because of this, the men told her that they would not take her. They had tired of trying to help the poor woman, so she stayed at Lotu [Lutu] Point. The woman's belly was quite large and she was approaching her time to give birth.

One day, the woman went to her garden to gather some food. When she went to the garden, she wanted to break some sugarcanes with her hands. However, she was unable to do so, because they were too strong. She cut a finger on her left hand. She dug the ground in her garden with her right hand and her blood filled two holes. When the two holes were filled, she covered them and went back to her home.

Some days passed and the woman went back to her garden. She was shocked to see papaya, sugarcane and banana peels lying about the garden. She turned and saw that the garden ground had been churned about, and she heard boys' voices. When she looked in the middle of the garden, she saw two boys playing in the dirt. The two holes that she had filled with her blood had become two little boys.

Every day, Mokwanyeyewe thought about going to the garden to see what the boys were doing. So, she left the garden and went home. Another day, she went to the garden and hid amongst the sugarcanes. When she was among the canes, the boys came and went up a banana plant that had ripe bananas. The woman jumped out of the sugarcanes and grabbed them both. The two boys were shocked and cried together. They thought that the woman was a ghost and that she would eat them on the spot.

However, they listened to the woman tell them that she was their mother. After they listened to this, they went with their mother to the village. The mother called them, *Gase* (Left Hand) and *Ando* (Right Hand).

Their mother took care of them well. Before long, they became very handsome men. Their mother showed them how to make a house, how to make bows and arrows, how to carve a canoe, and various other things.

Their mother carefully showed them all of the things that the ancestors had done and they understood all of these things. Their mother told them that if they wanted to catch fish, to only go to the Lae area and to spear or hook fish there.

She told them that they could not go to the beachside because there were bad things there. However, the two boys asked their mother to tell them what these bad things were. Their mother told them they were Samba and Kulik [Gulik].

They told their mother that they could fight now and that they were not afraid of such things. Their mother looked at them and said, "Yes, it's true that you're big men now and you can fight, but you must look after yourselves." Their mother told them where Kulik and Sambai [Samba] lived.

The two boys did not waste time. They prepared their things for fighting and they went to see the two things that their mother had always told them about.

First, they went to Samba. When they went to Samba's home, they made a loud noise, hit the canoe and called its name. They made Samba furious, so Samba went on top of the seawater. When Samba went up, the first brother, Ando (Right Hand) took his spear and threw it at Samba, but he missed.

His little brother, Gase (Left Hand) then raised his spear and nailed Samba, the bad clam, directly in the "eye." He pulled Samba up onto the canoe and they paddled off to see the other bad thing, Kulik. Kulim [Kulik] was a huge, strong, octopus. At the octopus' home, the two boys hit the side of their canoe and made a big racket. Kulik heard this, left its house under the sea and went up to look. Oh my, the big brother threw his spear directly at Kulik and missed again. Then little Gase got up, raised his spear and threw it hard directly at Kulik's eye.

After that, they put Kulik on top of their canoe and they paddled directly to Lutu Point to meet the third bad thing, the big wild pig, Bokwalam. At Lutu Point, the two brothers erected a long platform on the beach by the sea.

When they were ready on top of the platform, they made much noise, hitting logs and waking Bokwalam. When the bad pig heard this noise, oh my, it was furious and went down to the beach. The two brothers were ready on top of the platform. When the pig came and bumped their platform to make them fall down, the big brother, Ando, raised his spear and sent it towards Bokwalam. However, he missed for a third time. His spear just struck the coral rubble.

Now it was time for the little boy Gase. You already know that he was the left-hand man. Gase just raised his spear and threw it hard, directly at the wild pig, Bokwalam. Gase put his spear into Bokwalam's innards and the poor pig collapsed and was finished.

The two of them together pulled the pig onto the canoe. They took the three bad things towards the place where their mother lived. They sang, called out and were happy as they paddled vigorously towards their mother's home. Their mother heard them from afar and waited for them at the beach.

When their mother saw the three bad things dead on top of her sons' canoe, she was ecstatic. She told Samba and Kulik to throw them into the sea, except for Bokwalam, which was removed to the beach where they would eat it.

The two brothers took Kulik and Samba to the sea and threw them in. They returned, removed Bokwalam's skin, then cooked and ate it.

Some weeks after they killed these three bad things, they made a big garden and made a fire to burn off the rubbish. The men from Bukaua and Lae saw the rising smoke from the fire, so they asked themselves, "Hey, who's that over there making a fire?"

Later, they heard the story that the bad woman that they had left when they fled had given birth, and that her children took out Samba, Kulik and Bokwalam. Every person who had left their village at Lotu Point near Salamaua was very happy and they returned again to live with the two brothers and their mother.

Ambrose Maie
P. O. Box 1801
Buakap, Salamaua
Morobe Province

B16.1.4.1. Giant devastating boar; B16.5.3. Devastating shell-fish; B16.5.3+. Devastating octopus; G510.4. Hero overcomes devastating animal; L31. Youngest brother helps elder; P231. Mother and son; P251.5. Two brothers; R213. Escape from home; T534. Conception from blood; T545. Birth from ground; T570. Pregnancy; T587. Birth of twins; T685. Twins; Z71.1. Formulistic number: three

# Father Ruined the Meat

(Wantok 467, May 7, 1983, page 19)

Long, long ago, in a village in the Pindiu area, on the Finschhafen Peninsula, there lived a man with his wife and children. They lived in a village called Eslanda [**Esianda**, **Kube** People, **Morobe** Province].

The woman's husband often went to kill wild game in the forest. When he killed pigs for himself, he would kill them with his bow. Then he would kill pigs for wife and children, and he would just use his urine. When he brought the wild game back to the house, he would eat well. But when his wife and children wanted to eat their meat, it was spoiled.

He often did this sort of thing. One time, the father wanted to go to hunt game in the forest and the mother told the two children to follow him. The mother told the two children to find out what the father did to make the meat delicious all of the other times.

The two children walked and hid. They followed their father and entered the very deep forest. They saw their father chasing a pig and killing it with his urine. Later, the father followed a partially forested area and killed another pig with his bow.

The father heaved and carried the two pigs together and came to a hut that they had made in the deep forest. He cut the two pigs and cooked the meat in a fire.

When the pork was cooking on the fire, the father removed his two eyeballs and put them aside. The meat was ready, so he removed it and ate. He ate the meat of the pig that he had shot with the bow.

The father did not touch the pig that he had killed with urine. He would make his wife and children eat this pork. But the two children were hiding and watching what their father did.

The children ran back first to the village and reported to mother. The mother sent the last boy back to steal the father's two eyes. The boy approached the father and did not make much noise. He walked and stole the father's two eyes then took them back to his mother.

The mother put her husband's eyes inside a bamboo tube then buried it in the earth near the house. The poor father was blind, but he followed the trail and walked very carefully, arriving at the house. He sat and apologized to his wife and children, but he did not tell about what he had done to them.

The piece of bamboo by the house stayed there for many years and became very large. When the men, women and children walked to the gardens, they often heard the poor father calling out, "Jomebong! Jomebong." His two eyes inside the bamboo heard him calling and looked for a way to get out.

The father's two eyes ran from the base of the bamboo, went up to the top and then down again. The father lied to his first son and said, "What is it that makes the noise inside the bamboo, going up and down?" The boy replied to his father that he did not know what it was that was making the noise inside the bamboo.

One time, the wife of the poor father went to the garden and let the first boy watch the father at the village. The father asked, "My son? If you follow something that I say now, I'll give you a big present later."

The boy listened to his father and just stood by. When the mother went to the garden with the other children on another day, the first son did as the father said. He went to the mother's house.

The son stole the mother's stone axe then ran and cut the base of the bamboo. When the bamboo broke, the father's two eyes shot straight out and went to the father's face. Oh my, the old man was ecstatic!

The mother and the other children finished working in the garden then went to the village in the afternoon. The mother saw the boy sitting with the father and she was very angry. She did not speak to her husband or first son.

Another morning, the mother and the other children went to another garden. The father performed some of his strong sorcery. A strong wind and rain arose, then the ground churned and killed his wife and the other children.

The first son saw this and was terribly sorry. He transformed himself into a huge python. In turn, the old father was sorry for his son and he turned himself into a boulder that lay on the ground.

If you go to this village, Esanda [Esianda] now, you can see this boulder lying there. It is just the old man! The big python hides in the deep forest, so you will not see it.

Roy Botany
Papua New Guinea Scout Association, Buimo Troops
P. O. Box 254
Lae
Morobe Province

A974. Rocks from transformation of people to stone; A977.5. Origin of particular rock; D191B. Transformation: boy to serpent (snake); D231M. Transformation: man to stone; D489. Objects made larger—miscellaneous; D1002.1. Magic urine; D1402.18+. Urine kills animal; D1544.1. Magic spell controls earthquake; D2142.1. Wind produced by magic; D2143.1. Rain produced by magic; D2148. Earth magically caused to quake; D2161.3.1.1. Eyes torn out magically replaced; F541.11. Removable eyes; K300. Thefts and cheats—general; P210. Husband and wife; P231. Mother and son; P233. Father and son; P251.5. Two brothers; Q151. Life spared as reward; Q261. Treachery punished; Q411. Death as punishment; Q451.7. Blinding as punishment; R260. Pursuits; S11.3.3. Father kills son; S63+. Husband kills wife; W157. Dishonesty

# A Woman Married a *Masalai* from the Same Tribe
(Wantok 468, May 14, 1983, page 23)

This ancestor story comes from the ancestors of the Nesc Barapu Tribe in the Garaina District of **Morobe** Province [**Guhu-Samane** People].

Long, long ago, there lived a man who they called Masu among the Nese Barapu. He lived with his wife Satia. One time, Masu and Satia went to a mountain called Dumeu to hunt for wild game. They walked for two whole days and arrived at Mount Dumeu. They made a hut and slept inside it for the night.

Mount Dumeu was the place of a *masalai* snake called Dzoni Turango. Satia did not understand very well the story of this mountain. It was the first time that she had gone to this place.

Masu woke up quickly in the early morning and did not tell his wife. No, he left the woman sleeping and he went to hunt for game.

The sun rose brightly and poor Satia had to urinate badly. She quickly went to urinate in a hole in the ground near the mountain. Oh my, Satia made a big mistake!

This hole in the ground was the door to the *masalai* snake, Dzoni Turango. The *masalai* snake smelled the woman's urine, opened its eyes and saw Satia.

The *masalai* snake said, "Aha! Now this woman will die right on top of my chest. Where will she go?" The *masalai* closed its eyes again and slept in the hole in the ground.

In the evening, Masu brought some game back to the hut. He and Satia cooked the meat and ate some. They smoked some meat and left it. Then they slept that night.

The next morning, Masu woke up very early and went to hunt for some more game. Dzoni Turango turned into a real man and went to Satia. They became "friends" and slept together.

Dazoni [Dzoni] Turango told Satia that they should marry. Satia thought that Dazoni Turango was a real man and she agreed to this. In the afternoon, the *masalai* snake (Dazoni Turango) departed, and poor Masu carried the meat back to the hut.

Satia did not reveal this bad sin that she had done during the day. They saw that the meat was plentiful and they prepared to return to the village. Satia carried a net bag and Masu carried the multi-pronged arrows, spears, and axe. The clouds thundered and a heavy rain fell. The ground broke and a strong wind arose. Lightning flashed nearby.

The wind broke a tree that blocked Masu and Satia's path. The *masalai* snake did not want Satia to leave him. This is a kind of trick that *masalai*s use!

When Masu and Satia wanted to go out, the clouds thundered. However when Masu went to go out, the sun came out nicely and there was no rain or wind. This sort of thing happened many times and Satia now understood.

She thought about Dzoni Turango and told Masu to walk back to the village. Masu listened to his wife and was downcast. He held tightly to his wife and cried hard.

Masu was very sorry, but he had known about the *masalai*. He was afraid and divided the meat with their dogs. He rose and cried then returned to the village.

When Masu left, the *masalai* snake turned into a real man, then came and took Satia to his home. Satia stayed with the *masalai* snake (Dzoni Turango) for some time then she became pregnant. The bad *masalai* had "known" her on the sly!

One good time, Satia and Dzoni Turango worked at their garden near Mount Dumeu. A little bird called Biloli flew in the forest and went past Satia.

This bird, Biloli, called out and flew slowly back and forth. Satia noticed this bird. It was a totem bird from her tribe, Nese Barapu.

Satia called out, went to the bird and said, "O, Biloli, you are a bird and you can be happy and fly about. The *masalai* snake has ruined me, and my poor husband Masu has left me... and gone to the village. I'm completely lost here on this mountain."

This bird is a totem for Dzoni Turango also. Dzoni Turango heard Biloli talking and was terribly ashamed because Satia was also from his tribe. Oh my! The *masalai* snake was very wrong to have ruined his kin!

The *masalai* snake went very quietly to the garden and cut sugarcanes called <u>*doni mukowa*</u>. He pulled up many of these sugarcanes and put them in a very attractive net bag. He took Satia back to the village.

When they approached the village, Dzoni Turango told Satia, "If you give birth to a boy, you can take care of him. If you give birth to a girl, she belongs to me. The clouds will thunder and I'll be able to hear it. Then I'll come to get the girl at that time."

The people saw Satia and they came from the village. They were ecstatic. Satia's old husband, Masu, had married another woman.

When Masu saw his old wife, Satia, he was very happy that he now had two wives. They lived for some months, then Satia gave birth to a baby girl. Satia put the girl in the *masalai* snake's attractive net bag. She took the net bag with the girl in it and hung it on a tree by the house.

The clouds thundered, a heavy rain fell and a tremendous wind blew in the village. Everyone in the village went and hid in each of their houses. The *masalai* snake came quietly and carried the net bag with the girl to Mount Dumeu.

Many people from the Garaina area know that the Nese Barapu people are the same tribe as the *masalai* snake. And, this tribe, Nese Barapu, planted many sugarcanes with black skins that are red on the inside. This kind of sugar cane came from the *masalai* snake from Mount Dumeu.


Nime Adzawe and Khatawi Ekaro
Ruino Brothers Trading, Bulolo
P. O. Box 1474
Lae
Morobe Province



A2684.4K. Origin of sugar cane; B211.3. Speaking bird; B211.6.1. Speaking snake (serpent); B631.9. Human offspring of marriage of person and snake; B656.2. Marriage to serpent in human form; D191M. Transformation: man to serpent (snake); D391M. Transformation: serpent (snake) to man; D2142.1. Wind produced by magic; D2143.1. Rain produced by magic; D2148. Earth magically caused to quake; D2149.1. Thunderbolt magically produced; F401.3.8. Spirits in form of snake; F490+. Masalai; K1544. Husband unwittingly instrumental in wife's adultery; P210. Husband and wife; P232. Mother and daughter; P234. Father and daughter; R4. Surprise capture; T100. Marriage; T111. Marriage of mortal and supernatural being; T145.0.1. Polygyny; T481. Adultery; T570. Pregnancy; T580. Childbirth


## How Did Man Arise?
(Wantok 469, May 21, 1983, page 19)

Long ago in a village, there were only women. There was just one man who lived in another place. One time, the man went to hunt for wild game in the forest. He brought his two dogs with him. They hunted for game until it became dark.

When it was dark, the man and his two dogs looked for a place to sleep. They searched and searched for a place to sleep then they saw a huge log near the beach. The man went back to the forest to get his two dogs and some game that they had hunted.

They went to the log, then the man went inside it, made a fire and smoked his meat. Later, he felt sleepy and he wanted to sleep. His two dogs just stayed there. Not much later, the high tide came and pulled the huge log with the sleeping man out to sea.

The man's two dogs began to howl at him, but he did not hear them. The two dogs jumped into the sea. They swam and swam, but the tide was much too strong so the two dogs swallowed water and drowned.

The man slept very well and the sea carried him back near a beach. In the morning, he awoke and was disoriented on the beach. He walked and followed the shore then found a garden. He went inside the garden and sat down.

The garden in which the man sat belonged to two sisters. The man sat and hid at the base of some sugarcanes. Before long, the two sisters came to weed their garden. The sisters began weeding, then the first sister went closer to the sugarcanes where the man was hiding. The woman saw the man and screamed, but the man said, "Don't be afraid."

Later, the other sister also looked at the man. She was afraid too, but the man told both of them not to be afraid. He asked the sisters to come closer to him and they did so.

When they went closer, they asked him, "How did you get here?" The man told them that he had gone hunting for game in the forest with his two dogs when it became dark. They had looked for a place to sleep, so they went to the beach and found a huge tree. He and his dogs slept inside it. Late at night, the high tide pulled them out to sea. When the two dogs jumped into the sea, they swallowed seawater and drowned. After that, he was alone and went to the two sisters' garden.

After the man told this story to the sisters, the women told him that he could go to their village because there were no men there. The women also said that the man could marry them and they would take him to their village. The sisters just put him inside their house and the other women did not know to look for him.

They stayed there for a very long time and the first sister became pregnant. The second sister just went to get water, food and meat for them to eat.

The women of the village asked the second sister, "We never see your elder sister, where is she?" The second sister told them that she had boils on her breasts. The women said, "Then we should probably come to look at them this afternoon." However the second sister said, "No, you can't come. You're just sorceresses."

After a little while, the first sister gave birth to a boy. Some time later, the second sister also gave birth to a boy. The two boys grew up, then the two sisters told all of the women and they came to see the two boys, and they were happy.

The two boys became big men, they married the other women of the village and they also gave birth to many people. So now, we have many people in all of the places on the earth.

James Numbuk

P. O. Box 639

Wewak

East Sepik Province

A1280. First man (woman); F112. Journey to Land of Women; P210. Husband and wife; P230. Parents and children; P231. Mother and son; P233. Father and son; P252.1. Two sisters; T100. Marriage; T145.0.1. Polygyny; T570. Pregnancy; T580. Childbirth

## Komiaui Married a Cassowary
(Wantok 470, May 28, 1983, page 19)

Long, long ago, there were two brothers in a village. Their names were Suai and Komiaui. Suai was the big brother and Komiaui was the little brother. Their parents had died. All of their kin were married in the village, but they had not yet married.

One time, Suai told Komiaui, "Brother, I think we should stay here. Never mind making a garden that is deep in the forest."

So, they made a garden. After they finished planting, they returned to the village. They stayed for a fairly long time and then Suai sent Komiaui to go and look at their garden.

In the early morning, Komaiai [Komiaui] woke up, took his spear and went to the garden. He went close to the garden and heard a noise inside it. He went closer and saw cassowaries breaking apart the leafy greens, *aibika*, and taro leaves. He was angry and shot a cassowary with the spear. All of the other cassowaries ran away.

The cassowary that he had shot was in pain and was walking about very slowly. The spear was still inside the cassowary's leg. He followed the cassowary for a while then arrived at the home of the cassowaries. When Komiaui saw that he had approached the home of the cassowaries, he was afraid and hid nearby.

However, the cassowary that he was following knew this and told the leader. The cassowary that he had shot felt the pain in its leg and went to sleep.

The other cassowaries talked about when they were taking the leafy greens and taro leaves in the man's garden, and the man found them and shot one of them.

The leader of the cassowaries asked them where the man was. They said, "He just followed us and stayed there at night." Their leader said, "One of you, run and call for him to come to me." The man came and the cassowary leader scolded him.

The leader said, "Why did you shoot one of my children? I sent them to find food for us." The man said, "I'm sorry sir, I didn't know. They went inside our garden, broke up the new *aibika* and removed the taro leaves, so I shot one." The leader said, "That's alright. That was their mistake too. They ruined your new garden. Come here. We'll go and stay at the house."

So, the two of them went to stay at the cassowary leader's house. At night, the leader asked the man, "Are you married or not?" The boy said that he and his big brother were not yet married.

The leader said, "When we sleep, you'll hear a noise outside the house, but you can't get up. The noise will sound like, 'Tu yu tu tu tooooo!'"

After the noise ended, he awakened Komiaui and told him to go into another little room. Oh my! He was surprised to see a young woman laughing at him. Komiaui was very happy because this was his wife. He took her and they slept together. In the morning, they gave food to them and they went to Komiaui's village.

However at the village, Suai was waiting for his little brother until one day he thought hard. Suai thought that a wild pig had killed him. That very afternoon, Komiau [Komiaui] and his wife arrived.

When Suai saw his brother with the young woman, he was surprised and asked him, "Brother, where did you get this woman?" His little brother told the story of how he had gotten this woman. The big brother listened to him and was speechless. He said, "You were strong and found this woman. You'll marry and you can take care of me."

However, Suai was lying. They lived for a fairly long time and the big brother lusted for Komiau's wife, so he killed his little brother and married his wife.

My story is from my grandparent, Sukundai, from **Yamben** Village, in **East Sepik** Province, who told me this story [**Muniwara** People]. I wrote it down and sent it for you to print.

Vitus Uraningi
Turubu, Wewak
East Sepik Province

B211.3.17K. Speaking cassowary; B222+. Land of cassowaries; B242.2+. Leader of cassowaries; B652+. Marriage to cassowary in human form; D350+W. Transformation: cassowary to woman; P210. Husband and wife; P251.5. Two brothers; P263. Brother-in-law; P264. Sister-in-law; R260. Pursuits; S73.1.4. Fratricide motivated by love-jealousy; T92.10. Rival in love killed; T100. Marriage; W181. Jealousy

# Two Brothers Found Wives

(Wantok 471, June 4, 1983, page 19)

Long ago, in the time of the ancestors, there were two brothers in a village called **Hasrumraka**. Their big brother's name was Kempa and the little brother's name was Oru.

One time, the little brother, Oru took his brother and went into the deep forest to shoot birds. He walked and walked, then he saw a big bird and shot it. The bird carried the arrow and went down to the hand of an old woman. The old woman took the bird, removed the arrow then cooked and ate the bird.

Poor Oru tried hard to find the bird. He went and followed along, towards the old woman. The old woman told him that she had eaten the bird and that only the arrow was left. Oru told the old woman to give the arrow back. The old woman gave the arrow back to him.

The old woman asked Oru to sleep there and to go back to his home another day. She also told Oru to climb up a tree, cut a branch off, come down, and carve the branch for digging sweet potatoes. Oru heeded the old woman, so he went up and cut the tree branch. After Oru cut the branch, he watched it fall to the base of the tree, and then he saw two beautiful women standing there.

Oh my, Oru jumped down the tree and held the two women. He was very happy because of the old woman. Later, he took the two women and went to his village. When he arrived at the village, he told his brother that he had found the two women.

The big brother told Oru to give him one young woman, but the [little] brother told him, "Go find one yourself. I can't give you one." So, the big brother Kempa took his bow and went into the forest. He saw a big bird and shot it. It fell down by the old woman. The old woman removed the arrow from the bird, then cooked and ate it.

Kempa went to the old woman and asked her for the bird. The old woman told him that she had eaten the bird and that only the arrow was left. Kempa scolded the old woman. She told Kempa to climb up the tree, cut a branch, and carve it for digging sweet potatoes.

The boy was angry. He went up the tree and cut a branch, but it broke in the middle. He cut another correctly and when he saw it falling, he saw two women standing there. One of the two women had a crooked nose and the other was a beautiful woman. Then Kempa went down and took the two women back to the village. They lived happily together and raised many [sons] and daughters. Now in the

Highlands, you will see that it is filled with many men and women.

Iserel Tufi
P. O. Box 431
Kieta
North Solomons Province

A1663+. People with crooked noses; D431.2+W. Transformation: stick to woman; P210. Husband and wife; P230. Parents and children; P251.4+. One brother acts wisely, another acts unwisely; P251.5. Two brothers; T145.0.1. Polygyny; W181. Jealousy

## The Pythons in the New Guinea Walnut Tree

(Wantok 472, June 4, 1983, page 19)

Long ago, in **Boroman** Village, on **Karkar** Island, there was a man who lived with his wife [**Takia** People, **Madang** Province].

One day, the man traveled in the forest. He saw a New Guinea walnut tree that was bearing many ripe fruits. The flying foxes were coming and eating the fruits of this tree. The man quickly went to the village and thought about straightening his bow and arrows. He thought about shooting the flying foxes that night.

He waited at the village until it became dark, then he took his bow and arrows and went to the base of the tree. You know, it is the custom that when going into the forest to hunt for game, one does not explain to one's kin what one is doing. So, though he had straightened his bow and arrows, he had not explained what he would do to the children, the mother and father, or all his other kin. He just went into the forest.

He walked and walked on the trail. He just thought about what he was doing until he arrived at the base of the tree. When he looked up the tree, oh my! There was not a vacant branch or leaf on the tree. All of the branches and leaves of the tree were just filled with flying foxes. The tree was completely blackened by them.

The man trembled fiercely and climbed the tree very quickly. When he arrived at the crown of the tree, he saw a big hole there. The hole went very far down into the darkness. The poor man tried to find a place to stand, but there were not any good footings. He prepared to shoot the flying foxes. He found a place where there were no flying foxes. He stood near the hole and tried to shoot the flying foxes.

The good-for-nothing took an arrow and put it in the bowstring. He prepared to draw the bow back and he let one fly at a flying fox. He had aimed at a huge flying fox.

He pulled the bowstring back and he shot the huge flying fox.

He kept pulling the bowstring back; it came close to his chest. When the poor man tried to let go of the bowstring again, it did not work. The bowstring broke and the man fell down into the tree hole. He looked for a way to get out of the hole, but he was really stuck inside. This hole belonged to a python.

The pythons had also gone outside in the evening to look for food for themselves and the man had just fallen into their home. The poor man could not go outside and he stayed in the pythons' home until dawn broke. It was light and his kin at the village tried to find him, but they did not see him anywhere.

In the early morning of the next day, the man's kin woke up again and went to the forest to try to find him. However, they did not find him on this day. In the afternoon, his kin returned to their village and they said that they thought that a *masalai* had eaten him.

The poor man was still inside the walnut tree. In the morning, the pythons returned to their hole and they saw this man. Oh my, every vine had a python upon it. The little pythons were on the small vines of the walnut tree, and the big pythons were on the big vines. When the man had fallen down the hole, he had blocked the pythons' home, so the pythons stayed on the vines and branches of the tree.

The next morning, the pythons thought of finding a way to help him come outside, so they looked for a way to help him. The mother and father of the pythons encircled themselves below, the baby pythons encircled themselves above, and they raised him up and outside the hole of the walnut tree.

The man went down the tree and to the village where he told his kin this story. The man did not take pity upon the pythons that had helped him. He told the men of the village then they went to the walnut tree and cut it down. They often ate pythons at this time, just treating them as game meat. After they cut the tree down, they killed all of the pythons in the hole and ate them.

J. N. Hanslim
c/- L. Akoi, Ela Motors
P. O. Box 110
Madang
Madang Province

B31.4+. Giant flying fox; B336. Helpful animal killed (threatened) by ungrateful hero; B491.1. Helpful serpent; B540+. Snake rescuer; C490+. Tabu: telling specific hunting plans; P210. Husband and wife; P230. Parents and children; P231. Mother and son; P233. Father and son; R49.1. Captivity in tree; W154. Ingratitude

## A Bird-Woman Married a Man

(Wantok 473, June 18, 1983, page 19)

Long ago, there was a woman and her son. They lived for a while then her son grew to be a big man. The man's name was Les. He made a house and a garden.

One time, he was making a new garden. He burned the forest, cleared everything off, and prepared to plant some crops. When darkness arrived, he went to sleep at the house. In the morning, he and his mother went to work at the garden. However when they arrived at the garden, there were no taros or other things that Les had planted. Everything was gone. They were shocked and went back to the house. That night, Les told his mother that he alone would go to the garden and try to find out who it was that had stolen the new food plants that he planted.

Les went back. When he looked, he saw many women planting corn, sweet potatoes and taros. All of them were young, but one was more beautiful than the others were. Her skin was pure white, like the sun. Les watched this young woman then went slowly back to the house and slept.

In the morning, he explained this to his mother and they devised a plan. Les told his mother, "Tomorrow, you should call out as if I had died, then many women will come and cry for me. While I'm lying there, you must tie me with ropes, but don't make them too secure. You must bind me with vines that grow in the stream." He told his mother this and that when all of the women arrive, "You must cry and say that the bad ropes must break."

The mother did everything that Les had told her to do. The mother found two trees and hung Les on top of them. Les' mother cried, then many men and women came from every corner to cry. The beautiful woman who had made the garden also came. She cried and held Les' hand.

While the mother was crying, the bad rope broke then Les got up and grabbed the woman who was holding his hand. The second rope also broke and everyone ran about. Les held tightly onto the woman. The woman turned into a stone, then a tree, then a mountain, but Les kept holding her tightly.

Les continued to hold tightly onto the woman for about four hours. Then the woman told him that she was tired. She said, "Let go of me and we'll marry." Les let go of her and they lived happily in the house. However the woman promised, "If I do something wrong or incorrect, you can't say, 'You're a water-child.' or something that customarily sits on top of the water."

Les and the woman lived happily until the woman gave birth to a baby. The baby was four months old, and the mother gave the baby to Les then went outside. She did not return quickly and the baby cried for a very long time. Les became angry. Later, the woman went to the house and Les said, "Fucking child of birds and water! Where do you live now that you've come back?"

The woman listened to this and she began to cry. She cried until it became dark. Then they went to sleep in the house. At night, the woman tried to wake Les, but he was dead asleep.

The woman put the baby in a net bag and she began to follow a trail. Near this place was a pond. She lit a torch and walked away.

After the woman had departed, Les woke up and looked for her. He saw that the woman [was not] asleep in the house, so he went outside and saw the torchlight down beneath the pond. The man sped off to get his wife and bring her back. Les went into the water, but the water threw him back on top. He tried again to get his wife back, but he was unable.

Les went back to the house and cried and cried until dawn. In the morning, he woke up and went to the water to look for his wife. He dug the earth and went very far down, but it became dark and he went to sleep. In the early morning of the next day, he woke up and finished digging, but he did not find her. On the side of the water, the woman had found a tree and placed a big boulder there. Les left this place and went back to the house.

This is a true story. If you go to **Sirunki**, [you can see] the place where Les had dug [**Enga** People, **Enga** Province].

Aepa Karinyo

Laiagam

Enga Province

A977.5. Origin of particular rock; A983+. Origin of holes in ground; B652. Marriage to bird in human form; D215W. Transformation: woman to tree; D231W. Transformation: woman to stone; D291W. Transformation: woman to mountain; D361.1+. Forest Spirit Bride; D610. Repeated transformation; D921. Magic lake (pond); F527.7K+. White person; K1538+. Death feigned to capture bride; K1860. Deception by feigned death (sleep); P210. Husband and wife; P230. Parents and children; P231. Mother and son; Q325. Disobedience punished; R4. Surprise capture; R213. Escape from home; R260. Pursuits; T192. Marriage by force; T580. Childbirth; W126. Disobedience

## Why We Have Various Kinds of Foods Today

(Wantok 474, June 25, 1983, page 19)

Long, long ago, there was a man who lived on this land. He had two sons. One time, the brother of this man made a big feast at the time when men often ate wild tree fruits.

The man's two sons went to the place of this big party. When they returned to their village, the man's brother did not give any food to the two boys to bring back to their village to show their parents that they had been to the party.

The man's brother was furious and told the boys, "Tomorrow we'll go to the forest in the early morning." So in the early morning, they woke up and went to the forest. The boys' father chewed betel nuts and spat on bamboos, thus making a trail. They arrived at a mountain and the man told his sons, "Cut the forest and bring the forest here." They cleared the forest then the man took some sticks and pulled hard until there were twenty little sticks in a bundle.

Then he told the boys, "On the last day, the twentieth day, as these sticks mark the days, you must return to this forest." He told them that one stick would mark each day. He said, "On the second day, you must burn this part of the forest that you have cleared."

Then he told his sons, "Cut me now." But the boys said, "Why should we cut you?" Their father said, "My brother was angry at us, so I want to make you happy. So, I'm asking you to cut me."

The two sons listened to him and did as he wanted them to do. They cut him and later they cried for him. They left this place that they had cleared and they left the pieces of their father with the bamboos that they had worked at cutting all day. They were not able to go out because they were thinking about their father. Their mother did not know what had happened to her kin.

On the second day, they returned to the forest that they had cleared. They made a fire and burned the area. When they went back to their village, they went inside the house and just stayed there. On the twentieth day, they went back to the place that they had burned. When they arrived at the bamboos, the big brother chewed betel nuts and spat upon the bamboos then went inside. When they arrived at the place that they had cleared on top of the mountain, they saw various kinds of foods growing that they had never seen before.

They both took each of the kinds of food and tried them. In the afternoon, they took some and went to their mother at the house. When their mother tried these kinds of foods, she was very surprised at the how good they were. When she asked them how they had found these foods, they told her what had happened when they had killed their father and cut him up on the mountain.

Another day, they went with their mother to this part of the forest. The big brother chewed betel nuts and spat on the bamboos, then they went inside and took all of their things and went together. After they went inside the bamboos closed up again.

They began to make a little village at this place. They made a house. When they cut a tree, all of the trees just fell down as if men had cut them. They brought the tree to this place, but all of the other trees also came there. When they dug a hole, all of the postholes for the house were ready. They worked like this and their house was complete in just one day.

On the night of the Kigul Festival, they hit the signal drum. The people from the big village heard it and many of them asked, "That signal drum is coming from very far away, isn't it?" They did this for a while, then a prankster from this village went to sea in his canoe and saw the fire on the mountain. He called out to the two brothers and to their mother, "Where is the trail up to there?"

The big brother threw a little stone down the trail. The prankster went up and they gave him various kinds of foods. They told him, "Tomorrow, you must tell the men of the big village to come to the festival. The women of the village must also come with their husbands. The head woman of the village and her sister must also come together." In the morning, they divided the food and the men went back to the big village, but the head woman and her sister stayed in the little village. They married the two brothers. The big brother married the head woman and the little brother married her sister. On this trail now, we have coconuts, sweet potatoes, bananas and various other things that we eat today.

Marcel Topenia
Hutjena High School
P. O. Box 71
North Solomons Province

A2680. Origin of other plant forms; A2686.4.1. Origin of sweet potato; A2687.5. Origin of banana; A2681.5.1. Origin of coconut tree; D950.15. Magic bamboo tree; D985.5. Magic betel-nut; D1001. Magic spittle; D1935+. Work magically multiplied; E631.5. Reincarnation as plant; P210. Husband and wife; P231. Mother and son; P233. Father and son; P251.5. Two brothers; P252.1. Two sisters; P293. Uncle; P297. Nephew; S22+. Patricide; S139.7. Murder by slicing person into small pieces; T100. Marriage; W152. Stinginess


## Brother Tricked Brother

(Wantok 475, July 2, 1983, page 19)

Long, long ago, in a village they call **Waben [Olo People]** in the area near Aitape in **West Sepik [Province],** there were two friends. They were good friends since the time when they were little until the time when they had grown.

One of the friends was named Faive and the other Maive. They were both married, but neither had children.

One time, Faive traveled, looking for *kina* shell in the mangrove [swamps]. He took some, returned to the house and cooked them a unique way. After he boiled them, he removed the flesh, pulverized it and oiled it with coconut. Then, he put the meat inside *tulip* leaves and cooked it. When it was ready, he covered it with breadfruit leaves and cooked it in an earth oven beneath a fire.

Afterwards, he rested and had a smoke. When he finished chewing betel nuts and smoking, he uncovered his earth oven. He brought the food out and oh my! A wonderful smell emanated. Whoever would have been near would have just salivated.

At the exact time when he opened the food wrappings, his friend Faive came and smelled it then asked Maive, "Hey what are you cooking that smells so good?" However, his friend was a little greedy and replied, "Hey you, cool it. This is not something for you, I'll come talk to you later."

The two of them ate the food and Faive thought that the food was delicious, so he asked Maive, "This food is delicious. What kind of meat did you cook?" Maive told his friend, "It's something that opens and closes that they call *kina*. It lives in the mangroves." Faive was quite surprised and said, "[So] it's a *kina*, but how did you find it?" Maive told Faive, "I think you're really crazy. These are not small. The big ones live near the sea."

Then Maive told this story to Faive. First he must find a *kina*. Then when he gets it, he must grab it tightly and it will die. After it dies, Faive should take it to Maive and he will show him how to cook it.

So, Faive went to the mangroves near the sea then searched and searched. He saw one and he was ecstatic. He put his hands down, directly into the open mouth of the *kina* shell. When he [put his hands] inside, the kina closed its mouth, broke the bones on his hands and held him until he died.

Later, the people of the village found him. They burned him and he drifted in the sea near the mangroves. The bones of his hands were completely broken. Maive thought that he had tricked his friend, causing him to die, so he cried terribly for his friend.

Afterwards, people asked him why he was crying. He told them that he had tricked Faive into shoving his hands inside the *kina*. So, the *kina* had grabbed his hands and broken them, then he died.

After the men listened to Maive's story, they were furious and killed him too. Later, they made a platform on top of the mangroves and laid the two friends together upon the platform.

Katmon John
Aitape
Sandaun [West Sepik] Province

[There is apparently only one publicly accessible copy of this issue in Port Moresby. The story in this copy was poor.]

K890+. Deceived into sticking body part into giant clam; K2297. Treacherous friend; P210. Husband and wife; P310. Friendship; Q261. Treachery punished; Q411. Death as punishment; S110. Murders; V61.2. Dead burned on pyre; W151. Greed; W157. Dishonesty

## When the Rodents Arose from the Ground
(Wantok 476, July 16, 1983, page 19)

Long ago, there was an old woman. Her husband had died. She had one child and one cassowary. Her child went to work, so she lived with the cassowary. This cassowary often killed men.

One time, the old woman told the cassowary that a child would come to the house with a red basket and that the cassowary should not kill the child. After the old woman told the cassowary this, she went to the garden. The cassowary stayed at the house and the child arrived with the red basket.

The cassowary forgot then quickly jumped and kicked the old woman's child to death. The cassowary thought that it had killed another man, so it was elated and went to the child's mother. The child's mother thought that some other man wanted to steal something of hers.

The old woman was very happy with her cassowary when she went inside the house. But oh my, the old woman was shocked to see her child lying dead. She was speechless. She went inside the house, took a short stick and a short rope then went outside. She called out to her cassowary. She tightened the rope around the cassowary's leg and took the short stick and tried to break the cassowary's head. However, she missed and the cassowary jumped upon her, killing her.

The rope that the old woman had tied to the cassowary was also tied to her leg, so after the old woman died, the cassowary pulled her behind and went to a fruit tree. The fruit tree was full of ripe fruits. Two men had made a cassowary trap underneath it.

The cassowary pulled the old woman and was hungry. The cassowary saw a ripe fruit lying on the ground. When the cassowary gobbled the fruit, it was caught in the trap set by the two men.

Another day, one of the men who had made the trap said that he would go look at the trap to see if it had caught a cassowary. If there was a cassowary in the trap, he would kick the tree and his seedlings would move. He told his friend that if the tree seedlings [moved], they would cook [the cassowary] in an earth oven. After he told his friend this, he departed. When he arrived at the fruit tree and saw the cassowary in the trap, he was ecstatic. However when he wanted to get the cassowary, he also saw the old woman lying dead. He was afraid and wanted to run away. But no, he hit his head on the fruit tree and died.

His friend saw the tree sprouts move when the man hit his head, so he thought of what his friend had said, "If there was a cassowary in the trap, he would kick the base of the tree and his seedlings would move. He quickly climbed up a tree. He bent a big tree branch and fell on top of the fire that he had made to cook the cassowary. The fire burned and killed him.

The fire burned his belly, which exploded and fell onto the grass. A maternal kinsman of this second man saw the fire smoking and going very high. He thought that his maternal kin was cooking a cassowary, so he went to look for the two of them. He went and saw a big fire burning and his maternal kinsman who had fallen onto it. He looked at the grass and saw the man's belly, but he thought that it was the cassowary's belly that the two men had left.

He took the man's belly and ate it. After he ate it, he went to a house. He went inside the house then stood and died. However, before he died completely, he pointed with his axe and then he stood up, dead.

An old couple was hunting for wild game in the forest and they saw the house. They went inside and saw the dead man standing with his axe. They were speechless. They went outside the house and they ran away. They ran and ran into the deep forest. The old man saw a banana plant and told the old woman to sit and wait for him. He told the old woman, "If a man comes, pretend to cough and I'll come down from the banana plant then we'll run away."

After he said this, he went to tie up the bananas. The old woman sat and watched. The old man tied a wrapping around the bananas, and a banana leaf fell down on the old woman's face. The old woman got up and coughed. The old man thought that a man had come, so he jumped down the banana plant and ran away. The old woman thought that the old man was on top of the banana plant. She saw a

man approaching and she also ran away. She ran behind her old husband until they arrived at another house.

When they arrived at the house, it was dark and they slept. The old man turned and saw the old woman. He took a stone and bashed her face, killing her.

The old man could not walk. He sat and sat until he too died. Some days passed, then the bodies of the two old people became soft and fell to pieces. The pieces of flesh from the two old people grew legs, hands, mouths, noses, eyes, tails and later fur. They became many little rodents.

Some of these rodents ran around under the house, into the grasses, onto the trees, and in the forest. Some lived in the house. So now, we have many rodents all over the earth.

William Gand
Kerowagi Catholic Mission
P. O. Box 57
Kerowagi
Simbu Province

A1840. Creation of rodentia; D950+. Magic tree seedling; D1799.10K. Magic power produced by striking, kicking, or stamping foot; E612.13. Reincarnation as rat; G61. Relative's flesh eaten unwittingly; G91.2. Cannibalism causes death; N339+. Man dies after falling into fire; N339.13+. Accidental death by striking head against tree; N340. Hasty killing or condemnation (mistake); P210. Husband and wife; P230. Parents and children; P290+. Maternal kin; P310. Friendship; R220. Flights; R260. Pursuits; S22+. Matricide; S110. Murders; Z49.13+. Chain of deaths

## A Man Lost a Star Woman
(Wantok 47[7], July 16, 1983, page 27)

Long, long ago, there was a man named Sumi Sama. He lived in a village near Kagua in the **Southern Highlands** Province. He was a leader in **Sumi** [Village, **Kewa** People]. However, poor Sama was not married; he was single and a leader. At night, he often slept and heard some group that played sweet music and sang on Mount Sumi.

One day, he went to this mountain and carefully examined the place where the sweet music originated. He searched and searched, then he saw a tree that was very tall, more than 4000 meters, or something like that. The tree was extremely slippery from the base to the crown.

At the base of the tree, he saw a place where they dug the white clay and painted their faces with the clay. This kind of earth is used by the Highlands People to paint their faces for festivals. Sama saw this and said, "Oh, I know now. It's the star women who come down from this tree to get the white clay then go back up again." Later, he made a hole at the base of the tree and pointed his hand at the place where they dug the earth. Then he waited.

Sama waited and waited until darkness arrived. He was very prepared and he looked carefully at how the star women would arrive. Before long, he heard music, singing and laughing arising. All of the star women were coming down the tree, getting the clay, going back up the tree and painting their faces. The very last one was the leader of the star women. She descended and took some clay. After she took it, she turned to go back up the tree. Sama stood up and grabbed her. The woman called loudly for Sama to let her go. Sama told her, "I, Sama, am just standing and holding you. You can't go back now."

The star woman scared Sama. She turned into many things, such as snake, crocodile, wild pig, tree, stone, water, and thorny rattan. However, Sama still held tightly and said, "I'm holding you tightly. You can't go back." They fought like this in the darkness until the morning of the next day. Then the woman told Sama, "You're a good man. Every muscle in my legs and hands are in pain, so let me go now. I'm not a woman of this earth, but I know about you, Sama." Sama replied to her, "I, Sama, am holding you. You will be my wife now."

The star woman told Sama, "That's good, but you must make something for me later if I tell you to." Sama was not worried and took the star woman to live at Sumi Village for a very long time. The star woman also told Sama that if he did not listen to what she said, there would be something bad that would happen to them at some time.

They lived together for three weeks, then Sama heard that there would be a big festival at a village near Sumi. The star woman told Sama that if he went to the festival, he could not sing or dance with the other women. Later, she made a string from vines in the forest and tied it to the *tanget* leaves on Sama's backside. Later, she told Sama, "If this string breaks, then you have done wrong and something bad will happen to us."

Sama listened to his star wife and went to the festival. At the time of the festival, the people called and called, "Look, Sama our leader is coming now." A huge woman saw Sama, then she ran and took Sama's axe. They sang and walked.

They sang and walked. One, two, three, before long, the string on Sama's backside broke. Sama very quickly ran to the house and went to see the star woman. One, two, three, the woman went to a branch of the big tree and made a net bag. Sama called out, "Star woman, please come down." However, the woman climbed higher and higher up the tree.

Sama wanted to get the woman, but the woman went all of the way up and Sama could not get her back anymore. Sama began to make a ladder that went all of the way up the tree, but the star woman jumped on a stone that was very long until she reached the sky. Sama continued making the ladder and he jumped up, following the star woman. However when he wanted to hold the star woman's hand, he fell all of the way down to the hole in the stone. The poor man fell and died in the hole. His bones are still there.

Today, the men of Sumi village have often taken Sama's bones and made magic spells for playing gambling games. All of the bones are gone and only the skull remains.

Now, if you go to Kagua and Sumi, you can see the pandanus tree (*karuka*), the big ditch that they dug to make gardens and the blocks where Sama rests.

If Sama had not done wrong by this star woman, we would get women free. However, Sama ruined it for us men and we have to pay bride price with plenty of money.

Mathew Leme Rake
Nawok Plantation, P. O. Box 60
Kokopo
East New Britain Province

A1555.2. Origin of custom of purchasing wives; D114.3+W. Transformation: woman to sow (wild); D191W. Transformation: woman to serpent (snake); D194W. Transformation: woman to crocodile; D215.11K+W. Transformation: woman to rattan; D215W. Transformation: woman to tree; D231W. Transformation: woman to stone; D283W. Transformation: woman to water; D361.1+. Forest Spirit Bride; D610. Repeated transformation; D1007. Magic bone (human); D1184.2. Magic string; D1407. Magic object helps gambler win; D2120. Magic transportation; F52. Ladder to upper world; E761.3. Life token: tree (flower) fades; E761.7+. Life token: string slackens; F54.1. Tree stretches to sky; F215. Fairies live in star-world; P210. Husband and wife; Q243.2. Seduction punished; Q325. Disobedience punished; Q411. Death as punishment; R4. Surprise capture; R213. Escape from home; R260. Pursuits; T52. Bride purchased; T111. Marriage of mortal and supernatural being; T192. Marriage by force; W126. Disobedience

## The Father Got Rid of His Son
(Wantok 478, July 23, 1983, page 27)

Long ago, there was a married couple who lived in their village. The man's name was Donita and his wife's name was Kilikafo. They had five children; just one was boy and the others were girls.

One day, their parents made an earth oven. The father cut five pieces of bamboo, one for each of the children to fetch water. However, the father broke one of them at the base. He gave the good ones to the girls and the broken one to the little boy who was named Ketulo.

The children took the bamboos and went very far away to a stream to fetch water. The girls' bamboos were fine and they filled them quickly with water then carried them back to the village. Poor Ketulo tried to fill his bamboo but it never filled.

He worked at this for a very long time. At that time, his parents removed the food from the earth oven and they walked to another place that was far away.

Later, Ketulo saw that the bamboo had a hole in the base. He thought hard about how he could bring water to the house. He was terrified that his father would beat him. He was terrified but he still went to the house. When he arrived at the house, he found that his parents and sisters were not there. He looked where the earth oven was, saw some food and ate it. Later, he looked at where they slept. He opened the door of the bedroom, but they were not there. Oh my, when he saw that, he cried and cried.

The little boy kept looking and looking for them. He followed their footprints on the trail. He followed and followed them and went very far.

### Tricking the Child

The group walked on a long trail and became hungry, so they made a fire and cooked some sweet potatoes. They ate the sweet potatoes, left some on the trail and departed. Ketulo arrived later. He was also famished. He saw the place where they had made the fire and the pieces of food that they left on the trail. He took some pieces of food and ate them.

His parents and sisters walked and walked and arrived at a rope bridge that went across a river. After they hopped off the bridge, they cut the bridge ropes down. They hit the trail again and arrived at a big bridge. The poor little boy Ketulo arrived at the river. When he saw them going to the big bridge, he called out to them. He told his father that he had walked alone and had come to find them.

His father told him, "That's OK. We'll leave you there, but you can still find the way to get to us. Then you can come with us." His father threw a rope to him on the other side of the big river. When Ketulo caught the rope to get to the other side, his father cut it. The water carried him away. Before he went far, he arrived at the side of the river where his father had stood.

### The Father Thought His Son Was Dead

His father thought that the water had carried him far away to the place in the forest where they had made their house. The little boy arrived on the other side and he followed them, but he became confused in that part of the forest, so he climbed a big tree. He looked down and saw a fire and smoke. He went down the tree and went to get a good look at the fire. However he saw Lokulokuia, a crocodile, making the fire and sitting there.

The crocodile asked him what he was looking for. Ketulo said that he was looking for his parents. The crocodile told him that some enemies had killed her parents and sisters. Ketulo cried terribly and stayed with Lokulokuia.

Lokulokuia took care of him until he became a big man. One time, Lokulokuia heard that there would be a big festival at a nearby village. So, Lokulokuia told Ketulo that whoever was her child must go to the big festival and then return and tell about it.

### Wanting to Have Sex with a Woman

Lokuklokuia [Lokulokuia] adorned Ketulo very nicely and he went to the festival. He sang and danced, then a beautiful woman who had come to the festival found him. They held hands and sang and danced. They sang and danced fervently until it was almost dark. Then the woman left him and went to her house. The boy continued to sing and dance. His parents, who did not know that he was at this festival, arrived.

One of Ketulo's sisters also went to the festival and she saw him singing and dancing. She said, "Aia, look at that boy over there. He looks like my true brother." She was very troubled, so she cried and told her mother that she had seen a boy who looked like her brother.

Ketulo finished singing and dancing then went to the house and told his mother, Lokulokuia, that he nearly had sex with a woman. Lokulokuia died laughing at Ketulo. They continued to stay there for about six months. Later, the two of them again heard a message that there would be a big festival at the village that they had gone to before. Lokulokuia told Ketulo, "Now, if you go to this other festival, you must give it to whichever woman comes to sing and dance with you."

Ketulo listened to his mother and was ecstatic. He put on his finest adornments and went to the festival. He sang and danced while Lokulokuia changed her skin and became a very beautiful woman. She put on fine adornments and went to see Ketulo jumping at the festival.

### Fervently Singing and Dancing

Lokulokuia jumped and held Ketulo's hand then they sang and danced. They danced heatedly and Ketulo felt a need to defecate, so he told the woman (Lokulokuia), "Stay here. I'm going to take a dump first." He tricked the woman, went into the house and saw that her husband was not there. He opened the door, went inside and saw Lokulokuia's skin lying on the floor. He thought that the woman with whom he was dancing was just Lokulokuia. So, he took Lokulokuia's skin and burned it in a fire.

Later, he went back to the festival. He was furious at Lokulokuia, so he did not dance with her. He sang and danced with another woman. Lokulokuia saw this and thought hard. She went to the house and saw that her skin was no longer there. She just stood there and thought hard. She thought, "Ketulo found out my trick. When he comes back from the festival will we marry or not?"

Ketulo was singing and dancing. His parents and sister came to see him, and they tried to call his name. They called out, "Ketulo, that's you, huh?" Ketulo heard his name. He turned and looked at them then thought, "Who's that calling my name?" Later, he recognized them and they held him and cried with him. But later, Ketulo told his father, "Before, you just left me there. Then you left and I followed you to the big river, and you were not sorry for me. When I held onto the rope, you cut it and I fell down into the water. The water took me down into the deep forest. I cried, then went and found Lokulokuia. She took care of me and we lived together."

After he told them this, he took them to his house with Lokulokuia, and they found the woman (Lokulokuia) sitting there. He told his parents and sisters, "Look at this woman. She's my mother and she took care of me until I became a big man." Lokulokuia rose and told him, "I'm not your mother. I'm your wife."

Ketulo replied to her, "You're my mother, so how can we marry?" However, the woman was very insistent that they would marry. So, they married and made a house for themselves with the parents and Ketulo's sisters at Lokulokuia's home.

Simon Kefo
Vudai Agriculture College
P. O. Kerevat [Keravat], via Rabaul
East New Britain Province

B211.6.4K. Speaking crocodile; B535.0.14+. Crocodile as nurse for child; B656.3K+. Marriage to crocodile in human form; D397+W. Transformation: crocodile to woman; D531+. Transformation by removing skin; D793.2. Disenchantment made permanent by burning cast-off skin; H1023.2.4. Task: filling a bottomless water tube; K963. Rope cut and victim dropped; P210. Husband and wife; P231. Mother and son; P232. Mother and daughter; P233. Father and son; P234. Father and daughter; P253+. Four sisters and one brother; P261. Father-in-law; P262. Mother-in-law; P264. Sister-in-law; P272. Foster mother; P275. Foster son; R260. Pursuits; P265+. Daughter-in-law; S11.3.6. Father throws boy into river (sea); S142. Person thrown into the water and abandoned; S301. Children abandoned (exposed); T100. Marriage; T412+. Foster mother-son incest

## The *Masalai* Eagle

(Wantok 479, July 30, 1983, page 26)

Long ago, in the time of the ancestors, the people of **Ambunti** Village, in **East Sepik** Province were often afraid of a *masalai* eagle [**Manambu** People]. This eagle lived on the other side of a lake, near the village. It often ate men.

At this time, only the women worked hard in the village. At this place too, there were two sisters. They often worked in a garden on the other side of the lake.

One time, the two of them went to work in the garden. When they finished, they gathered some wild sugarcane (*pitpit*) leaves. When the big sister wanted to throw away some of them, she missed and the leaves cut her finger. She took a breadfruit leaf and let the blood run down into it. When the blood dried, they left and went to the village.

They decided that they would return to the garden in the next month. They forgot the garden, went to the lake, caught fish and returned to the house.

After a month, the big sister told the little sister that the next morning, they would go to the garden. They slept that night and in the morning, they woke up and paddled their canoe to the garden. When they arrived, oh my, were they surprised. The food plants were gone. The big sister told her little sister, "Sis, I'll hide in the garden. Go to the village and get an axe, then come back and we'll kill whatever finished off our food."

The big sister hid and waited to see something come to eat the garden food. She waited and waited for a very long time. Then she saw two small boys race by and try take some ripe bananas. But they missed and fell into a hole. This was a hole that the two sisters had dug at the base of the banana plant.

When the big sister saw this, she gnashed her teeth and went to see her sister. When she met her sister, they were very happy and danced. After they danced, they went to the hole to find the two boys. When they first arrived there, the big sister told the little sister that she would look after the big boy and the little sister would look after the little boy. They went and held them. The big sister told the little sister to make "grass" skirts for them.

One day, the *masalai* eagle went to another place and looked for men to eat. The sisters kept a careful eye on the two boys, lest the eagle eat them.

One time, the sisters asked the two boys where they had come from. The big boy listened, but he did not know how to reply, so he just made a sign in answer to the sisters.

The sisters took the two boys, went to the village and hid them in traditional mosquito netting. The boys stayed there until they grew up. They asked their two mothers, "Why are there no men in this village?" Their mothers told them that a huge *masalai* eagle often ate men. So, the brothers told their mothers to cut two wild betel nut palm trees so that they could make bows and arrows.

The mothers took the wild betel palms and brought them. The brothers made their bows at night. There was a very bright moon and they worked until they completed their two bows. Later, they told their mothers to cook some sago for them.

In the very early morning, before the first cock crowed, they took the canoe and paddled away. When they went ashore under a tree, dawn broke. It was very lucky that the bird had not seen them. The bird had flown to another place and eaten men.

Very quickly, they cut a very big and long piece of bamboo. The big brother took the bamboo and carried it with a rope up the tree. Then he sent the rope down to the ground and told his little brother, "When you see the *masalai* eagle come, you must pull this rope. I'll tie the rope to my hands and be hung up." So, he took the spear and lay on the bamboo at the *masalai* eagle's aerie. He also told his brother, "If I kill the eagle and throw it down, you should cut its neck and put its head in the canoe then we'll go back home."

The little brother watched beneath the tree. They waited and waited for a very long time. It was nearly evening, then the little brother looked up and saw the *masalai* eagle flying down. When the eagle was about to perch on its aerie, the little brother immediately pulled the rope. The big brother, who was lying on the bamboo, felt his hands shake.

He took his big and good arrow, and put it in the bow. When he drew the bow back, all of the bones and muscles in his body were taut. When he let go of the arrow, it shot out and pierced the *masalai* eagle in its neck. The eagle cried out terribly and fell down to the ground, shaking the ground. The little brother quickly cut its neck and put it in the canoe. Later, his brother descended and they sped back home in the canoe.

They arrived home, and their mothers were ecstatic. Their mothers hit the signal drum on the next morning and the women of the village gathered. The two mothers told all of the women that the two boys had taken out the *masa-lai* eagle. The big sister also told all of the young women to marry the two brothers. So, they married and raised boys and girls. They grew to be men and women and married, then raised more people, et cetera, et cetera.

Kerry Wangi

Malala High School

P. O. Box Alexishafen

Madang Province

[Note: the origin of the two brothers is not explicitly stated in this story, but see the stories in *Wantok* #422 and 466 for a similar conception-from-blood motif.]

A515.1.1. Twin culture heroes; B16.3. Devastating birds; B33. Man-eating birds; B872.1. Giant eagle; F401.3.7+. Spirit in form of an eagle; F490+. Masalai; G510.4. Hero overcomes devastating animal; P210. Husband and wife; L31. Youngest brother helps elder; P230. Parents and children; P231. Mother and son; P251.5. Two brothers; P252.1. Two sisters; P294. Aunt; P297. Nephew; T100. Marriage; T145.0.1. Polygyny; T534. Conception from blood; T587. Birth of twins; T685. Twins; Z210. Brothers as heroes

## A [Man] Tricked a Pomio Ancestral Ghost
(Wantok 480, August 6, 1983, page 27)

Long ago, in the time of the ancestors, the people of **Pomio** [Village] often heated sea water in tree bark to make salt for putting on leafy vegetables and other foods [**Mengen** People, **East New Britain** Province]. The men liked this salt.

One time, a leader from a village called Mile [**Mili**] wanted to make some salt to carry back to his village. He left Mile when it was still the middle of the night then walked and walked. He walked and walked until it was evening then he finally arrived at Pomio. His poor legs were completely cramped from the trail, so he went right to sleep. While he slept, he did not make a sound. It was as if he was dead. This was because the trail was very long and had mountains and valleys too. He slept well until the early morning then he awoke.

The sun had not yet risen high when he took the things for heating seawater and he left. When he arrived at the place for heating seawater, he put the things down and went to look for firewood. He piled the firewood up then he took the little sticks and made a platform for laying the tree bark. After the platform was finished, he put the tree bark on top of it. He poured the sea water into a coconut shell and spilled the water on the tree bark until it was completely filled. Then he made a big fire underneath the platform.

After that, he spilled water on some leaves. Then he put the bark back and filled it with more seawater. He did this until it was completely covered with salt.

The leader knew that the sun was setting, so he poured the salt into a bark [container] and went back to Pomio Village.

He slept there and in the very early morning, he went to his home at Mile. While he was walking there, he saw two cockatoos fighting in the trail. He ran quickly and grabbed the birds so that they would not escape. However, he only grabbed them by the feathers and they escaped. He put his bark container on the side of the trail and followed the two birds. However, the birds flew very high, so he returned.

While he was following the cockatoos, an ancestral ghost came. The ghost saw the package of salt and thought, "What is it that this man has covered up?" The ghost opened it and saw the salt. The ghost tried it. "Oh my, this is delicious," said the ghost. The ghost ate the salt until it was all gone. Then the ghost went inside the bark container and slept.

Before long, the ghost wanted to see if the man was coming. The leader took the cockatoo feathers and put them on his head, like a headdress. The poor man did not know that the ghost was there. He took the bark container and carried it. He did not know that he was carrying the ancestral ghost that had eaten his salt. The ghost's belly was swollen terribly and was near the breaking point.

The man passed three miles and he felt the bark container become terribly heavy. He said, "Oh my, the salt that I've carried from Pomio up here wasn't heavy, but now what?" He said, "I think I'll open it and see." Oh my, the ghost heard this and pretended to close its eyes. The man looked and knew it was the ancestral ghost. He said, "I'm going to shit first." The ghost felt the man put the container down and saw the man defecating. After the man defecated, he took the feathers from his hair and stood them in his feces. He did not return. No, he cut another trail and began to run. He did not fool around, he ran fast.

The ghost saw the feathers still standing in the feces and thought that the man was still there, but he was not. The ghost waited until the evening and said, "Oh my, that's a long time to take a shit, and he hasn't returned yet."

The ghost thought about eating the man. The ghost went to look for the man but only found the feces. The man was gone. The ghost looked around and did not see him. Then the ghost smelled his trail and sped away. The man had almost arrived at the village.

It was night, but the man was still running. He heard something behind him. He heard the ghost shouting, "Men, shut your doors." The man also shouted, "You, open your doors." However, the ghost was stronger than those who closed their doors were. The men heard the man's voice and they opened their doors. The man ran directly inside the house. Oh my, the ghost sped and just scratched the man's backside. The ghost was furious and said, "Man, you're a braggart. You tricked me. If you hadn't, you'd have been finished and I'd have put your bones on the trail."

Benson Gope

Vuvu, Box 67

Rabaul

East New Britain Province

E261.4. Ghost pursues man; E541. Revenants eat; E542. Dead man touches living; E568. Revenant lies down and sleeps; G11.10. Cannibalistic spirits; K525+. Escape by substituting feathers and excrement; K551.16+. Man escapes by ruse: must go to defecate; R210. Escapes; R260. Pursuits

## A Woman Gave Birth to an Eaglet
(Wantok 481, August 13, 1983, page 26)

Long ago, in a village in the Salamaua area in **Morobe** Province, there was a young and very beautiful woman. Men lusted for her all of the time.

At this village, there was also a *masalai* stone axe that was hung in the men's house. This men's house was completely forbidden for women and for ordinary men to enter.

One day, the young woman's parents went to work in the garden while she stayed alone in their house. After a while, the *masalai* axe turned into a man and deceived the young woman. He said, "Hey, granddaughter, come steer the canoe and we'll go spearfishing by the drifting log."

This log was not a small thing. It was huge. A flood had carried it down the Markham River to the shore. The sea had carried it to Salamaua Peninsula. Fish were often underneath this tree. The woman listened to the old man and they went to go spearfishing. Oh my, they did not fool around, they speared many fish by this drifting tree.

They were still there and the old *masalai* man told the young woman, "Granddaughter, I'll wait for you in the canoe. Go on top of the drifting tree and grab those crabs. I'll go back there and spear some more fish, then I'll come back to look for you."

The poor young woman grabbed the crabs. The *masalai* man had lied to her and sped off to the village, leaving her there. The old man quickly left the canoe with the fish inside it, went to the men's house, and turned back into the stone axe that was hanging up there.

In the afternoon, the young woman's parents returned from the garden and did not see her. They began to look for her. They called and called, but there was no answer back from the young woman. They went and looked at the place for fetching water, but she was not there. They asked the other people in their family, but they too did not know.

The married couple said to themselves, "Daughter is having her time of the month, and we have put forth a big taboo. However, she broke this taboo and walked around. The bad *masalai* has taken her out."

The poor young girl sat, waiting and waiting. She ate the crabs on the drifting log. She stayed there for some time and gave birth to an egg. She thought hard, "Should I throw away this egg or should I hold onto it, then let go of it if I find help?"

She looked after the egg. Later it hatched and an eaglet came out. The mother taught the eaglet the local language and the eaglet learned it as well as a real man.

The mother said, "Go to our village and look at the garden. Bring back a banana." The son listened to this and thought. When the eagle grew up and was strong, he also carried net bags of taro and followed the orders that his mother gave him. He brought a net bag of firewood and fire.

His mother was happy because the eagle often caught many fish too. They of them did not lack anything. One time, the mother asked her eagle son, "Son, can you carry me so that we can go to the village or not?" Her son replied, "Mama, I can carry you." So, she tested her son. She told the eagle to carry a heavy stone to her that weighed as much as she did. She said, "Carry it here and then I'll see if you can carry me."

The bad boy flew up and went to Lutu Peninsula then brought a huge stone back to their drifting tree home. Oh my, the tree almost sank in the sea. His mother was afraid and called out. The bad boy lifted it again and brought it back to a spot on Lutu Peninsula. This stone is still there. We call it *Hoc Songgahi Keng*. In the Bukawa [**Bukawac**] Language, this means, "The Stone that the Eagle Brought."

When the eagle returned to the drifting log, his mother was ready. She tied together two net bags and went inside them. The eagle put only two claws on them and carried his mother up like a helicopter hooks forty-four gallon gasoline drums. He swung off like nothing else. The mother was terrified that she would fall and die, but her son told her, "It's not as heavy as the stone that I first carried."

The eagle carried his mother to the village and the mother told him, "Son, don't put me down quickly when I tell you to do so. When I see your grandparents' house, I'll tell you. Then go straight down and leave me." The son followed his mother's orders.

When they came right to the woman's parents, the mother told her son and they went down slowly. He left his mother there at the house. The mother told her son, "Go up and perch on a big tree then I'll first tell the whole story to your grandparents."

The son went and perched and waited. The woman took fragrant flowers from around the house and crushed them. The smell wafted up above the house. Her [father] went outside to check on this and he was shocked to see his daughter standing there. Oh my, he could not believe that it was his daughter, so he called out to her mother to come down from the house. They talked and talked until she told them the whole story. Later, she told them, "If you want to see my son, then I'll call him here."

The woman called for her son to come down and the two grandparents looked at him. The grandparents cried. They were ecstatic and called out. All of the people came to see the two of them and were very happy.

The woman's son told everyone, "If you want to make a party for me and my mother, that's alright. You can go and just gather the [non-meat] food. I'll take care of finding the meat." The people of the village did not believe him, so he told them, "OK, you stay here and watch me first." He shot straight off, then a huge tuna [*Gymnosarda unicolor* (Allen & Swainston, 1992: 48-49)] jumped up and back down towards the sea. However, the eagle-son hooked it and brought it back like a helicopter carries a piece of lumber.

Everyone saw this and was speechless. The bad boy brought the fish and threw it down right before their eyes and they were elated.

Later, the leader of the village marked the day of the party. The eagle-son heard this and caught fish for one week prior, fish such as tuna, barracuda [*Sphyraena* spp. (Allen & Swainston, 1992: 48-49)], and turtles which filled the village. The village smelled awful from all of the seafood and from game from the forest too. The meat from the forest was from animals such as birds, wild pigs, birds of paradise, bandicoots, and many others.

They made a huge, happy party then put the rubbish in the men's house where the *masalai* axe resided. A fire burned the stone axe. When the axe burned, the *masalai* man came out, went up to the top of the house and told everyone, "I'm completely wrong. Now I'm finished by the fire." Now if you come to this peninsula, you'll find some new eagles living in this area.

Gideion Apeng

P. O. Box 1801

Lae

Morobe Province

A977.5. Origin of particular rock; B211.3.11K. Speaking eagle; B541.3. Bird rescues man from sea; B542.1.1. Eagle carries man to safety; B552. Man carried by bird; C141. Tabu: going forth during menses; C181+. Women may not enter men's house; C182. Uninitiated men may not enter men's house; D250+M. Transformation: man to axe; D434+M. Transformation: axe to man; F405.12+. Spirit killed by fire; F490+. Masalai; F495+. Stone-axe spirit; H1562.2.2+. Before undertaking rescue, eagle tests strength by lifting stone; K1616. Marooned man reaches home and outwits marooner; P210. Husband and wife; P231. Mother and son; P232. Mother and daughter; P234. Father and daughter; P291. Grandfather; P292. Grandmother; Q414. Punishment: burning alive; Q467K. Marooning at sea as punishment; R130. Rescue of abandoned or lost persons; S141.3+. Abandonment on log floating in sea; T554.10+. Woman gives birth to an eagle; T565. Woman lays an egg

## Hapleng Became a Leader

(Wantok 482, August 20, 1983, page 27)

Long ago, there was a trickster who lived in a village. His name was Hapleng. He befriended a very sweet and beautiful woman whom he thought of marrying.

However this woman did not want to marry him, so he thought very hard about what he could do to marry this woman. One day, he told himself, "Never mind, I'll try again."

In the very early morning, he woke up and went to the forest. He killed a marsupial (*kapul*), took out the guts and threw the body away. Then he went back to the village. At night, he carried the marsupial guts to his girlfriend. He hid them carefully so that the woman did not see them. Then the two of them *karim lek*ed. Late at night, the woman was dead asleep. Hapleng got up and rubbed the marsupial's guts on his face. He lay so that his face was close to her buttocks and her face was very close to his.

They lay like that until morning. When the woman's mother awoke and saw the man lying close to her daughter's buttocks, she said to him, "Hey, [future] in-law, why are you sleeping awkwardly near her butt?" Hapleng woke up and said, "Ugh, [future] in-law, bring some fire here and look carefully. I smell something like shit nearby." The old woman lit a torch to look at the man. Hapleng's face was full of feces. The two of them looked at the woman's "grass" skirt. Oh no, it was full of feces too. The old woman was speechless; she was mortified.

So she told her daughter, "You shat on the man's face, so you must marry him now." When Hapleng heard this, he

was very happy. He took the woman and they went to his village, then they married.

They lived there for a while and the woman gave birth to a baby boy. One day, the woman went to the garden and the man took care of the baby at the house. In the afternoon, the mother approached the house and the baby was crying. Hapleng was angry and told the baby, "Your mother rubbed marsupial shit on my face and I married her. She gave birth to you, why are you crying?" The baby's mother was nearby and she heard her husband say this. She said, "Ai! What are you saying to baby? You tricked my mother and you married me, huh?" Come and get me. I'll go live at my village. Come and get me."

Another day, the woman took her baby and went to her parents' home. She lived there for some time and married another man from the village.

One day, they held a huge festival at the woman's new husband's village. The trickster or loser, Hapleng, also went to see this festival. He looked and saw that the woman that he had married was working at the festival. After he saw this, he went and waited for her. When it was time for the earth ovens, Hapleng quickly hid and dressed like the woman's new husband.

Later, he came and stood near the door of the house where his [ex-]wife lived. He told her, "Give me the baby while you quickly cook the food." The woman did not look at him carefully and she gave the baby to him. Hapleng took the baby away and killed him. [The woman finished] covering the earth oven and went out and saw that her husband was not there. She thought that he had taken the baby to the dancing ground.

She went behind and asked her husband for the baby. Her husband said, "Whom did you give the baby to?" The woman said, "I prepared the earth oven and you took the baby. Where did you put the baby?" Her husband told her, "I didn't go to the house. I just stayed here until now. Whom did you give the baby to? Whom did you talk to?" However, the woman was insistent and the two of them fought. Some men told them, "During the day, we saw Hapleng come here. He's a terrible trickster. He probably took your baby and left." Then they went and searched, and the married couple uncovered the earth oven. They looked in the oven. Oh my, the baby was bloated and burned awfully.

Later, all of the men of the village took their bows and arrows, and followed this rogue. Hapleng had tricked them and he carried only an axe, but they did not know this.

Near seven o'clock at night, he went up a tree. The men came and surrounded the base of the tree. The woman's husband told the group that Hapleng had killed the baby, so he would go up the tree and shoot him. Hapleng went very far up to the crown of the tree and prepared to strike the man.

However, it was somewhat dark now and the man did not see Hapleng, so Hapleng took his spear [axe?] and struck the man right in his neck. The bamboo spear broke, and he fell down and died.

Haplang [Hapleng] told the man's kin not to cut [the tree], so they waited. He went and stood far away then asked them, "You're going to kill Hapleng or whom? Watch out that you don't kill one of your own kin. I, Hapleng have come."

The group of men listened to Hapleng, so they lit torches and looked carefully at their faces to see if they were relatives or not. They saw their kinsman lying dead. They carried him back to their village and Hapleng walked back to his village. Later, he became a big leader in his village and married another woman.

This story comes from **Bupkila** Village, Apa Kimi, **Western Highlands** [Province, **Wahgi** People].

Tonny Dilu

Watta Plantation

Rabaul

East New Britain Province

[Tonny Dilu wrote the ancestor story in *Wantok* #580. This story is similar.]

J1110. Clever persons; K914.3. Slaying under cover of darkness; K1810. Deception by disguise; K1350. Woman persuaded (or wooed) by trick; K1910. Marital impostors; K2150+. Sleeping girlfriend made to appear to have shat on boyfriend to force marriage; L160. Success of the unpromising hero (heroine); P210. Husband and wife; P231. Mother and son; P232. Mother and daughter; P233. Father and son; P262. Mother-in-law; P265. Son-in-law; P600+. Courtship customs: *karim lek*; Q411.3. Death of father (son, etc.) as punishment; R210. Escapes; R213. Escape from home; R260. Pursuits; R311. Tree refuge; S11.3.3. Father kills son; S139.2.2+. Corpse put into cooking pot or cooked; S139.4. Murder by mangling with axe; T50. Wooing; T100. Marriage; T580. Childbirth; X716.1H+. Befouling with excrement

## Two Beautiful Women Came Out of a Green Coconut

(Wantok 483, August 27, 1983, page 26)

Long, long ago, there were two brothers who lived in a village called Sibu [**Sipuru**] near Kista [Kieta] in **North Solomons** Province [**Nasioi** People]. Their names were Kopeu and Taingu. Kopeu was grown and Taingu was his elder.

They lived together for a very long time, but they did not know how they had grown because their parents had died when they were still young.

They lived there, and did not have food in their house. They were famished, and one morning, Taingu left the village and went to the beach. He pulled his canoe to the sea then he paddled out to sea. He paddled and paddled then he saw an island. In the afternoon, he arrived at the island.

He stood on the beach and saw a little house. At this time, Taingu was famished. He stood and saw an old woman walking out of the house. The old woman saw Taingu and said, "Good afternoon." Taingu replied to the old woman's greeting.

The old woman's skin was completely filled with sores. Every spot on her body had a sore. Also, her nose was full of mucus.

The old woman wanted to walk back and she called out for Taingu to go inside her house. Later, she gave food to Taingu that she had mixed with her mucus and pus. Taingu was wrecked from hunger, so he just ate the food until the hunger was completely gone.

That night, they slept in the old woman's house until the next day. In the morning, the old woman told Taingu to climb a coconut palm tree. She also told him not to throw the coconuts on the ground when he picked them. Taingu listened to the old woman, climbed the coconut tree and fetched two green coconuts. Then he descended and put the two coconuts inside his canoe. He said good-bye to the old woman and began to paddle back to his village.

When Taingu was in the middle of the sea, the sun made him very hot. He was in great need of cold water, but he had forgotten his two coconuts. Later, he remembered that the coconuts were in the canoe and he was very happy. He told himself, "Oh am I lucky. I thought that I'd be without water, but the old woman knew and gave me two coconuts."

He took a green coconut and broke it open. Oh my, he was shocked to see a young and beautiful woman approach him. He took the other coconut and broke it open. Another young woman arose. Oh my, Taingi [Taingu] was ecstatic.

In the afternoon, Taingu and his two wives went to his village. At the village, his brother saw his two wives and asked, "Hey Taingu, where did you get these two women? Can you give me one of them?" However Taingu replied, "I can't give you one of them. They're both mine." So, Kopeu then began to ask Taingu how he had gotten the women.

After Taingu told him, he went down to the beach and pulled his canoe to the sea. He began to paddle towards the island that Taingu had told him about. He paddled and paddled. When he went ashore on the island, he looked about and just saw the house. Later, he also saw the old woman. He asked the old woman, "Hey, are you the only one who lives on this island?" The old woman said, "Yes", and later called for him to go inside her house to eat.

However Kopeu told her, "Why are you calling out to me? I'm famished. If the food's bad, I'll clobber you."

The old woman brought the food and gave it to Kopeu. This food was full of pus and mucus from the old woman. So when Kopeu saw this, he shouted, "Hey, what are you, a woman or a ghost? I'm not your pig or dog. Why did you give me this slop." At night, Kopeu slept hungry. In the morning, the old woman told him to take two green coconuts. However Kopeu replied to her, "Never mind the green coconuts, I'll take ripe coconuts and make a soup at the village." The old woman was insistent that Kopeu take the green coconuts, but Kopeu ignored her and said, "Ha, shut up. I know what I'm doing."

Kopeu brought down ripe coconuts and put them in his canoe. Then he sped back towards his village. He paddled his canoe across the deep sea. After a while, it became very hot because the sun was very bright. Kopeu took a ripe coconut and broke it open. He saw the old woman that he had left on the island appear before him.

He took the other coconut and broke it open. Another old woman appeared. Kopeu had two old women, so he was furious and killed them both. Later, he threw their bodies into the sea.

He arrived at the village in the afternoon. Taingu and his two wives were still in the garden. Quickly, he shoved a spear underneath Taingu's bed. Near dark, Taingu and his two wives arrived at the village.

When they arrived, Taingu told his two wives, "You two cook, I'm completely exhausted. My bones ache from work. I'll go straighten my back first on the bed. When the food is ready, you must wake me." Taingu wanted to sleep on the bed, but no, the spear underneath the bed shot him right in the middle and he died.

The food was ready and the two women tried to wake him, but they later found that he had died. They began to cry. While they were crying, Kopeu came and told them, "Don't cry too much. I'm here and I'll marry you." However the women told him, "If you want to marry us, then make a bonfire and put our husband in it quickly."

Kopeu made the fire and put Taingu's body on top of it. The women cried and cried, then they jumped onto the fire and the fire burned them with their husband. Kopeu saw this and he too jumped into the fire and died.

Ronson Ameau
Okoranang Village
P. O. Box 227
Panguna
North Solomons Province

D431.11+W. Transformation: coconut to woman; K910+. Bed turned into death trap; M451.1. Death by suicide; N343.4. Lover commits suicide on finding beloved dead; P16.4.1. Suttee; P210. Husband and wife; P214.1. Wife commits suicide (dies) on death of husband; P251.4. Brothers scorn brother's wise counsel; P251.5. Two brothers; P263. Brother-in-law; P264. Sister-in-law; Q325. Disobedience punished; Q411. Death as punishment; S73.1.4. Fratricide motivated by love-jealousy; S110. Murders; S112. Burning to death; T92.10. Rival in love killed; T145.0.1. Polygyny; V61.2. Dead burned on pyre; W31. Obedience; W126. Disobedience; W181. Jealousy

## Dumbu Grabbed a Ghost Boy
(Wantok 484, September 3, 1983, page 23)

One night, the moon was bright and it shined as brightly as the sun. An old man named Dumbu walked in the moonlight and went towards another village called **Asip**, just near Salamaua [**Morobe** Province, **Kela** People].

He walked and walked and he heard something crash on top of a banana leaf. He thought that it was a man who made the noise and who was trying to kill him. Dumbu was holding a *limbum* [spear] and an axe made of [stone]. He said to himself, "If this man really wants to kill me, I'll nail him first with this spear and then I'll get him with the axe."

He moved quietly and approached the banana plant where the noise came from. He stood and carefully watched the top of the banana plant. He saw the head of a boy who was taking bananas and eating them. Dumbu thought hard, "Is that a real boy or a marsupial (*kapul*)?" He watched from the base of the banana plant because he wanted to see what it really was.

Poor Dumbu waited and waited, then a ghost came before him. However, he was not afraid and did not run away. He held his spear and kept staring at this place.

At dawn, he saw the ghost boy quietly crying. He got up and cut the banana plant down then the ghost boy fell on the ground. Dumbu quickly fell on top of the ghost. Oh my, the ghost boy got up and put his long finger [nails] into Dumbu's skin, and blood flowed.

Dumbu was furious. He told the ghost boy, "I want to take you and go to the house. Why are you so stubborn?" When the ghost heard this, he kicked old Dumbu's leg. He ran underneath his groin then struck his testicles and penis. He also broke off his loincloth.

Later, Dumbu told the good ghost boy that he wanted to take him to the house and not to be too stubborn. He tied his hands and legs with rattan. Then he cut the ghost boy's long finger and toe [nails], and he went to his village.

When they arrived at the village, all of the men, women and children gathered to see the ghost boy.

Dumbu asked his wife, "Mother, what do you think? Should we take care of this boy or not?" His wife replied to him, "If you bring him here, then you can take care of him." Oh my, was Dumbu angry now. He killed the ghost boy. All of the men, women and children came and scolded Dumbu, "Why did you kill the ghost boy?"

He told them that his wife did not want to take care of the ghost boy, so he had killed him. He also told them that his wife said that she thought he had married a woman from **Salamaua**, that this woman had given birth, and that Dumbu had brought her child. "So I'm furious."

Dumbu told the people that he had killed his boy and that he would cook and eat it. Later, he made a bonfire and cooked and ate the boy. After he finished eating, he told the people of his village, that the penis and testicles of the boy had thorns like the marsupial on the 5¢ coin of Australia [echidna]. Bumdu [Dumbu] also told the people that he ate the other parts of the boy's body first and left the penis and testicles for the very last. So he closed his eyes and said, "This is something for the very end."

Michael Mawi

Department of Forests

Box 87

Bulolo

Morobe Province

E422.1.8+. Revenant with long nails; E425.3. Revenant as child; E446. Ghost killed and thus finally laid; E461. Fight of revenant with living person; E542.1. Ghostly fingers leave mark on person's body; F515.2.2. Person with very long fingernails; F547.3.3+. Thorny penis; F547.7+. Thorny testicles; G72+. Parent eats would-be foster child; P210. Husband and wife; P271. Foster father; P275. Foster son; R4. Surprise capture; R10.3. Children abducted; S110. Murders; W167. Stubbornness; W181. Jealousy; X712.3.1H. Injury to testicles

## The Song and Dance of the Stars

(Wantok 485, September 10, 1983, page 23)

Long ago, on **Ali** Island, there lived two men who were very good friends [**Ali** People, **West Sepik** Province]. One day, they wanted to go spearfishing with torches at sea. In the afternoon, they met and talked about spearfishing at night.

While they were talking, a bad *masalai* was near the wild pandanus tree (*karuka*) and overheard them. At night, when the two friends were still asleep, the *masalai* came and called one of the men, then the two of them pulled down the canoe and went spearfishing. The *masalai* paddled from behind and the man was in the front. They worked at spearfishing.

The man thought that the one behind him was really his friend as they were spearing fish. They did this for a while and they arrived at the big village. The man wanted to check the fish inside the canoe, but there was not a single fish inside the canoe. So, he knew that this was not his friend. The one in the back was just a *masalai* who had eaten all of the fish.

The man thought and thought and then lied to the *masalai*, "Brother, stay here and wait for me. I'll swim ashore and look for a *limbum* [bucket] for us to put the fish in. The *masalai* waited and the man swam ashore. When he came ashore, he told the crabs on the beach, "If you hear a man calling out, tell him, '*Rual eang rawar sieng*,'" meaning the *limbum* is too hard.

Then the man ran and ran, then he saw two sister star-women. He was completely out of breath and he told them about the bad *masalai*.

The sisters quickly went up, sent a rope down and pulled the man up. The *masalai* waited and waited, becoming irate. Then the *masalai* went to follow the man. The *masalai* ran and ran, and he saw them pulling the man. He asked to be pulled too. So, the sisters took another rope, one that was bad, and sent it down to pull the *masalai*.

They pulled and pulled, then the rope broke. The poor *masalai* fell down to the ground and was finished. Before long, the ants just came and took the pieces of its flesh, fixing the *masalai* up again. Quickly, the *masalai* got up and killed the ants. Then the *masalai* said, "*Am arew esei esei ew keto ke ke*?" ("Whom should I kill? I'm here.") Then the *masalai* fled ran away.

At the man's village, his kin became worried and thought that he was dead. But no, the man was living with the star-sisters at their home. One day, the man was working in the garden and he heard the clouds thunder. It thundered and he cried. When he cried, one of the star-women saw this and went to tell the two sisters about him.

One afternoon, the two sisters called out for all of the star people to come and talk, and to bring this brother of theirs. Another day, all of the star people came with yams, taros, bananas and other things. At night, they would bring the man.

When it was almost the right time, they all gathered and called for the whirlwind to come. They took the presents, sang and danced together, then brought the man forth. It was nearly the dead of night when all of the star people turned into flying foxes then went and hung about near the man's house. He knocked on his door. His kin said, "Who's that? We're trying to find one of our lost kinsmen." So he replied, "Open the door, it's just me."

They heard his voice, opened the door and saw him standing there. Oh my, they held him and cried and cried. The man told them, "Go walk to all of the houses and tell the people that in the morning if they see flying foxes hanging near their houses or in the trees not to kill them. Leave them be."

So, everyone made a huge feast and was happy that the star people had called the whirlwind to come and bring the food to give to them. The two sister star-women were very troubled that they had lost their brother.

This man and everyone else took the yams, taros, and things then made a big celebration. This festival of the star people still exists in one village on Ali Island. This man taught his kin about this singing and dancing called *Jieng Taung*.

Gerry Y. Kola
Catholic Mission
Ali Island, P. O. Aitape
West Sepik Province

A1542.2. Origin of particular dance; B211.8.1K. Speaking crab; B336+. Helpful animal killed (threatened) by ungrateful ogre; B481.1. Helpful ant; B495.1. Helpful crab; D117.5K. Transformation: person to flying fox; D1520.28. Magic transportation in whirlwind; E30+. Resuscitation by being pieced back together by ants; F15. Visit to star-world; F51. Sky-rope; F215. Fairies live in star-world; F490+. Masalai; G550+. Rescue from ogre by star women; G560. Ogre deceived into releasing prisoner; H46.1+. Ogre recognized when it devours raw flesh; K1930. Treacherous impostors; P252.1. Two sisters; P273. Foster brother; P274. Foster sister; P310. Friendship; R100. Rescues; R260. Pursuits; W154. Ingratitude


## Dogs Killed their Master

(Wantok 486, September 17, 1983, page 23)

Long, long ago, in a village named Mopor [**Mapor** Village, **Waskia** People, **Madang** Province], there lived a man who was very clever at catching wild game. His name was Gilas. This clever hunter had many dogs. Gilas was married.

One morning, he woke up when it was still dark and explained to his wife what he would do. Gilas' wife understood well that when Gilas returned from the forest, he never came back empty-handed. Never. He always came with a pig or other wild game.

This morning, Gilas went to the forest with all his dogs to hunt for pigs in the forest. However at this time, Gilas did not shoot a pig. The dogs just worked hard. They went around and around and were famished. Gilas was hungry too. They had woken when it was still in the middle of the night. On their way, the grasses and tree leaves were wet and had stuck to Gilas' and the dogs' skins. They just kept going around and around. They did not kill a pig.

They went to look for a good place, then Gilas with his dogs went to sleep. One little dog woke up, went to Gilas and began to lick Gilas' skin. Gilas did not know this. The sun was warming him and he was dead asleep.

The big dogs saw this and thought that the little dog had killed him. So, the big dogs ran over and ate Gilas.

Poor Gilas did not have the strength to get rid of them. No, there were too many dogs gathered around Gilas, cutting him to pieces. One dog, Gilas' true friend, carried him to the village. The blood was still flowing when as he brought him.

Gilas' poor wife had prepared all of the food for the dogs and her husband. She was waiting. When she looked at the trail where her husband and the dogs usually came, she saw the dog carrying Gilas' head. She thought that this dog was carrying a pig. She kept watching as the dog carried Gilas' head and put it on his wife's [bed].

Gilas' wife went on top of the house and thought that she would see the head of a pig or another animal. But no, she was surprised to see Gilas' head. She began to cry and talk to herself. When the people of the village heard her crying and talking, they followed the blood from Gilas' head and arrived at the place where the dogs had torn him apart and eaten him.

The dogs had eaten every single piece of flesh. The men brought his leg and arm bones then buried them in a grave. Afterwards, the men killed all of Gilas' dogs with spears.

Mrs. Benny Lemot
Sisiak No. 3
Madang
Madang Province

J1110. Clever persons; N340+. Dogs kill owner, mistaking his sleep for death; P210. Husband and wife; Q211. Murder punished; Q411. Death as punishment; V61.3+. Dead buried

## An Ancestral Ghost Child Was the Father of the Barambu [Balambu] People

(Wantok 487, September 24, 1983, page 27)

There is a stream called Bama. At its source are some wild bananas. One day, a man left in the afternoon and saw marsupials (*kapul*) eating these bananas.

The man returned. He straightened a bow, cooked some food, and then took his things and walked up to the place where the wild bananas were. He watched carefully for the marsupials.

There was a nice, bright moon and he thought that the marsupials would come. But no, the wild women were coming raucously and devouring the wild bananas. The poor man had to urinate badly, so he kept watching as he urinated.

He was still standing there, and he saw a wild woman bringing her baby. When she saw the man's shoulder, she thought it was a tree and she hung the baby [in a net bag] upon the man's shoulder. The man saw this, took the wild woman's baby and sped off to the village.

When the wild woman came and did not see her baby, she smelled the man's trail and followed him to the village. However, when the man approached the village, he called out for all of the men to close their doors.

When the wild woman came and called out for the man to give back the baby, he did not want to do this. The man told the wild woman, "I didn't steal this baby of yours, you gave it to me. So, I can't gave it to you."

The wild woman said, "That's enough. You can take care of the baby, but you can't beat her. Don't send her to fetch water. Don't sent her out when it's raining at five or six o'clock in the afternoon." She said this and departed.

The baby was a girl and when she grew up, she was very beautiful. The man sent her to another man. When they married, they had three children.

One afternoon, a little child was crying and its father scolded it, "If you're a human child, you'll be heard." However it was an ancestral ghost's child, so it was not heard.

The child listened to this and waited for its mother. When its mother returned, the child repeated what its father had said. Its mother cried terribly. The mother took some things, then she and her child ran away. The other two children stayed with the father.

Now they are the group that is called mixed race (or "red skin"). If you travel to the Finschhafen area, you will see these people in a village called Barambu [**Balambu, Sio** People] [**Morobe** Province].

Gibson Fenerio

Mt. Hageng [Hagen

Western Highlands Province]

A991+. Origin of particular village; F567.1. Wild woman; P210. Husband and wife; P230. Parents and children; P231. Mother and son; P233. Father and son; P250. Brothers and sisters; P271. Foster father; P275+. Foster daughter; R10.3. Children abducted; R213. Escape from home; R260. Pursuits; T100. Marriage

## One *Masalai* with Good Eyes and One with Bad

(Wantok 488, October 1, 1983, page 27)

Long ago, by a river called Onepa in the **Garaina** [Village] area of **Morobe** Province, there were two *masalai*s [**Guhu-Samane** People]. One was named Neseia and the other was named Neseanga. These two voraciously ate the people of this area.

When the women wanted to go to the gardens, their husbands often carried axes, and bows and arrows, then followed their wives to the gardens. If the women went by themselves, the *masalai*s would eat them.

One time when the sun was burning hot, a boy took his spear and a net then went down to the Onepa River. He went to work at blocking a small branch of the river. As he was gathering the fish, the two friends [*masalai*s] came then stood and salivated. They salivated because this boy was quite fat. When the two of them said good day to the little boy, he looked up at them then wailed and trembled. However, his crying and shouting did not go far because they held him and tied him up.

They took the little boy, carried him to a gravesite and slept with him. In the morning, they carried him to their house. While they were walking, Neseia (who had good eyes) told Neseanga (who did not have good eyes) to go first. They began to argue. Later, the *masalai* with good eyes said that he would go first. "If something bad happens on the trail, then I won't know about you," he said to the *masalai* with the bad eyes. The *masalai* with bad eyes promised, "I'll put my hand on top of our meat [the boy]."

After they walked a long time, Nesenga [Neseanga], the *masalai* without eyesight, forgot what he had said and took his hand off the little boy.

When the ghost of the little boy's mother saw that the *masalai* had removed his hand and they were resting, she threw a rope down to her son and raised him to the crown of the tree. The two poor *masalai*s just carried the platform [that the boy had been tied to] back to their village.

When they arrived at the village, a boy asked, "What are you two carrying?" Neseanga said, "We're carrying a 'pig.' Take a look." The boy said, "But I don't see a pig on the platform." When Neseia heard this, he turned around. It was true that there was no pig there. Oh my, the two of them fought bitterly.

Neseia said, "That was why I told you to go first." After they finished arguing, they went back to look for the little boy. You know that for these *masalai*s, when they came close to a little boy, they smelled him.

However Neseia, who had good eyesight, could not smell well, so he did not smell the little boy. Neseanga, who could not see, smelled the little boy. Neseanga went and stood near the tree where the boy was lying. He told Neseia to look and see if the boy was there, and if so to tell him to go up. When Neseanga told him to go up, he was angry, but then he agreed, "If I go up, then you grab him or I'll kill you."

When Neseia came close to the boy, the boy told him, "If you kill and eat me, don't eat my head. My mother told me this." So Neseia asked why. The little boy said, "If you want to hear the source of this message, you must close your eyes."

When the *masalai* closed his eyes, the little boy shook him off. While he was falling, the little boy called out to the *masalai*'s friend that their meat was coming down. When Neseanga heard this, he thought that it was the little boy and he bashed in his friend's head and killed him.

Neseanga was sightless, and he had killed his friend. When the boy descended, he took the axe from Neseanga's hand and killed him. He cut both of their necks.

The people of the village had thought that this boy had died. However when they saw him coming back to the village, they were very happy and made a big feast. The skulls and bones of these two *masalai*s are still by the River Onepa in a cave.

K. Billy and D. Rakie
P. O. Box 170
Bulolo
Morobe Province

E323. Dead mother's friendly return; E379.1+. Return from dead to rescue someone from an ogre; F655. Extraordinary perception of blind men; F490+. Masalai; G501. Stupid ogre; G302.2.1. Kingdom of demons; G346. Devastating monster; G440. Ogre abducts person; G510.4+. Hero overcomes devastating ogre; G512.1+. Ogre killed with axe; K333.1. Blind Dupe; K721+. Dupe persuaded to close eyes, is pushed out of tree; K841. Substitute for execution obtained by trickery; N340. Hasty killing or condemnation (mistake); P231. Mother and son; P310. Friendship; R10. Abduction; R153.4. Mother rescues son; R260. Pursuits; R311. Tree refuge; S139.4. Murder by mangling with axe; V61.3+. Dead buried

# A Dead Man Took Care of His Son
(Wantok 489, October 8, 1983, page 27)

Long, long ago, in the time of the ancestors, there lived two old women. These two old women often stayed together in their village.

The name of this village is Maladum [**Melandum**] in the mountains by Kabum [Kabwum] in **Morobe** [Province, **Komba** People].

The place where the two old women lived did not have many people. The people lived far away in the mountains of Kabum. They did not have children in their youth. These women were like men, they were tall and stout. They had muscles just like men.

However now they were old. One of the old women was pregnant. She gave birth to a son. The woman and her old husband and the boy lived together. The other old woman died.

So, the three of them were left. The old mother became sick after a little while and she died. The poor old man took care of the baby.

The poor old father was very worried when the mother died. However, the baby did not know because he was too small when his mother had died. The father took the mother's body and buried her very near the house.

Later, the man was very troubled. Where could mother's milk be found for the baby? There were no other women with a little baby who lived nearby that could give milk to him. But the man had another idea to end his worries for his baby. At night, after the mother's death, the father made a bed for themselves near the door. The baby slept on the side by the door. At night the mother's ghost came up to the house and gave milk to the baby.

Every night, the mother's ghost would give milk to her baby. She did this until the baby grew up and became weaned. He became a big boy, and then a man. Then the mother's ghost left the father and son entirely. She just let them live there.

One day, the father and son went hunting for wild game in the forest. In the early morning, they traveled the mountains and they saw a marsupial (*kapul*) on top of a tree. The father was down on the ground and he shot it with his bow. They both carried it together.

It was nearly dark. They found many kinds of game and then went back towards the house. Near dusk, the old father saw a red marsupial again on top of a tree. The father shot his bow and [the marsupial] fell onto a tree branch. The father went up to remove the marsupial and bring it down to the ground. When he was on the tree, he wanted to get closer to the marsupial. It was too bad, because it was dark he could not see what he was holding very well. The old man missed at grabbing a tree branch. The father fell badly. Because he was old, he could not catch his breath, so he passed out and died.

The son was far away and did not know that his father and fallen and died. The father's ghost went and told the son, "Come on, let's go to the house now. It's completely dark in the forest." The father's ghost carried the bow and arrows and some of the meat. The son carried the rest of the meat, and they walked away.

The father's body was still at the base of the tree where he had fallen. How would the son find out? The ghost had fooled him well. The father's ghost did not want his son to worry too much because he was now alone. The ghost did not want him to see that his father was dead, so he had tricked him.

When they approached the house, the father's ghost told him to wait for him to go into the bushes to urinate. The son waited for a very long time. The ghost went to the place where the body had fallen. The ghost carried his body and put it in the middle of a trail that was far away. He avoided the son and took the body away. The son did not see him because the ghost had taken a ghostly smoke trail.

Later, the ghost accompanied the son and they walked away. Later still, the ghost tricked the son, "Oh sorry, I left my best arrow at the place where I pissed. Wait for me and I'll quickly get it." The ghost ran off, but he had lied. He brought his body back and put in the house at this time.

The ghost covered up his body well and put it amongst the firewood. The ghost was really his father. Nothing had changed. When it was time to eat, the ghost would clean and remove the skins from the taros or sweet potatoes and give the good ones to the son.

The ghost did this and the son thought a lot about this kind of behavior. It looked very unusual. His father had changed the way that he lived. This is what the son thought. The ghost took perfect care of him. He never got angry with him. The ghost did these kinds of things and the real father had died a fairly long time ago.

When the son cooked food, he would leave the good food for his father (the ghost). But the father's ghost always told him, "Never mind that, you eat as much of the good food as you want. I'm still troubled about your mother and I can't eat well."

One day, the two of them wanted to make an earth oven. The son prepared a huge pig to be cooked in the earth oven. He carved it up and put it into the earth oven with leafy vegetables .

When the food was ready, the son asked the father to uncover it. But no, the father told his son that he should uncover it.

So, the son worked at uncovering it. The father [ghost] went up to the house and carried his body, which was dressed finely, and put it in the middle of the house. Then the ghost disappeared completely. The son called and called up to the house. He saw his father's body, but it did not smell. The son was very worried and could not eat. He killed himself. This place no longer has people. The men, women and children are completely gone. The earth oven is there, just decaying.

Gims Kandom

P. O. Box 272

Kieta

North Solomons Province

E323.1.1. Dead mother returns to suckle child; E327+. Dead father returns to aid child; E327+. Dead father returns to prevent son from learning of his death; E425.1. Revenant as woman; E425.2. Revenant as man; F610.0.1. Remarkably strong woman; M451.1. Death by suicide; P210. Husband and wife; P231. Mother and son; P233+. Son commits suicide on death of father; T570. Pregnancy; T580. Childbirth; T611. Suckling of children; V61.3+. Dead buried

## How Mosquitoes Came to Kranget [Kranket] Island
(Wantok 490, October 15, 1983, page 31)

This is a true story from the ancestors who lived on Kranget [**Kranket**] Island in **Madang** [Province, **Gedaged** People].

Long, long ago, the people of Kranget Island in Madang [Province] did not know about mosquitoes. They knew their name, but they had never seen one with their own eyes.

One time, a very old grandfather from Kranget went to see his kin in the big village of **Biliau**, also in Madang Province [**Bilbil** People]. He paddled and paddled then arrived on the mainland. He put his canoe up and went to sit

in a house.  The old grandfather had taken fish with him
and he gave the fish to his kin.  His wife from Biliau
cooked the food then they sat and ate.  It was afternoon at
this time.

They sat for a while and then something sang out near
the ear of the old grandfather.  Before long, something bit
him and he was in pain.  It was as if a sago thorn had
stabbed him.  The poor old grandfather from Kranget Island
was quite surprised.

So the man from Kranget asked someone from Biliau,
"Friend what was it that sang in my ear then shot me like a
nail?"  The grandfather from Biliau said, "Friend, that's a
mosquito.  That nasty little thing often makes us sleep
poorly at night."

The old man from Kranget Island said, "Oh my, that's
a good thing to wake someone up at night.  I'd like to get
some to bring to the island with me."  The man from Biliau
told the man from Kranget that he would find many and put
them in a bamboo tube.  The two old men set a time to
meet.

The man from Kranget told the man from Biliau not to
speak out to the people of Kranget Island about the mosquitoes.  The old man from Kranget told the man from Biliau,
"Often, we will smoke fish, but people forget and fall dead
asleep every night, so the fish do not get properly smoked.
I want to bring the mosquitoes to my island where they can
bite and stab us like nails then awaken us.  After that the
people can watch after the fish all of the time.  We often fall
dead asleep by the side of the fish fire.  Sometimes, the fish
fall right into the fire or fall from the fish rack.  The mosquitoes must live on the island."

The old man from Kranget went back to the island.  He
paddled and paddled then arrived at the island in the late
afternoon, near dark.  His old wife went off the canoe and
brought the food, such as bananas, yams and leafy vegetables that they had brought from her old friend at Biliau.

At night, the old couple cooked the food and the old
man told the story of the mosquitoes and all of the things
that had happened when they went to Biliau.  When the old
woman listened to this story, she was very happy.  Some
days later, the old couple from Kranget went to Biliau.
They brought plenty of fish and gave them to the old couple
on the mainland.  They gave them the fish and took many
bamboo tubes filled with mosquitoes.

Later, everyone of Kranget heard about this.  The island completely emptied out to go to Biliau to buy mosquitoes with fish.  There was a very big meeting, the people of
Kranget Island and Biliau Village dressed very finely.

They put on their finest dress for this meeting and they
traded fish for bamboo tubes filled with mosquitoes.

After this meeting, the people of Kranget paddled in
their many canoes back to the island.  They chewed betel
nuts, sang and danced, because this meeting was like none
before.

Before, the people of Kranget and Biliau often just exchanged sago, yams, taros, and fish.  After this, Kranget Island was completely filled with mosquitoes.  The people
never slept like they did before.  The fish used to half-burn
and people used to fall into the fire or the fish platform.
This was because of the idea from the old man of Kranget.

Kanog Kushen
P. O. Box 406
Madang
Madang Province

A2584.1+. How mosquito arrived on certain island; J2050+. Mosquitoes
purchased to distribute on island to keep people awake at night; P210.
Husband and wife; P310. Friendship

## The Big Brother Took Good
## Care of His Two Young Siblings
(Wantok 491, October 22, 1983, page 30)

Long, long ago, in the time of the ancestors, there were
three children.  They were quite miserable.  Their parents
had died when they were still small.  They often gathered
scraps from the food that their paternal uncle's wife gave to
her children.

The youngest child would collect and eat the pieces of
bone and other food scraps that were left.  The uncle's wife
would give the best food to her own children.  However
when the uncle was at home, the woman was afraid and
would give a little bit of good food to the little boy.

The eldest brother was thirteen.  His name was Kaubir.
After him, was the sister who was ten.  Her name was
Maliwan.  The little boy was Tapur and was only three
years old.

The big brother worked hard at taking care of his little
brother and sister because their aunt never took care of
them well.  She often scolded the little boy and said various
things.  Tapur cried all of the time.  The big brother,
Kaubir, was often very troubled and he took his two siblings with him.  They would walk into the forest to look for
*tulip* leaves [to eat].

If they went through a bad place in the forest, Kaubir
would put his little brother on top of his shoulders and carry

him. The little sister, Maliwan, often carried a little broken net bag that she had found in the rubbish. They often went looking for *tulip* leaves, other leafy greens, and other foods in the forest. Then they would make a fire.

These poor children would sit and just cook the leafy greens without meat. They would cover the leaves with mushrooms that they had found in the forest, and then cook and eat them. When it became dark, they would walk back to the house. They would sleep in the house with their uncle's family.

Their aunt was a very selfish woman. The good meat went to her own children. The bones and scraps went to the three children. It happened like this every day. Her children would eat first. Later, she would give some to the three siblings.

Poor Kaubir, Tapur and their sister Maliwan did not worry. When they were famished, the big brother Kaubir would find some ripe coconuts and break them open to eat. Little Tapur cried often. Maliwan and Kaubir often carried him into the forest to look for *tulip* leaves or mushrooms to cook quickly and give to Tapur.

When the big brother wanted to take his uncle's knife or small axe to use and carry and go into the forest, their aunt would scold him. When he wanted to take a spear, it would be the same thing. She would say, "Your parents were complete trash. Now they're dead. They did not own anything."

However, this was not true because the uncle had taken everything of theirs: spears, bows, big axes, and knives. They had told Kaubir and Tapur that when they became big men, that they could use them. Everything that their mother had used, their aunt had taken from Maliwan and used.

The three of them often went barehanded looking for leafy vegetables. They did not have anything like a knife or a stone axe. They just worked like that.

Many years passed. Kaubir grew up to be about seventeen years old, and the sister also grew a little bigger. The little boy, Tapur, grew to about ten years old.

One morning, very early, Kaubir woke up his sister and his little brother. They got up quietly and went to get a broken-down canoe that often leaked. The big brother and sister looked for some clay and covered up [the holes] well. The girl steered the canoe. The little boy, Tapur sat in the middle of the canoe and the big brother sat in the front. They paddled and paddled downstream and looked for a place where their parents had taken Kaubir when he was little. It was a place in the forest where they had processed sago and killed many pigs.

They pulled their way with a stick. Then they could pull no further. This time, their uncle and aunt did not know that they had run away. The big brother had thought of this place before, but he did not know that it was real. He had thought that it was just a dream.

The current carried them, and the big brother saw the mouth of a small stream. They paddled and paddled up to this place. It was the place where their parents had made a hut before. It was the place where they often stayed for some days or about a week, then returned to the village with sago and pork from a pig that they had shot.

The poor children arrived that day and they just slept in the open. In the early morning, the big brother woke up and found the axe, knife, bow, and other things that the parents had used to hunt wild game and to eat sago. The house was filled with all of these things.

They cleaned the place. There were many *tulip* trees, and mushrooms filled the bases of the sago palm trees. There were coconut palms, some betel nut palms and many, many sago palms. The hut was ready to collapse because it was very old. They sat there in their new place. This was the place that their parents and grandparents had used to find food. It was their land.

The big brother cut sago palms. The sister, Maliwan, rinsed the sago pith. The little brother, Tapur, helped them cook the food and do small chores.

They lived at this place and grew to be adults. The sister, Maliwan, became a big woman. It was time for her to marry. She was about 22 or 23 years old. Kaubir was a big man too. The little brother, Tapur, had also grown. The three of them became strong and handsome people because they worked hard and did various kinds of chores.

Their uncle, his family, and the people of the village thought that they had died. They had completely forgotten them. One day, they realized that they must return to the village so that the big brother could marry and so that the sister, Maliwan, could also find a husband. She had become a smart and very muscular woman. They surpassed their uncle's children. They were smarter.

One day, they filled up the new canoe, the one that Kaubir had made, with sago, pork, betel nuts, coconuts, and many other kinds of foods. In the very early morning, after many years of living in this forest "village", they began to paddle back to the village.

The new canoe was well balanced and was more beautiful than all of the other canoes of the village. The big brother had become a big man. He sat in the middle of the canoe, rested and chewed betel nuts. When they approached the village, the little sister, who was now a big woman, sat and steered the canoe. Tapur was in the front. Their paddling was excellent. They had various adornments on their arms.

Their aunt stood near the stream. They saw them first and called to their family to come and look. They thought that they were people from another village. However the little brother, Tapur, called out to them, "Auntie, you're standing crookedly. What are you looking at? It's just me. Before you often just gave me garbage and bones. I and my two siblings have returned to the village now." The aunt was speechless. The uncle saw them and cried terribly. He had grown a beard in mourning for them. He had thought that they were dead, so he removed his beard.

Maliwan, the sister, married. The big brother Kaubir also married. Some time later, Tapur also married. Their story has gone to all of the villages of this area.

James Cansol
P. O. Box 639
Wewak
East Sepik Province

P210. Husband and wife; P230. Parents and children; P253.0.2. One sister and two brothers; P271. Foster father; P272. Foster mother; P293. Uncle; P294. Aunt; P297. Nephew; P298. Niece; P681+. Mourning customs: growing beard; R213. Escape from home; S12.6. Cruel mother refuses children food; S72. Cruel aunt; T100. Marriage; W151. Greed; W157. Dishonesty


## A Boy Tricked Two Girls

(Wantok 492, October 29, 1983, page 27)

Long, long ago, in the time of the ancestors, there was a couple who lived in a village. This couple did not have children.

They were married for many years, but they had not had any children until one time when they had a baby. This newborn baby was a boy.

At the very same time, another woman in this village gave birth to a baby girl. This woman already had another daughter. When the two daughters grew up, they looked exactly like twins. That was because the elder sister had not grown quickly.

The boy had grown up near the village. From the time that he was little, his parents had not explained to the other people of the village that he was a boy. No, they all thought that he was just a girl.

When the little boy grew up and began to walk around, his father gave him the name Manga. Manga's mother made a girl's "grass" skirt for Manga. That year, Manga traveled with the girls of the village. He traveled with them, played with them, and did the things that girls do in a group. He grew up with them.

The girls thought that he was a girl and so did their parents. He made good friends with the two girls who lived in the middle of the village, the ones who looked like twins.

Manga traveled to all of the places with the girls. Manga was very good friends with the two sisters. When the girls went to bathe or play in the water, Manga would play or bathe with his skirt on. He never removed it like the other girls did.

They would ask him, and Manga would tell them that his mother forbade him to bathe naked. His parents treated him very well because they had been without children for a long time. They treated him well when he was still little. They called him a girl and put him near the girls.

At the same time, they wanted him to grow up with the girls and to travel with them. Later, they could still promise a good wife for him.

One time, all of the girls of the village, Manga's group, went to play together, cook some food, and travel in the forest. Later, they went to bathe in the river. Manga did not remove his skirt. His breasts had not developed. The girls asked him, "Friend, why haven't your breasts come out? All of us, your girlfriends, have breasts. Also, you always play in the water with your skirt. You never remove it like we do."

### No Breasts

The young man, Manga, lied to them, "No, my father sang and danced at my food so that when I ate it, my breasts did not develop as quickly as yours. After some years I'll have them. My mother makes a new 'grass' skirt for me all of the time. She wants me to bathe with the skirt all of the time. So, this is what I always do."

It was nearly time for Manga to become a man and to look like a man. His parents prepared all of the things. This was a very big day. At night, his father taught Manga what he must do the next day.

He told him that it would be time for him to marry and that he could no longer travel with the women. It would be bad if he stayed any longer with women since they would quickly see that he was a man. Manga had become a very handsome young man.

In the afternoon, two girls, sisters, came up to the house, looking for Manga. They wanted to go hunting for wild game on the next day, like girls of the village often did. Manga's mother saw them and asked them about this.

They told Manga's mother that they wanted Manga to travel with them in the forest.

### Lying to Them

Manga's mother told them that only the two of them and Manga should go, that they should not go with the others. Manga's mother lied to them because Manga did not like the other girls of the village. If only the three of them went, that would be fine. At this time, Manga was sitting like a man in the house with his father.

He sat there and listened to all of the lies that his mother told the two sisters. That night, Manga's father sang and danced. He spat many kinds of ginger upon Manga, drenching him, and Manga became a real man. He was completely muscular, so when women would see him, they fell for him.

His father told him that the day when he takes the two young women with him, he must be careful. When they were ready to go and play in the water, Manga must eat his father's ginger then sing and dance there. That would make him look like a real man.

Another morning, the two sisters came to get Manga. Manga was still like a woman. All of the things went in a net bag that he put on his head. He fastened this to his "grass" skirt. They went off to the forest, like they always did. The two women really did not know that Manga was a man.

### Teaching

Manga's father had taught him what he should do. His father had given him two citrus fruits that he tied up well and covered with a small net bag. Manga put this down into a very big net bag and carried it on his head like women carry net bags.

They looked for *tulip* leaves and other kinds of foods in the forest. Then it was time for them to rest and go look for a stream in which to bathe. They all went to bathe. The two sisters removed their skirts, but Manga did not. Then they bathed. Manga took the ginger that his father had given him. He chewed it and spat it upon himself. Then he prepared to hold the citruses in his hands.

They played a game where one would go down into the water and then resurface. If the other woman hit the diver with the wild citrus, she would score a point for herself. This was a contest played all of the time at this village.

Manga told the two women that they should both go down into the water and then come up again. When they went down, Manga spat ginger on himself for a second time, then he became an excellent man. He stood on a log that was floating near where they were bathing. With the two domesticated citruses that his father had given him, he sang at his hands. Quickly, he tore off the skirt in which he had always bathed. Then he stood as a real man.

He held a citrus in each of his hands. The young sister drifted downstream and came up first. The big sister swam down and had not surfaced yet.

When the little sister surfaced, Manga hit her body with the citrus and called out, "You're mine." Then the big sister went above the water and he struck her with the citrus. Manga called out, "O ooooh, you're mine." Manga told them, "You two thought that I was a girl. No, you're my wives now."

The two of them both shouted and cried and cried. They went to the village and told their parents. Everyone in the village heard this news that Manga was a boy and that he had always pretended to be a girl.

Another girl who often traveled with Manga was happy. She said that it was good and that they would no longer travel with him. However, when they saw Manga with the two sisters who were his wives, they fell over because he had become a very handsome man in the village. Manga married the two sisters. The little sister who he had marked with the citrus became his first wife. The other woman was her big sister.

Jakias Kiate

Health Centre

Pimaga

Mendi

**Southern Highlands** Province

D11+. Magic masculinization; D967+. Magic ginger; D1001. Magic spittle; D1335. Object gives magic strength; D1781. Magic results from singing; D1781+. Magic results from dancing; D1830. Magic strength; D1860. Magic beautification; K1321. Seduction by man disguising as woman; P210. Husband and wife; P231. Mother and son; P232. Mother and daughter; P233. Father and son; P252.1. Two sisters; P310. Friendship; T100. Marriage; T145.0.1. Polygyny; T589.7. Simultaneous births; W157. Dishonesty

# A Ghost Found Her Grave

(Wantok 493, November 5, 1983, page 23)

Long, long ago, in the time of the ancestors, there was a married couple. They lived in a village that the ancestors called Kunmandikir in the **Kokopo** area [**Tolai** People, **East New Britain**]. This ancestral couple only had a son who was about six years old.

The mother's name was Kubar and the father's was Bange. One time, mother Kubar was terribly sick. She wanted some other kind of food and meat from the forest. She did not like the food that they gave her in the village.

Because she was terribly sick, father Bange wanted to find some good food to give to Kubar. He wanted to hunt some wild game in the forest because the poor mother had been very sick for a very long time. Her body was a complete wreck. They had to give her good food or she would die.

So, the father and son went into the forest to look for food that would satisfy the sick mother. They left and when they were in the deep forest, mother Kubar was in the village. However, while the father and son were hunting for food in the forest, mother Kubar died.

She had died and her body lay in the house, but the father and son did not know that the mother had died. Kubar's ghost rose up and followed the father and son into the forest.

She walked and walked, following them. The boy turned back and saw his mother's ghost following them. The boy was surprised and he called to his father that mother was following them. The father turned back and looked, but he did not see the mother. He was angry with the boy because he had lied to his father.

They set out again, walking and looking for food. The mother's ghost stood close behind the boy. The boy was surprised again and called to his father. This time, the father was completely fed up with this because when he turned to look, the mother was not there. He was angry and he hit his son who cried.

They continued looking for food and the mother's ghost continued to follow them. The fourth time that the mother stood by them, the father and son both saw her. This time, the mother's ghost did not leave them like before.

The mother's ghost told them, "I saw you coming through the forest, so I was sorry for you and followed you. My sickness is over now, but I was still a little weary so I didn't have the strength to walk on the forest trails with you. But now, I feel that I can walk and carry the net bag of food and that we can return to the village."

The two of them did not think that it was the mother's ghost. No, they thought that it was the mother who had followed them. This was because the ghost had confused them, lest the father think too much.

It was near dark, and they did not think about returning to the village. This was because the father thought that that there were no more people in the family at the village. The

three of them stayed together in the forest. If the mother were still sleeping in the village, then the father and son would have tried to go back to the house quickly.

But no, the ghost was with them and the father thought that it was really the mother with them. They went and cooked the food. They sat and ate in a forest hut at the place where people of the village often slept when they hunted for food. While they sat eating, the ghost ate very slowly so that the father and son would think that it was really the mother.

When they were sleeping late at night, a feral cat went to the hut and turned into a woman then explained to the man, "If your boy wants to piss or shit, you yourself must take him out of the hut. You must pretend and instead run away completely. That woman is not your mother. She's her ghost." Father Bange watched and listened to this. It was like a dream as he was sleeping at night in the forest hut.

At the same time, the boy needed to urinate. The mother's ghost insisted on taking the boy out to urinate, but the father was more insistent and he took the boy out to urinate. The father carried the boy and they ran away back to the village. The ghost woman waited and waited but they did not return. She took a big net bag and followed them. She wanted to put the boy into the net bag because the man had not given an explanation to her. She was not just a ghost, she was his wife.

The ghost woman did not walk. She was a ghost, not a real person who walked on legs. She was a ghost, so she tossed the net bag on top of her head. It hung down to her big, long "grass" skirt. Then the ghost flew and caught up to them. She wanted to put the little boy into the net bag and carry him away.

However, it was very lucky that the two of them had already arrived at the village. They found sadness. They were saddened and troubled when they found the mother's body lying in the house. They were troubled and they cried. They buried her body. The ghost did not return to the village. When the body was in the grave, the ghost stopped following the father and son.

Jacob Aina

P. T. R. College, P. O. Box 104

Kokopo

East New Britain Province

D342W. Transformation: cat to woman; E261.4. Ghost pursues man; E425.1. Revenant as woman; E441+. Ghost laid by burial; E541. Revenants eat; J1050. Attention to warnings; P210. Husband and wife; P231. Mother and son; P233. Father and son; R210. Escapes; R260. Pursuits; V61.3+. Dead buried; Z71.2. Formulistic number: four

# Andamai Found a Snake-Man

(Wantok 494, November 12, 1983, page 31)

Long, long ago, in the time of the ancestors, there lived a widow. She only had a little baby. The woman, whose name was Andamai, lived with her baby in a bad house, but the woman worked hard like a man. There was a taro garden and another garden that had sugarcanes and other kinds of things. When she went hunting for food in the forest for game such as marsupials (*kapul*), birds, or wildfowls, Andamai was better at hunting them than any man.

She was still alone with her little baby when she cut down big trees, chopped them up, carried them and threw them down. Sometimes, she would sharpen stone axes or traditional knives. Before, men only made knives and axes with stones. Andamai did not know how to count.

She and her little boy lived like that. One day, Andamai went alone into the forest. She saw a huge pig standing near the trail and walking towards her.

When the pig saw Andamai, it pranced belligerently (*samsam*) towards her. The poor woman was as strong as a man was, and she was smart. She was not skinny, she was a muscular woman. However, it was too late for her to get a spear and quickly kill the pig. Andamai always beat pigs or cassowaries.

However this time, the pig had her. The pig had two long tusks hanging outside its mouth. Andamai wanted to kill it with a spear, but it was too late. The pig knocked down Andamai, trampled her and was about to cut her.

But there was one man of the forest who often saw Andamai, and he was very sorry that she worked as hard as men did. He often lusted for this muscular woman. He thought hard about how he could marry her or seek her favors, but he was afraid.

This time, though, was a bad time. This man had to help Andamai or the pig would kill and eat her. So, the man went to help her. At this time he was lying on a tree and looking at Andamai. However, the woman did not see him.

Every time that Andamai went to look for food in the waters or forests or gardens, the man would follow her then hide and spy upon her. Andamai did not know that this man did this.

This man's name was Python. He was an enormous snake. Python jumped down and grabbed the pig that had almost killed Andamai. Andamai was half-dead, but the snake crushed the pig around its middle, breaking all its bones until the pig was pulverized. Blood flowed from its mouth and nose and it died.

Andamai did not know what had happened. She saw the huge snake, her eyes spun around and she fell asleep. She felt pain and there were big marks from when the pig had cut her. Her guts had almost fallen out at the time that she had seen Python.

Python turned into a very handsome man and became a type of man that Andamai had never seen before. He carried the woman up to his tree house that was on top of a huge tree branch. Andamai had not yet awoken and she did not look good. She had passed out, her eyes and head spun around. Python took some vines and gave her the medicinal liquid from the vines.

When Andamai woke up again, she saw the man sitting and watching her. When she saw the python-man, Andamai, she wanted to pass out again. She had never seen a man like this. She asked Python where she was and how she had gotten there. Was she looking at a huge python or not?

Andamai told Python that she thought a huge snake must have eaten her. Why was she on top of the tree? She was looking for her village.

Python told Andamai the whole story. He said not to be afraid of him. He told her that his name was Python and he wanted to marry her. He told her that he was often sorry for her because she worked hard. At the same time, he lusted for her.

The woman told Python that she had a baby, so Python could be a foster father. This did not trouble Python, he was just happy. Later, they went and lived together at this place in the forest. One night, Python turned back into a huge snake and lay close to Andamai. Andamai was surprised half-to-death and was terrified. She took the axe and almost cut the snake, but she was not quick enough. Python turned into a man.

Oh my, Andamai and the little boy did not really believe this. After a long time, they lived well during the time that Python was not a snake. When they went to look for food or worked, Python would turn into a snake and kill pigs, cassowaries and other animals. Andamai no longer worked hard like she did before and their home was overflowing with food.

Andamai became pregnant and gave birth to a baby boy. It was Python's son, but he did not look like a snake. It was a real boy. While he was growing to be a man, the snake acted as his father. The women of the village lusted after him. He and his half-brother lived well together.

Some years later, Python became very old and he died. The old mother and her two sons still lived together at this place. The two young men married two beautiful young women and they had children at this little forest hut on top of the tree. It became a big village of the ancestors. The old mother Andamai who had married the snake became blind and then she too died.

Kin Yusti

Department of Agriculture

Lae

Morobe Province

B491.1. Helpful serpent; B656.1. Marriage to python in human form; B631.9. Human offspring of marriage of person and snake; B871.1.2. Giant boar; B875.1. Giant serpent; D191M. Transformation: man to serpent (snake); D391M. Transformation: serpent (snake) to man; F610.0.1. Remarkably strong woman; F765+. Village on top of a tree; P210. Husband and wife; P230. Parents and children; P231. Mother and son; P233. Father and son; P271. Foster father; P275. Foster son; P290+. Half-brother; R161. Lover rescues his lady; T10. Falling in love; T100. Marriage; T570. Pregnancy; T580. Childbirth

## A Ghost Woman Tricked a Mother

(Wantok 495, November 19, 1983, page 23)

Long, long ago, in the time of the ancestors, there was an ancestral village. One day, the women of the village decided to go look for food on the next day.

They often met to speak in a particular place. Sometimes, they would send a message for their little children to come. This day, a woman went and asked her girlfriend if it would be all right for the two of them to look for fish. The woman was still nursing a little baby.

The two of them agreed. Underneath the house, a ghost was listening. The ghost heard everything that the women had decided. They had decided that one would wake up the other with her baby at the time of the third cock's crowing, near dawn.

The following day, very early in the morning, the third cock crowed. The ghost woman woke up the other woman with her little baby. The ghost looked just like her friend, the real woman, from the night that they had made the decision.

So, the mother, the baby and the ghost went to look for fish. They paddled a canoe towards the sea. They paddled and paddled, arriving at a reef.

They cast their fishing lines down into the sea and waited for the fish to come. They shot some spears. At the same time, the woman's real friend woke up in the village, but she had missed them. The woman's husband was surprised and thought hard, "Who is mother with?" He was troubled because he thought that she would have waited. It was bad that she had taken the baby and departed.

At sea, the ghost woman was steering the canoe, and the real woman and the baby were in the front of the canoe. The real woman gave the baby to the ghost woman to take care of while she watched and hauled in fish.

Then everything changed at that time. Before long, the ghost woman broke the little finger on the baby's left hand and the baby cried. The baby's mother asked why the baby was crying. The ghost said, "No, it's a piece of taro from last night that I ate. The sound is just like crying."

Then the ghost broke another finger. The baby cried again and the mother asked again. The ghost said something. This kept up until all of the fingers and toes were gone.

When the ghost removed the head of the baby from its neck, the baby stopped crying. The ghost threw the baby's head down towards the front of the canoe. The mother's fishing line snared the baby's head.

The mother thought that it was a fish. She tried pulling the fishing line up. No! It was her baby's head hanging on the hook. The mother was speechless. She held her breath and did not say anything. She said to herself, "Ah, I came with a ghost. I thought that it was a real woman that had come with me."

The mother was angry and wanted to kill the ghost, but how? She told the ghost that they must go ashore so she could defecate. However, she really wanted to run away from the ghost. They went ashore and onto the beach. The woman told the ghost to wait at the canoe. The woman ran away quickly. The ghost waited and waited. Then the ghost sped off, following the woman.

However, the real woman knew this and went up a big palm tree that was like a *limbum* palm. It had many fruits hanging from it. The woman went to the top of the tree. The fruits were much bigger than the betel nuts that come from Buka Island.

The ghost went and saw the real woman sitting on top of the tree, and she laughed hysterically. The ghost called up, "Where are you going today? I'm going to eat you and finish you off for good. I'll eat your bones and belly too. I'll do to you exactly what I did to the baby. You're just my meat. You'll fill my belly well."

Then the ghost went up the tree, and went very close to the woman. The woman thrashed her head with the tree fruits. The ghost fell down and blood shot from her head. She danced around at the base of the tree. Then the ghost went up again and came close to her. Right away, the woman hit her again with the fruits. The ghost fell down. The ghost called up to the woman that she could not die from fighting like this. They worked at singing hard and laughing together. The ghost told the real woman that when all of the fruits were gone, she would eat her. The ghost would go up and really eat her.

However at this time, the woman was also calling out to whomever was hunting for food to come to this part of the forest and help her. There was a man hunting for wild game, but he was far away and the woman's shouting sounded just like a bird. It was not clear.

The ghost called up to the woman again. The ghost said that this part of the forest was very far away from the village and men did not travel there. The ghost told the woman not to waste her time.

The woman sitting in the tree had many bundles of tree fruits hanging there. Some were ripe, others were green, and still others were young. They were hard as stones. When the woman shot them down and hit the ghost, blood just shot out from every place that she had hit her.

After a while, the fruit bundles were almost gone. The man heard her a little clearer. He heard that it was the shouting of a real person. He went very close and clearly heard the woman's voice.

The man who had been hunting for game looked for the woman who was a friend of his. The man went very close then stood and saw what the ghost was doing to the woman. The ghost was fervently dancing and singing at the base of the tree.

The ghost was not concerned about the pain. The fruits on top of the tree were almost gone. He saw that the woman was his friend's wife and that the ghost was underneath.

Finally, the ghost again went up the tree. This time, the fruits were young and the ghost did not feel pain when the woman struck her. At the same time, the woman called out for people to come to this part of the forest and help her.

The man jumped out and said, "Yes, I'm here at this part of the forest." The ghost turned back and went towards the man. But no, she became caught on the man's spear. The man put the spear right into her guts and cut her open. The woman came down slowly from the tree. The man took the ghost's guts, spread them around the trees, and cut up the ghost's body.

Later, the woman told the man the story about her baby and the ghost. The man took the woman back to the village. At this time in my village, when women decide to hunt for food, they must be quiet. They cannot talk loudly at night.

Peter Sale
Kandrian High School
P. O. Kandrian
West New Britain Province

C490+. Tabu: telling specific hunting plans; E261.4. Ghost pursues man; E402.1.1.4. Ghost sings; E425.1. Revenant as woman; E440+. Ghost laid by spear/arrow; E461. Fight of revenant with living person; E493. Dead men dance; E545. The dead speak; G11.10. Cannibalistic spirits; K551.16. Woman escapes by ruse: must go to defecate; K1930. Treacherous impostors; P210. Husband and wife; P230. Parents and children; P310. Friendship; Q211. Murder punished; Q411. Death as punishment; R100. Rescues; R260. Pursuits; R311. Tree refuge; S110+. Eaten alive; S139.2. Slain person dismembered; T611. Suckling of children

## A Manus Woman Tricked a *Masalai*

(Wantok 496, November 26, 1983, page 27)

Long ago, in the time of the ancestors, there was a village called **Droia** in **Manus** Province [**Kuruti** People]. There were four hundred women who lived in this village. These women often bathed together in a river called Werei. The women bathed at the head of the river.

There was a big boulder that stood near the Werei River. Inside the boulder was a big hole where a *masalai* named Lapanpowarei lived.

When the women went to bathe, they left their bamboo flutes at the base of a papaya tree. They blew these flutes and made music. Amongst these women was one named Pingop. She left her flute with all of the others too.

The *masalai* took Pingop's flute and hid it. Then the *masalai* shot papayas at the women who were bathing in the river.

The women found that something was hitting them and they were in pain. They were afraid and surprised. They went to get their flutes and go to a festival with them. They quickly ran away to this place.

Pingop tried to find her flute. The *masalai* was holding it and sitting and hiding. Pangaop [Pingop] was still searching. The women who had run away came returned to help her. Then the women tired and went back.

The *masalai* just looked at Pingop then went into the clearing with her flute. The woman was terrified but she was strong and said to the *masalai*, "I'd like to get my flute back."

The *masalai* told Pingop, "If you get a pig, I'll give you back the flute." So, the woman went and found a pig. She killed it and brought it back to the *masalai* man. However he was not happy, he swallowed the pig right away.

The *masalai* told the women to go find a crocodile and bring it back to give to him. The *masalai* would give her back the flute. "If you go and find one and bring it back, you'll get your flute." So quickly, the woman went and found a crocodile. She took a huge net and brought it to give to the *masalai*. This was a big crocodile and the *masalai* swallowed it slowly down into his belly. however, he was not filled up yet.

He asked the woman again to go and find a turtle. The woman went and found one then brought it to give to the *masalai*. The woman was very strong because the flute was her strength. The other women were doing plenty of work at this time, sitting, singing and dancing traditionally. The flutes were their strength. Men still had this strength too.

This is why she absolutely did not want to give the flute to the *masalai*. If he carried the flute with him, she would become weak over anything. Also, she would not look like other women of the village.

Ringop [Pingop] brought everything that the *masalai* told her to bring to him. However, one thing that Pingop did not know was that the *masalai* was making a song and dance for her to like him.

When Pingop returned to give him food, the *masalai* spat out all of the pieces of his love spell. After that, she brought the last food that the *masalai* had asked for. The woman wanted to talk to the *masalai* to get back her flute, but she slipped and fell right onto the *masalai*.

The *masalai* saw the woman's desire and asked her, "Do you want me to give you back your bamboo flute?" The woman said, "No, it is both of ours." The *masalai* asked Pingop, "Do you want to marry me too? If not, then you're afraid of me." The woman just agreed.

The *masalai* carried Pingop inside with him to the hole in the boulder. When they went inside, the woman saw where the *masalai* dwelled in this very nice place. His house was better than any other kind. The woman looked and trembled all over.

For many years, the woman lived with her *masalai* who was very lazy. The *masalai* ate a tremendous amount. He slept and was lazy, and he never did any work. The woman worked hard and was completely fed up. She wanted to run away and return to her village because she saw that the *masalai* had become very old.

The woman tired of him and thought of running away. The *masalai* found out and tried to do something so that she would not run away.

However, it was too late. Many years had passed and the woman was tired. One morning, the woman woke up quickly and ran away, above the cave. She went up to the ground, then arrived at the village. She made a house on top of a tree branch and sat there. At this time, the *masalai* was sleeping awkwardly.

Later, the *masalai* woke up and found that the woman was not in the house under the hole in the boulder. He went up to the ground and smelled the trail that the woman had taken then followed her.

The woman had made a ladder down from her house to the ground. Close to the middle of the ladder, she had cut it a little bit. Under the ladder, she had made a trench with sharp tree thorns and bamboos.

The *masalai* wanted to go up and get the woman. The *masalai* was furious and said to her that she did not explain this [her departure] to him. He would eat her so that she would not run away again.

The *masalai* tried to go up, but the ladder broke in the middle. He fell down on top of the tree thorns below and died. The woman cut the *masalai*'s body and gave the parts to the big birds to eat. Later, a tornado came and ruined the village, and everyone died. The woman was the very first to die during this bad time, but her stone house is still standing there.

Ronnie Mari
P. O. Box 84
Manus High School
Lorengau
Manus Province

A977. Origin of particular stones or groups of stones; A1000+. Village destroyed by tornado; B875.2. Giant crocodile; D1223.1. Magic flute; D1335+. Flute gives magic strength; D1781. Magic results from singing; D1781+. Magic results from dancing; D1900. Love induced by magic; D2142.1+. Tornado produced by magic; F490+. Masalai; F610.0.1. Remarkably strong woman; F910. Extraordinary swallowings; G81. Unwitting marriage to cannibal; G400. Person falls into ogre's power; G512+ Ogre killed by entrapment; G641K. Ogres live in cave(s); K300. Thefts and cheats—general; K735. Capture in pitfall; P210. Husband and wife; R210. Escapes; R260. Pursuits; R311. Tree refuge; S139.2. Slain person dismembered; T10. Falling in love; T111. Marriage of mortal and supernatural being; W111. Laziness; W125. Gluttony

## The Old Man Punished the Children
(Wantok 497, December 3, 1983, page 23)

Long, long ago, in the time of the ancestors, there was an old man. Every day, the old grandfather would go to work in his big banana garden.

The young boys of the village often found various kinds of bananas and brought them to give to the old man to plant. The old man excelled in the variety of his bananas, many of which other people in the village did not have.

Every day, the boys went to help him in the garden until the garden became like a banana plantation. Because of the boys' hard work, the old grandfather told them that he would give them ripe bananas from the best plant to eat.

After he said, this, he gave the very best ripe bananas to the boys. He made ripe banana soup and the small group of boys ate it inside the spirit house.

Some time later, the old man went to check on his garden. He found that some of the bananas were gone. These were bananas that a child had carried and that the old man had cleaned and prepared. He went to check another time and he saw that thieves had cut and stolen some bananas. This sort of thing happened every day and many bananas disappeared from the garden.

It was these little boys who had helped him before that were stealing the bananas. One day, the old man thought about going to hide in his garden hut. He hid quietly in his garden hut. One evening, near dusk, the little boys went to the garden to steal the bananas.

The old man sat and just watched. He did not do a thing and he let them go. Another evening, the boys came and took only the best bananas, just leaving the rubbish for the birds to eat in the garden.

The old grandfather was furious at these little boys. He did not say anything. He got up quietly and went back to the village. However this time, he no longer liked these little boys. They had turned on him and ruined him.

The old grandfather brought a big, beautiful, ripe banana to eat back at his house in the village. He put it in a huge pot. The banana was perfectly ripe. One day at the spirit house, he told the boys that he would make some new soup and prepare to make a new garden.

The old grandfather sang and danced at the soup. Then he put it close to the big ancestral signal drum in the spirit house. The boys gathered and ate.

When they began to eat, the old man struck the signal drum just one time. The boys flew around because they had turned into birds. The drum had turned them into birds. The signal drum turned into a huge boulder and the banana soup transformed into a strong rain and wind.

The big spirit house turned into a huge tree. The young men who had turned into birds lived high up on the tree. The old man looked for another village to live that had many other people.

He left his natal village for good lest the people looked for their children and became angry. They would accuse him. So, the old man went to another village that was very far from his natal village so that they could not find him.

The boys who had turned into birds lived on top of this tree in their village all of the time. These birds always traveled together. In the morning, they looked for food and in the afternoon, they would come and perch on the tree.

The boulder that was formerly the signal drum rolled down into the stream when the strong rain and wind arose from the banana soup. The boulder arrived at the stream and turned the stream into a big river. The boulder continued to roll, arriving at the sea and landing by the side of an island. The path that the boulder had taken was that of the big river. This boulder now stands on **Manam** Island in **Madang** [Province, **Manam** People].

The parents looked for their children and worried. They assumed that some group of people had killed them and the old man. After some years, the people forgot the children and the old man. The old man had gone to a new village with new, good people who never stole. Then he made a big banana garden again.

Gabriel Gebara

Office of Information

Vanimo

West Sepik Province

A934.11. River from transformation; A977.5. Origin of particular rock; D150B. Transformation: boy to bird; D450+. Transformation: house to tree; D450+. Transformation: soup to rain; D450+. Transformation: soup to wind; D480+. Transformation: stream to river; D1211. Magic drum; D471+. Transformation: drum to stone; D1781. Magic results from singing; D1781+. Magic results from dancing; K420. Thief loses his goods or is detected; P230. Parents and children; Q86. Reward for industry; Q212. Theft punished; Q281.1. Ungrateful children punished; Q551.3.2.2+. Punishment: transformation into bird; Q584.2. Transformation of a man to animal as fitting punishment; R210. Escapes; V112.1. Spirit huts; W154. Ingratitude

## Samborpia Became a Crocodile
(Wantok 498, December 10, 1983, page 26)

Long, long ago, there was man named Samborpia. Samborpia had two wives. The two women had children. The children and their mothers were skin and bones, they did not have any muscles on them.

Samborpia had a huge sore on his leg. He always went to a stream and put his leg in the water. When he put his leg into the water, the fish would swim and eat at his sore. He would sit for a long time, then remove his leg from the water.

When he removed his leg, the fish would be attached to his sore. Then he would remove the fish and put them in a fish basket. When the basket was completely filled, he would carry them back to his two wives. His wives would cook these fish and eat them.

Samborpia never ate these fish. No, he only ate other kinds of foods.

He did this many times. His two wives often thought about why it was that they often ate plenty of fish but that they were still just skin-and-bones. They decided that one of them would follow him and look at the place where he caught his fish.

In the morning, the man woke up and told the two women that he would go to find fish for them and their children. After he left, the first wife followed him.

The woman hid and saw her husband putting his leg down into the water. She sat and watched the man taking out his leg and removing the fish that were attached to the sore on his leg. The woman had a good look, then she very quietly and went back to the village. She explained to the other wife what she had seen their husband do.

In the afternoon, the man returned to the village and gave the fish to his two wives. The women did not cook the fish.

Samborpia tried to hurry them to cook the fish and eat, but the two women did not hurry. They said, "These are junk fish. We don't want to eat them."

Smborpia [Samborpia] was furious and said, "Who saw me?" The first wife said, "I saw you take the fish from your sore."

Samborpia said, "OK, I'll throw away these junk fish." Then he took the fish and threw them into the forest, and they did not have meat to eat with their food.

They lived there for a long time and Samborpia thought about returning to the stream. He went to the stream and carved a log to look like the head of a crocodile. After he finished carving the log, he made a basket and put the carved log into the basket.

He took some sago and put it inside the basket. After that, he put the basket into the water. However, the basket was not anchored and it drifted in the stream. Sombarpia [Samborpia] saw this and brought back the basket. He went and found a big stone. He brought it and put it in the neck of the basket. He tied the stone, then sang and danced and threw the basket back into the stream. The water carried the basket away.

The Samborpia stood up near the stream and said, "Crocodile, arise and swim on top of the water." The crocodile went on top of the water. Later, he said, "That's enough." Then the crocodile went down into the water again.

Samborpia saw this and he was happy. He told the crocodile, "Stay for another week and I'll come back again with my wives. If you see a woman carrying a net bag of laundry, you must eat her." Samborpia finished explaining this to the crocodile and went back to his house.

After some weeks, Samborpia told his wives that he would go hunting for fish in the stream. He said, "I saw lots of fish in the stream because the boys were playing in the stream and the water became very dirty. The fish are only in the clear areas."

However, it was not children playing in the stream that had made the water dirty. It was just Samborpia's crocodile.

Samborpia took his two wives to the stream and showed them. Oh my, the two women saw this and were very happy. They brought their nets and went inside the water.

The first wife stood and watched while the second wife worked at surrounding the fish. She saw the crocodile coming through the water and she thought that it was a huge fish coming around. The woman tried to surround the crocodile in the water.

The two of them worked like this for a long time, then the woman felt the crocodile and called out to the first wife, "OK, I'm chasing it towards you now. Watch carefully and catch it."

The first wife heard this and watched so as to grab the big "fish." But no, the crocodile just went and pulled the first wife down then ate her. The second wife saw this then jumped up onto the ground and trembled.

Samborpia said, "You two thought that I was just playing around with you. This was something that I spoke to you about that you've seen." The woman was afraid and did not speak. She just quietly took her net bag and the two of them went back to the village. From just this crocodile arose all of the other crocodiles on the earth. Before Samborpia created this crocodile, there were no crocodiles on the earth.

Dominic Apkims
**Amaki** Village [**Kwoma** People]
Mirsey Community School
Ambunti
**East Sepik** Province

A2146. Creation of crocodile; B212. Animal understands human speech; B491.3. Helpful crocodile; D445+. Transformation: image of crocodile vivified; D1781. Magic results from singing; D1781+. Magic results from dancing; D2150+. Catching fish with ulcer as bait; P210. Husband and wife; P230. Parents and children; Q411.14. Death as punishment for spying on uncanny persons; R260. Pursuits; S63+. Husband kills wife; T145.0.1. Polygyny

## Weipun Married the Flying Foxes' Wives

(Wantok 499, December 17, 1983, page 27)

In the time of the ancestors, long, long ago, only women filled **Walis** and **Tarawai** Islands in **East Sepik** Province [**Boiken** People].

These women were married to flying foxes. A man from the Yangoru area stepped on these two islands and changed the way of life of these women.

This man's name was Weipun. He was from a small village named **Sima** in the Yangoru area in the Sepik. Weipun was married and lived with his wife and kin.

One time, a big festival came up in another village near Sima. When Weipun wanted to go the festival, he explained this to his wife. He told his wife clearly that she must sleep in her bed at night and that Weipun's sister also must sleep in the bed with her.

Weipun's wife did not listen to him carefully and she let Weipun's sister sleep in Weipun's bed at night. When Weipun had had enough of the festival, he returned at night. He went directly to bed and slept.

Weipun turned his body in the bed and thought that his wife was sleeping near him. So, he slept with the woman in the bed. However, he was mistaken and committed a sin with his own sister.

Weipun's sister woke up and called out, "Hey brother, I'm your sister. I'm not your wife. You're mistaken!"

The man listened to his sister and he was terribly ashamed. He left the house and ran outside. Poor Weipun was wrong and he was completely ashamed. He looked for a way to leave the village for good.

Weipun took one of his dogs and went into the forest. He walked and walked then he arrived at the mouth of the Hawain River. It was dark again and a heavy rain fell.

Weipun found a hole at the base of a *nar* tree [*Pterocarpus indicus* (Soerianegara and Lemmens, 1993: 379)]. He went inside the tree hole and hid. He brought a big stone and placed it at the entrance of the hole.

He made a fire inside the hole and fell dead asleep. While he was still sleeping, a big flood uprooted the tree. The water carried the tree with him far asea.

Weipun was still asleep when the waves carried him and the tree away towards the shores of Walis Island. The waves carried the tree to rest on the beach. Poor Weipun was completely dead asleep and did not know that the tree had moved in the water and arrived at this place.

He arrived in the morning. He removed the stone from the door and went outside. He was surprised to see a different place. He saw that the sea surrounded this place and he knew that it was an island.

He walked around the beach. He became hungry because he was standing and walking from morning until afternoon.

He walked a little more then he saw a garden underneath the trees. He went inside the garden. He took some ripe bananas and some sugarcane then he ate them. After he ate, he went back inside the tree hole and slept.

In the morning, the two sisters who had made this garden went there and saw that someone had stolen food from their garden. They were furious and they went back to the village.

The next morning, Weipun returned to the garden and again took bananas and sugarcanes then carried them off to eat. After he ate, he went back inside the tree hole and slept.

When the two sisters returned to the garden, they saw what had happened to the food that they had worked hard at planting. They decided to find out who it was that had stolen food from their garden.

One sister hid amidst the sugarcanes and the other went back to the village. When the sister who was hiding in the sugarcanes saw Weipun walking around in the garden, she grabbed Weipun asked him, "Are you a man or a ghost?"

Weipun said, "I'm a man. And you, are you a woman or a ghost?" The woman said, "I'm a real woman."

The woman fulfilled her desires [i.e., had sex] with Weipun then told him to go inside the net bag. She would hide him in the firewood and carry him back to her house.

The woman did not tell her sister that she had a man in their house. She also did not explain this to the other women of the village. At night, the flying foxes would come to the women of the village, and this woman would kill and cook them. Her sister asked, "Hey, why the hell are you killing our husbands?"

Her sister lied to her and said, "I'm tired of them coming and holding my body so I'm killing them."

One day, the woman tightly shut the door to her room and went to the garden. Her sister could not go inside her room, so she went underneath the house and looked inside. She saw the man sitting down and making a net bag.

Pieces of twine fell down and the man pulled them pack into the house. The woman saw this. She went back up into the house and opened the door. She went inside and saw the man.

Later, her sister returned from the garden and saw that she had found out about the man. The sister was angry and she took the man outside the house to look at him. Then Weipun married all of the women of the village.

After some time, Weipun's first wife became pregnant. When she was about to give birth, Weipun was not in the village.

The woman felt a terrible pain and the other women did not know how to help her give birth. The woman went like this for a while, then she got up, broke open her belly and died.

When Weipun returned to the village, the other women told him what had happened to his first wife. He listened and told the women, "If later one of you wants to give birth, you must call out for me to come. Then I'll show you how to give birth."

After that, the women killed all of their flying-fox husbands and Weipun ate them. They gave birth to many babies and populated Walis and Tarawai Islands. Before, the women were married to flying foxes and because of this did not raise children. Later, they married Weipun and had many babies then there were many people on these two islands.

Baltazar Kasim
P. O. Box 602
Wewak
East Sepik Province

[See *Wantok* #299 for a similar story from Walis Island.]

A1011. Local deluges; A1021.0.4. Deluge: escape on floating tree; B601.14.1K. Marriage to flying foxes (in village without men); F112. Journey to Land of Women; F566.1+. Island of women only; J1745.2+. Ignorance of childbirth; M451.1. Death by suicide; P210. Husband and wife; P230. Parents and children; P252.1. Two sisters; P253. Sister and brother; P264. Sister-in-law; R213. Escape from home; S63+. Wife kills husband; S110. Murders; T100. Marriage; T145.0.1. Polygyny; T415. Brother-sister incest; T570. Pregnancy; T580. Childbirth; W157. Dishonesty

# The *Rokia Zava* [Log] Ruined a Friendship
### (Wantok 500, December 24, 1983, page 23)

Long, long ago, there were two good friends who lived in **Lufa** Village [**Yagaria** People, **Eastern Highlands** Province]. The two friends were very old men, and they just lived in a single house.

One of the old men had red skin and the other had black skin. The red-skinned man made a nice garden for himself near the house. He planted various kinds of taros inside this garden.

The red-skinned man took the base of a big tree, a *rokia zava* [lit., "tree branch"], and stood it at the top of the taro garden. He was following the ancestral custom where it is believed that a *rokia zava* will stand and look after the garden. It will protect other people from ruining the garden.

The black-skinned man made his garden far away in the forest and he did not worry about it. However every morning, noon, and night, he would go to defecate in the forest near the house. He would walk over and wipe his buttocks on the *rokia zava*.

This log had a small hole where the black-skinned man would wipe his buttocks. The black-skinned man always wiped his buttocks on this log. The poor red-skinned man did not know this.

The red-skinned man often weeded his garden, but he did not know about the erroneous ways of his friend with the *rokia zava*. The two of them lived well together, cooked food, sat and talked all of the time. They were content and did not get angry.

One day, the old red-skinned man went to check on the taros inside his garden. He walked from the bottom of the garden to the top. He looked at the *rokia zava* and saw the pieces of fecal matter attached to it.

The red-skinned man looked at this great affront and gnashed his teeth. He was furious, but he did not know which man or woman had made this affront on his log. He thought that the other people of the village wanted to taunt him.

So, the red-skinned man went and cut a strong piece of bamboo then made a little knife with the bamboo. Oh my, was the edge of the bamboo sharp! This was because the red-skinned man had taken a stone and sharpened the knife very well.

He took the bamboo knife and shoved it into the little hole in the *rokia zava*. He went to sleep, forgetting his friend, because he was still deeply troubled and did not want to talk to anyone.

The old black-skinned man woke up in the early morning and went near the house to defecate. He defecated and the walked directly towards the *rokia zava*. This was because he wanted to wipe his buttocks there.

Oh my! Oh my! The bamboo knife cut a hole right in the old black-skinned man's buttocks. It went up and down. Blood shot out and he was in great pain. The poor old black-skinned man screamed and screamed for his friend.

The red-skinned man heard his friend's screaming, quickly woke up and ran towards the garden. He saw the big mistake that his friend had done.  He jumped up and punched the black-skinned man.

The black-skinned man felt the pain in his buttocks, but he did not care.  He defended himself and punched his friend.  Then the two of them fought fiercely.

The old red-skinned man cursed the black-skinned man and said, "_Dayate, dayate humalaue_!"  This means, "That was something that I planted with my own hands."

The black-skinned man replied, "_Aigute, aigute humalaue_!"  This means, "That was something that I used to wiped my ass."

The two friends were still angry and they continued fighting through the evening.  Oh my, their fighting began in the early morning and went through the evening!  Their bodies were badly injured all over.  Their entire bodies were bloody and swollen.  Not one part of their bodies was uninjured.  Not one!

The two of them kicked and punched until they were completely exhausted.  They were out of breath and half-dead.  The black-skinned man collapsed and fell asleep on one side.  The red-skinned man also collapsed and he slept on the other side.

They slept soundly until dawn.  The old red-skinned man woke up and killed all of his red-skinned pigs then gave them to his friend.  The black-skinned man paid his debt and killed all of his black-skinned pigs then gave them to the red-skinned man.  They exchanged the pigs and shook hands.

They put to rest this dispute then held each other and cried.  They were sorry and cried for a very long time.  Later, they laughed again.  They met and carved the pork.  They heated stones and cooked the pork in earth ovens then told stories.

In the afternoon, they uncovered the earth ovens, sat together and ate.  They could not finish all of the pork because the old red-skinned man had removed many taros and cooked them with the pork.  They called out for people to come and take some of the pork.

Everyone laughed themselves half-to-death when they heard the story of this, "fight of _rokia zava_."  In my language, _rokia_ means "stick" and _zava_ means "tree."

Everyone celebrated with the red-skinned man and the black-skinned man because they all had some of the big feast.  They carried their food back to each of their homes.

Nowadays, some old men and women have not forgotten this story.  They tell about these two friends who lived in their house until they were very old.  The two of them died together on the same day.

Some people from some places inside the Lufa District of Eastern Highlands Province still tell this story to the young children.  It is true that you can hear or read this story and laugh, but this story has an important origin.  It is the kind of parable that old people explain to young people.

K. Baru Adove
Public Service Commission
Waigani, Port Moresby
[National Capital District]

D956. Magic stick of wood; F527.1. Red person; F527.5. Black man; F529.2. People without anuses; P310. Friendship; P600+. Stick put at top of garden for protection; P634.0.1+. Custom of exchanging food after reconciliation; Q222. Punishment for desecration of holy places (images, etc.); Q584.2. Transformation of a man to animal as fitting punishment; X740.1H+. Symbolic pedicatory rape while at stool; X716.1H+. Befouling with excrement

## The Single Man Who Tricked a Woman
(Wantok 501, January 7, 1984, page 23)

A very long time ago, there was a single man who lived with all of the other people in a village.  This man did not have a wife, and he still lived in his own house.  However, he often thought of and coveted a beautiful married woman in this village.

The man often went to many other villages to try to find a wife.  However, the women in the other villages became tired of seeing him and they scolded him when he flashed his private parts at them.

Often, he would look at one attractive, married woman in his village and he would salivate for her [lit., "swallow his spit"].  However, he could not find a way to meet this woman.  This sorry, single man often thought of her at night.  When he slept in his bed, he often turned and twisted his body just like a bedbug was eating him.  However it was not a bedbug; he was restless because he was dreaming of this woman.

Sometimes he saw the attractive married woman "befriend" another man, and he would become very angry.  The single man saw her doing this many times and he also wanted to try her body.  So, the man sat down and made a plan to visit this woman.

Not much later, he had his chance.  At this time, the attractive, married woman went into the forest with her little child.  They went to scrape and process sago and then to bring it home.  Because of this, the woman's husband went to another place.

The single man found out which path the woman and child had taken. The man sped away into the forest with his bow and arrows.

The single man did not waste any time. He went to hunt some game and killed a marsupial (*kapul*). He then climbed a tree that stood amidst of where the woman was going to be scraping sago.

After the man had climbed this tree, he used all of his strength to break one of its branches. The branch fell and landed in the path where the woman was going to be walking. The man went down and quickly ran into the forest with his bow and arrows.

The man broke up some branches and leaves then put them in the path. He broke up some branches that were the home to some large red ants, and he put the ants' nest close to the pile that he was making.

He took his bamboo knife and cut open the belly of the marsupial at the edge of the path. He pulled out the guts of the marsupial and rubbed its blood on his stomach. He took the marsupial guts and put it underneath his hand so that it looked like his own belly had been ruptured.

He broke open the ant's nest and let the ants bite him all over his body. He then went to the middle of the pile. He laid himself underneath the tree branch as if he was a dead man.

This trick of his was to make another person think that he had gone on top of the branch that had fallen. The person would think that the tree branch had broken his belly open and killed him. However this did not happen; the single man had made this sort of trick just for this attractive woman.

The man lay in the middle of the path just like a man who had died. He stuck his tongue out and closed his eyes shut. He ignored the ants that continued to bite his body. This rotten man did not care.

He heard the woman talking with her child. They were approaching, so he lay awkwardly just like a dead man. The woman came and saw him lying in the path with his belly broken open with blood coming out, she saw that ants had just ruined his body.

However as you know, the blood was really from the marsupial. The woman was shaking and was quite frightened. She told her young child to run and go home, to talk to another man and tell him to come bring this poor man back to the village.

When the child ran back towards home, the single man got up quickly and held the woman tightly. The poor woman was furious, but she could not cry out because the single man had captured her deep in the forest.

All of the men from the village came to look for the man who had died, but there was no one there. They looked around near the path, but there was nothing! So they went back to the village and had a long discussion.

The single man took the attractive woman to another place that was far from their village. They made themselves a house; they cleared some land and made a garden. He stayed with the woman, and he was truly happy. They lived at this new place for an entire year.

Everyone from the village thought that he had died in the forest, but they were wrong. The single man with the attractive woman now had a child. The man and woman left their new place and returned to their village.

Everyone in the village was surprised when they saw the poor man, but they were happy because the woman was carrying her attractive child. The woman's true husband had died, and the single man shouted with joy.

Philip Kawa
**Torembi** [**Sawos** People]
Wewak
**East Sepik** Province

K1862. Death feigned to meet lover; P210. Husband and wife; P230. Parents and children; R10. Abduction; T10. Falling in love; T192. Marriage by force; T481. Adultery; W181. Jealousy; X743H. Humor concerning exhibitionism

## The Two Brothers Found Yams
### (*Mami*) on Siassi [Island]
(Wantok 502, January 14, 1984, page 22)

Long, long ago, on **Siassi** Island, the people did not know about yams (*mami*) [**Mutu** People, **Morobe** Province]. They did not know that yams were something to eat. They thought that yam was just an ordinary vine in their forests.

There were two brothers who lived at this time. The two brothers did not have a father. Only their old mother lived with them. Their mother was very old and she only liked to eat meat.

One night, the two brothers wanted to sleep. The old mother told the first son, "Tomorrow, you and your little brother shall go to the forest and hunt for marsupials (*kapul*). I want to drink marsupial soup."

In the early morning, the brothers took their spears and stone axes then called their dogs. They left the village and went inside the forest.

They arrived at very big river. They crossed the water and went to the other side. They walked directly into the forest. One of their dogs could not cross the water, so it ran away back to the village.

The two brothers thought that all of their dogs had come with them and they did not look carefully at the dogs. They entered the deep forest and the big brother told his little brother, "Walk quietly. Don't talk or cut the trees or make noises. Just walk quietly behind me."

The two brothers walked, looking for marsupials. They walked and walked. The sun was completely obscured by clouds. It was high noon. The little brother told his big brother, "Can we rest a little?" His big brother said, "OK, let's rest a little and then look for game again."

When the two brothers sat down, all of their dogs came and sat close to them. However, one dog did not come. The two brothers thought that it was lost. The little brother was very worried about their dog, so he asked his brother to find their dog.

The big brother said that they must first try to call the dog. He got up and called out, but nothing happened. Then he broke wind very loudly.

All of the dogs that were sitting near them smelled his gas and they were racked with hunger. They thought that he wanted to defecate and so they came and stood close to the big brother. However after the smell was gone, the dogs howled and howled, then began to run back to the village.

It was nearly dark and the two brothers called the dogs to go back to the village. But they did not know that all of their dogs had already gone back to the village. They called and called, but the dogs did not arrive.

Darkness came and the two brothers looked for a place to sleep. They thought about making a forest hut for themselves. They did not have food and they thought that they would just go to sleep hungry. They made a bonfire with tree branches. The big brother went back into the forest a little distance to look for some good, big tree leaves to make a bed for sleeping.

They straightened their things and they sat for a little while, telling stories. Then they slept. Late at night, the little brother wanted to defecate, so he woke up very quietly and just went outside near the hut. However as he was defecating, a huge marsupial smelled his feces and came close the little boy's behind. The little brother was defecating and the big marsupial began to eat his feces.

After the marsupial finished all of the boy's feces on the ground, it got up and cleaned the little boy's buttocks. When the boy turned around to look, he saw this huge thing finishing off his feces.

So, the good-for-nothing left some of the feces inside himself and went inside the forest hut. He woke his brother and told him about the marsupial. The little brother had not cleaned his buttocks, so his feces smelled and the marsupial was waiting outside.

The brothers decided to kill the marsupial. The little brother told his brother, "You should go hide in the forest. I'll pretend to go and defecate. When the marsupial comes to eat my shit, you can come behind and kill it."

The big brother took his stone axe. He went first and hid in the forest. The little brother went outside again and defecated. The marsupial returned and began eating his feces. While the marsupial was devouring the feces, the big brother came from behind and put the axe directly through its head.

Then the little brother went inside the forest and cleaned his buttocks. At this time, he took a yam leaf and rubbed his buttocks. His big brother took the marsupial and carried it into their forest hut. The little brother returned to the hut and felt his buttocks itch. When he scratched, it felt much better. He told his big brother about the leaf and his brother said that they must wait until dawn, then they could look at the leaf.

In the early morning, they made a big fire and cooked the marsupial. Later, they went and found the leaf that the little brother had used to rub his buttocks. They saw that it was not from a tree. It was just from a vine. They began to dig the earth at the base of the vine.

They dug and dug then saw that there was food at the base of the yam vine. They removed the yam tuber and carried it off to cook. They finished cooking and the big brother was the first to try the yam.

The yam was delicious. The big brother was very happy that the yam tasted so good and he called out happily. The little brother also tried it and it was delicious. They carried some marsupial to their old mother at the village.

When they arrived at the house, they smelled that something was not right. They looked and saw that their old mother had died and was lying there. They cried terribly. The other people of Siassi Village heard this and came to their house. They saw the marsupial meat outside with the yam. Some of them cooked and ate it.

The brothers went outside and saw the other people eating the yam, singing, dancing and talking about this thing that was so delicious.

At this time, the people of Siassi knew that yams were something to be eaten. They went inside the forest to look for yams, and they also cooked and ate wild yams. At this time, many people carried the yam and *mami* roots back to the village and planted them.

Tom S. Mollo

c/- Const Steven Mais

Box 1910

Boroko

National Capital District

A2686.4.3. Origin of yams; B871.2+. Giant marsupial; P231. Mother and son; P251.5. Two brothers; X716H+. The escoumerda; X716.6H. Smell of breaking wind; X716.8H. Fortuitous breaking wind

## Two Birds that Killed Men

(Wantok 503, January 21, 1984, page 23)

Long, long ago, in the time of the ancestors, in Werman [**Wereman**] Village, near Wewak, **East Sepik** Province, there was a tree between two villages [**Sawos** People]. The two villages were Upper Werman and Lower Werman.

On this tree were two birds that lived there all of the time. The name of this kind of bird in my language is *gawi*.

The two birds would perch and watch the men, women and children of the two villages very carefully. When the men, women and children would leave their houses and walk away, the birds would fly down, snatch them and carry them up to the tree. After they ate the human flesh, they would just let the bones fall down to the base of the tree.

Down at the base of the tree, there was a pond. The people of the two villages did not have a way to get close to the tree or to go up and kill the two birds.

One night, the men of the two villages sat and met in the big spirit house. They tried to think of and discuss a way to kill the two birds. If they could not find a way, the two birds would finish off everyone who was living in these villages.

Two men spoke out that they would go up the tree and kill two birds. The men of the villages laughed at what these two men thought because the tree that the two birds lived on was not young. It was truly huge. It was so tall that it went up to the clouds. The base of the tree was immense and an ordinary man could not climb it.

One day, the men of the two villages traveled to the forests and gardens to look for food. In the afternoon, the men finished working and returned to the villages. They saw the two men carving a hand drum. They asked them about this, but they did not reply. They just slowly finished all of the work on this big hand drum on that day.

After they finished the hand drum, they told the men of the villages that they would go inside the huge hand drum. The men were to carry the hand drum and put it in the clearing where the two birds could see them.

That night, the two men cooked yams for themselves to eat for when they stayed inside the drum. The men of the villages did not sleep. They met and told stories to the two men.

Near dawn, the cock crowed and the two men went inside the big drum. One man put his head inside one hole of the drum and the other man put his head inside the other hole. They also carried two sticks to strike the drum.

They stayed tight inside the drum. Then the men closed the two openings of the drum with huge coconut shells.

They carried away the drum with the two men inside and put it directly in the middle of the clearing. They had done this when it was still dark because if it was light, the two birds would have finished off the two men.

Dawn broke then the two birds flew down, snatched the big drum and carried it up the tree. The other men saw this while they were sitting and hiding. They cowered and were frightened.

The two men felt that they were on top of the tree. They just waited until darkness came, then they would kill the birds.

They slept and when they were hungry, they ate the yams inside the drum. Night came and the *gawi* birds slept very close to the side of the drum.

Very quietly, the two men opened the ends of the drum and quickly went outside. The birds were not thinking. The men conquered and killed them.

The men took the two sticks for beating the drum and bashed the birds. One *gawi* fell down to a place where two women were rinsing sago.

The other bird fell down to the base of the tree. Then the two men on top of the tree called down to the men to make a ladder so that they could go down. The men were ecstatic and made a very long ladder.

The two men went to the ground and told the men of the villages where the birds had fallen. They took one of the birds. Later, they looked for the other. They searched and arrived at the place where the two women were rinsing sago. However, the two women had taken the bird and hidden it among the sago palm leaves. They lied to the men that they had not seen the bird.

The men searched and searched, but did not find the bird. They knew that the two women had hidden the bird. They were angry and killed the two women. The blood of the two women went down to a small stream and turned into a fish that we call _kavi_.

The men found the _gawi_ bird feathers and the blood that had gone amongst the sago. They found the bird among the sago leaves where the women had hidden it.

They took the bird and carried it to the villages. The people of the two Werman villages gathered and made a huge feast for the two men who had killed the two birds. This was because for many years, they never walked happily in this area where the tree was. They were always afraid of the two birds.

Now there is a marking where the tree stood by Werman Village. The sago trees still stand where they killed the two women. If you ask the old people of Werman Village, they will tell you the story and show you these places too.

Jack Lapui

Works and Supply, P. O. Box 106

Wewak

East Sepik Province

[There is a similar story in _Wantok_ #1159.]

A990. Other land features; B16.3+. Devastating bird killed; B33. Man-eating birds; B552. Man carried by bird; D447.3+. Transformation: blood to fish; F54.1. Tree stretches to sky; F813.3.2+. Gigantic nut; G510.4. Hero overcomes devastating animal; K753. Capture by hiding in disguised objects; Q263.1. Death as punishment for perjury; Q411. Death as punishment; V112.1. Spirit huts; W157. Dishonesty

## A Bee Took Care of a Boy
(Wantok 504, January 28, 1984, page 23)

Long ago, in the time of the ancestors, there were a man and his wife who lived with many other people on the mainland near the beach. This man and woman had a small son.

One morning, the man told his wife and child to go with him to find some food and leafy greens on an island. This island was fairly far from the mainland. The three of them paddled their canoe to the island.

There was a story going around the village that a huge _masalai_ snake watched over the island. This _masalai_ snake was short and fat. It had two huge heads. One was its real head and the other was a head on its tail.

This man and his wife understood this story, but the boy did not know about it. The three of them paddled the canoe and approached the island.

The snake smelled them, then went and hid near the beach that they were about to land upon. Oh my! The ma-_salai_ snake saw the man, the woman, and the fat little boy and it was very happy.

When the canoe went ashore, the _masalai_ snake's real head dived first and smashed the middle of the canoe, breaking it into two pieces. The bow of the canoe carried the father down towards the sea.

The _masalai_ snake's other head leapt and swallowed the other part of the canoe with the mother and boy. However, a big bee quickly flew by and pulled the boy from his mother's arms.

The bee carried the little boy and quickly flew to its house under a big tree on the island. The _masalai_ snake pulled the father and mother up on the beach and swallowed all of their flesh. All of their bones just lay on the beach.

The bee took care of the little boy very well. The boy still crawled around, he was not yet able to stand. The bee traveled to all of the places on the island, killing little birds and giving them to the baby.

When the baby wanted to go far away, the bee would fly and gently bite his hands or legs then pull him back. The poor baby would cry, but the bee thought of him and took care of him well. The bee also spoke and taught the baby how to make things.

The bee looked after the child on the island until he was about ten years old. The two of them still traveled the island and the bee taught the child how to take care of himself. The bee taught the boy how to look for food, how to hunt for wild game in the forest, and how to fight.

One morning, the boy told the bee to make a bow for him. This insect, the bee, was a very smart insect. It flew quickly into the forest. It chewed on a strong _limbum_ palm and broke it.

The bee flew and broke a strong vine then tied it to the piece of the _limbum_ palm. It tightened the vine on the two ends of the _limbum_ and the _limbum_ became like a bow. The bee then went and put it in the boy's hand.

The bee revealed the story of the _masalai_ snake that had eaten the boy's parents. The two of them decided to go and kill the snake. They prepared many arrows, lest the _masalai_ snake pulverize them.

In the very early morning, the bee told the boy to sit on top of its body and they would fly to the snake's house. The boy was ready with his bow. The bee sped off directly towards the _masalai_ snake's head.

The _masalai_ snake smelled the boy and stood by. The snake leapt up and shoved its mouth out to eat the bee and the boy, but it was too late. The boy let loose an arrow and shot the snake's head.

The torso of the snake swept the trees and grasses then went to surround the bee and the boy. "Get out of the way!" Immediately, four arrows flew from his bow and were planted into the snake's body. The other head at the snake's tail turned and jumped down to break the boy's head.

The *masalai* snake had nearly planted its two fangs into the boy's face, but the boy stretched his hands and quickly swung an arrow that anchored into the *masalai* snake's head. The snake bled profusely and the lay dead on the ground.

The poor boy was out of breath, but the bee did not rest yet. The bee carried the boy. They had tricked and killed the snake. They laughed and were very happy.

The bee and the boy walked to the beach and arrived at the place in the sand where the *masalai* snake had eaten his parents. They carried his parents' bones and went to the bee's house.

The boy helped the bee join all of the bones of the man and woman. The bee worked at obtaining mud for the mouth, arms, and legs, joining the earth with their bones. They worked and worked then the bee breathed inside them and the man and woman arose.

The man and woman were surprised and they saw the boy standing with the bee, laughing. The mother looked and knew that it was her son. She walked over and held him tightly, crying terribly. They were happy and cried together. The man also went over and held the bee tightly and shook the bee's hands a lot.

They laughed and walked together to the forest. They gathered plenty of food and game then went to cook it at the bee's house. They made a huge party. The men of the mainland came fishing with their canoes at night, and they saw a big fire on the island.

The people of the mainland often looked at the fire and the large amounts of smoke that frequently came from the island. However they thought that the *masalai* snake still lived there, so they did not want to go there to look at the island. It was just the man, woman, boy and bee who lived there.

The man thought about returning to the mainland, so he made a canoe. The bee helped him obtain various kinds of things and finished the work of making the canoe.

The poor bee was alone on the island, so the bee also wanted to go the mainland. The *masalai* snake had eaten the bees on the island, so the bee had no kin.

The man and bee worked hard until one year, they finished the canoe. Later, they took the canoe and paddled to the mainland. Everyone came and gathered to welcome him, his wife, their son, and the bee too.

However, the people of the mainland did not recognize the man and woman because they had gray hair. The boy had become a big man, but they told the little story and everyone was happy to get this family back.

The people were happy to eat, sing and dance. The poor bee flew away and looked for kin in the forest. The bee met some kin and they flew together back to the island. However the bee, who had been alone, often went to look at the boy who had been with him on the island.

Peter Sale

Kandrian High School

West New Britain Province

B15.1.2.1.1. Two-headed serpent; B16.5.1. Giant devastating serpent; B170+. Flight on bee; B211.4.2. Speaking bee; B481.3. Helpful bee; B535+. Bee as nurse for child; B873+. Giant bee; B875.1. Giant serpent; D935.2. Magic clay; D1005. Magic breath; E30. Resuscitation by arrangement of members; F490+. Masalai; G354.1. Snake as ogre; G510.4. Hero overcomes devastating animal; L111.4. Orphan hero; P210. Husband and wife; P231+. Son avenges mother; P233.6. Son avenges father; P275. Foster son; Q211. Murder punished; Q411. Death as punishment; R100. Rescues

## A Woman Disobeyed What Was Said

(Wantok 505, February 4, 1984, page 23)

Long, long ago, in the time of the ancestors, there was a village on **Manus** Island [**Manus** Province]. There was a woman who lived alone [i.e., only with her children] in this village.

One day, all of the men, women and children emptied out and went to a village for a huge festival. Many people from villages near and far gathered. The people of the mainland and the small islands filled up this village for the festival.

The woman had a baby who was not strong yet. Her two big sons went with their maternal kin so that they could learn the festival customs.

Their father had died. His grave was underneath the house. Also underneath the house was their big pig. This pig was still young. The father had set the time for it to be killed when the first son became a man.

The father had told the mother not to let the two sons travel with other kinsmen, that they must only travel with their paternal uncle. The father died and his ghost was angry with the children's maternal kin who had taken them to the festival.

Late at night, there was no talking and there was no children's crying at this village. Only the woman with her baby was there.

Then [it sounded like] the pig which lived underneath the house began to make noises. The woman thought that it was the pig, but no, it was her husband in the grave who was hitting and shaking the ground. The house shook and the pig called out again.

The woman was sleeping with her baby. She lit a torch and went down to check on the pig, but the pig was sleeping quietly.

Before, the woman [would] have gone and worked at the festival in the other village, making food and singing and dancing. She would have sung and danced. The woman had not gone because her husband had just died and if she had seen his friends at the festival she would have been troubled. So, she was mourning and troubled because of her husband. She just sat in the house. Also, she had a newborn baby. She had been pregnant when her husband had died.

The woman saw the pig sleeping quietly and she went back into the house. This time, she heard a very loud noise underneath the house. It was the dead man rising from the grave and walking upon the earth. He took the big pig. The pig squealed and squealed very loudly. Then it stopped squealing.

The dead man went outside then carried the huge pig down into the grave. The woman heard the ground rumbling underneath the house.

She thought that the pig was asleep because there was no more noise. However, the woman did not have the slightest idea that her husband had carried the pig on the path of the dead.

Near morning when it was still dark, the people were still wildly singing and dancing at the other village. The people bowed down then rose up again with their various adornments.

However, the two boys' maternal kin were not very happy at the festival. The two boys' eyes spun around in sleepiness. Their maternal uncle's wife sat and looked after the two of them. They slept close to her. Their maternal uncle sang and danced with the other people. Trouble was about to come to his sister's village and the two boy's maternal kin did not understand the festival very well.

At the village, the woman was sleeping with her baby. She listened for the cock's crowing and then she would know that it was near dawn. She just thought about her two sons who were at the festival with their maternal kin. She wanted dawn to come quickly and for them to return to the house so that she could see them again.

The woman slept and waited for them. Before long, the dead man made a loud noise underneath the house. He arose and came out of his grave. He walked and went directly up to the house.

The woman heard a noise at the house door. She called out, "Hey, this place doesn't have dogs. All of the dogs went to the festival with their owners. What is it that is making that noise at the door?"

The man just put his hand on the bed and cut the little baby. The woman was shocked and turned to see her husband. Then the man's face changed to look like that of a ghost. The woman saw this and she screamed and cried.

The man took his little baby then broke the baby into two pieces and ate them. Later, he spat the blood from the baby into the woman's face.

He told the woman that he would eat her too. The woman was afraid and began to run. She went to the festival site, but her brother was looking for time. His head was spinning around and his kin were trying to help him at the festival. His sister's troubles had taken him.

The woman screamed and cried while still running. Her husband carried the baby's bones in one hand and the pig bones in the other as he was chasing the woman. He shouted to her that her bones would be in between them and that he would carry them.

The woman ran and ran. She was almost out of breath. It was light and the path was clear. She met the first group of people who had left the village and she fell down. However, she was not dead. She got up later and told the story to her two children and her brother.

Later, they burned the house and the grave at the village. The woman and her two sons went to live with their maternal kin in their house.


Paul Hanai
Manus High School
Manus Province


B871.1.2.1. Giant hog; E221+. Dead husband's malevolent return; E222+. Dead father's malevolent return; E261.4. Ghost pursues man; E230. Return from dead to inflict punishment; E410. The unquiet grave; E425.2. Revenant as man; G11.10. Cannibalistic spirits; P210. Husband and wife; P231. Mother and son; P251.5. Two brothers; P253. Sister and brother; P290+. Maternal kin; P293+. Maternal uncle; P293+. Paternal uncle; P294+. Maternal aunt; P310. Friendship; Q325. Disobedience punished; Q411.3. Death of father (son, etc.) as punishment; R260. Pursuits; S11.3. Father kills child; S11.3.8. Father eats own children; S110. Murders; S139.2. Slain person dismembered; T570. Pregnancy; V61.3+. Dead buried; W126. Disobedience

## Kondumung's Mistake

(Wantok 506, February 11, 1984, page 26)

Long, long ago, in the time of the ancestors, there was no sun or moon. There were two mountains, Nunga and Auduka. The two mountains stood near the **Nebilyer** area in **Western Highlands** Province [**Hagen** People]. These two mountains thought about standing up together.

One night, Nunga asked a marsupial (*kapul*) to bring a message to Auduka. The name of the marsupial was Kondumung. Nunga told marsupial Kondumung, "I want you to tell Auduka that the two of us will meet and stand together on just one side."

Nunga told the marsupial to go tell the other mountain that at night when everyone would be asleep, they would slowly move and stand close together.

The marsupial walked slowly on the ground. The marsupial jumped up on a tree branch and went to give the information to the other mountain.

When the marsupial arrived at the Truk River, it was daylight. This was because the other mountain stood very far away. The marsupial was terrified that men would see it, so it jumped down to the river.

Mount Nunga thought that the other mountain had gotten the message. The mountain began to move very slowly towards where the other mountain stood. When Nunga arrived at Neiblyer [Nebilyer], dawn had arrived. The mountain saw this and was terrified that the men would find out that it was no longer standing at the usual place.

Immediately, the mountain moved back towards the place where it had been standing before. So now, you can see pieces of its "arms." Nunga arrived at the Nebilyer River, but the other mountain did not have the slightest idea about what Nunga had thought. This was because nobody had told the mountain. The marsupial that had carried the message became frightened when dawn broke and it went down to the Truk River.

So now, when people go walking around in the forests of Mount Auduka, they never call the name of the other mountain, Nunga. This is because Auduka would be angry and wreck the people's trails so that they could not find the way back to the village.

One time, an ancestor went up to Mount Auduka and called the name of Auduka. The man looked for his home, but the deep forest and grasses covered up the trail. The man did not have a way back to the village. For many days and nights, he tried to find his way back to the village.

He did not find a way. He worked at killing wild game in the forests of Mount Auduka, and he ate. He did this for a while then he became a real wild man. He tied tree leaves to make something like a loincloth. He would get very cold when strong winds rose up the mountain.

Many months passed and the man longed to search for a trail in the forests of this mountain. Also, at this time when he walked and searched for a trail, the ghosts of the mountain would call out from a corner, "Here's the trail! Come here."

But when he went go to the place, there was no trail there. He thought that the men of his village would look for him and call out again. But the ghosts from another corner called out, "Here's the trail! Come here." He did this, but the ghosts of the mountain befuddled him. The real trail had been completely blocked off. The man also thought that the ghosts had completely confused him.

Later, the man died and only his bones were left on the mountain. After this, the people knew that the man must have gone up Mount Auduka because the mountain would explode and make noise at night. This was just the cry and song of the ghosts of the mountain. They were happy to have eaten the meat of this man.

Now, the two mountains still stand far apart, just like before in the time of the ancestors. If the marsupial had gone quickly and delivered the message, the two mountains would be standing very close. But now this is not the case, they are at opposite ends.

Mr. T. Mang

P. O. Box 35

Mt. Hagen

Western Highlands Province

This was a story from the Tok Pisin Literature Contest. John Kolia [editor of the journal *Oral History* from 1972-1977] sent the story to *Wantok*.

A965. Origin of mountain chain; C430+. Tabu: uttering name of mountain; E481.3. Abode of dead in mountain; E545. The dead speak; F567. Wild man; F755.1. Speaking mountain; F755.6. Moving mountain; G11.10. Cannibalistic spirits

## Why Do Eagle, Flying Fox and Cockatoo Often Steal?

(Wantok 507, February 18, 1984, pages 26-27)

Long, long ago, in land of the **Mesem** People, a woman put her son into a net bag and hung the bag upon a tree branch. Then she weeded her yam garden [**Morobe** Province].

She was not watching the baby, so soon thereafter, a big eagle flew and snatched the net bag, pulling it up with the baby.

Oh my! The mother heard the baby crying from above. She looked up and saw the eagle carrying the baby and the net bag. The mother screamed and cried, but it was too late.

Quickly, a flying fox came and raised the net bag with the baby onto the eagle's back. A cockatoo also came.

The eagle told the cockatoo, "Fly away and arrange for a place for the baby to sit."

After the cockatoo did this, the two of them arrived and put the baby down there. The baby's first two teeth had come out.

The eagle became like a father, the flying fox like a mother, and the cockatoo like a brother to the baby. The mother went and found papayas, ripe bananas, and other fruits that were good for the baby to eat. These "birds" [the flying fox is a mammal] took care of the baby very well.

When the baby became a little bigger, the eagle father killed wild game such as pigs or marsupials (*kapul*) to give to the baby, and the baby would eat them.

The cockatoo would travel, looking for corn, beans, bananas, and other things to eat. Cockatoo would also eat these. Cockatoo would also give these things to [the others].

They did this for a while, then the little baby became a big man. The father stood and dressed his son while he sat there.

The eagle removed his tail feathers and affixed them nicely around his son's face. When the wind blew the feathers, it would make a noise.

In another village, there lived a man, his wife and two daughters. However, there was no man there to marry the two daughters.

The first daughter often went hunting for rats, bandicoots, and other marsupials to give to her parents and her little sister. They would cook and eat these. She would do this every day. One day, she went close to the big tree where the boy lived.

On this day, the woman went directly to the tree and looked for rats in the hole underneath the tree. The boy's father had decorated him with the cockatoo's feathers.

The wind blew the cockatoo feathers on the boy's face, making a noise. The shadow of the plumage fell directly upon the woman's breasts. The woman thought that it was tree leaves, so she removed some tree leaves.

She looked again at her breasts and it was still there. She tried to remove a branch, but the noise was still there. She was angry now and she removed all of the tree leaves that were near her.

She looked again and it was still there. She said, "What's wrong now?" When she said this, she looked up at the tree branch.

"You people! That's not a man, that's the sign of a real good-for-nothing!"

After she saw this, she shouted, "Oh sorry, my man, come down quickly." He said that no, he wanted her to come up. However, there was no way up, so she shouted and shouted until it was evening, and nearly dark.

She left the base of the tree and ran back to the village where she told her story to her parents about what she had seen. She said, "Please, quickly sharpen a stone axe. Then tomorrow in the early morning, we'll wake up and cut the tree down. Afterwards, I'll marry my man. Mama, you should prepare food for us, then papa will take down the big tree."

They finished all of their preparations that night and they slept. They awoke when it was still in the middle of the night and the departed. When they arrived at the big tree, the father looked up. It was too true! The man was adorned handsomely and sitting up there. The father quickly cut and cut the tree.

When the tree was about to break, the eagle father grabbed his son's hair and hoisted him up. The flying fox went underneath and helped the eagle raise their son. The cockatoo flew away, found a nice big tree and prepared a place for his brother to sit.

When the tree broke, the two "birds" raised the boy. The woman saw this and called out to them. The woman went and stood on a mountain then watched the "birds" perching on a big tree. When the woman saw this, she told her father to go back to their village.

The next day, they went to cut the big tree where the "birds" had perched. When the tree was about to fall, the "birds" got up and carried the boy to another tree. They did this until eight trees were gone.

At the last tree, the eagle father told the mother and the brother cockatoo, "Let's give this boy to them now. The poor people have worked very hard, cutting many trees. So let's give the boy to them and the woman will marry him."

Then the woman's father quickly cut the tree. When the tree was about to fall, the two "birds" raised the boy up and the tree fell down. Later, he came down gently to the village where the woman and her parents lived.

When the birds took the boy close to the ground, oh my, the woman was not quiet. She jumped and jumped, shouting, "Bring him down quickly."

The eagle and the flying fox came and stood the boy on the ground. The father eagle, mother flying fox, and brother cockatoo gave instructions to the woman.

The father eagle said, "I'm the father of this boy, so the payment for this man shall be for me to chase and kill a pig for you. I shall carry it for you to eat. I'll take a chicken from you, so you can't become angry. That's the payment for this boy."

The mother flying fox said, "I'm the mother of this boy. I'll go around your garden and eat ripe bananas, ripe papayas, and other foods. This is the payment for my son, so you can't be angry. Also, I'll hang on your bean plants, so you can't become angry and kill me. Do you understand?"

The man's kin finished speaking and flew away. The woman and her parents took the man then went to the village. The woman married this man and they lived together.

The man helped them make a house and gardens, and he did other kinds of work. They lived there for a while, then one day, the man's wife went to the garden. She worked at gathering foods such as leafy greens and beans.

She went close to the base of the beans and saw the man's mother, the flying fox, hanging on the bean vines. The woman forgot, and she killed the flying fox. She covered the flying fox, put her in the net bag and carried her back to the village. She took the flying fox and cooked her with yams and taros.

After she finished cooking, she divided the food up and gave some to her husband. The man saw the meat and asked his wife, "What kind of meat did you cook?" The woman said, "It's the meat that we often eat. It's flying fox."

Oh my, the man was speechless. He was out of breath and did not eat. He was sorry for his mother. He did not sleep. He cried and cried through the night and through the next morning too. In the early morning, the woman told the man, "Let's go to the garden to weed the yams and taros."

The man said, "You go. I'm sick. Later, when the sun is strong, I'll go see you."

He had lied to them, and they went off to their garden. When they had left for the garden, the man stood some spears on the ground. He stood on the roof of the house and jumped upon the spears.

The spears shot through his belly and he died lying on top of them. Later, the woman, the parents and the little sister return from the garden. They looked around the house and they saw the good-for-nothing lying dead. The woman ran to hold her husband's body and she cried.

The old man scolded his daughter, "That's your fault. The man was sorry for his mother, so he did this. When they brought the man, they gave you instructions. His mother told you, 'If I go to hang on the beans, don't kill me.' But you ignored this and killed her. Because of this, the man was sorry for his mother and he killed himself."

Afterwards, they just lived in the village. It was only they who lived there. Later, they died and there were no more people in this village.

Mr. Dofe
**Sibi** Village
M. B. T. Group, Box 146
Lae
Morobe Province

A2455+. Why cockatoo is thief; A2455+. Why eagle is thief; A2455+. Why flying fox is thief; B211.2.11K+. Speaking flying fox; B211.3+. Speaking cockatoo; B211.3.11K. Speaking eagle; B535+. Flying fox as nurse for child; B535.0.7+. Cockatoo as nurse for child; B535.0.7+. Eagle as nurse for child; B552. Man carried by bird; B552+. Person carried by flying fox; G61.1. Child recognizes relative's flesh when it is served to be eaten; M451.1. Death by suicide; P210. Husband and wife; P231. Mother and son; P231+. Son commits suicide on death of mother; P232. Mother and daughter; P234. Father and daughter; P252.1. Two sisters; P261. Father-in-law; P262. Mother-in-law; P265. Son-in-law; P265+. Daughter-in-law; P271. Foster father; P272. Foster mother; P273. Foster brother; P275. Foster son; R13.3.2. Eagle carries off youth; R260. Pursuits; S54+. Daughter-in-law kills mother-in-law; S110. Murders; T52. Bride purchased; T52+. Groom purchased; T100. Marriage; Z71.16.1. Formulistic number: eight

## Where Did Lime (Calcium Oxide) for Planting Yams Come From?

(Wantok 508a, February 25, 1984, page 26)

Long, long ago in a village, there was a woman who was having her monthly period and she went into the forest to look for bamboos. The bamboos that the woman found were the spears of a *masalai* cockatoo.

While the woman was searching for bamboos, she looked at the base of a *ton* tree and she saw some *ton* fruits. She took some and ate them. They tasted delicious. She looked up tree and she saw a cockatoo eating *ton* fruits.

The woman called out, "If you're a good cockatoo, then throw some *ton* fruits down at me." The cockatoo listened and threw some *ton* fruits at the woman.

It was becoming dark and the woman went to the village. She arrived at the village and began to share the bamboos and *ton* fruits with the people of the village. They ate, but they did not taste good, as they did when the woman had eaten them. After she finished eating, she went inside the house and slept.

While the people of the village slept, the *masalai* cockatoo turned into the woman's husband, went inside the woman's house, and worked at "befriending" her. The woman felt a man on top of her, so she got up and called out. The *masalai* cockatoo did this many times.

One night, the men of the village decided to see which man it was that often came to the woman at night. While they were watching, they saw the *masalai* cockatoo turn into a real man then try to go inside the woman's house. When they saw this, they got up and surrounded the *masalai*.

At dawn, they took the woman to the *masalai* cockatoo's home. When the men wanted to return to the village, they told a boy to watch the *masalai* and see what it would do to the woman.

The boy watched and he saw the *masalai* rise above the pond then tell the woman to close her eyes. The woman closed her eyes and the *masalai* cut off her two breasts.

The *masalai* struck the water. The water opened and the two of them went down. When the boy saw this, he went to the village and told everyone what the *masalai* had done. Everyone was sorry and cried terribly.

It was nearly dark. They beat the signal drum towards all of the villages, telling them to heat stones. After they finished heating the stones, they carried them to the pond and threw the stones down into the pond. They watched the *masalai* man ascend. They took him, cut him into little pieces and burned him.

After they burned him, they took the ashes, which were like lime (calcium oxide), and sent them to all of the villages. Now our villages carry this lime and use it for planting yams that otherwise would not grow well. The pond is still there.

If you travel to Kumbuhun [**Kumbuhum**] Village [**Mountain Arapesh** People, **East Sepik** Province], you can see this pond and the lime too.

R. Henry
Yangoru High School
East Sepik Province

A978.1+. Origin of lime (calcium oxide) from body of dead spirit; B212. Animal understands human speech; B469+. Helpful cockatoo; D150+M. Transformation: man to cockatoo; D350+M. Transformation: cockatoo to man; D921. Magic lake (pond); F401.3.7+. Spirit in form of cockatoo; F490+. Masalai; K1311. Seduction by masking as woman's husband; K1910. Marital impostors; Q411. Death as punishment; R4. Surprise capture; R260. Pursuits; S176.1K2+. Murder by cutting off breasts



## Heahun Showed the Way

(Wantok 508b, February 25, 1984, page 26)

Long, long ago in the time of the ancestors in the **Yangoru** area, the mountain called Turun did not exist [**Boiken** People, **East Sepik**].

At this time, the men of this area still dug the earth in all of the villages and in the Sepik River area too. They piled the dirt up at the place where this mountain is now.

They worked at doing this for a while, until a mountain arose. They had dug the earth at these places, and they walked upon the places around the Sepik River and the other places that are now there.

At these places that the men did not walk upon, there were hills such as those of Yangoru and Maprik. The mountain called Turun had a friend in the **Kairiru** Island area [**Kairiru** People]. The name of this mountain is Heahun.

Whenever Mount Turun wanted to chew betel nuts, he would call out to his wife, Nakaguwai, to come open up her vagina so that Turun could chew the betel nuts inside Nakaguwai [with] lime (calcium oxide). He did this all of the time. One time, Mount Heahun arrived at his home and asked him for lime.

Turun said, "I never eat betel nuts with lime." He called for his wife, Nakaguwai, who was in the garden.

Nakaguwai came, and her husband told her to chew betel nuts inside her vagina. When Heahun saw this, he got up and scolded Turun then gave him some real lime. Turun chewed the lime that Heahun had given him and he saw that the betel nut turned bright red [as it should].

When Heahun wanted to return to his home, he told Turun to kill some pigs, then the two of them could make a party. Before dawn, Turan [Turun] went and took his "dogs", which were lizards that are called *lewo* in my language, and went into the forest. When they entered the forest, they killed grasshoppers as if they were their pigs.

After they killed all of these, Turun let his "pigs" into a big playground [field]. He left the "pigs", then he went to the house and struck the sago palm leaf wall of the house as if it was a signal drum. However when he struck it, the sound of the wall did not go far.

When it was nearly dawn, Heahun arrived. He told Turun in his language that Turun had not beaten the signal drum.

However Turun said, "I beat the signal drum."

Heahun asked, "Where's your signal drum?" Turun showed him the house wall that he had used like a signal drum.

After they spoke, Heahun asked Turun for the pigs that Turun had tied up. Turun took him to the playground where he had left the things for his friends and kin.

Heahun looked and told Turun that he did not know about this kind of "pig", the grasshoppers that he gives to his friends and kin.

Heahun went back to his village. He took real pigs and dogs, and some foods such as taros, yams, sago. Then went to give them to Turun.

Turun saw Heahun bringing the food and he told Heahun, "I don't know about this kind of food. I rub my tongue on stones for food, I drink water, then I go to sleep."

Heahun listened to this, then he took some taros and yams and cooked them. After he finished cooking, he gave them to Turun and Turun ate them. After Heahun showed these things, the men of this area had them.

[Anonymous]

A962.5. Mountains made with the hand; A978+. Origin of lime (calcium oxide); A1831. Creation of dog; A1871. Creation of hog (pig); A2681+. Origin of sago; A2686.4.2. Origin of taro; A2686.4.3. Origin of yams; F755.1. Speaking mountain; F755.5+. Mountain has wife; P210. Husband and wife; P310. Friendship; X712.1H+. Origin of lime (calcium oxide): woman's genitals; X736.3H+. Symbolic cunnilinctus

## The Crocodile Katumu Desired the Woman from Bukibalikim

(Wantok 509, March 3, 1984, page 31)

Long ago, in the time of the ancestors, there was a village called Bukibalikim. In this village, there were two *masalais*. The name of the *masalai* man was Katumu and the name of the *masalai* woman was Nablamu.

One day, everyone went around to the gardens and looked for food. The only the boys stayed in the village. The sun was very hot, so the children went to the Ka-wi River to bathe.

Two *masalais* were in the water. When the sun was hot, they would tire and sleep by the water.

While the boys bathed, a strong rain and wind arose. The boys searched for a house in which to hide, but there was a cave and that is where all of the boys ran and sat in hiding.

When the boys were inside the cave, they smelled crocodile. However it was not a crocodile, it was the scales of a crocodile girl who was fourteen years old. When they sat down, the two *masalais* shook the boulder and the ground broke apart a little and fell on top of the boys' bodies.

They thought that it was the crocodile girl who had shaken the ground. However, the crocodile girl had not seen this and she surrounded the boys, making them frightened. No, a crocodile was also sitting with them in the cave.

The boys sat until the afternoon when the rain and wind stopped. What would they do? They hid in the cave and they covered themselves well. They did not look outside. It was evening.

The two crocodiles did not retreat. The girl and her little brother, the crocodile boy, knew the various tricks of the two *masalais*. The two crocodiles slowly left the boys' hiding place and left the cave.

When the two of them went out, they blocked all of the entrances to the cave. This caused the boys to look for a way to get out while they were inside the cave.

In the evening, the boys' parents began to search for them. The two crocodiles became people and spoke to them, "If you tie up pigs, chickens, and traditional shell rings, we'll tell you were your boys are."

The parents tied up thirty pigs, fifteen chickens, and twenty-three traditional rings. Later, the two of them took these things and the crocodile girl told the people where the boys were.

The two crocodiles carried the pigs, chickens and rings, and went to the two *masalais*. They told them the parents' story. The boys' parents were still standing outside the cave, screaming and crying for their boys.

Nablamu listened to the parents' crying and told her husband, Katumu that he must open the cave so that the boys could get out. But no, the *masalai* man was insistent that he wanted to eat all of the boys.

The *masalai* woman still tried to convince her husband. She told her husband that he must let them go because he had gotten a good ransom from their parents, which the brother and sister crocodile had brought.

But no, the *masalai* man was stronger. Nablamu was angry and turned her back on her husband. The parents were still screaming and crying by the entrance of the cave.

It did no good. The *masalai* man lubricated his mouth and swallowed the boys. He ate them and left one young woman who had gone with the boys. The woman was seventeen years old. The *masalai* man liked her very much. However he did not want to marry her, he wanted to eat her too.

The young woman had bracelets on her hands. These bracelets had *kina* shells inside them. These were the types of bracelets that women use when they adorn themselves for festivals.

The *masalai* man wanted the woman to look at the faces of her parents. He opened the cave door. The young woman called out to her parents that all of the children had been pulverized. She said, "I'm the last one and he's going to swallow me now. All of you go back home, there are no more children!"

Her two parents listened to this and they cried. All of the other parents also cried. Some people, whose children had been eaten by the *masalai*, cried and went back to the village.

The *masalai* swallowed the young woman who was the last one. Then he told his wife, Nablamu, to make a place to sleep because he had finished all of the children and he was exhausted. His belly was completely bloated.

While he slept, he felt his body become very hot. He went outside to the river and put his big belly into it. Before long, he felt his belly cool.

This was because the cold water went inside his belly. It went inside his belly because of the *kina* shells that the young woman had on her arms. The young woman and two big boys were not dead. The *masalai* had just swallowed them whole into his belly. The little boys had died; the *masalai* had crushed their bones.

The parents were happy, but some were sorry and worried. They cried for their children. Much later, the *masalai*'s belly broke open and he turned about in the river, nearly dying. When he died, a strong rain and wind arose, removing the big stones where the *masalai* woman lived.

The woman cut the *masalai*'s belly into two pieces, then all of the dead boys, the two big boys, and the young woman who had not died spilled out into the river. Their bodies were completely soft, so they sat on top of the sand until they regained their strength. Then they walked to the village. The three of them told the story of the *masalai*.

The *masalai* woman also died when she no longer had a place to live. She worried about her husband, Katumu, and this worrying killed her.

Kenny Kombuli
Jambi [**Yambi**] Mission [**Abelam** People]
Maprik
**East Sepik** Province

D397+B. Transformation: crocodile to boy; D397+G. Transformation: crocodile to girl; D906. Magic wind; D1552. Mountains or rocks open and close; D2142.1. Wind produced by magic; D2143.1. Rain produced by magic; F490+. Masalai; F911. Person (animal) swallowed without killing; G422. Ogre imprisons victim; G512. Ogre killed; P210. Husband and wife; P214.1. Wife commits suicide (dies) on death of husband; P231. Mother and son; P232. Mother and daughter; P233. Father and son; P234. Father and daughter; P253. Sister and brother; R45.3. Captivity in cave; R210. Escapes

# The Little Brother Ignored What He Was Told
(Wantok 510, March 10, 1984, page 26-27)

Long, long ago, in the time of the ancestors, there were two brothers who lived in a village. Their parents had died long before.

The brothers lived for a while, then one time the big brother told the little brother, "Hey, little brother! Tomorrow we'll wake up in the morning and go to the old village,. We'll look for coconuts to eat that we had left there, then we'll bring some here to the new village. You were still a boy when we left the old village, but now you've grown up. I'll take you to our old village and you'll see it."

The little brother said, "Oh that's good, big brother. I want to go see our old village. Let's go to our old village and see the coconuts then eat them at the old village."

So at night, they slept. In the morning, the brothers took their traditional knives, net bags, fire[-making equipment], bows and arrows. They walked and walked then they arrived at the old village.

They made a fire, hung their net bags on a tree, and put their bows and arrows there. They took their knives and they went into the forest.

They cut grasses and brush at the base of trees such as breadfruit, *tulip*, betel nut palm, banana, coconut and other kinds of food plants.

After the brothers cut the grasses and cleaned the brush around the food trees, the big brother told the little brother, "Hey, little brother, stand here and I'll go look for coconut seedlings to take to the village to plant. I'll also get some green coconuts to drink."

The little brother said, "OK, you can go look for coconut seedlings and bring green coconuts. I'll stay here and clean the bases of our food trees."

So, the little brother stood there and the big brother went to find coconut seedlings and green coconuts for drinking. The big brother gathered coconut seedlings, then he went up to fetch some green coconuts. After he fetched the green coconuts, he sat on top of the coconut palm and saw a big coconut.

## Marks on a Coconut
The brother saw that the big coconut had marks or holes around the middle of it, and he thought that a marsupial (*kapul*) had scraped it.

However, it was actually something that a ghost child had done at night. The child had removed some meat from the big coconut. The big brother went down, took the coconut seedlings and green coconuts, then carried them back to his little brother.

They cut the green coconuts. After they drank the coconut milk, the big brother told the little brother to go back to the village.

He told the little brother to carry the coconut seedlings to the village, then he himself would stay and watch the big coconut at night. He said that a marsupial had cut it and made marks in the middle of a big coconut.

However the little brother said, "Oh sorry big brother, you saw this, but you should show me the coconut. I'll watch it and you can go to the village."

They went and the big brother showed him, then the big brother told him to carry the coconut seedlings to the village. However, the little brother was insisted that he should watch the big coconut.

The big brother said, "No, you must go to the village."

The little brother said, "No, you go and I'll watch."

The brothers spoke like this for a while, then the little brother became furious and told the big brother, "Hey, would you like to get speared by me? Do you think I can't watch? I'm not a boy."

Then the big brother told him, "Hey little brother, don't get so angry. I told you that this is the old village. Bad ghosts have come here, and cut and made marks around the coconuts. We may think that these are marks from marsupials."

The little brother said, "You said that the ghost came and cut or made marks. Are you a man or woman, that you say it's a ghost?"

But the big brother said, "Hey brother, don't ignore what I say."

The little brother said, "Go to the village. It's dark now."

The little brother ignored what his big brother said, and the big brother went to the village. When it became dark, the little brother went to watch the big coconut.

He stayed for a little while. The ghost child and its mother arrived in the area then worked at cutting the big coconut. The cuttings from the coconut fell down to the place where the little brother was watching. The little brother was at the base of the coconut tree.

When the little brother felt the rubbish falling on top of himself, he raised his eyes and saw the ghost child. However, the moon was lit and he thought that it was a marsupial.

He said, "Now this marsupial's going to die."

He stretched the bow and arrow then shot the ghost child.

When the arrow entered the ghost child, the child called out, "O o o o mama, they've shot me."

Oh my, oh my, the little brother heard this and raced away. However it was too late, the mother ghost came, took the child, and threw it towards the little brother.

When she threw away the child, she asked the boy, "Are you going with him or not?"

The boy said, "No."

The mother found the ghost child and threw it towards the boy. It stuck to the little brother's back.

Then the child said, "Mother, I'll go with him now."

The mother ran back. The little brother tried to remove the ghost child, but he was completely unsuccessful. It was stuck fast to his back.

The little brother carried it and arrived at the village. He called out for his brother to come and remove the ghost or to cut it with a knife.

The big brother said, "OK, I told you that that was the old village and that there were no marsupials that cut big coconuts there. But you said, 'I'm a [man], not a [woman].' Now you've found out. I told you, but you ignored what I said. Now you've found out."

The ghost child was stuck to the little brother's back and ate his flesh. The ghost had almost removed the boy's belly and entrails.

Everyone, including his big brother, tried to beat off the ghost child who was eating him, but the ghost child did not feel pain, as a real people do.

When they beat the ghost, the real boy called out, "Hey you can't beat him, you're just beating me." All of the men and the big brother aimed at the ghost, but they could not defeat it.

The ghost child ate all of the flesh in his back and the little brother died. After he died, the ghost child let go and went down to the ground. When the ghost was on the ground, everyone including the big brother cut it into tiny pieces.

So now in this village, the big brothers listen to what the big people say, and the little brothers do not listen. They are usually stubborn and oblivious. They never listen to the big men or leaders of the village.

This is a story that my paternal aunt told me when I lived in **Maui** Village, near Lumi, **West Sepik** Province [**Olo** People].

William Sabien

H. A. W. 2 P. I. R.

Moem Barracks

East Sepik Province

A2850+. Why younger brothers are stubborn; E423. Revenant in animal form; E440+. Walking ghost laid by cutting into pieces; E262. Ghost rides on man's back; E425.1. Revenant as woman; E425.3. Revenant as child; E541. Revenants eat; E545. The dead speak; G11.10. Cannibalistic spirits; P231. Mother and son; P251.4. Brothers scorn brother's wise counsel; P251.5. Two brothers; Q325. Disobedience punished; Q411. Death as punishment; R40+. Entrapment by sitting on shoulders/back; R260. Pursuits; S110+. Eaten alive; S139.7. Murder by slicing person into small pieces; W167. Stubbornness; W126. Disobedience

## The Bad Boy Had His Revenge and He Became a Leader

(Wantok 511, March 17, 1984, page 26)

Long, long ago, in the time of the ancestors, there was a little boy who lived in the Sepik River area. The parents of this boy had died when he was still small. He was only about five years old. This boy lived with his maternal aunt. The aunt was married and also had a son, but the boy was older than this son was.

Whenever the aunt and her husband left the village to look for food or to work, their nephew would take care of the pigs and their son.

When his parents returned, their son would lie and say that his cousin had hit him and had not given food to him. The parents would become very angry at the poor boy.

He would run away and hide then cry terribly. But where could he go? There were no other kin to take care of him. This aunt was his only relative in the village. She and her husband would beat the boy terribly when their son gave his false reports to them.

He would cry and tell his aunt, "I never did that sort of thing. I always take care of him well. I give him food when he's hungry. I know that if I do this work, you'll give me food, otherwise you won't give me any."

The aunt often scolded him and told him not to tell lies where the people of the village would hear him. The woman and her husband only listened to and believe what their son said.

Another day, the parents went to look for food in the garden. The boy took care of his little cousin. The two of them went to look for some *galip* nuts in the forest. They took some *galip* nuts and worked at breaking them open and eating them.

It was nearly evening, so they knew that the parents would be coming back to the village. The little boy knew this and did not have anything to say to the parents.

### Hit His Hand

He hit his hand on a rock and began to cry. The parents arrived and saw him still crying. They asked him about this. He lied and said that the boy had hit him with a rock.

The boy wanted to tell them that his little cousin was lying, but the aunt took a big stick and beat him terribly. The bones in his back were nearly broken. Blood was flowing from his mouth and nose.

The boy cried and cried, then he just slept underneath the house. They did not give him food. The boy was very sorry [that he had no] parents and he cried.

The next day in the very early morning, before it was light, the boy woke up and walked into the forest. He did not know which trail that he was following. He just walked. He was not afraid of trouble or enemies coming to him. He thought that if he died, it would be good because he would see the faces of his parents.

The boy walked and walked. He felt hungry and he slept at the base of a tree. Later, he got back his strength and looked for cold water to drink before walking.

He walked and walked then arrived at a big mountain. As he stood watching, he saw smoke rising from very far away.

He followed the smoke, and it became dark. Then he arrived at this place. There, he found a very small house that had a very old woman who was alone on this mountain in the deep forest.

The boy looked inside the house and the old woman opened the door. The old woman saw him and asked, "What is a little boy like you doing here? Who did you come with?" The boy told the old woman that he had come alone and that he did not know where he was going.

### Giving Food

The old woman took him inside and gave him food. She asked the boy, "How did you know about this place? No man ever comes looking for food in this forest."

The boy sat down and told the story of what his aunt and uncle had done to him. The old woman listened and was very sorry. She cried for the boy.

The old woman said, "Don't worry. This forest of mine has plenty of food. I have no children and you can become my son. I'll take care of you and you'll stay here. You can't go back to the village."

So, the boy stayed with the old woman. Many years passed and the boy lived well. He loved the old woman as if she were his mother.

The boy often did various kinds of work. He worked in the garden, hunted wild game, and cleaned pigs and cassowaries. He was very smart about the ways of the forest and the mountain. He grew up and became very muscular.

The old woman became very old. It was nearly her time to die. The young man took care of her well. He looked for firewood and other things. The old woman often just sat in the house because her eyes were almost blind.

One morning, the old woman sat by the fire and thought. She knew that the young man must go back to the village and marry.

She called out for her son to come. She told him about what she was thinking, but the man listened and did not like what she said.

**Leaving the Old Woman**

The old woman tried to persuade him to return to the village and to marry. The man agreed, but he did not want to leave his old foster mother who had taken care of him well and raised him to be a man. The man thought for many days, then he agreed with the old woman.

One morning, they walked and walked, towards the beach. The old woman sang and danced then spat on the man's legs and arms to give him the strength to walk.

This woman was not an ordinary woman, she was a woman who could look into the souls of other people. She also knew songs and sorcery. The man had not known about the woman's powers. The old woman had not told him.

They walked and walked then went quickly to the beach. The beach was not near, it was very far. However the old woman had performed a song and dance, and they arrived quickly.

When they arrived at the beach, the old woman told him, "Go in this canoe until you arrive right at your village."

Then she said one last thing to the man, "My son, I'm giving you all of my power now. When you arrive at the village, many women will like you. You shall become the leader of the village. You shall have a big piece of land, a big house and many kinds of things. There will no longer be enemies coming after you. You can't return to look for me because I can't live any longer. This house and this place will look differently, and will not be the forest and mountain that you have walked on."

The old woman called out and a boulder came up from the water. Then she said something and the stone turned into what looked like canoe.

The man went down and stood on the canoe, which had money and various kinds of good things in it. However to the eyes of other people, the canoe looked like a stone. The man saw it as a canoe.

The man stood on the canoe, and the old woman threw out her hands and spilled ashes into a fire. What she did closed off the way back. The man looked back and he no longer saw the old woman's face. He was troubled and cried terribly for his foster mother.

The stone drifted and went directly to the beach near the village. The man took all of the things, went up to the village and made a new house.

The old woman's power had come into effect and made all of the work come very quickly. Many young women fell for him.

There were various things on the man's fence that other people did not have. Many people of the village would spill around his fence and ask him to help them.

He often helped the people without asking for recompense. However when his aunt, uncle and cousin came, the man would charge them shell money. He wanted that they should pay him back for the hard time that they had given him when he was a little boy.

The people of the village did not recognize him, not at all. Later, the aunt thought hard, "Why is it that we pay for things that other people get for free from this man?"

One day, the woman went and asked him. The man said, "It's because of the poor boy that you often beat half-to-death because of your son's lies. Now, I'm getting revenge. Whatever it is that you want on my fence, you must buy with an expensive gift. The others get it for free."

The woman listened to this and cried, she was very troubled. She went and told her husband. The man, woman and child were troubled and sorry. They took big pieces of shell money and brought them to the man for the trouble that they had given him when he was small.

However, the man did not want to take this shell money. He told the three of them, "We are enemies until you or I die."

The man married the beautiful daughter of the leader of a village that was fairly far away. The people of that village were enemies with his village. His marriage made the two villages become friendly. The man became a leader of his village. Many of the women of his own village were jealous for his wife.

The aunt's son was not married. His parents had become completely destitute and owned nothing of value. This was their punishment from the old woman's power.

The man and his family lived happily in this village. They were important people and leaders of the village.

N. Watae
Aitape
**West Sepik** Province

D452.1.13K. Transformation: stone to boat; D931.1.2. Magic ashes; D1001. Magic spittle; D1524.3. Magic stone serves as boat; D1641.2+. Stones move magically; D1711. Magician; D1721. Magic power from magician; D1774. Magic results from speaking; D1781. Magic results from singing; D1781+. Magic results from dancing; D1835+. Magic strength from spittle; D2122. Journey with magic speed; F841.1.1. Stone boat (ship); K2100. False accusation; L111.4.4. Mistreated orphan hero; P210. Husband and wife; P231. Mother and son; P233. Father and son; P272.1+. Sorceress foster mother; P275. Foster son; P295. Cousins; P294+. Maternal aunt; P293+. Maternal uncle; P297. Nephew; Q285. Cruelty punished; Q458. Flogging as punishment; Q595.4. Loss of money as punishment; R213. Escape from home; S70+. Cruel cousin; S71. Cruel uncle; S72. Cruel aunt; T10. Falling in love; T100. Marriage; W181. Jealousy


# A Woman Became a Man

(Wantok 512, March 24, 1984, pages 30-31)

Long, long ago, there was just a man and his wife who lived someplace in the **Asaro** Valley [People] of **Eastern Highlands** Province.

There were no other people who lived near this place. The ancestors did not know the name of the man and his wife, but in my story, I call the man Baundo and the woman Loime.

Baundo and Loime did not live happily together because Baundo was often angry and beat poor Loime all of the time. However, they lived together for a while. Loime became pregnant and then gave birth to a baby boy.

Baundo was very happy. Loime was happier still, but she was weary all of the time because Baundo often beat her whenever they argued about the smallest problem.

One time, Baundo explained to his wife that he would go hunt for wild game in the deep forest. He wanted the baby boy to eat meat and become a big man quickly. He told Loime that the two of them must make a little food and that they must be happy for their son.

Baundo took a stone axe, a bow and arrows, then went into the deep forest. He counted with his hands indicating that he would sleep in the deep forest for three entire weeks. He admonished his wife to take care of the baby well.

## Loime Ran Away

Baundo went into the forest and Loime was very happy because it was a good chance for her to run away to another place and to leave Baundo. She was angry because Baundo beat her all of the time and she was tired of it.

Loime cut the base of a long piece of bamboo and ensorcelled it. She sang and danced then called out quietly. She said a spell and poured the house, the garden, the pigs and dogs, and everything at their little home into the bamboo tube. However, she left one bundle of sugarcane standing there.

Loime put the little baby in an old broken net bag and hung the net bag with the baby on top of the bundle of standing sugarcanes. She performed her song and dance again then called out for the deep forest to cover up this little place of theirs. The place became deep forest; the trees and grasses covered it up.

She called out for a heavy rain to fall on this place then she escaped to another place that was very far away. She walked and walked for three days and then arrived at a hill.

This place looked the same as her old place with Baundo. She sang and danced again then everything came out of the bamboo and stood on the new hill.

The house, sugarcanes, garden, pigs and dogs inside the bamboo came outside and filled Loime's new small home. She happily sat down and laughed because she had run away from her husband who had beaten her all of the time.

Poor Baundo had gathered plenty of game and returned to be surprised because the place had changed. Why had the place changed such that there was no house, or anything else of his? The deep forest had taken over the place. Oh my! He was completely confused. A heavy rain also began to fall, and he found himself in a very bad situation.

## Baundo Was Angry

He was angry and walked around, looking about, trying to find his wife and baby. But where were they? Loime had run away!

Baundo heard the baby crying inside the deep forest and he worked hard to cut the forest, breaking the rattans and clearing the way to get to the baby.

He saw the baby sleeping inside a broken net bag on top of a bundle of sugarcanes. Oh my! He was very sorry to see the baby crying and shoving his arms and legs around.

He removed the baby from the net bag and held him to his shoulder. His tears fell down because he was very sorry for the baby. The heavy rain fell, getting him and the baby wet, but he ignored it. Baundo stood, carrying his baby, and he thought hard. He was furious that his wife had left the baby.

It was a little dark and the heavy rain let up. Baundo carried his baby and sat underneath the base of a tree. The baby was very hungry for food and was crying loudly.

Baundo broke the bones and meat of the game then let the baby eat. Baundo cut the tree leaves and made a bed for himself and the baby underneath this tree in the forest. They slept at this place for many days and nights.

### Calling Out to Loime

Every day, poor Baundo tried to call out to Loime, but she did not reply. Never mind. Baundo stopped being angry, but he thought about the baby and he took care of him.

He and the baby ate the meat until the meat was gone. Baundo had smoked the meat and put it inside some bamboo tubes. He would make a fire and heat the meat when the baby wanted to eat the meat.

When the meat was gone, Baundo and the baby each broke the sugarcanes in the bundle that Loime had left. They ate these sugarcanes for a while, then they too were finished. There was not much food nearby.

When the baby was hungry and cried for food, Baundo would break off the young leaves of bamboo shoots and give them to him. Many days passed and the baby became emaciated. Baundo saw that the baby was crying all of the time, so he was pained and very troubled by this.

One day, Baundo climbed a tall tree and looked around. He stood on top of it then tried to see other people or a nearby village, but he did not see anything.

Another time, Baundo climbed the tree and tried to look everywhere. That was it! He saw smoke from a fire coming from a mountain that was very far away. He saw that he must walk about three or four days before he would come to the place where the smoke was rising.

He jumped down, carried the baby with all of the other things, and walked towards the place where the smoke was rising. He walked and slept in the middle of the forest for three nights, then he arrived at the new place.

### Becoming a Man

This new place was Loime's home. When Baundo and the baby were still walking in the distance, Loime had seen the baby and gone inside the house. She changed and became a man. He then pretended to go weed the garden.

Loime heated stones and made an earth oven in the morning. The food was still in the ground. Baundo looked at this place and saw that it was exactly like his old home.

The house was the same. The dogs smelled Baundo's body; they ran and played around his legs.

Baundo saw that these dogs and pigs were his same dogs and pigs from the old place. However, he looked at the man and he changed his mind. He just thought of his stomach. He thought that the man had stolen his things and put them at this place.

Baundo was afraid because he believed that this man was a *masalai* or a sorcerer, so he did not speak. He did not know that this man was just his old wife, Loime. Baundo thought hard and stood near the house. He looked and walked around.

Loime pretended to work in the garden. He knew that Baundo understood that all of the things were the same as those at the old place. Baundo went close to Loime and wanted to talk.

Loime just turned and said, "Do you want something? Get out of here, this is my place. This is not a place for other men."

Baundo scratched his head. He was terrified and said, "I'm very sorry. My baby and I left our distant home and came here. The forest covered over my home, and my wife also ran away from me. So, I walked and looked for a new place with good food because my little baby has no food and often cries loudly. Would you have pity on me and the baby and let us stay with you here?"

Loime saw that the baby was emaciated and crying loudly. He was heartbroken, but his face was completely dry and he did not reply to Baundo.

In the afternoon, Loime removed food from the earth oven and went to sit in the house. He ate the sweet potatoes, leafy greens, and pork. He did not give any food to Baundo and the baby. Oh my! Baundo was famished. The baby was also famished and was crying.

### Sitting Nearby

Baundo and the baby went to sit near Loime's house and ogle the food. After Loime was sated and finished eating, he carried all of the food to give to the pigs. When Loime turned his face the other way, Baundo took some scraps of food from the pigs and ate. He also gave some scraps of food from the pigs to his little baby.

Loime knew what Baundo was doing, but he was not sorry, not at all. Another day, Loime hurried Baundo to weed the sugarcane garden. For this hard work, Loime left them some pieces of food.

When the baby cried for food, Baundo would break the sugarcanes where the insects had ruined them and give the pieces to the baby. This was because Loime had completely forbidden them from getting the good sugarcanes. Poor Baundo thought about the hard work, about leaving Loime's charity, and about giving food to the baby.

Another day, Loime told Baundo to cut plenty of firewood. He wanted to make an earth oven. Poor Baundo worked hard at getting the firewood, gathering stones, digging a hole and preparing everything.

On the third morning, Baundo worked at heating the stones in a fire. Later, he went to get yams, taros, sweet potatoes and leafy greens.

Baundo worked hard at arranging things, then the little baby lay down and cried hard. However, Loime did not think of carrying the baby, not at all. Baundo wanted to leave the work of cutting the taros, yams and sweet potatoes and go to help the baby. But Loime strongly forbade him and told him that he could not eat if he ignored him.

Baundo covered up the bamboo tubes of food. The Loime let Baundo kill six big pigs in the pigsty and cook them with the food. Poor Baundo's body was in pain, his heart ached. It would be bad if the baby did not get food, so he just worked.

The stones for the earth oven were extremely hot, so they put the covered food into the big hole and covered them with a little earth and some leaves. Loime sat on the ladder of the house and let Baundo do the hard work. In the afternoon, he hurried Baundo to uncover the earth oven from the ground.

### Furious

When they sat down and prepared to eat, Loime said, "Wait! You can't put your hands on the food yet. I'm going inside and getting something from the house first. After that we can eat the food."

Oh my! Loime was not a man any more! He had turned back into the real Loime who was Baundo's wife. Oh my… oh my! Baundo was furious at all of the work he had done and he wanted to curse Loime, but he was afraid because it was clear now that Loime had evil powers to perform sorcery.

Loime stood and talked sternly to Baundo, "You are the man who always beat me. Always, huh! How strong are you really? Now you feel it, huh! Don't be your egotistic self and hit me every day, OK?"

Baundo lowered his head and his tears flowed. He got up very slowly and went to put his two hands on Loime's shoulders. He cried and cried until he could cry no more. Loime went and carried the little baby then gave her breast to him. They sat down together and finished all of the food.

### Living in Harmony

They finished eating. Baundo sat with a heavy heart and thought hard. Loime told him to forget his troubles, because now they must live in harmony and think about raising the baby.

Baundo never hit his wife again. They lived there and raised many children. Later, the children grew up and married other clans from faraway villages then made families in Baundo and Loime's village. They became plentiful.

However, the men never beat the women. Only brainless men would beat women. So today, there are few men inside the Asaro Valley who become angry with women.

Men usually listen to what women say and live in harmony with them all of the time. This is because many men understand this story of the woman who transformed herself and let the man do the hard work.

My old grandparent, Aizeko, told this ancestor story and I wrote it down for everyone to read and think about.


Amos Mutupa

P. O. Box 6

Bogia

Madang Province


A1680+. Why husbands do not beat their wives in Asaro Valley; D11. Transformation woman to man; D12. Transformation: man to woman; D491.2.1. Compressible magic box; D683.2. Transformation by witch (sorceress); D941.1. Forest produced by magic; D1711. Magician; D1774. Magic results from speaking; D1781. Magic results from singing; D1781+. Magic results from dancing; D2136. Objects magically moved; D2143.1. Rain produced by magic; D2188.3. Village vanishes; P210. Husband and wife; P230. Parents and children; P231. Mother and son; P233. Father and son; Q285. Cruelty punished; Q438. Punishment: abandonment in forest; R213. Escape from home; R227.2. Flight from hated husband; S12. Cruel mother; S62. Cruel husband; S143. Abandonment in forest; T100. Marriage; T298. Reconciliation of separated couple; T570. Pregnancy; T580. Childbirth

# A Man Became a Turtle

(Wantok 513, March 31, 1984, page 26-27)

Long, long ago, in the time of the ancestors, there was a man who went fishing. This man left the village late at night. He carried his spears and walked towards the beach in the dead of night. This was turtle season. Many turtles went up to the beach late at night.

The man walked and turned over turtles [thus disabling them]. He found many little turtles and turned them over. He tied up their legs with ropes then tied them to a stick. Afterwards, he carried them back to the village.

He no longer thought about fishing because he had found many turtles. Another night, the man went back to the beach, gathered the turtles and carried them back to the village.

Many people from the village heard that the turtles were coming up the beach at night. Everyone spilled out of the village to hunt for turtles, but they each found only one turtle. This was because there were too many of them and they could not find many turtles. They did this all of the time until nearly a whole month had passed.

Out in the deep sea, there was a village underneath the sea where the turtles lived. The big mother turtle was worried because the young she-turtles went up to the beach to breathe and did not return to the village.

The people of the village often hunted them and took them to eat. At this time, the village stank with the smell of turtle meat. After the people ate the meat, they would throw the bones back into the sea.

One day, a turtle bone arrived at the turtle village underneath the sea. When the turtles saw this, they were very troubled. They called out for all of the turtles to go to a huge meeting.

They appointed a she-turtle as leader to go with the other young she-turtles. Then they went to sit on the beach. The turtles wanted to find out why the other turtles did not return to the village. Many hundreds of turtles departed. They did not know what would happen to them.

When the she-turtles sat upon the beach, they saw only one man walking and hunting for turtles. When he approached them, the young turtles that had gathered in one place saw him and slowly escaped down into the sea.

The man walked again and came to where the leader was sitting. The young she-turtle waited until she heard what the man would say.

The man saw the big turtle leader sitting there. He thought that it was a piece of a tree. Oh my, he walked over and bumped his leg on her.

The turtle got up and told the man, "Hey, didn't you see me sitting here while you were walking from over there?"

The man listened and was shocked. He quickly took the spear to shoot the turtle. The turtle was about to tell the man something more, but the man trembled in fear. He quickly shot the turtle somewhere on her leg.

However, the stubborn turtle did not die. Quickly, the turtles who were waiting in the water ran up on the beach and grabbed the man. The man thought about running away, but he was unable to do so. The turtles tied his legs and hands, then put him on the back of the big turtle leader who carried him far away into the deep sea. They went down beneath to their village. They told the man not to be afraid because they would not kill him.

Only the she-turtles lived in this village. They took him down, gave him their food, and the man turned completely into a he-turtle.

Many years passed, and the man who had turned into a turtle married a young she-turtle. Now, this village had he-turtles too.

One day, the old he-turtle wanted to go look for his old village. He went back above the water and sat on the beach where he saw a man walking towards him.

When the man came very close to the he-turtle, he called out to him. Then he became a real man.

The real man saw this and was surprised. He told the turtle-man, "We had forgotten completely about you. You died and now you've become a ghost."

The turtle man said, "No. I speak to you as a turtle-man."

Then he told his story to the real man, "I can't change back because I have turtle blood, so I can't change now."

He told the man, "Now listen to me. I want you to give recompense. If a she-turtle comes, then you must tie her legs and carry her to the village. However, you can't kill her. You must give your food to her. First, sing and dance at the food, then give her the food. At night, the turtle will become a real woman. I myself will bring her. This turtle is my daughter. You must take care of her well and she will become your wife."

Another night, the old turtle took his big daughter back to the place on the beach that he had marked. The father turtle watched then the real man came, grabbed his daughter and tied her legs.

The woman sat crying for her father, but the father told her that she would have a new village for a home and that she can tell the story of her home in the deep sea.

The father was worried for his daughter. He sat and watched as the man carried the turtle away. The father turtle went down to the water, and back under the sea.

Later, the real man went to the village and followed all of the instructions that the turtle-man had told him to do. Later, at night, the young she-turtle became a real woman.

The man married her and they had children. Later, the people found out the woman's story. They knew that her father had become a turtle and that he lived under the sea at the turtle village.

William Sabien

Wewak

East Sepik Province

[Mr. Sabien wrote the ancestor stories in *Wantok* #510, 517, 581, 637, 642, 657, and 771. He is probably from the **Olo** People, **West Sepik** Province.]

B211.6.3K. Speaking turtle; B226+. Kingdom of turtles; B655+. Marriage to turtle in human form; B875.3. Giant turtle; D193M. Transformation: man to tortoise (turtle); D390+M. Transformation: turtle to man; D390+W. Transformation: turtle to woman; D551. Transformation by eating; D1030. Magic food; D1781. Magic results from singing; D1781+. Magic results from dancing; F127.4K. Journey to land of turtles; P210. Husband and wife; P230. Parents and children; P234. Father and daughter; R13.4+. Abduction by turtle; R210. Escapes; T192. Marriage by force; W167. Stubbornness

# Bandur's Island

(Wantok 514, April 7, 1984, page 27)

Long, long ago, in the time of the ancestors, there was a place called Bunderlis in the **Manus** Province area. This place was a small island that was just a stone on top of the sea. There were no trees or people on it. There was just one marsupial (*kapul*) [probably the Admiralty cuscus, *Spilocuscus kraemeri* (Flannery (1995b: 104-105)] that lived there. The marsupial's name was Bandur.

Bandur was the true ancestor of this part of the sea, but Bandur was not a *masalai*. The people who lived nearby thought that Bandur was a woman. When their canoes paddled near the stone island, they would see smoke rising but they did not know that it was a marsupial on this island.

They often thought that it was huge woman who lived there. The ancestors never went very close to this island. When they fished at night, they would see the light from the fire. They would think that it was a woman who had lit the fire.

But no, it was just this marsupial Bandur. It was an unusually kind of marsupial because this island was only stone, without grasses, forest or trees. The island was not big, so it was just a piece of stone in the middle of the sea. One time, a woman and her husband went fishing by torch light at night. They paddled to a reef near the stone island. There was no moon that night. The current took them to the shores of this island in the pitch-blackness.

They thought that the canoe had gone ashore on the mainland, so the man told the woman that they should sleep a little, then at dawn they would go to the reef again.

The woman's eyes spun around and she slept in the canoe. The man went up to the shore of this island and walked around, to see what was nearby.

When it was darkest, he saw the mark of a man standing there. However it was not a man, it was just the marsupial. The marsupial turned into a beautiful and smart young woman who stood there.

It was pitch dark at this time. However, the place where Bandur, the marsupial woman, stood had an unusual light. It was as if the moon had come out from a cloud.

The man saw her then he went closer and glued his eyes upon her. This was because he had never seen such a woman before. Never. The woman's skin was lit like the moon. Her hair was completely soft and rested upon her two shoulders. The man's eyes spun around and around as he looked at his woman.

He walked very close then asked the woman where she came from, what the name of her village was, and what the names of her parents or grandparents were.

The woman very quietly told the man that she did not have grandparents, that she did not know her parents, and that her home was the island. The marsupial woman spoke quietly which made the man's eyes spin around, so he fell asleep. He slept on the shore until dawn. When he awoke in the morning, the woman was not there, and he was just sleeping on stone. His wife and the canoe were nearby.

The two of them just found the big stone drifting in the sea. The man could not tell if he was dreaming at night or whether it really happened.

He told the story to his wife. The woman did not believe him and she just laughed. They thought that they had found the mainland when they had seen the firelight at night, but they had not. They were lost. They caught many fish in the morning then they paddled back to the village.

Another night, the man told the woman that they would go back and fish by torch light again. Then something happened. This time, the marsupial confused the man and he did not travel. He slept in the canoe. The woman walked around on the shore and she met the woman.

The woman found the marsupial woman sitting there. She turned her back where she was sitting in the odd light. The woman thought that what her husband had told her must be true. She went to find out. When she approached, the marsupial woman did not look at her and she became angry.

She said, "Why do you and your husband come here? Aren't you happy that I gave you plenty of fish for you to bring to the village? You want to find out more about me, huh?"

When the marsupial woman turned to face the real woman, too bad, it was a marsupial's face on top of a woman's body. The body was very beautiful like the man had seen.

The real woman was afraid and called out back to the man. However when she turned to run back, her legs went down into the water and dawn broke. She was just standing on top of rocks.

The woman's husband heard his and came to ask for her. The woman told the story to her husband. He believed her, but he did not believe that the woman had looked like a marsupial. The man told his wife that he had seen a very beautiful woman.

However, she could not return to the canoe. She was still standing on the stone island and the stone was slowly sinking into the sea. The man called out for the woman to jump into the canoe, but she was unable to do so. The woman's legs were stuck fast to the stone and she sank completely into the sea. The man and the canoe spun around on top of the sea at this place. He cried and called out.

The man thought that the beautiful woman was a *masalai* and that this was the place about which the ancestors had told stories. The man cried hard and he went back to the village.

The marsupial twisted and pulled the man's thoughts so that he would not tell the people about Bandur, the marsupial woman's home. He just told them that a big shark had taken his wife when they were fishing on the reef.

The marsupial had put these words into the man's head. So when he arrived at the village, he just lied to the people about how his wife had died.

The poor man was troubled about his wife's death. At night, the marsupial would see the man as he slept. The marsupial wanted this man just as she had killed his wife on the stone.

Some years passed and the man forgot his deceased wife. He still often went around looking for food. The stone that went down with the woman, Bandurelis [Bunderlis] Island was no longer, it had gone beneath the sea.

One night, the man went fishing by torchlight, but he did not go to the place where his wife had died. He sat and rested in the canoe then put his fishing line down. He no longer stood with a spear.

The canoe went directly ashore on this stone island again. That night, the big stone had resurfaced. The marsupial confused the man's thinking. But this time, the man did something else. When he traveled in his sleep, he was stronger than the marsupial's powers.

He was asleep and the marsupial arrived at the man's canoe, which was ashore on the stone. Dawn arrived and the man saw the stone standing there. Oh my, he was terrified. He cried and thought of his wife. He thought that the stone would also take him down into the sea. But it was not to be.

While he was grieving and crying, he was surprised at the marsupial sitting at the stern of the canoe. The marsupial told the man, "Don't cry anymore."

The man was surprised and he took a spear to shoot the marsupial. The man was terrified to hear the marsupial speaking, and he was very confused.

The man was completely crazy. He took the spear and blasted it straight into the marsupial. The marsupial was impaled on the spear. After he had shot the marsupial, he shoved the spear with the marsupial down into the sea. The man's head spun around until he was half-dead in the canoe. He became sick because of the marsupial's ghost.

The marsupial turned back into the beautiful young woman that the man had seen before. She became a real woman and sat at the stern of the canoe. She paddled slowly to the village while the man was still asleep.

When the man's head cleared, he awoke. He found the woman sitting in the canoe and he almost died again. Later, the woman woke him and told him the story.

She told the man her name, Bandur. She said that before she was a marsupial, but that she was now a real woman. This is what she told him, "I still like you. I killed your wife." The man was happy, so he and Bandur paddled back to the village then Bandur became his wife.

Molen Sei
Riuriu Village
Manus Province

B20+. Marsupial-faced woman; B211.2.12K+. Speaking marsupial; B650+. Marriage to marsupial in human form; D179.6K+W. Transformation: woman to marsupial; D310+W. Transformation: marsupial to woman; D452.3+. Transformation: sand to rock; D2000+. Mind control; E265.1. Meeting ghost causes sickness; E656+. Reincarnation: marsupial to woman; F804. Floating rock (stone); F944.3. Island sinks into sea; F969.3. Marvelous light; K730. Victim trapped; P210. Husband and wife; Q211. Murder punished; Q411. Death as punishment; S131. Murder by drowning; T100. Marriage; W181. Jealousy; W151. Greed

## A Cassowary Stole a Boy
(Wantok 515, April 14, 1984, page 26)

Long ago, in the time of the ancestors, there was a married couple in **North Solomons** Province. They had a little boy who was one year old and was beginning to walk.

The married couple and their baby always went hunting for wild game or went to process sago.  One day, the three of them went into the forest to process sago.  When the baby tired, he would go to sit where his father was grating sago.

Near noon, the baby ate and his mother put him into a net bag where he slept.  The mother hung the net bag with the boy close to the place where she was standing.

The married couple worked at making sago until it was nearly evening.  The mother carried the sago to where her husband was standing and where the net bag with the boy was.  The mother did not waste time because she knew that the boy was sleeping alone in the net bag.

This time, when the mother had left the boy, a cassowary threw something like lime (calcium oxide) at the place where the boy was sleeping.  Something had also turned the married couple's thoughts so that they had forgotten their baby.

The cassowary had thrown away scraps then sung and danced at them.  Then she (the cassowary) had thrown them down to the water.

The cassowary had performed this song and dance, poisoning the water when it was still morning.  Later, the cassowary looked at the boy's face and wanted the boy very much.

In the afternoon, the married couple wanted to finish working, so they no longer thought about baby.  The woman did not think of the place where she had hung the net bag.

In the evening, the woman finished filling up the sago in net bags, then the two of them went back to the village.  The little baby still slept in the net bag at the place where the mother had hung him.  The lime that the cassowary had spilled in the area had made it so that the married couple could not see him.  The water that they had drunk had a poison in it, and the poison made them forget entirely about the baby.

They arrived at the village.  After they arrived at the village, a heavy rain and strong wind arose in the forest and village.  When their kin asked them about the baby, it was only then that they remembered.  They were shocked that they had forgotten.

She screamed and cried then threw the net bag of sago at the house.  The woman accusingly asked her husband, "I thought that you carried the baby with you."

The man was angry that the woman had said such a thing.  He thought that she had carried the baby in the net bag while they walked back.

They argued heatedly, then fought back and forth.  The man's kin were now very angry with them.  Then the two of them walked back to look for the baby.  However, the heavy rain and strong wind made it completely impassable.  The trees fell about, blocking the way.  The downpour made it completely dark.

In the forest, the cassowary carried the net bag with the baby and hid him at the base of the sago palm tree where the father had sat.  The kin of the village went searching and searching, but it was without success.  They thought that a wild pig or something had eaten the baby, or that a *masalai* had carried him away.

The little baby was crying, but the cassowary sang and he slept well.  After the parents and their kin went back to the village, the boy awoke.  The cassowary went to look for food to give to him.

The cassowary took care of the baby.  The cassowary often went to steal ripe bananas from the villager's gardens, then brought them to give to him.  The cassowary often fetched water to give to the baby.

The boy no longer knew about his parents.  The cassowary took him to her home.  The cassowary made a little house under the base of a big tree and they always lived in this house.  The parents forgot about him.

The boy grew to be a big man and the cassowary told him that he must no longer stay in the forest and that he must go back to his real home.

The cassowary told the man which trails to follow when he went back to the village.  The cassowary also told him that if he later wanted to hunt for game, there would be plenty of food near him when he walked in the forest.

The cassowary also told him that if he married, his wife could not go looking for food far in the forest.  She explained that she would tell the other cassowaries that they would supply food if she, his foster mother, were not nearby when he went into the forest.

The man now knew more about hunting for food in the forest.  He often jumped up trees.  He would jump along one tree branch onto another tree.  His foster mother, the cassowary, gave all kinds of songs and dances to him.  Their power went to him.

The man was ready to return to the village, but he did not know where it was.  The cassowary showed him the trail to follow to arrive at the village.  The man told the cassowary that he could never forget her whenever she came to see him.

The cassowary told the man the story of when she had taken him, "You were a very young boy.  I liked you very much and I stole you from your parents when they hung you up in a net bag. At that time, your parents were processing sago. Now you must go back to the village because your parents think that you died."

The cassowary finished the story and the man walked to his parents' village. In the middle of the trail, he met a very young woman. This young woman was the wife of a *masalai* that lived in the area.

The man spoke with the woman. He coaxed her to go with him to the village. The man stopped talking and tied a *tanget* leaf to the woman, indicating that he wanted to marry her. He told the woman that he would go to the village first, then he would return later and get her.

The young woman was really a *masalai*. The man spoke with her for a long time. The *masalai* man saw this and was terribly jealous. Quickly, he went to the big cave in the mountain. This cave was their home.

The *masalai*'s face was horrible. He also did not ask the man, no he did not. The woman was also afraid that her husband would become a complete *masalai*.

The man saw this and was terrified because his cassowary foster mother had told him to follow the trail directly to the village and not to dawdle. The man trembled a little at the young woman, but she was not a real woman. She was the *masalai*'s wife.

The man was afraid, so he quickly jumped up a tree and sat there. He waited for the *masalai* to leave first, then he would go down and leave. However it was not to be, the *masalai* sat there and waited.

He waited for a very long time, then the *masalai* began to cut the tree.

The man saw this and he jumped to another tree. The *masalai* crushed that tree too. The man jumped again to a third tree. But something happened, he was terrified and he had forgotten the powers that his cassowary mother had given to him.

This continued for a while, he jumped across the trees and approached the village. Then he jumped onto a coconut palm tree. The *masalai* saw that he had arrived by the village. The *masalai* was afraid of people, so he went back into the forest. The man was completely out of breath and he sat on top of the coconut tree. It was evening now and the man was sitting on top of the coconut tree.

The man took the coconuts and removed the husks with his teeth. He saw a young woman walking on the trail near the coconut tree and he called out to her.

The man looked down and he saw a woman carrying a huge basket on her back. Quietly, the man aimed and threw down a piece of coconut meat directly at the basket.

The woman was surprised and looked up the coconut tree, then the man waved at her. The woman saw this and went to tell her parents. The woman's parents and some other people gathered to look, then the man went down the coconut tree. He went down to the ground and he told his story to the villagers. Then the people told his two parents. The parents were very old and were sitting in the house. The man went to see them and he told the story, crying hard for them.

Now, it is completely forbidden for parents to carry babies with them when they work at processing sago in the forest.

Later, the man had [no] troubles. He and his wife found it easy to obtain food like his cassowary foster mother had promised.

Henry Qua

St. Joseph's High School, P. O. Box 105

Kieta

North Solomons Province

B211.3.17K. Speaking cassowary; B535.0.7+. Cassowary as nurse for child; C612+. Tabu: bringing baby into forest to make sago; D1246. Magic powder; D1737.1. Magic power from mother; D1781. Magic results from singing; D1781+. Magic results from dancing; D2000. Magic forgetfulness; D2142.1. Wind produced by magic; D2143.1. Rain produced by magic; F490+. Masalai; P210. Husband and wife; P231. Mother and son; P232. Mother and daughter; P233. Father and son; P234. Father and daughter; P272. Foster mother; P275. Foster son; R13.4K+. Cassowary abducts person; R260. Pursuits; R311. Tree refuge; S143. Abandonment in forest; W126. Disobedience; W181. Jealousy

## The Trail to Where the Sun Rises
(Wantok 516, April 21, 1984, page 26)

Long, long ago, there was an old mother and her young daughter who lived near the source of the River Anda and the River Puleng in the Kabwum area of Morobe Province.

The old mother worked in the garden every day, then she would carry a little food back to the house. The daughter would follow the river then catch fish, eels, crayfish and other kinds of game by the river. They would cook these foods and sit down in the evening at the house to eat.

Every day, the young woman would take a net bag then follow the two rivers and catch game by the river. However one day, she followed a branch of the river and did not find fish, eels or crayfish. No, she saw marsupials (*kapul*) drifting down the water.

So, she filled her net bag just with marsupials. Then she followed the two rivers to where they met. She followed the Anda River and found out that the marsupials did not come down this river.

She turned back and followed the Puleng River. She saw that the marsupials were drifting down this river. It looked as if the marsupials had just died, since blood was still coming from their bodies. The woman continued following the river, filling up her net bag until it was dark.

The woman marked the place where she was then she turned back and went to the house. Oh my, the net bag was bursting with marsupials!

The old mother was very happy to see so many marsupials. She asked her daughter where she had gotten so many marsupials. The daughter told her mother exactly where it was.

That night, they cooked the marsupials and ate their fill of marsupial meat with the other food, then they prepared to sleep.

When they were about to go to sleep, the daughter told the mother that she would go and get more marsupials on the next day. The daughter said that she would wake up when it was still the middle of the night then go to find out who it was that had killed the marsupials and thrown them into the Puleng River.

They prepared some food for the daughter to carry when she went looking for marsupials again. When she was about to leave, she told her old mother, "If I come to a *masalai*'s home, then I can't come back. If I go to a real man's home, then I'll come back." After she said this, she left to follow the Puleng River.

She walked and walked, then she came fairly close to the place. She saw the bloody marsupials drifting in the water. They had just recently been killed and thrown into the water, and they were drifting down. The woman thought that she had come close to the place. She said this and she kept walking. She heard the place where the two rivers met and she worried about the big place.

She stood close and was about to raise her head when she saw a huge stone house. Inside the house sat an old woman. The young woman walked quietly and went to the old woman.

When the old woman saw her, she was shocked and asked about her. She replied to the old woman, "I followed the marsupials that you threw away and I came to meet you."

The old woman told her, "Don't be afraid when my children come." She said that her children where various kinds of snakes. Some were short, some were long and some were huge.

She listened and before long, they came from far away. The huge brother of the pythons came first and called to his younger siblings. He called for all his siblings to come back to their mother's home.

When the old woman heard the python calling for his siblings to return to the house, she told the woman to go underneath her legs and to hide her face.

The python's kin arrived at the house and they smelled the woman inside. They threw down marsupials for their old mother to cook for them to eat. After they gave her the marsupials, they lay about their home.

The big python carried a big marsupial. The small snakes each carried a small marsupial that was their size, and the lizards carried rats.

Late at night, the big python transformed himself and became a handsome man. When the woman got up and saw him, oh my, she was very troubled. The two of them married. Before long, they had a son. His name was Uyong.

The boy became five years old. His mother always worked in the garden, and his father would go to the forest to hunt for wild game. He would stay and work in the garden with his mother.

One time, the father went to the forest and they stayed behind. The mother went to work planting taros, sugarcanes, bananas, and other things. Their son went to the head of the river. He worked at closing and opening the flow of the water.

The water would go down and remove the things that his mother had planted. Uyong did this many times and his mother became angry. The mother came up and scolded Uyong.

The mother said, "You're a stubborn snake child just like your father. You don't do any work in the garden. You're just acting stupidly. Later, you'll think about going around the deep forest and hunting game, just like your father."

Uyong was ashamed and cried terribly. He walked around, waiting for his father at the head of the forest trail. When the father came and found him, Uyong told about the bad things that his mother had said to him.

The father was very sorry to see his son crying and talking. The tears flowed from the son and the father's heart was completely broken when he saw his son.

The father carried him and they ran away from the mother. They left the place that they called Sambyo, cutting through the very deep forest and arriving at Mount Kromwel [Mount Cromwell or Mount Ulur]. They sat and rested on Mount Kromwel for a fairly long time while the mother waited for them in the garden.

The mother called out to Uyong repeatedly, but he did not reply, so she left all her things in the garden and followed the father's footsteps into the deep forest. She walked and called out to her son Uyong, but he did not reply to her shouting.

The father and son Uyong sat resting. They heard the mother's voice calling out and approaching them. Uyong heard his mother calling and wanted to reply, but his father forbade him. The father told Uyong that this calling was coming from a bird in the forest called *ningon kotingon*.

When the mother approached the father and son, the father carried the son and walked again to another place that was far away. When they went to sit and rest, the mother approached, but the father and son got up and walked to another place.

Uyong was sure that he heard his mother's voice, so he told his father to wait for her. However, the father lied to him about calling out behind them, that his neck was in pain. The mother was very sorry and began to cry.

The mother [cried] and sang at the same time, following them in the deep forest. She sang, "*Nane* Uyong, *kirite kimbamo taite tapamo*, *Nane Uyong*, Uyong!" This means, "Baby Uyong, you two stand, you two stand, you two sit, we sit, baby Uyong, Uyong!"

The father and baby Uyong arrived at Mount Sarawaget [Sarawaket], and they sat down again. However the mother's calling came closer to them, so they got up again and walked further to the peak of the mountain. The father spoke and turned Uyong into fuzzy grass.

The mother followed their footsteps up towards the summit. She wanted to find the way that the father had taken, but she was unable to do so. When she sat upon the fuzzy grass, she turned into a boulder.

This grass grows and covers a big area on the top of Mount Sarawaget. This grass also grows in many places, and in gardens too. It grows in places that were once deep forest.

The mother who became a boulder stands there like a big stone house with many wild sugarcanes (*pitpit*) growing on top of her neck. Water falls from the stone like mother's milk.

All of us people from Kabwum believe that this story is true because the sun usually rises at about five o'clock in the morning and first shines on this stone house with the fuzzy grasses at the Mount Sarawaget summit. Afterwards, the sun shoots its light down into Kabwum Valley.

Many people use the water that comes from the stone mother's breasts as medicine for children. Other women fill up the water and give it to children whose skin is peeling, and they use it when their mothers are dying. They believe that this water makes children stouter and stronger.

I, myself have seen this stone house with the fuzzy grasses, the wild sugarcanes, and the water that flows like mother's milk. I believe that this ancestor story is true.

This story comes from **Indagen** Village, Kabwum District, in **Morobe** Province [**Komba** People].

K. Hendingnare Mumengire
Indagen Village
c/- P & T [Post & Telecommunications]
Lae
Morobe Province

[See *Wantok* #748 for a similar story.]

A974. Rocks from transformation of people to stone; A977.5. Origin of particular rock; A2683. Origin of grass; B631. Human offspring from marriage to animal; B656.1. Marriage to python in human form; B875.1. Giant serpent; D223B. Transformation: boy to grass; D231W. Transformation: woman to stone; D391+M. Transformation: python to man; D671. Transformation flight; D1242.1. Magic water; D1500.1.18. Magic healing water; D1774. Magic results from speaking; P210. Husband and wife; P231. Mother and son; P232. Mother and daughter; P233. Father and son; P250. Brothers and sisters; R213. Escape from home; R260. Pursuits; T100. Marriage; T554.0.3K+. Woman gives birth to lizard; T554.7. Woman gives birth to a snake; W167. Stubbornness

## The Mistake of Watching the Moon
(Wantok 517, April 28, 1984, page 24)

Long, long ago, in the time of the ancestors, a man, his wife, and their two children lived in a village. One night, the man woke up and told his wife, "You and the children stay here. I'm going to watch the moon."

After the man said this, he took a net bag, some fire, a bow and arrows, and a traditional knife. Then he walked and walked until he arrived at the place where he thought he would be able to watch the moon.

He put down the fire, his net bag, and the bow and arrows. Then he took traditional [shell] ring money and a small image of a fish. But it was not really the image of a fish. In my language it is called *salam*.

Oh my, oh my, the good-for-nothing was dressed very finely. Then he took his hand drum and went back to the village. When he arrived at the village, his wife and children asked him, "Did you kill wild game or not?"

The man lied and said, "I'm very sorry, I didn't kill any game."

He did not tell them that he had sung through the night until dawn. He also had hidden his adornments in the forest before he had returned to the village.

The next night, he told his wife and children that he would go watch the moon. He left them, carrying his net bag, and arrived at the place where he had sung and danced before.

When he arrived, he took his adornments and put them on, then he began to sing and dance. He sang and danced until he was out of breath, then he sat down and chewed betel nuts. After he finished chewing, he got up, held the hand drum then sang and danced fervently again.

When dawn broke, the man hid his festive adornments. Then he carried his knife, bow and arrows, and net bag, and walked back to the village.

The wife and children thought that he had gone to watch in the forest and that he had killed an animal and brought it back. But no, they saw him arrive empty-handed.

They asked him, "Did you kill an animal or not?"

The man did not know that his wife had followed him. She had followed the forest trail and arrived at the place where he usually hid the things for his singing and dancing.

His wife had seen him take the things and decorate himself, then fervently sing and dance. His wife was very angry because she had seen this. She said, "Aha! Now I know the deceits of this lazy man. He lies to us and goes there to sing and dance."

After the woman saw this, she thought about tricking her husband. The woman took some mud and put it on her skin. She walked very quietly to where the man sang and danced.

There was a tree that was near there and the woman quietly climbed the tree. The man fervently sang and danced. The lizard skin on the drum almost broke.

The woman went up the tree. She changed her voice and called out, "Ha! My husband, you're singing and dancing. I'm going to eat you right up. You're my meat."

After the woman said this, she jumped down near the man. The man screamed terribly. He trembled fiercely. He ran away and fell down then screamed and ran some more.

He went and thought some more about his adornments. He heard the woman calling and he thought that it was really a ghost woman that was chasing him. As he was running away, he broke the ring money and _salam_.

His wife had already arrived at the house, washed off and removed the clay from her skin. She went inside the house and told her two children, "Your father has lied to us about going to hunt for game. He just goes to sing and dance in the forest."

Before long, they heard their father gasping and coming to the house. He banged on the door and yelled for them to open it. They heard him and they lied to him, telling him to pull hard.

Their father called out, "Open the door, a ghost woman is chasing me. Hurry and open the door!"

His big child went and opened the door for him. The father came inside the house and told his children to close the door.

They lied to him and asked, "Where's the ghost that's chasing you?"

Their father said that he was sitting and watching the moon when a ghost woman was sitting on top of a tree and looking at him. Then the ghost jumped down, chased him and tried to eat him.

In the morning, the man told his wife and two children, "Stay here and I'll go look for the things that I left in the forest. The ghost chased me and I did not think about getting these things."

After the man left, the mother told her children, "He's a liar. He wants to go look for the ring money, hand drum and _salam_. When he ran away last night, he probably broke these things and now he wants to check up on them."

The man arrived at the place where he had sung and danced at night. He saw that his things were broken and scattered about. The poor man saw this and was speechless. He was very troubled, so he just took the net bag, knife, bow and arrows, then walked back to his village.

When he arrived at the village, his wife cooked some food and stirred some sago. The man approached very quietly and sat down. When his wife leaned forward, he saw a piece of mud stuck to the side of one of her breasts.

When the man saw this, he knew that it was just his wife who had fooled him at night. The man was furious because he was troubled about the drum, _salam_, and ring money that broke when he had run away at night. He did not say anything, he just stayed there quietly. Then it was time for them to eat. His wife served the food and they sat to eat.

One time, the man told his children that he and their mother would go to the forest to gather _galip_ nuts. He called out to the children and he told them, "You stay here. Your mother and I will go to the forest to gather _galip_ nuts. Your maternal kin will want some and will send a message here."

The married couple walked and walked then arrived at the place where the _galip_ trees were. The man cut a piece of bamboo and put a hook on it. Then he worked at breaking the *galip* nuts on the tree. His wife went up the tree and worked at cutting the nuts.

While the man was hooking the *galip* nuts, he called out to his wife, "Hoi, where are you?"

The poor woman heard this and thought that the man was just asking so she replied, "I'm here. I'll move around so you can see."

Her husband saw this so he took his bamboo and shot the woman right in her shoulder. The bamboo went through to the other side. The woman called out once, but she fell down to the ground and died.

The man [who was also on the tree] saw her fall. He sent a lizard down to check on the woman. He told the lizard that if the woman was really dead, that the lizard should take some blood from her nose or mouth and show him.

The lizard took some blood and came to show the man. Then the man went down the *galip* tree, took his wife's body and put it at the base of the tree.

After he put his wife's body down, he took the *galip* nuts and put them around her body. When he finished, he cut off his wife's breasts and carried them back to the village.

He arrived at the village and told the two children, "Your mother carried the *galip* nuts to give to your maternal kin, so you must cook these edible mushrooms for me."

The children took the package that their father gave them and they carried it inside the house. They untied the rope and when they opened the package, they saw their mother's breasts inside it.

They saw this and they did not cook them. They left them. When it was still at night, they went to ask their maternal relative whether their mother had brought some *galip* nuts. However, their relative told them that their mother had not brought *galip* nuts to the house.

The children listened to this and the returned to their house. They slept until dawn, then they went to the place where their parents had gathered *galip* nuts.

When they arrived at this place, they saw their mother's body lying at the base of the *galip* tree. They saw the *galip* nuts around her body. They were troubled about their mother. They cried and cried.

They did not tell their father about this because they knew that their father was angry with their mother and that he had killed her.

They lived with their father for a while and the father thought that his children had forgotten their mother. One day, their father told them, "Children, tomorrow we'll go to the garden and burn the weeds."

In the morning, the three of them woke up together and went to the garden. They arrived at the garden and began gathering the weeds and lighting a fire. Their father planted taros, corn, yams, beans, *aibika*, and other foods.

They worked in the garden until noon. Their father continued to plant food and he became thirsty. He called out to his children, "Hoi, my neck's dry. Can you fetch me some water?"

His children just listened to him. They wanted to get revenge for their mother. They went inside the forest, and then the little sister told the big sister, "Now father must die."

They cut a piece of bamboo tube and the little sister looked for a centipede. She found one, brought it back and put it into the bamboo tube. The big sister cried for her father and put a grasshopper (*eilam*) inside the bamboo.

They filled it up with water and they brought it to the garden. They arrived at the garden and the big sister called out to their father, "Papa, come get your water and drink."

The little sister told her father that he must take the bamboo tube of water and drink it. The father took the tube of water from her hand and drank.

The father did not know about the centipede that the girl had put inside the water, and it went down into his belly. Later, he took the tube of water from the big girl and he also drank that.

This time, when he drank the water, the *elam* [*eilam*] went down with the water into his belly. He felt his legs, arms and neck itch, but he thought that it was just rubbish in the water that made his neck itch like that.

The *elam* and centipede did not die. The man stood for a little, then he felt a pain in his belly. It was the centipede eating the man's belly.

The two bugs ate at his belly until they arrived at his liver, then the man died. His two children took him and went to bury him in their garden. Later, they returned to their village.

My aunt told me this story when I lived in **Maui** Village near Lumi in **West Sepik** Province [**Olo** People].

William Jimmy Sabien

c/- Hubert Woflu

2 PIR B Coy

Moem Barracks

Wewak

East Sepik Province

[For a similar story see *Wantok* #310.]

B212. Animal understands human speech; B491.2. Helpful lizard; E261.4+. Imagined ghost pursues man; G61.1. Child recognizes relative's flesh when it is served to be eaten; K1833. Disguise as ghost; P210. Husband and wife; P232+. Daughter avenges mother; P234. Father and daughter; P252.1. Two sisters; P290+. Maternal kin; Q211. Murder punished; Q260. Deceptions punished; Q321. Laziness punished; Q411. Death as punishment; R260. Pursuits; S22+. Patricide; S63+. Husband kills wife; S111.8+. Murder by feeding poisonous invertebrates; S176+. Mutilation: breasts cut off; W111. Laziness; W157. Dishonesty

# The Man Who Became a Bird

(Wantok 518, May 5, 1984, page 20)

Long, long ago in the time of the ancestors, there was a village called **Moniyau**. By this village, there were two birds. One usually went inside the village and the other usually went in the forest near the village.

The little bird that lived in the village was named Baiayrin. The big one in the forest was named Dangand. The little bird had nicely colored feathers on its body. The feathers were long and looked very beautiful. However, the big bird in the forest by the village did not have [much] food. The bird often worked hard to find food, and its feathers were missing here and there.

The little bird in the village was cared for by a man who gave it good food all of the time. They often gave it coconut milk and many ripe bananas. The bird's owner also sang and danced for it, giving water and food to it. This made the bird grow beautiful and stronger.

If some man wanted to steal the bird, it would call out, "Papa, papa." Then the bird's owner would know that there were people who wanted to steal or hold the bird.

One day, the bird that lived in the forest smelled the food that the little bird's owner had given to it. The big bird flew near the house and saw the little bird eating.

The big bird very quietly walked into the house. When the little bird saw this, it did not call out to its owner. This was because the big bird told it in the local language that it was [its] sister.

The little bird shared its food, and the big bird ate. Later, the big bird saw that the little bird's feathers were more beautiful and it was very jealous.

The big bird asked the little bird, "How did you get your feathers?" The big bird asked this because it thought that it must get many feathers on its body. However, the big bird had no feathers: it was nearly bald.

The big bird was not worried any more because it had hidden and stolen before, and it saw that the little bird's owner often sang and gave food to the little bird. So, it knew why the little bird had beautiful feathers and why it looked beautiful and strong. It was also because the little bird never looked for food in the forest like the big bird who worked hard at finding food.

The big bird found this out and thought about going to steal the little bird's food, then to take away the little bird's power and its beautiful feathers too.

When the big bird finished eating with the little bird, it walked out a little from the house then turned and said, "You no longer have power and strength. I've taken your power and strength. You shall get my feathers and you'll be nearly bald. Your beautiful feathers will come to me."

The little bird heard this and called out, "Papa, papa." When the owner arrived, he saw the big bird perching high up on a tree branch near their house.

The big bird called down to the little bird's owner, "I took your child's power because I ate some of its food. Your child will no longer look good. All of you people in this village will hunt for my feathers and try to remove me from all of the places in the forest because I alone will have beautiful feathers."

The people of the village had often used the little bird's feathers from its owner to put on their heads or to decorate themselves for festivals.

Now, the man no longer had such a business. The power departed with the bird into the forest. Men always search the corners of the forest to grab the bird, but without success.

Every day, the little bird sat and looked very sad in the house. It did not have strength or beautiful feathers anymore. The people of the village found out that this had happened to the village bird.

A little later, the little bird was in pain. Its owner no longer gave it good food and coconut milk. Its skin became bald because its feathers no longer grew.

The little bird was very angry. One night, while its owner slept, it cut and cut the cage in which it lived then it went outside to fly in the forest. That night it went to live outside. It had never thought that it lived in a cage because it never thought about escaping. The singing, dancing, food and water from its owner made it just like his child.

The man's strength also resided in the bird. When the little bird left the house and escaped to the forest, its owner went crazy. The man began to speak like a bird. Later, he called out, "Papa, papa," just like the little bird had called out. Later, every night that he slept, bird feathers began to grow on his skin. His skin changed very slowly and became like that of a bird.

The little bird carried a poison, and its strength left completely for the forest. The little bird carried the poison and shoved it into a tree hole. When the poison smelled its strongest, the man from the village changed further. One night he went to sleep. In the morning, he woke up and the man's head had changed, becoming almost like that of a bird.

The people of the village saw this and were afraid that the man had become very sick and had turned into a *masalai*. His wife saw that his arms and legs had turned into those of a bird, so she left him. She ran away from him completely and went to another village.

After that, the man lived entirely alone. One night, the little bird returned to the house and saw the man. The bird said, "You never gave me good food. That caused me great pain. Now everyone in the village shuns you."

That night, the man turned completely into a bird and flew into the forest. The people did not know whether the man had just left or whether he had run away and turned into a *masalai*. He had turned into a bird, and he flew near his wife's house every day.

[Anonymous]

B172. Magic bird; B211.3. Speaking bird; B500. Magic power from animals; D150M. Transformation: man to bird; D413+. Transformation: beautiful bird to ugly bird; D413+. Transformation: ugly bird to beautiful bird; D551. Transformation by eating; D681. Gradual transformation; D1335.1. Magic strength-giving food; L300. Triumph of the weak; P210. Husband and wife; Q551.3.2.2+. Punishment: transformation into bird; Q584.2. Transformation of a man to animal as fitting punishment; R213. Escape from home; W181. Jealousy


## The *Masalai* Took a Baby
(Wantok 519, May 12, 1984, page 20)

Long, long ago, there was a place on top of a mountain. The name of this place is Mokun. There was a married couple that lived in this place. The man's name was Narua and the woman's name was Yan. They lived very well in their little home. However, they had a big problem because they did not have children. They had a big place with land and forest, but they worried about having children.

They often worked in a garden, made sago, and hunted for wild game in the forest. They did this sort of thing every day, then one night they sat and talked about children. They talked and talked, then a *masalai* man came underneath the house and overheard them talking about children.

The *masalai* sat well and listened, then he got up and left. The married couple talked and talked, then they went back and slept. In the morning, they awoke and went to the forest.

They found much game in the forest, then they returned home in the late afternoon. Yan cooked the food, then they ate and slept. At night, the *masalai* came quietly, went inside and slept with the woman. The *masalai* turned into a real man when he went to the woman, so that the woman would think that it was her husband.

Every night, the *masalai* would turn into a real man and the go to Yan. After a while, the woman became pregnant. Her husband saw this and was very happy because it had been a long time that they had not had any children and they were very troubled by this.

The man, Narua, often worked very hard, going to the forest and hunting game, bringing it back, cooking it and giving to his wife to eat. After a while, when it was nearly time for the woman to give birth, the man said, "I have a very big worry. You must give birth to a baby boy."

His wife, Yan, listened and said, "I don't know what it will be. It will be the first time that I'll have given birth."

Her husband told her not to worry too much because it would be their first child. If it were a baby girl, then that would also be all right.

They finished sitting and talking, then they went to sleep. The *masalai* came and watched. Yan was very happy. The *masalai* said, "I'm very sorry Narua. It's not your baby. It's my baby. I'll take it to my home and look after it."

In the morning, Yan woke up and told her husband, "Don't go into the forest. You must just stay at home because I feel like I'll be giving birth soon."

Her husband listened and did not go to the forest. He just stayed at home. When his wife felt that she would give birth, she told her husband to take her to the birthing place.

The woman gave birth and saw that it was a boy. She was very happy and brought the baby to show to her husband. Her husband was very happy and jumped for joy.

They went back to their house. They began to talk about what name to give to the baby. The husband, Narua, listened and gave the name Kamosal to the baby boy.

Yan and her husband were very happy for their baby and they took care of him very well. They lived for a while, and the baby grew up.

One day, they did not have sago, so the parents sat and decided to go cut a sago palm on the next day. In the morning, they awoke and went to make sago. The father found a sago palm tree and he cut it down. Then they worked at pulverizing the pith.

His wife carried a basket that they filled with the pulverized sago. At this time, she had put her baby inside a baby's basket while she worked.

The *masalai* man came and turned into a pig.  He looked for scraps close to the place where they were making sago.  The pig worked at eating the scraps while watching the married couple and the baby.  Before long, the pig saw Yan carrying baby Kamosol [Kamosal] and hanging the basket up on a tree branch close to the place where she worked rinsing the sago.

The *masalai* saw this then sang and danced, which completely confused her about her baby.  She just worked diligently at rinsing the sago.  When she heard her husband calling out again to carry sago to be rinsed, she got up and left the baby.

After Yan left, the *masalai* immediately turned into a real man then grabbed the baby and was very happy.  He held Kamasal [Kamosol], put him back inside the net bag [basket], then stood and watched.

When Yan brought the sago back to rinse, she no longer thought about the baby.  She just worked at rinsing the pulverized sago.  Her husband also did not think about their baby.  He also worked at pounding the sago and calling out for his wife to carry it.

The married couple bent down at their work [i.e., worked hard] until the work was finished.  Afterwards, Yan carried her basket and the other things, then she and her husband walked back to their house.

When they arrived home, Narua thought of the baby and began to ask Yan, "You brought baby.  Where did you put him?"

Yan heard this and was surprised.  She told her husband, "I'm very sorry.  I left the baby at the place where I worked rinsing sago."  Oh my, Narua heard this and was furious.

He told Yan, "Light a torch, then go back to that place and look for baby."

They took torches and lit them.  They walked back to the place where they had processed sago.  They arrived there and they could not find the baby.  They searched and searched, but to no avail.  They were both angry and kept searching until dawn broke.  They cried together then went back home.

Old Timari told this story and I wrote it down.

Solar Tommy
**Yimas** Village [**Yimas** People]
Amboin
**East Sepik** Province

D94+M. Transformation: ogre to man; D136M. Transformation: man to swine; D336.1M. Transformation: pig to man; D1781. Magic results from singing; D1781+. Magic results from dancing; D2000. Magic forgetfulness; K1311. Seduction by masking as woman's husband; K1910. Marital impostors; K1920. Substituted children; P210. Husband and wife; P231. Mother and son; P233. Father and son; R10.3. Children abducted; R11. Abduction by monster (ogre); T570. Pregnancy; T580. Childbirth

## The Boys Who Conquered Masumura

(Wantok 520, May 19, 1984, page 20)

Long, long ago, in the time of the ancestors, in the area near Finsafen [Finschhafen], there was a *masalai* named Masumura [**Morobe** Province].  This *masalai* dwelled inside a hole in the ground.

One day, all of the men, women and children wanted to make a garden, so they went into the forest.  They arrived there, and the parents began to cut the forest while the children played.  While they played, the children saw Masumura's hole.

They thought that it was a rat's hole or that some animal had dug it.  The bad *masalai* was hungry and slept soundly.  Oh my, the children did not think that it was Masumura's hole, so they began to dig around the hole and to shout.

When Masumura heard that there were people nearby, he was happy and said, "Hey, am I dreaming or what?  That's meat."  Then he wanted to go outside.

Then he went outside and cut all of the children with their parents in the middle, just like a flash.  There was only woman left.  She was afraid and hid at the base of some sugarcane.  Once the *masalai* had departed, the woman wanted to run away, but a sugarcane leaf cut her hand and blood gushed out.  It flowed out like water.  The woman was very worried that she was bleeding.

She took a wild taro leaf and put it on her hand.  The wild taro leaf stanched the bleeding, then she went to the village.  At this time, there were no other women in the village, and she was alone.

The next day, she went back to the garden.  When she arrived, she saw that her blood had turned into two little fish.  The woman then went back to the village.

Another day, she returned and saw that the fish had turned into two little children.  She was happy and she took them to her house.

The two children were boys.  The woman took care of them until they grew to be big men.  Then she told the story of how Masumura had killed and eaten their fellow tribespeople.

The men were furious at the *masalai*, and they told their mother, "We'll kill him."  The mother told them, "No, he'll eat us."

They persisted and they told their mother that they would learn a way to kill the *masalai*. So, their mother taught them to make bows and to sharpen arrows. The two of them finished making everything, then they asked their mother to show them the place where the *masalai* dwelled.

They shouted and talked loudly, and their mother scolded them, "What if the *masalai* hears you, he'll come here. Don't talk so much now."

The boys [men] became strong enough to make everything and they told their mother, "Now, we'll fight with him."

They made six fences and put all of their spears on each of the six fences.

They told their mother, "You must hide well otherwise Masumura will eat you." The mother departed then the two of them called out, "Masumura, you're the kind of man who can't eat the two of us."

They went inside the first fence. Quickly, the bad man arrived and said, "Ha, I'll eat you two animals right up."

When he said this, the first fence broke and the two boys jumped behind the second fence.

Oh my, a big fight began with smoke and dust being kicked up. They fought and the two of them worked at shooting Masumura, but it was not enough. The *masalai* said, "Ha... I'll eat you two animals right up." Then the second fence broke.

The two boys jumped over the third fence and only three more fences were left. They were afraid, but they did not flinch at fighting. Masumura's body had various holes and arrow marks, and blood was flowing. The two of them were so hot that sweat was just pouring from them. Masumura was not worried. They continued, and the fourth fence also broke.

It was too bad when they arrived at the sixth fence, Masumura's strength was finished. The two of them drew back their arrows and shot him right in the belly. The arrows went straight through to his liver. He fell down to the ground and died. The two of them called out that they had killed the *masalai* Masumura.

Their mother was ecstatic. They sent a message to the other villages. The people from the other villages gathered in one place and made a big party with singing and dancing to congratulate the two boys and their mother.

Gerlin Benen Aze
Mendi Mobile Base
Mendi
Southern Highlands Province

[See the ancestor stories in *Wantok* #635, 672, and 721. These stories also have a *masalai* named Masumura. This story probably comes from the **Kâte** People]

A515.1.1. Twin culture heroes; D370B. Transformation: fish to boy; D447.3+. Transformation: blood to fish; F490+. Masalai; F490+. Masumura; G346.0.1+. Devastating monster which lives in hole in ground; G510.4+. Hero overcomes devastating ogre; G512.1+. Ogre killed with spear/arrow; G641K. Ogres live in cave(s); P230. Parents and children; P231. Mother and son; P251.5. Two brothers; S118.1. Murder by cutting adversary in two; T534. Conception from blood; T587. Birth of twins; T685. Twins; Z71.4. Formulistic number: six; Z210. Brothers as heroes; Z356. Unique survivor

## The Birds Who Helped a Man
(Wantok 521a, May 26, 1984, page 20)

Long, long ago, there was a *masalai* man. He killed many people and kept eating them.

One time, a man and his wife were working in a garden. They worked and worked, and the hot sun made them terribly thirsty for water. The woman was dying of thirst, so she sent the man to fetch water in the forest.

After the man went to get water in the forest, it was not long when a man came with water in his hands. The man was a *masalai*. He had transformed himself to appear like the woman's husband, and went to her. Too bad, the woman saw him and thought that he was really her husband.

The *masalai* man just picked up the woman and ran away. The poor husband came and saw that his wife was not there. He took their things and went back to the village. He arrived and asked his wife's kin about her, but they said, "We haven't seen your wife."

At this time, an old man lived there. The old man was very surprised and told the young man that a *masalai* man often lived there who killed and ate people. When the man heard this, he cried and cried then went to the place where his wife lived.

After a while, the man told all of the men to find her. If a man found his wife, he would kill all his pigs and give all his garden food to him. At this time, all of the men tried, but they could not find his wife.

One time, the man traveled in the forest to find some birds to help him. When he went a little farther, he heard some talking, "What are you looking for?"

The man was surprised and said, "I'm looking for my wife. When he turned around, he saw little birds perched on a tree branch. The little birds alit and told the man, "We'll help you find your wife."

The man listened to this and he took them to the place. When the man took them there, the little birds told him, "Your wife is on the other side of the big sea. If you give a bag to us, we'll go get her."

However the man was afraid and said, "You'll drop my wife in the sea." The little birds said, "We can carry her to you quite well."

The man pulled up a stone to be flown to the other side of the sea and back. The little birds carried it in a net back to the other side of the sea and brought it back. The man was happy and told the birds to go.

The little birds flew again and went to the other side. They flew down to the *masalai*'s house. They flew inside and took the woman out.

The woman was terrified and said, "You're too small." The birds told her, "Your husband sent us to come and bring you." The woman was afraid but she slowly went into the net bag, and the birds carried her back to the village.

When they arrived at the village, the people were elated to see her. Her husband was ecstatic, so he killed many pigs, removed much food from the garden, and made a big feast.

He made a big earth oven and made food for the little birds too. When the food was ready, some of the little birds ate pork and others ate yams.

The birds that ate yams became white. Those that ate pork turned mottled, black and white. So if you look, you will see that some birds are black and white.

Sinai Talian
Mt. Hagen High School
Western Highlands Province

A2411.2. Origin of color of bird; B211.3. Speaking bird; B450. Helpful birds; B541.3. Bird rescues man from sea; B552. Man carried by bird; D94+M. Transformation: ogre to man; D551.2.7+. Transformation by eating yam; D551.3. Transformation by eating flesh; F490+. Masalai; H1562.2.2+. Before undertaking rescue, bird tests strength by lifting stone; G346. Devastating monster; K1910. Marital impostors; P210. Husband and wife; P290+. Maternal kin; Q53. Reward for rescue; R11. Abduction by monster (ogre); R110. Rescue of captive; S110. Murders

## Marsupials (*Kapul*) and Dogs Are Enemies
(Wantok 521b, May 26, 1984, page 20)

Long, long ago, in the time of the ancestors, there was a marsupial (*kapul*) and a dog who were good friends. Every afternoon, they would meet on a good piece of ground and then sing and dance.

The dog and marsupial never had troubles because they were good friends. One time at about three o'clock in the afternoon, a dog wanted to go drink water. The dog drank a little and thought that it was quite delicious. The dog had smelled something very good.

A little later, the dog followed the smell towards the source of the water. The dog followed and followed, then found a dead marsupial there. The dog ate a piece of the marsupial, then cut it and gave some to its dog friends.

The dogs ate the marsupial and they thought that the marsupial was very delicious. One afternoon, the dogs decided to have a meeting. They said that they should sing and dance, then later they would eat the marsupials.

They finished speaking, then later in the afternoon, they pretended to sing and dance at the place that they usually did.

Then two marsupials began to sing and dance. After they finished, another dog got up and sang, "In the afternoon, I want to eat you. Where do you think you're going with your singing and dancing?"

They sang back and forth, then the dogs and marsupial fought. So now, marsupials run away from dogs.

Jack L. Pai
B. C. L. [Bougainville Copper Limited], B-39
Panguna
North Solomons Province

A2494.4+. Enmity between dog and marsupial; B211.1.7. Speaking dog; B214.1+. Singing marsupial; B214.1.4. Singing dog; B263+. War between dogs and marsupials; B293+. Dance of dogs; B293+. Dance of marsupials; P310. Friendship

## The *Masalai* Broke a Heart
(Wantok 522, June 2, 1984, page 20)

Long, long ago, in the time of the ancestors in the **Southern Highlands** Province, there was a village called Ekari [**Egari** Village, **Mendi** People]. There was a young man who lived with his two sisters in this village.

One day, the brother went to hunt for marsupials (*kapul*) in the forest. The big sister went to the garden, and the little sister stayed alone in the house.

When the two of them had departed, a *masalai* who lived on the mountain by Ekari Village transformed its appearance to be that of the big sister. The *masalai* brought many marsupials to the little sister. Among these marsupials was one that was red-skinned and had beautiful fur.

The *masalai* went to the girl and told her that she must cook the marsupials quickly before they spoil. The girl listened to her and she butchered the [red] marsupial then she cooked it well. The *masalai* woman told the girl, "Eat the marsupial meat now."

The girl did not know that the woman was a *masalai* from the mountain who had changed her appearance into that of her big sister. At this time, her big sister was still working in the garden and her brother was still hunting for wild game in the forest.

The *masalai* had put a magic love spell upon the marsupial. If the girl ate it, she would follow the trail and walk to find the *masalai*. The poor girl did not know this, so she cooked the marsupial then ate it.

While the girl was eating, the *masalai* transformed to appear as her big brother then waited by the stream near their house. This was not a river; it was a stream that was channeled with bamboos. It brought the mountain water to their house.

The *masalai* had turned into the girl's brother and stood there. When the girl finished eating the marsupial, she brought the scraps near the water. She wanted to drink some water and wash her hands. However, she was surprised to see the *masalai* who had turned into her brother standing there.

The girl looked at him and was not afraid because she thought that he was her brother. The man told her to follow him closely. The *masalai* man took a stick and put it on top of her right breast.

The girl saw that this was not normal, so she was angry because her brother had done this. She was angry and wanted to swing it on top of him, but she did not do this. The man just left. The girl ran away and cried at the house because of the bad thing that her brother had done to her.

She cried at the house. Her real brother was hunting for game in the forest. He returned to the village in the evening. Shortly thereafter, the big sister returned to the house with yams, taros, sweet potatoes, pandanus fruits (*marita*), and leafy greens.

The girl spoke heatedly about her brother. She told her big sister what had happened. Their brother searched for his real position and for something to say.

He told her that he had been in the forest all day long. He had not been in the forest near the village. He told them that he had climbed many mountains and crossed many rivers while he was hunting for game.

Their brother told the girl that she was lying or that she was sleeping and dreaming in the sun and had seen her brother's spirit in the village. However all his talking was for naught, the girl just sat and cried.

The *masalai* was in the area by the house and heard the angry talk between the two sisters and the brother. At night, the *masalai* gave a dream to the girl's brother and big sister that the *masalai* wanted their young sister.

In the morning when they awoke, the two of them did not speak. The brother let the dream stay in his head. The big sister did the same thing. In the dream, the *masalai* had told them that he himself had appeared as the big brother and hit the girl on her breast with the stick.

The two of them were terrified and did not want to speak. The brother did not know that the big sister had also had the same dream. The sister also did not know that the brother had this dream. This dream just stayed in their thoughts.

The woman slept at night and the *masalai* came to their house. The *masalai* put something near the place where the woman slept. The next morning, she woke up and did know this. She jumped up and walked away.

The woman was hooked in her thoughts for this man who was far away. The man thought of her from another place that was many mountains and rivers away. If she wanted to go to the man, she would have to walk for many days and nights.

This man who was in the woman's soul was just the *masalai* man. The woman did not see the man's face, but her heart thought of a good man who lived in a faraway place. The woman's thoughts were fixed, never mind that it was far away, that the trails were bad, and that she would meet many difficulties or enemies. She would walk to this place until she found the kind of man who was in her thoughts.

The *masalai* was still far away. One day, the woman said good-bye to her big sister and her big brother. She wanted to walk away. The two of them insisted that they did not want to let her go, but the woman was persistent too. The brother and sister did not know which man it was that the sister was going to, or where she was going.

When the two of them stopped her, their young sister just sat down and cried because the *masalai* had broken her heart. The two of them had given all of their good words, so they let her go look for this man that she loved.

The big brother and sister walked with her. They walked and walked and walked. After many days and nights, their two bodies were exhausted. The two of them stayed at this place. The woman who had the *masalai*'s power in her kept walking to find this man.

Nearly one month had passed and the woman was still walking to find him. However the whole time, the *masalai* was walking near her as she was looking for the man who had burned her heart. The *masalai* had turned into a bird, a lizard, a snake, and other kinds of animals to show the way for the woman to walk.

When she left her big brother and sister in the middle of the trail, she had told them, "If I go and find the man that I love, and I'm not worried about him, I'll make a bonfire and you'll see the smoke. This smoke will mean that I'm alright, that I've found him and that I'm living well. I'll return to see you with my husband. You must make a bonfire so that I'll see the smoke and know that you're alright. Never mind that the place is very far away, I'll still make a fire."

They knew that if she lived with them, she would worry. Her worrying for this man would kill her. Because of this, she had spoken to them and walked away. She walked and walked then arrived at the place of the *masalai*s. The place was just like a village.

The *masalai* men married real woman and lived there. When the *masalai*s turned into real men, they would become more handsome. The village was filled only with good, beautiful woman from the area. The *masalai*s had placed a love spell upon them and pulled them in to marry them, just like this woman had followed this man.

When the woman arrived, she looked at the man's face and she passed out. The man was just a *masalai*, but he had performed various kinds of tricks and love spells upon her. The *masalai* held the woman's hand and took her to the village. He showed her all of the other *masalai*s and women.

Later, the woman found out that it was a *masalai* village, but that the women were real women who had married the *masalai*s. She also found out that it was this *masalai* who had turned into her brother when she was standing, drinking water and washing her hands. When the she had, the brother and sister thought of their dreams. They thought that the *masalai* must have changed their sister's thoughts and caused her to go find the *masalai* and marry him.

Later, the woman married this *masalai* man. She did what she had promised when she left her big sister and brother. She and her husband made a bonfire on top of a mountain. The big sister was in the garden and saw the smoke that was far away. The fire was lit brightly and the smoke covered everywhere even though the *masalai*s were far from their home.

The brother and sister burned a big area of sword grass on a mountain to show the woman and her husband that they were also well, and that they had seen their smoke. Everything that their sister had promised happened. The woman, her *masalai* husband, and their baby walked to see the woman's big sister and brother after about two years.

Agnes Osil

Mendi

Southern Highlands Province

D11. Transformation woman to man; D94+W. Transformation: spirit to woman; D100+. Transformation: spirit to animal; D150.0.1K+. Transformation: spirit to bird; D191+. Transformation: spirit to serpent (snake); D197. Transformation: spirit to lizard; D610. Repeated transformation; D1032. Magic meat; D1427. Magic object compels one to follow; D1810.8.2. Information received through dream; D1900. Love induced by magic; F121. Journey to world of spirits; F460. Mountain-spirits; F490+. Masalai; K1315. Seduction by impostor; P210. Husband and wife; P230. Parents and children; P253.0.2+. Two sisters and one brother; P263. Brother-in-law; P264. Sister-in-law; P293. Uncle; P294. Aunt; T10. Falling in love; T111. Marriage of mortal and supernatural being

## Two Women Became Birds of Paradise
(Wantok 523, June 9, 1984, page 20)

Long, long ago, there was a man who lived in a village near a hill. The man had two wives. The man usually just stayed at home. The two women always went to hunt for food, but the man never ate this food. If he spoke to them about eating pork, they would go bring some, then he would throw it away like trash. Afterwards, he would call for another kind of food. He kept doing this and the two women became exhausted.

When he asked them for food, they scolded him and said, "What kind of food do you really want to eat? You haven't eaten any of the kinds of food that we've brought. You always throw it away like trash." The place where he threw the trash was full of food and it stank terribly.

The man worked his wives very hard and they became mad at him. One time, the women worked very hard and they were mad at him. He told them, "Now would you get two dogs and go to the forest to hunt for some bandicoots for me to eat?" The two of them thought it was true so they caught some bandicoots and brought them back, but he did not want them and he threw them on the trash heap. The bandicoots and other foods were rotting, and had many insects.

After a while, he told them that he wanted to eat dog. The two of them killed a dog, cooked it and brought it to him. However he did not eat it. He did as before and the two of them were very angry.

One time, he told them that he wanted to eat a piglet. They told him, "We only have one dog and it is not enough. You tricked us into killing the other dog and you did not eat it."

They were angry and they took just the one dog into the forest. The dog surrounded a piglet and bit it. They took it back to the village, cooked it and gave it to him, but he did not eat it. He told them that he wanted to eat the last dog. They listened to him and they killed and cooked the good dog. They thought that the man would eat it, but when they brought it to him, he did not eat. The two dogs were dead and the two women did not have any more dogs for hunting food.

One day, the man told them to hunt for a cassowary for him to eat. They told him, "We don't have any more dogs to help us hunt for food." So, the man told them to go fishing.

They listened to him, they took a net and went to a river to look for fish. They caught fish and went to the house. They cooked the fish well with leafy greens and brought it to him, but he did not eat it. The two women's hearts were burning.

They searched for a way to leave him. The next day, they told him, "Stay here, we're going to bathe." However, they left and went to work cutting a *mangas* tree. They finished cutting it then they put it in the river and went back to the house. The next day, they went back and put the *mangas* tree in the sun to dry.

When the *mangas* tree was dry, they quietly took it to the house and made wings for themselves. The first woman made colored wings and the second woman made wings without colors. After they were done, they tied on their wings.

One time, the man went to bathe, so the two of them hurried and tried to fly. The first woman flew and sat on part of a tree, then returned. The second woman also tried. Then they tied the wings again and put them on. While the man was bathing, the women burned all of the man's banana plants until there were none.

One [day], the man told them, "You two [go] for food." They told him, "We have brought you every kind of food, but you have never eaten. We don't have dogs to help us hunt for food."

This was the last time that they talked with him. While he slept, they quickly took their wings, put them on, and

they flew. They called out together and sat on the branch of a *tulip* tree. They flew again and sat on a tall *limbum* palm tree and sang.

The man heard this and wanted to see. He looked up and saw his two wives. Then he called out for them to come down. He called loudly. He got up, ate the various rotting foods and told them, "You two come down. I'm eating this food."

They did not come down. The man looked for a bow but none were there. He made an armlet and cooked two pieces of sago in a bamboo tube of water, then he was ready. It was not yet dawn when he began to climb the *limbum* tree. He climbed and climbed until sunset, then he slept.

This *limbum* tree was very tall and he slept three nights on the tree. It was nearly dawn again when he woke up and approached them. When he saw them sitting, he took a spear made of *limbum* and prepared to shoot them. But no, they grabbed him, pulled him, and beat him terribly. The man fell down and died.

They flew down and burned down their house completely. Then they flew up again. They sat and sang that their husband was dead. They flew away to the deep forest and became birds of paradise.

So now, you can see that there are two kinds of bird of paradise. One is colorful and the other is not. One woman had made her wings colored and this is the beautiful bird of paradise. The other did not color her wings, and this bird of paradise is not colored.

If you go to the forest, you will see this. If you do not go, you cannot see that there are two kinds of bird of paradise. [There are actually many species of bird of paradise.] Michael T.

**Waskuk** Village [**Wogamusin** People]
**East Sepik** Province

A1970+. Creation of bird of paradise; A2411.2+. Origin of color of bird of paradise; D150+W. Transformation: woman to bird of paradise; F54.1. Tree stretches to sky; F1021.1. Flight on artificial wings; P210. Husband and wife; Q285. Cruelty punished; Q411. Death as punishment; R213. Escape from home; R227.2. Flight from hated husband; R260. Pursuits; S62. Cruel husband; S63+. Wife kills husband; S110. Murders; T145.0.1. Polygyny; W31. Obedience

# A Woman Came from a Stick
(Wantok 524, June 16, 1984, page 20)

Long, long ago, in the time of the ancestors, there were two brothers who lived in a village called **Elamel**. They made a huge garden and they found various kinds of foods, taros, sweet potatoes, yams, bananas, sugarcanes, and leafy vegetables.

The garden was huge and it had various foods in it. They made a big fence around the entire garden. Their fence was superior and went very high.

Because of this, there were no wild pigs to smell the food, go inside the garden, and remove the brothers' food. The fence was big and tall. One branch of it often broke down when there was a strong wind or when big wild pigs went and shoved it.

This happened all of the time because the two brothers also did other kinds of work with other men of the village, so they did not look at their garden every day.

About a week later, the brothers went to the garden. They saw that another area of the garden fence had broken down. They took some new wood and make a good fence again with new ropes, rattans, and strong wood.

Some weeks later, they went to see the garden. This time, many yams, taros and sweet potatoes were ready to be harvested. The smell of the food made the wild pigs knock the fence, so the fence was broken.

The two brothers were not married. When the men did heavy work in the village, the women would go check on the gardens, perform small chores, and straighten the gardens.

The little brother saw that the fence was broken, so he worked at collecting old wood and ropes. Then they would cut new wood and make the fence good again.

The big brother went to find some very strong wood. He walked very far to cut some trees that are like ironwood trees.

He walked and walked then arrived at a place where men from the village had never been. He saw a garden from which smoke was rising. He walked quietly to see who was making a garden so far from the village.

He approached and he saw a very old man removing the grasses from his garden. He had never seen this old man before and he did not recognize him. The old man was ancient and he had a long white beard down his chest. His head was full of white hairs too.

The big brother saw this old man and wanted to turn back, but the old man had already been watching him for a while. He knew whenever a man approached. The old man was not an ordinary man, he had powers of observation.

The old man called out to him, "Son, come here. Don't be afraid of me." He walked closer to the old man. The old man asked him what it was that he was looking for.

He told his story to the old man about his garden food and his little brother. The old man told him, "Come and stay with me tonight. You can return to your village another day."

He was afraid, but he was too afraid to run away from the old man. He thought that the old man was a dead man or a *masalai*. The old man told him that everyone in his village had died during a raid.

The old man had hidden, so he had not died when the enemies came to kill all of the men, women, children, pigs, and dogs of his village. He hid and just quietly worked at a garden.

The old man took the young man and they arrived at a boulder. The old man hit the boulder with a stick then the door of the stone opened. They walked inside the boulder. They cooked and ate, then they slept. In the morning, the old man hit the stone and the door opened again. He told the young man to go bathe in the nearby stream.

At night they sat and ate in the boulder. The old man told various stories to the young man. The big brother told the old man that he and his little brother were not yet married, so their life was hard. There were no women to check on their garden when they did other kinds of hard work in the village.

In the morning, the man went to the stream to bathe. The old man looked for two sticks that were as strong as ironwood. He performed a song and dance, then he positioned the sticks.

When the young man arrived, the old man told him, "These two sticks are your strength. Carry them carefully and don't put them just anywhere. Take them and stand one in the garden. The other you can carry home."

The old man also told him, "I've put a mark in the exact center of the stick. You must take this stick to the village and put it inside your house. Then you must break or cut the stick where the mark is and always leave it in the house."

The man prepared to leave the old man. The old man told him not to turn and look back to try to see him. This was because the old man had given his power to the young man. When the young man began to walk back to his village, the old man turned into a boulder.

The man arrived at the garden and stood up a stick like the old man had told him to do. When he stood the stick up in the garden, a huge, strong fence stood around the garden. The wood and ropes of the fence were very strong and lasted for many years until the two brothers removed the old food plants and planted new food plants in the garden.

Later, the man arrived in the village and brought the good news to his brother that the garden food would do well and that there was now a strong fence. However, the man did not know what the other stick was for. He took it and cut it well in the middle where the mark was. He left the pieces in the house.

Then he went to see his little brother and he told his story about the old man. When the little brother went up into the house, he saw that two sticks had turned into two very young women who were preparing food to be cooked. The women sat and laughed when they saw him.

The young women surprised him very much. He quickly went down and told his brother. He thought that his big brother had brought the women with him.

The power of the old man had done this and two sticks became people. The two men married these women, and the women always went to check on the garden. The brothers no longer worried much about the garden.

Elekolae and Henry Hotto
Gerehu
National Capital District

D231M. Transformation: man to stone; D431.2+W. Transformation: stick to woman; D956. Magic stick of wood; D1552.1. Mountain opens at blow of divining rod; D1781. Magic results from singing; D1781+. Magic results from dancing; D1825.2. Magic power to see distant objects; D1830. Magic strength; P210. Husband and wife; P251.5. Two brothers; P263. Brother-in-law; P264. Sister-in-law; T100. Marriage


## The Man in the Clouds Taught a Lesson

(Wantok 525, June 23, 1984, page 19)

Long, long ago, in the time of the ancestors, the parents and other adults went back and forth, doing their work. They went to look for adornments for a festival on this day. Only the young women stayed to look after the little children in the village.

It always worked like that, the adults would go to work and the young women would take care of the little children. In the afternoon, near the time when the parents were to return to the village, there was a bird perched on top of a tree in the front of a house. It sang down towards a young woman in the house.

Whenever the woman went to fetch water or firewood, it would sing down to her. However, she did not know that it was a real man singing. She thought that it was a bird singing.

One day, the woman's parents went to work. The young woman looked after her little brother. When the bird sang to her, she replied, "Hey, why are you singing? You're just a bird. I can eat you with the new food that my parents will bring."

The bird listened to her and just thought about it. Another afternoon, the young women of the village traveled. This woman also traveled with them in the village. It was nearly dark and she was about to go inside the house when the bird sang to her again.

The woman looked up and called out to the bird again, "Hey, shut your mouth. I can just cook your sorry flesh and eat it with the new food that my parents brought."

The bird said, "Is that so? I'll try you next round." This was because the woman was always mocking the bird like this. The woman was very young, and nearing the time for marriage. She was her parents' first child.

One day, the parents went to work, then returned. The young women were still sitting and talking at the house of another woman's house when they heard thunder. They were caught completely off-guard when the rain and wind came. They immediately ran back to their houses.

The young woman ran towards her house. It was dark now. When the rain and wind came, it became completely dark. When she ran close to the house, lightning flashed and the clouds thundered.

The place became light and completely clear. The woman saw the house ladder very clearly. She thought that it was the ladder to her house, but no, it was the ladder belonging to the man who sang down to her like a bird.

The man up in the clouds sat in his house and had a good look at the woman. The woman climbed the man's ladder, up to his house in the clouds.

The woman thought that she was climbing the ladder to her house, but she missed hers because the man in the clouds had stood his ladder in front of hers.

The woman climbed up and up then felt her legs cramping. The bird was no longer a bird. It had become a real man and sat in his house in the clouds with his wife. He looked at the young woman climbing the ladder. The strong rain and strong wind ended, but the place was dark. There was a light rain and a gentle breeze.

The woman climbed and called out, "Why did you move this ladder up so high?" The man in the house called down like a bird to the woman, "Come up."

The woman heard him and was afraid. She looked down and no longer saw the ladder. The ladder just disappeared before her eyes. However when she looked up, she saw that the ladder kept going.

She did not know where the ladder was going. She did not see the man's house either. She went up and cried at the same time. She did not know where she was.

She climbed and climbed until she arrived at the door of the house. The young woman was completely exhausted because she had gone very high up the long ladder.

When the woman arrived at the house door, the man sat in the house and just laughed. He held the woman's hand. The woman was terrified and cried harder. The man told her not to be afraid.

The man told her, "Whenever I saw you walking by your house, I would speak down to you in the voice of a bird. You always called out to me that you could eat my flesh with the good new food that your parents would bring to the house for you. It was just me who had called out to you like a bird."

The man and his wife were aged. They were the ones who made the rain. Their house was in the clouds where there were no people to see them.

The man told her, "I was the one who threw the ladder down to you because you are a beautiful young woman. I have no sons to take my place. There is no way for you to run back to your parents, but you can sit here and look down and see your parents and the people in the village. You can see whatever they do."

When the woman heard this, she then became the old man's wife. She cried hard until it was dark. The man told his old wife to make a sleeping place for the young woman. The woman just cried and cried. Her two eyes swelled up and she went to sleep. She did not eat at all.

The next morning, she awoke then sat in the house and looked down. She saw her village, her house, and the people too. How could she return? The place looked very far and she lived in the clouds at a completely different place.

Her parents and the people below could not see her, but she could see them. She worried and cried again, then she slept. In the afternoon, she woke up and felt hungry. The old woman gave food to her. The woman saw that the food was like snakes.

The woman did not want to eat it. The man told her, "We usually eat this kind of food. The good food that you wanted to eat with my flesh is not here. You must just eat this kind of food."

The woman was ruined with hunger, so she just ate a little, then she slept.

Some time later, she began to eat the kind of food that the old couple gave her. The man overcame the woman's thoughts with his power. The woman married the old man. She forgot her parents, the other people, and her friends too. However, she often looked down and saw them going around the village.

The old couple and the young woman lived together. The young woman gave birth to a baby boy. When the baby became a little bigger, his parents told him the story of his grandparents. Then he too stood on the house and looked down at the people in his mother's village.

One day, a heavy rain and strong wind arose again. The old man threw his ladder down right in front of the ladder of the woman's parents' house. They went down, but the parents had forgotten her. They thought that an enemy had killed her. When they went down to the village, many, many years had passed.

The old man had adorned his young wife and son with traditional decorations. They went down and arrived at her parent's house.

Parents teach their daughters not to talk back to birds when they sing lest the birds become men like the man who lives in the clouds.

Andrew Koim

Arawa

North Solomons Province

A287. Rain-god; B211.3. Speaking bird; C490+. Tabu: speaking to birds; D350M. Transformation: bird to man; D863. Magic object mysteriously disappears; D2142.1. Wind produced by magic; D2143.1. Rain produced by magic; D2149.1. Thunderbolt magically produced; D2000+. Mind control; F12.1. Journey to sky-god; F52. Ladder to upper world; K1328. Disguise as animal to seduce woman; K1840. Deception by substitution; P210. Husband and wife; P231. Mother and son; P232. Mother and daughter; P233. Father and son; P234. Father and daughter; P253. Sister and brother; P291. Grandfather; P292. Grandmother; P310. Friendship; R14. Deity (demigod) abducts person; T111.2+. Mortal marries person in sky; T145.0.1. Polygyny; T192. Marriage by force; T580. Childbirth

## Children Were Killed by a Stone
(Wantok 526, June 30, 1984, page 20)

Before, in the time of the ancestors, in **Meregese** Village, in the Turubu [Terebu] Village area, by Wewak, there lived two families [**Bungain** or **Kaiep** People, **East Sepik** Province; Terebu Village was original Kaiep-speaking but is now predominantly Bungain-speaking (Laycock, 1973: 35-36)].

The first family's father's name was Sio, the mother's name was Kiwe. They had a son, Huwa, and a daughter, Maijo. The father of the second family was Bowi and the mother was Wabijon. Their son was Heibo and their daughter was Wo.

One day, the four children decided to go fishing in the river called Wihuwa. They decided that they would go on the next morning. The next morning, they took their hooks and food scraps for the hooks, then they went to the Wihuwa River where they went fishing.

While they were fishing in the river, a heavy rain fell, and they looked for a place to hide. Huwa told them that they must just run to the village. But no, Heibo told them that they must hide inside a big cave. [Huwa said], "My sister and I will go back to the village in the rain."

Huwa and his sister, Maijo, walked back to the village. Heibo and his sister, Wo, hid inside the cave. Heibo and his sister Wo were safe inside the cave. However a very heavy rain fell, and the water flooded from the mountains, removing small stones. The flood made the big stones fall down and covered the exit. Heibo and Wo did not have a way to get outside.

The rain stopped and the two children still sat inside the cave. The children's parents were waiting and waiting, then they asked the other two children, "Did you see Heibo and Wo or not?" Huwa and Maijo, from the first family, then told the story to the parents of the second family, "We went fishing together in the Wihuwa River. When the heavy rain fell, only the two of us [returned]. Heibo was insistent and they went to hide in the cave. The two of us left them and just came to the house."

When Heibo and Wo's parents heard this, they were very worried. They went to the place where the big cave was, but the cave was covered over where Heibo and Wo were. They could not come outside.

The parents yelled and called the children's names. The children heard them and replied, but how could the two of them remove the stones? The stones were huge. The parents tried unsuccessfully. They cried together and went back to the village.

The two parents revealed the news to the people of the village. They cooked a pig and brought it near the cave. One man knew a song and dance. He sang and danced for the cave to open up and give way.

However it did not work, the cave was still blocked. Everyone tied a rope to a stone and tried pulling it. They pulled and pulled, and the rope broke. Then they tied another rope and this one also broke. They looked for a huge rope and tied this to the stone, but the stone was not an ordinary stone and the third rope broke.

The people were tired and exhausted. Their hands were sore and they just went back to the village. That night, everyone sat and gathered, talking about what they could do.

They looked for the best diviner in the village. In the morning, they carried pigs, coconuts, betel nuts, and shell money from the village to decorate the stone. The diviner sang and danced, but nothing happened. The good, strong *tanget* plants that the diviner used for his singing and dancing had no effect on opening the cave. Nothing happened.

There was a very small hole where the two children inside could see people standing outside. Heibo called out to them from inside, "We're hungry and we're eating our own loincloth and 'grass' skirt. We're having trouble breathing. I think that my little sister is nearly dying."

The parents heard this and they cried. The parents of the first family and the children's friends, Huwa and Maijo, were also very troubled. They tried to dig at the hole to make another way to the cave. But whenever the people dug into the place where the two children were, the stone would cover it up again.

It had been nearly a month when the boy called out to their parents, telling them that Wo had died. Every night, the two parents sat near the place by the stone. They kept looking for a way to do something, but nothing happened.

After some time, they did not go there anymore because they thought that if the stone saw them, it could not open. This is what they thought, so they did not go there.

One day, the two of them called into the cave. Heibo did not reply. The parents knew that Heibo had died. The people of the village sat near the cave and cried for the two children. Their friends from the first family, Huwa and Maijo, cried and put white clay upon their heads and bodies.

They decorated the stone like a grave for the two children. Then they went back to the village. After six months had passed, the parents went back to burn the gravesite. They saw that the entrance of the cave had opened.

They explained this to the people of the village. Everyone sang, danced and cried together, and went around the place. Heibo's friend, Huwa, and Wo's friend, Maijo, went inside. They carried the bones of their friends outside the cave.

At night, they placed the bones of Heibo and Wo in the middle of the village on a platform. They sang and danced then had a huge feast. The next morning, they buried Heibo's bones and made a real grave in the village.

This is a true ancestor story.  David Dereme Kalbe's grandparent told it to him and he sent it to *Wantok Newspaper*.

David Dereme
P & T [Post & Telecommunications] Corps Line
Arawa
North Solomons Province

D1552. Mountains or rocks open and close; D1711. Magician; P210. Husband and wife; P231. Mother and son; P232. Mother and daughter; P233. Father and son; P234. Father and daughter; P310. Friendship; P253. Sister and brother; P681+. Mourning customs: earth on body; R45.3. Captivity in cave; R51.1. Prisoners starved; V61.3+. Dead buried

## Urin — The Man Who Arose from Blood
(Wantok 527, July 7, 1984, page 20)

Long ago, in the time of the ancestors, there was a man named Urin who lived in the forests of **Yangoru** in **East Sepik** Province [**Boiken** People].  A mother had not given birth to this man.  No, he just came from the blood of a woman.

Sairawa was the name of the woman from whom Urin had come.  One day, Sairawa went to the garden and worked until the afternoon.  When it was time to go back to the village, she cut some sugarcane and gathered other small foods to carry back to the village.

Sairawa cut the sugarcanes, and the stone knife that she used missed, cutting her hand.  Sairawa felt a terrible pain.  Blood shot out from her hand.  She took a vine and tied up her hand to stop the blood.  However, she had lost a lot.  When the blood had come out of her hand, it made a hole in the ground where it dripped.  Later, she covered the hole with earth and put a heavy stone on top of it.

She did this because she did not [want] wild pigs or snakes to remove the earth and drink her blood.  It was now evening, so she took the net bags of food and went back to her house.

Some time later, she made a new garden.  She just left the old garden there.  However after a while, she returned to it to get some food.

After about one year, Sairawa had forgotten the old garden.  She worked hard at the new garden.  Then after about another year, the woman went to check on the bananas and other foods that were still in the garden.

Oh my!  The woman was surprised to see a man standing right in the middle of the hole that she had covered with her blood.  She saw that the man was very tall.  When Sairawa saw this, she became afraid and ran away, back towards home.

The man told her, "Don't be afraid, my good mother.  I'd like you to find a huge, heavy log and bring it near the hole where I'm standing.  The woman heard this and looked for a huge, new log.  She pulled and pulled then put it near the man.

Urin's two legs were stuck fast to the ground.  He held the log and he pulled his two legs hard.  He left the hole and stood on the ground.  Sairawa saw that Urin was even taller.  He was taller than a banana plant [3-6 meters].

Urin told Sairawa, "Don't be afraid because I'm your child.  I came from the blood that dripped down from your hand."

His mother, Sairawa, was speechless.  She moved back and just thought about whether Urin was telling the truth or lying.  It would be bad if he was a *masalai* or a ghost.  Urin told his mother that they should go to the village.

They stayed in the garden until the afternoon.  They arrived at the house when it was completely dark.  She spoke, and no one saw Urin go inside the house that she lived in with her husband.

Sairawa was as strong as her husband was now.  The husband was ecstatic and went to see Urin.  His heart went out to him and he was even happier.  He went to strike the signal drum.  All of the men of the village came to gather.  Sairawa's husband told the people the good news and the source of his happiness.

The men listened and they did not believe it, but each of them went up to the house and saw Urin sitting inside.  They did not see how tall he was because he was not standing.  The next week, they gathered firewood, food, yams (*yam* and *mami*), taros, sweet potatoes, betel nuts, betel peppers, ripe coconuts, chickens, and pigs.  They made a big feast.  They sang and danced that day until dark.  After one week, all of the places were happy that the new man had come to their village.

They sang and danced until late at night, then the people of the village told Urin's father to tell him to join them in singing and dancing.  When Urin went to join them at singing and dancing, oh my, everyone looked like short hand drums.  This man, Urin, was much taller than everyone else was.  He was the tallest in the village.

The people looked at Urin and were happy.  They turned their heads and bent far down, as they sang and danced.  Urin's mother, Sairawa, put on a new "grass" skirt with her sister then they sang and danced near Urin to show their happiness for their child.

Later, when everyone went to plant yams (*yam* and *mami*) in the gardens, Urin usually just went there. He did not plant yams with his own hands yet. He thought that if he planted yams with his own hands, he would be planting his own spirit and this would cause his death.

When the people asked him what he was afraid of, Urin told them that only the leader of the village had the power to plant yams and no one else. These kinds of yams would not produce well.

He also told them that they could plant their own spirits in a hole in the ground with the yams. The people listened to what he said. Urin was a special man in the village, and they believed what he said. So, the people appointed some leaders who had the power to do this kind of work, and Urin alone did not plant yams.

Later, he married many women. Urin's children only lived in one village and they became our many ancestors.

Emil Saufie

Box 8

Yangoru

East Sepik Province

A523. Giant as culture hero; A1590+. Origin of yam planting customs; D2150+. Magic associated with planting yams; F531. Giant; P210. Husband and wife; P230. Parents and children; P231. Mother and son; P233. Father and son; P294. Aunt; P297. Nephew; T100. Marriage; T145.0.1. Polygyny; T534. Conception from blood; T545. Birth from ground; T615. Supernatural growth

## Enemies Stopped Fighting

(Wantok 528, July 14, 1984, page 19)

Long ago, in the time of the ancestors, women usually did all of the work of finding firewood and food, fetching water, cooking food, and taking care of children. The men usually worried about big things like enemies taking their land. This was life in the Highlands, but now life has changed a little.

One day, some women of the village went to the forest to look for leafy greens. These women were all from the same tribe. There was another woman who was pregnant and who followed them. She belonged to another tribe that was hostile to this group of people. It was nearly time for the woman to give birth.

The women went searching for food, and they followed a stream up a mountain. There were three women who went together. The woman who was pregnant went to the forest later. She tried to hide and follow them, and they did not know this. The three women did not know about her and they did not see that she was pregnant either.

The woman was ashamed to stay in her village because the people of the village often mocked her and spoke behind her back. They said that when she would give birth, they would kill her and her baby. They said that they would tie her and her baby to a tree and that large red ants would eat them and urinate upon them.

So, the woman who was pregnant on the trail just walked around in the forest until it was dark. At night, she would go sleep in garden huts. When she saw people of her village, she would go to the gardens or to look for food in the forest. The woman usually went to hide in the forest.

This time, she went to befriend the women from the other village and travel with them. She walked into the forest until the day that she gave birth and killed the baby. She buried the baby in the area of the big river.

Later, she cleaned and carefully washed the place where she had given birth to the baby. She went to sleep in a garden hut. This was where the women found her. The garden hut belonged to one of these women.

All of the women had found pandanus nuts (*karuka*) and bamboo sprouts. They sat down, cooked and ate. Then they heard the woman. They saw her sleeping. One woman took her traditional stone knife and wanted to cut the woman's neck.

The woman told them that she was looking for food in the forest and that a snake had bitten her. Because of this, her head spun around and she fell asleep. She lied to them that she was in terrible pain and was about to die, so she had gone to sleep in the hut.

One of the women listened to this, took a *salat* leaf and rubbed it on the woman's skin [for healing purposes], but it did nothing. The woman was just lying to them. She did not tell the woman that she had just given birth then killed and buried the baby by the river.

The women did not know this, so they just went back to the village and did not talk about what had happened. They did not know about this woman and what had happened to her. The woman lived in the hut, then later she ran away to another village. She married a new husband and lived in a village that was far away.

One time, a husband and his wife went to this place in the forest near the site of the baby boy's grave. They saw that there was a very young man bathing in the river and sitting on top of a stone near the grave. They watched and went closer, but the man did not stay when they went to the place where they had seen him. They thought that it was a man from their village, but they did not get a good look at his face. The man was the ghost of the little boy to whom the woman had given birth, killed and buried at this place.

The couple went to this place another time. At that time, they heard a little child crying. They went close to the child and they heard the ghost crying like a baby. However when they went closer, the crying stopped.

This sort of thing happened many, many times. Another time, they went there and they saw a little boy laughing, singing and dancing near the stone. They heard his voice and when they went a little closer, they saw a little boy singing and dancing fervently. When they went closer, the boy was no longer there. He was still singing and dancing on top of his grave.

That day, they went back to the village. They thought and spoke, "What kind of ancestral ghost does this kind of thing?" They did not speak about this to the other people of the village.

One day, the man went alone into the forest because he wanted to find out who it really was that lived by the stone. He went and watched near the stone. He stayed very near, but nothing happened. The little boy's ghost turned into a young man and went up to the real man. The man was surprised to see him. He took his bow and arrows then prepared to shoot. He thought that the young man was an enemy but he was not.

The ghost told him not to be afraid. The real man did not know that it was a ghost. The boy's ghost told him to follow him to the grave. Near the stone, the ghost told the man to stay awhile first, then dig the earth because something good was in the ground.

The man dug down. When he raised his head to ask, the boy was no longer there. The man looked for him but to no avail. He continued to dig then found the bones and skull of the baby that the woman had killed and buried.

When the man found this, he was afraid and left the bones there without covering them with dirt. He got up and ran off hastily. He was completely out of breath. The ghost boy was in the middle of the trail and told him the story, "My mother is named... She is now married to a man in this village." He gave the name of the village. "I'm a child of the trail, so mother gave birth to me, killed me and buried me here. This is my grave and those are my bones. I want for people to know my story, so I went to you and your wife when you came by this river."

The boy's ghost finished speaking then left. The man saw everything as if it were a dream. When the man arrived at the village, the ghost's power took him and he nearly died. They gave him cold water and he revived.

The man told his people and the people of the woman's old village about this story. The woman's people thought that the woman had died, but she had not. She had married in a village that was far away.

Louis Amili
**Kakemuto** Village [**Yagaria** People]
Lufa
**Eastern Highlands** Province

E231. Return from dead to reveal murder; E261.4. Ghost pursues man; E265.1. Meeting ghost causes sickness; E402.1.1.4. Ghost sings; E425.2. Revenant as man; E425.3. Revenant as child; E410. The unquiet grave; E493. Dead men dance; E540+. The dead laugh; E545. The dead speak; E599.13. Dead person bathes; P210. Husband and wife; P231. Mother and son; R213. Escape from home; R220. Flights; R260. Pursuits; S12.2+. Cruel mother kills son; S110. Murders; T100. Marriage; T570. Pregnancy; T580. Childbirth; V61.3+. Dead buried; W157. Dishonesty

## The *Masalai*'s Skin
(Wantok 529, July 21, 1984, page 20)

Before, in the time of the ancestors, snakes were the real food of people. They would cut the snakes and cook them on a fire like eels. Some would make snake soup in a clay pot then eat it. They often mixed snake meat with leafy greens from the forest and had very good food.

At this time, there were two brothers. One time, they killed a snake and made soup. However it was not a real snake, they just had the skin of a snake. The snake had shed its skin and the two boys had taken it.

That day, the two brothers, Nayan and his little brother Namuni, looked for food in the forest and saw the skin of a huge snake. The skin was like a small net at the base of a tree. They took it and filled a big basket with pandanus (*karuka*) nuts that the little brother Namuni held. Namuni carried the snake's skin and they went to look for food in the forest.

They walked and walked until it was nearly evening. They had found some edible grasses, wild taro leaves, and *salat*. They went to get yams and taros from the garden, then they returned to the village.

That night, they made a huge amount of soup. They put the snake's skin into the water until it was completely soft. They cooked it with all of the greens, taros and yams. The put in just a little bit of *salat* leaves to make the soup hot.

They broke up the food and [garnished] the leafy greens with the snakeskin and some insects that they had found in the forest. They divided the food and gave some soup to their kin. That night, they gorged on soup. Their bodies were exhausted and they went to sleep. The big brother, Nayan, had eaten the side of the snake's skin that was near the head. At night, when he slept and snored, it was exactly like the sound of a snake hissing.

The little brother, Namuni, awoke at night when he heard Nayan snoring. When he awoke, he told his brother to sleep well. This was because when he was snoring, the sound was very loud and a man standing outside could hear it perfectly clearly.

The snake's skin that the two brothers had used to make soup and had eaten was not from a small snake. It was huge. It was a *masalai* in this area. The snake had a huge head like a coconut. It had two long ears hanging down. It had teeth like that of a dog. It had two long fangs for eating people, pigs and dogs. Its two big eyes were red and very long. If you measured their sizes, they would be about fifty feet long. The middle of its body was like a four-gallon drum.

Nayan and Namuni did not know that it was the skin of a *masalai*. They had thought that it was an ordinary snake's skin lying around, so when they had found it they were very happy. They had made a large amount of food for a party with the snake's skin soup.

In the morning, the two brothers went to the garden. When they finished working in the garden, the little brother, Namuni, went to look for a little food to bring home. Nayan rested and slept in the garden hut.

While he was sleeping, the huge *masalai* snake whose skin they had eaten slithered quietly into the garden. A black cloud covered this place in the garden and the two brothers thought that it would rain. They did not think much about this, so they just stayed there.

The *masalai* sat under the house and just showed its head towards the big brother who was lying there.

The big brother saw the *masalai*'s head and he thought that he was dreaming. But no, he opened his eyes and looked directly at the head of the *masalai*. The head just lay there with its two long ears hanging down. The *masalai*'s face looked terrible. Nayan saw this and screamed in terror. Immediately, the *masalai*'s head moved back into hiding.

The snake's body hid in the forest. The little brother Namuni walked and walked, back to the garden, where he saw a log that he jumped over. However, he did not see that it was really the body of the snake.

The *masalai* also saw Namuni going by and it quickly lay quietly. The place where the *masalai* stayed was completely dark. The *masalai* slithered slowly, and the dark-

ness, clouds and wind followed where the *masalai* went. The two brothers did not know about this. They took the food and went back to the village.

Beginning at this time, the big brother, Nayan, would see the *masalai*'s head in his dreams every night. He was often afraid and screamed frightfully. At night, he would breathe heavily and hiss like a snake. The little brother was worried for his big brother. He thought that his big brother was ill, but they did not discover the cause of the illness.

Some weeks passed and the big brother went to check on the garden. His little brother did not go with him. Nayan weeded the garden well and removed all of the rubbish. The garden looked excellent. The man worked quickly and did all of the work well. Before, he had not worked hard like this.

After he finished working, he picked taros and yams, cut sugarcanes and gathered leafy greens. He waited for the sun to cool, then he would walk back to the village. He went to lie down and rest in the garden hut.

Before long, he was surprised. He thought that it was evening because the place was dark. However it was not evening, the *masalai* had come and was lying in wait nearby. Nayan saw that darkness covered the place completely. A heavy rain fell down and a strong wind arose.

Nayan thought that he had slept for a very long time. He saw that the place was dark and he said that he would not sleep, but return to the village in the morning. However, this was not to be. When he looked out, the *masalai*'s head was there.

Nayan heard the snake and trembled in fear. He screamed and cried for his brother, but there was no way to run away from the *masalai*. His legs and arms were completely exhausted.

The *masalai* told Nayan that the rain, wind, darkness and clouds followed wherever the *masalai* went. The *masalai* often hid as it traveled because of these things lest the people notice it in a clearing. After the *masalai* said this, it rose up and swallowed Nayan down into its belly.

Later, Namuni's brother saw that Nayan had not arrived in the village, so he went to look for him. Nayan's food was gathered in the garden and the garden was cleaned and weeded, but he could not find Nayan.

Namuni looked for his brother and called out, but there was no answer. Later, he saw a big mark that had been made from pulling a big log. The grasses and small trees were broken and lying about. Namuni thought that his brother must have encountered enemies. He saw a little blood and water lying about. Namuni cried for his brother and put earth on his head and body. Then he cried and went back to the village.

Later, at night Nayan's ghost came in a dream and told his story to Namuni. He told of the *masalai*'s anger and of his death. He told Namuni and the other kin to go to an area that Nayan had marked where they should kill a pig. If they did not do this, the *masalai* would follow them and eat them.

They followed the dream and the *masalai* no longer pursued them. After this, they no longer ate snakeskins. When the people of this area walk into the forest and see a snake's skin lying around, they walk far away to avoid it.

Mathew Tepe Ambusi
**Togemas** Village [**Enga** People]
P. O. Box 195
Wabag
**Enga** Province

B91+. Serpent with dog's head; B211.6.1. Speaking snake (serpent); B875.1. Giant serpent; C221.1+. Tabu: eating snake's skin; C920. Death for breaking tabu; D908. Magic darkness; D1030. Magic food; D1810.8.2. Information received through dream; D2142.1. Wind produced by magic; D2143.1. Rain produced by magic; D2147. Magic control of clouds; E326. Dead brother's friendly return; E363.3. Ghost warns the living; F490+. Masalai; F512+. Unusually large eyes; F541.6.2. Person has red eye; G354.1. Snake as ogre; P251.5. Two brothers; P681+. Mourning customs: earth on body; Q411. Death as punishment; R260. Pursuits; S110. Murders; V12.4.3. Pig as sacrifice

## Ghosts Took a Man

(Wantok 530, July 28, 1984, page 20)

Long ago, in the time of the ancestors, there lived a man who hunted birds [flying foxes]. He usually took a big net and tied it to the trees on top of a mountain. He caught many flying foxes with this net.

In this forest, there were two men who had died. They had tried to take some birds when their net had pulled them up, where they hung and died. Their ghosts flew around like birds in this area. When the men went to put their nets there at night, the two birds would fly and cut the nets.

Sometimes, they would break the nets completely and just leave them hanging there. In the morning, the people would go and find them like this. Many times the two birds would break the nets and just leave them with many holes. However, there were real birds that would become caught in the nets, and the people would pull the nets down to take the birds.

One day, the man who was the champion at catching birds left with his net. He went up two huge mountains.

No man had ever gone to this part of the forest before. The man went up very high to the summit of the two huge mountains. He looked to the other side and he saw an excellent place to tie his net.

He cut some trees and cleared a good little area where he would sleep and watch the birds. Then he tied his net. The place where he tied his net was very good because it was the valley between the two mountains.

There were many trees standing that were full of ripe fruits. At night, many flying foxes would scramble for food or tree fruits. The man stayed in a very good place. All of the other places were filled with other men with their nets.

At night, the man straightened everything out and sat very quietly. The area was completely clear because there was a bright moon. The man saw a tremendous number of flying foxes coming and hanging on the net until the net almost broke from their weight. The man pulled the net down, took the flying foxes and piled them up. He tied them up and put them in bundles.

He hoisted the net up again in this area. The same thing happened a second time. He pulled the net down and tied up the flying foxes.

The third time that he hoisted the net, it was almost dawn. He was elated because he wanted to show the flying foxes that he had caught in the net to the other men. When he went back to the village, he would tell his friends.

However, the third time was a loss. He sat and watched, and a strong chill took him. The light was no longer clear because the moon had set. The man sat, but there were no more [flying foxes] coming to hang on his net.

He was sleepy and his eyes spun around. He tied a piece of rope from the net around his leg and he slept. If there were many birds hanging on the net, then the rope would move around and he would wake up. The flying foxes bypassed the net and two huge birds flew there. It was dawn now.

The two birds had the head and face of a bird and the legs and head [?] of a man. They also had the wings of a flying fox. The two birds were the ghosts of the two men who had died before in this forest.

The birds just came and hung upon the net. They pulled the net strongly and broke two holes in the net, then flew back again. The man felt the strong movements and was surprised. He looked up and saw that his net had two big holes.

He was worried. He wanted to pull the net down and return to the village because it was completely light now. However, it was not to be. Before long, the two ghost birds flew back again. They went and grabbed the net and pulled it completely away.

The rope was still tied to the man's leg, so the birds pulled the man and carried him away. The man hung off the rope and the two birds flew off. He screamed very loudly and the men of this part of the forest heard him. The other men were ready to walk back to the village and they did not know that this man was screaming because he was still in the part of the forest [that was far away].

The two birds carried him to the place where they were staying. The man kept calling and calling to be let go. Later, he also flew like a flying fox and became like the other two men. His legs, arms, head and face were those of a flying fox.

The men of this village no longer go to this part of the forest. Many people no longer eat flying foxes because they often think of the three ghost birds.

Goluk Lapun

Sinai Bitol Gold Mines

Wau

Morobe Province

B20+. Man-flying fox; B31.6. Other giant birds; B40+. Bird-flying fox; B50. Bird-men; B552. Man carried by bird; C221.1+. Tabu: eating flying fox; C612. Forbidden forest; D117.5KM. Transformation: man to flying fox; E230. Return from dead to inflict punishment; E423+. Revenant as flying fox; E423.3. Revenant as bird; R13.3. Person carried off by bird


## The Eagle's Child

(Wantok 531, August 4, 1984, page 18)

Long ago, in the time of the ancestors, in the area near Wapenamanda in **Enga** Province, there was a village named **Yuka** [**Enga** People]. There lived a man who was married to two wives. At this time, the two women were pregnant.

The man left the women and walked very far away to the area of the Baiya [**Baiyer**] River [**Kyaka** People, **Eastern Highlands** Province]. There was a big festival and they had killed many pigs. Many, many people filled the area. The two women were pregnant, so they could not go to this festival.

Before the man had walked on this long trail, he explained something carefully to his two wives. He told them, "If one of you gives birth to a boy, then he must be killed, I don't like boys. If one of you gives birth to a girl, then take care of her well."

The man left for the big festival at Baiya River, and the first wife gave birth to a baby girl. She was overjoyed be-cause she knew that her husband would also be happy for their daughter.

However, the second wife gave birth to a boy, and this wife was very worried because the husband would not be happy when he returned to the village.

The woman told the first wife that she had given birth to a boy and that she would throw him into the Lamande River. However in the morning, the second wife brought her new baby into the deep forest.

She took the baby to the place where there were many wild dogs, pigs and other wild animals. She saw a clearing underneath a big tree. The mother cried and cried. She made a bed for the baby with some big leaves.

The mother put some pig fat on the leaves so that when the baby cried for milk, he would eat the pig fat. She left the baby there and cried on the way back to the village.

Before long, after the mother had left the area, a big eagle flew and perched on top of a branch of the big tree under which the baby was lying. The eagle heard the little baby crying underneath the tree, then flew down near to where the baby was crying.

The eagle lifted the big leaves and saw the baby crying there. Very gently, the eagle carried the baby and put him on her wing then flew away.

The eagle flew off and put the baby on top of her little house, which was on the branch of a big tree. The eagle made a little bed and put the baby to sleep there. The eagle laughed at the little baby when she thought about what the little baby would become.

The baby slept while the eagle flew away then perched near where a man was carrying pork in a big bag. The eagle flew down, stole the pork and flew back to the house on top of the tree. The eagle tore up the meat until it was soft. Then the eagle gave it with ripe bananas that she had stolen from some people's garden. The eagle sat and gave the food to the baby, then gave him a little water.

The eagle took care of the baby, and he grew a little bigger. He still lived in the tree house. He never worried about a thing. There was always plenty of food because his eagle mother often stole bananas and meat from villagers. The eagle would fly down and steal from people as they were carrying things along the trails.

The boy became a big man and no longer lived in the house on top of the tree. The eagle told her son, "You are no longer a little boy, you are a man now. I can't look for food for you any longer, but here is land for you. You can make a garden for yourself here. I'll live on top of the tree in the old house and watch you all of the time."

The eagle then gave a name to the man. His name was Kevel Tandi. The eagle who had taken care of Keven [Kevel] like a father and mother also thought that it was now time for Kevel to marry.

Under the big tree where the eagle lived, Kevel made a big food garden and a big pigpen. The pigpen began with two pigs that the eagle had stolen from other men and carried to Kevel. One was a boar and the other was a sow. They grew to be quite large.

The eagle told her son that another morning she would go to a place that was very far away, and that she could not get to the place quickly to find something. The eagle told her son that she would go find something very powerful for him.

In the morning of the next day, the eagle awoke and flew away. The eagle flew around many villages, spying carefully on the streams, gardens, and forests. The eagle wanted to find a good and smart woman to become her son's wife.

The eagle did not find anyone in many villages. The eagle went by many streams, mountains, forests, and gardens, but the eagle found none. Then the eagle arrived at a garden that was many thousands of kilometers away from her home with Kevel. The eagle saw some young women working in the garden. The eagle went down to a nearby tree branch and spied carefully upon the women.

When the work was finished, the women walked back towards the village. The eagle saw one very young and beautiful woman amongst them. The eagle saw that the woman had worked very hard. The eagle flew down, snatched the woman and carried her up and away. The other women saw this. They screamed and cried, but it was too late. The eagle had snatched her and carried her far away. They flew away and arrived at the place where Kevel Tandi was.

The eagle took the woman and put her on top of the house in the tree, not in Kevel Tandi's house on the ground. The eagle told the man to go up the ladder to the house. When Kevel went up and saw the woman sitting there, his eyes popped open.

The eagle told him, "This is your wife. I traveled for a long time and very far away to find her. What do you think of her now?"

Tandi replied, "Mama and papa, I'm speechless. I lusted for her the first moment that I put eyes upon her."

The eagle asked the woman, and the woman replied, "I've never seen this kind of man before. I'm speechless, so I'll marry him."

They married and they lived there. The woman went down to the man's house. She saw the pig pen and food garden; the eagle was speechless [lit., "her tongue was very short"]. The woman was much happier because if she had married a man from her own village, she would not have had so many kinds of things.

The two of them lived there, and the woman was very smart about husbanding the pigs, and giving food. She often worked very hard taking care of other things, as well as the food and work in their big garden.

They lived there for many years. The eagle was very happy to see her son begin a family when Kevel's wife gave birth to a baby boy.

The eagle was not as smart as before. The eagle was old and the feathers on her two wings were old, so the eagle usually just perched in the house.

One day, the eagle called out to her son and told him the story of when she had found him. The son was very saddened and cried for the eagle.

The eagle told him that when she died, Kevel must bury her body where Kevel's mother had cast him away. This place marks two things: the eagle's grave, and the place where Kevel's mother had cast him away, where the eagle had taken him.

The son and the family lived many years then his mother died. Kevel Tandi followed all of the instructions that his mother had told him, but he did not know his real mother and father. The place where he lived became populous, and the other villagers saw and understood this.

Sia Napita
P. O. Box 795
Arawa
North Solomons Province

[See *Wantok* #1161 for a similar story.]

B211.3.11K. Speaking eagle; B535.0.7+. Eagle as nurse for child; B552. Man carried by bird; B871.1.2.1. Giant hog; D2121. Magic journey; K300. Thefts and cheats—general; L111.2. Foundling hero; P210. Husband and wife; P231. Mother and son; P232. Mother and daughter; P233. Father and son; P234. Father and daughter; P262. Mother-in-law; P265+. Daughter-in-law; P272. Foster mother; P275. Foster son; R13.3.2. Eagle carries off youth; S11. Cruel father; S12. Cruel mother; S143. Abandonment in forest; T15. Love at first sight; T100. Marriage; T145.0.1. Polygyny; T570. Pregnancy; T580. Childbirth

## The Money Tree

(Wantok 532, August 11, 1984, page 18)

Long, long ago, there were two girls who lived by themselves after their mother had died. One was six years old and the other was three years old.

The two of them were very unfortunate: they were still very small when their mother had died. Their father had died even earlier. When the mother died, they had thought that their mother was just sleeping and that she would get up again. They sat near their mother and they tried to wake her. The younger one cried and said, "Mama, wake up and give me food. I'm hungry." However the mother could not get up again: she was gone for good.

They stayed there until the next day came. The bigger girl saw that their mother could not get up again, so she held her mother and cried. Later, she saw that her little sister was completely famished, so she went to look for food that her mother had found earlier and was in the house. She gave the food to her sister.

It was nearly night time when an old [man] approached their house. He heard the crying of the two little girls. He went closer and called to them. The bigger girl told him that their mother had died and was lying there. She told the old man, "Our mother has been sleeping since yesterday and has not woken yet."

The old [man] went up and saw that the woman's skin was getting soft. He slowly made a hole then carried the woman down and buried her. The two children cried and cried. The little girl's eyes swelled up. She was completely famished and she went to sleep. The other one, who was six years old, cried and cried. She went to sleep near her sister.

The old [man] did not think about them. Later, he found out that they did not have any kin to take after them. The old man took all his things and went to live with them and to take care of them.

That night, after the old man had buried their mother, the mother came in a dream to her elder daughter. She told her, "At my head will grow a tree. After six months, something like a sprout will arise, then it will get bigger. This will not be an ordinary tree, it will be a Malay apple tree. It will be a special Malay apple tree because money will come from the tree for you and your little sister."

She examined the dream in the morning and she told the old man what her mother had told her at night. She told the old man what she had said. The old man listened and told her not to tell anyone.

After six months, the tree sprout began to come up right where the old man had buried the mother. The tree became big and bore fruits (Malay apples). The two girls and the old man tended the mother's grave well. They always adorned it and put soil on top of the tree. The tree grew very quickly.

The first Malay apple was ripe and the big girl went to get it. The old man watched. She thought that it was just an ordinary Malay apple, but when she broke it open, money spilled out. It was then that the old man told her about the dream he had had.

Whenever the Malay apples were ripe, they were just filled with money. The old man and the two girls had much money. They lived well at the house and had good food. The old man did not give coconut milk to the little girl anymore.

The place where they lived became a town. There is light, power, houses with galvanized iron roofs, and traffic lights. They often wear nice clothing too. These were the clothes that the girls' mother had given them. When the girls and the old man had everything, and the girls had grown into big women, they married and had children. Then the tree died.

Andrew Koim

Arawa

North Solomons Province

D1663.6+. Magic tree gives money; D1810.8.2. Information received through dream; E323. Dead mother's friendly return; E631. Reincarnation in plant (tree) growing from grave; L111.4.2. Orphan heroine; P210. Husband and wife; P230. Parents and children; P232. Mother and daughter; P252.1. Two sisters; P271. Foster father; P275+. Foster daughter; T100. Marriage; V61.3+. Dead buried


## Pekenatu [Pekenatun] and Pindalu [Pindalua]

(Wantok 533, August 18, 1984, page 20)

In the time of yore, there was a woman who lived with her little granddaughter on **Ponam** Island, **Manus** Province [**Ponam** People]. The old woman's name was Nagulua and her granddaughter's name was Pindalua.

Pindalua's parents had left her, and old granny Nagulua took care of her. Every day, Nagulua would leave Pindalua sleeping on a bed in her house. Nagalua would go to the garden to work then bring food back to the village.

One time, Nagulua left Pindalua sleeping and went to the garden. She slept in the house in the morning until the time when the sun reached the middle of the sky and she was very hungry.

Pindalua awoke and left the bed to look for food. She saw her old grandmother's net bag hanging on a piece of wood inside the house. She checked the bag and took out a nice piece of fruit from inside the bag.

Pindalua thought that the fruit was an ordinary one, but it was not. The fruit was her old granny's husband. Pindalua was hungry, so she just broke the fruit with a bamboo knife.

When the fruit broke into two pieces, much red blood spilled out. The blood flowed and followed old Nagulua's footsteps to the garden. Nagulua saw the blood and was furious because she knew that her little granddaughter had killed her husband.

Nagulua took her stone axe and cut a piece of thorny rattan, then brought it to the village. She thrashed Pindalua's buttocks violently with the rattan. She did this to Pindalua until she was half-dead.

Nagulua's temper cooled off again. She cooked some food as the sun was setting. She and the little granddaughter sat and ate together. They finished eating, then they slept.

The next morning, Nagulua carried a net bag of things for working in the garden then walked off to the garden. The little girl Pindalua awoke and gathered all her "grass" skirts, mats, baskets, and other kinds of adornments. She put all of these things inside a huge net bag.

Pindalua carried the net bag, left the village and walked towards the beach. She was very sorry to leave the village, but she was angry with her old granny who had beaten her, so she ran away.

She walked by the beach area. She walked and walked then arrived at a big house made of stone. This house belonged to a man named Pekenatun. This man, Pekenatun, had ten wives.

Pindalua went and stood near Pekenatun's big canoe and she waited. A heavy rain fell and a strong wind arose. Pindalua sat down and the rain drenched her.

After the rain and wind ended, Pekenatun went outside to remove the rainwater that had filled his canoe. However, he did not see Pindalua.

Pekenatun stood and smelled something good. This smell came from Pindalua's nice "grass" skirt. But Pekenatun did not know where the smell was originating.

Pekenatun removed the rainwater from the canoe then walked back to his house. Pindalua called out Pekenatun's name, so the leader turned his head and looked back. However, he did not see Pindalua because his eyes were not adjusted to the light yet [lit., "his eyes were still dark"].

Pindalua called out again and told Pekenatun to look closer [lit., "remove the darkness from his eyes"]. Pekenatun rubbed his hands on his eyes and saw the girl Pindalua standing near him.

Pindalua told her story to him, and Pekenatun promised to take care of her. Pekenatun told Pindalua to stand near the canoe until it was dark. Pekenatun went and removed his first wife from the house.

Pekenatun's first wife took her things and went to sleep with the second wife in another house. When it was dark, Pekenatun went to get Pindalua and bring her to the first wife's house. Pindalua used this house as if it were her own.

Pekenatun did not want his ten wives to find out about Pindalua, so he forbade his wives from going inside the house where Pindalua slept. Pekenatun shut the door and all of the windows of the house.

Pekenatun's ten wives could not carry food into Pindalua's house. The women had to bring the food to Pekenatun first, then he himself would bring it to Pindalua. This is what they did for many weeks.

One time, Pekenatun took his big canoe and went fishing with some men in the sea. They voyaged the sea for three days and three nights. Pindalu just stayed in the house.

On the fourth day, Pekenatun's first and second wives thought bad thoughts and made a decision. They wanted to find out what it was that their husband had forbidden them to see in the first wife's house.

**Opening the Door**

The first and second wives went and opened the house door. They saw the young girl sleeping on the bed, but the two women were not angry. They went back and told the other eight women to cook food at each of their houses.

When the food was ready, Pekenatun's ten wives carried the food and gathered in front of Pindalua. They thought that Pindalua was Pekenatun's new wife and they were happy, so they showed their good traditional manners and gave food to the new woman.

The ten women left the food and went back to their houses. However, poor Pindalua was ashamed and felt like trash. She ran away from the house and walked on the beach.

She walked on the reef and went to the outer part. She saw Pekenatun's big canoe that was still in the sea. The canoe was very far from where Pindalua was standing, but Pindalua opened her mouth and shouted loudly to Pekenatun.

She shouted in my language, "Pekenatu-*o*, *aluwewe* *sunamesu*-*s*-*sia* *lorima* *laima* *lori*... Pekenatun!" She walked on the reef and went to the outer part. She shouted two more times. The wind carried her voice and Pekenatun heard her shouting.

Pekenatun heard Pindalua's voice clearly. He told all his workers to sit quietly and listen to the shouting. Some workers laughed and said that it was a bird calling. However, they listened carefully and they heard the third shout come clearly like the voice of a girl.

Pekenatun stood on top of the canoe and saw a girl standing on the reef who was waving her hands. He hurried the workers to pull in all of the nets and fishing lines, then paddle the canoe directly to the place where Pindalua was standing.

The canoe was still going when a strong wind arose. The sea became choppy and very rough. The Pekenatun's canoe began to drift on top of the sea like a piece of trash.

His workers were terrified, but Pekenatun told them strongly that they must stay calm. He told them to prepare to jump and swim to the beach if the canoe capsizes.

The strong waves carried the canoe up, spun it around, then down, and the canoe broke into two pieces. Pekenatun and all his workers raced to swim ashore. However, the sea drowned some of the workers.

Pekenatun thought hard about Pindalua and swam strongly, breaking through the sea, and arriving at the reef. The reef cut Pekenatun all over his body. Blood flowed and the sea salt burned his open wounds. But he was unconcerned.

He walked on the reef and arrived at the beach then jumped onto the sand. The workers who had not drowned were still coming ashore. But Pekenatun had forgotten the men and he walked close to Pindalu [Pindalua].

When Pekenatun put his hands out to grab Pindalu, he missed because Pindalu had run away and leapt up a callophylum tree. She climbed the tree and stood on a branch. She called out for Pekenatun to try to grab her.

Pekenatun jumped and went up the callophylum tree, following Pindalu. However, she fooled him and went up to the crown of the tree. The poor leader kept following her.

Pekenatun approached Pindalu at the crown, but when Pekenatun was about to hold Pindalu's hand, the girl jumped from the crown of the tree and dived directly into the mouth of a clam. The clam shut its mouth and covered Pindalu's body.

Too bad, Pekenatun did not see Pindalu shove her head back up again. Pekenatun's heart was broken. He looked

down and wanted to jump after Pindalu into the sea, but he did not do so. A few of his tears fell, and he carefully jumped down from the crown of the tree to the ground.

Pekenatun had taken care of Pindalu and promised that they would marry because Pindalu was a beautiful girl. It looked as if her breasts would be budding after another year. Pekenatun wanted to make Pindalu his first wife, but his promise failed because Pindalua had died and rested inside the mouth of a clam.

Poor Pekenatun put his head down and walked on the beach until he arrived at his house. His ten wives saw him and were surprised, but they did not speak.

Pekenatun's body was still bloody, but he walked quietly inside his house. He did not speak or call out to his wives. The women did not want to approach him because they knew that a big mistake had made Pindalu run away.

Pekenatun continued to live with his ten wives, but he did not walk happily as before. He looked as if part of his heart and his strength had been lost.

Steven S. Saragum
Section 19, Lot 17
Arawa
North Solomons Province

B874.6. Giant clam; D1643+. Blood travels by itself; F911.4.1.1+. Person swallowed by great clam; P210. Husband and wife; P292.1. Grandmother as foster mother; Q211. Murder punished; Q458. Flogging as punishment; R213. Escape from home; R220. Flights; R260. Pursuits; S110. Murders; T81. Death from love; T117.7+. Marriage to a fruit; T145.0.1. Polygyny; W126. Disobedience

## A Pig Ruined the Garden
(Wantok 534, August 25, 1984, page 19)

Long, long ago, in the time of the ancestors, two brothers lived in a place called **Lambega**. There was not another man, woman or child who lived with them, so they fenced in a big piece of forest and made an enormous garden.

In this garden, they planted sweet potatoes, yams, taros, bananas, leafy greens, and other kinds of food. Oh my, there was an enormous amount of yams and taros. They were never hungry. Never.

They had a good life. There was so much food in the garden that it just fell down and rotted. They did not have any worries because they had everything in abundance.

One time, after the brothers had finished working in the garden, they went back to the house and cooked food. After they finished eating, they went to sleep.

Night came, and the two brothers were dead asleep. An enormous pig left its hiding place and went directly for the men's garden. The pig pushed and pushed at the fence until it broke and fell down.

The pig went inside the garden and dug at all of the kinds of food that the brothers had in the garden. The pig did not fool around. It would have ruined all of the food if the sun had not risen. But the sun was about to rise, so the pig left the garden and went back to its hiding place.

After it was light and the sun had risen high, the two brothers left their house and went to their garden. Oh my, they did not speak when they saw the garden.

Their necks were dried and blocked up. The little brother was furious. Quickly, he went back to the house, prepared a string for his bow and made spears. When he saw the big brother walking back from the garden, the little brother hid the bow and arrows then pretended to just be sitting.

The big brother brought some food that the pig had unearthed, so they cooked this food. Later, they slept. While the big brother was asleep, the little brother got up very quietly, took his bow and arrows, then went to the garden to watch.

He sat very quietly. Before long, he heard the noise from a pig coming towards him. All of the hair on the little brother stood up. He was terrified.

The pig did not go anywhere else. It went directly to the place where it had broken on the previous night. It bashed the fence down again and went inside. When it went inside, it began to dig at the food. It dug and dug until it came to the place where the bad boy [man] was.

The boy drew back the bow very far. He stretched it and held it. When the pig came closer to him, he let go, but the arrow raced out and stuck to the side of the pig.

The pig was in great pain. It squealed terribly. The pig just squealed. It did not fall. It ran off quickly into the forest.

When the pig left, the boy removed the fence rope and walked back to the house. Then he pretended to sleep. Oh my, before dawn, in the very early morning, the pig's owner went and stood at the door of the boys' house.

When the brothers awoke, the man spoke to them, "Boys, you poorly shot my pig last night. Whoever shot this pig must come with me and remove the arrow from the pig's body. After that, you can return."

So, the little brother prepared his bow and arrows and went with the pig's owner. When the little brother and the pig's owner left, the big brother was very troubled and cried.

The little brother and this man walked and walked, then arrived at a big river. The sides of the river were covered only with stones. They walked down to a small trail, then they walked over a rope bridge.

The path was not good because the bridge went to the top of the man's long house. This house was substantial. They went to the top of the house and then passed over to the other side.

When they arrived at the hut where the pigs slept, the pig's owner told the little brother, "Hey, the pig that you shot is here, so go inside and remove [the arrow]."

When the boy opened the door and looked, oh my, the bad pig was sleeping awkwardly. So, the brother told the pig's owner to shut the door well and close all of the little holes of the hut. The pig's owner followed the boy's instructions and closed up the whole hut.

When the man closed the hut completely, he called out to all his kin that he had the man who had shot the pig and that this wrongdoer was imprisoned inside the hut. He told all of the men to go gather leafy greens and other foods, then they would kill the boy and eat him.

The bad boy waited and waited, then when he knew that all of the men were gone in their gardens, he quickly killed the pig. He butchered the pig completely and prepared all of the pork. Then he saw that the pig's heart was still beating. When he saw this, he stood and looked around the village. Two very beautiful women stood directly where he was. When he saw the women, he was terrified.

However the women told him, "This is a very bad place. We'll go wait on the other side of the river. When you finish your work, you must quickly come see us because they'll kill you if you don't come with us quickly."

After they said this, the boy quickly went out and put the pork on top of each house. When he finished, he took his bow and arrows then walked down to one of the long houses. A little boy saw him and called out.

Oh my, the boy's father, mother and many kinsmen began to spill down to try to kill the little brother. However, the boy did not miss. He gave an arrow to each of them and followed the path that the two women had taken. He arrived at the big river where the women were already standing on the other side. They just sent a rope to him and he sped over to meet them.

Then the boy and the two women cut the rope, and they ran away quickly to his home. The enemies no longer had a way to follow them. The three of them walked and arrived at the boy's house where they saw the big brother waiting there. The poor big brother was crying loudly. He rubbed dirt on his skin and cried.

Later, they killed a big pig, removed all of the food from the garden and made a huge feast. They divided everything in the house, the garden, the pigs, and the dogs. The little brother took part and the big brother took part.

The little brother gave one woman to his big brother and he had one for himself. The two of them took care of the two women until they grew up, then they married and raised big families.

Henry Hotto Anamu Hribela
Gorobe Street
Badili
National Capital District

B871.1.2. Giant boar; G11.18. Cannibal tribe; P210. Husband and wife; P230. Parents and children; P251.5. Two brothers; P263. Brother-in-law; P264. Sister-in-law; P681+. Mourning customs: earth on body; Q211.6. Killing an animal revenged; Q429.1. Punishment: culprit eaten by cannibals; R49+. Captivity in pigsty; R210. Escapes; T100. Marriage

## The Enemies of Kanganamun

(Wantok 535, September 1, 1984, page 19)

Long, long ago, there were two brothers who lived in a village called Kanganamun [**Kanganaman** Village, **Iatmul** People, **East Sepik** Province]. This village is near the Sepik River. The two brothers were Wapawi and Namawi. Wapawi was the big brother and Namawi was the little brother. Wapawi was married, but his little brother Namawi was single.

Wapawi was very knowledgeable about hunting wild game. He always left the village and went to hunt game in the deep forest. However, his wife was not very good. She was a woman who fooled around.

When Wapawi went to hunt for game in the deep forest, the other men of this village would fool around with his wife. This sort of thing happened often but Wapawi did not find out about this.

One day, Wapawi took his hunting gear and walked far away to the mountains. His wife and little brother stayed in the village. Namawi also did not know about his brother's wife.

Namawi was tired of doing other work, so he went to sleep in the men's house. He slept well on top of a bed. Many of the village leaders met in this men's house.

These leaders gossiped and told various stories. They thought that Namawi was dead asleep, so they told the story of the various things that they had done with Wapawi's wife. However the little brother, Namawi pretended to sleep while his eyes were shut and he listened to the various stories being told about his big brother's wife.

The leaders sent one man to bring firewood back into the men's house. The firewood was already lit. The leaders wanted to find out whether Namawi was really asleep, or whether he was just pretending with his eyes shut and eavesdropping on the bad stories. A leader blew on the fire and put the firewood on top of Namawi's leg. He felt a great pain on his leg, but he clenched his teeth, tensed up and pretended to be dead asleep.

When Namawi did not rise, a leader got up again and scratched his belly with his finger. The leader wanted Namawi to feel the stroking on his belly and open his eyes. But no, Namawi lied there as if he was dead asleep. All of the leaders really believed that he was dead asleep and that he did not hear the bad stories that they told near him.

The leaders revealed the stories of the various bad things that they had done to Wapawi's wife. After one man finished his story, the next revealed his. Poor Namawi pretended to sleep as he heard all of the words that the leaders told. He committed these stories to memory. Later, after all of the men finished their bad stories, Namawi opened his eyes and pretended that he had been dead asleep.

Two days later, the big brother, Wapawi returned to the village. He had a tremendous amount of game, but his little brother did not show that he was happy to see his big brother. This was because of the bad things that he had heard about his brother's wife, which had made him terribly ashamed.

Namawi did not sit down quietly at Wapawi's house. He told all of the stories. Poor Wapawi listened to the bad stories about his wife. Oh my! He was furious, but he did not show his anger to him.

Wapawi thought of something to ruin the men of the village who had befouled his wife. He and his little brother made a house on top of a coconut palm tree. They took all of their belongings and carried them up to the tree house.

There was a lake that was near Kanganamun, and there was a big *masalai* crocodile that lived in this lake. The *masalai* crocodile often listened to what men said.

Wapawi had a strong thought to make the *masalai* crocodile ruin the village. He and his little brother decided to get revenge on everyone from Kanganamun.

Wapawi and Namawi took a big stalk of betel nuts from their garden then took it to the lake. They paddled their canoe to the exact center of the lake. They broke a piece of a stalk of betel nuts and threw it into the water. They knew that the *masalai* crocodile lived in this area.

The *masalai* crocodile saw the stalk of betel nuts and sent a little crocodile child up to the surface. Wapawi asked the crocodile, "Are you the father crocodile or what?" The crocodile turned its head to show that it was not the father crocodile.

Wapawi told the crocodile child to go down again and to send the father crocodile to the surface. Before long, the father crocodile came to the surface and rested close to the side of the canoe. He put his head closer and listened to everything that Wapawi said.

Wapawi revealed all of his worries and troubles to the *masalai* crocodile. He wanted the *masalai* crocodile to send a flood down to the village with everyone late at night. Wapawi revealed all of this, then he put the big stalk of betel nuts on the back of the *masalai* crocodile. The *masalai* crocodile carried the betel nut stalk back down into the water.

Wapawi and his little brother paddled the canoe back. They put the canoe by the side of the lake and they returned to the village.

The sun was setting and darkness was approaching. Wapawi and his little brother took all of their little things and went up to the house at the top of the coconut palm. Wapawi's wife and the other people stayed in the village and slept in their houses.

In the dead of night, the water at the *masalai* crocodile's home broke loose from the lake and spilled down to the village. The people of village were dead asleep and they did not know that the water was moving towards the village.

Only one woman woke up and went outside. She stood on the house urinating and she heard the noise of the water underneath the house. The place was pitch dark and she could not see well. The water was moving and still climbing higher.

This woman felt the water moving and coming closer to the side of the house. She was surprised and screamed to the people in the other houses. All of the men, women and children cried and screamed then went back and forth, trying to leave the houses. But it was too late.

The flood swelled and rose quickly. It knocked over everything inside the village. All of the men, women, children, pigs, dogs and other animals drowned and died. There was not one person left alive.

However, Wapawi and Namawi slept well in the house that they had made on top of the coconut palm. When they left their house and went down, they saw that the village was completely empty. Wapawi was happy because the men who had done the bad things with his wife were dead.

His wife was also dead, and the flood had carried everything back into the lake.

Wapawi and his little brother went to look for a wife in another village. They married and raised new families. Their families became plentiful and they lived again in this village.

If you go to Kanganamun Village, you will see that the lake is still there.

David Yaman
Nuvigo
Wewak
East Sepik Province

A1011. Local deluges; A1015.2. Spirit causes deluge; A1018. Flood as punishment; A1023. Escape from deluge on tree; B212. Animal understands human speech; B491.3. Helpful crocodile; B875.2. Giant crocodile; F401.3+. Spirit in crocodile form; F490+. Masalai; K1501. Cuckold; K1868. Deception by pretending sleep; P210. Husband and wife; P230. Parents and children; P251.5. Two brothers; P263. Brother-in-law; P264. Sister-in-law; Q241. Adultery punished; Q428.1. Drowning as punishment for adultery; R311. Tree refuge; S131. Murder by drowning; T100. Marriage; T481. Adultery

## The Village of the *Masalai* Fish
### (Wantok 536, September 8, 1984, page 19)

Long, long ago, in my village, there was a man named Sassemb. One day, he awoke and left our village to go to another village that is near ours. He slept with his friends for just one night, then in the morning he woke up and wanted to go back to our village, **Nungori [Boiken** People, **East Sepik** Province].

While Sassem [Sassemb] was walking, he went down to a river named Munjan [Munguma]. When Sassemb approached the river, he came close to a pond and was surprised to see that it was filled with the fish that we call grouper or cod. These fish were swimming back and forth in the pond. When Sassemb saw the fish, he quivered in desire to spear them.

In the time of the ancestors, they only had bamboo spears and small nets for catching fish in the water. Sassemb wanted very much to catch the fish, so he quickly left his things there, took his little net and went down to the water.

The fish were swimming back and forth, and the good-for-nothing saw this. He held his little net and began to swim behind the fish. He followed one of the fish for a while, but he could not grab it. Whenever he approached, the fish would trick him and swim back to the other side.

Sassemb did this for a while. He did not know that the fish had taken him into a *masalai*'s hole [cave]. These fish were not real fish. No, they were *masalai* fish.

When Sassemb approached these fish, he felt like he could no longer swim. He was surprised to see a village because this place looked exactly like a human settlement.

Sassemb saw this and was very worried. He thought hard, "Where am I really?"

Immediately, an old woman came to him and asked, "How did you get here?"

Sassemb told the old woman that he had swum around with the fish and arrived at this place. The old woman replied to the good-for-nothing, "Those things are not your fish. Those are just my little sows. There are no fish here for you to chase or kill. You're very wrong to want to kill my piglets."

The old woman finished scolding Sassemb then told him, "You must go back now. If you don't, the men will return from the forest and kill you…"

The man listened to this and was terrified. On this day, all of the men of the village had gone to the forest to hunt for wild pigs. If they stayed there, they would kill Sassemb on the next day.

The old woman asked him again, "Where do you want to go now?" The poor man was speechless because he did not know how to leave this village of the *masalai*s. He just stood there.

The old woman said, "I'm sorry for you, so I'll make a way for you to return. If I don't do this and leave you here, the men will come find you, then kill you."

The man listened to this and just stood there. The old woman told Sassemb, "Close your eyes." The good-for-nothing listened to the old woman and closed his eyes.

The old woman took a leaf from a *ton* tree. But she did not do this exactly, she took the stem or spine of the leaf that had fallen and dried. She took this and sang and danced towards it. The old woman struck the place where Sassemb was standing, and immediately the stone [cave] opened again. Then the old woman told Sassembo [Sassemb] to open his eyes again.

When he opened his eyes again, he saw that his way was clear. The old woman told him, "Go now. Don't stay here any longer." Sassemb got up and walked away, leaving the old woman.

He walked and walked and came to a village. This place is the one that still belongs to us from Nungori. The name of this place is Juraung. If you go near our village, you will see this place where he arrived.

When Sassemb arrived, he planted some *purpur* and *tanget* plants. If you are someone from the villages of Numindogum, Haumbuge [Haumbugwe], or Handara and you see this, then you can just go to this place, Jiraung [Juraung] by Nungori Village. We often call it Pon Nungori Sachi.

Paul S. Woginguma

Nungori

Wewak

East Sepik Province

D955. Magic leaf; D956. Magic stick of wood; D1552.1. Mountain opens at blow of divining rod; D1781. Magic results from singing; D1781+. Magic results from dancing; F124. Journey to land of demons; F420.1.3.2. Water-spirit as fish; F490+. Masalai; F760+. Village inside cave; R110. Rescue of captive; R260. Pursuits

## Big Leg's Mistake
(Wantok 537, September 15, 1984, page 20)

Long, long ago, in the time of the ancestors, there were various kinds of people. In the area by Madang, there was an island that had a man with one huge leg [**Bilbil** or **Gedaged** People?, **Madang** Province]. This man's leg had swollen and become very large. The people of this island called him Big Leg.

One morning on the mainland, a man and his wife went to the garden. They walked to the garden hut and the man told his wife, "Stay in the garden hut. I'll go get some betel nuts and peppers from over there, then I'll return." The woman stayed there and made a fire. Smoke rose from the fire.

On the island, Big Leg saw the smoke rising. He thought, "There must be another village on the mainland by the beach. There must be more beautiful women over there. Is the smoke coming from far away? Are they men or women? I'll go and see."

Big Leg took his canoe and paddled slowly. One of his legs was enormous and the other was puny. He was afraid of becoming stuck at sea and drowning, because the weight of his leg could sink him. Before, when he was a boy, he had never swum out from the village into the sea. He had never swum once.

He sat and paddled to the place where the smoke rose. He went ashore on the beach and walked quietly. He saw a woman sitting near a fire and cooking some food.

The good-for-nothing was ecstatic. The woman's husband was getting betel nuts and peppers, and he was not worried about her because this was not the first time for them to walk into the forest.

Big Leg stood in hiding and he looked at what the woman was making. He was a little afraid that her husband was nearby. He hid to find out whether the woman had come alone or not. Later, when he did not see another man, the good-for-nothing just ran out and pulled the woman by her hand while he shut her mouth.

Big Leg told her, "If you call out, I'll kill you. You must shut up if you want to see the moon, the sun, or your parents." He took the woman out to the beach and put her in the canoe. He paddled back to his island.

They arrived on the island and he took the woman to his parents. The parents saw the woman and they were very happy because the island did not have women that liked him. This was because he had a big leg.

Big Leg's father beat the signal drum to announce that there would be a festival to celebrate his marriage. Big Leg's mother adorned the woman. Big Leg's father adorned him. However, the woman was not happy... she just cried.

When his mother asked the woman why she was crying, the woman replied, "I'm so happy because this is the first time that I've seen a man that I'll marry. In the place where I live, we've never seen a man. Only women live there."

Big Leg asked his mother whether his woman was all right. The mother sent a message to Big Leg, "Son, you must be happy. The woman loves you and is very happy to marry you. Their village does not have men and she was happy to see you and to marry you. She is crying because she is so happy."

Big Leg listened to this and told his father, "You must adorn me well, and put on all kinds of adornments on my bad leg to hide it so that the woman can't see it. She'll lust for me even more when I sing and dance." However, it was just a lie. The woman was worried and cried for her husband on the mainland that she had left.

In the garden on the mainland, the woman's husband returned to see that his wife was not there. However, he saw the ashes of the fire that she had thrown on her way when Big Leg had dragged her off. The woman's husband followed these marks until he arrived at the beach.

He saw the place where the canoe had landed and he saw his wife's footprints. He saw Big Leg's footprints too. He saw that one leg was tiny and the other leg was huge.

The man thought, "A *masalai* must have carried my wife into the water." He sat and looked across the sea, and he cried. Then he got up and walked back to the village.

That night on the island, they had a big celebration. All of the men, women and children filled Big Leg's home. Big Leg's parents prepared a big feast. The people gathered to eat, smoke, laugh and beat the hand drums. Oh my, they were happy.

However, the woman sat and worried. She cried harder. Big Leg's mother told her to go befriend Big Leg, and to sing and dance with him. So, they sang and danced together. The woman only sang and danced a little, then she went and sat back down.

Big Leg's mother saw this, so she also left the dance area to find her new daughter-in-law. The woman was sitting and crying harder. She cried through the night and her two eyes became terribly red and swollen. But you know, that night, the people and the mother too did not understand that the woman was worried.

Big Leg wanted the woman to see how well he sang and danced, so he did not go around singing and dancing like the other men. He just stood in one place near where his wife and mother were sitting.

He showed them how well he danced even though his huge leg made it very hard for him to kneel down and dance. Big Leg turned and asked his mother, "Do you see this? Aren't my adornments are beautiful?"

The mother replied, "You're very handsome with all your adornments. They leave me speechless."

Big Leg did not sing and dance as much, but he still stood with his back to all of the men. He faced his mother and wife. He struck his hand drum, bent his knees, lied down, and arose again. He asked his mother again, "My wife, isn't my singing and dancing stylish?"

The mother replied, "Oh my! That looks just like you. She tells me that she loves only you and that she's sitting very close to you to see how you sing and dance."

However, it was not true. The woman just sat there and did not want to see this big-legged man. She cried for the good husband that she had left at home.

Later, Big Leg still felt bad, so he wanted to see his wife and tell her about her Big Leg. He went to hold her hand. He told her, "Get up and look at all of the married people singing and dancing together. Get up and hold my hand, then sing and dance when I beat the hand drum. We'll sing and dance around happily with all of the other people."

The woman listened and arose, then they sang and danced together. Big Leg was very happy that the woman held his hand. He beat the hand drum, bent his knees, lay down, and then rose again. However, the woman just sang very quietly. She began to think that this was a good time for her to run away. She began to think of a way to escape.

They sang and danced until dawn, then everyone went back to their houses to sleep. They were exhausted because they had sung, danced, and eaten through the night. So, everyone collapsed and slept.

Big Leg and his wife and parents also slept. Big Leg told his mother, "I'm exhausted, so I'll sleep. You must look at the woman. Whatever she wants, you must give her. You must take care of her."

The mother told him, "Son, don't worry." However, the mother did not follow through on what she had told her son. Before long, the mother also was snoring. She had also fallen dead asleep.

Then the woman got up very quietly, ran and hid in the forest. She went and took the canoe, then very quickly paddled away from the island. The woman paddled well and arrived quickly at the garden. She followed the garden trail and arrived at the hut. She saw her real husband, held him and cried. Later, she told the story to her husband about what had happened to her.

The man listened to this and was furious. He told his wife, "Don't cry anymore, you've returned. Now I'll watch carefully. If this Big Leg comes to look for you, he'll be shot right through with my spear. Then I'll tie a *tanget* plant to mark that I've killed a man."

On the island, Big Leg woke up to find that the woman was not there. He was furious at his mother. He and his father beat the poor old mother. Big Leg was furious. He told his mother, "I'll get the woman back. I know which way she went. She said that her village has no men. I'll go with the some single men from the village to the woman's village and bring more women back to the island."

On the mainland, the woman and the man decided to go to the garden. The man told the woman, "You must make a bonfire so that the smoke rises high, and so that Big Leg will see it and come. I'll hide carefully. When he comes to get you, you must walk in the front and let Big Leg go behind you. I'll see him clearly and shoot him dead with the spear."

The woman listened carefully to what he said, then they went back to the garden. The woman made a bonfire and sat in the garden hut. She pretended to cook food. The woman was dressed finely, so that Big Leg would lust for her.

On the island, Big Leg saw the smoke and lusted for her [lit., "swallowed his spit"]. He dressed finely as if for a festival. Big Leg took a canoe and paddled quietly away.

He went up to the woman, held her and asked, "Why did you run away?"

The woman replied, "I ran away because I was worried about my mother, so I paddled the canoe to see her. I hadn't gone to the village, so I was worried and cried. It was good to come and talk with her. So now I've come to wait for you."

Big Leg heard this and was happy. He held the woman's hand. He told the woman, "Get up, let's go now. I saw the smoke and I knew that it was you here. So, I came to fetch you."

They got up and left. However, the woman's husband was lying in wait. The woman followed her husband's instructions and went first while Big Leg walked behind her.

The woman's husband aimed carefully at the small piece of forest behind the base of a big tree. When Big Leg passed by it, the man threw the spear hard and it went directly through Big Leg's chest. The spear went through his back.

Big Leg fell down and just spoke a little, "You worthless lying woman. It was a trap."

The woman's husband jumped over to Big Leg and said, "Ah friend, where are you going? You ruined my wife, but now you'll see the moon, the sun and your parents. Where are you going now?"

The man put another spear through Big Leg's head and finished him off. They carried his corpse with the spears and put it in the canoe. They told Big Leg's corpse, "You can't go wandering about. You must carefully steer your canoe to your island home."

The canoe with the corpse drifted directly towards his home and landed on the beach. Later, the people found Big Leg's body with the two spears still stuck into his body.

The people of the island saw this and were terrified. They thought that the men of the opposite shore must have killed him. It was at this time too that they knew that there were men who lived there and not just women.

Dale Magando

Bumayoung Lutheran High School

Lae

Morobe Province

D1523.2. Self-propelling (ship) boat; D1774. Magic results from speaking; F517+. Person with one large leg; K914. Murder from ambush; P210. Husband and wife; P231. Mother and son; P233. Father and son; P261. Father-in-law; P262. Mother-in-law; P265+. Daughter-in-law; Q213. Abduction punished; Q411. Death as punishment; Q458. Flogging as punishment; R10. Abduction; R210. Escapes; R260. Pursuits; S110. Murders; T192. Marriage by force; W157. Dishonesty

## The Dogs' Wives

(Wantok 538, September 22, 1984, page 18)

Long, long ago, in the time of the ancestors, there was a village without men. The women of the village only married dogs, but no children came from these dog marriages.

The women always went to the gardens and made sago. The dogs would go to the forest and kill pigs. If the wild game were too heavy to pull back to the village, they would leave it there and tell their wives to go bring the pigs back to the village. Later, they would butcher and divide the meat among the dogs' wives.

The married couples always lived like this. When some dogs went to hunt for pigs, cassowaries, or other game, other dogs would jump up a huge, tall coconut palm tree that went out across the water. They would scramble to the top of this tree, they would sing, "*Yabun wimar... ee wimar... eh*," and then quickly jump down into the water. They would swim ashore, and then go back up the coconut palm, sing and jump down into the water again.

One time, two women were still in the forest rinsing sago. One of them cut down a sago palm tree, cleaned off the bark, then removed and scraped the sago pith.

The other woman cleared an area for rinsing the sago, then erected a trough for rinsing it. The two women processed sago. In a place that was very far away, there was a real man. He had left his village to look for food in the forest.

The man shot a huge Victoria crowned pigeon [*Goura victoria*] with his bow and arrow. However, the pigeon spun and spun around with the arrow, flying very far away. It went over about four mountains, then the pigeon lost its breath and fell down near the place where the women were rinsing sago. The pigeon fell down at the top of the small stream that the women were using to rinse the sago.

One woman saw that the water was not flowing strongly, so she called out to the other woman, "Hey, come here and take a look at the water. How are we going to rinse the sago now?"

The other woman who was scraping the sago went and looked. The other woman told her friend, "I'll wait here and you go look. There's probably a big tree branch that fell down or a piece of earth that broke off and blocked the water."

But no, it was the two wings of the pigeon and its body that blocked up the stream. The big pigeon had fallen right in the middle of the little stream.

The woman took the bird and carried it back. The other woman saw this bird and did not believe it. She said,

"Who do you think shot that pigeon? It has an arrow in it. We women never shoot birds like this. Who could have shot it? Our dog husbands don't know how to do this. Oh never mind, go back and scrape the sago. We'll finish quickly, then leave before the afternoon winds arise and it becomes hard to find the way back."

The woman who was rinsing the sago hid the pigeon well underneath a *limbum* palm tree near where she was working. The other woman finished the sago that she was scraping.

The man who had shot the pigeon followed the forest towards the place where the pigeon had fallen. He passed the four [mountains], then arrived at the place where the two women were processing sago.

However, he did not reveal himself to the two of them. He hid very quietly and just watched the women. Oh my, he was very surprised to see how hard the women worked at processing the sago.

Later, he very quietly climbed a big tree that had many vines attached to it, so that the women would see him. He sat on a tree branch. The man had a feather headdress in his hair.

The man hid well and feathers made a noise in the wind. The shadow of the feathers moved back and forth in the water. One of the women saw this and was surprised. She was terrified.

She looked up the tree, but she did not see anything like a headdress. She called to the other woman, "Hey, come here. I was rinsing the sago and I saw the image of a headdress on a man's head. I saw it here."

They looked around, but they did not find him. They said, "This is not a men's place... how did they get here? We've never seen a men's place." They stayed and finished the sago work.

Later, the man went down the tree very quietly. He very slowly came before the women. One of the women saw him and was shamed by the man. She just stood there. The man told her, "Don't be ashamed. I'm looking for a pigeon that I shot which flew around here. Have you seen it or not?"

She called out to the other woman to come and meet him. The women said that they had hidden the pigeon. The man told the women, "I'll help you scrape the sago."

The women replied, "No. Please, we want you to just sit down. We're still doing this hard work. We don't have men at the village."

The women both lowered their heads in shame and whispered, "We're married to dogs. There are no men in the village. Every woman is married to a dog."

The man listened to this and sat quietly. The two women did not want him to do any work. After the women finished making sago, the three of them prepared to go back to the village.

They told the man that the two of them would carry the sago and go to the house first to see if there were dogs or other women from the village. One of the women would take the man inside the house.

The two women followed the trail. One went first, the other hid and stood with the man in the forest near the house. The first woman saw that no one was there. She called out for them to come quietly to the house. For two nights, the dogs came to the house and sniffed near the traditional bags in which people slept to keep out mosquitoes [probably **East Sepik** Province (e.g., see Gewertz, 1983: 3)]. The two women's two dog husbands smelled the man and wanted to call out.

The two women got up and told the two dogs, "Why? That's pig meat... or cassowary that you always kill in the forest. That meat isn't for you. Come on, get out! Clear the area and sleep down below until we call for you to come for food."

The two dogs left and just sniffed around the place and called out. [The women said], "You two are always just jumping in the water and never thinking about hunting for [game]. So, that's why it's staying under the house." However, the two dogs knew that there must be a real man there because they continued to smell him. The man stayed inside the bag while the women cooked food and gave it to him inside the net [bag] to eat.

The man sang and danced [at some things], then he told the women to take these things. He told them to carry them and put them underneath the ropes on the coconut palm where the dogs scramble and jump into the water. One of the women carried these things and followed the man's instructions. So, just like every day, the dogs scrambled up the coconut palm, sang and jumped into the water.

Just one old bitch was sitting and watching as the other dogs sang on top of the coconut palm then jumped into the water. The old dog sat watching as all of the dogs filled the top of the coconut palm that lay across the water. Their heaviness made one of the ropes at the base of the tree break and crash.

The old bitch called out, "Hey you, take it easy. I heard a rope break at the base of the tree. Did you hear it or not?"

The dogs listened and called, "Hey watch your mouth. What? Is this new to us or what?"

The second time that they filled the coconut palm, they stood and sang together, "_Yambun_ _wimari_... _ee_... _wimari_... _ah_." Then another rope at the base of the coconut palm broke.

The old dog turned and called again. They cursed the old dog terribly, "You're bad. Call out, call out, for what? You don't have a face. It's full of scabies. You lazy old good-for-nothing, shut your mouth lest we come kill you and throw you down into the water."

So then, all of the ropes at the base of the coconut palm began to break. Almost all of them were broken and the palm tree was again full of dogs. The coconut palm was very heavy that afternoon. The dogs sang again and were about to jump when the coconut palm fell down with all of the dogs into the water. The dogs could not swim because the man's singing and dancing had killed them. They all drowned.

The old bitch just sat there and cried, "You ignored me and then you died, glug... glug... glug. Who shall I live with now? Glug... glug."

Then the real women of the village went to kill the old bitch. The man married the two women and had children. After this, real people lived in this village.

Mathias Uba

Gali [Galai Settlement] Block

Kimbe

West New Britain Province

B31.6+. Giant pigeon; B211.1.7. Speaking dog; B214.1.4. Singing dog; B601.2. Marriage to dog; D800. Magic object; D1781. Magic results from singing; D1781+. Magic results from dancing; D2061. Magic murder; J652. Inattention to warnings; P210. Husband and wife; P230. Parents and children; Q411. Death as punishment; Q321. Laziness punished; Q428. Punishment: drowning; Q582. Fitting death as punishment; S63+. Wife kills husband; S131. Murder by drowning; T100. Marriage; T145.0.1. Polygyny; W111. Laziness; W157. Dishonesty


## The Ground Swallowed People
(Wantok 539, September 29, 1984, page 27)

Long, long ago, the women and children never went into the men's house. The men in the men's house would make a carving of a man and erect him by the men's house.

When the men went to a new garden to get food, they would take the food, walk slowly back to the men's house, and put all of the food by the legs of this wooden man. The men of the village would customarily slaughter a pig.

The men would do this because they wanted the statue to bless their new garden. The statue's blessing would come forth and the people would not be short of food during times of famine. Pigs would also be more plentiful and girls would not encounter enemies. This statue belonged to the men at this time. It was completely forbidden for women or children to look at this god.

One time, there was a woman who lived alone in her house. She had thought hard because the men always took big net bags [of food] to please this god. So, the woman also wanted to see their god.

The woman went to the men's house. She went by the house and called out, "Hey, if there's a man in the house, come down now." A boy heard her and came outside.

The woman saw this boy and said, "I gave some food inside a net bag to my husband yesterday. He did not bring my net bag back, so I came to get the bag now."

The boy listened to this and went inside the house. He came out again with the net bag. But the woman said, "That's not mine."

The boy went inside the house again and came out with another net bag. However the woman said, "No. Go look carefully. My net bag must be inside." They did this for a while until the boy had found nearly all of the net bags in the house. However, the woman had not yet seen her net bag.

The woman scolded the boy terribly. After she did this, the little boy went inside the house and brought outside various kinds of things that belonged to all of the men. The woman looked carefully at all of the things that were hidden inside the men's house, but the woman's thoughts did not stop with the net bag. No, she had a great desire to see their god's face. Finally, the poor boy went inside and carried the men's god outside.

The woman said, "Thank you very much. Thank you very much. I have seen our god." Then the woman left the men's house and went back to her house.

The boy was alone again and thought hard. The leaders of the village had put a strong taboo upon women and children against looking at their god's face. However, this woman had seen the god. What would happen now?

The god waited patiently for all of the men, women and children who were walking around, seeing their friends or who were in the gardens, to return to the village. The god wanted everyone in the village to be in one place. Then the god would show them his wrath.

Everyone slept well that night. When dawn broke and the sun rose a little, the god sent forth a tremendous downpour. Not a single man could go to the garden or the forest because of this rain. Everyone just stayed in the houses.

The god sent an eagle flying across the sky. All of the rats saw the big bird flying above and were terrified. The

rats dug through the earth, trying to hide. However when the rats dug the earth, they broke it up and made huge holes.

The clouds thundered and the rain came down like never before. This made everyone even more terrified, so they just stayed in the houses. The big village broke apart into pieces and all of the houses capsized into the Timba [Timbe] River. When the ground broke apart, two brothers took their bows and arrows then shot all of the pigs and dogs. When they did this, all of the stones and trees broke apart, and the ground broke apart further.

The earth devoured everyone who jumped into the Timbe River. The two brothers tried to escape, but the god shoveled them into the mud and they died. The ground broke apart and entered the Timbe River. When the ground entered one side, two lakes arose.

The house posts that belonged to all of these people are still there. Everyone who went to this place saw the house posts standing there. The posts began to rot in 1960.

The name of this village that broke apart was Dundunlomon [**Dalugilomon**]. The men of Songin [**Songgin**] Village in the Kabwum District of **Morobe** Province heard this story and told all of the men near them [**Timbe** People].

James Mala
Tauramba Pharmacy
Port Moresby
National Capital District

A920.1.0.1. Origin of particular lake; A1011. Local deluges; A1015. Flood caused by gods or other superior beings; C311.1.8. Tabu: looking at deity; C923. Death by drowning for breaking tabu; D1347.4. Magic statue gives fecundity; D1402.19. Magic statue kills; D2074.1.3. Birds magically called; D2143.1. Rain produced by magic; D2149.1. Thunderbolt magically produced; D2148. Earth magically caused to quake; D2151.8. Magic flood; F969.7. Famine; P210. Husband and wife; P251.5. Two brothers; Q411. Death as punishment; V1.11.3. Worship of wooden idol

## Surataura's Prank
(Wantok 540, October 6, 1984, page 23)

Long, long ago, there were two good friends who lived in a village. The name of the first man was Surataura and the name of his friend was Kuwoko.

Every day, these two men were good friends to each other. They traveled to all of the places in their region. After they would help their parents, they would meet, travel, do various kinds of work, and do the things that young men do.

There was a big festival in the two friends' village one day. The people from another village came to meet and compete at singing and dancing. At this time in the past, young women would lust for the young men who could beat their hand drums alluringly.

Surataura adorned his body and he looked very handsome. His hand drum sounded very loud because he had a good marsupial (*kapul*) skin on the opening of his drum.

Poor Kuwoko had a drum, but he did not have a marsupial skin to stretch across its opening. So, he went to ask Surataura. Kuwoko asked Surataura, "Friend, where did you get this marsupial skin?"

Surataura replied, "Hey friend, you must go talk to your mother and remove the skin from her knee. You must take this piece of skin from her knee and stretch it across the mouth of your drum. Then your hand drum will sound louder."

Kuwoko went and firmly asked his old mother, then cut the skin from his mother's knee. Kuwoko took the skin from his mother's knee and departed. His old mother's knee bled profusely and she died.

Surataura and Kuwoko stayed at the festival that night until the next morning. Then everyone walked around the village. Kuwoko arrived at his house and was shocked.

Kuwoko saw his old mother lying dead. He went back and scolded Surataura, "Friend, you lied to me and I killed my mother."

However, Kuwoko was not angry and did not fight with his friend. He was sorry for his friend's mother. Kuwoko carried his mother and buried her. He thought hard about getting revenge against his friend.

Kuwoko thought of a good way to ruin his friend. He made a big fence and created a garden inside it. Surataura helped Kuwoko erect the fence and dig the earth to plant the food. Their friendship was not over yet.

Kuwoko adorned himself well and went to work in his new garden. Then he adorned himself and sang and danced. He jumped and burned the grass inside the garden.

However, he was not afraid of the light and smoke from the fire. He jumped around, and the light and smoke of the fire engulfed him.

When the light of the fire came close to him, he would quickly jump down into a hole and hide. He would jump up, sing and dance when the fire was lit near the hole in which he stayed. He made this hole the place where he stayed. He did this sort of thing often and confused Surataura.

Surataura jumped and asked Kuwoko, "How is it that the fire has not burned your body?"

Kuwoko said, "You must sing and dance then jump back and forth when the fire approaches you. The fire can't burn you if you sing and dance and stand right in the middle of the fire."

Surataura believed what his friend said and just followed the instructions. However the fire burned his arms, legs, head, nose, face, ears, and every part of his body. The fire completely burned his clothing. All his skin was burned and in terrible pain.

He lay down, turning his body back and forth, but the pain did not stop. He arose and ran to the river. He jumped into the river and lay there until his whole body cooled off.

Poor Surataura saw that his whole body was burned and completely black when he left the river. He now understood that his friend had lied to him.

Surataura went and told Kuwoko, "I thought that you told the truth, so I followed everything that you said. But the fire burned me and completely ruined me, so I can't be your friend anymore. Because you are still a handsome man and my skin is poor and ruined, women will not like me."

The friendship ended at this time. Surataura ran away and lived at another place. Kuwoko had run away because he was ashamed of his ruined friend. The two of them changed their bodies and became little grasshoppers.

There is a small black grasshopper that often jumps around stones. It has various kinds of trash stuck to its skin. This grasshopper is just Surataura.

The other kind of grasshopper often digs holes inside the ground [probably the ground cricket, family Gryllacrididae]. You can always see this kind of grasshopper carrying its food and taking it inside its hole. This grasshopper is Kuwoko.

The grasshopper kin of Kuwoko are clean and have good colors on their skins. However, Surataura's grasshopper kin have completely black skins because the ashes from the fire had burned the skin of their leader long, long ago. If you see this kind of grasshopper, you will think that it is ashes from a fire, but no, it's Suratura [Surataura].

Mathias Uba

Block Number 1489, Galai [Settlement Block] One

Kimbe

West New Britain Province

[This story is probably from the **East Sepik** Province. Mr. Uba also wrote the ancestor story in *Wantok* #538.]

A2064. Creation of grasshopper; D183.2M. Transformation: man to cricket; D183.2+M. Transformation: man to grasshopper; K891.4+. Dupe tricked into burning self; K940.2+. Man tricked into killing his mother; K2297. Treacherous friend; P231. Mother and son; P310. Friendship;

Q261. Treachery punished; Q414. Punishment: burning alive; R220. Flights; S22+. Matricide; S110. Murders; V61.3+. Dead buried; W157. Dishonesty


## The Crocodile Took Bajingei

(Wantok 541, October 13, 1984, page 35)

Long, long ago, in the time of the ancestors, there was a canoe. The canoe's name was Bajingei. A crocodile ancestral spirit had sunk [a canoe] which went to the bottom of Kondabi Lake. This place is near **Apan**, by Walu [**Malu**] Village, Ambunti, **East Sepik** Province [**Manambu** People].

This Kondobi [Kondabi] Lake is still there. The place where the canoe went down has grasses and pandanus trees (*karuka*) growing in the middle of the water. These are marks left from the canoe, Bajingei.

The father of this canoe came from the Nambul/Samblap Clan. This is a true story that happened long ago, but nowadays, children often hear this ancestor story.

The story goes as follows. A man carved a new canoe. The canoe was so long that twenty men paddled it. The tree from which he carved it was the second largest ironwood tree.

This man had no children, so when he finished the canoe, he put various crocodile markings at the bow of the canoe. The two sides of the canoe were filled with the markings of those of a Sepik spirit house.

The women and children did not approach this canoe. The canoe's father gave the name Bajingei to the canoe. He did not have children, so he gave a real man's name to his canoe. When the children of the village saw this canoe, they felt their bodies rise up in fear from a distance.

After about three days, the father of the canoe burned [the hollow of] the canoe carefully [to finish its construction] and adorned it with various kinds of *tanget* and *purpur* plants. The men of the village asked him for his canoe so that they could take the dogs and go to hunt for pigs in the [forest].

This day was the first time that the canoe's father and some leaders brought the dogs and went to Kondabi Lake. When they went ashore, the canoe's father tied a strong, new rattan to the bow and another two to the stern.

The canoe's father let one young man watch the canoe because the Bajingei canoe was like his child and he took excellent care of it. He let the young man stay and watch the canoe lest something bad happen to the canoe while the men were hunting for pigs.

The canoe's father and the other men left for the forest with the dogs to hunt for pigs. While they were in the forest, the crocodile ancestral spirit that was underneath the lake saw the new canoe and lusted for it. This was because the canoe had the marks of a crocodile on it.

The crocodile thought, "Now I'll get that canoe and bring it down as my own." So the crocodile sent his soldiers, the little fish and the crocodiles to the surface of the water. They asked the canoe to go down beneath the water with them. They told the canoe that their king below insisted that it to go down with them.

Bajingei was not an ordinary canoe. It was a canoe called *sakival mitikal*. This happens when a real man, full of adornments, sings and dances in the traditional manner of his father, then he adorns and spits upon it. When this happens, and girls and young men see it from far away, and their skin jumps in fear.

So, the crocodile ancestral spirit sent crayfish up who asked, "Why are you staying there? The king below the lake wants us to go down together."

The canoe said, "No. Why should I go down? I already have a father. He is in the forest and he told me to wait here, so I'm just staying here."

The crayfish went down and told their king, "The canoe did not want to come." So, the crocodile sent the scorpionfish [order Scorpaeniformes; note: these are saltwater fish], crabs, eels, mullet [family Mugilidae], pearl perch, hermit crabs or snails, herring [a saltwater fish], tilapia, turtles, and small crocodiles too. However, the canoe was insistent and did not want to go down. These animals just brought the message back to their king.

The young man was staying on a tree branch and carefully watched the fish talking with the canoe. He could not believe this, so he just stayed there and watched.

The king sent a huge crocodile up to the surface to again ask the canoe. However, the canoe told it that it had a father and did not want to leave him, and that it was still waiting for its father. The big crocodile listened to this, went back and told its crocodile king.

The big king crocodile ancestral spirit asked his second, who was named Sap. When Sap went to the surface, the water began to roil and spin. The water also swelled and roiled when Sap came up to the canoe.

Sap asked the canoe, "All of the king's soldiers came to the surface and asked you, but you didn't want to come. I'm the king's second in command, so now I've come to get you. Let's go down together."

Bajingei the canoe replied, "I'm very sorry. There's no way for me to go down. I already told the people (fish)

when they asked. I'm waiting for my father. When he comes back from the forest, we'll go back to the village."

Sap just descended, and the water roiled and went descended with him. The king ancestral crocodile listened to Sap and he said, "Is that so? The canoe did not want to come with you. So, I myself will go to the surface and ask what the canoe thinks. The canoe will have no more power. I'll take the canoe down with me. All of you must prepare and watch for this."

The crocodile ancestral spirit Kupawal went to the surface. He usually lived in the place called Kupatangir. When he went to the surface, oh my, the water swelled and surrounded the canoe, making it look like breakers in the sea.

He went to the surface and told the canoe, "I've come now to get you. I sent all my soldiers to work, and I just stayed at Kupatangir. What kind of canoe are you to pull me to the surface here? I've come to the surface, so now we'll go down."

First he asked the canoe, "Who are you? Who is your kin?" The canoe said that its name was Bajingei. The young man was watching this and called out to the canoe's father and the other men who had taken the dogs to hunt for pigs in the forest.

The power of Kupawal, the crocodile ancestral spirit, took the canoe. The ropes on the stern broke. Then the second rattan rope broke. The young man saw this and called out again.

When this enemy came to his child, the canoe's father did not want to hunt for pigs. He tried to hurry the other men to go back quickly to the lake. They left the forest quickly and walked off. He heard the young man calling out. It was like the sound of a faraway bird.

They walked quickly with the dogs and the pigs that they had killed. When they arrived at the lake, only the prow (or nose) of the [canoe] was standing and dancing in the middle of the water.

The father of Bajingei the canoe saw this. He screamed and cried terribly. He jumped in the water and swam out to hold Bajingei's nose as he cried.

He cried and spoke, "You're not a canoe. You're my real child. Why did you leave me? Who wanted to steal you from me?"

The canoe's father spoke and cried at the same time. This kind of talking, called _ia-wayavi_, ended.

The other men stood and watched. They called out to the canoe's father, "That's enough now. Come back to the ground, then we'll see what the canoe does."

The crocodile ancestral spirit held the canoe so that only the nose danced on the surface. He wanted to give time for the canoe's father to see it for the last time before the canoe went down.

Bajingei's father carried two pigs, swam out and tied a rope to the canoe's prow. He stopped crying and carried a long decorated gourd containing lime (calcium oxide). This was only used in the spirit house. He broke the gourd and spilled the lime that was used by men when they were by the fence of the spirit house or at a festival only for leaders.

The father of the canoe did this, then he swam back to the shore, sat and cried. The other men watched. The crocodile ancestral spirit brought the canoe, danced and went down to his place in the lake. This is the place called Daguawli. Then he traveled to all of the places, and brought the canoe back to the place where he lived. The prow of the canoe went down very slowly until it was all of the way down. The water swelled and roiled when Banjingei [Bajingei] and Kupawal went below the water.

Now the canoe's marks are there. The grasses and pandanus trees stand behind the canoe's marks in Kondabi Lake. When the people of Malu and Apan go fishing or do other work at this lake, they still think of this. However, they do not talk about the canoe. Some are afraid and never go close to the place where the canoe is located. They are terrified that they would not find food or fish on that day and would just go back to the village empty-handed.

Before, this lake was not there because the Sepik River went down through there. However the ground broke, new ground arose, and an ox-bow lake formed.

This area of the Sepik River clogged up and the river broke through a new path. This clogged up area became Kondabi Lake. When the canoe went down, its father blocked off this part of the Sepik River.

John Naul
Malu Village
Ambunti
East Sepik Province

A920.1.0.1. Origin of particular lake; A990. Other land features; B211.5. Speaking fish; B211.6.4K. Speaking crocodile; B211.8K+. Speaking crayfish; B240.15. Crocodile as king of animals; B875.2. Giant crocodile; C400. Speaking tabu; C610. The one forbidden place; C933.2. Luck in fishing lost for breaking tabu; D1001. Magic spittle; D1121. Magic boat; D1610.11. Speaking ship; D1781. Magic results from singing; D1781+. Magic results from dancing; P230. Parents and children; R10. Abduction; R260. Pursuits; V112.1. Spirit huts

# Kopesi Got Revenge

(Wantok 542, October 20, 1984, page 23)

Long, long ago, there was a girl who did not have legs. When her mother gave birth to her, her parents saw that she had come out well except that she did not have her legs. So, she just lived in their house in the village.

Her parents gave the name Kopesi to their daughter. They took care of her very well because she was born like this. The child would always just stay in the house, and the parents would go to the garden or the forest to look for their food. When Kopesi was twelve years old, she was a very beautiful girl.

One time, the parents left Kopesi in the village and went to the garden. While she was in the village, a woman came and saw her. This woman had four legs and her name was Ovorinang.

Ovorinang saw Kopesi sitting and she said, "Friend, what are you doing sitting here?"

Kopesi replied, "I have no legs, so I sit in the village. My parents left for the garden."

The woman Ovornang [Ovorinang] listened to this and said, "Don't worry, I'll give you two legs, then we'll go to my garden."

Kopesi listened and was very happy. Ovorinang gave her the two legs and Kopesi put them on. Then they walked to the garden. When they arrived at the garden, Ovorinang fooled Kopesi into thinking that she was working. Instead, she went into the forest and had sex with men.

Poor Kopesi broke her bones weeding Ovorinang's garden until the afternoon. Then the woman, Ovarinang [Ovorinang], arrived and told Kopesi to give her two legs back. Kopesi listened and returned the woman's legs. She took them and walked back to the village. Poor Kopesi did not have legs to walk back to the village, so she worked at pulling and pulling her torso back to the village. Rattan thorns and other vines and grasses poked her skin. She arrived at the place where they fetched water and had no more strength, so she just lay there.

When her parents returned from the [garden in the] forest, they found her lying there, so they asked her, "Kopesi, why are you lying there?"

Kopesi told them the story about how Ovoranang had come and tricked her when she was alone in the forest. The parents listened and were furious. They told their daughter, "Next time, don't listen to this woman lest she fool you again."

They took Kopesi back to their house. They lived there for some time, then the woman Ovoraning [Ovorinang] came around again to Kopesi's home while she was alone in the village.

Ovorinang arrived there and saw Kopesi. She told her, "Friend, I've come to take you with me to look for *galip* nuts in the forest."

However, Kopesi was not happy to see this woman. She said, "Before, you came and tricked me, then you took back your legs and left me in the forest. My parents found me and were furious. So now, I can't follow you again."

Ovorinang lied to Kopesi and flattered him. She said, "Now look at this. I'll give you these two legs." When Kopesi heard this, she was very happy because she thought that the woman was telling the truth. She listened and put on Ovorinang's two legs, then they walked into the forest.

When they arrived at the place where the *galip* trees were located, Ovorinang lied to Kopesi that she wanted to defecate. So, Kopesi began to gather the *galip* nuts. Ovorinang just pretended to defecate and went to see her men friends inside the forest.

Kopesi kept working at gathering the *galip* nuts until afternoon. Then the woman Ovorinang came back to Kopesi and asked her, "Where are the *galip* nuts?" Kopesi showed her the *galip* nuts and they brought them back towards the village. When they approached the river again, Ovorinang told Kopesi to return her legs.

Poor Kopesi did not have legs now, so she pulled and pulled her torso closer to the river, then she lay down. Her parents arrived and saw her like this, and they were furious. They knew that the woman Ovorinang had lied to their child again. They told Kopesi, "Now, let's look for this woman, but don't listen to her lies."

The next day, the parents wanted to go finish their work in the garden. The father took Kopesi to an area by the house where he tied her up amongst the sugarcanes. Then the mother and father went into the forest.

Kopesi stayed there and heard the woman Ovorinang approaching and calling out to her. Kopesi replied, "Papa tied me up in the sugarcanes. I can't come with you."

Ovorinang listened and went to get her friend [Kopesi]. She gave her the two legs and they walked to the garden. When they arrived at the garden, Ovorinang fooled her again and went inside the forest to look for her men friends. Kopesi worked very hard in the garden by herself.

In the afternoon, Ovorinang arrived and told Kopesi that they would go back to the village. When they approached the river, Ovorinang took back the legs again. Poor Kopesi pulled her trunk and arrived at the river.

Her parents arrived and saw her again, and they were completely exasperated. The father was furious and told his daughter, "Tomorrow, you'll be completely different."

He finished scolding his daughter, then they went back to the village. Kopesi's mother cooked the food, then they ate and slept. Very early in the morning, at about half past five, the father awoke and arranged his things.

He took coconut oil, a "grass" skirt and paints, and adorned his daughter Kopesi well. The father took armbands, the shell money of the **North Solomons** [Province]. They killed a _mimis_ [?] and adorned the child very well so that she looked beautiful. Then the father took her and sat her down directly in front of the house.

The father told her, "If Ovorinang comes to see you and asks, 'What are you doing that you have come like this?' You must reply and say, 'My parents are angry with me. They're going to cook me in a clay pot. That's why I look this way.'"

After the father taught his daughter this, he and the mother went to the garden. Kopesi sat, and later the trickster woman Ovorinang arrived at her house.

Ovorinang saw her and said, "Friend Kopesi, you look beautiful. What are you doing that you look so beautiful?" Kopesi told her that her parents would be cooking her in a clay pot until she becomes something else.

Ovorinang listened and told Kopesi, "I also want to become beautiful. I think you should cook me too." Kopesi listened to this and said, "Give me the legs first, then I'll get up and show you." The trickster woman did not think any more. She just gave her legs to Kopesi, telling her to work quickly.

Kopesi went and took a big pot then came outside. She told her friend to go inside and sit in the pot. Then she took a piece of rope and tied up Ovorinang well. Then she made a fire.

While the fire was heating the pot, Ovorinang cried out, "Hey, the fire's burning me."

However Kopesi told her, "You be quiet and he'll put the adornments on your body." The fire burned Ovorinang's body well and she cried out, but Kopesi did not listen. She taught her a lesson, and put more firewood onto the fire.

After a while, Ovorinang died inside the pot. When Ovorinang was done with, Kopesi went and called to the men in the forest to come and eat the meat. The men sat down and ate and ate, then they saw Ovarinang's head and they knew that they were eating their woman, Ovorinang.

Kopesi was very happy now because she had two legs and walked around as she pleased. She lived well and often helped her parents by doing whatever kind of work they had in the village or in the garden.

B. Pirung
P. O. Box 109
Kieta
North Solomons Province

[B. Pirung wrote the ancestor story in _Wantok_ #601. He or she is probably from the **Nasioi** People.]

F517+. Person with four legs; F517+. Removable legs; F517.0.3K. Person without legs; G61.1+. Person recognizes lover's flesh when it is served to be eaten; J1110. Clever persons; K499.10+. Person pretends to go to work, but goes out to have sex; K551.16. Woman escapes by ruse: must go to defecate; K843+. Dupe persuaded to be killed in order to look more beautiful; L112.11.1K+. Legless child as hero; P210. Husband and wife; P232. Mother and daughter; P234. Father and daughter; Q414. Punishment: burning alive; T580. Childbirth

# Nol Became a _Masalai_'s Son
(Wantok 543, October 27, 1984, page 27)

Long, long ago, in the time of the ancestors, in the **Sinasina** Village area of the **Simbu** [Province] mountains, there lived a sorceress [**Sinasina** People]. Her name was Bleku. Bleku lived in a house in a part of the forest where people never traveled. They were afraid of this sorceress.

Bleku had a strong desire to obtain a child. Because she did not have a child, all of the mountains and forests did not received rain. Bleku had blocked the rain from falling until she obtained a child. So, even the small streams were completely dry in the entire area.

There was no food in the gardens either, so there was a famine in the whole area. One time, a small group of children from the village went to many places to look for food. They did not find any food, so they became tired and breathless.

Among this young group was a very young boy whose name was Nol. He was completely out of breath as well as overheated. He told the older children, "Go ahead. I'll stay underneath the base of this tree. When you return, then take me back to the village with you."

So they let him stay, and only the bigger children continued to look for food. They went very far away. The boy stayed under the base of the tree and rested.

Then Bleku, the sorceress, walked along and arrived at this place in the forest. She saw the little boy Nol sleeping underneath the base of the tree. Quickly, Bleku went and grabbed him. She was happy to carry him. She sang, danced and called out, "Go ahead rain, come forth now. I have a child now."

Oh my, a tremendous downpour fell. It rained like never before. Everywhere, the people were happy and sent a message to go to the mountain peaks.

Bleku carried little Nol inside her home in a cave and gave him various kinds of food. Nol was famished and had never seen these kinds of foods before, so he just ate and ate.

He kept eating until his belly filled and became completely bloated. After eating, he slept. As he slept, the sorceress took a small bamboo flute and spoke to it, "If my child wants to run away, you must come forth and make music so that I hear it quickly and come to search for him."

Bleku tied the flute well to [his] hair then went to look for food in the surrounding mixed forest. She worked at hunting pigs so that they could make a huge feast to celebrate Nol, her new son.

Nol slept for a while, then he woke up and saw that he was in a cave and that it was pitch black. Quickly, he got up and ran away. His friends had returned and were looking for him. They did not find him, so they went back to the village and explained what had happened to his parents.

The little boy, Nol, tried to find his friends. He walked and walked, but it was too late because Bleku had returned and found him.

Nol could not run away because when he slept in the *masalai* woman Bleku's house, she had put the little bamboo flute in his hair. Nol did not know that this flute was in the hair. So when he had run away from the cave to look for his friends, the little bamboo flute was in his hair. Nol did not know that this flute was in his hair.

When Nol had run away from the cave to find his friend, the little bamboo flute cried out. The wind went through the flute and music came forth. The *masalai* woman Bleku heard this when she was still far away. She quickly ran back to get Nol.

Nol was looking for his friends and was walking in the forest. When Bleku came before Nol's eyes, she had changed her face into that of his mother from the village.

Then she told Nol, "Come here and let's go home now. We've been trying to find you." Nol thought that it was really his mother, so Bleku held Nol's hand and they walked back to Belku's [Bleku's] home.

Bleku knew that Nol's friends had returned to tell Nol's parents. She had spied upon them a long time ago. It would not be long when they would go look for Nol in every part of the forest. So, Bleku wanted to take Nol to her home quickly and change Nol's thoughts so that he no longer thought about his parents and his real home.

Bleku and Nol returned to the cave. Inside the home, there was good food. The game that Bleku had hunted was cooking. The smell of the food went outside the home and Nol felt hungry again. He went inside and Bleku gave him food. While they were walking back home, Nol's thinking had become confused. He no longer asked about the *masalai*'s home.

Nol sat and gorged himself, then he slept. Outside the cave, throughout the forests of the area, his parents and everyone from the village were calling out and looking for Nol. They did this for about one week. Some men slept in the forest hut and looked for Nol night and day.

However, Bleku had performed her song and dance and the door of the cave stayed completely dark. Only Bleku could look outside and see that people were looking for Nol. Nol did not know that people were trying to find him.

They searched and searched, but to no avail. They decided that Nol must have died, so they went back to the village. Bleku locked up Nol for a very long time. Nol stopped thinking about the village and his parents. He thought that he was completely entrapped inside the cave.

Bleku sang and danced then Nol became a real man. However, the smoke hid him whenever he went walking around. He would go to his parent's village and the other people of the village never saw him. This was because the smoke obscured him up to their eyes.

Nol himself could see clearly and he spoke to them. When he spoke, the people or his parents, would hear a bird calling, or a grasshopper or other insect crying out. His voice had changed and people did not know that the sound was from Nol's speaking.

When he went to hold his parents, the hair on their bodies would stand up. They did not know that this was a sign that Nol was holding them. He often did these things to the people of the village, but they had forgotten him long ago. They thought that he had died.

When his parents did hard work, Nol would go help them. However he would always go back to live with Bleku. The *masalai* woman had entirely become his mother. Bleku was happy with her son, so this area has rain and sun, and all of the foods grow very well, better than before.

Elijah Omele
Klai Nimbre Village
Goroka
Eastern Highlands Province

A1420+. Why food supply is plentiful; D42.2. Spirit takes shape of man; D683.2. Transformation by witch (sorceress); D908. Magic darkness;

D1223.1. Magic flute; D1317.7+. Magic flute gives alarm; D1361.1+. Magic smoke of invisibility; D1711. Magician; D1781. Magic results from singing; D1781+. Magic results from dancing; D1890. Magic aging; D1983. Invisibility conferred on person; D2000+. Magic confusion; D2143.1.2. Rain produced by singing; D2143.1.2+. Rain produced by dancing; D2143.2. Drought produced by magic; F490+. Masalai; F969.7. Famine; K1900. Impostures; P210. Husband and wife; P231. Mother and son; P233. Father and son; P272.1+. Sorceress foster mother; P275. Foster son; P310. Friendship; R45.3. Captivity in cave; R210. Escapes; R260. Pursuits

## Dogs Try to Find Their Real Skins

(Wantok 544, November 3, 1984, page 31)

Long, long ago, there were many hundred thousands of dogs on the earth. It looked as if the dogs had taken over the earth. One good thing was that they were people's best friends. They were also the best friends of wild game, flying birds and earth-bound birds.

The group of dogs had leaders that were like village chiefs (*luluai*) and assistant village chiefs (*tultul*) who ran things so that life in the village worked well. It was just like how we have government officials and village councilors in the village.

The dogs had a chairman who ran village meetings. There were also policemen to take care of law and order in the village.

They would appoint times for their meetings, but if something important happened in the village, they would call a meeting quickly.

When they did work in the village such as building a house for a villager, all would work hand-in-hand and finish the job in just one day. When they hunted for wild game, all of the he-dogs would go to the forest while the bitches would go process sago. Later, in the afternoon, they would all gather and make a big feast. If one was sick or if an enemy had killed one of them, they would all go together and mourn for the body.

You would feel sorry for yourself if you lived during this time of the dogs, oh my! You would think of removing your human skin and becoming one of the dogs. This was because their life was completely different — it was much better than the customs and life of us humans.

However one time, the earth turned. An important message went around to all of the places that the next morning at eight o'clock there would be an important meeting in their big meeting house. The chairman wanted everyone to come.

This was not really a day for holding a meeting. However, the chairman had sent a message to all of the councilors, village chiefs, and assistant village chiefs to meet in each of their group houses to explain to all that the meeting would be at eight o'clock in the morning.

The message went to all of the group houses. The next morning before it was eight o'clock, everyone came to meet at the meeting place.

Two of the dog policemen were in control and standing at the sides of the door. They were checking who had not come. They said that everyone had come in time for the big meeting.

However, before all of the dogs went inside to get their seats in the meeting house, each of them removed their skins and threw them up and around to the others.

After they all took their seats, the chairman opened their meeting at exactly eight o'clock in the morning. There were wild cries all around. At this time too, there was something flowing like water.

One dog sat and looked at the time on his hand[watch] then stood to excuse himself to the chairman, "Excuse me, mis… mister chairman." "Yessss boy. Can I help you?" said the chairman.

"Excuse me, misss… mister chairman, we've missed the food bell. What time will we go out to eat?" "Shut up, you!" said the chairman, "Did you come to eat or did you come for the meeting? Shut your dirty mouth and stay still or I'll send my officer to slap your mouth."

"Hey, I'm not angry, but look, many of us are very angry." "Shut up and stay still," said the chairman, "I told you to shut your mouth and stay still." The chairman said, "I told you to shut your stinking mouth and stay still. Are you a man or a wild pig?!" "Hey, don't call me a wild pig or I'll come and break your head with this chair. You fucking swine! Your belly's like that of a cow."

That was the end of the meeting. A fight broke out and all of the dogs broke ranks. Some went on the side of the chairman and some went on the side of the other one. Oh my, there had never been a fight like this before. It was tremendous. All of the chairs and tables were broken about. Many of the dogs ran away, leaving the village of the fight with their faces swollen.

However when they left the fight, not one of them took their real skins when they ran away. Each of them ran with the skins of the others.

Later, when they arrived at each of their group houses, they discovered that the skins that they had put on were not their real skins. So then, they went around looking for their real skins.

Try to watch carefully at dogs' wanderings in your area or if you travel to other places. You will see that when one dog walks up to meet another, it will first smell the other's buttocks and skin. If it smells like it is a friend's skin and not its own, it will leave and look for another. However, if it smells its real skin on the other dog, what do you think will happen? It will know this and two clouds will explode. You will see dust coming and you will think that earth will be near its last days.

Rex Namah
**Redi**
**Simbu** Province

A1000+. Earth will end when dogs find their real skins; A2471.1.1. Why dogs sniff at one another; B211.1.7. Speaking dog; B221+. Dog society; B241.2.7. King of dogs; B266. Animals fight; D531+. Transformation by removing skin; P310. Friendship; R220. Flights

## Kimaru and the Red Insects

(Wantok 545, November 10, 1984, page 31)

Before, in the time of the ancestors in the **Bundi** area of **Madang** Province, in the mountains of a village called **Emegari**, the red insects were called the men of this area [**Gende** People]. In my language, they call these red insects *nogorubu kena*.

These red insects were fighting men. When they went to fight, they often killed more than ten villages of their enemies. Emegari Village and **Tisawe** Village were two places that often pushed back and forth (*samsam*) at war. They often completely destroyed everything over the smallest thing.

They became the people of these three areas. However, the real origin of the Bundi was from these two villages. All of the men of Emegari Village were in the same clan as those in Tisawe. All of the girls ran between these three places.

There was one man who was a true leader. He was the leader of all fights. If the men of Tisawe grabbed an enemy during this man's time, he would cut the enemy's neck.

This man's name was Kimaru Korogia. He had much hair, and his hair spun around. He always rubbed tree oil on his hair. His hair went past his two shoulders and down his back.

This man, Kimaru Korogia, demanded recognition for every fight. Whether he fought with the enemies or not, the other men would grab an enemy and bring the enemy to him. Then Kimaru would cut his head off and he would be recognized for this. He would then tie a *tanget* leaf to a long rope and hang it up in the spirit house.

Kimaru would butcher the meat of this man. Then he would cook the meat with taros, sweet potatoes, pandanus fruits (*marita*), and make a large amount of soup. When he drank this soup, the fighters would dance fervently and sing while Kimaru was contented with his big pot of soup.

The pot was huge and made of clay. When he was not able to finish the soup, he would share it with his second-in-command who was also a leader.

Kimaru no longer worried about his daughters. They all had run away because the enemies killed his wives and children all of the time. However when the enemies killed one of Kimaru's wives, he would marry another woman. He always married young women whose breasts were still firm.

The girls of the village were completely tired of this and ran away. However Tisawe, the fighter, was not worried. They would go to steal the young women from other nearby villages or from enemy villages then bring them for Kimaru to marry. This behavior brought troubles and caused the men of Tisawe to fight again.

Kimaru's custom of eating men's flesh happened all of the time, so he became very sick. One time, he broke open an enemy's head and cut it up into small pieces, then he put it into a pot. He stirred it with leaves and sticks from wild taro. Then he ate.

His belly became completely bloated, so he slept inside the men's house. The men's house was jam-packed with bows and arrows, and bones and skulls of the enemies that Timaru [Kimaru] and his clan had killed.

Kimaru slept, then he began to hear his belly explode like thunder. His belly slowly expanded. The meat that he had butchered and made into soup for himself churned and churned in his belly.

The next night, he did not sleep well. His belly was still swollen and became like the big pot that he used to cook soup. His belly was swollen nearly up to his shoulders, so that he just looked like a man's head.

His intestines were terribly swollen. This was because he had a boil. Kimaru told his second-in-command to shoot the boil so that his belly would deflate a little. At night, he was in terrible pain and could not sleep.

The second-in-command sharpened a bamboo [spear] and lanced the boil. But he missed the pus and only blood came out. Later, the blood stopped flowing a little at the place of the boil and the real man's [eaten man's] flesh began to come out. The head from the pot including the man's ears was inside Kimaru's belly was showing.

Kimaru died. His belly deflated. The place near his breast looked like the man's head too. This happened because the opening of the pot had the man's two ears.

After Kimaru died, all of the men of Tisawe no longer thought about fighting. Their strength was gone. They did not fight back-and-forth as they had done before and their new daughters no longer ran away. Now in Bundi, people live together.

Gabriel Doa [Andbruk]
Esso PNG
Lae
Morobe Province

B16.6. Devastating insects; B224. Kingdom of insects; B246. King of insects; G11.18. Cannibal tribe; G91.2. Cannibalism causes death; G346. Devastating monster; G352+. Insect as ogre; P210. Husband and wife; P234. Father and daughter; R10. Abduction; R220. Flights; S133. Murder by beheading; T100. Marriage; T145.0.1. Polygyny; T192. Marriage by force; V112.1. Spirit huts

## A Snake Went inside a Boil

(Wantok 546, November 17, 1984, page 23)

Long ago, in the time of the ancestors, two women went looking for food and firewood in the forest. They found much firewood. When they went to look for more in the very deep forest, they piled the firewood at the base of a tree and departed.

At this time, the women were still gathering leafy greens, such as *tulip*, and pandanus fruits (*marita*). They tried to hunt marsupials (*kapul*), the favorite food of the people in this area.

It was nearly noon, and the sun was very hot. Amidst some boulders, there was a good, clear stream that ran down a small valley.

One woman told her friend, "Let's tie the firewood with a rope and pile it up. We'll bathe, then after [we've] cooled off, we'll take the firewood and walk back to the village."

The other woman, who had a boil on her back, told her friend, "I just carried a bundle of firewood on top of my head. Tomorrow, I'll return and get my other bundles. I can't carry them on my back."

Her friend agreed and they went to bathe in the cold water. The water was perfectly clear and clean. They bathed well and cooled off.

The woman with the boil on her back saw something among the boulders in the water, near the place where they

had bathed. The woman looked down and saw a short snake. This snake was fat and very awkward.

The woman found a tree leaf then covered the head and mouth of the snake. She held the snake by its head. The snake had just shed its skin, so its body was very soft. The woman was very happy and tied the snake with a rope. She told the other woman who was bathing.

The woman returned to the nearby forest to cut bamboo. She cut just one piece and returned to get the snake to put inside the bamboo. She closed the opening of the bamboo with a new tree leaf.

She put the bamboo with the snake in her net bag. Then the two women carried their firewood and walked back towards the village.

The bamboo with the snake rested well inside the net bag with the leafy greens that the woman had filled it with. These things did not hurt the boil on the woman's back too much.

She had put a big bundle of firewood on her head. The other woman had slung two bundles with rope on her back. She had tied the other bundle carefully and carried it on her head. The net bags of food were on top of the two firewood bundles on her back. She did this so that the other woman would not have too heavy a load.

They left some firewood there because they would return the next day. The woman with the boil would also get her kin to go and help her with the firewood.

They walked slowly and told stories as they went along. The other woman carried a heavy load, so they walked very slowly. It was afternoon, the time when people usually returned to the village after working in the gardens or going to the forest.

The woman felt the site of the boil itching a little. She felt a movement coming from the boil, so she asked her friend, "Hey, put down the firewood on your head and see what's moving around." When the other woman looked, she screamed and cried.

The woman saw the tail of the snake just hanging out. At the site of the boil was a big hole with a sore. The woman cried and wanted to grab the snake's tail, but the snake quickly pulled its tail inside.

While they had been walking along, the snake in the bamboo tube had smelled the woman's boil and shoved its head inside. When the tree leaves that covered the bamboo had fallen off, the snake left the net bag and went to eat the boil on her back. It had eaten and eaten until only its tail was hanging outside. When the other woman had wanted to pull it, it was too late.

They threw down all of the firewood and walked quickly back to the village. At the village, the woman told her husband and her kin that she would die because a snake was inside her body.

The men of the village did not know what to do now. That night, the woman cooked much food because she knew that she was about to die.

The snake ate everything inside the woman's belly, then ate the food that was in her. After that, it ate the veins and arteries, then it ate the woman's liver and the woman died.

The woman had put the snake in her bag and carried it to the village. She had done this so that later, the two women would cut, cook and eat the snake with *tulip* leaves that they had collected in the forest.

When the woman died, they cut open her body and took the snake out. The snake was not dead. It had eaten everything inside the woman's body and had become big and engorged.

Later, the men buried the woman in a grave. They gathered the firewood and piled it up well in the middle of the village. At night, the woman's husband cut the snake with an axe and put it on top of the firewood. He put more firewood on top of this, lit the fire and burned the snake.

Rosa Kapa
**Gumine** [Village, **Golin** People]
**Simbu** Province

G328+. Snake enters boil/wound and devours victim; P210. Husband and wife; P310. Friendship; V61.3+. Dead buried

## A Ghost Helped a Pregnant Woman

(Wantok 547, November 24, 1984, page 23)

Long, long ago, there was a little stream by Sapanaut [**Japanaut**] Village, in the Sepik River area [**Iatmul** People, **East Sepik** Province]. The name of this stream was Kilvan. This stream went through the Dagugun Clan's land.

There was a big fig tree that stood by this stream. A forest ghost dwelled at the base of this fig tree. The name of the ghost was Yavudabui. He was the Dagugun's kin.

One time when the Sepik River was flooded, the water overflowed its banks and went into the Kilvan Stream. The fish filled this stream, so the Dagugun women brought nets and caught many, many fish.

At this time, there was a young Dagugun man who was newly married in the village. His wife was pregnant, so this woman did not go to catch fish.

The newly married man's kin did not help him with his wife. The newlyweds did not have any fish to cook and eat, so the young pregnant woman took her net anyway and went to catch fish.

She often caught fish in the stream near the fig tree. She was not worried about the ghost Yavudabui who lived at the base of the fig tree. She just went fishing there for three whole weeks. She was pregnant, but she was not worried. She was just happy to be catching fish.

On the fourth week, the woman slept and felt a great pain in her belly. She thought that it was just an ordinary pain in her belly, so she told her husband in the morning that she would go check on the net by the fig tree.

The woman's husband cut firewood and waited by the house. When the woman was pulling in the fish by the fig tree, she felt the pain become stronger in her belly.

The pain overcame the poor woman and she lost her strength. She could not stand firmly or walk, so she gently put her legs out and sat at the base of the tree.

There were no other men or women nearby. She cried softly from the pain for a while, then she gave birth. However, the ghost Yavudabui and his wife, who were inside their house, were watching this woman. Yavudabui's house was inside the base of the fig tree.

Yavudabui watched for a while, then he felt very sorry for the young woman who had given birth. He told his wife to go help the young woman. So, Yavudabui's wife walked out and stood near the young woman.

When the young woman saw Yavudabui's wife, she was terrified. She had just given birth and was holding the newborn. She was afraid that the ghost woman would eat the new baby.

However, Yavudabui's wife gave a careful explanation to the young woman, and the woman believed her. The young woman carried her baby and followed the ghost woman up to Yavudabui's house.

The ladder to the house was just made of rope. The young woman worked hard, carrying the baby and holding the rope, as she went up to the house door. She placed her legs very slowly and went up to the verandah of the house.

The ghost Yavudabui was sitting there. He asked the young woman, "To which clan do you belong?" The young woman said, "I belong to the Dagugun Clan." "So, don't be afraid. You must just be happy here. You came directly to your home. We who live here are the same clan as you who live outside."

Yavudabui finished speaking, then went and killed a chicken. He gave it to the young woman and her baby. The young woman cooked the chicken. She and the little baby ate the chicken.

Yavudabui let the young woman and the baby sleep in the house. He promised that the woman's husband would come on the next afternoon and take her back to the village. However, Yavudabui was just talking nonsense and did not let the woman go outside.

The young woman's husband waited and waited until the next afternoon, then he left to find his wife. He approached the fig tree and saw much blood at the base of the tree. He thought that enemies had killed his wife at this place.

The poor young man walked and walked, then went around the area of the fig tree and cried. However, his wife was up in the Yavudabui's house where she saw her husband. The woman was very sorry for her husband because the man had seen the blood at the base of the fig tree and was crying and mournful. The young man believed that enemies had killed his wife, so he went back to the village.

The ghost Yavudabui and his wife took care of the young woman and her little baby well. They lived in this house for two whole years. The little boy kicked his legs and walked around.

Yavudabui saw that the boy could walk now and he was ready to send him and his mother back to the village. So, Yavudabui killed two pigs and filled two net bags with plenty of food for the young woman.

Yavudabui spoke clearly to the young woman, "I must give you much food to bring away lest the clan think that I'm a pauper."

At twelve o'clock noon the next day, Yavudabui sent the young woman and her son to the village. The young woman put the pork and food inside a canoe, and the little boy sat at the bow of the canoe. The mother sat at the stern.

The young woman and her son paddled and followed the Sepik River for a little while, then arrived at the village. At this time, the woman's husband was working in the garden by the river. The young woman saw her husband. However, her husband did not recognize his wife and son.

The young man thought hard. He thought, "This young woman looks exactly like my wife." He thought that his wife had died, so he did not speak.

The woman and child paddled the canoe ashore and approached the place where the man was standing. The man walked closer and looked harder at the woman and child.

The woman surprised the man. She said, "Look at your son. He's sitting at the bow of the canoe."

It was true. The man was ecstatic and jumped around. He held his son and tears flowed.

The man made a big feast and killed many of his pigs. All of the other people gathered and were happy for the woman and her son who had left and returned. The woman's young husband took much pork and brought to the base of the fig tree.

Simeon Kevu

P. O. Box 1276

Lae

Morobe Province

E276. Ghosts haunt tree; E320. Dead relative's friendly return; F81.1.2+. Journey to land of dead; P210. Husband and wife; P231. Mother and son; P233. Father and son; R49.1. Captivity in tree; T570. Pregnancy; T580. Childbirth

## Abut and the *Masalai* Woman
(Wantok 548, December 1, 1984, page 27)

In Mansuat [**Mensuat**] Village, in the Biwat area, in **East Sepik** Province, there was a man named Abut [**Bisis** People]. One time, the women of the village wanted to go fishing in a stream, so they asked Abut to bring them to the forest. Abut's sister was among these women, she was Kaigan's wife.

At about six o'clock in the morning, they left the village and walked into the forest. They arrived at the stream, then Abut left the women there and walked directly to a place called Yambinobot [**Yaminbot** Village, **Mekmek** People] to get his bows.

When he arrived at Yambimbot [Yaminbot], it was about twelve o'clock noon. He went to get his bows and wanted to return, but the men of Yambimbot Village told him to eat first. So Abut sat and ate, then at about two o'clock, he left Yambimbot and went back towards the village.

Abut followed the trail to the village. While he was still walking along the trail, the women left the forest and arrived back at the village. He arrived at the place where they said that they would meet him. He saw his sister, Kaigan's wife, just waiting there.

Abut wanted to go past her, but she told him, "Brother sit and eat a little first. The women left you and went back. Only I thought about you and waited here. Here's your sago. Sit and eat."

However, Abut did not want to do this. He thought that before, his [sister] never called out for him to eat. Then he thought that he did not want to stand there, so he walked away quietly.

The woman kept telling him to eat, but Abut was insistent that he had already eaten and that he did not want any food. The woman was persistent and Abut tried to ignore her talking while the two of them walked away. They walked together and talked for a while until they arrived at a place in the trail where a tree had broken and fallen down, blocking the trail.

Abut saw this and jumped on top of the tree. He stood there and saw the woman walking behind him. The woman arrived at the tree, but she did not jump on top of it. She walked around the tree to its crown. Oh my, when Abut saw this, he knew that it was not a real woman following him, it was a *masalai* woman.

He began to run now. While he was running, he looked behind. The woman had gone around the tree and was coming down the trail. She too began to run, following Abut.

Abut ran and ran, then he looked and saw a man walking towards him. He was completely out of breath and called out to the man to stand and help him. However the man saw this, so he got up and turned, then sped back towards the village.

This man's name was Mukuai. Abut called out, "Hey, Mukuai, stand and help me." But no, Mujuai [Mukuai] kept going. When the two of them arrived at the village, Mukuai ran directly home, but poor Abut fell down in a ditch half-dead because all of the wind was knocked out of him.

All of the men of the village ran out and saw Abut. They asked him what it was that was chasing him when he had run and fallen down. He just said a few words, "I'll tell you later."

The *masalai* woman was following Abut. When she saw the men coming to get Abut out of the ditch, she did not approach them. She said, "That's alright that he's not alone. Many men live there. Later, I'll ruin one of them." So, she just left and stood among the men.

When Abut was all right again, he told the men that the *masalai* woman had fooled him in the forest and chased him back to the village. One of the men, whose name was Marinokuan, laughed and said, "He's testing you boys, but he can't do it to me." He did not know that the *masalai* woman was standing among them and listening to what he said.

One time, this man, Marinokuan, wanted to go to the forest and look at his bird blind that was on top of a big, tall fig tree. He left his wife in the village and walked alone into the forest.

When he arrived at his bird blind, he went inside and prepared the spears at each of the holes of the blind. He finished his preparations then he wanted to just sit down. He saw his wife approaching.

The woman called up to him, "I'm was tired of staying at the house, so I followed you here to the forest." Poor Marinokuan listened and called down for the woman to come up to the bird blind.

The woman went up the tree and into the bird blind. The woman was carrying some food and told Marinokuan to eat. After he ate, the woman sat close to him. He became aroused, and the two of them slept together.

When they finished, the woman got up and changed her face. She laughed and said, "Hah, you thought that I was your wife!" The man was speechless because he knew that the *masalai* woman had fooled him.

The *masalai* woman told him, "When you return to the village, you must tell your real wife that you've been ruined."

So Marinokuan left the bird blind and went back down to the ground. He walked and walked to the village. He arrived in the village and went directly to his house. He went inside the kitchen and told his wife to make a fire for him to lie near.

His wife made a fire, then Marinokuan went and lay near the fire. He told his wife, "Go cut all of the betel nuts and kill all my pigs. I'm ruined. A *masalai* woman had sex with me."

Marinokuan's wife followed her husband's instructions. She went to cut all of the betel nuts and kill all her husband's pigs. When she returned to the house, she saw that her husband was dead.

Masai Manum told this story. Morris Manum wrote it down and sent it.

Morris Manum
c/- Augustine Abut
Wewak Timber
P. O. Box 219
Madang Province

D94+W. Transformation: spirit to woman; F402.1.10. Spirit pursues person; F441.6.3. Sexual relations with wood-spirit fatal; F490+. Masalai; K800. Fatal deception; K1311+. Seduction by masking as man's wife; K1900. Impostures; K1910. Marital impostors; P210. Husband and wife; P253. Sister and brother; R220. Flights; R260. Pursuits

## The Man Who Became a Jimbir Pig

(Wantok 549, December 8, 1984, page 23)

Long ago, there was a man who often put on a pig's skin and went to kill many, many pigs for the big feasts that were often held in his village.

One day, the people of the village wanted to make a huge festival. They told the people of the other nearby villages to come to the big festival.

A man who was going to this festival first asked his maternal relative to go kill a pig. This relative had power that the other people of the village did not know about.

The maternal relative often went to the forest to a place where he had hidden a pig's skin. He would put on the pigskin, sing and dance, then turn into a real pig.

The man who was going to the festival went first to his maternal relative and asked, "You are a man who knows much about how to hunt and kill pigs, so I want you to go hunt some pigs then we'll compensate you."

The maternal relative said, "Don't worry. When do you want the pigs?" The man told his maternal relative that he wanted the pigs right away, so the relative went into the forest and put on his pigskin. He killed many, many pigs.

He carried them and piled them up in one part of the forest. The man removed his skin and put it away, then he walked like a real man back to the village. He told his relative and the girls to go carry the pigs to the village. They butchered the pigs, made an earth oven, and ate at the big festival.

The people of the village did this often. Whichever man in the village had a large task and wanted to make a feast would go ask this man to kill pigs. Later, they would pay him with traditional wealth.

The people of the village did not know that he had special powers, that he put on pigskin and killed other pigs. They just thought that the man had "good blood" and that he excelled at killing pigs.

The man would put on the pigskin, then he would go to all of the corners of the forest regardless of whether there was very dense forest where there were many thorny rattans or other vines, or whether there was a swamp or a large mountain. The man would turn into a pig and go forth.

Sometimes, he would arrive at the home of the pigs and speak with the father of the pigs who was the boar who ruled all pigs. He would ask whether the father pig could give some pigs to him. The father pig would tell him, "Don't worry. Just go walking into the forest and there will be some pigs. Just hunt and kill them."

The man often killed pigs, then he would leave them there at only one place. The men of the village would go directly to the place where the man had marked. They would butcher the pigs and the women would carry them back to the village.

For many years, this man was the best at killing pigs. Then one day, the man's maternal relative thought about how he had killed so many pigs while the other men of the village had not.

He thought to himself, "Now if he returns into the forest, I'll follow him and see what it is that he does to kill so many pigs all of the time."

One day, the man wanted to go to the forest again. In the afternoon, he sat and sharpened his spears. The maternal relative asked him, "Are you just sharpening your spears or will you be walking into the forest?"

The man replied, "Kinsman, some people asked me to go hunt one or two pigs, so tomorrow I'll go walking a little into the forest."

In the early morning, the man departed. His maternal relative sat watching and then he followed him. He explained to his wife that he was going to wake up quietly and just depart. He wanted to find out how his kinsman killed so many more pigs than any other man in the village did.

When he arrived in the forest, he hid and saw the man put on the pigskin. Quickly, he turned into a pig and trotted through the forest.

His maternal relative watched and thought, "So it's true, this man has a kind of power that enables him to excel at killing pigs. Now I know."

He finished watching then walked back to the village. Later, the other man also returned to the village and sent the women to go carry the pigs that he had killed and put in the forest.

Another day, the maternal relative who had hidden and spied walked into the forest. He arrived at the place where his maternal relative hid the pigskin.

The man took the pigskin and put it on top of his body. He sped off to hunt for pigs. However, he did not kill any pigs. This was because the pigskin was not something that belonged to him. It belonged to another man. Only that man had the power to put on the pigskin and remove it again.

The man traveled to all of the places in the forest. Later, near evening, he returned to the place where he had taken the pigskin. He wanted to remove it, but he was unable to do so. The skin was completely stuck. He turned and turned on the dirt and grasses, but he could not remove the pigskin.

The man became a pig completely. At the village, his wife waited until it was dark. The next morning, the man's wife was worried. She went to his maternal relative and told him what had happened.

The man listened and went to the place where he usually put the pigskin, but the skin was not there. He returned and explained to the people that his maternal relative must have hidden and seen his power, then turned into a pig.

Philippa Kurai
Kimbe
West New Britain Province

["Jimbir" is the name of a pig from long ago among the **Manambu** People, **East Sepik** Province. See the stories by D. Takendu in *Oral History* 5(5): 2-53, 1977.]

B221+. Kingdom of swine; D114.3.2M. Transformation: man to boar; D336.1M. Transformation: pig to man; D531. Transformation by putting on skin; D791.2. Disenchantment by only one person; D1449+. Magic skin gives hunting power; D1781. Magic results from singing; D1781+. Magic results from dancing; P210. Husband and wife; P290+. Maternal kin; Q212. Theft punished; Q551.3.2+. Punishment: transformation into pig; R260. Pursuits

## The Mistake of Eating Eel

(Wantok 550, December 15, 1984, page 23)

Long ago, in the time of the ancestors, there was a *masalai* eel that lived in a lake. One time, the women of the village went and looked for food near the water.

One woman saw the huge eel and was terrified. She saw that it was still far away. She thought that it was a snake and called out to the other women who were working at gathering *tulip* leaves near the lake.

The woman stood and watched the big *masalai* eel shooting beneath the water. Part of the eel's body was on top of the water, but its head was still beneath the water.

The women were terrified. They quickly left the area and went back to the village. They arrived there and explained to their husbands what had happened. In the afternoon, all of the men of the village gathered and shared their thoughts about how to get the big *masalai*.

A leader of the village told all of the men at the meeting, "Long ago, before you were born, we often went to find food in that area, but we never found any marsupials (*kapul*), birds, pigs or small cassowaries. This is because of the *masalai* that lives in the water. This *masalai* often hides the food in a clearing while we miss it and go walking in another part of the forest."

He also said, "Even if the sun would shine brightly for many months, this water would not dry up, not even a little like other lakes would. We have been too afraid to go to this place. However tomorrow in the early morning before dawn, you shall go and finish off all of the bad things that live in that lake."

That night, the men sharpened their arrows carefully and readied their bows. Then they were well prepared to leave in the early morning. The next morning, before dawn, all of the men of the village spilled out towards the lake.

They took three young girls with them because the *masalai* eel would see the three beautiful girls then come up to the clearing from the water. If the eel saw the men, it would hide.

They hid around the nearby forest, but the *masalai* eel knew that the men were nearby. It had smelled them long before while they were approaching the eel's lake.

However, when the eel saw the finely dressed beautiful girls who were standing by the water, the *masalai* came out from hiding and shot its tail up near the girls.

The girls screamed in terror. Then the men spat ginger and went down towards the water. They entered the water, but the ground was muddy. They took sticks and spears and tried to find the *masalai*.

All of the men stood in a row and fenced in one side of the water. They went together with the spears and sticks. They shot the sticks down and they dug through the muck.

They approached the place, which was very deep at one corner. They joined their long sticks together with ropes. At the end of the sticks they tied their spears. They worked at spearing the ground with them.

Then one man shot the *masalai* eel right in its head. When the *masalai* felt this, it turned and twisted. The man stayed on the ground, threw a spear and fell down very badly.

The other men went and helped him. They took more spears and shot them down at this place. Then they had a direct hit on the eel and pulled it up. They brought it up and speared it all over its body.

The *masalai* eel died. They made a small platform and carried the eel to the village. That afternoon, the men butchered the eel meat and cooked it in bamboo tubes.

That night, all of the men, women and children gathered in one place. They cooked bananas and sweet potatoes in an earth oven then mixed it with the eel meat. The people were happy, they sang and danced. The men beat the signal drums and hand drums.

That night, they feasted, danced and sang until daybreak. Afterwards, they went to sleep around their houses. A flock of birds approached the village, circled around the village then flew back again.

The people slept and lazed about because the meat of the *masalai* eel had made them exhausted. Later, they heard the clouds thunder and felt a large earthquake. They stopped sleeping. Everyone awoke, opened their eyes and trembled.

They were afraid and just stayed inside their houses. They watched the earth break apart at all of the corners of the village; a big flood arose. They saw their little village drifting in the middle of the water.

Before long, they saw that the mainland was very far away. The little island drifted to the middle of the sea and became **Karkar** Island [**Madang** Province]. The village is **Dumad** [**Takia** People].

So, the people of Boran Village [**Matiu Number 2**] on this island never eat eel. They believe that if they eat eel, all of the pigs would die. Eating eel is a big tabu at this place. These people ate the *masalai* eel before at Boran Village in the time of the ancestors.

Boran Village used to be on the mainland. However, their mistake of eating the *masalai* eel made their village break apart and become Karkar Island.

Steven Foluy
Bareodige Village
North Coast
Madang Province

A955+. Island separated from mainland; A1018. Flood as punishment; B874.2. Giant eel; C221.1.3.2. Tabu: eating eel; D967+. Magic ginger; D1001. Magic spittle; D2148. Earth magically caused to quake; D2149.1. Thunderbolt magically produced; D2151.8. Magic flood; F420.1.3.2+. Water-spirit as eel; F490+. Masalai; P210. Husband and wife; Q211. Murder punished; Q552.25. Earthquake as punishment


# Lapa Kella Wronged the Sail Kusi Clan

(Wantok 551, December 22, 1984, page 27)

Long, long ago, in the time of the ancestors, there was a bird that lived in one part of the forest. The name of this bird was Lapa Kella. Whenever the bird slept, he stayed inside a cave. There were no people who lived near this part of the forest. The people lived very far away.

The bird was famished. First he looked for food, but he could not find any, so he became hungrier. Then the bird flew to a place where there was a garden. He wanted to steal ripe bananas, but he saw a woman working there who was weeding her garden.

The bird was famished and he wanted to fill his belly, but he saw the woman and was terrified that the woman might break one of his wings. The bird watched the bananas and stayed near where the woman was working.

Near the garden, there was a huge tree that was fruiting, but these were not fruits that a bird could eat. The bird had been famished for a long time, so he tried eating these fruits.

The bird tried the fruits. The fruits tasted delicious, like no other. The bird sated himself on the food until he was bloated. The discarded parts of the fruits fell down around the base of the tree, but some of them fell down on top of a little baby that was sleeping under the tree.

The baby felt pained. The bird was surprised to hear the baby crying. The baby's mother had put him to sleep in a net bag and hung the bag underneath the tree. The mother did not hear the baby crying. She was working hard, weeding the garden.

Lapa Kella went down and lifted up the baby with the net bag and carried the baby to the cave that was his home. The baby's net bag was not too heavy because Lapa was not small. He was a huge bird.

Lapa put the baby to sleep and the baby stopped crying. The bird made a nice bed from dried grasses and leaves, then the baby slept well there.

The bird flew again to another place. The bird stole some pork fat and some other things. When the baby awoke, Lapa gave the baby the pork fat as if it was milk, and the baby drank it.

Lapa did this all of the time. The bird would fly and steal meat, ripe bananas, wildfowl eggs from the forest, and chickens from the villages too.

Some men often found Lapa stealing food and they wanted to shoot him down. But no, Lapa's long talons gripped the food well and Lapa would quickly fly away. The men would always miss.

The bird did this sort of thing, giving various kinds of foods to the baby until he became a boy and then a big man. He could not stay in the cave any longer.

Another time, Lapa flew to a village and stole axes, bows, arrows, and other things. The bird took these things back to the man to use and work with.

Lapa took his son and showed him these things. Then the bird told him how to hold his legs. The man held one of Lapa's legs then the bird carried him and stood him on the ground.

Lapa taught him they ways of making gardens and houses, and other kinds of hard work that people do. He erected a huge house. By the house there was a big garden with various kinds of foods growing. He and Lapa lived happily in this house.

One day, Lapa flew up to a mountain. The bird sat on top of a tree and saw many, many women working in their gardens. Because some days had passed, Lapa saw his son working very hard alone in the garden. A hard, sharp thorn from a vine stabbed his hand and he screamed in pain.

Lapa saw him in pain and was angry, but the bird thought and stayed quietly. Then the bird flew and perched on a tree. There was water running under this tree. The young women from the gardens were gulping water here. The last young woman came to drink water.

Just before the woman went to drink water, Lapa threw some trash down into the water. The woman saw that the water was dirty and she was reluctant to drink. She looked up the tree and saw the huge bird throwing trash down. The young woman threw a stone and blasted the bird, but he was not a real bird, he was Lapa!

The bird pretended to die and fell down asleep on the ground. The woman was about to go and hold the bird when he flew far away. The bird had tricked her and let the young woman follow him up to the source of the stream.

The woman entered the deep forest where Lapa and his son's big garden was located. The woman was afraid and she looked around. The young man, the son of Lapa, saw the woman and called out for her to go into the house.

Oh my! The woman was surprised when the man asked her because something had pulled her to his home with the bird. The woman told him about the bird and the man listened. He told the woman to go with him to his house.

Inside the house, the woman saw the huge bird lying by the fire. The woman asked the young man, but the man turned and told a story about some other things.

Rain was falling and the woman wanted to go back to her home. However, the rain was very heavy and blocked the way, so the woman slept in the house in the deep forest.

In the morning, the man and woman awoke. They saw a huge pig sleeping at the door. The woman was surprised, but the man understood that his father had stolen the pig and brought it there.

They butchered the pig and cooked it in an earth oven with other food. They sat together and ate. The young woman did not think any more about going home quickly. This was because she lusted for this young man and the good things at this place.

They lived together and then the woman asked the man to take her to her home. However, the young man did not know where the woman's village was, and the woman was also confused about the way to go.

However, Lapa knew. So, his son asked Lapa to go first and show the way to him and the woman. They walked until they arrived at the woman's home.

The people of the village saw the woman arrive with the handsome young man and they were surprised. Many of them were happy, but the woman's siblings and parents were not happy.

Some of the woman's kin thought that the man had raped her and hidden her, so they wanted to shoot him with bows and arrows. However, the young woman thought of the man and forbade her kin from doing this.

The woman explained that she had followed a huge bird and entered the deep forest. The young man had taken care of her, but the woman's parents were still angry. They told their daughter that she must go back with her husband.

The woman's kin wanted the young man to pay a bride price. They would be happy for such a payment. So, the woman and the man returned to the man's home.

Lapa, the bird, was staying at the house. He took a huge pig and three little pigs. He took these pigs with plenty of other food and placed them by the house.

His son and the woman saw that these things were ready, and they were surprised. There was even a rope that tied the pigs to a wooden post.

Some days later, the woman's kin went to get their payment. They also took four pigs with them. The first pig was very big. They wanted the man to take their pigs. The man's kin would give pigs and other payments to the woman's kin.

They gathered together and agreed on the payments. They understood that the woman was married to this young man. Later, they killed the pigs and divided the meat among themselves.

Lapa wanted the first big pig from the woman's kin very much. He asked his son whether he could butcher this pig, but the son forbade him. Lapa's son scolded him three times. Old Lapa was angry.

He himself wanted to butcher the pig, but his son did not want this. It would be bad if the woman's kin saw this huge bird cutting the pig with his talons and then they gossiped.

The son completely ignored what his father said. He held one of his father's legs and threw his body into the forest. Lapa flew and perched on a tree by the house and stared. The son was sorry and called out for his father to come butcher the pig, but the father was angry and refused.

Then he called out, "Ke-ke-ke-ke-ke," and flew to the top of a mountain. His old house and his son were still there. He called out again, "_Sail-kusi, sail-kusi, sail-kusi_!"

This phrase, _sail-kusi_, means, "You won't have the strength to fight, make gardens, fight men, or do other things. Your descendants will be completely lost." The son understood this. He sat and tears fell. He cried and cried.

The woman's kin saw this and were sorry. They let their daughter stay with her husband and they carried all of their things back to the village.

This bird, Lapa Kella called out and flew though the deep forest to the top of a mountain. Then he left completely and never returned.

His son and the bride live entirely at this place. Later, they raised many children. Their clan took the name, "Sail Kusi." The Sail Kusi Clan is still in existence.

John Pokia
Wake Youth Group
P. O. Box 243
Kieta
North Solomons Province

[Mr. Pokia wrote the ancestor story in _Wantok_ #558. He is from between the **Southern Highlands** and **Enga** Provinces (**Huli**, **Mendi** or **Katinja** People).]

A1640+. Origin of Sail Kusi Clan; B31.6. Other giant birds; B211.3. Speaking bird; B535.0.7. Bird as nurse for child; B552. Man carried by bird; K300. Thefts and cheats—general; K1860. Deception by feigned death (sleep); M411.1. Curse by parent; P210. Husband and wife; P230. Parents and children; P232. Mother and daughter; P233. Father and son; P234. Father and daughter; P261. Father-in-law; P262. Mother-in-law; P265. Son-in-law; P271. Foster father; P275. Foster son; R13.3. Person carried off by bird; R260. Pursuits; T10. Falling in love; T52. Bride purchased; T100. Marriage; Z71.1. Formulistic number: three

## Why the Rain Falls

(Wantok 552, January 5, 1985, page 23)

Long ago, in the time of the ancestors, there were just two men's heads in one area. A big bad time arose in this place where the two heads lived.

There was a strong sun for many months without the slightest rain falling. The area where the two heads lived was completely dry and burning hot. There was not the smallest stream nearby to which the two heads could roll and cool off.

They stayed there until they thought that they would die. Then one day, the heads thought that the water must be where the sun rises. So when it was still early in the morning, the two heads went away. They rolled and rolled into the forest, into the sword grasses, over bare earth, persistently trying to find water.

In the forest where they turned and rolled, they arrived at a huge road. This road looked like many hundred men had rolled big ironwood logs across it.

Every part of the forest and sword-grassland was completely nailed to the ground. This was the road that the men's heads followed. At the place where there was a mountain, the heads went along the side.

They rolled and rolled for nearly a week, but there was no place for them to stop. Every place was completely dry and very hard, then a strong wind arose. They went a very long way. While they were going along, the villagers who lived on some mountains heard thunder. They thought that heavy rain and strong winds would come, but it would not.

The heads kept going towards a place that was cooler. One head turned and told his friend, "I feel cooler now. I think the water must be close."

The two heads were men. They had the eyes, ears, mouths, and heads of men. However, they did not have necks, legs, or arms. They rolled and arrived at a small stream. This stream was dry, but there was still a little water that looked like a puddle.

The heads both went down to the water and felt cold. One went back up to the ground. He did this because he was afraid that he could gain weight and be stuck in the water forever.

He went up and took a ginger (_gorgor_) leaf, and then wrapped it into a cup, so that he could draw water for himself to drink.

The other head was still below in the water. He was drinking and drinking until he was completely filled and his eyes spun around. Then he wanted to go up, but he was unable to do so. The head was heavy. He rolled and rolled around the puddle, making the water go down completely.

His friend, who was still on the ground, looked and did not see the head in the water anymore. He was more concerned that if he went down too, he would go the same way. He was afraid and he cried for his friend. He rolled and rolled then arrived at a small, nearby mountain that he made his new home.

Every time he went to the water where his friend was, he would only use the leaf to draw water. Then he would return. He always did this. The two heads still do this. Now, the two heads are broken. One lives on the mountain and the other lives at the source of the stream.

The man's head on the mountain often thinks back about his friend in the water. In the morning, he wakes up then worries and cries. When it is sunny, he looks for food. In the afternoon, he returns to his home and worries again for his friend and cries again. Because of this, we see the rain fall on top of the mountain area every afternoon and morning [a common occurrence in the tropics].

Because the other head is in the water, much [cold] water flows down even if the sun shines for many months.

Mathew Uba

Block 1489, Galai [Settlement Block] 1

Kimbe

West New Britain Province

[Mr. Uba also wrote the ancestor story in *Wantok* #538. He is probably from **East Sepik** Province.]

A1131.1. Rain from tears; D1610.5. Speaking head; F501. Person consisting only of head; P310. Friendship

## The Ghost Man of the Mountain

(Wantok 553, January 12, 1985, page 23)

Long, long ago, in a part of the forest on a mountain called Tuweifu, the men of Rawete [**Rauwetei**] Village often went to make their camps to hunt for marsupials (*sikau*) [**Olo** People, **West Sepik** Province]. At the place where the people made camps, there lived a ghost man. His name was Huwou.

This ghost man, Huwou, often chased men who tried to go sleep on the mountain and hunt for marsupials. He always did this, so the men hunting for marsupials never found any wild game.

One time, the men of Rawete Village were angry and decided to kill Huwou, so they went to the mountain where they would erect a house and then prepare to kill the ghost man.

After they erected the house, they made a bonfire, cooked breadfruits and also heated stones. They hung up three stalks of betel nuts on the door of the house. One of the stalks was good and the other two were bad.

While the men sat by the fire, it started to become dark. The insects of the forest began to sing, and other sounds of the forest arose as well. Before long, they heard the ghost man Huwou approaching the house where they were sitting.

The ghost man knocked on the door and asked the men whether he could go inside the house. The men inside the house replied, "If you finish the three stalks of betel nuts that are hanging outside the house, we'll open the door and you can come inside the house."

Huwou listened to this and removed the three stalks of betel nuts. He did not care whether the betel nuts were bad, he swallowed them and called out for the men to let him inside the house.

However, the men inside the house said, "No, we won't let you come inside the house until you finish the breadfruits."

The men took a breadfruit and broke it in the middle. They threw one piece out and Huwou swallowed it like water. Then they threw another piece outside and it just vanished inside the ghost's mouth.

When the men saw this, they took another big breadfruit and threw it outside. They had not broken this breadfruit, but the ghost did not care and just swallowed the second breadfruit.

The men saw this and winched up the house door a crack. They told Huwou, "Lie down and shove your two legs inside first because that is how we go inside the house."

The poor ghost man listened and thought that the men were telling the truth. He lay down and shoved his legs inside the house, then very slowly he worked at shoving his body inside.

When his two legs were inside the door, the men winched the door up a little more until the man's belly was directly under the house door. Then the men threw the door back down and trapped his belly.

The door was stuck. The men jumped down and took ropes, tying one leg to one doorpost and the other leg to the other post. The poor ghost man did not have a way to escape.

The men very quickly took the stones that they had heated in the fire and shoved them up the ghost's rectum until he was dead.

After the ghost Huwou was dead, the men took him and shoved him inside the house. Then all of the men left the house and went outside. They took the fire and lit the house. The ghost man burned with the house. The men ran away back to their village.

Now, on this place on the mountain where the men had killed this *masalai* [ghost], there is an ironwood post still standing. This is a post from the house that the men had made when they killed the ghost.

When the men of Rawete Village go to this place, they are not able to return to the village because they become confused and walk aimlessly until they enter the very deep forest.

Daniel Wamtau

Rawete

Lumi

West Sepik Province

C612. Forbidden forest; C612+. Forbidden mountain; E261.4. Ghost pursues man; E425.2. Revenant as man; E446.2. Ghost laid by burning body; E541. Revenants eat; F408.3. Spirits dwell at tabu place; F387. Fairy captured; F490+. Masalai; F910. Extraordinary swallowings; K1111. Dupe puts hand (paws) into cleft of tree (wedge, vise); R260. Pursuits; S112+. Murder by putting hot stones up rectum; Z71.1. Formulistic number: three

## Baili Oddo Became a *Masalai* Snake

(Wantok 554, January 19, 1985, page 23)

Long ago, there was a man whose name was Baili Oddo. He was from **Garu** Village [**Bola** People] and he had married a woman from **Kandoka** Village [**Kove** People, **West New Britain** Province].

The married couple lived for many years and had many children. Later, the man often cursed and beat his wife, and ridiculed her parents. The woman was always troubled but she just stayed there.

After a while, the woman grew tired of this treatment by her husband. So one day, she woke up and carried her little baby towards the beach. They took a canoe and paddled to her village.

The woman arrived at her parents' house and she cried to them about the bad things that her husband had often done to her. The father told her their good story and the daughter told them about all of the ridicule that her husband had given them.

The woman's father listened then told his daughter, "I've heard all your troubles. I have one thought for your husband. You and your baby sleep now. Tomorrow, you'll return to the village and tell your husband. Then you'll come next week and we'll do some traditional work. You must bring all of the children together."

The woman and her child slept. In the morning, they awoke and returned to the man's village. The woman told her husband that her father wanted them all to go see him in his village.

On the week that the father had appointed, the woman, her husband and their children took the canoe and paddled to the woman's village.

They arrived at the village. The woman's father went to the forest. When he arrived in the forest, he stood and called out to the *masalai* snake, "Snake, snake, where are you? I'm your son. I want you to come out of your hole and give a little piece of your fat for me to give to the man who ridiculed me and who beat my daughter all of the time."

The snake came out of its cave then the man covered it up well with leaves and took it back to the village. They cooked it with pig fat in an earth oven. When it was time to eat, the woman's father took the *masalai*'s fat and gave it right to his son-in-law, Baili Oddo. He did not know that this was the fat of a *masalai*, so he just ate it.

After they finished eating, they prepared to return to the village. Baili Oddo told his daughter and the others to go and get their canoe and paddle back to the village.

While they were paddling back to the village, he began to cough and the *masalai*'s fat began to come out of his nose and mouth. Baili Oddo became breathless from coughing. He turned to his wife and said, "Your father poisoned me with the *masalai* snake's fat. Now I'm turning into a snake and I'll be leaving all of you."

Then he told his wife, "You must take care of our children well." The woman listened and she began to cry. Then Baili Oddo began to turn into a snake.

The woman and the children saw this and were terrified. However he told them, "Don't be afraid of me. Paddle quickly and I'll be down there. I'll be just beneath the sea."

Then Baili Oddo went down into the sea. However he felt that he could not go, so he went back up and told them, "Paddle and go a little farther. This is not my place." So, his wife and children paddled farther.

They paddled and paddled then Baili Oddo told them again, "That's enough. Stop the canoe and I'll go down here. Wait for me. If I go down completely, then paddle quickly to the village because I'll be testing my powers as a snake."

When their father did not resurface, they paddled very quickly towards their village. They arrived at their house and a heavy rain and strong wind arose. The waves rose and became very choppy. They knew that it was just their father, Baili Oddo, who was testing his powers and causing these things to happen. They were not worried because they were in the village when these things were happening.

Anthon Bob Kadiko
Goma No. 2
Dami Village
P. O. Talasea
West New Britain Province

B91.5. Sea-serpent; B211.6.1. Speaking snake (serpent); B491.1. Helpful serpent; D191M. Transformation: man to serpent (snake); D551.3+. Transformation by eating fat; D2074.1+. Snake magically called; D2142.1. Wind produced by magic; D2143.1. Rain produced by magic; D2151.3. Magic control of waves; F401.3.8. Spirits in form of snake; F490+. Masalai; P210. Husband and wife; P230. Parents and children; P232. Mother and daughter; P234. Father and daughter; P291. Grandfather; P292. Grandmother; P261. Father-in-law; P262. Mother-in-law; P265. Son-in-law; Q285. Cruelty punished; Q297. Slander punished; Q551.3. Punishment: transformation; S62. Cruel husband

## Nokoro Called Out to a Ghost

(Wantok 555, January 26, 1985, page 23)

Long, long ago, around 1938 or 1939, there lived a man named Nokoro. His wife had died and he worked hard taking care of the children by himself.

When his wife had died, they had three daughters. Nokoro worked very hard at cooking food, working in the garden, and hunting wild game for his three daughters. Some of his kin in the village often helped him with food and other things because Nokoro was widowed and worked hard at taking care of the children.

One morning, he awoke and prepared to go into the deep forest to hunt for marsupials (*kapul*). He did not explain to his brothers in the village that he wanted to go hunting for game. He just woke up quietly, carried his bow, arrows and net bag then walked into the forest.

He walked and walked then arrived at Mount Viboro, then he went down to the Bia River. He followed the Bia River closely until he arrived at the source of the river. He cut across to Mount Hokopia Siliopa, walked around it, then arrived at the Ipi River.

Oh my, the good-for-nothing, just thought of one thing. He wanted very much to find game and he wanted to catch the largest marsupial in the deep forest to bring back to his children. So, he kept going into the deep forest to try to fulfill his desire.

Before long, the good-for-nothing knocked out a marsupial. He put the marsupial on his shoulder and kept going into the deep forest. Oh my, Nokoro kept going and going until he arrived at the places marked Soriapeto, Yuro and Naio in the very deep forest. He caught his breath there and thought hard about returning to his village.

When he looked up at the sun, he saw that the sun was right in the middle of the sky. The ancestors often looked at the sun to tell the time of day. So when he saw that the sun was in the middle of the sky, he turned around and thought of returning to the village.

Going back, he followed the other side of the mountain. He cut through the middle of the Hamu River, and the Ipi River again. He did not find any marsupials there, so he kept walking and walking until he was at the side of Mount Hokopia Silipoa again.

He left this place on the mountain, then his dog found a tree hole. His dog began to wag its tail and bark, then pace back and forth at this tree.

Nokoro saw this and cut a small branch. He shoved it inside the tree hole. A marsupial was inside the tree when Nokoro shoved the stick inside. The marsupial screamed and ran up to the crown of the tree. Nokoro had shoved the stick inside, but the marsupial would not come down to where he could see and kill it.

Nokoro climbed the tree and blocked all of the holes that he saw on the tree. He went up and up, until he arrived at the crown of the tree. When Nokoro was at the crown of the tree, he looked around at the villages, Yuro, Mioi, Diliato, Wenao, Wario,

Homua, and other villages. Oh my, the view was very clear and his eyes could see very far away. When Noroko saw these villages, he became very sad because when his wife was still alive, the two of them had walked together to these places hunting for game and other food. Noroko thought of this and he stopped thinking about what had appeared in the tree.

He forgot completely about the fire that he had made in the tree. The wind arose and brought the fire up to his legs, giving him a surprise. When he looked down, he saw that the base of the tree was engulfed in flames. He did not have a way to get down to the ground.

Nokoro tried to think of a way to save his life. He urinated and defecated downwards to try to put out the fire, but he could not put out the flames. When he had walked around on the ground, Nokoro had walked as a real man.

However when the fire completely surrounded him on the tree, he would become a bird.

He was worried about his three daughters. He knew that they would not have a way to evade enemies. The fire went very high and began to burn his skin, so he started to call out.

Nokoro screamed and called the names of everyone in his family, including his three daughters. He called their names, then he cried and screamed for his wife who had died, "Oh, Jei's mother, if your ghost is with me, then help me with this accident. Who will take care of our three daughters? You know that I have always worked hard getting meat and other foods. If you're with me, then you must help me. Who will take care of our daughters?"

Nokoro called out like this, then he stopped crying. He thought about jumping down to a tree that grew near the one that he was on.

He closed his eyes tightly and jumped to the other tree. He did not care if he died, so he fell down like a leaf on the other tree. Nokoro felt like he was holding a tree branch and he did not think any more. He went down quickly to the base of the tree then caught his breath again.

When Noroko descended the tree, he did not think about what had happened to him. He just thought about running away from the fire. When he went down and trampled the earth again, he caught his breath because his spirit had run away.

Nokoro had put his hands in the middle of the tree and descended as if he had been pushed down. Now he held the base of a tree and caught his breath on the ground.

His body had been burned badly by the flames. When he had descended the tree, his skin became ruined. The tree had scraped him badly.

He did not have anything. He had left the bow, arrows, net bag, and marsupial that he had killed at the base of the tree. He left the bowstring and walked slowly on the trail back to the village.

Nokoro's skin looked as if red paint had been spilled upon his body. He did not have a scrap of clothing on his body because everything had torn off when he had sped down the tree. He walked bare-assed back to the village.

Nokoro returned to his house very late at night. His daughters had waited for him for a long time and they had thought that he had encountered an enemy on the trail. When they heard their father standing outside the house, they called out for the eldest daughter to go and open the house door.

The children heard their father's voice and they were very happy to see him. The eldest daughter opened the door and wanted to see her father, but her father said, "Stay far away from me. My body's been ruined."

Nokoro went inside the house very quietly and tried to sleep, but he could not sleep because his body was in great pain. He screamed and cried until daybreak.

In the morning, a message went around for all his kin to gather together. They thought that Nokoro would die, so they cried, held him, and mourned. However, Nokoro did not die. He lived and became better again. After this accident, Nokoro never traveled in the forest again.

If you travel or work in Karimui, you will hear this story about Nokoro. If you go to Yur [Yuro], you can see this mountain. This mountain is really there. It stands behind a large mountain. The place where the fire burned Noroko is still there too.

Noroko lived for a long time, longer than many men in his village did. He married three women and had many, many children. His children also married and had their children, and Noroko saw his grandchildren.
His grandchildren also married and had children, and Noroko saw them as well. He saw three generations after himself then he died in 1983.

This story comes from Karamui [**Karimui**] Village, between the **Simbu** and Gulf Provinces [**Mikaru** People], and from **Yuro** Village in Karimui Naio.

Kisowai

P. O. Box 6510

Boroko

National Capital District

E322. Dead wife's friendly return; E380. Ghost summoned; J2183.6. Short-sightedness in case of fire; P210. Husband and wife; P230. Parents and children; P234. Father and daughter; P251. Brothers; P252.2. Three sisters; T100. Marriage; T145.0.1. Polygyny

## The Man Who Married a *Masalai*'s Daughter
(Wantok 556, February 2, 1985, page 23)

In the time of yore, there was a man and his son who lived in the deep forest. There were no others who lived with them in the little place where they lived.

One time, the father told his son, "Now, let's go through the forest and hunt for marsupials (*kapul*)." The father took his bow and arrows out and straightened them, then they left the house and walked away. The father carried the bow and arrows, and the son carried the food.

They walked and arrived at a pond. They saw a big marsupial sitting on top of a tree. The father told his son to watch from below, while he would climb the tree.

The father went up the tree to the place on a branch that was directly over the pond. He did not look carefully at the branch because his eyes were just looking at the marsupial. He was close to where the marsupial was. He bent the dry tree branch. The tree branch broke and fell down into the pond, but his ghost immediately jumped up and stood on another tree branch.

The man's son turned and saw his father's ghost. He asked him, "Papa, what happened?" The father's spirit lied and said, "I shot the marsupial and it fell in the water."

The poor boy thought that the man was really his father, so he waited at the base of the tree until the ghost came down. They stopped hunting for marsupials after this, and began to walk back home.

They walked and walked. In the middle of the trail, the father's ghost lied to the boy and said, "My good arrow fell on the trail. I'll go back and get it." He lied to the boy, so the poor boy waited on the trail. The ghost went back on the trail on which they had traveled.

The ghost returned quickly to the place where the boy's father had fallen. The ghost took the man's corpse and brought it near the place by the house where they kept firewood. Then the ghost covered up the body well with banana leaves and went back to the place where the boy was waiting.

They walked back to the house, but the ghost did not explain what had happened to the boy. The boy thought that the ghost was really his father.

They lived well at their house. They traveled together and they did the same work that the boy had done before with his father. However when they cooked and sat to eat, the ghost ate the skins and gave the meat to the boy.

The father always did this, so one time, the boy asked his father, "Papa, why do you always eat just the skins and give me the meat to eat?"

The father told him, "I'm old, so if you just eat well, you'll grow big quickly."

They lived like this for a while, then the child became a big man. One time, they killed a pig, and they wanted to cook it in an earth oven. The father's ghost told his son to dig the earth for the oven. The boy said, "Why should I dig the earth?"

The father's ghost told him, "Don't think, just dig the hole." The boy listened to him, then dug the hole. When the earth oven was ready, they removed the food and brought it inside the house.

Later, the father's ghost told the boy, "Go up to the place where we keep firewood and carry the bundle that is inside the big banana leaves back down."

The boy listened to the ghost and went up to get the bundle, but he wanted to look. The poor son saw his father's corpse. Then he thought back to the time when the two of them had gone into the forest to hunt marsupials. He cried and carried the bundle outside, then buried it in a hole. Afterwards, he went inside to see his father's ghost.

His father's ghost told him the story, then he just disappeared. The boy was troubled. Later he took a piece of pork that they had cooked and he ate it. He smoked the rest of the pork and put it away.

He was alone in this area. One time, he saw a nice tree growing on top of a mountain near his house, and he thought about going to cut it.

In the morning, he awoke and went to cut the tree, then he sang and danced. A *masalai*'s daughter was walking around near this place and heard the singing. The *masalai* woman followed the sound of the singing until she arrived at the man's house.

The *masalai* woman hid among the sugarcanes and watched. The man finished singing, then he walked back to his house. When he approached the house, he saw some sugarcanes that were broken about. He went to tie up the sugarcanes, but when he looked inside the canes, he saw the woman.

The man asked her, "Where did you come from? Are you a man's daughter or a ghost's daughter?"

The woman lied and said, "I'm a man's daughter."

The man listened to this and he was very happy to take the woman to his house. They stayed there and the man told the story of his father and of how his father's ghost had taken care of him. The woman lived there and they married.

After the woman gave birth to their first child, they were ecstatic. The man told his wife to send a message to her kin to come look at the baby. The woman's old mother heard this and came.

The married couple did not know that the old *masalai* woman was thinking of ruining their child. So when the old woman came to live with them, they left the baby with her and they went into the forest to look for leafy greens and firewood.

When the parents had left for the forest, the old *masalai* woman cut off the child's finger and ate it. The baby was in pain and cried. The parents heard this and returned to the house.

The old *masalai* lied and said that a bamboo [leaf] from the house had cut the baby's hand, making it cry. The married couple knew that the old woman must have been lying to them. While the old woman was sleeping at night, they woke up very quietly and killed her. They carried her and threw her down into a bad place.

So now, there is a bad place in the **Kabwum** area that has two springs shooting straight out from it [**Selepet** People, **Morobe** Province]. This marks the two crying eyes of the old *masalai* woman.

G. L. Evong
C. T. C. Box 60
Panguna
North Solomons Province

A941.0.1. Origin of a particular spring; E327+. Dead father returns to prevent son from learning of his death; E425.2. Revenant as man; F490+. Masalai; G512. Ogre killed; P210. Husband and wife; P230. Parents and children; P232. Mother and daughter; P233. Father and son; P262. Mother-in-law; P265. Son-in-law; P292. Grandmother; S22+. Matricide; S41. Cruel grandmother; S110. Murders; T100. Marriage; T115. Man marries ogre's daughter; T580. Childbirth

# The Festival for Pulling the *Garamut* Tree/Signal Drum

(Wantok 557, February 9, 1985, page 23)

Long, long ago, in **Yaweng** Village in the Drekikir [Dreikikir] area of **East Sepik** Province, there were two brothers who took their dogs and traveled in the forest [**Urat** People].

They had killed some pigs and marsupials (*kapul*) and they were still going around. When they entered the deep forest, they became famished so they talked about turning back and going home.

While they walked back, they saw a breadfruit tree that had many fruits on it. They also saw smoke from a fire near where the breadfruit tree was standing.

The brothers saw this and they were very happy. The big brother told his little brother, "Go get some fire and return. I'll go up the tree and get some breadfruit."

The little brother listened to his big brother and walked to the place where the smoke was rising, but he did not know that the smoke was not really smoke from a fire. No, it was smoke from a *masalai* named Rikim.

When the little brother walked over there and saw the smoke, he thought that some men were making a garden for themselves by making a fire, causing the smoke to rise. He followed the smoke and he saw that the smoke was rising from amidst some wild sugarcanes (*tiktik*).

He went amidst the wild sugarcanes and saw an old man sitting there. The little brother asked him, "Grandfather, I'd like to take some fire from you." The old man said, "That's alright. Go inside the house and get some fire."

The young man went inside the house and saw the fire. He took a piece and walked back to the place where his brother was working at gathering breadfruits.

The little brother went to his big brother and they made a fire, then they cooked the breadfruits. When the breadfruits were ready, they sat and prepared to eat.

When they were ready to eat, the ground began to shake. They heard the *masalai* call out, "Hey, who is it that came and took a piece of my skin away?"

The big brother heard this and knew that it was just a ghost making this noise. He asked his little brother, "Where exactly did you get the fire?" The little brother told him that he had gotten the fire from the house of an old man who was amidst some wild sugar canes.

His brother listened and said, "That was a *masalai*. We must run away now." While they were running away, the little brother felt that he could run no further because all his strength was gone. The *masalai* had done this and the poor boy had absolutely no strength.

He told his big brother, "I can't walk. My arms and legs are dead."

The big brother listened and began to cry. He knew that the *masalai*'s power had taken his brother, and that his arms and legs had no strength to run away from this place.

The little brother told his big brother, "Don't worry about me. Leave me here and run back to the village. If you also stay, the *masalai* will come find us then finish off both of us. Run to the village and tell the people so that they'll know."

The two of them were still there when they heard the noise coming again. The sound was coming closer to them. The big brother listened and he was angry. He was carrying a piece of bamboo and he quickly sharpened it. Then he gave the bamboo to his little brother.

The big brother told his little brother, "When the python comes and swallows you, break its belly open with this piece of bamboo then it will die." After he taught his brother this, he quickly went up the breadfruit tree and tried to hide.

While he was hiding, he saw the snake speeding towards the place where his brother was lying. While the snake sped along, it bumped and knocked over the grasses and small trees along its way.

Then the *masalai* python arrived at the place where the boy was lying. The little brother held the piece of bamboo in his hand and kept his arms against his chest. Then he turned and lay down. He put his chest down on the ground.

He did this so that the snake could not see the piece of bamboo that he hid in his hand.

The snake came and swallowed the boy right down. Before long, the snake began to turn around crazily. The boy had put the piece of bamboo directly at the python's neck and pulled it all of the way down its belly. The bamboo had cut all of the way from the snake's neck to its belly.

The python's belly was completely open and it was dying. Quickly, the boy jumped out again. The snake turned and twisted then went back to its home among the wild sugarcanes, where it died.

At the place where the snake turned around, a lake arose. The two brothers had long ago fled to their village. When they arrived, they called out for the men to come, then they told them about the *masalai* snake.

Only one man was not in the village on this day, so he did not hear the brothers' story. In the very early morning, he awoke and went to the forest to hunt for wild game. While he was walking around, he arrived at the lake.

Oh my, was he surprised. He said, "Where did this lake come from? Long, long ago, there was no lake in this place, and we often came here to hunt game."

The man was terrified when he wanted to see how the lake arose. He went to look around the lake. He was shocked to see a gigantic snake's head lying there. He went closer and looked carefully. He saw that the snake was dead. He was completely afraid and ran away, directly to the village.

He arrived at the village and told the people about the big, dead snake that was by the lake that had arisen. The men told him about the two brothers who had killed the *masalai* snake.

The men of the village listened and decided to go see the snake. So the next day, the men of the village woke up and went to see it. They wanted to stretch it out and measure the length of the snake.

The men of another village also came to help them, but there were not enough men to stretch the snake out. Something anchored it so that it would not move even a little. The ropes that the men used to pull the snake just broke.

They did this and failed, then they sent a message to the Urat People, the **Urim** [People], Kombia Number 1 [**Kombio Number 1** Village, **Abelam** People], and **Kombio Number 2** [Abelam People] villages. The people from these villages came to try to move the snake, but they still could not do it.

The people from these places worked at cooking food and carrying it to their kin who were working very hard at trying to pull the snake. When they were beginning to lose their breath from pulling the snake, the *masalai*'s kin decided to go pull the snake towards them.

When the kin arrived, the men saw the two of them and asked them, "Where did you two come from? You can't pull this snake." The boy listened to this and said, "No. The two of us are just walking around." The men listened to this and they kept pulling the snake.

The two of them left the group and went fairly far away. The boy told his sister to make a fire and cook taros, then he would arrange their way. The two of them were far from the other people when they arrived at this place.

Then someone told the two children to come. One of the children was a boy and the other a girl. So, they put their two taros inside the girl's *limbum* basket for her to carry. Then the two of them went to the place where the people had gathered. Along the way, the little boy pulled a string [or vine] while they were walking along.

The other people were eating sago with some good meat. They did not think about giving any meat to these two. They said, "This is not food for children."

The children's taro was ready, so they ate. The little boy said, "Grandpa, we want to bring you out so the people will see you."

After he explained this to the *masalai*, he told his sister, "I'm going to tie this string, then I'll bring part of it out. Afterwards, you and I shall pull it."

The boy took the string and walked down to the water. The men saw him and asked, "Hey, where are you going?" The boy replied, "I want to go see the snake."

The men said, "You bad, shitty boy." They saw the piece of string that he was carrying and they died laughing. Some of them spat on him, and beat him and his sister.

The two of them did not care. They said, "We just want to try." So, the boy went and tied his piece of string to the head of the snake, then pulled the string. Oh my, they died laughing. They just stood and watched the brother and sister.

The boy went and gave a piece of the [string] to his sister, then they both held the string. They sang and danced and called their *masalai*'s name. When they pulled the [string], the snake began to move and come out of the water.

They pulled the snake out completely and everyone was surprised. Everyone went down and helped the two children pull the snake out and put it into the clearing. All of the people from the five places spilled out to see this *masalai* snake.

Now, the people of the Drekikir area hold a festival for the two children who pulled the snake out. Nowadays, the people also perform this song and dance at the time when they pull the *garamut* tree [used as to make signal drums]. They also use this vine that the children had taken to pull the snake to pull the *garamut* tree from the forest.

Willie Wokumel
Raval Settlement
Kavieng
New Ireland Province

A920.1.0.1. Origin of particular lake; A1540. Origin of religious ceremonials; A1542.2. Origin of particular dance; A1543. Origin of religious songs (chants); B875.1. Giant serpent; D191M. Transformation: man to serpent (snake); D1184.2. Magic string; D1766.7. Magic results from uttering powerful name; D1781. Magic results from singing; D1781+. Magic results from dancing; D1835.5. Magic strength results from songs; D1835.5+. Magic strength results from dances; D1837. Magic weakness; D2148. Earth magically caused to quake; F490+. Masalai; F911.7. Serpent swallows man; F912.2. Victim kills swallower from within by cutting; G354.1. Snake as ogre; L300. Triumph of the weak; P251.5. Two brothers; P253. Sister and brother; P291. Grandfather; R210. Escapes; R220. Flights; R311. Tree refuge; R260. Pursuits

# The Yamap [Yamaip] Clan [Almost] Finished off the Temo [Timotop] Clan

(Wantok 558, February 16, 1985, page 23)

In the time of the ancestors, there were twelve brothers who lived someplace. There were no other people who lived there. It was just the twelve brothers.

The twelve brothers were not married because there were no women who lived near their home. The eleven elder brothers were becoming old, but the youngest was only sixteen years old.

One day, the first brother wanted to go to the forest to hunt marsupials (*kapul*). He fetched his bow and arrows and other things for walking into the forest, then he departed. After two weeks passed, the brother had not returned home. His brothers waited a long time, so they began to worry. The second brother said that he would go and look for their big brother.

The second brother left his younger brothers at their home and he too went into the forest, leaving completely. The brothers waited at home for two weeks, but he did not return home.

Then the third brother left to look for the two elder brothers, and the same thing also happened to him. They all were in the forest and had not returned home. The brothers waited and waited, then they sent the fourth brother to look for the others.

When the fourth brother did not return home, the fifth brother left home to look for the other brothers. They did this until all of the brothers had left home except for the last boy who was now entirely alone.

He saw that all his brothers had left for the forest and he was very troubled, so he cried for them. He thought hard for a while, then he fetched his things to walk into the forest.

He took some sweet potatoes and leafy greens. He killed one of their pigs that they had husbanded. He butchered the pig into two pieces. He cooked one in an earth oven, and he put down the other. When the earth oven was ready, he ate some, then he tied up the rest and carried it with the other food.

## Dressed Finely

He dressed finely, carried his things and walked away. He walked and walked until the sun was beginning to set. Then he arrived at a clearing near the forest trail that he was following.

He put his load down and looked for things to make a little place for himself to sleep. While he was going around this area, he saw a very old house that was standing.

The young boy arrived at the house and saw that the house did not look like a house that men would make. The house was broken-down. He wanted to look inside the house. He saw that a fire was lit there, and an old white-haired woman was sitting by the fire.

The woman was extremely old. Her two eyes were blind and her legs and arms were completely ruined. Oh my, the boy saw this old woman and he was very sorry for her.

The boy took his things and went inside the old woman's house. He asked the old woman if he could help her. The old woman heard him and spoke to him. She told him, "I live here and I always hear men walking up and down the trail, but none of them come near me. When they see me they spit at me, so I'm ashamed and I never go outside the house. You're a very good boy to come and see me."

The old woman asked the boy why it was that he had come to this place. The boy told the old woman that his name was Itali Tamban and that he was trying to find all his brothers who had left their home and not returned.

The woman listened to the boy's story and spoke, "I know that many men walk along this trail, but I never know where they go."

Later, the boy removed the food that he had taken with him, then they ate and slept. In the very early morning, the youth woke up, took his axe and went to cut trees to make a house for the old woman. He carried the wood back and began making a house for her.

### Making a Bed

After the house was finished, the boy made a bed and other things inside the house. The old woman was elated because of Itali Tamban. She told Itali, "You must go to a mountain and take back two round stones with two strong sticks for making crossed braces."

The boy listened to the old woman and brought back these things. Then the old woman told him to heat the stones in a fire. When the two stones were very hot, the old woman told the boy to take the stones and tie them well with the braces and rope.

The old woman told him, "Follow this trail and you'll arrive at a big tree. At the base of the tree, you'll find the bones of your brothers piled there. A big *masalai* killed and ate them. Leave the bones and leap up the tree. You'll see a hole in the middle and the *masalai* will open its mouth to eat you. You must throw these two stones down into the *masalai*'s big mouth then jump down and come back here."

After the boy heard this, he spoke to the old woman, took the two stones and walked away. When he arrived at the base of the big tree, he saw his brothers' bones piled there.

He avoided them and went up the tree. The big *masalai* heard him, came outside and opened its mouth to eat the boy, but the boy immediately threw the two stones into the *masalai*'s mouth.

The *masalai* was injured and did not come out. The boy jumped down to the ground and ran back to the old woman. He arrived and told the old woman that he had thrown the stones down into the *masalai*'s mouth.

They slept that night and heard the *masalai* crying and crying until it died. In the morning, the boy told the old woman that he must return to his home because he knew that his brothers were dead and because he had killed the *masalai* who had killed them.

### Giving Thanks

The old woman gave her thanks to the boy, then he left the old woman and returned to his home.

This is a true story. From then until now, they call the *masalai*'s clan "Yamaip," the old woman's clan "Yalipun," and the boy's clan "Timotop."

In the area where the *masalai* died, the Yamaip Clan often slaughter pigs and marsupials then bring them to the place where the *masalai* died. They usually mark one day each year to do this.

When the Yamaip Clan do this, the old woman's clan, Yalipun, and the boy's clan, Timotop, never go near this area. This is because the two clans are enemies with the Yalipun.

Now the young people know that ordinary men are forbidden from going to this place. In 1966, a policeman went to this place. Later, he came back, slept at night, then woke up and went around crazily shooting some men. The kin of these men were angry and killed this policeman.

This story is from the area between **Southern Highlands** and **Enga** Provinces [**Huli**, **Mendi** or **Katinja** People].

John Pokia

W. Y. G. Kieta

North Solomons Province

A1540. Origin of religious ceremonials; A1675+. Origin of enmity between clans; C630. Tabu: the one forbidden time; C610. The one forbidden place; C949.1. Insanity for breaking tabu; F490+. Masalai; G100. Giant ogre; G363+. Ogre with enormous mouth; G512.3.1. Ogre killed by throwing hot stones (metal) into his throat; K951.1. Murder by throwing hot stones in the mouth; P251.3.1. Brothers strive to avenge each other; P251.6.7. Twelve brothers; Q40. Kindness rewarded; Q211. Murder punished; Q215. Cannibalism punished; Q411. Death as punishment; R260. Pursuits; S112. Burning to death; V12.4+. Marsupial as sacrifice; V12.4.3. Pig as sacrifice; V70. Religious feasts and fasts; W27. Gratitude

## A Ghost Tricked a Man
(Wantok 559, February 23, 1985, page 23)

Long, long ago, in a place called Tais Wara [lit., "Swamp Water"], there lived two brothers. In this place, there were many ponds that were near their home.

One day, the big brother told his little brother, "Tomorrow morning, we'll go scoop the water and catch fish."

While the brothers talked, a ghost man was hiding near the house. The ghost had heard the two brothers' decision. The ghost listened, then left them and returned to his house.

In the very early morning, the ghost changed his face and became like the little brother. He went to the big brother and woke him up, "Big brother, why are you sleeping? The sun's rising now, and we won't be able to catch fish if other people see us in the water."

The big brother woke up then took their spears, fire, and sago. When he was getting the sago, the ghost told him, "You should take plenty of sago so that we'll catch many fish in the water."

So, the big brother took six packages of sago, then they left the house and walked towards the swamp. They walked and walked until they were far from their home. The big brother did not know that his little brother was not with him. He was going around with a ghost.

They arrived at the swamp and the big brother put the things down. They went down and scooped out the water, then they took the fish that were thrashing about in the water.

They worked at catching the fish, even the ghost did. Although the ghost also worked at catching the fish, he did not put the whole fish down. He ate the heads of the fish and put the rest down in a pile.

He did this for a while, then the big brother turned and watched. When he saw the man eating the fish heads, he began to think, "I must have come with a ghost."

The brother looked carefully at the man and he saw that one of the ghost's ears was erect. Then the man knew that it was a ghost. The poor man thought hard, then went to get the fish.

After a little while, the ghost told the brother, "Stay here while I go into the forest. I'll be back."

The ghost went inside the forest and affixed a small ghost to a tree leaf, then carried it back and put it down. The brother saw this and asked the ghost, "What did you put inside the leaf?"

The ghost lied to the brother, "Nothing. I went inside the forest and found some mushrooms, so I brought them back for us to eat with fish and sago."

After he said this, he told the brother that he would return into the forest. Then the ghost went back into the forest and brought out a fairly big one again.

When the big brother saw this bundle, he asked the ghost about it. The ghost angrily said, "I'm tired of you asking so many questions. I brought some edible grasses for us to cook and eat with the fish and mushrooms."

He said this, then he returned to the forest. When he returned, he carried a bundle out again. He kept doing this until he had brought many ghosts out of the forest. The last time he went into the forest, he brought out a huge ghost.

When the fish was ready, the brother opened the bundles to check and see what kind of food was inside them. When he looked, he only saw bad things piled inside the bundles. The brother just got up and left the area then sped back home. He ran and ran until he saw his home.

The ghost had gone back inside the forest to bring his kin out and he did not know that the man had opened the bundles and seen the bad things. The ghost returned with another big ghost. Then he began to look for the man.

However, the man had already fled. He was completely out of breath and no longer thought about the fish or his spears. He ran until he arrived at their house and he collapsed half-dead at the house door.

After he got his breath back, he began to look for his little brother. He went and found his brother working in the garden. The big brother told the story to his little brother, "A bad man had changed his face, so I thought that I had just gone with you. I went with him and he did things that told me that a ghost was tricking me, so I ran away and came here."

The brother finished telling the story, then they went back to their house. After this, they watched very carefully that ghosts did not come to trick them again.

Chandrew Aboy
**Utai** Community School [**Kwomtari** People]
Amanab
**West Sepik** Province

D42.2. Spirit takes shape of man; E425.2. Revenant as man; F542. Remarkable ears; H46.1+. Revenant recognized when it devours raw flesh; K1900. Impostures; P251.5. Two brothers; R220. Flights

## A Man Cut off His Wife's Hand
(Wantok 560, March 2, 1985, page 27)

Long, long ago, in the time of the ancestors, there lived a man and his wife on an island called Pilio [**Pilelo**]. This is a very beautiful island in **West New Britain** Province [**Arawe** People].

The married couple lived well on their island. They had a garden and they always worked there. They would gather food, then return home. When they wanted meat, they would go to the reef and catch fish and other seafood in the sea.

The woman's husband was a very hard worker. After a while, the woman gave birth to a baby boy. They called this baby Agap. The married couple was very happy for their baby, and they lived well together until Agap became a big man.

One day, the three of them wanted to go to the garden, but the mother felt a little ill, so she stayed home while the father and son went without her. However the woman only pretended to be sick, so she went to sit down at the beach.

While she was sitting on the beach, she saw an old man walking towards her. This man was dressed very finely with traditional adornments. When the man came close, the woman was terrified and wanted to run away. However, the man's adornments caught her eye, and she sat down half-dead.

The old man approached the woman and told her, "Don't be afraid and run away." The woman just lay there. The old man told her, "When you return to the house, you must do all of the work with only one hand."

The woman listened to the old man and she went back to her house. When she returned to the house, she sat again and thought hard about what the man had said.

She thought back to the old man and to the time when she had come to the beach. The woman thought, "If I listen to that man and use only one hand, I'll also get many traditional adornments like him."

In the afternoon, when her husband and son returned from the garden, the woman just kept quiet. She did not tell them about the man who had approached her on the beach and told her what to do.

They lived there for a while, and the woman always did work with only one of her hands. Her husband and son never noticed this behavior.

One day, the three of them went to work in their garden. They worked and worked, and the man saw that his wife was not working very smartly. So, he went behind her to check on her. He saw that his wife was using just one of her hands.

The man saw this and thought that she must have gotten a nail in one of her hands, or that her hand was in pain and that she was using just one hand to work.

When they returned to the house in the afternoon, the man's wife cooked and did other work. The man did not think too much about this because he thought that his wife's hand was in pain and that she was just using the other hand.

Afterwards, the man often looked carefully when his wife was working. Just like before, he often saw his wife using only one of her hands to work. Now the man began to think hard, "I must ask her why she always uses only one hand to work."

That night, after they cooked and ate, the man asked his wife why she always used only one of her hands to work. His wife told him about the time when she was sick and the old man had come and told her to use only one of her hands to work.

The woman finished telling her husband what the old man had told her, but she did not know that her husband was very angry with her. So in the very early morning, the woman woke up and walked down to sit on the beach.

Her husband woke up very quietly and took a knife. He went down to the beach and cut one of the woman's hands right off. After he did this, he went back to the house, took their son, Agap, and they left her. The poor woman sat with her hand on the beach.

Charles Kalus
Pilio [Island]
West New Britain Province

P210. Husband and wife; P231. Mother and son; P233. Father and son; Q260. Deceptions punished; Q451.1. Hands cut off as punishment; R213. Escape from home; S62. Cruel husband; S161. Mutilation: cutting off hands (arms); S430. Disposal of cast-off wife; T580. Childbirth; W157. Dishonesty

## The Man Who Changed His Skin
(Wantok 561, March 9, 1985, page 23)

Long, long ago, in the time of the ancestors, there was a man who often changed his skin to be covered with scales from ringworm. Some time afterwards, he would change back to his good skin.

Whenever his skin was scabrous, he would smell truly awful and no one would want to approach him. His skin would smell awful when the sun warmed the scabs on his skin.

At the time of festivals, the man that I am telling you about, the good-for-nothing, would turn into the Angel Lucifer. He would become a very handsome, strong and smart man. He would outdo [lit., "cut down"] all of the other men of the village.

Whenever there was a festival, the man would scrape off the scales from his skin. When all of the bad blood came out, the good-for-nothing would lie by the fire.

When the people of the village began to sing and dance, this bad man would get up, remove his bad skin and put it inside a *limbum* basket. Then he would put all his adornments on and become very stylish. He would expertly sing and dance among the other men of the village.

I tell all you married woman and you single women too, that this rotten good-for-nothing was completely nuts. He often screamed at himself. But the rotten good-for-nothing would stylishly chew betel nuts, betel peppers and lime (calcium oxide) amongst them, then the breasts of the young women would go out [to him]. He would sing and dance until near dawn.

At dawn, he would turn about, dance and sing towards the house. Immediately, he would take his bad skin and wear it. Then he would scrape the scabs until blood flowed. Afterwards, he would sleep awkwardly by the fire.

While he slept, he would see people who had gone to the festival returning to their houses. The man would ask them, "Are you finished singing and dancing?"

They would reply, "Yes, we've finished singing and dancing."

The he would say, "Good, I want to come, but my bad skin offends people by its smell, so I can't come."

When the mothers heard this, they were sorry for him, so they each gave him betel nuts and betel peppers. He often lied to the people like this.

However men often asked, "Who's that young man who often comes to sing and dance, and who makes our women fall for him? What area is he from?"

They often tried hard to find out who this man was. However, they never knew that it was the rotten good-for-nothing whose skin smelled who was this youth.

One time, the people of another village called for the scabrous man's clan to go to a festival at their village. Everyone prepared and dressed to go to this village. The rotten man sat and told his kin, "That's OK, go ahead. I'll stay and watch the house." They were very sorry for him.

The whole clan spilled out to the festival. At the village, there was one young woman who was sick. Her parents had left and she was alone in the house.

When everyone had left, the bad man went to the stream to wash carefully. Then he returned to the house. He removed his scabs, and when he wanted to put on his adornments, he made a mistake. The young woman had been quietly looking at this man. The young woman gnashed her teeth, then left the house.

The man dressed very finely, then he followed the rest of the clan to the festival. The young woman slept in the house and just thought about this man.

The man arrived at the site of the festival, then he sang and danced fervently. He turned and turned at the site of the festival. When it was near dawn, the man immediately wanted to hide and run back to the house then put on his old scabrous skin. However, a problem arose.

The woman who had seen him took his scabrous skin and burned it in a fire. She was the one who had spied upon him when he had removed his bad skin.

Later, the man quickly returned to the stream and looked for his skin, but it was not there. He went to wash first, then the young woman went out to the clearing.

She asked the man, "Hey what are you looking for? Is that still you? All of us tried hard to find out who that man was. Where are you going now? You've lied too much. You don't have scabby skin now. I burned your skin in a fire. Now where are you going? You're my man now. You'll marry me."

The man was speechless. He sat quietly. The woman went and held his hand. They chewed betel nuts together. Later, the woman's parents came looking for her. They found her near the stream. They saw their daughter sitting with this man.

Later, everyone in the village listened to the news about this man. The woman told her parents that they often thought that he was the ringworm man whose skin was rotten and smelly. But no, he was not this kind of man. He was a handsome man whom they had tried hard to find. It was just this man sitting there with his real skin.

This story also went to all of the other villages. The people of the villages marked the day to gather for a feast for their wedding party.

This story comes from **Wagi** Village in **Madang** Province [**Tangu** People].

Patricia Daubana and Ignatius Dubanau

P. O. Box 785

Lae

Morobe Province

D52.2. Ugly man becomes handsome; D531+. Transformation by removing skin D793.2. Disenchantment made permanent by burning cast-off skin; D1337.2.5. Magic skin makes person appear ugly; F687. Remarkable fragrance (odor) of person; K1930. Treacherous impostors; P210. Husband and wife; P232. Mother and daughter; P234. Father and daughter; T100. Marriage

## A Ghost Woman Ate a Baby
(Wantok 562, March 16, 1985, page 27)

One day, in the time of the ancestors, long ago, a woman named Marayang traveled in the forest gathering mangos. The woman had taken her baby with her to gather mangos.

They found a huge mango tree. It was mango season too, so this mango tree was loaded with many fruits. The woman put her little baby at the base of the mango tree.

She made a little bed with tree leaves and the baby slept there. Then the woman went up the tree. She worked at gathering ripe mangos and filling the net bag that she had carried up with herself. She let some of the mangos fall about to be gathered later.

While she was above the ground, a ghost woman turned into a real woman from the village and sat near the baby. The baby's mother was on the mango tree and did not know this. She did not see this either because the leaves of the [mango tree] obscured the baby.

The ghost woman carried the baby who was sleeping. She tried to break one of its fingers to eat. The baby was in pain and cried loudly.

Its mother, Marayang, heard this and replied, "Hey, why are you crying? I'm just about ready to come down." However, the baby ceased crying.

The woman quickly jumped to another branch of the mango tree with her net bag of mangos. When she stood at that place, it was clear, so she looked down to the ground and saw her baby. But no! She also saw this woman there. The woman was holding the baby's hand.

Marayang was surprised to see the ghost woman there, but she did not think that the woman was a ghost. After the ghost woman did not speak, Marayang was clear in her thoughts that it was a ghost woman.

She sat up there and called down to the ghost woman, "Hey, what are you doing to my baby that's making it cry so much?"

The ghost woman looked up at Marayang and told her, "Come down and I'll eat both of you... I was beginning with your baby, where are you going?"

Marayang was biding her time. There was no way to get down now. She just sat on the mango tree branch, worried and cried for her baby.

She called out to whichever people in this part of the forest might hear and help her. But no, Marayang's cries went unheeded day and night.

The poor woman looked at the ghost eating the legs, arms and all of the parts of her baby. The ghost held the baby's head up to its mother and said, "Look at your baby's head. I'm going to swallow it now. You too, I'm going to swallow your head like this. So where are you going?"

The ghost woman opened her mouth and swallowed the baby's head straight down. Marayang sat on the mango tree and was speechless because the worrying was killing her and because she was angry with the ghost.

After the ghost swallowed the baby's head, she went and gathered leaves and vines from the forest. She adorned herself, then sang and danced fervently at the base of the mango tree.

She sang and danced towards the woman and told her, "Where are you going? I'm going to swallow your head too. Which one of your friends or kin is coming here to help you? I'm here, but no one's going to find you here. I've confused their thoughts so that they can't think of you. Because they won't come looking for you, you'll die and go down into my mouth just like your own baby."

So now, Marayang looked for any possible way to get down to the ground. She thought that she must fight hard with the ghost and run away. The ghost sang and danced, then wanted to go up the mango tree to get her.

The ghost jumped up to a place near where the woman was. Quickly, the woman took a huge unripe mango and hammered the ghost's head. The ghost cowered and went down to the ground.

The ghost went up again near Marayang. Quickly, she took another mango and blasted the ghost's brains. Blood shot out of the ghost's head and the ghost went back down to the base of the mango tree. The ghost kept it up, and the woman hit her with mangos until all of the mangos near the woman were gone.

Then she jumped on top of another branch. She ran out of all of the mangos on this branch too. The ghost felt sore and blood flowed from her body. However, this was not an ordinary woman. No, the ghost would not die quickly.

Those who are ghosts are insensitive. The ghost went up the mango tree again, and went very close. Marayang held two big very ripe mangos in her hands. These were from her net bag.

The ghost approached and put her hands up to pull the woman's legs. The woman put the ripe mangos right into the ghost's eyes. The next time, she took mangos that weren't ripe and blasted the ghost's head with many of them. The ghost went down and the woman quickly followed her down.

She hit the ghost with mangos, kicked her, and hammered her head against the base of the tree. The ghost was put in her place. Marayang quickly ran back to her village. The ghost got up and followed her, but it was too late, the woman had arrived home.

When she arrived at the village, she fell down and fainted for a short time. This was because she was afraid, worried and completely out of breath. Later, she told the people of the village the story of the ghost and her baby.

Deri Jacob
**Maiamsariang** Village [**Adzera** People]
Kaiapit
**Morobe** Province

D1781. Magic results from singing; D1781+. Magic results from dancing; D2000. Magic forgetfulness; E261.4. Ghost pursues man; E425.1. Revenant as woman; E493. Dead men dance; E546. The dead sing; G11.10. Cannibalistic spirits; K1930. Treacherous impostors; P230. Parents and children; R210. Escapes; R260. Pursuits; R311. Tree refuge; S110+. Eaten alive

## Boanouo Tahia — Son of a Pig

(Wantok 563, March 23, 1985, page 23)

Long ago, in the time of the ancestors, in the Bao area, in my village, **Laipo**, in **West New Britain** [Province], a pig gave birth to a real boy along with her other piglets [**Psohoh** People].

One ancestral mother, named Kare-Kamia, was looking for firewood in the forest when she found this baby. While she was working at tying her firewood, she heard the sound of piglets squealing for milk in the nearby forest. She also heard the cries of this baby boy.

The mother pig told her piglets, "Move back, so that Banouo [Boanouo] Tahia can also have milk." When the woman heard this from the mother pig's mouth, she threw away all her firewood, quickly ran back to the village and told her husband.

The two of them went back quietly to this part of the forest. They stood and watched quietly. They saw the mother pig and the piglets with the baby boy sleeping near the piglets.

The two of them hid and watched for a very long time. They saw the mother pig leave her children and walk around, searching for food. Quickly, the man went and carried the baby boy, then he and his wife ran back to the village. They were terrified that the mother pig would see them and chase them.

While they carried the baby away, the little pigs cried for their brother. They squealed and cried so that their mother would hear then come back to see them.

However it was too late, the married couple had stolen him and run away. Before long, the people of the village heard about the baby's story. The leading men and women of the village were angry with the married couple.

They said, "Why did you bring this baby *masalai* here? He'll ruin the village."

The married couple told the people that he was not a *masalai*'s baby. He was a real baby. They did not tell the real story that a pig had given birth to the baby. When the people had said the two of them that he was a pig's baby, the married couple concealed all of their truthful speech from them.

When the mother pig found out that her baby was gone, she cried terribly and the piglets also cried with their mother. Then the father of the baby went to the mother pig and told her not to cry.

The father of the baby had the head and face of a man and the body of a pig. He was huge. He was the *masalai* owner of this land.

He told the mother pig and the piglets, "Don't cry. These two people and the people of the village will go down into my mouth."

One night, he went towards the village and sat near the village. The next morning, he went and saw his baby with the woman in the village.

The father pig returned home and looked up to the clouds. He kept looking up at the clouds until it was nearly dusk. Then he called out loudly. The people of the village heard this cry, which was like birds singing before rainfall.

He stayed there a little longer, then he called up to the clouds. He called out to the rain and wind, and for a bad time to come. He called out again. On the third time that he called, the people saw the clouds become dark and they saw that the rain would fall.

When the people heard the calling, the woman who had stolen the baby replied, "Ah, why is there always that sound? Before long a heavy rain will fall every day but just now the sun is about to rise. We want to go find food and make gardens for having a good time."

The fourth time that the *masalai* called out, a tornado arose. The people left the houses and went outside. They were terrified that the houses would fall and be covered over.

The people of the village saw the trees, the coconut palms near the houses, and the nearby forest lying flat like tree branches about to break and fall down. The banana plants and sugarcanes fell about.

The men called for the mothers to hold the children carefully and not to let them go to the bases of the coconut palms, under the houses or under other trees. Then they saw a house fall. This was the house that belonged to the married couple that had stolen the pig's baby.

Later, they saw a very heavy rain falling. The rain poured and poured, making the place completely dark. After a little while longer, a great earthquake arose.

The people were afraid and began to speak, "Oh my, we've never seen such an awful time before. Why has this happened?"

Every house in the village fell down. The people were worried and the children and mothers cried terribly. The rain poured down and the village was completely ruined from the water. The flood from the rain made the place look like a lake.

Everyone gathered and stood on just one hill. The wind came, the rain fell, and the earth trembled, forcing them to stay there.

The woman and her husband held their baby. The water began to recede from the village. When the people looked for their homes, the woman heard the baby crying. When the baby cried, it turned into the cry of the piglets that the woman had first heard in the forest.

The people heard this and they were terrified. They said, "Kill him. Kill that baby. He's not a real baby. What did we say before? He's a *masalai*."

One man was furious and took a knife to kill the baby. When he went close to the baby, the baby became like his father. His head and face were human but his body was that of a pig.

Everyone found his or her homes. Then the baby's father came out to the village clearing, took his son and departed. Then the bad time ended.

The *masalai* pig father told the people, "You haven't ruined my son. If you had ruined him, you would all have gone down into my mouth. You didn't know that I'm the owner of this land that you live on. If you take care of it well, I shall leave you be. I just gave you a bad time to feel [what I can do]."

After this, the people of the village no longer wanted to hunt pigs. Also, they never ate pigs after this.

Henry Nuli

Mora-Mora Vocational School

Hoskins

West New Britain Province

A1000+. Village destroyed by tornado; A1011. Local deluges; A1681.2+. Why Psohoh People do not eat pork; B29.3. Man-hog; B211.2+. Speaking boar; B871.1.2. Giant boar; C221.1.1.5. Tabu: eating pork; C841.4. Tabu: hunting a pig; D114.3.2B. Transformation: boy to boar; D682. Partial transformation; D1544.1. Magic spell controls earthquake; D1774. Magic results from speaking; D2142.1. Wind produced by magic; D2143.1. Rain produced by magic; D2148. Earth magically caused to quake; F490+. Masalai; G352.2. Wild boar as ogre; P210. Husband and wife; P231. Mother and son; P233. Father and son; P271. Foster father; P272. Foster mother; P275. Foster son; Q213. Abduction punished; Q595. Loss or destruction of property as punishment; R10.3. Children abducted; R153.3. Father rescues son(s); T566. Human son of animal parents; T611. Suckling of children; Z71.2. Formulistic number: four

## Tabuagele Raped a Woman

(Wantok 564, March 30, 1985, page 27)

Long, long ago, there was a strong *masalai* named Tabuagele. He had four huge eyes. He lived in a cave near the beach near Baai [**Baia**] Village in **East New Britain** Province [**Melamela** People].

Nowadays, the villagers call the place where Tabuagele lived, Pakanaveu. This place has many stones. There are many snakes from the reef, both big and small, that fill this place.

The people of the village call these big reef snakes, "*amangau*." The little snakes are called, "*abalivo*." The people are terrified of the *amangau* because they can bite people.

If you are a new person who wants to go bathe in the sea by Pakanaveu, you must be careful. You must go with some man or woman who has kin from the Tabuagele Clan. Then the *masalai*s from this area will see this and will not try to ruin you.

If you go by yourself to bathe in the sea from this part of the beach, you will become sick and vomit blood. This is because while you are bathing near Pakanaveu Beach, the reef snakes will swim very close to you. You cannot see or feel their bodies pass through yours.

These snakes will swim and rub their bodies against yours, then swim close to your belly. These snakes are black and white, red and white, yellow and black, and the big snakes have black on their skins.

One time, there was a big meeting and a big feast that they called Balabalaguan, which took place in **Talwat** Village [**Tolai** People]. The people of Talwat sent a message about the Balabalaguan. They also asked that the people from Baai should bring a wooden mask (*tumbuan*) and a ceremonial headdress (*dukduk*) with them.

Iavatau is the name of the mask and Tomarinair is the name of the headdress. The women and children of Baai prepared the food for the earth oven in the morning, then they readied their other things to bring to the Balabalaguan.

In the afternoon, the women and children put all of their things in canoes and paddled to Talwat. The leaders and young men walked briskly with Iavatau and Tomarinair on the trail to Talwat.

On this day, the people of Baai left a very beautiful young woman back in the village. This was because the woman was menstruating, so it was completely forbidden for her to go to the Balabalaguan.

It was very difficult for this woman to go outside and walk on a long trail. In the evening, she felt very bad because she had lost much blood.

She did not want to stay inside the house any longer, so she walked along the part of the beach called Pakanaveu. She thought about bathing in the sea and removing the blood from her body.

She removed the "grass" skirt from her body and jumped into the sea. She swam back and forth in the sea. She did not know that Tabuagele's four big eyes saw her there. She also did not know that Amangau and Balivo [Abalivo] had joined her.

It was late evening, and the blood from her body was no longer flowing. So, she went up to the beach and tied on her "grass" skirt. She returned to the house and slept.

When she was dead asleep, the *masalai* Tabuagele went to her bed and slept with her until dawn. In the early morning, some people who had gone to Talwat returned. They were completely exhausted and out of breath. They wanted very much to shut their eyes and sleep. But no, they found out that their kin, the young woman who had stayed back in the village, was dead. They screamed and cried back and forth, "Adovot Tabuagele!!!"

John Tiamon

Hohola

Port Moresby [National Capital District]

C141. Tabu: going forth during menses; C615. Forbidden body of water; C920. Death for breaking tabu; C940. Sickness or weakness for breaking tabu; D1980. Magic invisibility; F408.3. Spirits dwell at tabu place; F471.2. Incubus; F490+. Masalai; F512+. Unusually large eyes; F512.2.1. Persons (animals) with four (six) eyes; T475.2.1. Intercourse with sleeping girl

# Women Burned the Spirit House

(Wantok 565, April 6, 1985, page 23)

Long, long ago, in Mansuat [**Mensuat**] Village in **East Sepik** Province, there was a big spirit house [**Bisis** People]. Every man of the village slept in this house. The women and children slept in their own houses because it was forbidden for them to go inside the men's spirit house.

The men who slept in the spirit house never took care of their wives and children. The poor women of this village often worked very hard taking care of their children. The men would just father the children and leave them for the women to take care of.

The men always went to the forest to kill pigs, cassowaries and marsupials (*kapul*). Then they would return to the village, but they would not give any meat to the women, none at all.

The men would hide well and do this sort of thing lest the women of the village would see their detestable habits. They did this often. When they left the spirit house and went to the forest, they would leave two men to watch the spirit house. The names of these two men were Jari and Matugain.

## Jari and Matugain

These two men, Jari and Matugain, were not tall men, they were short. When the other men left the spirit house, these two men would just stay inside. They did not go outside for even a short time.

When the women and children went to the spirit house to see the men, these two men, Jari and Matugain, would scold them terribly. This spirit house had very tight security because the men did not want their wives to see the despicable, greedy things that they did.

Among all of the women of this village, there were two who were leaders. The names of these two women were Cariak and Muriark. These two women often gathered the other women and told about what their husbands did to them.

## One Law

During the day, their children would play in the village, and in the afternoon, they would go back to the houses and cry hungrily to their mothers.

Their mothers would say, "You have no fathers to take care of you." When the children would hear this from their mothers, they would be very troubled and stop crying. The men of the spirit house never rested from hunting wild game in the forest.

Cariark [Cariak] and Muriark knew that their husbands must have been hiding something that they did not want the women to discover. They often very tried hard to discover out what it was.

There was another law that the men of the spirit house had made. This law of theirs was as follows, not one man who lived in the spirit house could give a piece of meat to women or children. The law was that if one of the men did this, the other men would kill him.

The men were afraid of this law and they never gave meat to their wives or children. The two guardians of the spirit house, Jari and Matuguain [Matugain], always just stayed in the house. They never went out of the house, even if they had to defecate or urinate.

When they wanted to defecate or urinate, they would just do it inside the spirit house. After they defecated inside the spirit house, they would cover it up with leaves and put it down. Then in the evening, when the other men returned to the spirit house, the two of them would go down to the ground and throw away their feces.

However one day, one of the men from the spirit house was very sorry for his child, so he took a small piece of meat and hid it. He took it to give to his child. His poor child did not eat this meat because its mother took it and hid it.

In the early morning, all of the men of the spirit house awoke and left for the forest to hunt game. This woman woke up and took the piece of meat that her husband had hidden and carried to give to their child. She took the piece of meat and went directly to their two leaders, Cariark and Muriark.

Cariak and Muriark saw this piece of meat, so they called out for all of the other women of the village to come and begin talking about what they must do to the two men who led the spirit house.

The women spoke about going into the spirit house. Then Cariark and Muriark sent the women to the forest to get the tree fruits that women gather in the forest. These look like wild mangos. They carried many of these tree fruits back to the village.

Then when they arrived at the village, Cariark and Muriark led all of the women to the spirit house to see Jari and Matugain. The women carried the tree fruits with them.

When Jari and Matugain saw the women, they tried to chase them away, but they were unable to do so. The women were persistent and ignored the two men, Jari and his in-law Matuguain, and went inside the spirit house. Then all of the women spilled into their husbands' spirit house.

### Seeing the Racks

Oh my, oh my, when they went inside the spirit house, they saw racks of meat all over the house. The place was completely filled with meat that the men had smoked carefully and piled up.

Then the women turned and told Jari and Matuguain, "So, you men have hidden this meat from us, huh?" Jari and Matuguain listened and trembled.

Then the two of them told the women, "We're good men, but your husbands prevented us from giving meat to you." The women did not listen to what the men said.

They turned, then Cariark with some other women held Jari and Muriark, while the other women grabbed Matuguain. They removed their loincloths and laid them on the floor of the spirit house.

Then the women brought out the tree fruits that they had taken from the forest. They began to shove them up the men's shit-holes. They kept shoving the tree fruits up there until the men's tongues came out and they died.

After the women killed the men, they ruined everything inside the spirit house. After they ruined everything, they carried some big torches, put them inside the spirit house and returned to their houses.

After they returned to their houses, Cariark and Muriark gathered all of the women and told them, "Go to each of your houses and stir the sago. Then cut off enough of a portion for yourself, leaving a big piece inside the pot. After you eat your portion, kill all your children and put them inside the pot with the sago. After you do this, come see us."

The poor women were very troubled about doing this to their children, but they listened to what their leaders told them to do. On this day, a terrible cry came from the village. All of the women cried terribly when they killed their children. They killed all of their children. Not one was left.

### Furious

Some of the women were furious at what Cariark and Muriark had told them to do to their children. Only Cariark left her beautiful baby alone. The women were angry with her and said, "Why did you tell us to kill our children, but you yourself left your baby alone?"

It was nearly evening, and the women went down to the spirit house. They burned the spirit house, and they began to walk towards the forest. While they were walking, they saw Cariark still carrying her baby, so the women cursed her fiercely.

They cursed and cursed her, but Cariark still did not want to kill her baby. While they were still walking, Cariark looked and saw a fig tree standing.

So, Cariark went underneath the fig tree and hung the baby up [in a net bag] on the tree. Then she said, "If there is a person who lives in this fig tree, then come down and take this baby."

After she said this, she left the tree and walked away. Before long, she saw an ancestral ghost woman descend the fig tree and take her baby.

The women's husbands were in the forest and they saw an enormous amount of smoke rising from their village. They left the pigs, cassowaries, and other game, then ran back to their village.

When they arrived at the village, they saw that the fire had finished their spirit house. They were troubled and they cried terribly when they saw that it was ruined and that their children were dead inside the pots. They became eagles and flew around this fire.

So now when the forest is on fire, or when men make a new garden and burn the forest, we see these eagles flying around. It is just these men who had become eagles.

I am from Mansuat Village in the Angoram District of East Sepik Province.

Benjamin Manowak
c/- Steven Amenasik
Wewak Timbers
P. O. Box 291
Madang
Madang Province

A2471.3+. Why eagle hovers over fire; C830+. Tabu: giving meat to women or children; C830+. Tabu: women or children entering spirit house; C920. Death for breaking tabu; D152.2M. Transformation: man to eagle; E320+. Dead relative's friendly return to adopt child; P210. Husband and wife; P230. Parents and children; P263. Brother-in-law; P272. Foster mother; Q276. Stinginess punished; Q402. Punishment of children for parents' offenses; Q411. Death as punishment; Q486.1. Criminal's house burned down; Q553.4. Death of children as punishment; S11+. Cruel father refuses children food; S12.2. Cruel mother kills child; S62+. Cruel husband refuses wife food; S100+. Murder by putting hot stones up rectum; S139.2.2+. Corpse put into cooking pot or cooked; V112.1. Spirit huts; W152. Stinginess; X740.1H+. Symbolic pedicatory rape

## The *Masalai*s of Gagwekalo

(Wantok 566, April 13, 1985, page 24)

Long ago, in the time of the ancestors, in **Aying** Village in the Buang area, there lived a man and his family [**Mapos Buang** People, **Morobe** Province].

One day, the man spoke to his wife about going to the Wagau River. The man said that he would go the Mount Gagwekalo. He told his wife to prepare food for him to carry.

The man awoke in the morning and walked up the mountain. Then he walked to straighten the branches of the yams in their garden. The yams had grown and their branches were going all over, so he worked at putting sticks in the ground and tying the branches to the sticks.

While the man was working, a *masalai* woman walked close to the garden and coughed a little. The coughing surprised the man. He turned and looked around to see who had coughed. He was surprised to see his wife carrying the baby, coming towards him and then standing there.

However, it was not really his wife. It was the *masalai* who had turned into the man's wife. The woman called out to the man, "Hey, come carry the baby while I go do some work too." The man listened and thought that it was really his wife that was calling. The man went and carried the baby who was hanging in a net bag from a tree branch.

The *masalai* woman went and helped the man do much work in the garden. She gathered some beans, leafy greens called _gelen_, some other foods, and filled up a net bag.

The woman him, "Come and follow baby and me. We'll go first and cook food for us." The man agreed, and the two of them left him in the garden.

The man worked in the garden until the evening. It was nearly dark, so he got up and walked to Aying Village. At the village, his real wife and baby were cooking soup. They served the food and sat to eat.

The man wanted to eat, but he felt some sand in the leafy greens. He asked his wife, "What kind of sand is this? Did the sand that's stuck to the greens come from the yams that we removed from the garden?"

The woman replied, "No. I think the sand is from the Wagau River. We washed the greens there."

The man did not say anything. He just sat and ate. Later, he went to his brother and told him about the *masalai* woman who had come to him in his garden on the mountain. The brothers decided that they would go watch the *masalai* woman, then they would follow and kill her.

The next day, in the early morning, the two brothers went to the garden on top of Mount Gagwekalo. They arrived at the garden, and the little brother hid in the nearby forest. The big brother was the man whom the *masalai* woman had seen working in the garden before.

The *masalai* woman put her baby into a net bag and walked back to the garden. The two of them worked at fencing in the garden. Then the baby in the net bag began to cry.

The woman went close to the garden gate and called out for the man to carry the net bag and to hang it on a tree branch in the middle of the garden.

The man walked close to the *masalai* woman. When the woman wanted to put one leg and her head inside the garden, oh no. Quickly, the second brother who was hiding went and cut the *masalai* woman's neck. The brothers killed her and cut her into very small pieces.

When the *masalai* baby in the net bag saw the men kill its mother, it stretched the net bag hard and broke it. The baby wanted to run and eat the two men. The men turned and saw this then just laughed. They killed the *masalai* baby too, then they returned to the village.

At night, the other *masalai*s did not see the faces of the mother *masalai* and her baby in their village. They saw that she was [not there], so they followed her smell to the man's garden, where they found the two of them.

The two men had pulverized the bodies of the mother and baby, mixed the corpses with vines and leaves, and covered them up well with dirt. They had covered up the bodies with garden rubbish at the place where they had killed the mother and baby so that there was no sign of them. The *masalai*s searched unsuccessfully. They knew that two men must have killed the mother and baby *masalai*s.

So, the *masalai*s sent a message to the two men and the other people of Aying Village that if they wanted to fight, they could have a fight with the *masalai*s.

Then one day, the *masalai* men and the real men met in Ayingbaremb Valley by this mountain. The *masalai*s gathered on one side and the real men gathered on the other side.

A real man blew a bamboo flute, then the *masalai*s pranced belligerently (*samsam*) towards the real men. The *masalai*s used their long toenails, fingernails, and teeth to fight. The men used their spears to fight.

The two sides were both strong. However, many of the *masalai*s died because the real men were far away and were able to shoot their spears from a distance. The *masalai*s had one way to finish off the men. They wanted to get close and eat them, so they left the great battle.

The leader of the *masalai*s saw this and called out to the real men, "OK, you win the fight. You've killed many of us, including women and children. However, you must watch the women and children carefully on this mountain because that is our place. If you bring dogs to hunt for wild game, you won't find pigs, cassowaries or any kind of game."

The people of Aying Village no longer go up Mount Gagwekalo. This was an ancestor story from this area.

Ken Siling
Mainyada L. S. B.
P. O. Box 89
Bulolo
Morobe Province

C612+. Forbidden mountain; D94+W. Transformation: ogre to woman; F408.3. Spirits dwell at tabu place; F490+. Masalai; F515.2.2. Person with very long fingernails; F544.3.5. Remarkably long teeth; G512. Ogre killed; G512.1+. Ogre killed with spear/arrow; K1910. Marital impostors; P210. Husband and wife; P230. Parents and children; P251.5. Two brothers; Q262. Impostor punished; Q411. Death as punishment; S110. Murders; S139.2. Slain person dismembered

## An Old Woman Was the Origin of Various Foods

(Wantok 567, April 20, 1985, page 20)

Long, long ago, in my area, by Talasea, the ancestors did not have foods such as taro, cassava, banana or other foods.

The people of the village always worked very hard, going to the forest, looking for wild yams and tree fruits to eat.

One day, the parents wanted to go looking for food in the forest, so they told their children, "Stay in the village. We'll go into the forest to look for some food for us."

The parents left the village and went into the forest. The children just stayed there. Some played and others just sat in their houses.

The children were there and an old woman went to them. The name of this old woman was Pae. When the children saw her, oh my, they were terrified and ran to their houses. They had never seen this old woman before, so they were terrified.

The old woman saw the children running away, so she called to them, "Hey you, don't be afraid of me. I'm one of your ancestors. Come outside of your houses and I'll tell you something good."

The children listened to what the old woman said, then they began to go outside their houses. They went slowly and sat near the old woman.

All of the children sat down, and the old woman told them, "Go into the houses and bring firewood here. We'll make a big earth oven."

The children listened and they asked the old woman, "What is it that we'll cook in the earth oven?"

The old woman replied, "You'll cook me." Then the old woman sent the children to bring leaves back to the village. The children went and brought leaves. They put them by the place where they had put the firewood."

Then the old woman told them, "Now, all of you must listen to me. When the fire cools a little, then you must cover me up and cook me in the earth oven. Then when the earth oven is ready, you must uncover it and you'll see all kinds of food inside of it."

The children listened to the old woman and they made a fire. When the fire cooled a little, they covered the old woman and cooked her in the earth oven. When the earth oven was ready, they removed the fire and opened it up. Oh my, oh my, the children saw various good foods inside the earth oven.

Then the children sat down and ate the good foods until their parents came to the village. The children showed the foods to their parents, and they too ate. After the food was gone, the children told them to throw away their trashy food of the forest ghosts.

The children told the story to the parents about the old woman who had come to the village and showed them the good food. Then the people of this area had good food such as taros, yams, bananas and other foods.

My father told this story to me and I wrote it down.

Anton [Bob] Kadiko
**Dami** Village [**Bola** People]
P. O. Talasea
**West New Britain** Province

A2686.4.1+. Origin of cassava; A2686.4.2. Origin of taro; A2687.5. Origin of banana; E276+. Ghosts haunt forest; E631.5+. Reincarnation as sweet potato; E631.5+. Reincarnation as yam; E631.5.7K. Reincarnation as banana plants; P210. Husband and wife; P230. Parents and children; R220. Flights; S112. Burning to death

## A *Masalai* Ruined Dikiti's Eyes

(Wantok 568, April 27, 1985, page 20)

Long ago, in the time of the ancestors, there were two brothers who lived in a village. Yarimu was the big brother and Dikiti was the little brother. Yarimu was married, but Dikiti was still single

Yarimu was a real man. He was married, had a family and lived like the man of the village. However, his little brother Dikiti had an unusual power with his two eyes. Dikiti could have been married by this time, but the power of eyes caused women not to like him.

This was how Dikiti walked around every day. When he traveled, he would look at women as if they were real women. However, when Dikiti approached them, his eyes would see the women as snakes or centipedes. Dikiti would look for them and ask himself, "Hey, where did these women whom I just saw go?"

There was one woman at the village whom the big brother Yarimu and his family wanted Dikiti to marry. The woman was young, and smart at making gardens and hunting for food. The woman's parents agreed for Dikiti to marry her.

However, this problem always happened. When Dikiti approached women and wanted to talk with them, he would see the women turn into centipedes or snakes. Dikiti could only see them from far away, and the women would also see Dikiti.

They would be far away from each other, and they would call back and forth. When the man or woman went close, Dikiti's two eyes would change again then turn the person into a centipede. However, the woman would see Dikiti well.

This is how it always happened. The man would send a message for him to go between him and the woman. Then when the two of them wanted to talk, they would still be far away and talking to each other. If they stood close, he could not see the woman.

This behavior made him very troubled. First he thought that the woman had ensorcelled him, so he tried to look at other women too, but the same thing happened.

Yarimu's wife was the same too. Dikiti usually only approached men because he usually saw men well. He could sit down near them, and talk and eat with them.

Dikiti saw that his friends were married and had children. He was troubled. Every night, he would think about what he could do for himself.

Why was it that he could not see women close-up, and he could not touch their skin or hold their hands? Why did the women just disappear and turn into snakes or centipedes?

Dikiti never slept. Thinking about women occupied him and made him worry. It was killing him. Another day, he went up to a mountain and performed various songs and dances to all of the places that were sacred to him.

The *masalai*s gathered, and happily sang and danced with him. However, Dikiti did not know what was really happening to his life. Later, the *masalai*s told him that he had drunk urine from a stream once when he had gone hunting for food in the forest.

The stream that Dikiti had drunk from had urine from a *masalai* in it. The water had changed his two eyes so that when he went approached women, he would see the women turn to snakes.

However, it was too late now for the *masalai*s to remove the poison from his eyes. Dikiti had become a *masalai*. His eyes could not see women close-up, and he could not marry real women.

The woman did not know that Dikiti had become a *masalai*. She thought that Dikiti had died in the forest. Whenever the woman went into the forest, Dikiti would become a centipede or snake and approach her. At first the woman was afraid, but later, she found out and she cried terribly for Dikiti.

[Anonymous]

[See the ancestor story in *Wantok* #573. This story also has two brothers named Yarimu and Dikiti. It comes from **Masara** Village, **Emerum** People, **Madang** Province.]

D94+M. Transformation: man to ogre/spirit; D191M. Transformation: man to serpent (snake); D191M. Transformation: man to serpent (snake); D191W. Transformation: woman to serpent (snake); D192.2W. Transformation: woman to centipede; D993. Magic eye; D1002.1. Magic urine; F490+. Masalai; P210. Husband and wife; P230. Parents and children; P232. Mother and daughter; P234. Father and daughter; P251.5. Two brothers; P263. Brother-in-law; P264. Sister-in-law; P310. Friendship; T80. Tragic love

## Women Killed a Man's Head

(Wantok 569, May 4, 1985, page 20)

Long, long ago, there was a village called Koiya [**Kauwo**], near Mount Ialibu that was filled with young women [**Wiru** People, **Southern Highlands** Province]. In this village, there were no men, only women.

One day, the young women filed off to the forest to look for food. They paired off and walked around the forest, looking for ant eggs.

All of the women left except for one woman who stayed behind. This woman was very beautiful, and the other women of the village were jealous of her, so she did not have partners very often.

On this day, the woman who was alone traveled into forest. When she went to a place where the sword grass was piled high, she thought that it was an ant nest, so she shoved a stick that she was holding inside. If the ants fled, she could take their eggs.

But no, a man's head jumped outside and jumped onto one of her breasts. The woman was surprised and screamed and cried. The head was stuck like a baby drinking mother's milk.

The woman tried to remove him, and did various things to the head to get him from her breast. Then the other women heard the screaming and went to help her.

Inside the forest, the women did various kinds of things to remove the man's head from the woman's breast. However it was to no avail, the head was stuck fast. The woman felt like her breast would break or that the man would eat her.

A big woman who had gone with the others stopped the women from doing these things. She took a net bag and shoved the head inside it. The young woman carried it in front of her and went to the village. The man's head was inside the net bag and still attached to her breast.

All of the women returned to the village. Their sister was in the middle as they were walking. They did not carry food either because of this bad thing that had happened.

The old women of the village saw this. They gathered and spoke about finding a way to kill the man's head. They said that if they killed the man's head, it would leave the poor woman's breast.

One very old woman told the others, "All of you must gather firewood and pile it in just one place. Then we'll make a big fire and have a big feast tonight."

All of the women listened and followed the old woman's instructions. The young woman with the head on her breast just sat down in the house.

Then the women sang and danced happily together. They put on various kinds of festive adornments. They gathered firewood, sweet potatoes, pandanus fruits (*marita*), wild sugarcane (*pitpit*), leafy greens, and five whole pigs.

They killed one pig first then carried the pork to give to the head. When the man's head saw the pork and smelled its blood, oh my, he opened his eyes very wide.

Then the old woman told the other women, "When I make a sign, then you must light the fire quickly."

The old woman appointed one big, strong woman to kill the head and carry it to the fire.

The old woman turned and spoke in a different language. She asked the head who was still hanging from the young woman, "Where are you from? Mount Ialibu? Where?"

The man's head moved up and down, meaning yes.

The old woman asked again, "Are you a *masalai* from Ialibu?"

The head said, "No."

The old woman asked, "Are you a dead man?"

The head replied, "No."

The old woman asked again, "Are you a real man that wants to marry this young woman?"

The head said, "Yes."

The old woman asked, "Do you come from a place where there are men like you?"

The headman replied, "Yes."

All of the women listened to this and were afraid. They told the old woman that they must run away from this place. Then the old woman told the women that they must think about the big feast that would come later.

The food was ready, so they served the food to the women. They raised the young woman very high and put food near the head. When there was much pork was near the head, the head very quickly left the breast, went down, and opened his mouth to eat the pork.

The strong woman had taken a big spear and was ready nearby. When the head was about to open his mouth and eat the meat, the strong woman loosed the spear into his mouth.

The old woman gave the sign and the women lit the fire. The strong woman swung the spear with the man's head inside the fire. The head trembled and spun around with the spear in the fire.

The fire was very bright and the women burned the head to a crisp. They sang and danced around the fire. They did not know that that the place where the man's head came from was a place that was filled with men's heads.

The bonfire burned the head and it also burned the other heads that were far away. This was because their blood was the same and when one head was in the fire, the other heads also felt the fire burning them and spinning them around.

While the women sang, danced and jumped together, a big explosion surprised them. Inside the fire, the head was completely burned to ashes, but the brain was not burned well, then it exploded.

Afterwards, far away in the village of the men's heads, they also exploded at the same time after they had rolled and turned on the ground from the pain of the fire burning them. However, there was no fire that burned them.

The women were surprised and afraid. They ran away and went to the place where the old woman lived. The old woman told the women, "Don't be afraid. There are no enemies such as the men's heads because all of the heads died with the one that burned in the fire."

The woman who had the man's head biting her breast was also terrified, but after the old woman said this, she was happy again. However, before long, the women saw a flood with blood from the other heads go to the place of the bonfire. Every place was covered with water.

The little place where the women lived, where they had burned the head was still dry land. This place is now where Mount Ialibu stands.

Peter Kay

Longere Village

Pangia

Southern Highlands Province

A1011. Local deluges; A1012.3. Flood from blood; D2061.2.2. Murder by sympathetic magic; F501+. Man consisting only of head attaches to woman's breast; F566.1+. Village of women only; K925. Victim pushed into fire; P252. Sisters; Q414. Punishment: burning alive; R331K. Mountain refuge; S112. Burning to death; W181. Jealousy

# Hand Drums Confused Two Women

(Wantok 570, May 11, 1985, page 20)

In a village named Begesin [**Bagasin**] in the Usino area of **Madang** Province, there lived two young women [**Girawa** People]. Their names were Tukuame and Munda. Many young men of the village often tried to marry them. But they were unsuccessful. The two women were very stubborn.

One day, the men of the village were constructing a pigsty. The men of this village sent a message to the other villages to come to a big festival and feast at Begesin Village. They decided that whoever excelled at singing and dancing could carry away these two women.

Everyone in all of the villages near Usino received the message that day. At the beginning of this time, there also lived a young man in **Ginam** Village. He straightened and prepared his adornments well for the day of the festival.

The young man's name was Akuai Trago. Many people asked him to prepare their decorations. This was because he well knew all of the little things to do to make decorations.

Akuai prepared his own adornments, then he also prepared the adornments of another man. The next day, it would be time for everyone to gather at the site of the festival. That night, Akuai went to the forest and cut a piece of bamboo.

This bamboo was perfectly straight and was pure green. That night, Akuai quietly pulled this excellent bamboo to the village. He watched carefully so that the surface of the bamboo did not become ruined. He carried it and put it inside the pigsty that had been decorated well for the big day.

After he put the good bamboo there, he stood nearby and said some words. Then he left the pigsty and walked outside a little. Before long, he heard a big explosion like the firing of a gun.

The good-for-nothing Akuai wanted to turn and look, but no, a young man was standing there. The man had appeared when the bamboo broke. The bamboo was no longer there.

Oh my, Akuai saw the man and ran to grab him. The young man also held Akuai and said, "Hey brother, thank you very much for bringing me here. Now we're brothers."

Akuai told the man, "We're brothers now. Your name is Mundagawa and I'm Akuai."

Dawn was breaking and many men, women and children had prepared their decorations and were walking towards the festival. The two men walked away. However, no one knew where Mundagawa had come from. They saw him and thought that he was a man from another village who had also come to the festival gathering. They walked and walked. Near the Ramu River, they saw a very old couple. The old couple was bent over, their eyes were sunken, their bodies were broken, and they had white hair.

The people's hearts burst with happiness because of going to the festival, but they did not cast their eyes towards the old couple. When the old couple called to the passersby to give them a hand, they did not look at them.

They turned back and called out, "Never mind calling out, you two are old and worthless. Your time has passed many years and months ago. Now it's our time."

The old couple sat, watched and ate by the Ramu River. They did not care about what the people had said to them.

Then Akuai and Mundagawa walked and walked, and the old couple called out to them. The young men turned back and went back to sit and tell stories with the old people.

The men sat and ate with the old couple, then the old man gave them casuarina tree sap [lit., "milk and blood"]. Then he told the men, "When you arrive at the festival, put the casuarina sap on your hand drums. This is so that the sound of the drums will be better than those of any other person."

Akuai and Mundagawa followed the old man's instructions. They would apply the casuarina sap, but the festival was still some time in the future. The people sang and danced through the night.

The men decided to put the casuarina sap on their hand drums now. They blew upon the sap until it dried. When they beat their drums, everyone heard it clearly. The two women heard it and looked for the sound.

From where was the sound of the hand drums coming? The two women looked directly at Akuai and Mundagawa. They went and held the men's hands then sang and danced. When the women's mother saw this, she cried. She knew that she would lose her two daughters. She cried. The beautiful "grass" skirt that she had tied onto one of them, she had cut into two parts. She put one part on Tukuame and the other on Munda.

The father saw that she was sad, but he was happy to see that the handsome young men would marry his daughters. He would use one "grass" skirt in the traditional manner, to tie to Akuai's hand. The other would be tied to Mundagawa's right hand.

He removed the shell that was hanging from his right ear and hung it on Akuai's right ear. The father put the

shell from his left ear on Mundagawa's left ear. He put the big shell on his head onto Mundagawa's head. He removed the strong *tambu* shell from his back and put in on Akuai's neck.

The mother carried two beautiful new net bags that she had made for the two women, and she put them on top of their heads. The festival was still going on through the night. A big fire was in the middle. Nearby, the women and men made a small fire and sat down to chew betel nuts, smoke and tell stories.

Very close by, they erected a big piece of bamboo that they had broken to look like a torch. It was dawn and they butchered the pigs, dividing them among the villages. The betel nuts, betel peppers, yams, coconuts, and other foods went all around.

The two men with the women went up to the old couple near the Ramu River. Akuai took the big sister Tukuame. Mundagawa took the little sister Munda.

The old couple saw them and was elated. They knew that the sound of the hand drums with the casuarina sap had confused Tukumae [Tukuame] and Munda's thinking, and they had fallen for the two men.

They had known that after the festival, the two men would return to them with the two women. All of the young men of the near and far villages had put on fine adornments and traditional forest scents.

The father of the two women was the leader of all of the clans in the Usino area, so a big contest had arisen [to marry his two daughters].

The old man told a story to the two men, and then he gave red grass to Akuai. Akuai and his wife Tukuame, followed him up to the Negera River. Mundagawa took white grass. He and his wife, Munda, followed the Negra [Negera] River down towards the sea.

Now, on top of Mount Akuai and Mount Tukuame are **Bundi** Village and the Bundi [**Gende**] People. Mundagawa and Munda went down the Negera River to live and begin the **Usino** [People].

Gabriel Doa [Andbruk]
Wait [White] Stone area
Emegari Village, Bundi
Madang Province

A1611+. Origin of Bundi People; A1611+. Origin of Gende People; D431.10M. Transformation: sections of bamboo to man; D974. Magic plant-sap; D1355.1. Love-producing music; D1774. Magic results from speaking; P210. Husband and wife; P232. Mother and daughter; P234. Father and daughter; P251.5. Two brothers; P252.1. Two sisters; P261. Father-in-law; P262. Mother-in-law; P265. Son-in-law; Q40. Kindness rewarded; T10. Falling in love; W167. Stubbornness

## The Dog Got Back at the Old Woman

(Wantok 571, May 18, 1985, page 20)

Long, long ago, in somewhere in the mountains of Kainantu, there was a village called **Ritega** [**Eastern Highlands** Province]. In this village, there lived an old woman and her dog.

They did not live with other people. No, they lived by themselves in their small house that was far from where other people lived. This house of theirs was about three miles away from the other houses.

The old woman often took care of her dog well, so the dog was happy and always took care of the old woman well by chasing *masalai*s and sorcerers who approached to their house.

The old woman had eight children. They were married and had their own children. The old woman's children lived with other people in village communal houses.

The old woman's sons brought their pigs to her, and she husbanded their pigs in a pigsty that was near her house. The men's wives always brought food for the pigs and for the old woman too. They would bring the food to their house. Because of this, the old woman was never short of food.

The old woman's children would always come to kill their pigs, and they would leave some meat and two big pieces of fat from the bellies for their old mother. The old woman would the meat well, then she and her dog could eat for about four weeks.

One time, there was a great enemy who came between the old woman and her dog. This is how the problem came about. Once, the old woman's children did not kill their pigs. The poor old woman and her dog had not eaten meat for a long time. The old woman thought about killing one of her children's pigs and cooking it, but then she thought not to, so she just stayed there with her dog.

One morning, one of her children came and told her that he had come to kill a pig for them to cook in an earth oven. The old woman's child took a huge pig and killed it.

They killed the pig, then they cooked it in an earth oven. The man divided the meat. The liver, belly, and fat were what his mother liked very much, so he put these inside his old mother's house. Then the son took the rest of the pork and returned home.

The old woman trembled with excitement because of the meat, then she did something reprehensible to her dog. She did not think of her poor dog, not at all. The old woman ignored the dog. She sat and ate the pork alone until it was completely dark.

While the old woman was eating meat, the poor dog was sitting and just staring. The old woman did not think of the dog, she alone swallowed the meat. Slowly, she rose and scolded the dog, "I always take care of you well, but you never kill wild game and bring it to me. You just think of yourself and never of me. Now you'll know your mistake."

The old woman thought that the dog could not understand what she said, but the dog listened. It just lay there quietly and thought, "OK old woman, let's see. Is it because of your strength or my strength that we live well in this forested area so far from the other houses?"

So at about eight o'clock at night, the dog removed the ashes from its skin and went outside. When the dog went out, it went directly to the communal house of the *masalai*s and called for all of the *masalai*s to gather.

When the *masalai*s gathered, the dog told them, "You always go around the house that I live in with the old woman. You go there to kill her, but I'm there and I chase you. You're afraid of me, but now I agree that you can go to the house and kill the old woman."

Oh my, when the *masalai*s heard this, they were very happy. They followed the dog back to the house. When they arrived at the house, the dog told the *masalai*s to wait outside while the dog went inside to see whether the old woman was sleeping.

The dog went inside the house and saw the old woman sleeping awkwardly because she had eaten the pork until her belly was bloated and she was half-dead. The dog saw this, quietly went back outside, and then told the *masalai*s to go inside the house and bring the woman out.

The *masalai*s listened and went inside the house. Some carried her legs and some carried her in the middle. They began taking her outside.

When they carried her out, the old woman felt it. She slowly opened her eyes and saw the *masalai*s carrying her outside. Oh my, the old woman just screamed. The *masalai*s were surprised. They left her and ran away. The old woman just got up and pulled her axe out, then swung at the dog's head. The poor dog cried out and fell dead.

Dawn came and the old woman called out to the communal house. When the people heard her, they all woke up and ran to see her.

Then the old woman's children took all her goods and she went with the other people to the communal house. The old woman lived there until her death.

Reuben K. Nassoh

Kainantu

Eastern Highlands Province

B211.1.7. Speaking dog; F490+. Masalai; G580+. Ogres frightened away by screaming; P231. Mother and son; P262. Mother-in-law; P265+. Daughter-in-law; Q281. Ingratitude punished; Q281+. Betrayal punished; Q411. Death as punishment; R220. Flights; W125. Gluttony; W152. Stinginess; W154. Ingratitude

## Yomba Transformed a
## Ghost into a Real Person

(Wantok 572, May 25, 1985, page 20)

Long ago, in the time of the ancestors, there was a man named Yomba who lived in the Nuku area. Yomba often traveled in the forest looking for food or went working in the garden in the sun. When the sun went down, Yomba would hear the birds sing and he would walk back to the house.

One day, Yomba went to the garden. He worked and he saw that the sun was still bright. Yomba kept working, then he saw the clouds about to gather and cover the sun. He heard the clouds thunder and he took a little piece of ginger that was in his net bag. He chewed it and he spat it up towards the clouds. He called the name of the mountain so that the spirit of the mountain would blow the clouds far away.

Quickly, Yomba shot a pig with a spear then carried the piglet with other garden food to the village. However, when he came to the other side of the mountain, a heavy rain began to fall. Yomba could not cross the river because the river was flooded.

The rain moved and arrived at the place where Yomba was. Yomba saw that the area had become completely dark, then the rain fell down, the clouds thundered and many tree branches fell about.

Yomba saw the big mountain standing there. Yomba carried the garden food and tied it with vines into two big bundles along with the pig. He went to sit under cover and to wait until the rain stopped.

However, Yomba did not see that there was a small trail directly behind the base of the tree that went down to the ground. Under this tree was a big cave that was completely open. This was some people's house. Their place was clear, but the people had covered the entrance with rubbish so that it looked like an ordinary place.

Yomba sat until it was completely dark. The rain and wind did not stop. Yomba thought to himself, "Never mind, I'll sleep here at the base of the tree. Tomorrow, I'll walk back to the house."

That night, a woman carried her son in a net bag along with food, and was walking near the base of the tree. They began to remove the rubbish that was by the ladder of the house that was in the big cave. The little boy trampled old Yomba who was sleeping.

The woman also smelled the blood of a young pig. The mother and son were not real people like Yomba. They were ghosts. They wanted to go down to their underground house.

The boy trampled on Yomba and felt that his skin was hot. This was because ghosts' skins are cold, whether it is sunny or rainy.

The boy told his mother, "There's an enemy. I felt the hot blood shooting through his legs." Yomba heard this and got up. The two of them saw this and opened the stone cave door. They brought old Yomba who carried the bundles of food and the piglet with him.

The three of them went together down into the ghosts' house. The ghost woman cooked the food. She butchered the pig and left it.

Yomba told the woman to cook the pork and the leafy greens. The woman replied that she could not cook it. No, they would leave it like that, then eat it.

Yomba shut his mouth, but he thought, "Oh my, I thought this was a real woman. She and her son are ghosts. The boy and mother eat. They don't eat with their mouths. They put the food in the back of their heads near their necks. All of the food, the piglet meat and the new food, is just gone. All of the meat and the pig's belly are just gone. Yomba himself just ate ripe bananas and sugarcanes."

Yomba looked at the pork; the belly was gone. He just opened his mouth and did not say anything. Yomba thought hard and looked for a way to escape from this place.

Luckily, the next day when the rain and wind had stopped, the ghost woman told her son to look after Yomba while she went to search for food.

When the woman departed, Yomba chewed a little ginger and spat a tiny amount on the ghost boy. He thought that it would confuse him while he carried him up to the ground. So, he put him on his shoulder and walked away. However before they walked away, Yomba chewed the ginger and spat it all over. He performed a kind of dance and song, then spat around the door of this house in the forest.

He sang and danced at everything in the house, then blew on himself and the bow. Old Yomba was not an ordinary man, so his singing and dancing made his two legs traverse the long distance up from the house.

He told this story to everyone in the village. They prepared various kinds of songs and dances so that the ghost woman and her ghost kin could not see her boy's face.

The men sang and danced. They put betel nuts, betel peppers, and ginger in a pile together. They blew on the village and it changed completely. The village was hidden in smoke when the ghosts came to get the child. They tried to see the village and the child, but they were unable to do so. The leaders of the village had blown the smoke, and the smoke blocked off the ghosts completely.

Old Yomba stopped worrying. He put on various adornments and gave away various foods. Yomba performed a dance and song, and the little boy turned into a real boy in the village.

The boy no longer thought of his ghost mother. Yomba told him that he could not look for food or make a garden or go into the part of the forest where his mother lived.

Yomba completely forbade him from doing this. He told his ghost son to go to the other side of the river and not to the side of the mountain.

After a while, the man did not know that he was a ghost child, and he did not know that he was not Yomba's son. Later, the man married and had children. One of the man's children turned into a ghost to take the place of his father. At this time Yomba died.

Elias Yomolot
Imbi-ip [**Imbiyip**] Village [**Yahang** People]
Nuku
**West Sepik** Province

D42.2. Spirit takes shape of man; D44+B. Transformation: boy to ghost; D967+. Magic ginger; D985.5. Magic betel-nut; D985.5+. Magic betel-pepper; D1001. Magic spittle; D1271+. Magic smoke; D1548. Magic object controls weather; D1711. Magician; D1766.7. Magic results from uttering powerful name; D1781. Magic results from singing; D1781+. Magic results from dancing; D1980. Magic invisibility; D2000+. Magic confusion; D2122. Journey with magic speed; E422.1.3+. Cold revenants; E425.1. Revenant as woman; E425.3. Revenant as child; E541+. Revenants eat from back of head; F460. Mountain-spirits; H46.1+. Revenant recognized when it devours raw flesh; P230. Parents and children; P231. Mother and son; P271. Foster father; P275. Foster son; R10.3. Children abducted; R260. Pursuits; T100. Marriage

# How Did Yams (*Yam* and *Mami*) Arise?

(Wantok 573, June 1, 1985, page 28)

Long, long ago, in my village, there were two brothers. The names of these brothers were Dikiti and Yarimu. Dikiti was the little brother and Yarimu was the name of the big brother. The two brothers were very handsome men, but there was one small problem with Dikiti, the little brother.

Dikiti never defecated because his shit-hole was completely blocked. It was true that he often ate, but the food would just go down and rot in his belly.

Only the big brother, Yarimu, was married. Poor Dikiti was not married because he was the kind of man who did not have a shit-hole, so he lived alone.

One day, Yarimu and his wives worked at cutting an ironwood tree near the stream. Dikiti was walking around and he became thirsty for water. He went down to the stream and drank. He saw the ironwood tree bark drifting on the water.

When Dikiti saw this, he took a piece of the bark and smelled the sweet smell of ironwood. He looked again and saw many pieces of ironwood bark still drifting down to where he was standing.

Dikiti followed the ironwood bark upstream. He walked and walked, then approached the place where Yarimu and his wives were cutting the ironwood tree. Then they saw him.

Yarimu told his wives, "Go and hide. Dikiti is approaching." Yarimu's wives listened, got up and then turned into snakes and centipedes, which lay about.

Dikiti walked and arrived at this place. Oh my, he saw the big snakes and centipedes lying around and he screamed terribly.

Yarimu saw this and he called out, "Hey, why are you screaming?" Then his wives turned back into women again and laughed hysterically at Dikiti.

They said, "Hey are you the man with whom we played and frightened?" Dikiti told the women that he had thought that they were real snakes and centipedes, so he was frightened and had screamed.

The women asked him whether he wanted to eat ironwood [fruits]. Dikiti told them that he did, so the women listened and piled ironwood [fruits] upon him. The good-for-nothing sat quietly and began to eat the ironwood [fruits].

While Dikiti sat eating, his brother Yarimu got up quietly and went fairly far away, where he dug a water hole.

He hid his spear and then he returned and sat with his brother.

Dikiti gorged himself on the ironwood [fruits] until he became thirsty for water. He got up and told his brother, "I want to drink water."

Yarimu listened and said, "Come, I found a good water hole that is nearby."

The brothers walked to the water hole. When they arrived, the big brother Yarimu told him, "Dikiti, you must lie down and go down low, then drink the water."

When Dikiti lay down, his buttocks were near the breaking point. This was because the man did not have a shit-hole, so his buttocks were jam-packed.

Quietly, Yarimu got up, took his spear and shoved it right into Dikiti's buttocks. Oh my, the man's buttocks broke apart. The feces and blood spilled right out. The blood and feces flowed and flowed until it all came out. Then Yarimu took his brother and went to his house and to his wives.

Yarimu went and put his brother in the house, then he went to sleep. While Dikiti was in his brother's house, the sore on his buttocks had not yet healed, so he just slept. At this time too, it looked as if there was no food in Yarimu's house.

One time, he felt a little better and was lying inside the house. He saw Yarimu's wife wafting the smell of sword grass. Then she went to fetch water to boil.

However while the water was boiling, the meat and other food just appeared. Oh my, Dikiti was surprised to see the food appear just like water. But he did not speak. He just shut his mouth and ate what was given to him.

Yarimu's wives did this all of the time. At mealtime, the women would waft the smell of sword grass, fetch water, and boil it. Then food would just appear.

Dikiti did not worry about living at this place because his brother and his brother's wives worked at taking care of him well. After a while, the sore on his buttocks healed. One time, he told his brother Yarimu that he wanted to return home.

Yarimu told him, "Little boy, come hold these things." Yarimu gave him two coconuts and a bamboo tube of water. After he gave these things to Dikiti, he told him, "When you walk off and you feel like shitting, you must put just the bamboo tube of water down, then hold the two coconuts in your hands."

Dikiti listened to his brother. He carried the things and walked back to his home. While he was still walking on the trail, he felt the need to defecate. So, he put the two coconuts down on the trail and went inside the forest to defecate.

While he was sitting and defecating, he heard two women laughing. Dikiti listened, then got up and went back to see who was laughing. He saw two very beautiful women standing on the trail where he had put the two coconuts.

Dikiti saw this and wanted to talk with them, but the two women just laughed and walked away. The poor man called out to them, but they kept laughing and began to run from him.

The women ran and ran until they went down to the stream underneath the smell of sword grass. Dikiti followed them and he saw the women going down to the stream. He also walked there and wafted the smell of sword grass to look for the two women.

When Dikiti wafted the sword-grass smell, a bird shot right into Dikiti's eye. Dikiti walked around in confusion and fell on the other side of the stream. Then two pigs came to this stream and killed Dikiti.

Dikiti lay there dead. Then yams (*yam* and *mami*) began to spill out from this stream because the sword-grass smell had blocked up the hole. The water was in a clear place, and the food spilled out.

One of Yarimu's wives went to see this and called out to all to the others, "Hey all of you must come. This place is ruined now."

Yarimu and his other wives listened to the shouting and ran to the place of the sword-grass smell to see that Dikiti was lying dead.

They tried to dam the stream, but they could not do so. The yams were still spilling out. So now, the people of the Wasara [**Galisakan**] area have plenty of yams in their villages [**Emerum** People, **Madang** Province]. This is the story that explains how yams came to our villages.

Mathew Maikua
P. S. C. Hostel, P. O. Box 213
Madang
Madang Province

[See also *Wantok* #568 for a story about Yarimu and Dikiti.]

B873+. Giant centipede; B875.1. Giant serpent; D191W. Transformation: woman to serpent (snake); D192.2W. Transformation: woman to centipede; D380W. Transformation: centipede to woman; D391W. Transformation: serpent (snake) to woman; D431.11+W. Transformation: coconut to woman; D965.12. Magic grass; D1030.1. Food supplied by magic; F529.2. People without anuses; P210. Husband and wife; P263. Brother-in-law; P264. Sister-in-law; P251.5. Two brothers; R260. Pursuits; T145.0.1. Polygyny; X740.1H+. Symbolic pedicatory rape

# Two Brothers Killed the Old Ghosts

(Wantok 574, June 8, 1985, page 28)

Long, long ago, there were two brothers who lived in a village. The names of these brothers were Alo and Rabae. The brothers were not ordinary men. Whenever they went to the forest, they did not fool around at killing marsupials (*kapul*). They always killed many marsupials when they traveled in the forest, so they were very happy in their village.

One time, the moon was bright and the two brothers decided to go hunt for marsupials in the forest again. They carried their bows, arrows and axes, then they began to walk off into a dense forest that was far from the village. The marsupials were very plentiful at this place.

As the two brothers walked along the trail, they shot marsupials along the way. They did not like to carry many things, so they put the marsupials down for themselves to get on their return to the village.

The two brothers worked at killing marsupials. They did not see what was following them along this trail. An old woman was going behind them. Whenever the two brothers killed marsupials and put them down, the old woman would eat them.

The two brothers came close to a tree, and Alo told Rabae, "You stand below and watch. I'll climb the tree and shoot marsupials. Then you take them and collect them at one place."

Alo finished explaining to his brother, then he ascended tree. However, Rabae had not heard that Alo had said to look for his marsupials. It was late at night, and Alo was carrying a bundle of arrows. He climbed the tree and began to shoot the marsupials.

He worked at shooting the marsupials from the branches below. He threw them down and followed the other branches of the tree. He trembled at killing the marsupials, and did not look down to see the places where the marsupials had fallen.

When Alo arrived at the crown of the tree, his arrows were almost gone. It looked like there were just two arrows left. One branch of the tree went very far out, and the good-for-nothing saw a marsupial going along that branch.

So, he aimed directly at it and shot the marsupial. When he looked down at the ground, the man was shocked to see an old woman eating all of the marsupials.

The old woman said, "I'm so sorry that I've worked very hard at finding you, but now you're here. Now I'll kill you and eat you." Alo looked down and saw that the woman's two teeth were huge. She fastened her net back and went to stand at the base of the tree.

The old woman called out for her husband to come to the base of the tree too. The man's teeth were just like those of the woman.

The woman's husband arrived and asked his wife, "What did you do to find this good wild game [i.e., the man] for us?"

The old woman replied, "He always came here, finishing off our wild game, so that's how I found him."

Her husband listened and he told the man on top of the tree, "Hey, was it you that always came here and finished off our game inside the forest, you that we've tried so hard to find? Now where are you going?"

Poor Alo listened and was terrified: he urinated and defecated. He called out to his brother Rabae, but his brother had run back to the village long ago. The deep forest was very far away, and no one heard the poor man's shouts from the top of the tree.

The old woman told her husband, "I'm going up the tree. Watch carefully lest the man jump down and run away." Poor Alo listened and did not know what to do. His arrows were gone and he was just sitting on the tree branch. He had thrown down his bow, but he still held his axe.

When the woman approached the place where Alo was sitting, the good-for-nothing cut off her head which then fell down to the base of the tree. She told her husband to climb the tree.

He climbed the tree until he approached Alo. However, Alo again cut off his head. His head also went down to the base of the tree.

The two old ghosts tried to move, but they were unable to do so. The woman told her husband to watch the base of the tree. She ran back to their house and brought a huge net bag.

The net bag was huge, like a fishing net. The woman took the net bag and covered up the whole tree. Alo was sitting up there. The woman climbed the tree again. Alo wanted to cut her, but she was still climbing. Alo became afraid and jumped down to the base of the tree.

He fell right into the net bag, and the woman's husband tied the mouth of the net bag very quickly. His wife descended and the two of them carried Alo in the net bag to their house.

They carried him and put the net bag on top of the fireplace. Oh my, the smoke ruined the poor man. He was completely out of air and near death.

The couple's two children came and said, "We want to see him too. Remove him from the net bag." However, their parents told them that it was a marsupial.

In the morning, they told the children, "We're going to get vegetables, firewood, and leaves to make an earth oven… We can't return to the house quickly. You must not touch the marsupial, or it will eat you."

The parents left the children there and went to look for these things. The boys sat and played with rope. They made various things, and one of them said, "We know everything except for one thing that we don't know."

The good-for-nothing was lying inside the net bag and he heard the children talking. He called to them, "I know this thing. If you want me to teach you, then come and remove me from the net bag first. Then I'll show you."

The children listened to this, then raced to remove the net bag and bring it down. The man came out of the net bag and told them, "Now I'll teach you, but your father has an axe." The boys said, "Yes." Alo told them to go and bring ginger (*gorgor*) leaves too.

Then he told the children to go out with him to the big tree. The man put the things on top of the tree and told the children, "Go and lie on top of the tree, then I'll teach you about this thing that you're trying to find. When you're asleep, you'll hear noises. Don't open your eyes."

When the children were lying in a row, Alo began to cut their necks. After he cut them, he cut the children into little pieces and threw their bodies around the forest.

Then he went inside the house and hid inside a big gourd (*sel kambang*) that the ancestors used to store tree oil.

He sat there and heard the parents returning to the house. They saw that their children were not there, but that blood was spilled all over the trail and at the tree by the house. They looked at the blood and thought that their children had eaten the bad marsupial, then had run away to hide.

They called out and searched for their children for a while, then they saw the legs and arms of the children lying around the forest by the house. They ran back to the house and saw the place where the net bag had been hung. They saw that the net bag ropes were loose, and they knew that the man had probably just come out of the net bag and killed their children.

The two of them sniffed around to find Alo. His smell was still strong inside the house, so the man told the woman, "Look carefully. He's still inside the house. He hasn't run away."

The woman searched and searched then arrived at the place where the gourd was. When the woman looked in-side, Alo took some marsupial's teeth and removed the old [ghost] woman's two eyes. The old woman fell back.

The old man was trying to find Alo too. He called from inside to his wife, but his wife did not reply at all. The old man went inside the house again to check on her. When he went inside, he saw that his wife was lying awkwardly.

He began to look for the man inside the house again. When he arrived at the place where the gourd stood, he looked inside. Alo sprung up and removed the old man's two eyes and he fell near where his wife was lying.

Quickly, Alo came out of the gourd and took a big pig from the old couple. He went to the place where they had long before prepared to cook him in an earth oven. He butchered the pig and cooked it in the earth oven. Then he went back to their house.

He went inside and took their good things: the stone axes, bows, tree oil, *kina* shells, and pigs. He carried them to the trail that was very far from the house. After he put them there, he went back again and uncovered the earth oven.

Alo only ate the pig's guts. He tied up all of the meat with leaves and filled a net bag. When he was finished, he went to the house. He fastened the old couple's house door tightly. He took a big, strong rope and tied it well, then he went outside. He took some big tree branches and piled them up around the house, then he lit them on fire.

The fire burned the house along with the old couple. Then the man carried the things and walked back to his village. When he was far away, he heard shouting behind him, "That's alright you can go ahead. One day we'll come to see you."

Alo sped along, he went back directly until he came to his village. He went up to the house and saw his brother, Rabae, just lying there. He was close to dying. His two eyes were completely shut and he was just lying there.

His brother Rabae was not sick. He was worried because he had thought that the old couple had killed Alo. So, every day, he just sat and cried.

When Alo returned to the village, Rabae was elated. Alo removed the things that he had brought and his brother put them away. They butchered the pork and they ate. Alo told the story to his brother about the old couple.

Rabae listened to the story and was angry with the old ghost couple. He said, "That's alright. You've returned. Let them come and we'll see them."

A little rain fell that day. When they arrived, the old couple ate through the first fence that was around the house. The two brothers shot at them, but the old couple kept coming.  They broke through the second fence.  They cut the third fence, then the fourth, and on and on until they arrived at the last fence.

The brothers saw this and they began to run to the other side of a bridge.  The old couple broke the last fence and they began to run to the bridge to kill the two brothers.  The two men saw this and they just watched.  When the old couple came to the center of the bridge, the men cut the ropes and trees [that supported the bridge].

The bridge broke and the old couple fell down into the river.  The old couple fell into the water and became fish.  The brothers had no way to return to the village, so they became birds.

This kind of bird never flies near the ground.  No, it always flies high in the clouds.  The name of this bird in my language is *puluma*.

Kete Pondopa
**Kira** Village [**Kewa** People]
Kagua
**Southern Highlands** Province

A1970. Creation of miscellaneous birds; D150M. Transformation: man to bird; D170M. Transformation: man to fish; D170W. Transformation: woman to fish; D1610.5. Speaking head; E261.4. Ghost pursues man; E402.1.1.1. Ghost calls; E425.1. Revenant as woman; E425.2. Revenant as man; E425.3. Revenant as child; E437.2. Ghost laid in body of water; E446.3+. Ghost laid by dismemberment; E783.1. Head cut off and successfully replaced; E783.5. Vital head speaks; F544.3.5. Remarkably long teeth; G11.10. Cannibalistic spirits; G441. Ogre carries victim in bag (basket); K812. Victim burned in his own house (or hiding place); K826+. Dupe killed after being persuaded to close eyes; K914. Murder from ambush; P210. Husband and wife; P251.5. Two brothers; P231. Mother and son; P233. Father and son; Q213. Abduction punished; Q402. Punishment of children for parents' offenses; Q411. Death as punishment; Q553.4. Death of children as punishment; R11. Abduction by monster (ogre); R210. Escapes; R220. Flights; R260. Pursuits; S112.0.2. House (hostel) burned with all inside; S118.2. Murder by cutting throat; S139.2. Slain person dismembered; S165. Mutilation: putting out eyes; S180+. Smoking person over fire; W157. Dishonesty

## A Flood Ruined a Village

(Wantok 575, June 15, 1985, page 20)

Long, long ago, in my village, there was a big python that lived at the base of a tree.

One day, the children of the village went and played at the place where the python lived.  They raced around and threw green coconuts down to the place where the snake lived.

When the boys threw the coconuts down, the snake rounded up the coconuts and brought them to the place where it slept.  It did this for a while, then the children on top of the coconut palm saw that their green coconuts were just disappearing.

They began to look for what it was that had done this to their coconuts.  One boy went down, close to the hole in the tree.  He saw the big python lying there with the green coconuts that they had been throwing down for a long time.

The boy shouted and ran away.  His other friends also went to look.  They too shouted and ran back to the village.  They explained to the people of the village about the big python.

When the leaders heard about the big python lying near the village, oh my, were they happy.  They broke ginger (*gorgor*) leaves.  They carried them back to the place where the snake was lying.  They did not kill the snake.  No, they tied it up with the ginger leaves and carried it back to the village.

In the afternoon, the leaders called out to the men, women and children to come and gather.  They told them of the huge feast that they would make and eat with the snake.  They worked at getting everything in order in the village, then they slept.

In the morning, all of the men, women and children woke up and went to get the food, betel nuts, betel peppers, and other things for the big feast.  They appointed two girls and their two brothers to watch the python.

When everyone left the village, the python changed into a very young man and went towards them.  Oh my, the four of them were shocked and they trembled together.  However the snake told them, "I'm not a snake.  I'm a real man like you, so you don't need to be afraid of me."

He told the two boys to go fetch the betel nuts and peppers, and a piece of leaf from a banana plant called *amorenem*.  The boys went and fetched the things that he had asked for, and brought them back to give to him.

The snake-man took the betel nuts and peppers then chewed them.  He spat on the banana leaf.  He did this because when the men saw him, they would see that he was a real man and not a snake that had chewed and spat betel nuts.

He told the girls, "If the men ask you to kill me, then tell them to give my belly to you."  He pointed to a very tall coconut palm tree and told them, "If something happens, then take the two boys with some fire and all of you go up that coconut tree."

The snake finished speaking with them, and they rested.  In the afternoon, all of the men, women and children returned to the village with various foods and leafy greens that they had taken to eat with their meat.

When all of them had returned to the village, the two girls told them that it was not a real snake, but a man. They showed the people the betel nut spittle that the snake had spat long before. When the men listened to this, they laughed hysterically at the two girls.

They said, "You two probably dreamt this, or maybe your boyfriends came to stay with you, ate the betel nuts, and spat it around. Then you two wanted to lie to us."

They said this, then they killed the python. They butchered the snake meat for everyone in the village. The two girls took the snake's guts then they carried them down to the river.

They washed the snake's guts and removed the feces. When they looked inside the guts, they found that it was filled with traditional adornments. They found the teeth of dogs and flying foxes. They took these things and adorned the two young boys who had been with them when the snake had become a man.

In the afternoon, everyone came and gathered together. They began to eat their good meat. When they began to eat, a strong wind and rain began to arise. A big flood also began to come to this village. It covered all of the men, women, children, houses, pigs, dogs and other things in the village.

On the previous day, the four had had climbed and sat upon the coconut palm that the snake had pointed out. After two days, they took a green coconut and threw it down to see if the flood had receded or not. However, the coconut showed that it had not yet receded.

They threw one more green coconut down. They saw that the flood had receded a little, but they did not go down to the ground quickly. They still sat on the tree and waited.

Then two *masalai* stones came and pulverized the bones of the men, women, children, and other things in the village. After this, two big chickens came down and swept all of the bones into the forest. While they swept the place and walked around, they spoke, "*Manag gu bar pu. Manag gu bar pu.*"

This means, "Where are you going, nowhere, huh." Then the village was clean again and the two girls and their brothers came down from the coconut tree. The boys made a house and they lived together there.

They lived there for a while, then the two boys became big men. They changed and married. Each woman married the other's brother. They raised children and their village became big again.

This was the story of the snake and my own clan that is called Rangai.

John Masabi
Saint Fidelis College, Kap
Aleksisafen [Alexishafen]
Madang Province

A1011. Local deluges; A1018. Flood as punishment; A1640+. Origin of Rangai Clan; B91.6. Serpent causes flood; B211.3.2.1. Speaking chicken; B872.8K. Giant rooster; B875.1. Giant serpent; D391M. Transformation: serpent (snake) to man; D931. Magic rock (stone); D2142.1. Wind produced by magic; D2143.1. Rain produced by magic; D2151.8. Magic flood; F490+. Masalai; F495. Stone-spirit; J652. Inattention to warnings; P210. Husband and wife; P230. Parents and children; P253. Sister and brother; P263. Brother-in-law; P264. Sister-in-law; P230. Parents and children; P310. Friendship; Q211.6. Killing an animal revenged; Q428. Punishment: drowning; R311. Tree refuge; T100. Marriage

[The story in *Wantok* #576 is the same as that in #426.]


# Do Not Covet Food
### (Wantok 577, June 29, 1985, page 20)

Long, long ago, in the time of the ancestors, there lived a brother and a sister. Their parents had died and they lived by themselves.

The girl was grown and nearly ready to marry. However, the poor boy was still small, and his sister took care of him all of the time.

They lived for a while, then the woman married. She took her little brother to live with her in her husband's house. While they lived there, the woman took care of her brother very well.

After the woman cooked the food, she would put a big piece of taro or yam and some meat on her brother's plate. For herself and her husband, they would eat small pieces of taro and meat or whatever she had cooked.

The woman did this for a long time and her husband became very angry. The man often thought badly of his little brother-in-law. The woman also saw that her husband was not happy with her brother.

Then one day, the woman's husband told his brother-in-law, "Brother-in-law, let's go to the garden and cut some new forest."

The woman listened and thought hard. She told her husband, "Never mind that. Go to the garden alone and leave the boy here with me to help me do other work."

The man was angry and scolded his wife. The poor little boy did not know what was wrong. He thought that she wanted to stop him.

The woman's husband and his brother-in-law left for the forest and the woman sat and thought, "I know that my husband has taken the boy to the forest to kill him."

In the afternoon, the woman finished cooking and sat waiting by the house door. She sat and watched, then she saw her husband coming alone.

She asked him, "Where's my brother?" Her husband said, "Huh? He left me in the forest and walked back to the village."

The woman listened to what her husband said, but she did not believe it. She firmly thought that he must have killed her little brother.

Darkness came and the woman still sat by their house door. While she was sitting and mourning, a star flew to her. The woman was completely mournful and said, "I'm so sad. That man killed my brother and returned to the village."

The star listened, then went around and around the place where the woman was mourning. The woman sat for a while, then she rose and took a traditional rope and a net bag that we people of **Kieta** call *tora* [**Nasioi** People, **North Solomons** Province]. She also took a pandanus (*karuka*) mat and followed the star.

They went and went until they arrived at the place where her husband and little brother had cut the forest. The star flew until it sat right on the little boy's body.

The woman's husband had killed his little brother-in-law and covered him with leaves. When the woman raised the leaves, she saw her brother's body lying there.

That night, the woman sat near her brother's body and cried. She took her *tora* and the rope, then made a knapsack for her brother's body.

The woman did not want to return to the village to see her husband. She thought, "Never mind that my brother stinks on my back [in the knapsack], I can't be a good wife any more."

Night and day, the woman traveled and sang dirges for her brother. She traveled to faraway places and she always would sing dirges inside the forest. Her brother's body rotted on her back.

One time, a man took his dogs, then traveled and hunted for wild game in the forest. The woman had traveled in the forest for a very long time, and her brother's body had finished rotting on her back because it had been so long.

The man went around looking for game in the forest and heard the mournful singing. He thought, "Who is that singing so sweetly?"

The man listened to the woman's voice approaching. He went and hid in the forest, watching. When the woman's singing came closer, the man smelled the decay and saw the very beautiful woman singing and walking closer.

When the woman approached him, the man came out and said, "Hey, you're my true wife."

The woman was shocked and cowered. She said, "I'm not a good woman. I'm a rubbish woman. My husband killed my brother, and I'm carrying his corpse around like this."

The woman told the story of what had happened to her life with her husband and her little brother. The man listened and did not care about the smell. He told the woman to come closer and hide herself at one part of the forest, then he would return to the village.

When he arrived at the village, his two wives asked him, "Where's our meat?" The man lied and told them, "The dogs tired of hunting for game, so we returned to the village. Tomorrow, I'll return to the forest."

The next day, the man woke up in the early morning and went back to the place in the forest where he had hidden the woman. He took the woman and washed her with a shrub (*purpur*), other aromatic grasses and leaves to remove the rotting smell.

In the afternoon, the man returned to the village. His two wives asked him again about the game. They said, "What kind of man are you? Before, you often brought meat back to the house. Now you've completely slacked off and come back empty-handed."

The women scolded the man for a while, and the man told them, "Rest easy. I found a woman in the forest and I want to bring her here, but it would be bad if you scolded her. I hid her and I went to see her."

His wives listened and laughed then told him, "Go bring her here with us and the three of us will be friends." The man listened to this and was very happy, so he went to the forest and brought the woman to his house.

The man's two wives treated the woman well and were very sorry for her when they heard the story that her first husband had killed her brother.

The next day, they went to the garden, and the man's two wives gave taros and yams (*yam* and *mami*) to the woman to plant in her own garden. However their husband said, "You three must make one huge garden and plant many food plants. When the food is ripe, we'll make a huge festival and call out for the people of the village to come. I want to see the man who killed your little brother."

The women listened to this and made a huge garden. They planted various foods in the garden. They always worked hard in this garden of theirs.

When the food in the garden was ready, they sent a message to all of the villages to come to the big festival at their home. All of the villages came to this big festival and sang and danced until dawn.

In the morning, the man called to his three wives to come and stand up. The man asked the woman to show him who it was that had killed her brother.

They walked and walked then came to the very last group. The woman recognized her first husband. She told the man. The man very quietly took his bow and shot him. The man fell down dead.

Everyone saw this and cut the man into small pieces. That was a story from our area, "Don't covet the food that a sister gives to her brother lest you kill your in-law and your wife leaves you."

Viavent Jerry
P. O. Box 109
Kieta
North Solomons Province

C280+. Tabu: coveting food given by wife to brother-in-law; D1314.13+. Star reveals corpse; K811.1. Enemies invited to banquet and killed; P253. Sister and brother; P263. Brother-in-law; S55+. Cruel brother-in-law; Q211. Murder punished; Q411. Death as punishment; R213. Escape from home; S63+. Wife kills husband; S110. Murders; S139.2. Slain person dismembered; T100. Marriage; T145.0.1. Polygyny; W157. Dishonesty; W195. Envy

## The Stubborn *Masalai* Had a Bad Time

(Wantok 578, July 6, 1985, page 24)

Long, long ago, in the time of the ancestors, there lived two *masalai*s, a man and a woman. The name of the *masalai* man was Okung and the woman's name was Anasi. Their house was beneath a cave, high on top of a mountain.

Below this area, at the base of the mountain was a big river. This river was a place where people from a nearby village bathed, drank water, and did various other things.

Often, the children of the village would go bathing until their eyes were bloodshot, then they would return to their houses. However, when the children would return to the village, one of them would be missing. The children would not know that one of themselves had disappeared.

After they would arrive in the village, the parents would find out and think that the child had died, that the child was somewhere else, or that an ancestral ghost from the forest had confused the child.

Every day, the children went to bathe in the river. When it was time for them to return, they got ready. Whoever was the last to leave the water became lost.

It was the *masalai* man who lived up in his mountain house who swung his long spear down to the river. He would hook the child and bring the child up to the house.

The *masalai* man, Okung, would tell his wife, Anasi, to cook the children in a big pot and then the two of them would eat the children. The *masalai*s' pot was made of stone. The food in the pot would be ready quickly with just a little fire.

This is how it went all of the time. Then Anasi told her husband, "Hey, you can't do this sort of thing all of the time. If the people of the village find out that we're killing their children, they'll come to kill us."

Okung told his wife, "You talk a lot because you never eat and fill yourself with this good meat, huh? Just shut up and cook the food."

The people of the village found out that great enemies had come upon their children. For many nights and days, the men would gather by a fireplace in the village and talk about finding out what it was that was killing their children.

They were very troubled because they never found their bodies either. The children just disappeared.

They decided that one man would just hide and watch when some children would go to the river to see what would happen to them. The next day, a boy took a bamboo tube and went to fill it at the river.

After the boy filled the tube with water, he wanted to turn around and go back to the village. The *masalai* Okung's long spear came down from the mountain, hooked the boy and brought him up. The boy did not make a sound. He was hanging dead from the spear.

The man was hiding and he saw everything clearly. He saw the boy hanging dead from the spear when the *masalai* had pulled him to the top of the mountain. His blood just flowed down. The bamboo with the water in it spilled about.

The man saw this, so he quickly took the empty tube and ran back to the village. He fell before the eyes of the other people and cried.

He told the people, "It was not a pretty picture that I saw in the water. No! The *masalai* on top of the mountain killed the little boy just like an animal."

They decided on that day to go get the *masalai* couple who had feasted upon them. At this time, they marked for death the couple that had finished off all of the children of the village.

They decided to go to the villages that were both near and far. They would have a big, happy festival and eat together. They sent the message out to their kin and fellow tribesman from near and far.

The big day approached. The leader of the village with some people went to ask Okung and Anasi to come to have a good time.

They went to the river and called up the mountain. Okung listened and replied that he was very happy that they had asked him and his wife. However the *masalai*'s wife, Anansi [Anasi], was not happy. She was very worried.

Anasi told Okung, "Look, what do I always tell you? They called out to us so that they can kill us."

Okung told his wife, "Don't worry. I have the power to kill them. Come and we'll eat the good food that they've prepared."

However, Anasi did not feel well. She was not happy to go on this big day. She brought her worries with her.

The two of them arrived at the village and sat upon a platform that the people had made for them. Underneath, near the platform, was a huge hole that the people had dug. However, they had covered the hole well with grasses and dirt so that people could not see it.

They heated stones in a big fire. The stones were still red hot in the fire. The men called out to Okung, "Okung, can you help us push these stones. They're too heavy." Okung said, "OK."

He rose and went to help them. The fire was near the place where the hole was. When he put his head and hands down to push the stones, the men gathered together and immediately pushed Okung down into the hole that they had prepared.

Okung was turning around in the hole. Quickly, the men pushed the fire and hot stones down into the hole. The stones cooked and pulverized Okung. Okung tried all manners of his powers, but he was completely lost. The people of the village had won.

Okung's wife, Anasi saw what had happened. She was terrified and cried, but the men told her that they could not kill her. It was not her fault. It was only Okung's fault.

They let her go back to her home on top of the mountain. The people sang and danced. They ate happily until the next day when the people from far away went back.

So because of this, more children were raised in this village. The *masalai* woman, Anasi, became a good friend of the villagers because when they went hunting for wild game in the forests of the mountain, the game was plentiful and easy for the people to shoot.

This was because Anasi still closed the animals' eyes with the power of ancestral ghosts or *masalais*.

Tubawai Abbai
Nago Nago [**Nagovisi** People]
Wakupa [**Bakupa** Village]
Sovere [Sovele Roman Catholic Mission]
[**North Solomons** Province]

D2062.2. Blinding by magic; F490+. Masalai; G512.2. Ogre stoned to death; G512.3. Ogre burned to death; J652. Inattention to warnings; K735.1. Mats over holes as pitfall; K811.1. Enemies invited to banquet and killed; P210. Husband and wife; P230. Parents and children; Q55+. Reward for sparing life; Q141.2. Plentiful game animals (fish) as reward; Q211. Murder punished; Q414.0.12. Burning as punishment for murder; S112. Burning to death; W167. Stubbornness

# Kemkapukere Killed a Snake

(Wantok 579, July 13, 1985, page 20)

Long, long ago, in Keruma [**Kerum**] Village in **Simbu** Province, there lived a man named Kemkapukere. When it was time to fight with enemies, Kemkapukere was a real man at fighting. When he went to fight, he would kill ten to twelve enemies. His arrows never missed the mark.

Kemkapukere was renowned for killing wild game and birds too. Whenever he went into the forest, he did not fool around at killing marsupials (*kapul*), birds, wild pigs, or other animals.

One day, Kemkapukere went to hunt for birds at a place called Mauboumanei. He arrived there and he saw a huge fig tree standing. At the base of the fig tree was a big hole where various birds often drank water.

### Seeing the Birds

Oh my, Kemkapukere saw the birds there and thought of making a small bird blind by the water hole. He saw the various kinds of birds with their multi-colored feathers. He trembled and wanted to kill all of them.

He held arrows in one hand and his bow in the other. He jumped, sang and danced around because he was elated to have found this place where the birds were so plentiful.

He returned home to Keruma. He awoke in the early morning when it was still dark. He carried the bow and arrows with his stone axe then returned to the place where the birds were. Kemkapukere arrived at this place then cut some saplings and made a small round hut near the base of the fig tree.

After he made the hut, he cut a piece of bamboo and shoved it towards where the birds usually drank water. The bamboo was for him to shove his arrows to kill the birds when they came to drink water.

So every morning, the man would abstain from drinking water. He would leave his house when it was still early morning, and go to watch the birds. His wife would shove sweet potatoes into the fire and he would carry these off to eat while he watched the birds.

### Around the Forest

In the early morning, the birds would travel the forest and eat tree fruits. When they became thirsty, they would fly over and drink water at this puddle at the base of the fig tree.

Kemkapukere would chew ginger and spit it into the puddle, so that the birds only liked to drink this water.

Kemkapukere watched and killed many, many birds. In the afternoon, he carried the birds back to the house. He and his wife would cook them in an earth oven then eat them. He always went to watch the birds, kill them and bring them back.

One morning, he awoke very early and went to watch the birds. He watched and watched until noon, but not one bird had drunk from the water at this place.

The good-for-nothing waited and waited, then he became furious. The sun was very strong now and the man was furious. He just sat and waited.

The father [or owner] of the birds was a giant snake who came to this hole and saw the man, Kemkapukere, sitting and watching for the birds.

The snake came and began to surround the hut where the man was sitting. The snake surrounded the house, then shoved his head inside the door where the man was sitting and waiting.

### The Giant Snake

Poor Kemkapukere saw the huge snake and was speechless. The snake's mouth was enormous, so he trembled terribly.

The snake spoke, "So it was just you who always came here to finish off my birds, huh?" The man listened and had nothing to say.

The snake told him, "Give me all of your arrows now." Kemkapukere listened to this and slowly gave all of his arrows to the snake. The snake swallowed all of the arrows.

After the snake swallowed them, he told Kemkapukere, "Give me your armlets, your loincloth, and your belt that fastens your 'grass' skirt." The man listened to this and he removed all of these things that the snake had asked him

for. He gave all of these things to the snake. Just like the arrows, the snake swallowed all of these things.

Then the snake told the man, "Come now." The poor man was completely silent and walked towards the snake's mouth. The snake swallowed him right down.

However, Kemkapukere was not an ordinary man. When the snake had told him to give away his things, the man had removed his bamboo knife from the net bag and hidden it well in his hand. So when the snake shad wallowed him, he was holding his bamboo knife.

While the snake slithered through the forest, the man began to cut the snake's belly to find a way out. The snake slithered and slithered until the snake was nearly dying. They were at a bad place where there was a waterfall. Below which, there was a pond.

### The Snake Was Ready

They approached this place and the snake was ready to go down to the bad place. Kemkapukere cut through and opened the snake belly completely. Then the snake fell, and the man jumped out with his knife, some meat, some grass and some bones of the snake.

Later, Kemkapukere killed a big white pig. He took the pig's blood and mixed it with the bones and meat of the snake. He carried this to a particular place and buried it. This marked this place as sacred (tabu) where his descendants can see and know this story.

This snake is the same as our ancestor. The snake's name is Mamegilkuwa, and this place is Mamenulkuom. This story comes from the Elimbara area, Suave [**Chuave** People], Simbu Province.


Moses Morry
P. O. Box 2610
Boroko
National Capital District


A992. Origin of sacred places; B211.6.1. Speaking snake (serpent); B242+. Serpent as king of birds; B875.1. Giant serpent; F911.7. Serpent swallows man; F912.2. Victim kills swallower from within by cutting; P210. Husband and wife

# Hapleng the Trickster
(Wantok 580, July 20, 1985, page 20)

Long ago, there was a trickster who lived in a village. This man's name was Hapleng. He befriended a very sweet and beautiful woman, and he thought of marrying her. However the woman did not want to marry Hapleng, so Hapleng thought very hard for a way to marry this woman.

One day, Hapleng said, "Never mind, I'll keep trying."

In the very early morning, he woke up and went to the forest. He killed a marsupial (*kapul*), took its guts and threw away the meat. At night, he carried the marsupial's guts and went to the woman's house. He hid them carefully so that the woman did not see them. Then the two of them *karim lek*ed.

### Dead Asleep

Very late at night, the woman was dead asleep. Hapleng took the marsupial's guts and rubbed them on his face while he was still close to the woman.

At dawn, they saw that the place where Hapleng had slept was full of feces. Purpur [lit., "Grass Skirt"], the woman, was attached to it and had slept in it too. She was full of feces, and the place smelled very foul.

The old woman saw the feces and told her daughter, "Look, you shat upon him. So now you must marry him."

When Hapleng heard this, he was elated. The woman was speechless and terribly ashamed as she sat there. Her mother told her, "Go on, go with Hapleng. You've ruined him. This is very shameful and we, your parents, don't want to carry this shame. So you must marry Hapleng now."

Hapleng was happy inside his soul, but he did not show it very much to his new wife. All of his worries were over now.

He thought to himself, "The woman is too strong and doesn't like me. I think her parents like me a lot, so they let me marry their daughter."

So, Hapleng married this woman and they went to his village. Hapleng and his wife lived happily. They found food and made a garden together. Then the woman became pregnant, and gave birth to a boy. One day, the mother went to the garden while Hapleng and the baby stayed in the house.

### Garden Work

The mother worked in the garden until the evening. She took the food and firewood then went home. When she approached, the mother hard the baby crying.

The mother heard Hapleng speaking sternly to the baby, "Your mother rubbed marsupial shit on my face, then I married her and she gave birth to you. Why are you crying?"

The woman stayed nearby and listened to everything that Hapleng said. The mother replied, "Ah ha, what did you say to the baby? You tricked my mother and you married me, huh? Now come and get me. I'll go live in my village, and you'll come get me?"

The next day, the woman took the baby and ran away. She lived in her parents' village. She lived there for a long time, and Hapleng did not come to get her and the baby back. After she lived there a long time, she married another man. This man was from another village.

One day, they had a huge festival at the village of the second husband. The trickster or loser, Hapleng, also went to this festival.

### Seeing the Woman

He looked and saw his ex-wife singing and dancing. Hapleng waited for her. When the time came to eat the food from the big earth oven, Hapleng quickly went and hid then dressed like the woman's second husband.

After Hapleng had dressed, he went and stood at the door of the house where the woman was sitting. He told the woman, "I'll hold baby while you quickly cook the food in the earth oven." The woman did not recognize him and gave the baby to Hapleng.

Hapleng took the baby. He went and killed him, then covered him up in an earth oven. The woman went and saw her husband, thinking that he had taken the baby with him to the dancing grounds.

She went behind and asked her husband for the baby. Her husband said, "To whom did you give the baby?" The woman replied, "I went to cook at the earth oven, and you took him. Where did you put him?"

The man told her, "I didn't go to the house. I've just been here at the dancing grounds until now. Now, to whom did you give the baby?"

The woman was persistent and the two of them fought. Some of the clan told them that during the day, they had seen Hapleng in the dancing grounds. The woman said, "It's true, Hapleng gave me a bundle, but I thought that it was you because he was dressed like you."

The two of them uncovered the earth oven. They removed the bundle that he had given to her too.

### Uncovering the Bundle

When they uncovered the big bundle, it was too bad, the baby had been cooked with the leafy greens that were on top of the food that they had put in the earth oven.

Later, the people saw this. They took their bows, arrows and axes then followed this man, Hapleng. Later at night, they found Hapleng going up a tree. He was sitting and hiding. [The second husband said], "That man killed my baby, so I'll go up and kill him now."

However Hapleng had gone up near the crown of the big, tall tree. He was ready with an axe in his hand. His spear was also at the ready.

But it was too dark, so the men did not see where Hapleng was. When the man came close, Hapleng aimed carefully and shot him with the spear in his neck.

Hapleng spoke to the man's kin. He told them that they could not cut the tree until Hapleng went down to the ground. However, the men thought that it was the woman's husband who had climbed the tree who was speaking.

But no, it was just Hapleng. He went down quickly and stood far away. He asked the men, "Who did you kill? Was it Hapleng, or did you kill one of your own kin? It was me, Hapleng, that came down."

The people listened to this and they lit the torches. When all of the torches were lit, they saw that the man was not Hapleng. No, it was the woman's husband, their kinsman, who had fallen dead with the spear in his neck.

Hapleng hid very carefully in the forest. He saw the people carrying the man and walking back to their village. Hapleng also walked back to his own village. Later, he married another woman. He became a leader of his village.

This story comes from **Bupkila** Village, **Western Highlands** Province [**Wahgi** People].

Tonny Dilu

Watta Plantation

Rabaul

East New Britain Province

[Tonny Dilu also wrote a similar ancestor story in *Wantok* #482.]

J1110. Clever persons; K1350. Woman persuaded (or wooed) by trick; K1810. Deception by disguise; K2150+. Sleeping girlfriend made to appear to have shat on boyfriend to force marriage; L160. Success of the unpromising hero (heroine); P210. Husband and wife; P231. Mother and son; P232. Mother and daughter; P233. Father and son; P234. Father and daughter; P261. Father-in-law; P262. Mother-in-law; P265. Son-in-law; P600+. Courtship customs: *karim lek*; Q411.3. Death of father (son, etc.) as punishment; R220. Escapes; R260. Pursuits; R311. Tree refuge; S11.3.3. Father kills son; S110. Murders; S139.2.2+. Corpse put into cooking pot or cooked; T50. Wooing; T100. Marriage; T570. Pregnancy; T580. Childbirth; X716.1H+. Befouling with excrement

## A Ghost Tricked a Woman
(Wantok 581, July 27, 1985, page 20)

Long, long ago, in the time of the ancestors, there were two women who lived in a village. These two women usually called each other Borwane.

This name, Borwane, is as if the two of them had eaten a round *galip* nut. Inside the *galip* nut, the meat is in two halves, so the two women spoke as if they were like the galip nut. In my language, the name of this *galip* nut is *bouril*.

So these two women, or Borwane, would travel together and do their work together. If one of them were working in the garden, the other would also work with her. They would always travel together. There was not one time when one of them left the others and traveled by herself. Never.

One night, the two women sat and told stories in the house. One of them told her friend, "Tomorrow, we'll wake up very early in the morning and go beat vines in the stream [to poison fish]. When the sun rises, we'll collect the fish. Then later, we'll go looking for breadfruits."

The two Borwane agreed to this then went to sleep. They had also decided which of them would wake up first and wake the other Borwane.

While they were talking, they did not know about the bones of a ghost that the village leaders had hung upon a coral tree. The ghost had listened carefully to what they said.

Did the two friends know that something bad had heard what they said? They did not know because the leaders of the village did not tell the youth of the village that the ghost's bones were there. This was so that they would not gossip about them and cause men from other villages to come and take the bones.

If the other group took the bones and brought them to a *masalai* place, all of the men, women and children of the village would die. This was why the leaders did not speak to the village about where they had hung the ghost's bones.

It was close to dawn and the birds called out. The ghost awoke, left her bones on the coral tree, and went down. The ghost went to one of the two Borwane. The ghost went to the house of the second woman and awoke her.

The real woman woke up and asked her, "Is dawn here? Don't wake me if it's still nighttime."

The ghost replied in the exact voice of her friend, "Why are you still sleeping? Oh my, it's almost time for the sun to rise now."

The poor real woman listened and thought that she was really her Borwane who had come to wake her. So she arose, took her betel nuts and betel peppers, then filled her net bag. She also took her bundle of sago and went outside the house.

She told the ghost, "Let's go now lest the sun rise and the people of the village see us."

The two of them left the village. They walked and walked until they came to the stream where they had wanted to catch fish. Then the sun rose completely.

The real woman hung up her net bag on a tree branch, went into the forest, and began to gather vines. The ghost woman also went to help her remove the poison vines and bring them back.

Then the real woman went downstream and worked at beating the vines. The ghost woman went and beat the vines upstream. They beat the vines for a while until the sun became a little stronger. Then they went out of the stream, and sat and waited for the fish to die.

While they sat, the ghost woman asked the real woman for betel nuts and betel peppers. The real woman went and fetched the betel nuts and peppers, then they sat and chewed them.

After they rested, they went down to the stream and began to remove the fish that had died and those that were stunned in the water. Oh my, were the fish plentiful in this stream. The women did well fishing there.

So when they went back up, the real woman made three whole bundles of fish. The ghost woman only had one bundle because she was eating the fish while she was taking them from the water. The poor real woman did not know that the ghost was eating the raw fish.

Then they took the fish and carried some to be cooked. They made a fire and began to cook the fish. The real woman cooked her fish well, but the ghost woman did not cook her fish well.

The real woman saw this and said, "Borwane, your fish are not cooked well. Put them back in the fire until they're done."

The ghost woman listened and said, "If you cook the fish well, they'll get dry. You must just pretend to cook them in the fire. Then when you eat them, the fish oil will still be there."

The ghost said this and continued to pretend to cook her fish. She removed them quickly from the fire. The real woman waited until her own fish were quite done.

When all of the fish were done, the real woman arose and took her package of sago. Then they sat to eat. The real woman ate slowly, and the ghost woman just swallowed her fish plain.

The real woman saw this and said, "Hey, Borwane, where do you want to go that you're eating so quickly? Be careful that the fish bones don't get stuck in your neck."

The ghost woman listened to this and replied, "Borwane, you should eat quickly too, then we'll look for breadfruits."

However the real woman said, "I'm afraid of getting the fish bones stuck in my throat, so I'm eating slowly. I think that you're like a ghost, you eat so quickly."

The real woman was just kidding. She did not know that the woman that she had gone with was actually a ghost.

The ghost woman finished her food and asked the real woman for some betel nuts and peppers. The real woman said, "Borwane, go get the net bag that I hung up on the tree branch, and you'll find the betel nuts and peppers."

When the ghost woman went to raise her hand to bring the net bag down, the real woman saw that her armpit was bright red.

The real woman saw this and began to think hard. She said to herself, "Oh my, oh my, I'm crazy. I came with that ghost woman. She's not my friend." The woman thought this while she was sitting.

The ghost woman brought the net bag and they chewed betel nuts. The real woman slyly looked at the ghost woman's eyes and saw that her eyes looked like those of a ghost: they were bright red. The real woman saw this and began to think, "How shall I run away from this ghost and return to the village?"

They finished chewing betel nuts and talked about going to find breadfruits. The real woman asked the ghost woman how many bundles of fish she had caught. The real woman showed the ghost her three bundles.

The ghost woman showed the real woman just the one bundle. The real woman saw this and asked, "Borwane, many fish died in the river, so why did you just get one bundle?"

The ghost woman said, "I tired of getting all of the fish." The real woman listened, but she did not know that the ghost woman was lying to her. This was because she thought that the ghost woman had eaten quickly and because the fish that she had cooked were not cooked well. The real woman also knew that the ghost must have eaten raw fish.

When they were ready to go look for breadfruits, the real woman thought of running away. So, she lied to the ghost woman, "Borwane, I'm dying to take a shit. Sit and wait for me while I go inside the forest to shit."

The ghost woman listened to this and said, "Don't worry. I'll wait for you here. After you shit, we'll go look for breadfruits."

However, the real woman did not go to defecate. She just went inside the forest and began to run away. She saw a green grasshopper that had a hard back. She told the grasshopper, "If you hear someone calling to me, you must reply, 'Ho, Borwan [Borwane], I'm still shitting!'"

The woman explained this to the grasshopper, then she sped right back to the village. She did not think about falling or about thorns in the forest stabbing her, the good-for-nothing just sped back.

The ghost woman was sitting and waiting then called out, "Borwane?" The grasshopper heard this and replied, "Borwane, I'm still shitting." The ghost woman listened to this and thought that the real woman had replied to her, so she sat quietly.

After a while, the ghost woman called out again, "Borwane... Borwane, why are you taking so long in the forest?"

The grasshopper heard this and replied to the ghost's shouting, "Borwane, I'm still shitting."

The ghost woman listened to this and was furious. She arose and went inside the part of the forest where the woman had gone to defecate.

She went there and called out again, "Borwane, where are you?" The grasshopper replied, "Borwane, I'm still shitting."

The ghost woman listened to this and tried to find the woman. She saw the grasshopper sitting on a tree. Oh my, the ghost woman was furious and just swallowed the grasshopper.

The ghost was still angry, so she sniffed around to find out where the woman had fled. She smelled the direction, then she began to follow the woman to the village.

The poor woman went and went then became completely out of breath. When she was almost at the village, the ghost woman caught up to her.

The ghost beat the woman and the woman fell down half-dead in the middle of the village. The people of the village were shocked. Her real friend, was surprised to see her Borwane half-dead.

Then the leaders of the village took tree bark and ginger. They chewed these and spat them upon the woman. They washed her with cold ginger then the woman sat up and told the story to them about what had happened to her.

The men of the village listened to this story and went to get the ghost's bones. They carried them and threw them in the pond. Then they cut the coral tree down to the ground.

So, in the time of the ancestors, they would hang up bones, or carry them and throw them into a pond. Also, the name Borwane is still used by us.

If two women chew betel nuts from two halves [of the nut], one will call the other this. The same thing is true for *talis* nuts and for [other] *galip* nuts.

My maternal aunt told this story to me when I lived in **Wanu** Village [**West Sepik** Province, **Olo** People].

William J. Sabien
Marinkis Plantation
P. O. Box 41
Kinim
Karkar Island
Madang Province

B211.4+. Speaking grasshopper; B335. Helpful animal killed by hero's enemy; B486.2+. Helpful cricket/grasshopper; D42.2. Spirit takes shape of man; E422.2.1. Revenant red; E422.1.11.4. Revenant as skeleton; E425.1. Revenant as woman; E261.4. Ghost pursues man; E437.2. Ghost laid in body of water; E541. Revenants eat; E545. The dead speak; F419.4K. Spirits eat food raw; K551.16. Woman escapes by ruse: must go to defecate; K1930. Treacherous impostors; P311.0.1+. Friends share same name; R220. Flights; R260. Pursuits

## Posere Killed a Bad *Masalai*
### (Wantok 582, August 3, 1985, page 20)

Long, long ago, there was an island in **Manus** Province where a brother and sister lived. Their parents had died, so their grandmother took them and looked after them.

However, the old woman was not a good grandmother. When the two children were with her, the old woman would think of killing them.

One day, she sent the two children to bathe in the sea. She told them to bathe until the sun went down. The two children listened to what the old woman said, and they went to bathe. They bathed until the sun set and the salt burned their eyes badly. They returned to their grandmother's house. They lay down, badly hurt, and went so sleep.

The old woman saw them and was very happy. Quietly, she went to get some thorns from a citrus tree [for a needle] and some string for making net bags. She sewed up children's eyes with the string, then she tied them with rope.

Afterwards, the old woman carried the children down to the beach and put them inside a canoe. She paddled very far asea and threw the children down into the sea.

However, the two children did not drown. They drifted and drifted until the sea carried them to the shore of a small beach on an island. They arrived on the island in the early morning. This island was completely deserted.

There was a very bad *masalai* who lived on this island. The *masalai* often ate men, women, and children as well as the animals that arrived on this island. The *masalai*'s nose was very sensitive, and it smelled things for him to kill and eat.

Behind this island was a small island which had bay and mangrove trees growing on it. When the brother and sister drifted to this island, the big brother, who was named Posere, landed on the branch of a mangrove tree.

Posere felt that he had landed on an island. He cut the rope from his hands. He was surprised that his eyes were shut, so he gently put his hands up and removed the string that his evil grandmother had sewn them with.

Then he helped his sister, Niasere, remove the string from her hands and eyes. After they removed this, they saw the bad bananas of the *masalai*, and they knew that the current had carried them to the *masalai*'s island.

They saw this and they knew that if they were not smart, the *masalai* would kill and eat them. Quickly, they went inside the forest and found an aromatic shrub (*purpur*) used for festivals, and they rubbed their skins with this. They did this so that the *masalai* could not detect their scent.

They dressed finely with some more leaves from this aromatic shrub, and they walked off to find the place where the *masalai* dwelled. They walked and walked until they arrived at the place where the *masalai* dwelled.

The *masalai*'s house was on land. The good-for-nothing slept very well because on the previous day he had killed many animals. He had eaten them until his belly was completely bloated, then he had gone to sleep.

The brother and sister saw this and began to dig a hole by the steps of the house. They dug the hole and went down far. The width of the hole was the size of the *masalai*.

After they dug the hole, they got up and went into the forest to cut pieces of green bamboo. They sharpened the bamboos well and planted bases of the bamboos in the hole with the sharp ends upward.

After they aligned the bamboo well, they got up then sang and danced. They called the names of various snakes from the mainland and also from the forest of this island. The snakes heard the singing and they went to this place. The two of them put the snakes down into the hole.

After the snakes were down there, they went and brought big, long tree branches, then lined them up by the hole. They [placed] banana leaves on the branches. After this, they threw dirt and covered the banana leaves.

After their hard work, they prepared to wake the bad *masalai*. They sang and danced then told the *masalai* to wake up and come get his good meat now.

The *masalai* was sleeping and began to feel hungry. When the *masalai* wanted to get up, it heard the siblings' singing. The *masalai* immediately got up and walked towards them. The *masalai* was famished and did not think about walking slowly. The *masalai* trampled through his strong house and down his ladder to see the brother and sister.

When the *masalai* trampled the last step of the ladder, and was about to put its leg down on the ground. The ground just broke and the great weight of the *masalai* made it fall directly into the hole.

The *masalai* fell down and planted its back upon the sharp bamboos inside the hole. The snakes began to bite him too. The brother and sister saw this and they began to throw rocks down into the hole, breaking the *masalai*'s skull and bones.

The *masalai* died inside this hole, then the brother and sister took dirt and sand, filling the hole. They covered the hole well, then they sat to rest. Later, Posere beat the *masalai*'s signal drum, informing the people of the other islands that the *masalai* was dead.

The people of the other islands heard this and were very happy. This was because the *masalai* had always killed people who went to its island. They were very happy that Posere had killed their enemy.

All of them cooked food in earth ovens, killed animals and brought them in canoes, then paddled to this island. They arrived on the island and began to beat the signal drum, then they sang and danced fervently.

They made Posere the leader of this island. His sister, Niasere, was very happy for her brother. The two of them lived on this island. Later, they found friends, married and raised their families.

Kasiana Tiamon

D. P. I. [Department of Primary Industries], Marine Fisheries

Wewak

East Sepik Province

B491.1. Helpful serpent; D1781. Magic results from singing; D1781+. Magic results from dancing; D2074.1. Animals magically called; F490+. Masalai; G512+. Ogre killed by snakes; G512.1. Ogre killed with knife (sword); G512.2. Ogre stoned to death; K735. Capture in pitfall; L111.4.1. Orphan hero lives with grandmother; L111.4.4. Mistreated orphan hero; P272. Foster mother; P210. Husband and wife; P230. Parents and children; P253. Sister and brother; P275. Foster son; P275+. Foster daughter; P292.1. Grandmother as foster mother; Q211. Murder punished; Q215. Cannibalism punished; Q411. Death as punishment; S12+. Mother throws child into river (sea); S12.4+. Cruel mother sews child's eyes shut; S36+. Cruel foster mother; S41. Cruel grandmother; S110. Murders; T100. Marriage

## A Woman Gave Birth to a Baby Snake

(Wantok 583, August 10, 1985, page 24)

Long ago, in Ngarutumoa [**Naratumwa**] Village, there were a man and his wife who lived with some of their families [**Adzera** People, **Morobe** Province].

They lived there for a while and the woman became pregnant. After the ninth month, the woman still had not given birth. Her belly was huge and they thought that it was time for her to give birth, but it was not the time.

Her husband asked her, "Hey, when will you give birth to the baby? Your belly's very big now, and many months have passed."

The woman listened and said, "I don't know. It's probably twins. It's been a very long time."

The woman's husband told her to just stay in the village and not to go to the forest or garden or to do heavy work. The man thought a lot about his wife. It would be bad if his wife died because her belly was huge.

The poor man did all of the work by himself, getting food from the garden and hunting for wild game in the forest. His wife just stayed in their house.

They lived like this for a while, then one night the woman began to feel a pain, and she told her husband. Then, when it was still that night, the woman gave birth to a baby boy and a snake.

Oh my, it was a baby boy and a snake. They gave the name Sampai to the snake. The man and his wife took care of this snake very well along with their baby until the two of them grew up. When the snake became very large, its middle was like an automobile's rubber tire.

The couple and their children lived well in their village. Then, the time for a battle was approaching. Their father told Sampai, "There will be a big fight coming, so we'll go and hide you in the forest." The name of this forest that they were to hide Sampai is called Ngarungufing.

They told the snake to get ready. It was morning and they got up to walk into the forest. The father and mother, their boy, and some other people from Tumoa [Naratumwa] Village walked off first. The snake, Sampai, came after them.

When they approached the Nagarungufing [Ngarungufing] forest, some men went first and put a tree across the trailhead that they would take them into the forest. They held their stone axes and stood at the ready.

The parents and their boy went and jumped over the tree. They waited for Sampai on the other side. Poor Sampai approached the tree. However, when Sampai went over the tree, oh no, a man jumped and cut off Sampai's tail.

When they cut the snake's tail, it sped away into the very deep forest. It went completely out of Ngarungufing and went to another forest that is called Garamimin in the Warisain Village area. Now, the snake Sampai still lives in this area.

The snake's middle is huge, like a forty-four gallon drum. This is a story that the people of the Markham Valley believe because they saw it with their own eyes.

William Ayam
Hohola
National Capital District

B875.1. Giant serpent; P210. Husband and wife; P230. Parents and children; P231. Mother and son; P233. Father and son; P250. Brothers and sisters; R210. Escapes; R213. Escape from home; T554.7. Woman gives birth to a snake; T574. Long pregnancy; T587+. Birth of twins: one human, one snake


## Wirikaira Found a Lake

(Wantok 584, August 17, 1985, page 24)

Long ago, there was a lake in a forest called Namodian in the **Gomia** area of **Simbu** Province [**Chuave** People]. There was not a single man or woman who had found this lake. One time, a great fight came between the Kinogu and the Gomia clans in this forest. It was then that they found this lake.

The two clans, Gomia and Kinogu, fought and approached this lake. However, they did not know that it was there because it was filled with grasses and the water was beneath the grasses.

As they fought, the Konogu [Kinogu] pushed the Gomia back, and went close to the water. An old man named Wirikaira from the Gomia Clan trampled the grass. The ground was completely soft and the water took Wirikaira down. Wirikaira did not know how to swim in the water, so he did not resurface. The grass covered him over.

After the fight ended, all of the men went back home. The Gomia looked for old Wirikaira who had not returned to the village. His kin thought that the enemies had killed him at the battle scene.

The next morning, the men of Gomia searched for him at the site of the big battle. Some men followed the path that the old man had run, and they saw the lake there. Some places were filled with forest and grasses, and this had obscured the lake.

They found the place where Wirikaira had fallen. His family had thought that Wirikaira had died underwater, so they cried near the water.

The men cleared this place where the water had taken the old man down. They waited and saw the men trying to find Wirikaira's body. While his family was waiting, they were shocked to see old Wirikaira rising up from the water.

The old man carried sugarcanes and bananas for planting. When his wives saw this, they were afraid and got up to run away. They thought that this was Wirikaira's ghost coming up from the water.

However, Wirikaira called out for them to return for him to tell his story. He told them that he was not dead. He had just slept underwater with some of the clan.

However his daughters were even more afraid, so they took their elders back to the village. Wirikaira went to the village and he told the story to the villagers.

Wirikaira told the story of the water taking him down. In the place where he went underwater, there was a very big door. There was a man who was in charge of this door. The man opened the door and quickly took him inside.

Inside, there was a village. The man took Wirikaira inside a house. Wirikaira told the story of how he had seen many houses and very nice things underwater.

He said that he slept just one night inside this house. The next morning, the people of the village gathered sugarcanes and bananas for Wirikaira to carry back with him.

The underwater people told Wirikaira, "When you go up to your village, you must hold tightly onto these bananas and sugarcanes that we've given to you. Later, you must plant them and they'll grow well because these are things to be eaten."

After they finished speaking, they held his two legs while the bananas and sugarcanes hung about from his arms and sides. The people held Wirikaira's two legs and swung him up above the water.

His family was sitting and crying by the water when they had seen old Wirikaira shooting up above the water with the sugarcanes and bananas hanging around his body that were to be planted.

After this time, there were sugarcanes and bananas growing in the gardens in the Gomia People's area of Simbu Province. Wirikaira's story is very important among the Gomia. Later, the Kinogu People found out that the Gomia had bananas and sugarcanes. The Kinongu [Kinogu] Clan did not have these. This knowledge brought more fighting because the Kinogu often stole sugarcanes and bananas from the Gomia's gardens.

This lake became the Gomia People's property, and it is the only lake in the area. Whichever clan wanted to do work there or just use the water of the lake would cause a big fight to arise again.

Now, we Gomia People often go looking for small fish in this lake in the Namodian forest.

Inoch Morris

Pokora

Gomia Village

Simbu Province

A2684.4K. Origin of sugar cane; A2687.5. Origin of banana; F725.5.1. Visit to people of village under lake; P210. Husband and wife; P232. Mother and daughter; P234. Father and daughter; Q212. Theft punished; T145.0.1. Polygyny

## When Bat Became Frog's Enemy
(Wantok 585, August 24, 1985, page 23)

Long ago, in the time of the ancestors, Frog and Bat were very good friends. They would travel everywhere together. Sometimes, if Frog could not go to a mountainous place, Bat would carry Frog and fly there.

When they went to a faraway place to search for food, or around to other places, Bat would carry Frog and fly away. But for the easy places, or the places near water, Bat would go down to the ground then sit and walk with Frog.

One day, they decided to go to the garden on the following day. The next morning, they stayed in the garden. When the sun became very hot, at about noon, they made a fire. Frog arranged some edible grasses to be cooked.

Bat flew away to look for food. When Bat returned to the garden, they sat together and cooked their food in the fire. They talked about working in the garden and they ate.

### Garden
However even though they ate much food, they felt hungry again before long. Frog and Bat were two who ate very similarly. This time, they sat and ate in the garden. They thought of a way to try to prevent their finishing the food in such a short time.

Bat told Frog, "Stay here and I'll go alone to look for something in the forest, then I'll return very quickly."

Frog said, "OK, go ahead." Bat brought two vines back to Frog.

Bat told Frog, "Friend, you know that we usually eat very similarly, and we're similarly hungry. So, we also shit similarly. We must tie these to ourselves."

Bat told Frog, "I'll sew up your ass and make it smaller. You'll feel it a little and you won't be able to eat much because you won't have a place to shit. After that you'll sew up my ass just like yours."

Then the two of them began. Bat took a vine and sewed up Frog's cloaca. Bat sewed up Frog's shit-path and left just a tiny hole. Oh my, Frog felt a terrible pain.

On about the third day, Frog felt a very bad sore on its rear end. This caused Frog to eat very little. Later, after some days, Frog ate just a little. Frog only defecated a little too, through the small cloaca that Bat had sewn up and left. This made Frog's belly hard and completely blocked up, so Frog could only eat a little bit.

Later, Frog began to sew up Bat's anus. However, Frog did not leave even a little space. Frog sewed it up entirely so that there was not even a little hole for the feces to exit.

Oh my, this sent Bat to searching. Later, when Bat ate, it was very hard to defecate. Bat felt terrible because its belly was filled, and this caused a terrible pain.

Bat screamed and rolled around. The pain was just like a fire. Bat screamed, "Aya, I'm going to die now. Frog, Why did you do this to me? I didn't sew up your ass completely. You did something terrible to me."

Bat screamed and screamed until it found a way to defecate. Bat was angry with Frog and chased after Frog. However, Frog quickly jumped and hid under a stone where Bat could not go to find him.

Bat rolled and rolled. Bat's belly was in pain. Bat vomited all of the food that had turned into feces from its mouth. Thereafter, Bat only vomited from its mouth.

So now, frogs have a small space to defecate, and bats always just vomit the waste from their mouths. When bats fly up and see frogs, they quickly fly down and snatch them in their two legs, then eat the frogs. It was because of this mistake that frogs and bats broke apart. They are no longer good friends, they are bitter enemies.

Perison Koimb
Ramu Sugar
Gusap
Lae
Morobe Province

A2364+. Why frog has small cloaca; A2494.16.1+. Enmity between frog and bat; A2470+. Why bat vomits; B211.2.11K. Speaking bats; B211.7.1. Speaking frog; P310. Friendship; S160+. Anus sewn up

# A Man Ate His Own Wife

(Wantok 586, August 31, 1985, page 22)

Long, long ago, in the time of the ancestors, there was a tree that was filled with fruits and was near a big boulder. Many of these fruits were ripe.

After some time passed, a man was hunting for wild game in this forest. He saw that this tree was completely filled with ripe fruits. The man was elated. He pulled out some grasses and put them on top of the tree. This was so that whoever looked at this would see that this tree was already claimed.

Then the man returned to the village. Later, a ghost man went to this tree. He was furious. He asked, "Who put these grasses on top of the fruit tree? Whose tree is this?" The ghost removed the grasses that the man had tied. He, the ghost, took a new vine with grasses and tied these to the fruit tree.

The next morning, the man went to see the fruit tree. He saw the grasses that the ghost had put there. He was irate, and he removed the grasses. He took some new ones and tied these to the tree again. The two of them did this for a while, and the real man became completely fed up.

One day, the real man was furious about what had been happening all of the time. So, he sent some young boys from the village to this place.

He told each of them that they must bring a little handbag or net bag and leave. So when they arrived at the tree, they would get some ripe fruit.

The little boys saw that this tree was loaded with ripe fruits. They trembled with joy and went up the tree. They harvested the fruits and filled their bags.

At this time, while they were harvesting the fruits, the ghost man and his wife were inside their house down inside a cave. The ghost man was making a spear and his wife was making her net bag for him.

One of the fruits fell down and entered the cave. It fell close to the place where the ghost man was. He took the fruit, broke it in the middle and ate it. Another fruit fell, then the two of them took it and ate it. Then a third fruit fell, and they ate this one too.

The ghost man told his wife that he would go up and check on what was happening because there must be some people stealing the fruits, causing some to fall near them.

The ghost man took his stick and went up. He saw the boys watching him. They quickly became afraid, jumped down to the ground and ran away. However, there was one boy who was very high up the tree. It was too late for him to flee.

The ghost went up to the boy and called to him, "You! Where are you going now?" The boy replied, "I'll jump to the nearby trees and escape."

The ghost took an axe and cut all of the nearby trees. Then he asked the little boy again, "Now you're going to die. Where are you going?"

The boy replied, "I'll fall down into the deep forest and grasses that are nearby then you won't be able to catch me."

The ghost finished off all of the forest and removed all of the grasses that were nearby. The ghost called out, "Now you have no place to escape."

The boy replied, "There's still the hair on top of your head. I'll fall on top of that."

The ghost listened and removed all of the hair on top of his head.

The boy told the ghost, "Now I have no way to escape, so open that big bag and hold it so I can jump into the bag."

The ghost listened to this and put a small bamboo knife that was very sharp into the bag. He told the boy to jump down. The boy jumped down into the bag. Quickly, the ghost tied up the opening of the bag. He carried the boy inside the bag down into the house in the cave.

The ghost told his wife that some wild game was in the bag, so she must watch the game in the bag carefully. The ghost man went to find leafy greens. When he returned to the house, the two of them would kill the boy and cook him. They would season him with the greens and eat him.

However the woman had constructed the net bag very well, so she did not carefully watch the bag with the boy inside of it. The little boy looked for something to cut the bag but he did not find anything. He was hot and running out of breath, then he found the bamboo knife.

He took the knife and cut the bag. Quickly, he took the big spear that the ghost had made before. The boy struck the ghost woman hard and she died.

The boy cut up the ghost woman and cooked her in an earth oven. The boy changed everything and pretended to be sitting and making a net bag like the ghost man's old wife.

The ghost man went back to the house and the boy sat like his old wife. He changed his voice a little and told the ghost, "Go get your food and eat. I already made the earth oven and it's ready."

The boy spoke exactly like the ghost man's wife. The man removed the food and sat and gorged himself on his wife's flesh. He only spoke about eating quickly. The little boy quickly and quietly backed away to the back of the house, then he ran away.

When he was fairly far away, the boy called out, "Hey, look at that! You're the ghost who ate his own wife!"

The boy went to his clan and told them the story. They took their bows and arrows then got ready. When the ghost man came to the village, the boy's clan saw him and shot all of their arrows into him, then the ghost man died.

Avei Deeft
**Isontenu** Village [**Agarabi** People]
Kainantu
**Eastern Highlands** Province

E425.1. Revenant as woman; E425.2. Revenant as man; E440+. Ghost laid by spear/arrow; G11.10. Cannibalistic spirits; G61. Relative's flesh eaten unwittingly; G441. Ogre carries victim in bag (basket); K1836. Disguise of man in woman's dress; P210. Husband and wife; Q213. Abduction punished; Q411. Death as punishment; R10.3. Children abducted; R11. Abduction by monster (ogre); R210. Escapes; R220. Flights; R260. Pursuits; S110. Murders

## Why Is it that Marsupials (*Kapul*) are Meat for Dogs?
(Wantok 587, September 7, 1985, page 21)

Long, long ago, dogs and marsupials (*kapul*) were good friends. They were always together and they were never angry.

Every six months, the dogs and marsupials would have a big festival in a village called **Kindan**. This village is in the Lagaip area of **Southern Highlands** Province. [Lagaip is in Enga Province.]

One time, the leader of the dogs and marsupials called out for them to make a festival at Kindam [Kindan]. The leader had explained that all of the dogs and marsupials must come with their elders. They could not leave the elders, so they all left their villages and went to the festival at Kindan.

This village was huge. There were no trees or streams. There was only just a little sword grass in this village.

When the time of the festival arrived, the sun was bright and the village was very hot. There was not one good place to hide. One dog was very thirsty for water and tried to find a place to drink. The dog went and found a small water hole then drank there. The water was very sweet, but the dog did not know why this water was sweeter than other waters. The dog wanted to find out.The dog followed the stream for this water hole and arrived at its source. The dog saw a dead marsupial lying there. The marsupial's blood was spilling into the source of the stream. The dog put its nose towards the water and sniffed. Oh my, the dead marsupial smelled wonderful, so the dog tried eating some of the marsupial's flesh. The marsupial's flesh was delicious, so the dog finished all of it. Later, the dog walked back to the site of the festival.

The dog stood in the middle of the festival and whispered to all of the dogs. The dog told them that marsupial meat was good food for them. The dog told them to each grab a marsupial when the festival ended. The dogs should each kill a marsupial.

While the dog was whispering, one marsupial heard what was said. The marsupial sang, "*Yu mede poo le wielele. Pitamo kado kedapoko epe. Eamanya papo lo-we!*" This song means, "If there is wind when it is dark, I'll run up a good vine going up a tree."

This was the last song. The dogs each grabbed a marsupial and ate them. Many marsupials saw this and ran about, going up tree vines.

Now, if you go to Kindan Village, you will see the clearing where the dogs and marsupials were. This is where they had the festival. But now, dogs and marsupials are enemies, so marsupials are afraid and just hide on top of trees.

Ms. Miriame and [Robert?]
Kaki
P. O. Box 796
Panguna
North Solomons Province

[The ancestor story in *Wantok* #724 is similar to this one.]

A2494.4+. Enmity between dog and marsupial; B211.1.7. Speaking dog; B214.1+. Singing marsupial; P310. Friendship


## Agum and Amom Challenged Aronta

(Wantok 588, September 14, 1985, page 35)

In the time of the ancestors, long ago, there were two brothers who lived in **Legam** Village, near the Mankon River in the Buang area of **Morobe** Province [**Buang** People]. The first brother was Agum and the second was Amom.

Agum and Amom lived on one side of the river, and a *masalai* woman named Aronta lived on the other side. The old woman, Aronta, had a big garden that was full of taros, bananas, yams, sweet potatoes, wild sugarcanes (*pitpit*), sugarcanes, and many other kinds of food. There was so much food that it just rotted.Agum and Amom did not know that Aronta lived on the other side of the river. One

time, they left Legam and walked downriver. Agum saw smoke from a fire rising on the other side of the river.

The two brothers walked close to Aronta's home. The place was very clear, and they saw Aronta standing there. They were afraid of Ronta [Aronta], but they walked closer.

They saw Aronta very clearly. Aronta did not look like a *masalai* woman. No, she was like a real woman. However, her finger and toenails were very long and she had long hair on her head and body. The two brothers stood and watched. They were afraid that Ronta would kill them. They walked back to their village.

They lived in the village for some years. Amom became a big man and he grew a beard. The two of them decided to return and kill Ronta.

They pretended to make a bridge across the river to Aronta's home. On the third day, they were completely ready to fight. They took a *limbum* palm tree and made spears from it. On the third day, they walked to the false-bridge and approached Aronta's house.

Agum and Amom walked quietly, then stood under the house. Before long, Agum saw long hair hanging from the house that went halfway to the ground. This was Aronta's pubic hair.

The two brothers broke a stick. They grabbed the hair and twisted it with the stick. The hair went around the stick very tightly. They pulled the stick and removed some of Aronta's hair. Oh my, was Aronta surprised, she felt a terrible pain. She jumped up and down because many of her pubic hairs had broken off, and she was in great pain.

Aronta called out, "Who's the man that's irritating me for a fight?"

Agum went and stood in the clearing then said, "Aronta, you're going to die now. My brother and I have come to fight you."

Aronta told them to wait and she would get her fighting gear. She went inside the house. She took her two long teeth and put them in her mouth. She took two *limbum* shields for deflecting spears.

She went outside the house and opened her mouth. Her two long teeth broke everything around. She jumped down to the ground and chased Agum and Amom.

Agum threw a spear towards Aronta's face. But the spear missed and just fell down. At this time, a cloud thundered and a heavy rain fell. A strong wind arose and a flood covered the place where they were standing.

The flood crushed all of the areas around Legam and went down to the **Bumatu** area and to the mouth of Buang River. Aronta did not care that the place was ruined. She chased Agum and Amom then arrived at the Mankon River.

Agum ran and fooled Ronta who was behind him. Amom went first and stood on one side of the bridge. Agum fooled Aronta and went to the exact middle of the bridge. He ran quickly to the other side with Amom.

Aronta kept running and Amom cut the rope of the bridge. The bridge broke with Aronta and went down into the Mankon River. The water carried her down. Then Aronta bashed her mouth on a boulder. One of her teeth broke. She tried hard to swim and cross the flooded river, but the poor woman had no more strength.

Agum and Amom walked on the side of the river and followed Aronta downstream. They arrived at the place where the Mase River and Yeis River meet. However, Aronta put her legs on a good footing and stood upon the ground again.

Aronta arose and ran after the two brothers again. They began to fight again, and they went upriver. Agum's spears were completely gone because he had thrown many and missed.

Amom gave his spears to Agum, but Agum missed and just threw the spears away. There was one last spear belonging to Amom.

Agum stretched and swung the last spear into Aronta's chest. Oh my, Aronta screamed, swinging her arms and legs around, trying to remove the spear. But no, the spear pierced her heart and she fell half-dead onto the ground.Agum removed the spear and stabbed Aronta's head. Why was Aronta still alive? Aronta tried to stand again, but she fell down and died.

Agum and Amom left Aronta at the place where she had fallen, and they walked upriver. However, their arms and legs were exhausted and they were out of breath.

They walked for a little while, then they sat down. Afterwards, they became two mountains that are in this area. These two mountains are near Legam and Bumatu.

If people go to this area today, they will see these two mountains standing there. The people of this area call these two mountains Agum and Amom, after the names of these two brothers.

Arim Nipaya
Magem Village
Buang
Morobe Province

A965. Origin of mountain chain; A1011. Local deluges; A1617. Origin of place-name; D291M. Transformation: man to mountain; D2142.1. Wind produced by magic; D2143.1. Rain produced by magic; D2149.1. Thunderbolt magically produced; D2151.8. Magic flood; F490+. Masalai; F515.2.2. Person with very long fingernails; F513.1+. Removable teeth; F544.3.5. Remarkably long teeth; F547.6.1. Remarkably long pubic hair; G214.1. Witch with long teeth; G219.3. Witch has long nails; G219.4. Witch with very long hair; K983.2. Dupes lured onto tree-trunk bridge; fall to death; L31. Youngest brother helps elder; P251.5. Two brothers; R260. Pursuits

## The Sister Fought like a Man
(Wantok 589, September 21, 1985, page 35)

Long ago, in the time of the ancestors, there was a young man and his sister who lived in a village. The brother always took care of his sister well. He often told her to make gardens, search for food, take care of the garden food, and take care of their little pig well.

One day, the brother told the sister that he would go to search for food. He would go very far away to search for the food. He would not come back quickly if he did not find any.

He told his sister to take care of the sweet potatoes and the little pig well. Then he fetched plenty of firewood.

There was a big tree that stood by their house. He told his sister to fence the tree well, and watch the tree because they would get firewood from it later. He told her to watch carefully that the others do not cut their firewood.

After he said this, he walked away to look for food. The woman stayed and followed her brother's instructions, but the brother did not return home quickly. It had been a long time, about five days. The woman was waiting and was a little worried about her brother.

The woman was short of firewood and food too. It was the sixth day. The woman cut the firewood that was still standing at the base of the tree that her brother had [put there].

She cut and cut the firewood into small pieces. She cooked her food, then ate. At night, she slept, and her brother still had not returned home. While she was sleeping that night, she heard an explosion outside of the house.

The woman woke up and quietly walked out to look. She saw a man trying to cut the big tree that she had fenced off for her own firewood.

She was furious. She quietly walked back inside the house so the thief could not see her. The woman took a bow and arrows then shot right at him. An arrow got him in his guts and he died.

The woman saw this and was terrified. She trembled and cried for her big brother. She sat inside late that night. She was very upset. She looked down the big trail and listened for the sound of her brother walking.

She did this because she had caused much trouble. The next morning, the people would find out about what she had done and kill her too.

While she was worrying and crying, her brother arrived at the house very late that night. The sister saw him and cried then told the story to him.

She told him, "I followed your instructions. I saw and killed that man. Now his kin will come to kill us just for that worthless firewood."

The brother told his sister not to cry and worry anymore. He said, "Little sister, I told you that you would fight like a man, and you did just as I told you."

He told his sister the way that they must follow to fight with the kin of the dead man who was still lying outside their house.

The brother told his sister, "You must listen carefully. Now you must look like a man. You'll put on a loincloth. On top of your skin, you'll wear the skin of a cassowary. This cassowary skin will cover your breasts. Then you'll put bird of paradise [feathers] on your head. Cassowary bones will hang from your neck. Afterwards, put on two armbands and two leg-bands. You'll carry a bow and arrows, and act just like a man. The man's kin are plentiful and we are just two. I'll put on grandfather's clothing that he used before he died. We must fight with the enemies."

In the very early morning, the two of them sharpened arrows, worked on the bows and fixed some axes. They made big bundles of bows and arrows to hide in the forest. They hid some nearby and they hid some fairly far away on the trail. They put others close to the house. They would fight and run to the arrows on the trail.

That morning, the man's kin found out. They knew that the brother and sister must have killed him. They brought together the clan to kill these two.

However, the two of them were standing at the ready. The clan did not know that the man's sister had become a man. Her face was adorned with earth.

They thought that the man must have hidden his sister and that another man was helping him fight against them.

They fought strongly. The brother and sister gave it to them, thrusting arrows at them. The two of them shot arrows at them, pushing them back and back behind the trail where they had prepared the arrows.

The fight continued and the two were not done for. They killed some of the others because they had prepared well and because they were lying in wait. The man's kin had thought that it would be easy to kill the brother and sister because they did not have any kin to help them.

The two of them fought and fought, and then all of the arrows were gone. They left and made a hut. They made it in the forest and just stayed there for the night. The brother walked around quietly and stealthily. He went back to the house and brought food back into the forest.

That night, they just ate what they could. The next day, they walked around hungrily, looking for forest food and for a new place to go. They would never return to their old home.They saw a huge tree. The sister waited underneath the tree. The brother went very high up the tree and saw smoke rising far away in the place where the sun rises.

He went down and told his sister that they would follow the forest to the place where the smoke was rising. They slept for two nights, walked for three days, and arrived at this place.

The woman hid somewhere in the forest while the man went alone to see what kind of people lived at this place. He found only one old man. This man knew how to make love charms or sorcery. After the old man heard the man's story, he told him to call out to his sister.

The old man said, "Don't worry, you two, no one will harm you anymore. You're my children. You'll carry my power. Wherever you walk, you'll never fall into harm."

The two of them lived with him. The woman married and left to live with a man from a nearby village. The brother married a woman and lived with his old foster father. The brother lived with the old man. Later the old man died and the brother had these kinds of powers too.

Andrew Koim

Arawa

North Solomons Province

D1711. Magician; D1721. Magic power from magician; F610.0.1. Remarkably strong woman; K1837. Disguise of woman in man's clothes; L111.4. Orphan hero; L111.4.2. Orphan heroine; P253. Sister and brother; Q212. Theft punished; P210. Husband and wife; P261. Father-in-law; P265+. Daughter-in-law; P271.1. Magician as foster father; P275. Foster son; P275+. Foster daughter; P600+. Virilocality; Q212. Theft punished; Q411.13. Death as punishment for thievery; R213. Escape from home; S110. Murders; T100. Marriage

## The Old Woman Ate Boys
(Wantok 590, October 5, 1985, page 24)

Long ago, in the time of the ancestors, there was an old woman and her husband who lived in a small place. Their home was near many sago palm trees and swamps.

The name of the old woman was Ampufafua, the name of her husband was Yanangotof. The other people lived in a big village. Their houses were fairly far from the place where the old man and woman had made their house.

There was a big mango tree that grew directly in the middle of the big village, and one that grew in the middle of the old couple's place. When it was mango season, the big trees would bear very well.

One time, the mangos were bearing well. The mangos were ripe and falling around the ground. There were not many people around this area, so the mangos just rotted.

One day, a man from the big village walked into the forest with his dog and arrived at the big mango tree. The man saw that the mangos were ripe and just falling to the ground. He gathered the mangos and went back to the village.

When he arrived at the village, he told his kin in the village about the forest where he had found the big mango tree. His children and other boys of the village listened and trembled to go get the mangos at the tree.

One day, a boy from the village woke up in the very early morning. He took his net bag and walked off to find the mango tree. The boy walked and walked until he arrived at the base of the mango tree.

Oh my, the mangos had fallen and filled the base of the tree. The boy packed his net bag and put it at the base of the tree. He climbed the tree until he arrived at the crown. He took some ripe mangos then sat and ate.

While the boy was eating mangos, the old woman Ampufafua walked over and arrived at the base of the mango tree. She looked around, seeing that the boy's net bag was packed with mangos and was lying at the base of the tree.

The old woman called out, "Hey, who's the thief that came to steal my mangos?" While she called out like this, the boy on top of the tree listened and trembled. The mangos that he was eating fell right down to the place where the woman was standing.

The old woman looked up and saw the boy sitting on top of the tree. Oh my, the old woman was elated and called up, "Hey, my meat, come down quickly and bring your mangos back home. Why are you lying on top of the tree?"

The old woman finished calling then began to remove her mucus and she put it around the base of the mango tree. She did this because she wanted the boy to trample her mucus and become stuck to the ground so that she could come and kill him easily.

The old woman then waited at the base of the mango tree. She thought that the little boy would come down and that she would kill him.

However, the boy was not an ordinary person. He had some of his own powers too. When he saw the old woman removing her mucus around the tree, he turned into a mouse and just followed the mango tree until he found vines that were attached to it. He jumped to a tree that was fairly far away from the mango tree.

Then he went down very quietly and fled to his village. The old woman, Amapufafua [Ampufafua], waited and waited until she tired. Then she rose and looked up. She could not see the boy.

[The old woman went to the village.]

The old woman listened and asked the boys what time their parents would return to the village. The boys told her that their parents would return in the evening.

The old woman was very happy. She flattered the boys well and told them, "Oh, that's too bad, my grandsons. It's not good for you to be here alone. All of you go inside this net bag and I'll carry you to my house. There's much food there and there's also good water where you can play and bathe.

The boys listened to this and thought that the nice old woman was telling the truth. All of them jumped into the big net bag. The old woman tied the opening of the bag tightly and carried them off to her home.

When they arrived at her home, her old man Yanagotof [Yanangotof] was sitting and sharpening his spears. Very gently, the woman hung up the net bag with them in it, and she quickly went to the garden. She gathered leafy greens and other food to season the children.

When the old woman departed for the garden, the children inside the net bag were crying and making much noise. The old man was sharpening his spears and heard the children's cries. He went to see what it was, and he saw the boys piled inside the net bag.

The old man, Yanangotof, was very sorry for them, so he gently took his bamboo knife and cut the net bag. The bag broke then the children jumped out and ran back to their village.

When they arrived at the village, they told their story to the people of the village about the old woman who had come and tricked them. The men listened to this and were furious. They decided to go to the place where the old couple lived and to kill the old woman.

In the early morning, the men awoke then carried their spears and wooden shields to fight with the old woman. The old woman knew that the men of the village would come looking for her, so she was also ready.

The strong warriors went first and met this woman, Ampufafua, then began to fight with her. The woman was very strong and fought with the men for a while. They could not kill her quickly. She had long arms and extraordinarily long fingernails, so she could scratch the strong men who were fighting. However, the men of the village remained strong. They fought until their spears were gone and the old woman was dead.

Then they turned and fought her husband. However, the man had already turned into a snake and had gone down to hide in the swamp. The men of the village burned the couple's house and they returned to their village.

Now, if women from my village go fishing in small streams or swamps, they will see this snake, *yanangotof* inside the water.

I heard this ancestor story from my father, and I wrote it down.

Bingin Wangkeng
**Munum** Village [**Wampar** People]
Lae
**Morobe** Province

A2145. Creation of snake (serpent); D117.1B. Transformation: boy to mouse; D191M. Transformation: man to serpent (snake); D1001+. Magic mucus; F515.2.2. Person with very long fingernails; F516.3+. Long-armed person; F610.0.1. Remarkably strong woman; G219.3. Witch has long nails; G441. Ogre carries victim in bag (basket); G530.1+. Help from ogress' husband; G550. Rescue from ogre; K711. Deception into entering bag; P210. Husband and wife; P230. Parents and children; Q213. Abduction punished; Q411. Death as punishment; R4. Surprise capture; R10.3. Children abducted; R11. Abduction by monster (ogre); R110. Rescue of captive; R210. Escapes; R220. Flights; R260. Pursuits; S110. Murders

## Walini Turned into Stone

(Wantok 591, October 12, 1985, page 22)

Long ago, in the time of the ancestors, there were two brothers who lived in **Yapai** Village on top of the mountains in the Enga area [**Enga** People?, **Enga** Province].

The name of the first brother was Kuaka. His little brother was Walini. Their parents had died and they lived alone. Kuaka was a big man, but poor Walini was still little.

Walini never traveled to places because he was too small to travel in the forest or to do heavy work. So only the big brother, Kuaka, did the hard work for themselves.

One early morning, Kauka [Kuaka] told his little brother, "Stay in the village. I'll go look for some food for us. I'll be back in the evening."

Kuaka left the village and went into the forest. However, Kuaka did not follow the trails into the mountains that he had always taken. This day, he cut through a new forest trail.

He walked and walked then found a huge boulder. Inside the boulder was a house where people slept. Kuaka went inside the cave and saw various things as well as piles of food.

Kuaka did not know whose house it was, but he took the food and filled his net bag with it. Then he quickly returned to the village.

The next day, he returned. He went into the mixed-forest and went inside the big cave. He took some good food such as pork and cassowary meat, filling his net bag. Then he carried it back to the village.

The owner of the house was surprised that someone was stealing food from his house. Before, this sort of thing had never happened. He was worried about his food, so he sat and thought about finding the thief.

One time, Kuaka told his little brother that he must not eat the meat so quickly. The little brother did not know where the meat came from. He thought that his big brother, Kuaka, had killed wild game in the forest and brought much meat back for them to eat. He did not know that Kuaka had stolen the meat.

One day, Kuaka told his little brother Walini to go to this part of the forest. Kuaka told him which trail he must follow, and where he would find the boulder.

Kuaka told Walini that under the boulder was a big cave and a house. The entrance was small. Kuaka told Walini to look around carefully lest men or birds see him go in the house inside the cave.

Walini listened and left for this forest. He went inside the cave. He saw the piles of food. The owner of the house was angry and he wanted to grab the thief, so he had piled the good food high.

When Walini went inside the house, he saw the food. Oh my, he trembled and sat and ate. He gorged himself. He had not listened carefully to what his big brother had told him, that he must fill the net bag with food and leave the house quickly. He trembled at the food, sat and ate.

Then he heard thunder and the place shook. Little Walini felt the earthquake and he was terrified. He ran and sat with his eyes and ears closed in a corner.

When he wanted to open his eyes, oh my, he saw a big, tall man walking towards the cave. Oh my, he was huge. Walini was terrified and just sat there.

When the man walked, he would cause the clouds to thunder and the earth to shake. Walini was half-dead with fear. He had no way to escape, so he hid in a small corner amid the shadows inside the house.

The *masalai* saw that his food was not there, so he was furious. He said something and the door of the cave shut tightly. The little brother was trapped inside now. Then he became a stone.

The big brother looked for him to no avail. He called out to the boulder, but the cave door was stuck tight. Kuaka called out to Walini, but his words did not go past the boulder. The boulder just echoed Kuaka's voice. Kuaka was troubled and cried. He went back to the village.

So now, if you go near this boulder and call out, the boulder will echo what you say. This boulder is called Kuaka, after the ancestor Kuaka in this story.

The people who live on top of Mount Kuaka are called the Walini People. This is from the name of the ancestor who was the little brother that turned to stone.

Robert Kaki

Panguna

North Solomons Province

A1195. Origin of echo; A1617. Origin of place-name; D231B. Transformation: boy to stone; D1552.2. Mountain opens to magic formula (Open Sesame); D1774. Magic results from speaking; F490+. Masalai; F531.3+. Giant's walking causes earthquake; F531.3+. Giant's walking causes thunder; J1050. Attention to warnings; K300. Thefts and cheats—general; P251.4+. One brother acts wisely, another acts unwisely; P251.5. Two brothers

## A Python Swallowed a Man

(Wantok 592, October 19, 1985, page 32)

In the time of the ancestors, long ago, a man went into the forest. He went to check on a new sago area that he had fenced off so that wild pigs that smelled the sago would become stuck on the fence. Then the man could kill them.

The man and his wife belonged to an ancestral village called **Yakeltim** in **West Sepik** [Province, **Awun** People].

At night, the man told his wife that in the very early morning, before it was light, he would walk into the forest and check on the fence that he had erected by the sago palm trees.

In the morning, the man went with his bow and arrows. He waited a little, then when it was near dawn, he heard something like the sound of a pig approaching from a place near the sago palms.

However when the man came very close, he did not see a pig there. No, he did not see the gigantic python coiled behind the fence.

When the man came closer, the python arose and bound his two arms. The python surrounded the man's two arms until he could not turn or move them.

Then the snake broke all of the man's bones and swallowed him. The snake's belly was bloated and it looked exactly like an ancestral spirit.

The snake lay there. It did not make the slightest movement because it was completely exhausted. Later, it moved very slowly and went to sleep by the water.

The man's wife was waiting and the sun rose. It became close to noon. She waited through the afternoon. At night, she noticed that her husband had not returned to the house, so she called out to their two dogs.

She told the dogs, "Your master hasn't returned to the house and I'm worried. A wild pig must have killed and eaten him, so you must follow your master's trail and go after him."

The woman gave some food to the dogs. A man in the woman's family took the dogs and followed the man into the forest. They followed the forest trail and arrived at the place where the man had made the fence, but they did not see him. Then the dogs sniffed out the place where the big python was lying.

The dogs both barked and ran there. The way that the python had gone down to the water looked like a big trail. It looked like a trail that had been made by men dragging a big tree.

The dogs barked and went right to the python. They barked loudly until the man came to this place. The man saw that the snake was still coiled inside the water. The snake's belly was greatly swollen. The man knew that this monster snake must have swallowed the man, causing its belly to become engorged.

He called to the dogs, then the three of them returned to the village. They arrived at the village and sent a message for all of the men to come. The men brought stone axes, bows and arrows, then they walked off to the place where the python was lying. They arrived by the water, and the python was lying there. They surrounded the water.

All of the men stood by with their arrows., then one of the men beat pieces of wood. The python heard this and raised its head from the water.

The men went closer and saw the place where the snake's head was. All of the men were ready. The man beat the wood again, then all of the men shouted, sang and danced.

The snake listened and raised its head to move. When the snake straightened its body to slither, all of the men shot their arrows at its head, middle and tail.

The snake died and the men made a big stretcher. Six men carried the snake back to the village. Later, they cut the snake's belly, removed the man's body and buried him. They butchered the snake and burned it in a bonfire.

Larry Kinon
Mark Trading Company
P. O. Box 23
Wewak
East Sepik Province

B875.1. Giant serpent; F911.7. Serpent swallows man; P210. Husband and wife; V61.3+. Dead buried

## Two Boulders Found a Place
(Wantok 593, October 26, 1985, page 24)

Long ago, in the time of the ancestors, there were two men who lived in the mountains where the Sepik River originates. These two men found that their space was [too] small.

The men were from two different families. The name of the first man was Tunjimelia, from the Sarak Tribe. The other was Kolungudimi from the Samblap Tribe.

. This place where the two men lived was called **Sakitip**. Their descendants shortened the men's names to be Kolung and Tunjs. They were not boys.

One time, a heavy rain and strong wind arose, and the place became completely dark from clouds. The men, Tunjs and Kolung, became two big boulders.

They began to roll because they felt very hot and they wanted to find a cool place. The source of the Sepik River was the place where they had begun to roll.

They rolled and rolled then arrived at a small stream where the Sepik River begins. They rested in the water, but there was no room. The water did not flow enough to cover them, so they kept looking for a place to stand. They left this place, and kept going down the Sepik River, looking for a bigger place to rest.

They arrived at a resting-place, but the owner of this place, who was underwater, did not like the two men staying there. This was because if they stayed there, they would cover the entire resting space.

The two of them rolled and rolled, going down the Sepik River. They arrived at another place on the Sepik. The crocodile father who was the *masalai* of this place did not want them to stay. So, the two of them kept going down, following the flooded Sepik, trying to find a big place where they could both stay.

However at every place, the owner did not want them to stay. Tujimlea [Tunjimelia] and Kolungudimi followed the Sepik onward. They arrived at the mouth at **Kopar** [Village, **Kopar** People], where the Sepik River meets the sea. This is the area of the **Murik** [People, **East Sepik Province**].

They kept looking along the sea, and at every place where they wanted to stand, there was an owner who did not want the two men there.

Tunjis [Tunjs] and Kolung kept going to the place where the sun rises. They were still looking for a place, but they could not find one. The two men were different stones that other *masalai*s under the Sepik River and the deep sea did not like to be near.

Tunjs and Kolung kept going until they found a huge bay. They wanted to go inside the bay, but the owners of this area forbade them.

They told them to make their home in the middle of the sea. They gave them just one space. Then the two stones planted themselves there.

Today, this place where the two stones are located is called Simpson Harbor, in **Rabaul** [Town, **Tolai** People]. The two big stones stand outside the bay of Rabaul [Simpson Harbor], and they are called "Beehives" [Dawapia Rocks].

From this ancestor story come the names of the two boulders that stand in Rabaul Harbor, Tunjimeli and Kolungudimi.

Yuaneng Sissu
Maliau Village
Wapanamb area, Sepik River
East Sepik Province

A955. Origin of islands; A977. Origin of particular stones or groups of stones; D231M. Transformation: man to stone; D1641.2. Stones remove themselves; F401.3+. Spirit in crocodile form; F490+. Masalai

## The Power of the Marsupial (*Kapul*) Kondomong Helped a Sister and Was the Origin of People
(Wantok 594, November 2, 1985, page 23)

Long ago, there were five young women. They lived in a place where there were no men for them. Four of the women were big and the fifth was very young.

They had built their own house and they made a huge garden. They often obtained their own food and they each husbanded their own pigs.

The women happily worked in the garden and took care of the pigs. Before long, the women went to sleep. In the very early morning, they heard the sound of a bamboo flute from a nearby mountain. They heard the sound of the flute, but they were still sleeping, so they forgot about it. However the next morning, the flute sounded again.

The first sister told her other sisters, "I want to go and see this thing, so I want you to help me kill a pig. Then I can go."

The other sisters agreed, so they killed a pig that the woman carried off with her. The woman walked away, and when she arrived at the mountain, oh my! She was shocked to see a handsome young man. The woman stood there elated.

The man saw her and asked, "Where did you come from?" "Oh, I heard the sound of that bamboo flute, and I came here," the woman replied.

The man approved and carried her to his house. However her poor sisters were waiting and waiting. Their sister did not return, so they went to sleep.

They slept until the next morning when they again heard this sound. The second woman did the same thing, killing the pig, taking things, and walking away. It was too bad, the poor woman did not return. The next day, another sister went and the same thing happened: she did not return.

All of the women departed, except the last of them, who stayed. The poor, youngest one had no friends with her. So, she did the same thing as her elder sisters. She killed her pig and carried it away.

When she arrived at the man's place, he asked her the same thing. The young woman replied, "Many of my good sisters went, but they did not return, so I followed them."

The man said, "OK, come and the two of us will go." The two of them walked away. When they arrived at a big river, the man just left her there in confusion.

The young woman looked upriver and saw a marsupial (*kapul*) there. The name of this marsupial was Kondomong.

The woman asked Kondomong, "Are you a real marsupial or just a man? If you're a man, can you take me to the other side of the river?"

Oh my! When the marsupial heard this, he quickly put his tail in the water, [blocking it]. The big river dried up completely, and the woman walked to the other side. The young woman took the spine of the pig, cut off a leg and gave it to Kondomong.

Kondomong replied, "Many young women went by here, but I don't know where they went. They probably just died. Also, they never did this for me. So, go and sleep with this man, give birth, and husband pigs. However, you must do this when you go to the man's house. He will tell you to climb a tree. After you jump up there, he'll call out for you to look down. When you see a pond, he will ask you its name. You must say, 'Bunabunalep.' Also, when he asks your pig's name, you must say, 'Galuagaluamong.' And when he asks his own name, say, 'Tentenyau.' After this, he will call for you to come down."

The young woman listened to Kondomong and departed. When she arrived at the house, an old man was blowing his mucus about. He told the young woman to do things.

Oh my, when the young woman did all of these things, the poor old man became a young handsome man. They married, lived happily and had many children.

Before, there were no people, but it was from the power of Kondomong that we are here now.

Barkley Koi

Panguna

North Solomons Province

A1280. First man (woman); B211.2.12K+. Speaking marsupial; B430+. Helpful marsupial; B871.2+. Giant marsupial; D1881. Magic self-rejuvenation; H300. Tests connected with marriage; J1050. Attention to warnings; P210. Husband and wife; P230. Parents and children; P252.2+. Five sisters; Q93. Reward for supernatural help; R260. Pursuits; T56.1.1. Bride attracted by flute; T100. Marriage

## The Ancestral Ghost's Very First Trick!
(Wantok 595, November 9, 1985, page 27)

Long, long ago, there were two brothers who lived in a village. Their parents had died. The big brother was about eighteen years old and his name was Kimala.

The big brother, Lesa, often traveled in the forest and hunted for wild game for themselves. The little brother, Kimara [Kimala], stayed in the village, taking care of their garden and house. They lived like this for a very long time.

One day, there was no meat inside their house. It was the dry season too, so they did not find any game. They just slept at night [without eating]. In the early morning Lesa woke up, took a bow, an axe, and his two dogs and went into the forest.

Lesa went very far away into the deep forest to hunt for game because he thought that since it was the dry season, there would not be any game near where they lived. When he entered the deep forest, oh my, he killed many marsupials (*kapul*) and some other animals too. He also killed a cassowary.

When he had enough animals, he thought that it was time to return to the village. He carried the animals that he had killed, walked away, and arrived at a mountain that was between the forest and the village.

When Lesa arrived at the mountain, he put his things down and caught his breath. He smoked and listened to something making a noise behind himself. Lesa turned and saw an old man walking towards him.

The man walked very quietly towards the place where Lesa was sitting and smoking. However, it was not a real man. No, it was an ancestral ghost from the forest!

Lesa arose and asked him, "Where did you come from?" The old man said, "I came from my village to hunt for game in the forest, but I didn't find any animals, so I'm going back now."

Lesa saw that the man was old and he was very sorry when he heard that the man had not found any game. Lesa gave him some of his meat. Then, a bird, that is called _yaesaka_ in my language, came very close and perched on the branch of a small tree.

The ancestral ghost told him, "Hey, my kin, shoot that bird." Lesa drew back his bow and shot the bird in its chest. The bird fell down to the base of a tree. Lesa went to get it and bring it back to the ancestral ghost. But no, the ancestral ghost had stolen his meat and departed. Then Lesa knew that it was an ancestral ghost who had stolen the meat and tricked him into shooting the bird.

Lesa was furious at the ancestral ghost. He carried just the one bird that he had shot, and walked back to the village. At the village, his little brother Kimala was preparing leafy greens, stones and firewood for an earth oven. However, Lesa went to Kimala with just the one bird. Lesa told the story to Kimala and the two of them were furious together at the ancestral ghost.

Later, Lesa went back to the forest to hunt for food again. The ancestral ghost turned into a beautiful woman and did the same things as before.

The ancestral ghost, who had turned into a woman, again stole Lesa's meat then quickly ran away. This time too, Lesa returned empty-handed to the village and told the story to Kimala. They were angry again.

The third time, the two of them thought of looking for this ancestral ghost. They spun a string until it was very long.

So, Lesa carried this string with him into the forest while he hunted for game. However, this time he [the ghost] missed. The bad man (the ancestral ghost) transformed himself and became another man. He met Lesa on another mountain.

Lesa tied the string to the leg of a marsupial that he had killed, and the other end of the string to his net bag. The two of them sat and talked. A bird flew and perched on the branch of a tree that was very close to them.

The ghost man told Lesa, "Hey, my kin, shoot that bird." This time, Lesa was not worried. Lesa drew back his bow and shot the bird. It landed fairly far away.

Lesa was not worried because he had made a trick. He walked slowly and looked for the bird that he had shot. He carried it back to the place where he was sitting with the ancestral ghost. However, Lesa did not see the ghost man sitting there anymore with the meat. Only his net bag was there.

Lesa followed the piece of string that he had tied to the net bag and to the marsupial's leg that the ancestral ghost had carried away. Lesa followed the string for a long way. Lesa saw the string go to a stone.

Lesa went past the stone. He followed another trail and arrived at a small habitation. He approached and saw a small house standing amidst sword grass. Lesa saw smoke rising outside the house.

Lesa walked quietly and approached the house. He drew back his bow. He saw the ancestral ghost sitting and cooking the marsupial that he had stolen from Lesa.

Lesa drew his bow back very far and let an arrow fly. It went right into the ghost man's guts. The ghost died. Lesa cut the ancestral ghost into small pieces. He burned the pieces on a bonfire. Lesa went inside the house and saw a young woman sitting there, cooking food.

Lesa asked the woman, "How did you come to be here?" The woman replied, "The ancestral ghost man confused me and I've lived here with him."

Lesa told the woman to put all of the things into a net bag. He took the woman with him, and they walked back to the village. Kimala was very happy to see the beautiful woman. The woman and Lesa married. The three of them lived in this village and raised a family.

Kenny Sangia
Ela Motors
Lae
Morobe Province

E425.1. Revenant as woman; E425.2. Revenant as man; E425.2.1. Revenant as old man; E440+. Ghost laid by spear/arrow; E593.5+. Ghost steals food; K341. Owner's interest distracted while goods are stolen; P210. Husband and wife; P230. Parents and children; P251.5. Two brothers; P263. Brother-in-law; P264. Sister-in-law; Q212. Theft punished; Q411. Death as punishment; R220. Flights; R260. Pursuits; S110. Murders; S139.2. Slain person dismembered; T100. Marriage; W11. Generosity

# A Flood Drowned People

(Wantok 596, November 16, 1985, page 20)

Long, long ago, a very old woman lived in a village. The people of this village called her Ramingain. She was a woman who made black magic, evil spells, and sorcery (*sanguma*). She lived alone, among the people of this village. They never gave her food, firewood, or any help at all.

Old Ramingain never cared about this very much. She was very old. She could take care of herself better. Her eyes were completely blind and her teeth were all gone. Her arms, legs and body were very weak, so she just sat in the house. Her time for walking around was over.

This is how the story goes. One time, all of the leaders of this village held a meeting. It was a very big meeting. They spoke about making a party. They wanted to have a good time, where the people would prepare a large festival and be happy.

They decided to make this big festival one week after the day of their meeting. They gave time for their wives to make adornments for the festival and gather enough food.

## Frail Body

The men went to the forest to hunt for wild game to prepare for the big day. They found many, many animals, and the food piled up. The decorations were all ready, and the people just waited for the appointed day of the festival.

When the day arrived, all of the men, women, and youths were very happy. They did not think about old Ramingain who could not see or do the joyous things on that day with the other people of the village. Her body was frail and she just lay in the house.

Ramingaim [Ramingain] was very troubled that she could not be happy with the other people of her village. The poor woman just sat inside her house and cried, so that the people of the village could not see her.

On the last day, a young man and his sister were returning from the forest after they had hunted some game for themselves. They approached the old woman's house. They heard her crying, and the young man's sister asked her brother, "Hey, do you hear the old woman crying inside her house?"

## Old Woman Crying

The woman's brother put his ear out and also heard Ramingain crying. However she was crying very softly, so that people would not hear her. The brother turned and told his sister, "I think it would be good for us to find out what the poor old woman would like, and to try to help her."

They went inside Ramingain's house. The brother went first and helped old Ramingain's hand. He asked her what it was that caused her to worry and cry.

Old Ramingain felt the man holding her hand and asked, "Who are you that has come into my house?" The brother replied, "It's just me with my little sister. We were returning from the forest after finding food and game for the big festival when we heard you crying. So, we came inside the house to try to help you."

Old Ramingaim cried harder and replied to the brother, "I heard that tomorrow there would be a huge festival here in our village. So, I thought that I couldn't do anything to celebrate with you. I'm sad that no one in the village thought of helping me with food and meat, so I'm just crying over this."

The brother and his sister were sorry again for old Ramingain. They told her that they would try to help her with food and meat.

## Festival

The two of them stayed with old Ramingain until the big festival began. The people of the village made a huge feast on the day of the festival. However at old Ramingain's house, the brother, sister and the old woman cooked food for themselves to eat.

In the afternoon, while the festival was in the village, the three who were at the old woman's house ate. Then it was time for old Ramingain to reveal her troubles to the brother and sister. She told them that she was not happy with the people of their village, and that she would make black magic and kill everyone that night.

Old Ramingain told the two youths, "At night, when you go with the people at the site of the festival, I'll begin my song and ruin the people. However when you two go, I'll explain this to you. You must put plenty of food in a basket for yourselves to take to the festival."

## A Signal

"You'll get a signal from me when I'm about to destroy these people. You must go up a very tall coconut palm tree, and bring the basket of food with you. I'll send a flood down to all of the men, women and children who are having fun at this festival," old Ramingain told them.

When the two of them left the old woman's house, they did not forget about what she had told them. They went to the site of the huge festival. They saw the men, women and children dancing fervently.

They had heard some of the songs that would bring the disaster from the old woman when they had left her house. These songs would call out to all of the small places of water that were near their village to come gather at the place where the men, women and children were celebrating.

It was late at night now. Old Ramingain called out for the waters to come underground where the people were singing, dancing and celebrating. The people did not know what was coming to them. They saw the ground churning and becoming soft. They thought that the children had urinated. They hit the children and told them that they could not urinate around that area again. They kept singing and dancing.

However, when the brother and sister saw the water coming up from the ground, they thought of old Ramingain. They took their basket of food and climbed a very tall coconut tree. They heard the people beating the hand drums, singing and laughing with gusto.

After a short while, the water pushed forth up to the knees of the people who were singing and dancing. The host of the party asked, "Hey what's all this?" They thought about what was happening, then the water went up to their bellies. The children were afraid. They were crying and swimming around.

A little while later, the water went above the adult's heads. Many children and old people died, and the male leaders tried to swim. However after a short while, the water covered all of the houses and trees. These men were also lost. The water covered them and they died. This happened because of old Ramingain's anger.

Old Ramingain could not escape either. The water drowned her too. However, she sang for the water not to cover the tops of the coconut palms. So, her *masalai* listened to this and the two youths did not die. The water did not cover them over.

Every place was just flooded with water. The two of them were hungry now because they had stayed on the coconut tree for a long time and they had eaten the basket of food that old Ramingaim had told them to take with them.

They left the coconut tree and went down. They found out that they were the only ones in the village. Later, the brother married his sister, and they had many children.

There are some people who say now that sometimes they hear a cock still crowing underneath this lake. They also say that you can hear the men, women and children of this lake. So, it is forbidden for men, women and children to travel in this area. The story is that they [the people under the lake] can confuse you, and you will stay in this part of the forest for many days.



Patrick K. Noris
Kimbe Concrete Product
P. O. Box 120
Kimbe
West New Britain Province

A920.1.0.1. Origin of particular lake; A1011. Local deluges; A1018. Flood as punishment; C615.1. Forbidden lake (pool); D1242.1. Magic water; D1711. Magician; D1781. Magic results from singing; D2151.8. Magic flood; F490+. Masalai; P210. Husband and wife; P230. Parents and children; P253. Sister and brother; Q2. Kind and unkind; Q40. Kindness rewarded; Q280. Unkindness punished; Q411. Death as punishment; Q428. Punishment: drowning; R311. Tree refuge; T100. Marriage; T415.5. Brother-sister marriage; W10. Kindness; W11. Generosity

## A Son Found His Father's Eyes

(Wantok 597, November 23, 1985, page 24)

Long ago, in the time of the ancestors, there was a man who lived in the deep forests of Mount Kubor, by **Minj** in **Western Highlands** Province [**Wahgi** People].

The name of this man was Angaipal. There was no other man or woman who knew him because he lived on the summit of the mountain where it was terribly cold.

The man was very good at making gardens and trapping various kinds of animals. One time, he looked for a marsupial (*kapul*) trail for placing traps. The good-for-nothing looked and found a good marsupial trail.

He laid traps and returned to his house. In the very early morning, he awoke and walked off to see whether the traps held wild game or not. He walked and arrived at the new trap that he had laid the day before. The good-for-nothing looked and saw a ghost bird hanging there.

Poor Angaipal was very afraid. He lowered his head and went to run back to his house, but the ghost bird saw him and called out for Angaipal to come remove the trap. Angaipal put his game down and went to quickly remove the ghost bird from the trap.

When the ghost bird was free, it removed Angaipal's two eyes. The ghost bird put a cucumber in the man's right eye socket, and it planted a gourd (*kambang*) in the left eye socket.

Poor Angaipal was crazy and completely confused, but he knew the tail. He took a stick and walked very slowly back to his house.

Many months passed, then the cucumber and gourd became big and grew long. They bore fruit that hung from a tree.

However at the bases of the cucumber and gourd were Angaipal's eyes. At this time, all of the women of the sword-grass lands decided to go to the deep forest to look for vines to make net bags.

The next day was a good time, so the women gathered and left for the deep forest in the early morning. They found many, many vines, then they went very close to old Angaipal's house.

Oh my! The women saw many cucumbers and gourds hanging about. They felt terribly hungry, so they took them and ate them. One woman hung her net bag with her baby on a tree fork, and she quickly gathered some cucumbers.

When the woman went close and picked a big cucumber, the man shouted loudly, saying that something was on his body, causing him pain. [He said,] "Who's doing this?" All of the women heard this and ran back to the village. However, the other woman had forgotten that she had hung her baby on the tree and she also went back to the village.

The baby slept well until the afternoon, then he felt hungry and began to cry. Angaipal heard the baby crying. He arose then slowly went and heard the baby crying close to him. He felt with his hands and held the net bag with the baby. He thought that it was a baby girl, but later he took the baby to the house, felt its body and discovered that it was a boy. The old man was elated. Angaipal took very care of the baby well, and he became a real man. His name was Pukpia.

One time, Pukpia asked his father, "Why don't you want to tell me who it was that removed your eyes?"

Angaipal said, "I don't want to tell you because something bad will happen to you just like it did to me." Pukpia said, "I'm a man and I'm strong." So the father told his story, and the son listened.

Pukpia went and set a trap to try to catch the ghost bird, then he returned to the house. When he returned, he sharpened his spears and axe. Then in the very early morning, he walked off to see the trap. When Pukpia arrived there, he saw the ghost bird hung in the trap.

The ghost bird called out, "Come quickly and release me. Why have you set a trap on my trail? This is my trail!" Pukpia said, "I'll remove you if you first show me where my father's eyes are."

However the ghost bird replied, "If you remove me first, then I'll show you." Pukpia said, "No, that's too bad. I can't remove you. If you tell me about my father's eyes, then I will."

So the ghost bird told Pukpia, "Go to the Minj River waterfall. Underneath the Minj River, you'll see two packages, one wrapped with ginger leaves (*gorgor*) and one wrapped with wild sugarcane (*pitpit*) leaves. Take these to your father and remove the cucumber from his right eye.

Put the eye in from the ginger package, then remove the gourd from his left eye and open the wild sugarcane leaves. You'll find his left eye, then put it back. After you put his eyes back, blow on them and he'll see again."

Then Pukpia killed the ghost bird, cut it into tiny pieces and threw them around. Pukpia jumped to the Minj River. He found his father's eyes and took them to the house. Pukpia put his father's eyes back and he could see again.

They lived happily together, and now there is no ghost bird that lives in the forest of Mount Kubor by Minj.

Oliver Okame

Delta Development Company, P. O. Box 7001

Boroko

National Capital District

B211.3. Speaking bird; D1005. Magic breath; D2161.3.1.1. Eyes torn out magically replaced; E423.3. Revenant as bird; E446. Ghost killed and thus finally laid; F512+. Person has plants growing from eye sockets; P231. Mother and son; P233. Father and son; P271. Foster father; P275. Foster son; Q285.3. Cruel mutilation punished; Q411. Death as punishment; Q451.7. Blinding as punishment; R4. Surprise capture; R220. Flights; S110. Murders; S143. Abandonment in forest; S165. Mutilation: putting out eyes

## A Mangy Dog Killed a Ghost Man
(Wantok 598, November 30, 1985, page 24)

Long, long ago, there were two men who hunted for wild game together who lived in a village. One night, they decided to hunt for game in the very early morning. They talked about getting their dogs and hunting for wild pigs in the deep forest. While the two men were deciding this, a ghost man was hiding by the house and heard what they said.

In the very early morning, the first man took his five dogs and walked off to meet his friend at the other house. However the other friend was not ready yet, he was still sleeping. The ghost man took his place and was waiting on the trail.

The ghost man fooled the first man well, but the first man asked him a hard question. The ghost man said that he really was his friend, so the two of them went together into the deep forest.

They walked and came to the midst of the very deep forest. The dogs surrounded a big pig then began to bark and chase the pig back and forth. The real man and the ghost man both killed the pig with their spears and axes.

This pig was big and very heavy, so the men cut a long tree [for a pole] with some strong forest vines and tied the legs of the pig.

The real man carried the part of the pole that was near the pig's head. The ghost man carried the side that was near the pig's tail. Then they walked back home.

The poor real man did not know that his "friend" behind him was a ghost. They walked along, and the ghost man removed the pig's right testicle then ate it. The ghost man's mouth and teeth made crunching sounds.

The real man heard this and asked about it. The ghost man replied that he was eating wild vegetables and that the vegetables in his mouth were making the sound.

Before long, the ghost man ate the pig's other testicle. The man in front heard this and again asked his "friend" behind him. The ghost man said the same thing as before.

They walked until they arrived at a river. They put the pig down, sat on the ground and rested. Then the real man saw that some of the pig's skin and flesh had been removed, and that there was some blood coming from the place where the pig's testicles had hung.

He saw that a piece of the pig's flesh had been removed, but he did not say anything. He knew that the other man was a ghost. He thought of a way to escape. He was not afraid.

The real man told his "friend" that they must butcher the pig and put it into bamboo tubes. He said that the pig was too heavy to carry across the river and get home. So, they cut pieces of bamboo that were near the river.

The real man told the ghost man to go bathe. He said, "Hey, friend, go and bathe. I'll put the meat into twenty bamboo tubes for you and twenty for me too. Then I'll cook the meat in a fire and watch over it. After you wash up, come to the fire, and I'll go down and bathe."

The ghost man went to bathe. The real man dug up plenty of mud and filled twenty bamboo tubes. He shoved just one big piece of meat into the mouth of the bamboo tubes to fool the ghost man. Then he took the pork and filled his own twenty tubes.

While the ghost man was still bathing, the real man chased his dogs to the other side of the river. He chased them back towards the village.

The man and the dogs walked a little. It was hot on the trail. He hung up his twenty tubes on a tree, then he chased four of the dogs back to the village. He let one small mangy dog stay with him.

The ghost man finished bathing and went up to the sandy shore. He saw his twenty bamboo tubes lying by the side of the fire. He saw the pork at the mouth of one of the tubes and salivated. This was because he had bathed and he was ready to eat.

Then he broke open a bamboo tube. He saw that there was only one piece of meat at the mouth of the tube, but that the rest was just filled with mud.

He broke the other tubes until he came to the last. All of the tubes were the same, a piece of meat and the rest filled with mud. Oh my, the ghost was furious, and he sped off. He ran after the man from the village who was on the trail.

The ghost man smelled the mangy dog and kept following this smell. The mangy dog did not hide well; it hid by the trail. The ghost man jumped to grab the dog and kill it.

However, the mangy dog had a good trick. It jumped to the other side. The ghost man missed and fell awkwardly on the ground. The mangy dog turned around behind the ghost and bit his testicles.

The mangy dog planted its teeth hard and pulled the ghost man's testicles. The ghost man screamed, but the mangy dog did not leave his body. The dog pulled the ghost man's body hard and the ghost lost his strength.

The dog's master ran with a spear and planted the spear into the ghost's head and belly. The ghost trembled and stopped making noise. He was dead.

The man was very happy with his mangy dog because the dog had helped him kill the bad ghost. So, the man removed a tube of pork. He broke the tube and let the mangy dog finish all of the pork. When all of the meat was gone, they walked back home.

On this day, the man gave a great thanks to the mangy dog. Every day of the following year, he did not forget about giving good food to this dog. He took care of this dog well and always bathed him in the water.

This man also had learned something. The ancestors told him that it is completely forbidden to tell stories at night about what one will do on the next day. This is because there are various things that will listen to this talking. If a man wants to go hunt for game, he will just rise quietly with his friend or brother and leave.

The reason for this is that people saw that ghost men and women often tricked many people. However, dogs know that real men smell one way and that ghosts and game smell differently.

Der Iamunare
P. O. Box 656
Mt. Hagen
Western Highlands Province

B421. Helpful dog; C401+. Tabu: speaking of plans at night; E261.4. Ghost pursues man; E425.2. Revenant as man; E440+. Ghost laid by spear/arrow; H46.1+. Revenant recognized when it devours raw flesh; K1840. Deception by substitution; K1900. Impostures; L310. Weak overcomes strong in conflict; P310. Friendship; R220. Flights; R260. Pursuits; S176.1. Mutilation: emasculation; W27. Gratitude; X712.3.1H. Injury to testicles

## A Cassowary Befouled a Man

(Wantok 599, December 7, 1985, page 23)

Long ago, in the time of the ancestors, there was a village called **Ami** in the Oksampin area, in the mountains of **West Sepik** [Province, **Oksapmin** People].

In Ami Village, there was a man who lived with his family. One day, the man told his kin that he would go hunt for wild game and other food in the forest.

The man departed. He walked into the very deep forest. He heard the sound of pigs or cassowaries or something. He listened carefully and heard birds singing about.

He walked a little and approached the base of a big tree. He saw large cassowary eggs there. The man was elated to see these eggs.

He said, "This is very good. Now I won't go back empty-handed. The cassowary's eggs are plentiful and good." However the man changed his mind, "I should probably wait here, then the mother cassowary will return for her eggs."

A short distance from the eggs, the man made a small forest hut with tree leaves and vines. He waited. He waited and waited, then he grew slightly impatient.

He took his bow and arrows then returned the village. He saw his family, ate with them, and told the story of what had happened in the forest. His wife cooked a cassowary egg then the two of them sat, ate and talked.

At night, he told his wife, "Listen, tomorrow I'll return to this place where I took the cassowary's egg. I know that the mother cassowary will look for her eggs, so I'll return to the hut underneath the fig tree."

His wife told him, "You must be very careful. Cassowaries often kill men. Also, watch out for wild pigs."

The next morning, the man walked and went directly to this place in the forest. That day, the man went around and around the forest, hunting for some more game.

Night was approaching, so the man half-slept and listened for whether the mother cassowary would come. Before long, he saw the cassowary walking over and lying on top of the nest.

The cassowary turned about because she was laying more eggs. When the man saw this, he thought, "Should I

hide and jump on top of the cassowary or should I shoot her with a spear?"

But no, he felt that it would be good for him to grab her, tie her legs with rope and carry her to the village. The man hid carefully, and very slowly walked forward. Quickly, the man jumped on top of the cassowary from behind, grabbing her. When the cassowary felt this, she was surprised and sped off, carrying the man on her back as she ran.

The cassowary ran off and the man kept holding on to her neck as he hung off of her back. The cassowary carried him into the deep forest, underneath thorny vines and fuzzy [urticating] grasses. The man kept holding on.

The cassowary ran and beat her back on the base of a tree to remove him. It did not work, the man kept holding on from on top of the cassowary. She carried him to a place with many kinds of vines.

It was too bad. The man's skin was not like before. Blood was shooting about, his skin was removed. It looked like a fire had burned him all over. This was because of the thorny vines, because of the base of the tree, and because of the various urticating grasses that had gotten the man while the cassowary carried him with her.

Then the cassowary went to a swampy area. The whole area was mud covered with water. The cassowary ran with her load, the man, on top of her.

The cassowary could not lift her legs now. She went down and was stuck. The man went down into the water and swam slowly to solid ground.

The man walked very slowly. He cut through the forest and came to a clearing. While he walked, he marked the way, so that whoever came later would be able to follow this trail.

The man arrived at an old garden belonging to some people. He sat and rested. Then he walked again. He could not call out because his throat was very sore and his skin was in terrible condition.

He heard some people in another garden talking. The man followed the sound and went towards them. They saw him and they were very sorry for him. They carried him to the village.

He told the story of the cassowary that had befouled him. He told the men of the village to follow the trail that he had taken to them. The men took bows and arrows then walked off.

They arrived at the flooded area and saw the cassowary still standing there. Where could she run? Her two legs were stuck in the muck.

The men did not kill her. They cut some vines, some rattans, and some trees. They said, "Are you the cassowary that befouled and ruined one of our men? Today, you'll die. You've beaten us enough. You've shown off to only one man."

Then they went closer. One man tied a vine noose, threw it on the cassowary and pulled. Quickly, the noose went around the cassowary's long neck and harnessed her.

Then the men went slowly, held the two legs and bound them with vines. They carried her up onto the firm ground, then tied the cassowary up to a good log with strong rattans.

They switched off as they carried her to the village because the big mother cassowary was very heavy. They butchered her, and a very big piece went to the man who had been wrecked by her.

This was the beginning of when it was cautioned against men of the village doing this: it is completely forbidden to grab cassowaries or pigs because cassowaries and pigs can kill men.

Okat Kewani
Ongu Store
Aitape
West Sepik Province

C841+. Tabu: grabbing cassowary by neck; C841+. Tabu: grabbing wild pig by neck; F989.4+. Man rides on back of fleeing cassowary; P210. Husband and wife; R260. Pursuits


## Blood Became a Baby

(Wantok 600, December 14, 1985, page 18)

Long ago, in the time of the ancestors, there was a married couple who lived in the place that we now call southern Bougainville [**Buin** or **Siwai** People?, **North Solomons** Province]. The couple did not have children, but the couple did have many gardens. They were very hard workers.

Every day, they would go to the gardens. While the woman worked in the gardens, the man would hunt for wild game in the forest.

One time, the man did hard work in the many gardens, and the woman looked for *tulip* leaves and other food in the nearby forest.

This day, they went to the gardens again. And so, like every evening they would return to the house. The woman's husband became very sick because he had worked too hard in their many gardens. That night, the man died.

Then the woman found herself alone. She slept that night, and the man's ghost came in her dreams.

The man's ghost came to her in a dream and said, "Don't worry anymore about me. You're alone and strong. Take care of everything that I've left you."

He told the woman, "Your gardens will grow well. There will be no enemies. Whatever you plant will always bear good food. I'll always stand by you like your god. Never mind that I've left you and am far away now."

Late that night, she awoke and was still troubled. She stopped crying, then slept thinking about what she had seen in her dream.

One day, the woman went to the garden and worked until the bright sun baked her. She became very thirsty for water. She cut a sugarcane, and the sugarcane leaf cut one of her fingers.

Quickly, she cut a taro leaf. She covered the blood with the taro leaf, and buried it in the ground. The sugarcane juice that the woman drank quenched her thirst.

One week later, the woman returned to the garden to check up on the place where she had buried her blood. She dug down and found an egg there. The woman did not think about this, she just covered it with earth again.

When the woman was still in the garden, her husband came to her in a short dream. He told her not to go back to the village, and that she must sleep in their old garden hut that night.

The woman made a fire and cooked a little food for herself. She ate the food by the fire. She was not worried or afraid. She and her husband sometimes had done this sort of thing in the garden hut. Her husband's ghost looked after her wherever she went. The woman cooked and ate, then she went to sleep.

She dreamt again, and her husband told her that the next morning she would see a new kind of thing growing in the garden. The woman slept.

The next morning, she awoke and saw a little baby boy crying on top of the place where she had buried her blood. The woman saw the baby and carried him. She was elated. She looked for water, but did not find any, so she cut sugarcanes and bathed the baby with the sugarcane juice.

The woman no longer went back to the village. Her husband instructed her in dreams that she must stay in the garden hut as if it were her home.

She went and took all of her things from her house in the village. Her new home was her garden hut. The woman took care of the baby alone until he grew up. He became a big man and helped his old mother with all of the work in the garden.

Alois Kavi and John Iuaru
Malmal High School
Madang
Madang Province

D457.1.14K. Transformation: blood to eggs; D1810.8.2. Information received through dream; E321. Dead husband's friendly return; E363.2. Ghost returns to protect the living; P210. Husband and wife; P231. Mother and son; T534. Conception from blood; T542. Birth of human being from an egg


# Do Not Covet Your Little Brother

(Wantok 601, December 21, 1985, Page 35)

Long ago, there were two brothers who lived together in a village. The big brother was a young man and he was the stronger of the two. He was married and lived with his wife. The little brother was not yet old enough to get a wife, so he lived with his parents in a large house.

If you had seen the behavior of these two brothers, you would have seen that the little brother was more skilled than his elder brother was. The younger brother was better at painting and decorating all of the traditional material, including bows and arrows. The big brother did not have this kind of knowledge or ability.

Everyone in the village knew that the little brother excelled at making good bows and well-decorated arrows. They knew that he excelled at making all kinds of decorations.

One fine day, the little brother went into the forest to find some birds so that his mother could make some good soup in the afternoon.

That same day, the big brother's wife went to work in her garden, and the big brother went to another place with the other men for a big festival.

The little brother went deep into the forest to find some truly wild birds. He arrived at his big brother's garden and he stopped there. His big brother's wife was weeding there.

The little brother had shot a bird with his arrow. The bird fell inside his brother's garden where his sister-in-law was exerting herself.

His sister-in-law, who was working among the taros, trembled when the arrow came down close to her. She grabbed it and hid it. She saw that the colors and decorations on the arrow were excellent. She wanted to know who was the owner of this arrow.

She also thought that if these kinds of decorations were on her skin, she would become a truly beautiful woman. She wanted the owner of this arrow to put these kinds of markings onto her skin too.

She was looking and thinking about the arrow when the little brother walked into the garden. He was just following the path that his arrow had taken. He came crashing through when the woman turned and saw him.

"I was trying to find my arrow with a bird that I shot, have you seen my arrow?"

"It's here. I'm holding your arrow right here. Come and get it," said the woman.

When the little brother came to get the arrow, his sister-in-law told him to make the same kinds of decorations on her body that were on the arrow.

He replied, "No, you are my big brother's wife and I can't paint decorations on your body."

"No, don't worry about your big brother, you should make these colors and decorations on my body. My husband can't see us now."

His sister-in-law flattered him so well that he did not have anything more to say, and he forgot entirely about his big brother.

"If my brother gets angry about these decorations, you can't tell him who painted them on your body. This is a secret between the two of us."

The woman replied, "Don't worry, I'll make up another story and he won't be able to find out who it was that painted my body."

She told her brother-in-law to make the marks on her belly, on her back and even on the inside of her thighs. She told him that she wanted these because she dearly desired his pictures and decorations.

When the boy painted and cut his sister-in-law's skin with a piece of bamboo [i.e., tattooed her], he began to fear that his brother would find out that he had put these decorations on his wife and that he would not like it.

The woman was persistent, and her brother-in-law tattooed the marks on the inside of her thighs.

Blood flowed all over her skin, but she told the little brother to cut even more marks. So, when they finished their tattoo work, the little brother ran back to his parents' house and the woman went back to her own house.

When she arrived at her house, the woman did not chop and cook food [as is customary]. No, she went to sleep.

When the big brother finished the festival at the other place, he carried with him food and meat, such as pork. When he returned home, he called out for his wife to take care of all of the food that he had brought, but his wife replied that bamboo had poked her and that she was unable to work.

The woman made up the story like this: a piece of bamboo that an ant was carrying in the garden broke off when she had wanted to go outside [of the garden hut]. The bamboo jabbed her belly and other parts of her body.

The husband knew that his wife was trying to lie to him, so he went inside the house to see what was wrong with his wife.

She tried to hide her skin, but her husband found out that there were marks on her. He wanted to find out who had painted these marks upon her.

The big brother beat the village signal drum. He called out for all of the men in the village to come and meet at the leaders' meeting house. He brought many clusters of betel nuts. He shared them with all of the young and old men who came. He told the assembly that he wanted them to put their wooden objects into a big basket that he would place on the side.

This story comes from the **Buin** area [**Buin** People, **North Solomons** Province]. The man placed a big basket on the side and the other men put their decorated objects inside the basket.

The big brother saw that his little brother also put his finished markings inside the basket. He looked at all of the markings, and he saw that the markings of his brother were the same kind as those that were on his wife's skin.

He was truly angry because he now knew that his little brother had made the marks on his wife and that he had even put them on the inside of her thighs. So, he now thought that he would kill his little brother.

One day he told his little brother that he would follow him to the sea. They could fish for their elders and for his wife.

The two of them went far out to sea where they could not see land. They had brought ripe coconuts with them so that they could both drink the milk and eat the meat of the coconuts.

Far asea, the big brother broke open a coconut and half of it fell in the water. He asked his little brother to swim in the sea and fetch the piece of coconut.

When the little brother entered the sea to get the coconut, the big brother quickly paddled off leaving the little brother adrift. The little brother saw this and then knew that his big brother wanted to kill him.

The little brother was angry and began to eat the coconut that he was holding. At this time, some fish saw some pieces of coconut that he had spit out, so they came to look for the coconut.

When the little brother saw the fish, he gave them little pieces but he asked them to carry him to the big fish. They carried him to another place, then they departed. Later, a big fish ate a piece of coconut and carried the boy closer to land, but then the fish left him.

Finally, a big turtle swam and came to eat a piece of coconut. When the turtle heard the little brother's story, he became angry at the big brother, so he carried this boy to the beach near his village, then left him there.

Before the turtle returned to the sea, the little boy told the turtle, "When my parents see me, they will make a huge feast."

He pointed to a big stone and said, "Look at this stone. When I want you and the fish to come, I'll point to this stone. Now, go and inform all of the other fish who helped me to get ready for this big feast."

When the boy arrived at the village, his parents were very happy. The boy's father made a great effort to prepare food for everyone in the village, the other leaders, and the friends of the little boy. When all of the preparations were ready, the boy's father told him to call out to his friends to come to this party.

The boy went down to the beach. He hit the stone and talked to the turtle. Quickly, the turtle and all of the fish who had helped him in the sea came ashore. When they were all ashore on the beach, they all turned into real men and went to the boy's house.

The big feast began and the boy's father told everyone that he was very happy that his child had returned from the sea. The party lasted until dawn. All of the girls went to sleep while the men from the sea and the men of the land continued to dance and sing.

At this time, the little brother went above his big brother. He told the village that he now wanted to return his obligation to his big brother.

So, the two of them fought. Then all of the men who were at the party divided into two groups. The group from the sea helped the little brother and the group from the land stood with the big brother.

The fight broke up and the group from the sea trampled all of the taros at the party. They were angry because the big brother's wife had been hiding in the middle of taro and she was the one who had started all of the trouble.

B. Pirung
Sirowa [Sirowai]
P. O. Box 109
Kieta
N. S. P. [Not Solomons Province]

B470. Helpful fish; B491.5. Helpful turtle (tortoise); B541.1. Escape from sea on fish's back; B551.5. Turtle (tortoise) carries person across river (ocean); D370M. Transformation: fish to man; D390+M. Transformation:

turtle to man; P210. Husband and wife; P231. Mother and son; P233. Father and son; P251.5. Two brothers; P251.5.3. Hostile brothers; P263. Brother-in-law; P264. Sister-in-law; P310. Friendship; Q53. Reward for rescue; Q380+. Tattooing of wife punished; Q467K. Marooning at sea as punishment; S142. Person thrown into the water and abandoned; W157. Dishonesty; W181. Jealousy

# Amaita Surpassed His Boastful Friends

. (Wantok 602, December 28, 1985, page 20)

Long ago, in the time of the ancestors, there was a young, single man who lived alone. The people of the village liked this man very much because the he was a hard worker. He had a garden where he planted various kinds of foods. He was also very smart at hunting for wild game in the forest.

He was a very hard worker at all of the collective work of the village, but he was not one to boast, to be stubborn or to gossip. Many people respected him very much. They often told the other young men not to be stubborn, that they must try to follow the good ways of this man.

The other young men were often very happy. They usually would intensely lust after the women of the village. The one young man did not do this; he stayed there by himself.

This man's name was Amaita. Amaita did not like to think too much about going around boastfully or about looking for women.

The people of the village liked his manners very much. They often coveted him. There were some parents who wanted their daughters to marry Amaita.

The young women did not like him because they thought that Amaita was [not] smart. Amaita did not usually show them his good deeds, nor did he go around gabbing.

The young women of the village usually just went to the boastful men. They thought that Amaitai [Amaita] was a weakling. Many young men married the young women of the village, but Amatai [Amaita] stayed single. His entire age group was married and had children.

Some years passed and some men were sorry that Amatai had no wife. He was a good man who worked very hard. They thought that Amatai was not strong, or that he was far from asking women who liked him. They thought that he was afraid or ashamed.

Some of his good friends shared their thoughts about finding a woman for Amatai. They knew that Amatai was a hard worker and that he excelled at finding food. He usually did his own work.

His friends found a very beautiful woman, but the woman was from another village. They did not know the habits of this woman. When Amatai saw this woman, he fell in love with her because she was a very young and beautiful.

A decision was made, and Amatai married her. They lived happily as newlyweds. The woman never did the slightest work. She usually just sat and ate.

Amatai did not care. He was always working in the garden or hunting for food in the forest. The woman did not change at all. She just sat in the house while he did everything. The woman just sat and gobbled food.

The man saw this and thought hard. He thought that his friends must have tricked him. Amatai was furious and evicted the woman. He took another useless woman. This woman had ringworm.

Amatai said, "I don't care. My first wife was from another village. My friends just carried her and put her in my house."

He saw that this ringworm woman was a very hard worker, and that she belonged to his own village. She did not look very nice compared to his first wife.

Amatai thought of a scheme. He took the ringworm woman to a stream that came down the mountain. There was no one else in the stream. The woman went down and bathed. Some time later, she cleaned her skin with leaves from a breadfruit tree and removed all of the ringworm scabs from her skin.

There was no longer any ringworm on her skin. The woman became very beautiful. Her skin became reddish. Oh my, when Amatai saw this, he was elated. He did not care that there were no red-skinned women in the village. His ringworm wife had changed and become very beautiful.

The two of them went back to the village. Together, they took the food from the forest and the garden. Then they arrived at the village. When the people of the village saw the woman, they asked, "Amatai must have found a third wife, huh? Oh my, she's beautiful and her skin is red. There are no other red-skinned women here. Where did he find her?"

They did not yet understand that it was the poor ringworm woman. The men of the village did not want Amatai to scavenge around their own village [for women]. Later, they discovered what had happened. They could not believe that the ringworm woman had changed and become a very beautiful woman.

She looked more beautiful than did the young women that Amatai's friends had married. The women were jealous of this woman and Amatai's friends were jealous of him too.

Amatai lived with his wife. The woman had a beautiful baby. The people said, "Look at that rotten good-for-nothing. He worked hard and he lives well. He's not stubborn or boastful. His friends played a trick upon him, but he still came out ahead. Now, he has a beautiful wife and baby."

Kisawai Waboro
**Yaro** Village [**Mikaru** or **Pawaia** People]
Karimui
**Simbu** Province

D1500.1.4.2+. Magic healing breadfruit leaf removes ringworm; D1866.1. Beautification by bathing; D1866.2. Beautification by removal of skin; F527.1. Red person; P210. Husband and wife; P230. Parents and children; P310. Friendship; T10. Falling in love; T100. Marriage; T145.7+. Man's first wife beautiful but lazy, his second ugly but diligent; W111. Laziness; W117. Boastfulness; W167. Stubbornness; W195. Envy